# JOHN
# LE CARRÉ

# JOHN LE CARRÉ

## TINKER TAILOR SOLDIER SPY

## THE HONOURABLE SCHOOLBOY

## SMILEY'S PEOPLE

OCTOPUS BOOKS

*Tinker Tailor Soldier Spy* first published in Great Britain
in 1974 by Hodder and Stoughton Limited
*The Honourable Schoolboy* first published in Great Britain in
1977 by Hodder and Stoughton Limited
*Smiley's People* first published in Great Britain in 1979 by
Hodder and Stoughton Limited

This edition first published in Great Britain in 1990 by
Peerage Books
an imprint of
The Octopus Group Limited
Michelin House
81 Fulham Road
London SW3 6RB

ISBN 1 85052 170 0

Printed and bound in the United Kingdom by Bath Press

# CONTENTS

# TINKER
# TAILOR
# SOLDIER SPY

# ONE

The truth is, if old Major Dover hadn't dropped dead at Taunton races Jim would never have come to Thursgood's at all. He came in mid-term without an interview, late May it was though no one would have thought it from the weather, employed through one of the shiftier agencies specialising in supply teachers for prep schools, to hold down old Dover's teaching till someone suitable could be found. 'A linguist,' Thursgood told the common room, 'a temporary measure,' and brushed away his forelock in self-defence. 'Priddo.' He gave the spelling 'P-R-I-D' – French was not Thursgood's subject so he consulted the slip of paper – 'E-A-U-X, the first name James. I think he'll do us very well till July.' The staff had no difficulty in reading the signals. Jim Prideaux was a poor white of the teaching community. He belonged to the same sad bunch as the late Mrs Loveday who had a Persian lamb coat and stood in for junior divinity until her cheques bounced, or the late Mr Maltby, the pianist who had been called from choir practice to help the police with their enquiries, and for all anyone knew was helping them to this day, for Maltby's trunk still lay in the cellar awaiting instructions. Several of the staff, but chiefly Marjoribanks, were in favour of opening that trunk. They said it contained notorious missing treasures: Aprahamian's silver-framed picture of his Lebanese mother, for instance; Best-Ingram's Swiss army penknife and Matron's watch. But Thursgood set his creaseless face resolutely against their entreaties. Only five years had passed since he had inherited the school from his father, but they had taught him already that some things are best locked away.

Jim Prideaux arrived on a Friday in a rainstorm. The rain rolled like gun-smoke down the brown combes of the Quantocks, then raced across the empty cricket fields into the sandstone of the crumbling façades. He arrived just after lunch, driving an old red Alvis and towing a second-hand caravan that had once been blue. Early afternoons at Thursgood's are a tranquil time, a brief truce in the running fight of each school day. The boys are sent to rest in their dormitories, the staff sit in the common room over coffee reading newspapers or correcting boys' work. Thursgood reads a novel to his mother. Of the whole school therefore only little Bill Roach actually saw Jim arrive, saw the steam belching from the Alvis' bonnet as it wheezed its way down the pitted drive, windscreen wipers going full pelt and the caravan shuddering through the puddles in pursuit.

Roach was a new boy in those days and graded dull, if not actually deficient. Thursgood's was his second prep school in two terms. He was a fat round child with asthma and he spent large parts of his rest kneeling on the end of his bed, gazing through the window. His mother lived grandly in Bath; his father was agreed to be the richest in the school, a distinction which cost the son dear. Coming from a broken home Roach was also a natural watcher. In

Roach's observation Jim did not stop at the school buildings but continued across the sweep to the stable yard. He knew the layout of the place already. Roach decided later that he must have made a reconnaissance or studied maps. Even when he reached the yard he didn't stop but drove straight on to the wet grass, travelling at speed to keep the momentum. Then over a hummock into the Dip, head first and out of sight. Roach half expected the caravan to jack-knife on the brink, Jim took it over so fast, but instead it just lifted its tail and disappeared like a giant rabbit into its hole.

The Dip is a piece of Thursgood folklore. It lies in a patch of waste land between the orchard, the fruithouse and the stable yard. To look at, it is no more than a depression in the ground, grass covered, with hummocks on the northern side, each about boy-height and covered in tufted thickets which in summer grow spongy. It is these hummocks that give the Dip its special virtue as a playground and also its reputation, which varies with the fantasy of each new generation of boys. They are the traces of an open-cast silver mine, says one year and digs enthusiastically for wealth. They are a Romano-British fort, says another, and stages battles with sticks and clay missiles. To others the Dip is a bomb-crater from the war and the hummocks are seated bodies buried in the blast. The truth is more prosaic. Six years ago, and not long before his abrupt elopement with a receptionist from the Castle Hotel, Thursgood's father had launched an appeal for a swimming pool and persuaded the boys to dig a large hole with a deep and a shallow end. But the money that came in was never quite enough to finance the ambition, so it was frittered away on other schemes, such as a new projector for the art school, and a plan to grow mushrooms in the school cellars. And even, said the cruel ones, to feather a nest for certain illicit lovers when they eventually took flight to Germany, the lady's native home.

Jim was unaware of these associations. The fact remains that by sheer luck he had chosen the one corner of Thursgood's academy which as far as Roach was concerned was endowed with supernatural properties.

Roach waited at the window but saw nothing more. Both the Alvis and the caravan were in dead ground and if it hadn't been for the wet red tracks across the grass he might have wondered whether he had dreamed the whole thing. But the tracks were real, so when the bell went for the end of rest he put on his Wellingtons and trudged through the rain to the top of the Dip and peered down and there was Jim dressed in an army raincoat and a quite extraordinary hat, broad-brimmed like a safari hat but hairy, with one side pinned up in a rakish piratical curl and the water running off it like a gutter.

The Alvis was in the stable yard; Roach never knew how Jim spirited it out of the Dip, but the caravan was right down there, at what should have been the deep end, bedded on platforms of weathered brick, and Jim was sitting on the step drinking from a green plastic beaker, and rubbing his right shoulder as if he had banged it on something, while the rain poured off his hat. Then the hat lifted and Roach found himself staring at an extremely fierce red face, made still fiercer by the shadow of the brim and by a brown moustache washed into fangs by the rain. The rest of the face was criss-crossed with jagged cracks, so deep and crooked that Roach concluded in another of his flashes of imaginative genius that Jim had once been very hungry in a tropical place and filled up again since. The left arm still lay across his chest, the right shoulder was still drawn high against his neck. But the whole tangled shape of him had stiffened, he was like an animal frozen against its background: a stag, thought Roach on a hopeful impulse, something noble.

'Who the hell are you?' asked a very military voice.

'Sir, Roach, sir. I'm a new boy.'

For a moment longer, the brick face surveyed Roach from the shadow of the hat. Then, to his intense relief, its features relaxed into a wolfish grin, the left hand, still clapped over the right shoulder, resumed its slow massage while at the same time he managed a long pull from the plastic beaker.

'New boy, eh?' Jim repeated into the beaker, still grinning. 'Well that's a turn up for the book, I will say.'

Rising now, and turning his crooked back on Roach, Jim set to work on what appeared to be a detailed study of the caravan's four legs, a very critical study which involved much rocking of the suspension, and much tilting of the strangely garbed head, and the emplacement of several bricks at different angles and points. Meanwhile the spring rain was clattering down on everything: his coat, his hat and the roof of the old caravan. And Roach noticed that throughout these manoeuvres Jim's right shoulder had not budged at all but stayed wedged high against his neck like a rock under the mackintosh. Therefore he wondered whether Jim was a sort of giant hunchback and whether all hunch backs hurt as Jim's did. And he noticed as a generality, a thing to store away, that people with bad backs take long strides, it was something to do with balance.

'New boy, eh? Well *I'm* not a new boy,' Jim went on, in altogether a much more friendly tone, as he pulled at a leg of the caravan. 'I'm an old boy. Old as Rip Van Winkle if you want to know. Older. Got any friends?'

'No, sir,' said Roach simply, in the listless tone which schoolboys always use for saying 'no', leaving all positive response to their interrogators. Jim however made no response at all, so that Roach felt an odd stirring of kinship suddenly, and of hope.

'My other name's Bill,' he said. 'I was christened Bill but Mr Thursgood calls me William.'

'Bill, eh. The unpaid Bill. Anyone ever call you that?'

'No, sir.'

'Good name, anyway.'

'Yes, sir.'

'Known a lot of Bills. They've all been good 'uns.'

With that, in a manner of speaking, the introduction was made, Jim did not tell Roach to go away so Roach stayed on the brow peering downward through his rain-smeared spectacles. The bricks, he noticed with awe, were pinched from the cucumber frame. Several had been loose already and Jim must have loosened them a bit more. It seemed a wonderful thing to Roach that anyone just arrived at Thursgood's should be so self-possessed as to pinch the actual fabric of the school for his own purposes, and doubly wonderful that Jim had run a lead off the hydrant for his water, for that hydrant was the subject of a special school rule: to touch it at all was a beatable offence.

'Hey you, Bill. You wouldn't have such a thing as a marble on you by any chance?'

'A-sir-what-sir?' Roach asked, patting his pockets in a dazed way.

'Marble, old boy. Round glass marble, little ball. Don't boys play marbles any more? We did when I was at school.'

Roach had no marble but Aprahamian had had a whole collection flown in from Beirut. It took Roach about fifty seconds to race back to the school, secure one against the wildest undertakings and return panting to the Dip. There he hesitated, for in his mind the Dip was already Jim's and Roach required leave to descend it. But Jim had disappeared into the caravan, so having waited a moment Roach stepped gingerly down the bank and offered the marble through the doorway. Jim didn't spot him at once. He was sipping from the beaker and staring out of the window at the black clouds as they tore this way and that over the Quantocks. This sipping movement, Roach noticed, was actually quite difficult, for Jim could not easily swallow standing up straight, he had to tilt his whole twisted trunk backward to achieve the angle. Meanwhile the rain came on really hard again, rattling against the caravan like gravel.

'Sir,' said Roach but Jim made no move.

'Trouble with an Alvis is, no damn springs,' said Jim at last, more to the window than to his visitor. 'You drive along with your rump on the white line, eh? Cripple anybody.' And, tilting his trunk again, he drank.

'Yes, sir,' said Roach, much surprised that Jim should assume he was a driver.

Jim had taken off his hat. His sandy hair was close cropped, there were patches where someone had gone too low with the scissors. These patches were mainly on one side, so that Roach guessed that Jim had cut his hair himself with his good arm, which made him even more lopsided.

'I brought you a marble,' said Roach.

'Very good of you. Thanks, old boy.' Taking the marble he slowly rolled it round his hard, powdery palm and Roach knew at once that he was very skilful at all sorts of things; that he was the kind of man who lived on terms with tools and objects generally. 'Not level, you see, Bill,' he confided, still intent upon the marble. 'Skew-whiff. Like me. Watch,' and turned purposefully to the larger window. A strip of aluminium beading ran along the bottom, put there to catch the condensation. Laying the marble in it, Jim watched it roll to the end and fall on the floor.

'Skew-whiff,' he repeated. 'Kipping in the stern. Can't have that, can we? Hey, hey, where'd you get to, you little brute?'

The caravan was not a homely place, Roach noticed, stooping to retrieve the marble. It might have belonged to anyone, though it was scrupulously clean. Not even a picture of his wife, thought Roach, who had not yet met a bachelor, with the exception of Mr Thursgood. The only personal things he could find were a webbing kitbag hanging from the door, a set of sewing things stored beside the bunk and a homemade shower made from a perforated biscuit tin and neatly welded to the roof. And on the table one bottle of colourless drink, gin or vodka, because that was what his father drank when Roach went to his flat for weekends in the holidays.

'East-west looks okay but north-south is undoubtedly skew-whiff,' Jim declared, testing the other window ledge. 'What are you good at, Bill?'

'I don't know, sir,' said Roach woodenly.

'Got to be good at something surely, everyone is. How about football? Are you good at football, Bill?'

'No, sir,' said Roach.

'Are you a swat, then?' Jim asked carelessly, as he lowered himself with a short grunt onto the bed, and took a pull from the beaker. 'You don't look a swat I must say,' he added politely. 'Although you're a loner.'

'I don't know,' Roach repeated and moved half a pace towards the open door.

'What's your best thing, then?' He took another long sip. 'Must be good at something, Bill, everyone is. My best thing was ducks and drakes. Cheers.'

Now this was an unfortunate question to ask of Roach just then for it occupied most of his waking hours. Indeed he had recently come to doubt whether he had any purpose on earth at all. In work and play he considered himself seriously inadequate; even the daily routine of the school, such as making his bed and tidying his clothes, seemed to be beyond his reach. Also he lacked piety, old Mrs Thursgood had told him so, he screwed up his face too much at chapel. He blamed himself very much for these shortcomings but most of all he blamed himself for the break-up of his parents' marriage, which he should have seen coming and taken steps to prevent. He even wondered whether he was more directly responsible, whether for instance he was abnormally wicked or divisive or slothful, and that his bad character had wrought the rift. At his last school he had tried to explain this by screaming and feigning fits of cerebral palsy, which his aunt had. His parents conferred, as they frequently did in their reasonable way, and changed his school. Therefore this chance question, levelled at him in the cramped caravan by a creature at least halfway to divinity, a fellow solitary at that, brought him suddenly very near disaster. He felt the heat charging to his face, he watched his spectacles mist over and the caravan begin to dissolve into a sea of grief. Whether Jim noticed this, Roach never knew, for suddenly he had turned his crooked back on him, moved away to the table and was helping himself from the plastic beaker while he threw out saving phrases.

'You're a good watcher, anyway, I'll tell you that for nothing, old boy. Us singles always are, no one to rely on, what? No one else spotted me. Gave me a real turn up there, parked on the horizon. Thought you were a juju man. Best watcher in the unit, Bill Roach is, I'll bet. Long as he's got his specs on. What?'

'Yes,' Roach agreed gratefully, 'I am.'

'Well, you stay here and watch, then,' Jim commanded, clapping the safari hat back on his head, 'and I'll slip outside and trim the legs. Do that?'

'Yes, sir.'

'Where's damn marble?'

'Here, sir.'

'Call out when she moves, right? North, south, whichever way she rolls. Understand?'

'Yes, sir.'

'Know which way's north?'

'That way,' said Roach promptly and stuck out his arm at random.

'Right. Well, you call when she rolls,' Jim repeated and disappeared into the rain. A moment later Roach felt the ground swaying under his feet and heard another roar either of pain or anger, as Jim wrestled with an off-side prop.

In the course of that same summer term, the boys paid Jim the compliment of a nickname. They had several shots before they were happy. They tried Trooper, which caught the bit of military in him, his occasional, quite harmless cursing and his solitary rambles in the Quantocks. All the same Trooper didn't stick, so they tried Pirate and for a while Goulash. Goulash because of his taste for hot food, the smell of curries and onions and paprika that greeted them in warm puffs as they filed past the Dip on their way to

Evensong. Goulash for his perfect French which was held to have a slushy quality. Spikely of Five B could imitate it to a hair: 'You heard the question, Berger. What is Emile looking at?' – a convulsive jerk of the right hand – 'Don't gawp at me, old boy, I'm not a juju man. *Qu'est-ce qu'il regarde, Emile, dans le tableau que tu as sous le nez? Mon cher Berger*, if you do not very soon summon one lucid sentence of French, *je te mettrai tout de suite à la porte, tu comprends*, you beastly toad?'

But these terrible threats were never carried out, neither in French nor English. In a quaint way, they actually added to the aura of gentleness which quickly surrounded him, a gentleness only possible in big men seen through the eyes of boys.

Yet Goulash did not satisfy them either. It lacked the hint of strength contained. It took no account of Jim's passionate Englishness, which was the only subject where he could be relied on to waste time. Toad Spikely had only to venture one disparaging comment on the monarchy, extol the joys of some foreign country, preferably a hot one, for Jim to colour sharply and snap out a good three minutes' worth on the privilege of being born an Englishman. He knew they were teasing him but he was unable not to rise. Often he ended his homily with a rueful grin, and muttered references to red herrings and red marks too, and red faces when certain people would have to come in for extra work and miss their football. But England was his love; when it came down to it, no one suffered for her.

'Best place in the whole damn world!' he bellowed once. 'Know why? Know why, toad?'

Spikely did not, so Jim seized a crayon and drew a globe. To the west, America, he said, full of greedy fools fouling up their inheritance. To the east, China-Russia, he drew no distinction: boiler suits, prison camps and a damn long march to nowhere. In the middle . . .

Finally they hit on Rhino.

Partly this was a play on Prideaux, partly a reference to his taste for living off the land and his appetite for physical exercise which they noted constantly. Shivering in the shower queue first thing in the morning they would see the Rhino pounding down Combe Lane with a rucksack on his crooked back as he returned from his morning march. Going to bed they could glimpse his lonely shadow through the perspex roof of the fives court as the Rhino tirelessly attacked the concrete wall. And sometimes on warm evenings from their dormitory windows they would covertly watch him at golf, which he played with a dreadful old iron, zigzag across the playing fields, often after reading to them from an extremely English adventure book: Biggles, Percy Westerman or Jeffrey Farnol, grabbed haphazard from the dingy library. At each stroke they waited for the grunt as he started his backswing and they were seldom disappointed. They kept a meticulous score. At the staff cricket match he made seventy-five before dismissing himself with a ball deliberately lofted to Spikely at square leg. 'Catch, toad, catch it, go on. Well done, Spikely, good lad, that's what you're there for.'

He was also credited, despite his taste for tolerance, with a sound understanding of the criminal mind. There were several examples of this, but the most telling occurred a few days before the end of term, when Spikely discovered in Jim's waste basket a draft of the next day's examination paper, and rented it to candidates at five new pence a time. Several boys paid their shilling and spent an agonized night memorising answers by torchlight in their dormitories. But when the exam came round Jim presented a quite different paper.

'You can look at this one for nothing,' he bellowed as he sat down. And having hauled open his *Daily Telegraph* calmly gave himself over to the latest counsels of the juju men, which they understood to mean almost anyone with intellectual pretension, even if he wrote in the Queen's cause.

There was lastly the incident of the owl, which had a separate place in their opinion of him since it involved death, a phenomenon to which children react variously. The weather continuing cold, Jim brought a bucket of coal to his classroom and one Wednesday lit it in the grate, and sat there with his back to the warmth, reading a *dictée*. First some soot fell which he ignored, then the owl came down, a full-sized barn owl which had nested up there, no doubt, through many unswept winters and summers of Dover's rule, and was now smoked out, dazed and black from beating itself to exhaustion in the flue. It fell over the coals and collapsed in a heap on the wooden floorboard with a clatter and a scuffle, then lay like an emissary of the devil, hunched but breathing, wings stretched, staring straight out at the boys through the soot which caked its eyes. There was no one who was not frightened; even Spikely, a hero, was frightened. Except for Jim, who had in a second folded the beast together and taken it out of the door without a word. They heard nothing, though they listened like stowaways, till the sound of running water from down the corridor as Jim evidently washed his hands. 'He's having a pee,' said Spikely, which earned a nervous laugh. But as they filed out of the classroom they discovered the owl still folded, neatly dead and awaiting burial on top of the compost heap beside the Dip. Its neck, as the braver ones established, was snapped. Only a gamekeeper, declared Sudeley, who had one, would know how to kill an owl so well.

Among the rest of the Thursgood community, opinion regarding Jim was less unanimous. The ghost of Mr Maltby the pianist died hard. Matron, siding with Bill Roach, pronounced him heroic and in need of care: it was a miracle he managed with that back. Marjoribanks said he had been run over by a bus when he was drunk. It was Marjoribanks also, at the staff match where Jim so excelled, who pointed out the sweater. Marjoribanks was not a cricketer but he had strolled down to watch with Thursgood.

'Do you think that sweater's kosher,' he asked in a high, jokey voice, 'or do you think he pinched it?'

'Leonard, that's very unfair,' Thursgood scolded, hammering at the flanks of his Labrador. 'Bite him, Ginny, bite the bad man.'

By the time he reached his study, however, Thursgood's laughter had quite worn off and he became extremely nervous. Bogus Oxford men he could deal with, just as in his time he had known classics masters who had no Greek and parsons who had no divinity. Such men, confronted with proof of their deception, broke down and wept and left, or stayed on half pay. But men who withheld genuine accomplishment, these were a breed he had not met but he knew already that he did not like them. Having consulted the university calendar, he telephoned the agency, a Mr Stroll of the house of Stroll and Medley.

'What precisely do you want to know?' Mr Stroll asked with a dreadful sigh.

'Well, nothing *precisely*.' Thursgood's mother was sewing at a sampler and seemed not to hear. 'Merely that if one asks for a written *curriculum vitae* one likes it to be complete. One doesn't like gaps. Not if one pays one's fee.'

At this point Thursgood found himself wondering rather wildly whether he had woken Mr Stroll from a deep sleep to which he had now returned.

'Very patriotic bloke,' Mr Stroll observed finally.

'I did not employ him for his patriotism.'

'He's been in dock,' Mr Stroll whispered on, as if through frightful draughts of cigarette smoke. 'Laid up. Spinal.'

'Quite so. But I assume he has not been in hospital for the whole of the last twenty-five years. *Touché*,' he murmured to his mother, his hand over the mouthpiece and once more it crossed his mind that Mr Stroll had dropped off to sleep.

'You've only got him till the end of term,' Mr Stroll breathed. 'If you don't fancy him, chuck him out. You asked for temporary, temporary's what you've got. You said cheap, you've got cheap.'

'That's as may be,' Thursgood retorted gamely. 'But I've paid you a twenty guineas fee, my father dealt with you for many years and I'm entitled to certain assurances. You've put here – may I read it to you? – you've put here *Before his injury, various overseas appointments of a commercial and prospecting nature.* Now that is hardly an enlightening description of a lifetime's employment, is it?'

At her sewing his mother nodded her agreement. 'It is *not*,' she echoed aloud.

'That's my first point. Let me go on a little –'

'Not too much, darling,' warned his mother.

'I happen to know he was up at Oxford in thirty-eight. Why didn't he finish? What went wrong?'

'I seem to recall there was an interlude round about then,' said Mr Stroll after another age. 'But I expect you're too young to remember it.'

'He can't have been in prison *all* the time,' said his mother after a very long silence still without looking up from her sewing.

'He's been somewhere,' said Thursgood morosely, staring across the windswept gardens towards the Dip.

All through the summer holidays, as he moved uncomfortably between one household and another, embracing and rejecting, Bill Roach fretted about Jim, whether his back was hurting, what he was doing for money now that he had no one to teach and only half a term's pay to live on; worst of all whether he would be there when the new term began, for Bill had a feeling he could not describe that Jim lived so precariously on the world's surface that he might at any time fall off into a void; for he feared that Jim was like himself, without a natural gravity to hold him on. He rehearsed the circumstances of their first meeting, and in particular Jim's enquiry regarding friendship, and he had a holy terror that just as he had failed his parents in love, so he had failed Jim, largely owing to the disparity in their ages. And that therefore Jim had moved on and was already looking somewhere else for a companion, scanning other schools with his pale eyes. He imagined also that, like himself, Jim had had a great attachment that had failed him, and which he longed to replace. But here Bill Roach's speculation met a dead end: he had no idea how adults loved each other.

There was so little he could do that was practical. He consulted a medical book and interrogated his mother about hunchbacks and he longed but did not dare to steal a bottle of his father's vodka and take it back to Thursgood's as a lure. And when at last his mother's chauffeur dropped him at the hated steps, he did not pause to say goodbye but ran for all he was worth to the top of the Dip, and there to his immeasurable joy was Jim's caravan in its same spot at the bottom, a shade dirtier than before, and a fresh patch of earth beside it, he supposed for winter vegetables. And Jim sitting on the step grinning up at him, as if he had heard Bill coming and got the grin of welcome ready before he appeared at the brink.

That same term, Jim invented a nickname for Roach. He dropped Bill and called him Jumbo instead. He gave no reason for this and Roach, as is common in the case of christenings, was in no position to object. In return, Roach appointed himself Jim's guardian; a regent-guardian, was how he thought of the appointment; a stand-in replacing Jim's departed friend, whoever that friend might be.

# TWO

Unlike Jim Prideaux, Mr George Smiley was not naturally equipped for hurrying in the rain, least of all at dead of night. Indeed, he might have been the final form for which Bill Roach was the prototype. Small, podgy and at best middle-aged, he was by appearance one of London's meek who do not inherit the earth. His legs were short, his gait anything but agile, his dress costly, ill-fitting and extremely wet. His overcoat, which had a hint of widowhood about it, was of that black, loose weave which is designed to retain moisture. Either the sleeves were too long or his arms too short for, as with Roach, when he wore his mackintosh, the cuffs all but concealed the fingers. For reasons of vanity he wore no hat, believing rightly that hats made him ridiculous. 'Like an egg cosy,' his beautiful wife had remarked not long before the last occasion on which she left him, and her criticism as so often had endured. Therefore the rain had formed in fat, unbanishable drops on the thick lenses of his spectacles, forcing him alternately to lower or throw back his head as he scuttled along the pavement which skirted the blackened arcades of Victoria Station. He was proceeding west, to the sanctuary of Chelsea where he lived. His step, for whatever reason, was a fraction uncertain, and if Jim Prideaux had risen out of the shadows demanding to know whether he had any friends, he would probably have answered that he preferred to settle for a taxi.

'Roddy's such a windbag,' he muttered to himself as a fresh deluge dashed itself against his ample cheeks, then trickled downward to his sodden shirt. 'Why didn't I just get up and leave?'

Ruefully, Smiley once more rehearsed the reasons for his present misery, and concluded with a dispassion inseparable from the humble part of his nature that they were of his own making.

It had been from the start a day of travail. He had risen too late after working too late the night before, a practice which had crept up on him since retirement last year. Discovering he had run out of coffee, he queued at the grocer's till he ran out of patience also, then haughtily decided to attend to his personal administration. His bank statement, which had arrived with the morning's post, revealed that his wife had drawn the lion's share of his monthly pension: very well, he decreed, he would sell something. The response was irrational for he was quite decently off, and the obscure City bank responsible for his pension paid it with regularity. Wrapping up an early edition of Grimmelshausen, nevertheless, a modest treasure from his Oxford days, he solemnly set off for Heywood Hill's bookshop in Curzon Street where he occasionally contracted friendly bargains with the proprietor. On the way he became even more irritable and from a callbox sought an appointment with his solicitor for that afternoon.

'George, how can you be so vulgar?' Nobody divorces Ann. Send her flowers and come to lunch.'

This advice bucked him up and he approached Heywood Hill with a merry heart only to walk slap into the arms of Roddy Martindale emerging from Trumper's after his weekly haircut.

Martindale had no valid claim on Smiley either professionally or socially. He worked on the fleshy side of the Foreign Office and his job consisted of lunching visiting dignitaries whom no one else would have entertained in his woodshed. He was a floating bachelor with a grey mane and that nimbleness which only fat men have. He affected buttonholes and pale suits, and he pretended on the flimsiest grounds to an intimate familiarity with the large backrooms of Whitehall. Some years ago, before it was disbanded, he had adorned a Whitehall working party to coordinate intelligence. In the war, having a certain mathematical facility, he had also haunted the fringes of the secret world; and once, as he never tired of telling, worked with John Landsbury on a Circus coding operation of transient delicacy. But the war, as Smiley sometimes had to remind himself, was thirty years ago.

'Hullo, Roddy,' said Smiley. 'Nice to see you.'

Martindale spoke in a confiding upper-class bellow of the sort which, on foreign holidays, had more than once caused Smiley to sign out of his hotel and run for cover.

'My dear boy, if it isn't the maestro himself! They told me you were locked up with the monks in St Gallen or somewhere, poring over manuscripts! Confess to me at once. I want to know all you've been doing, every little bit. Are you well? Do you love England still? How's the delicious Ann?' His restless gaze flicked up and down the street before lighting on the wrapped volume of Grimmelshausen under Smiley's arm. 'Pound to a penny that's a present for her. They tell me you spoil her outrageously.' His voice dropped to a mountainous murmur: 'I say, you're not back on the beat are you? Don't tell me it's all cover, George, *cover*?' His sharp tongue explored the moist edges of his little mouth, then, like a snake, vanished between its folds.

So, fool that he was, Smiley bought his escape by agreeing to dine that same evening at a club in Manchester Square to which they both belonged but which Smiley avoided like the pest, not least because Roddy Martindale was a member. When evening came he was still full of luncheon at the White Tower where his solicitor, a very self-indulgent man, had decided that only a great meal would recover George from his doldrums. Martindale, by a different route, had reached the same conclusion and for four long hours over food Smiley did not want they had bandied names as if they were forgotten footballers. Jebedee, who was Smiley's old tutor: '*Such* a loss to us, bless him,' Martindale murmured, who so far as Smiley knew had never clapped eyes on Jebedee. 'And what a talent for the game, eh? One of the real greats, I always say.' Then Fielding, the French medievalist from Cambridge: 'Oh, but what a *lovely* sense of humour. Sharp, mind, sharp!' Then Sparke from the School of Oriental Languages and lastly Steed-Asprey, who had founded that very club in order to escape from bores like Roddy Martindale.

'I knew his poor brother, you know. Half the mind and twice the brawn, bless him. Brain went all the other way.'

And Smiley through a fog of drink had listened to this nonsense, saying 'yes' and 'no' and 'what a pity' and 'no, they never found him' and once, to his abiding shame, 'oh come, you flatter me,' till with lugubrious inevitability Martindale came to more recent things, the change of power and Smiley's withdrawal from the service.

Predictably, he started with the last days of Control: 'Your old boss, George, bless him, the only one who ever kept his name a secret. Not from you, of course, he never had *any* secrets from you, George, did he? Close as thieves, Smiley and Control were, so they say, right to the end.'

'They're very complimentary.'

'Don't flirt, George. I'm an old trooper, you forget. You and Control were just like that.' Briefly the plump hands made a token marriage. 'That's why you were thrown out, don't deceive me, that's why Bill Haydon got your job. That's why he's Percy Alleline's cup bearer and you're not.'

'If you say so, Roddy.'

'I do. I say more than that. *Far* more.'

As Martindale drew closer Smiley caught the odour of one of Trumper's most sensitive creations.

'I say something else: Control never died at all. He's been seen.' With a fluttering gesture he silenced Smiley's protests. 'Let me finish. Willy Andrewartha walked straight into him in Jo'burg airport, in the waiting room. Not a ghost. Flesh. Willy was at the bar buying a soda for the heat, you haven't seen Willy recently but he's a balloon. He turned round and there was Control beside him dressed up like a ghastly Boer. The moment he saw Willy he bolted. How's that? So now we know. Control never died at all. He was driven out by Percy Alleline and his three-piece band so he went to ground in South Africa, bless him. Well, you can't blame him, can you? You can't blame a man for wanting a drop of peace in the evening of his life. I can't.'

The monstrosity of this, reaching Smiley through a thickening wall of spiritual exhaustion, left him momentarily speechless.

'That's ridiculous! That's the most idiotic story I every heard! Control is dead. He died of a heart attack after a long illness. Besides he hated South Africa. He hated everywhere except Surrey, the Circus and Lord's Cricket Ground. Really, Roddy, you mustn't tell stories like that.' He might have added: I buried him myself at a hateful crematorium in the East End, last Christmas eve, alone. The parson had a speech impediment.

'Willy Andrewartha was always the most God-awful liar,' Martindale reflected, quite unruffled. 'I said the same to him myself: "The sheerest nonsense, Willy, you should be ashamed of yourself".' And straight on as if never by thought or word had he subscribed to that silly view: 'It was the

Czech scandal that put the final nail into Control's coffin, I suppose. That poor fellow who was shot in the back and got himself into the newspapers, the one who was so thick with Bill Haydon always, so we hear. *Ellis*, we're to call him, and we still do, don't we, even if we know his real name as well as we know our own.'

Shrewdly Martindale waited for Smiley to cap this, but Smiley had no intention of capping anything so Martindale tried a third tack.

'Somehow I can never quite believe in Percy Alleline as Chief, can you? Is it age, George, or is it just my natural cynicism? Do tell me, you're so good at people. I suppose power sits poorly on those we've grown up with. Is that a clue? There are so few who can carry it off for me these days and poor Percy's such an *obvious* person, I always think, specially after that little serpent, Control. That heavy good fellowship; how can one take him seriously? One has only to think of him in the old days lolling in the bar of the Travellers', sucking away on that log pipe of his and buying drinks for the moguls; well, really, one does like one's perfidy to be subtle, don't you agree? Or don't you care as long as it's successful? What's his knack, George, what's his secret recipe?' He was speaking most intently, leaning forward, his eyes greedy and excited. Only food could otherwise move him so deeply. 'Living off the wits of his subordinates; well, maybe that's leadership these days.'

'Really, Roddy, I can't help you,' said Smiley weakly. 'I never knew Percy as a force, you see. Only as a –' He lost the word.

'A striver,' Martindale suggested, eyes glistening. 'With his sights on Control's purple, day and night. Now he's wearing it and the mob loves him. So who's his strong left arm, George? Who's earning him his reputation? Wonderfully well he's doing, we hear it from all sides. Little reading rooms at the Admiralty, little committees popping up with funny names, red carpet for Percy wherever he goes in the Whitehall corridors, junior ministers receiving special words of congratulation from on high, people one's never heard of getting grand medals for nothing. I've seen it all before, you know.'

'Roddy, I can't help you,' Smiley insisted, making to get up. 'You're out of my depth, truly.' But Martindale was physically restraining him, holding him at the table with one damp hand while he talked still faster.

'So who's the cleverboots? Not Percy, that's for sure. And don't tell me the Americans have started trusting us again either.' The grip tightened. 'Dashing Bill Haydon, our latter-day Lawrence of Arabia, bless him; there you are, it's Bill, your old rival.' Martindale's tongue poked out its head again, reconnoitred and withdrew, leaving a thin smile like a trail. 'I'm told that you and Bill shared *everything* once upon a time,' he said. 'Still he never was orthodox, was he? Genius never is.'

'Anything further you require, Mr Smiley?' the waiter asked.

'Then it's Bland: the shopsoiled white hope, the redbrick don.' Still he would not release him. 'And if those two aren't providing the speed, it's someone in retirement, isn't it? I mean someone pretending to be in retirement, don't I? And if Control's dead, who is there left? Apart from you.'

They were putting on their coats. The porters had gone home, they had to fetch them for themselves from the empty brown racks.

'Roy Bland's not redbrick,' Smiley said loudly. 'He was at St Antony's College Oxford, if you want to know.'

Heaven help me, it was the best I could do, thought Smiley.

'Don't be silly, dear,' Martindale snapped. Smiley had bored him: he looked sulky and cheated; distressing downward folds had formed on the lower contours of his cheeks. 'Of course St Antony's is redbrick, it makes no difference there's a little bit of sandstone in the same street, even if he was your protégé. I expect he's Bill Haydon's now – don't tip him, it's my party not yours. Father to them all Bill is, always was. Draws them like bees. Well, he has the glamour, hasn't he, not like some of us. Star quality I call it, one of the few. I'm told the women literally bow down before him, if that's what women do.'

'Good night, Roddy.'

'Love to Ann, mind.'

'I won't forget.'

'Well, don't.'

And now it was pouring with rain, Smiley was soaked to the skin and God as a punishment had removed all taxis from the face of London.

# THREE

'Sheer lack of willpower,' he told himself, as he courteously declined the suggestions of a lady in the doorway, 'One calls it politeness whereas in fact it is nothing but weakness. You *featherhead*, Martindale. You pompous, bogus, effeminate, non-productive . . . ' He stepped widely to avoid an unseen obstacle. 'Weakness,' he resumed, 'and an inability to live a self-sufficient life independent of institutions' – a puddle emptied itself neatly into his shoe – 'and emotional attachments which have long outlived their purpose. *Viz* my wife, *viz* the Circus, *viz* living in London. Taxi!'

Smiley lurched forward but was already too late. Two girls, giggling under one umbrella, clambered aboard in a flurry of arms and legs. Uselessly pulling up the collar of his black overcoat he continued his solitary march. 'Shopsoiled white hope,' he muttered furiously. 'Little bit of sandstone in the street. You bombastic, inquisitive, impertinent –'

And then of course he remembered far too late that he had left the Grimmelshausen at his club.

'Oh damn!' he cried *sopra voce*, halting in his tracks for greater emphasis. 'Oh damn, oh *damn*, oh damn.'

He would sell his London house: he had decided. Back there under the awning, crouched beside the cigarette machine, waiting for the cloudburst to end, he had taken this grave decision. Property values in London had risen out of proportion, he had heard it from every side. Good. He would sell and with a part of the proceeds buy a cottage in the Cotswolds. Burford? Too much traffic. Steeple Aston, that was a place. He would set up as a mild eccentric, discursive, withdrawn, but possessing one or two lovable habits such as muttering to himself as he bumbled along pavements. Out of date perhaps, but who wasn't these days? Out of date, but loyal to his own time. At a certain moment, after all, every man chooses: will he go forward, will he go back? There was nothing dishonourable in not being blown about by every little modern wind. Better to have worth, to entrench, to be an oak of one's own generation. And if Ann wanted to return, well, he would show her the door.

Or not show her the door according to, well, how much she wanted to return.

Consoled by these visions Smiley arrived at the King's Road, where he paused on the pavement as if waiting to cross. To either side, festive boutiques. Before him, his own Bywater Street, a cul-de-sac exactly one hundred and seventeen of his own paces long. When he had first come to live here these Georgian cottages had a modest, down-at-heel charm, with young couples making do on fifteen pounds a week and a tax-free lodger hidden in the basement. Now steel screens protected their lower windows and for each house three cars jammed the kerb. From long habit Smiley passed these in review, checking which were familiar, which were not; of the unfamiliar, which had aerials and extra mirrors, which were the closed vans that watchers like. Partly he did this as a test of memory, a private Kim's game to preserve his mind from the atrophy of retirement, just as on other days he learnt the names of the shops along his bus route to the British Museum; just as he knew how many stairs there were to each flight of his own house and which way each of the twelve doors opened.

But Smiley had a second reason which was fear, the secret fear that follows every professional to his grave. Namely, that one day, out of a past so complex that he himself could not remember all the enemies he might have made, one of them would find him and demand the reckoning.

At the bottom of the street a neighbour was exercising her dog; seeing him, she lifted her head to say something but he ignored her, knowing it would be about Ann. He crossed the road. His house was in darkness, the curtains were as he had left them. He climbed the six steps to the front door. Since Ann's departure, his cleaning woman had also left: no one but Ann had a key. There were two locks, a Banham deadlock and a Chubb Pipekey, and two splinters of his own manufacture, splits of oak each the size of a thumbnail, wedged into the lintel above and below the Banham. They were a hangover from his days in the field. Recently, without knowing why, he had started using them again; perhaps he didn't want her to take him by surprise. With the tips of his fingers he discovered each in turn. The routine over, he unlocked the door, pushed it open and felt the midday mail slithering over the carpet.

What was due? he wondered. *German Life and Letters*? *Philology*? *Philology*, he decided; it was already overdue. Putting on the hall light he stooped and peered through his post. One 'account rendered' from his tailor for a suit he had not ordered but which he suspected was one of those presently adorning Ann's lover; one bill from a garage in Henley for her petrol (what, pray, were they doing in Henley, broke, on the ninth of October?); one letter from the bank regarding a local cashing facility in favour of the Lady Ann Smiley at a branch of the Midland Bank in Immingham.

And what the devil, he demanded of this document, are they doing in Immingham? Who ever had a love affair in Immingham, for goodness' sake? Where *was* Immingham?

He was still pondering the question when his gaze fell upon an unfamiliar umbrella in the stand, a silk one with a stitched leather handle and a gold ring with no initial. And it passed through his mind with a speed which has no place in time that since the umbrella was dry it must have arrived there before six fifteen when the rain began, for there was no moisture in the stand either. Also that it was an elegant umbrella and the ferrule was barely scratched though it was not new. And that therefore the umbrella belonged to someone agile, even young, like Ann's latest swain. But that since its owner had known about the wedges and known how to put them back once he was inside the house, and had the wit to lay the mail against the door after disturbing and no doubt reading it, then most likely he knew Smiley too; and was not a lover but a professional like himself, who had at some time worked closely with him and knew his handwriting, as it is called in the jargon.

The drawing room door was ajar. Softly he pushed it further open.

'Peter?' he said.

Through the gap he saw by the light of the street two suède shoes, lazily folded, protruding from one end of the sofa.

'I'd leave that coat on if I were you, George, old boy,' said an amiable voice. 'We've got a long way to go.'

Five minutes later, dressed in a vast brown travelling coat, a gift from Ann and the only one he had that was dry, George Smiley was sitting crossly in the passenger seat of Peter Guillam's extremely draughty sports car, which he had parked in an adjoining square. Their destination was Ascot, a place famous for women and horses. And less famous perhaps as the residence of Mr Oliver Lacon of the Cabinet Office, a senior adviser to various mixed committees and a watch-dog of intelligence affairs. Or, as Guillam had it less reverentially, Whitehall's head prefect.

While at Thursgood's school, wakefully in bed, Bill Roach was contemplating the latest wonders which had befallen him in the course of his daily vigil over Jim's welfare. Yesterday Jim had amazed Latzy. Thursday he had stolen Miss Aaronson's mail. Miss Aaronson taught violin and scripture, Roach courted her for her tenderness. Latzy the assistant gardener was a DP, said Matron, and DPs spoke no English, or very little. DP meant Different Person, said Matron, or anyway foreign from the war. But yesterday Jim had spoken to Latzy, seeking his assistance with the car club, and he had spoken to him in DP, or whatever DPs speak, and Latzy had grown a foot taller on the spot.

The matter of Miss Aaronson's mail was more complex. There were two envelopes on the staffroom sideboard Thursday morning after chapel when Roach called for his form's exercise books, one addressed to Jim and one to Miss Aaronson. Jim's was typewritten. Miss Aaronson's was handwritten, in a hand not unlike Jim's own. The staffroom, while Roach made these observations, was empty. He helped himself to the exercise books and was quietly taking his leave when Jim walked in by the other door, red and blowing from his early walk.

'On your way, Jumbo, bell's gone,' stooping over the sideboard.

'Yes, sir.'

'Foxy weather, eh Jumbo?'

'Yes, sir.'

'On your way, then.'

At the door, Roach looked round. Jim was standing again, leaning back to open the morning's *Daily Telegraph*. The sideboard was empty. Both envelopes had gone.

Had Jim written to Miss Aaronson and changed his mind? Proposing marriage, perhaps? Another thought came to Bill Roach. Recently, Jim had acquired an old typewriter, a wrecked Remington which he had put right with his own hands. Had he typed his own letter on it? Was he so lonely that he wrote himself letters, and stole other people's as well? Roach fell asleep.

# FOUR

Guillam drove languidly but fast. Smells of autumn filled the car, a full moon was shining, strands of mist hung over open fields and the cold was irresistible. Smiley wondered how old Guillam was and guessed forty, but in that light he could have been an undergraduate sculling on the river; he moved the gear lever with a long flowing movement as if he were passing it through water. In any case, Smiley reflected irritably, the car was far too young for Guillam. They had raced through Runnymede and begun the run up Egham Hill. They had been driving for twenty minutes and Smiley had asked a dozen questions and received no answer worth a penny, and now a nagging fear was waking in him which he refused to name.

'I'm surprised they didn't throw you out with the rest of us,' he said, not very pleasantly, as he hauled the skirts of his coat more tightly round him. 'You had all the qualifications: good at your work, loyal, discreet.'

'They put me in charge of scalphunters.'

'Oh my Lord,' said Smiley with a shudder, and, pulling up his collar round his ample chins, he abandoned himself to that memory in place of others more disturbing: Brixton, and the grim flint schoolhouse that served the scalphunters as their headquarters. The scalphunters' official name was Travel. They had been formed by Control on Bill Haydon's suggestion in the pioneer days of the cold war, when murder and kidnapping and crash blackmail were common currency, and their first commandant was Haydon's nominee. They were a small outfit, about a dozen men, and they were to handle the hit-and-run jobs that were too dirty or too risky for the residents abroad. Good intelligence work, Control had always preached, was gradual and rested on a kind of gentleness. The scalphunters were the exception to his own rule. They weren't gradual and they weren't gentle either, thus reflecting Haydon's temperament rather than Control's. And they worked solo, which was why they were stabled out of sight behind a flint wall with broken glass and barbed wire on the top.

'I asked whether "lateralism" was a word to you.'

'It most certainly is not.'

'It's the 'in' doctrine. We used to go up and down. Now we go along.'

'What's that supposed to mean?'

'In your day the Circus ran itself by regions. Africa, satellites, Russia, China, South East Asia, you name it; each region was commanded by its own juju man, Control sat in heaven and held the strings. Remember?'

'It strikes a distant chord.'

'Well today everything operational is under one hat. It's called London Station. Regions are out, lateralism is in. Bill Haydon's Commander London Station, Roy Bland's his number two, Toby Esterhase runs between them like a poodle. They're a service within a service. They share their own secrets and don't mix with the proles. It makes us more secure.'

'It sounds a very good idea,' said Smiley, studiously ignoring the innuendo.

As the memories once more began seething upward into his conscious mind, an extraordinary feeling passed over him: that he was living the day twice, first with Martindale in the club, now again with Guillam in a dream. They passed a plantation of young pine trees. The moonlight lay in strips between them.

Smiley began, 'Is there any word of –' Then he asked, in a more tentative tone, 'What's the news of Ellis?'

'In quarantine,' said Guillam tersely.

'Oh I'm sure. Of course. I don't mean to pry. Merely, can he get around and so on? He did recover; he can walk? Backs can be terribly tricky, I understand.'

'The word says he manages pretty well. How's Ann, I didn't ask.'

'Fine. Just fine.'

It was pitch dark inside the car. They had turned off the road and were passing over gravel. Black walls of foliage rose to either side, lights appeared, then a high porch, and the steepled outline of a rambling house lifted above the treetops. The rain had stopped, but as Smiley stepped into the fresh air he heard all round him the restless ticking of wet leaves.

Yes, he thought, it was raining when I came here before; when the name Jim Ellis was headline news.

They had washed and in the lofty cloakroom inspected Lacon's climbing kit mawkishly dumped on the Sheraton chest of drawers. Now they sat in a half circle facing one empty chair. It was the ugliest house for miles around and Lacon had picked it up for a song. 'A Berkshire Camelot,' he had once called it, explaining it away to Smiley, 'built by a teetotal millionaire.' The drawing room was a great hall with stained-glass windows twenty feet high and a pine gallery over the entrance. Smiley counted off the familiar things: an upright piano littered with musical scores, old portraits of clerics in gowns, a wad of printed invitations. He looked for the Cambridge University oar and found it slung over the fireplace. The same fire was burning, too mean for the enormous grate. An air of need prevailing over wealth.

'Are you enjoying retirement, George?' Lacon asked, as if blurting into the

ear trumpet of a deaf aunt. 'You don't miss the warmth of human contact? I
rather would, I think. One's work, one's old buddies.'

He was a string bean of a man, graceless and boyish: church and spy
establishment, said Haydon, the Circus wit. His father was a dignitary of the
Scottish church and his mother something noble. Occasionally the smarter
Sundays wrote about him, calling him 'new-style' because he was young. The
skin of his face was clawed from hasty shaving.

'Oh I think I manage very well really, thank you,' said Smiley politely. And
to draw it out: 'Yes. Yes, I'm sure I do. And you? All goes well with you?'

'No big changes, no. All very smooth. Charlotte got her scholarship to
Roedean, which was nice.'

'Oh good.'

'And your wife, she's in the pink and so on?'

His expressions were also boyish.

'Very bonny, thank you,' said Smiley, trying gallantly to respond in kind.

They were watching the double doors. From far off they heard the jangle
of footsteps on a ceramic floor. Smiley guessed two people, both men. The
doors opened and a tall figure appeared half in silhouette. For the fraction of
a moment Smiley glimpsed a second man behind him, dark, small and
attentive; but only the one man stepped into the room before the doors were
closed by unseen hands.

'Lock us in please,' Lacon called, and they heard the snap of the key. 'You
know Smiley, don't you?'

'Yes, I think I do,' said the figure as he began the long walk towards them
out of the far gloom. 'I think he once gave me a job, didn't you, Mr Smiley?'

His voice was as soft as a southerner's drawl but there was no mistaking the
colonial accent. 'Tarr, sir. Ricki Tarr from Penang.'

A fragment of firelight illuminated one side of the stark smile and made a
hollow of one eye. 'The lawyer's boy, remember? Come on, Mr Smiley, you
changed my first nappies.'

And then absurdly they were all four standing and Guillam and Lacon
looked on like godparents while Tarr shook Smiley's hand once, then again,
then once more for the photographs.

'How are you, Mr Smiley? It's real nice to see you, sir.'

Relinquishing Smiley's hand at last he swung away in the direction of his
appointed chair, while Smiley thought: Yes, with Ricki Tarr it could have
happened. With Tarr, anything could have happened. My God, he thought;
two hours ago I was telling myself I would take refuge in the past. He felt
thirsty and supposed it was fear.

Ten? Twelve years ago? It was not his night for understanding time.
Among Smiley's jobs in those days was the vetting of recruits: no one was
taken on without his nod, no one trained without his signature on the
schedule. The cold war was running high, scalphunters were in demand, the
Circus's residences abroad had been ordered by Haydon to look out for likely
material. Steve Mackelvore from Djakarta came up with Tarr. Mackelvore
was an old pro with cover as a shipping agent and he found Tarr angry
drunk, kicking round the docks looking for a girl called Rose who had walked
out on him.

According to Tarr's story he was mixed up with a bunch of Belgians running guns between the islands and up-coast. He disliked Belgians and he was bored with gunrunning and he was angry because they'd stolen Rose. Mackelvore reckoned he would respond to discipline and was young enough to train for the type of mailfist operation that the scalphunters undertook from behind the walls of their glum Brixton schoolhouse. After the usual searches Tarr was forwarded to Singapore for a second look, then to the Nursery at Sarratt for a third. At that point Smiley came into the act as moderator at a succession of interviews, some hostile. Sarratt Nursery was the training compound, but it had space for other uses.

Tarr's father was an Australian solicitor living in Penang, it seemed. The mother was a small-time actress from Bradford who came East with a British drama group before the war. The father, Smiley recalled, had an evangelical streak and preached in local gospel halls. The mother had a small criminal record in England but Tarr's father either didn't know or didn't care. When the war came the couple evacuated to Singapore for the sake of their young son. A few months later Singapore fell and Ricki Tarr began his education in Changi jail under Japanese supervision. In Changi the father preached God's charity to everyone in sight, and if the Japs hadn't persecuted him his fellow prisoners would have done the job for them. With Liberation the three of them went back to Penang. Ricki tried to read for the law but more often broke it and the father turned some rough preachers loose on him to beat the sin out of his soul. Tarr flew the coop to Borneo. At eighteen he was a fully paid-up gunrunner playing all seven ends against the middle around the Indonesian islands, and that was how Mackelvore stumbled on him.

By the time he had graduated from the Nursery, the Malayan emergency had broken. Tarr was played back into gunrunning. Almost the first people he bumped into were his old Belgian friends. They were too busy supplying guns to the Communists to bother where he had been and they were shorthanded. Tarr ran a few shipments for them in order to blow their contacts, then one night got them drunk, shot four of them including Rose and set fire to their boat. He hung around Malaya and did a couple more jobs before being called back to Brixton and refitted for special operations in Kenya – or, in less sophisticated language, hunting Mau Mau for bounty.

After Kenya, Smiley pretty much lost sight of him, but a couple of incidents stuck in his memory because they might have become scandals and Control had to be informed. In sixty-four Tarr was sent to Brazil to make a crash offer of a bribe to an armaments minister known to be in deep water. Tarr was too rough; the minister panicked and told the press. Tarr had Dutch cover and no one was wiser except Netherlands intelligence, who were furious. In Spain a year later, acting on a tip-off supplied by Bill Haydon, Tarr blackmailed – or burned, as the scalphunters would say – a Polish diplomat who had lost his heart to a dancer. The first yield was good, Tarr won a commendation and a bonus. But when he went back for a second helping the Pole wrote a confession to his ambassador and threw himself, with or without encouragement, out of a high window.

In Brixton, they used to call him accident-prone. Guillam, by the expression on his immature but aging face, as they sat in their half circle round the meagre fire, called him a lot worse than that.

'Well, I guess I'd better make my pitch,' Tarr said pleasantly as he settled his easy body into the chair.

# FIVE

'It happened around six months ago,' Tarr began.

'April,' Guillam snapped. 'Just keep it precise, shall we, all the way along?'

'April, then,' Tarr said equably. 'Things were pretty quiet in Brixton. I guess there must have been half a dozen of us on stand-by. Pete Sembrini, he was in from Rome, Cy Vanhofer had just made a hit in Budapest' – he gave a mischievous smile – 'Ping-Pong and snooker in the Brixton waiting room. Right, Mr Guillam?'

'It was the silly season.'

When out of the blue, said Tarr, a flash requisition from Hong Kong residency.

'They had a low-grade Soviet trade delegation in town, chasing up electrical goods for the Moscow market. One of the delegates was stepping wide in the nightclubs. Name of Boris, Mr Guillam has the details. No previous record. They'd had the tabs on him for five days, and the delegation was booked in for twelve more. Politically it was too hot for the local boys to handle but they reckoned a crash approach might do the trick. The yield didn't look that special but so what? Maybe we'd just buy him for stock, right, Mr Guillam?'

Stock meant sale or exchange with another intelligence service: a commerce in small-time defectors handled by the scalphunters.

Ignoring Tarr, Guillam said: 'South East Asia was Tarr's parish. He was sitting around with nothing to do so I ordered him to make a site inspection and report back by cable.'

Each time someone else spoke Tarr sank into a dream. His gaze settled upon the speaker, a mistiness entered his eyes and there was a pause like a coming back before he began again.

'So I did what Mr Guillam ordered,' he said, 'I always do, don't I, Mr Guillam? I'm a good boy really, even if I am impulsive.'

He flew the next night, Saturday March 31st, with an Australian passport describing him as a car salesman and two virgin Swiss escape passports hidden in the lining of his suitcase. These were contingency documents to be filled in as circumstances demanded: one for Boris, one for himself. He made a car rendezvous with the Hong Kong resident not far from his hotel, the Golden Gate on Kowloon.

Here Guillam leaned over to Smiley and murmered:

'Tufty Thesinger, buffoon. Ex-major, King's African Rifles. Percy Alleline's appointment.'

Thesinger produced a report on Boris's movements based on one week's surveillance.

'Boris was a real oddball,' Tarr said, 'I couldn't make him out. He'd been boozing every night without a break. He hadn't slept for a week and Thesinger's watchers were folding at the knees. All day he trailed round after the delegation, inspecting factories, chiming in at discussions and being the bright young Soviet official.'

'How young?' Smiley asked.

Guillam threw in: 'His visa application gave him born Minsk forty-six.'

'Evening time, he'd go back to the Alexandra Lodge, an old shanty house out in North Point where the delegation had holed out. He'd eat with the crew, then around nine he'd ease out the side entrance, grab a taxi and belt over to the mainline night spots on Kowloon side. His favourite haunt was the Cat's Cradle in Queen's Road, where he bought drinks for local businessmen and acted like Mr Personality. He might stay there till midnight. From the Cradle he cut back through the tunnel to Wanchai, to a place called Angelika's where the drink was cheaper. Alone. Angelika's is a café with a hell-hole in the basement where the sailors and the tourists go, and Boris seemed to like that. He'd have three or four drinks and keep the receipts. Mainly he drank brandy but now and then he'd have a vodka to vary his diet. He'd had one tangle with a Eurasian girl along the way and Thesinger's watchers got after her and bought the story. She said he was lonely and sat on the bed moaning about his wife for not appreciating his genius. That was a real breakthrough,' he added sarcastically as Lacon noisily swooped on the little fire and stirred it, one coal against the other, into life. 'That night I went down to the Cradle and took a look at him. Thesinger's watchers had been sent to bed with a glass of milk. They didn't want to know.'

Sometimes as Tarr spoke an extraordinary stillness came over his body as if he were hearing his own voice played back to him.

'He arrived ten minutes after me and he brought his own company, a big blond Swede with a Chinese broad in tow. It was dark so I moved into a table nearby. They ordered Scotch, Boris paid and I sat six feet away watching the lousy band and listening to their conversation. The Swede asked Boris where he was staying, and Boris said the Excelsior which was a damn lie because he was staying at the Alexandra Lodge with the rest of the church outing. All right, the Alexandra is down the list: the Excelsior sounds better. About midnight the party breaks up. Boris says he's got to go home and tomorrow's a busy day. That was the second lie because he was no more going home than – what's the one, Jekyll and Hyde, right! – the regular doctor who dressed up and went on the razzle. So Boris was who?'

For a moment no one helped him.

'Hyde,' said Lacon to his scrubbed red hands. Sitting again, he had clasped them on his lap.

'Hyde,' Tarr repeated. 'Thank you, Mr Lacon; I always saw you as a literary man. So they settle the bill and I traipse over to Wanchai to be there ahead of him when he hits Angelika's. By this time I'm pretty sure I'm in the wrong ball game.'

On dry long fingers, Tarr studiously counted off the reasons: first, he never knew a Soviet delegation that didn't carry a couple of security gorillas whose job it was to keep the boys out of the fleshpots. So how did Boris slip the leash night after night? Second, he didn't like the way Boris pushed his foreign currency around. For a Soviet official that was against nature, he insisted: 'He just doesn't have any damn currency. If he does, he buys beads for his squaw. And three, I didn't like the way he lied. He was a sight too glib for decency.'

So Tarr waited at Angelika's, and sure enough half an hour later his Mr Hyde turned up all on his own. 'He sits down and calls for a drink. That's all he does. Sits and drinks like a damn wallflower!'

Once more it was Smiley's turn to receive the heat of Tarr's charm: 'So what's it all about, Mr Smiley? See what I mean? It's *little* things I'm noticing,' he confided, still to Smiley. 'Just take the way he sat. Believe me, sir, if we'd been in that place ourselves we couldn't have sat better than Boris. He had the pick of the exits and the stairway, he had a fine view of the main entrance and the action, he was right-handed and he was covered by a left-hand wall. Boris was a professional, Mr Smiley, there was no doubt of it whatsoever. He was waiting for a connect, working a letter-box maybe, or trailing his coat and looking for a pass from a mug like me. Well, now listen: it's one thing to burn a small-time trade delegate. It's quite a different ball game to swing your legs at a Centre-trained hood, right, Mr Guillam?'

Guillam said: 'Since the reorganization scalphunters have no brief to trawl for double agents. They must be turned over to London Station on sight. The boys have a standing order over Bill Haydon's own signature. If there's even a smell of the opposition, abandon.' He added, for Smiley's special ear: 'Under lateralism our autonomy is cut to the bone.'

'And I've been in double-double games before,' Tarr confessed in a tone of injured virtue. 'Believe me, Mr Smiley, they are a can of worms.'

'I'm sure they are,' said Smiley and gave a prim tug at his spectacles.

Tarr cabled Guillam 'no sale', booked a flight home and went shopping. However, since his flight didn't leave till Thursday he thought that before he left, just to pay his fare, he might as well burgle Boris's room.

'The Alexandra's a real ramshackle old place, Mr Smiley, off Marble Road, with a stack of wooden balconies. As for the locks, why, sir, they give up when they see you coming.'

In a very short time therefore Tarr was standing inside Boris's room with his back against the door, waiting for his eyes to grow accustomed to the dark. He was still standing there when a woman spoke to him in Russian drowsily from the bed.

'It was Boris's wife,' Tarr explained. 'She was crying. Look, I'll call her Irina, right? Mr Guillam has the details.'

Smiley was already objecting; wife was impossible, he said. Centre would never let them both out of Russia at the same time, they'd keep one and send the other –

'Common-law marriage,' Guillam said drily. 'Unofficial but permanent.'

'There's a lot that are the other way round these days,' said Tarr with a sharp grin at no one, least of all at Smiley, and Guillam shot him another foul look.

# SIX

From the outset of this meeting Smiley had assumed for the main a Buddha-like inscrutability from which neither Tarr's story nor the rare interjections of Lacon and Guillam could rouse him. He sat leaning back with his short legs bent, head forward and plump hands linked across his generous stomach.

His hooded eyes had closed behind the thick lenses. His only fidget was to polish his glasses on the silk lining of his tie, and when he did this his eyes had a soaked, naked look which was embarrassing to those who caught him at it. His interjection, however, and the donnish, inane sound which followed Guillam's explanation, now acted like a signal upon the rest of the gathering, bringing a shuffling of chairs and a clearing of throats.

Lacon was foremost: 'George, what are your drinking habits? Can I get you a Scotch or anything?' He offered drink solicitously, like aspirin for a headache. 'I forgot to say it earlier,' he explained. 'George, a bracer: come. It's winter, after all. A nip of something?'

'I'm fine, thank you,' Smiley said.

He would have liked a little coffee from the percolator but somehow he didn't feel able to ask. Also he remembered it was terrible.

'Guillam?' Lacon proceeded. No; Guillam also found it impossible to accept alcohol from Lacon.

He didn't offer anything to Tarr, who went straight on with his narrative.

Tarr took Irina's presence calmly, he said. He had worked up his fallback before he entered the building and now he went straight into his act. He didn't pull a gun or slap his hand over her mouth or any of that tripe, as he put it, but he said he had come to speak to Boris on a private matter, he was sorry and he was damn well going to sit there till Boris showed up. In good Australian, as became an outraged car salesman from down under, he explained that while he didn't want to barge into anyone's business he was damned if he was going to have his girl and his money stolen in a single night by a lousy Russian who couldn't pay for his pleasures. He worked up a lot of outrage but managed to keep his voice down and then he waited to see what she did.

And that, said Tarr, was how it all began.

It was eleven thirty when he made Boris's room. He left at one thirty with a promise of a meeting next night. By then the situation was all the other way: 'We weren't doing anything improper, mind. Just pen friends, right, Mr Smiley?'

For a moment, that bland sneer seemed to lay claim to Smiley's most precious secrets.

'Right,' he assented vapidly.

There was nothing exotic about Irina's presence in Hong Kong and no reason why Thesinger should have known of it, Tarr explained. Irina was a member of the delegation in her own right. She was a trained textile buyer: 'Come to think of it, she was a sight better qualified than her old man, if I can call him that. She was a plain kid, a bit blue-stocking for my taste, but she was young and she had one hell of a pretty smile when she stopped crying.' Tarr coloured quaintly. 'She was good company,' he insisted, as if arguing against a trend. 'When Mr Thomas from Adelaide came into her life she was at the end of the line from worrying what to do about the demon Boris. She thought I was the Angel Gabriel. Who could she talk to about her husband who wouldn't turn the dogs on him? She'd no chums on the delegation, she'd no one else she trusted even back in Moscow, she said. Nobody who hadn't been through it would ever know what it was like trying to keep a ruined relationship going while all the time you're on the move.' Smiley was once more in a deep trance. 'Hotel after hotel, city after city, not even allowed to speak to the natives in a natural way or get a smile from a stranger, that's how she described her life. She reckoned it was a pretty miserable state of affairs,

Mr Smiley, and there was a lot of God-thumping and an empty vodka bottle beside the bed to show for it. Why couldn't she be like normal people? she kept saying. Why couldn't she enjoy the Lord's sunshine like the rest of us? She loved sightseeing, she loved foreign kids, why couldn't she have a kid of her own? A kid born free, not in captivity. She kept saying that: born in captivity, born free. "I'm a jolly person, Thomas. I'm a normal, sociable girl. I like people: why should I deceive them when I like them?" And then she said, the trouble was that long ago she had been chosen for the work that made her frozen like an old woman and cut her off from God. So that's why she'd had a drink and why she was having a cry. She'd kind of forgotten her husband by then, she was apologizing for having a fling, more.' Again he faltered. 'I could scent it, Mr Smiley. There was gold in her. I could scent it from the start. Knowledge is power, they say, sir, and Irina had the power, same as she had quality. She was hellbent maybe, but she could still give her all. I can sense generosity in a woman where I meet it, Mr Smiley. I have a talent for it. And this lady was all set to be generous. Jesus, how do you describe a hunch? Some people can smell water under the ground . . .'

He seemed to expect some show of sympathy so Smiley said, 'I understand,' and plucked at the lobe of his ear.

Watching Smiley with a strange dependence in his expression, Tarr kept silent a stretch longer. 'First thing next morning I cancelled my flight and changed my hotel,' he said finally.

Abruptly Smiley opened his eyes wide. 'What did you tell London?'

'Nothing.'

'Why not?'

'Because he's a devious fool,' said Guillam.

'Maybe I thought Mr Guillam would say "Come home Tarr",' he replied, with a knowing glance at Guillam that was not returned. 'You see, long ago when I was a little boy I made a mistake and walked into a honey-trap.'

'He made an ass of himself with a Polish girl,' said Guillam. 'He sensed her generosity too.'

'I knew Irina was no honey-trap but how could I expect Mr Guillam to believe me? No way.'

'Did you tell Thesinger?'

'Hell, no.'

'What reason did you give London for postponing your flight?'

'I was due to fly Thursday. I reckoned no one back home would miss me till Tuesday. Specially with Boris being a dead duck.'

'He didn't give a reason and the housekeepers posted him absent without leave on the Monday,' said Guillam. 'He broke every rule in the book. And some that aren't. By the middle of that week even Bill Haydon was beating his wardrums. And I was having to listen,' he added tartly.

However that was, Tarr and Irina met next evening. They met again the evening after that. The first meeting was in a café and it limped. They took a lot of care not to be seen because Irina was frightened stiff, not just of her husband but of the security guards attached to the delegation, the gorillas as Tarr called them. She refused a drink and she was shaking. The second evening Tarr was still waiting on her generosity. They took the tram up to Victoria Peak, jammed between American matrons in white socks and eyeshades. The third he hired a car and drove her round the New Territories till she suddenly got the heebies about being so close to the Chinese border, so they had to run for harbour. Nevertheless she loved that trip and often spoke of the tidy beauty of it, the fish ponds and the paddy fields. Tarr also liked the trip because it proved to both of them that they weren't being watched. But Irina still had not unpacked, as he put it.

'Now I'll tell you a damn odd thing about this stage of the game. At the start, I worked Thomas the Aussie to death. I fed her a lot of smoke about a sheep station outside Adelaide and a big property in the high street with a glass front and "Thomas" in lights. She didn't believe me. She nodded and fooled around and waited till I'd said my piece, then she said "Yes, Thomas," "No, Thomas," and changed the subject.'

On the fourth evening he drove her into the hills overlooking North Shore and Irina told Tarr that she had fallen in love with him and that she was employed by Moscow Centre, she and her husband both, and that she knew Tarr was in the trade, too; she could tell by his alertness and the way he listened with his eyes.

'She'd decided I was an English colonel of intelligence,' said Tarr with no smile at all. 'She was crying one minute and laughing the next and in my opinion she was three-quarters of the way to being a basket case. Half, she talked like a pocket-book loony heroine, half like a nice up-and-down suburban kid. The English were her favourite people. Gentlemen, she kept saying. I'd brought her a bottle of vodka and she drank half of it in about fifteen seconds flat. Hooray for English gentlemen. Boris was the lead and Irina was the back-up girl. It was a his-and-hers act, and one day she'd talk to Percy Alleline and tell him a great secret all for himself. Boris was on a trawl for Hong Kong businessmen and had a postbox job on the side for the local Soviet residency. Irina ran courier, boiled down the microdots and played radio for him on a high-speed squirt to beat the listeners. That was how it read on paper, see? The two nightclubs were rendezvous and fallback for his local connect, in that order. But all Boris really wanted to do was drink and chase the dancing girls and have depressions. Or else go for five-hour walks because he couldn't stand being in the same room with his wife. All Irina did was wait around crying and getting plastered and fancy herself sitting alone at Percy's fireside telling him all she knew. I kept her there talking, up on the hill, sitting in the car. I didn't move because I didn't want to break the spell. We watched the dusk fall on the harbour and the lovely moon come up there, and the peasants slipping by with their long poles and kerosene lamps. All we needed was Humphrey Bogart in a tuxedo. I kept my foot on the vodka bottle and let her talk. I didn't move a muscle. Fact, Mr Smiley. Fact,' he declared, with the defencelessness of a man longing to be believed, but Smiley's eyes were closed and he was deaf to all appeal.

'She just completely let go,' Tarr explained, as if it were suddenly an accident, a thing he had had no part in. 'She told me her whole life-story from birth to Colonel Thomas; that's me. Mummy, Daddy, early loves, recruitment, training, her lousy half marriage, the lot. How her and Boris were teamed at training and had been together ever since: one of the great unbreakable relationships. She told me her real name, her workname and the cover names she'd travelled and transmitted by, then she hauled out her handbag and started showing me her conjuring set: recessed fountain pen, signal plan folded up inside; concealed camera, the works. "Wait till Percy sees that," I tell her – playing her along, like. It was production-line stuff, mind, nothing coach-built, but grade one material all the same. To round it off she starts barking the dirt about the Soviet Hong Kong set up: legmen, safe houses, letter-boxes, the lot. I was going crazy trying to remember it all.'

'But you did,' said Guillam shortly.

Yes, Tarr agreed; near on, he did. He knew she hadn't told him the whole truth, but he knew truth came hard to a girl who'd been a hood since puberty and he reckoned that for a beginner she was doing pretty nice.

'I kind of felt for her,' he said with another flash of that false confessiveness. 'I felt we were on the same wavelength, no messing.'

'Quite so,' said Lacon in a rare interjection. He was very pale, but whether that was anger or the effect of the grey light of early morning creeping through the shutters, there was no way to tell.

## SEVEN

'Now I was in a queer situation. I saw her next day and the day after and I reckoned that if she wasn't already schizoid she was going to be that way damn soon. One minute talking about Percy giving her a top job in the Circus working for Colonel Thomas, and arguing the hell with me about whether she should be a lieutenant or a major. Next minute saying she wouldn't spy for anybody ever again and she was going to grow flowers and rut in the hay with Thomas. Then she had a convent kick: Baptist nuns were going to wash her soul. I nearly died. Who the hell ever heard of Baptist nuns, I ask her? Never mind, she says, Baptists are the greatest, her mother was a peasant and knew. That was the second biggest secret she would ever tell me. "What's the biggest, then?" I ask. No dice. All she's saying is, we're in mortal danger, bigger than I could possibly know: there's no hope for either of us unless she has that special chat with Brother Percy. "What danger, for Christ's sake? What do you know that I don't?" She was vain as a cat but when I pressed her she clammed up and I was frightened to death she'd belt home and sing the lot to Boris. I was running out of time too. Then it was Wednesday already and the delegation was due to fly home to Moscow Friday. Her tradecraft wasn't all lousy but how could I trust a nut like that? You know how women are when they are in love, Mr Smiley. They can't hardly –'

Guillam had already cut him off. 'You just keep your head down, right?' he ordered, and Tarr sulked for a space.

'All I knew was, Irina wanted to defect – talk to Percy as she called it. She had three days left and the sooner she jumped the better for everybody. If I waited much longer she was going to talk herself out of it. So I took the plunge and walked in on Thesinger, first thing while he was opening up the shop.'

'Wednesday the eleventh,' Smiley murmured. 'In London the early hours of the morning.'

'I guess Thesinger thought I was a ghost. "I'm talking to London, personal for head of London Station," I said. He argued like hell but he let me do it. I sat at his desk and coded up the message myself from a one-time pad while Thesinger watched me like a sick dog. We had to top and tail it like trade code because Thesinger has export cover. That took me an extra half hour. I was nervy, I really was. Then I burnt the whole damn pad and typed the message on the ticker machine. At that point there wasn't a soul on earth but me who knew what the numbers meant on that sheet of paper, not Thesinger, nobody but me. I applied for full defector treatment for Irina on emergency procedure. I held out for all the goodies she'd never even talked about: cash, nationality, a new identity, no limelight and a place to live. After all, I was her business representative in a manner of speaking, wasn't I, Mr Smiley?'

Smiley glanced up as if surprised to be addressed. 'Yes,' he said quite kindly. 'Yes, I suppose in a manner of speaking that's what you were.'

'He also had a piece of the action, if I know him,' said Guillam under his breath.

Catching this or guessing the meaning of it, Tarr was furious.

'That's a damn lie!' he shouted, colouring deeply. 'That's a –' After glaring at Guillam a moment longer, he went back to his story.

'I outlined her career and her access, including jobs she'd had at Centre. I asked for inquisitors and an Air Force plane. She thought I was asking for a personal meeting with Percy Alleline on neutral ground but I reckoned we'd cross that bridge when we were past it. I suggested they should send out a couple of Esterhase's lamplighters to take charge of her, maybe a tame doctor as well.'

'Why lamplighters?' Smiley asked sharply. 'They're not allowed to handle defectors.'

The lamplighters were Toby Esterhase's pack, based not in Brixton but in Acton. Their job was to provide the support services for mainline operations: watching, listening, transport and safe houses.

'Ah well, Toby's come up in the world since your day, Mr Smiley,' Tarr explained. 'They tell me even his pavement artists ride around in Cadillacs. Steal the scalphunters' bread out of their mouths too, if they get the chance, right, Mr Guillam?'

'They've become the general footpads for London Station,' Guillam said shortly. 'Part of lateralism.'

'I reckoned it would take half a year for the inquisitors to clean her out, and for some reason she was crazy about Scotland. She had a great wish to spend the rest of her life there in fact. With Thomas. Raising our babies in the heather. I gave it to the London Station address group, I graded it flash and by hand of officer only.'

Guillam put in: 'That's the new formula for maximum limit. It's supposed to cut out handling in the coding rooms.'

'But not in London Station?' said Smiley.

'That's their affair.'

'You heard Bill Haydon got that job, I suppose?' said Lacon, jerking round on Smiley. 'Head of London Station? He's effectively their chief of operations, just as Percy used to be when Control was there. They've changed all the names, that's the thing. You know how your old buddies are about names. You ought to fill him in, Guillam, bring him up to date.'

'Oh I think I have the picture, thank you,' Smiley said politely. Of Tarr, with a deceptive dreaminess, he asked: 'She spoke of a great secret, you said?'

'Yes, sir.'

'Did you give any hint of this in your cable to London?'

He had touched something, there was no doubt of it; he had found a spot where touching hurt, for Tarr winced, and darted a suspicious glance at Lacon, then at Guillam.

Guessing his meaning, Lacon at once sang out a disclaimer: 'Smiley knows nothing beyond what you have so far told him in this room,' he said. 'Correct, Guillam?' Guillam nodded yes, watching Smiley.

'I told London the same as she'd told me,' Tarr conceded grumpily, like someone who has been robbed of a good story.

'What form of words, precisely?' Smiley asked. 'I wonder whether you remember that?'

'"Claims to have further information crucial to the well-being of the Circus, but not yet disclosed." Near enough, anyhow.'

'Thank you. Thank you very much.'

They waited for Tarr to continue.

'I also requested Head of London Station to inform Mr Guillam here that I'd landed on my feet and wasn't playing hookey for the hell of it.'

'Did that happen?' Smiley asked.

'Nobody said anything to me,' said Guillam drily.

'I hung around all day for an answer but by evening it still hadn't come. Irina was doing a normal day's work. I insisted on that, you see. She wanted to stage a light dose of fever to keep her in bed but I wouldn't hear of it. The delegation had factories to visit on Kowloon and I told her to tag along and look intelligent. I made her swear to keep off the bottle. I didn't want her involved in amateur dramatics at the last moment. I wanted it normal right up to when she jumped. I waited till evening then cabled a flash follow-up.'

Smiley's shrouded gaze fixed upon the pale face before him. 'You had an acknowledgement, of course?' he asked.

'"We read you." That's all. I sweated out the whole damn night. By dawn I still didn't have an answer. I thought: maybe that RAF plane is already on its way. London's playing it long, I thought, tying all the knots before they bring me in. I mean when you're that far away from them you *have* to believe they're good. Whatever you think of them, you *have* to believe that. And I mean now and then they are, right, Mr Guillam?'

No one helped him.

'I was worried about Irina, see? I was damn certain that if she had to wait another day she would crack. Finally the answer did come. It wasn't an answer at all. It was a stall:

'"Tell us what sections she worked in, names of former contacts and acquaintances inside Moscow Centre, name of her present boss, date of intake into Centre." Jesus I don't know what else. I drafted a reply fast because I had a three o'clock date with her down by the church –'

'What church?' Smiley again.

'English Baptist.' To everyone's astonishment, Tarr was once again blushing. 'She liked to visit there. Not for services, just to sniff around. I hung around the entrance looking natural but she didn't show. It was the first time she'd broken a date. Our fallback was for three hours later on the hilltop, then a one minute fifty descending scale back at the church till we met up. If she was in trouble she was going to leave her bathing suit on her window-sill. She was a swimming nut, swam every day. I shot round to the Alexandra: no bathing suit. I had two and a half hours to kill. There was nothing I could do any more except wait.'

Smiley said: 'What was the priority of London Station's telegram to you?'

'Immediate.'

'But yours was flash?'

'Both of mine were flash.'

'Was London's telegram signed?'

Guillam put in: 'They're not any more. Outsiders deal with London Station as a unit.'

'Was it decipher yourself?'

'No,' said Guillam.

They waited for Tarr to go on.

'I kicked around Thesinger's office but I wasn't too popular there, he doesn't approve of scalphunters and he has a big thing going on the Chinese mainland which he seemed to think I was going to blow for him. So I sat in a café and I had this idea I just might go down to the airport. It was an idea: like you might say, "maybe I'll go to a movie." I told the cab driver to go like hell. I didn't even argue the price. It got like a panic. I barged the Information queue and asked for all departures to Russia or connections in. I went nearly mad going through the flight lists, yelling at the Chinese clerks, but there wasn't a plane since yesterday and none till six tonight. But now I had this hunch. I had to know. What about charters, what about the unscheduled flights, freight, casual transit? Had nothing, but *really* nothing, been routed for Moscow since yesterday morning? Then this little girl comes through with the answer, one of the Chinese hostesses. She fancies me, see. She's doing me a favour. An unscheduled Soviet plane had taken off two hours ago. Only four passengers boarded. The centre of attraction was a woman invalid. A lady. In a coma. They had to cart her to the plane on a stretcher and her face was wrapped in bandages. Two male nurses went with her and one doctor, that was the party. I called the Alexandra as a last hope. Neither Irina nor her fake husband had checked out of their room but there was no reply. The lousy hotel didn't even know they'd left.'

Perhaps the music had been going on a long time and Smiley only noticed it now. He heard it in imperfect fragments from different parts of the house: a scale on a flute, a child's tune on a recorder, a violin piece more confidently played. The many Lacon daughters were waking up.

# EIGHT

'Perhaps she *was* ill,' said Smiley stolidly, speaking more to Guillam than anyone else. 'Perhaps she *was* in a coma. Perhaps they were real nurses who took her away. By the sound of her she was a pretty good mess, at best.' He added, with half a glance at Tarr: 'Ater all, only twenty-four hours had elapsed between your first telegram and Irina's departure. You can hardly lay it at London's door on that timing.'

'You can *just*,' said Guillam, looking at the floor. 'It's extremely fast, but it does just work, if somebody in London –' They were all waiting. 'If somebody in London had very good footwork. And in Moscow too, of course.'

'Now that's exactly what I told myself, sir,' said Tarr proudly, taking up Smiley's point and ignoring Guillam's. 'My very words, Mr Smiley. Relax, Ricki, I said, you'll be shooting at shadows if you're not damn careful.'

'Or the Russians tumbled to her,' Smiley insisted. 'The security guards found out about your affair and removed her. It would be a wonder if they *hadn't* found out, the way you two carried on.'

'Or she told her husband,' Tarr suggested. 'I understand psychology as well as the next man, sir. I know what can happen between a husband and wife when they have fallen out. She wishes to annoy him. To goad him, to obtain a reaction, I thought. "Want to hear what I've been doing while you've been out boozing and cutting the rug?" – like that. Boris peels off and tells the gorillas, they sandbag her and take her home. I went through all those possibilities, Mr Smiley, believe me. I really worked on them, truth. Same as any man does whose woman walks out on him.'

'Let's just have the story, shall we?' Guillam whispered, furious.

Well now, said Tarr, he would agree that for twenty-four hours he went a bit berserk: 'Now I don't often get that way, right, Mr Guillam?'

'Often enough.'

'I was feeling pretty physical. Frustrated, you could almost say.'

His conviction that a considerable prize had been brutally snatched away from him drove him to a distracted fury which found expression in a rampage through old haunts. He went to the Cat's Cradle, then to Angelika's and by dawn he had taken in half a dozen other places besides, not to mention a few girls along the way. At some point he crossed town and raised a spot of dust around the Alexandra. He was hoping to have a couple of words with those security gorillas. When he sobered down he got thinking about Irina and their time together, and he decided before he flew back to London to go round their dead letter-boxes to check whether by any chance she had written to him before she left.

Partly it was something to do. 'Partly I guess I couldn't bear to think of a letter of hers kicking around in a hole in the wall while she sweated it out in the hot seat,' he added, the ever-redeemable boy.

They had two places where they dropped mail for one another. The first was not far from the hotel on a building site.

'Ever seen that bamboo scaffolding they use? Fantastic. I've seen it twenty storeys high and the coolies swarming over it with slabs of precast concrete.' A bit of discarded piping, he said, handy at shoulder height. It seemed most likely, if Irina was in a hurry, that the piping was the letter-box she would use, but when Tarr went there it was empty. The second was back by the church, 'in under where they stow the pamphlets,' as he put it. 'This stand was part of an old wardrobe, see. If you kneel in the back pew and grope around, there's a loose board. Behind the board there's a recess full of rubbish and rat's mess. I tell you, it made a real lovely drop, the best ever.'

There was a short pause, illuminated by the vision of Ricki Tarr and his Moscow Centre mistress kneeling side by side in the rear pew of a Baptist church in Hong Kong.

In this dead letter-box, Tarr said, he found not a letter but a whole damn diary. The writing was fine and done on both sides of the paper so that quite often the black ink came through. It was fast urgent writing with no erasures. He knew at a glance that she had maintained it in her lucid periods.

'This isn't it, mind. This is only my copy.'

Slipping a long hand inside his shirt he had drawn out a leather purse attached to a broad thong of hide. From it he took a grimy wad of paper.

'I guess she dropped the diary just before they hit her,' he said. 'Maybe she was having a last pray at the same time. I made the translation myself.'

'I didn't know you spoke Russian,' said Smiley – a comment lost to everyone but Tarr, who at once grinned.

'Ah, now, a man needs a qualification in this profession, Mr Smiley,' he explained as he separated the pages. 'I may not have been too great at law but a further language can be decisive. You know what the poets say, I expect?' He looked up from his labours and his grin widened. '"To possess another language is to possess another soul." A great king wrote that, sir, Charles the Fifth. My father never forgot a quotation, I'll say that for him, though the funny thing is he couldn't speak a damn thing but English. I'll read the diary aloud to you if you don't mind.'

'He hasn't a word of Russian to his name,' said Guillam. 'They spoke English all the time. Irina had done a three-year English course.'

Guillam had chosen the ceiling to look at, Lacon his hands. Only Smiley was watching Tarr, who was laughing quietly at his own little joke.

'All set?' he enquired. 'Right then, I'll begin. "Thomas, listen, I am talking to you." She called me by my surname,' he explained. 'I told her I was Tony but it was always Thomas, right? "This diary is my gift for you in case they take me away before I speak to Alleline. I would prefer to give you my life, Thomas, and naturally my body, but I think it more likely that this wretched secret will be all I have to make you happy. Use it well!"' Tarr glanced up. 'It's marked Monday. She wrote the diary over the four days.' His voice had become flat, almost bored. '"In Moscow Centre there is more gossip than our superiors would wish. Especially the little fellows like to make themselves grand by appearing to be in the know. For two years before I was attached to the Trade Ministry I worked as a supervisor in the filing department of our headquarters in Dzerzhinsky Square. The work was so boring, Thomas, the atmosphere was not happy and I was unmarried. We were encouraged to be suspicious of one another; it is such a strain never to give your heart, not once. Under me was a clerk named Ivlov. Though Ivlov was not socially or in rank my equal the oppressive atmosphere brought out a mutuality in our temperaments. Forgive me, sometimes only the body can speak for us, you should have appeared earlier, Thomas! Several times Ivlov and I worked night shifts together and eventually we agreed to defy regulations and meet outside the building. He was blond, Thomas, like you, and I wanted him. We met in a café in a poor district of Moscow. In Russia we are taught that Moscow has no poor districts but this is a lie. Ivlov told me that his real name was Brod but he was not a Jew. He brought me some coffee sent to him illicitly by a comrade in Teheran, he was very sweet, also some stockings. Ivlov told me that he admired me greatly and that he had once worked in a section responsible for recording the particulars of all the foreign agents employed by Centre. I laughed and told him that no such record existed, it was an idea of dreamers to suppose that so many secrets would be in one place. Well, we were both dreamers I suppose.'"

Again Tarr broke off: 'We get a new day,' he announced. 'She kicks off with a lot of "good morning Thomas's," prayers and a bit of love-talk. A woman can't write to the air, she says, so she's writing to Thomas. Her old man's gone out early, she's got an hour to herself. Okay?'

Smiley grunted.

"'On the second occasion with Ivlov I met him in the room of a cousin of Ivlov's wife, a teacher at Moscow State University. No-one else was present. The meeting, which was extremely secret, involved what in a report we would call an incriminating act. I think, Thomas, you yourself once or twice committed such an act! Also at this meeting Ivlov told me the following story to bind us in ever closer friendship. Thomas, you must take care. Have you heard of Karla? He is an old fox, the most cunning in the Centre, the most secret, even his name is not one that Russians understand. Ivlov was extremely frightened to tell me this story, which according to Ivlov concerned a great conspiracy, perhaps the greatest we have. The story of Ivlov is as follows. You should tell it only to *most trustworthy people*, Thomas, because of its extremely conspiratorial nature. You must tell no one in the Circus, for no one can be trusted until the riddle is solved. Ivlov said it was not true that he once worked on agent records. He had invented this story only to show me the great depth of his knowledge concerning the Centre's affairs and to assure me that I was not in love with a nobody. The truth was he had worked for Karla as a helper in one of Karla's great conspiracies and he had actually been stationed in England in a conspiratorial capacity, under the cover of being a driver and assistant coding clerk at the Embassy. For this task he was provided with the workname Lapin. Thus Brod became Ivlov and Ivlov became Lapin: of this poor Ivlov was extremely proud. I did not tell him what Lapin means in French. That a man's wealth should be counted by the number of his names! Ivlov's task was to service a mole. A mole is a deep penetration agent so called because he burrows deep into the fabric of Western imperialism, in this case an Englishman. Moles are very precious to the Centre because of the many years it takes to place them, often fifteen or twenty. Most of the English moles were recruited by Karla before the war and came from the higher bourgeoisie, even aristocrats and nobles who were disgusted with their origins, and became secretly fanatic, much more fanatic than their working-class English comrades who are slothful. Several were applying to join the Party when Karla stopped them in time and directed them to special work. Some fought in Spain against Franco Fascism and Karla's talent-spotters found them there and turned them over to Karla for recruitment. Others were recruited in the war during the alliance of expediency between Soviet Russia and Britain. Others afterwards, disappointed that the war did not bring Socialism to the West . . . ." It kind of dries up here,' Tarr announced without looking anywhere but at his own manuscript. 'I wrote down: "dries up." I guess her old man came back earlier than she expected. The ink's all blotted. God knows where she stowed the damn thing. Under the mattress maybe.'

If this was meant as a joke, it failed.

'"The mole whom Lapin serviced in London was known by the code name Gerald. He had been recruited by Karla and was the object of extreme conspiracy. The servicing of moles is performed only by comrades with a very high standard of ability, said Ivlov. Thus while in appearance Ivlov-Lapin was at the Embassy a mere nobody, subjected to many humiliations on account of his apparent insignificance, such as standing with women behind the bar at functions, by right he was a great man, the secret assistant to Colonel Gregor Viktorov whose workname at the Embassy is Polyakov."'

Here Smiley made his one interjection, asking for the spelling. Like an actor disturbed in midflow, Tarr answered rudely: 'P-o-l-y-a-k-o-v, got it?'

'Thank you,' said Smiley with unshakable courtesy, in a manner which conveyed conclusively that the name had no significance for him whatever. Tarr resumed.

'"Viktorov is himself an old professional of great cunning, said Ivlov. His cover job is cultural attaché and that is how he speaks to Karla. As Cultural Attaché Polyakov he organises lectures to British universities and societies concerning cultural matters in the Soviet Union, but his nightwork as Colonel Gregor Viktorov is briefing and debriefing the mole Gerald on instruction from Karla at Centre. For this purpose Colonel Viktorov-Polyakov uses legmen and poor Ivlov was for a while one. Nevertheless it is Karla in Moscow who is the real controller of the mole Gerald."'

'Now it really changes,' said Tarr. 'She's writing at night and she's either plastered or scared out of her pants because she's going all over the damn page. There's talk about footsteps in the corridor and the dirty looks she's getting from the gorillas. Not transcribed, right, Mr Smiley?' And, receiving a small nod, he went on: '"The measures for the mole's security were remarkable. Written reports from London to Karla at Moscow Centre even after coding were cut in two and sent by separate couriers, others in secret inks underneath orthodox Embassy correspondence. Ivlov told me that the mole Gerald produced at times more conspiratorial material than Viktorov-Polyakov could conveniently handle. Much was on undeveloped film, often thirty reels in a week. Anyone opening the container in the wrong fashion at once exposed the film. Other material was given by the mole in speeches, at extremely conspiratorial meetings, and recorded on special tape that could only be played through complicated machines. This tape was also wiped clean by exposure to light or to the wrong machine. The meetings were of the crash type, always different, always sudden, that is all I know except that it was the time when the Fascist aggression in Vietnam was at its worst; in England the extreme reactionaries had again taken the power. Also that according to Ivlov-Lapin the mole Gerald was a high functionary in the Circus. Thomas, I tell you this because, since I love you, I have decided to admire all English, you most of all. I do not wish to think of an English gentleman behaving as a traitor, though naturally I believe he was right to join the workers' cause. Also I fear for the safety of anyone employed by the Circus in a conspiracy. Thomas, I love you, take care with this knowledge, it could hurt you also. Ivlov was a man like you, even if they called him Lapin . . ."' Tarr paused diffidently. 'There's a bit at the end which . . .'

'Read it,' Guillam murmured.

Lifting the wad of paper slightly sideways, Tarr read in the same flat drawl; '"Thomas, I am telling you this also because I am afraid. This morning when I woke he was sitting on the bed, staring at me like a madman. When I went downstairs for coffee the guards Trepov and Novikov watched me like animals, eating very carelessly. I am sure they had been there hours, also from the Residency Avilov sat with them, a boy. Have you been indiscreet, Thomas? Did you tell more than you let me think? Now you see why only Alleline would do. You need not blame yourself, I can guess what you have told them. In my heart I am free. You have seen only the bad things in me, the drink, the fear, the lies we live. But deep inside me burns a new and blessed light. I used to think that the secret world was a separate place and that I was banished for ever to an island of half people. But Thomas it is not separate. God has shown me that it is here, right in the middle of the real world, all round us, and we have only to open the door and step outside to be free. Thomas, you must always long for the light which I have found. It is called love. Now I shall take this to our secret place, and leave it there while there is still time. Dear God I hope there is. God give me sanctuary in His Church. Remember it: I loved you there also."' He was extremely pale and his hands, as he pulled open his shirt to return the diary to its purse, were trembling and moist. 'There's a last bit,' he said. 'It goes: "Thomas, why could you remember so few prayers from your boyhood? Your father was a great and good man." Like I told you,' he explained, 'she was crazy.'

Lacon had opened the blinds and now the full white light of day was pouring into the room. The windows looked on to a small paddock where Jackie Lacon, a fat little girl in plaits and a hard hat, was cautiously cantering her pony.

# NINE

Before Tarr left, Smiley asked a number of questions of him. He was gazing not at Tarr but myopically into the middle distance, his pouchy face despondent from the tragedy.

'Where is the original of that diary?'

'I put it straight back in the dead letter-box. Figure it this way, Mr Smiley: by the time I found the diary Irina had been in Moscow twenty-four hours. I guessed she wouldn't have a lot of breath when it came to the interrogation. Most likely they'd sweated her on the plane, then a second going over when she touched down, then question one as soon as the big boys had finished their breakfast. That's the way they do it to the timid ones: the arm first and the questions after, right? So it might be only a matter of a day or two before Centre sent along a footpad to take a peek round the back of the church, okay?' Primly again: 'Also I had my own welfare to consider.'

'He means that Moscow Centre would be less interested in cutting his throat if they thought he hadn't read the diary,' said Guillam.

'Did you photograph it?'

'I don't carry a camera. I bought a dollar notebook. I copied the diary into the notebook. The original I put back. The whole job took me four hours flat.' He glanced at Guillam, then away from him. In the fresh daylight, a deep inner fear was suddenly apparent in Tarr's face. 'When I got back to the hotel, my room was a wreck; they'd even stripped the paper off the walls. The manager told me, "Get the hell out". He didn't want to know.'

'He's carrying a gun,' said Guillam. 'He won't part with it.'

'You're damn right I won't.'

Smiley offered a dyspeptic grunt of sympathy: 'These meetings you had with Irina: the dead letter-boxes, the safety signals and fallbacks. Who proposed the tradecraft: you or she?'

'She did.'

'What were the safety signals?'

'Body talk. If I wore my collar open she knew I'd had a look around and I reckoned the coast was clear. If I wore it closed, scrub the meeting till the fallback.'

'And Irina?'

'Handbag. Left hand, right hand. I got there first and waited up somewhere she could see me. That gave her the choice: whether to go ahead or split.'

'All this happened more than six months ago. What have you been doing since?'

'Resting,' said Tarr rudely.

Guillam said: 'He panicked and went native. He bolted to Kuala Lumpur, then lay up in one of the hill villages. That's his story. He has a daughter called Danny.'

'Danny's my little kid.'

'He shacked up with Danny and her mother,' said Guillam, talking, as was his habit, clean across anything Tarr said. 'He's got wives scattered across the globe but she seems to lead the pack just now.'

'Why did you choose this particualar moment to come to us?'

Tarr said nothing.

'Don't you want to spend Christmas with Danny?'

'Sure.'

'So what happened? Did something scare you?'

'There was rumours,' said Tarr sullenly.

'What sort of rumours?'

'Some Frenchman turned up in KL telling them all I owed him money. Wanted to get some lawyer hounding me. I don't owe anybody money.'

Smiley returned to Guillam. 'At the Circus he's still posted as a defector?'

'Presumed.'

'What have they done about it so far?'

'It's out of my hands. I heard on the grapevine that London Station held a couple of war parties over him a while back but they didn't invite me and I don't know what came of them. Nothing, I should think, as usual.'

'What passport's he been using?'

Tarr had his answer ready: 'I threw away Thomas the day I hit Malaya. I

reckoned Thomas wasn't exactly the flavour of the month in Moscow and I'd
do better to kill him off right there. In KL I had them run me up a British
passport, name of Poole.' He handed it to Smiley. 'It's not bad for the money.'

'Why didn't you use one of your Swiss escapes?'

Another wary pause.

'Or did you lose them when your hotel room was searched?'

Guillam said: 'He cached them as soon as he arrived in Hong Kong.
Standard practice.'

'So why didn't you use them?'

'They were numbered, Mr Smiley. They may have been blank but they
were numbered. I was feeling a mite windy, frankly. If London had the
numbers, maybe Moscow did too, if you take my meaning.'

'So what did you do with your Swiss escapes?' Smiley repeated pleasantly.

'He says he threw them away,' said Guillam. 'He sold them more likely. Or
swapped them for that one.'

'How? Threw them away how? Did you burn them?'

'That's right, I burned them,' said Tarr, with a nervy ring to his voice, half a
threat, half fear.

'So when you say this Frenchman was enquiring for you –'

'He was looking for Poole.'

'But who else ever heard of Poole, except the man who faked this passport?'
Smiley asked, turning the pages. Tarr said nothing. 'Tell me how you
travelled to England,' Smiley suggested.

'Soft route from Dublin. No problem.' Tarr lied badly under pressure.
Perhaps his parents were to blame. He was too fast when he had no answer
ready, too aggressive when he had one up his sleeve.

'How did you get to Dublin?' Smiley asked, checking the border stamps on
the middle page.

'Roses.' He had recovered his confidence. 'Roses all the way. I've got a girl
who's an air hostess with South African. A pal of mine flew me cargo to the
Cape, at the Cape my girl took care of me then hitched me a free ride to
Dublin with one of the pilots. As far as anyone back East knows I never left
the peninsula.'

'I'm doing what I can to check,' said Guillam to the ceiling.

'Well you be damn careful, baby,' Tarr snapped down the line to Guillam.
'Because I don't want the wrong people on my back.'

'Why did you come to Mr Guillam?' Smiley enquired, still deep in Poole's
passport. It had a used, well-thumbed look, neither too full nor too empty.
'Apart from the fact that you were frightened, of course.'

'Mr Guillam's my boss,' said Tarr virtuously.

'Did it cross your mind he might just turn you straight over to Alleline?
After all, you're something of a wanted man as far as the Circus top brass is
concerned, aren't you?'

'Sure. But I don't figure Mr Guillam's any fonder of the new arrangement
than you are Mr Smiley.'

'He also loves England,' Guillam explained with mordant sarcasm.

'Sure. I got homesick.'

'Did you ever consider going to anyone else but Mr Guillam? Why not one
of the overseas residencies, for instance, where you were in less danger? Is
Mackelvore still head man in Paris?' Guillam nodded. 'There you are, then:

you could have gone to Mr Mackelvore. He recruited you, you can trust him: he's old Circus. You could have sat safely in Paris instead of risking your neck over here. Oh dear God. Lacon quick!'

Smiley had risen to his feet, the back of one hand pressed to his mouth as he stared out of the window. In the paddock Jackie Lacon was lying on her stomach screaming while a riderless pony careered between the trees. They were still watching as Lacon's wife, a pretty woman with long hair and thick winter stockings, bounded over the fence and gathered the child up.

'They're often taking tumbles,' Lacon remarked, quite cross. 'They don't hurt themselves at that age.' And scarcely more graciously: 'You're not responsible for everyone, you know, George.'

Slowly they settled again.

'And if you had been making for Paris,' Smiley resumed, 'which route would you have taken?'

'The same till Ireland then Dublin-Orly I guess. What do you expect me to do: walk on the damn water?'

At this Lacon coloured and Guillam with an angry exclamation rose to his feet. But Smiley seemed quite unbothered. Taking up the passport again he turned slowly back to the beginning.

'And how did you get in touch with Mr Guillam?'

Guillam answered for him, speaking fast: 'He knew where I garage my car. He left a note on it saying he wanted to buy it and signed it with his workname Trench. He suggested a place to meet and put in a veiled plea for privacy before I took my trade elsewhere. I brought Fawn along to babysit –'

Smiley interrupted: 'That was Fawn at the door just now?'

'He watched my back while we talked,' Guillam said. 'I've kept him with us ever since. As soon as I'd heard Tarr's story, I rang Lacon from a callbox and asked for an interview. George, why don't we talk this over among ourselves?'

'Rang Lacon down here or in London?'

'Down here,' said Lacon.

There was a pause till Guillam explained: 'I happened to remember the name of a girl in Lacon's office. I mentioned her name and said she had asked me to speak to him urgently on an intimate matter. It wasn't perfect but it was the best I could think of on the spur of the moment.' He added, filling the silence, 'Well damn it, there was no *reason* to suppose the phone was tapped.'

'There was every reason.'

Smiley had closed the passport and was examining the binding by the light of a tattered reading lamp at his side. 'This is rather good, isn't it?' he remarked lightly. 'Really very good indeed. I'd say that was a professional product. I can't find a blemish.'

'Don't worry, Mr Smiley,' Tarr retorted, taking it back, 'it's not made in Russia.' By the time he reached the door his smile had returned. 'You know something?' he said, addressing all three of them down the aisle of the long room. 'If Irina is right, you boys are going to need a whole new Circus. So if we all stick together I guess we could be in on the ground floor.' He gave the door a playful tap. 'Come on, darling, it's me, Ricki.'

'Thank you! It's all right now! Open up, please,' Lacon shouted and a moment later the key was turned, the dark figure of Fawn the babysitter flitted into view and the four footsteps faded into the big hollows of the house, to the distant accompaniment of Jackie Lacon's crying.

# TEN

On another side of the house, away from the pony paddock a grass tennis court was hidden among the trees. It was not a good tennis court; it was mown seldom. In spring the grass was sodden from the winter and no sun got in to dry it, in summer the balls disappeared into the foliage and this morning it was ankle deep in frosted leaves that had collected here from all over the garden. But round the outside, roughly following the wire rectangle, a footpath wandered between some beech trees and here Smiley and Lacon wandered also. Smiley had fetched his travelling coat but Lacon wore only his threadbare suit. For this reason perhaps he chose a brisk, if uncoordinated, pace which with each stride took him well ahead of Smiley so that he had constantly to hover, shoulders and elbows lifted, waiting till the shorter man caught up. Then he promptly bounded off again, gaining ground. They completed two laps in this way before Lacon broke the silence.

'When you came to me a year ago with a similar suggestion, I'm afraid I threw you out. I suppose I should apologize. I was remiss.' There was a suitable silence while he pondered his dereliction. 'I instructed you to abandon your enquiries.'

'You told me they were unconstitutional,' Smiley said mournfully, as if he were recalling the same sad error.

'Was that the word I used? Good Lord, how very pompous of me!'

From the direction of the house came the sound of Jackie's continued crying.

'You never had any, did you?' Lacon piped at once, his head lifted to the sound.

'I'm sorry?'

'Children. You and Ann.'

'No.'

'Nephews, nieces?'

'One nephew.'

'On your side?'

'Hers.'

Perhaps I never left the place, he thought, peering around him at the tangled roses, the broken swings and sodden sandpits, the raw, red house so shrill in the morning light. Perhaps we're still here from last time.

Lacon was apologizing again: 'Dare I say I didn't absolutely trust your motives? It rather crossed my mind that Control had put you up to it, you see. As a way of hanging on to power and keeping Percy Alleline out' – swirling away again, long strides, wrists outward.

'Oh no, I assure you Control knew nothing about it at all.'

'I realize that now. I didn't at the time. It's a little difficult to know when to trust you people and when not. You do live by rather different standards, don't you? I mean you have to. I accept that. I'm not being judgmental. Our aims are the same after all, even if our methods are different' – bounding over a cattle ditch – 'I once heard someone say morality was method. Do you hold with that? I suppose you wouldn't. You would say that morality was vested in the aim, I expect. Difficult to know what one's aims *are*, that's the trouble, specially if you're British. We can't expect you people to determine our *policy* for us, can we? We can only ask you to further it. Correct? Tricky one, that.'

Rather than chase after him, Smiley sat on a rusted swing seat and huddled himself more tightly in his coat, till finally Lacon stalked back and perched beside him. For a while they rocked together to the rhythm of the groaning springs.

'Why the devil did she choose Tarr?' Lacon muttered at last, fiddling his long fingers. 'Of all people in the world to choose for a confessor, I can imagine none more miserably unsuitable.'

'I'm afraid you'll have to ask a woman that question, not us,' said Smiley, wondering again where Immingham was.

'Oh indeed,' Lacon agreed lavishly. 'All that's a complete mystery. I'm seeing the Minister at eleven,' he confided in a lower tone, 'I have to put him in the picture. Your parliamentary cousin,' he added, forcing an intimate joke.

'Ann's cousin actually,' Smiley corrected him, in the same absent tone. 'Far removed I may add, but cousin for all that.'

'And Bill Haydon is also Ann's cousin? Our distinguished Head of London Station.' They had played this game before as well.

'By a different route, yes, Bill is also her cousin.' He added quite uselessly: 'She comes from an old family with a strong political tradition. With time it's rather spread.'

'The tradition?' – Lacon loved to nail an ambiguity.

'The family.'

Beyond the trees, Smiley thought, cars are passing. Beyond the trees lies a whole world, but Lacon had this red castle and a sense of Christian ethic that promises him no reward except a knighthood, the respect of his peers, a fat pension and a couple of charitable directorships in the City.

'Anyway I'm seeing him at eleven.' Lacon had jerked to his feet and they were walking again. Smiley caught the name 'Ellis' floating backward to him on the leafy morning air. For a moment, as in the car with Guillam, an odd nervousness overcame him.

'After all,' Lacon was saying, 'we both held perfectly honourable positions. You felt that Ellis had been betrayed and you wanted a witch-hunt. My Minister and I felt there had been gross incompetence on the part of Control – a view which to put it mildly the Foreign Office shared – and we wanted a new broom.'

'Oh I quite understand *your* dilemma,' said Smiley, more to himself than to Lacon.

'I'm glad. And don't forget, George: you were Control's man. Control preferred you to Haydon and when he lost his grip towards the end and launched that whole extraordinary adventure it was you who fronted for him. No one but you, George. It's not every day that the head of one's secret service embarks on a private war against the Czechs.' It was clear that the memory still smarted. 'In other circumstances I suppose Haydon might have gone to the wall, but you were in the hot seat and –'

'And Percy Alleline was the Minister's man,' said Smiley, mildly enough for Lacon to slow himself and listen.

'It wasn't as if you had a suspect, you know! You didn't point the finger at anyone! A directionless enquiry can be extraordinarily destructive!'

'Whereas a new broom sweeps cleaner.'

'Percy Alleline? All in all he has done extremely well. He has produced intelligence instead of scandal, he has stuck to the letter of his charter and won the trust of his customers. He has not yet, to my knowledge, invaded Czechoslovak territory.'

'With Bill Haydon to field for him, who wouldn't?'

'Control, for one,' said Lacon with punch.

They had drawn up at an empty swimming pool and now stood staring into the deep end. From its grimy depths Smiley fancied he heard again the insinuating tones of Roddy Martindale: 'Little reading rooms at the Admiralty, little committees popping up with funny names . . .'

'Is that special source of Percy's still running?' Smiley enquired. 'The Witchcraft material or whatever it's called these days?'

'I didn't know you were on the list,' Lacon said, not at all pleased. 'Since you ask, yes. Source Merlin's our mainstay and Witchcraft is still the name of his product. The Circus hasn't turned in such good material for years. Since I can remember, in fact.'

'And still subject to all that special handling?'

'Certainly, and now that this has happened I've no doubt that we shall take even more rigorous precautions.'

'I wouldn't do that if I were you. Gerald might smell a rat.'

'That's the point, isn't it?' Lacon observed quickly. His strength was improbable, Smiley reflected. One minute he was like a thin, drooping boxer whose gloves were too big for his wrists; the next he had reached out and rocked you against the ropes, and was surveying you with Christian compassion. 'We can't move. We can't investigate because all the instruments of enquiry are in the Circus's hands, perhaps in the mole Gerald's. We can't watch, or listen, or open mail. To do any one of those things would require the resources of Esterhase's lamplighters, and Esterhase, like anyone else, must be suspect. We can't interrogate, we can't take steps to limit a particular person's access to delicate secrets. To do any of these things would be to run the risk of alarming the mole. It's the oldest question of all, George. Who can spy on the spies? Who can smell out the fox without running with him?' He made an awful stab at humour: 'Mole, rather,' he said, in a confiding aside.

In a fit of energy Smiley had broken away and was pounding ahead of Lacon down the path that led towards the paddock.

'Then go to the competition,' he called. 'Go to the security people. They're the experts, they'll do you a job.'

'The Minister won't have that. You know perfectly well how he and Alleline feel about the competition. Rightly too, if I may say so. A lot of ex-colonial administrators ploughing through Circus papers: you might as well bring in the army to investigate the navy!'

'That's no comparison at all,' Smiley objected.

But Lacon as a good civil servant had his second metaphor ready: 'Very well, the Minister would rather live with a damp roof than see his castle pulled down by outsiders. Does that satisfy you? He has a perfectly good point, George. We do have agents in the field and I wouldn't give much for their chances once the security gentlemen barge in.'

Now it was Smiley's turn to slow down.

'How many?'

'Six hundred, give or take a few.'

'And behind the Curtain?'

'We budget for a hundred and twenty.' With numbers, with facts of all sorts, Lacon never faltered. They were the gold he worked with, wrested from the grey bureaucratic earth. 'So far as I can make out from the financial returns, almost all of them are presently active.' He took a long bound. 'So I can tell him you'll do it, can I?' he sang, quite casually, as if the question were mere formality, tick the appropriate box. 'You'll take the job, clean the stables? Go backwards, go forwards, do whatever is necessary? It's your generation after all. Your legacy.'

Smiley had pushed open the paddock gate and slammed it behind him. They were facing each other over its rickety frame. Lacon, slightly pink, wore a dependent smile.

'Why do I say Ellis?' he asked conversationally. 'Why do I talk about the Ellis affair when the poor man's name was Prideaux?'

'Ellis was his workname.'

'Of course. So many scandals in those days, one forgets the details.' Hiatus. Swinging of the right forearm. Lunge. 'And he was Haydon's friend, not yours?'

'They were at Oxford together before the war.'

'And stablemates in the Circus during and after. The famous Haydon-Prideaux partnership. My predecessor spoke of it interminably.' He repeated: 'But you were never close to him?'

'To Prideaux? No.'

'Not a cousin, I mean?'

'For Heaven's sake,' Smiley breathed.

Lacon grew suddenly awkward again, but a dogged purpose kept his gaze on Smiley. 'And there's no emotional or other reason which you feel might debar you from the assignment? You must speak up, George,' he insisted anxiously, as if speaking up were the last thing he wanted. He waited a fraction, then threw it all away: 'Though I see no real case. There's always a part of us that belongs to the public domain, isn't there? The social contract cuts both ways, you always knew that I'm sure. So did Prideaux.'

'What does that mean?'

'Well, good Lord, he was shot, George. A bullet in the back is held to be quite a sacrifice, isn't it, even in your world?'

Alone, Smiley stood at the further end of the paddock, under the dripping trees, trying to make sense of his emotions while he reached for breath. Like an old illness, his anger had taken him by surprise. Ever since his retirement he had been denying its existence, steering clear of anything that could touch it off: newspapers, former colleagues, gossip of the Martindale sort. After a lifetime of living by his wits and his considerable memory, he had given himself full time to the profession of forgetting. He had forced himself to pursue scholarly interests which had served him well enough as a distraction while he was at the Circus, but now that he was unemployed were nothing, absolutely nothing. He could have shouted: Nothing!

'Burn the lot,' Ann had suggested helpfully, referring to his books. 'Set fire to the house. But don't rot.'

If by rot, she meant conform, she was right to read that as his aim. He had tried, really tried, as he approached what the insurance advertisements were pleased to call the evening of his life, to be all that a model *rentier* should be; though no one, least of all Ann, thanked him for the effort. Each morning as he got out of bed, each evening as he went back to it usually alone, he had reminded himself that he never was and never had been indispensable. He had schooled himself to admit that in those last wretched months of Control's career, when disasters followed one another with heady speed, he had been guilty of seeing things out of proportion. And if the old professional Adam rebelled in him now and then and said: You *know* the place went bad, you *know* Jim Prideaux was betrayed – and what more eloquent testimony is there than a bullet, two bullets in the back? – Well, he had replied, suppose he did? And suppose he was right? 'It is sheer vanity to believe that one, fat, middle-aged spy is the only person capable of holding the world together,' he would tell himself. And other times: 'I never heard of anyone yet who left the Circus without some unfinished business.'

Only Ann, though she could not read his workings, refused to accept his findings. She was quite passionate, in fact, as only women can be on matters of business, really driving him to go back, take up where he had left off, never to veer aside in favour of the easy arguments. Not of course that she knew anything, but what woman was ever stopped by a want of information? She felt. And despised him for not acting in accordance with her feelings.

And now, at the very moment when he was near enough beginning to believe his own dogma, a feat made no easier by Ann's infatuation for an out-of-work actor, what happens but that the assembled ghosts of his past – Lacon, Control, Karla, Alleline, Esterhase, Bland, and finally Bill Haydon himself – barge into his cell and cheerfully inform him, as they drag him back to this same garden, that everything which he had been calling vanity is truth?

'Haydon,' he repeated to himself, no longer able to stem the tides of memory. Even the name was like a jolt. 'I'm told that you and Bill shared *everything* once upon a time,' said Martindale. He stared at his chubby hands, watching them shake. Too old? Impotent? Afraid of the chase? Or afraid of what he might unearth at the end of it? 'There are always a dozen reasons for doing nothing,' Ann liked to say – it was a favourite apologia, indeed, for many of her misdemeanours – 'there is only one reason for doing *something*. And that's because you want to.' Or have to? Ann would furiously deny it: coercion, she would say, is just another word for doing what you want; or for not doing what you are afraid of.

Middle children weep longer than their brothers and sisters. Over her mother's shoulder, stilling her pains and her injured pride, Jackie Lacon watched the party leave. First, two men she had not seen before, one tall, one short and dark. They drove off in a small green van. No one waved to them, she noticed, or even said goodbye. Next, her father left in his own car; lastly a blond good-looking man and a short fat one in an enormous overcoat like a pony blanket made their way to a sports car parked under the beech trees. For a moment she really thought there must be something wrong with the fat one, he followed so slowly and so painfully. Then, seeing the handsome man hold the car door for him, he seemed to wake, and hurried forward with a lumpy skip. Unaccountably, this gesture upset her afresh. A storm of sorrow seized her and her mother could not console her.

# ELEVEN

Peter Guillam was a chivalrous fellow whose conscious loyalties were determined by his affections. The others had been made over long ago to the Circus. His father, a French businessman, had spied for a Circus *réseau* in the war while his mother, an Englishwoman, did mysterious things with codes. Until eight years ago, under the cover of a shipping clerk, Guillam himself had run his own agents in French North Africa, which was considered a murderous assignment. He was blown, his agents were hanged, he entered the long middle age of the grounded pro. He devilled in London, sometimes for Smiley, ran a few home-based operations including a network of girl-friends who were not, as the jargon has it, inter-conscious and when Alleline's crowd took over he was shoved out to grass in Brixton, he supposed because he had the wrong connections, among them Smiley. That, resolutely, was how until last Friday he would have told the story of his life. Of his relationship with Smiley he would have dwelt principally upon the end.

Guillam was living mainly in London docks in those days, where he was putting together low-grade Marine networks from whatever odd Polish, Russian and Chinese seamen he and a bunch of talent-spotters occasionally managed to get their hands on. Between-whiles he sat in a small room on the first floor of the Circus and consoled a pretty secretary called Mary and he was quite happy except that no one in authority would answer his minutes. When he used the phone he got engaged or no answer. He had heard vaguely there was trouble, but there was always trouble. It was common knowledge for instance that Alleline and Control had locked horns but they had been doing little else for years. He also knew, like everyone else, that a big operation had aborted in Czechoslovakia, that the Foreign Office and the Defence Ministry had jointly blown a gasket and that Jim Prideaux, head of the scalphunters, the oldest Czecho hand, and Bill Haydon's life-long stringer, had been shot up and put in the bag. Hence, he assumed, the loud silence and the glum faces. Hence also Bill Haydon's manic anger, of which the news spread like a nervous thrill through all the building: like God's wrath, said Mary, who loved a full-scale passion. Later he heard the catastrophe called Testify. Testify, Haydon told him much later, was the most incompetent bloody operation ever launched by an old man for his dying glory, and Jim Prideaux was the price of it. Bits made the newspapers, there were Parliamentary questions and even rumours, never officially confirmed, but British troops in Germany had been put on full alert.

Eventually by sauntering in and out of other people's offices he began to realise what everyone else had realized some weeks before. The Circus wasn't just silent, it was frozen. Nothing was coming in, nothing was going out; not at the level at which Guillam moved, anyhow. Inside the building people in authority had gone to earth and when pay day came round there were no buff envelopes in the pigeon-holes because, according to Mary, the house-keepers had not received the usual monthly authority to issue them. Now and then somebody would say they had seen Alleline leaving his club and he looked furious. Or Control getting into his car and he looked sunny. Or that Bill Haydon had resigned on the grounds that he had been overruled or undercut, but Bill was always resigning. This time, said the rumour, the grounds were somewhat different, however: Haydon was furious that the

Circus would not pay the Czech price for Jim Prideaux's repatriation; it was said to be too high in agents, or prestige. And that Bill had broken out in one of his fits of chauvinism, and declared that any price was fair to get one loyal Englishman home: give them everything, only get Jim back.

Then one evening Smiley peered round Guillam's door and suggested a drink. Mary didn't realize who he was and just said 'hullo' in her stylish classless drawl. As they walked out of the Circus side by side Smiley wished the janitors good night with unusual terseness, and in the pub in Wardour Street he said 'I've been sacked,' and that was all.

From the pub they went to a wine bar off Charing Cross, a cellar with music playing and no one there. 'Did they give any reason?' Guillam enquired. 'Or is it just because you've lost your figure?'

It was the word 'reason' that Smiley fixed on. He was by then politely but thoroughly drunk, but reason, as they walked unsteadily along the Thames embankment, reason got through to him:

'Reason as logic, or reason as motive?' he demanded, sounding less like himself than Bill Haydon, whose pre-war Oxford Union style of polemic seemed in those days to be in everybody's ears. 'Or reason as a way of life?' They sat on a bench. 'They don't have to give *me* reasons. I can write my own damn reasons. And that is not the same,' he insisted as Guillam guided him carefully into a cab, gave the driver the money and the address, 'that is not the same as the half-baked tolerance that comes from no longer caring.'

'Amen,' said Guillam, fully realizing as he watched the cab pull into the distance that by the rules of the Circus their friendship, such as it was, had that minute ended. Next day Guillam learned that more heads had rolled and that Percy Alleline was to stand in as nightwatchman with the title of acting chief and that Bill Haydon, to everyone's astonishment, but most likely out of persisting anger with Control, would serve under him; or as the wise ones said, over him.

By Christmas, Control was dead: 'They'll get you next,' said Mary, who saw these events as a second storming of the Winter Palace, and she wept when Guillam departed for the siberias of Brixton, ironically to fill Jim Prideaux's slot.

Climbing the four steps to the Circus that wet Monday afternoon, his mind bright with the prospect of felony, Guillam passed these events in review and decided that today was the beginning of the road back.

He had spent the previous night at his spacious flat in Eaton Place in the company of Camilla, a music student with a long body and a sad, beautiful face. Though she was not more than twenty, her black hair was streaked with grey, as if from a shock she never talked about. As another effect, perhaps, of the same undescribed trauma, she ate no meat, wore no leather and drank nothing alcoholic; only in love, it seemed to Guillam, she was free of these mysterious restraints.

He had spent the morning alone in his extremely dingy room in Brixton photographing Circus documents, having first drawn a subminiature camera from his own operational stores, a thing he did quite often to keep his hand in. The storeman had asked 'daylight or electric?' and they had a friendly discussion about film grain. He told his secretary he didn't want to be disturbed, closed his door and set to work according to Smiley's precise instructions. The windows were high in the wall. Even sitting, he could see only the sky and the tip of the new school up the road.

He began with works of reference from his personal safe. Smiley had given him priorities. First the staff directory, on issue to senior officers only, which supplied the home addresses, telephone numbers, names, and worknames of all home-based Circus personnel. Second, the handbook on staff duties, including the fold-in diagram of the Circus's reorganisation under Alleline. At its centre lay Bill Haydon's London Station, like a giant spider in its own web. 'After the Prideaux fiasco,' Bill had reputedly fumed, 'we'll have no more damned private armies, no more left hand not knowing what the right hand is doing.' Alleline, Guillam noticed, was billed twice: once as Chief, once as 'Director Special Sources'. According to rumour it was those sources which kept the Circus in business. Nothing else, in Guillam's view, could account for the Circus's inertia at working level and the esteem it enjoyed in Whitehall. To these documents, at Smiley's insistence, he added the scalphunters' revised charter, in the form of an Alleline letter beginning 'Dear Guillam', and setting out in detail the diminution of his powers. In several cases, the winner was Toby Esterhase, head of Acton lamplighters, the one out-station which had actually grown fatter under lateralism.

Next he moved to his desk and photographed, also on Smiley's instruction, a handful of routine circulars which might be useful as background reading. These included a belly-ache from Admin on the state of safe houses in the London Area ('*Kindly* treat them as if they were your *own*') and another about the misuse of unlisted Circus telephones for private calls. Lastly a very rude personal letter from documents warning him 'for the last time of asking' that his workname driving licence was out of date, and that unless he took the trouble to renew it 'his name would be forwarded to housekeepers for appropriate disciplinary action.'

He put away the camera and returned to his safe. On the bottom shelf lay a stack of lamplighter reports issued over Toby Esterhase's signature and stamped with the codeword 'Hatchet'. These supplied the names and cover jobs of the two or three hundred identified Soviet intelligence officers operating in London under legal or semi-legal cover; trade, Tass, Aeroflot, Radio Moscow, consular and diplomatic. Where appropriate they also gave the dates of lamplighter investigations and names of branch lines, which is jargon for contacts thrown up in the course of surveillance and not necess-arily run to earth. The reports came in a main annual volume and monthly supplements. He consulted the main volume first, then the supplements. At eleven twenty he locked his safe, rang London Station on the direct line and asked for Lauder Strickland of Banking section.

'Lauder, this is Peter from Brixton, how's trade?'

'Yes, Peter, what can we do for you?'

Brisk and blank. We of London Station have more important friends, said the tone.

It was a question of washing some dirty money, Guillam explained, to finance a ploy against a French diplomatic courier who seemed to be for sale. In his meekest voice he wondered whether Lauder could possibly find the time for them to meet and discuss it. Was the project London Station cleared? Lauder demanded. No, but Guillam had already sent the papers to Bill by shuttle. Lauder Strickland came down a peg; Guillam pressed his cause: 'There are one or two tricky aspects, Lauder, I think we need your sort of brain.'

Lauder said he could spare him half an hour.

On his way to the West End he dropped his films at the meagre premises of a chemist's called Lark, in the Charing Cross Road. Lark, if it was he, was a very fat man with tremendous fists. The shop was empty.

'Mr Lampton's films, to be developed,' said Guillam. Lark took the package to the back room and when he returned he said 'All done' in a gravel voice, then blew out a lot of breath at once, as if he were smoking, which he wasn't. He saw Guillam to the door and closed it behind him with a clatter. Where on God's earth does George find them? Guillam wondered. He had bought some throat pastilles. Every move must be accountable, Smiley had warned him: assume that the Circus has the dogs on you twenty-four hours a day. So what's new about that? Guillam thought; Toby Esterhase would put the dogs on his own mother if it brought him a pat on the back from Alleline.

From Charing Cross he walked up to Chez Victor for lunch with his head man Cy Vanhofer and a thug calling himself Lorimer who claimed to be sharing his mistress with the East German ambassador in Stockholm. Lorimer said the girl was ready to play ball but she needed British citizenship and a lot of money on delivery of the first take. She would do anything, he said: spike the ambassador's mail, bug his rooms 'or put broken glass in his bath', which was supposed to be a joke. Guillam reckoned Lorimer was lying and he was inclined to wonder whether Vanhofer was too, but he was wise enough to realize that he was in no state to say which way anyone was leaning just then. He liked Chez Victor but had no recollection of what he ate and now as he entered the lobby of the Circus he knew the reason was excitement.

'Hullo, Bryant.'

'Nice to see you, sir. Take a seat, sir, please, just for a moment, sir, thank you,' said Bryant, all in one breath, and Guillam perched on the wooden settle thinking of dentists and Camilla. She was a recent and somewhat mercurial acquisition; it was a while since things had moved quite so fast for him. They met at a party and she talked about truth, alone in a corner over a carrot juice. Guillam, taking a long chance, said he wasn't too good at ethics so why didn't they just go to bed together? She considered for a while, gravely; then fetched her coat. She'd been hanging around ever since, cooking nut rissoles and playing the flute.

The lobby looked dingier than ever. Three old lifts, a wooden barrier, a poster for Mazawattee tea, Bryant's glass-fronted sentry box with a Scenes of England calendar and a line of mossy telephones.

'Mr Strickland *is* expecting you, sir,' said Bryant as he emerged, and in slow motion stamped a pink chit with the time of day: fourteen fifty-five, P. Bryant, Janitor. The grille of the centre lift rattled like a bunch of dry sticks.

'Time you oiled that thing, isn't it?' Guillam called as he waited for the mechanism to mesh.

'We keep asking,' said Bryant, embarking on a favourite lament. 'They never do a thing about it. You can ask till you're blue in the face. How's the family, sir?'

'Fine,' said Guillam, who had none.

'That's right,' said Bryant. Looking down Guillam saw his creamy head vanish between his feet. Mary called him strawberry and vanilla, he remembered: red face, white hair and mushy.

In the lift he examined his pass. 'Permit to enter LS' ran the headline. 'Purpose of visit: Banking Section. This document to be handed back on leaving.' And a space marked 'host's signature,' blank.

'Well met, Peter. Greetings. You're a trifle late I think, but never mind.'

Lauder was waiting at the barrier, all five foot nothing of him, white collared and secretly on tiptoe to be visited. In Control's day this floor had been a thoroughfare of busy people. Today a barrier closed the entrance and a rat-faced janitor scrutinized his pass.

'Good God, how long have you had that monster?' Guillam asked, slowing down before a shiny new coffee-machine. A couple of girls, filling beakers, glanced round and said, 'Hullo, Lauder,' looking at Guillam. The tall one reminded him of Camilla: the same slow-burning eyes, censuring male insufficiency.

'Ah, but you've no notion how many man-hours it saves,' Lauder cried at once. 'Fantastic. Quite fantastic,' and all but knocked over Bill Haydon in his enthusiasm.

He was emerging from his room, an hexagonal pepper pot overlooking New Compton Street and the Charing Cross Road. He was moving in the same direction as they were but at about half a mile an hour, which for Bill indoors was full throttle. Outdoors was a different matter; Guillam had seen that too, on training games at Sarratt, and once on a night drop in Greece. Outdoors he was swift and eager; his keen face, in this clammy corridor shadowed and withdrawn, seemed in the free air to be fashioned by the outlandish places where he had served. There was no end to these: no operational theatre, in Guillam's admiring eyes, that did not bear the Haydon imprint somewhere. Over and again in his own career he had made the same eerie encounter with Bill's exotic progress. A year or two back, still working on marine intelligence and having as one of his targets the assembly of a team of coast watchers for the Chinese ports of Wenchow and Amoy, Guillam discovered to his amazement that there were actually Chinese stay-behind agents living in those very towns, recruited by Bill Haydon in the course of some forgotten war-time exploit, rigged out with cached radios and equipment, with whom contact might be made. Another time, raking through war records of Circus strongarm men, more out of nostalgia for the period than present professional optimism, Guillam stumbled twice on Haydon's work-name in as many minutes: in forty-one he was running French fishing smacks out of the Helford Estuary; in the same year, with Jim Prideaux as his stringer, he was laying down courier lines across southern Europe from the Balkans to Madrid. To Guillam, Haydon was of that unrepeatable, fading Circus generation, to which his parents and George Smiley also belonged – exclusive and in Haydon's case blue-blooded – which had lived a dozen leisured lives to his own hasty one, and still, thirty years later, gave the Circus its dying flavour of adventure.

Seeing them both, Haydon stood rock still. It was a month since Guillam had spoken to him; he had probably been away on unexplained business. Now, against the light of his own open doorway, he looked strangely black and tall. He was carrying something, Guillam could not make out what it was, a magazine, a file, or a report; his room, split by his own shadow, was an undergraduate mayhem, monkish and chaotic. Reports, flimsies and dossiers lay heaped everywhere; on the wall a baize noticeboard jammed with post-cards and press cuttings; beside it, askew and unframed, one of Bill's old paintings, a rounded abstract in the hard flat colours of the desert.

'Hullo, Bill,' said Guillam.

Leaving his door still open – a breach of housekeeper regulations – Haydon fell in ahead of them, still without a word. He was dressed with his customary dottiness. The leather patches of his jacket were stitched on like diamonds, not squares, which from behind gave him a harlequin look. His spectacles were jammed into his lank grey forelock like goggles. For a moment they followed him uncertainly, till without warning he suddenly turned himself round, all of him at once like a statue being slowly swivelled on its plinth, and fixed his gaze on Guillam. Then grinned, so that his crescent eyebrows went straight up like a clown's, and his face became handsome and absurdly young.

'What the hell are you doing here, you pariah?' he enquired pleasantly.

Taking the question seriously Lauder started to explain about the Frenchman and the dirty money.

'Well, mind you lock up the spoons,' said Bill, talking straight through him. 'Those bloody scalphunters will steal the gold out of your teeth. Lock up the girls too,' he added as an afterthought, his eyes still on Guillam, 'if they'll let you. Since when did scalphunters wash their own money? That's our job.'

'Lauder's doing the washing. We're just spending the stuff.'

'Papers to me,' Haydon said to Strickland, with sudden curtness. 'I'm not crossing any more bloody wires.'

'They're already routed to you,' said Guillam. 'They're probably in your in-tray now.'

A last nod sent them on ahead, so that Guillam felt Haydon's pale blue gaze boring into his back all the way to the next dark turning.

'Fantastic fellow,' Lauder declared, as if Guillam had never met him. 'London Station could not be in better hands. Incredible ability. Incredible record. Brilliant.'

Whereas you, thought Guillam savagely, are brilliant by association. With Bill, with the coffee-machine, with banks. His meditations were interrupted by Roy Bland's caustic Cockney voice, issuing from a doorway ahead of them.

'Hey Lauder, hold on a minute: have you seen Bloody Bill anywhere? He's wanted urgently.'

Followed at once by Toby Esterhase's faithful mid-European echo from the same direction: 'Immediately Lauder, actually, we have put out an alert for him.'

They had entered the last cramped corridor. Lauder was perhaps three paces on and was already composing his answer to this question as Guillam arrived at the open doorway and looked in. Bland was sprawled massively at his desk. He had thrown off his jacket and was clutching a paper. Arcs of sweat ringed his armpits. Tiny Toby Esterhase was stooped over him like a head waiter, a stiff-backed miniature ambassador with silvery hair and a crisp unfriendly jaw, and he had stretched out one hand towards the paper as if to recommend a speciality. They had evidently been reading the same documents when Bland caught sight of Lauder Strickland passing.

'Indeed I have seen Bill Haydon,' said Lauder, who had a trick of rephrasing questions to make them sound more seemly. 'I suspect Bill is on his way to you this moment. He's a way back there down the corridor; we were having a brief word about a couple of things.'

Bland's gaze moved slowly to Guillam and settled there; its chilly appraisal was uncomfortably reminiscent of Haydon's. 'Hullo, Pete,' he said. At this Tiny Toby straightened up and turned his eyes also directly towards Guillam: brown and quiet like a pointer's.

'Hi,' said Guillam, 'what's the joke?'

Their greeting was not merely frosty, it was downright hostile. Guillam had lived cheek by jowl with Toby Esterhase for three months on a very dodgy operation in Switzerland and Toby had never smiled once, so his stare came as no surprise. But Roy Bland was one of Smiley's discoveries, a warm-hearted impulsive fellow for that world, red-haired and burly, an intellectual primitive whose idea of a good evening was talking Wittgenstein in the pubs round Kentish Town. He'd spent ten years as a Party hack, plodding the academic circuit in Eastern Europe, and now like Guillam he was grounded, which was even something of a bond. His usual style was a big grin, a slap on the shoulder and a blast of last night's beer; but not today.

'No joke, Peter old boy,' said Roy, mustering a belated smile. 'Just surprised to see you, that's all. We're used to having this floor to ourselves.'

'Here's Bill,' said Lauder, very pleased to have his prognostication so promptly confirmed. In a strip of light, as he entered it, Guillam noticed the queer colour of Haydon's cheeks. A blushing red, daubed high on the bones, but deep, made up of tiny broken veins. It gave him, thought Guillam in his heightened state of nervousness, a slightly Dorian Gray look.

His meeting with Lauder Strickland lasted an hour and twenty minutes, Guillam spun it out that long, and throughout it his mind went back to Bland and Esterhase and he wondered what the hell was eating them.

'Well, I suppose I'd better go and clear all this with the Dolphin,' he said at last. 'We all know how she is about Swiss banks.' The housekeepers lived two doors down from Banking. 'I'll leave this here,' he added and tossed the pass on to Lauder's desk.

Diana Dolphin's room smelt of fresh deodorant; her chainmail handbag lay on the safe beside a copy of the *Financial Times*. She was one of those groomed Circus brides whom no one ever marries. Yes, he said wearily, the operational papers were already on submission to London Station. Yes, he understood that freewheeling with dirty money was a thing of the past.

'Then we shall look into it and let you know,' she announced, which meant she would go and ask Phil Porteous who sat next door.

'I'll tell Lauder then,' said Guillam, and left.

Move, he thought.

In the men's room he waited thirty seconds at the basins, watching the door in the mirror and listening. A curious quiet had descended over the whole floor. Come on, he thought, you're getting old, move. He crossed the corridor, stepped boldly into the duty officers' room, closed the door with a slam and looked round. He reckoned he had ten minutes and he reckoned that a slammed door made less noise in that silence than a door surreptitiously closed. Move.

He had brought the camera but the light was awful. The net curtained window looked onto a courtyard full of blackened pipes. He couldn't have risked a brighter bulb even if he'd had one with him, so he used his memory. Nothing much seemed to have changed since the take-over. In the daytime the place was used as a rest-room for girls with the vapours and to judge by the smell of cheap scent it still was. Along one wall lay the Rexine divan which at night made into a rotten bed; beside it the first-aid chest with the red cross peeling off the front, and a clapped-out television. The steel cupboard stood in its same place between the switchboard and the locked telephones and he made a beeline for it. It was an old cupboard and he could have opened it with a tin opener. He had brought his picks and a couple of light alloy tools. Then he remembered that the combination used to be 31-22-11 and he tried it, four anti, three clock, two anti, clockwise till she springs. The dial was so jaded it knew the way. When he opened the door dust rolled out of the bottom in a cloud, crawled a distance then slowly lifted towards the dark window. At the same moment he heard what sounded like a single note played on a flute: it came from a car, most likely, braking in the street outside; or the wheel of a file trolley squeaking on linoleum; but for that moment it was one of those long, mournful notes which made up Camilla's practice scales. She played exactly when she felt like it. At midnight, in the early morning or whenever. She didn't give a damn about the neighbours; she seemed quite nerveless altogether. He remembered her that first evening: 'Which is your side of the bed? Where shall I put my clothes?' He prided himself on his delicate touch in such things but Camilla had no use for it, technique was already a compromise, a compromise with reality, she would say an escape from it. All right, so get me out of this lot.

The duty logbooks were on the top shelf in bound volumes with the dates pasted on the spines. They looked like family account books. He took down the volume for April and studied the list of names on the inside cover, wondering whether anyone could see him from the dupe-room across the courtyard, and if they could, would they care? He began working through the entries, searching for the night of the tenth and eleventh when the signals traffic between London Station and Tarr was supposed to have taken place. Hong Kong was nine hours ahead, Smiley had pointed out: Tarr's telegram and London's first answer had both happened out of hours.

From the corridor came a sudden swell of voices and for a second he even fancied he could pick out Alleline's growling border brogue lifted in humourless banter, but fancies were two a penny just now. He had a cover story and a part of him believed it already. If he was caught, the whole of him would believe it and if the Sarratt inquisitors sweated him he had a fallback, he never travelled without one. All the same he was terrified. The voices died, and the ghost of Percy Alleline with them. Sweat was running over his ribs. A girl tripped past humming a tune from *Hair*. If Bill hears you he'll murder you, he thought, if there's one thing that sends Bill spare it's humming. 'What are you doing here, you pariah?'

Then to his fleeting amusement he actually heard Bill's infuriated roar, echoing from God knows what distance: 'Stop that moaning. Who *is* the fool?'

Move. Once you stop you never start again: there is a special stage-fright that can make you dry up and walk away, that burns your fingers when you touch the goods and turns your stomach to water. Move. He put back the April volume and drew four others at random, February, June, September and October. He flicked through them fast, looking for comparisons, returned them to the shelf and dropped into a crouch. He wished to God the dust would settle. Why didn't someone complain? Always the same when a lot of people use one place: no one's responsible, no one gives a hoot. He was looking for the night janitors' attendance lists. He found them on the bottom shelf, jammed in with the teabags and the condensed milk: sheafs of them in envelope-type folders. The janitors filled them in and brought them to you twice in your twelve hours' tour of duty: at midnight and again at six a.m. You vouched for their correctness – God knows how, since the night staff were scattered all over the building – signed them off, kept the third copy and chucked it in the cupboard, no one knew why. That was the procedure before the Flood, and it seemed to be the procedure now.

Dust and teabags on one shelf, he thought. How long since anyone made tea?

Once again he fixed his sights on April 10th/11th. His shirt was clinging to his ribs. What's happened to me? Christ, I'm over the hill. He turned forward and back, forward again, twice, three times, then closed the cupboard on the lot. He waited, listened, took a last worried look at the dust then stepped boldly across the corridor, back to the safety of the men's room. On the way the clatter hit him: coding machines, the ringing of the telephones, a girl's voice calling 'Where's that damn float, I had it in my hand,' and that mysterious piping again, but no longer like Camilla's in the small hours. Next time I'll get her to do the job, he thought savagely; without compromise, face to face, the way life should be.

In the men's room he found Spike Kaspar and Nick de Silsky standing at the hand basins and murmuring at each other into the mirror: legmen for Haydon's Soviet networks, they'd been around for years, known simply as the Russians. Seeing Guillam they at once stopped talking.

'Hullo, you two. Christ you really *are* inseparable.'

They were blond and squat and they looked more like Russians than the real ones. He waited till they'd gone, rinsed the dust off his fingers then drifted back to Lauder Strickland's room.

'Lord save us, that Dolphin does talk,' he said carelessly.

'Very able officer. Nearest thing to indispensable we have around here. Extremely competent, you can take my word for it,' said Lauder. Looking closely at his watch before he signed the chit, he led Guillam back to the lifts. Toby Esterhase was at the barrier, talking to the unfriendly young janitor.

'You are going back to Brixton, Peter?' His tone was casual, his expression as usual impenetrable.

'Why?'

'I have a car outside actually. I thought maybe I could run you. We have some business out that way.'

Run you: Tiny Toby spoke no known language perfectly, but he spoke them all. In Switzerland Guillam had heard his French and it had a German accent; his German had a Slav accent and his English was full of stray flaws and stops and false vowel sounds.

'It's all right, Tobe, I think I'll just go home. Night.'

'Straight home? I would run you, that's all.'

'Thanks, I've got shopping to do. All those bloody god-children.'

'Sure,' said Toby as he hadn't any, and stuck in his little granite jaw in disappointment.

What the hell does he want? Guillam thought again. Tiny Toby and Big Roy both: why were they giving me the eye? Was it something they were reading or something they ate?

Out in the street he sauntered down the Charing Cross Road peering at the windows of the bookshops while his other mind checked both sides of the pavement. It had turned much colder, a wind was getting up and there was a promise to people's faces as they bustled by. He felt elated. Till now he had been living too much in the past, he decided. Time to get my eye in again. In Zwemmers he examined a coffee-table book called *Musical Instruments Down the Ages* and remembered that Camilla had a late lesson with Doctor Sand, her flute teacher. He walked back as far as Foyles, glancing down the bus queues as he went. Think of it as abroad, Smiley had said. Remembering the duty room and Roy Bland's fishy stare, Guillam had no difficulty. And Bill too: was Haydon party to their same suspicion? No. Bill was his own category, Guillam decided, unable to resist a surge of loyalty to Haydon. Bill would share nothing that was not his own in the first place. Set beside Bill, those other two were pygmies.

In Soho he hailed a cab and asked for Waterloo Station. At Waterloo from a reeking phone box he telephoned a number in Mitcham, Surrey, and spoke to Inspector Mendel, formerly of Special Branch, known to both Guillam and Smiley from other lives. When Mendel came on the line he asked for Jenny and heard Mendel tell him tersely that no Jenny lived there. He apologized and rang off. He dialled the time and feigned a pleasant conversation with the automatic announcer because there was an old lady outside waiting for him to finish. By now he should be there, he thought. He rang off and dialled a second number in Mitcham, this time a callbox at the end of Mendel's avenue.

'This is Will,' said Guillam.

'And this is Arthur,' said Mendel cheerfully. 'How's Will?' He was a quirkish, loping tracker of a man, sharp-faced and sharp-eyed, and Guillam had a very precise picture of him just then, leaning over his policeman's notebook with his pencil poised.

'I want to give you the headlines now in case I go under a bus.'

'That's right, Will,' said Mendel consolingly. 'Can't be too careful.'

He gave his message slowly, using the scholastic cover they had agreed on as a last protection against random interception: exams, students, stolen papers. Each time he paused he heard nothing but a faint scratching. He imagined Mendel writing slowly and legibly and not speaking till he had it all down.

'I got those happy snaps from the chemist by the by,' said Mendel finally, when he had checked it all back. 'Come out a treat. Not a miss among them.'

'Thanks. I'm glad.'

But Mendel had already rung off.

I'll say one thing for moles, thought Guillam: it's a long dark tunnel all the way. As he held open the door for the old lady he noticed the telephone receiver lying on its cradle, how the sweat crawled over it in drips. He considered his message to Mendel, he thought again of Roy Bland and Toby Esterhase staring at him through the doorway, he wondered quite urgently where Smiley was, and whether he was taking care. He returned to Eaton Place needing Camilla badly, and a little afraid of his reasons. Was it really age that was against him suddenly? Somehow, for the first time in his life, he had sinned against his own notions of nobility. He had a sense of dirtiness, even of self-disgust.

# TWELVE

There are old men who go back to Oxford and find their youth beckoning to them from the stones. Smiley was not one of them. Ten years ago he might have felt a pull. Not now. Passing the Bodleian he vaguely thought: I worked there. Seeing the house of his old tutor in Parks Road, he remembered that before the war in its long garden Jebedee had first suggested he might care to talk to 'one or two people I know in London.' And hearing Tom Tower strike the evening six he found himself thinking of Bill Haydon and Jim Prideaux, who must have arrived here the year that Smiley went down and were then gathered up by the war; and he wondered idly how they must have looked together then, Bill the painter, polemicist and socialite; Jim the athlete, hanging on his words. In their heyday together in the Circus, he reflected, that distinction had all but evened out: Jim grew nimble at the brainwork and Bill in the field was no man's fool. Only at the end, the old polarity asserted itself: the workhorse went back to his stable, the thinker to his desk.

Spots of rain were falling but he couldn't see them. He had travelled by rail and walked from the station, making detours all the way: Blackwell's, his old college, anywhere, then north. Dusk had come here early because of the trees.

Reaching a cul-de-sac he once more dawdled, once more took stock. A woman in a shawl rode past him on a pushbike, gliding through the beams of the streetlamps where they pierced the swathes of mist. Dismounting, she pulled open a gate and vanished. Across the road a muffled figure was walking a dog, man or woman he couldn't tell. Otherwise the road was empty, so was the phone box. Then abruptly two men passed him, talking loudly about God and war. The younger one did most of the talking. Hearing the older one agree, Smiley supposed he was the don.

He was following a high paling that bulged with shrubs. The gate of number fifteen was soft on its hinges, a double gate but only one side used. When he pushed it, the latch was broken. The house stood a long way back; most of the windows were lit. In one, high up, a young man stooped over a desk. At another, two girls seemed to be arguing, at a third, a very pale woman was playing the viola but he couldn't hear the sound. The ground-floor windows were also lit but the curtains were drawn. The porch was tiled, the front door was panelled with stained glass; on the jamb was pinned an old notice: 'After 11 p.m. use side door only.' Over the bells, more notices: 'Prince three rings', 'Lumby two rings', 'Buzz: out all evening, see you, Janet.' The bottom bell said 'Sachs' and he pressed it. At once dogs barked and a woman started yelling.

'Flush, you stupid boy, it's only a dunderhead. Flush, shut up you fool. Flush!'

The door opened part way, held on a chain; a body swelled into the opening. While Smiley in the same instant gave his whole effort to seeing who else was inside the house, two shrewd eyes, wet like a baby's appraised him, noted his briefcase and his spattered shoes, flickered upward to peer past his shoulder down the drive, then once more looked him over. Finally the white face broke into a charming smile, and Miss Connie Sachs, formerly queen of research at the Circus, registered her spontaneous joy.

'George Smiley,' she cried, with a shy trailing laugh as she drew him into the house. 'Why you lovely darling man, I thought you were selling me a Hoover bless you and all the time it's George!'

She closed the door after him, fast.

She was a big woman, bigger than Smiley by a head. A tangle of white hair framed her sprawling face. She wore a brown jacket like a blazer and trousers with elastic at the waist and she had a low belly like an old man's. A coke fire smouldered in the grate. Cats lay before it and a mangy grey spaniel, too fat to move, lounged on the divan. On a trolley were the tins she ate from and the bottles she drank from. From the same adaptor she drew the power for her radio, her electric ring and her curling tongs. A boy with shoulder-length hair lay on the floor, making toast. Seeing Smiley he put down his brass trident.

'Oh Jingle darling, *could* it be tomorrow?' Connie implored. 'It's not often my oldest, oldest lover comes to see me.' He had forgotten her voice. She played with it constantly, pitching it at all odd levels. 'I'll give you a whole free hour, dear, all to himself: will you? One of my dunderheads,' she explained to Smiley, long before the boy was out of earshot. 'I still teach, I don't know why. *George*,' she murmured, watching him proudly across the room as he took the sherry bottle from his briefcase and filled two glasses. 'Of all the lovely darling men I ever knew. *He walked*,' she explained to the spaniel. 'Look at his boots. Walked all the way from London, didn't you George? Oh *bless*, God bless.'

It was hard for her to drink. Her arthritic fingers were turned downward as if they had all been broken in the same accident, and her arm was stiff. 'Did you walk alone, George?' she asked, fishing a loose cigarette from her blazer pocket. 'Not accompanied, were we?'

He lit the cigarette for her and she held it like a peashooter, fingers along the top, then watched him down the line of it with her shrewd, pink eyes. 'So what does he want from Connie, you bad boy?'

'Her memory.'

'What part?'

'We're going back over some old ground.'

'Hear that, Flush?' she yelled to the spaniel. 'First they chuck us out with an old bone then they come begging to us. Which *ground*, George?'

'I've brought a letter for you from Lacon. He'll be at his club this evening at seven. If you're worried you're to call him from the phone box down the road. I'd prefer you not to do that, but if you must he'll make the necessary impressive noises.'

She had been holding him but now her hands flopped to her sides and for a good while she floated round the room, knowing the places to rest and the holds to steady her and cursing, 'Oh damn George Smiley and all who sail in him.' At the window, perhaps out of habit, she parted the edge of the curtain but there seemed to be nothing to distract her.

'Oh George, damn you so,' she muttered. 'How could you let a *Lacon* in? Might as well let in the competition, while you're about it.'

On the table lay a copy of the day's *Times*, crossword uppermost. Each square was inked in laboured letters. There were no blanks.

'Went to the footer today,' she sang from the dark under the stairs as she cheered herself up from the trolley. 'Lovely Will took me. My favourite dunderhead, wasn't that super of him?' Her little-girl voice, it went with an outrageous pout. 'Connie got *cold*, George. Froze solid, Connie did, toes an' all.'

He guessed she was crying so he fetched her from the dark and led her to the sofa. Her glass was empty so he filled it half. Side by side on the sofa they drank while Connie's tears ran down her blazer on to his hands.

'Oh George,' she kept saying. 'Do you know what she told me when they threw me out? That personnel cow?' She was holding one point of Smiley's collar, working it between her finger and thumb while she cheered up. 'You know what the cow said?' Her sergeant-major voice: '"You're losing your sense of proportion, Connie. It's time you got out into the real world." I *hate* the real world, George. I like the Circus and all my lovely boys.' She took his hands, trying to interlace her fingers with his.

'Polyakov,' he said quietly, pronouncing it in accordance with Tarr's instruction, 'Aleksey Aleksandrovich Polyakov, Cultural Attaché, Soviet Embassy London. He's come alive again, just as you predicted.'

A car was drawing up in the road, he heard only the sound of the wheels, the engine was already switched off. The footsteps, very lightly.

'Janet, smuggling in her boyfriend,' Connie whispered, her pink-rimmed eyes fixed on his while she shared his distraction. 'She thinks I don't know. Hear that? Metal quarters on his heels. Now wait.' The footsteps stopped, there was a small scuffle. 'She's giving him the key. He thinks he works it more quietly than she can. He can't.' The lock turned with a heavy snap. 'Oh you men,' Connie breathed with a hopeless smile. 'Oh George. Why do you have to drag up Aleks?' And for a while she wept for Aleks Polyakov.

Her brothers were dons, Smiley remembered; her father was a professor of something. Control had met her at bridge and invented a job for her.

She began her story like a fairy-tale: 'Once upon a time there was a defector called Stanley, way back in sixty-three,' and she applied to it the same spurious logic, part inspiration, part intellectual opportunism, born of a wonderful mind which had never grown up. Her formless white face took on the grandmother's glow of enchanted reminiscence. Her memory was as compendious as her body and surely she loved it more, for she had put everything aside to listen to it: her drink, her cigarette, even for a while Smiley's passive hand. She sat no longer slouched but strictly, her big head to one side as she dreamily plucked the white wool of her hair. He had assumed she would begin at once with Polyakov, but she began with Stanley; he had forgotten her passion for family trees. Stanley, she said; the inquisitors' covername for a fifth-rate defector from Moscow Centre. March sixty-three. The scalphunters bought him secondhand from the Dutch and shipped him to Sarratt and probably if it hadn't been the silly season and if the inquisitors hadn't happened to have time on their hands, well who knows whether any of it would ever have come to light? As it was, Brother Stanley had a speck of gold on him, one teeny speck, and they found it. The Dutch missed it but the inquisitors found it and a copy of their report came to Connie: 'Which was a whole *other* miracle in itself,' Connie bellowed huffily, 'considering that everyone, and *specially* Sarratt, made an absolute *principle* of leaving research off their distribution lists.'

Patiently Smiley waited for the speck of gold, for Connie was of an age where the only thing a man could give her was time.

Now Stanley had defected while he was on a mailfist job in the Hague, she explained. He was by profession an assassin of some sort and had been sent to Holland to murder a Russian émigré who was getting on Centre's nerves.

Instead, he decided to give himself up. 'Some *girl* had made a fool of him,' said Connie with great contempt. 'The Dutch set him a honey-trap, my dear, and he barged in with his eyes wide shut.'

To prepare him for the mission Centre had posted him to one of their training camps outside Moscow for a brush-up in the black arts: sabotage and silent killing. The Dutch, when they had him, were shocked by this and made it the focal point of their interrogation. They put his picture in the newspapers and had him drawing pictures of cyanide bullets and all the other dreary weaponry which Centre so adored. But at the Nursery the inquisitors knew that stuff by heart so they concentrated on the camp itself, which was a new one, not much known. 'Sort of millionaires' Sarratt,' she explained. They made a sketch-plan of the compound, which covered several hundred acres of forest and lakeland, and put in all the buildings Stanley could remember: laundries, canteens, lecture huts, ranges, all the dross. Stanley had been there several times and remembered a lot. They thought they were about finished when Stanley went very quiet. He took a pencil and in the north west corner he drew five more huts and a double fence round them for the guard dogs, bless him. These huts were new, said Stanley, built in the last few months. You reached them by a private road; he had seen them from a hilltop when he was out walking with his instructor, Milos. According to Milos (who was Stanley's *friend*, said Connie with much innuendo) they housed a special school recently founded by Karla for training military officers in conspiracy.

'So, my dear, there we were,' Connie cried. 'For *years* we'd been hearing rumours that Karla was trying to build a private army of his own inside Moscow Centre but, poor lamb, he hadn't the power. We knew he had agents scattered round the globe and *naturally* he was worried that as he grew older and more senior he wouldn't be able to manage them alone. We knew that like everyone else he was *dreadfully* jealous of them and couldn't bear the idea of handing them over to the legal residencies in the target countries. Well *naturally* he wouldn't: you know how he hated residencies: overstaffed, insecure. Same as he hated the old guard. Flat-earthers, he called them. Quite right. Well now he had the power and he was doing something about it, as any real man would. March sixty-three,' she repeated in case Smiley had missed the date.

Then nothing, of course. 'The usual game: sit on your thumbs, get on with other work, whistle for a wind.' She sat on them for three years, until Major Mikhail Fedorovich Komarov, Assistant Military Attaché in the Soviet Embassy in Tokyo, was caught *in flagrante* taking delivery of six reels of top secret intelligence procured by a senior official in the Japanese Defence Ministry. Komarov was the hero of her second fairy-tale: not a defector but a soldier with the shoulder boards of the artillery.

'And medals, my dear! Medals galore!'

Komarov himself had to leave Tokyo so fast that his dog got locked in his flat and was later found starved to death, which was something Connie could *not* forgive him for. Whereas Komarov's Japanese agent was of course duly interrogated and by a happy chance the Circus was able to buy the report from the Toka.

'Why, George, come to think of it, it was you who arranged the deal!'

With a quaint moue of professional vanity, Smiley conceded that it might well have been.

The essence of the report was simple. The Japanese defence official was a mole. He had been recruited before the war in the shadow of the Japanese invasion of Manchuria, by one Martin Brandt, a German journalist who seemed to be connected with the Comintern. Brandt, said Connie, was one of Karla's names in the nineteen-thirties. Komarov himself had never been a member of the official Tokyo residency inside the Embassy, he'd worked solo with one legman and a direct line to Karla, whose brother officer he had been in the war. Better still, before he arrived in Tokyo he had attended a special training course at a new school outside Moscow set up specially for Karla's hand-picked pupils. 'Conclusion,' Connie sang. 'Brother Komarov was our first and also *not* very distinguished graduate of the Karla training school. He was shot, poor lamb,' she added, with a dramatic fall of her voice. 'They never *hang*, do they: too impatient, the little horrors.'

Now Connie had felt able to go to town, she said. Knowing what signs to look for, she tracked back through Karla's file. She spent three weeks in Whitehall with the army's Moscow-gazers combing Soviet army posting bulletins for disguised entries until, from a host of suspects, she reckoned she had three new, identifiable Karla trainees. All were military men, all were personally acquainted with Karla, all were ten to fifteen years his junior. She gave their names as Bardin, Stokovsky and Viktorov, all colonels.

At the mention of the third name a dullness descended over Smiley's features, and his eyes turned very tired, as if he were staving off boredom.

'So what became of them all?' he asked.

'Bardin changed to Sokolov then Rusakov. Joined the Soviet Delegation to the United Nations in New York. No overt connection with the local residency, no involvement in bread-and-butter operations, no coat-trailing, no talent-spotting, a good solid cover job. Still there for all I know.'

'Stokovsky?'

'Went illegal, set up a photographic business in Paris as Grodescu, French Rumanian. Formed an affiliate in Bonn, believed to be running one of Karla's West German sources from across the border.'

'And the third? Viktorov?'

'Sunk without trace.'

'Oh dear,' said Smiley, and his boredom seemed to deepen.

'Trained and disappeared off the face of the earth. May have died of course. One does *tend* to forget the natural causes.'

'Oh indeed,' Smiley agreed, 'oh quite.'

He had that art, from miles and miles of secret life, of listening at the front of his mind; of letting the primary incidents unroll directly before him while another, quite separate faculty wrestled with their historical connection. The connection ran through Tarr to Irina, through Irina to her poor lover who was so proud of being called Lapin, and of serving one Colonel Gregor Viktorov 'whose workname at the Embassy is Polyakov'. In his memory, these things were like part of a childhood; he would never forget them.

'Were there photographs, Connie?' he asked glumly. 'Did you land physical descriptions at all?'

'Of Bardin at the United Nations, naturally. Of Stokovsky, perhaps. We had an old press picture from his soldiering days but we could never quite nail the verification.'

'And of Viktorov who sank without trace?' Still, it might have been any name. 'No pretty pictures of him, either?' Smiley asked, going down the room to fetch more drink.

'Viktorov, Colonel Gregor,' Connie repeated with a fond distracted smile. 'Fought like a terrier at Stalingrad. No, we never had a photograph. Pity.

They said he was yards the best.' She perked up: 'Though of course we don't *know* about the others. Five huts and a two-year course: well my dear, that adds up to a sight more than three graduates after all these years!'

With a tiny sign of disappointment, as if to say there was nothing so far in that whole narrative, let alone in the person of Colonel Gregor Viktorov, to advance him in his laborious quest, Smiley suggested they should pass to the wholly unrelated phenomenon of Polyakov, Aleksey Aleksandrovich, of the Soviet Embassy in London, better known to Connie as dear Aleks Polyakov, and establish just where he fitted in to Karla's scheme of things and why it was that she had been forbidden to investigate him further.

# THIRTEEN

She was much more animated now. Polyakov was not a fairy-tale hero, he was her lover Aleks, though she had never spoken to him, probably never seen him in the flesh. She had moved to another seat closer to the reading lamp, a rocking chair that relieved certain pains: she could sit nowhere for long. She had tilted her head back so that Smiley was looking at the white billows of her neck and she dangled one stiff hand coquettishly, recalling indiscretions she did not regret; while to Smiley's tidy mind her speculations, in terms of the acceptable arithmetic of intelligence, seemed even wilder than before.

'*Oh* he was so good,' she said. 'Seven long years Aleks had been here before we even had an inkling. Seven years, my dear, and not so much as a *tickle*! Imagine!'

She quoted his original visa application those nine years ago: Polyakov, Aleksey Aleksandrovich, graduate of Leningrad State University, Cultural Attaché with second secretary rank, married but not accompanied by wife, born third of March nineteen twenty-two in the Ukraine, son of a transporter, early education not supplied. She ran straight on, a smile in her voice as she gave the lamplighters' first routine description: 'Height five foot eleven, heavy build, colour of eyes green, colour of hair black, no other visible distinguishing marks. Jolly giant of a bloke,' she declared with a laugh. 'Tremendous joker. Black quiff, here, over the right eye. I'm sure he was a bottom pincher though we never caught him at it. I'd have offered him one or two bottoms of our own if Toby had played ball, which he wouldn't. Not that Aleksey Aleksandrovich would have fallen for *that*, mind. Aleks was *far* too fly,' she said proudly. 'Lovely voice. Mellow like yours. I often used to play the tapes twice, just to listen to him speaking. Is he really still around, George? I don't even like to ask, you see. I'm afraid they'll all change and I won't know them any more.'

He was still there, Smiley assured her. The same cover, the same rank.

'And still occupying that dreadful little suburban house in Highgate that Toby's watchers hated so? Forty, Meadow Close, top floor. Oh it was a *pest* of a place. I love a man who really lives his cover, and Aleks did. He was the busiest culture vulture that Embassy ever had. If you wanted something done fast, lecturer, musician, you name it, Aleks cut through the red tape faster than any man.'

'How did he manage that, Connie?'

'Not how *you* think, George Smiley,' she sang as the blood shot to her face. '*Oh* no. Aleksey Aleksandrovich was nothing but what he said he was, so there, you ask Toby Esterhase or Percy Alleline. Pure as the driven snow, he was. Unbesmirched in any shape or form, Toby will put you right on that!'

'Hey,' Smiley murmured, filling her glass. 'Hey, steady, Connie. Come down.'

'*Fooey*,' she shouted, quite unmollified. 'Sheer unadulterated *fooey*. Aleksey Aleksandrovich Polyakov was a six-cylinder Karla-trained hood if ever I saw one, and they wouldn't even listen to me! "You're seeing spies under the bed," says Toby. "Lamplighters are fully extended," says Percy,' – her Scottish brogue – '"We've no place for luxuries here." Luxuries my foot!' She was crying again. 'Poor George,' she kept saying. 'Poor George. You tried to help out but what could you do? You were on the down staircase yourself. Oh George, don't go hunting with the Lacons. Please don't.'

Gently he guided her back to Polyakov, and why she was so sure he was Karla's hood, a graduate of Karla's special school.

'It was Remembrance Day,' she sobbed. 'We photographed his medals, 'course we did.'

Year one again, year one of her eight-year love affair with Aleks Polyakov. The curious thing was, she said, that she had her eye on him from the moment he arrived:

'"Hullo," I thought. "I'm going to have a bit of fun with you."'

Quite why she thought that she didn't know. Perhaps it was his self-sufficiency, perhaps it was his poker walk, straight off the parade ground: 'Tough as a button. Army written all over him.' Or perhaps it was the way he lived: 'He chose the one house in London those lamplighters couldn't get within fifty yards of.' Or perhaps it was his work: 'There were three cultural attachés already, two of them were hoods and the only thing the third did was cart the flowers up to Highgate cemetery for poor Karl Marx.'

She was a little dazed so he walked her again, taking the whole weight of her when she stumbled. Well, she said, at first Toby Esterhase agreed to put Aleks on the A list and have his Acton lamplighters cover him for random days, twelve out of every thirty, and each time they followed him he was as pure as the driven snow.

'My dear, you'd have thought I'd rung him up and told him: "Aleks Aleksandrovich, mind your p's and q's because I'm putting Tiny Toby's dogs on you. So just you live your cover and no monkey business."'

He went to functions, lectures, strolled in the park, played a little tennis and short of giving sweets to the kids he couldn't have been more respectable. Connie fought for continued coverage but it was a losing battle. The machinery ground on and Polyakov was transferred to the B list: to be topped up every six months or as resources allowed. The six-monthly top-ups produced nothing at all, and after three years he was graded Persil: investigated in depth and found to be of no intelligence interest. There was nothing Connie could do, and really she had almost begun to live with the assessment when one gorgeous November day lovely Teddy Hankie telephoned her rather breathlessly from the Laundry at Acton to say Aleks Polyakov had blown his cover and run up his true colours at last. They were splashed all over the mast-head.

'Teddy was an old *old* chum. Old Circus and a perfect pet, I don't care if he's ninety. He'd finished for the day and was on his way home when the Soviet Ambassador's Volga drove past going to the wreath-laying ceremony, carrying the three service attachés. Three others were following in a second car. One was Polyakov and he was wearing more medals than a Christmas tree. Teddy shot down to Whitehall with his camera and photographed them across the street. My dear *everything* was on our side: the weather was perfect, a bit of rain and then some lovely evening sunshine, he could have got the smile on a fly's backside at three hundred yards. We blew up the photographs and there they were: two gallantry and four campaign. Aleks Polyakov was a war veteran and he'd never told a soul in seven years. Oh I was excited! I didn't even need to plot the campaigns. "Toby," I said – I rang him straight away – "You just listen to me for a moment, you Hungarian poison dwarf. This is one of the occasions when ego has finally got the better of cover. I want you to turn Aleks Aleksandrovich *inside out* for me, no if's or but's, Connie's little hunch has come home trumps."'

'And what did Toby say?'

The grey spaniel let out a dismal sigh, and dropped off to sleep again.

'Toby?' Connie was suddenly very lonely. 'Oh, Tiny Toby gave me his dead fish voice and said Percy Alleline was now head of operations, didn't he? It was Percy's job, not his, to allocate resources. I knew straight away something was wrong but I thought it was Toby.' She fell silent. 'Damn fire,' she muttered morosely. 'You only have to turn your back and it goes out.' She had lost interest. 'You know the rest. Report went to Percy. "So what?" Percy says. "Polyakov used to be in the Russian army. It was a biggish army and not everybody who fought in it was Karla's agent.' Very funny. Accused me of unscientific deduction.' 'Whose expression is that?' I said to him. "It's not *de*duction at all," he says, "it's *in*duction." "My dear Percy, wherever have you been learning words like that, you sound just like a beastly doctor or someone." My *dear*, he was cross! As a sop, Toby puts the dogs on Aleks and nothing happens. "Spike his house," I said. "His car, everything! Rig a mugging, turn him inside out, put the listeners on him! Fake a mistaken identity, search him. Anything, but for God's *sake* do something because it's a pound to a rouble Aleks Polyakov is running an English mole!" So Percy sends for me, all lofty,' – The brogue again – '"You're to leave Polyakov alone. You're to put him out of your silly woman's mind, do you understand? You and your blasted Polly-whatsisname are becoming a damned nuisance, so lay off him." Follows it up with a rude letter. "We spoke and you agreed," copy to head cow. I wrote "yes repeat no" on the bottom and sent it back to him.' She switched to her sergeant-major voice: '"You're losing your sense of proportion, Connie. Time you went out into the real world."'

Connie was having a hangover. She was sitting again, slumped over her glass. Her eyes had closed and her head kept falling to one side.

'Oh God,' she whispered, waking up again. 'Oh my Lordy be.'

'Did Polyakov have a legman?' Smiley asked.

'Why should he? He's a culture vulture. Culture vultures don't need legmen.'

'Komarov had one in Tokyo. You said so.'

'Komarov was military,' she said sullenly.

'So was Polyakov. You saw his medals.'

He held her hand, waiting. Lapin the rabbit, she said, clerk driver at the Embassy, twerp. At first she couldn't work him out. She suspected him of being one Ivlov alias Brod but she couldn't prove it and no one would help her anyway. Lapin the rabbit spent most of his day padding round London looking at girls and not daring to talk to them. But gradually she began to pick up the connection. Polyakov gave a reception, Lapin helped pour the drinks. Polyakov was called in late at night, and half an hour later Lapin turned up presumably to unbutton a telegram. And when Polyakov flew to Moscow Lapin the rabbit actually moved into the Embassy and slept there till he came back: 'He was doubling up,' said Connie firmly. 'Stuck out a mile.'

'So you reported that too?'

''Course I did.'

'And what happened?'

'Connie was sacked and Lapin went hippety-lippety home,' Connie said with a giggle. She yawned. 'Hey ho,' she said. 'Halcyon days. Did I start the landslide, George?'

The fire was quite dead. From somewhere above them came a thud, perhaps it was Janet and her lover. Gradually, Connie began humming, then swaying to her own music.

He stayed, trying to cheer her up. He gave her more drink and finally it brightened her.

'Come on,' she said, 'I'll show you *my* bloody medals.'

Dormitory feasts again. She had them in a scuffed attaché case which Smiley had to pull out from under the bed. First a real medal in a box and a typed citation calling her by her workname Constance Salinger and putting her on the Prime Minister's list.

''Cos Connie was a good girl,' she explained, her cheek against his. 'And loved all her gorgeous boys.'

Then photographs of past members of the Circus: Connie in Wren's uniform in the war, standing between Jebedee and Old Bill Magnus the wrangler, taken somewhere in England; Connie with Bill Haydon one side and Jim Prideaux the other, the men in cricket gear and all three looking very-nicely-thank you, as Connie put it, on the summer course at Sarratt, the grounds stretching out behind them, mown and sunlit and the sight screens glistening. Next an enormous magnifying glass with signatures engraved on the lens: From Roy, from Percy, from Toby and lots of others, 'To Connie with love and never say goodbye!'

Lastly Bill's own special contribution: a caricature of Connie lying across the whole expanse of Kensington Palace Gardens while she peered at the Soviet Embassy through a telescope: 'With love and fond memories, dear, dear, Connie.'

'They still remember him here, you know. The golden boy. Christ Church common room has a couple of his paintings. They take them out quite often. Giles Langley stopped me in the High only the other day: did I ever hear from Haydon? Don't know what I said: Yes. No. Does Giles's sister still do safe houses, do you know?' Smiley did not. '"We miss his flair," says Giles, "they don't breed them like Bill Haydon any more." ' Giles must be a hundred and

eight in the shade. Says he taught Bill modern history in the days before
Empire became a dirty word. Asked after Jim, too. "His alter ego we might
say, hem hem, hem hem." You never liked Bill, did you?' Connie ran on
vaguely, as she packed it all away again in plastic bags and bits of cloth. 'I
never knew whether you were jealous of him or he was jealous of you. Too
glamorous, I suppose. You always distrusted looks. Only in men, mind.'

'My dear Connie, don't be absurd,' Smiley retorted, off guard for once. 'Bill
and I were perfectly good friends. What on earth makes you say that?'

'Nothing.' She had almost forgotten it. 'I heard once he had a run round
the park with Ann, that's all. Isn't he a cousin of hers or something? I always
thought you'd have been so good together, you and Bill, if it could have
worked. You'd have brought back the old spirit. Instead of that Scottish
twerp. Bill rebuilding Camelot' – her fairy-tale smile again – 'and George –'

'George picking up the bits,' said Smiley, vamping for her, and they
laughed, Smiley falsely.

'Give me a kiss, George. Give Connie a kiss.'

She showed him through the kitchen garden, the route her lodgers used,
she said he would prefer it to the view of the filthy new bungalows the
Harrison pigs had flung up in the next door garden. A thin rain was falling,
the few stars glowed big and pale in the mist; on the road lorries rumbled
northward through the night. Clasping him Connie grew suddenly
frightened.

'You're very naughty, George. Do you hear? Look at me. Don't look that
way, it's all neon lights and Sodom. Kiss me. All over the world beastly people
are making our time into nothing, why do you help them? Why?'

'I'm not helping them, Connie.'

''Course you are. Look at me. It was a good time, do you hear? A real time.
Englishmen could be proud then. Let them be proud now.'

'That's not quite up to me, Connie.'

She was pulling his face on to her own, so he kissed her full on the lips.

'Poor loves.' She was breathing heavily, not perhaps from any one emotion
but from a whole mess of them, washed around in her like mixed drinks.
'Poor loves. Trained to Empire, trained to rule the waves. All gone. All taken
away. Bye-bye world. You're the last George, you and Bill. And filthy Percy a
bit.' He had known it would end like this; but not quite so awfully. He had had
the same story from her every Christmas at the little drinking parties that
went on in corners round the Circus. 'You don't know Millponds, do you?'
she was asking.

'What's Millponds?'

'My brother's place. Beautiful Palladian house, lovely grounds, near
Newbury. One day a road came. Crash. Bang. Motorway. Took all the
grounds away. I grew up there, you see. They haven't sold Sarratt, have they?
I was afraid they might.'

'I'm sure they haven't.'

He longed to be free of her but she was clutching him more fiercely, he
could feel her heart thumping against him.

'If it's bad, don't come back. Promise? I'm an old leopard and I'm too old to
change my spots. I want to remember you all as you were. Lovely, lovely boys.'

He did not like to leave her there in the dark, swaying under the trees, so he
walked her halfway back to the house, neither of them talking. As he went
down the road he heard her humming again, so loud it was like a scream. But
it was nothing to the mayhem inside him just then, the currents of alarm and

anger and disgust at this blind night walk with God knew what bodies at the end.

He caught a stopping train to Slough where Mendel was waiting for him with a hired car. As they drove slowly towards the orange glow of the city, he listened to the sum of Peter Guillam's researches. The duty officers' ledger contained no record of the night of the tenth and eleventh of April, said Mendel. The pages had been excised with a razor blade. The janitors' returns for the same night were also missing, as were the signals' returns.

'Peter thinks it was done recently. There's a note scribbled on the next page saying "All enquiries to Head of London Station." It's in Esterhase's hand-writing and dated Friday.'

'*Last* Friday?' said Smiley, turning so fast that his seat belt let out a whine of complaint. 'That's the day Tarr arrived in England.'

'It's all according to Peter,' Mendel replied stolidly.

And finally, that concerning Lapin alias Ivlov, and Cultural Attaché Aleksey Aleksandrovich Polyakov, both of the Soviet Embassy in London, Toby Esterhase's lamplighter reports carried no adverse trace whatever. Both had been investigated, both were graded Persil: the cleanest category available. Lapin had been posted back to Moscow a year ago.

In a briefcase, Mendel had also brought Guillam's photographs, the result of his foray at Brixton developed and blown up to full plate size. Close to Paddington Station, Smiley got out and Mendel handed the case to him through the doorway.

'Sure you don't want me to come with you?' Mendel asked

'Thank you. It's only a hundred yards.'

'Lucky for you there's twenty-four hours in the day, then.'

'Yes, it is.'

'Some people sleep.'

'Good night.'

Mendel was still holding onto the briefcase. 'I may have found the school,' he said. 'Place called Thursgood's near Taunton. He did half a term's supply work in Berkshire first, then seems to have hoofed it to Somerset. Got a caravan, I hear. Want me to check?'

'How will you do that?'

'Bang on his door. Sell him a Hoover, get to know him socially.'

'I'm sorry,' said Smiley, suddenly worried. 'I'm afraid I'm jumping at shadows. I'm sorry, that was rude of me.'

'Young Guillam's jumping at shadows too,' said Mendel firmly. 'Says he's getting funny looks around the place. Says there's something up and they're all in it. I told him to have a stiff drink.'

'Yes,' said Smiley after further thought. 'Yes, that's the thing to do. Jim's a pro,' he explained. 'A fieldman of the old school. He's good, whatever they did to him.'

Camilla had come back late. Guillam had understood her flute lesson with Sand ended at nine, yet it was eleven by the time she let herself in, and he was accordingly short with her, he couldn't help it. Now she lay in bed with her grey-black hair spread over the pillow watching him as he stood at the unlit window staring in the square.

'Have you eaten?' he said.

'Doctor Sand fed me.'

'What on?'

Sand was a Persian, she had told him.

No answer. Dreams, perhaps? Nut steak? Love? In bed she never stirred except to embrace him. When she slept she barely breathed; sometimes he would wake and watch her, wondering how he would feel if she were dead.

'Are you fond of Sand?' he asked.

'Sometimes.'

'Is he your lover?'

'Sometimes.'

'Maybe you should move in with him instead of me.'

'It's not like that,' said Camilla. 'You don't understand.'

No. He didn't. First there had been a loving couple necking in the back of a Rover, then a lonely queer in a trilby exercising his Sealyham, then a pair of girls made an hour-long call from a phone box outside his front door. There need be nothing to any of it, except that the events were consecutive, like a changing of the guard. Now a van had parked and no one got out. More lovers, or a lamplighters' night team? The van had been there ten minutes when the Rover drove away.

Camilla was asleep. He lay awake beside her, waiting for tomorrow when, at Smiley's request, he intended to steal the file on the Prideaux affair, otherwise known as the Ellis scandal or – more locally – Operation Testify.

# FOURTEEN

It had been, till that moment, the second happiest day of Bill Roach's short life. The happiest was shortly before the dissolution of his household, when his father discovered a wasps' nest in the roof and recruited Bill to help him smoke them out. His father was not an outdoor man, not even handy, but after Bill had looked up wasps in his encyclopaedia they drove to the chemist together and bought sulphur, which they burned on a charger under the eaves, and did the wasps to death.

Whereas today had seen the formal opening of Jim Prideaux's car club rally. Till now they had only stripped the Alvis down, refurbished her and put her together again but today as the reward they had laid out, with the help of Latzy the DP, a slalom of straw bales on the stony side of the drive, then each in turn had taken the wheel and with Jim as timekeeper puffed and shunted through the gates to the tumult of their supporters. 'Best car England ever made,' was how Jim had introduced his car. 'Out of production, thanks to socialism.' She was now repainted, she had a racing Union Jack on the bonnet, and she was undoubtedly the finest, fastest car on earth. In the first round Roach had come third out of fourteen, and now in the second he had reached the chestnut trees without once stalling, and was all set for the home lap and a record time. He had never imagined anything could give him so much pleasure. He loved the car, he loved Jim and he even loved the school, and for the first time in his life he loved trying to win. He could hear Jim yelling 'Easy, Jumbo' and he could see Latzy leaping up and down with the improvised chequered flag, but as he clattered past the post he knew already that Jim wasn't watching him any more but glaring down the course towards the beech trees.

'Sir, how long, sir?' he asked breathlessly and there was a small hush.

'Timekeeper!' sang Spikely, chancing his luck. 'Time please, Rhino.'

'Was very good, Jumbo,' Latzy said, also looking at Jim.

For once, Spikely's impertinence, like Roach's entreaty, found no response. Jim was staring across the field, towards the lane that formed the eastern border. A boy named Coleshaw stood beside him, whose nickname was Cole Slaw. He was a lag from IIIB, and famous for sucking up to staff. The ground lay very flat just there before lifting to the hills; often after a few days' rain it flooded. For this reason there was no good hedge beside the lane but a post-and-wire fence; and no trees either, just the fence, the flats, and sometimes the Quantocks behind, which today had vanished in the general whiteness. The flats could have been a marsh leading to a lake, or simply to the white infinity. Against this washed-out background strolled a single figure, a trim, inconspicuous pedestrian, male and thin-faced, in a trilby hat and grey raincoat, carrying a walking stick which he barely used. Watching him also, Roach decided that the man wanted to walk faster but was going slowly for a purpose.

'Got your specs on, Jumbo?' asked Jim, staring after this same figure who was about to draw level with the next post.

'Yes, sir.'

'Who is he, then? Looks like Solomon Grundy.'

'Don't know, sir.'

'Never seen him before?'

'No, sir.'

'Not staff, not village. So who is he? Beggarman? Thief? Why doesn't he look this way, Jumbo? What's wrong with us? Wouldn't you, if you saw a bunch of boys flogging a car round a field? Doesn't he like cars? Doesn't he like boys?'

Roach was still thinking up an answer to all these questions when Jim started speaking to Latzy in DP, using a murmured level sort of tone which at once suggested to Roach that there was a complicity between them, a special foreign bond. The impression was strengthened by Latzy's reply, plainly negative, which had the same unstartled quietness.

'Sir, please sir, I think he's to do with the church, sir,' said Cole Slaw. 'I saw him talking to Wells Fargo, sir, after the service.'

The vicar's name was Spargo and he was very old. It was Thursgood legend that he was in fact the great Wells Fargo in retirement. At this intelligence, Jim thought a while and Roach, furious, told himself that Coleshaw was making the story up.

'Hear what they talked about, Cole Slaw?'

'Sir, no, sir. They were looking at pew lists, sir. But I could ask Wells Fargo, sir.'

'*Our* pew lists? Thursgood pew lists?'

'Yes, sir. School pew lists. Thursgood's. With all the names, sir, where we sit.'

And where the staff sit too, thought Roach sickly.

'Anybody sees him again, let me know. Or any other sinister bodies, understand?' Jim was addressing them all, making light of it now. 'Don't hold with odd bods hanging about the school. Last place I was at we had a whole damn gang. Cleared the place out. Silver, money, boys' watches, radios, God knows what they didn't pinch. He'll pinch the Alvis next. Best car England ever made and out of production. Colour of hair, Jumbo?'

'Black, sir.'

'Height, Cole Slaw?'

'Sir, six foot, sir.'

'Everybody looks six foot to Cole Slaw, sir,' said a wit, for Coleslaw was a midget, reputedly fed on gin as a baby.

'Age, Spikely, you toad?'

'Ninety-one, sir.'

The moment dissolved in laughter, Roach was awarded a re-drive and did badly, and the same night lay in an anguish of jealousy that the entire car club, not to mention Latzy, had been recruited wholesale to the select rank of watcher. It was poor consolation to assure himself that their vigilance would never match his own; that Jim's order would not outlive the day; or that from now on Roach must increase his efforts to meet what was clearly an advancing threat.

The thin-faced stranger disappeared, but next day Jim paid a rare visit to the churchyard; Roach saw him talking to Wells Fargo, before an open grave. Thereafter Bill Roach noticed a steady darkening of Jim's face, and an alertness which at times was like an anger in him, as he stalked through the twilight every evening, or sat on the hummocks outside his caravan, indifferent to the cold or wet, smoking his tiny cigar and sipping his vodka as the dusk closed on him.

# FIFTEEN

The Hotel Islay in Sussex Gardens – where, on the day after his visit to Ascot, George Smiley under the name of Barraclough had set up his operational headquarters – was a very quiet place considering its position, and perfectly suited to his needs. It lay a hundred yards south of Paddington Station, one of a terrace of elderly mansions cut off from the main avenue by a line of plane trees and a parking patch. The traffic roared past it all night. But the inside, though it was a firebowl of clashing wallpapers and copper lampshades, was a place of extraordinary calm. Not only was there nothing going on in the hotel: there was nothing going on in the world either, and this impression was strengthened by Mrs Pope Graham, the proprietor, a major's widow with a terribly langorous voice which imparted a sense of deep fatigue to Mr Barraclough or anyone else who sought her hospitality. Inspector Mendel, whose informant she had been for many years, insisted that her name was common Graham. The Pope had been added for grandeur or out of deference to Rome.

'Your father wasn't a Greenjacket, was he, dear?' she enquired, with a yawn, as she read Barraclough in the register. Smiley paid her fifty pounds' advance for a two-week stay and she gave him room eight because he wanted to work. He asked for a desk and she gave him a rickety card table, Norman the boy brought it. 'It's Georgian,' she sighed, supervising its delivery. 'So you will love it for me, won't you, dear? I shouldn't lend it to you really, it was the major's.'

To the fifty, Mendel privately had added a further twenty on account from his own wallet, dirty oncers as he called them, which he later recovered from Smiley. 'No smell to nothing, is there?' he told her.

'You could say so,' Mrs Pope Graham agreed, demurely stowing the notes among her nether garments.

'I'll want every scrap,' Mendel warned, seated in her basement apartment over a bottle of the one she liked. 'Times of entry and exit, contacts, life-style, and most of all' – he lifted an emphatic finger – 'most of all, more important than you can possibly know, this is, I'll want suspicious persons taking an interest or putting questions to your staff under a pretext.' He gave her his state-of-the-nation look. 'Even if they say they're the Guards Armoured and Sherlock Holmes rolled into one.'

'There's only me and Norman,' said Mrs Pope Graham, indicating a shivery boy in a black overcoat to which Mrs Pope Graham had stitched a velvet collar of beige. 'And they'll not get far with Norman, will they, dear, you're too sensitive.'

'Same with his incoming letters,' said the Inspector. 'I'll want postmarks and times posted where legible, but not tampering or holding back. Same with his objects.' He allowed a hush to fall as he eyed the substantial safe which formed such a feature of the furnishings. 'Now and then, he's going to ask for objects to be lodged. Mainly they'll be papers, sometimes books. There's only one person allowed to look at those objects apart from him' – he pulled a sudden, piratical grin – 'Me. Understand? No one else can even know you've got them. And don't fiddle with them or he'll know because he's sharp. It's got to be expert fiddling. I'm not saying any more,' Mendel concluded; though he did remark to Smiley, soon after returning from Somerset, that if twenty quid was all it cost them, Norman and his protectress were the cheapest babysitting service in the business.

In which boast he was pardonably mistaken, for he could hardly be expected to know of Jim's recruitment of the entire car club; nor the means by which Jim was able subsequently to trace the path of Mendel's wary investigations. Nor could Mendel, or anyone else, have guessed the state of electric alertness to which anger, and the strain of waiting, and perhaps a little madness, had seemingly brought him.

Room eight was on the top floor. Its window looked on to the parapet. Beyond the parapet lay a side street with a shady bookshop and a travel agency called the Wide World. The hand towel was embroidered 'Swan Hotel

Marlow'. Lacon stalked in the same evening carrying a fat briefcase containing the first consignment of papers from his office. To talk they sat side by side on the bed while Smiley played a transistor wireless to drown the sound of their voices. Lacon took this mawkishly; he seemed somehow too old for the picnic. Next morning on his way to work Lacon reclaimed the papers and returned the books which Smiley had given him to pad out his briefcase. In this role Lacon was at his worst. His manner was offended and off-hand; he made it clear he detested the irregularity. In the cold weather, he seemed to have developed a permanent blush. But Smiley could not have read the files by day because they were on call to Lacon's staff and their absence would have caused an uproar. Nor did he want to. He knew better than anyone that he was desperately short of time. Over the next three days this procedure varied very little. Each evening on his way to take the train from Paddington, Lacon dropped in his papers and each night Mrs Pope Graham furtively reported to Mendel that the sour gangly one had called again, the one who looked down his nose at Norman. Each morning, after three hours' sleep and a disgusting breakfast of undercooked sausage and overcooked tomato – there was no other menu – Smiley waited for Lacon to arrive, then slipped gratefully into the cold winter's day to take his place among his fellow men.

They were extraordinary nights for Smiley alone up there on the top floor. Thinking of them afterwards, though his days between were just as fraught and on the surface more eventful, he recalled them as a single journey, almost a single night. 'And you'll do it?' Lacon had piped shamelessly in the garden. 'Go forwards, go backwards?' As Smiley retraced path after path into his own past, there was no longer any difference between the two: forwards or backwards, it was the same journey and its destination lay ahead of him. There was nothing in that room, no object among that whole magpie collection of tattered hotel junk, that separated him from the rooms of his recollection. He was back on the top floor of the Circus, in his own plain office with the Oxford prints, just as he had left it a year ago. Beyond his door lay the low-ceilinged anteroom where Control's grey-haired ladies, the mothers, softly typed and answered telephones; while here in the hotel an undiscovered genius along the corridor night and day tapped patiently at an old machine. At the anteroom's far end – in Mrs Pope Graham's world there was a bathroom there, and a warning not to use it – stood the blank door that led to Control's sanctuary: an alley of a place, with old steel cupboards and old red books, a smell of sweet dust and jasmine tea. Behind the desk, Control himself, a carcass of a man by then, with his lank grey forelock and his smile as warm as a skull.

This mental transposition was so complete in Smiley that when his telephone rang – the extension was an extra, payable in cash – he had to give himself time to remember where he was. Other sounds had an equally confusing effect on him, such as the rustle of pigeons on the parapet, the scraping of the television mast in the wind, and in rain the sudden river gurgling in the roof valley. For these sounds also belonged to his past, and in Cambridge Circus were heard by the fifth floor only. His ear selected them no doubt for that very reason: they were the background jingle of his past. Once in the early morning, hearing a footfall in the corridor outside his room, Smiley actually went to the bedroom door expecting to let in the Circus night coding clerk. He was immersed in Guillam's photographs at the time, puzzling out from far too little information the likely Circus procedure under lateralism for handling an incoming telegram from Hong Kong. But instead of the clerk he found Norman barefooted in pyjamas. Confetti was strewn over the carpet and two pairs of shoes stood outside the opposite door, a man's and a girl's, though no one at the Islay, least of all Norman, would ever clean them.

'Stop prying and go to bed,' said Smiley. And when Norman only stared: 'Oh do go away, will you?' – And nearly, but he stopped himself in time – 'you grubby little man.'

'Operation Witchcraft,' read the title on the first volume which Lacon had brought to him that first night. 'Policy regarding distribution of Special Product.' The rest of the cover was obliterated by warning labels and handling instructions, including one which quaintly advised the accidental finder to 'return the file UNREAD' to the Chief Registrar at the Cabinet Office. 'Operation Witchcraft,' read the second. 'Supplementary estimates to the Treasury, special accomodation in London, special financing arrangements, bounty etc.' 'Source Merlin,' read the third, bound to the first with pink ribbon. 'Customer Evaluations, cost effectiveness, wider exploitation, see also Secret Annexe.' But the secret annexe was not attached, and when Smiley asked for it there was a coldness.

'The Minister keeps it in his personal safe,' Lacon snapped.

'Do you know the combination?'

'Certainly not,' he retorted, now furious.

'What is the title of it?'

'It can be of no possible concern to you. I entirely fail to see why you should waste your time chasing after this material in the first place. It's highly secret and we have done everything humanly possible to keep the readership to the minimum.'

'Even a secret annexe has to have a title,' said Smiley mildly.

'This has none.'

'Does it give the identity of Merlin?'

'Don't be ridiculous. The Minister would not want to know, and Alleline would not want to tell him.'

'What does wider exploitation mean?'

'I refuse to be interrogated, George. You're not family any more, you know. By rights I should have you specially cleared as it is.'

'Witchcraft-cleared?'

'Yes.'

'Do we have a list of people who have been cleared in that way?'

It was in the policy file, Lacon retorted, and all but slammed the door on him before coming back, to the slow chant of 'Where have all the flowers gone?' introduced by an Australian disc-jockey. 'The Minister – ' He began again. 'He doesn't like devious explanations. He has a saying: he'll only believe what can be written on a postcard. He's very impatient to be given something he can get his hands on.'

Smiley said: 'You won't forget Prideaux, will you? Just anything you have on him at all; even scraps are better than nothing.'

With that Smiley left Lacon to glare a while, then make a second exit: 'You're not going fey are you, George? You realize that Prideaux had most likely never even *heard* of Witchcraft before he was shot? I really do fail to see why you can't stick with the primary problem instead of rootling around in

. . . .' But by this time he had talked himself out of the room.

Smiley turned to the last of the batch: 'Operation Witchcraft, correspondence with Department.' Department being one of Whitehall's many euphemisms for the Circus. This volume was conducted in the form of official minutes between the Minister on the one side, and on the other – recognizable at once by his laborious schoolboy hand – Percy Alleline, at that time still consigned to the bottom rungs of Control's ladder of beings.

A very dull monument, Smiley reflected, surveying these much-handled files, to such a long and cruel war.

# SIXTEEN

It was this long and cruel war which in its main battles Smiley now relived as he embarked upon his reading. The files contained only the thinnest record of it; his memory contained far more. Its protagonists were Alleline and Control, its origins misty. Bill Haydon, a keen if saddened follower of those events, maintained that the two men learned to hate each other at Cambridge during Control's brief spell as a don and Alleline's as an undergraduate. According to Bill, Alleline was Control's pupil and a bad one, and Control taunted him, which he certainly might have.

The story was grotesque enough for Control to play it up: 'Percy and I are blood brothers I hear. We romped together in punts, imagine!' He never said whether it was true.

To half-legends of that sort Smiley could add a few hard facts from his knowledge of the two men's early lives. While Control was no man's child, Percy Alleline was a lowland Scot and a son of the Manse; his father was a Presbyterian hammer and if Percy did not have his faith, he had surely inherited the faculty of bullish persuasion. He missed the war by a year or two and joined the Circus from a City company. At Cambridge he had been a bit of a politician (somewhat to the right of Genghis Khan, said Haydon who was himself, Lord knows, no milk and water Liberal) and a bit of an athlete. He was recruited by a figure of no account called Maston who for a short time contrived to build himself a corner in counter intelligence. Maston saw a great future in Alleline and, having peddled his name furiously, fell from grace. Finding Alleline an embarrassment, Circus packed him off to South America where he did two full tours under consular cover without returning to England.

Even Control admitted that Percy did extremely well there, Smiley recalled. The Argentinians, liking his tennis and the way he rode, took him for a gentleman – Control speaking – and assumed he was stupid, which

Percy never quite was. By the time he handed over to his successor he had put together a string of agents along both seaboards and was spreading his wings northward as well. After home leave and a couple of weeks' briefing he was moved to India where his agents seemed to regard him as the reincarnation of the British Raj. He preached loyalty to them, paid them next to nothing and when it suited him sold them down the river. From India he went to Cairo. That posting should have been difficult for Alleline, if not impossible; for the Middle East till then had been Haydon's favourite stamping ground. The Cairo networks looked on Bill quite literally in the terms which Martindale had used of him that fateful night in his anonymous dining-club: as a latter-day Lawrence of Arabia. They were all set to make life hell for his successor. Yet somehow Percy bulldozed his way through, and if he had only steered clear of the Americans, might have gone down in memory as a better man than Haydon. Instead there was a scandal and an open row between Percy and Control.

The circumstances were still obscure: the incident occurred long before Smiley's elevation as Control's high chamberlain. With no authority from London, it appeared, Alleline had involved himself in a silly American plot to replace a local potentate with one of their own. Alleline had always had a fatal reverence for the Americans. From Argentina he had observed with admiration their rout of left-wing politicians around the hemisphere; in India he had delighted in their skill at dividing the forces of centralisation. Whereas Control, like most of the Circus, despised them and all their works, which he frequently sought to undermine.

The plot aborted, the British oil companies were furious and Alleline, as the jargon happily puts it, had to leave in his socks. Later, Alleline claimed that Control had urged him on, then pulled the rug out from under; even, that he had deliberately blown the plot to Moscow. However it was, Alleline reached London to find a posting order directing him to the Nursery where he was to take over the training of greenhorn probationers. It was a slot normally reserved for run-down contract men with a couple of years to go before their pension. There were just so few jobs left in London those days for a man of Percy's seniority and talents, explained Bill Haydon, then head of personnel.

'Then you'll damn well have to invent me one,' said Percy. He was right. As Bill frankly confessed to Smiley some while later, he had reckoned without the power of the Alleline lobby.

'But who are these people?' Smiley used to ask. 'How can they force a man on you when you don't want him?'

'Golfers,' Control snapped. Golfers and conservatives, for Alleline in those days was flirting with the opposition and was received with open arms, not least by Miles Sercombe, Ann's lamentably unremoved cousin, and now Lacon's Minister. Yet Control had little power to resist. The Circus was in the doldrums and there was loose talk of scrapping the existing outfit entirely and starting elsewhere with a new one. Failures in that world occur traditionally in series but this had been an exceptionally long run. Product had slumped; more and more of it had turned out to be suspect. In the places where it mattered Control's hand was none too strong.

This temporary incapacity did not mar Control's joy in the drafting of Percy Alleline's personal charter as Operational Director. He called it Percy's Fool's Cap.

There was nothing Smiley could do. Bill Haydon was in Washington by then, trying to negotiate an intelligence treaty with what he called the fascist puritans of the American agency. But Smiley had risen to the fifth floor and one of his tasks was to keep petitioners off Control's back. So it was to Smiley that Alleline came to ask: 'Why?' Would call on him in his office when Control was out, invite him to that dismal flat of his having first sent his paramour to the cinema, interrogate him in his plaintive brogue. 'Why?' He even invested in a bottle of malt whisky which he forced on Smiley liberally while sticking to the cheaper brand himself.

'What have I done to him, George , that's so damn special? We'd a brush or two, what's so unusual to that, if you'll tell me? Why does he pick on me? All I want is a place at the top table. God knows my record entitles me to that!'

By top table he meant the fifth floor.

The charter which Control had drafted for him, and which at a glance had a most impressive shape, gave Alleline the right to examine all operations before they were launched. The small print made this right conditional upon the consent of the operational sections and Control made sure that this was not forthcoming. The charter invited him to 'co-ordinate resources and break down regional jealousies', a concept Alleline had since achieved with the establishment of London Station. But the resources sections, such as the lamplighters, the forgers, the listeners and the wranglers, declined to open their books to him and he lacked the powers to force them. So Alleline starved, his trays were empty from lunchtime onwards.

'I'm mediocre, is that it? We've all to be geniuses these days, prima donnas and no damn chorus; old men at that.' For Alleline, though it was easily forgettable in him, was still a young man to be at the top table, with eight or ten years to brandish over Haydon and Smiley, and more over Control.

Control was immovable: 'Percy Alleline would sell his mother for a knighthood and this service for a seat in the House of Lords.' And later, as his hateful illness began creeping over him: 'I refuse to bequeath my life's work to a parade horse. I'm too vain to be flattered, too old to be ambitious and I'm ugly as a crab. Percy's quite the other way and there are enough witty men in Whitehall to prefer his sort to mine.'

Which was how, indirectly, Control might be said to have brought Witch-craft upon his own head.

'George, come in here,' Control snapped one day over the buzzer. 'Brother Percy's trying to twist my tail. Come in here or there'll be bloodshed.'

It was a time, Smiley remembered, when unsuccessful warriors were returning from foreign parts. Roy Bland had just flown in from Belgrade, where with Toby Esterhase's help he had been trying to save the wreck of a dying network; Paul Skordeno, at that time head German, had just buried his best Soviet agent in East Berlin, and as to Bill, after another fruitless trip he was back in the pepper pot fuming about Pentagon arrogance, Pentagon idiocy, Pentagon duplicity; and claiming that 'the time had come to do a deal with the bloody Russians instead'.

And in the Islay it was after midnight; a late guest was ringing the bell. Which will cost him ten bob to Norman, thought Smiley, for whom the revised British coinage was still something of a puzzle. With a sigh, he drew towards him the first of the Witchcraft files, and having vouchsafed a gingerly lick to his right finger and thumb, set to work matching the official memory with his own.

'We spoke,' wrote Alleline, only a couple of months after that interview, in a slightly hysterical personal letter to Ann's distinguished cousin the Minister and entered on Lacon's file. 'Witchcraft reports derive from a source of extreme sensitivity. To my mind no existing method of Whitehall distribution meets the case. The despatch box system which we used for GADFLY fell down when keys were lost by Whitehall customers, or in one disgraceful case when an overworked Under Secretary gave his key to his personal assistant. I have already spoken to Lilley of naval intelligence who is prepared to put at our disposal a special reading room in the Admiralty main building where the material is made available to customers and watched over by a senior janitor of this service. The reading room will be known, for cover purposes, as the conference room of the Adriatic Working Party or the AWP room for short. Customers with reading rights will not have passes, since these also are open to abuse. Instead they will identify themselves personally to my janitor' – Smiley noted the pronoun – 'who will be equipped with an indoctrination list illustrated with customers' photographs.'

Lacon, not yet convinced, to the Treasury through his odious master, the Minister, on whose behalf his submissions were invariably made: 'Even allowing that this is necessary, the reading room will have to be extensively rebuilt.

(1) Will you authorize cost?

(2) If so the cost should seem to be borne by the Admiralty. Department will covertly reimburse. ·

(3) There is also the question of extra janitors, a further expense . . .'

And there is a question of Alleline's greater glory, Smiley commented as he slowly turned the pages. It shone already like a beacon everywhere: Percy is heading for the top table and Control might already be dead.

From the stairwell, came the sound of rather beautiful singing. A Welsh guest, very drunk, was wishing everyone goodnight.

Witchcraft, Smiley recalled – his memory again, the files knew nothing so plainly human – Witchcraft was by no means Percy Alleline's first attempt, in his new post, at launching his own operation; but since his charter bound him to obtain Control's approval, its predecessors had been stillborn. For a while, for instance, he had concentrated on tunnelling. The Americans had built audio tunnels in Berlin and Belgrade, the French had managed something similar against the Americans. Very well, under Percy's banner the Circus would get in on the market. Control looked on benignly, an inter-services committee was formed (known as the Alleline Committee), a team of boffins from Nuts and Bolts made a survey of the foundations of the Soviet Embassy in Athens, where Alleline counted on the unstinted support of the latest military regime which, like its predecessors, he greatly admired. Then very gently Control knocked over Percy's bricks and waited for him to come up with something new. Which, after several shots between, was exactly what Percy was doing that grey morning when Control peremptorily summoned Smiley to the feast.

Control was sitting at his desk, Alleline was standing at the window, between them lay a plain folder, bright yellow and closed.

'Sit over there and take a look at this nonsense.'

Smiley sat in the easy chair and Alleline stayed at the window resting his big elbows on the sill, staring over the rooftops to Nelson's Column and the spires of Whitehall beyond.

Inside the folder was a photograph of what purported to be a high-level Soviet naval dispatch fifteen pages long.

'Who made the translation?' Smiley asked, thinking that it looked good enough to be Roy Bland's work.

'God,' Control replied. 'God made it, didn't he, Percy? Don't ask him anything, George, he won't tell you.'

It was Control's time for looking exceptionally youthful. Smiley remembered how he had lost weight, how his cheeks were pink, and how those who knew him little tended to congratulate him on his good appearance. Only Smiley, perhaps, ever noticed the tiny beads of sweat which even in those days habitually followed his hairline.

Precisely, the document was an appreciation, allegedly prepared for the Soviet High Command, of a recent Soviet naval exercise in the Mediterranean and Black Sea. In Lacon's file it was entered simply as Report No. I, under the title: 'Naval'. For months the Admiralty had been screaming at the Circus for anything relating to this exercise. It therefore had an impressive topicality which at once, in Smiley's eyes, made it suspect. It was detailed but it dealt with matters which Smiley did not understand even at a distance: shore-to-sea strike power, radio activation of enemy alert procedures, the higher mathematics of the balance of terror. If it was genuine it was gold dust but there was no earthly reason to suppose it was genuine. Every week the Circus processed dozens of unsolicited so-called Soviet documents. Most were straight pedlar material. A few were deliberate plants by allies with an axe to grind, a few more were Russian chickenfeed. Very rarely one or other turned out to be sound, but usually after it had been rejected.

'Whose initials are these?' Smiley asked, referring to some annotations pencilled in Russian in the margin. 'Does anyone know?'

Control tilted his head at Alleline. 'Ask the authority. Don't ask me.'

'Zharov,' said Alleline. 'Admiral, Black Sea Fleet.'

'It's not dated,' Smiley objected.

'It's a draft,' Alleline replied complacently, his brogue richer than usual. 'Zharov signed it Thursday. The finished despatch with those amendments went out on circulation Monday, dated accordingly.'

Today was Tuesday.

'Where does it come from?' Smiley asked, still lost.

'Percy doesn't feel able to tell,' said Control.

'What do our own evaluators say?'

'They've not seen it,' said Alleline, 'and what's more they're not going to.'

Control said icily: 'My brother in Christ, Lilley, of naval intelligence, has passed a preliminary opinion, however, has he not, Percy? Percy showed it to him last night – over a pink gin, was it, Percy, at the Travellers'?'

'At the Admiralty.'

'Brother Lilley, being a fellow Caledonian of Percy's, is as a rule sparing in his praise. However when he telephoned me half an hour ago he was positively fulsome. He even congratulated me. He regards the documents as genuine and is seeking our permission – Percy's, I suppose I should say – to apprise his fellow sealords of its conclusions.'

'Quite impossible,' said Alleline. 'It's for his eyes only, at least for a couple more weeks.'

'The stuff is so hot,' Control explained, 'that it has to be cooled off before it can be distributed.'

'But where does it come from?' Smiley insisted.

'Oh Percy's dreamed up a covername, don't you worry. Never been slow on covernames, have we, Percy?'

'But what's the access? Who's the case officer?'

'You'll enjoy this.' Control promised, aside. He was extraordinarily angry. In their long association Smiley could not remember him so angry. His slim, freckled hands were shaking and his normally lifeless eyes were sparkling with fury.

'Source Merlin,' Alleline said, prefacing the announcement with a slight but very Scottish sucking of the teeth, 'is a highly placed source with access to the most sensitive levels of Soviet policy-making.' And as if he were royalty: 'We have dubbed his product Witchcraft.'

He had used the identical form of words, Smiley noticed, in a top secret and personal letter to a fan at the Treasury, requesting for himself greater discretion in *ad hoc* payments to agents.

'He'll be saying he won him at the football pool next,' Control warned, who despite his second youth had an old man's inaccuracy when it came to popular idiom. 'Now get him to tell you why he won't tell you.'

Alleline was undeterred. He too was flushed, but with triumph, not disease. He filled his big chest for a long speech, which he delivered entirely to Smiley, tonelessly, rather as a Scottish police sergeant might give evidence before the courts.

'The identity of Source Merlin is a secret which is not mine to divulge. He's the fruit of a long cultivation by certain people in this service. People who are bound to me, as I am to them. People who are not at all entertained, either, by the failure rate around this place. There's been too much blown. Too much lost, wasted, too many scandals. I've said so many times but I might as well have spoken to the wind for all the damn care he paid me.'

'He's referring to me,' Control explained from the sidelines. 'I am *he* in this speech, you follow, George?'

'The ordinary principles of tradecraft and security have gone to the wall in this service. Need to know: where is it? Compartmentation at all levels: where is it, George? There's too much regional back-biting, stimulated from the top.'

'Another reference to myself,' Control put in.

'Divide and rule, that's the principle at work these days. Personalities who should be helping to fight communism are all at one another's throats. We're losing our top partners.'

'He means the Americans,' Control explained.

'We are losing our livelihood. Our self-respect. We've had enough.' He took back the report and jammed it under his arm. 'We've had a bellyful, in fact.'

'And like everyone who's had enough,' said Control as Alleline noisily left the room, 'he wants more.'

Now for a while Lacon's files, instead of Smiley's memory, once more took up the story. It was typical of the atmosphere of those last months that, having been brought in on the affair at the beginning, Smiley should have received no subsequent word of how it had developed. Control detested failure, as he detested illness, and his own failures most. He knew that to recognize failure was to live with it; that a service that did not struggle did not survive. He detested the silk-shirt agents, who hogged large chunks of the budget to the detriment of the bread-and-butter networks in which he put his faith. He loved success, but he detested miracles if they put the rest of his endeavour out of focus. He detested weakness as he detested sentiment and religion, and he detested Percy Alleline who had a dash of most of them. His way of dealing with them was literally to close the door: to withdraw into the dingy solitude of his upper rooms, receive no visitors and have all his phone calls fed to him by the mothers. The same quiet ladies fed him jasmine tea and the countless office files which he sent for and returned in heaps. Smiley would see them piled before the door as he went about his own business of trying to keep the rest of the Circus afloat. Many were old, from the days before Control led the pack. Some were personal, the biographies of past and present members of the service.

Control never said what he was doing. If Smiley asked the mothers, or if Bill Haydon sauntered in, favourite boy, and made the same enquiry, they only shook their heads or silently raised their eyebrows towards paradise: 'A terminal case,' said these gentle glances. 'We are humouring a great man at the end of his career.' But Smiley – as he now patiently leafed through file after file, and in a corner of his complex mind rehearsed Irina's letter to Ricki Tarr – Smiley knew, and in a quite real way took comfort from the knowledge, that he was not after all the first to make this journey of exploration; that Control's ghost was his companion into all but the furthest reaches; and might even have stayed the whole distance if Operation Testify, at the eleventh hour, had not stopped him dead.

Breakfast again and a much subdued Welshman not drawn by undercooked sausage and overcooked tomato.

'Do you want these back,' Lacon demanded, 'or have you done with them? They can't be very enlightening since they don't even contain the reports.'

'Tonight, please, if you don't mind.'

'I suppose you realize you look a wreck.'

He didn't realize, but at Bywater Street when he returned there Ann's pretty gilt mirror showed his eyes red-rimmed and his plump cheeks clawed with fatigue. He slept a little, then went his mysterious ways. When evening came Lacon was actually waiting for him. Smiley went straight on with his reading.

For six weeks, according to the files, the naval dispatch had no successor. Other sections of the Ministry of Defence echoed the Admiralty's enthusiasm for the original dispatch, the Foreign Office remarked that 'this document sheds an extraordinary sidelight on Soviet aggressive thinking', whatever that meant; Alleline persisted in his demands for special handling of the material but he was like a general with no army. Lacon referred frostily to 'the somewhat delayed follow-up', and suggested to his Minister that he should 'defuse the situation with the Admiralty'. From Control, according to the file, nothing. Perhaps he was lying low and praying it would blow over. In the lull a Treasury Moscow-gazer sourly pointed out that Whitehall had seen plenty of this in recent years: an encouraging first report, then silence or, worse, a scandal.

He was wrong. In the seventh week Alleline announced publication of three new Witchcraft reports all on the same day. All took the form of secret Soviet interdepartmental correspondence, though the topics differed widely.

Witchcraft No. 2, according to Lacon's summary, described tensions inside Comecon and spoke of the degenerative effect of Western trade deals on its weaker members. In Circus terms, this was a classic report from Roy Bland territory, covering the very target which the Hungarian-based Aggravate network had been attacking in vain for years. 'Excellent *tour d'horizon*,' wrote a Foreign Office customer, 'and backed by good collateral.'

Witchcraft No. 3 discussed revisionism in Hungary and Kadar's renewed purges in political and academic life: the best way to end loose talk in Hungary, said the author of the paper, borrowing a phrase coined by Khrushchev long before, would be to shoot some more intellectuals. Once again this was Roy Bland territory. 'A salutary warning,' wrote the same Foreign Office commentator, 'to all those who like to think the Soviet Union is going soft on satellites.'

These two reports were both in essence background, but Witchcraft No. 4 was sixty pages long and held by the customers to be unique. It was an immensely technical Soviet Foreign Service appreciation of the advantages and disadvantages of negotiating with a weakened American president. The conclusion, on balance, was that by throwing the President a bone for his own electorate, the Soviet Union could buy useful concessions in forthcoming discussions on multiple nuclear warheads. But it seriously questioned the desirability of allowing the United States to feel too much the loser, since this could tempt the Pentagon into a retributive or pre-emptive strike. The report was from the very heart of Bill Haydon territory. But as Haydon himself wrote in a touching minute to Alleline – promptly copied without Haydon's knowledge to the Minister and entered on the Cabinet Office file – in twenty-five years of attacking the Soviet nuclear target he had not laid his hands on anything of this quality.

'Nor,' he concluded, 'unless I am extremely mistaken, have our American brothers-in-arms. I know that these are early days, but it does occur to me that anyone taking this material to Washington could drive a very hard bargain in return. Indeed, if Merlin maintains the standard, I would venture to predict that we could buy anything there is to have in the American agency's shop.'

Percy Alleline had his reading room; and George Smiley made himself a coffee on the derelict burner beside the wash-stand. Midway the meter ran out and in a temper he called for Norman and ordered five pounds' worth of shillings.

# SEVENTEEN

With mounting interest Smiley continued his journey through Lacon's meagre records from that first meeting of protagonists until the present day. At the time, such a mood of suspicion had gripped the Circus that even between Smiley and Control the subject of Source Merlin became taboo. Alleline brought up the Witchcraft reports and waited in the anteroom while the mothers took them to Control, who signed them at once in order to demonstrate that he had not read them. Alleline took back the file, poked his head round Smiley's door, grunted a greeting, and clumped down the staircase. Bland kept his distance, and even Bill Haydon's breezy visits, traditionally a part of the life up there, of the talking shop which Control in the old days had liked to foster among his senior lieutenants, became fewer and shorter, then ceased entirely.

'Control's going potty,' Haydon told Smiley with contempt. 'And if I'm not mistaken he's also dying. It's just a question of which gets him first.'

Ths customary Tuesday meetings were discontinued, and Smiley found himself constantly harassed by Control either to go abroad on some blurred errand, or to visit the domestic out-stations – Sarratt, Brixton, Acton and the rest – as his personal envoy. He had a growing feeling that Control wanted him out of the way. When they talked, he felt the heavy strain of suspicion between them, so that even Smiley seriously wondered whether Bill was right and Control was unfit for his job.

The Cabinet Office files made it clear that those next three months saw a steady flowering of the Witchcraft operation, without any help from Control. Reports came in at the rate of two or even three a month and the standard, according to the customers, continued excellent, but Control's name was seldom mentioned and he was never invited to comment. Occasionally the evaluators produced quibbles. More often they complained that corroboration was not possible since Merlin took them into uncharted areas: could we not ask the Americans to check? We could not, said the Minister. Not yet, said Alleline; who in a confidential minute seen by no one, added: 'When the time is ripe we shall do more than barter our material for theirs. We are not interested in a one-time deal. Our task is to establish Merlin's track record beyond all doubt. When that is done, Haydon can go to market . . .'

There was no longer any question of it. Among the chosen few who were admitted to the chambers of the Adriatic Working Party, Merlin was already a winner. His material was accurate, often other sources confirmed it retrospectively. A Witchcraft committee formed with the Minister in the chair. Alleline was vice-chairman. Merlin had become an industry, and Control was not even employed. Which was why in desperation he had sent out Smiley with his beggar's bowl: 'There are three of them and Alleline,' he said. 'Sweat them, George. Tempt them, bully them, give them whatever they eat.'

Of those meetings also, the files were blessedly ignorant, for they belonged in the worst rooms of Smiley's memory. He had known already by then that there was nothing in Control's larder that would satisfy their hunger.

It was April. Smiley had come back from Portugal, where he had been burying a scandal, to find Control living under siege. Files lay strewn over the floor; new locks had been fitted to the windows. He had put the tea cosy over his one telephone and from the ceiling hung a baffler against electronic eavesdropping, a thing like an electric fan which constantly varied its pitch. In the three weeks Smiley had been away, Control had become an old man.

'Tell them they're buying their way in with counterfeit money,' he ordered, barely looking up from his files. 'Tell them any damn thing. I need time.'

'There are three of them and Alleline,' Smiley now repeated to himself, seated at the major's card table and studying Lacon's list of those who had been Witchcraft-cleared. Today there were sixty-eight licensed visitors to the Adriatic Working Party's reading room. Each, like a member of the Communist Party, was numbered according to the date of his admission. The list had been retyped since Control's death; Smiley was not included. But the same four founding fathers still headed the list: Alleline, Bland, Esterhase and Bill Haydon. Three of them and Alleline, Control had said.

Suddenly Smiley's mind, open as he read to every inference, every oblique connection, was assailed by a quite extraneous vision: of himself and Ann walking the Cornish cliffs. It was the time immediately after Control's death, the worst time Smiley could remember in their long, puzzled marriage. They were high on the coast, somewhere between Lamorna and Porthcurno, they had gone there out of season ostensibly for Ann to take the sea air for her cough. They had been following the coast path, each lost in his thoughts: she to Haydon, he supposed, he to Control, to Jim Prideaux and Testify, and the whole mess he had left between him on retirement. They shared no harmony. They had lost all calmness in one another's company; they were a mystery to each other, and the most banal conversation could take strange, uncontrollable directions. In London, Ann had been living wildly, taking anyone who would have her. He knew only that she was trying to bury something that hurt or worried her very much; but he knew no way to reach her.

'If *I* had died,' she demanded suddenly, 'rather than Control, say, how would you feel towards Bill?'

Smiley was still pondering his answer when she threw in: 'I sometimes think I safeguard your opinion of him. Is that possible? That I somehow keep the two of you together. Is that possible?'

'It's possible.' He added: 'Yes, I suppose I'm dependent on Bill in a way.'

'Is Bill still important in the Circus?'

'More than he was, probably.'

'And he still goes to Washington, wheels and deals with them, turns them upside down?'

'I expect so. I hear so.'

'Is he as important as you are?'

'I suppose.'

'I suppose,' she repeated. 'I expect. I hear. Is he *better* then? A better performer than you, better at the arithmetic? Tell me. Please tell me. You must.'

She was strangely excited. Her eyes, tearful from the wind, shone desperately upon him, she had both hands on his arm, and like a child was dragging on him for an answer.

'You've always told me that men aren't to be compared,' he replied awkwardly. 'You've always said, you didn't think in that category of comparison.'

'Tell me!'

'All right: no, he's not better.'

'As good?'

'No.'

'And if I wasn't there, what would you think of him then? If Bill were not my cousin, not my anything? Tell me. Would you think more of him, or less?'

'Less, I suppose.'

'Then think less *now*. I divorce him from the family, from our lives, from everything. Here and now. I throw him into the sea. There. Do you understand?'

He understood only: go back to the Circus, finish your business. It was one of a dozen ways she had of saying the same thing.

Still disturbed by this intrusion on his memory, Smiley stood up in rather a flurry and went to the window, his habitual lookout when he was distracted. A line of seagulls, half a dozen of them, had settled on the parapet. He must have heard them calling, and remembered that walk to Lamorna.

'I cough when there are things I can't say,' Ann had told him once. What couldn't she say then? he asked glumly of the chimney pots across the street. Connie could say it, Martindale could say it; so why couldn't Ann?

'Three of them and Alleline,' Smiley muttered aloud. The seagulls had gone, all at once, as if they had spotted a better place. 'Tell them they're buying their way in with counterfeit money.' And if the banks accept the money? If the experts pronounce it genuine, and Bill Haydon praises it to the skies? And the Cabinet Office files are full of plaudits for the brave new men of Cambridge Circus, who have finally broken the jinx?

He had chosen Esterhase first because Toby owed Smiley his career. Smiley had recruited him in Vienna, a starving student living in the ruins of a museum of which his dead uncle had been curator. He drove down to Acton and bearded him at the Laundry across his walnut desk with its row of ivory telephones. On the wall, kneeling Magi, questionable Italian 17th century. Through the window, a closed courtyard crammed with cars and vans and motorbikes, and rest-huts where the teams of lamplighters killed time between shifts. First Smiley asked Toby about his family: there was a son who went to Westminster and a daughter at medical school, first year. Then he put it to Toby that the lamplighters were two months behind on their worksheets and when Toby hedged he asked him outright whether his boys had been doing any special jobs recently, either at home or abroad, which for good reasons of security Toby didn't feel able to mention in his returns.

'Who would I do that for, George?' Toby had asked, dead-eyed. 'You know in my book that's completely illegal.' And idiom, in Toby's book, had a way of being ludicrous.

'Well, I can see you doing it for Percy Alleline, for one,' Smiley suggested, feeding him the excuse: 'After all, if Percy *ordered* you to do something and not to record it, you'd be in a very difficult position.'

'What sort of something, though, George, I wonder?'

'Clear a foreign letter-box, prime a safe house, watch someone's back, spike an embassy. Percy's Director of Operations, after all. You might think he was acting on instructions from the fifth floor. I can see that happening quite reasonably.'

Toby looked carefully at Smiley. He was holding a cigarette, but apart from lighting it he hadn't smoked it at all. It was a hand-rolled affair, taken from a silver box, but once lit it never went into his mouth. It swung around, along the line or away to the side; sometimes it was poised to take the plunge, but it never did. Meanwhile Toby made his speech: one of Toby's personal statements, supposedly definitive about where he stood at this point in his life.

Toby liked the service, he said. He would prefer to remain in it. He felt sentimental about it. He had other interests and at any time they could claim him altogether, but he liked the service best. His trouble was, he said, promotion. Not that he wanted it for any greedy reason. He would say his reasons were social.

'You know, George, I have so many years' seniority I feel actually quite embarrassed when these young fellows ask me to take orders from them. You know what I mean? Acton, even: just the name of Acton for them is ridiculous.'

'Oh,' said Smiley mildly. 'Which young fellows are these?'

But Esterhase had lost interest. His statement completed, his face settled again into its familiar blank expression, his doll's eyes fixed on a point in the middle distance.

'Do you mean Roy Bland?' Smiley asked. 'Or Percy? Is Percy young? Who, Toby?'

It was no good, Toby regretted: 'George, when you are overdue for promotion and working your fingers to the bones, anyone looks young who's above you on the ladder.'

'Perhaps Control could move you up a few rungs,' Smiley suggested, not much caring for himself in this role.

Esterhase's reply struck a chill. 'Well actually, you know George, I am not too sure he is able these days. Look here, I give Ann something' – opening a drawer – 'When I heard you were coming I phone a couple of friends of mine, something beautiful I say, something for a faultless woman, you know I never forget her since we met once at Bill Haydon's cocktail?'

So Smiley carried off the consolation prize – a costly scent smuggled, he assumed, by one of Toby's homing lamplighters – and took his beggar bowl to Bland, knowing as he did so that he was coming one step nearer to Haydon.

Returning to the major's table, Smiley searched through Lacon's files till he came to a slim volume marked 'Operation Witchcraft, direct subsidies', which recorded the earliest expenses incurred through the running of Source Merlin. 'For reasons of security it is proposed,' wrote Alleline in yet another personal memo to the Minister, this one dated almost two years ago, 'to keep the Witchcraft financing *absolutely separate* from all other Circus imprests. Until some proper cover can be found, I am asking you for *direct subventions from Treasury funds* rather than mere supplementaries to the Secret Vote which in due course *are certain to find their way into the mainstream of Circus accounting*. I shall then account to you personally.'

'Approved,' wrote the Minister a week later, 'provided always . . . '

There were no provisions. A glance at the first row of figures showed Smiley all he needed to know: already by May of that year, when that interview at Acton took place, Toby Esterhase had personally made no fewer than eight trips on the Witchcraft budget, two to Paris, two to the Hague, one to Helsinki and three to Berlin. In each case the purpose of the journey was curtly described as 'Collecting product'. Between May and November, when Control faded from the scene, he made a further nineteen. One of these took him to Sofia, another to Istanbul. None required him to be absent for more than three full days. Most took place at weekends. On several such journeys, he was accompanied by Bland.

Not to put too fine an edge on it, Toby Esterhase, as Smiley had never seriously doubted, had lied in his teeth. It was nice to find the record confirming his impression.

Smiley's feelings towards Roy Bland at that time were ambivalent. Recalling them now, he decided they still were. A don had spotted him, Smiley had recruited him; the combination was oddly akin to the one which had brought Smiley himself into the Circus net. But this time there was no German monster to fan the patriotic flame, and Smiley had always been a little embarrassed by protestations of anti-communism. Like Smiley, Bland had no real childhood. His father was a docker, a passionate trade unionist, and a Party member. His mother died when Bland was a boy. His father hated education as he hated authority and when Bland grew clever the father took it into his head that he had lost his son to the ruling class and beat the life out of him. Bland fought his way to grammar school and in the holidays worked his fingers, as Toby would say, to the bones, in order to raise the extra fee. When Smiley met him in his tutor's rooms at Oxford, he had the battered look of someone just arrived from a bad journey.

Smiley took him up, and over several months edged closer to a proposition, which Bland accepted largely, Smiley assumed, out of animosity towards his father. After that he passed out of Smiley's care. Subsisting on odd grants undescribed, Bland toiled in the Marx Memorial Library and wrote leftist papers for tiny magazines that would have died long ago had the Circus not subsidized them. In the evenings he argued the toss at smoky meetings in pubs and school halls. In the vacations he went to the Nursery, where a fanatic called Thatch ran a charm-school for outward-bound penetration agents, one pupil at a time. Thatch trained Bland in tradecraft and carefully nudged his progressive opinions nearer to his father's Marxist camp. Three years to the day after his recruitment, partly thanks to his proletarian pedigree, and his father's influence at King Street, Bland won a year's appointment as assistant lector in economics at the University of Poznan. He was launched.

From Poland he applied successfully for a post at the Budapest Academy of Sciences and for the next eight years he lived the nomadic life of a minor left-wing intellectual in search of light, often liked but never trusted. He stayed in Prague, returned to Poland, did a hellish two semesters in Sofia and six in Kiev where he had a nervous breakdown, his second in as many months. Once more the Nursery took charge of him, this time to dry him out. He was passed as clean, his networks were given to other fieldmen and Roy himself was brought into the Circus to manage, mainly from a desk, the networks he had recruited in the field. Recently, it had seemed to Smiley, Bland had become very much Haydon's colleague. If Smiley chanced to call on Roy for a chat, like as not Bill was lounging in his armchair surrounded by papers, charts and cigarette smoke; if he dropped in on Bill it was no surprise to find Bland, in a sweat-soaked shirt, padding heavily back and forth across the carpet. Bill had Russia, Bland the satellites; but already in those early days of Witchcraft, the distinction had all but vanished.

They met at a pub in St John's Wood, May still, half past five on a dull day and the garden empty. Roy brought a child, a boy of five or so, a tiny Bland, fair, burly and pink-faced. He didn't explain the boy but sometimes as they talked he shut off and watched him where he sat on a bench away from them, eating nuts. Nervous breakdowns or not Bland still bore the imprimatur of the Thatch philosophy for agents in the enemy camp: self-faith, positive participation, Pied-Piper appeal and all those other uncomfortable phrases which in the high day of the cold war culture had turned the Nursery into something close to a moral rearmament centre.

'So what's the deal?' Bland asked affably.

'There isn't one really, Roy. Control feels that the present situation is unhealthy. He doesn't like to see you getting mixed up in a cabal. Nor do I.'

'Great. So what's the deal?'

'What do you want?'

On the table, soaked from the earlier rainfall, was a cruet set left over from lunchtime with a bunch of paper-wrapped cellulose toothpicks in the centre compartment. Taking one, Bland spat the paper on to the grass and began working his back teeth with the fat end.

'Well, how about a five-thousand-quid backhander out the reptile fund?'

'And a house and a car?' said Smiley, making a joke of it.

'And the kid to Eton,' Bland added, and winked across the concrete paving to the boy while he went on working with the toothpick. 'I've paid, see, George. You know that. I don't know what I've bought with it but I've paid a hell of a lot. I want some back. Ten years solitary for the fifth floor, that's big money at any age. Even yours. There must have been a reason why I fell for all the *spiel* but I can't quite remember what it was. Must be your magnetic personality.'

Smiley's glass was still going so Bland fetched himself another from the bar, and something for the boy as well.

'You're an educated sort of swine,' he announced easily as he sat down again. 'An artist is a bloke who can hold two fundamentally opposing views and still function: who dreamed that one up?'

'Scott Fitzgerald,' Smiley replied, thinking for a moment that Bland was proposing to say something about Bill Haydon.

'Well, Fitzgerald knew a thing or two,' Bland affirmed. As he drank, his slightly bulging eyes slid sideways towards the fence, as if in search of someone. 'And I'm definitely functioning, George. As a good socialist I'm going for the money. As a good capitalist, I'm sticking with the revolution, because if you can't beat it spy on it. Don't look like that, George. It's the name of the game these days: you scratch my conscience, I'll drive your Jag, right?' He was already lifting an arm as he said this. 'With you in a minute!' he called across the lawn. 'Set one up for me!'

Two girls were hovering the other side of the wire fence.

'Is that Bill's joke?' Smiley asked, suddenly quite angry.

'Is what?'

'Is that one of Bill's jokes about materialist England, the pigs-in-clover society?'

'Could be,' said Bland and finished his drink. 'Don't you like it?'

'Not too much, no. I never knew Bill before as a radical reformer. What's come over him all of a sudden?'

'That's not radical,' Bland retorted, resenting any devaluation of his socialism, or of Haydon. 'That's just looking out the bloody window. That's just England now, man. Nobody wants that, do they?'

'So how do you propose,' Smiley demanded, hearing himself at his pompous worst, 'to destroy the acquisitive and competitive instincts in western society, without also destroying . . .'

Bland had finished his drink; and the meeting too. 'Why should you be bothered? You've got Bill's job. What more do you want? Long as it lasts.'

And Bill's got my wife, Smiley thought, as Bland rose to go: and, damn him, he's told you.

The boy had invented a game. He had laid the table on its side and was rolling an empty bottle on to the gravel. Each time he started the bottle higher up the table top. Smiley left before it smashed.

Unlike Esterhase, Bland had not even bothered to lie. Lacon's files made no bones of his involvement with the Witchcraft operation:

'Source Merlin,' wrote Alleline, in a minute dated soon after Control's departure, 'is in every sense a committee operation . . . I cannot honestly say which of my three assistants deserves most praise. The energy of Bland has been an inspiration to us all . . .' He was replying to the Minister's suggestion that those responsible for Witchcraft should be honoured in the New Year's list. 'While Haydon's operational ingenuity is at times little short of Merlin's own,' he added. The medals went to all three; Alleline's appointment as Chief was confirmed, and with it his beloved knighthood.

# EIGHTEEN

Which left me Bill, thought Smiley.

In the course of most London nights, there is one respite from alarm. Ten, twenty minutes, thirty, even an hour, and not a drunk groans or a child cries or a car's tyres whine into collision. In Sussex Gardens it happens around three. That night it came early, at one, as Smiley stood once more at his dormer window peering down like a prisoner at Mrs Pope Graham's sand patch, where a Bedford van had recently parked. Its roof was daubed with slogans: Sydney ninety days, Athens non stop, Mary Lou here we come. A light glowed inside and he presumed some children were sleeping there in unmarried bliss. Kids, he was supposed to call them. Curtains covered the windows.

Which left me Bill, he thought, still staring at the closed curtains of the van and its flamboyant globe-trotting proclamations; which left me Bill, and our friendly little chat in Bywater Street, just the two of us, old friends, old comrades at arms, 'sharing everything', as Martindale had it so elegantly, but Ann sent out for the evening so that the men could be alone. Which left me Bill, he repeated, and felt the blood rise, and the colours of his vision heighten, and his sense of moderation begin its dangerous slide.

Who was he? Smiley had no focus on him any more. Each time he thought of him, he drew him too large, and different. Until Ann's affair with him he thought he knew Bill pretty well: both his brilliance and its limitations. He was of the pre-war set that seemed to have vanished for good, which managed to be disreputable and high-minded at the same time. His father was a high court judge, two of his several beautiful sisters had married into the aristocracy; at Oxford he favoured the unfashionable right rather than the fashionable left, but never to the point of strain. From his late teens he had been a keen explorer and amateur painter of brave, if over-ambitious stamp: several of his paintings now hung in Miles Sercombe's fatuous palace in Carlton Gardens. He had connections in every embassy and consulate across the Middle East and he used them ruthlessly. He took up remote languages with ease, and when thirty-nine came, the Circus snapped him up, they had had their eye on him for years. He had a dazzling war. He was ubiquitous and charming; he was unorthodox and occasionally outrageous. He was probably heroic. The comparison with Lawrence was inevitable.

And it was true, Smiley conceded, that Bill in his time had fiddled with substantial pieces of history; had proposed all sorts of grand designs for restoring England to influence and greatness – like Rupert Brooke he seldom spoke of Britain. But Smiley in his rare moments of objectivity could remember few that ever got off the ground.

It was the other side of Haydon's nature, by contrast, which as a colleague he had found easier to respect: the slow-burning skills of the natural agent runner, his rare sense of balance in the playing back of double agents, and the mounting of deception operations: his art of fostering affection, even love, though it ran against the grain of other loyalties.

As witness, thank you, my wife.

Perhaps Bill really *is* out of scale, he thought hopelessly, still grappling for a sense of proportion. Picturing him now, and putting him beside Bland, Esterhase, even Alleline, it did truthfully seem to Smiley that all of them were to a great or small extent imperfect imitations of that one original, Haydon. That their affections were like steps towards the same unobtainable ideal of the rounded man, even if the idea was itself misconceived, or misplaced; even if Bill was utterly unworthy of it. Bland in his blunt impertinence, Esterhase in his lofty artificial Englishness, Alleline with his shallow gift of leadership: without Bill they were a disarray. Smiley also knew, or thought he knew – the idea came to him now as a mild enlightenment – that Bill in turn was also very little by himself: that while his admirers – Bland, Prideaux, Alleline, Esterhase, and all the rest of the supporters' club – might find in him completeness, Bill's real trick was to use them, to live through them to complete himself; here a piece, there a piece, from their passive identities: thus disguising the fact that he was less, far less, than the sum of his apparent qualities . . . and finally submerging this dependence beneath an artist's arrogance, calling them the creatures of his mind . . .

'That's quite enough,' said Smiley aloud.

Withdrawing abruptly from this insight, dismissing it irritably as yet another theory about Bill, he cooled his overheated mind with the recollection of their last meeting.

'I suppose you want to grill me about bloody Merlin,' Bill began. He looked tired and nervy; it was his time for commuting to Washington. In the old days he would have brought an unsuitable girl and sent her to sit with Ann upstairs while they talked their business; expecting Ann to bolster his genius to her, thought Smiley cruelly. They were all of the same sort: half his age, bedraggled art school, clinging, surly; Ann used to say he had a supplier. And once to shock he brought a ghastly youth called Steggie, an assistant barman from one of the Chelsea pubs with an open shirt and a gold chain round his midriff.

'Well they do say you write the reports,' Smiley explained.

'I thought that was Bland's job,' said Bill with his foxy grin.

'Roy makes the translations,' said Smiley. 'You draft the covering reports; they're typed on your machine. The material's not cleared for typists at all.'

Bill listened carefully, brows lifted, as if at any moment he might interrupt with an objection or a more congenial topic, then hoisted himself from the deep armchair and ambled to the bookcase, where he stood a full shelf higher than Smiley. Fishing out a volume with his long fingers he peered into it, grinning.

'Percy Alleline won't do,' he announced, turning a page. 'Is that the premise?'

'Pretty well,'

'Which means that Merlin won't do either. Merlin would do if he were *my* source, wouldn't he? What would happen if bloody Bill here pottered along to Control and said he'd hooked a big fish and wanted to play him alone? "That's very nifty of you, Bill boy," Control would say. "You do it just the way you want, Bill boy, 'course you do. Have some filthy tea." He'd be giving me a medal by now instead of sending you snooping round the corridors. We used to be rather a classy bunch. Why are we so vulgar these days?'

'He thinks Percy's on the make,' Smiley said.

'So he is. So am I. I want to be head boy. Did you know that? Time I made something of myself, George. Half a painter, half a spy, time I was *all* something. Since when was ambition a sin in our beastly outfit?'

'Who runs him, Bill?'

'Percy? Karla does, who else? Lower-class bloke with upper-class sources, must be a bounder. Percy's sold out to Karla, it's the only explanation.' He had developed the art, long ago, of deliberately misunderstanding. 'Percy's our house mole,' he said.

'I meant who runs Merlin? Who *is* Merlin? What's going on?'

Leaving the bookcase Haydon took himself on a tour of Smiley's drawings. 'This is a Callot, isn't it?' – unhooking a small gilt frame and holding it to the light – 'It's nice.' He tilted his spectacles to make them magnify. Smiley was certain he had looked at it a dozen times before. 'It's *very* nice. Doesn't anyone think *my* nose should be out of joint? I am supposed to be in charge of the Russian target, you know. Given it my best years, set up networks, talent-spotters, all mod cons. You chaps on the fifth floor have forgotten what it's like to run an operation where it takes you three days to post a letter and you don't even get an answer for your trouble.'

Smiley, dutifully: Yes, I have forgotten. Yes, I sympathize. No, Ann is nowhere in my thoughts. We are colleagues after all and men of the world, we are here to talk about Merlin and Control.

'Along comes this upstart Percy, damn Caledonian street-merchant, no shadow of class, shoving a whole wagonload of Russian goodies. Bloody annoying, don't you think?'

'Very.'

'Trouble is, my networks aren't very good. Much easier to spy on Percy than – ' He broke off, tired of his own thesis. His attention had settled on a tiny van Mieris head in chalk. 'And I fancy this *very* much,' he said.

'Ann gave it me.'

'Amends?'

'Probably.'

'Must have been quite a sin. How long have you had it?'

Even now, Smiley remembered noticing how silent it was in the street. Tuesday? Wednesday? And he remembered thinking, 'No, Bill. For you I have so far received no consolation prize at all. As of this evening you don't even rate a pair of bedroom slippers.' Thinking but not saying.

'Is Control dead yet?' Haydon asked.

'Just busy.'

'What does he do all day? He's like a hermit with the clap, scratching around all on his own in that cave up there. All those bloody files he reads, what's he about for God's sake? Sentimental tour of his unlovely past, I'll bet. He looks sick as a cat. I suppose that's Merlin's fault too, is it?'

Again Smiley said nothing.

'Why does he eat with the cooks? Why doesn't he join us instead of grubbing around for truffles up there? What's he after?'

'I didn't know he was after anything,' said Smiley.

'Ah, stop flirting around. Of course he is. I've got a source up there, one of the mothers, didn't you know? Tells me indiscretions for chocolate. Control's been toiling through personal dossiers of old Circus folk heroes, sniffing out the dirt, who was pink, who was a queen. Half of them are under the earth already. Making a study of all our failures: can you imagine? And for why? Because we've got a success on our hands. He's mad, George. He's got the big itch: senile paranoia, take my word for it. Ann ever tell you about wicked Uncle Fry? Thought the servants were bugging the roses to find out where he'd hidden his money. Get away from him, George. Death's a bore. Cut the cord, move down a few floors. Join the proles.'

Ann had still not returned so they sauntered side by side down the King's Road looking for a cab while Bill enunciated his latest vision of politics, and Smiley said 'Yes, Bill,' 'No, Bill,' and wondered how he was going to break it to Control. He forgot now which particular vision it was. The year before, Bill had been a great hawk. He had wanted to run down conventional forces in Europe and replace them outright with nuclear weapons. He was about the only person left in Whitehall who believed in Britain's independent deterrent. This year, if Smiley remembered rightly, Bill was an aggressive English pacifist and wanted the Sweden solution but without the Swedes.

No cab came, it was a beautiful night, and like old friends they went on walking, side by side.

'By the by, if you ever want to sell that Mieris, let me know, will you? I'll give you a bloody decent price for it.'

Thinking Bill was making another bad joke, Smiley rounded on him, at last prepared to be angry. Haydon was not even conscious of his interest. He was gazing down the street, his long arm raised at an approaching cab.

'Oh Christ, look at them,' he shouted irritably. 'Full of bloody Jews going to Quag's.'

'Bill's backside must look like a damn gridiron,' Control muttered next day. 'The years he's spent sitting on the fence.' For a moment he stared at Smiley in an unfocused way, as if looking through him to some different, less fleshly prospect; then ducked his eyes and seemed to go on reading. 'I'm glad he's not *my* cousin,' he said.

The following Monday, the mothers had surprising news for Smiley. Control had flown to Belfast for discussions with the army. Later, checking the travel imprests, Smiley nailed the lie. No one in the Circus had flown to Belfast for discussions that month but there was a charge for a first-class return to Vienna and the issuing authority was given as G. Smiley.

Haydon, also looking for Control, was cross: 'So now what's the pitch? Dragging Ireland into the net, creating an organizational diversion, I suppose. Jesus, your man's a bore!'

The light in the van went out but Smiley continued to gaze at its garish roof. How do they live? he wondered. What do they do for water, money? He tried to fathom the logistics of a troglodyte life in Sussex Gardens: water, drains, light. Ann would work them out all right; so would Bill.

Facts. What were the facts?

Facts were that one balmy pre-Witchcraft summer evening I returned unexpectedly from Berlin to find Bill Haydon stretched on the drawing-room floor of my house in Bywater Street and Ann playing Liszt on the gramophone. Ann was sitting across the room from him in her dressing gown, wearing no make-up. There was no scene, everyone behaved with painful naturalness. According to Bill he had dropped by on his way from the airport, having just flown in from Washington; Ann had been in bed but insisted on getting up to receive him. We agreed it was a pity we hadn't shared a car from Heathrow. Bill left, I asked 'What did he want?' And Ann said 'A shoulder to cry on'. Bill was having girl trouble, wanted to pour out his heart, she said.

'There's Felicity in Washington who wants a baby and Jan in London who's having one.'

'Bill's?'

'God knows. I'm sure Bill doesn't.'

Next morning, without even wishing to, Smiley established that Bill had been back in London two days, not one. Following the episode Bill showed an uncharacteristic deference towards Smiley and Smiley reciprocated with acts of courtesy which normally belong to a newer friendship. In due course Smiley noticed that the secret was out, and he was still mystified by the speed with which that had happened. He supposed Bill had boasted to someone, perhaps Bland. If the word was correct, Ann had broken three of her own rules. Bill was Circus and he was Set – her word for family and ramifications. On either count he would be out of bounds. Thirdly, she had received him at Bywater Street, an agreed violation of territorial decencies.

Withdrawing once more into his own lonely life, Smiley waited for Ann to say something. He moved into the spare room and arranged for himself plenty of evening engagements in order that he would not be too aware of her comings and goings. Gradually it dawned on him that she was deeply unhappy. She lost weight, she lost her sense of play, and if he didn't know her better he would have sworn she was having a bad bout of the guilts, even of self-disgust. When he was gentle with her she fended him off; she showed no interest in Christmas shopping and developed a wasting cough which he knew was her signal of distress. If it had not been for Operation Testify, they would have left for Cornwall earlier. As it was, they had to postpone the trip till January, by which time Control was dead, Smiley was unemployed, the scale had tipped: and Ann to his mortification was covering the Haydon card with as many others as she could pull from the pack.

So what happened? Did she break off the affair? Did Haydon? Why did she never speak of it? Did it matter anyway, one among so many? He gave up. Like the Cheshire Cat, the face of Bill Haydon seemed to recede as soon as he advanced upon it, leaving only the smile behind. But he knew that somehow Bill had hurt her deeply, which was the sin of sins.

# NINETEEN

Returning with a sigh to the unlovable card-table, Smiley resumed his reading of Merlin's progress since his own enforced retirement from the Circus. The new regime of Percy Alleline, he at once noticed, had immediately produced several favourable changes in Merlin's lifestyle. It was like a maturing, a settling down. The night dashes to European capitals ceased, the flow of intelligence became more regular and less nervy. There were headaches, certainly. Merlin's demands for money – requirements, never threats – continued, and with the steady decline in the value of the pound these large payments in foreign currency caused the Treasury much agony. There was even a suggestion at one point, never pursued, that 'since we are the country of Merlin's choice, he should be ready to shoulder his portion of our financial vicissitudes'. Haydon and Bland exploded, apparently: 'I have not the face,' wrote Alleline with rare frankness to the Minister, 'to mention this subject to my staff again.'

There was also a row about a new camera, which at great expense was broken into tubular components by Nuts and Bolts section and fitted into a standard lamp of Soviet manufacture. The lamp, after screams of pain, this time from the Foreign Office, was spirited to Moscow by diplomatic bag. The problem was then the drop. The residency could not be informed of Merlin's identity, nor did it know the contents of the lamp. The lamp was unwieldy, and would not fit the boot of the resident's car. After several shots, an untidy handover was achieved but the camera never worked and there was bad blood between the Circus and its Moscow residency as a result. A less ambitious model was taken by Esterhase to Helsinki where it was handed – thus Alleline's memo to the Minister – to 'a trusted intermediary whose frontier crossing would go unchallenged'.

Suddenly, Smiley sat up with a jolt.

'We spoke,' wrote Alleline to the Minister, in a minute dated February 27th this year. 'You agreed to submit a supplementary estimate to the Treasury for a London house to be carried on the Witchcraft budget.'

He read it once, then again more slowly. The Treasury had sanctioned sixty thousand pounds for the freehold and another ten for furniture and fittings. To cut costs, it wanted its own lawyers to handle the conveyance. Alleline refused to reveal the address. For the same reason there was an argument about who should keep the deeds. This time the Treasury put its foot down and its lawyers drew up instruments to get the house back from Alleline should he die or go bankrupt. But he still kept the address to himself, as also the justification for this remarkable, and costly, adjunct to an operation that was supposedly taking place abroad.

Smiley searched eagerly for an explanation. The financial files, he quickly confirmed, were scrupulous to offer none. They contained only one veiled reference to the London house, and that was when the rates were doubled: Minister to Alleline: 'I assume the London end is still necessary?' Alleline to Minister: 'Eminently. I would say more than ever. I would add that the circle of knowledge has not widened since our conversation.' What knowledge?

It was not till he went back to the files which appraised the Witchcraft product that he came on the solution. The house was paid for in late March. Occupancy followed immediately. From the same date exactly, Merlin began to acquire a personality, and it was shaped here in the customers' comments. Till now, to Smiley's suspicious eye, Merlin had been a machine: faultless in tradecraft, eerie in his access, free of the strains that make most agents such hard going. Now suddenly he was having a tantrum.

'We put to Merlin your follow-up question about the prevailing Kremlin view on the sale of Russian oil surpluses to the United States. We suggested to him, at your request, that this was at odds with his report last month that the Kremlin is presently flirting with the Tanaka government for a contract to sell Siberian oil on the Japanese market. Merlin saw no contradiction in the two reports and declined to forecast which market might ultimately be favoured.'

Whitehall regretted its temerity.

'Merlin will not repeat not add to his report on the repression of Georgian nationalism and the rioting in Tbilisi. Not being himself a Georgian, he takes the traditional Russian view that all Georgians are thieves and vagabonds, and better behind bars . . .'

Whitehall agreed not to press.

Merlin had suddenly drawn nearer. Was it only the acquisition of a London house which gave Smiley this new sense of Merlin's physical proximity? From the remote stillness of a Moscow winter, Merlin seemed suddenly to be sitting here before him in the tattered room; in the street outside his window, waiting in the rain, where now and then, he knew, Mendel kept his solitary guard. Here out of the blue was a Merlin who talked and answered back and gratuitously offered his opinions: a Merlin who had time to be met. Met here in London? Fed, entertained, debriefed in a sixty-thousand-pound house while he threw his weight about and made jokes about Georgians? What was this circle of knowledge which had now formed itself even within the wider circle of those initiated into the secrets of the Witchcraft operation?

At this point, an improbable figure flitted across the stage: one JPR, a new recruit to Whitehall's growing band of Witchcraft evaluators. Consulting the indoctrination list, Smiley established that his full name was Ribble, and that he was a member of Foreign Office Research Department. J. P. Ribble was puzzled.

JPR to the Adriatic Working Party (AWP): 'May I respectfully draw your attention to an apparent discrepancy concerning dates? Witchcraft No. 104 (Soviet-French discussions on joint aircraft production) is dated April 21st.

According to your covering minute, Merlin had this information directly from General Markov on the day after the negotiating parties agreed to a secret exchange of notes. But on that day, April 21st, according to our Paris Embassy, Markov was still in Paris and Merlin, as witness your report No. 109, was himself visiting a missile research establishment outside Leningrad . . .'

The minute cited no fewer than four similar 'discrepancies', which put together suggested a degree of mobility in Merlin that would have done credit to his miraculous namesake.

J. P. Ribble was told in as many words to mind his own business. But in a separate minute to the Minister, Alleline made an extraordinary admission which shed an entirely new light on the nature of the Witchcraft operation.

'Extremely secret and personal. We spoke. Merlin, as you have known for some time, is not one source but several. While we have done our best for security reasons to disguise this fact from your readers, the sheer volume of material makes it increasingly difficult to continue with this fiction. Might it not be time to come clean, at least on a limited basis? By the same token it would do the Treasury no harm to learn that Merlin's ten thousand Swiss francs a month in salary, and a similar figure for expenses and running costs, are scarcely excessive when the cloth has to be cut so many ways.'

But the minute ended on a harsher note: 'Nevertheless, even if we agree to open the door this far, I regard it as paramount that knowledge of the existence of the London house, and the purpose for which it is used, remain absolutely at a minimum. Indeed, once Merlin's plurality is published among our readers, the delicacy of the London operation is increased.'

Totally mystified, Smiley read this correspondence several times. Then, as if struck by a sudden thought he looked up, his face a picture of confusion. So far away were his thoughts, indeed, so intense and complex, that the telephone rang several times inside the room before he responded to the summons. Lifting the receiver, he glanced at his watch; it was six in the evening, he had been reading barely an hour.

'Mr. Barraclough? This is Lofthouse from finance, sir.'

Peter Guillam, using the emergency procedure, was asking by means of the agreed phrases for a crash meeting and he sounded shaken.

# TWENTY

The Circus archives were not accessible from the main entrance. They rambled through a warren of dingy rooms and half landings at the back of the building, more like one of the secondhand bookshops which proliferate round there, than the organized memory of a large department. They were reached by a dull doorway in the Charing Cross Road jammed between a picture-framer and an all-day café that was out of bounds to staff. A plate on the door read 'Town and Country Language School, Staff Only' and another 'C and L Distribution Ltd.' To enter you pressed one or other bell and waited for Alwyn, an effeminate Marine who spoke only of weekends. Till Wednesday or so he spoke of the weekend past, after that he spoke of the weekend to come. This morning, a Tuesday, he was in a mood of indignant unrest.

'Here, what about that storm then?' he demanded as he pushed the book across the counter for Guillam to sign. 'Might as well live in a lighthouse. All Saturday, all Sunday. I said to my friend: "Here we are in the middle of London and listen to it." Want me to look after that for you?'

'You should have been where I was,' said Guillam, consigning the brown canvas grip into Alwyn's waiting hands. 'Talk about listen to it, you could hardly stand upright.'

Don't be over-friendly, he thought, talking to himself.

'Still I do like the country,' Alwyn confided, stowing the grip in one of the open lockers behind the counter. 'Want a number then? I'm supposed to give you one, the Dolphin would kill me if she knew.'

'I'll trust you,' said Guillam. Climbing the four steps he pushed open the swing doors to the reading room. The place was like a makeshift lecture hall: a dozen desks all facing the same way, a raised area where the archivist sat. Guillam took a desk near the back. It was still early – ten ten by his watch – and the only other reader was Ben Thruxton of research, who spent most of his time here. Long ago, masquerading as a Latvian dissident, Ben had run with revolutionaries through the streets of Moscow calling death to the oppressors. Now he crouched over his papers like an old priest, white-haired and perfectly still.

Seeing Guillam standing at her desk, the archivist smiled. Quite often, when Brixton was dead, Guillam would spend a day here searching through old cases for one that could stand refiring. She was Sal, a plump, sporting girl who ran a youth club in Chiswick and was a judo black belt.

'Break any good necks this weekend?' he asked, helping himself to a bunch of green requisition slips.

Sal handed him the notes she kept for him in her steel cupboard.

'Couple. How about you?'

'Visiting aunts in Shropshire, thank you.'

'Some aunts,' said Sal.

Still at her desk he filled in slips for the next two references on his list. He watched her stamp them, tear off the flimsies, and post them through a slot on her desk.

'D corridor,' she murmured, handing back the top copies. 'The two-eights are halfway on your right, the three-ones are next alcove down.'

Pushing open the far door, he entered the main hall. At the centre an old lift like a miner's cage carried files into the body of the Circus. Two bleary juniors were feeding it, a third stood by to operate the winch. Guillam moved slowly along the shelves reading the fluorescent number cards.

'Lacon swears he holds no file on Testify at all,' Smiley had explained in his usual worried way. 'He has a few resettlement papers on Prideaux and nothing else.' And in the same lugubrious tone: 'So I'm afraid we'll have to find a way of getting hold of whatever there is in Circus Registry.'

For 'getting hold', in Smiley's dictionary, read 'steal'.

One girl stood on a ladder. Oscar Allitson the collator was fitting a laundry basket with wrangler files, Astrid the maintenance man was mending a radiator. The shelves were wooden, deep as bunks and divided into pigeon-holes by panels of ply. He already knew that the Testify reference was four-four eight-two E, which meant alcove forty-four, where he now stood. E stood for extinct and was used for dead operations only. Guillam counted to the eighth pigeon-hole from the left. Testify should be second from the left but there was no way of making certain because the spines were unmarked. His reconnaissance complete, he drew the two files he had requested, leaving the green slips in the steel brackets provided for them.

'There won't be much, I'm sure,' Smiley had said, as if thinner files were easier. 'But there ought to be something, if only for appearances.' That was another thing about him that Guillam didn't like just then: he spoke as if you followed his reasoning, as if you were inside his mind all the time.

Sitting down he pretended to read but passed the time thinking of Camilla. What was he supposed to make of her? Early this morning as she lay in his arms she told him she had once been married. Sometimes she spoke like that: as if she'd lived about twenty lives. It was a mistake, so they packed it in.

'What went wrong?'

'Nothing. We weren't right for each other.'

Guillam didn't believe her.

'Did you get a divorce?'

'I expect so.'

'Don't be damn silly, you must know whether you're divorced or not!'

His parents handled it, she said; he was foreign.

'Does he send you money?'

'Why should he? He doesn't owe me anything.'

Then the flute again, in the spare room, long questioning notes in the half light while Guillam made coffee. Is she a fake or an angel? He'd half a mind to pass her name across the records. She had a lesson with Sand in an hour.

Armed with a green slip with a four-three reference, he returned the two files to their places and positioned himself at the alcove next to Testify.

'Dry run uneventful,' he thought.

The girl was still up her ladder. Allitson had vanished but the laundry basket was still there. The radiator had already exhausted Astrid and he was sitting beside it reading the *Sun*. The green slip read four-three four-three and he found the file at once because he had already marked it down. It had a pink jacket like Testify. Like Testify it was reasonably thumbed. He fitted the green slip into the bracket. He moved back across the aisle, again checked Allitson and the girls, then reached for the Testify file and replaced it very fast with the file he had in his hand.

'I think the vital thing, Peter' – Smiley speaking – 'is not to leave a gap. So what I suggest is, you requisition a comparable file, *physically* comparable I mean, and pop it into the gap which is left by – '

'I get you,' Guillam said.

Holding the Testify file casually in his right hand, title inward to his body, Guillam returned to the reading room and again sat at his desk. Sal raised her eyebrows and mouthed something. Guillam nodded that all was well, thinking that was what she was asking, but she beckoned him over. Momentary panic. Take the file with me or leave it? What do I usually do? He left it on the desk.

'Juliet's going for coffee,' Sal whispered. 'Want some?'

Guillam laid a shilling on the counter.

He glanced at the clock, then at his watch. Christ, stop looking at your damn watch! Think of Camilla, think of her starting her lesson, think of those aunts you didn't spend the weekend with, think of Alwyn not looking in your bag. Think of anything but the time. Eighteen minutes to wait. 'Peter, if you have the smallest reservation, you really mustn't go ahead with it. Nothing is as important as that.' Great, so how do you spot a reservation, when thirty teenage butterflies are mating in your stomach, and the sweat is like a secret rain inside your shirt? Never, he swore, never had he had it this bad.

Opening the Testify file he tried to read it.

It wasn't all that thin, but it wasn't fat either. It looked pretty much like a token volume, as Smiley had said: the first serial was taken up with a description of what wasn't there. 'Annexes 1 to 8 held London Station, cross refer to PFs ELLIS Jim, PRIDEAUX Jim, HAJEK Vladimir, COLLINS Sam, HABOLT Max . . .' and Uncle Tom Cobley and All. 'For these files, consult H/London Station or CC,' standing for Chief of Circus and his appointed mothers. Don't look at your watch, look at the clock and do the arithmetic, you idiot. Eight minutes. Odd to be pinching files about one's predecessor. Odd to have Jim as a predecessor, come to think of it, and a secretary who held a wake over him without ever mentioning his name. The only living trace Guillam had ever found of him, apart from his workname on the files, was his squash racquet jammed behind the safe in his room, with J. P. hand-done in poker work on the handle. He showed it to Ellen, a tough old biddy who could make Cy Vanhofer quail like a schoolboy, and she broke into floods of tears, wrapped it and sent it to the housekeepers by the next shuttle with a personal note to the Dolphin insisting that it be returned to him 'if humanly possible'. How's your game these days, Jim, with a couple of Czech bullets in your shoulder bone?

Still eight minutes.

'Now if you could contrive,' said Smiley, 'I mean if it wouldn't be too much bother, to take your car in for a service at your local garage. Using your home phone to make the appointment, of course, in the *hope* that Toby is listening . . .'

In the hope. Mother of pearl. And all his cosy chats with Camilla? Still eight minutes.

The rest of the file seemed to be Foreign Office telegrams, Czech press cuttings, monitoring reports on Prague radio, extracts from a policy file on the resettlement and rehabilitation of blown agents, draft submissions to the Treasury and a post-mortem by Alleline which blamed Control for the fiasco. Sooner you than me George.

In his mind, Guillam began measuring the distance from his desk to the rear door where Alwyn dozed at the reception counter. He reckoned it was five paces and he decided to make a tactical staging post. Two paces from the door stood a chart chest like a big yellow piano. It was filled with oddments of reference: large-scale maps, back copies of *Who's Who*, old Baedekers. Putting a pencil between his teeth he picked up the Testify file, wandered to the chest, selected a telephone directory of Warsaw and began writing names on a sheet of paper. My hand! a voice screamed inside him: my hand is shaking all over the page, look at those figures, I might be drunk! Why has no one noticed? The girl Juliet came in with a tray and put a cup on his desk. He blew her a distracted kiss. He selected another directory, he thought for Poznan, and laid it beside the first. When Alwyn came through the door he didn't even look up.

'Telephone, sir,' he murmured.

'Oh to hell,' said Guillam deep in the directory. 'Who is it?'

'Outside line, sir. Someone rough. The garage, I think, regarding your car. Said he'd got some bad news for you,' said Alwyn, very pleased.

Guillam was holding the Testify file in both hands, apparently cross-referring with the directory. He had his back to Sal and he could feel his knees shaking against his trouser legs. The pencil was still jammed in his mouth. Alwyn went ahead and held the swing door for him and he passed through it reading the file: like a damned choirboy, he thought. He waited for lightning to strike him, Sal to call murder, old Ben the superspy to leap suddenly to life, but it didn't happen. He felt much better: Alwyn is my ally, I trust him, we are united against the Dolphin, I can move. The swing doors closed, he went down the four steps and there was Alwyn again, holding open the door to the telephone cubicle. The lower part was panelled, the upper part glass. Lifting the receiver he laid the file at his feet and heard Mendel tell him he needed a new gear box, the job could cost anything up to a hundred quid. They'd worked this up for the benefit of the housekeepers or whoever read the transcripts, and Guillam kept it going nicely to and fro till Alwyn was safely behind his counter, listening like an eagle. It's working, he thought, I'm flying, it's working after all. He heard himself say: 'Well, at least get on to the main agents first and find out how long they'll take to supply the damn thing. Have you got their number?' And irritably: 'Hang on.'

He half opened the door and kept the mouthpiece jammed against his backside because he was very concerned that this part should not go on tape. 'Alwyn, chuck me that bag a minute will you?'

Alwyn brought it over keenly, like the first-aid man at a football match. 'All right, Mr Guillam, sir? Open it for you, sir?'

'Just dump it there, thanks.'

The bag was on the floor outside the cubicle. Now he stooped, dragged it inside and unzipped it. At the middle, among his shirts and a lot of newspaper, were three dummy files, one buff, one green, one pink. He took out the pink file and his address book and replaced them with the Testify file. He closed the zip, stood up and read Mendel a telephone number, actually the right one. He rang off, handed Alwyn the bag and returned to the reading room with the dummy file. He dawdled at the chart chest, fiddled with a couple more directories, then sauntered to the archive carrying the dummy file. Allitson was going through a comedy routine, first pulling then pushing the laundry basket.

'Peter, give us a hand will you, I'm stuck.'

'Half a sec.'

Recovering the four-three file from the Testify pigeon-hole, he replaced it with the dummy, restored it to its rightful place in the four-three alcove and removed the green slip from the bracket. God is in his Heaven and the first night was a wow. He could have sung out loud: God is in his Heaven and I can still fly.

He took the slip to Sal, who signed it and put it on a spike as she always did. Later today she would check. If the file was in its place she would destroy both the green slip and the flimsy from the box, and not even clever Sal would remember that he had been alongside the four-four alcove. He was about to return to the archive to give old Allitson a hand when he found himself looking straight into the brown, unfriendly eyes of Toby Esterhase.

'Peter,' said Toby in his not quite perfect English. 'I am so sorry to disturb you but we have a tiny crisis and Percy Alleline would like quite an urgent word with you. Can you come now? That would be very kind.' And at the door, as Alwyn let them out: 'Your opinion he wants actually,' he remarked with the officiousness of a small but rising man. 'He wishes to consult you for an opinion.'

In a desperately inspired moment Guillam turned to Alwyn and said, 'There's a midday shuttle to Brixton. You might just give Transport a buzz and ask them to take that thing over for me, will you?'

'Will do, sir,' said Alwyn. 'Will do. Mind the step, sir.'

And you pray for me, thought Guillam.

# TWENTY-ONE

'Our Shadow Foreign Secretary,' Haydon called him. The janitors called him Snow White because of his hair. Toby Esterhase dressed like a male model but the moment he dropped his shoulders or closed his tiny fists he was unmistakably a fighter. Following him down the fourth-floor corridor, noting the coffee machine again, and Lauder Strickland's voice explaining that he was unobtainable, Guillam thought: 'Christ, we're back in Berne and on the run.'

He'd half a mind to call this out to Toby, but decided the comparison was unwise.

Whenever he thought of Toby, that was what he thought of: Switzerland eight years ago, when Toby was just a humdrum watcher with a growing reputation for informal listening on the side. Guillam was kicking his heels after North Africa, so the Circus packed them both off to Berne on a one-time operation to spike a pair of Belgian arms dealers who were using the Swiss to spread their wares in unpopular directions. They rented a villa next door to the target house and the same night Toby opened up a junction box and rearranged things so that they overheard the Belgians' conversations on their own phone. Guillam was boss and legman and twice a day he dropped the tapes on the Berne residency, using a parked car as a letter-box. With the same ease Toby bribed the local postman to give him a first sight of the Belgians' mail before he delivered it, and the cleaning lady to plant a radio mike in the drawing room where they held most of their discussions. For diversion they went to the Chikito and Toby danced with the youngest girls. Now and then he brought one home but by morning she was always gone and Toby had the windows open to get rid of the smell.

They lived this way for three months and Guillam knew him no better at the end than on the first day. He didn't even know his country of origin. Toby was a snob and knew the places to eat and be seen. He washed his own clothes and at night he wore a net over his Snow White hair, and on the day the police hit the villa and Guillam had to hop over the back wall, he found Toby at the Bellevue Hotel munching *patisseries* and watching the *thé dansant*. He listened to what Guillam had to say, paid his bill, tipped first the band-leader, then Franz the head porter, then led the way along a succession of corridors and staircases to the underground garage where he had cached the escape car and passports. There also, punctiliously, he asked for his bill. 'If you ever want to get out of Switzerland in a hurry,' thought Guillam, 'you pay your bills first.' The corridors were endless, with mirror walls and Versailles chandeliers, so that Guillam was following not just one Esterhase but a whole delegation of them.

It was this vision that came back to him now, though the narrow wooden staircase to Alleline's rooms was painted mud green and only a battered parchment lampshade recalled the chandeliers.

'To see the Chief,' Toby announced portentously to the young janitor who beckoned them through with an insolent nod. In the anteroom at four grey typewriters sat the four grey mothers in pearls and twinsets. They nodded to Guillam and ignored Toby. A sign over Alleline's door said 'engaged'. Beside it, a six-foot wardrobe safe, new. Guillam wondered how on earth the floor took the strain. On its top, bottles of South African sherry, glasses, plates. Tuesday, he remembered: London Station's informal lunch meeting.

'I'll have no phone calls, please, ladies,' said Toby elaborately, holding back the door for Guillam. 'We are having a conference.'

One of the mothers said: 'We heard.'

It was a war party.

Alleline sat at the head of the table in the megalomaniac's carving chair, reading a two-page document, and he didn't stir when Guillam came in. He just growled: 'Down there with you. By Paul. Below the salt,' and went on reading with heavy concentration.

The chair to Alleline's right was empty and Guillam knew it was Haydon's by the posture-curve cushion tied to it with string. To Alleline's left sat Roy Bland, also reading, but he looked up as Guillam passed and said 'Wotcher, Peter' then followed him all the way down the table with his bulging pale eyes. Next to Bill's empty chair sat Mo Delaware, London Station's token woman, in bobbed hair and a brown tweed suit. Across from her, Phil Porteous, the head housekeeper, a rich servile man with a big house in suburbia. When he saw Guillam he stopped his reading altogether, ostentatiously closed the folder, laid his sleek hands over it and smirked.

'Below the salt means next to Paul Skordeno,' said Phil, still smirking.

'Thanks. I can see it.'

Across from Porteous came Bill's Russians, last seen in the fourth-floor men's room, Nick de Silsky and his boyfriend Kaspar. They couldn't smile and for all Guillam knew they couldn't read either because they had no papers in front of them, they were the only ones who hadn't. They sat with their four thick hands on the table as if somebody was holding a gun behind them, and they just watched him with their four brown eyes.

Downhill from Porteous sat Paul Skordeno, now reputedly Roy Bland's fieldman on the satellite networks, though others said he ran between wickets for Bill. Paul was thin and mean and forty with a pitted brown face and long arms. Guillam had once paired with him on a tough-guy course at the Nursery and they had all but killed each other.

Guillam moved the chair away from him and sat down, so Toby sat next along like the other half of a bodyguard. What the hell do they expect me to do? thought Guillam: make a dash for freedom? Everyone was watching Alleline fill his pipe when Bill Haydon upstaged him. The door opened and at first no one came in. Then a slow shuffle and Bill appeared, clutching a cup of coffee in both hands, the saucer on top. He had a striped folder jammed under his arm and his glasses were over his nose for a change, so he must have done his reading elsewhere. They've all been reading it except me, thought Guillam, and I don't know what it is. He wondered whether it was the same document that Esterhase and Toby were reading yesterday and decided on no evidence at all that it was; that yesterday it had just come in; that Toby had brought it to Roy and that he had disturbed them in their first excitement; if excitement was the word.

Alleline had still not looked up. Down the table Guillam had only his rich black hair to look at, and a pair of broad tweedy shoulders. Mo Delaware was pulling at her forelock while she read. Percy had two wives, Guillam remembered, as Camilla once more flitted through his teeming mind, and both were alcoholics, which must mean something. He had met only the London edition. Percy was forming his supporters' club and gave a drinks party at his sprawling panelled flat in Buckingham Palace Mansions. Guillam arrived late and he was taking off his coat in the lobby when a pale blonde woman loomed timidly towards him holding out her hands. He took her for the maid wanting his coat.

'I'm Joy,' she said in a theatrical voice, like 'I'm Virtue' or 'I'm Continence'. It wasn't his coat she wanted but a kiss. Yielding to it, Guillam inhaled the joint pleasures of '*Je Reviens*' and a high concentration of inexpensive sherry.

'Well now, young Peter Guillam' – Alleline speaking – 'are you ready for me finally or have you other calls to make about my house?' He half looked up and Guillam noticed two tiny triangles of fur on each weathered cheek. 'What are you getting up to out there in the sticks these days?' – turning a page – 'apart from chasing the local virgins, if there are any in Brixton which I severely doubt – if you'll pardon my freedom, Mo – and wasting public money on expensive lunches?'

This banter was Alleline's one instrument of communication, it could be friendly or hostile, reproachful or congratulatory, but in the end it was like a constant tapping on the same spot.

'Couple of Arab ploys look quite promising. Cy Vanhofer's got a lead to a German diplomat. That's about it.'

'Arabs,' Alleline repeated, pushing aside the folder and dragging a rough pipe from his pocket. 'Any bloody fool can burn an Arab, can't he, Bill? Buy a whole damn Arab cabinet for half a crown if you've a mind to.' From another pocket Alleline took a tobacco pouch, which he tossed easily onto the table. 'I hear you've been hobnobbing with our late-lamented Brother Tarr. How is he these days?'

A lot of things went through Guillam's mind as he heard himself answer. That the surveillance on his flat did not begin till last night, he was sure of it. That over the weekend he was in the clear unless Fawn the captive babysitter had doubled, which would have been hard for him. That Roy Bland bore a close resemblance to the late Dylan Thomas, Roy had always reminded him of someone and till this moment he'd never been able to pin down the connection, and that Mo Delaware had only passed muster as a woman because of her brownie mannishness. He wondered whether Dylan Thomas had had Roy's extraordinary pale blue eyes. That Toby Esterhase was helping himself to a cigarette from his gold case, and that Alleline didn't as a rule allow cigarettes but only pipes, so Toby must stand pretty well with Alleline just now. That Bill Haydon was looking strangely young and that Circus rumours about his love life were not after all so laughable: they said he went both ways. That Paul Skordeno had one brown palm flat on the table and the thumb slightly lifted in a way that hardened the hitting surface on the outside of the hand. He thought also of his canvas case: had Alwyn put it on the shuttle? Or had he gone off for his lunch leaving it in Registry, waiting to be inspected by one of these new young janitors bursting for promotion? And Guillam wondered not for the first time just how long Toby had been hanging around Registry before he noticed him.

He selected a facetious tone: 'That's right, Chief. Tarr and I have tea at Fortnum's every afternoon.'

Alleline was sucking his empty pipe, testing the packing of the tobacco.

'Peter Guillam,' he said deliberately, in his pert brogue. 'You may not be aware of this, but I am of an extremely forgiving nature. I am positively seething with goodwill, in fact. All I require is the matter of your discussion with Tarr. I do not ask for his head, nor any other part of his damned anatomy, and I will restrain my impulse personally to strangle him. Or you.' He struck a match and lit his pipe, making a monstrous flame. 'I would even go so far as to consider hanging a gold chain about your neck and bringing you into the palace from hateful Brixton.'

'In that case I can't wait for him to turn up,' said Guillam.

'And there's a free pardon for Tarr till I get my hands on him.'

'I'll tell him. He'll be thrilled.'

A great cloud of smoke rolled out over the table.

'I'm very disappointed with you, young Peter. Giving ear to gross slanders of a divisive and insidious nature. I pay you honest money and you stab me in the back. I consider that extremely poor reward for keeping you alive. Against the entreaties of my advisers, I may tell you.'

Alleline had a new mannerism, one that Guillam had noticed often in vain men of middle age: it involved taking hold of a tuck of flesh under the chin, and massaging it between finger and thumb in the hope of reducing it.

'Tell us some more about Tarr's circumstances just now,' said Alleline. 'Tell us about his emotional state. He has a daughter, has he not? A wee daughter name of Danny. Does he talk of her at all?'

'He used to.'

'Regale us with some anecdotes about her.'

'I don't know any. He was very fond of her, that's all I know.'

'Obsessively fond?' His voice rose suddenly in anger. 'What's that shrug for? What the hell are you shrugging at me like that for? I'm talking to you about a defector from your own damn section, I'm accusing you of playing hookey with him behind my back, of taking part in damn-fool parlour games when you don't know the stakes involved, and all you do is shrug at me down the table. There's a *law*, Peter Guillam, against consorting with enemy agents. Maybe you didn't know that. I've a good mind to throw the book at you!'

'But I haven't been seeing him,' said Guillam as anger came also to his rescue. 'It's not me who's been playing parlour games. It's you. So get off my back.'

In the same moment he sensed the relaxation round the table, like a tiny descent into boredom, like a general recognition that Alleline had shot off all his ammunition and the target was unmarked. Skordeno was fidgeting with a bit of ivory, some lucky charm he carried round with him. Bland was reading again and Bill Haydon was drinking his coffee and finding it terrible, for he made a sour face at Mo Delaware and put down the cup. Toby Esterhase, chin in hand, had raised his eyebrows and was gazing at the red cellophane which filled the Victorian grate. Only the Russians continued to watch him unblinkingly, like a pair of terriers not wanting to believe that the hunt was over.

'So he used to chat to you about Danny, eh? And he told you he loved her,' said Alleline, back at the document before him. 'Who's Danny's mother?'

'A Eurasian girl.'

Now Haydon spoke for the first time. 'Unmistakably Eurasian, or could she pass for something nearer home?'

'Tarr seems to think she looks full European. He thinks the kid does too.'

Alleline read aloud: 'Twelve years old, long blonde hair, brown eyes, slim. Is that Danny?'

'I should think it could be. It sounds like her.'

There was a long silence and not even Haydon seemed inclined to break it.

'So if I told you,' Alleline resumed, choosing his words extremely carefully: 'if I told you that Danny and her mother were due to arrive three days ago at London Airport on the direct flight from Singapore, I may take it you would share our perplexity.'

'Yes, I would.'

'You would also keep your mouth shut when you got out of here. You'd tell no one but your twelve best friends?'

From not far away came Phil Porteous's purr: 'The source is extremely secret, Peter. It may sound to you like ordinary flight information but it isn't that at all. It's ultra, *ultra* sensitive.'

'Ah well, in that case I'll try to keep my mouth *ultra* shut,' said Guillam to Porteous and while Porteous coloured, Bill Haydon gave another schoolboy grin.

Alleline came back. 'So what would you make of this information? Come on Peter' – the banter again – 'Come on, you were his boss, his guide, philosopher and his friend, where's your psychology for God's sake? Why is Tarr coming to England?'

'That's not what you said at all. You said Tarr's girl and her daughter Danny were expected in London three days ago. Perhaps she's visiting relations. Perhaps she's got a new boyfriend. How should I know?'

'Don't be obtuse, man. Doesn't it occur to you that where little Danny is, Tarr himself is unlikely to be far behind? If he's not here already, which I'm inclined to believe he is, that being the manner of men to come first and bring their impedimenta later. Pardon me, Mo Delaware, a lapse.'

For the second time Guillam allowed himself a little temperament. 'Till now it had not occurred to me, no. Till now Tarr was a defector. Housekeepers' ruling as of seven months ago. Right or wrong, Phil? Tarr was sitting in Moscow and everything he knew should be regarded as blown. Right, Phil? That was also held to be a good enough reason for turning the lights out in

Brixton and giving one chunk of our workload to London Station and another to Toby's lamplighters. What's Tarr supposed to be doing now: redefecting to us?'

'Redefecting would be a damned charitable way of putting it, I'll tell you that for nothing,' Alleline retorted, back at the paper before him. 'Listen to me. Listen exactly, and remember. Because I've no doubt that like the rest of my staff you've a memory like a sieve, all you prima donnas are the same. Danny and her mother are travelling on fake British passports in the name of Poole, like the harbour. The passports are Russian fakes. A third went to Tarr himself, the well known *Mister* Poole. Tarr is already in England but we don't know where. He left ahead of Danny and her mother and came here by a different route, our investigations suggest a black one. He instructed his wife or mistress or whatever' – he said this as if he had neither – 'pardon again, Mo, to follow him in one week, which they have not yet done, apparently. This information only reached us yesterday so we've a lot of footwork to do yet. Tarr instructed them, Danny and her mother, that if by chance he failed to make contact with them, they should throw themselves on the mercy of one Peter Guillam. That's you, I believe.'

'If they were due three days ago what's happened to them?'

'Delayed. Missed their plane. Changed their plans. Lost their tickets. How the hell do I know?'

'Or else the information's wrong,' Guillam suggested.

'It isn't,' Alleline snapped.

Resentment, mystification: Guillam clung to them both. 'All right. The Russians have turned Tarr round. They've sent his family over – God knows why, I'd have thought they'd put them in the bank – and they've sent him too. Why's it all so hot? What sort of plant can he be when we don't believe a word he says?'

This time, he noticed with exhilaration, his audience was watching Alleline; who seemed to Guillam to be torn between giving a satisfactory but indiscreet answer, or making a fool of himself.

'Never mind what sort of plant! Muddying pools. Poisoning wells, maybe. That damn sort. Pulling the rug out when we're all but home and dry.' His circulars read that way too, thought Guillam. Metaphors chasing each other off the page. 'But just you remember this. At the first peep, before the first peep, at the first whisper of him or his lady or his wee daughter, young Peter Guillam, you come to one of us grown-ups. Anyone you see at this table. But not another damn soul. Do you follow that injunction perfectly? Because there are more damn wheels within wheels here than you can possibly guess or have any right to know . . .'

It became suddenly a conversation in movement. Bland had plugged his hands into his pockets and slouched across the room to lean against the far door. Alleline had relit his pipe and was putting out the match with a long movement of his arm while he glowered at Guillam through the smoke. 'Who are you courting these days, Peter, who's the lucky wee lady?' Porteous was sliding a sheet of paper down the table for Guillam's signature. 'For you, Peter, if you please.' Paul Skordeno was whispering something into the ear of one of the Russians, and Esterhase was at the door giving unpopular orders to the mothers. Only Mo Delaware's brown, unassuming eyes still held Guillam in their gaze.

'Read it first, won't you,' Porteous advised silkily.

Guillam was halfway through the form already: 'I certify that I have today been advised of the contents of Witchcraft report No. 308, Source Merlin,' ran the first paragraph. 'I undertake not to divulge any part of this report to other members of the Service, nor will I divulge the existence of Source Merlin. I also undertake to report at once any matter which comes to my notice which appears to bear on his material.'

The door had stayed open and, as Guillam signed, the second echelon of London Station filed in, led by the mothers with trays of sandwiches: Diana Dolphin, Lauder Strickland looking taut enough to blow up, the girls from distribution and a sour-faced old warhorse called Haggard, who was Ben Thruxton's overlord. Guillam left slowly, counting heads because he knew Smiley would want to know who was there. At the door, to his surprise, he found himself joined by Haydon, who seemed to have decided that the remaining festivities were not for him.

'Stupid bloody cabaret,' Bill remarked, waving vaguely at the mothers. 'Percy's getting more insufferable every day.'

'He does seem to,' said Guillam heartily.

'How's Smiley these days? Seen much of him? You used to be quite a chum of his, didn't you?'

Guillam's world, which was showing signs till then of steadying to a sensible pace, plunged violently. 'Afraid not,' he said, 'he's out of bounds.'

'Don't tell me you take any notice of that nonsense,' Bill snorted. They had reached the stairs. Haydon went ahead.

'How about you?' Guillam called. 'Have you seen much of him?'

'And Ann's flown the coop,' said Bill, ignoring the question. 'Pushed off with a sailor boy or a waiter or something.' The door to his room was wide open, the desk was heaped with secret files. 'Is that right?'

'I didn't know,' said Guillam. 'Poor old George.'

'Coffee?'

'I think I'll get back, thanks.'

'For tea with Brother Tarr?'

'That's right. At Fortnum's. So long.'

In Archives Section, Alwyn was back from lunch. 'Bag's all gone, sir,' he said gaily. 'Should be over in Brixton by now.'

'Oh damn,' said Guillam, firing his last shot. 'There was something in it I needed.'

A sickening notion had struck him: it seemed so neat and so horribly obvious that he could only wonder why it had come to him so late. Sand was Camilla's husband. She was living a double life. Now whole vistas of deceit opened before him. His friends, his loves, even the Circus itself, joined and re-formed in endless patterns of intrigue. A line of Mendel's came back to him, dropped two nights ago as they drank beer in some glum suburban pub: 'Cheer up, Peter, old son. Jesus Christ only had twelve, you know, and one of them was a double.'

Tarr, he thought. That bastard Ricki Tarr.

# TWENTY-TWO

The bedroom was long and low, once a maid's room, built into the attic. Guillam was standing at the door; Tarr sat on the bed motionless, his head tilted back against the sloped ceiling, hands to either side of him, fingers wide. There was a dormer window above him and from where Guillam stood he could see long reaches of black Suffolk countryside, and a line of black trees traced against the sky. The wallpaper was brown with large red flowers. The one light hung from a black oak truss, lighting their two faces in strange geometric patterns, and when either of them moved, Tarr on the bed or Smiley on the wooden kitchen chair, they seemed by their movement to take the light with them a distance before it resettled.

Left to himself Guillam would have been very rough with Tarr, he had no doubt of it. His nerves were all over the place and on the drive down he had touched ninety before Smiley sharply told him to go steady. Left to himself he would have been tempted to beat the daylights out of Tarr and if necessary he would have brought Fawn in to lend a hand; driving, he had a very clear picture of opening the front door of wherever Tarr lived and hitting him in the face several times, with love from Camilla and her ex-husband, the distinguished doctor of the flute. And perhaps in the shared tension of the journey Smiley had received the same picture telepathically for the little he said was clearly directed to talking Guillam down. 'Tarr has not lied to us, Peter. Not in any material way. He has simply done what agents do the world over: he has failed to tell us the whole story. On the other hand he has been rather clever.' Far from sharing Guillam's bewilderment, he seemed curiously confident, even complacent, to the extent of allowing himself a sententious aphorism from Steed Asprey on the arts of double cross; something about not looking for perfection, but for advantage, which again had Guillam thinking about Camilla. 'Karla has admitted us to the inner circle,' Smiley announced, and Guillam made a bad joke about changing at Charing Cross. After that Smiley contented himself with giving directions and watching the wing mirror.

They had met at Crystal Palace, a van pickup with Mendel driving. They drove to Barnsbury, straight into a car body repair shop at the end of a cobbled alley full of children. There they were received with discreet rapture by an old German and his son, who had stripped the plates off the van almost before they got out of it and led them to a souped-up Vauxhall ready to drive out of the far end of the workshop. Mendel stayed behind with the Testify file which Guillam had brought from Brixton in his night-bag; Smiley said, 'Find the A12.' There was very little traffic but short of Colchester they hit a cluster of lorries and Guillam suddenly lost patience. Smiley had to order him to pull in. Once they met an old man driving at twenty in the fast lane. As they overtook him on the inside he veered wildly towards them, drunk or ill, or just terrified. And once with no warning they hit a fog wall, it seemed to fall on them from above. Guillam drove clean through it, afraid to brake because of black ice. Past Colchester they took small lanes. On the signposts were names like Little Horkesley, Wormingford and Bures Green, then the signposts stopped and Guillam had a feeling of being nowhere at all.

'Left here and left again at the dower house. Go as far as you can but park short of the gates.'

They reached what seemed to be a hamlet but there were no lights, no people and no moon. As they got out the cold hit them and Guillam smelt a cricket field and woodsmoke and Christmas all at once; he thought he had never been anywhere so quiet or so cold or so remote. A church tower rose ahead of them, a white fence ran to one side, and up on the slope stood what he took to be the rectory, a low rambling house, part thatched, he could make out the fringe of gable against the sky. Fawn was waiting for them; he came to the car as they parked, and climbed silently into the back.

'Ricki's been that much better today, sir,' he reported. He had evidently done a lot of reporting to Smiley in the last few days. He was a steady, soft-spoken boy with a great will to please, but the rest of the Brixton pack seemed to be afraid of him, Guillam didn't know why. 'Not so nervy, more relaxed I'd say. Did his pools this morning, loves the pools Ricki does, this afternoon we dug up fir trees for Miss Ailsa, so's she could drive them into market. This evening we had a nice game of cards and early bed.'

'Has he been out alone?' asked Smiley.

'No, sir.'

'Has he used the telephone?'

'Gracious no, sir, not while I'm around, and I'm sure not while Miss Ailsa was either.'

Their breath had misted the windows of the car, but Smiley would not have the engine on so there was no heater and no de-mister.

'Has he mentioned his daughter Danny?'

'Over the weekend he did a lot. Now he's sort of cooled off about them. I think he's shut them out of his mind in view of the emotional side.'

'He hasn't talked about seeing them again?'

'No, sir.'

'Nothing about arrangements for meeting when all this is over?'

'No, sir.'

'Or bringing them to England?'

'No, sir.'

'Nor about providing them with documents?'

'No, sir.'

Guillam chimed in irritably: 'So what has he talked about, for heaven's sake?'

'The Russian lady, sir. Irina. He likes to read her diary. He says when the mole's caught, he's going to make Centre swap him for Irina. Then we'll get her a nice place, sir, like Miss Ailsa's but up in Scotland where it's nicer. He says he'll see me right, too. Give me a big job in the Circus. He's been encouraging me to learn another language to increase my scope.'

There was no telling, from the flat voice behind them in the dark, what Fawn made of this advice.

'Where is he now?'

'In bed, sir.'

'Close the doors quietly.'

Ailsa Brimley was waiting in the front porch for them: a grey-haired lady of sixty with a firm, intelligent face. She was old Circus, Smiley said, one of Lord Lansbury's coding ladies from the war, now in retirement but still formidable. She wore a trim brown suit. She shook Guillam by the hand and said 'How do you do', bolted the door and when he looked again she had gone. Smiley led the way upstairs. Fawn should wait on the lower landing in case he was needed.

'It's Smiley,' he said, knocking on Tarr's door. 'I want a chat with you.'

Tarr opened the door fast. He must have heard them coming, he must have been waiting just the other side. He opened it with his left hand, holding the gun in his right, and he was looking past Smiley down the corridor.

'It's only Guillam,' said Smiley.

'That's what I mean,' said Tarr. 'Babies can bite.'

They stepped inside. He wore slacks and some sort of cheap Malay wrap. Spelling cards lay spread over the floor and in the air hung a smell of curry which he had cooked for himself on a ring.

'I'm sorry to be pestering you,' said Smiley with an air of sincere commiseration. 'But I must ask you again what you did with those two Swiss escape passports you took with you to Hong Kong.'

'Why?' said Tarr at last.

The jauntiness was all gone. He had a prison pallor, he had lost weight and as he sat on the bed with the gun on the pillow beside him, his eyes sought them out nervously, each in turn, trusting nothing.

Smiley said: 'Listen. I want to believe your story. Nothing is altered. Once we know, we'll respect your privacy. But we have to know. It's terribly important. Your whole future stands by it.'

And a lot more besides, thought Guillam, watching; a whole chunk of devious arithmetic was hanging by a thread, if Guillam knew Smiley at all.

'I told you, I burned them. I didn't fancy the numbers. I reckoned they were blown. Might as well put a label round your neck: "Tarr, Ricki Tarr, Wanted," soon as use those passports.'

Smiley's questions were terribly slow in coming. Even to Guillam it was painful waiting for them in the deep silence of the night.

'What did you burn them with?'

'What the hell does that matter?'

But Smiley apparently did not feel like giving reasons for his enquiries, he preferred to let the silence do its work, and he seemed confident that it would. Guillam had seen whole interrogations conducted that way: a laboured catechism swathed in deep coverings of routine, wearying pauses as each answer was written down in longhand and the suspect's brain besieged itself with a thousand questions to the interrogator's one; and his hold on his story weakened from day to day.

'When you bought your British passport in the name of Poole,' Smiley asked, after another age, 'did you buy any other passports from the same source?'

'Why should I?'

But Smiley did not feel like giving reasons.

'Why should I?' Tarr repeated. 'I'm not a damn collector for Christ's sake, all I wanted was to get out from under.'

'And protect your child,' Smiley suggested, with an understanding smile. 'And protect her mother too, if you could. I'm sure you gave a lot of thought to that,' he said in a flattering tone. 'After all, you could hardly leave them behind to the mercy of that inquisitive Frenchman, could you?'

Waiting, Smiley appeared to examine the lexicon cards, reading off the words longways and sideways. There was nothing to them: they were random words. One was mis-spelt, Guillam noticed 'epistle' with the last two letters back to front. What's he been doing up there, Guillam wondered, in that stinking fleapit of a hotel? What furtive little tracks has his mind been following, locked away with the sauce bottles and the commercial travellers?

'All right,' said Tarr sullenly, 'so I got passports for Danny and her mother. Mrs. Poole, Miss Danny Poole. What do we do now; cry out in ecstasy?'

Again it was the silence that accused.

'Now why didn't you tell us that before?' Smiley asked, in the tone of a disappointed father. 'We're not monsters. We don't wish them harm. Why didn't you tell us? Perhaps we could even have helped you,' and went back to his examination of the cards. Tarr must have used two or three packs, they lay in rivers over the coconut carpet. 'Why didn't you tell us?' he repeated. 'There's no crime in looking after the people one loves.'

If they'll let you, thought Guillam, with Camilla in mind.

To help Tarr answer, Smiley was making helpful suggestions: 'Was it because you dipped into your operational expenses to buy these British passports? Was that the reason you didn't tell us? Good heavens, no one here is worried about money. You've brought us a vital piece of information. Why should we quarrel about a couple of thousand dollars?' And the time ticked away again without anyone using it.

'Or was it,' Smiley suggested, 'that you were ashamed?'

Guillam stiffened, his own problems forgotten.

'Rightly ashamed in a way, I suppose. It wasn't a very gallant act, after all, to leave Danny and her mother with blown passports, at the mercy of that so-called Frenchman who was looking so hard for Mr Poole, was it? While you yourself escaped to all this VIP treatment? It is horrible to think of,' Smiley agreed, as if Tarr, not he, had made the point. 'It is horrible to contemplate the lengths Karla would go to in order to obtain your silence. Or your services.'

The sweat on Tarr's face was suddenly unbearable. There was too much of it, it was like tears all over. The cards no longer interested Smiley, his eye had settled on a different game. It was a toy, made of two steel rods like the shafts of a pair of tongs. The trick was to roll a steel ball along them. The further you rolled it the more points you won when it fell into one of the holes underneath.

'The other reason you might not have told us, I suppose, is that you burnt them. You burnt the *British* passports, I mean, not the Swiss ones.'

Go easy, George, thought Guillam, and softly moved a pace nearer to cover the gap between them. Just go easy.

'You knew that Poole was blown, so you burnt the Poole passports you had bought for Danny and her mother, but you kept your own because there was no alternative. Then you made travel bookings for the two of them in the name of Poole in order to convince everybody that you still believed in the Poole passports. By everybody, I think I mean Karla's footpads, don't I? You doctored the Swiss escapes, one for Danny, one for her mother, took a chance that the numbers wouldn't be noticed, and you made a different set of arrangements which you didn't advertise. Arrangements which matured earlier than those you made for the Pooles. How would that be? Such as staying out East but somewhere else, like Djakarta: somewhere you have friends.'

Even from where he stood, Guillam was too slow. Tarr's hands were at Smiley's throat, the chair toppled and Tarr fell with him. From the heap, Guillam selected Tarr's right arm and flung it into a lock against his back, bringing it very near to breaking as he did so. From nowhere Fawn appeared, took the gun from the pillow and walked back to Tarr as if to give him a hand. Then Smiley was straightening his suit and Tarr was back on the bed, dabbing the corner of his mouth with a handkerchief.

Smiley said: 'I don't know where they are. As far as I know, no harm has come to them. You believe that, do you?'

Tarr was staring at him, waiting. His eyes were furious, but over Smiley a kind of calm had settled, and Guillam guessed it was the reassurance he had been hoping for.

'Maybe you should keep a better eye on your own damn woman and leave mine alone,' Tarr whispered, his hand across his mouth. With an exclamation, Guillam sprang forward but Smiley restrained him.

'As long as you don't try to communicate with them,' Smiley continued, 'it's probably better that I shouldn't know. Unless you want me to do something about them. Money or protection or comfort of some sort?'

Tarr shook his head. There was blood in his mouth, a lot of it, and Guillam realised Fawn must have hit him but he couldn't work out when.

'It won't be long now,' Smiley said. 'Perhaps a week. Less if I can manage it. Try not to think too much.'

By the time they left, Tarr was grinning again, so Guillam guessed that the visit, or the insult to Smiley or the smash in the face, had done him good.

'Those football pool coupons,' Smiley said quietly to Fawn as they climbed into the car: 'You don't post them anywhere, do you?'

'No, sir.'

'Well let's hope to God he doesn't have a win,' Smiley remarked in a most unusual fit of jocularity, and there was laughter all round.

The memory plays strange tricks on an exhausted, over-laden brain. As Guillam drove, one part of his conscious mind upon the road and another still wretchedly grappling with even more gothic suspicions of Camilla, odd images of this and other long days drifted freely through his memory. Days of plain terror in Morocco as one by one his agent lines went dead on him, and every footfall on the stair had him scurrying to the window to check the street; days of idleness in Brixton when he watched that poor world slip by and wondered how long before he joined it. And suddenly the written report was there before him on his desk: cyclostyled on blue flimsy because it was traded, source unknown and probably unreliable, and every word of it came back to him in letters a foot high.

*According to a recently released prisoner from Lubianka, Moscow Centre held a secret execution in the punishment block in July. The victims were three of its own functionaries. One was a woman. All three were shot in the back of the neck.*

'It was stamped "internal",' Guillam said dully. They had parked in a layby beside a roadhouse hung with fairy lights. 'Somebody from London Station had scribbled on it: *Can anyone identify the bodies?*'

By the coloured glow of the lights, Guillam watched Smiley's face pucker in disgust.

'Yes,' he agreed at last. 'Yes, well now the woman was Irina, wasn't she? Then there was Ivlov and then there was Boris, her husband, I suppose.' His voice remained extremely matter of fact. 'Tarr mustn't know,' he continued, as if shaking off lassitude. 'It is vital that he should have no wind of this. God knows what he would do, or not do, if he knew that Irina was dead.' For some moments neither moved; perhaps for their different reasons neither had the strength just then, or the heart.

'I ought to telephone,' said Smiley, but he made no attempt to leave the car.
'George?'
'I have a phone call to make,' he muttered. 'Lacon.'
'Then make it.'

Reaching across him, Guillam pushed open the door. Smiley clambered out, walked a distance over the tarmac, then seemed to change his mind and came back.

'Come and eat something,' he said through the window, in the same preoccupied tone. 'I don't think even Toby's people would follow us in here.'

It was once a restaurant, now a transport café with trappings of old grandeur. The menu was bound in red leather and stained with grease. The boy who brought it was half asleep.

'I hear the *coq au vin* is always reliable,' said Smiley with a poor effort at humour, as he returned from the telephone booth in the corner. And in a quieter voice, that fell short and echoed nowhere: 'Tell me, how much do you know about Karla?'

'About as much as I know about Witchcraft, and Source Merlin, and whatever else it said on the paper I signed for Porteous.'

'Ah well now that's a very good answer, as it happens. You meant it as a rebuke, I expect, but, as it happens, the analogy was most apt.' The boy reappeared, swinging a bottle of Burgundy like an Indian club. 'Would you please let it breathe a little?'

The boy stared at Smiley as if he were mad.

'Open it and leave it on the table,' said Guillam curtly.

It was not the whole story Smiley told. Afterwards Guillam did notice several gaps. But it was enough to lift his spirits from the doldrums where they had strayed.

# TWENTY-THREE

'It is the business of agent runners to turn themselves into legends,' Smiley began, rather as if he were delivering a trainee lecture at the Nursery. 'They do this first to impress their agents. Later they try it out on their colleagues and in my personal experience make rare asses of themselves in consequence. A few go so far as to try it on themselves. Those are the charlatans and they may be got rid of quickly, there's no other way.'

Yet legends were made and Karla was one of them. Even his age was a mystery. Most likely Karla was not his real name. Decades of his life were not accounted for, and probably never would be, since the people he worked with had a way of dying off or keeping their mouths shut.

'There's a story that his father was in the Okhrana and later reappeared in the Cheka. I don't think it's true but it may be. There's another that he worked as a kitchen boy on an armoured train against Japanese Occupation troops in the East. He is said to have learnt his tradecraft from Berg – to have been his ewe lamb in fact – which is a bit like being taught music by . . . oh, name a great composer. So far as I am concerned, his career began in Spain in thirty-six, because that at least is documented. He posed as a White Russian journalist in the Franco cause and recruited a stable of German agents. It was a most intricate operation and for a young man remarkable. He popped up next in the Soviet counter-offensive against Smolensk in the autumn of forty-one as an intelligence officer under Konev. He had the job of running networks of partisans behind the German lines. Along the way he discovered that his radio operator had been turned round and was transmitting radio messages to the enemy. He turned him back and from then on played a radio game which had them going in all directions.'

That was another part of the legend, said Smiley: at Yelnya, thanks to Karla, the Germans shelled their own forward line.

'And between these two sightings,' he continued, 'in thirty-six and forty-one, Karla visited Britain, we think he was here six months. But even today we don't know – that's to say I don't know – under what name or cover. Which isn't to say Gerald doesn't. But Gerald isn't likely to tell us, at least not on purpose.'

Smiley had never talked to Guillam this way. He was not given to confidences or long lectures; Guillam knew him as a shy man, for all his vanities, and one who expected very little communication.

'In forty-eight-odd, having served his country loyally, Karla did a spell in prison and later in Siberia. There was nothing personal about it. He simply happened to be in one of those sections of Red Army intelligence which in some purge or other ceased to exist.'

And certainly, Smiley went on, after his post-Stalin reinstatement, he went to America; because when the Indian authorities in the summer of fifty-five arrested him in Delhi on vague immigration charges, he had just flown in from California. Circus gossip later linked him with the big treason scandals in Britain and the States.

Smiley knew better: 'Karla was in disgrace again. Moscow was out for his blood, and we thought we might persuade him to defect. That was why I flew to Delhi. To have a chat with him.'

There was a pause while the weary boy slouched over and enquired whether everything was to their satisfaction. Smiley with great solicitude assured him that it was.

'The story of my meeting with Karla,' he resumed, 'belonged very much to the mood of the period. In the mid-fifties Moscow Centre was in pieces on the floor. Senior officers were being shot or purged wholesale and its lower ranks were seized with a collective paranoia. As a first result, there was a crop of defections among Centre officers stationed overseas. All over the place, Singapore, Nairobi, Stockholm, Canberra, Washington, I don't know where, we got this same steady trickle from the residencies: not just the big fish but the legmen, drivers, cypher clerks, typists. Somehow we had to respond – I don't think it's ever realized how much the industry stimulates its own inflation – and in no time I became a kind of commercial traveller, flying off one day to a capital city, the next to a dingy border outpost – once even to a ship at sea – to sign up defecting Russians. To seed, to stream, to fix the terms, to attend to debriefing and eventual disposal.'

Guillam was watching him all the while but even in that cruel neon glow Smiley's expression revealed nothing but a slightly anxious concentration.

'We evolved, you might say, three kinds of contract for those whose stories held together. If the client's access wasn't interesting we might trade him to another country and forget him. Buy him for stock, as you would say, much as the scalphunters do today. Or we might play him back into Russia: that's assuming his defection had not already been noticed there. Or if he was lucky we took him; cleaned him of whatever he knew and resettled him in the West. London decided usually. Not me. But remember this. At that time Karla, or Gerstmann as he called himself, was just another client. I've told his story back to front; I didn't want to be coy with you, but you have to bear in mind now, through anything that happened between us, or didn't happen which is more to the point, that all I or anyone in the Circus knew when I flew to Delhi was that a man calling himself Gertsmann had been setting up a radio link between Rudnev, head of illegal networks at Moscow Centre, and a Centre-run apparatus in California that was lying fallow for want of a means of communication. That's all. Gertsmann had smuggled a transmitter across the Canadian border and lain up for three weeks in San Francisco breaking in the new operator. That was the assumption, and there was a batch of test transmissions to back it up.'

For these test transmissions between Moscow and California, Smiley explained, a book code was used: 'Then one day Moscow signalled a straight order – '

'Still on the book code?'

'Precisely. That is the point. Owing to a temporary inattention on the part of Rudnev's cryptographers, we were ahead of the game. The wranglers broke the code and that's how we got out information. Gerstmann was to leave San Francisco at once and head for Delhi for a rendezvous with the Tass correspondent, a talent-spotter who had stumbled on a hot Chinese lead and needed immediate direction. Why they dragged him all the way from San Francisco to Delhi, why it had to be Karla and no one else – well that's a story for another day. The only material point is that when Gerstmann kept the rendezvous in Delhi, the Tass man handed him an aeroplane ticket and told him to go straight home to Moscow. No questions. The order came from Rudnev personally. It was signed with Rudnev's workname and it was brusque even by Russian standards.'

Whereupon the Tass man fled, leaving Gerstmann standing on the pavement with a lot of questions and twenty-eight hours until take-off.

'He hadn't been standing there long when the Indian authorities arrested him at our request and carted him off to Delhi jail. As far as I remember we had promised the Indians a piece of the product. I *think* that was the deal,' he remarked, and like someone suddenly shocked by the faultiness of his own memory fell silent and looked distractedly down the steamy room. 'Or perhaps we said they could have him when we'd done with him. Dear oh dear.'

'It doesn't really matter,' Guillam said.

'For once in Karla's life, as I say, the Circus was ahead of him,' Smiley resumed, having taken a sip of wine and made a sour face. 'He couldn't know it but the San Francisco network which he had just serviced had been rolled up hide and hair the day he left for Delhi. As soon as Control had the story from the wranglers he traded it to the Americans on the understanding that they missed Gerstmann but hit the rest of the Rudnev network in California. Gerstmann flew on to Delhi unaware, and he was still unaware when I arrived at Delhi jail to sell him a piece of insurance, as Control called it. His choice was very simple. There could not be the slightest doubt, on present form, that Gerstmann's head was on the block in Moscow, where to save his own neck Rudnev was busy denouncing him for blowing the San Francisco network. The affair had made a great splash in the States and Moscow was very angry at the publicity. I had with me the American press photographs of the arrest; even of the radio set Karla had imported and the signals plans he had cached before he left. You know how prickly we all become when things get into the papers.'

Guillam did; and with a jolt remembered the Testify file which he had left with Mendel earlier that evening.

'To sum it up, Karla was the proverbial cold war orphan. He had left home to do a job abroad. The job had blown up in his face, but he couldn't go back: home was more hostile than abroad. We had no powers of permanent arrest, so it was up to Karla to ask us for protection. I don't think I had ever come across a clearer case for defection. I had only to convince him of the arrest of the San Francisco network – wave the press photographs and cuttings from my briefcase at him – talk to him a little about the unfriendly conspiracies of brother Rudnev in Moscow, and cable the somewhat overworked inquisitors in Sarratt, and with any luck I'd make London by the weekend. I rather think I had tickets for Sadlers Wells. It was Ann's great year for ballet.'

Yes, Guillam had heard about that too, a twenty-year old Welsh Apollo, the season's wonder boy. They had been burning up London for months.

The heat in the jail was appalling, Smiley continued. The cell had an iron table at the centre and iron cattle rings let into the wall. 'They brought him manacled, which seemed silly because he was so slight. I asked them to free his hands and when they did, he put them on the table in front of him and watched the blood come back. It must have been painful but he didn't comment on it. He'd been there a week and he was wearing a calico tunic. Red. I forget what red meant. Some piece of prison ethic.' Taking a sip of wine, he again pulled a face, then slowly corrected the gesture as the memories once more bore in upon him.

'Well, at first sight, he made little impression on me. I would have been hard put to it to recognise in the little fellow before me the master of cunning we have heard about in Irina's letter, poor woman. I suppose it's also true that my nerve-ends had been a good deal blunted by so many similar encounters in the last few months, by travel, and well by – well, by things at home.'

In all the time Guillam had known him, it was the nearest Smiley had ever come to acknowledging Ann's infidelities.

'For some reason, it hurt an awful lot.' His eyes were still open but his gaze had fixed upon an inner world. The skin of his brow and cheeks was drawn smooth as if by exertion of his memory; but nothing could conceal from Guillam the loneliness evoked by this one admission. 'I have a theory which I suspect is rather immoral,' Smiley went on, more lightly. 'Each of us has only a quantum of compassion. That if we lavish our concern on every stray cat, we never get to the centre of things. What do you think of it?'

'What did Karla look like?' Guillam asked, treating the question as rhetorical.

'Avuncular. Modest, and avuncular. He would have looked very well as a priest: the shabby, gnomic variety one sees in small Italian towns. Little wiry chap, with silvery hair, bright brown eyes and plenty of wrinkles. Or a schoolmaster, he could have been a schoolmaster: tough, whatever that means, and sagacious within the limits of his experience: but the small canvas, all the same. He made no other initial impression, except that his gaze was straight and it fixed on me from early in our talk. If you can call it a talk, seeing that he never uttered a word. Not one, the whole time we were together; not a syllable. Also it was stinking hot and I was travelled to death.'

Out of a sense of manners rather than appetite, Smiley set to work on his food, eating several mouthfuls joylessly before resuming his narrative. 'There,' he muttered, 'that shouldn't offend the cook. The truth is, I was slightly predisposed against Mr Gerstmann. We all have our prejudices and radio men are mine. They're a thoroughly tiresome lot in my experience, bad fieldmen and overstrung, and disgracefully unreliable when it comes down to doing the job. Gerstmann, it seemed to me, was just another of the clan. Perhaps I'm looking for excuses for going to work on him with less' – he hesitated – 'less care, less caution, than in retrospect would seem appropriate.' He grew suddenly stronger. 'Though I'm not at all sure I need make any excuses,' he said.

Here Guillam sensed a wave of unusual anger, imparted by a ghostly smile that crossed Smiley's pale lips. 'To hell with it,' Smiley muttered.

Guillam waited, mystified.

'I also remember thinking that prison seemed to have taken him over very fast in seven days. He had that white dust in the skin and he wasn't sweating. I was, profusely. I trotted out my piece, as I had a dozen times that year already, except that there was obviously no question of his being played back into Russia as our agent. "You have the alternative. It's no one else's business but your own. Come to the West and we can give you, within reason, a decent life. After questioning, at which you are expected to cooperate, we can help you to a new start, a new name, seclusion, a certain amount of money. On the other hand you can go home and I suppose they'll shoot you or send you to a camp. Last month they sent Bykov, Shur and Muranov. Now why don't you tell me your real name?" Something like that. Then I sat back and wiped away the sweat and waited for him to say, "Yes, thank you". He did nothing. He didn't speak. He simply sat there stiff and tiny under the big fan that didn't work, looking at me with his brown, rather jolly eyes. Hands out in front of him. They were very calloused. I remember thinking I must ask him where he had been doing so much manual labour. He held them – like this – resting on the table, palms upwards and fingers a little bent, as if he were still manacled.'

The boy, thinking that by this gesture Smiley was indicating some want, came lumbering over and Smiley again assured him that all was doubly well, and the wine in particular was exquisite, he really wondered where they had it from; till the boy left grinning with secret amusement and flapped his cloth at an adjoining table.

'It was then, I think, that an extraordinary feeling of unease began to creep over me. The heat was really getting to me. The stench was terrible and I remember listening to the *pat pat* of my own sweat falling onto the iron table. It wasn't just his silence; his physical stillness began to get under my skin. Oh, I had known defectors who took time to speak. It can be a great wrench, for somebody trained to secrecy even towards his closest friends suddenly to open his mouth and spill secrets to his enemies. It also crossed my mind that the prison authorities might have thought it a courtesy to soften him up before they brought him to me. They assured me they hadn't, but of course one can never tell. So at first I put his silence down to shock. But this stillness, this intense, watchful stillness, was a different matter. Specially when everything inside me was so much in motion: Ann, my own heartbeats, the effects of heat and travel . . .'

'I can understand,' said Guillam quietly.

'Can you? Sitting is an eloquent business, any actor will tell you that. We sit according to our natures. We sprawl and straddle, we rest like boxers between rounds, we fidget, perch, cross and uncross our legs, lose patience, lose endurance. Gerstmann did none of those things. His posture was finite and irreducible, his little jagged body was like a promontory of rock; he could have sat that way all day, without stirring a muscle. Whereas I –' Breaking out in an awkward, embarrassed laugh, Smiley tasted the wine again, but it was no better than before. 'Whereas I longed to have something before me, papers, a book, a report. I think I am a restless person; fussy, variable. I thought so then, anyway. I felt I lacked philosophic repose. Lacked philosophy, if you like. My work had been oppressing me much more than I realized; till now. But in that foul cell I really felt aggrieved. I felt that the entire responsibility for fighting the cold war had landed on my shoulders. Which was tripe, of course, I was just exhausted and a little bit ill.' He drank again.

'I tell you,' he insisted, once more quite angry with himself. 'No one has any business to apologize for what I did.'

'What did you do?' Guillam asked with a laugh.

'So anyway there came this gap,' Smiley resumed, disregarding the question. 'Hardly of Gerstmann's making, since he was all gap anyway; so of mine, then. I had said my piece; I had flourished the photographs, which he ignored – I may say, he appeared quite ready to take my word for it that the San Francisco network was blown. I restated this part, that part, talked a few variations, and finally I dried up. Or rather sat there sweating like a pig. Well any fool knows that if ever that happens, you get up and walk out: "Take it or leave it," you say. "See you in the morning"; anything. "Go away and think for an hour."

'As it was, the next thing I knew I was talking about Ann.' He left no time for Guillam's muffled exclamation. 'Oh not about *my* Ann, not in as many words. About *his* Ann. I assumed he had one. I had asked myself, lazily no doubt, what would a man think of in such a situation, what would I? And my mind came up with a subjective answer: his woman. Is it called projection or substitution? I detest those terms but I'm sure one of them applies. I exchanged my predicament for his, that is the point, and as I now realize I began to conduct an interrogation with myself – he didn't speak, can you imagine? There were certain externals, it is true, to which I pinned the approach. He *looked* connubial; he *looked* like half a union; he *looked* too complete to be alone in all his life. Then there was his passport, describing Gerstmann as married; and it is a habit in all of us to make our cover stories, our assumed personae, at least parallel with the reality.' He lapsed again into a moment of reflection. 'I often thought that. I even put it to Control: we should take the opposition's cover stories more seriously, I said. The more identities a man has, the more they express the person they conceal. The fifty-year-old who knocks five years off his age. The married man who calls himself a bachelor; the fatherless man who gives himself two children . . . Or the interrogator who projects himself into the life of a man who does not speak. Few men can resist expressing their appetites when they are making a fantasy about themselves.'

He was lost again, and Guillam waited patiently for him to come back. For while Smiley might have fixed his concentration upon Karla, Guillam had fixed his on Smiley; and just then would have gone anywhere with him, turned any corner in order to remain beside him and hear the story out.

'I also knew from the American observation reports that Gerstmann was a chain-smoker: Camels. I sent out for several packs of them – *packs* is the American word? – and I remember feeling very strange as I handed money to a guard. I had the impression, you see, that Gerstmann saw something symbolic in the transaction of money between myself and the Indian. I wore a money belt in those days. I had to grope and peel off a note from a bundle. Gerstmann's gaze made me feel like a fifth-rate imperialist oppressor.' He smiled. 'And that I assuredly am *not*. Bill, if you like. Percy. But not I.' He called to the boy, in order to send him away: 'May we have some water, please? A jug and two glasses? Thank you.' Again he picked up the story: 'So I asked him about Mrs Gerstmann.

'I asked him: where was she? It was a question I would dearly have wished answered about Ann. No reply but the eyes unwavering. To either side of him, the two guards, and their eyes seemed so light by comparison. She must make a new life, I said; there was no other way. Had he no friend he could count on to look after her? Perhaps we could find methods of getting in touch with her secretly? I put it to him that his going back to Moscow would do nothing for her at all. I was listening to myself, I ran on, I couldn't stop. Perhaps I didn't want to. I was really thinking of leaving Ann you see, I thought the time had come. To go back would be a quixotic act, I told him, of no material value to his wife, or anyone, quite the reverse. She would be ostracized; at best, she would be allowed to see him briefly before he was shot. On the other hand, if he threw in his lot with us, we might be able to trade her; we had a lot of stock in those days remember, and some of it was going back to Russia as barter; though why in God's name we should have used it up for that purpose is beyond me. Surely, I said, she would prefer to know him safe and well in the West, with a fair chance that she herself would join him, than shot or starving to death in Siberia? I really harped upon her: his expression encouraged me. I could have sworn I was getting through to him, that I had found the chink in his armour: when of course all I was doing – all I was doing was showing him the chink in mine. And when I mentioned Siberia, I touched something. I could feel it, like a lump in my own throat, I could feel in Gerstmann a shiver of revulsion. Well, naturally I did,' Smiley commented sourly; 'since it was only recently that he had been an inmate. Finally, back came the guard with the cigarettes, armfuls of them, and dumped them with a clatter on the iron table. I counted the change, tipped him, and in doing so again caught the expression in Gerstmann's eyes; I fancied I read amusement there, but really I was no longer in a state to tell. I noticed that the boy refused my tip; I suppose he disliked the English. I tore open a packet and offered Gerstmann a cigarette. "Come," I said, "you're a chain-smoker, everyone knows that. And this is your favourite brand." My voice sounded strained and silly, and there was nothing I could do about it. Gerstmann stood up and politely indicated to the warders that he would like to return to his cell.'

Taking his time, Smiley pushed aside his half eaten food, over which white flakes of fat had formed like seasonable frost.

'As he left the cell he changed his mind and helped himself to a packet of cigarettes and the lighter from the table, my lighter, a gift from Ann. "To George from Ann with all my love." I would never have dreamed of letting him take it in the ordinary way; but this was not the ordinary way. Indeed I thought it thoroughly appropriate that he should take her lighter; I thought it, Lord help me, expressive of the bond between us. He dropped the lighter and the cigarettes into the pouch of his red tunic, then put out his hand for hand-cuffs. I said: "Light one now if you want." I told the guards: "Let him light a cigarette, please." But he didn't make a movement. "The intention is to put you on tomorrow's plane to Moscow unless we come to terms," I added. He might not have heard me. I watched the guards lead him out, then returned to my hotel, someone drove me, to this day I couldn't tell you who. I no longer knew what I felt. I was more confused and more ill than I would admit, even to myself. I ate a poor dinner, drank too much and ran a soaring temperature. I lay on my bed sweating, dreaming about Gerstmann. I wanted him terribly to stay. Light-headed as I was, I had really set myself to keep him, to remake his life, if possible to set him up again with his wife in idyllic circumstances. To make him free; to get him out of the war for good. I wanted him desperately not to go back.' He glanced up with an expression of self-irony. 'What I am saying is, Peter: it was Smiley, not Gerstmann who was stepping out of the conflict that night.'

'You were ill,' Guillam insisted.

'Let us say tired. Ill or tired; all night, between aspirin and quinine and treacle visions of the Gerstmann marriage resurrected, I had a recurring image. It was of Gerstmann, poised on the sill, staring down into the street with those fixed brown eyes: and myself talking to him, on and on, "Stay, don't jump, stay." Not realizing of course that I was dreaming of my own insecurity, not his. In the early morning a doctor gave me injections to bring down the fever. I should have dropped the case, cabled for a replacement. I should have waited before going to the prison, but I had nothing but Gerstmann in mind: I needed to hear his decision. By eight o'clock I was already having myself escorted to the accommodation cells. He was sitting stiff as a ramrod on a trestle bench; for the first time, I guessed the soldier in him, and I knew that like me he hadn't slept all night. He hadn't shaved and there was a silver down on his jaw which gave him an old man's face. On other benches, Indians were sleeping, and with his red tunic and this silvery light colouring he looked very white among them. He was holding Ann's lighter in his hand; the packet of cigarettes lay beside him on the bench, untouched. I concluded that he had been using the night, and the foresworn cigarettes, to decide whether he could face prison and interrogation, and death. One look at his expression told me that he had decided he could. I didn't beseech him,' Smiley said, going straight on. 'He would never have been swayed by histrionics. His plane left in the mid-morning; I still had two hours. I am the worst advocate in the world but in those two hours I tried to summon all the reasons I knew for his not flying to Moscow. I believed, you see, that I had seen something in his face that was superior to mere dogma; not realizing that it was my own reflection. I had convinced myself that Gerstmann ultimately was accessible to ordinary human arguments coming from a man of his own age and profession and, well, durability. I didn't promise him wealth and women and Cadillacs and cheap butter, I accepted that he had no use for those things. I had the wit by then, at least, to steer clear of the topic of his wife. I didn't make speeches to him about freedom, whatever that means, or the essential good will of the West: besides, they were not favourable days for selling that story, and I was in no clear ideological state myself. I took the line of kinship. "Look," I said, "we're getting to be old men, and we've spent our lives looking for the weaknesses in one another's systems. I can see through Eastern values just as you can through our Western ones. Both of us, I am sure, have experienced *ad nauseam* the technical satisfactions of this wretched war. But now your own side is going to shoot you. Don't you think it's time to recognize that there is as little worth on your side as there is on mine? Look," I said, "in our trade we had only negative vision. In that sense, neither of us has anywhere to go. Both of us when we were young, subscribed to *great* visions –" Again I felt an impulse in him – Siberia – I had touched a nerve – "but not any more. Surely?" I urged him just to answer me this: did it not occur to him that he and I by different routes might well have reached the same conclusions about life? Even if my conclusions were what he would call unliberated, surely our workings were identical? Did he not believe for example that the political generality was meaningless? That only the particu-lar in life had value for him now? That in the hands of politicians grand designs achieve nothing but new forms of the old misery? And that therefore his life, the saving of it from yet another meaningless firing squad, was more important – morally, ethically more important – than the sense of duty, or obligation, or commitment, or whatever it was that kept him on this present path of self-destruction? Did it not occur to him to question – after all the travels of his life – to question the integrity of a system that proposed cold-bloodedly to shoot him down for misdemeanours he had never committed? I begged him – yes I did beseech him, I'm afraid, we were on the way to the airport, he still had not addressed a word to me – I begged him to consider whether he really believed; whether faith in the system he had served was honestly possible to him at this moment.'

For a while now, Smiley sat silent.

'I had thrown psychology to the winds, such as I possess; tradecraft too. You can imagine what Control said. My story amused him, all the same; he loved to hear of people's weakness. Mine especially, for some reason.' He had resumed his factual manner. 'So there we are. When the plane arrived I climbed aboard with him, and flew part of the distance: in those days it wasn't all jet. He was slipping away from me and I couldn't do anything to stop him. I'd given up talking but I was there if he wanted to change his mind. He didn't. He would rather die than give me what I wanted; he would rather die than disown the political system to which he was committed. The last I saw of him, so far as I know, was his expressionless face framed in the cabin window of the aeroplane, watching me walk down the gangway. A couple of very Russian-looking thugs had joined us and were sitting in the seats behind him and there was really no point in my staying. I flew home, and Control said: "Well I hope to God they do shoot him," and restored me with a cup of tea. That filthy China stuff he drinks, lemon jasmine or whatever, he sends out for it to that grocer's round the corner. I mean he used to. Then he sent me on three months' leave without the option. "I like you to have doubts," he said. "It tells me where you stand. But don't make a cult of them or you'll be a bore." It was a warning. I heeded it. And he told me to stop thinking about the Americans so much; he assured me that he barely gave them a thought.'

Guillam gazed at him, waiting for the resolution. 'But what do *you* make of it?' he demanded, in a tone that suggested he had been cheated of the end. 'Did Karla ever really think of staying?'

'I'm sure it never crossed his mind,' said Smiley with disgust. 'I behaved like a soft fool. The very archetype of a flabby Western liberal. But I would rather be my kind of fool than his for all that. I am sure,' Smiley repeated vigorously, 'that neither my arguments nor his own predicament at Moscow Centre would ultimately have swayed him in the least. I expect he spent the night working out how he would outgun Rudnev when he got home. Rudnev was shot a month later, incidentally. Karla got Rudnev's job and set to work reactivating his old agents. Among them Gerald, no doubt. It's odd to reflect that all the time he was looking at me, he could have been thinking of Gerald. I expect they've had a good laugh about it since.'

The episode had one other result, said Smiley. Since his San Francisco experience Karla had never once touched illegal radio. He cut it right out of his handwriting: 'Embassy links are a different matter. But in the field his agents aren't allowed to go near it. And he still has Ann's cigarette lighter.'

'Yours,' Guillam corrected him.

'Yes. Yes, mine. Of course. Tell me,' he continued, as the waiter took away his money, 'was Tarr referring to anyone in particular when he made that unpleasant reference to Ann?'

'I'm afraid he was. Yes.'

'The rumour is as precise as that?' Smiley enquired. 'And it goes that far down the line? Even to Tarr?'

'Yes.'

'And what does it say precisely?'

'That Bill Haydon was Ann Smiley's lover,' said Guillam, feeling that coldness coming over him which was his protection when he broke bad news, such as: you're blown; you're sacked; you're dying.

'Ah. I see. Yes. Thank you.'

There was a very awkward silence.

'And there was, is there a Mrs Gerstmann?' Guillam asked.

'Karla once made a marriage with a girl in Leningrad, a student. She killed herself when he was sent to Siberia.'

'So Karla is fireproof,' Guillam asked finally. 'He can't be bought and he can't be beaten?'

They returned to the car.

'I must say that was rather expensive for what we had,' Smiley confessed. 'Do you think the waiter robbed me?'

But Guillam was not disposed to chat about the cost of bad meals in England. Driving again, the day once more became a nightmare to him, a milling confusion of half-perceived dangers, and suspicions.

'So who's Source Merlin?' he demanded. 'Where could Alleline have had that information from, if not from the Russians themselves?'

'Oh, he had it from the Russians all right.'

'But for God's sake, if the Russians sent Tarr –'

'They didn't. Nor did Tarr use the British passports, did he? The Russians got it wrong. What Alleline had was the proof that Tarr had fooled them. That is the vital message we have learned from that whole storm in a teacup.'

'So what the hell did Percy mean about "muddying pools"? He must have been talking about Irina, for heaven's sake.'

'And Gerald,' Smiley agreed.

Again they drove in silence, and the gap between them seemed suddenly unbridgeable.

'Look: I'm not quite there myself, Peter,' Smiley said quietly. 'But nearly I am. Karla's pulled the Circus inside out; that much I understand, so do you. But there's a last clever knot, and I can't undo it. Though I mean to. And if you want a sermon, Karla is not fireproof because he's a fanatic. And one day, if I have anything to do with it, that lack of moderation will be his downfall.'

It was raining as they reached Stratford tube station; a bunch of pedestrians was huddled under the canopy.

'Peter, I want you to take it easy from now on.'

'Three months without the option?'

'Rest on your oars a bit.'

Closing the passenger door after him, Guillam had a sudden urge to wish Smiley goodnight or even good luck, so he leaned across the seat and lowered the window and drew in his breath to call. But Smiley was gone. He had never known anyone who could disappear so quickly in a crowd.

Through the remainder of that same night, the light in the dormer window of Mr Barraclough's attic room at the Islay Hotel burned uninterrupted. Unchanged, unshaven, George Smiley remained bowed at the major's table, reading, comparing, annotating, cross-referring, all with an intensity which, had he been his own observer, would surely have recalled for him the last days of Control on the fifth floor at Cambridge Circus. Shaking the pieces, he consulted Guillam's leave rosters and sick lists going back over the last year and set these beside the overt travel pattern of Cultural Attaché Aleksey Aleksandrovich Polyakov, his trips to Moscow, his trips out of London as reported to the Foreign Office by Special Branch and the immigration authorities. He compared these again with the dates when Merlin apparently supplied his information and, without quite knowing why he was doing it, broke down the Witchcraft reports into those which were demonstrably topical at the time they were received, and those which could have been banked a month, two months before, either by Merlin or his controllers, in order to bridge empty periods: such as think pieces, character studies of prominent members of the administration, scraps of Kremlin tittle-tattle which could have been picked up any time and saved for a rainless day. Having listed the topical reports, he set down their dates in a single column and threw out the rest. At this point, his mood could best be compared with that of a scientist who senses by instinct that he is on the brink of a discovery and is awaiting any minute the logical connection. Later, in conversation with Mendel, he called it 'shoving everything into a test tube and seeing if it exploded.' What fascinated him most, he said, was the very point which Guillam had made regarding Alleline's grim warnings about muddied pools: he was looking, in other terms, for the 'last clever knot' which Karla had tied in order to explain away the precise suspicions to which Irina's letter had given shape.

He came up with some curious preliminary findings. First, that on the nine occasions when Merlin had produced a topical report, either Polyakov had been in London or Toby Esterhase had taken a quick trip abroad. Second, that over the crucial period following Tarr's adventure in Hong Kong this year, Polyakov was in Moscow for urgent cultural consultations; and that soon afterwards Merlin came through with some of his most spectacular and topical material on the 'ideological penetration' of the United States, including an appreciation of Centre's coverage of the major American intelligence targets.

Backtracking again, he established that the converse was also true: that the reports he had discarded on the grounds that they had no close attachment to recent events were those which most generally went into distribution while Polyakov was in Moscow or on leave.

And then he had it.

No explosive revelation, no flash of light, no cry of 'Eureka', phone calls to Guillam, Lacon, 'Smiley is a world champion.' Merely that here before him, in the records he had examined and the notes he had compiled, was the corroboration of a theory which Smiley and Guillam and Ricki Tarr had that day from their separate points of view seen demonstrated: that between the mole Gerald and the Source Merlin there was an interplay that could no longer be denied; that Merlin's proverbial versatility allowed him to function as Karla's instrument as well as Alleline's. Or should he rather say, Smiley reflected – tossing a towel over his shoulder and hopping blithely into the corridor for a celebratory bath – as Karla's agent. And that at the heart of this plot lay a device so simple that it left him genuinely elated by its symmetry. It had even a physical presence: here in London, a house, paid for by the Treasury, all sixty thousand pounds of it; and often coveted no doubt, by the many luckless taxpayers who daily passed it by, confident they could never afford it and not knowing that they had already paid for it. It was with a lighter heart than he had known for many months that he took up the stolen file on Operation Testify.

# TWENTY-FOUR

To her credit, Matron had been worried about Roach all week, ever since she had spotted him alone in the washroom, ten minutes after the rest of his dormitory had gone down to breakfast, still in his pyjama trousers, hunched over a basin while he doggedly cleaned his teeth. When she questioned him, he avoided her eye. 'It's that wretched father of his,' she told Thursgood. 'He's getting him down again.' And by the Friday: 'You *must* write to the mother and tell her he's having a spell.'

But not even Matron, for all her motherly perception, would have hit on plain terror as the diagnosis.

Whatever could he do, he a child? That was his guilt. That was the thread that led directly back to the misfortune of his parents. That was the predicament that threw upon his hunched shoulders the responsibility night and day for preserving the world's peace. Roach the watcher – 'best watcher in the whole damn unit', to use Jim Prideaux's treasured words – had finally watched too well. He would have sacrificed everything he possessed, his money, his leather photograph case of his parents, whatever gave him value in the world, if it would buy him release from the knowledge which had consumed him since Sunday evening.

He had put out signals. On Sunday night, an hour after lights out, he had gone noisily to the lavatory, probed his throat, gagged and finally vomited. But the dormitory monitor, who was supposed to wake and raise the alarm – 'Matron, Roach's been sick' – slept stubbornly through the whole charade. Roach clambered miserably back into bed. From the callbox outside the staffroom next afternoon, he had dialled the menu for the day and whispered strangely into the mouthpiece, hoping to be overheard by a master, and taken for mad. No one paid him any attention. He had tried mixing up reality with dreams, in the hope that the event would be converted into something he had imagined; but each morning as he passed the Dip he saw again Jim's crooked figure stooping over the spade in the moonlight; he saw the black shadow of his face under the brim of his old hat, and heard the grunt of effort as he dug.

Roach should never have been there. That also was his guilt: that the knowledge was acquired by sin. After a 'cello lesson on the far side of the village, he had returned to school with deliberate slowness in order to be too late for evensong, and Mrs Thursgood's disapproving eye. The whole school was worshipping, all but himself and Jim: he heard them sing the *Magnificat* as he passed the church, taking the long route so that he could skirt the Dip, where Jim's light was glowing. Standing in his usual place, Roach watched Jim's shadow move slowly across the curtained window. He's turning in early, he decided with approval, as the light suddenly went out; for Jim had recently been too absent for his taste, driving off in the Alvis after rugger and not returning till Roach was asleep. Then the caravan door opened and closed and Jim was standing at the vegetable patch with a spade in his hand and Roach in great perplexity was wondering what on earth he should be wanting to dig for in the dark. Vegetables for his supper? For a moment Jim stood stock still, listening to the *Magnificat*, then glared slowly round and straight at Roach, though he was out of sight against the blackness of the hummocks. Roach even thought of calling to him; but felt too sinful on account of missing chapel.

Finally Jim began measuring. That at least was how it seemed to Roach. Instead of digging he had knelt at one corner of the patch and laid the spade on the earth, as if aligning it with something which was out of sight to Roach: for instance the church spire. This done, Jim strode quickly to where the blade lay, marked the spot with a thud of his heel, took up the spade and dug fast, Roach counted twelve times; then stood back, taking stock again. From the church, silence; then prayers. Quickly stooping, Jim drew a package from the ground, which he at once smothered in the folds of his duffel coat. Seconds later, and much faster than seemed possible, the caravan door slammed, the light went on again, and in the boldest moment of his life Bill Roach tiptoed down the Dip to within three feet of the poorly curtained window, using the slope to give himself the height he needed to look in.

Jim stood at the table. On the bunk behind him lay a heap of exercise books, a vodka bottle and an empty glass. He must have dumped them there to make space. He had a penknife ready but he wasn't using it. Jim would never have cut string if he could avoid it. The package was a foot long and made of yellowy stuff like a tobacco pouch. Pulling it open, he drew out what seemed to be a monkey wrench wrapped in sacking. But who would bury a monkey wrench, even for the best car England ever made? The screws or bolts were in a separate yellow envelope; he spilled them on to the table and examined each in turn. Not screws: pen tops. Not pen tops either; but they had sunk out of sight.

And not a monkey wrench, not a spanner, nothing but absolutely nothing for the car.

Roach had blundered wildly to the brow. He was running between the hummocks, making for the drive, but running slower than he had ever run before; running through sand and deep water and dragging grass, gulping the night air, sobbing it out again, running lopsidedly like Jim, pushing now with this leg, now with the other, flailing with his head for extra speed. He had no thought for where he was heading. All his awareness was behind him; fixed on the black revolver and the bands of chamois leather; on the pen tops that turned to bullets as Jim threaded them methodically into the chamber, his lined face tipped towards the lamplight, pale and slightly squinting in the dazzle.

# TWENTY-FIVE

'I won't be quoted, George,' the Minister warned in his lounging drawl. 'No minutes, no packdrill. I got voters to deal with. You don't. Nor does Oliver Lacon, do you Oliver?'

He had also, thought Smiley, the American violence with auxiliary verbs: 'Yes, I'm sorry about that,' he said.

'You'd be sorrier still if you had my constituency,' the Minister retorted.

Predictably, the mere question of where they should meet had sparked a silly quarrel. Smiley had pointed out to Lacon that it would be unwise to meet at his room in Whitehall since it was under constant attack by Circus personnel, whether janitors delivering despatch boxes or Percy Alleline dropping in to discuss Ireland. Whereas the Minister declined both the Islay Hotel and Bywater Street on the arbitrary grounds that they were insecure. He had recently appeared on television and was proud of being recognized. After several more calls back and forth they settled for Mendel's semi-detached Tudor residence in Mitcham where the Minister and his shiny car stuck out like a sore thumb. There they now sat, Lacon, Smiley and the Minister, in the trim front room with net curtains and fresh salmon sandwiches, while their host stood upstairs watching the approaches. In the lane, children tried to make the chauffeur tell them who he worked for.

Behind the Minster's head ran a row of books on bees. They were Mendel's passion, Smiley remembered: he used the word 'exotic' for bees that did not come from Surrey. The Minister was a young man still, with a dark jowl that looked as though it had been knocked off-true in some unseemly fracas. His head was bald on top, which gave him an unwarranted air of maturity, and a terrible Eton drawl. 'All right, so what are the decisions?' He also had the bully's art of dialogue.

'Well first, I suppose, you should damp down whatever recent negotiations you've been having with the Americans. I was thinking of the untitled secret annexe which you keep in your safe,' said Smiley, 'the one that discusses the further exploitation of Witchcraft material.'

'Never heard of it,' said the Minister.

'I quite understand the incentives, of course; it's always tempting to get one's hands on the cream of that enormous American service, and I can see the argument for trading them Witchcraft in return.'

'So what are the arguments *against*?' the Minister enquired as if he was talking to his stockbroker.

'If the mole Gerald exists,' Smiley began. Of all her cousins, Ann had once said proudly, Miles Sercombe was without a single redeeming feature. For the first time, Smiley really believed she was right. He felt not only idiotic but incoherent. 'If the mole exists, which I assume is common ground among us.' He waited, but no one said it wasn't. 'If the mole exists,' he repeated, 'it's not only the Circus which will double its profits by the American deal. Moscow Centre will too, because they'll get from the mole whatever you buy from the Americans.'

In a gesture of frustration the Minister slapped his hand on Mendel's table, leaving a moist imprint on the polish.

'God damn it I do *not* understand,' he declared. 'That Witchcraft stuff is bloody marvellous! A month ago it was buying us the moon. Now we're disappearing up our orifices and saying the Russians are cooking it for us. What the hell's happening?'

'Well, I don't think that's quite as illogical as it sounds as a matter of fact. After all, we've run the odd Russian network from time to time, and though I say it myself we ran them rather well. We gave them the best material we could afford. Rocketry, war planning. You were in on that yourself' – this to Lacon, who threw a jerky nod of agreement. 'We tossed them agents we could do without, we gave them good communications, safed their courier links, cleared the air for their signals so that we could listen to them. That was the price we paid for running the opposition – what was your expression? – "for knowing how they briefed their commissars". I'm sure Karla would do as much for us if he was running our networks. He'd do more, wouldn't he, if he had his eye on the American market too?' He broke off and glanced at Lacon. 'Much, much more. An American connection, a big American dividend I mean, would put the mole Gerald *right* at the top table. The Circus too by proxy of course. As a Russian, one would give almost anything to the English if . . . well, if one could buy the Americans in return.'

'Thank you,' said Lacon quickly.

The Minister left, taking a couple of sandwiches with him to eat in the car and failing to say goodbye to Mendel, presumably because he was not a constituent.

Lacon stayed behind.

'You asked me to look out for anything on Prideaux,' he announced at last.

'Well I find that we do have a few papers on him after all.'

He had happened to be going through some files on the internal security of the Circus, he explained, 'Simply to clear my decks.' Doing so, he had stumbled on some old positive vetting reports. One of them related to Prideaux.

'He was cleared absolutely, you understand. Not a shadow. However,' – an odd inflexion of his voice caused Smiley to glance at him – 'I think it might interest you all the same. Some tiny murmur about his time at Oxford. We're all entitled to be a bit pink at that age.'

'Indeed yes.'

The silence returned, broken only by the soft tread of Mendel upstairs.

'Prideaux and Haydon were really very close indeed, you know,' Lacon confessed. 'I hadn't realized.'

He was suddenly in a great hurry to leave. Delving in his briefcase, he hauled out a large plain envelope, thrust it into Smiley's hand and went off to the prouder world of Whitehall; and Mr Barraclough to the Islay Hotel, where he returned to his reading of Operation Testify.

# TWENTY-SIX

It was lunchtime next day. Smiley had read and slept a little, read again and bathed and as he climbed the steps to that pretty London house he felt pleased because he liked Sam.

The house was brown brick and Georgian, just off Grosvenor Square. There were five steps and a brass doorbell in a scalloped recess. The door was black with pillars either side. He pushed the bell and he might as well have pushed the door, it opened at once. He entered a circular hallway with another door the other end, and two large men in black suits who might have been ushers at Westminster Abbey. Over a marble chimney piece horses pranced and they might have been Stubbs. One man stood close while he took off his coat; the second led him to a bible desk to sign the book.

'Hebden,' Smiley murmured as he wrote, giving a workname Sam could remember. 'Adrian Hebden.'

The man who had his coat repeated the name into a house telephone: 'Mr Hebden, Mr Adrian Hebden.'

'If you wouldn't mind waiting one second, sir,' said the man by the bible desk. There was no music and Smiley had the feeling there should have been; also a fountain.

'I'm a friend of Mr Collins as a matter of fact,' said Smiley. 'If Mr Collins is available. I think he may even be expecting me.'

The man at the telephone murmured 'Thank you' and hung it on the hook. He led Smiley to the inner door and pushed it open. It made no sound at all, not even a rustle on the silk carpet.

'Mr Collins is over there, sir,' he murmured respectfully. 'Drinks are with the courtesy of the house.'

The three reception rooms had been run together, with pillars and arches to divide them optically, and mahogany panelling. In each room was one table, the third was sixty feet away. The lights shone on meaningless pictures of fruit in colossal gold frames, and on the green baize tablecloths. The curtains were drawn, the tables about one third occupied, four or five players to each, all men, but the only sound was the click of the ball in the wheel, and the click of chips as they were redistributed, and the very low murmur of the croupiers.

'Adrian Hebden,' said Sam Collins, with a twinkle in his voice. 'Long time no see.'

'Hullo, Sam,' said Smiley and they shook hands.

'Come to my lair,' said Sam and nodded to the only other man in the room who was standing, a very big man with blood pressure and a chipped face. The big man nodded too.

'Care for it?' Sam enquired as they crossed a corridor draped in red silk.

'It's very impressive,' said Smiley politely.

'That's the word,' said Sam. 'Impressive. That's what it is.' He was wearing a dinner jacket. His office was done in Edwardian plush, his desk had a marble top and ball-and-claw feet, but the room itself was very small and not at all well ventilated, more like the back room of a theatre, Smiley thought, furnished with left-over props.

'They might even let me put in a few pennies of my own later, give it another year. They're toughish boys, but very go-ahead, you know.'

'I'm sure,' said Smiley.

'Like we were in the old days.'

'That's right.'

He was trim and light-hearted in his manner and he had a trim black moustache. Smiley couldn't imagine him without it. He was probably fifty. He had spent a lot of time out East, where they had once worked together on a catch-and-carry job against a Chinese radio operator. His complexion and hair were greying but he still looked thirty-five. His smile was warm and he had a confiding, messroom friendliness. He kept both hands on the table as if he were at cards and he looked at Smiley with a possessive fondness that was paternal or filial or both.

'If chummy goes over five,' he said, still smiling, 'give me a buzz, Harry, will you? Otherwise keep your big mouth shut, I'm chatting up an oil king.' He was talking into a box on his desk. 'Where is he now?'

'Three up,' said a gravel voice. Smiley guessed it belonged to the chipped man with blood pressure.

'Then he's got eight to lose,' said Sam blandly. 'Keep him at the table, that's all. Make a hero of him.' He switched off and grinned. Smiley grinned back.

'Really, it's a great life,' Sam assured him. 'Better than selling washing machines, anyway. Bit odd, of course, putting on the dinner jacket at ten in the morning. Reminds me of diplomatic cover.' Smiley laughed. 'Straight, too, believe it or not,' Sam added with no change to his expression. 'We get all the help we need from the arithmetic.'

'I'm sure you do,' said Smiley, once more with great politeness.

'Care for some music?'

It was canned and came out of the ceiling. Sam turned it up as loud as they could bear.

'So what can I do you for?' Sam asked, the smile broadening.

'I want to talk to you about the night Jim Prideaux was shot. You were duty officer.'

Sam smoked brown cigarettes that smelt of cigar. Lighting one, he let the end catch fire, then watched it die to an ember. 'Writing your memoirs, old boy?' he enquired.

'We're reopening the case.'

'What's this *we*, old boy?'

'I, myself and me, with Lacon pushing and the Minister pulling.'

'All power corrupts but some must govern and in that case Brother Lacon will reluctantly scramble to the top of the heap.'

'It hasn't changed,' said Smiley.

Sam drew ruminatively on his cigarette. The music switched to phrases of Noël Coward.

'It's a dream of mine, actually,' said Sam Collins through the noise. 'One of these days Percy Alleline walks through that door with a shabby brown suitcase and ask for a flutter. He puts the whole of the secret vote on red and loses.'

'The record's been filleted,' said Smiley. 'It's a matter of going to people and asking what they remember. There's almost nothing on the file at all.'

'I'm surprised,' said Sam. Over the phone he ordered sandwiches. 'Live on them,' he explained. 'Sandwiches and canapés. One of the perks.'

He was pouring coffee when the red pinlight glowed between them on the desk.

'Chummy's even,' said the gravel voice.

'Then start counting,' said Sam and closed the switch.

He told it plainly but precisely, the way a good soldier recalls a battle, not to win or lose any more, but simply to remember. He had just come back from abroad, he said, a three-year stint in Vientiane. He'd checked in with personnel and cleared himself with the Dolphin; no one seemed to have any plans for him so he was thinking of taking off for the South of France for a month's leave when MacFadean, that old janitor who was practically Control's valet, scooped him up in the corridor and marched him to Control's room.

'This was which day exactly?' said Smiley.

'October 19th.'

'The Thursday.'

'The Thursday. I was thinking of flying to Nice on Monday. You were in Berlin. I wanted to buy you a drink but the mothers said you were *occupé* and when I checked with Movements they told me you'd gone to Berlin.'

'Yes, that's true,' Smiley said simply. 'Control sent me there.'

To get me out of the way, he might have added; it was a feeling he had had even at the time.

'I hunted round for Bill but Bill was also in baulk. Control had packed him up-country somewhere,' said Sam, avoiding Smiley's eye.

'On a wild goose chase,' Smiley murmured. 'But he came back.'

Here Sam tipped a sharp, quizzical glance in Smiley's direction, but he added nothing on the subject of Bill Haydon's journey.

'The whole place seemed dead. Damn nearly caught the first plane back to Vientiane.'

'It pretty much *was* dead,' Smiley confessed, and thought: except for Witchcraft.

And Control, said Sam, looked as though he'd had a five-day fever. He was surrounded by a sea of files, his skin was yellow and as he talked he kept breaking off to wipe his forehead with a handkerchief. He scarcely bothered with the usual fan-dance at all, said Sam. He didn't congratulate him on three good years in the field, or make some snide reference to his private life which was at that time messy; he simply said he wanted Sam to do weekend duty instead of Mary Masterman, could Sam swing it?

'"Sure I can swing it," I said. "If you want me to do duty officer, I'll do it." He said he'd give me the rest of the story on Saturday. Meanwhile I must tell no one. I mustn't give a hint anywhere in the building, even that he'd asked me this one thing. He needed someone good to man the switchboard in case there was a crisis, but it had to be someone from an outstation or someone like me who'd been away from head office for a long time. And it had to be an old hand.'

So Sam went to Mary Masterman and sold her a hard-luck story about not being able to get the tenant out of his flat before he went on leave on Monday; how would it be if he did her duty for her and saved himself the hotel? He took over at nine on Saturday morning with his toothbrush and six cans of beer in a briefcase which still had palm tree stickers on the side. Geoff Agate was slated to relieve him on Sunday evening.

Once again Sam dwelt on how dead the place was. Back in the old days, Saturdays were much like any other day, he said. Most regional sections had a deskman working weekends, some even had night staff, and when you took a tour of the building you had the feeling that, warts and all, this was an outfit that had a lot going. But that Saturday morning the building might have been evacuated, said Sam; which in a way, from what he heard later, it had been – on orders from Control. A couple of wranglers toiled on the second floor, the radio and code rooms were going strong but those boys worked all the hours anyway. Otherwise, said Sam, it was the big silence. He sat around waiting for Control to ring but nothing happened. He fleshed out another hour teasing the janitors whom he reckoned the idlest lot of so-and-so's in the Circus. He checked their attendance lists and found two typists and one desk officer marked in but absent, so he put the head janitor, a new boy called Mellows, on report. Finally he went upstairs to see if Control was in.

'He was sitting all alone, except for MacFadean. No mothers, no you, just old Mac peeking around with jasmine tea and sympathy. Too much?'

'No, just go on please. As much detail as you can remember.'

'So then Control peeled off another veil. Half a veil. Someone was doing a special job for him, he said. It was of great importance to the Service. He kept saying that: to the Service. Not Whitehall or sterling or the price of fish, but us. Even when it was all over I must never breathe a word about it. Not even to you. Or Bill or Bland or anyone.'

'Nor Alleline?'

'He never mentioned Percy once.'

'No,' Smiley agreed. 'He scarcely could at the end.'

'I should regard him for the night as Director of Operations. I should see myself as cut-out between Control and whatever was going on in the rest of the building. If anything came in, a signal, a phone call, however trivial it seemed, I should wait till the coast was clear, then whip upstairs and hand it to

Control. No one was to know, now or later, that Control was the man behind the gun. In no case should I phone him or minute him; even the internal lines were taboo. Truth, George,' said Sam, helping himself to a sandwich.

'Oh I do believe you,' said Smiley with feeling.

If outgoing telegrams had to be sent, Sam should once more act as Control's cut-out. He need not expect much to happen till this evening; even then it was most unlikely anything would happen. As to the janitors and people like that, as Control put it, Sam should do his damnedest to act natural and look busy.

The séance over, Sam returned to the duty room, sent out for an evening paper, opened a can of beer, selected an outside telephone line and set about losing his shirt. There was steeplechasing at Kempton, which he hadn't watched for years. Early evening, he took another walk around the lines and tested the alarm pads on the floor of the general registry. Three out of the fifteen didn't work and by this time the janitors were really loving him. He cooked himself an egg and when he'd eaten it he trotted upstairs to take a pound off old Mac and give him a beer.

'He'd asked me to put him a quid on some nag with three left feet. I chatted with him for ten minutes, went back to my lair, wrote some letters, watched a rotten movie on the telly, then turned in. The first call came just as I was getting to sleep. Eleven twenty exactly. The phones didn't stop ringing for the next ten hours. I thought the switchboard was going to blow up in my face.'

'Arcadi's five down,' said a voice over the box.

'Excuse me,' said Sam, with his habitual grin, and leaving Smiley to the music slipped upstairs to cope.

Sitting alone, Smiley watched Sam's brown cigarette slowly burning away in the ashtray. He waited, Sam didn't return, he wondered whether he should stub it out. Not allowed to smoke on duty, he thought; house rules.

'All done,' said Sam.

The first call came from the Foreign Office resident clerk on the direct line, said Sam. In the Whitehall stakes, you might say, the Foreign Office won by a curled lip.

'The Reuters headman in London had just called him with a story of a shooting in Prague. A British spy had been shot dead by Russian security forces, there was a hunt out for his accomplices and was the FO interested? The duty clerk was passing it to us for information. I said it sounded bunkum, and rang off just as Mike Meakin of wranglers came through to say that all hell had broken out on the Czech air: half of it was coded, but the other half was *en clair*. He kept getting garbled accounts of a shooting near Brno. Prague or Brno? I asked. Or both? Just Brno. I said keep listening and by then all five buzzers were going. Just as I was leaving the room, the resident clerk came back on the direct. The Reuters man had corrected his story, he said: for Prague read Brno. I closed the door and it was like leaving a wasps' nest in your drawing room. Control was standing at his desk as I came in. He'd heard me coming up the stairs. Has Alleline put a carpet on those stairs, by the way?'

'No,' said Smiley. He was quite impassive. 'George is like a swift,' Ann had once told Haydon in his hearing. 'He cuts down his body temperature till it's the same as the environment. Then he doesn't lose energy adjusting.'

'You know how quick he was when he looked at you. He checked my hands to see whether I had a telegram for him and I wished I'd been carrying something but they were empty. "I'm afraid there's a bit of a panic," I said. I gave him the gist, he looked at his watch, I suppose he was trying to work out what should have been happening if everything had been plain sailing. I said "Can I have a brief, please?" He sat down, I couldn't see him too well, he had that low green light on his desk. I said again, "I'll need a brief. Do you want me to deny it? Why don't I get someone in?" No answer. Mind you, there wasn't anyone to get, but I didn't know that yet. "I must have a brief." We could hear footsteps downstairs and I knew the radio boys were trying to find me. "Do you want to come down and handle it yourself?" I said. I went round to the other side of the desk, stepping over these files, all open at different places; you'd think he was compiling an encyclopaedia. Some of them must have been pre-war. He was sitting like this.'

Sam bunched his fingers, laid the tips to his forehead and stared at the desk. His other hand was laid flat, holding Control's imaginary fob watch. "Tell MacFadean to get me a cab then find Smiley." "What about the operation?" I asked. I had to wait all night for an answer. "It's deniable," he says. "Both men had foreign documents. No one could know they were British at this stage." "They're only talking about one man," I said. Then I said, "Smiley's in Berlin." That's what I think I said anyway. So we have another two-minute silence. "Anyone will do. It makes no difference." I should have been sorry for him I suppose but just then I couldn't raise much sympathy. I was having to hold the baby and I didn't know a damn thing. MacFadean wasn't around so I reckoned Control could find his own cab and by the time I got to the bottom of the steps I must have looked like Gordon of Khartoum. The duty harridan from monitoring was waving bulletins at me like flags, a couple of janitors were yelling at me, the radio boy was clutching a bunch of signals, the phones were going, not just my own, but half a dozen of the direct lines on the fourth floor. I went straight to the duty room and switched off all the lines while I tried to get my bearings. The monitor – what's that woman's name for God's sake, used to play bridge with the Dolphin?'

'Purcell. Molly Purcell.'

'That's the one. Her story was at least straightforward. Prague radio was promising an emergency bulletin in half an hour's time. That was a quarter of an hour ago. The bulletin would concern an act of gross provocation by a Western power, an infringement of Czechoslovakia's sovereignty,and an outrage against freedom-loving people of all nations. Apart from that,' said Sam drily, 'it was going to be laughs all the way. I rang Bywater Street of course, then I made a signal to Berlin telling them to find you and fly you back by yesterday. I gave Mellows the main phone numbers and sent him off to find an outside line and get hold of whoever was around of the top brass. Percy was in Scotland for the weekend and out to dinner. His cook gave Mellows a number, he rang it, spoke to his host. Percy had just left.'

'I'm sorry,' Smiley interrupted. 'Rang Bywater Street, what for?' he was holding his upper lip between his finger and thumb, pulling it out like a deformity, while he stared into the middle distance.

'In case you'd come back early from Berlin,' said Sam.

'And had I?'

'No.'

'So who did you speak to?'

'Ann.'

Smiley said: 'Ann's away just now. Could you remind me how it went, that conversation?'

'I asked for you and she said you were in Berlin.'

'And that was all?'

'It was a crisis, George,' Sam said in a warning tone.

'So?'

'I asked her whether by any chance she knew where Bill Haydon was. It was urgent. I gathered he was on leave but might be around. Somebody once told me they were cousins.' He added: 'Besides, he's a friend of the family, I understood.'

'Yes. He is. What did she say?'

'Gave me a shirty "*no*" and rang off. Sorry about that, George. War's war.'

'How did she sound?' Smiley asked after letting the aphorism lie between them for some while.

'I told you: shirty.'

Roy was at Leeds University talent-spotting, said Sam, and not available.

Between calls, Sam was getting the whole book thrown at him. He might as well have invaded Cuba: 'The military were yelling about Czech tank movements along the Austrian border, the wranglers couldn't hear themselves think for the radio traffic round Brno, and as for the Foreign Office, the resident clerk was having the vapours and yellow fever all in one. First Lacon then the Minister were baying at the doors and at half past twelve we had the promised Czech news bulletin, twenty minutes late but none the worse for that. A British spy named Jim Ellis, travelling on false Czech papers and assisted by Czech counter-revolutionaries, had attempted to kidnap an unnamed Czech general in the forest near Brno, and smuggle him over the Austrian border. Ellis had been shot but they didn't say killed, other arrests were imminent. I looked Ellis up in the workname index and found Jim Prideaux. And I thought, just as Control must have thought: If Jim is shot and has Czech papers, how the hell do they know his workname, and how do they know he's British? Then Bill Haydon arrived, white as a sheet. Picked up the story on the tickertape at his club. He turned straight round and came to the Circus.'

'At what time was that exactly?' Smiley asked, with a vague frown. 'It must have been rather late.'

Sam looked as if he wished he could make it easier. 'One fifteen,' he said.

'Which is late, isn't it, for reading club tickertapes?'

'Not in my world, old boy.'

'Bill's the Savile, isn't he?'

'Don't know,' said Sam doggedly. He drank some coffee. 'He was a treat to watch, that's all I can tell you. I used to think of him as an erratic sort of devil. Not that night, believe me. All right, he was shaken. Who wouldn't be? He arrived knowing there'd been a God-awful shooting party and that was about all. But when I told him that it was Jim who'd been shot, he looked at me like a madman. Thought he was going to go for me. "Shot. Shot how? Shot dead?" I shoved the bulletins into his hand and he tore through them one by one –'

'Wouldn't he have known already from the tickertape?' Smiley asked, in a small voice. 'I thought the news was everywhere by then: Ellis shot. That was the lead story, wasn't it?'

'Depends which news bulletin he saw, I suppose,' Sam shrugged it off. 'Anyway, he took over the switchboard and by morning he'd picked up what few pieces there were and introduced something pretty close to calm. He told

the Foreign Office to sit tight and hold its water, he got hold of Toby
Esterhase and sent him off to pull in a brace of Czech agents, students at the
London School of Economics. Bill had been letting them hatch till then, he
was planning to turn them round and play them back into Czecho. Toby's
lamplighters sandbagged the pair of them and locked them up in Sarratt.
Then Bill rang the Czech head resident in London and spoke to him like a
sergeant major: threatened to strip him so bare he'd be the laughing stock of
the profession, if a hair of Jim Prideaux's head was hurt. He invited him to
pass that on to his masters. I felt I was watching a street accident and Bill was
the only doctor. He rang a press contact and told him in strict confidence that
Ellis was a Czech mercenary with an American contract; he could use the
story unattributably. It actually made the late editions. Soon as he could, he
slid off to Jim's rooms to make sure he'd left nothing around that a journalist
might pick on if a journalist were clever enough to make the connection, Ellis
to Prideaux. I guess he did a thorough cleaning-up job. Dependants,
everything.'

'There weren't any dependants,' Smiley said. 'Apart from Bill, I suppose,'
he added, half under his breath.

Sam wound it up:

'At eight o'clock Percy Alleline arrived, he'd cadged a special plane off the
air force. He was grinning all over. I didn't think that was very clever of him,
considering Bill's feelings, but there you are. He wanted to know why I was
doing duty so I gave him the same story I'd given Mary Masterman: no flat.
He used my phone to make a date with the Minister and was still talking when
Roy Bland came in, hopping mad and half plastered, wanting to know who
the hell had been messing on his patch and practically accusing me. I said
"Christ, man, what about old Jim? You could pity him while you were about
it," but Roy's a hungry boy and likes the living better than the dead. I gave
him the switchboard with my love, went down to the Savoy for breakfast and
read the Sundays. The most any of them did was run the Prague radio
reports and a pooh-pooh denial from the Foreign Office.'

Finally Smiley said: 'After that you went to the South of France?'

'For two lovely months.'

'Did anyone question you again – about Control, for instance?'

'Not till I got back. You were out on your ear by then, Control was ill in
hospital.' Sam's voice deepened a little. 'He didn't do anything *silly*, did he?'

'He just died. What happened?'

'Percy was acting head-boy. He called for me and wanted to know why I'd
done duty for Masterman and what communication I'd had with Control. I
stuck to my story and Percy called me a liar.'

'So that's what they sacked you for: lying?'

'Alcoholism. The janitors got a bit of their own back. They'd counted five
beer cans in the waste basket in the duty officer's lair and reported it to the
housekeepers. There's a standing order: no booze on the premises. In the
due process of time a disciplinary body found me guilty of setting fire to the
Queen's dockyards so I joined the bookies. What happened to you?'

'Oh, much the same. I didn't seem to be able to convince them I wasn't
involved.'

'Well, if you want anyone's throat cut,' said Sam, as he saw him quietly out
through a side door into a pretty mews, 'give me a buzz.' Smiley was sunk in
thought. 'And if you ever want a flutter,' Sam went on, 'bring along some of
Ann's smart friends.'

'Sam, listen. Bill was making love to Ann that night. No, listen. You phoned her, she told you Bill wasn't there. As soon as she'd rung off, she pushed Bill out of bed and he turned up at the Circus an hour later knowing that there had been a shooting in Czecho. If you were giving me the story from the shoulder – on a postcard – that's what you'd say?'

'Broadly.'

'But you didn't tell Ann about Czecho when you phoned her –'

'He stopped at his club on the way to the Circus.'

'If it was open. Very well: then why didn't he know that Jim Prideaux had been shot?'

In the daylight, Sam looked briefly old, though the grin had not left his face. He seemed about to say something, then changed his mind. He seemed angry, then thwarted, then blank again. 'Cheeribye,' he said. 'Mind how you go,' and withdrew to the permanent night-time of his elected trade.

# TWENTY-SEVEN

When Smiley had left the Islay for Grosvenor Square that morning the streets had been bathed in harsh sunshine and the sky was blue. Now as he drove the hired Rover past the unlovable façades of the Edgware Road, the wind had dropped, the sky was black with waiting rain and all that remained of the sun was a lingering redness on the tarmac. He parked in St John's Wood Road, in the forecourt of a new tower block with a glass porch, but he did not enter by the porch. Passing a large sculpture describing, as it seemed to him, nothing but a sort of cosmic muddle, he made his way through icy drizzle to a descending outside staircase marked 'exit only'. The first flight was of terrazzo tile and had a banister of African teak. Below that, the contractor's generosity ceased. Rough-rendered plaster replaced the earlier luxury and a stench of uncollected refuse crammed the air. His manner was cautious rather than furtive, but when he reached the iron door he paused before putting both hands to the long handle, and drew himself together as if for an ordeal. The door opened a foot and stopped with a thud, to be answered by a shout of fury, which echoed many times like a shout in a swimming pool.

'Hey, why you don't look out once?'

Smiley edged through the gap. The door had stopped against the bumper of a shiny car, but Smiley wasn't looking at the car. Across the garage two men in overalls were hosing down a Rolls-Royce in a cage. Both were looking in his direction.

'Why you don't come other way?' the same angry voice demanded. 'You tenant here? Why you don't use tenant lift? This stair for fire.'

It was not possible to tell which of them was speaking, but whichever it was he spoke in a heavy Slav accent. The light in the cage was behind them. The shorter man held the hose.

Smiley walked forward, taking care to keep his hands clear of his pockets. The man with the hose went back to work, but the taller stayed watching him through the gloom. He wore white overalls and he had turned the collar points upwards, which gave him a rakish air. His black hair was swept back and full.

'I'm not a tenant, I'm afraid,' Smiley conceded. 'But I wonder if I might just speak to someone about renting a space. My name's *Carmichael*,' he explained in a louder voice. 'I've bought a flat up the road.'

He made a gesture as if to produce a card; as if his documents would speak better for him than his insignificant appearance. 'I'll pay in advance,' he promised. 'I could sign a contract or whatever is necessary, I'm sure. I'd want it to be above board, naturally. I can give references, pay a deposit, anything within reason. As long as it's above board. It's a Rover. A new one. I won't go behind the Company's back because I don't believe in it. But I'll do anything else within reason. I'd have brought it down, but I didn't want to presume. And, well, I know it sounds silly but I didn't like the look of the ramp. It's so new, you see.'

Throughout this protracted statement of intent, which he delivered with an air of fussy concern, Smiley had remained in the downbeam of a bright light strung from the rafter: a supplicant, rather abject figure, one might have thought, and easily visible across the open space. The attitude had its effect. Leaving the cage, the white figure strode towards a glazed kiosk, built between two iron pillars, and with his fine head beckoned Smiley to follow. As he went, he pulled the gloves off his hands. They were leather gloves, handstitched and quite expensive.

'Well, you want mind out how you open door,' he warned in the same loud voice. 'You want use lift, see, or maybe you pay couple pounds. Use lift you don't make no trouble.'

'Max, I want to talk to you,' said Smiley once they were inside the kiosk. 'Alone. Away from here.'

Max was broad and powerful with a pale boy's face, but the skin of it was lined like an old man's. He was handsome and his eyes were very still. He had altogether a rather deadly stillness.

'Now? You want talk now?'

'In the car. I've got one outside. If you walk to the top of the ramp you can get straight into it.'

Putting his hand to his mouth Max yelled across the garage. He was half a head taller than Smiley and had a roar like a drum major's. Smiley couldn't catch the words. Possibly they were Czech. There was no answer but Max was already unbuttoning his overalls.

'It's about Jim Prideaux,' Smiley said.

'Sure,' said Max.

They drove up to Hampstead and sat in the shiny Rover, watching the kids breaking the ice on the pond. The rain had held off after all; perhaps because it was so cold.

Above ground Max wore a blue suit and a blue shirt. His tie was blue but carefully differentiated from the other blues: he had taken a lot of trouble to get the shade. He wore several rings and flying boots with zips at the side.

'I'm not in it any more. Did they tell you?' Smiley asked. Max shrugged. 'I thought they would have told you,' Smiley said.

Max was sitting straight; he didn't use the seat to lean on, he was too proud. He did not look at Smiley. His eyes were turned fixedly to the pool and the kids fooling and skidding in the reeds.

'They don't tell me nothing,' he said.

'I was sacked,' said Smiley. 'I guess at about the same time as you.'

Max seemed to stretch slightly then settle again. 'Too bad, George. What you do: steal money?'

'I don't want them to know, Max.'

'You private, I private too,' said Max and from a gold case offered Smiley a cigarete which he declined.

'I want to hear what happened,' Smiley went on. 'I wanted to find out before they sacked me but there wasn't time.'

'That why they sack you?'

'Maybe.'

'You don't know so much, huh?' said Max, his gaze nonchalantly on the kids.

Smiley spoke very simply, watching all the while in case Max didn't understand. They could have spoken German but Max wouldn't have that, he knew. So he spoke English and watched Max's face.

'I don't know anything, Max. I had no part in it at all. I was in Berlin when it happened, I knew nothing of the planning or the underground. They cabled me, but when I arrived in London it was too late.'

'Planning,' Max repeated. 'That was some planning.' His jaw and cheeks became suddenly a mass of lines and his eyes turned narrow, making a grimace or a smile. 'So now you got plenty time, eh George? Jesus, that was some planning.'

'Jim had a special job to do. He asked for you.'

'Sure. Jim ask for Max to babysit.'

'How did he get you? Did he turn up in Acton and speak to Toby Esterhase, and say "Toby, I want Max"? How did he get you?'

Max's hands were resting on his knees. They were groomed and slender, all but the knuckles which were very broad. Now, at the mention of Esterhase he turned the palms inwards and made a light cage of them as if he had caught a butterfly.

'What the hell?' Max asked.

'So what did happen?'

'Was private,' said Max. 'Jim private, I private. Like now.'

'Come,' said Smiley. 'Please.'

Max spoke as if it was any mess: family or business or love. It was a Monday evening in mid-October, yes, the sixteenth. It was a slack time, he hadn't been abroad for weeks and he was fed up. He had spent all day making a reconnaissance of a house in Bloomsbury where a pair of Chinese students was supposed to live; the lamplighters were thinking of mounting a burglary against their rooms. He was on the point of returning to the Laundry in Acton to write his report when Jim picked him up in the street with a chance-encounter routine and drove him up to Crystal Palace, where they sat in the car and talked, like now, except they spoke Czech. Jim said there was a special job going, something so big, so secret that no one else in the Circus, not even Toby Esterhase, was allowed to know that it was taking place. It came from the top of the tree and it was hairy. Was Max interested?

'I say: "Sure, Jim. Max interested." The he ask me: "Take leave. You go to Toby, you say: Toby, my mother sick, I got to take some leave." I don't got no mother. "Sure," I say, "I take leave. How long for, please, Jim?"'

The whole job shouldn't last more than the weekend, said Jim. They should be in on Saturday and out on Sunday. Then he asked Max whether he had any current identities running for him: best would be Austrian, small trade, with driving licence to match. If Max had none handy at Acton, Jim would get something put together in Brixton.

'Sure, I say. I have Hartmann, Rudi, from Linz, Sudeten émigré.'

So Max gave Toby a story about girl trouble up in Bradford and Toby gave Max a ten-minute lecture on the sexual mores of the English; and on the Thursday, Jim and Max met in a safe house which the scalphunters ran in those days, a rackety old place in Lambeth. Jim had brought the keys. A three-day hit, Jim repeated, a clandestine conference outside Brno. Jim had a big map and they studied it. Jim would travel Czech, Max would go Austrian. They would make their separate ways as far as Brno. Jim would fly from Paris to Prague, then train from Prague. He didn't say what papers he would be carrying himself but Max presumed Czech because Czech was Jim's other side, Max had seen him use it before. Max was Hartmann Rudi trading in glass and ovenware. He was to cross the Austrian border by van near Mikulov, then head north to Brno, giving himself plenty of time to make a six-thirty rendezvous on Saturday evening in a side street near the football ground. There was a big match that evening starting at seven. Jim would walk with the crowd as far as the side street them climb into the van. They agreed times, fallbacks and the usual contingencies; and besides, said Max, they knew each other's handwriting by heart.

Once out of Brno they were to drive together along the Bilovice road as far as Krtiny, then turn east towards Racice. Somewhere along the Racice road they would pass on the left side a parked black car, most likely a Fiat. The first two figures of the registration would be nine nine. The driver would be reading a newspaper. They would pull up, Max would go over and ask whether he was all right. The man would reply that his doctor had forbidden him to drive more than three hours at a stretch. Max would say it was true that long journeys were a strain on the heart. The driver would then show them where to park the van and take them to the rendezvous in his own car.

'Who were you meeting, Max? Did Jim tell you that as well?'

No, that was all Jim told him.

As far as Brno, said Max, things went pretty much as planned. Driving from Mikulov he was followed for a while by a couple of civilian motorcyclists who interchanged every ten minutes, but he put that down to his Austrian number plates and it didn't bother him. He made Brno comfortably by mid-afternoon, and to keep things shipshape he booked into the hotel and drank a couple of coffees in the restaurant. Some stooge picked him up and Max talked to him about the vicissitudes of the glass trade and his girl in Linz who'd gone off with an American. Jim missed the first rendezvous but he made the fallback an hour later. Max supposed at first the train was late but Jim just said 'Drive slowly,' and he knew then that there was trouble.

This was how it was going to work, said Jim. There'd been a change of plan. Max was to stay right out of it. He should drop Jim short of the rendezvous, then lie up in Brno till Monday morning. He was not to make contact with any of the Circus's trade routes: no one from Aggravate, no one from Plato, least of all with the Prague residency. If Jim didn't surface at the hotel by eight on Monday morning, Max should get out any way he could. If Jim did surface, Max's job would be to carry Jim's message to Control: the message could be very simple, it might be no more than one word. When he got to London, he should go to Control personally, make an appointment through old McFadean, and give him the message, was that clear? If Jim didn't show up, Max should take up life where he left off and deny everything, inside the Circus as well as out.

'Did Jim say why the plan had changed?'

'Jim worried.'

'So something had happened to him on his way to meet you?'

'Maybe. I say Jim: "Listen Jim, I come with you. You worried, I be babysitter, I drive for you, shoot for you, what the hell?" Jim get damn angry, okay?'

'Okay,' said Smiley.

They drove to the Racice road, and found the car parked without lights facing a track over a field, a Fiat, nine nine on the number plates, black. Max stopped the van and let Jim out. As Jim walked towards the Fiat, the driver opened the door an inch in order to work the courtesy light. He had a newspaper opened over the steering wheel.

'Could you see his face?'

'Was in shadow.'

Max waited, presumably they exchanged word codes, Jim got in, the car drove away over the track, still without lights. Max returned to Brno. He was sitting over a schnapps in the restaurant when the whole town started rumbling. He thought at first the sound came from the football stadium, then he realized it was lorries, a convoy racing down the road. He asked the waitress what was going on and she said there had been a shooting in the woods, counter-revolutionaries were responsible. He went out to the van, turned on the radio and caught the bulletin from Prague. That was the first he had heard of a general. He guessed there were cordons everywhere, and anyway he had Jim's instructions to lie up in the hotel till Monday morning.

'Maybe Jim send me message. Maybe some guy from resistance come to me.'

'With this one word,' said Smiley quietly.

'Sure.'

'He didn't say what sort of word it was?'

'You crazy,' said Max. It was either a statement or a question.

'A Czech word or an English word or a German word?'

No one came, said Max, not bothering to answer craziness.

On Monday he burned his entry passport, changed the plates on his van and used his West German escape. Rather than head south he drove southwest, ditched the van and crossed the border by bus to Freistadt which was the softest route he knew. In Freistadt he had a drink and spent the night with a girl because he felt puzzled and angry and he needed to catch his breath. He got to London on Tuesday night and despite Jim's orders he thought he'd better try and contact Control: 'That was quite damn difficult,' he commented.

He tried to telephone but only got as far as the mothers. MacFadean wasn't around. He thought of writing but he remembered Jim, and how no one else in the Circus was allowed to know. He decided that writing was too dangerous. The rumour at the Acton Laundry said that Control was ill. He tried to find out what hospital, but couldn't.

'Did people at the Laundry seem to know where you'd been?'

'I wonder.'

He was still wondering when the housekeepers sent for him and asked to look at his Rudi Hartmann passport. Max said he had lost it, which was after all pretty near true. Why hadn't he reported the loss? He didn't know. When had the loss occurred? He didn't know. When did he last see Jim Prideaux? He couldn't remember. He was sent down to the Nursery at Sarratt but Max felt fit and angry and after two or three days the inquisitors got tired of him or somebody called them off.

'I go back Acton Laundry. Toby Esterhase give me hundred pound, tell me go to hell.'

A scream of applause went up round the pond. Two boys had sunk a great slab of ice and now the water was bubbling through the hole.

'Max, what happened to Jim?'

'What the hell?'

'You hear these things. It gets around among the émigrés. What happened to him? Who mended him, how did Bill Haydon buy him back?'

'Emigrés don't speak Max no more.'

'But you have heard, haven't you?'

This time it was the white hands that told him. Smiley saw the spread of fingers, five on one hand, three on the other and already he felt the sickness before Max spoke.

'So they shoot Jim from behind. Maybe Jim was running away, what the hell? They put Jim in prison. That's not so good for Jim. For my friends also. Not good.' He started counting: 'Pribyl,' he began, touching his thumb. 'Bukova Mirek, from Pribyl's wife the brother.' He took a finger. 'Also Pribyl's wife.' A second finger, a third: 'Kolin Jiri, also his sister, mainly dead. This was network Aggravate.' He changed hands. 'After network Aggravate come network Plato. Come lawyer Rapotin, come Colonel Landkron, and typists Eva Krieglova and Hanka Bilova. Also mainly dead. That's damn big price, George,' – holding the clean fingers close to Smiley's face – 'that's damn big price for one Englishman with bullet-hole.' He was losing his temper. 'Why you bother, George? Circus don't be no good for Czecho. Allies don't be no good for Czecho. No rich guy don't get no poor guy out of prison! You want know some history? How you say "*Märchen*," please George?'

'Fairy-tale,' said Smiley.

'Okay, so don't tell me no more damn fairy-tale how English got to save Czecho no more!'

'Perhaps it wasn't Jim,' said Smiley after a long silence. 'Perhaps it was someone else who blew the networks. Not Jim.'

Max was already opening the door. 'What the hell?' he asked.

'Max,' said Smiley.

'Don't worry, George. I don't got no one to sell you to. Okay?'

'Okay.'

Sitting in the car still, Smiley watched him hail a taxi. He did it with a flick of the hand as if he were summoning a waiter. He gave the address without bothering to look at the driver. Then rode off sitting very upright again, staring straight ahead of him, like royalty ignoring the crowd.

As the taxi disappeared, Inspector Mendel rose slowly from the bench, folded together his newspaper, walked over to the Rover.

'You're clean,' he said. 'Nothing on your back, nothing on your conscience.'

Not so sure of that, Smiley handed him the keys to the car then walked to the bus stop, first crossing the road in order to head west.

# TWENTY-EIGHT

His destination was in Fleet Street, a ground-floor cellar full of wine barrels. In other areas three thirty might be considered a little late for a pre-luncheon aperitif, but as Smiley gently pushed open the door a dozen shadowy figures turned to eye him from the bar. And at a corner table, as unremarked as the plastic prison arches or the fake muskets on the wall, sat Jerry Westerby with a very large pink gin.

'Old boy,' said Jerry Westerby shyly, in a voice that seemed to come out of the ground. 'Well I'll be damned. Hey, Jimmy!' His hand, which he laid on Smiley's arm while he signalled for refreshment with the other, was enormous and cushioned with muscle, for Jerry had once been wicket-keeper for a county cricket team. In contrast to other wicket-keepers he was a big man, but his shoulders were still hunched from keeping his hands low. He had a mop of sandy grey hair and a red face and he wore a famous sporting tie over a cream silk shirt. The sight of Smiley clearly gave him great joy, for he was beaming with pleasure.

'Well I'll be damned,' he repeated. 'Of all the amazing things. Hey, what are you doing these days?' – dragging him forcibly into the seat beside him. 'Sunning your fanny, spitting at the ceiling? Hey –' a most urgent question – 'what'll it be?'

Smiley ordered a Bloody Mary.

'It isn't complete coincidence, Jerry,' Smiley confessed. There was a slight pause between them which Jerry was suddenly concerned to fill.

'Listen, how's the demon wife? All well? That's the stuff. One of the great marriages that one, always said so.'

Jerry Westerby himself had made several marriages but few that had given him pleasure.

'Do a deal with you, George,' he proposed, rolling one great shoulder towards him. 'I'll shack up with Ann and spit at the ceiling, you take my job and write up the women's ping-pong. How's that? God bless.'

'Cheers,' said Smiley good-humouredly.

'Haven't seen many of the boys and girls for a while, matter of fact,' Jerry confessed awkwardly with another unaccountable blush. 'Christmas card from old Toby last year, that's about my lot. Guess they've put me on the shelf as well. Can't blame them.' He flicked the rim of his glass. 'Too much of this stuff, that's what it is. They think I'll blab. Crack up.'

'I'm sure they don't,' said Smiley, and the silence reclaimed them both.

'Too much wampum not good for braves,' Jerry intoned solemnly. For years they had had this Red Indian joke running, Smiley remembered with a sinking heart.

'*How*,' said Smiley.

'*How*,' said Jerry, and they drank.

'I burnt your letter as soon as I'd read it,' Smiley went on in a quiet, unbothered voice. 'In case you wondered. I didn't tell anyone about it at all. It came too late anyway. It was all over.'

At this, Jerry's lively complexion turned a deep scarlet.

'So it wasn't the letter you wrote me that put them off you,' Smiley continued in the same very gentle voice, 'if that's what you were thinking. And after all, you did drop it in to me by hand.'

'Very decent of you,' Jerry muttered. 'Thanks. Shouldn't have written it. Talking out of school.'

'Nonsense,' said Smiley as he ordered two more. 'You did it for the good of the Service.'

To himself, saying this, Smiley sounded like Lacon. But the only way to talk to Jerry was to talk like Jerry's newspaper: short sentences; facile opinions.

Jerry expelled some breath and a lot of cigarette smoke. 'Last job, oh, year ago,' he recalled with a new airiness. 'More. Dumping some little packet in Budapest. Nothing to it really. Phone box. Ledge at the top. Put my hand up. Left it there. Kid's play. Don't think I muffed it or anything. Did my sums first, all that. Safety signals. "Box ready for emptying. Help yourself." The way they taught us, you know. Still, you lads know best, don't you. You're the owls. Do one's bit that's the thing. Can't do more. All part of a pattern. Design.'

'They'll be beating the doors down for you soon,' said Smiley consolingly. 'I expect they're resting you up for a season. They do that, you know.'

'Hope so,' said Jerry with a loyal, very diffident smile. His glass shook slightly as he drank.

'Was that the trip you made just before you wrote to me?' Smiley asked.

'Sure. Same trip actually, Budapest, then Prague.'

'And it was in Prague that you heard this story? The story you referred to in your letter to me?'

At the bar a florid man in a black suit was predicting the imminent collapse of the nation. He gave us three months he said, then curtains.

'Rum chap, Toby Esterhase,' said Jerry.

'But good,' said Smiley.

'Oh my God, old boy, first rate. Brilliant, my view. But rum, you know. *How*.' They drank again, and Jerry Westerby loosely poked a finger behind his head, in imitation of an Apache feather.

'Trouble is,' the florid man at the bar was saying, over the top of his drink, 'we won't even know it's happened.'

They decided to lunch straight away, because Jerry had this story to file for tomorrow's edition: the West Brom striker had flipped his lid. They went to a curry house where the management was content to serve beer at tea time and they agreed that if anyone bumped into them Jerry would introduce George as his bank manager, a notion which tickled him repeatedly throughout his hearty meal. There was background music which Jerry called the connubial flight of the mosquito, and at times it threatened to drown the fainter notes of his husky voice; which was probably just as well. For while Smiley made a brave show of enthusiasm for the curry, Jerry was launched, after his initial reluctance, upon quite a different story, concerning one Jim Ellis: the story which dear old Toby Esterhase had refused to let him print.

Jerry Westerby was that extremely rare person, the perfect witness. He had no fantasy, no malice, no personal opinion. Merely: the thing was rum. He couldn't get it off his mind and come to think of it, he hadn't spoken to Toby since.

'Just this card you see, "Happy Christmas, Toby," – picture of Leadenhall Street in the snow.' He gazed in great perplexity at the electric fan. 'Nothing *special* about Leadenhall Street, is there, old boy? Not a spy house or a meeting place or something, is it?'

'Not that I know of,' said Smiley, with a laugh.

'Couldn't think why he chose Leadenhall Street for a Christmas card. Damned odd, don't you think?'

Perhaps he just wanted a snowy picture of London, Smiley suggested; Toby after all was quite foreign in lots of ways.

'Rum way to keep in touch, I must say. Used to send me a crate of Scotch regular as clockwork.' Jerry frowned and drank from his krug. 'It's not the Scotch I mind,' he explained with that puzzlement that often clouded the greater visions of his life, 'buy my own Scotch any time. It's just that when you're on the outside, you think everything has a meaning so presents are important, see what I'm getting at?'

It was a year ago, well, December. The Restaurant Sport in Prague, said Jerry Westerby, was a bit off the track of your average Western journalist. Most of them hung around the Cosmo or the International, talking in low murmurs and keeping together because they were jumpy. But Jerry's local was the Sport and ever since he had taken Holotek the goalie along after winning the match against the Tartars, Jerry had had the big hand from the barman, whose name was Stanislaus, or Stan.

'Stan's a perfect prince. Does just what he damn well pleases. Makes you suddenly think Czecho's a free country.'

Restaurant, he explained, meant bar. Whereas bar in Czecho meant nightclub, which was rum. Smiley agreed that it must be confusing.

All the same, Jerry always kept an ear to the ground when he went there, after all it was Czecho and once or twice he'd been able to bring back the odd snippet for Toby or put him on to the track of someone.

'Even if it was just currency dealing, black-market stuff. All grist to the mill, according to Tobe. These little scraps add up – that's what Tobe said, anyway.'

Quite right, Smiley agreed. That was the way it worked.

'Tobe was the owl, what?'

'Sure.'

'I used to work straight to Roy Bland, you see. Then Roy got kicked upstairs so Tobe took me over. Bit unsettling actually, changes. Cheers.'

'How long had you been working to Toby when this trip took place?'

'Couple of years, not more.'

There was a pause while food came and krugs were refilled and Jerry

Westerby with his enormous, hands shattered a popadam on to the hottest curry on the menu, then spread a crimson sauce over the top. The sauce, he said, was to give it bite. 'Old Khan runs it up for me specially,' he explained aside. 'Keeps it in a deep shelter.'

So anyway, he resumed, that night in Stan's bar there was this young boy with the pudding-bowl haircut and the pretty girl on his arm.

'And I thought: "Watch out, Jerry boy, that's an army haircut." Right?'

'Right,' Smiley echoed, thinking that in some ways Jerry was a bit of an owl himself.

It turned out the boy was Stan's nephew and very proud of his English: 'Amazing what people will tell you if it gives them a chance of showing off their languages.' He was on leave from the army and he'd fallen in love with this girl, he'd eight days to go and the whole world was his friend, Jerry included. Jerry particularly, in fact, because Jerry was paying for the booze.

'So we're all sitting hugger-mugger at the big table in the corner, students, pretty girls, all sorts. Old Stan had come round from behind the bar and some laddie was doing a fair job with a squeeze box. Bags of *Gemütlichkeit*, bags of booze, bags of noise.'

The noise was specially important, Jerry explained, because it let him chat to the boy without anyone else paying attention. The boy was sitting next to Jerry, he'd taken a shine to him from the start. He had one arm slung round the girl and one arm round Jerry.

'One of those kids who can touch you without giving you the creeps. Don't like being touched as a rule. Greeks do it. Hate it, personally.'

Smiley said he hated it too.

'Come to think of it, the girl looked a bit like Ann,' Jerry reflected. 'Foxy, know what I mean? Garbo eyes, lots of oomph.'

So while everyone was carrying on singing and drinking and playing kiss-in-the-ring, this lad asked Jerry whether he would like to know the truth about Jim Ellis.

'Pretended I'd never heard of him,' Jerry explained to Smiley. '"Love to," I said. "Who's Jim Ellis when he's at home?" And the boy looks at me as if I'm daft and says, "A British spy." Only no one else heard you see, they were all yelling and singing saucy songs. He had the girl's head on his shoulder but she was half cut and in her seventh heaven, so he just went on talking to me, proud of his English, you see.'

'I get it,' said Smiley.

'"British spy." Yells straight into my ear-hole. "Fought with Czech partisans in the war. Came here calling himself Hajek and was shot by the Russian secret police." So I just shrugged and said, "News to me, old boy." Not pushing, you see. Mustn't ever be pushy, ever. Scares them off.'

'You're absolutely right,' said Smiley wholeheartedly, and for an interlude patiently parried further questions about Ann, and what it was like to love, really love the other person all your life.

'I am a conscript,' the boy began, according to Jerry Westerby. 'I have to serve in the army or I can't go to university.' In October he had been on basic training manoeuvres in the forests near Brno. There was always a lot of military in the woods there; in summer the whole area was closed to the public for a month at a time. He was on a boring infantry exercise that was supposed to last two weeks but on the third day it was called off for no reason and the troops were ordered back to town. That was the order: pack now and get back to barracks. The whole forest was to be cleared by dusk.

'Within hours, every sort of daft rumour was flying around,' Jerry went on. 'Some fellow said the ballistics research station at Tisnov had blown up. Somebody else said the training battalions had mutinied and were shooting up the Russian soldiers. Fresh uprising in Prague, Russians taken over the government, the Germans had attacked, God knows what hadn't happened. You know what soldiers are. Same everywhere, soldiers. Gossip till the cows come home.'

The reference to the army moved Jerry Westerby to ask after certain acquaintances from his military days, people Smiley had dimly known, and forgotten. Finally they resumed.

'They broke camp, packed the lorries and sat about waiting for the convoy to get moving. They'd gone half a mile when everything stopped again and the convoy was ordered off the road. Lorries had to duckshuffle into the trees. Got stuck in the mud, ditches, every damn thing. Chaos apparently.'

It was the Russians, said Westerby. They were coming from the direction of Brno and they were in a very big hurry and everything that was Czech had to get out of the light or take the consequences.

'First came a bunch of motorcycles tearing down the track with lights flashing and the drivers screaming at them. Then a staff car and civilians, the boy reckoned six civilians altogether. Then two lorry-loads of special troops armed to the eyebrows and wearing combat paint. Finally a truck full of tracker dogs. All making a most Godawful row. Not boring you am I, old boy?'

Westerby dabbed the sweat from his face with a handkerchief and blinked like someone coming round. The sweat had come through his silk shirt as well; he looked as if he had been under a shower. Curry not being a food he cared for, Smiley ordered two more krugs to wash away the taste.

'So that was the first part of the story. Czech troops out, Russian troops in. Got it?'

Smiley said yes, he thought he had his mind round it so far.

Back in Brno, however, the boy quickly learned that his unit's part in the proceedings was nowhere near done. Their convoy was joined up with another and the next night for eight or ten hours they tore round the countryside with no apparent destination. They drove west to Trebic, stopped and waited while the signals section made a long transmission, then they cut back south-east nearly as far as Znojmo on the Austrian border, signalling like mad as they went; no one knew who had ordered the route, no one would explain a thing. At one point they were ordered to fix bayonets, at another they pitched camp, then packed up all their kit again and pushed off. Here and there they met up with other units; near Breclav marshalling-yards, tanks going round in circles, once a pair of self-propelled guns on pre-laid track. Everywhere the story was the same: chaotic, pointless activity. The older hands said it was a Russian punishment for being Czech. Back in Brno again, the boy heard a different explanation. The Russians were after a British spy called Hajek. He'd been spying on the research station and tried to kidnap a general and the Russians had shot him.

'So the boy asked, you see,' said Jerry. 'Sassy little devil, asked his sergeant: "If Hajek is already shot, why do we have to tear round the countryside creating an uproar?" And the sergeant told him, "Because it's the army." Sergeants all over the world, what?'

Very quietly Smiley asked: 'We're talking about two nights, Jerry. Which night did the Russians move into the forest?'

Jerry Westerby screwed up his face in perplexity. 'That's what the boy wanted to tell me, you see, George. That's what he was trying to put over in Stan's bar. What all the rumours were about. The Russians moved in on Friday. They didn't shoot Hajek till Saturday. So the wise lads were saying: there you are, Russians were waiting for Hajek to turn up. Knew he was coming. Knew the lot. Lay in wait. Bad story, you see. Bad for our reputation, see what I mean? Bad for big chief. Bad for tribe. *How.*'

'*How,*' said Smiley, into his beer.

'That's what Toby felt too, mind. We saw it the same way, we just reacted differently.'

'So you told all to Toby,' said Smiley lightly, as he passed Jerry a large dish of dal. 'You had to see him anyway to tell him you'd dropped the package for him in Budapest, so you told him the Hajek story too.'

Well, that was just it, said Jerry. That was the thing that had bothered him, the thing that was rum, the thing that made him write to George actually. 'Old Tobe said it was tripe. Got all regimental and nasty. First he was mustard, clapping me on the back and Westerby for Mayor. He went back to the shop and next morning he threw the book at me. Emergency meeting, drove me round and round the park in a car, yelling blue murder. Said I was so plastered these days I didn't know fact from fiction. All that stuff. Made me a bit shirty, actually.'

'I expect you wondered who he'd been talking to in between,' said Smiley sympathetically. 'What did he say *exactly*,' he asked, not in any intense way but as if he just wanted to get it all crystal clear in his mind.

'Told me it was most likely a put-up ploy. Boy was a provocateur. Disruption job to make the Circus chase its own tail. Tore my ears off for disseminating half-baked rumours. I said to him, George: "Old boy," I said, "Tobe, I was only reporting, old boy. No need to get hot under the collar. Yesterday you thought I was the cat's whiskers. No point in turning round and shooting the messenger. If you've decided you don't like the story, that's your business." Wouldn't sort of listen any more, know what I mean? Illogical, I thought it was. Bloke like that. Hot one minute and cold the next. Not his best performance, know what I mean?'

With his left hand Jerry rubbed the side of his head, like a schoolboy pretending to think. '"Okie dokie," I said, "forget it. I'll write it up for the rag. Not the part about the Russians getting there first. The other part. *Dirty work in the forest,* that sort of tripe." I said to him: "If it isn't good enough for the Circus, it'll do for the rag." Then he went up the wall again. Next day some owl rings the old man. Keep that baboon Westerby off the Ellis story. Rub his nose in the D notice: formal warning. "All further references to Jim Ellis alias Hajek against the national interest, so put 'em on the spike." Back to women's ping-pong. Cheers.'

'But by then you'd written to me,' Smiley reminded him.

Jerry Westerby blushed terribly. 'Sorry about that,' he said. 'Got all xenophobe and suspicious. Comes from being on the outside: you don't trust your best friends. Trust them, well, less than strangers.' He tried again: 'Just that I thought old Tobe was going a bit haywire. Shouldn't have done it, should I? Against the rules.' Through his embarrassment he managed a painful grin. 'Then I heard on the grapevine that the firm had given you the heaveho, so I felt an even bigger damn fool. Not hunting alone, are you, old boy? Not . . .'

He left the question unasked; but not perhaps unanswered.

As they parted, Smiley took him gently by the arm.

'If Toby should get in touch with you, I think it better if you don't tell him we met today. He's a good fellow but he does tend to think people are ganging up on him.'

'Wouldn't dream of it, old boy.'

'And if he does get in touch in the next few days,' Smiley went on – in that remote contingency, his tone suggested – 'you could even warn me, actually. Then I can back you up. Don't ring *me*, come to think of it, ring this number.'

Suddenly, Jerry Westerby was in a hurry; that story about the West Brom striker couldn't wait. But as he accepted Smiley's card he did ask with a queer, embarrassed glance away from him: 'Nothing untoward going on is there, old boy? No dirty work at the crossroads?' The grin was quite terrible. 'Tribe hasn't gone on the rampage or anything?'

Smiley laughed and lightly laid a hand on Jerry's enormous, slightly hunched shoulder.

'Any time,' said Westerby.

'I'll remember.'

'I thought it was you, you see: you who telephoned the old man.'

'It wasn't.'

'Maybe it was Alleline.'

'I expect so.'

'Any time,' said Westerby again. 'Sorry, you know. Love to Ann.' He hesitated.

'Come on, Jerry, out with it,' said Smiley.

'Toby had some story about her. I told him to stuff it up his shirt front. Nothing to it, is there?'

'Thanks, Jerry. So long. *How*.'

'I knew there wasn't,' said Jerry, very pleased, and lifting his finger to denote the feather, padded off into his own reserves.

# TWENTY-NINE

Waiting that night, alone in bed at the Islay but not yet able to sleep, Smiley took up once more the file which Lacon had given him in Mendel's house. It dated from the late Fifties, when like other Whitehall departments the Circus was being pressed by the competition to take a hard look at the loyalty of its staff. Most of the entries were routine: telephone intercepts, surveillance reports, enless interviews with dons, friends and nominated referees. But one document held Smiley like a magnet; he could not get enough of it. It was a letter, entered baldly on the index as 'Haydon to Fanshawe, February 3rd, 1937'. More precisely it was a handwritten letter, from the undergraduate Bill Haydon to his tutor Fanshawe, a Circus talent-spotter, introducing the young Jim Prideaux as a suitable candidate for recruitment to British intelligence. It was prefaced by a wry *explication de texte*. The Optimates were 'an upper-class Christ Church club, mainly old Etonian,' wrote the unknown author. Fanshawe (P. R. de T. Fanshawe, Légion d'Honneur, OBE, Personal File so and so) was its founder, Haydon (countless cross-references) was in that year its leading light. The political complexion of the Optimates, to whom Haydon's father had also in his day belonged, was unashamedly conservative. Fanshawe, long dead, was a passionate empire man and 'the Optimates were his private selection tank for The Great Game', ran the preface. Curiously enough, Smiley dimly remembered Fanshawe from his own day: a thin eager man with rimless spectacles, a Neville Chamberlain umbrella and an unnatural flush to his cheeks as if he were still teething. Steed-Asprey called him the fairy godfather.

'My dear Fan, I suggest you stir yourself to make a few enquiries about the young gentleman whose name is appended on the attached fragment of human skin.' [Inquisitors' superfluous note: Prideaux.] 'You probably know Jim – if you know him at all – as an *athleticus* of some accomplishment. What you do not know but ought to is that he is no mean linguist nor yet a total idiot either . . . '

[Here followed a biographical summary of surprising accuracy: . . . Lycée Lakanal in Paris, put down for Eton never went there, Jesuit day-school Prague, two semesters Strasbourg, parents in European banking, small aristo, live apart . . . ]

'Hence our Jim's wide familiarity with parts foreign, and his rather parentless look, which I find irresistible. By the way: though he is made up of all different bits of Europe, make no mistake: the completed version is devoutly our own. At present, he is a bit of a striver and a puzzler, for he has just noticed that there is a World Beyond the Touchline and that world is me. 'But you must first hear how I met him.

'As you know, it is my habit (and your command) now and then to put on Arab costume and go down to the bazaars, there to sit among the great unwashed and give ear to the word of their prophets, that I may in due course better confound them. The juju man *en vogue* that evening came from the bosom of Mother Russia herself: one Academician Khlebnikov presently attached to the Soviet Embassy in London, a jolly, rather infectious little fellow, who managed some quite witty things among the usual nonsense. The bazaar in question was a debating club called the Populars, our rival, dear Fan, and well known to you from other forays I have occasionally made. After the sermon a wildly proletarian coffee was served, to the accompaniment of a dreadfully democratic bun, and I noticed this large fellow sitting alone at the back of the room, apparently too shy to mingle. His face was slightly familiar from the cricket field; it turns out we both played in some silly scratch team without exchanging a word. I don't quite know how to describe him. He has it, Fan. I am serious now.'

Here the handwriting, till now ill-at-ease, spread out as the writer got into his stride:

'He has that heavy quiet that commands. Hard-headed, quite literally. One of those shrewd quiet ones that lead the team without anyone noticing. Fan, you know how hard it is for me to *act*. You have to remind me all the time, intellectually remind me, that unless I sample life's dangers I shall never know its mysteries. But Jim acts from instinct . . . he is functional . . . He's my other half, between us we'd make one marvellous man, except that neither of us can sing. And Fan, you know that feeling when you just have to go out and find someone new or the world will die on you?'

The writing steadied again.

'"Yavas Lagloo," says I, which I understand is Russian for meet me in the woodshed or something similar, and he says "Oh hullo," which I think he would have said to the Archangel Gabriel if he'd happened to be passing.

'"What is your dilemma?" says I.

'"I haven't got one," says he, after about an hour's thought.

'"Then what are you doing here? If you haven't a dilemma how did you get in?"

'So he gives a big placid grin and we saunter over to the great Khlebnikov, shake his tiny paw for a while then toddle back to my rooms. Where we drink. And drink. And Fan, He drank everything in sight. Or perhaps I did, I forget. And come the dawn, do you know what we did? I will tell you, Fan. We walked solemnly down to the Parks, I sit on a bench with a stopwatch, big Jim gets into his running kit and lopes twenty circuits. Twenty. I was quite exhausted.

'We can come to you any time, he asks nothing better than to be in my company or that of my wicked, divine friends. In short, he has appointed me his Mephistopheles and I am vastly tickled by the compliment. By the by, he is virgin, about eight foot tall and built by the same firm that did Stonehenge. Do not be alarmed.'

The file died again. Sitting up, Smiley turned the yellowed pages impatiently, looking for stronger meat. The tutors of both men aver (twenty years later) that it is inconceivable that the relationship between the two was 'more than purely friendly' . . . Haydon's evidence was never called . . . Jim's tutor speaks of him as 'intellectually omnivorous after long starvation' – dismisses any suggestion that he was 'pink'. The confrontation which takes place at Sarratt begins with long apologies, particularly in view of Jim's superb war record. Jim's answers breathe a pleasing straightforwardness after the extravagance of Haydon's letter. One representative of the competition present, but his voice is seldom heard. No, Jim never again met Khlebnikov or anyone representing himself as his emissary . . . No, he never spoke to him but on that one occasion. No, he had no other contact with communists or Russians at that time, he could not remember the name of a single member of the Populars . . .

Q:(*Alleline*)     Shouldn't think that keeps you awake, does it?

A:     As a matter of fact, no. (*laughter*)

Yes, he had been a member of the Populars just as he had been a member of his college drama club, the philatelic society, the modern language society, the Union and the historical society, the ethical society and the Rudolph Steiner study group . . . It was a way of getting to hear interesting lectures, and of meeting people; particularly the second. No, he had never distributed left-wing literature, though he did for a while take *Soviet Weekly* . . . No, he had never paid dues to any political party, at Oxford or later, as a matter of fact he had never even used his vote . . . One reason why he joined so many clubs at Oxford was that after a messy education abroad he had no natural English contemporaries from school . . .

By now the inquisitors are one and all on Jim's side; everyone is on the same side against the competition and its bureaucratic meddling.

Q:(*Alleline*)      As a matter of interest, since you were overseas so much, do you mind telling us where you learned your off-drive? (*laughter*)

A:                Oh, I had an uncle actually, with a place outside Paris. He was cricket mad. Had a net and all the equipment. When I went there for holidays he bowled at me non-stop.

[Inquisitors' note: Comte Henri de Sainte-Yvonne, dec. 1941, PF. AF64-7.] End of interview. Competition representative would like to call Haydon as a witness but Haydon is abroad and not available. Fixture postponed *sine die* . . .

Smiley was nearly asleep as he read the last entry on the file, tossed in haphazard long after Jim's formal clearance had come through from the competition. It was a cutting from an Oxford newspaper of the day giving a review of Haydon's one-man exhibition in June 1938 headed *Real or Surreal? An Oxford Eye*. Having torn the exhibition to shreds the critic ended on this gleeful note: 'We understand that the distinguished Mr James Prideaux took time off from his cricket in order to help hang the canvasses. He would have done better, in our opinion, to remain in the Banbury Road. However, since his role of Dobbin to the arts was the only heartfelt thing about the whole occasion, perhaps we had better not sneer too loud . . .'

He dozed, his mind a controlled clutter of doubts, suspicions and certainties. He thought of Ann, and in his tiredness cherished her profoundly, longing to protect her frailty with his own. Like a young man he whispered her name aloud and imagined her beautiful face bowing over him in the half light, while Mrs Pope Graham yelled prohibition through the key-hole. He thought of Tarr and Irina, and pondered uselessly on love and loyalty; he thought of Jim Prideaux and what tomorrow held. He was aware of a modest sense of approaching conquest. He had been driven a long way, he had sailed backwards and forwards; tomorrow, if he was lucky, he might spot land: a peaceful little desert island, for instance. Somewhere Karla had never heard of. Just for himself and Ann. He fell asleep.

# THIRTY

In Jim Prideaux's world Thursday had gone along like any other, except that some time in the small hours of the morning the wound in his shoulder bone started leaking, he supposed because of the inter-house run on Wednesday afternoon. He was woken by the pain, and by the draught on the wet of his back where the discharge flowed. The other time this happened he had driven himself to Taunton General but the nurses took one look at him and slapped him into emergency to wait for doctor somebody and an X-ray, so he filched his clothes and left. He'd done with hospitals and he'd done with medicos. English hospitals, other hospitals, Jim had done with them. They called the discharge a track.

He couldn't reach the wound to treat it, but after last time he had hacked himself triangles of lint and stitched strings to the corners. Having put these handy on the draining board and prepared the hibitane, he cooked hot water, added half a packet of salt and gave himself an improvised shower, crouching to get his back under the jet. He soaked the lint in the hibitane, flung it across his back, strapped it from the front and lay face down on the bunk with a vodka handy. The pain eased and a drowsiness came over him, but he knew if he gave way to it he would sleep all day, so he took the vodka bottle to the window and sat at the table correcting Five B French while Thursday's dawn slipped into the Dip and the rooks started their clatter in the elms.

Sometimes he thought of the wound as a memory he couldn't keep down. He tried his damnedest to patch it over and forget but even his damnedest wasn't always enough.

He took the correcting slowly because he liked it, and because correcting kept his mind in the right places. At six-thirty, seven, he was done so he put on some old flannel bags and a sports coat and walked quietly down to the church, which was never locked. There he knelt a moment in the centre aisle of the Curtois ante-chapel, which was a family monument to the dead from two wars, and seldom visited by anyone. The cross on the little altar had been carved by sappers at Verdun. Still kneeling Jim groped cautiously under the pew until his fingertips discovered the line of several pieces of adhesive tape; and, following these, a casing of cold metal. His devotions over, he bashed up Combe Lane to the hilltop, jogging a bit to get a sweat running, because the warm did him wonders while it lasted, and rhythm soothed his vigilance. After his sleepless night and the early morning vodka, he was feeling a bit light-headed, so when he saw the ponies down the combe, gawping at him with their fool faces, he yelled at them in bad Somerset – 'Git 'arn there! Damned old fools, take your silly eyes off me!' – before pounding down the lane again for coffee, and a change of bandage.

First lesson after prayers was Five B French and there Jim all but lost his temper: he doled out a silly punishment to Clements, the draper's son, and had to take it back at the end of class. In the common room he went through another routine, of the sort he had followed in the church: quickly, mindlessly, no fumble and out. It was a simple enough notion, the mail check, but it worked. He'd never heard of anyone who used it, among the pros, but then pros don't talk about their game. 'See it this way,' he would have said. 'If the opposition is watching you, it's certain to be watching your mail, because the mail's the easiest watch in the game: easier still if the opposition is the home side and has the cooperation of the postal service. So what do you do? Every week, from the same post-box, at the same time, at the same rate, you post one envelope to yourself and a second to an innocent party at the same address. Shove in a bit of trash – charity Christmas card literature, come-on from local supermarket – be sure to seal envelope, stand back and compare times of arrival. If your letter turns up later than the other feller's you've just felt someone's hot breath on you, in this case Toby's.'

Jim called it, in his odd, chipped vocabulary, water-testing, and once again the temperature was unobjectionable. The two letters clocked in together, but Jim arrived too late to pinch back the one addressed to Marjoribanks, whose turn it was to act as unwitting running mate. So having pocketed his own, Jim snorted at the *Daily Telegraph* while Marjoribanks with an irritable 'Oh, to hell' tore up a printed invitation to join the Bible Reading Fellowship. From there, school routine carried him again till junior rugger versus St Ermin's, which he was billed to referee. It was a fast game and when it was over his back acted up again, so he drank vodka till first bell, which he'd promised to take for young Elwes. He couldn't remember why he'd promised, but the younger staff and specially the married ones relied on him a lot for odd jobs and he let it happen. The bell was an old ship's tocsin, something Thursgood's father had dug up and now part of the tradition. As Jim rang it he was aware of little Bill Roach standing right beside him, peering up at him with a white smile, wanting his attention, as he wanted it half a dozen times each day.

'Hullo there, Jumbo, what's your headache this time?'

'Sir, please, sir.'

'Come on, Jumbo, out with it.'

'Sir, there's someone asking where you live, sir,' said Roach.

Jim put down the bell.

'What sort of someone, Jumbo? Come on, I won't bite you, come on, hey . . . hey! What sort of someone? Man someone? Woman? Juju man? Hey! Come on, old feller,' he said softly, crouching to Roach's height. 'No need to cry. What's the matter then? Got a temperature?' He pulled a handkerchief from his sleeve. 'What sort of someone?' he repeated in the same low voice.

'He asked at Mrs McCullum's. He said he was a friend. Then he got back into his car, it's parked in the church yard, sir.' A fresh gust of tears: 'He's just sitting in it.'

'Get the hell away, damn you!' Jim called to a bunch of seniors grinning in a doorway. 'Get the hell!' He went back to Roach. 'Tall friend? Sloppy tall kind of fellow, Jumbo? Eyebrows and a stoop? Thin feller? Bradbury, come here and stop gawping! Stand by to take Jumbo up to Matron! Thin feller?' he asked again, kind but very steady.

But Roach had run out of words. He had no memory any more, no sense of size or perspective; his faculty of selection in the adult world had gone. Big men, small men, old, young, crooked, straight, they were a single army of indistinguishable dangers. To say no to Jim was more than he could bear: to say yes was to shoulder the whole awful responsibility of disappointing him. He saw Jim's eyes on him, he saw the smile go out and felt the merciful touch of one big hand upon his arm.

'Attaboy, Jumbo. Nobody ever watched like you, did they?'

Laying his head hopelessly against Bradbury's shoulder, Bill Roach closed his eyes. When he opened them he saw through his tears that Jim was already halfway up the staircase.

Jim felt calm; almost easy. For days he had known there was someone. That also was part of his routine: to watch the places where the watchers asked. The church, where the ebb and flow of the local population is a ready topic; county hall, register of electors; tradesmen, if they kept customer accounts; pubs, if the quarry didn't use them: in England he knew these were the natural traps which watchers automatically patrolled before they closed on you. And sure enough in Taunton two days ago, chatting pleasantly with the assistant librarian, Jim had come across the footprint he was looking for. A stranger, down from London apparently, had been interested in village wards, yes, a political gentleman – well more in the line of political research, he was, professional, you could tell – and one of the things he wanted, fancy that now, was the up-to-date record of Jim's very village, yes, the voters' list, they were thinking of making a door-to-door survey of a really out of the way community, specially new immigrants. Yes, fancy that, Jim agreed and from then on made his dispositions. He bought railway tickets to places: Taunton Exeter, Taunton London, Taunton Swindon, all valid one month; because he knew that if he were on the run again, tickets would be hard to come by. He had uncached his old identities and his gun and hid them handily above ground; he dumped a suitcase full of clothes in the boot of the Alvis, and kept the tank full. These precautions made sleep a possibility; or would have done, before his back.

'Sir, who won, sir?'

Prebble, a new boy, in dressing gown and toothpaste, on his way to surgery. Sometimes boys spoke to Jim for no reason, his size and crookedness were a challenge.

'Sir, the match, sir, versus St Ermin's.'

'St *Vermins*,' another boy piped. 'Yes, sir, who won actually?'

'Sir, *they* did, sir,' Jim barked. 'As you'd have known *sir* if you'd been watching *sir*,' and swinging an enormous fist at them in a slow feinted punch, he propelled both boys across the corridor to Matron's dispensary.

'Night, sir.'

'Night, you toads,' Jim sang and stepped the other way into the sick bay for a view of the church and the cemetery. The sick bay was unlit, it had a look and a stink he hated. Twelve boys lay in the gloom dozing between supper and temperatures.

'Who's that?' asked a hoarse voice.

'Rhino,' said another. 'Hey Rhino, who won against St Vermins?'

To call Jim by his nickname was insubordinate but boys in sick bay feel free from discipline.

'Rhino? Who the hell's *Rhino*? Don't know him. Not a name to me,' Jim snorted, squeezing between two beds. 'Put that torch away, not allowed. Damn walkover, that's who won. Eighteen to nothing for Vermin's.' That window went down almost to the floor. An old fireguard protected it from boys. 'Too much damn fumble in the three-quarter line,' he muttered, peering down.

'I hate rugger,' said a boy called Stephen.

The blue Ford was parked in the shadow of the church, close in under the elms. From the ground floor it would have been out of sight but it didn't look hidden. Jim stood very still, a little back from the window, studying it for tell-tale signs. The light was fading fast but his eyesight was good and he knew what to look for: discreet aerial, second inside mirror for the legman, burn marks under the exhaust. Sensing the tension in him, the boys became facetious.

'Sir, is it a bird, sir? Is she any good, sir?'

'Sir, are we on fire?'

'Sir, what are her legs like?'

'Gosh, sir, don't say it's Miss *Aaronson*?' At this everyone started giggling because Miss Aaronson was old and ugly.

'Shut up,' Jim snapped, quite angry. 'Rude pigs, shut up.' Downstairs in assembly Thursgood was calling senior roll before prep.

Abercrombie? Sir. Astor? Sir. Blakeney? Sick, sir.

Still watching, Jim saw the car door open and George Smiley climb cautiously out, wearing a heavy overcoat.

Matron's footsteps sounded in the corridor. He heard the squeak of her rubber heels and the rattle of thermometers in a paste pot.

'My good Rhino, whatever are you doing in my sick bay? And close that curtain, you bad boy, you'll have the whole lot of them dying of pneumonia. William Merridew, sit up at once.'

Smiley was locking the car door. He was alone and he carried nothing, not even a briefcase.

'They're screaming for you in Grenville, Rhino.'

'Going, gone,' Jim retorted briskly and with a jerky 'Night, all,' he humped his way to Grenville dormitory where he was pledged to finish a story by John Buchan. Reading aloud, he noticed that there were certain sounds he had trouble pronouncing, they caught somewhere in his throat. He knew he was sweating, he guessed his back was seeping and by the time he had finished there was a stiffness round his jaw which was not just from reading aloud. But all these things were small symptoms beside the rage which was mounting in him as he plunged into the freezing night air. For a moment, on the overgrown terrace, he hesitated, staring at the church. It would take him three minutes, less, to untape the gun from underneath the pew, shove it into the waistband of his trousers, left side, butt inward to the groin . . .

But instinct advised him 'no', so he set course directly for the caravan, singing 'Hey diddle diddle' as loud as his tuneless voice would carry.

# THIRTY-ONE

Inside the motel room, the state of restlessness was constant. Even when the traffic outside went through one of its rare lulls the windows continued vibrating. In the bathroom the tooth glasses also vibrated, while from either wall and above them they could hear music, thumps and bits of conversation or laughter. When a car arrived in the forecourt, the slam of the door seemed to happen inside the room, and the footsteps too. Of the furnishings, everything matched. The yellow chairs matched the yellow pictures and the yellow carpet. The candlewick bedspreads matched the orange paintwork on the doors, and by coincidence the label on the vodka bottle. Smiley had arranged things properly. He had spaced the chairs and put the vodka on the low table and now as Jim sat glaring at him he extracted a plate of smoked salmon from the tiny refrigerator, and brown bread already buttered. His mood in contrast to Jim's was noticeably bright, his movements swift and purposeful.

'I thought we should at least be comfortable,' he said, with a short smile, setting things busily on the table. 'When do you have to be at school again? Is there a particular time?' Receiving no answer he sat down. 'How do you like teaching? I seem to remember you had a spell of it after the war, is that right? Before they hauled you back? Was that also a prep school? I don't think I knew.'

'Look at the file,' Jim barked. 'Don't you come here playing cat and mouse with me, George Smiley. If you want to know things, read my file.'

Reaching across the table Smiley poured two drinks and handed one to Jim.

'Your personal file at the Circus?'

'Get it from housekeepers. Get it from Control.'

'I suppose I should,' said Smiley doubtfully. 'The trouble is Control's dead and I was thrown out long before you came back. Didn't anyone bother to tell you that when they got you home?'

A softening came over Jim's face at this, and he made in slow motion one of those gestures which so amused the boys at Thursgood's. 'Dear God,' he muttered, 'so Control's gone,' and passed his left hand over the fangs of his moustache, then upward to his moth-eaten hair. 'Poor old devil,' he muttered. 'What did he die of, George? Heart? Heart kill him?'

'They didn't even tell you this at the debriefing?' Smiley asked.

At the mention of a debriefing, Jim stiffened and his glare returned.

'Yes,' said Smiley. 'It was his heart.'

'Who got the job?'

Smiley laughed. 'My goodness, Jim, what *did* you all talk about at Sarratt, if they didn't even tell you that?'

'God damn it, who got the job? Wasn't you, was it, threw you out! Who got the job, George?'

'Alleline got it,' said Smiley, watching Jim very carefully, noting how the right forearm rested motionless across the knees. 'Who did you want to get it? Have a candidate, did you, Jim?' And after a long pause: 'And they didn't tell you what happened to the Aggravate network, by any chance? To Pribyl, to his wife, and brother-in-law? Or to the Plato network? Landkron, Eva Krieglova, Hanka Bilova? You recruited some of those, didn't you, in the old days before Roy Bland? Old Landkron even worked for you in the war.'

There was something terrible just then about the way Jim would not move forward and could not move back. His red face was twisted with the strain of indecision and the sweat had gathered in studs over his shaggy ginger eyebrows.

'God damn you, George, what the devil do you want? I've drawn a line. That's what they told me to do. Draw a line, make a new life, forget the whole thing.'

'Which *they* is this, Jim? Roy? Bill, Percy?' He waited. 'Did they tell you what happened to Max, whoever they were? Max is all right, by the way.' Rising, he briskly refreshed Jim's drink, then sat again.

'All right, come on, so what's happened to the networks?'

'They're blown. The story is you blew them to save your own skin. I don't believe it. But I have to know what happened.' He went straight on: 'I know Control made you promise by all that's holy, but that's finished. I know you've been questioned to death and I know you've pushed some things so far down you can hardly find them any more or tell the difference between truth and cover. I know you've tried to draw a line under it and say it didn't happen. I've tried that, too. Well, after tonight you can draw your line. I've brought a letter from Lacon and if you want to ring him he's standing by. I don't want to silence you. I'd rather you talked. Why didn't you come and see me at home when you got back? You could have done. You tried to see me before you left, so why not when you got back? Wasn't just the rules that kept you away.'

'Didn't anyone get out?' Jim said.

'No. They seem to have been shot.'

They had telephoned Lacon and now Smiley sat alone sipping his drink. From the bathroom he could hear the sound of running taps and grunts as Jim sluiced water in his face.

'For God's sake let's get somewhere we can breathe,' Jim whispered, as if it were a condition of his talking. Smiley picked up the bottle and walked beside him as they crossed the tarmac to the car.

They drove for twenty minutes; Jim took the wheel. When they parked they were on the plateau, this morning's hilltop free of fog, and a long view down the valley. Scattered lights reached into the distance. Jim sat as still as iron, right shoulder high and hands hung down, gazing through the misted windscreen at the shadow of the hills. The sky was light and Jim's face was cut sharp against it. Smiley kept his first questions short. The anger had left Jim's voice and little by little he spoke with greater ease. Once, discussing Control's tradecraft, he even laughed, but Smiley never relaxed, he was as cautious as if he were leading a child across the street. When Jim ran on, or bridled, or showed a flash of temper, Smiley gently drew him back until they were level again, moving at the same pace and in the same direction. When Jim hesitated, Smily coaxed him forward over the obstacle. At first, by a mixture of instinct and deduction, Smiley actually fed Jim his own story.

For Jim's first briefing by Control, Smiley suggested, they had made a rendezvous outside the Circus? They had. Where? At a service flat in St James's, a place proposed by Control. Was any one else present? No one. And to get in touch with Jim in the first place, Control had used MacFadean, his personal janitor? Yes, old Mac came over on the Brixton shuttle with a note asking Jim for a meeting that night. Jim was to tell Mac yes or no and give him back the note. He was on no account to use the telephone, even the internal line, to discuss the arrangement. Jim had told Mac yes and arrived at seven.

'First, I suppose, Control cautioned you?'

'Told me not to trust anyone.'

'Did he name particular people?'

'Later,' said Jim. 'Not at first. At first, he just said: trust nobody. Specially nobody in the mainstream. George?'

'Yes.'

'They were shot all right, were they? Landkron, Krieglova, the Pribyls? Straight shooting?'

'The secret police rolled up both networks the same night. After that no one knows, but next of kin were told they were dead. That usually means they are.'

To their left a line of pine trees like a motionless army climbed out of the valley.

'And then I suppose Control asked you what Czech identities you had running for you,' Smiley resumed. 'Is that right?'

He had to repeat the question.

'I told him Hajek,' said Jim finally. 'Vladimir Hajek, Czech journalist based on Paris. Control asked me how much longer the papers were good for. "You never know," I said. "Sometimes they're blown after one trip."' His voice went suddenly louder, as if he had lost his hold on it. 'Deaf as an adder, Control was, when he wanted to be.'

'So then he told you what he wanted you to do,' Smiley suggested.

'First, we discussed deniability. He said if I was caught, I should keep Control out of it. A scalphunter ploy, bit of private enterprise. Even at the time I thought: Who the hell will ever believe that? Every word he spoke was letting blood,' said Jim. 'All through the briefing I could feel his resistance to telling me anything. He didn't want me to know but he wanted me well briefed. "I've had an offer of service," Control says. "Highly placed official, covername Testify." "Czech official?" I ask. "On the military side," he says. "You're a military-minded man, Jim, you two should hit it off pretty well." That's how it went, the whole damn way. I thought, If you don't want to tell me, don't, but stop dithering.'

After more circling, said Jim, Control announced that Testify was a Czech general of artillery. His name was Stevcek; he was known as a pro-Soviet hawk in the Prague defence hierarchy, whatever that was worth; he had worked in Moscow on liaison, he was one of the very few Czechs the Russians trusted. Stevcek had conveyed to Control, through an intermediary whom Control had personally interviewed in Austria, his desire to talk to a ranking officer of the Circus on matters of mutual interest. The emissary must be a Czech speaker, somebody able to make decisions. On Friday October 20th Stevcek would be inspecting the weapon research station at Tisnov, near Brno, about a hundred miles north of the Austrian border. From there he would be visiting a hunting lodge for the weekend, alone. It was a place high up in the forests not far from Racice. He would be willing to receive an emissary there on the evening of Saturday 21st. He would also supply an escort to and from Brno.

Smiley asked: 'Did Control have any suggestions about Stevcek's motive?'

'A girlfriend,' Jim said. 'Student he was going with, having a last spring, Control said: twenty years' age difference between them. She was shot during the uprising of summer sixty-eight. Till then, Stevcek had managed to bury his anti-Russian feelings in favour of his career. The girl's death put an end to all that: he was out for their blood. For four years he'd lain low acting friendly and salting away information that would really hurt them. Soon as we gave him assurances and fixed the trade routes, he was ready to sell.'

'Had Control checked any of this?'

'What he could. Stevcek was well enough documented. Hungry desk general with a long list of staff appointments. Technocrat. When he wasn't on courses he was sharpening his teeth abroad: Warsaw, Moscow, Peking for a year, spell of military attaché in Africa, Moscow again. Young for his rank.'

'Did Control tell you what you were to expect in the way of information?'

'Defence material. Rocketry. Ballistics.'

'Anything else?' said Smiley, passing the bottle.

'Bit of politics.'

'Anything else?'

Not for the first time, Smiley had the distinct sense of stumbling not on Jim's ignorance, but on the relic of a willed determination not to remember. In the dark, Jim Prideaux's breathing became suddenly deep and greedy. He had lifted his hands to the top of the wheel and was resting his chin on them, peering blankly at the frosted windscreen.

'How long were they in the bag before being shot?' Jim demanded to know.

'I'm afraid a lot longer than you were,' Smiley confessed.

'Holy God,' said Jim. With a handkerchief taken from his sleeve, he wiped away the sweat and whatever else was glistening on his face.

'The intelligence Control was hoping to get out of Stevcek,' Smiley prompted, ever so softly.

'That's what they asked me at the interrogation.'

'At Sarratt?'

Jim shook his head. 'Over there.' He nodded his shaggy head towards the hills. 'They knew it was Control's operation from the start. There was nothing I could say to persuade them it was mine. They laughed.'

Once again Smiley waited patiently till Jim was ready to go on.

'Stevcek,' said Jim. 'Control had this bee in his bonnet: Stevcek would provide the answer, Stevcek would provide the key. "What key?" I asked. "What key?" Had his bag, that old brown music case. Pulled out charts, annotated all in his own handwriting. Charts in coloured inks, crayons. "Your visual aid," he says. "This is the fellow you'll be meeting." Stevcek's career plotted year by year: took me right through it. Military academies, medals, wives. "He's fond of horses," he says. "You used to ride yourself, Jim. Something else in common, remember it." I thought: That'll be fun, sitting in Czecho with the dogs after me, talking about breaking thoroughbred mares.'

He laughed a little strangely so Smiley laughed too.

'The appointments in red were for Stevcek's Soviet liaison work. Green were his intelligence work. Stevcek had had a finger in everything. Fourth man in Czech army intelligence, chief boffin on weaponry, secretary to the national internal security committee, military counsellor of some sort to the Praesidium, Anglo-American desk in the Czech military intelligence set-up. Then Control comes to this patch in the mid-Sixties, Stevcek's second spell in Moscow, and it's marked in green and red fifty-fifty. Ostensibly Stevcek was attached to the Warsaw Pact Liaison staff as a colonel general, says Control, but that was just cover. "He'd nothing to do with the Warsaw Pact Liaison staff. His real job was in Moscow Centre's England section. He operated under the workname of Minin," he says. "His job was dovetailing Czech efforts with Centre's. This is the treasure," Control says. "What Stevcek really wants to sell us is the name of Moscow Centre's mole inside the Circus.'"

It might be only one word, Smiley thought, remembering Max, and felt again that sudden wave of apprehension. In the end, he knew, that was all it would be: a name for the mole Gerald, a scream in the dark.

"'There's a rotten apple, Jim,' Control said, 'and he's infecting all the others.'" Jim was going straight on. His voice had stiffened, his manner also. 'Kept talking about elimination, how he'd backtracked and researched and was nearly there. There were five possibilities, he said. Don't ask me how he dug them up. "It's one of the top five," he says. "Five fingers to a hand." He gave me a drink and we sat there like a pair of schoolboys making up a code, me and Control. We used Tinker, Tailor. We sat there in the flat putting it together, drinking that cheap Cyprus sherry he always gave. If I couldn't get out, if there was any fumble after I'd met Stevcek, if I had to go under-ground, I must get the one word to him even if I had to go to Prague and chalk it on the Embassy door or ring the Prague resident and yell it at him down the phone. Tinker, Tailor, Soldier, Sailor. Alleline was Tinker, Haydon was Tailor, Bland was Soldier and Toby Esterhase was Poorman. We dropped Sailor because it rhymed with Tailor. You were Beggarman,' Jim said.

'Was I now? And how did you take to it, Jim, to Control's theory? How did the idea strike you, over-all?'

'Damn silly. Poppycock.'

'Why?'

'Just damn silly,' he repeated in a tone of military stubbornness. 'Think of any one of you – mole – *mad*!'

'But did you believe it?'

'No! Lord alive, man, why do you –'

'Why not? Rationally we always accepted that sooner or later it would happen. We always warned one another: be on your guard. We've turned enough members of other outfits: Russians, Poles, Czechs, French. Even the odd American. What's so special about the British, all of a sudden?'

Sensing Jim's antagonism, Smiley opened his door and let the cold air pour in.

'How about a stroll?' he said. 'No point in being cooped up when we can walk around.'

With movement, as Smiley anticipated, Jim found a new fluency of speech.

They were on the western rim of the plateau, with only a few trees standing and several lying felled. A frosted bench was offered but they ignored it. There was no wind, the stars were very clear, and as Jim took up his story they went on walking side by side, Jim adjusting always to Smiley's pace, now away from the car, now back again. Occasionally they drew up, shoulder to shoulder, facing down the valley.

First Jim described the recruitment of Max and the manoeuvres he went through in order to disguise his mission from the rest of the Circus. He let it leak that he had a tentative lead to a high-stepping Soviet cypher clerk in Stockholm, and booked himself to Copenhagen in his old workname, Ellis. Instead, he flew to Paris, switched to his Hajek papers and landed by scheduled flight at Prague airport at ten on Saturday morning. He went through the barriers like a song, confirmed the time of his train at the terminus, then took a walk because he had a couple of hours to kill and thought he might watch his back a little before he left for Brno. That autumn there had been freak bad weather. There was snow on the ground and more falling.

In Czecho, said Jim, surveillance was not usually a problem. The security services knew next to nothing about street watching, probably because no administration in living memory had ever had to feel shy about it. The tendency, said Jim, was still to throw cars and pavement artists around like Al Capone, and that was what Jim was looking for: black Skodas and trios of squat men in trilbies. In the cold, spotting these things is marginally harder because the traffic is slow, the people walk faster and everyone is muffled to the nose. All the same, till he reached Masaryk Station, or Central as they're pleased to call it these days, he had no worries. But at Masaryk, said Jim, he got a whisper, more instinct than fact, about two women who'd bought tickets ahead of him.

Here, with the dispassionate ease of a professional, Jim went back over the ground. In a covered shopping arcade beside Wenceslas Square he had been overtaken by three women, of whom the one in the middle was pushing a pram. The woman nearest the kerb carried a red plastic handbag and the woman on the inside was walking a dog on a lead. Ten minutes later two other women came towards him, arm in arm, both in a hurry, and it crossed his mind that if Toby Esterhase had had the running of the job, an arrangement like this would be his handwriting; quick profile changes from the pram, back-up cars standing off with shortwave radio or bleep, with a second team lying back in case the forward party overran. At Masaryk, looking at the two women ahead of him in the ticket queue, Jim was faced with the knowledge that it was happening now. There is one garment that a watcher has neither time nor inclination to change, least of all in sub-Arctic weather, and that is his shoes. Of the two pairs offered for his inspection in the ticket queue Jim recognized one: fur-lined plastic, black, with zips on the outside and soles of thick brown composition which slightly sang in the snow. He had seen them once already that morning, in the Sterba passage, worn with different top clothes by the woman who had pushed past him with the pram. From then on, Jim didn't suspect. He knew, just as Smiley would have known.

At the station bookstall, Jim bought himself a *Rude Pravo* and boarded the Brno train. If they had wanted to arrest him they would by now have done so. They must be after the branchlines: that is to say, they were following Jim in order to house his contacts. There was no point in looking for reasons, but Jim guessed that the Hajek identity was blown and they'd primed the trap the moment he booked himself on the plane. As long as they didn't know he had flushed them, he still had the edge, said Jim; and for a moment Smiley was back in occupied Germany, in his own time as a field agent, living with terror in his mouth, naked to every stranger's glance.

He was supposed to catch the thirteen eight arriving Brno sixteen twenty-seven. It was cancelled so he took some wonderful stopping train, a special for the football match, which called at every other lamp-post, and each time Jim reckoned he could pick out the hoods. The quality was variable. At Chocen, a one-horse place if ever he saw one, he got out and bought himself a sausage and there were no fewer than five, all men, spread down the tiny platform with their hands in their pockets, pretending to chat to one another, and making damn fools of themselves.

'If there's one thing that distinguishes a good watcher from a bad one,' said Jim, 'it's the gentle art of doing damn all convincingly.'

At Svitavy two men and a woman entered his carriage and talked about the big match. After a while Jim joined the conversation: he had been reading up the form in his newspaper. It was a club replay, and everyone was going crazy about it. By Brno nothing more had happened so he got out and sauntered through shops and crowded areas where they had to stay close for fear of losing him.

He wanted to lull them, demonstrate to them that he suspected nothing. He knew now that he was the target of what Toby would call a grand slam operation. On foot they were working teams of seven. The cars changed so often he couldn't count them. The overall direction came from a scruffy green van driven by a thug. The van had a loop aerial and a chalk star scrawled high on the back where no child could reach. The cars, where he picked them out, were declared to one another by a woman's handbag on the gloveboard and a passenger sun visor turned down. He guessed there were other signs but those two were good enough for him. He knew from what Toby had told him that jobs like this could cost a hundred people and were unwieldy if the quarry bolted. Toby hated them for that reason.

There is one store in Brno main square that sells everything, said Jim. Shopping in Czecho is usually a bore because there are so few retail outlets for each state industry, but this place was new and quite impressive. He bought children's toys, a scarf, some cigarettes and tried on shoes. He guessed his watchers were still waiting for his clandestine contact. He stole a fur hat and a white plastic raincoat and a carrier bag to put them in. He loitered at the men's department long enough to confirm that two women who formed the forward pair were still behind him but reluctant to come too close. He guessed they had signalled for men to take over, and were waiting. In the men's lavatory he moved very fast. He pulled the white raincoat over his overcoat, stuffed the carrier bag into the pocket and put on the fur hat. He abandoned his remaining parcels then ran like a madman down the emergency staircase, smashed open a fire door, pelted down an alley, strolled up another which was one-way, stuffed the white raincoat into the carrier bag, sauntered into another store which was just closing, and there bought a black raincoat to replace the white one. Using the departing shoppers for cover he squeezed into a crowded tram, stayed aboard till the last stop but one, walked for an hour and made the fallback with Max to the minute.

Here he described his dialogue with Max and said they nearly had a standing fight.

Smiley asked: 'It never crossed your mind to drop the job?'

'No. It did not,' Jim snapped, his voice rising in a threat.

'Although, right from the start, you thought the idea was poppycock?' There was nothing but defence in Smiley's tone. No edge, no wish to score: only a wish to have the truth, clear under the night sky. 'You just kept marching. You'd seen what was on your back, you thought the mission absurd, but you still went on, deeper and deeper into the jungle.'

'I did.'

'Had you perhaps changed your mind about the mission? Did curiosity draw you after all, was that it? You wanted passionately to know who the mole was, for instance? I'm only speculating, Jim.'

'What's the difference? What the hell does my motive matter in a damn mess like this?'

The half moon was free of cloud and seemed very close. Jim sat on the bench. It was bedded in loose gravel and while he spoke he occasionally picked up a pebble and flicked it backhand into the bracken. Smiley sat beside him, looking nowhere but at Jim. Once, to keep him company, he took a pull

of vodka and thought of Tarr and Irina drinking on their own hilltop in
Hong Kong. It must be a habit of the trade, he decided: we talk better when
there's a view.

Through the window of the parked Fiat, said Jim, the word code passed off
without a hitch. The driver was one of those stiff, muscle-bound Czech
Magyars with an Edwardian moustache and a mouthful of garlic. Jim didn't
like him but he hadn't expected to. The two back doors were locked and there
was a row about where he should sit. The Magyar said it was insecure for Jim
to be in the back. It was also undemocratic. Jim told him to go to hell. He
asked Jim whether he had a gun and Jim said no, which was not true, but if
the Magyar didn't believe him, he didn't dare say so. He asked whether Jim
had brought instructions for the General? Jim said he had brought nothing.
He had come to listen.

Jim felt a bit nervy, he said. They drove and the Magyar said his piece.
When they reached the lodge there would be no lights and no sign of life.
The General would be inside. If there was any sign of life, a bicycle, a car, a
dog, if there was any sign that the hut was occupied, then the Magyar would
go in first and Jim would wait in the car. Otherwise Jim should go in alone and
the Magyar would do the waiting. Was that clear?

Why didn't they just go in together? Jim asked. Because the General didn't
want them to, said the Magyar.

They drove for half an hour by Jim's watch, heading north-east at an
average of thirty kilometres an hour. The track was winding and steep and
tree-lined. There was no moon and he could see very little except occasionally
against the skyline more forest, more hilltops. The snow had come from the
north, he noticed; it was a point that was useful later. The track was clear but
rutted by heavy lorries. They drove without lights. The Magyar had begun
telling a dirty story and Jim guessed it was his way of being nervous. The
smell of garlic was awful. He seemed to chew it all the time. Without warning
he cut the engine. They were running downhill, but more slowly. They had
not quite stopped when the Magyar reached for the handbrake and Jim
smashed his head against the window-post and took his gun. They were at the
opening to a side-path. Thirty yards down this path lay a low wooden hut.
There was no sign of life.

Jim told the Magyar what he would like him to do. He would like him to
wear Jim's fur hat and Jim's coat and take the walk for him. He should take it
slowly, keeping his hands linked behind his back, and walking at the centre of
the path. If he failed to do either of those things Jim would shoot him. When
he reached the hut he should go inside and explain to the General that Jim
was indulging in an elementary precaution. Then he should walk slowly back,
report to Jim that all was well, and the General was ready to receive him. Or
not, as the case might be.

The Magyar didn't seem very happy about this but he didn't have much
choice. Before he got out Jim made him turn the car round and face it down
the path. If there was any monkey business, Jim explained, he would put on
the headlights and shoot him along the beam, not once, but several times, and
not in the legs. The Magyar began his walk. He had nearly reached the hut
when the whole area was floodlit: the hut, the path and a large space around.
Then a number of things happened at once. Jim didn't see everything
because he was busy turning the car. He saw four men fall out of the trees,
and, so far as he could work out, one of them sandbagged the Magyar.
Shooting started but none of the four paid it any attention, they were

standing back while somebody took photographs. The shooting seemed to be
directed at the clear sky behind the floodlights. It was very theatrical. Flares
exploded, Very lights went up, even tracer, and as Jim raced the Fiat down
the track he had the impression of leaving a military tattoo at its climax. He
was almost clear – he really felt he *was* clear – when from the woods to his right
someone opened up with a machine-gun at close quarters. The first burst
shot off a back wheel and turned the car over. He saw the wheel fly over the
bonnet as the car took to the ditch on the left. The ditch might have been ten
foot deep but the snow let him down kindly. The car didn't burn so he lay
behind it and waited, facing across the track hoping to get a shot at the
machine-gunner. The next burst came from behind him and threw him up
against the car. The woods must have been crawling with troops. He knew
that he had been hit twice. Both shots caught him in the right shoulder and it
seemed amazing to him, as he lay there watching the tattoo, that they hadn't
taken off the arm. A klaxon sounded, maybe two or three. An ambulance
rolled down the track and there was still enough shooting to frighten the
game for years. The ambulance reminded him of those old Hollywood fire
engines, yet the ambulance boys stood gazing at him without a care in the
world. He was losing consciousness as he heard a second car arrive, and men's
voices, and more photographs were taken, this time of the right man.
Someone gave orders but he couldn't tell what they were because they were
given in Russian. His one thought, as they dumped him on the stretcher and
the lights went out, concerned going back to London. He imagined himself in
the St James's flat, with the coloured charts and the sheaf of notes, sitting in
the armchair and explaining to Control how in their old age the two of them
had walked into the biggest sucker's punch in the history of the trade. His
only consolation was that they had sandbagged the Magyar, but looking back
Jim wished very much he'd broken his neck for him: it was a thing he could
have managed very easily, and without compunction.

# THIRTY-TWO

The describing of pain was to Jim an indulgence to be dispensed with. To
Smiley, his stoicism had something awesome about it, the more so because he
seemed unaware of it. The gaps in his story came mainly where he passed out,
he explained. The ambulance drove him, so far as he could fathom, further
north. He guessed this from the trees when they opened the door to let the
doctor in: the snow was heaviest when he looked back. The surface was good
and he guessed they were on road to Hradec. The doctor gave him an
injection; he come round in prison hospital with barred windows high up,

and three men watching him. He came round again after the operation in a different cell with no windows at all, and he thought probably the first questioning took place there, about seventy-two hours after they'd patched him up, but time was already a problem and of course they'd taken away his watch.

They moved him a lot. Either to different rooms, depending on what they were going to do with him, or to other prisons depending on who was questioning him. Sometimes they just moved to keep him awake, walking him down cell corridors at night. He was also moved in lorries, and once by a Czech transport plane, but he was trussed for the flight and hooded, and passed out very soon after they took off. The interrogation which followed this flight was very long. Otherwise he had little sense of progression from one questioning to another and thinking didn't get it any straighter for him, rather the reverse. The thing that was still strongest in his memory was the plan of campaign he formed while he waited for the first interrogation to begin. He knew silence would be impossible and for his own sanity, or survival, there had to be a dialogue, and at the end of it they had to think he had told them what he knew, all he knew. Lying in hospital he prepared his mind into lines of defence behind which, if he was lucky, he could fall back stage by stage until he had given the impression of total defeat. His forward line, he reckoned, and his most expendable, was the bare bones of Operation Testify. It was anyone's guess whether Stevcek was a plant, or had been betrayed. But whichever was the case, one thing was certain: the Czechs knew more about Stevcek than Jim did. His first concession therefore would be the Stevcek story, since they had it already; but he would make them work for it. First he would deny everything and stick to his cover. After a fight he would admit to being a British spy and give his workname Ellis so that if they published it, the Circus would at least know he was alive and trying. He had little doubt that the elaborate trap and the photographs augured a lot of ballyhoo. After that, in accordance with his understanding with Control, he would describe the operation as his own show, mounted without the consent of his superiors and calculated to win him favour. And he would bury, as deep as they could go and deeper, all thoughts of a spy inside the Circus.

'No mole,' said Jim, to the black outlines of the Quantocks. 'No meeting with Control, no service flat in St James's.'

'No Tinker, Tailor.'

His second line of defence would be Max. He proposed at first to deny that he had brought a legman at all. Then he might say he had brought one but he didn't know his name. Then, because everyone likes a name, he would give them one: the wrong one first, then the right one. By that time Max must be clear, or underground, or caught.

Now came in Jim's imagination a succession of less strongly held positions: recent scalphunter operations, Circus tittle-tattle, anything to make his interrogators think he was broken and talking free and that this was all he had, they had passed the last trench. He would rack his memory for back scalphunter cases, and if necessary he would give them the names of one or two Soviet and satellite officials who had recently been turned or burned; of others who in the past had made a one-time sale of assets and, since they had not defected, might now be considered to be in line for burning or a second bite. He would throw them any bone he could think of, sell them if necessary the entire Brixton stable. And all this would be the smokescreen to disguise what seemed to Jim to be his most vulnerable intelligence, since they would certainly expect him to possess it: the identity of members of the Czech end of the Aggravate and Plato networks.

'Landkron, Krieglova, Bilova, the Pribyls,' said Jim.

Why did he choose the same order for their names? Smiley wondered.

For a long time Jim had had no responsibility for these networks. Years earlier, before he took over Brixton, he had helped establish them, recruited some of the founder members; since then a lot had happened to them in the hands of Bland and Haydon of which he knew nothing. But he was certain that he still knew enough to blow them both sky high. And what worried him most was the fear that Control, or Bill, or Percy Alleline, or whoever had the final say these days, would be too greedy, or too slow, to evacuate the networks by the time Jim, under forms of duress he could only guess at, had no alternative but to break completely.

'So that's the joke,' said Jim, with no humour whatever. 'They couldn't have cared less about the networks. They asked me half a dozen questions about Aggravate then lost interest. They knew damn well that Testify wasn't my private brain-child and they knew all about Control buying the Stevcek pass in Vienna. They began exactly where I wanted to end: with the briefing in St James's. They didn't ask me about a legman, they weren't interested in who had driven me to the rendezvous with the Magyar. All they wanted to talk about was Control's rotten-apple theory.'

One word, thought Smiley again, it might be just one word. He said: 'Did they actually know the St James's address?'

'They knew the brand of the bloody sherry, man.'

'And the charts?' asked Smiley quickly. 'The music case?'

'No.' He added: 'Not at first. No.'

Thinking inside out, Steed Asprey used to call it. They knew because the mole Gerald had told them, thought Smiley. The mole knew what the housekeepers had succeeded in getting out of old MacFadean. The Circus conducts its post mortem: Karla has the benefit of its findings in time to use them on Jim.

'So I suppose by now you were beginning to think Control was right: there *was* a mole,' said Smiley.

Jim and Smiley were leaning on a wooden gate. The ground sloped sharply away from them in a long sweep of bracken and fields. Below them lay another village, a bay and a thin ribbon of moonlit sea.

'They went straight to the heart of it. "Why did Control go it alone? What did he hope to achieve?" "His comeback," I said, So they laugh: "With tinpot information about military emplacements in the area of Brno? That wouldn't even buy him a square meal in his Club." "Maybe he was losing his grip," I said. If Control was losing his grip, they said, who was stamping on his fingers? Alleline, I said, that was the buzz; Alleline and Control were in competition to provide intelligence. But in Brixton we only got the rumours, I said. "And what is Alleline producing that Control is *not* producing?" "I don't know." "But you just said that Alleline and Control are in competition to provide intelligence." "It's rumour. I don't know." Back to the cooler.'

Time, said Jim, at this stage lost him completely. He lived either in the darkness of the hood, or in the white light of the cells. There was no night or day, and to make it even more weird they kept the noises going most of the time.

They were working him on the production-line principle, he explained: no sleep, relays of questions, a lot of disorientation, a lot of muscle, till the interrogation became to him a slow race between going a bit dotty, as he called it, and breaking completely. Naturally, he hoped he'd go dotty but that wasn't something you could decide for yourself, because they had a way of bringing you back. A lot of muscle was done electrically.

'So we start again. New tack. "Stevcek was an important general. If he asked for a senior British officer, he could expect him to be properly informed about all aspects of his career. Are you telling us you did not inform yourself?" "I'm saying I got my information from Control." "Did you read Stevcek's dossier at the Circus?" "No." "Did Control?" "I don't know." "What conclusions did Control draw from Stevcek's second appointment in Moscow? Did Control speak to you about Stevcek's role in the Warsaw Pact Liaison Committee?" "No." They stuck to that question and I suppose I stuck to my answer because after a few more no's they got a bit crazy. They seemed to lose patience. When I passed out they hosed me down and had another crack.'

Movement, said Jim. His narrative had become oddly jerky. Cells, corridors, car . . . at the airport, VIP treatment and a mauling before the aeroplane . . . on the flight, dropped off to sleep and was punished for it: 'Came round in a cell again, smaller, no paint on the walls. Sometimes I thought I was in Russia. I worked out by the stars that we had flown east. Sometimes I was in Sarratt, back on the interrogation resistance course.'

For a couple of days they let him alone. Head was muzzy. He kept hearing the shooting in the forest and he saw the tattoo again, and when finally the big session started, the one he remembered as the marathon, he had the disadvantage of feeling half defeated when he went in.

'Matter of health much as anything,' he explained, very tense now.

'We could make a break if you wanted,' Smiley said, but where Jim was, there were no breaks, and what he wanted was irrelevant.

That was the long one, Jim said. Sometime in the course of it, he told them about Control's notes and his charts and the coloured inks and crayons. They were going at him like the devil and he remembered an all-male audience, at one end of the room, peering like a lot of damn medicos and muttering to one another, and he told them about the crayons just to keep the talk alive, to make them stop and listen. They listened but they didn't stop.

'Once they had the colours they wanted to know what the colours meant. "What did blue mean?" "Control didn't have blue." "What did red mean? What did red stand for? Give us an example of red on the chart. What did red mean? What did red mean?" Then everybody clears out except a couple of guards and one little frosty fellow, stiff back, seemed to be head boy. The guards take me over to a table and this little fellow sits beside me like a bloody gnome with his hands folded. He's got two crayons in front of him, red and green, and a chart of Stevcek's career.'

It wasn't that Jim broke exactly, he just ran out of invention. He couldn't think up any more stories. The truths which he had locked away so deeply were the only things that suggested themselves.

'So you told him about the rotten apple,' Smiley suggested. 'And you told him about Tinker, Tailor.'

Yes, Jim agreed, he did. He told him that Control believed Stevcek could identify a mole inside the Circus. He told him about the Tinker, Tailor code and who each of them was, name by name.

'What was his reaction?'

'Thought for a bit then offered me a cigarette. Hated the damn thing.'

'Why?'

'Tasted American. Camel, one of those.'

'Did he smoke one himself?'

Jim gave a short nod. 'Bloody chimney,' he said.

Time, after that, began once more to flow, said Jim. He was taken to a camp, he guessed outside a town, and lived in a compound of huts with a double perimeter of wire. With the help of a guard he was soon able to walk; one day they even went for a stroll in the forest. The camp was very big: his own compound was only a part of it. At night he could see the glow of a city to the east. The guards wore denims and didn't speak so he still had no way of telling whether he was in Czecho or in Russia, but his money was heavily on Russia, and when the surgeon came to take a look at his back he used a Russian-English interpreter to express his contempt for his predecessor's handiwork. The interrogation continued sporadically, but without hostility. They put a fresh team on him but it was a leisurely crowd by comparison with the first eleven.

One night he was taken to a military airport and flown by RAF fighter to Inverness. From there he went by small plane to Elstree, then by van to Sarratt; both were night journeys.

Jim was winding up fast. He was already launched on his experiences at the Nursery, in fact, when Smiley asked: 'And the head man, the little frosty one: you never saw him again?'

Once, Jim conceded; just before he left.

'What for?'

'Gossip.' Much louder. 'Lot of damned tripe about Circus personalities, matter of fact.'

'Which personalities?'

Jim ducked that question. Tripe about who was on the up staircase, he said, who was on the down. Who was next in line for Chief: '"How should I know?" I said. "Bloody janitors hear it before Brixton does."'

'So who came in for the tripe precisely?'

Mainly Roy Bland, said Jim sullenly. How did Bland reconcile his left-wing leanings with the work of the Circus? He hasn't got any left-wing leanings, said Jim, that's how. What was Bland's standing with Esterhase and Alleline? What did Bland think of Bill's paintings? Then how much Roy drank and what would become of him if Bill ever withdrew his support for him? Jim gave meagre answers to these questions.

'Was anyone else mentioned?'

'Esterhase,' Jim snapped, in the same taut tone. 'Bloody man wanted to know how anyone could trust a Hungarian.'

Smiley's next question seemed, even to himself, to cast an absolute silence over the whole black valley.

'And what did he say about me?' He repeated: 'What did he say about me?'

'Showed me a cigarette lighter. Said it was yours. Present from Ann. "With all my love". Her signature. Engraved.'

'Did he mention how he came by it? What did he say, Jim? Come on, I'm not going to weaken at the knees just because some Russian hood made a bad joke about me.'

Jim's answer came out like an army order. 'He reckoned that after Bill Haydon's fling with her, she might care to redraft the inscription.' He swung away towards the car. 'I told him,' he shouted furiously. 'Told him to his wrinkled little face. You can't judge Bill by things like that. Artists have totally different standards. See things we can't see. Feel things that are beyond us. Bloody little man just laughed. "Didn't know his pictures were that good," he said. I told him, George. "Go to hell. Go to bloody hell. If you had one Bill Haydon in your damned outfit, you could call it set and match." I said to him: "Christ Almighty," I said, "what are you running over here? A service or the bloody Salvation Army?"'

'That was well said,' Smiley remarked at last, as if commenting on some distant debate. 'And you'd never seen him before?'

'Who?'

'The little frosty chap. He wasn't familiar to you – from long ago for instance? Well, you know how we are. We're trained to see a lot of faces, photographs of Centre personalities, and sometimes they stick. Even if we can't put a name to them any more. This one didn't anyway. I just wondered. It occurred to me you had a lot of time to think,' he went on, conversationally. 'You lay there recovering, waiting to come home, and what else had you to do, but think?' He waited. 'So what did you think of, I wonder? The mission. Your mission, I suppose.'

'Off and on.'

'With what conclusions? Anything useful? Any suspicions, insights, any hints for me to take away?'

'Damn all, thank you,' Jim snapped, very hard. 'You know me, George Smiley, I'm not a juju man, I'm a –'

'You're a plain field man who lets the other chaps do his thinking. Nevertheless: when you know you have been led into a king-sized trap, betrayed, shot in the back, and have nothing to do for months but lie or sit on a bunk, or pace a Russian cell, I would guess that even the most dedicated man of action' – his voice had lost none of its friendliness – 'might put his mind to wondering how he landed in such a scrape. Let's take Operation Testify a minute,' Smiley suggested to the motionless figure before him. 'Testify ended Control's career. He was disgraced and he couldn't pursue his mole, assuming there was one. The Circus passed into other hands. With a sense of timeliness, Control died. Testify did something else too. It revealed to the Russians – through you, actually – the exact reach of Control's suspicions. That he'd narrowed the field to five, but apparently no further. I'm not suggesting you should have fathomed all that for yourself in your cell, waiting. After all you had no idea, sitting in the pen, that Control had been thrown out – though it might have occurred to you that the Russians laid on that mock battle in the forest in order to raise a wind. Did it?'

'You've forgotten the networks,' said Jim dully.

'Oh, the Czechs had the networks marked down long before you came on the scene. They only rolled them up in order to compound Control's failure.'

The discursive, almost chatty tone with which Smiley threw out these theories found no resonance in Jim. Having waited in vain for him to volunteer some word, Smiley let the matter drop. 'Well let's just go over your reception at Sarratt, shall we? To wrap it up?'

In a rare moment of forgetfulness he helped himself to the vodka bottle before passing it to Jim.

To judge by his voice, Jim had had enough. He spoke fast and angrily, with that same military shortness that was his refuge from intellectual incursions.

For four days Sarratt was limbo, he said: 'Ate a lot, drank a lot, slept a lot. Walked round the cricket ground.' He'd have swum, but the pool was under repair, as it had been six months before: damned inefficient. He had a medical, watched television in his hut and played a bit of chess with Cranko, who was running reception.

Meanwhile he waited for Control to show up, but he didn't. The first person from the Circus to visit him was the resettlement officer, talking about a friendly teaching agency, next came some pay wallah to discuss his pension entitlement, then the doctor again to assess him for a gratuity. He waited for the inquisitors to appear but they never did, which was a relief because he didn't know what he would have told them until he had the green light from Control and he'd had enough of questions. He guessed Control was holding them off. It seemed mad that he should keep from the inquisitors what he had already told the Russians and the Czechs but until he heard from Control, what else could he do? When Control still sent no word, he formed notions of presenting himself to Lacon and telling his story. Then he decided that Control was waiting for him to get clear of the Nursery before he contacted him. He had a relapse for a few days and when it was over Toby Esterhase turned up in a new suit, apparently to shake him by the hand and wish him good luck. But in fact to tell him how things stood.

'Bloody odd fellow to send, but he seemed to have come up in the world. Then I remembered what Control said about only using chaps from outstations.'

Esterhase told him that the Circus had very nearly gone under as a result of Testify and that Jim was currently the Circus's number one leper. Control was out of the game and a reorganisation was going on in order to appease Whitehall.

'Then he told me not to worry,' said Jim.

'In what way not worry?'

'About my special brief. He said a few people knew the real story, and I needn't worry because it was being taken care of. All the facts were known. Then he gave me a thousand quid in cash to add to my gratuity.'

'Who from?'

'He didn't say.'

'Did he mention Control's theory about Stevcek? Centre's spy inside the Circus?'

'The facts were known,' Jim repeated, glaring. 'He *ordered* me not to approach anyone or try to get my story heard because it was all being taken care of at the highest level and anything I did might spoil the kill. The Circus was back on the road. I could forget Tinker, Tailor and the whole damn game: moles, everything. "Drop out," he said. "You're a lucky man, Jim," he kept saying. "You've been ordered to become a lotus-eater." I could forget it. Right? Forget it. Just behave as if it had never happened.' He was shouting. 'And that's what I've been doing: obeying orders and forgetting!'

The night landscape seemed to Smiley suddenly innocent; it was like a great canvas on which nothing bad or cruel had ever been painted. Side by side, they stared down the valley over the clusters of lights to a tor raised against the horizon. A single tower stood at its top and for a moment it marked for Smiley the end of the journey.

'Yes,' he said. 'I did a bit of forgetting too. So Toby actually mentioned

Tinker, Tailor to you. However did he get hold of *that* story, unless . . . And no word from Bill?' he went on. 'Not even a postcard.'

'Bill was abroad,' said Jim shortly.

'Who told you that?'

'Toby.'

'So you never saw Bill: since Testify, your oldest, closest friend, he disappeared.'

'You heard what Toby said. I was out of bounds. Quarantine.'

'Bill was never much of a one for regulations, though, was he?' said Smiley, in a reminiscent tone.

'And you were never one to see him straight,' Jim barked.

'Sorry I wasn't there when you called on me before you left for Czecho,' Smiley remarked after a small pause. 'Control had pushed me over to Germany to get me out of the light and when I came back – what was it that you wanted, exactly?'

'Nothing. Thought Czecho might be a bit hairy. Thought I'd give you the nod, say goodbye.'

'Before a mission?' cried Smiley in mild surprise. 'Before such a *special* mission?' Jim showed no sign that he had heard. 'Did you give anyone else the nod? I suppose we were all away. Toby, Roy – Bill, did he get one?'

'No one.'

'Bill was on leave, wasn't he? But I gather he was around all the same.'

'No one,' Jim insisted, as a spasm of pain caused him to lift his right shoulder and rotate his head. 'All out,' he said.

'That's very unlike you Jim,' said Smiley in the same mild tone, 'to go round shaking hands with people before you go on vital missions. You must have been getting sentimental in your old age. It wasn't . . .' he hesitated. 'It wasn't advice or anything that you wanted, was it? After all, you did think the mission was poppycock, didn't you? And that Control was losing his grip. Perhaps you felt you should take your problem to a third party? It all had rather a mad air, I agree.'

Learn the facts, Steed Asprey used to say, then try on the stories like clothes.

With Jim locked in a furious silence they returned to the car.

At the motel Smiley drew twenty postcard-sized photographs from the recesses of his greatcoat and laid them out in two lines across the ceramic table. Some were snaps, some portraits; all were of men and none of them looked English. With a grimace Jim picked out two and handed them to Smiley. He was sure of the first, he muttered, less sure of the second. The first was the headman, the frosty gnome. The second was one of the swine who watched from the shadows while the thugs took Jim to pieces. Smiley returned the photographs to his pocket. As he topped up their glasses for a nightcap, a less tortured observer than Jim might have noticed a sense not of triumph but of ceremony about him; as though the drink were putting a seal on something.

'So when was the last time you saw Bill, actually? To talk to,' Smiley asked, just as one might about any old friend. He had evidently disturbed Jim in other thoughts, for he took a moment to lift his head and catch the question.

'Oh, round about,' he said carelessly. 'Bumped into him in the corridors I suppose.'

'And to talk to? Never mind.' For Jim had returned to his other thoughts.

Jim would not be driven all the way to school. Smiley had to drop him short, at the top of the tarmac path that led through the graveyard to the church. He had left some work-books in the ante-chapel, he said. Momentarily, Smiley felt disposed to disbelieve him, but could not understand why. Perhaps because he had come to the opinion that after thirty years in the trade, Jim was still a rather poor liar. The last Smiley saw of him was that lopsided shadow striding towards the Norman porch as his heels cracked like gunshot between the tombs.

Smiley drove to Taunton and from the Castle Hotel made a string of telephone calls. Though exhausted he slept fitfully between visions of Karla sitting at Jim's table with two crayons, and Cultural Attaché Polyakov alias Viktorov, fired by concern for the safety of his mole Gerald, waiting impatiently in the interrogation cell for Jim to break. Lastly of Toby Esterhase bobbing into Sarratt in place of the absent Haydon, cheerfully advising Jim to forget all about Tinker, Tailor, and his dead inventor, Control.

The same night Peter Guillam drove west, clean across England to Liverpool, with Ricki Tarr as his only passenger. It was a tedious journey in beastly conditions. For most of it Tarr boasted about the rewards he would claim, and the promotion, once he had carried out his mission. From there he talked about his women: Danny, her mother, Irina. He seemed to envisage a *ménage à quatre* in which the two women would jointly care for Danny, and for himself.

'There's a lot of the mother in Irina. That's what frustrates her, naturally.' Boris, he said, could get lost, he would tell Karla to keep him. As their destination approached, his mood changed again and he fell silent. The dawn was cold and foggy. In the suburbs they had to drop to a crawl and cyclists overtook them. A reek of soot and steel filled the car.

'Don't hang about in Dublin, either,' said Guillam suddenly. 'They expect you to work the soft routes so keep your head down. Take the first plane out.'

'We've been through all that.'

'Well I'm going through it all again,' Guillam retorted. 'What's Mackelvore's workname?'

'For Christ's sake,' Tarr breathed, and gave it.

It was still dark when the Irish ferry sailed. There were soldiers and police everywhere: this war, the last, the one before. A fierce wind was blowing off the sea and the going looked rough. At the dockside, a sense of fellowship briefly touched the small crowd as the ship's lights bobbed quickly into the gloom. Somewhere a woman was crying, somewhere a drunk was celebrating his release.

He drove back slowly, trying to work himself out: the new Guillam who starts at sudden noises, has nightmares and not only can't keep his girl but makes up crazy reasons for distrusting her. He had challenged her about Sand, and the hours she kept, and about her secrecy in general. After listening with her grave brown eyes fixed on him she told him he was a fool, and left. 'I am what you think I am,' she said, and fetched her things from the bedroom. From his empty flat he telephoned Toby Esterhase inviting him for a friendly chat later that day.

## THIRTY-THREE

Smiley sat in the Minister's Rolls, with Lacon beside him. In Ann's family the car was called the black bed-pan, and hated for its flashiness. The chauffeur had been sent to find himself breakfast. The Minister sat in the front and everyone looked forward down the long bonnet, across the river to the foggy towers of Battersea Power Station. The Minister's hair was full at the back, and licked into small black horns around the ears.

'If you're right,' the Minister declared, after a funereal silence, 'I'm not saying you're not, but if you are, how much porcelain will he break at the end of the day?'

Smiley did not quite understand.

'I'm talking about scandal. Gerald gets to Moscow. Right, so then what happens? Does he leap on a soapbox and laugh his head off in public about all the people he's made fools of over here? I mean Christ, we're all in this together, aren't we? I don't see why we should let him go just so's he can pull the bloody roof down over our heads and the competition sweep the bloody pool.'

He tried a different tack. 'I mean to say, just because the Russians know our secrets doesn't mean everyone else has to. We got plenty of other fish to fry apart from them, don't we? What about all the black men: are they going to be reading the gory details in the Wallah-Wallah News in a week's time?'

Or his constituents, Smiley thought.

'I think that's always been a point the Russians accept,' said Lacon. 'After all, if you make your enemy look a fool, you lose the justification for engaging him.' He added: 'They've never made use of their opportunities so far, have they?'

'Well, make sure they toe the line. Get it in writing. No, don't. But you tell them what's sauce for the goose is sauce for the gander. We don't go round publishing the batting order at Moscow Centre, so they can bloody well play ball too, for once.'

Declining a lift, Smiley said the walk would do him good.

It was Thursgood's day for duty and he felt it badly. Headmasters, in his opinion, should be above the menial tasks, they should keep their minds clear for policy and leadership. The flourish of his Cambridge gown did not console him, and as he stood in the gymnasium watching the boys file in for morning line-up, his eye fixed on them balefully, if not with downright hostility. It was Marjoribanks, though, who dealt the death-blow.

'He said it was his mother,' he explained, in a low murmur to Thursgood's left ear. 'He'd had a telegram and proposed to leave at once. He wouldn't even stay for a cup of tea. I promised to pass on the message.'

'It's monstrous, absolutely monstrous,' said Thursgood.

'I'll take his French if you like. We can double up Five and Six.'

'I'm furious,' said Thursgood. 'I can't think, I'm so furious.'

'And Irving says he'll take the rugger final.'

'Reports to be written, exams, rugger finals to play off. What's supposed to be the matter with the woman? Just a flu, I suppose, a seasonal flu. Well we've all got that, so have our mothers. Where does she live?'

'I rather gathered from what he said to Sue that she was dying.'

'Well that's *one* excuse he won't be able to use again,' said Thursgood, quite unmollified, and with a sharp bark quelled the noise and read the roll.

'Roach?'

'Sick, sir.'

That was all he needed to fill his cup. The school's richest boy having a nervous breakdown about his wretched parents, and the father threatening to remove him.

## THIRTY-FOUR

It was almost four o'clock on the afternoon of the same day. 'Safe houses I have known,' thought Guillam, looking round the gloomy flat. He could write of them the way a commercial traveller could write about hotels: from your five-star hall of mirrors in Belgravia with Wedgwood pilasters and gilded oakleaves, to this two-room scalphunters' shakedown in Lexham Gardens, smelling of dust and drains, with a three-foot fire extinguisher in the pitch-dark hall. Over the fireplace, cavaliers drinking out of pewter. On the nest of tables, sea shells for ashtrays, and in the grey kitchen, anonymous instructions to Be Sure and Turn Off the Gas Both Cocks. He was crossing the hall when the house bell rang, exactly on time. He lifted the phone and heard Toby's distorted voice howling in the earpiece. He pressed the button and heard the clunk of the electric lock echoing in the stairwell. He opened the front door but left it on the chain till he was sure Toby was alone.

'How are we?' said Guillam cheerfully, letting him in.

'Fine actually, Peter,' said Toby, pulling off his coat and gloves.

There was tea on a tray: Guillam had prepared it, two cups. To safe houses belongs a certain standard of catering. Either you are pretending you live there, or that you are adept anywhere; or simply that you think of everything. In the trade, naturalness is an art, Guillam decided. That was something Camilla could not appreciate.

'Actually it's quite strange weather,' Esterhase announced, as if he had really been analysing its qualities. Safe house small talk was never much better. 'One walks a few steps and is completely exhausted already. So we are expecting a Pole?' he said, sitting down. 'A Pole in the fur trade who you think might run courier for us?'

'Due here any minute.'

'Do we know him? I had my people look up the name but they found no trace.'

My people, thought Guillam: I must remember to use that one. 'The Free Poles made a pass at him a few months back and he ran a mile,' he said. 'Then

Karl Stack spotted him round the warehouses and thought he might be useful to the scalphunters.' He shrugged. 'I liked him but what's the point? We can't even keep our own people busy.'

'Peter, you are very generous,' said Esterhase reverently, and Guillam had the ridiculous feeling he had just tipped him. To his relief the front-door bell rang and Fawn took up his place in the doorway.

'Sorry about this, Toby,' Smiley said, a little out of breath from the stairs. 'Peter, where shall I hang my coat?'

Turning him to the wall, Guillam lifted Toby's unresisting hands and put them against it, then searched him for a gun, taking his time. Toby had none.

'Did he come alone?' Guillam asked. 'Or is there some little friend waiting in the road?'

'Looked all clear to me,' said Fawn.

Smiley was at the window, gazing down into the street. 'Put the light out a minute, will you?' he said.

'Wait in the hall,' Guillam ordered, and Fawn withdrew, carrying Smiley's coat. 'Seen something?' he asked Smiley, joining him at the window.

Already the London afternoon had taken on the misty pinks and yellows of evening. The square was Victorian residential; at the centre, a caged garden, already dark. 'Just a shadow, I suppose,' said Smiley with a grunt, and turned back to Esterhase. The clock on the mantelpiece chimed four. Fawn must have wound it up.

'I want to put a thesis to you, Toby. A notion about what's going on. May I?'

Esterhase didn't move an eyelash. His little hands rested on the wooden arms of his chair. He sat quite comfortably, but slightly to attention, toes and heels of his polished shoes together.

'You don't have to speak at all. There's no risk to listening, is there?'

'Maybe.'

'It's two years ago. Percy Alleline wants Control's job, but he has no standing in the Circus. Control has made sure of that. Control is sick and past his prime but Percy can't dislodge him. Remember the time?'

Esterhase gave a neat nod.

'One of those silly seasons,' said Smiley in his reasonable voice. 'There isn't enough work outside so we start intriguing around the service, spying on one another. Percy's sitting in his room one morning with nothing to do. He has a paper appointment as operational director, but in practice he's a rubber stamp between the regional sections and Control, if that. Percy's door opens and somebody walks in. We'll call him Gerald, it's just a name. "Percy," he says, "I've stumbled an a major Russian source. It could be a gold mine." Or perhaps he doesn't say anything till they're outside the building, because Gerald is very much a field man, he doesn't like to talk with walls and telephones around. Perhaps they take a walk in the park or a drive in a car. Perhaps they eat a meal somewhere, and at this stage there isn't much Percy can do but listen. Percy's had very little experience of the European scene, remember, least of all Czecho or the Balkans. He cut his teeth in South America and after that he worked the old possessions: India, the Middle East. He doesn't know a lot about Russians or Czechs or what you will, he's inclined to see red as red and leave it at that. Unfair?'

Esterhase pursed his lips and frowned a little, as if to say he never discussed a superior.

'Whereas Gerald is an expert on those things. His operational life has been spent weaving and ducking round the Eastern markets. Percy's out of his depth but keen. Gerald's on his home ground. This Russian source, says Gerald, could be the richest the Circus has had for years. Gerald doesn't want to say too much but he expects to be getting some trade samples in a day or two and when he does, he'd like Percy to run his eye over them just to get a notion of the quality. They can go into source details later. "But why me?" says Percy. "What's it all about?" So Gerald tells him. "Percy," he says. "Some of us in the regional sections are worried sick by the level of operational losses. There seems to be a jinx around. Too much loose talk inside the Circus and out. Too many people being cut in on distribution. Out in the field, our agents are going to the wall, our networks are being rolled up or worse, and every new ploy ends up a street accident. We want you to help us put that right." Gerald is not mutinous, and he's careful not to suggest that there's a traitor inside the Circus who's blowing all the operations, because you and I know that once talk like that gets around the machinery grinds to a halt. Anyway the last thing Gerald wants is a witch-hunt. But he does say that the place is leaking at the joints, and that slovenliness at the top is leading to failures lower down. All balm to Percy's ear. He lists the recent scandals and he's careful to lean on Alleline's own Middle East adventure, which went so wrong and nearly cost Percy his career. Then he makes his proposal. This is what he says. In my thesis, you understand; it's just a thesis.'

'Sure, George,' said Toby, and licked his lips.

'Another thesis would be that Alleline was his own Gerald, you see. It just happens that I don't believe it: I don't believe Percy is capable of going out and buying himself a top Russian spy and manning his own boat from then on. I think he'd mess it up.'

'Sure,' said Esterhase, with absolute confidence.

'So this, in my thesis, is what Gerald says to Percy next. "We – that is, myself and those like-minded souls who are associated with this project – would like you to act as our father-figure, Percy. We're not political men, we're operators. We don't understand the Whitehall jungle. But you do. You handle the committees, we'll handle Merlin. If you act as our cut-out, and protect us from the rot that's set in, which means in effect limiting knowledge of the operation to the absolute minimum, we'll supply the goods." They talk over ways and means in which this might be done, then Gerald leaves Percy to fret for a bit. A week, a month, I don't know. Long enough for Percy to have done his thinking. One day Gerald produces the first sample. And of course it's very good. Very, very good. Naval stuff as it happens, which couldn't suit Percy better because he's very well in at the Admiralty, it's his supporters' club. So Percy gives his naval friends a sneak preview and they water at the mouth. "Where does it come from? Will there be more?" There's plenty more. As to the indentity of the source – well that's a big, big mystery at this stage, but so it should be. Forgive me if I'm a little wide of the mark here and there but I've only the file to go by.'

The mention of a file, the first indication that Smiley might be acting in some official capacity, produced in Esterhase a discernible response. The habitual licking of the lips was accompanied by a forward movement of the head and an expression of shrewd familiarity, as if Toby by all these signals was trying to indicate that he too had read the file, whatever file it was, and entirely shared Smiley's conclusions. Smiley had broken off to drink some tea.

'More for you, Toby?' he asked, over his cup.

'I'll get it,' said Guillam with more firmness than hospitality. 'Tea, Fawn,' he called through the door. It opened at once and Fawn appeared on the threshold, cup in hand.

Smiley was back at the window. He had parted the curtain an inch, and was staring into the square.

'Toby?'

'Yes, George?'

'Did you bring a babysitter?'

'No.'

'No one?'

'George, why should I bring babysitters if I am just going to meet Peter and a poor Pole?'

Smiley returned to his chair. 'Merlin as a source,' he resumed. 'Where was I? Yes, well conveniently Merlin wasn't just one source, was he, as little by little Gerald explained to Percy and the two others he had by now drawn into the magic circle. Merlin was a Soviet agent all right, but rather like Alleline he was also the spokesman of a dissident group. We love to see ourselves in other people's situations, and I'm sure Percy warmed to Merlin from the start. This group, this caucus of which Merlin was the leader, was made up of, say, half a dozen like-minded Soviet officials, each in his way well-placed. With time, I suspect, Gerald gave his lieutenants, and Percy, a pretty close picture of these sub-sources, but I don't know. Merlin's job was to collate their intelligence and get it to the West, and over the next few months he showed remarkable versatility in doing just that. He used all manner of methods, and the Circus was only too willing to feed him the equipment. Secret writing, microdots stuck over full-stops on innocent-looking letters, dead letter-boxes in Western capitals, filled by God knows what brave Russian, and dutifully cleared by Toby Esterhase's brave lamplighters. Live meetings even, arranged and watched over by Toby's babysitters' – a minute pause as Smiley glanced again towards the window – 'a couple of drops in Moscow that had to be fielded by the local residency, though they were never allowed to know their benefactor. But no clandestine radio; Merlin doesn't care for it. There was a proposal once – it even got as far as the Treasury – to set up a permanent long-arm radio station in Finland, just to service him, but it all foundered when Merlin said: "Not on your nellie." He must have been taking lessons from Karla, mustn't he? You know how Karla hates radio. The great thing is, Merlin has mobility: that's his biggest talent. Perhaps he's in the Moscow Trade Ministry and can use the travelling salesmen. Anyway, he has the resources and he has the leads out of Russia. And that's why his fellow conspirators look to him to deal with Gerald and agree the terms, the financial terms. Because they do want money. Lots of money. I should have mentioned that. In that respect, secret services and their customers are like anyone else, I'm afraid. They value most what costs most, and Merlin costs a fortune. Ever bought a fake picture?'

'I sold a couple once,' said Toby with a flashy, nervous smile, but no one laughed.

'The more you pay for it, the less inclined you are to doubt it. Silly, but there we are. It's also comforting for everyone to know that Merlin is venal. That's a motive we all understand, right, Toby? Specially in the Treasury. Twenty thousand francs a month into a Soviet bank: well, there's no knowing who wouldn't bend a few egalitarian principles for money like that. So

Whitehall pays him a fortune, and calls his intelligence priceless. And some of it *is* good,' Smiley conceded. 'Very good, I do think, and so it should be. Then one day, Gerald admits Percy to the greatest secret of all. The Merlin caucus has a London end. It's the start, I should tell you now, of a very, very clever knot.'

Toby put down his cup and with his handkerchief primly dabbed the corners of his mouth.

'According to Gerald, a member of the Soviet Embassy here in London is actually ready and able to act as Merlin's London representative. He is even in the extraordinary position of being able to use, on rare occasions, the Embassy facilities to talk to Merlin in Moscow, to send and receive messages. And if every imaginable precaution is taken, it is even possible now and then for Gerald to arrange clandestine meetings with this wonder-man, to brief and debrief him, to put follow-up questions and receive answers from Merlin almost by return of post. We'll call this Soviet official Aleksey Aleksandrovich Polyakov, and we'll pretend he's a member of the cultural section of the Soviet Embassy. Are you with me?'

'I didn't hear anything,' said Esterhase. 'I gone deaf.'

'The story is, he's been a member of the London Embassy quite a while – nine years to be precise – but Merlin's only recently added him to the flock. While Polyakov was on leave in Moscow, perhaps?'

'I'm not hearing nothing.'

'Very quickly Polyakov becomes important, because before long Gerald appoints him linchpin of the Witchcraft operation and a lot more besides. The dead drops in Amsterdam and Paris, the secret inks, the micro-dots: they all go on all right, but at less of a pitch. The convenience of having Polyakov right on the doorstep is too good to miss. Some of Merlin's best material is smuggled to London by diplomatic bag: all Polyakov has to do is slit open the envelopes and pass them to his counterpart in the Circus: Gerald or whomever Gerald nominates. But we must never forget that this part of the Merlin operation is deathly, deathly secret. The Witchcraft committee itself is of course secret too, but large. That's inevitable. The operation is large, the take is large, processing and distribution alone require a mass of clerical supervision: transcribers, translators, codists, typists, evaluators and God knows what. None of that worries Gerald at all, of course: he likes it in fact, because the art of being Gerald is to be one of a crowd. Is the Witchcraft committee led from below? From the middle or from the top? I rather like Karla's description of committees, don't you? Is it Chinese? A committee is an animal with four back legs.

'But the London end – Polyakov's leg – that part is confined to the original magic circle. Skordeno, de Silsky, all the pack: they can tear off abroad and devil like mad for Merlin away from home. But here in London, the operation involving brother Polyakov, the way that knot is tied, that's a very special secret, for very special reasons. You, Percy, Bill Haydon and Roy Bland. You four are the magic circle. Right? Now let's just speculate about how it works, in detail. There's a house, we know that. All the same, meetings there are very elaborately arranged, we can be sure of that, can't we? Who meets him, Toby? Who has the handling of Polyakov? You? Roy? Bill?'

Taking the fat end of his tie, Smiley turned the silk lining outwards and began polishing his glasses. 'Everyone does,' he said, answering his own question. 'How's that? Sometimes Percy meets him. I would guess Percy represents the authoritarian side with him: "Isn't it time you took a holiday? Have you heard from your wife this week?" Percy would be good at that. But the Witchcraft committee uses Percy sparingly. Percy's the big gun and he must have rarity value. Then there's Bill Haydon; Bill meets him. That would happen more often, I think. Bill's impressive on Russia and he has entertainment value. I have a feeling that he and Polyakov would hit it off pretty well. I would think Bill shone when it came to the briefing and the follow-up questions, wouldn't you? Making certain that the right messages went to Moscow? Sometimes he takes Roy Bland with him, sometimes he sends Roy on his own. I expect that's something they work out between themselves. And Roy of course is an economic expert, as well as top man on satellites, so there'll be lots to talk about in that department also. And sometimes – I imagine birthdays, Toby, or at Christmas, or special presentations of thanks and money – there's a small fortune written down to entertainment, I notice, let alone bounties – sometimes, to make the party go, you all four trot along, and raise your glasses to the king across the water: to Merlin, through his envoy, Polyakov. Finally I suppose Toby himself has things to talk to friend Polyakov about. There's tradecraft to discuss, there are the useful snippets about goings-on inside the Embassy, which are so handy to the lamplighters in their bread-and-butter surveillance operations against the residency. So Toby also has his solo sessions. After all, we shouldn't overlook Polyakov's local potential, quite apart from his role as Merlin's London representative. It's not every day we have a tame Soviet diplomat in London eating out of our hands. A little training with a camera and Polyakov could be very useful just at the straight domestic level. Provided we all remember our priorities.'

His gaze had not left Toby's face. 'I can imagine that Polyakov might run to quite a few reels of film, can't you? And that one of the jobs of whoever was seeing him might be to replenish his stock: take him little sealed packets. Packets of film. Unexposed film, of course, since it came from the Circus. Tell me Toby, could you please, is Lapin a name to you?'

A lick, a frown, a smile, a forward movement of the head: 'Sure, George, I know Lapin.'

'Who ordered the lamplighter reports on Lapin destroyed?'

'I did, George.'

'On your own initiative?'

The smile broadened a fraction. 'Listen, George, I made some rungs up the ladder these days.'

'Who said Connie Sachs had to be pushed downhill?'

'Look I think it was Percy, okay? Say it was Percy, maybe Bill. You know how it is in a big operation. Shoes to mend, pots to clean, always a thing going.' He shrugged. 'Maybe it was Roy, huh?'

'So you take orders from all of them,' said Smiley lightly. 'That's very indiscriminate of you, Toby. You should know better.'

Esterhase didn't like that at all.

'Who told you to cool off Max, Toby? Was it the same three people? Only I have to report all this to Lacon, you see. He's being awfully pressing just at the moment. He seems to have the Minister on his back. Who was it?'

'George, you been talking to the wrong guys.'

'One of us has,' Smiley agreed pleasantly. 'That's for sure. They also want to know about Westerby: just who put the muzzle on him. Was it the same person who sent you down to Sarratt with a thousand quid in notes and a brief to put Jim Prideaux's mind at rest? It's only facts I'm after, Toby, not scalps. You know me, I'm not the vindictive sort. Anyway, what's to say you're not a very loyal fellow? It's just a question of who to.' He added: 'Only they do badly want to know, you see. There's even some ugly talk of calling in the competition. Nobody wants that, do they? It's like going to solicitors when you've had a row with your wife: an irrevocable step. Who gave you the message for Jim about Tinker, Tailor? Did you know what it meant? Did you have it straight from Polyakov, was that it ?'

'For God's sake,' Guillam whispered. 'Let me sweat the bastard.'

Smiley ignored him. 'Let's keep talking about Lapin. What was his job over here?'

'He worked for Polyakov.'

'His secretary in the cultural department?'

'His legman.'

'But my dear Toby: what on earth is a cultural attaché doing with his own legman?'

Esterhase's eyes were on Smiley all the time. He's like a dog, thought Guillam, he doesn't know whether to expect a kick or a bone. They flickered from Smiley's face to his hands, then back to his face, constantly checking the tell-tale places.

'Don't be damn silly, George,' Toby said carelessly. 'Polyakov is working for Moscow Centre. You know that as well as I do.' He crossed his little legs and, with a resurgence of all his former insolence, sat back in his chair and took a sip of cold tea.

Whereas Smiley, to Guillam's eye, appeared momentarily set back; from which Guillam in his confusion drily inferred that he was doubtless very pleased with himself. Perhaps because Toby was at last doing the talking.

'Come on, George,' Toby said. 'You're not a child. Think how many operations we ran this way. We buy Polyakov, okay? Polyakov's a Moscow hood but he's our Joe. But he's got to pretend to his own people that he's spying on us. How else does he get away with it? How does he walk in and out of that house all day, no gorillas, no babysitters, everything so easy? He comes down to our shop so he got to take home the goodies. So we give him goodies. Chickenfeed, so he can pass it home and everyone in Moscow clap him on the back and tell him he's a big guy, happens every day.'

If Guillam's head by now was reeling with a kind of furious awe, Smiley's seemed remarkably clear.

'And that's pretty much the standard story, is it, among the four initiated?'

'Well, standard I wouldn't know,' said Esterhase, with a very Hungarian movement of the hand, a spreading of the palm and a tilting either way.

'So who is Polyakov's agent?'

The question, Guillam saw, mattered very much to Smiley: he had played the whole long hand in order to arrive at it. As Guillam waited, his eyes now on Esterhase, who was by no means so confident any more, now on Smiley's mandarin face, he realized that he too was beginning to understand the shape of Karla's clever knot, as Smiley had called it – and of his own gruelling interview with Alleline.

'What I'm asking you is very simple,' Smiley insisted. 'Notionally, who is Polyakov's agent inside the Circus? Good heavens, Toby, don't be obtuse. If Polyakov's cover for meeting you people is that he is spying on the Circus, then he must have a Circus spy, mustn't he? So who is he? He can't come back to the Embassy after a meeting with you people, loaded with reels of Circus chickenfeed, and say, "I got this from the boys." There has to be a story, and a good one at that: a whole history of courtship, recruitment, clandestine meetings, money and motive. Doesn't there? Heavens, this isn't just

Polyakov's cover story: it's his lifeline. It's got to be thorough. It's got to be
convincing; I'd say it was a very big issue in the game. So who is he?' Smiley
enquired pleasantly. 'You? Toby Esterhase masquerades as a Circus traitor in
order to keep Polyakov in business? My hat, Toby, that's worth a whole
handful of medals.'

They waited while Toby thought.

'You're on a damn long road, George,' Toby said at last. 'What happens you
don't reach the other end?'

'Even with Lacon behind me?'

'You bring Lacon here. Percy, too; Bill. Why you come to the little guy? Go
to the big ones, pick on them.'

'I thought you *were* a big guy these days. You'd be a good choice for the part,
Toby. Hungarian ancestry, resentment about promotion, reasonable access
but not too much . . . quick-witted, likes money . . . with you as his agent,
Polyakov would have a cover story that really sits up and works. The big three
give you the chickenfeed, you hand it to Polyakov, Centre thinks Toby is all
theirs, everyone's served, everyone's content. The only problem arises when
it transpires that you've been handing Polyakov the crown jewels and getting
Russian chickenfeed in return. If that *should* turn out to be the case, you're
going to need pretty good friends. Like us. That's how my thesis runs – just to
complete it. That Gerald is a Russian mole, run by Karla. And he's pulled the
Circus inside out.'

Esterhase looked slightly ill. 'George, listen. If you're wrong, I don't want
to be wrong too, get me?'

'But if he's right you want to be right,' Guillam suggested, in a rare
interruption. 'And the sooner you're right the happier you'll be.'

'Sure,' said Toby, quite unaware of any irony. 'Sure. I mean George you got
a nice idea, but Jesus, there's two sides to everyone, George, agents specially,
and maybe it's you who got the wrong one. Listen: who ever called Witchcraft
chicken-feed? No one. Never. It's the best. You get one guy with a big mouth
starts shooting the dirt, and you dug up half London already. Get me? Look,
I do what they tell me. Okay? They say act the stooge for Polyakov, I act him.
Pass him this film, I pass it. I'm in a very dangerous situation,' he explained.
'For me, very dangerous indeed.'

'I'm sorry about that,' said Smiley at the window, where through a chink in
the curtain he was once more studying the square. 'Must be worrying for you.'

'Extremely,' Toby agreed, 'I get ulcers, can't eat. Very bad predicament.'

For a moment to Guillam's fury they were all three joined in a sympathetic
silence over Toby Esterhase's bad predicament.

'Toby, you wouldn't be lying about those babysitters, would you?' Smiley
enquired, still from the window.

'George, I cross my heart, I swear you.'

'What would you use for a job like this? Cars?'

'Pavement artists. Put a bus back by the air terminal, walk them through,
turn 'em over.'

'How many?'

'Eight, ten. This time of year six maybe. We got a lot ill. Christmas,' he said
morosely.

'And one man alone?'

'Never. You crazy. One man! You think I run a toffee shop these days?'

Leaving the window, Smiley sat down again.

'Listen, George, that's a terrible idea you got there, you know that? I'm a patriotic fellow: Jesus,' Toby repeated.

'What is Polyakov's job in the London residency?' Smiley asked.

'Polly works solo.'

'Running his master spy inside the Circus?'

'Sure. They take him off regular work, give him a free hand so's he can handle Toby, master spy. We work it all out, hours on end I sit with him. "Listen," I say. "Bill is suspecting me, my wife is suspecting me, my kid got measles and I can't pay the doctor." All the crap that agents give you, I give it to Polly, so's he can pass it home for real.'

'And who's Merlin?'

Esterhase shook his head.

'But at least you've heard he's based in Moscow,' Smiley said. 'And a member of the Soviet Intelligence establishment, whatever else he isn't?'

'That much they tell me,' Esterhase agreed.

'Which is how Polyakov can communicate with him. In the Circus's interest of course. Secretly, without his own people becoming suspicious?'

'Sure,' Toby resumed his lament, but Smiley seemed to be listening to sounds that were not in the room.

'And Tinker, Tailor?'

'I don't know what the hell it is. I do what Percy tell me.'

'And Percy told you to square Jim Prideaux?'

'Sure. Maybe was Bill, or Roy maybe; listen, it was Roy. I got to eat, George, understand? I don't cut my throat two ways, follow me?'

'It is the perfect fix: you see that, don't you, Toby, really?' Smiley remarked in a quiet, rather distant way. 'Assuming it *is* a fix. It makes everyone wrong who's right: Connie Sachs, Jerry Westerby . . . Jim Prideaux . . . even Control. Silences the doubters before they've even spoken out . . . the permutations are infinite, once you've brought off the basic lie. Moscow Centre must be allowed to think she has an important Circus source; Whitehall on no account must get wind of the same notion. Take it to its logical conclusion and Gerald would have us strangling our own children in their beds. It would be beautiful in another context,' he remarked almost dreamily. 'Poor Toby: yes, I do see. What a time you must have been having, running between them all.'

Toby had his next speech ready: 'Naturally if there is anything I can do of a practical nature, you know me, George, I am always pleased to help, no trouble. My boys are pretty well trained, you want to borrow them, maybe we can work a deal. Naturally I have to speak to Lacon first. All I want, I want to get this thing cleared up. For the sake of the Circus, you know. That's all I want. The good of the firm. I'm a modest man, I don't want anything for myself, okay?'

'Where's this safe house you keep exclusively for Polyakov?'

'Five, Lock Gardens, Camden Town.'

'With a caretaker?'

'Mrs McCraig.'

'Lately a listener?'

'Sure.'

'Is there built-in audio?'

'What you think?'

'So Millie McCraig keeps house and mans the recording instruments.'

She did, said Toby, ducking his head with great alertness.

'In a minute I want you to telephone her and tell her I'm staying the night and I'll want to use the equipment. Tell her I've been called in on a special job and she's to do whatever I ask. I'll be round about nine. What's the procedure for contacting Polyakov if you want a crash meeting?'

'My boys have a room on Haverstock Hill. Polly drives past the window each morning on the way to the Embassy, each night going home. If they put up a yellow poster protesting against traffic, that's the signal.'

'And at night? At weekends?'

'Wrong number phone call. But nobody likes that.'

'Has it ever been used?'

'I don't know.'

'You mean you don't listen to his phone?'

No answer.

'I want you to take the weekend off. Would that raise eyebrows at the Circus?' Enthusiastically, Esterhase shook his head. 'I'm sure you'd prefer to be out of it anyway, wouldn't you?' Esterhase nodded. 'Say you're having girl trouble or whatever sort of trouble you're in these days. You'll be spending the night here, possibly two. Fawn will look after you, there's food in the kitchen. What about your wife?'

While Guillam and Smiley looked on, Esterhase dialled the Circus and asked for Phil Porteous. He said his lines perfectly: a little self-pity, a little conspiracy, a little joke. Some girl who was passionate about him up north, Phil, and threatening wild things if he didn't go and hold her hand.

'Don't tell me, I know it happens to you every day, Phil. Hey, how's that gorgeous new secretary of yours? And listen, Phil, if Mara phones from home, tell her Toby's on a big job, okay? Blowing up the Kremlin, back on Monday. Make it nice and heavy, huh? Cheers, Phil.'

He rang off and dialled a number in north London. 'Mrs M., hullo, this is your favourite boyfriend, recognize the voice? Good. Listen I'm sending you a visitor tonight, an old, old friend, you'll be surprised. She hates me,' he explained to them, his hand over the mouthpiece. 'He wants to check the wiring,' he went on. 'Look it all over, make sure it's working okay, no bad leaks, all right?'

'If he's any trouble,' Guillam said to Fawn with real venom as they left, 'bind him hand and foot.'

In the stairwell, Smiley lightly touched his arm. 'Peter, I want you to watch my back. Will you do that for me? Give me a couple of minutes, then pick me up on the corner of Marloes Road, heading north. Stick to the west pavement.'

Guillam waited, then stepped into the street. A thin drizzle lay on the air, which had an eerie warmness like a thaw. Where lights shone, the moisture shifted in fine clouds, but in shadow he neither saw nor felt it: simply, a mist blurred his vision, making him half-close his eyes. He completed one round of the gardens then entered a pretty mews well south of the pick-up point. Reaching Marloes Road he crossed to the western pavement, bought an 002evening paper and began walking at a leisurely rate past villas set in deep gardens. He was counting off pedestrians, cyclists, cars, while out ahead of him, steadily plodding the far pavement he picked out George Smiley, the very prototype of the homegoing Londoner. 'Is it a team?' Guillam had asked. Smiley could not be specific. 'Short of Abingdon Villas, I'll cross over,' he said. 'Look for a solo. But look!'

As Guillam watched, Smiley pulled up abruptly, as if he had just remembered something, stepped perilously into the road and scuttled between the angry traffic to disappear at once through the doors of an off licence. As he did so, Guillam saw, or thought he saw, a tall crooked figure in a dark coat step out after him, but at that moment a bus drew up, screening both Smiley and his pursuer; and when it pulled away, it must have taken his pursuer with it, for the only survivor on that strip of pavement was an older man in a black plastic raincoat and cloth cap lolling at the bus-stop while he read his evening paper; and when Smiley emerged from the off licence with his brown bag, he did not so much as lift his head from the sporting pages. For a short while longer, Guillam trailed Smiley through the smarter reaches of Victorian Kensington as he slipped from one quiet square to another, sauntered into a mews and out again by the same route. Only once, when Guillam forgot Smiley and out of instinct turned upon his own tracks, did he have a suspicion of a third figure walking with them: a fanged shadow thrown against the broadloom brickwork of an empty street, but when he started forward, it was gone.

The night had its own madness after that; events ran too quickly for him to fasten on them singly. Not till days afterwards did he realize that the figure, or the shadow of it, had struck a chord of familiarity in his memory. Even then, for some time, he could not place it. Then one early morning, waking abruptly, he had it clear in his mind: a barking, military voice, a gentleness of manner heavily concealed, a squash racquet jammed behind the safe of his room in Brixton, which brought tears to the eyes of his unemotional secretary.

# THIRTY-FIVE

Probably the only thing which Steve Mackelvore did wrong that same evening, in terms of classic tradecraft, was blame himself for leaving the passenger door of his car unlocked. Climbing in from the driver's side, he put it down to his own negligence that the other lock was up. Survival, as Jim Prideaux liked to recall, is an infinite capacity for suspicion. By that purist standard Mackelvore should have suspected that in the middle of a particularly vile rush-hour, on a particularly vile evening, in one of those blaring side-streets that feed into the lower end of the Elysées, Ricki Tarr would unlock the passenger door and hold him up at gunpoint. But life in the Paris residency these days did little to keep a man's wits sharp, and most of Mackelvore's working day had been taken up with filing his weekly expenses and completing his weekly returns of staff for the housekeepers. Only lunch, a longish affair with an insecure anglophile in the French security labyrinth, had broken the monotony of that Friday.

His car, parked under a lime tree that was dying of exhaust fumes, had an extra-territorial registration and CC pasted on the back, for the residency cover was consular though no one took it seriously. Mackelvore was a Circus elder, a squat, white-haired Yorkshireman with a long record of consular appointments which in the eyes of the world had brought him no advancement. Paris was the last of them. He did not care particularly for Paris, and he knew from an operational lifetime in the Far East that the French were not for him. But as a prelude to retirement it could not be bettered. The allowances were good, the billet was comfortable, and the most that had been asked of him in the ten months he had been here was to welfare the occasional agent in transit, put up a chalkmark here and there, play postman to some ploy by London Station, and show a time to the visiting firemen.

Until now, that was, as he sat in his own car with Tarr's gun jammed against his rib-cage, and Tarr's hand resting affectionately on his right shoulder, ready to wrench his head off if he tried any monkey business. A couple of feet away, girls hurried past on their way to the Metro and six feet beyond that the traffic had come to a standstill: it could stay that way for an hour. None was faintly stirred by the sight of two men having a cosy chat in a parked car.

Tarr had been talking ever since Mackelvore sat down. He needed to send a message to Alleline, he said. It would be personal and decypher yourself and Tarr would like Steve to work the machine for him while Tarr stood off with the gun.

'What the hell have you been up to, Ricki?' Mackelvore complained, as they walked arm in arm back to the residency. 'The whole Service is looking for you, you know that, don't you? They'll skin you alive if they find you. We're supposed to do bloodcurdling things to you on sight.'

He thought of turning into the hold and smacking Tarr's neck but he knew he hadn't the speed, and Tarr would kill him.

The message would run to about two hundred groups, said Tarr, as Mackelvore unlocked the front door and put on the lights. When Steve had transmitted them they would sit on the machine and wait for Percy's answer. By tomorrow, if Tarr's instinct was correct, Percy would be coming over to Paris hot-foot to have a conference with Ricki. This conference would also take place in the residency, because Tarr reckoned it was marginally less likely that the Russians would try to kill him on British consular premises.

'You're berserk, Ricki. It's not the Russians who want to kill you. It's us.'

The front room was called Reception, it was what remained of the cover. It had an old wooden counter and out of date Notices to British Subjects hanging on the grimy wall. Here, with his left hand, Tarr searched Mackelvore for a weapon but found none. It was a courtyard house and most of the sensitive stuff was across the yard: the cypher room, the strong room and the machines.

'You're out of your mind, Ricki,' Mackelvore warned monotonously, as he led the way through a couple of empty offices and pressed the bell to the cypher room. 'You always thought you were Napoleon Bonaparte and now it's got you completely. You'd too much religion from your Dad.'

The steel message hatch slid back and a mystified, slightly silly face appeared in the opening. 'You can go home, Ben boy. Go home to your missus but stay close to your phone in case I need you, there's a lad. Leave the books where they are and put the keys in the machines. I'll be talking to London presently, under my own steam.'

The face withdrew and they waited while the boy unlocked the door from inside: one key, two keys, a spring lock.

'This gentleman's from out East, Ben,' Mackelvore explained as the door opened. 'He's one of my most distinguished connections.'

'Hullo, sir,' said Ben. He was a tall, mathematical-looking boy with spectacles and an unblinking gaze.

'Get along with you, Ben. I'll not dock it against your duty pay. You've the weekend free on full rates, and you'll not owe me time either. Off you go, then.'

'Ben stays here,' said Tarr.

In Cambridge Circus the lighting was quite yellow and from where Mendel stood, on the third floor of the clothes shop, the wet tarmac glistened like cheap gold. It was nearly midnight and he had been standing three hours. He stood between a net curtain and a clothes-horse. He stood the way coppers stand the world over, weight on both feet equally, legs straight, leaning slightly backward over the line of balance. He had pulled his hat low and turned up his collar to keep the white of his face from the street, but his eyes as they watched the front entrance below him glittered like a cat's eyes in a coal hole. He would wait another three hours or another six: Mendel was back on the beat, the scent of the hunt was in his nostrils. Better still, he was a night bird; the darkness of that fitting room woke him wonderfully. Such light as reached him from the street lay upside down in pale pieces on the ceiling. All the rest, the cutting benches, the bolts of cloth, the draped machines, the steam iron, the signed photographs of princes of the blood, these were there because he had seen them on his reconnaissance that afternoon; the light did not reach them and even now he could barely make them out.

From his window he covered most of the approaches: eight or nine unequal roads and alleys which for no good reason had chosen Cambridge Circus as their meeting point. Between them, the buildings were gimcrack, cheaply fitted out with bits of empire: a Roman bank, a theatre like a vast desecrated mosque. Behind them, high-rise blocks advanced like an army of robots. Above, a pink sky was slowly filling with fog.

Why was it so quiet? he wondered. The theatre had long emptied but why didn't the pleasure trade of Soho, only a stone's throw from his window, fill the place with taxis, groups of loiterers? Not a single fruit lorry had rumbled down Shaftesbury Avenue on its way to Covent Garden.

Through his binoculars Mendel once more studied the building straight across the road from him. It seemed to sleep even more soundly than its neighbours. The twin doors of the portico were closed and no light was visible in the ground floor windows. Only on the fourth floor, out of the second window from the left, a pale glow issued and Mendel knew it was the duty officer's room, Smiley had told him. Briefly he raised the glasses to the roof, where a plantation of aerials made wild patterns against the sky; then down a floor to the four blackened windows of the radio section.

'At night everyone uses the front door,' Guillam had said. 'It's an economy measure to cut down on janitors.'

In those three hours, only three events had rewarded Mendel's vigil: one an hour is not much. At half past nine a blue Ford Transit delivered two men carrying what looked like an ammunition box. They unlocked the door for themselves and closed it as soon as they were inside, while Mendel murmured his commentary into the telephone. At ten o'clock the shuttle arrived:

Guillam had warned him of this too. The shuttle collected hot documents from the out-stations and stored them for safekeeping at the Circus over the weekend. It called at Brixton, Acton and Sarratt in that order, said Guillam, lastly at the Admiralty, and it made the Circus by about ten. In the event it arrived on the dot of ten, and this time two men from inside the building came out to help unload; Mendel reported that too, and Smiley acknowledged with a patient 'thank you'.

Was Smiley sitting down? Was he in the darkness like Mendel? Mendel had a notion he was. Of all the odd coves he had known, Smiley was the oddest. You thought, to look at him, that he couldn't cross the road alone, but you might as well have offered protection to a hedgehog. Funnies, Mendel mused. A lifetime of chasing villains and how do I end up? Breaking and entering, standing in the dark and spying on the Funnies. He'd never held with Funnies till he met Smiley. Thought they were an interfering lot of amateurs and college boys; thought they were unconstitutional; thought the best thing the Branch could do, for its own sake and the public's, was say 'yes, sir, no, sir' and lose the correspondence. Come to think of it, with the notable exception of Smiley and Guillam, that's exactly what he thought tonight.

Shortly before eleven, just an hour ago, a cab arrived. A plain licensed London hackney cab, and it drew up at the theatre. Even that was something Smiley had warned him about: it was the habit within the service not to take taxis to the door. Some stopped at Foyles, some in Old Compton Street or at one of the shops; most people had a favourite cover destination and Alleline's was the theatre. Mendel had never seen Alleline but he had their description of him and as he watched him through the glasses he recognized him without a doubt, a big, lumbering fellow in a dark coat, even noticed how the cabby had pulled a bad face at his tip and called something after him as Alleline delved for his keys.

The front door is not secured, Guillam had explained, it is only locked. The security begins inside once you have turned left at the end of the corridor. Alleline lives on the fifth floor. You won't see his windows light up but there's a skylight and the glow should catch the chimney stack. Sure enough, as he watched, a patch of yellow appeared on the grimy brickwork of the chimney: Alleline had entered his room.

And young Guillam needs a holiday, thought Mendel. He'd seen *that* happen before, too: the tough ones who crack at forty. They lock it away, pretend it isn't there, lean on grown-ups who turn out not to be so grown up after all, then one day it's all over them, and their heroes come tumbling down and they're sitting at their desks with the tears pouring on to the blotter.

He had laid the receiver on the floor. Picking it up, he said: 'Looks like Tinker's clocked in.'

He gave the number of the cab, then went back to waiting.

'How did he look?' Smiley murmured.

'Busy,' said Mendel.

'So he should be.'

That one won't crack, though, Mendel decided with approval; one of your flabby oak trees, Smiley was. Think you could blow him over with one puff but when it comes to the storm he's the only one left standing at the end of it. At this point in his reflections a second cab drew up, squarely at the front entrance, and a tall slow figure cautiously climbed the steps one at a time like a man who takes care of his heart.

'Here's your Tailor,' Mendel murmured into the telephone. 'Hold on, here's Soldier-boy too. Proper gathering of the clans by the look of it. I say, take it easy.'

An old Mercedes 190 shot out of Earlham Street, swung directly beneath his window, and held the curve with difficulty as far as the northern outlet of the Charing Cross Road, where it parked. A young heavy fellow with ginger hair clambered out, slammed the door and clumped across the street to the entrance without taking the key out of the dash. A moment later another light went up on the fourth floor as Roy Bland joined the party.

All we need to know now is who comes out, thought Mendel.

# THIRTY-SIX

Lock Gardens, which presumably drew its name from the Camden and Hampstead Road Locks nearby, was a terrace of four flat-fronted 19th century houses built at the centre of a crescent, each with three floors and a basement and a strip of walled back garden running down to the Regent's Canal. The numbers ran two to five: number one had either fallen down or never been built. Number five made up the north end and as a safe house it could not have been improved, for there were three approaches in thirty yards and the canal towpath offered two more. To the north lay Camden High Street for joining traffic; south and west lay the parks and Primrose Hill. Better still, the neighbourhood possessed no social identity and demanded none. Some of the houses had been turned into one-roomed flats, and had ten door bells laid out like a typewriter. Some were got up grandly and had only one. Number five had two: one for Millie McCraig and one for her lodger Mr Jefferson.

Mrs McCraig was churchy and collected for everything, which was incidentally an excellent way of keeping an eye on the locals, though that was scarcely how they viewed her zeal. Jefferson, her lodger, was known vaguely to be foreign and in oil and away a lot. Lock Gardens was his *pied-à-terre*. The neighbours, when they bothered to notice him, found him shy and respectable. They would have formed the same impression of George Smiley if they happened to spot him in the dim light of the porch at nine that evening as Millie McCraig admitted him to her front room and drew the pious curtains.

She was a wiry Scottish widow with brown stockings and bobbed hair and the polished, wrinkled skin of an old man. In the interest of God and the Circus she had run Bible Schools in Mozambique and a seaman's mission in Hamburg and though she had been a professional eavesdropper for twenty years since then, she was still inclined to treat all menfolk as transgressors.

Smiley had no way of telling what she thought. Her manner, from the moment he arrived, had a deep and lonely stillness; she showed him round the house like a châtelaine whose guests had long since died.

First the semi-basement where she lived herself, full of plants and that medley of old postcards, brass table tops and carved black furniture which seems to attach itself to travelled British ladies of a certain age and class. Yes, if the Circus wanted her at night they rang her on the basement phone. Yes, there was a separate line upstairs, but it was only for outgoing calls. The basement phone had an extension in the upstairs dining room. Then up to the ground floor, a veritable shrine to the costly bad taste of the house-keepers: loud Regency stripes, gilded reproduction chairs, plush sofas with roped corners. The kitchen was untouched and squalid. Beyond it lay a glass outhouse, half conservatory, half scullery, which looked down to the rough garden and the canal. Strewn over the tiled floor: an old mangle, a copper and crates of tonic water.

'Where are the mikes, Millie?' Smiley had returned to the drawing room.

They were in pairs, Millie murmured, bedded behind the wallpaper, two pairs to each room on the ground floor, one to each room upstairs. Each pair was connected with a separate recorder. He followed her up the steep stairs. The top floor was unfurnished, save for an attic bedroom which contained a grey steel frame with eight tape machines, four up, four down.

'And Jefferson knows all about this?'

'Mr Jefferson,' said Millie primly, 'is run on a basis of trust.' That was the nearest she came to expressing her disapproval of Smiley, or her devotion to Christian ethics.

Downstairs again, she showed him the switches which controlled the system. An extra switch was fitted in each finger panel. Any time Jefferson or one of the boys, as she put it, wanted to go over to record, he had only to get up and turn down the left-hand light switch. From then on, the system was voice-activated; that is to say, the tape-deck did not turn unless somebody was speaking.

'And where are you while all this goes on, Millie?'

She remained downstairs, she said, as if that were a woman's place.

Smiley was pulling open cupboards, lockers, walking from room to room. Then back to the scullery again, with its view to the canal. Taking out a pocket torch he signalled one flash into the darkness of the garden.

'What are the safety procedures?' Smiley asked, as he thoughtfully fingered the end light switch by the drawing-room door.

Her reply came in a liturgical monotone: 'Two full milk bottles on the doorstep, you may come in and all's well. No milk bottles and you're not to enter.'

From the direction of the sunroom came a faint tapping. Returning to the scullery Smiley opened the glazed door and after a hastily murmured conversation reappeared with Guillam.

'You know Peter, don't you, Millie?'

Millie might, she might not, her little hard eyes had fixed on him with scorn. He was studying the switch panel, feeling in his pocket as he did so.

'What's he doing? He's not to do that. Stop him.'

If she was worried, said Smiley, she should ring Lacon on the basement phone. Millie McCraig didn't stir, but two red bruises had appeared on her leathery cheeks and she was snapping her fingers in anger. With a small screwdriver Guillam had cautiously removed the screws from either side of the plastic panel, and was peering at the wiring behind. Now, very carefully, he turned the end switch upside down, twisting it on its wires, then screwed the plate back in position, leaving the remaining switches undisturbed.

'We'll just try it,' said Guillam, and while Smiley went upstairs to check the tape deck, Guillam sang 'Old Man River' in a low Paul Robeson growl.

'Thank you,' said Smiley with a shudder, coming down again, 'that's more than enough.'

Millie had gone to the basement to ring Lacon. Quietly, Smiley set the stage. He put the telephone beside an armchair in the drawing room, then cleared his line of retreat to the scullery. He fetched two bottles of milk from the Coca-Cola ice-box in the kitchen and placed them on the doorstep to signify, in the eclectic language of Millie McCraig, that you may come in and all's well. He removed his shoes and left them in the scullery, and having put out all the lights, took up his post in the armchair just as Mendel made his connecting call.

On the canal towpath, meanwhile, Guillam had resumed his vigil of the house. The footpath is closed to the public one hour before dark: after that it can be anything from a trysting place for lovers to a haven for down and outs; both, for different reasons, are attracted by the darkness of the bridges. That cold night Guillam saw neither. Occasionally an empty train raced past, leaving a still greater emptiness behind. His nerves were so taut, his expectations so varied, that for a moment he saw the whole architecture of that night in apocalyptic terms: the signals on the railway bridge turned to gallows, the Victorian warehouses to gigantic prisons, their windows barred and arched against the misty sky. Closer at hand, the ripple of rats and the stink of still water. Then the drawing room lights went out; the house stood in darkness except for the chinks of yellow to either side of Millie's basement window. From the scullery a pin of light winked at him down the unkempt garden. Taking a pen torch from his pocket he slipped out the silver hood, sighted it with shaking fingers at the point from which the light had come, and signalled back. From now on they could only wait.

Tarr tossed the incoming telegram back to Ben, together with the one-time pad from the safe.

'Come on,' he said, 'earn your pay. Unbutton it.'

'It's personal for you,' Ben objected. 'Look. "Personal from Alleline decypher yourself." I'm not allowed to touch it. It's the tops.'

'Do as he asks, Ben,' said Mackelvore, watching Tarr.

For ten minutes no word passed between the three men. Tarr was standing across the room from them, very nervous from the waiting. He had jammed the gun in his waistband, butt inward to the groin. His jacket lay over a chair. The sweat had stuck his shirt to his back all the way down. Ben was using a ruler to read off the number groups, then carefully writing his findings on the block of graph paper before him. To concentrate he put his tongue against his teeth, and now he made a small click as he withdrew it. Putting aside his pencil, he offered Tarr the tearsheet.

'Read it aloud,' Tarr said.

Ben's voice was kindly, and a little fervent. '"Personal for Tarr from Alleline decypher yourself. I positively require clarification and/or trade samples before meeting your request. Quote information vital to safeguarding of the Service unquote does not qualify. Let me remind you of your bad position here following your disgraceful disappearance stop urge you confide Mackelvore immediately repeat immediately stop Chief.'"

Ben had not quite finished before Tarr began laughing in a strange, excited way.

'That's the way, Percy boy!' he cried. 'Yes repeat no! Know why he's stalling, Ben, darling? He's sizing up to shoot me in the bloody back! That's how he got my Russki girl. He's playing the same tune, the bastard.' He was ruffling Ben's hair, shouting at him, laughing 'I warn you Ben: there's some damn lousy people in this outfit, so don't you trust the one of them, I'm telling you, or you'll never grow up strong!'

Alone in the darkness of the drawing room Smiley also waited, sitting in the housekeeper's uncomfortable chair, his head propped awkwardly against the earpiece of the telephone. Occasionally he would mutter something and Mendel would mutter back, most of the time they shared the silence. His mood was subdued, even a little glum. Like an actor he had a sense of approaching anti-climax before the curtain went up, a sense of great things dwindling to a small, mean end; as death itself seemed small and mean to him after the struggles of his life. He had no sense of conquest that he knew of. His thoughts, as often when he was afraid, concerned people. He had no theories or judgments in particular. He simply wondered how everyone would be affected; and he felt responsible. He thought of Jim and Sam and Max and Connie and Jerry Westerby and personal loyalties all broken; in a separate category he thought of Ann and the hopeless dislocation of their talk on the Cornish cliffs; he wondered whether there was any love between human beings that did not rest upon some sort of self-delusion; he wished he could just get up and walk out before it happened, but he couldn't. He worried, in a quite paternal way, about Guillam, and wondered how he would take the late strains of growing up. He thought again of the day he buried Control. He thought about treason and wondered whether there was mind-less treason in the same way, supposedly, as there was mindless violence. It worried him that he felt so bankrupt; that whatever intellectual or philoso-phical precepts he clung to broke down entirely now that he was faced with the human situation.

'Anything?' he asked Mendel, into the telephone.

'A couple of drunks,' said Mendel, 'singing "see the jungle when it's wet with rain".'

'Never heard of it.'

Changing the telephone to his left side he drew the gun from the wallet pocket of his jacket, where it had already ruined the excellent silk lining. He discovered the safety catch and for a moment played with the idea that he didn't know which way was on and which way off. He snapped out the magazine and put it back, and remembered doing this hundreds of times on the trot, in the night range at Sarratt before the war; he remembered how you always shot with two hands, sir, one to hold the gun and one the magazine, sir; and how there was a piece of Circus folklore which demanded that he should lay his finger along the barrel and pull the trigger with his second. But when he tried it the sensation was ridiculous and he forgot about it.

'Just taking a walk,' he murmured, and Mendel said, 'Righty ho.'

The gun still in his hand he returned to the scullery, listening for a creak in the floorboards that might give him away, but the floor must have been concrete under the tatty carpet; he could have jumped and caused not even a vibration. With his torch he signalled two short flashes, a long delay then two more. At once Guillam replied with three short.

'Back again.'

'Got you,' said Mendel.

He settled, thinking glumly of Ann: to dream the impossible dream. He put the gun in his pocket. From the canal side, the moan of a hooter. At night? Boats moving at night? Must be a car. What if Gerald has a whole emergency procedure which we know nothing about? A callbox to callbox, a car pick-up? What if Polyakov has after all a legman, a helper whom Connie never identified. He'd been through that already. This system was built to be watertight, to accommodate meetings in all contingencies. When it comes to tradecraft, Karla is a pedant.

And his fancy that he was being followed? What of that? What of the shadow he never saw, only felt, till his back seemed to tingle with the intensity of his watcher's gaze; he saw nothing, heard nothing, only felt. He was too old not to heed the warning. The creak of a stair that had not creaked before; the rustle of a shutter when no wind was blowing; the car with a different number plate but the same scratch on the offside wing: the face on the underground that you know you have seen somewhere before: for years at a time these were signs he had lived by; any one of them was reason enough to move, change towns, identities. For in that profession there is no such thing as coincidence.

'One gone,' said Mendel suddenly. 'Hullo?'

'I'm here.'

Somebody had just come out of the Circus, said Mendel. Front door but he couldn't be certain of the identification. Mackintosh and hat. Bulky and moving fast. Must have ordered a cab to the door and stepped straight into it.

'Heading north, your way.'

Smiley looked at his watch. Give him ten minutes, he thought. Give him twelve, he'll have to stop and phone Polyakov on the way. Then he thought: don't be silly, he's done that already from the Circus.

'I'm ringing off,' said Smiley.

'Cheers,' said Mendel.

On the footpath, Guillam read three long flashes. The mole is on his way.

In the scullery Smiley had once more checked his thoroughfare, shoved some deck chairs aside and pinned a string to the mangle to guide him because he saw badly in the dark. The string led to the open kitchen door, the kitchen led to the drawing room and dining room both, it had the two doors side by side. The kitchen was a long room, actually an annexe to the house before the glass scullery was added. He had thought of using the dining room but it was too risky and besides from the dining room he couldn't signal to Guillam. So he waited in the scullery, feeling absurd in his stockinged feet, polishing his spectacles because the heat of his face kept misting them. It was much colder in the scullery. The drawing room was close and overheated but the scullery had these outside walls, and this glass and this concrete floor beneath the matting, which made his feet feel wet. The mole arrives first, he thought, the mole plays host: that is protocol, part of the pretence that Polyakov is Gerald's agent.

A London taxi is a flying bomb.

The comparison rose in him slowly, from deep in his unconscious memory. The clatter as it barges into the crescent, the metric tick-tick as the bass notes die. The cut-off: where has it stopped, which house, when all of us in the street are waiting in the dark, crouching under tables or clutching pieces of string, which house? Then the slam of the door, the explosive anti-climax: if you can hear it, it's not for you.

But Smiley heard it, and it was for him.

He heard the tread of one pair of feet on the gravel, brisk and vigorous. They stopped. It's the wrong door, Smiley thought absurdly, go away. He had the gun in his hand, he had dropped the catch. Still he listened, heard nothing. You're suspicious, Gerald, he thought. You're an old mole, you can sniff there's something wrong. Millie, he thought: Millie has taken away the milk bottles, put up a warning, headed him off. Millie's spoilt the kill. Then he heard the latch turn, one turn, two, it's a Banham lock, he remembered, my God we must keep Banham's in business. Of course: the mole had been patting his pockets; looking for his key. A nervous man would have had it in his hand already, would have been clutching it, cossetting it in his pocket all the way in the taxi; but not the mole. The mole might be worried but he was not nervous. At the same moment as the latch turned, the bell chimed: housekeeper's taste again, high tone, low tone, high tone. That will mean it's one of us, Millie had said; one of the boys, her boys, Connie's boys, Karla's boys. The front door opened, someone stepped into the house, he heard the shuffle of the mat, he heard the door close, he heard the light switches snap and saw a pale line appear under the kitchen door. He put the gun in his pocket and wiped the palm of his hand on his jacket, then took it out again and in the same moment he heard a second flying bomb, a second taxi pulling up, and footsteps fast: Polyakov didn't just have the key ready, he had his taxi money ready too: do Russians tip, he wondered, or is tipping undemocratic? Again the bell rang, the front door opened and closed, and Smiley heard the double chink as two milk bottles were put on the hall table in the interest of good order and sound tradecraft.

Lord save me, thought Smiley in horror as he stared at the old Coca-Cola ice box beside him, it never crossed my mind: suppose he had wanted to put them back in the fridge?

The strip of light under the kitchen door suddenly brighter as the drawing room lights were switched on. An extraordinary stillness descended over the house. Holding the string, Smiley edged forwards over the icy floor. Then he heard voices. At first they were indistinct. Or perhaps they always begin in a low tone. Now Polyakov came nearer: he was at the trolley, pouring drinks.

'What is our cover story in case we are disturbed?' he asked in good English.

Lovely voice, Smiley remembered, mellow like yours, I often used to play the tapes twice just to hear him speaking. Connie you should hear him now.

From the further end of the room still, a muffled murmur answered each question. Smiley could make nothing of it. 'Where shall we regroup?' 'What is our fallback?' 'Have you anything on you that you would prefer me to be carrying during our talk, bearing in mind I have diplomatic immunity?'

It must be a catechism, Smiley thought, part of Karla's school routine.

'Is the switch down? Will you please check? Thank you. What will you drink?'

'Scotch,' said Haydon, 'a bloody great big one.'

With a feeling of utter disbelief, Smiley listened to the familiar voice reading aloud the very telegram which Smiley himself had drafted for Tarr's use only forty-eight hours ago.

Then for a moment one part of Smiley broke into open revolt against the other. The wave of angry doubt which had swept over him in Lacon's garden, and ever since had pulled against his progress like a worrying tide, drove him now on to the rocks of despair, and then to mutiny: I refuse. Nothing is worth the destruction of another human being. Somewhere the path of pain and betrayal must end. Until that happened, there was no future: there was only a continued slide into still more terrifying versions of the present. This man was my friend and Ann's lover, Jim's friend and for all I know Jim's lover too; it was the treason, not the man, that belonged to the public domain.

Haydon had betrayed. As a lover, a colleague, a friend; as a patriot; as a member of that inestimable body which Ann loosely called the Set: in every capacity, Haydon had overtly pursued one aim and secretly achieved its opposite. Smiley knew very well that even now he did not grasp the scope of that appalling duplicity; yet there was a part of him that rose already in Haydon's defence. Was not Bill also betrayed? Connie's lament rang in his ears: 'Poor loves. Trained to Empire, trained to rule the waves . . . You're the last, George, you and Bill.' He saw with painful clarity an ambitious man born to the big canvas, brought up to rule, divide and conquer, whose visions and vanities all were fixed, like Percy's, upon the world's game; for whom the reality was a poor island with scarcely a voice that would carry across the water. Thus Smiley felt not only disgust; but, despite all that the moment meant to him, a surge of resentment against the institutions he was supposed to be protecting: 'The social contract cuts both ways, you know,' said Lacon. The Minister's lolling mendacity, Lacon's tight-lipped moral complacency, the bludgeoning greed of Percy Alleline: such men invalidated any contract: why should anyone be loyal to them?

He knew, of course. He had always known it was Bill. Just as Control had known, and Lacon in Mendel's house. Just as Connie and Jim had known, and Alleline and Esterhase, all of them tacitly shared that unexpressed half-knowledge which like an illness they hoped would go away if it was never owned to, never diagnosed.

And Ann? Did Ann know? Was that the shadow that fell over them that day on the Cornish cliffs?

For a space, that was how Smiley stood: a fat, barefooted spy, as Ann would say, deceived in love and impotent in hate, clutching a gun in one hand, a bit of string in the other, as he waited in the darkness. Then, gun still in hand, he tiptoed backward as far as the window, from which he signalled five short flashes in quick succession. Having waited long enough to read the acknowledgment, he returned to his listening post.

Guillam raced down the canal tow-path, the torch jolting wildly in his hand, till he reached a low-arched bridge and a steel stairway which led upward in zigzags to Gloucester Avenue. The gate was closed and he had to climb it, ripping one sleeve to the elbow. Lacon was standing at the corner of Princess Road, wearing an old country coat and carrying a briefcase.

'He's there. He's arrived,' Guillam whispered. 'He's got Gerald.'

'I won't have bloodshed,' Lacon warned. 'I want absolute calm.'

Guillam didn't bother to reply. Thirty yards down the road Mendel was waiting in a tame cab. They drove for two minutes, not so much, and stopped the cab short of the crescent. Guillam was holding Esterhase's doorkey. Reaching number five, Mendel and Guillam stepped over the gate rather than risk the noise of it and kept to the grass verge. As they went, Guillam glanced back and thought for a moment he saw a figure watching them, man or woman he couldn't tell, from the shadow of a doorway across the road; but when he drew Mendel's attention to the spot there was nothing there, and Mendel ordered him quite roughly to calm down. The porch light was out. Guillam inserted the key, felt the lock ease as he turned it. Damn fool, he thought triumphantly, why didn't you drop the latch? He pushed open the door an inch and hesitated. He was breathing slowly, filling his lungs for action. Mendel moved forward another bound. In the street two young boys went by, laughing loudly because they were nervous of the night. Once more Guillam looked back but the crescent was clear. He stepped into the hall. He was wearing suède shoes and they squeaked on the parquet, there was no carpet. At the drawing room door he listened long enough for the fury to break in him at last.

His butchered agents in Morocco, his exile to Brixton, the daily frustration of his efforts as daily he grew older and youth slipped through his fingers; the drabness that was closing round him; the truncation of his power to love, enjoy and laugh; the constant erosion of the plain, heroic standards he wished to live by; the checks and stops he imposed on himself in the name of tacit dedication; he could fling them all in Haydon's sneering face. Haydon, once his confessor; Haydon, always good for a laugh, a chat and a cup of burnt coffee; Haydon, a model on which he built his life.

More, far more. Now that he saw, he knew. Haydon was more than his model, he was his inspiration, the torch-bearer of a certain kind of antiquated romanticism, a notion of English calling which – for the very reason that it was vague and understated and elusive – had made sense of Guillam's life till now. In that moment, Guillam felt not merely betrayed; but orphaned. His suspicions, his resentments for so long turned outwards on the real world – on his women, his attempted loves – now swung upon the Circus and the failed magic which had formed his faith. With all his force he shoved open the door and sprang inside, gun in hand. Haydon and a heavy man with a black forelock were seated either side of a small table. Polyakov – Guillam recognized him from the photographs – was smoking a very English pipe. He wore a grey cardigan with a zip down the front, like the top half of a track suit. He had not even taken the pipe from his mouth before Guillam had Haydon by the collar. With a single heave he lifted him straight out of his chair. He had thrown away his gun and was hurling Haydon from side to side, shaking him like a dog, shouting. Then suddenly there seemed no point. After all, it was only Bill and they had done a lot together. Guillam had drawn back long before Mendel took his arm, and he heard Smiley, politely as ever inviting 'Bill and Colonel Viktorov', as he called them, to raise their hands and place them on their heads till Percy Alleline arrived.

'There was no-one out there, was there, that you noticed?' Smiley asked of Guillam, while they waited.

'Quiet as the grave,' said Mendel, answering for both of them.

# THIRTY-SEVEN

There are moments which are made up of too much stuff for them to be lived at the time they occur. For Guillam and all those present, this was one. Smiley's continued distraction and his frequent cautious glances from the window; Haydon's indifference, Polyakov's predictable fit of indignation, his demands to be treated as became a member of the Diplomatic Corps – demands which Guillam from his place on the sofa tersely threatened to meet – the flustered arrival of Alleline and Bland, more protestations and the pilgrimage upstairs where Smiley played the tapes, the long glum silence that followed their return to the drawing room; the arrival of Lacon and finally of Esterhase and Fawn, Millie McCraig's silent ministrations with the teapot: all these events and cameos unrolled with a theatrical unreality which, much like the trip to Ascot an age before, were intensified by the unreality of the hour of the day. It was also true that these incidents, which included at an early point the physical constraint of Polyakov, and a stream of Russian abuse directed at Fawn for hitting him, heaven knows where, despite Mendel's vigilance, were like a silly subplot against Smiley's only purpose in convening the assembly: to persuade Alleline that Haydon offered Smiley's one chance to treat with Karla, and to salve, in humanitarian if not professional terms, whatever was left of the networks which Haydon had betrayed. Smiley was not empowered to conduct these transactions, nor did he seem to want to; perhaps he reckoned that between them Esterhase and Bland and Alleline were better placed to know what agents were still theoretically in being. In any event he soon took himself upstairs, where Guillam heard him once more restlessly padding from one room to the other as he continued his vigil from the windows.

So while Alleline and his lieutenants withdrew with Polyakov to the dining room to conduct their business alone, the rest of them sat in silence in the drawing room, either looking at Haydon or deliberately away from him. He seemed unaware that they were there. Chin in hand, he sat apart from them in a corner, watched over by Fawn, and he looked rather bored. The conference ended, they all trooped out of the dining room and Alleline announced to Lacon, who insisted on not being present at the discussions, that an appointment had been made three days hence at this address, by which time 'the Colonel will have had a chance to consult his superiors.' Lacon nodded. It might have been a board meeting.

The departures were even stranger than the arrivals. Between Esterhase and Polyakov in particular, there was a curiously poignant farewell. Esterhase, who would always rather have been a gentleman than a spy, seemed determined to make a gallant occasion of it, and offered his hand, which Polyakov struck petulantly aside. Esterhase looked round forlornly for Smiley, perhaps in the hope of ingratiating himself further with him, then shrugged and flung an arm across Bland's broad shoulder. Soon afterwards they left together. They didn't say goodbye to anybody, but Bland looked dreadfully shaken and Esterhase seemed to be consoling him, though his own future at that moment could hardly have struck him as rosy. Soon afterwards a radio cab arrived for Polyakov and he too left without a nod to anyone. By now, the conversation had died entirely; without the Russian present, the show became wretchedly parochial. Haydon remained in his familiar bored

pose, still watched by Fawn and Mendel, and stared at in mute embarrassment by Lacon and Alleline. More telephone calls were made, mainly for
cars. At some point Smiley reappeared from upstairs and mentioned Tarr.
Alleline phoned the Circus and dictated one telegram to Paris saying that he
could return to England with honour, whatever that meant: and a second to
Mackelvore saying that Tarr was an acceptable person; which again seemed
to Guillam a matter of opinion.

Finally, to the general relief, a windowless van arrived from the Nursery
and two men got out whom Guillam had never seen before, one tall and
limping, the other doughy and ginger-haired. With a shudder he realized
they were inquisitors. Fawn fetched Haydon's coat from the hall, went
through the pockets and respectfully helped him into it. At this point, Smiley
gently interposed himself and insisted that Haydon's walk from the front
door to the van should take place without the hall light on, and that the escort
should be large. Guillam, Fawn, even Alleline were pressed into service, and
finally with Haydon at its centre the whole motley group shuffled through
the garden to the van.

'It's simply a precaution,' Smiley insisted. No one was disposed to argue
with him. Haydon climbed in, the inquisitors followed, locking the grille from
inside. As the doors closed Haydon lifted one hand in an amiable if dismissive
gesture directed at Alleline.

So it was only afterwards that separate things came back to Guillam and
single people came forward for his recollection; the unqualified hatred, for
instance, directed by Polyakov against everyone present from poor little
Millie McCraig upwards, and which actually distorted him: his mouth curved
in a savage, uncontrollable sneer, he turned white and trembled, but not
from fear and not from anger. It was just plain hatred, of the sort that
Guillam could not visit on Haydon, but then Haydon was of his own kind.

For Alleline, in the moment of his defeat, Guillam discovered a sneaking
admiration: Alleline at least had shown a certain bearing. But later Guillam
was not so sure whether Percy realized, on that first presentation of the facts,
quite what the facts were: after all, he was still Chief, and Haydon was still his
Iago.

But the strangest thing to Guillam, the insight that he took away with him
and thought over much more deeply than was commonly his policy, was that
despite his banked-up anger at the moment of breaking into the room, it
required an act of will on his own part, and quite a violent one at that, to
regard Bill Haydon with much other than affection. Perhaps, as Bill would
say, he had finally grown up. Best of all, on the same evening, he climbed the
steps to his flat and heard the familiar notes of Camilla's flute echoing in the
well. And if Camilla that night lost something of her mystery, at least by
morning he had succeeded in freeing her from the toils of doublecross to
which he had latterly consigned her.

In other ways also, over the next few days, his life took on a brighter look.
Percy Alleline had been dispatched on indefinite leave; Smiley had been
asked to come back for a while and help sweep up what was left. For Guillam
himself there was talk of being rescued from Brixton. It was not till much,
much later that he learned that there had been a final act: and he put a name
and a purpose to that familiar shadow which had followed Smiley through
the night streets of Kensington.

# THIRTY-EIGHT

For the next two days George Smiley lived in limbo. To his neighbours, when they noticed him, he seemed to have lapsed into a wasting grief. He rose late and pottered round the house in his dressing gown, cleaning things, dusting, cooking himself meals and not eating them. In the afternoon, quite against the local bye-laws he lit a coal fire and sat before it reading among his German poets or writing letters to Ann which he seldom completed and never posted. When the telephone rang he went to it quickly, only to be disappointed. Outside the window the weather continued foul, and the few passers-by – Smiley studied them continuously – were huddled in Balkan misery. Once Lacon called with a request from the Minister that Smiley should 'stand by to help clear up the mess at Cambridge Circus, were he called upon to do so' – in effect to act as nightwatchman till a replacement for Percy Alleline could be found. Replying vaguely, Smiley again prevailed on Lacon to take extreme care of Haydon's physical safety while he was at Sarratt.

'Aren't you being a little dramatic?' Lacon retorted. 'The only place he can go is Russia and we're sending him there anyway.'

'When? How soon?'

The details would take several more days to arrange. Smiley disdained, in his state of anticlimactic reaction, to ask how the interrogation was progressing meanwhile, but Lacon's manner suggested that the answer would have been 'badly'. Mendel brought him more solid fare.

'Immingham railway station's shut,' he said. 'You'll have to get out at Grimsby and hoof it or take a bus.'

More often Mendel simply sat and watched him as one might an invalid.

'Waiting won't make her come, you know,' he said once. 'Time the mountain went to Mohammed. Faint heart never won fair lady, if I may say so.'

On the morning of the third day, the door bell rang and Smiley answered it so fast that it might have been Ann, having mislaid her key as usual. It was Lacon. Smiley was required at Sarratt, he said; Haydon insisted on seeing him. The inquisitors had got nowhere and time was running out. The understanding was that if Smiley would act as confessor, Haydon would give a limited account of himself.

'I'm assured there has been no coercion,' Lacon said.

Sarratt was a sorry place after the grandeur which Smiley remembered. Most of the elms had gone with the disease; pylons burgeoned over the old cricket field. The house itself, a sprawling brick mansion, had also come down a lot since the heyday of the cold war in Europe and most of the better furniture seemed to have disappeared, he supposed into one of Alleline's houses. He found Haydon in a nissen hut hidden among the trees.

Inside, it had the stink of an Army guardhouse, black-painted walls and high-barred windows. Guards manned the rooms to either side and they received Smiley respectfully, calling him sir. The word, it seemed, had got around. Haydon was dressed in denims, he was trembling and he complained of dizziness. Several times he had to lie on his bed to stop the nose bleeds. He had grown a half-hearted beard: apparently there was a dispute about whether he was to be allowed a razor.

'Cheer up,' said Smiley. 'You'll be out of here soon.'

He had tried, on the journey down, to remember Prideaux, and Irina, and the Czech networks, and he even entered Haydon's room with a vague notion of public duty: somehow, he thought, he ought to censure him on behalf of right-thinking men. He felt instead rather shy; he felt he had never known Haydon at all, and now it was too late. He was also angry at Haydon's physical condition, but when he taxed the guards they professed mystification. He was angrier still to learn that the additional security precautions he had insisted on had been relaxed after the first day. When he demanded to see Craddox, head of Nursery, Craddox was unavailable and his assistant acted dumb.

Their first conversation was halting and banal.

Would Smiley please forward the mail from his club, and tell Alleline to get a move on with the horsetrading with Karla? And he needed tissues, paper tissues for his nose. His habit of weeping, Haydon explained, had nothing to do with remorse or pain, it was a physical reaction to what he called the pettiness of the inquisitors who had made up their minds that Haydon knew the names of other Karla recruits, and were determined to have them before he left. There was also a school of thought which held that Fanshawe of the Christ Church Optimates had been acting as a talent-spotter for Moscow Centre as well as for the Circus, Haydon explained: 'Really, what can one do with asses like that?' He managed, despite his weakness, to convey that his was the only level head around.

They walked in the grounds and Smiley established with something close to despair that the perimeter was not even patrolled any more, either by night or day. After one circuit, Haydon asked to go back to the hut, where he dug up a piece of floorboard and extracted some sheets of paper covered in hieroglyphics. They reminded Smiley forcibly of Irina's diary. Squatting on the bed he sorted through them, and in that pose, in that dull light, with his long forelock dangling almost to the paper, he might have been lounging in Control's room, back in the Sixties, propounding some wonderfully plausible and quite inoperable piece of skulduggery for England's greater glory. Smiley did not bother to write anything down, since it was common ground between them that their conversation was being recorded anyway. The statement began with a long apologia, of which he afterwards recalled only a few sentences:

'We live in an age where only fundamental issues matter . . .

'The United States is no longer capable of undertaking its own revolution . . .

'The political posture of the United Kingdom is without relevance or moral viability in world affairs . . . '

With much of it, Smiley might in other circumstances have agreed: it was the tone, rather than the music, which alienated him.

'In capitalist America economic repression of the masses is institutionalised to a point which not even Lenin could have foreseen.

'The cold war began in 1917 but the bitterest struggles lie ahead of us; as America's deathbed paranoia drives her to greater excesses abroad . . .'

He spoke not of the decline of the West, but of its death by greed and constipation. He hated America very deeply, he said, and Smiley supposed he did. Haydon also took it for granted that secret services were the only real measure of a nation's political health, the only real expression of its subconscious.

Finally he came to his own case. At Oxford, he said, he was genuinely of the right, and in the war, it scarcely mattered where one stood as long as one was fighting the Germans. For a while, after forty-five, he said, he had remained content with Britain's part in the world, till gradually it dawned on him just how trivial this was. How and when was a mystery. In the historical mayhem of his own lifetime he could point to no one occasion: simply he knew that if England were out of the game, the price of fish would not be altered by a farthing. He had often wondered which side he would be on if the test ever came; after prolonged reflection he had finally to admit that if either monolith had to win the day, he would prefer it to be the East.

'It's an aesthetic judgment as much as anything,' he explained, looking up. 'Partly a moral one, of course.'

'Of course,' said Smiley politely.

From then on, he said, it was only a matter of time before he put his efforts where his convictions lay.

That was the first day's take. A white sediment had formed on Haydon's lips, and he had begun weeping again. They agreed to meet tomorrow at the same time.

'It would be nice to go into the detail a little if we could, Bill,' Smiley said as he left.

'Oh and look, tell Jan, will you?' Haydon was lying on the bed, staunching his nose again. 'Doesn't matter a hoot what you say, long as you make it final.' Sitting up, he wrote out a cheque and put it in a brown envelope. 'Give her that for the milk bill.'

Realizing perhaps that Smiley was not quite at ease with this brief, he added: 'Well, I can't take her with me, can I? Even if they let her come, she'd be a bloody millstone.'

The same evening, following Haydon's instructions, Smiley took a tube to Kentish Town and unearthed a cottage in an unconverted mews. A flat-faced girl in jeans opened the door to him; there was a smell of oil paint and baby. He could not remember whether he had met her at Bywater Street so he opened with: 'I'm from Bill Haydon. He's quite all right but I've got various messages from him.'

'Jesus,' said the girl softly. 'About bloody time and all.'

The living room was filthy. Through the kitchen door he saw a pile of dirty crockery and he knew she used everything until it ran out, then washed it all at once. The floor boards were bare except for long psychedelic patterns of snakes and flowers and insects painted all over them.

'That's Bill's Michelangelo ceiling,' she said conversationally. 'Only he's not going to have Michelangelo's bad back. Are you government?' she asked, lighting a cigarette. 'He works for government, he told me.' Her hand was shaking and she had yellow smudges under her eyes.

'Oh look, first I'm to give you that,' said Smiley, and delving in an inside pocket handed her the envelope with the cheque.

'Bread,' said the girl, and put the envelope beside her.

'Bread,' said Smiley, answering her grin, then something in his expression, or the way he echoed that one word, made her take up the envelope and rip it open. There was no note, just the cheque, but the cheque was enough: even from where Smiley sat, he could see it had four figures.

Not knowing what she was doing, she walked across the room to the fireplace and put the cheque with the grocery bills in an old tin on the mantelpiece. She went into the kitchen and mixed two cups of Nescafé, but she only came out with one.

'Where is he?' she said. She stood facing him. 'He's gone chasing after that snotty little sailor boy again. Is that it? And this is the pay-off, is that it? Well you bloody tell him from me . . .'

Smiley had had scenes like this before, and now absurdly the old words came back to him.

'Bill's been doing work of national importance. I'm afraid we can't talk about it, and nor must you. A few days ago he went abroad on a secret job. He'll be away some while. Even years. He wasn't allowed to tell anyone he was leaving. He wants you to forget him. I really am most awfully sorry.'

He got that far before she burst out. He didn't hear all she said, because she was blurting and screaming, and when the baby heard her it started screaming too, from upstairs. She was swearing, not at him, not even particularly at Bill, just swearing dry-eyed and demanding to know who the hell, who the bloody bloody hell believed in government any more? Then her mood changed. Round the walls, Smiley noticed Bill's other paintings, mainly of the girl: few were finished, and they had a cramped, condemned quality by comparison with his earlier work.

'You don't like him, do you? I can tell,' she said. 'So why do you do his dirty work for him?'

To this question also there seemed no immediate answer. Returning to Bywater Street, he again had the impression of being followed, and tried to telephone Mendel with the number of a cab which had twice caught his eye, asking him to make immediate enquiries. For once, Mendel was out till after midnight: Smiley slept uneasily and woke at five. By eight he was back at Sarratt, to find Haydon in festive mood. The inquisitors had not bothered him; he had been told by Craddox that the exchanges had been agreed and he should expect to travel tomorrow or the next day. His requests had a valedictory ring; the balance of his salary and the proceeds of any odd sales made on his behalf should be forwarded to him care of the Moscow Narodny Bank who would also handle his mail. The Arnolfini Gallery in Bristol had a few pictures of his, including some early water colours of Damascus, which he coveted. Could Smiley please arrange? Then, the cover for his disappearance.

'Play it long,' he advised. 'Say I've been posted, lay on the mystery, give it a couple of years then run me down . . .'

'Oh I think we can manage something, thank you,' Smiley said.

For the first time since Smiley had known him, Haydon was worried about clothes. He wanted to arrive *looking* like someone, he said: first impressions were so important. 'Those Moscow tailors are unspeakable. Dress you up like a bloody beadle.'

'Quite,' said Smiley, whose opinion of London tailors was no better.

Oh and there was a boy, he added carelessly, a sailor friend, lived in Notting Hill. 'Better give him a couple of hundred to shut him up. Can you do that out of the reptile fund?'

'I'm sure.'

He wrote out an address. In the same spirit of good fellowship, Haydon then entered into what Smiley had called the details.

He declined to discuss any part of his recruitment nor of his lifelong relationship with Karla. 'Lifelong?' Smiley repeated quickly. 'When did you meet?' The assertions of yesterday appeared suddenly nonsensical, but Haydon would not elaborate.

From about nineteen fifty onwards, if he was to be believed, Haydon had made Karla occasional selected gifts of intelligence. These early efforts were confined to what he hoped would directly advance the Russian cause over the American; he was 'scrupulous not to give them anything harmful to ourselves' as he put it, or harmful to our agents in the field.

The Suez adventure in fifty-six finally persuaded him of the inanity of the British situation and of the British capacity to spike the advance of history while not being able to offer anything by way of contribution. The sight of the Americans sabotaging the British action in Egypt was, paradoxically, an additional incentive. He would say therefore that from fifty-six on, he was a committed, full-time Soviet mole with no holds barred. In sixty-one he formally received Soviet citizenship, and over the next ten years two Soviet medals – quaintly, he would not say which, though he insisted that they were 'top stuff'. Unfortunately, overseas postings during this period limited his access; and since he insisted on his information being acted upon wherever possible – 'rather than being chucked into some daft Soviet archive' – his work was dangerous as well as uneven. With his return to London, Karla sent him Polly (which was evidently the house name for Polyakov) as a helpmate, but Haydon found the constant pressure of clandestine meetings difficult to sustain, particularly in view of the quantity of stuff he was photographing.

He declined to discuss cameras, equipment, pay or tradecraft during this pre-Merlin period in London, and Smiley was conscious all the while that even the little Haydon was telling him was selected with meticulous care from a greater and perhaps somewhat different truth.

Meanwhile both Karla and Haydon were receiving signals that Control was smelling a rat. Control was ill, of course, but clearly he would never willingly give up the reins while there was a chance that he was making Karla a present of the service. It was a race between Control's researches and his health. Twice, he had very nearly struck gold – again, Haydon declined to say how – and if Karla had not been quick on his feet, the mole Gerald would have been trapped. It was out of this nervy situation that first Merlin, and finally Operation Testify, were born. Witchcraft was conceived primarily to take care of the succession: to put Alleline next to the throne and hasten Control's demise. Secondly, of course, Witchcraft gave Centre absolute autonomy over the product flowing into Whitehall. Thirdly – and in the long run most important, Haydon insisted – it brought the Circus into position as a major weapon against the American target.

'How much of the material was genuine?' Smiley asked.

Obviously the standard varied according to what one wanted to achieve, said Haydon. In theory, fabrication was very easy: Haydon had only to advise Karla of Whitehall's areas of ignorance and the fabricators would write for them. Once or twice, for the hell of it, said Haydon, he had written the odd report himself. It was an amusing exercise to receive, evaluate and distribute one's own work. The advantages of Witchcraft in terms of tradecraft were of course inestimable. It placed Haydon virtually out of Control's reach, and gave him a cast-iron cover story for meeting Polly whenever he wished. Often months would pass without their meeting at all. Haydon would photograph Circus documents in the seclusion of his room – under cover of preparing Polly's chickenfeed – hand it over to Esterhase with a lot of other rubbish and let him cart it down to the safe house in Lock Gardens.

'It was a classic,' Haydon said simply. 'Percy made the running, I slip-streamed behind him, Roy and Toby did the legwork.'

Here Smiley asked politely whether Karla had ever thought of having

Haydon actually take over the Circus himself: why bother with a stalking horse at all? Haydon stalled and it occurred to Smiley that Karla, like Control, might well have considered Haydon better cast as a subordinate.

Operation Testify, said Haydon, was rather a desperate throw. Haydon was certain that Control was getting very warm indeed. An analysis of the files he was drawing produced an uncomfortably complete inventory of the operations which Haydon had blown, or otherwise caused to abort. He had also succeeded in narrowing the field to officers of a certain age and rank . . .

'Was Stevcek's original offer genuine, by the way?' Smiley asked.

'Good Lord no,' said Haydon, actually shocked. 'It was a fix from the start. Stevcek existed, of course. He was a distinguished Czech general. But he never made an offer to anyone.'

Here Smiley sensed Haydon falter. For the first time, he actually seemed uneasy about the morality of his behaviour. His manner became noticeably defensive.

'Obviously, we needed to be certain Control would rise and how he would rise . . . and who he would send. We couldn't have him picking some half-arsed little pavement artist: it had to be a big gun to make the story stick. We knew he'd only settle for someone outside the mainstream and someone who wasn't Witchcraft cleared. If we made it a Czech, he'd have to choose a Czech speaker, naturally.'

'Naturally.'

'We wanted old Circus: someone who could bring down the temple a bit.'

'Yes,' said Smiley, remembering that heaving, sweating figure on the hilltop: 'Yes, I see the logic of that.'

'Well, damn it, I got him back,' snapped Haydon.

'Yes, that was good of you. Tell me, did Jim come to see you before he left on that Testify mission?'

'Yes, he did, as a matter of fact.'

'To say what?'

For a long, long while Haydon hesitated, then did not answer. But the answer was written there all the same, in the sudden emptying of his eyes, in the shadow of guilt that crossed his thin face. He came to warn you, Smiley thought; because he loved you. To warn you; just as he came to tell me that Control was mad, but couldn't find me because I was in Berlin. Jim was watching your back for you right till the end.

Also, Haydon resumed, it had to be a country with a recent history of counter-revolution: Czecho was honestly the only place.

Smiley appeared not quite to be listening.

'Why did you bring him back?' he asked. 'For friendship's sake? Because he was harmless and you held all the cards?'

It wasn't just that, Haydon explained. As long as Jim was in a Czech prison (he didn't say Russian) people would agitate for him, and see him as some sort of key. But once he was back, everyone in Whitehall would conspire to keep him quiet: that was the way of it with repatriations.

'I'm surprised Karla didn't just shoot him. Or did he hold back out of delicacy towards you?'

But Haydon had drifted away again into half-baked political assertions.

Then he began speaking about himself, and already to Smiley's eye, he seemed quite visibly to be shrinking to something quite small and mean. He was touched to hear that Ionesco had recently promised us a play in which the hero kept silent and everyone round him spoke incessantly. When the psychologists and fashionable historians came to write their apologias for him, he hoped they would remember that that was how he saw himself. As an artist, he had said all he had to say at the age of seventeen, and one had to do something with one's later years. He was awfully sorry he couldn't take some of his friends with him. He hoped Smiley would remember him with affection.

Smiley wanted at that point to tell him that he would not remember him in those terms at all, and a good deal more besides, but there seemed no point and Haydon was having another nose bleed.

'Oh, I'm to ask you to avoid publicity by the way. Miles Sercombe made quite a thing of it.'

Here Haydon managed a laugh. Having messed up the Circus in private, he said, he had no wish to repeat the process in public.

Before he left, Smiley asked the one question he still cared about.

'I'll have to break it to Ann. Is there anything particular you want me to pass on to her?'

It required discussion for the implication of Smiley's question to get through to him. At first, he thought Smiley had said 'Jan,' and couldn't understand why he had not yet called on her.

'Oh *your* Ann,' he said, as if there were a lot of Anns around.

It was Karla's idea, he explained. Karla had long recognised that Smiley was the biggest threat to the mole Gerald. 'He said you were quite good.'

'Thank you.'

'But you had this one price: Ann. The last illusion of the illusionless man. He reckoned that if I was known to be Ann's lover around the place you wouldn't see very straight when it came to other things.' His eyes, Smiley noticed, had become very fixed. Pewtery, Ann called them. 'Not to strain it or anything, but if it was possible, join the queue. Point?'

'Point,' said Smiley.

For instance, on the night of Testify, Karla was adamant that if possible Haydon should be dallying with Ann. As a form of insurance.

'And wasn't there in fact a small hitch that night?' Smiley asked, remembering Sam Collins, and the matter of whether Ellis had been shot. Haydon agreed that there had been. If everything had gone according to plan, the first Czech bulletins should have broken at ten thirty. Haydon would have had a chance to read his club tickertape after Sam Collins had rung Ann, and before he arrived at the Circus to take over. But because Jim had been shot, there was a fumble at the Czech end and the bulletin was released after his club had closed.

'Lucky no one followed it up,' he said, helping himself to another of Smiley's cigarettes. 'Which one was I by the way?' he asked conversationally. 'I forget.'

'Tailor. I was Beggarman.'

By then Smiley had had enough, so he slipped out, not bothering to say goodbye. He got into his car and drove for an hour anywhere, till he found himself on a side road to Oxford doing eighty, so he stopped for lunch and headed for London. He still couldn't face Bywater Street so he went to a cinema, dined somewhere and got home at midnight slightly drunk to find both Lacon and Miles Sercombe on the doorstep, and Sercombe's fatuous Rolls, the black bed-pan, all fifty foot of it, hoved up on the kerb in everyone's way.

They drove to Sarratt at a mad speed, and there, in the open night under a clear sky, lit by several hand torches and stared at by several white-faced inmates of the Nursery, sat Bill Haydon on a garden fence facing the moonlit cricket field. He was wearing striped pyjamas under his overcoat; they looked more like prison clothes. His eyes were open and his head was propped unnaturally to one side, like the head of a bird when its neck had been expertly broken.

There was no particular dispute about what had happened. At ten thirty Haydon had complained to his guards of sleeplessness and nausea: he proposed to take some fresh air. His case being regarded as closed, no one thought to accompany him and he walked out into the darkness alone. One of the guards remembered him making a joke about 'examining the state of the wicket.' The other was too busy watching the television to remember anything. After half an hour they became apprehensive so the senior guard went off to take a look while his assistant stayed behind in case Haydon should return. Haydon was found where he was now sitting; the guard thought at first that he had fallen asleep. Stooping over him, he caught the smell of alcohol – he guessed gin or vodka – and decided that Haydon was drunk, which surprised him since the Nursery was officially dry. It wasn't till he tried to lift him that his head flopped over, and the rest of him followed as dead weight. Having vomited (the traces were over there by the tree) the guard propped him up again and sounded the alarm.

Had Haydon received any messages during the day? Smiley asked.

No. But his suit had come back from the cleaners and it was possible a message had been concealed in it – for instance inviting him to a rendezvous.

'So the Russians did it,' the Minister announced with satisfaction to Haydon's unresponsive form. 'To stop him peaching, I suppose. Bloody thugs.'

'No,' said Smiley. 'They take pride in getting their people back.'

'Then who the hell *did*?'

Everyone waited on Smiley's answer, but none came. The torches went out and the group moved uncertainly towards the car.

'Can we lose him just the same?' the Minister asked on the way back.

'He was a Soviet citizen. Let them have him,' said Lacon, still watching Smiley in the darkness.

They agreed it was a pity about the networks. Better see whether Karla would do the deal anyhow.

'He won't,' said Smiley.


Recalling this in the seclusion of his first class compartment, Smiley had the curious sensation of watching Haydon through the wrong end of a telescope. He had eaten very little since last night, but the bar had been open for most of the journey.

Leaving King's Cross he had had a wistful notion of liking Haydon, and respecting him: Bill was a man, after all, who had had something to say and had said it. But his mental system rejected this convenient simplification. The more he puzzled over Haydon's rambling account of himself, the more conscious he was of the contradictions. He tried at first to see Haydon in the romantic newspaper terms of a Thirties intellectual, for whom Moscow was the natural Mecca. 'Moscow was Bill's discipline,' he told himself. 'He needed the symmetry of an historical and economic solution.' This struck him as too sparse, so he added more of the man whom he was trying to like: 'Bill was a romantic and a snob. He wanted to join an elitist vanguard and lead the masses out of the darkness.' Then he remembered the half-finished canvases in the girl's drawing room in Kentish Town: cramped, overworked and condemned. He remembered also the ghost of Bill's authoritarian father – Ann had called him simply the Monster – and he imagined Bill's Marxism making up for his inadequacy as an artist, for his loveless childhood. Later of course it hardly mattered if the doctrine wore thin. Bill was set on the road and Karla would know how to keep him there. Treason is very much a matter of habit, Smiley decided, seeing Bill again stretched out on the floor in Bywater Street, while Ann played him music on the gramophone.

Bill had loved it, too. Smiley didn't doubt that for a moment. Standing at the middle of a secret stage, playing world against world, hero and playwright in one: oh, Bill had loved that all right.

Smiley shrugged it all aside, distrustful as ever of the standard shapes of human motive, and settled instead for a picture of one of those wooden Russian dolls that open up, revealing one person inside the other, and another inside him. Of all men living, only Karla had seen the last little doll inside Bill Haydon. When was Bill recruited, and how? Was his right wing stand at Oxford a pose, or was it paradoxically the state of sin from which Karla summoned him to grace?

Ask Karla: pity I didn't.

Ask Jim: I never shall.

Over the flat East Anglian landscape as it slid slowly by, the unyielding face of Karla replaced Bill Haydon's crooked deathmask. 'But you had this one price: Ann. The last illusion of the illusionless man. He reckoned that if I were known to be Ann's lover around the place you wouldn't see me very straight when it came to other things.'

Illusion? Was that really Karla's name for love? And Bill's?

'Here,' said the guard very loudly, and perhaps for the second time. 'Come on with it, you're for Grimsby then aren't you?'

'No, no: Immingham.' Then he remembered Mendel's instructions and clambered onto the platform.

There was no cab in sight, so having enquired at the ticket office, he made his way across the empty forecourt and stood beside a green sign marked 'Queue.' He had hoped she might collect him, but perhaps she hadn't received his wire. Ah well; the post office at Christmas: who could blame them? He wondered how she would take the news about Bill; till, remembering her frightened face on the cliffs in Cornwall, he realized that by then Bill was already dead for her. She had sensed the coldness of his touch, and somehow guessed what lay behind it.

Illusion? he repeated to himself. Illusionless?

It was bitterly cold; he hoped very much that her wretched lover had found her somewhere warm to live.

He wished he'd brought her fur boots from the cupboard under the stairs.

He remembered the copy of Grimmelshausen, still uncollected at Martindale's Club.

Then he saw her: her disreputable car shunting towards him down the lane marked 'Buses only' and Ann at the wheel staring the wrong way. Saw her get out, leaving the indicators winking, and walk into the station to enquire: tall and puckish, extraordinarily beautiful, essentially another man's woman.

For the rest of that term, Jim Prideaux behaved in the eyes of Roach much as his mother had behaved when his father went away. He spent a lot of time on little things, like fixing up the lighting for the school play and mending the soccer nets with string, and in French he took enormous pains over small inaccuracies. But big things, like his walks and solitary golf, these he gave up altogether, and in the evenings stayed in and kept clear of the village. Worst of all was his staring, empty look when Roach caught him unawares, and the way he forgot things in class, even red marks for merit: Roach had to remind him to hand them in each week.

To support him, Roach took the job of dimmer man on the lighting. Thus at rehearsals Jim had to give him a special signal, to Bill and no one else. He was to raise his arm and drop it to his side, when he wanted the footlights to fade.

With time, Jim seemed to respond to treatment, however. His eye grew clearer and he became alert again, as the shadow of his mother's death withdrew. By the night of the play he was more light-hearted than Roach had ever known him. 'Hey Jumbo, you silly toad, where's your mac, can't you see it's raining?' he called out, as tired but triumphant they trailed back to the main building after the performance. 'His real name is Bill,' he heard him explain to a visiting parent. 'We were new boys together.'

The gun, Bill Roach had finally convinced himself, was after all a dream.

# THE
# HONOURABLE
# SCHOOLBOY

For Jane, who bore the brunt, put up with my presence and absence alike, and made it all possible.

# FOREWORD

I offer my warm thanks to the many generous and hospitable people who found time to help me with my research for this novel.

In Singapore, Alwyne (Bob) Taylor, the *Daily Mail* correspondent; Max Vanzi of UPI; and Bruce Wilson of the *Melbourne Herald.*

In Hong Kong, Sydney Liu of *Newsweek;* Bing Wong of *Time;* H.D.S. Greenway of the *Washington Post;* Anthony Lawrence of the BBC; Richard Hughes, then of the *Sunday Times;* Donald A. Davis and Vic Vanzi of UPI; and Derek Davies and his staff at the *Far Eastern Economic Review,* notably Leo Goodstadt. I must also acknowledge with gratitude the exceptional co-operation of Major-General Penfold and his team at the Royal Hong Kong Jockey Club, who gave me the run of Happy Valley Racecourse and showed me much kindness without once seeking to know my purpose. I wish I could also name the several officials of the Hong Kong Government, and members of the Royal Hong Kong Police, who opened doors for me at some risk of embarrassment to themselves.

In Phnom Penh my genial host Baron Walther von Marschall took marvellous care of me, and I could never have managed without the wisdom of Kurt Furrer and Madame Yvette Pierpaoli, both of Suisindo Shipping and Trading Co., and presently in Bangkok.

But my special thanks must be reserved for those who put up with me the longest: for my friend David Greenway of the *Washington Post,* who allowed me to follow in his distinguished shadow through Laos, north-east Thailand and Phnom Penh. To him, to Bing Wong, and to certain Hong Kong Chinese friends who I believe will prefer to remain anonymous, I owe a great debt.

Last there is the great Dick Hughes, whose outward character and mannerisms I have shamelessly exaggerated for the part of old Craw. Some people, once met, simply elbow their way into a novel and sit there till the writer finds them a place, Dick is one. I am only sorry I could not obey his urgent exhortation to libel him to the hilt. My cruellest efforts could not prevail against the affectionate nature of the original.

And since none of these good people had any more notion than I did, in those days, of how the book would turn out, I must be quick to absolve them from my misdemeanours.

Terry Mayers, a veteran of the British Karate Team, advised me on certain alarming skills. For Miss Nellie Adams, for her stupendous bouts of typing, no praise is enough.

CORNWALL,
20TH FEBRUARY, 1977.

I and the public know
What all schoolchildren learn,
Those to whom evil
is done Do evil in return.

W. H. AUDEN

# PART ONE

## Winding the Clock

# ONE

## *how the circus left town*

Afterwards, in the dusty little corners where London's secret servants drink together, there was an argument about where the Dolphin case history should really begin. One crowd, led by a blimpish fellow in charge of microphone transcription, went so far as to claim that the fitting date was sixty years ago when 'that arch-cad Bill Haydon' was born into the world under a treacherous star. Haydon's very name struck a chill into them. It does so even today. For it was this same Haydon who, while still at Oxford, was recruited by Karla the Russian as a 'mole', or 'sleeper', or in English, agent of penetration, to work against them. And who with Karla's guidance entered their ranks and spied on them for thirty years or more. And whose eventual discovery – thus the line of reasoning – brought the British so low that they were forced into a fatal dependence upon their American sister service, whom they called in their own strange jargon 'the Cousins'. The Cousins changed the game entirely, said the blimpish fellow: much as he might have deplored power tennis or bodyline bowling. And ruined it too, said his seconds.

To less flowery minds, the true genesis was Haydon's unmasking by George Smiley and Smiley's consequent appointment as caretaker chief of the betrayed service, which occurred in the late November of 1973. Once George had got Karla under his skin, they said, there was no stopping him. The rest was inevitable, they said. Poor old George: but what a mind under all that burden!

One scholarly soul, a researcher of some sort, in the jargon a 'burrower', even insisted, in his cups, upon January 26th 1841 as the natural date, when a certain Captain Elliot of the Royal Navy took a landing party to a fog-laden rock called Hong Kong at the mouth of the Pearl River and a few days later proclaimed it a British colony. With Elliot's arrival, said the scholar, Hong Kong became the headquarters of Britain's opium trade to China and in consequence one of the pillars of the imperial economy. If the British had not invented the opium market – he said, not entirely serious – then there would have been no case, no ploy, no dividend: and therefore no renaissance of the Circus following Bill Haydon's traitorous depredations.

Whereas the hard men – the grounded fieldmen, the trainers and the case officers who made their own murmured caucus always – they saw the question solely in operational terms. They pointed to Smiley's deft footwork in tracking down Karla's paymaster in Vientiane; to Smiley's handling of the girl's parents; and to his wheeling and dealing with the reluctant barons of

Whitehall, who held the operational purse strings, and dealt out rights and permissions in the secret world. Above all, to the wonderful moment when he turned the operation round on its own axis. For these pros, the Dolphin case was a victory of technique. Nothing more. They saw the shotgun marriage with the Cousins as just another skilful bit of tradecraft in a long and delicate poker game. As to the final outcome: to hell. The king is dead, so long live the next one.

The debate continues wherever old comrades meet, though the name of Jerry Westerby, understandably, is seldom mentioned. Occasionally, it is true, somebody does, out of foolhardiness or sentiment or plain forgetfulness, dredge it up, and there is atmosphere for a moment; but it passes. Only the other day a young probationer just out of the Circus's refurbished training school at Sarratt – in the jargon again, 'the Nursery' – piped it out in the under-thirties bar, for instance. A watered-down version of the Dolphin case had recently been introduced at Sarratt as material for syndicate discussions, even playlets, and the poor boy, still very green, was fairly brimming with excitement to discover he was in the know: 'But my *God*,' he protested, enjoying the kind of fool's freedom sometimes granted to naval midshipmen in the wardroom, 'my *God*, why does nobody seem to recognize Westerby's part in the affair? If *anybody* carried the load, it was Jerry Westerby. He was the spearhead. Well, wasn't he? Frankly?' Except, of course, he did not utter the name 'Westerby', nor 'Jerry' either, not least because he did not know them; but used instead the cryptonym allocated to Jerry for the duration of the case.

Peter Guillam fielded this loose ball. Guillam is tall and tough and graceful, and probationers awaiting first posting tend to look up to him as some sort of Greek god.

'Westerby was the stick that poked the fire,' he declared curtly, ending the silence. 'Any fieldman would have done as well, some a damn sight better.'

When the boy still did not take the hint, Guillam rose and went over to him and, very pale, snapped into his ear that he should fetch himself another drink, if he could hold it, and thereafter guard his tongue for several days or weeks. Whereupon, the conversation returned once more to the topic of dear old George Smiley, surely the last of the *true* greats, and what was he doing with himself these days, back in retirement? So many lives he had led; so much to recollect in tranquillity, they agreed.

'George went five times round the moon to our one,' someone declared loyally, a woman.

Ten times, they agreed. Twenty! *Fifty!* With hyperbole, Westerby's shadow mercifully receded. As in a sense, so did George Smiley's. Well, George had a marvellous innings, they would say. At his age what could you expect?

Perhaps a more realistic point of departure is a certain typhoon Saturday in mid-1974, three o'clock in the afternoon, when Hong Kong lay battened down waiting for the next onslaught. In the bar of the Foreign Correspondents' Club, a score of journalists, mainly from former British colonies – Australian, Canadian, American – fooled and drank in a mood of violent idleness, a chorus without a hero. Thirteen floors below them, the old trams and double deckers were caked in the mud-brown sweat of building dust and smuts from the chimney-stacks in Kowloon. The tiny ponds outside the highrise hotels prickled with slow, subversive rain. And in the men's room, which provided the Club's best view of the harbour, young Luke the Californian was ducking his face into the handbasin, washing the blood from his mouth.

Luke was a wayward, gangling tennis player, an old man of twenty-seven who until the American pullout had been the star turn in his magazine's Saigon stable of war reporters. When you knew he played tennis it was hard to think of him doing anything else, even drinking. You imagined him at the net, uncoiling and smashing everything to kingdom come; or serving aces between double faults. His mind, as he sucked and spat, was fragmented by drink and mild concussion – Luke would probably have used the war-word 'fragged' – into several lucid parts. One part was occupied with a Wanchai bar girl called Ella for whose sake he had punched the pig policeman on the jaw and suffered the inevitable consequences: with the minimum necessary force, the said Superintendent Rockhurst, known otherwise as the Rocket, who was this minute relaxing in a corner of the bar after his exertions, had knocked him cold and kicked him smartly in the ribs. Another part of his mind was on something his Chinese landlord had said to him this morning when he called to complain of the noise of Luke's gramophone, and had stayed to drink a beer.

A scoop of some sort definitely. But what sort?

He retched again, then peered out of the window. The junks were lashed behind the barriers and the Star Ferry had stopped running. A veteran British frigate lay at anchor and Club rumours said Whitehall was selling it.

'Should be putting to sea,' he muttered confusedly, recalling some bit of naval lore he had picked up in his travels. 'Frigates put to sea in typhoons. Yes, *sir.*'

The hills were slate under the stacks of black cloudbank. Six months ago the sight would have had him cooing with pleasure. The harbour, the din, even the skyscraper shanties that clambered from the sea's edge upward to the Peak: after Saigon, Luke had ravenously embraced the whole scene. But all he saw today was a smug, rich British rock run by a bunch of plum-throated traders whose horizons went no further than their belly-lines. The Colony had therefore become for him exactly what it was already for the rest of the journalists: an airfield, a telephone, a laundry, a bed. Occasionally – but never for long – a woman. Where even experience had to be imported. As to the wars which for so long had been his addiction: they were as remote from Hong Kong as they were from London or New York. Only the Stock Exchange showed a token sensibility, and on Saturdays it was closed anyway.

'Think you're going to live, ace?' asked the shaggy Canadian cowboy, coming to the stall beside him. The two men had shared the pleasures of the Tet offensive.

'Thank you, dear, I feel perfectly topping,' Luke replied, in his most exalted English accent.

Luke decided it really was important for him to remember what Jake Chiu had said to him over the beer this morning, and suddenly like a gift from Heaven it came to him.

'I remember!' he shouted. 'Jesus, cowboy, I remember! Luke, you remember! My brain! It works! Folks, give ear to Luke!'

'Forget it,' the cowboy advised. 'That's badland out there today, ace. Whatever it is, forget it.'

But Luke kicked open the door and charged into the bar, arms flung wide. 'Hey! Hey! *Folks!*'

Not a head turned. Luke cupped his hands to his mouth.

'Listen you drunken bums, I got *news*. This is fantastic. Two bottles of Scotch a day and a brain like a razor. Someone give me a bell.'

Finding none, he grabbed a tankard and hammered it on the bar rail, spilling the beer. Even then, only the dwarf paid him the slightest notice.

'So what's happened, Lukie?' whined the dwarf, in his queeny Greenwich Village drawl. 'Has Big Moo gotten hiccups again? I can't bear it.'

Big Moo was Club jargon for the Governor and the dwarf was Luke's chief of bureau. He was a pouchy, sullen creature with disordered hair that wept in black strands over his face, and a silent way of popping up beside you. A year back, two Frenchmen, otherwise rarely seen here, had nearly killed him for a chance remark he had made on the origins of the mess in Vietnam. They took him to the lift, broke his jaw and several of his ribs, then dumped him in a heap on the ground floor and came back to finish their drinks. Soon afterwards the Australians did a similar job on him when he made a silly accusation about their token military involvement in the war. He suggested that Canberra had done a deal with President Johnson to keep the Australian boys in Vung Tau which was a picnic, while the Americans did the real fighting elsewhere. Unlike the French, the Australians didn't even bother to use the lift. They just beat the hell out of the dwarf where he stood, and when he fell they added a little more of the same. After that, he learned when to keep clear of certain people in Hong Kong. In times of persistent fog for instance. Or when the water was cut to four hours a day. Or on a typhoon Saturday.

Otherwise the Club was pretty much empty. For reasons of prestige, the top correspondents steered clear of the place anyway. A few businessmen, who came for the flavour pressmen give, a few girls, who came for the men. A couple of television war tourists in fake battle-drill. And in his customary corner, the awesome Rocker, Superintendent of Police, ex-Palestine, ex-Kenya, ex-Malaya, ex-Fiji, an implacable warhorse with a beer, one set of slightly reddened knuckles, and a weekend copy of the *South China Morning Post*. The Rocker, people said, came for the class. And at the big table at the centre, which on weekdays was the preserve of United Press International, lounged the Shanghai Junior Baptist Conservative Bowling Club, presided over by mottled old Craw the Australian, enjoying its usual Saturday tournament. The aim of the contest was to pitch a screwed-up napkin across the room, and lodge it in the wine rack. Every time you succeeded, your competitors bought you the bottle, and helped you drink it. Old Craw growled the orders to fire and an elderly Shanghainese waiter, Craw's favourite, wearily manned the butts and served the prizes. The game was not a zestful one that day, and some members were not bothering to throw. Nevertheless this was the group Luke selected for his audience.

'Big Moo's *wife's* got hiccups!' the dwarf insisted. 'Big Moo's wife's horse has got hiccups! Big Moo's wife's horse's *groom's* got hiccups! Big Moo's wife's horse's –'

Striding to the table Luke leapt straight on to it with a crash, breaking several glasses and cracking his head on the ceiling in the process. Framed up there against the south window in a half crouch he was out of scale to everyone: the dark mist, the dark shadow of the Peak behind it, and this giant filling the whole foreground. But they went on pitching and drinking as if they hadn't seen him. Only the Rocker glanced in Luke's direction, once, before licking a huge thumb and turning to the cartoon page.

'Round three,' Craw ordered, in his rich Australian accent. 'Brother Canada, prepare to fire. *Wait*, you slob. Fire.'

A screwed-up napkin floated toward the rack, taking a high trajectory. Finding a cranny it hung a moment, then flopped to the ground. Egged on by the dwarf, Luke began stamping on the table and more glasses fell. Finally he wore his audience down.

'Your Graces,' said old Craw with a sigh. 'Pray silence for my son. I fear he would have parley with us. Brother Luke, you have committed several acts of war today and one more will meet with our severe disfavour. Speak clearly and concisely omitting no detail, however slight, and thereafter hold your water, sir.'

In their tireless pursuit of legends about one another, old Craw was their Ancient Mariner. Craw had shaken more sand out of his shorts, they told each other, than most of them would ever walk over; and they were right. In Shanghai, where his career had started, he had been teaboy and city editor to the only English-speaking journal in the port. Since then, he had covered the Communists against Chiang Kai-shek and Chiang against the Japanese and the Americans against practically everyone. Craw gave them a sense of history in this rootless place. His style of speech, which at typhoon times even the hardiest might pardonably find irksome, was a genuine hangover from the Thirties, when Australia provided the bulk of journalists in the Orient; and the Vatican, for some reason, the jargon of their companionship.

So Luke, thanks to old Craw, finally got it out.

'Gentlemen! – Dwarf, you damn Polack, leave go my foot! – Gentlemen.' He paused to dab his mouth with a handkerchief. 'The house known as High Haven is for sale and his Grace Tufty Thesinger has flown the coop.'

Nothing happened but he didn't expect much anyway. Journalists are not given to cries of amazement nor even incredulity.

'High Haven,' Luke repeated sonorously, 'is up for grabs. Mr Jake Chiu, the well-known and popular real estate entrepreneur, more familiar to you as my personal irate landlord, has been charged by Her Majesty's majestic government to *dispose* of High Haven. To wit, peddle. Let me go, you Polish bastard, I'll kill you!'

The dwarf had toppled him. Only a flailing, agile leap saved him from injury. From the floor, Luke hurled more abuse at his assailant. Meanwhile, Craw's large head had turned to Luke, and his moist eyes fixed on him a baleful stare that seemed to go on for ever. Luke began to wonder which of Craw's many laws he might have sinned against. Beneath his various disguises, Craw was a complex and solitary figure, as everyone round the table knew. Under the willed roughness of his manner lay a love of the East which seemed sometimes to string him tighter than he could stand, so that there were months when he would disappear from sight altogether, and like a sulky elephant go off on his private paths until he was once more fit to live with.

'Don't burble, your Grace, do you mind?' said Craw at last, and tilted back his big head imperiously. 'Refrain from spewing low-grade bilge into highly salubrious water, will you, Squire? High Haven's the spookhouse. Been the spookhouse for years. Lair of the lynx-eyed Major Tufty Thesinger formerly of Her Majesty's Rifles, presently Hong Kong's Lestrade of the Yard. Tufty wouldn't fly the coop. He's a hood, not a tit. Give my son a drink, Monsignor,' – this to the Shanghainese barman – 'he's wandering.'

Craw intoned another fire order and the Club returned to its intellectual pursuits. The truth was, there was little new to these great spy-scoops by

Luke. He had a long reputation as a failed spook-watcher, and his leads were invariably disproved. Since Vietnam, the stupid lad saw spies under every carpet. He believed the world was run by them, and much of his spare time, when he was sober, was spent hanging round the Colony's numberless battalions of thinly-disguised China-watchers and worse, who infested the enormous American Consulate up the hill. So if it hadn't been such a listless day, the matter would probably have rested there. As it was, the dwarf saw an opening to amuse, and seized it:

'Tell us, Lukie,' he suggested, with a queer upward twisting of the hands, 'are they selling High Haven with *contents* or *as found*?'

The question won him a round of applause. Was High Haven worth more with its secrets or without?

'Do they sell it with *Major Thesinger*?' the South African photographer pursued, in his humourless sing-song, and there was more laughter still, though it was no more affectionate. The photographer was a disturbing figure, a crewcut and starved, and his complexion was pitted like the battlefields he loved to haunt. He came from Cape Town, but they called him Deathwish the Hun. The saying was, he would bury all of them, for he stalked them like a mute.

For several diverting minutes now, Luke's point was lost entirely under a spate of Major Thesinger stories and Major Thesinger imitations in which all but Craw joined. It was recalled that the Major had made his first appearance on the Colony as an importer, with some fatuous cover down among the Docks; only to transfer, six months later, quite improbably, to the Services' list and, complete with his staff of pallid clerks and doughy, well-bred secretaries, decamp to the said spookhouse as somebody's replacement. In particular his *tête-à-tête* luncheons were described, to which, as it now turned out, practically every journalist listening had at one time or another been invited. And which ended with laborious proposals over brandy, including such wonderful phrases as: 'Now look here old man if you should ever bump into an interesting Chow from over the river, you know – one with *access*, follow me? – just you remember High Haven!' Then the magic telephone number, the one that 'rings spot on my desk, no middlemen, tape recorders, nothing, right?' – which a good half dozen of them seemed to have in their diaries: 'Here, pencil this one on your cuff, pretend it's a date or a girlfriend or something. Ready for it? Hong Kongside five-zero-two-four . . .'

Having chanted the digits in unison, they fell quiet. Somewhere a clock chimed for three fifteen. Luke slowly stood up and brushed the dust from his jeans. The old Shanghainese waiter gave up his post by the racks and reached for the menu in the hope that someone might eat. For a moment, uncertainty overcame them. The day was forfeit. It had been so since the first gin. In the background a low growl sounded as the Rocker ordered himself a generous luncheon:

'And bring me a cold beer, *cold*, you hear, boy? Muchee coldee. Chop chop.' The Superintendent had his way with natives and said this every time. The quiet returned.

'Well, there you are, Lukie,' the dwarf called, moving away. 'That's how you win your Pulitzer, I guess. Congratulations, darling. Scoop of the year.'

'Ah, go impale yourselves, the bunch of you,' said Luke carelessly and started to make his way down the bar to where two sallow girls sat, army daughters on the prowl. 'Jake Chiu showed me the damn letter of instruction, didn't he? On Her Majesty's damn Service, wasn't it? Damn crest on the top, lion screwing a goat. Hi sweethearts, remember me? I'm the kind man who bought you the lollipops at the fair.'

'Thesinger don't answer,' Deathwish the Hun sang mournfully from the telephone. 'Nobody don't answer. Not Thesinger, not his duty man. They disconnected the line.' In the excitement, or the monotony, no one had noticed Deathwish slip away.

Till now, old Craw the Australian had lain dead as a dodo. Now, he looked up sharply.

'Dial it again, you fool,' he ordered, tart as a drill sergeant.

With a shrug, Deathwish dialled Thesinger's number a second time, and a couple of them went to watch him do it. Craw stayed put, watching from where he sat. There were two instruments. Deathwish tried the second, but with no better result.

'Ring the operator,' Craw ordered, across the room to them. 'Don't stand there like a pregnant banshee. Ring the operator, you African ape!'

Number disconnected, said the operator.

'Since when, man?' Deathwish demanded, into the mouthpiece.

No information available, said the operator.

'Maybe they got a new number, then, right, man?' Deathwish howled into the mouthpiece, still at the luckless operator. No one had ever seen him so involved. Life for Deathwish was what happened at the end of a viewfinder: such passion was only attributable to the typhoon.

No information available, said the operator.

'Ring Shallow Throat,' Craw ordered, now quite furious. 'Ring every damned striped-pants in the Colony!'

Deathwish shook his long head uncertainly. Shallow Throat was the official government spokesman, a hate-object to them all. To approach him for anything was bad face.

'Here, give him to me,' said Craw and rising to his feet shoved them aside to get to the phone and embark on the lugubrious courtship of Shallow Throat. 'Your devoted Craw, sir, at your service. How's your Eminence in mind and health? Charmed, sir, charmed. And the wife and veg, sir? All eating well, I trust? No scurvy or typhus? Good. Well now, perhaps you'll have the benison to advise me why the hell Tufty Thesinger's flown the coop?'

They watched him, but his face had set like rock, and there was nothing more to read there.

'And the same to you, sir!' he snorted finally and slammed the phone back on its cradle so hard the whole table bounced. Then he turned to the old Shanghainese waiter. 'Monsignor Goh, sir, order me a petrol donkey and oblige! Your Graces, get off your arses, the pack of you!'

'What the hell for?' said the dwarf, hoping to be included in the command.

'For a story, you snotty little Cardinal, for a story your lecherous, alcoholic Eminences. For wealth, fame, women and longevity!'

His black mood was indecipherable to any of them.

'But what did Shallow Throat say that was so damn bad?' the shaggy Canadian cowboy asked, mystified.

The dwarf echoed him. 'Yeah, so what did he say, Brother Craw?'

'He said *no comment*,' Craw replied with fine dignity, as if the words were the vilest slur upon his professional honour.

So up the Peak they went, leaving only the silent majority of drinkers to their peace: restive Deathwish the Hun, long Luke, then the shaggy Canadian cowboy, very striking in his Mexican revolutionary moustache, the dwarf, attaching as ever, and finally old Craw and the two army girls: a plenary session of the Shanghai Junior Baptist Conservative Bowling Club, therefore, with ladies added – though the Club was sworn to celibacy. Amazingly, the jolly Cantonese driver took them all, a triumph of exuberance over physics. He even consented to give three receipts for the full fare, one for each of the journals represented, a thing no Hong Kong taxi-driver had been known to do before or since. It was a day to break all precedents. Craw sat in the front wearing his famous soft straw hat with Eton colours on the ribbon, bequeathed to him by an old comrade in his will. The dwarf was squeezed over the gear lever, the other three men sat in the back, and the two girls sat on Luke's lap, which made it hard for him to dab his mouth. The Rocker did not see fit to join them. He had tucked his napkin into his collar in preparation for the Club's roast lamb and mint sauce and a lot of potatoes.

'And another beer! But *cold* this time, hear that, boy? *Muchee coldee*, and bring it *chop chop*.'

But once the coast was clear, the Rocker also made use of the telephone, and spoke to Someone in Authority, just to be on the safe side, though they agreed there was nothing to be done.

The taxi was a red Mercedes, quite new, but nowhere kills a car faster than the Peak, climbing at no speed forever, airconditioners at full blast. The weather continued awful. As they sobbed slowly up the concrete cliffs they were engulfed by a fog thick enough to choke on. When they got out it was even worse. A hot, unbudgeable curtain had spread itself across the summit, reeking of petrol and crammed with the din of the valley. The moisture floated in hot fine swarms. On a clear day they would have had a view both ways, one of the loveliest on earth: northward to Kowloon and the blue mountains of the New Territories which hid from sight the eight hundred million Chinese who lacked the privilege of British rule; southward to Repulse and Deep Water Bays and the open China Sea. High Haven after all had been built by the Royal Navy in the Twenties in all the grand innocence of that service, to receive and impart a sense of power. But that afternoon, if the house had not been set among the trees, and in a hollow where the trees grew tall in their effort to reach the sky, and if the trees had not kept the fog out, they would have had nothing to look at but the two white concrete pillars with the bell-buttons marked 'day' and 'night' and the chained gates they supported. Thanks to the trees, however, they saw the house clearly, though it was set back fifty yards. They could pick out the drainpipes, fire escapes and washing lines and they could admire the green dome which the Japanese army had added during their four years' tenancy.

Hurrying to the front in his desire to be accepted, the dwarf pressed the bell marked 'day'. A speaker was let into the pillar and they all stared at it, waiting for it to say something or, as Luke would have it, puff out pot-smoke. At the roadside, the Cantonese driver had switched on his radio full and it was playing a whining Chinese love song, on and on. The second pillar was blank except for a brass plate announcing the Inter Services Liaison Staff, Thesinger's threadbare cover. Deathwish the Hun had produced a camera and was photographing as methodically as if he were on one of his native battlefields.

'Maybe they don't work Saturdays,' Luke suggested, while they continued to wait, at which Craw told him not to be bloody silly: spooks worked seven days a week and round the clock, he said. Also they never ate, apart from Tufty.

'*Good* afternoon to you,' said the dwarf.

Pressing the night bell, he had put his twisted red lips to the vents of the speaker and affected an upper-class English accent, which to give him credit he managed surprisingly well.

'My name is Michael Hanbury-Steadly-Heamoor, and I'm personal bumboy to Big Moo. I should like, *pliss*, to speak to Major Thesinger on a matter of some urgency, *pliss* there is a mushroom-shaped cloud the Major may not have noticed, it *appearce* to be forming over the *Pearl* River and it's spoiling Big Moo's golf. *Thenk* you. Will you kindly open the gate?'

One of the blonde girls gave a titter.

'I didn't know he was a *Steadly*-Heamoor,' she said.

Abandoning Luke, they had tethered themselves to the shaggy Canadian's arm, and spent a lot of time whispering in his ear.

'He's Rasputin,' said one of the girls admiringly, stroking the back of his thigh. 'I've seen the film. He's the spitten image, aren't you, Canada?'

Now everybody had a drink from Luke's flask while they regrouped and wondered what to do. From the direction of the parked cab, the driver's Chinese love song continued dauntlessly, but the speakers on the pillars said nothing at all. The dwarf pressed both bells at once, and tried an Al Capone threat.

'Now see here, Thesinger, we know you're in there. You come out with your hands raised, uncloaked, throw down your dagger – *hey watch it, you stupid cow!*'

The imprecation was addressed neither to the Canadian, nor to old Craw – who was sidling towards the trees, apparently to meet a call of nature – but to Luke, who had decided to beat his way into the house. The gateway stood in a muddy service bay sheltered by dripping trees. On the far side was a pile of refuse, some new. Sauntering over to this in search of an illuminating clue, Luke had unearthed a piece of pig iron made in the shape of an S. Having carted it to the gate, though it must have weighed thirty pounds or more, he was holding it two-handed above his head and driving it against the staves, at which the gate tolled like a cracked bell.

Deathwish had sunk to one knee, his hollowed face clawed into a martyr's smile as he shot.

'Counting five, Tufty,' Luke yelled, with another shattering heave. 'One . . . ' He struck again. 'Two . . . '

Overhead an assorted flock of birds, some very large, lifted out of the trees and flew in slow spirals, but the thunder of the valley and the boom of the gate drowned their screams. Their taxi-driver was dancing about, clapping and laughing, his love song forgotten. Stranger still, in view of the menacing weather, an entire Chinese family appeared, pushing not one pram but two, and they began laughing also, even the smallest child, holding their hands across their mouths to conceal their teeth. Till suddenly the Canadian cowboy let out a cry, shook off the girls and pointed through the gates.

'For Lord's sakes what the heck's Craw doing? Old buzzard's jumped the wire.'

By now, whatever sense of normal scale there might have been had vanished. A collective madness had seized everyone. The drink, the black day, the claustrophobia, had gone to their heads entirely. The girls fondled the Canadian with abandon, Luke continued his hammering, the Chinese were hooting with laughter, until with divine timeliness the fog lifted, temples of blue-black cloud soared directly above them, and a torrent of rain crashed into the trees. A second longer and it hit them, drenching them in the first swoop. The girls, suddenly half naked, fled laughing and shrieking for the Mercedes, but the male ranks held firm – even the dwarf held firm – staring through the films of water at the unmistakable figure of Craw the Australian, in his old Etonian hat, standing in the shelter of the house under a rough porch that looked as if it were made for bicycles, though no one but a lunatic would bicycle up the Peak.

'Craw!' they screamed. 'Monsignor! The bastard's scooped us!'

The din of the rain was deafening, the branches seemed to be cracking under its force. Luke had thrown aside his mad hammer. The shaggy cowboy went first, Luke and the dwarf followed, Deathwish with his smile and his camera brought up the tail, crouching and hobbling as he continued photographing blindly. The rain poured off them as it wanted, sloshing in red rivulets round their ankles as they followed Craw's trail up a slope where the screech of bullfrogs added to the row. They scaled a bracken ridge, slithered to a halt before a barbed wire fence, clambered through the parted strands and crossed a low ditch. By the time they reached him, Craw was gazing at the green cupola, while the rain despite the straw hat ran busily off his jaw, turning his trim fawn suit into a blackened, shapeless tunic. He stood as if mesmerised, staring upward. Luke, who loved him best, spoke first.

'Your Grace? Hey, wake up! It's me: Romeo. Jesus Christ, what the hell's eating him?'

Suddenly concerned, Luke gently touched his arm. But still Craw didn't speak.

'Maybe he died standing up,' the dwarf suggested, while grinning Deathwish photographed him on this happy off-chance.

Like an old prizefighter, Craw slowly rallied. 'Brother Luke, we owe you a handsome apology, sir,' he muttered.

'Get him back to the cab,' said Luke, and began clearing a way for him, but the old boy refused to move.

'Tufty Thesinger. A good scout. Not a flyer – not sly enough for flight – but a good scout.'

'Tufty Thesinger rest in peace,' said Luke impatiently. 'Let's go. Dwarf, move your ass.'

'He's stoned,' said the cowboy.

'Consider the clues, Watson,' Craw resumed, after another pause for meditation, while Luke tugged at his arm and the rain came on still faster. 'Remark first the empty cages over the window, whence airconditioners have been untimely ripped. Parsimony, my son, a commendable virtue, especially if I may say so, in a spook. Notice the dome, there? Study it carefully, sir. Scratch marks. Not, alas, the footprints of a gigantic hound, but the scratch marks of wireless aerials removed by the frantic, roundeye hand. Ever heard of a spookhouse without a wireless aerial? Might as well have a cathouse without a piano.'

The rainfall had reached a crescendo. Huge drops thumped around them like shot. Craw's face was a mix of things which Luke could only guess at. Deep in his heart it occurred to him that Craw really might be dying. Luke had seen little of natural death, and was very much on the alert for it.

'Maybe they just got rock-fever and split,' he said, trying again to coax him to the car.

'Very possibly, your Grace, very possibly indeed. It is certainly the season for rash, ungovernable acts.'

'Home,' said Luke, and pulled firmly at his arm. 'Make a path there, will you? Stretcher party.'

But the old man still lingered stubbornly for a last look at the English spookhouse flinching in the storm.

The Canadian cowboy filed first and his piece deserved a better fate. He wrote it that night, while the girls slept in his bed. He guessed the story would go best as a magazine piece rather than straight news, so he built it round the Peak in general and only used Thesinger as a peg. He explained how the Peak was traditionally Hong Kong's Olympus – 'the higher you lived on it, the higher you stood in society' – and how the rich British opium traders, Hong Kong's founding fathers, fled there to avoid the cholera and fever of the town; how even a couple of decades ago a person of Chinese race required a pass before he could set foot there. He described the history of High Haven, and lastly its reputation, fostered by the Chinese-language press, as a witches' kitchen of British Imperialist plots against Mao. Overnight the kitchen had closed and the cooks had vanished.

'Another conciliatory gesture?' he asked. 'Appeasement? All part of Britain's low-profile policy towards the Mainland? Or simply one more sign that in South East Asia, as everywhere else in the world, the British were having to come down from their mountain top?'

His mistake was to select a heavy English Sunday paper which occasionally ran his pieces. The D-Notice forbidding all reference to these events was there ahead of him. 'Regret your nice Havenstory unplaced,' the editor cabled, and shoved it straight on the spike. A few days later, returning to his room, the cowboy found it ransacked. Also for several weeks, his telephone developed a sort of laryngitis, so that he never used it without including an obscene reference to Big Moo and his retinue.

Luke went home full of ideas, bathed, drank a lot of black coffee and set to work. He telephoned airlines, government contacts, and a whole host of pale, over-brushed acquaintances in the US Consulate, who infuriated him with arch and Delphic answers. He pestered furniture removal firms which specialized in handling government contracts. By ten that night he had, in his own words to the dwarf, whom he also telephoned several times, 'proof-cooked-five-different-ways' that Thesinger, his wife, and all the staff of High Haven, had left Hong Kong by charter in the early hours of Thursday morning, bound for London. Thesinger's boxer dog, he learned by a happy chance, would follow by air cargo later in the week. Having made a few notes, Luke crossed the room, settled to his typewriter, bashed out a few lines, and dried up, as he knew he would. He began in a rush, fluently:

'Today a fresh cloud of scandal hangs over the embattled and non-elected government of Britain's one remaining Asian colony. Hot on the latest revelation of graft in the police and civil service comes word that the Island's most hush-hush establishment, High Haven, base for Britain's cloak-and-dagger ploys against Red China, has been summarily shut down.'

There, with a blasphemous sob of impotence, he stopped and pressed his face into his open hands. Nightmares: those he could stand. To wake, after so much war, shaking and sweating from unspeakable visions, with his nostrils

filled with the stink of napalm on human flesh: in a way, it was a consolation to
him to know that after all that pressing down, the floodgates of his feeling
had burst. There had been times, experiencing those things, when he longed
for the leisure to recover his powers of disgust. If nightmares were necessary
in order to restore him to the ranks of normal men and women, then he could
embrace them with gratitude. But not in the worst of his nightmares had it
occurred to him that having written the war, he might not be able to write the
peace. For six night hours Luke fought with this awful deadness. Sometimes
he thought of old Craw, standing there with the rain running off him,
delivering his funeral oration: maybe *that* was the story? But whoever hung a
story on the strange humour of a fellow hack?

Nor did the dwarf's own hashed-out version meet with much success,
which made him very scratchy. On the face of it, the story had everything
they asked for. It spoofed the British, it had *spy* written large, and for once it
got away from the notion of America as the hangman of South East Asia. But
all he had for a reply, after a five-day wait, was a terse instruction to stay on his
rostrum and leave off trying to play the trumpet.

Which left old Craw. Though a mere sideshow by comparison with the
thrust of the main action, the timing of what Craw did, and did not do,
remains to this day impressive. He filed nothing for three weeks. There was
small stuff he should have handled but he didn't bother. To Luke, who was
seriously concerned for him, he seemed at first to continue his mysterious
decline. He lost his bounce and his love of fellowship entirely. He became
snappish and at times downright unkind, and he barked bad Cantonese at
the waiters; even at his favourite, Goh. He treated the Shanghai Bowlers as if
they were his worst enemies, and recalled alleged slights they had long
forgotten. Sitting alone at his window seat, he was like an old boulevardier
fallen on hard times, waspish, inward, slothful. Then one day he disappeared
and when Luke called apprehensively at his apartment the old amah told him
that 'Whisky Papa runrun London fastee'. She was a strange little creature
and Luke was inclined to doubt her. A dull North German stringer for *der
Spiegel* reported sighting Craw in Vientiane, carousing at the Constellation
bar, but again Luke wondered. Craw-watching had always been something of
an insider sport, and there was prestige in adding to the general fund.

Till a Monday came, and around midday the old boy strolled into the Club
wearing a new beige suit and a very fine buttonhole, all smiles and anecdotes
once more, and went to work on the High Haven story. He spent money,
more than his paper would normally have allowed him. He ate several jovial
lunches with well-dressed Americans from vaguely titled United States.
agencies, some of them known to Luke. Wearing his famous straw hat, he
took each separately to quiet, well-chosen restaurants. In the Club, he was
reviled for diplomat-crawling, a grave crime, and this pleased him. Next, a
China-watchers' conference summoned him to Tokyo, and with hindsight it
is fair to assume he used that visit to check out other parts of the story that was
shaping for him. Certainly he asked old friends at the conference to unearth
bits of fact for him when they got home to Bangkok, or Singapore, or Taipei
or wherever they came from, and they obliged because they knew he would
have done the same for them. In an eerie way, he seemed to know what he
was looking for before they found it.

The result appeared in its fullest version in a Sydney morning newspaper which was beyond the long arm of Anglo-American censorship. By common consent it recalled the master's vintage years. It ran to two thousand words. Typically, he did not lead with the High Haven story at all, but with the 'mysteriously empty wing' of the British Embassy in Bangkok, which till a month ago had housed a strange body called 'The Seato Coordination Unit', as well as a Visa Section boasting six second secretaries. Was it the pleasures of the Soho massage parlours, the old Australian enquired sweetly, which lured the Thais to Britain in such numbers that six second secretaries were needed to handle their visa applications? Strange, too, he mused, that since their departure, and the closure of that wing, long queues of aspirant travellers had *not* formed outside the Embassy. Gradually – he wrote at ease, but never carelessly – a surprising picture unfolded before his readers. He called British intelligence 'the Circus'. He said the name derived from the address of that organization's secret headquarters, which overlooked a famous inter-section of London streets. The Circus had not merely pulled out of High Haven, he said, but out of Bangkok, Singapore, Saigon, Tokyo, Manila, and Djakarta as well. And Seoul. Even solitary Taiwan was not immune, where an unsung British Resident was discovered to have shed three clerk-drivers and two secretarial assistants only a week before the article went to press.

'A hoods' Dunkirk,' Craw called it, 'in which Charter DC8s replaced the Kentish fishing fleets.'

What had prompted such an exodus? Craw offered several nimble theor-ies. Were we witnessing yet one more cut in British government spending? The writer was sceptical. In times of travail, Britain's tendency was to rely more, not less, on spies. Her entire empire history urged her to do so. The thinner her trade routes, the more elaborate her clandestine efforts to protect them. The more feeble her colonial grip, the more desperate her subversion of those who sought to loosen it. No: Britain might be on the breadline but the spies would be the last of her luxuries to go. Craw set up other possibilities and knocked them down. A gesture of *détente* toward Mainland China? he suggested, echoing the cowboy's point. Certainly Britain would do anything under the sun to keep Hong Kong clear of Mao's anti-colonial zeal – short of giving up her spies. Thus old Craw arrived at the theory he liked best:

'Right across the Far Eastern chequerboard,' he wrote, 'the Circus is performing what is known in the spy-trade as a duck-dive.'

But why?

The writer now quoted his 'senior American prebends of the intelligence church militant in Asia'. American intelligence agents generally, he said, and not just in Asia, were 'hopping mad about lax security in the British organizations'. They were hopping highest about the recent discovery of a top Russian spy – he threw in the correct tradename 'mole' – inside the Circus's London headquarters: a British traitor, whom they declined to name, but who in the words of the senior prebends had 'compromised every Anglo-American clandestine operation worth a dime for the last twenty years'. Where was the mole now? the writer had asked his sources. To which, with undiminished spleen, they had replied: 'Dead. In Russia. And hopefully both.'

Craw had never wanted for a wrap-up, but this one, to Luke's fond eye, had a real sense of ceremony about it. It was almost an assertion of life itself, if only of the secret life.

'*Is Kim the boy spy vanished for good, then, from the legends of the East?*' he asked. '*Shall the English pundit never again stain his skin, slip into native costume and silently take his place beside the village fires? Do not fear,*' he insisted. '*The British will be back! The time-honoured sport of spot-the-spook will be with us once again! The spy is not dead: he sleepeth.*'

The piece appeared. In the Club, it was fleetingly admired, envied, forgotten. A local English-language paper with strong American connections reprinted it in full, with the result that the mayfly after all enjoyed another day of life. The old boy's charity benefit, they said: a doffing of the cap before he passes from the stage. Then the overseas network of the BBC ran it, and finally the Colony's own torpid radio network ran a version of the BBC's version, and for a full day there was debate about whether Big Moo had decided to take the muzzle off the local news services. Yet even with this protracted billing, nobody, not Luke, not even the dwarf, saw fit to wonder how the devil the old man had known the back way into High Haven.

Which merely proved, if proof were ever needed, that journalists are no quicker than anybody else at spotting what goes on under their noses. It was a typhoon Saturday after all.

Within the Circus itself, as Craw had correctly called the seat of British intelligence, reactions to Craw's piece varied according to how much was known by those who were doing the reacting. In Housekeeping Section, for instance, which was responsible for such tatters of cover as the Circus could gather to itself these days, the old boy released a wave of pent-up fury which can only be understood by those who have tasted the atmosphere of a secret department under heavy siege. Even otherwise tolerant spirits became savagely retributive. Treachery! Breach of contract! Block his pension! Put him on the watch list! Prosecution the moment he returns to England! Down the market a little, those less rabid about their security took a kindlier view, though it was still uninformed. Well, well, they said a little ruefully, that was the way of it: name us a joe who didn't blow his top now and then, and specially one who'd been left in ignorance for as long as poor old Craw had. And after all, he'd disclosed nothing that wasn't generally available, now had he? Really those housekeeper people should show a *little* moderation. Look how they went for poor Molly Meakin the other night, sister to Mike and hardly out of ribbons, just because she left a bit of blank stationery in her waste basket!

Only those at the inmost point saw things differently. To them, old Craw's article was a discreet masterpiece of disinformation: George Smiley at his best, they said. Clearly, the story had to come out, and all were agreed that censorship at any time was objectionable. Much better, therefore, to let it come out in the manner of our choosing. The right timing, the right amount, the right tone: a lifetime's experience, they agreed, in every brushstroke. But that was not a view which passed outside their set.

Back in Hong Kong – clearly, said the Shanghai Bowlers, like the dying, the old boy had had a prophetic instinct of this – Craw's High Haven story turned out to be his swansong. A month after it appeared he had retired, not from the Colony but from his trade as a scribbler and from the Island too. Renting a cottage in the New Territories, he announced that he proposed to expire under a slanteye heaven. For the Bowlers he might as well have chosen Alaska. It was just too damn far, they said, to drive back when you were drunk. There was a rumour – untrue, since Craw's appetites did not run in that direction – that he had got himself a pretty Chinese boy as a companion. That was the dwarf's work: he did not like to be scooped by old men. Only Luke refused to put him out of mind. Luke drove out to see him one mid-morning after night-shift. For the hell of it, and because the old buzzard meant a lot to him. Craw was happy as a sandboy, he reported: quite his former vile self, but a bit dazed to be bearded by Luke without warning. He had a friend with him, not a Chinese boy, but a visiting fireman whom he introduced as George: a podgy, ill-sighted little body in very round spectacles who had apparently dropped in unexpectedly. Aside, Craw explained to Luke that this George was a backroom boy on a British newspaper syndicate he used to work for in the dark ages.

'Handles the geriatric side, your Grace. Taking a swing through Asia.'

Whoever he was, it was clear that Craw stood in awe of the podgy man, for he even called him 'your Holiness'. Luke had felt he was intruding and left without getting drunk.


So there it was. Thesinger's moonlight flit, old Craw's near death and resurrection; his swansong in defiance of so much hidden censorship; Luke's restless preoccupation with the secret world; the Circus's inspired exploitation of a necessary evil. Nothing planned, but as life would have it, a curtain-raiser to much that happened later. A typhoon Saturday; a ripple on the plunging, fetid, sterile, swarming pool which is Hong Kong; a bored chorus, still without a hero. And, curiously, a few months afterwards, it fell once more to Luke, in his role of Shakespearean messenger, to announce the hero's coming. The news came over the house wire while he was on stand-by and he published it to a bored audience with his customary fervour:

'Folks! Give ear! I have news! Jerry Westerby's back on the beat, men! Heading out East again, hear me, stringing for that same damn comic!'

'His *lordship*!' the dwarf cried at once in mock ecstasy. 'A *desh of blue blood, I say*, to raise the vulgar tone! *Oorah for quality, I say*.' With a profane oath, he threw a napkin at the wine rack. 'Jesus,' he said, and emptied Luke's glass.

# TWO

## *the great call*

On the afternoon the telegram arrived, Jerry Westerby was hacking at his typewriter on the shaded side of the balcony of his rundown farmhouse, the sack of old books dumped at his feet. The envelope was brought by the black-clad person of the postmistress, a craggy and ferocious peasant who with the ebbing of traditional forces had become the headman of the ragtag Tuscan hamlet. She was a wily creature but today the drama of the occasion had the better of her, and despite the heat she fairly scampered up the arid track. In her ledger the historic moment of delivery was later put at six past five, which was a lie but gave it force. The real time was five exactly. Indoors Westerby's scrawny girl, whom the village called the orphan, was hammering at a stubborn piece of goat's meat, vehemently, the way she attacked everything. The greedy eye of the postmistress spotted her, at the open window and from a good way off: elbows stuck out all ways and her top teeth jammed on to her lower lip: scowling, no doubt, as usual.

'Whore,' thought the postmistress passionately, 'now you have what you have been waiting for.'

The radio was blaring Verdi: the orphan would hear only classical music, as the whole village had learned from the scene she had made at the tavern the evening when the blacksmith tried to choose rock music on the juke box. She had thrown a pitcher at him. So what with the Verdi, and the typewriter and the goat, said the postmistress, the row was so deafening that even an Italian would have heard it.

Jerry sat like a locust on the wood floor, she recalled – maybe he had one cushion – and he was using the book-sack as a footstool. He sat splay-footed, typing between his knees. He had bits of flyblown manuscript spread round him, which were weighted with stones against the red-hot breezes which plagued his scalded hilltop, and a wicker flask of the local red at his elbow, no doubt for the moments, known even to the greatest artists, when natural inspiration failed him. He typed the eagle's way, she told them later amid admiring laughter: much circling before he swooped. And he wore what he always wore, whether he was loafing fruitlessly around his bit of paddock, tilling the dozen useless olive trees which the rogue Franco had palmed off on him, or paddling down to the village with the orphan to shop, or sitting in the tavern over a sharp one before embarking on the long climb home: buckskin boots which the orphan never brushed, and were consequently worn shiny at the toe, ankle socks which she never washed, a filthy shirt, once white, and grey shorts that looked as though they had been frayed by hostile dogs, and which an honest woman would long ago have mended. And he greeted her with that familiar burry rush of words, at once bashful and enthusiastic, which she did not understand in detail, but only generally, like a news broadcast, and could copy, through the black gaps of her decrepit teeth, with surprising flashes of fidelity.

'Mama Stefano, gosh, super, must be boiling. Here, sport, wet your whistle,' he exclaimed, while he slopped down the brick steps with a glass of

wine for her, grinning like a schoolboy, which was his nickname in the village:
the schoolboy, a telegram for the schoolboy, urgent from London! In nine
months no more than a wad of paperback books and the weekly scrawl from
his child, and now out of a blue sky this monument of a telegram, short like a
demand, but fifty words prepaid for the reply! Imagine, fifty, the cost alone!
Only natural that as many as possible should have tried their hand at reading
it.

They had choked at first over *honourable*: 'The *honourable* Gerald Westerby.'
Why? The baker, who had been a prisoner-of-war in Birmingham, produced
a battered dictionary: *having honour, title of courtesy given to the son of a nobleman.*
Of course. Signora Sanders, who lived across the valley had already declared
the schoolboy to be of noble blood. The second son of a press baron, she had
said, *Lord* Westerby a newspaper proprietor, dead. First the paper had died,
then its owner – thus Signora Sanders, a wit, they had passed the joke round.
Next *regret*, which was easy. So was *advise*. The postmistress was gratified to
discover, against all expectation, how much good Latin the English had
assimilated despite their decadence. The word *guardian* came harder for it
led to *protector*, thence inevitably to unsavoury jokes among the menfolk,
which the postmistress stamped on angrily. Till at last, step by step, the code
was broken and the story out. The schoolboy had a guardian, meaning a
substitute father. This *guardian* lay dangerously ill in hospital, demanding to
see the schoolboy before he died. He wanted nobody else. Only honourable
Westerby would do. Quickly they filled in the rest of the picture for themselves: the sobbing family gathered at the bedside, the wife prominent and
inconsolable, refined priests administering the last sacraments, valuables
being locked away, and all over the house, in corridors, back kitchens, the
same whispered word: Westerby – where is honourable Westerby?

Lastly the telegram's signatories remained to be interpreted. There were
three and they called themselves *solicitors*, a word which triggered one more
swoop of dirty innuendo before *notary* was arrived at, and faces abruptly
hardened. Holy Maria. If three notaries were involved, then so were large
sums of money. And if all three had insisted upon signing, and prepaid that
fifty word reply to boot, then not just large but mountainous sums! Acres!
Wagon loads! No wonder the orphan had clung to him so, the whore!
Suddenly everyone was clamouring to make the hill climb. Guido's
Lambretta would take him as far as the water tank, Mario could run like a fox.
Manuela the chandler's girl had a tender eye, the shadow of bereavement sat
well on her. Repulsing all volunteers – and handing Mario a sharp cuff for
the presumption – the postmistress locked the till and left her idiot son to
mind the shop, though it meant twenty sweltering minutes and – if that
cursed furnace of a wind was blowing up there – a mouthful of red dust for
her toil.

They had not made enough of Jerry at first. She regretted this now, as she
laboured through the olive groves, but the error had its reasons. First, he had
arrived in winter when the cheap buyers come. He arrived alone, but wearing
the furtive look of someone who has recently dumped a lot of human cargo,
such as children, wives, mothers: the postmistress had known men in her
time, and she had seen that wounded smile too often not to recognize it in
Jerry: 'I am married but free,' it said, and neither claim was true. Second, the
scented English major brought him, a known pig who ran a property agency
for exploiting peasants: yet another reason to spurn the schoolboy. The
scented major showed him several desirable farmhouses, including one in

which the postmistress herself had an interest – also, by coincidence, the finest – but the schoolboy settled instead for the pederast Franco's hovel stuck on this forsaken hilltop she was now ascending: the devil's hill, they called it; the devil came up here when hell became too cool for him. Slick Franco of all people, who watered his milk and his wine and spent his Sundays simpering with popinjays in the town square! The inflated price was half a million lire of which the scented major tried to steal a third, merely because there was a contract.

'And everyone knows why the major favoured slick Franco,' she hissed through her frothing teeth, and her pack of supporters made knowing noises 'tch-tch' at each other, till she angrily ordered them to shut up.

Also, as a shrewd woman, she distrusted something in Jerry's make-up. A hardness buried in the lavishness. She had seen it with Englishmen before, but the schoolboy was in a class by himself, and she distrusted him; she held him dangerous through his restless charm. Today of course one could put down those early failings to the eccentricity of a noble English writer, but at the time, the postmistress had shown him no such indulgence. 'Wait till the summer,' she had warned her customers in a snarl, soon after his first shambling visit to her shop – pasta, bread, flykiller. 'In the summer he'll find out what he's bought, the cretin.' In the summer, slick Franco's mice would storm the bedroom, Franco's fleas would devour him alive and Franco's pederastic hornets would chase him round the garden and the devil's red-hot wind would burn his parts to a frazzle. The water would run out, he would be forced to defecate in the fields like an animal. And when winter came round again the scented pig major could sell the house to another fool, at a loss to everyone but himself.

As to celebrity, in those first weeks the schoolboy showed not a shred of it. He never bargained, he had never heard of discounts, there was not even pleasure in robbing him. And when, in the shop, she drove him beyond his few miserable phrases of kitchen Italian, he did not raise his voice and bawl at her like the real English but shrugged happily and helped himself to whatever he wanted. A *writer*, they said; well, who was not? Very well, he bought quires of foolscap from her. She ordered more, he bought them. Bravo. He possessed books: a mildewed lot, by the look of them, which he carried in a grey jute sack like a poacher's and before the orphan came they would see him striding off into the middle of nowhere, the book-sack slung over his shoulder, for a reading session. Guido had happened on him in the Contessa's forest, perched on a log like a toad and leafing through them one after another, as if they were all one book and he had lost his place. He also possessed a typewriter of which the filthy cover was a patchwork of worn out luggage labels: bravo again. Just as any longhair who buys a paintpot calls himself an artist: *that* sort of writer. In the spring the orphan came and the postmistress hated her too.

A red-head, which was halfway to whoredom for a start. Not enough breast to nurse a rabbit, and worst of all a fierce eye for arithmetic. They said he found her in the town: whore again. From the first day, she had not let him out of her sight. Clung to him like a child. Ate with him, and sulked; drank with him, and sulked; shopped with him, picking up the language like a thief, till they became a minor local sight together, the English giant and his sulking wraith whore, trailing down the hill with their rush basket, the schoolboy in his tattered shorts grinning at everyone, the scowling orphan in her whore's sackcloth with nothing underneath, so that though she was plain as a scorpion the men stared after her to see her hard haunches rock through the fabric. She walked with all her fingers locked round his arm and her cheek against his shoulder, and she only let go of him to pay out meanly from the purse she now controlled. When they met a familiar face, he greeted it for both of them, flapping his vast free arm like a Fascist. And God help the man who, on the rare occasion when she went alone, ventured a fresh word or a wolf call: she would turn and spit like a gutter-cat, and her eyes burned like the devil's.

'And now we know why!' cried the postmistress, very loud, as, still climbing, she mounted a false crest. 'The orphan is after his inheritance. Why else would a whore be loyal?'

It was the visit of Signora Sanders to her shop which caused Mama Stefano's dramatic reappraisal of the schoolboy's worth, and of the orphan's motive. The Sanders was rich and bred horses further up the valley, where she lived with a lady friend known as the man-child who wore close-cut hair and chain belts. Their horses won prizes everywhere. The Sanders was sharp and intelligent and frugal in a way Italians liked, and she knew whomever was worth knowing of the few moth-eaten English scattered over the hills. She called ostensibly to buy a ham, a month ago it must have been, but her real quest was for the schoolboy. Was it true? she asked: 'Signor *Gerald* Westerby, and living here in the village? A large man, pepper and salt hair, athletic, full of energy, an aristocrat, shy?' Her father the general had known the family in England, she said; they had been neighbours in the country for a spell, the schoolboy's father and her own. The Sanders was considering paying him a visit: what were the schoolboy's circumstances? The postmistress muttered something about the orphan, but the Sanders was unperturbed:

'Oh the Westerbys are *always* changing their women,' she said with a laugh, and turned toward the door.

Dumbfounded, the postmistress detained her, then showered her with questions.

But who was he? What had he done with his youth? A journalist, said the Sanders, and gave what she knew of the family background; the father a flamboyant figure, fair-haired like the son, kept racehorses, she had met him again not long before his death and he was still a man. Like the son he was never at peace: women and houses, changing them all the time; always roaring at someone, if not at his son then at someone across the street. The postmistress pressed harder. But in his own right: was the schoolboy distinguished in his own right? Well, he had certainly worked for some distinguished newspapers, put it that way, said the Sanders, her smile mysteriously broadening.

'It is not the English habit, as a rule, to accord distinction to journalists,' she explained, in her classic, Roman way of talking.

But the postmistress needed more, far more. His writing, his book, what was all *that* about? So long! So much thrown away! Basketsful, the rubbish carter had told her – for no one in his right mind would light a fire up there in summertime. Beth Sanders understood the intensity of isolated people, and knew that in barren places their intelligence must fix on tiny matters. So she tried, she really tried to oblige. Well, he certainly had *travelled* incessantly, she said, coming back to the counter and putting down her parcel. Today all journalists were travellers, of course, breakfast in London, lunch in Rome, dinner in Delhi, but Signor Westerby had been exceptional even by that standard. So perhaps it was a travel book, she ventured.

But *why* had he travelled? the postmistress insisted, for whom no journey was without a goal: *why*?

For the wars, the Sanders replied patiently: for wars, pestilence and famine. 'What else had a journalist to do these days, after all, but report life's miseries?' she asked.

The postmistress shook her head wisely, all her senses fixed upon the revelation: the son of a blond equestrian lord who bellowed, a mad traveller, a writer in distinguished newspapers! And was there a particular theatre? she asked – a corner of God's earth – in which he was a specialist? He was mostly in the East, the Sanders thought, after a moment's reflection. He had been everywhere, but there is a kind of Englishman for whom only the East is home. No doubt that was why he had come to Italy. Some men go dull without the sun.

And some women, too, the postmistress shrieked, and they had a good laugh.

Ah the East, said the postmistress, with a tragic slanting of the head – war upon war, why didn't the Pope stop it? As Mama Stefano ran on this way, the Sanders seemed to remember something. She smiled slightly at first, and her smile grew. An exile's smile, the postmistress reflected, watching her: she is like a sailor remembering the sea.

'He used to drag a sackful of books around,' she said. 'We used to say he stole them from the big houses.'

'He carries it now!' the postmistress cried, and told how Guido had stumbled on him in the Contessa's forest, the schoolboy reading on the log.

'He had notions of becoming a *novelist*, I believe,' the Sanders continued, in the same vein of private reminiscence: 'I remember his father telling us. He was *frightfully* angry. Roared all over the house.'

'The schoolboy? The *schoolboy* was angry?' Mama Stefano exclaimed, now quite incredulous.

'No, no. The father.' The Sanders laughed aloud. In the English social scale, she explained, novelists rated even worse than journalists. 'Does he also paint still?'

'Paint? He is a painter?'

He tried, said the Sanders, but the father forbade that also. Painters were the lowest of *all* creatures, she said, amid fresh laughter: only the successful ones were remotely tolerable.

Soon after this multiple bombshell the blacksmith – the same blacksmith who had been the target of the orphan's pitcher – reported having seen Jerry . and the girl at the Sanders' stud, twice in one week, then three times, also eating there. And that the schoolboy had shown a great talent for horses, lunging and walking them with natural understanding, even the wildest. The orphan took no part, said the blacksmith. She sat in the shade with the man-child either reading from the book-sack or watching him with her jealous, unblinking eyes; waiting, as they all now knew, for the guardian to die. And today the telegram!

Jerry had seen Mama Stefano from a long way off. He had that instinct, there was a part of him that never ceased to watch: a black figure hobbling inexorably up the dust-path like a lame beetle in and out of the ruled shadows of the cedars, up the dry watercourse of slick Franco's olive groves, into their own bit of Italy as he called it, all two hundred square metres of it, but big enough to hit a tethered tennis-ball round a pole on cool evenings when they felt athletic. He had seen very early the blue envelope she was waving, and he had even heard the sound of her mewing carrying crookedly over the other sounds of the valley: the Lambrettas and the bandsaws. And his first gesture, without stopping his typing, was to steal a glance at the house to make sure the girl had closed the kitchen window to keep out the heat and the insects. Then, just as the postmistress later described, he went quickly down the steps to her, wine glass in hand, in order to head her off before she came too near.

He read the telegram slowly, once, bending over it to get the writing into shadow, and his face as Mama Stefano watched it became gaunt, and private, and an extra huskiness entered his voice as he laid one huge, cushioned hand on her arm.

'*La sera*,' he managed, as he guided her back along the path. He would send his reply this evening, he meant. '*Molto grazie*, Mama. Super. Thanks very much. Terrific.'

As they parted she was still chattering wildly, offering him every service under the sun, taxis, porters, phone calls to the airport, and Jerry was vaguely patting the pockets of his shorts for small or large change: he had momentarily forgotten, apparently, that the girl looked after the money.

The schoolboy had received the news with bearing, the postmistress reported to the village. Graciously, to the point of escorting her part of the way back; bravely, so that only a woman of the world – and one who knew the English – would have read the aching grief beneath; distractedly, so that he had neglected to tip her. Or was he already acquiring the extreme parsimony of the very rich?

But how did the *orphan* behave? they asked. Did she not sob and cry to the Virgin, pretending to share his distress?

'He has yet to tell her,' the postmistress whispered, recalling wistfully her one short glimpse of her, sideview, hammering at the meat: 'He has yet to consider her position.'

The village settled, waiting for the evening, and Jerry sat in the hornet field, gazing at the sea and winding the book-bag round and round, till it reached its limit, and unwound itself.

First there was the valley, and above it stood the five hills in a half ring, and above the hills ran the sea which at that time of day was no more than a flat brown stain in the sky. The hornet field where he sat was a long terrace shored by stones, with a ruined barn at one corner which had given them shelter to picnic and sunbathe unobserved until the hornets nested in the wall. She had seen them when she was hanging out washing, and run in to Jerry to tell him, and Jerry had unthinkingly grabbed a bucket of mortar from slick Franco's place and filled in all their entrances. Then called her down so that she could admire his handiwork: my man, how he protects me. In his memory he saw her exactly: shivering at his side, arms huddled across her body, staring at the new cement and listening to the crazed hornets inside and whispering, 'Jesus, Jesus,' too frightened to budge.

Maybe she'll wait for me, he thought.

He remembered the day he met her. He told himself that story often, because good luck was rare in Jerry's life, where women were concerned, and when it happened he liked to roll it around the tongue, as he would say. A Thursday. He'd taken his usual lift to town, in order to do a spot of shopping, or maybe to see a fresh set of faces and get away from the novel for a while; or maybe just to bolt from the screaming monotony of that empty landscape, which more often was like a prison to him, and a solitary one at that; or conceivably he might just hook himself a woman, which occasionally he brought off by hanging round the bar of the tourist hotel. So he was sitting reading in the trattoria in the town square – a carafe, plate of ham, olives – and suddenly he became aware of this skinny, rangy kid, red-head, sullen face and a brown dress like a monk's habit and a shoulder bag made out of carpet stuff.

'Looks naked without a guitar,' he'd thought.

Vaguely, she reminded him of his daughter Cat, short for Catherine, but only vaguely because he hadn't seen Cat for ten years, which was when his first marriage fell in. Quite why he hadn't seen her, he could even now not precisely say. In the first shock of separation, a confused sense of chivalry told him Cat did better to forget him. 'Best if she writes me off. Put her heart where her home is.' When her mother remarried, the case for self-denial seemed all the stronger. But sometimes he missed her very badly, and most likely that was why, having caught his interest, the girl held it. Did Cat go round like that, alone and spiked with tiredness? Had Cat got her freckles still, and a jaw like a pebble? Later, the girl told him she'd jumped the wall. She'd got herself a governess job with some rich family in Florence. Mother was too busy with the lovers to worry about the kids, but the husband had lots of time for the governess. She'd grabbed what cash she could find and bolted and here she was: no luggage, the police alerted, and using her last chewed banknote to buy herself one square meal before perdition.

There was not a lot of talent in the square that day – there never was – and by the time she sat down, that kid had got just about every able-bodied fellow in town giving her the treatment, from the waiters upward, purring 'beautiful missus' and much rougher stuff besides, of which Jerry missed the precise drift, but it had them all laughing at her expense. Then one of them tried to tweak her breast, at which Jerry got up and went over to her table. He was no great hero, quite the reverse in his secret view, but a lot of things were going around in his mind, and it might just as well have been Cat who was getting shoved into a corner. So yes: anger. He therefore clapped one hand on the shoulder of the small waiter who had made the dive for her, and one hand on the shoulder of the big one who had applauded such bravado, and he explained to them, in bad Italian, but in a fairly reasonable way, that they really must stop being pests, and let the beautiful missus eat her meal in peace. Otherwise he would break their greasy little necks. The atmosphere wasn't too good after that, and the little one seemed actually to be squaring for a fight, for his hand kept travelling toward a back pocket, and hitching at his jacket, till a final look at Jerry changed his mind for him. Jerry dumped some money on the table, picked up her bag for her, went back to collect his booksack, and led her by the arm, all but lifting her off the ground, across the square to the Apollo.

'Are you English?' she asked on the way.

'Pips, core, the lot,' Jerry snorted furiously, which was the first time he saw her smile. It was a smile definitely worth working for: her bony little face lit up like an urchin's through the grime.

So, simmered down a bit, Jerry fed her, and with the advent of calm he began spinning the tale a bit, because after all those weeks without a focus it was natural he should make an effort to amuse. He explained that he was a newshound out to grass and now writing a novel, that it was his first shot, that he was scratching a long-standing itch, and that he had a dwindling pile of cash from a comic that had paid him redundancy – which was a giggle, he said, because he had been redundant all his life.

'Kind of golden handshake,' he said. He had put a bit down for the house, loafed a bit, and now there was precious little gold left over. That was the second time she smiled. Encouraged, he touched on the solitary nature of the creative life: 'But, Christ, you wouldn't believe the sweat of really, well *really* getting it all to come *out*, sort of thing . . . '

'Wives?' she asked, interrupting him. For a moment, he had assumed she was tuning to the novel. Then he saw her waiting, suspicious eyes, so he replied cautiously: 'None active,' as if wives were volcanoes, which in Jerry's world they had been. After lunch as they drifted, somewhat plastered, across the empty square, with the sun pelting straight down on them, she made her one declaration of intent.

'Everything I own is in this bag, got it' she asked. It was the shoulder bag, made out of carpet stuff. 'That's the way I'm going to keep it. So just don't anybody give me anything I can't carry. Got it?'

When they reached his bus stop she hung around, and when the bus came she climbed aboard after him and let Jerry buy her a ticket, and when she got out at the village she climbed the hill with him, Jerry with his book-sack, the girl with her shoulder bag, and that's how it was. Three nights and most of the days she slept and on the fourth night she came to him. He was so unprepared for her that he had actually left his bedroom door locked: he had a bit of a thing about doors and windows, especially at night. So that she had to hammer on the door and shout, 'I want to come into your bloody cot for Christ's sake!' before he opened up.

'Just never lie to me,' she warned, scrambling into his bed as if they were sharing a dormitory feast. 'No words, no lies. Got it?'

As a lover, she was like a butterfly, he remembered: could have been Chinese. Weightless, never still, so unprotected he despaired of her. When the fireflies came out, the two of them knelt on the window-seat and watched them, and Jerry thought about the East. The cicadas shrieked and the frogs burped, and the lights of the fireflies ducked and parried round a central pool of blackness, and they would kneel there naked for an hour or more, watching and listening, while the hot moon drooped into the hill-crests. They never spoke on those occasions, nor reached any conclusions that he was aware of. But he gave up locking his door.

The music and the hammering had stopped, but a din of church bells had started, he supposed for evensong. The valley was never quiet, but the bells sounded heavier because of the dew. He sauntered over to the swingball, teasing the rope away from the metal pillar, then with his old buckskin boot kicked at the grass around the base, remembering her lithe little body flying from shot to shot and the monk's habit billowing.

'*Guardian* is the big one,' they had said to him. '*Guardian* means the road back,' they had said. For a moment longer Jerry hesitated, gazing downward again into the blue plain where the very road, not figurative at all, led shimmering and straight as a canal toward the city and the airport.

Jerry was not what he would have called a thinking man. A childhood spent listening to his father's bellowing had taught him early the value of big ideas, and big words as well. Perhaps that was what had joined him to the girl in the first place, he thought. That's what she was on about: 'Don't give me anything I can't carry.'

Maybe. Maybe not. She'll find someone else. They always do.

*It's time*, he thought. Money gone, novel stillborn, girl too young: come on. It's *time*.

Time for what?

*Time*! Time she found herself a young bull instead of wearing out an old one. Time to let the wanderlust stir. Strike camp. Wake the camels. On your way. Lord knows, Jerry had done it before once or twice. Pitch the old tent, stay a little, move on; sorry, sport.

It's an order, he told himself. Ours not to reason. Whistle goes, the lads rally. End of argument. *Guardian*.

Rum how he'd had a feeling it was coming, all the same, he thought, still staring into the blurred plain. No great presentiment, any of that tripe: simply, yes, a sense of time. It was due. A sense of season. In place of a gay upsurge of activity, however, a sluggishness seized hold of his body. He suddenly felt too tired, too fat, too sleepy ever to move again. He could have lain down just here, where he stood. He could have slept on the harsh grass till she woke him or the darkness came.

Tripe, he told himself. Sheer tripe. Taking the telegram from his pocket, he strode vigorously into the house, calling her name:

'Hey, sport! Old thing! Where are you hiding? Spot of bad news.' He handed it to her. 'Doomsville,' he said, and went to the window rather than watch her read it.

He waited till he heard the flutter of the paper landing on the table. Then he turned round because there was nothing else for it. She hadn't said anything but she had wedged her hands under her armpits and sometimes her body-talk was deafening. He saw how the fingers waved blindly about, trying to lock on to something.

'Why not shove off to Beth's place for a bit?' he suggested. 'She'll have you like a shot, old Beth. Thinks the world of you. Have you long as you like, Beth would.'

She kept her arms folded till he went down the hill to send his telegram. By the time he came back, she had got his suit out, the blue one they had always laughed about – his prison gear, she called it – but she was trembling and her face had turned white and ill, the way it went when he dealt with the hornets. When he tried to kiss her, she was cold as marble, so he let her be. At night they slept together and it was worse than being alone.

Mama Stefano announced the news at lunchtime, breathlessly. The honourable schoolboy had left, she said. He wore his suit. He carried a grip, his typewriter and the book-sack. Franco had taken him to the airport in the van. The orphan had gone with them but only as far as the sliproad to the autostrada. When she got out she didn't even say goodbye: just sat beside the road like the trash she was. For a while, after they dumped her, the schoolboy had remained very quiet and inward. He scarcely noticed Franco's ingenious and pointed questions, and he pulled at his tawny forelock a lot – the Sanders had called it pepper and salt. At the airport, with an hour to kill before the plane left, they had a flask together, also a game of dominoes, but when Franco tried to rob him for the fare, the schoolboy showed an unusual harshness, haggling at last like the true rich.

Franco had told her, she said: her bosom friend. Franco, maligned as a pederast. Had she not always defended him, Franco the elegant, Franco, the father of her idiot son? They had had their differences – who had not? – but let them only name for her, if they could, in the whole valley, a more upright, diligent, graceful, better dressed man than Franco, her friend and lover!

The schoolboy had gone back for his inheritance, she said.

THREE

# Mr George Smiley's horse

Only George Smiley, said Roddy Martindale, a fleshy Foreign Office wit, could have got himself appointed captain of a wrecked ship. Only Smiley, he added, could have compounded the pains of that appointment by choosing the same moment to abandon his beautiful, if occasionally errant, wife.

At first or even second glance George Smiley was ill-suited to either part, as Martindale was quick to note. He was tubby and in small ways hopelessly unassertive. A natural shyness made him from time to time pompous, and to men of Martindale's flamboyance his unobtrusiveness acted as a standing reproach. He was also myopic, and to see him in those first days after the holocaust, in his round spectacles and his civil servant weeds, attended by his slender, tight-mouthed cupbearer Peter Guillam, discreetly padding the marshier by-paths of the Whitehall jungle; or stooped over a heap of papers at any hour of day or night in his scruffy throne-room on the fifth floor of the Edwardian mausoleum in Cambridge Circus which he now commanded, you would think it was he, and not the dead Haydon, the Russian spy, who deserved the tradename 'mole'. After such long hours of work in that cavernous and half-deserted building, the bags beneath his eyes turned to bruises, he smiled seldom, though he was by no means humourless, and there were times when the mere exertion of rising from his chair seemed to leave him winded. Reaching the upright position, he would pause, mouth slightly open, and give a little, fricative 'uh' before moving off. Another mannerism had him polishing his spectacles distractedly on the fat end of his tie, which left his face so disconcertingly naked that one very senior secretary – in the jargon, these ladies were known as 'mothers' – was on more than one occasion assailed by a barely containable urge, of which psychiatrists would have made all sorts of heavy weather, to start forward and shelter him from the impossible task he seemed determined to perform.

'George Smiley isn't just cleaning the stable,' the same Roddy Martindale remarked, from his luncheon table at the Garrick. 'He's carrying his horse up the hill as well. Haw haw.'

Other rumours, favoured mainly by departments which had entered bids for the charter of the foundered service, were less respectful of his travail.

'George is living on his reputation,' they said, after a few months of this. 'Catching Bill Haydon was a fluke.'

Anyway, they said, it had been an American tip-off, not George's *coup* at all: the Cousins should have had the credit, but they had waived it diplomatically. No, no, said others, it was the Dutch. The Dutch had broken Moscow Centre's code and passed the take through liaison: ask Roddy Martindale – Martindale, of course, being a professional trafficker in Circus misinformation. And so, back and forth, while Smiley, seemingly oblivious, kept his counsel and dismissed his wife.

They could hardly believe it.

They were stunned.

Martindale, who had never loved a woman in his life, was particularly affronted. He made a positive *thing* of it at the Garrick.

'The gall! Him a complete nobody and her half a Sawley! Pavlovian, that's what I call it. Sheer Pavlovian cruelty. After years of putting up with her perfectly healthy peccadilloes – driving her to them, you mark my words – what does the little man do? Turns round and with quite *Napoleonic* brutality kicks her in the teeth! It's a scandal. I shall tell everyone it's a scandal. I'm a tolerant man in my way, not unworldy I think, but Smiley has gone too far. Oh yes.'

For once, as occasionally occurred, Martindale had the picture straight. The evidence was there for all to read. With Haydon dead and the past buried, the Smileys had made up their differences and together, with some small ceremony, the united couple had moved back into their little Chelsea house in Bywater Street. They had even made a stab at being in society. They had gone out, they had entertained in the style befitting George's new appointment; the Cousins, the odd Parliamentary Minister, a variety of Whitehall barons all dined and went home full; they had even for a few weeks made a modestly exotic couple around the higher bureaucratic circuit. Till overnight, to his wife's unmistakable discomfort, George Smiley had removed himself from her sight, and set up camp in the meagre attics behind his throne-room in the Circus. Soon the gloom of the place seemed to work itself into the fabric of his face, like dust into the complexion of a prisoner. While in Chelsea, Ann Smiley pined, taking very hardly to her unaccustomed rôle of wife abandoned.

Dedication, said the knowing. Monkish abstinence. George is a saint. And at *his* age.

Balls, the Martindale faction retorted. Dedication to *what*? What was there left, in that dreary red-brick monster, that could possibly command such an act of self-immolation? What was there *anywhere*, in beastly Whitehall or, Lord help us, in beastly *England*, that could command it any more?

Work, said the knowing.

But *what* work? came the falsetto protests of these self-appointed Circus-watchers, handing round, like Gorgons, their little scraps of sight and hearing. What did he do up there, shorn of three-quarters of his staff, all but a few old biddies to brew his tea, his networks blown to smithereens? His foreign residencies, his reptile fund frozen solid by the Treasury – they meant his operational accounts – and not a friend in Whitehall or Washington to call his own? Unless you counted that loping prig Lacon at the Cabinet Office to be his friend, always so determined to go down the line for him at every conceivable opportunity. And naturally *Lacon* would put up a fight for him: what else had he? The Circus was Lacon's power base. Without it, he was – well, what he was already, a capon. Naturally *Lacon* would sound the battle cry.

'It's a scandal,' Martindale announced huffily, as he cropped his smoked eel and steak-and-kidney and the club's own claret, up another twenty pence a crack. 'I shall tell everybody.'

Between the villagers of Whitehall and the villagers of Tuscany, there was sometimes surprisingly little to choose.

Time did not kill the rumours. To the contrary they multiplied, taking colour from his isolation, and calling it obsession.

It was remembered that Bill Haydon had not merely been George Smiley's colleague, but Ann's cousin and something more besides. Smiley's fury against him, they said, had not stopped at Haydon's death: he was positively dancing on Bill's grave. For example, George had personally supervised the clearing of Haydon's fabled pepper-pot room overlooking the Charing Cross Road, and the destruction of every last sign of him, from his indifferent oil-paintings by his own hand to the leftover oddments in the drawers of his desk; even the desk itself, which he had ordered sawn up, and burned. And when *that* was done, they maintained, he had called in Circus workmen to tear down the partition walls. Oh yes, said Martindale.

Or, for another example, and frankly a most unnerving one, take the photograph which hung on the wall of Smiley's dingy throne-room, a passport photograph by the look of it, but blown up far beyond its natural size, so that it had a grainy and some said spectral look. One of the Treasury boys spotted it during an ad-hoc conference about scrapping the operational bank accounts.

'Is that Control's portrait by the by?' he had asked of Peter Guillam, purely as a bit of social chit chat. No sinister intent behind the question. Well surely one was allowed to *ask*? Control, other names still unknown, was the legend of the place. He had been Smiley's guide and mentor for all of thirty years. Smiley had actually buried him, they said: for the very secret, like the very rich, have a tendency to die unmourned.

'No, it bloody well *isn't* Control,' Guillam the cupbearer had retorted, in that off-hand, supercilious way of his. 'It's Karla.'

And who was Karla when he was at home?

Karla, my dear, was the workname of the Soviet case officer who had recruited Bill Haydon in the first place, and had the running of him thereafter: 'A different sort of legend *entirely*, to say the least,' said Martindale, all a-quiver. 'It seems we've a real vendetta on our hands. How puerile can you get, I wonder?'

Even Lacon was a mite bothered by that picture.

'Now seriously, why do you hang him there, George?' he demanded, in his bold, head-prefect's voice, dropping in on Smiley one evening on his way home from the Cabinet Office. 'What does he mean to you, I wonder? Have you thought about that one? It isn't a little macabre, you don't think? The victorious enemy? I'd have thought he would get you down, gloating over you all up there?'

'Well, Bill's *dead*,' said Smiley, in that elliptical way he had sometimes of giving a clue to an argument, rather than the argument itself.

'And Karla's alive, you mean?' Lacon prompted. 'And you'd rather have a live enemy than a dead one? Is that what you mean?'

But questions of George Smiley, at a certain point had a habit of passing him by; even, said his colleagues, of appearing to be in bad taste.

An incident which provided more substantial fare around the Whitehall bazaars concerned the 'ferrets', or electronic sweepers. A worse case of favouritism could not be remembered anywhere. My *God* those hoods had a nerve sometimes! Martindale, who had been waiting a year to have *his* room done, sent a complaint to his Under-Secretary. By hand. To be opened personally by. So did his Brother-in-Christ at Defence and so, nearly, did Hammer of Treasury, but Hammer either forgot to post his, or thought better of it at the last moment. It wasn't just a question of priorities, not at all. Not even of principle. *Money* was involved. *Public* money. Treasury had already had half the Circus rewired on George's insistence. His paranoia about eavesdropping knew no limits, apparently. Add to that, the ferrets were short-staffed, there had been industrial disputes about unsocial hours – oh, any number of angles! Dynamite, the whole subject.

Yet what had happened in the event? Martindale had the details at his manicured fingertips. George went to Lacon on a Thursday – the day of the freak heatwave, you remember, when everyone practically *expired*, even at the Garrick – and by the Saturday – a Saturday, *imagine* the overtime! – the brutes were swarming over the Circus, enraging the neighbours with their din, and tearing the place apart. A more *gross* case of blind preference had not been met with since – since, well, they allowed Smiley to have back that mangy old Russian researcher of his, Sachs, Connie Sachs, the don woman from Oxford, against all reason, calling her a mother when she wasn't.

Discreetly, or as discreetly as he could manage, Martindale went to quite some lengths to find out whether the ferrets had actually discovered anything, but met a blank wall. In the secret world, information is money, and by that standard at least, though he might not know it, Roddy Martindale was a pauper, for the inside to this inside-story was known only to the smallest few. It was true that Smiley called on Lacon in his panelled room overlooking St. James's Park on the Thursday; and that the day was uncommonly hot for autumn. Rich shafts of sunlight poured on to the representational carpet, and the dust-specks played in them like tiny tropical fish. Lacon had even removed his jacket, though of course not his tie.

'Connie Sachs has been doing some arithmetic on Karla's handwriting in analogous cases,' Smiley announced.

'*Handwriting?*' Lacon echoed, as if handwriting were against the regulations.

'Tradecraft. Karla's habits of technique. It seems that where it was operable, he ran moles and sound-thieves in tandem.'

'Once more now in English, George, do you mind?'

Where circumstances allowed, said Smiley, Karla had liked to back up his agent operations with microphones. Though Smiley was satisfied that nothing had been said within the building which would compromise any 'present plans' as he called them, the implications were unsettling.

Lacon was getting to know Smiley's handwriting too.

'Any collateral for that rather academic theory?' he enquired, examining Smiley's expressionless features over the top of his pencil, which he held between his two index fingers, like a rule.

'We've been making an inventory of our own audio stores,' Smiley confessed with a puckering of his brow. 'There's a quantity of house equipment missing. A lot seems to have disappeared during the alterations of sixty-six.' Lacon waited, dragging it out of him. 'Haydon was on the building committee responsible for having the work carried out,' Smiley ended, as a final sop. 'He was the driving force, in fact. It's just – well, if the Cousins ever got to hear of it, I think it would be the last straw.'

Lacon was no fool, and the Cousins' wrath just when everyone was trying to smooth their feathers was a thing to be avoided at any cost. If he had had his way, he would have ordered the ferrets out the same day. Saturday was a compromise and without consulting anybody he despatched the entire team, all twelve of them, in two grey vans painted 'Pest Control'. It was true that they tore the place apart, hence the silly rumours about the destruction of the pepper-pot room. They were angry because it was the weekend, and perhaps therefore needlessly violent: the tax they paid on overtime was frightful. But their mood changed fast enough when they bagged eight radio microphones in the first sweep, every one of them Circus standard-issue from audio stores. Haydon's distribution of them was classic, as Lacon agreed when he called to make his own inspection. One in a drawer of a disused desk, as if innocently left there and forgotten about, except that the desk happened to be in the coding room. One collecting dust on top of an old steel cupboard in the fifth-floor conference room – or, in the jargon, rumpus room. And one, with typical Haydon flair, wedged behind the cistern in the senior officers' lavatory next door. A second sweep, to include load-bearing walls, threw up three more embedded in the fabric during the building work. Probes, with plastic snorkel-straws to pipe the sound back to them. The ferrets laid them out like a game-line. Extinct, of course, as all the devices were, but put there by Haydon nevertheless, and tuned to frequencies the Circus did not use.

'Maintained at Treasury cost, too, I declare,' said Lacon, with the driest of smiles, fondling the leads which had once connected the probe microphones with the mains power supply. 'Or used to be, till George rewired the place. I must be sure to tell Brother Hammer. He'll be thrilled.'

Hammer, a Welshman, being Lacon's most persistent enemy.

On Lacon's advice Smiley now staged a modest piece of theatre. He ordered the ferrets to reactivate the radio-microphones in the conference room and to modify the receiver on one of the Circus's few remaining surveillance cars. Then he invited three of the least bending Whitehall desk-jockeys, including the Welsh Hammer, to drive in a half-mile radius round the building, while they listened to a pre-scripted discussion between two of Smiley's shadowy helpers sitting in the rumpus room. Word for word. Not a syllable out of place.

After which, Smiley himself swore them to absolute secrecy, and for good measure made them sign a declaration, drafted by the housekeepers expressly to inspire awe. Peter Guillam reckoned it would keep them quiet for about a month.

'Or less if it rains,' he added sourly.

Yet if Martindale and his colleagues in the Whitehall outfield lived in a state of primaeval innocence about the reality of Smiley's world, those closer to the throne felt equally removed from him. The circles around him grew smaller as they grew nearer, and precious few in the early days, reached the centre. Entering the brown and dismal doorway of the Circus, with its temporary barriers manned by watchful janitors, Smiley shed none of his habitual privacy. For nights and days at a time, the door to his tiny office suite stayed closed and his only company was Peter Guillam, and a hovering dark-eyed factotum named Fawn, who had shared with Guillam the job of babysitting Smiley during the smoking-out of Haydon. Sometimes Smiley disappeared by the back door with no more than a nod, taking Fawn, a sleek, diminutive creature, with him and leaving Guillam to field the phone calls and get hold of him in emergency. The mothers likened his behaviour to the last days of Control, who had died in harness, thanks to Haydon, of a broken heart. By the organic processes of a closed society, a new word was added to the jargon. The unmasking of Haydon now became the *fall* and Circus history was divided into *before the fall* and *after* it. To Smiley's comings and goings, the physical *fall* of the building itself, three-quarters empty and, since the visit of the ferrets, in a wrecked condition, lent a sombre sense of ruin which at low moments became symbolic to those who had to live with it. What the ferrets destroy they do not put together: and the same, they felt perhaps, was true of Karla, whose dusty features, nailed there by their elusive chief, continued to watch over them from the shadows of his Spartan throne-room.

The little they did know was appalling. Such humdrum matters as personnel, for example, took on a horrific dimension. Smiley had blown staff to dismiss, and blown residencies to dismantle; poor Tufty Thesinger's in Hong Kong for one, though being pretty far removed from the anti-Soviet scene, Hong Kong was one of the last to go. Round Whitehall, a terrain which like Smiley they deeply distrusted, they heard of him engaged in bizarre and rather terrible arguments over terms of severance and resettlement. There were cases, it seemed – poor Tufty Thesinger in Hong Kong once more supplied the readiest example – where Bill Haydon had deliberately encouraged the over-promotion of burnt-out officers who could be counted on not to mount private initiatives. Should they be paid off at their natural value, or at the inflated one which Haydon had mischievously set on them? There were others where Haydon for his own preservation had confected reasons for dismissal. Should they receive full pension? Had they a claim to reinstatement? Perplexed young Ministers, new to power since the elections, made brave and contradictory rulings. In consequence a sad stream of deluded Circus field officers, both men and women, passed through Smiley's hands, and the housekeepers were ordered to make sure that for reasons of security and perhaps aesthetics, none of these returnees from foreign residencies should set foot inside the main building. Nor would Smiley tolerate any contact between the damned and the reprieved. Accordingly with grudging Treasury support from the Welsh Hammer, the housekeepers opened a temporary reception point in a rented house in Bloomsbury, under cover of a language school (Regret No Callers Without Appointment) and manned it with a quartet of pay-and-personnel officers. This body became inevitably the Bloomsbury Group, and it was known that sometimes for a spare hour or so

Smiley made a point of slipping down there and, rather in the manner of a hospital visitor, offering his condolences to faces frequently unknown to him. At other times, depending on his mood, he would remain entirely silent, preferring to perch unexplained and Buddha-like in a corner of the dusty interviewing room.

What drove him? What was he looking for? If anger was the root, then it was an anger common to them all in those days. They could be sitting together in the raftered rumpus room after a long day's work, joking and gossiping; but if someone should let slip the names of Karla or his mole Haydon, a silence of angels would descend on them, and not even cunning old Connie Sachs, the Moscow-gazer, could break the spell.

Even more affecting in the eyes of his subordinates were Smiley's efforts to save something of the agent networks from the wreck. Within a day of Haydon's arrest, all nine of the Circus's Soviet and East European networks had gone cold. Radio links stopped dead, courier lines dried up and there was every reason to say that, if there had been any genuinely Circus-owned agents left among them, they had been rolled up overnight. But Smiley fiercely opposed that easy view, just as he refused to accept that Karla and Moscow Centre between them were invincibly efficient, or tidy, or logical. He pestered Lacon, he pestered the Cousins in their vast annexes in Grosvenor Square, he insisted that agent radio frequencies continue to be monitored, and despite bitter protest by the Foreign Office – Roddy Martindale as ever to the fore – he had open-language messages put out by the overseas services of the BBC ordering any live agent who should happen to hear them and know the codeword, to abandon ship immediately. And, little by little, to their amazement, came tiny flutterings of life, like garbled messages from another planet.

First, the Cousins, in the person of their suspiciously bluff local station chief Martello, reported from Grosvenor Square that an American escape line was passing two British agents, a man and a woman, to the old holiday resort of Sochi on the Black Sea, where a small boat was being fitted in readiness for what Martello's quiet men insisted on calling an 'exfiltration assignment'. By his description, he was referring to the Churayevs, linchpins of the *Contemplate* network which had covered Georgia and the Ukraine. Without waiting for Treasury sanction, Smiley resurrected from retirement one Roy Bland, a burly ex-Marxist dialectician and sometime field agent, who had been the network's case officer. To Bland, who had come down heavily in the fall, he entrusted the two Russian leashdogs de Silsky and Kaspar, also in mothballs, also former Haydon protégés, to make up a standby reception party. They were still sitting in their RAF transport plane when word came through that the couple had been shot dead as they were leaving harbour. The exfiltration assignment had fallen through, said the Cousins. In sympathy, Martello personally telephoned Smiley with the news. He was a kindly man, by his own lights, and, like Smiley, old school. It was night-time, and raining furiously.

'Now don't go taking this too hardly, George,' he warned in his avuncular way. 'Hear me? There's fieldmen and there's deskmen and it's up to you and me to see that the distinction is preserved. Otherwise we all go crazy. Can't go down the line for every one of them. That's generalship. So you just remember that.'

Peter Guillam, who was at Smiley's shoulder when he took the call, swore later that Smiley showed no particular reaction: and Guillam knew him well.

Nevertheless, ten minutes later, unobserved by anybody, he was gone, and his voluminous mackintosh was missing from its peg. He returned after dawn, drenched to the skin, still carrying the mackintosh over his arm. Having changed, he returned to his desk, but when Guillam, unbidden, tiptoed in to him with tea, he found his master, to his embarrassment, sitting rigidly before an old volume of German poetry, fists clenched either side of it, while he silently wept.

Bland, Kaspar and de Silsky begged for reinstatement. They pointed to little Toby Esterhase, the Hungarian, who had somehow gained readmittance, and demanded the same treatment, in vain. They were stood down and not spoken of again. To injustice belongs injustice. Though tarnished, they might have been useful, but Smiley would not hear their names; not then; not later; not ever. Of the immediate post-fall period, that was the lowest point. There were those who seriously believed – inside the Circus as well as out – that they had heard the last beat of the secret English heart.

A few days after this catastrophe, as it happened, luck handed Smiley a small consolation. In Warsaw in broad daylight a Circus head agent on the run picked up the BBC signal and walked straight into the British Embassy. Thanks to ferocious lobbying by Lacon and Smiley between them, he was flown home to London the same night disguised as a diplomatic courier, Martindale notwithstanding. Mistrusting his cover story Smiley turned the man over to the Circus inquisitors who, deprived of other meat, nearly killed him but afterwards declared him clean. He was resettled in Australia.

Next, still at the very genesis of his rule, Smiley was compelled to pass judgement on the Circus's blown domestic outstations. His instinct was to shed everything: the safe houses, now totally unsafe; the Sarratt Nursery, where traditionally the briefing and training of agents and new entrants was conducted; the experimental audio laboratories in Harlow; the stinks-and-bangs school in Argyll; the water school in the Helford Estuary, where passé sailors practised the black arts of small-boat seacraft like the ritual of some lost religion; and the longarm radio transmission base at Canterbury. He would even have done away with the wranglers' headquarters in Bath where the code-breaking went on.

'Scrap the lot,' he told Lacon, calling on him in his rooms.

'And then what?' Lacon enquired, puzzled by his vehemence, which since the Sochi failure was more marked in him.

'Start again.'

'I see,' said Lacon, which meant, of course, that he didn't. Lacon had sheets of Treasury figures before him, and was studying them while he spoke.

'The Sarratt Nursery, for some reason which I fail to understand, is carried on the *military* budget,' he observed reflectively. 'Not on your reptile fund at all. The Foreign Office pays for Harlow – and I'm sure has long forgotten the fact – Argyll is under the wing of the Ministry of Defence, who most certainly won't know of its existence, the Post Office has Canterbury and the Navy has Helford. Bath, I'm pleased to say, is also supported from Foreign Office funds, over the particular signature of Martindale, appended six years ago and similarly faded from official memory. So they don't eat a thing. Do they?'

'They're dead wood,' Smiley insisted. 'And while they exist we shall never replace them. Sarratt went to the devil long ago, Helford is moribund, Argyll is farcical. As to the wranglers, for the last five years they've been working practically full time for Karla.'

'By Karla you mean Moscow Centre?'

'I mean the department responsible for Haydon and half a dozen –'

'I know what you mean. But I think it safer to stay with institutions if you don't mind. In that way we are spared the embarrassment of personalities. After all, that's what institutions are *for*, isn't it?' Lacon tapped his pencil rhythmically on his desk. Finally he looked up, and considered Smiley quizzically. 'Well, well, you *are* the root-and-bough man these days, George. I dread to think what would happen if you were ever to wield your axe round *my* side of the garden. Those outstations are gilt-edged stock. Do away with them now and you'll never get them back. Later, if you like, when you're on the road again, you can cash them in and buy yourself something better. You mustn't sell when the market's low, you know. You must wait till you can take a profit.'

Reluctantly, Smiley bowed to his advice.

As if all these headaches were not enough, there came one bleak Monday morning when a Treasury audit pointed up serious discrepancies in the conduct of the Circus reptile fund over the period of five years before it was frozen by the fall. Smiley was forced to hold a kangaroo court, at which an elderly clerk in Finance Section, hauled from retirement, broke down and confessed to a shameful passion for a girl in Registry who had led him by the nose. In a ghastly fit of remorse, the old man went home and hanged himself. Against all Guillam's advice, Smiley insisted on attending the funeral.

Yet it is a matter of record that from these quite dismal beginnings, and indeed from his very first weeks in office, George Smiley went over to the attack.

The base from which this attack was launched was in the first instance philosophical, in the second theoretical, and only in the last instance, thanks to the dramatic appearance of the egregious gambler Sam Collins, human.

The philosophy was simple. The task of an intelligence service, Smiley announced firmly, was not to play chase games but to deliver intelligence to its customers. If it failed to do this, those customers would resort to other, less scrupulous sellers or, worse, indulge in amateurish self-help. And the service itself would wither. Not to be seen in the Whitehall markets was not to be desired, he went on. Worse: unless the Circus produced, it would also have no wares to barter with the Cousins, nor with other sister services with whom reciprocal deals were traditional. Not to produce was not to trade, and not to trade was to die.

Amen, they said.

His theory – he called it his *premise* – on how intelligence could be produced with no resources, was the subject of an informal meeting held in the rumpus room not two months after his accession, between himself and the tiny inner circle which made up, to a point, his team of confidants. They were in all five: Smiley himself; Peter Guillam, his cupbearer; big, flowing Connie Sachs, the Moscow-gazer; Fawn, the dark-eyed factotum, who wore black gym-shoes and manned the Russian-style copper samovar and gave out biscuits; and lastly Doc di Salis, known as the Mad Jesuit, the Circus's head China-watcher. When God had finished making Connie Sachs, said the wags, He needed a rest, so He ran up Doc di Salis from the remnants. The Doc was a patchy, grubby little creature, more like Connie's monkey than her counterpart, and his features, it was true, from the spiky silver hair that strayed over his grimy collar, to the moist mis-shapen fingertips which picked like chicken beaks at everything around them, had an unquestionably ill-begotten look. If Beardsley had drawn him, he would have had him chained and hirsute, peeping round the corner of her enormous caftan. Yet di Salis was a notable orientalist, a scholar, and something of a hero too, for he had spent a part of the war in China, recruiting for God and the Circus, and another part in Changi jail, for the pleasure of the Japanese. That was the team: the Group of Five. In time it expanded, but to start with these five alone made up the famous cadre, and afterwards, to have been one of them, said di Salis, was 'like holding a Communist Party card with a single-figure membership number'.

First, Smiley reviewed the wreck, and that took some while, in the way that sacking a city takes some while, or liquidating great numbers of people. He simply drove through every back alley the Circus possessed, demonstrating quite ruthlessly how, by what method, and often exactly when, Haydon had laid bare its secrets to his Soviet masters. He had of course the advantage of his own interrogation of Haydon, and of the original researches which had led him to Haydon's discovery. He knew the track. Nevertheless, his peroration was a minor *tour de force* of destructive analysis.

'So no illusions,' he ended tersely. 'This service will never be the same again. It may be better, but it will be different.'

Amen again, they said, and took a doleful break to stretch their legs.

It was odd, Guillam recalled later, how the important scenes of those early months seemed all to play at night. The rumpus room was long and raftered, with high dormer windows which gave on to nothing but orange night sky and a coppice of rusted radio aerials, war relics which no one had seen fit to remove.

The *premise*, said Smiley when they had resettled, was that Haydon had done nothing against the Circus that was not directed, and that the direction came from one man personally: Karla.

His premise was, that in briefing Haydon, Karla was exposing the gaps in Moscow Centre's knowledge; that in ordering Haydon to suppress certain intelligence which came the Circus's way, in ordering him to downgrade or distort it, to deride it, or even to deny it circulation altogether, Karla was indicating the secrets he did not want revealed.

'So we can take the backbearings, can't we, darling?' murmured Connie Sachs, whose speed of uptake put her as usual a good length ahead of the rest of the field.

'That's right, Con. That's exactly what we can do,' said Smiley gravely. 'We can take the backbearings.' He resumed his lecture, leaving Guillam for one more mystified than before.

By minutely charting Haydon's path of destruction – his pugmarks as he called them – by exhaustively recording his selection of files; by reassembling, after aching weeks of research if necessary, the intelligence culled in good faith by Circus outstations, and balancing it, in every detail, against the intelligence distributed by Haydon to the Circus's customers in the Whitehall market place, it would be possible to take *backbearings* – as Connie so rightly called them – and establish Haydon's, and therefore Karla's, point of departure, said Smiley.

Once a correct backbearing had been taken, surprising doors of opportunity would open, and the Circus, against all outward likelihood, would be in a position to go over to the initiative – or, as Smiley put it – 'to *act*, and not merely to *react*.'

The premise, to use Connie Sachs's joyous description later, meant: 'Looking for another bloody Tutankhamun, with George Smiley holding the light and us poor Charlies doing the digging.'

At that time, of course, Jerry Westerby was not even a twinkle in their operational eye.

They went into battle next day, huge Connie to one corner, the crabbed little di Salis to his. As di Salis said, in a nasal, deprecating tone, which had a savage force: 'At least we do finally know why we're here.' Their families of pasty burrowers carved the archive in two. To Connie and 'my Bolshies' as she called them, went Russia and the Satellites. To di Salis and his 'yellow perils', China and the Third World. What fell between – source reports on the nation's theoretical Allies, for instance – was consigned to a special wait-bin for later evaluation. They worked, like Smiley himself, impossible hours. The canteen complained, the janitors threatened to walk out, but gradually the sheer energy of the burrowers infected even the ancillary staff and they shut up. A bantering rivalry developed. Under Connie's influence, backroom boys and girls who till now had scarcely been seen to smile, learned suddenly to chaff each other in the language of their great familiars in the world outside the Circus. Czarist imperialist running dogs drank tasteless coffee with divisive, deviationist chauvinist Stalinists and were proud of it. But the most impressive blossoming was unquestionably in di Salis, who interrupted his nocturnal labours with short but vigorous spells at the ping-pong table, where he would challenge all comers, leaping about like a lepidopterist after rare specimens. Soon the first fruits appeared, and gave them fresh impetus. Within a month, three reports had been nervously distributed, under extreme limitation, and even found favour with the sceptical Cousins. A month later a hardbound summary wordily entitled *Interim report on lacunae in Soviet intelligence regarding Nato sea to air strike capacity*, earned grudging applause from Martello's parent factory in Langley, Virginia, and an exuberant phone call from Martello himself.

'George, I *told* those guys!' he yelled, so loud that the telephone line seemed an unnecessary extravagance. 'I told them: "The Circus will deliver." Did they believe me? Did they hell!'

Meanwhile, sometimes with Guillam for company, sometimes with silent Fawn to babysit, Smiley himself conducted his own dark peregrinations and marched till he was half dead with tiredness. And still without reward, kept marching. By day, and often by night as well, he trailed the home counties and points beyond, questioning past officers of the Circus and former agents out to grass. In Chiswick, perched meekly in the office of a cut-price travel agent and talking in murmurs to a former Polish colonel of cavalry resettled as a clerk there, he thought he had glimpsed it; but like a mirage, the promise dissolved as he advanced on it. In a secondhand radio shop in Sevenoaks, a Sudeten Czech held out the same hope to him, but when he and Guillam hurried back to confirm the story from Circus records, they found the actors dead and no one left to lead him further. At a private stud in Newmarket, to Fawn's near-violent fury, he suffered insult at the hand of a tweedy and opinionated Scot, a protégé of Smiley's predecessor Alleline, all in the same elusive cause. Back home, he called for the papers, only once more to see the light go out.

For this was the last and unspoken conviction of the premise which Smiley had outlined in the rumpus room: that the snare with which Haydon had trapped himself was not unique. That in the end-analysis, it was not Haydon's paperwork which had caused his downfall, not his meddling with reports, nor his 'losing' of inconvenient records. It was Haydon's panic. It was Haydon's spontaneous intervention in a field operation, where the threat to himself, or perhaps to another Karla agent, was suddenly so grave that his one hope was to suppress it despite the risk. This was the trick which Smiley longed to find repeated. And this was the question which, never directly, but by inference, Smiley and his helpers in the Bloomsbury reception centre canvassed:

'Can you remember any incident during your service in the field when in your opinion you were unreasonably restrained from following an operational lead?'

And it was dapper Sam Collins, in his dinner jacket, with his brown cigarette and his trim moustache and his Mississippi dandy's smile, summoned for a quiet chat one day, who breezed in to say: 'Come to think of it, yes, old boy, I can.'

But behind this question again, and Sam's crucial answer, stalked the formidable person of Miss Connie Sachs and her pursuit for Russian gold.

And behind Connie again, as ever, the permanently misted photograph of Karla.

'*Connie's got one, Peter,*' she whispered to Guillam over the internal telephone late one night. '*She's got one, sure as boots.*'

It was not her first find by any means, nor her tenth, but her devious instinct told her straight away it was 'the genuine article, darling, mark old Connie's words'. So Guillam told Smiley and Smiley locked up his files and cleared his desk and said: 'All right, let her in.'

Connie was a huge, crippled, cunning woman, a don's daughter, a don's sister, herself some sort of academic, and known to the older hands as Mother Russia. The folklore said Control had recruited her over a rubber of bridge while she was still a debutante, on the night Neville Chamberlain promised 'peace in our time'. When Haydon came to power in the slipstream of his protector Alleline, one of his first and most prudent moves was to have Connie put out to grass. For Connie knew more about the byways of Moscow Centre than most of the wretched brutes, as she called them, who toiled there, and Karla's private army of moles and recruiters had always been her very special joy. Not a Soviet defector, in the old days, but his debriefing report had passed through Mother Russia's arthritic fingers; not a coat-trailer who had manoeuvred himself alongside an identified Karla talent-spotter, but Connie greedily rehearsed him in every detail of the quarry's choreography; not a scrap of hearsay over nearly forty years on the beat which had not been assumed into her pain-racked body, and lodged there among the junk of her compendious memory, to be turned up the moment she rummaged for it. Connie's mind, said Control once, in a kind of despair, was like the back of one enormous envelope. Dismissed, she went back to Oxford and the devil. At the time Smiley reclaimed her, her only recreation was *The Times* crossword and she was running at a comfortable two bottles a day. But that night, that modestly historic night, as she hauled her great frame along the fifth floor corridor toward George Smiley's inner room, she sported a clean grey caftan, she had daubed a pair of rosy lips not far from her own, and she had taken nothing stronger than a vile peppermint cordial all day long – of which the reek lingered in her wake – and a sense of occasion, they all decided afterwards, was stamped on her from the first. She carried a heavy plastic shopping bag, for she would countenance no leather. In her lair on a lower floor, her mongrel dog, christened Trot, and recruited on a wave of remorse for its late predecessor, whimpered disconsolately from beneath her desk, to the lively fury of her room-mate di Salis, who would often privily lash at the beast with his foot; or in more jovial moments, content himself with reciting to Connie the many tasty ways in which the Chinese prepared their dogs for the pot. Outside the Edwardian dormers, as she passed them one by one, a racing late-summer rain was falling, ending a long drought, and she saw it – she told them all later – as symbolic, if not Biblical. The drops rattled like pellets on the slate roof, flattening the dead leaves which had settled there. In the anteroom the mothers continued stonily with their business, accustomed to Connie's pilgrimages, and not liking them the better for it.

'*Darlings*,' Connie murmured, waving her bloated hand to them like royalty. 'So loyal. So *very* loyal.'

There was one step downward into the throne-room – the uninitiated tended to stumble on it despite the faded warning notice – and Connie with her arthritis negotiated it as if it were a ladder while Guillam held her arm. Smiley watched her, plump hands linked on his desk, as she began solemnly unpacking her offerings from the carrier: not eye of newt, nor the finger of a birth-strangled babe – Guillam speaking once more – but files, a string of them, flagged and annotated, the booty of yet another of her impassioned skirmishes through the Moscow Centre archive, which until her return from the dead a few months before had, thanks to Haydon, lain mouldering for all of three long years. As she pulled them out, and smoothed the notes which she had pinned on them like markers in her paperchase, she smiled that brimming smile of hers – Guillam again, for curiosity had obliged him to down tools and come and watch – and she was muttering 'there you little devil' and 'now where did *you* get to, you wretch?' not to Smiley or Guillam, of course, but to the documents themselves, for Connie had the affectation of assuming everything was alive and potentially recalcitrant, whether it was Trot her dog or a chair that obstructed her passage, or Moscow Centre, or finally Karla himself.

'A *guided tour*, darlings,' she announced, 'that's what Connie's been having. *Super* fun. Reminded me of Easter, when Mother hid painted eggs round the house and sent us gals off hunting for them.'

For perhaps three hours after that, interspersed with coffee and sandwiches and other unwanted treats which dark Fawn insisted on bringing to them, Guillam struggled to follow the twists and impulsions of Connie's extraordinary journey, to which her subsequent research had by now supplied the solid basis. She dealt Smiley papers as if they were playing cards, shoving them down and snatching them back with her crumpled hands almost before he had had a chance to read them. Over it all she was keeping up what Guillam called 'her fifth-rate conjurer's patter', the abracadabra of the obsessive burrower's trade. At the heart of her discovery, so far as Guillam could make out, lay what Connie called a Moscow Centre *goldseam*; a Soviet laundering operation to move clandestine funds into open-air channels. The charting of it was not complete. Israeli liaison had supplied one section, the Cousins another, Steve Mackelvore, head resident in Paris, now dead, a third. From Paris the trail turned East, by way of the Banque de l'Indochine. At this point also, the papers had been put up to Haydon's London Station, as the operational directorate was called, together with a recommendation from the Circus's depleted Soviet Research Section that the case be thrown open to full-scale enquiry in the field. London Station killed the suggestion stone dead.

'Potentially prejudicial to a highly delicate source,' wrote one of Haydon's minions, and that was that.

'File and forget,' Smiley muttered, distractedly turning pages. 'File and forget. We always have good reasons for doing nothing.'

Outside, the world was fast asleep.

'*Exactly*, dear,' said Connie very softly, as if she were afraid to wake him.

Files and folders were by then strewn all over the throne-room. The scene looked a lot more like a disaster than a triumph. For an hour longer, Guillam and Connie gazed silently into space or at Karla's photograph while Smiley conscientiously retraced her steps, his anxious face stooped to the reading lamps, its pudgy lines accentuated by the beam, his hands skipping over the papers, and occasionally lifting to his mouth so that he could lick his thumb. Once or twice he started to glance at her, or open his mouth to speak, but Connie had the answer ready before he put his question. In her mind, she was walking beside him along the path. When he had finished, he sat back, and took off his spectacles and polished them, not on the fat end of the tie for once, but on a new silk handkerchief in the top pocket of his black jacket, for he had spent most of the day cloistered with the Cousins on another fence-mending mission. While he did this, Connie beamed at Guillam and mouthed '*Isn't he a love?*' – a favourite dictum when she was talking of her Chief, which drove Guillam nearly mad with rage.

Smiley's next utterance had the ring of mild objection.

'All the same, Con, a formal search request *did* go out from London Station to our residency in Vientiane.'

'Happened before Bill had time to get his hoof on it,' she replied.

Not seeming to hear, Smiley picked up an open file and held it to her across the desk.

'And Vientiane *did* send a lengthy reply. It's all marked up in the index. We don't seem to have that. Where is it?'

Connie had not bothered to receive the offered file.

'In the *shredder*, darling,' she said, and beamed contentedly at Guillam.

The morning had come. Guillam strolled round switching out the lights. The same afternoon, he dropped in at the quiet West End gaming club where, in the permanent night-time of his elected trade, Sam Collins endured the rigours of retirement. Expecting to find him overseeing his usual afternoon game of chemin-de-fer, Guillam was surprised at being shown to a sumptuous room marked 'management'. Sam was roosting behind a fine desk, smiling prosperously through the smoke of his habitual brown cigarette.

'What the hell have you done, Sam?' Guillam demanded in a stage whisper, affecting to look round nervously. 'Taken over the Mafia? Jesus!'

'Oh that wasn't necessary,' said Sam with the same raffish smile. Slipping a mackintosh over his dinner jacket, he led Guillam down a passage and through a fire door into the street, where the two men hopped into the back of Guillam's waiting cab, while Guillam still secretly marvelled at Sam's newfound eminence.

Fieldmen have different ways of showing no emotion and Sam's was to smile, smoke slower, and fill his eyes with a dark glow of particular indulgence, fixing them intently on his partner in discussion. Sam was an Asian hand, old Circus, with a lot of time behind him in the field: five years in Borneo, six in Burma, five more in Northern Thailand and latterly three in the Laotian capital of Vientiane, all under natural cover as a general trader. The Thais had sweated him twice but let him go, he'd had to leave Sarawak in his socks. When he was in the mood, he had stories to tell about his journeying among the northern hill tribes of Burma and the Shans, but he was seldom in the mood. Sam was a Haydon casualty. There had been a moment, five years back, when Sam's lazy brilliance had made him a serious contender for promotion to the fifth floor – even, said some, to the post of Chief itself, had not Haydon put his weight behind the preposterous Percy Alleline. So, in place of power, Sam was left to moulder in the field until Haydon contrived to recall him, and have him sacked for a trumped-up misdemeanour.

'Sam! How good of you! Take a pew,' said Smiley, all conviviality for once. 'Will you drink? Where are you in your day? Perhaps we should be offering you breakfast?'

At Cambridge, Sam had taken a dazzling First, thus confounding his tutors, who till then had dismissed him as a near idiot. He had done it, the dons afterwards told each other consolingly, entirely on memory. The more worldly tongues told a different tale, however. According to them, Sam had trailed a love affair with a plain girl at the Examination Schools, and obtained from her, among other favours, a preview of the papers.

# FOUR

## *the castle wakes*

Now at first Smiley tested the water with Sam – and Sam, who liked a poker hand himself, tested the water with Smiley. Some fieldmen, and particularly the clever ones, take a perverse pride in not knowing the whole picture. Their art consists in the deft handling of loose ends and stops there stubbornly. Sam was inclined that way. Having raked a little in his dossier, Smiley tried him out on several old cases which had no sinister look at all, but which gave a clue to Sam's present disposition and confirmed his ability to remember accurately. He received Sam alone because with other people present it would have been a different game: either more or less intense, but different. Later, when the story was out in the open and only follow-up questions remained, he did summon Connie and Doc di Salis from the nether regions, and let Guillam sit in too. But that was later, and for the time being Smiley plumbed Sam's mind alone, concealing from him entirely the fact that all casepapers had been destroyed, and that since Mackelvore was dead, Sam was at present the only witness to certain key events.

'Now Sam, do you remember at all,' Smiley asked, when he finally judged the moment right, 'a request that came in to you in Vientiane once, from here in London, concerning certain money drafts from Paris? Just a standard request it would have been, asking for "unattributable field enquiries, please, to confirm or deny" – that sort of thing? Ring a bell by any chance?'

He had a sheet of notes before him, so that this was just one more question in a slow stream. As he spoke, he was actually marking something with his pencil, not looking at Sam at all. But in the same way that we hear better with our eyes closed, Smiley did sense Sam's attention harden: which is to say, Sam stretched out his legs a little, and crossed them, and slowed his gestures almost to a halt.

'Monthly transfers to the Banque de l'Indochine,' said Sam, after a suitable pause. 'Hefty ones. Paid out of a Canadian overseas account with their Paris affiliate.' He gave the number of the account. 'Payments made on the last Friday of every month. Start date January seventy-three or thereabouts. It rings a bell, sure.'

Smiley detected immediately that Sam was settling to a long game. His memory was clear but his information meagre: more like an opening bid than a frank reply.

Still stooped over the papers, Smiley said: 'Now can we just wander over the course here a little, Sam. There's some discrepancy on the filing side, and I'd like to get your part of the record straight.'

'Sure,' said Sam again and drew comfortably on his brown cigarette. He was watching Smiley's hands, and occasionally, with studied idleness, his eyes – though never for too long. Whereas Smiley, for his part, fought only to keep his mind open to the devious options of a fieldman's life. Sam might easily be defending something quite irrelevant. He had fiddled a little bit on his expenses, for example, and was afraid he'd been caught out. He had fabricated his report rather than go out and risk his neck: Sam was of an age, after all, where a fieldman looks first to his own skin. Or it was the opposite situation: Sam had ranged a little wider in his enquiries than Head Office had sanctioned. Hard pressed, he had gone to the pedlars rather than file a nil return. He had fixed himself a side-deal with the local Cousins. Or the local security services had blackmailed him – in Sarratt jargon, the angels had put a burn on him – and he had played the case both ways in order to survive and smile and keep his Circus pension. To read Sam's moves, Smiley knew that he must stay alert to these and countless other options. A desk is a dangerous place from which to watch the world.

So, as Smiley proposed, they wandered. London's request for field enquiries, said Sam, reached him in standard form, much as Smiley had described. It was shown to him by old Mac who, until his Paris posting, was the Circus's linkman in the Vientiane Embassy. An evening session at their safe house. Routine, though the Russian aspect stuck out from the start, and Sam actually remembered saying to Mac that early: 'London must think it's Moscow Centre reptile money,' because he had spotted the cryptonym of the

Circus's Soviet Research Section mixed in with the prelims on the signal. (Smiley noted that Mac had no busines showing Sam the signal.) Sam also remembered Mac's reply to his observation: 'They should never have given old Connie Sachs the shove,' he had said. Sam had agreed whole-heartedly.

As it happened, said Sam, the request was pretty easy to meet. Sam already had a contact at the Indochine, a good one, call him Johnny.

'Filed here, Sam?' Smiley enquired politely.

Sam avoided answering that question directly and Smiley respected his reluctance. The fieldman who files all his contacts with Head Office, or even clears them, was not yet born. As illusionists cling to their mystique, so fieldmen for different reasons are congenitally secretive about their sources.

Johnny was reliable, said Sam emphatically. He had an excellent track record on several arms-dealing and narcotics cases, and Sam would swear by him anywhere.

'Oh, you handled those things too, did you, Sam?' Smiley asked respectfully.

So Sam had moonlighted for the local narcotics bureau on the side, Smiley noted. A lot of fieldmen did that, some even with Head Office consent: in their world, they likened it to selling off industrial waste. It was a perk. Nothing dramatic, therefore, but Smiley stored away the information all the same.

'Johnny was okay,' Sam repeated, with a warning in his voice.

'I'm sure he was,' said Smiley with the same courtesy.

Sam continued with his story. He had called on Johnny at the Indochine and sold him a cock-and-bull cover to keep him quiet, and a few days later, Johnny, who was just a humble counter-clerk, had checked the ledgers and unearthed the dockets and Sam had the first leg of the connection cut and dried. The routine went this way, said Sam:

'On the last Friday of each month a telexed money order arrived from Paris to the credit of a Monsieur Delassus presently staying at the Hotel Condor, Vientiane, payable on production of passport, number quoted.' Once again, Sam effortlessly recited the figures. 'The bank sent out the advice, Delassus called first thing on the Monday, drew the money in cash, stuffed it in a briefcase and walked out with it. End of connection,' said Sam.

'How much?'

'Started small and grew fast. Then went on growing, then grew a little more.'

'Ending where?'

'Twenty-five thousand US in big ones,' said Sam without a flicker.

Smiley's eyebrows lifted slightly. 'A month?' he said, in humorous surprise.

'The big table,' Sam agreed and lapsed into a leisurely silence. There is a particular intensity about clever men whose brains are under-used, and sometimes there is no way they can control their emanations. In that sense, they are a great deal more at risk, under the bright lights, than their more stupid colleagues. 'You checking me against the record, old boy?' Sam asked.

'I'm not checking you against anything, Sam. You know how it is at times like this. Clutching at straws, listening to the wind.'

'Sure,' said Sam sympathetically and, when they had exchanged further glances of mutual confidence, once more resumed his narrative.

So Sam checked at the Hotel Condor, he said. The porter there was a stock sub-source to the trade, everybody owned him. No Delassus staying there, but the front desk cheerfully admitted to receiving a little something for

providing him with an accommodation address. The very next Monday –
which happened to follow the last Friday of the month, said Sam – with the
help of his contact Johnny, Sam duly hung around the bank 'cashing
travellers' cheques and whatnot', and had a grandstand view of the said
Monsieur Delassus marching in, handing over his French passport, counting
the money into a briefcase and retreating with it to a waiting taxi.

Taxis, Sam explained, were rare beasts in Vientiane: Anyone who was
anyone had a car and a driver, so the presumption was that Delassus didn't
want to be anyone.

'So far so good,' Sam concluded, watching with interest while Smiley wrote.

'So far so *very* good,' Smiley corrected him. Like his predecessor Control,
Smiley never used pads: just single sheets of paper, one at a time, and a glass
top to press on, which Fawn polished twice a day.

'Do I fit the record or do I deviate?' asked Sam.

'I'd say you were right on course, Sam,' Smiley said. 'It's the *detail* I'm
enjoying. You know how it is with records.'

The same evening, Sam said, hugger-mugger with his linkman Mac once
more, he took a long cool look at the rogues' gallery of local Russians, and was
able to identify the unlovely features of a Second Secretary (Commercial) at
the Soviet Embassy, Vientiane, mid-fifties, military bearing, no previous
convictions, full names given but unpronounceable and known therefore
around the diplomatic bazaars as 'Commercial Boris'.

But Sam, of course, had the unpronounceable names ready in his head and
spelt them out for Smiley slowly enough for him to write them down in block
capitals.

'Got it?' he enquired helpfully.

'Thank you, yes.'

'Somebody left the card index on a bus, have they, old boy?' Sam asked.

'That's right,' Smiley agreed, with a laugh.

When the crucial Monday came round again a month later, Sam went on,
he decided he would tread wary. So instead of gum-shoeing after Commercial Boris himself he stayed home and briefed a couple of locally based
leashdogs who specialized in pavement work.

'A lace curtain job,' said Sam. 'No shaking the tree, no branch lines, no
nothing, Laotian boys.'

'Our own?'

'Three years at the mast,' said Sam. 'And *good*,' added the fieldman in him,
for whom all his geese are swans.

The said leashdogs watched the briefcase on its next journey. The taxi, a
different one from the month before, took Boris on a tour of the town and
after half an hour dropped him back near the main square, not far from the
Indochine. Commercial Boris walked a short distance, ducked into a second
bank, a local one, and paid the entire sum straight across the counter to the
credit of another account.

'So tra-la,' said Sam, and lit a fresh cigarette, not bothering to conceal his
amused bewilderment that Smiley was rehearsing verbally a case so fully
documented.

'Tra-la indeed,' Smiley murmured, writing hard.

After that, said Sam, they were home and dry. Sam lay low for a couple of
weeks to let the dust settle, then put in his girl assistant to deliver the final
blow.

'Name?'

Sam gave it. A home-based senior girl, Sarratt trained, sharing his commercial cover. This senior girl waited ahead of Boris in the local bank, let him complete his paying-in-forms, then raised a small scene.

'How did she do that, Sam?' Smiley enquired.

'Demanded to be served first,' said Sam with a grin. 'Brother Boris being a male chauvinist pig, thought he had equal rights and objected. Words passed.'

The paying-in slip lay on the counter, said Sam, and while the senior girl did her number she read it upside down: twenty-five thousand American dollars to the credit of the overseas account of a mickey-mouse aviation company called Indocharter Vientiane, SA: 'Assets, a handful of clapped-out DC3s, a tin hut, a stack of fancy letter paper, one dumb blonde for the front office and a wildcat Mexican pilot known round town as Tiny Ricardo on account of his considerable height,' said Sam. He added: 'And the usual anonymous bunch of diligent Chinese in the back room, of course.'

Smiley's ears were so sharp at that moment that he could have heard a leaf fall; but what he heard, metaphorically, was the sound of barriers being erected, and he knew at once, from the cadence, from the tightening of the voice, from the tiny facial and physical things which made up an exaggerated show of throwaway, that he was closing on the heart of Sam's defences.

So in his mind he put in a marker, deciding to remain with the mickey-mouse aviation company for a while.

'Ah,' he said lightly, 'you mean you knew the firm already?'

Sam tossed out a small card. 'Vientiane's not exactly your giant metropolis, old boy.'

'But you knew of it? That's the point.'

'Everybody in town knew Tiny Ricardo,' said Sam, grinning more broadly than ever, and Smiley knew at once that Sam was throwing sand in his eyes. But he played Sam along all the same.

'So tell me about Ricardo,' he suggested.

'One of the ex-Air America clowns. Vientiane was stiff with them. Fought the secret war in Laos.'

'And lost it,' Smiley said, writing again.

'Single-handed,' Sam agreed, watching Smiley put aside one sheet and take another from his drawer. 'Ricardo was local legend. Flew with Captain Rocky and that crowd. Credited with a couple of joyrides into Yunnan province for the Cousins. When the war ended he kicked around a bit then took up with the Chinese. We used to call those outfits Air Opium. By the time Bill hauled me home they were a flourishing industry.'

Still Smiley let Sam run. As long as Sam thought he was leading Smiley from the scent, he would talk the hindlegs off a donkey; whereas if Sam thought Smiley was getting too close, he would put up the shutters at once.

'Fine,' he said amiably, therefore, after yet more careful writing. 'Now let's go back to what Sam did next, may we? We have the money, we know whom it's paid to, we know who handles it. What's your next move, Sam?'

Well, if Sam remembered rightly he took stock for a day or two. There were *angles*, Sam explained, gathering confidence: there were little things that caught the eye. First, you might say, there was the Strange Case of Commercial Boris. Boris, as Sam had indicated, was held to be a bona fide Russian diplomat, if such a thing existed: no known connection with any other firm. Yet he rode around alone, had sole signing rights over a pot of money, and in Sam's limited experience, either one of these things spelt *hood* on one hand.

'Not just hood, a blasted supremo. A red-toothed four-square paymaster, colonel or upwards, right?'

'What other *angles*, Sam?' Smiley asked, keeping Sam on the same long rein; still making no effort to go for what Sam regarded as the centre of things.

'The money wasn't mainstream,' said Sam. 'It was oddball. Mac said so. I said so. We all said so.'

Smiley's head lifted even more slowly than before.

'Why?' he asked, looking very straight at Sam.

'The above-the-line Soviet residency in Vientiane ran three bank accounts round town. The Cousins had all three wired. They've had them wired for years. They knew every cent the residency drew and even, from the account number, whether it was for intelligence gathering or subversion. The residency had its own money-carriers, and a triple-signature system for any drawing over a thousand bucks. Christ, George, I mean it's all in the record, you know!'

'Sam, I want you to pretend that record doesn't exist,' said Smiley gravely, still writing. 'All will be revealed to you in due season. Till then, bear with us.'

'Whatever you say,' said Sam, breathing much more easily, Smiley noticed: he seemed to feel he was on firmer ground.

It was at this point that Smiley proposed they get old Connie to come and lend an ear, and perhaps Doc di Salis too, since South East Asia was after all Doc's patch. Tactically, he was content to bide his time with Sam's little secret; and strategically, the force of Sam's story was already of burning interest. So Guillam was sent to whip them in while Smiley called a break and the two men stretched their legs.

'How's trade?' Sam asked politely.

'Well, a *little* depressed,' Smiley admitted. 'Miss it?'

'That's Karla is it?' said Sam, studying the photograph.

Smiley's tone became at once donnish and vague.

'Who? Ah yes, yes it is. Not much of a likeness I'm afraid, but the best we can do as yet.'

They might have been admiring an early water-colour.

'You've got some personal thing about him, haven't you?' said Sam ruminatively.

At this point Connie, di Salis and Guillam filed in, led by Guillam, with little Fawn needlessly holding open the door.

With the enigma temporarily set aside, therefore, the meeting became something of a war party: the hunt was up. First Smiley recapitulated for Sam, incidentally making it clear in the process that they were *pretending* there were no records – which was a veiled warning to the newcomers. Then Sam took up the tale where he had left off: about the *angles*, the little things that caught the eye; though really, he insisted, there was not a lot more to say. Once the trail led to Indocharter, Vientiane SA, it stopped dead.

'Indocharter was an overseas Chinese company,' said Sam with a glance at Doc di Salis. 'Mainly Swatownese.'

At the name 'Swatownese' di Salis gave a cry, part laughter, part lament. 'Oh they're the *very* worst,' he declared – meaning the most difficult to crack.

'It was an overseas Chinese outfit,' Sam repeated for the rest of them, 'and the loony bins of South East Asia are jam-packed with honest fieldmen who have tried to unravel the life-style of hot money once it entered the maw of the overseas Chinese.' Particularly, he added, of the Swatownese or Chiu Chow, who were a people apart, and controlled the rice monopolies in Thailand, Laos and several other spots as well. Of which league, said Sam, Indocharter, Vientiane SA, was classic. His trade cover had evidently allowed him to investigate it in some depth.

'First, the *société anonyme* was registered in Paris,' he said. 'Second, the *société*, on reliable information, was the property of a discreetly diversified overseas Shanghainese trading company based on Manila, which was itself owned by a Chiu Chow company registered in Bangkok, which in turn paid its dues to a totally amorphous outfit in Hong Kong called China Airsea, quoted on the local Stock Exchange, which owned everything from junk-fleets to cement factories to racehorses to restaurants. China Airsea was by Hong Kong standards a blue chip trading house, long-established and in good standing,' said Sam, 'and probably the only connection between Indocharter and China Airsea was that somebody's fifth elder brother had an aunt who was at school with one of the shareholders and owed him a favour.'

di Salis gave another swift, approving nod, and linking his awkward hands, thrust them over one crooked knee and drew it to his chin.

Smiley had closed his eyes and seemed to have dozed off. But in reality he was hearing precisely what he had expected to hear: when it came to the full staffing of the firm of Indocharter, Sam Collins trod very lightly round a certain personality.

'But I think you mentioned there were also two *non*-Chinese in the firm, Sam,' Smiley reminded him. 'A dumb blonde, you said, and a pilot. Ricardo.'

Sam lightly brushed the objection aside.

'Ricardo was a madcap march hare,' he said. 'The Chinese wouldn't have trusted him with the stamp money. The real work was all done in the back room. If cash came in, that's where it was handled, that's where it was lost. Whether it was Russian cash, opium cash or whatever.'

di Salis, pulling frantically at one ear-lobe, was prompt to agree: 'Reappearing at will in Vancouver, Amsterdam or Hong Kong or wherever it suited somebody's very Chinese purpose,' he declared, and writhed in pleasure at his own perception.

Once again, thought Smiley, Sam had got himself off the hook. 'Well, well,' he said. 'And how did it go from there, Sam, in your authorized version?'

'London scrubbed the case.'

From the dead silence, Sam must have realized in a second that he had touched a considerable nerve. His sign language indicated as much: for he did not peer round at their faces, or register any curiosity at all. Instead, out of a sort of theatrical modesty, he studied his shiny evening shoes and his elegant dress socks, and drew thoughtfully on his brown cigarette.

'When did they do that then, Sam?' asked Smiley.

Sam gave the date.

'Go back a little. Still forgetting the record, right? How much did London know of your enquiries as you went along? Tell us that. Did you send progress reports from day to day? Did Mac?'

If the mothers next door had set a bomb off, said Guillam afterwards, nobody would have taken his eyes off Sam.

Well, said Sam easily, as if humouring Smiley's whim, he was an old dog. His principle in the field had always been to do it first and apologize afterwards. Mac's too. Operate the other way round and soon you have London refusing to let you cross the street without changing your nappies first, said Sam.

'So?' said Smiley patiently.

So the first word they sent London on the case was, you might say, their last. Mac acknowledged the enquiry, reported the sum of Sam's findings and asked for instructions.

'And London? What did London do, Sam?'

'Sent Mac a top priority shriek pulling us both off the case and ordering him to cable back immediately confirming I had understood and obeyed the order. For good measure they threw in a rocket telling us not to fly solo again.'

Guillam was doodling on the sheet of paper before him: a flower, then petals, then rain falling on the flower. Connie was beaming at Sam as if it were his wedding day, and her baby eyes were brimming tears of excitement. di Salis as usual was jiggling and fiddling like an old engine but his gaze also, as much as he could fix it anywhere, was upon Sam.

'You must have been rather cross,' said Smiley.

'Not really.'

'Didn't you have any wish to see the case through? You'd made a consider-able strike.'

'I was irked, sure.'

'But you went along with London's instructions?'

'I'm a soldier, George. We all are in the field.'

'Very laudable,' said Smiley, considering Sam once more, how he lounged smooth and charming in his dinner jacket.

'Orders is orders,' said Sam, with a smile.

'Indeed. And when you eventually got back to London, I wonder,' Smiley went on, in a controlled, speculative way, 'and you had your "welcome-home-well-done" session with Bill, did you happen to mention the matter, casually, at all, to Bill?'

'Asked him what the hell he thought he was up to,' Sam agreed, just as leisurely.

'And what did Bill have to answer there, Sam?'

'Blamed the Cousins. Said they had got in on the act ahead of us. Said it was their case and their parish.'

'Had you any reason to believe that?'

'Sure. Ricardo.'

'You guessed he was the Cousins' man?'

'He'd flown for them. He was on their books already. He was a natural. All they had to do was keep him in play.'

'I thought we were agreed that a man like Ricardo would have no access to the real operations of the company?'

'Wouldn't stop them using him. Not the Cousins. Still be their case, even if Ricardo was a bummer. The hands-off pact would apply either way.'

'Let's go back to the moment when London pulled you off the case. You received the order, "Drop everything." You obeyed. But it was some while yet before you returned to London, wasn't it? Was there an aftermath of any kind?'

'Don't quite follow you, old boy.'

Once again, at the back of his mind, Smiley made a scrupulous record of Sam's evasion.

'For example your friendly contact at the Banque de l'Indochine. Johnny.

You kept up with him, of course?'

'Sure,' said Sam.

'And did Johnny happen to mention to you, as a matter of history, what happened to the goldseam after you'd received your hands-off telegram? Did it continue to come in month by month, just as it had before?'

'Stopped dead. Paris turned the tap off. No Indocharter, no nothing.'

'And Commercial Boris, of no previous convictions? Does he live happily ever after?'

'Went home.'

'Was he due to?'

'Done three years.'

'They usually do more.'

'Specially the hoods,' Sam agreed, smiling.

'And Ricardo, the madcap Mexican flyer whom you suspect of being the Cousins' agent: what became of him?'

'Died,' said Sam, eyes on Smiley all the while. 'Crashed up on the Thai border. The boys put it down to an overload of heroin.'

Pressed, Sam had that date, too.

'Was there moaning at the bar about that, so to speak?'

'Not much. General feeling seemed to be that Vientiane would be a safer place without Ricardo emptying his pistol through the ceiling of the White Rose or Madame Lulu's.'

'Where was that feeling expressed, Sam?'

'Oh, at Maurice's place.'

'Maurice?'

'Constellation Hotel. Maurice is the proprietor.'

'I see. Thank you.'

Here there was a definite gap, but Smiley seemed disinclined to fill it. Watched by Sam and his three assistants and Fawn the factotum, Smiley plucked at his spectacles, tilted them, straightened them and returned his hands to the glass top desk. Then he took Sam all the way through the story again, rechecked dates and names and places, very laboriously in the way of trained interrogators the world over, listening by long habit for the tiny flaws and the chance discrepancies and the omissions and the changes of emphasis, and apparently not finding any. And Sam, in his sense of false security, let it all happen, watching with the same blank smile with which he watched cards slip across the baize, or the roulette wheel tease the white ball from one bay to another.

'Sam, I wonder whether you could possibly manage to stay the night with us?' Smiley said, when they were once more just the two of them. 'Fawn will do you a bed and so on. Do you think you could swing that with your club?'

'My dear fellow,' said Sam generously.

Then Smiley did a rather unnerving thing. Having handed Sam a bunch of magazines, he phoned for Sam's personal dossier, all volumes, and with Sam sitting there before him he read them in silence from cover to cover.

'I see you're a ladies' man,' he remarked at last, as the dusk gathered at the window.

'Here and there,' Sam agreed, still smiling. 'Here and there.' But the nervousness was quite apparent in his voice.

When night came, Smiley sent the mothers home and issued orders through Housekeeping Section to have archives cleared of all burrowers by eight at the latest. He gave no reason. He let them think what they wanted. Sam should lie up in the rumpus room to be on call, and Fawn should keep him company and not let him stray. Fawn took this instruction literally. Even when the hours dragged out and Sam appeared to doze, Fawn stayed folded like a cat across the threshold, but with his eyes always open.

Then the four of them cloistered themselves in Registry – Connie, di Salis, Smiley and Guillam – and began the long, cautious paperchase. They looked first for the operational casepapers which properly should have been housed in the South East Asian cut, under the dates Sam had given them. There was no card in the index and there were no casepapers either, but this was not yet significant. Haydon's London Station had been in the habit of waylaying operational files and confining them to its own restricted archive. So they plodded across the basement, feet clapping on the brown linoleum tiles, till they came to a barred alcove like an antechapel where the remains of what was formerly London Station's archive were laid to rest. Once again they found no card, and no papers.

'Look for the telegrams,' Smiley ordered, so they checked the signals ledgers, both incoming and outgoing, and for a moment Guillam at least was ready to suspect Sam of lying, till Connie pointed out that the relevant traffic sheets had been typed with a different typewriter: a machine, as it later turned out, which had not been acquired by housekeepers till six months after the date on the paper.

'Look for floats,' Smiley ordered.

Circus floats were duplicated copies of main serials which Registry ran off when casepapers threatened to be in constant action. They were banked in loose-leaf folders like back-numbers of magazines and indexed every six weeks. After much delving Connie Sachs unearthed the South East Asian folder covering the six-week period immediately following Collins's trace request. It contained no reference to a suspected Soviet goldseam and none to Indocharter, Vientiane SA.

'Try the PFs,' said Smiley, with a rare use of initials, which he otherwise detested. So they trailed to another corner of Registry and sorted through drawers of cards, looking first for personal files on Commercial Boris, then for Ricardo, then under aliases for Tiny, believed dead, whom Sam had apparently mentioned in his original ill-fated report to London Station. Now and then Guillam was sent upstairs to ask Sam some small point, and found him reading *Field* and sipping a large Scotch, watched unflinchingly by Fawn, who occasionally varied his routine – Guillam learned later – with press-ups, first on two knuckles of each hand, then on his fingertips. In the case of Ricardo they mapped out phonetic variations and ran them across the index also.

'Where are the organizations filed?' Smiley asked.

But of the *société anonyme* known as Indocharter, Vientiane, the organizations index contained no card either.

'Look up the liaison material.'

Dealings with the Cousins in Haydon's day were handled entirely through the London Station Liaison Secretariat, of which he himself for obvious reasons had personal command and which held its own file copies of all inter-service correspondence. Returning to the antechapel, they once more drew a blank. To Peter Guillam the night was taking on surreal dimensions. Smiley had become all but wordless. His plump face turned to rock. Connie, in her excitement, had forgotten her arthritic aches and pains and was hopping around the shelves like a teenager at the ball. Not by any means a born paper man Guillam scrambled after her pretending to keep up with the pack, and secretly grateful for his trips up to Sam.

'We've *got* him, George, darling,' Connie kept saying under her breath. 'Sure as boots we've *got* the beastly toad.'

Doc di Salis had danced away in search of Indocharter's Chinese directors – Sam, astonishingly had the names of two still in his head – and was wrestling with these first in Chinese, then in Roman script, and finally in Chinese commercial code. Smiley sat in a chair reading the files on his knee like a man in a train, doughtily ignoring the passengers. Sometimes he lifted his head, but the sounds he heard were not from inside the room. Connie, on her own initiative, had launched a search for cross-references to files with which the casepapers should theoretically have been linked. There were subject files on mercenaries, and on freelance aviators. There were method files on Centre's techniques for laundering agent payments, and even a treatise, which she herself had written long ago, on the subject of below-the-line paymasters responsible for Karla's illegal networks functioning unbeknown to the mainstream residencies. Commerical Boris's unpronounceable last names had not been added to the appendix. There were background files on the Banque de l'Indochine and its links with the Moscow Narodny Bank, and statistical files on the growing scale of Centre's activities in South East Asia, and study files on the Vientiane residency itself. But the negatives only multiplied, and as they multiplied they proved the affirmative. Nowhere in their whole pursuit of Haydon had they come upon such a systematic and wholesale brushing-over of the traces. It was the backbearing of all time.

And it led inexorably east.

Only one clue that night pointed to the culprit. They came on it somewhere between dawn and morning while Guillam was dozing on his feet. Connie sniffed it out, Smiley laid it silently on the table, and three of them peered at it together under the reading light as if it were the clue to buried treasure: a clip of destruction certificates, a dozen in all, with the authorizing cryptonym scribbled in black felt-tip along the middle line, giving a pleasing effect of charcoal. The condemned files related to 'top secret correspondence with H/ Annexe' – that was to say, with the Cousins' Head of Station, then as now Smiley's Brother-in-Christ Martello. The reason for destruction was the same as Haydon had given to Sam Collins for abandoning field enquiries in Vientiane: '*Risk of compromising delicate American operation.*' The signature consigning the files to the incinerator was in Haydon's workname.

Returning upstairs, Smiley invited Sam once more to his room. Sam had removed his bow tie, and the stubble of his jaw against his open-necked white shirt made him a lot less smooth.

First, Smiley sent Fawn out for coffee. He let it arrive and he waited till Fawn had flitted away again before pouring two cups, black for both of them, sugar for Sam, a saccharine for Smiley on account of his weight problem. Then he settled in a soft chair at Sam's side rather than have a desk between them, in order to affiliate himself to Sam.

'Sam, I think I ought to hear a little about the girl,' he said, very softly, as if he were breaking sad news. 'Was it chivalry that made you miss her out?'

Sam seemed rather amused. 'Lost the files have you, old boy?' he enquired, with the same men's-room intimacy.

Sometimes, in order to obtain a confidence, it is necessary to impart one.

*John le Carré*

'*Bill* lost them,' Smiley replied gently.

Elaborately, Sam lapsed into deep thought. Curling one card-player's hand he surveyed his fingertips, lamenting their grimy state.

'That club of mine practically runs itself these days,' he reflected. 'I'm getting bored with it to be frank. Money, money. Time I had a change, made something of myself.'

Smiley understood, but he had to be firm.

'I've no resources, Sam. I can hardly feed the mouths I've hired already.'

Sam sipped his black coffee ruminatively, smiling through the steam.

'Who is she, Sam? What's it all about? No one minds how bad it is. It's water under the bridge, I promise you.'

Standing, Sam sank his hands in his pockets, shook his head, and rather as Jerry Westerby might have done, began meandering round the room, peering at the odd gloomy things that hung on the wall: group war photographs of dons in uniform; a framed and handwritten letter from a dead prime minister; Karla's portrait again, which this time he studied from very close, on and on.

'"Never throw your chips away,"' he remarked, so close to Karla that his breath dulled the glass. 'That's what my old mother used to tell me. "Never make a present of your assets. We get very few in life. Got to dole them out sparingly." Not as if there isn't a game going, is it?' he enquired. With his sleeve he wiped the glass clean. 'Very hungry mood prevails in this house of yours. Felt it the moment I walked in. The big table, I said to myself. Baby will eat tonight.'

Arriving at Smiley's desk, he sat himself in the chair as if testing it for comfort. The chair swivelled as well as rocked. Sam tried both movements. 'I need a search request,' he said.

'Top right,' said Smiley, and watched while Sam opened the drawer, pulled out a yellow flimsy and laid it on the glass to write.

For a couple of minutes, Sam composed in silence, pausing occasionally for artistic consideration, then writing again.

'Call me if she shows up,' he said and, with a facetious wave to Karla, made his exit.

When he had gone, Smiley took the form from the desk, sent for Guillam and handed it to him without a word. On the staircase Guillam paused to read the text.

'Worthington Elizabeth alias Lizzie, alias Ricardo Lizzie.' That was the top line. Then the details: 'Age about twenty-seven. Nationality British. Status, married, details of husband unknown, maiden name also unknown. 1972/3 common-law wife of Ricardo Tiny, now dead. Last known place of residence Vientiane, Laos. Last known occupation: typist-receptionist with Indocharter Vientiane SA. Previous occupations: nightclub hostess, whisky saleswoman, high-class tart.'

Performing its usual dismal rôle these days Registry took about three minutes to regret 'no trace repeat no trace of subject'. Beyond this, the Queen Bee took issue with the term 'high-class'. She insisted that 'superior' was the proper way to describe that kind of tart.

Curiously enough, Smiley was not deterred by Sam's reticence. He seemed happy to accept it as part and parcel of the trade. Instead, he requested copies of all source reports which Sam had originated from Vientiane or elsewhere over the last ten years odd, and which had escaped Haydon's clever knife. And thereafter, in leisure hours, such as they were, he browsed through these, and allowed his questing imagination to form pictures of Sam's own murky world.

At this hanging moment in the affair, Smiley showed a quite lovely sense of tact, as all later agreed. A lesser man might have stormed round to the Cousins and asked as a matter of the highest urgency that Martello look out the American end of the destroyed correspondence and grant him a sight of it, but Smiley wanted nothing stirred. Molly Meakin was a prim, pretty graduate, a little blue-stocking perhaps, a little inward, but already with a modest name as a capable desk-officer, and Old Circus by virtue of both her brother and her father. At the time of the fall she was still a probationer, cutting her milk teeth in Registry. After it she was kept on as skeleton staff and promoted, if that is the word, to Vetting Section, whence no man, let alone woman, says the folklore, returns alive. But Molly possessed, perhaps by heredity, what the trade calls a natural eye. While those around her were still exchanging anecdotes about exactly where they were and what they were wearing when the news of Haydon's arrest was broken to them, Molly was setting up an unobtrusive and unofficial channel to her opposite number at the Annexe in Grosvenor Square, which by-passed the laborious procedures laid down by the Cousins since the fall. Her greatest ally was routine. Molly's visiting day was a Friday. Every Friday she drank coffee with Ed, who manned the computer; and talked classical music with Marge, who doubled for Ed; and sometimes she stayed for old-tyme dancing or a game of shuffleboard or ten-pin bowling at the Twilight Club in the Annexe basement. Friday was also the day, quite incidentally, when she took along her little shopping-list of trace requests. Even if she had none outstanding, Molly was careful to invent some in order to keep the channel open, and on this particular Friday, at Smiley's behest, Molly Meakin included the name of Tiny Ricardo in her selection.

'But I don't want him sticking out in any way, Molly,' said Smiley anxiously.

'Of course not,' said Molly.

For smoke, as she called it, Molly chose a dozen other R's and when she came to Ricardo she wrote down 'Richards query Rickard query Ricardo, profession teacher query aviation instructor,' so that the real Ricardo would only be thrown up as a possible identification. Nationality Mexican query Arab, she added: and she threw in the extra information that he might anyway be dead.

It was once more late in the evening before Molly returned to the Circus. Guillam was exhausted. Forty is a difficult age at which to stay awake, he decided. At twenty or at sixty the body knows what it's about, but forty is an adolescence where one sleeps to grow up or to stay young. Molly was twenty-three. She came straight to Smiley's room, sat down primly with her knees pressed tight together, and began unpacking her handbag, watched intently by Connie Sachs, and even more intently by Peter Guillam, though for different reasons. She was sorry she'd been so long, she said severely, but Ed had insisted on taking her to a re-run of *True Grit*, a great favourite in the Twilight Club, and afterwards she had had to fight him off, but hadn't wished to give offence, least of all tonight. She handed Smiley an envelope and he opened it, and drew out a long buff computer card. So did she fight him off or not? Guillam wanted to know.

'How did it play?' was Smiley's first question.

'Quite straightforward,' she replied.

'What an extraordinary-looking script,' Smiley exclaimed next. But as he went on reading his expression changed slowly to a rare and wolfish grin.

Connie was less restrained. By the time she had passed the card to Guillam, she was laughing outright.

'Oh *Bill*! Oh you wicked lovely man! Talk about pointing everyone in the wrong direction! Oh the devil.'

In order to silence the Cousins, Haydon had reversed his original lie. Deciphered, the lengthy computer printout told the following enchanting story.

Anxious lest the Cousins might have been duplicating the Circus's enquiries into the firm of Indocharter, Bill Haydon, in his capacity as Head of London Station, had sent to the Annexe a pro-forma hands-off notice, under the standing bilateral agreement between the services. This advised the Americans that Indocharter, Vientiane SA was presently under scrutiny by London and that the Circus had an agent in place. Accordingly, the Americans consented to drop any interest they might have in the case in exchange for a share of the eventual take. As an aid to the British operation, the Cousins did however mention that their link with the pilot Tiny Ricardo was extinct.

In short, as neat an example of playing both ends against the middle as anybody had ever met with.

'Thank you, Molly,' said Smiley politely, when everyone had had a chance to marvel. 'Thank you very much indeed.'

'Not at all,' said Molly, prim as a nursemaid. 'And Ricardo is definitely dead, Mr Smiley,' she ended, and she quoted the same date of death which Sam Collins had already supplied. With that, she snapped together the clasp of her handbag, pulled her skirt over her admirable knees, and walked delicately from the room, well observed once more by Peter Guillam.

A different pace, a different mood entirely, now overtook the Circus. The frantic search for a trail, any trail, was over. They could march to a purpose, rather than gallop in all directions. The amiable distinction between the two families largely fell away: the bolshies and the yellow perils became a single unit under the joint direction of Connie and the Doc, even if they kept their separate skills. Joy after that, for the burrowers, came in bits, like waterholes on a long and dusty trek, and sometimes they all but fell at the wayside. Connie took no more than a week to identify the Soviet paymaster in Vientiane who had supervised the transfer of funds to Indocharter, Vientiane SA – the Commerical Boris. He was the former soldier Zimin, a longstanding graduate of Karla's private training school outside Moscow. Under the previous alias of Smirnov, this Zimin was on record as having played paymaster to an East German *apparat* in Switzerland six years ago. Using the name Kursky, he had surfaced before that in Vienna. As a secondary skill he offered sound-stealing and entrapment, and some said he was the same Zimin who had sprung the successful honey-trap in West Berlin against a certain French senator who later sold half his country's secrets down the river. He had left Vientiane exactly a month after Sam's report had hit London.

After that small triumph, Connie set herself the apparently impossible task of defining what arrangements Karla, or his paymaster Zimin, might have made to replace the interrupted goldseam. Her touchstones were several. First, the known conservatism of enormous intelligence establishments, and their attachment to proven traderoutes. Second, Centre's presumed need, since large payments were involved, to replace the old system with a new one fast. Third, Karla's complacency, both before the fall, when he had the Circus tethered, and since the fall, when it lay gasping and toothless at his feet. Lastly, quite simply, she relied upon her own encyclopaedic grasp of the subject. Gathering together the heaps of unprocessed raw material which had lain deliberately neglected during the years of her exile, Connie's team made huge arcs through the files, revised, conferred, drew charts and diagrams, pursued the individual handwriting of known operators, had migraines, argued, played ping-pong, and occasionally, with agonizing caution, and Smiley's express consent, undertook timid investigations in the field. A friendly contact in the City was persuaded to visit an old acquaintance who specialized in off-shore Hong Kong companies. A Cheapside currency broker opened his books to Toby Esterhase, the sharp-eyed Hungarian survivor who was all that remained of the Circus's once glorious travelling army of couriers and pavement artists. So it went on, at a snail's pace: but at least the snail knew where it wanted to go. Doc di Salis, in his distant way, took the overseas Chinese path, working his passage through the arcane connections of Indocharter, Vientiane SA, and its elusive echelons of parent companies. His helpers were as uncommon as himself, either language students or elderly recycled China hands. With time they acquired a collective pallor, like inmates of the same dank seminary.

Meanwhile, Smiley himself advanced no less cautiously, if anything down yet more devious avenues, and through a greater number of doors.

Once more he sank from view. It was a time of waiting and he spent it in attending to the hundred other things that needed his urgent attention. His brief burst of teamwork over, he withdrew to the inner regions of his solitary world. Whitehall saw him; so did Bloomsbury still; so did the Cousins. At other times the throne-room door stayed closed for days at a time, and only dark Fawn the factotum was permitted to flit in and out in his gym shoes, bearing steaming cups of coffee, plates of biscuits and occasional written memoranda, to or from his master. Smiley had always loathed the telephone, and now he would take no calls whatever, unless in Guillam's view they concerned matters of great urgency, and none did. The only instrument Smiley could not switch off controlled the direct line from Guillam's desk, but when he was in one of his moods he went so far as to put a teacosy over it in an effort to quell the ring. The invariable procedure was for Guillam to say that Smiley was out, or in conference, and would return the call in an hour's time. He then wrote out a message, handed it to Fawn, and eventually, with the initiative on his side, Smiley would ring back. He conferred with Connie, sometimes with di Salis, sometimes with both, but Guillam was not required. The Karla file was transferred from Connie's Research Section to Smiley's personal safe for good; all seven volumes. Guillam signed for them and took them into him, and when Smiley lifted his eyes from the desk and saw them, the quiet of recognition came over him, and he reached forward as if to receive an old friend. The door closed again, and more days passed.

'Any word?' Smiley would ask occasionally of Guillam. He meant: 'Has Connie rung?'

The Hong Kong residency was evacuated around this time, and too late Smiley was advised of the housekeepers' elephantine efforts at repressing the

High Haven story. He at once drew Craw's dossier, and again called Connie in for consultation. A few days later Craw himself appeared in London for a forty-eight hour visit. Guillam had heard him lecture at Sarratt and detested him. A couple of weeks afterwards, the old man's celebrated article finally saw the light of day. Smiley read it intently, then passed it to Guillam, and for once he actually offered an explanation for his action: Karla would know very well what the Circus was up to, he said. Backbearings were a time-honoured pastime. However, Karla would not be human if he didn't sleep after such a big kill.

'I want him to hear from everyone just how dead we are,' Smiley explained.

Soon this broken-wing technique was extended to other spheres, and one of Guillam's more entertaining tasks was to make sure that Roddy Martindale was well supplied with woeful stories about the Circus's disarray.

And still the burrowers toiled. They call it afterwards the phoney peace. They had the map, Connie said later, and they had the directions, but there were still mountains to be moved in spoonfuls. Waiting, Guillam took Molly Meakin to long and costly dinners but they ended inconclusively. He played squash with her and admired her eye, he swam with her and admired her body, but she warded off closer contact with a mysterious and private smile, turning her head away and downward while she went on holding him.

Under the continued pressure of idleness Fawn the factotum took to acting strangely. When Smiley disappeared and left him behind, he literally pined for his master's return. Catching him by surprise in his little den one evening, Guillam was shocked to find him in a near foetal crouch, winding a handkerchief round and round his thumb like a ligature, in order to hurt himself.

'For God's sake, it's nothing personal, man!' Guillam cried. 'George doesn't need you for once, that's all. Take a few days' leave or something. Cool off.'

But Fawn referred to Smiley as the Chief, and looked askance at those who called him George.

It was toward the end of this barren phase that a new and wonderful gadget appeared on the fifth floor. It was brought in suitcases by two crewcut technicians and installed over three days: a green telephone destined, despite his prejudices, for Smiley's desk and connecting him directly with the Annexe. It was routed by way of Guillam's room, and linked to all manner of anonymous grey boxes which hummed without warning. Its presence only deepened the general mood of nervousness: what use was a machine, they asked each other, if they had nothing to put into it?

But they had something.

Suddenly the word was out. What Connie had found she wasn't saying, but news of the discovery ran like wildfire through the building: 'Connie's *home*! The burrowers are *home*! They've found the new goldseam! They've traced it all the way through!'

Through what? To whom? Where did it end? Connie and di Salis still kept mum. For a day and a night they trailed in and out of the throne-room laden with files, no doubt once more in order to show Smiley their workings.

Then Smiley disappeared for three days and Guillam only learned much later that 'in order to screw down every bolt' as he called it, he had visited both Hamburg and Amsterdam for discussions with certain eminent bankers of his acquaintance. These gentlemen spent a great while explaining to him that the war was over and they could not possibly offend against their code of ethics, and then they gave him the information he so badly needed: though it was only the final confirmation of all that the burrowers had deduced. Smiley returned, but Peter Guillam still remained shut out, and he might well have continued in this private limbo indefinitely, had it not been for dinner at the Lacons.

Guillam's inclusion was pure chance. So was the dinner. Smiley had asked Lacon for an afternoon appointment at the Cabinet Office, and spent several hours in cahoots with Connie and di Salis preparing for it. At the last moment Lacon was summoned by his parliamentary masters, and proposed pot-luck at his ugly mansion at Ascot instead. Smiley detested driving and there was no duty car. In the end, Guillam offered to chauffeur him in his draughty old Porsche, having first put a rug over him which he was keeping in case Molly Meakin consented to a picnic. On the drive, Smiley attempted small-talk, which came hard to him, but he was nervous. They arrived in rain and there was muddle on the doorstep about what to do with the unexpected underling. Smiley insisted that Guillam would make his own way and return at ten-thirty: the Lacons that he *must* stay, and there was simply *masses* of food.

'It's up to you,' said Guillam to Smiley.

'Oh, of course. No I mean really, if it's all right with the Lacons, naturally,' said Smiley huffily and in they went.

So a fourth place was laid, and the overcooked steak was cut into bits till it looked like dry stew, and a daughter was despatched on her bicycle with a pound to fetch a second bottle of wine from the pub up the road. Mrs Lacon was doe-like and fair and blushing, a child bride who had become a child mother. The table was too long for four. She set Smiley and her husband one end and Guillam next to her. Having asked him whether he liked madrigals, she embarked on an endless account of a concert at her daughter's private school. She said it was absolutely *ruined* by the rich foreigners they were taking in to balance the books. Half of them couldn't sing in a Western way at all:

'I mean who wants one's child brought up with a lot of Persians when they all have six wives apiece?' she said.

Stringing her along, Guillam strove to catch the dialogue at the other end of the table. Lacon seemed to be bowling and batting at once.

'First, you petition *me*,' he boomed. 'You are doing that now, very properly. At this stage, you should give no more than a preliminary outline. Traditionally Ministers like nothing that cannot be written on a postcard. Preferably a *picture* postcard,' he said, and took a prim sip at the vile red wine.

Mrs Lacon, whose intolerance had a beatific innocence about it, began complaining about Jews.

'I mean they don't even eat the same *food* as we do,' she said. 'Penny says they get special herring things for lunch.'

Guillam again lost the thread till Lacon raised his voice in warning.

'Try to keep *Karla* out of this, George. I've asked you before. Learn to say *Moscow* instead, will you? They don't like personalities – however dispassionate your hatred of him. Nor do I.'

'Moscow then,' Smiley said.

'It's not that one *dislikes* them,' Mrs Lacon said. 'They're just different.'

Lacon picked up some earlier point. 'When you say a *large* sum, how large is large?'

'We are not yet in a position to say,' Smiley replied.

'Good. More enticing. Have you no panic factor?'

Smiley didn't follow that question any better than Guillam.

'What alarms you most about your discovery, George? What do you fear for, here, in your rôle of watchdog?'

'The security of a British Crown Colony?' Smiley suggested, after some thought.

'They're talking about Hong Kong,' Mrs Lacon explained to Guillam. 'My uncle was Political Secretary. On Daddy's side,' she added. 'Mummy's brothers never did anything brainy at all.'

She said Hong Kong was nice but smelly.

Lacon had become a little pink and erratic. 'Colony – my God, hear that, Val?' he called down the table, taking time off to educate her. 'Richer than we are by half, I should think, and from where *I* sit, enviably more secure as well. A full twenty years their Treaty has to run, even if the Chinese enforce it. At this rate, they should see us out in comfort!'

'Oliver thinks we're *doomed*,' Mrs Lacon explained to Guillam excitedly, as if she were admitting him to a family secret, and shot her husband an angelic smile.

Lacon resumed his former confiding tone, but he continued to blurt and Guillam guessed he was showing off to his squaw.

'You would also make the point to me wouldn't you – as background to the postcard as it were – that a major Soviet intelligence presence in Hong Kong would be an appalling embarrassment to the Colonial government in her relations with Peking?'

'Before I went as far as that –'

'On whose magnanimity,' Lacon pursued, 'she depends from hour to hour for her survival, correct?'

'It's because of these very implications –' Smiley said.

'Oh Penny, you're naked!' Mrs Lacon cried indulgently.

Providing Guillam with a glorious respite, she bounded off to calm an unruly small daughter who had appeared at the doorway. Lacon meanwhile had filled his lungs for an aria.

'We are therefore not only protecting Hong Kong from the *Russians* – which is bad enough, I grant you, but perhaps not *quite* bad enough for some of our higher-minded Ministers – we are protecting her from the wrath of Peking, which is universally held to be awful, right Guillam? *However* –' said Lacon, and to emphasize the *volte face* went so far as to arrest Smiley's arm with his long hand so that he had to put down his glass – '*however*,' he warned, as his erratic voice swooped and rose again, 'whether our masters will swallow all that is quite another matter altogether.'

'I would not consider asking them to until I had obtained corroboration of our data,' Smiley said sharply.

'Ah, but you can't, can you?' Lacon objected, changing hats. 'You can't go beyond domestic research. You haven't the charter.'

'Without a reconnaissance of the information –'

'Ah, but what does that *mean*, George?'

'Putting in an agent.'

Lacon lifted his eyebrows and turned away his head, reminding Guillam irresistibly of Molly Meakin.

'Method is not my affair, nor are the details. Clearly you can do nothing to embarrass since you have no money and no resources.' He poured more wine, spilling some. 'Val!' he yelled. 'Cloth!'

'I do have *some* money.'

'But not for that purpose.' The wine had stained the table cloth. Guillam poured salt on it while Lacon lifted the cloth and shoved his napkin ring under it to spare the polish.

A long silence followed, broken by the slow pat of wine falling on the parquet floor. Finally Lacon said: 'It is entirely up to you to define what is chargeable under your mandate.'

'May I have that in writing?'

'No, sir.'

'May I have your authority to take what steps are needed to corroborate the information?'

'No, sir.'

'But you won't block me?'

'Since I know nothing of method, and am not required to, it is hardly my province to dictate to you.'

'But since I make a formal approach –' Smiley began.

'Val, *do* bring a cloth! Once you make a formal approach I shall wash my hands of you entirely. It is the Intelligence Steering Group, not myself, who determines your scope of action. You will make your pitch. They will hear you out. From then on it's between you and them. I am just the midwife. Val, bring a cloth, it's everywhere!'

'Oh, it's my head on the block, not yours,' said Smiley, almost to himself. 'You're impartial. I know all about that.'

'*Oliver's* not impartial,' said Mrs Lacon gaily as she returned with the girl over her shoulder, brushed and wearing a nightdress. 'He's *terrifically* in favour of you, aren't you, Olly?' She handed Lacon a cloth and he began mopping. 'He's become a real *hawk* these days. Better than the Americans. Now say good night to everyone, Penny, come on.' She was offering the child to each of them in turn. 'Mr Smiley first . . . Mr Guillam, now Daddy . . . How's Ann, George, not off to the country again, I hope?'

'Oh very bonny, thank you.'

'Well, make Oliver give you what you want. He's getting *terribly* pompous, aren't you, Olly?'

She danced off, chanting her own rituals to the child.

'Hitty pitty *without* the wall . . . hitty pitty *within* the wall . . . and *bumps* goes Pottifer!'

Lacon proudly watched her go.

'Now, will you bring the Americans into it, George?' he demanded airily. 'That's a great catchpenny, you know. Wheel in the Cousins and you'd carry the committee without a shot fired. Foreign Office would eat out of your hand.'

'I would prefer to stay my hand on that.'

The green telephone, thought Guillam, might never have existed.

Lacon ruminated, twiddling his glass.

'Pity,' he pronounced finally. 'Pity. No Cousins, no panic factor . . . ' He gazed at the dumpy unimpressive figure before him. Smiley sat hands linked, eyes closed, seemingly half asleep. 'And no credibility either,' Lacon went on, apparently as a direct comment upon Smiley's appearance. 'Defence won't lift a finger for you, I'll tell you that for a start. Nor will the Home Office. The Treasury's a toss-up, and the Foreign Office – depends who they send to the meeting and what they had for breakfast.' Again he reflected. 'George.'

'Yes?'

'Let me send you an advocate. Somebody who can ride point for you, draft your submission, carry it to the barricades.'

'Oh I think I can manage thank you!'

'Make him rest more,' Lacon advised Guillam in a deafening whisper as they walked to the car. 'And try and get him to drop those black jackets and stuff. They went out with bustles. Goodbye, George! Ring me tomorrow if you change your mind and want help. Now drive carefully, Guillam. Remember you've been drinking.'

As they passed through the gates Guillam said something very rude indeed but Smiley was too deep inside the rug to hear.

'So it's Hong Kong then?' Guillam said, as they drove.

No answer, but no denial either.

'And who's the lucky fieldman?' Guillam asked, a little later, with no real hope of getting an answer. 'Or is that all part of foxing around with the Cousins?'

'We're not foxing around with them at all,' Smiley retorted, stung for once. 'If we cut them in, they'll swamp us. If we don't we've no resources. It's simply a matter of balance.'

Smiley dived back into the rug.

But the very next day, lo and behold, they were ready.

At ten, Smiley convened an operational directorate. Smiley talked, Connie talked, di Salis fidgeted and scratched himself like a verminous court tutor in a Restoration comedy, till it was his own turn to speak out, in his cracked, clever voice. The same evening still, Smiley sent his telegram to Italy: a real one, not just a signal, codeword Guardian, copy to the fast growing file. Smiley wrote it out, Guillam gave it to Fawn, who whisked it off triumphantly to the all-night post office at Charing Cross. From the air of ceremony with which Fawn departed, one might have supposed that the little buff form was the highest point so far of his sheltered life. This was not so. Before the fall, Fawn had worked under Guillam as a scalphunter based in Brixton. By actual trade, though, he was a silent killer.

# FIVE

## *a walk in the park*

Throughout that whole sunny week Jerry Westerby's leave-taking had a bustling, festive air which never once let up. If London was holding its summer late, then so, one might have thought, was Jerry. Stepmothers, vaccinations, travel touts, literary agents and Fleet Street editors; Jerry, though he loathed London like the pest, took them all in his cheery pounding stride. He even had a London persona to go with the buckskin boots: his suit, not Savile Row exactly, but a suit undeniably. His prison gear, as the orphan called it, was a washable, blue-faded affair, the creation of a twenty-four hour tailor named 'Pontschak Happy House of Bangkok', who guaranteed it *unwrinkable* in radiant silk letters on the tag. In the mild midday breezes it billowed as weightlessly as a frock on Brighton pier. His silk shirt from the same source had a yellowed locker-room look recalling Wimbledon or Henley. His tan, though Tuscan, was as English as the famous cricketing tie which flew from him like a patriotic flag. Only his expression, to the very discerning, had that certain watchfulness, which also Mama Stefano the postmistress had noticed, and which the instinct describes as 'professional', and leaves at that. Sometimes, if he anticipated waiting, he carted the book-sack with him, which gave him a bumpkin air: Dick Whittington had come to town.

He was based, if anywhere, in Thurloe Square where he lodged with his stepmother, the third Lady Westerby, in a tiny frilly flat crammed with huge antiques salvaged from abandoned houses. She was a painted, hen-like woman, snappish as old beauties sometimes are, and would often curse him for real or imagined crimes, such as smoking her last cigarette, or bringing in mud from his caged rambles in the park. Jerry took it all in good part. Sometimes, returning as late as three or four in the morning but still not sleepy, he would hammer on her door to wake her, though most often she was awake already; and when she had put on her make-up, he set her on his bed in her frou-frou dressing gown with a king-sized *crême de menthe frappé* in her little claw, while Jerry himself sprawled over the whole floor-space, among a magic mountain of junk, getting on with what he called his packing. The mountain was made of everything that was useless: old press cuttings, heaps of yellowed newspapers, legal deeds tied in green ribbon, and even a pair of custom-made riding boots, tree'd, but green with mildew. In theory Jerry was deciding what he would need of all this for his journey, but he seldom got much further than a keepsake of some kind, which set the two of them on a chain of memories. One night for example he unearthed an album of his earliest stories.

'Hey Pet, here's a good one! Westerby really rips the mask off this one! Make your heart beat faster does it, sport? Get the old blood stirring?'

'You should have gone into your uncle's business,' she retorted, turning the pages with great satisfaction. The uncle in question was a gravel king, whom Pet used freely to emphasize old Sambo's improvidence.

Another time they found a copy of the old man's will from years back – 'I, Samuel, also known as Sambo, Westerby' – jammed in with a bunch of bills and solicitors' correspondence addressed to Jerry in his function as executor, all stained with whisky, or quinine, and beginning 'We regret'.

'Bit of a turn-up, that one,' Jerry muttered uncomfortably, when it was too late to re-bury the envelope in the mountain. 'Reckon we could bung it down the old whatnot, don't you, sport?'

Her boot-button eyes glowed furiously.

'Aloud,' she ordered, in a booming theatrical voice, and in no time they were wandering together through the insoluble complexities of trusts that endowed grandchildren, educated nephews and nieces, the income to this wife for her lifetime, the capital to so-and-so on death or marriage; codicils to reward favours, others to punish slights.

'Hey, know who that was? Dread cousin Aldred, the one who went to jug! Jesus, why'd he want to leave *him* money? Blow it in one night!'

And codicils to take care of the racehorses, who might otherwise come under the axe: 'My horse Rosalie in Maison Laffitte, together with two thousand pounds a year for stabling . . . my horse Intruder presently under training in Dublin, to my son Gerald for their respective lifetimes, on the understanding he will support them to their natural deaths . . .'

Old Sambo, like Jerry, dearly loved a horse.

Also for Jerry: stock. Only for Jerry: the company's stock in millions. A mantle, power, responsibility; a whole grand world to inherit and romp around in – a world offered, promised even, then withheld: 'my son to manage all the newspapers of the group according to the style and codes of practice established in my lifetime.' Even a bastard was owned to: a sum of twenty thousands, free of duty payable to Miss Mary Something of the Green, Chobham, the mother of my acknowledged son Adam. The only trouble was: the cupboard was bare. The figures on the account sheet wasted steadily away from the day the great man's empire tottered into liquidation. Then changed to red and grew again into long blood-sucking insects swelling by a nought a year.

'Ah well, Pet,' said Jerry, in the unearthly silence of early dawn, as he tossed the envelope back on the magic mountain. 'Shot of him now, aren't you, sport?' Rolling on to his side, he grabbed the pile of faded newspapers – last editions of his father's brainchildren – and, as only old pressmen can, fumbled his way through all of them at once. 'Can't go chasing the dolly birds where *he* is, can he, Pet?' – a huge rustle of paper – 'Wouldn't put it past him, mind. Wouldn't be for want of trying, I daresay.' And in a quieter voice, as he turned back to glance at the little still doll on the edge of his bed, her feet barely reaching the carpet: 'You were always his *tai-tai*, sport, his number one. Always stuck up for you. Told me. "Most beautiful girl in the world, Pet is." Told me. Very words. Bellowed it at me across Fleet Street once. "Best wife I ever had."'

'Damn devil,' said his stepmother in a soft, sudden rush of pure North Country dialect, as the creases collected like a surgeon's pins round the red seam of her lips. 'Rotten devil, I hate every inch of him.' And for a while they stayed that way, neither of them speaking, Jerry lying pottering with his junk and yanking at his forelock, she sitting, joined in some kind of love for Jerry's father.

'You should have sold ballast for your Uncle Paul,' she sighed, with the insight of a much deceived woman.

On their last night Jerry took her out to dinner, and afterwards, back in Thurloe Square, she served him coffee in what was left of her Sèvres service. The gesture led to disaster. Wedging his broad forefinger unthinkingly into the handle of his cup, Jerry broke it off with a faint *putt* which mercifully escaped her notice. By dexterous palming, he contrived to conceal the damage from her until he was able to gain the kitchen and make a swap. God's wrath is inescapable, alas. When Jerry's plane staged in Tashkent – he had wangled himself a concession on the trans-Siberian route – he found to his surprise that the Russian authorities had opened a bar at one end of the waiting room: in Jerry's view amazing evidence of the country's liberalisation. Groping in his jacket pocket for hard currency to pay for a large vodka, he came instead on the pretty little porcelain question-mark with its snapped off edges. He forswore the vodka.

In business matters he was equally amenable, equally compliant. His literary agent was an old cricketing acquaintance, a snob of uncertain origins called Mencken, known as Ming, one of those natural fools for whom English society and the publishing world in particular are ever ready to make a comfortable space. Mencken was bluff and gusty and sported a grizzled beard, perhaps in order to suggest he wrote the books he hawked. They lunched in Jerry's club, a grand, grubby place which owed its survival to amalgamation with humbler clubs, and repeated appeals through the post. Huddled in the half-empty dining room, under the marble eyes of empire builders, they lamented Lancashire's lack of fast bowlers. Jerry wished Kent would 'hit the damn ball, Ming, not peck at it.' Middlesex, they agreed, had some good young ones coming on: but 'Lord help us, *look* at the way they pick 'em,' said Ming, shaking his head and cutting his food all at once.

'Pity you ran out of steam,' Ming bawled, to Jerry and anyone else who cared to listen. 'Nobody's brought off the eastern novel recently, my view. Greene managed it, if you can take Greene, which I can't, too much popery. Malraux if you like philosophy, which I don't. Maugham you can *have*, and before that it's back to Conrad. Cheers. Mind my saying something?' Jerry filled Ming's glass. 'Go easy on the Hemingway stuff. All that grace under pressure, love with your balls shot off. They don't like it, my view. It's been *said*.'

Jerry saw Ming to his cab.

'Mind my saying something?' Mencken repeated. 'Longer sentences. Moment you journalist chappies turn your hand to novels you write too short. Short paragraphs, short sentences, short chapters. You see the stuff in column inches, 'stead of across the page. Hemingway was just the same. Always trying to write novels on the back of a matchbox. Spread yourself, my view.'

'Cheero, Ming. Thanks.'

'Cheero, Westerby. Remember me to your old father, mind. Must be getting on now, I suppose. Still it comes to us all.'

Even with Stubbs, Jerry near enough preserved the same sunny temper; though Stubbs, as Connie Sachs would have said, was a known toad.

Pressmen, like other travelling people, make the same mess everywhere and Stubbs, as the group's managing editor, was no exception. His desk was littered with tea-stained proofs and ink-stained cups and the remains of a ham sandwich that had died of old age. Stubbs himself sat scowling at Jerry from the middle of it all as if Jerry had come to take it away from him.

'Stubbsie. Pride of the profession,' Jerry murmured, shoving open the door, and leaned against the wall with his hands behind him, as if to keep them in check.

Stubbs bit something hard and nasty on the tip of his tongue before returning to the file he was studying at the top of the muck on his desk. Stubbs made all the weary jokes about editors come true. He was a resentful man with heavy grey jowls and heavy eyelids that looked as though they had been rubbed with soot. He would stay with the Daily until the ulcers got him, and then they would send him to the Sunday. Another year, he would be farmed out to the women's magazines to take orders from children till he had served his time. Meanwhile he was devious, and listened to incoming phone calls from correspondents without telling them he was on the line.

'Saigon,' Stubbs growled, and with a chewed ballpoint marked something in a margin. His London accent was complicated by a half-hearted twang left over from the days when Canadian was the Fleet Street sound. 'Christmas three years back. Ring a bell?'

'What bell's that, old boy?' Jerry asked, still pressed against the wall.

'A *festive* bell,' said Stubbs, with a hangman's smile. 'Fellowship and good cheer in the bureau, when the group was fool enough to maintain one out there. A Christmas party. You gave it.' He read from a file. '"To Christmas luncheon, Hotel Continental. Saigon." Then you list the guests, just the way we ask you to. Stringers, photographers, drivers, secretaries, messenger boys, hell do I know? Cool seventy pounds changed hands in the interest of public relations and festive cheer. Recall that?' He went straight on. 'Among the guests you have Smoothie Stallwood entered. He was *there*, was he? Stallwood? His usual act? Oiling up to the ugliest girls, saying the right things?'

Waiting, Stubbs nibbled again at whatever it was he had on the tip of his tongue. But Jerry propped up the wall, ready to wait all day.

'We're a left-wing group,' said Stubbs, launching on a favourite dictum. 'That means we disapprove of fox-hunting and rely for our survival on the generosity of one illiterate millionaire. Records say Stallwood ate his Christmas lunch in Phnom Penh, lashing out hospitality on dignitaries of the Cambodian government, God help him. I've spoken to Stallwood, and he seems to think that's where he was. Phnom Penh.'

Jerry slouched over to the window and settled his rump against an old black radiator. Outside, not six feet from him, a grimy clock hung over the busy pavement, a present to Fleet Street from the founder. It was mid-morning but the hands were stuck at five to six. In a doorway across the street, two men stood reading a newspaper. They wore hats, and the newspaper obscured their faces, and Jerry reflected how lovely life would be if watchers only looked like that in reality.

'Everybody screws this comic, Stubbsie,' he said thoughtfully after another longish silence. 'You included. You're talking about three bloody years ago. Stuff it, sport. That's my advice. Pop it up the old back passage. Best place for that one.'

'It's not a comic, it's a rag. Comic's a colour supplement.'

'Comic to me, sport. Always was, always will be.'

'Welcome,' Stubbs intoned with a sigh. 'Welcome to the Chairman's choice.' He took up a printed form of contract. 'Name: Westerby, Clive Gerald,' he declaimed, pretending to read from it. 'Profession: aristocrat. Welcome to the son of old Sambo.' He tossed the contract on the desk. 'You take the both. The Sunday and the Daily. Seven day coverage, wars to tit-shows. No tenure or pension, expenses at the meanest possible level. Laundry in the field only and that doesn't mean the whole week's wash. You get a cable card but don't use it. Just airfreight your story and telex the number of the waybill and we'll put it on the spike for you when it arrives. Further payment by results. The BBC is also graciously pleased to take voice interviews from you at the usual derisory rates. Chairman says it's good for prestige, whatever the hell that means. For syndication –'

'Allelujah,' said Jerry in a long outward breath.

Ambling back to the desk, he took up the chewed ballpoint, still wet from Stubbs's lick, and without a glance at its owner, or the wording of the contract, scrawled his signature in a slow zigzag along the bottom of the last page, grinning lavishly. At the same moment, as if summoned to interrupt this hallowed event, a girl in jeans unceremoniously kicked open the door and dumped a fresh sheaf of galley on the desk. The phones rang – perhaps they had been ringing for some while – the girl departed, balancing absurdly on her enormous platform heels, an unfamiliar head poked around the door and yelled 'old man's prayer meeting, Stubbsie', an underling appeared and moments later Jerry was being marched down the chicken run: administration, foreign desk, editorial, pay, diary, sports, travel, the ghastly women's magazines. His guide was a twenty-year-old bearded graduate and Jerry called him 'Cedric' all the way through the ritual. On the pavement he paused, rocking slightly heel to toe and back, as if he were drunk, or punchdrunk.

'*Super*,' he muttered, loud enough for a couple of girls to turn and stare at him as they passed. 'Excellent. Marvellous. Splendid. Perfect.' With that, he dived into the nearest watering-hole, where a bunch of old hands were propping up the bar, mainly the industrial and political caucus, boasting about how they nearly had a page-five lead.

'Westerby! It's the Earl himself! It's the *suit*! The same suit! And the Earlybird's inside it, for Christ's sake!'

Jerry stayed until 'time' was called. He drank frugally, nevertheless, for he liked to keep a clear head for his walks in the park with George Smiley.

To every closed society there is an inside and an outside, and Jerry was on the outside. To walk in the park with George Smiley, in those days, or – free of the professional jargon, to make a clandestine rendezvous with him; or as Jerry himself might have expressed it, if he ever, God forbid, put a name to the larger issues of his destiny, 'to take a dive into his other, better life' – required him to saunter from a given point of departure, usually some rather under-populated area like the recently extinguished Covent Garden, and arrive still on foot at a given destination at a little before six, by which time, he assumed, the Circus's depleted team of pavement-artists had taken a look at his back and declared it clean. On the first evening his destination was the embankment side of Charing Cross underground station, as it was still called that year, a busy scrappy spot where something awkward always seems to be happening to the traffic. On the last evening it was a multiple bus stop on the southern pavement of Piccadilly where it borders Green Park. There were in all four occasions, two in London and two at the Nursery. The Sarratt stuff was operational – the obligatory re-bore in tradecraft, to which all fieldmen must periodically submit – and included much to be memorized, such as phone numbers, word codes and contact procedures; such as open-code phrases for insertion into plain language telex messages to the comic, such as fallbacks and emergency action in certain, it was hoped, remote contingencies. Like many sportsmen Jerry had a clear, easy memory for facts and when the inquisitors tested him they were pleased. Also they rehearsed him in the strong-arm stuff, with the result that his back bled from hitting the worn matting once too often.

The sessions in London consisted of one very simple briefing and one very short farewell.

The pickups were variously contrived. At Green Park, by way of a recognition signal, he carried a Fortnum & Mason carrier-bag and managed, however long the bus queue became, by a series of grins and shuffles, to remain neatly at the back of it. Hovering at the embankment, on the other hand, he clutched an out-of-date copy of *Time* magazine, bearing by coincidence the nourished features of Chairman Mao on the cover, of which the red lettering and border on a white field stood out strongly in the slanting sunlight. Big Ben struck six and Jerry counted the chimes, but the ethic of such meetings requires they do not happen on the hour nor on the quarter, but in the vaguer spaces in-between, which are held to be less conspicuous. Six o'clock was the autumn witching hour, when the smells of every wet and leaf-blown country cricket field in England were wafted up-river with the damp shreds of dusk, and Jerry passed the time in a pleasurable half-trance, scenting them thoughtlessly and keeping his left eye, for some reason, wedged tight shut. The van, when it lumbered up to him, was a battered green Bedford with a ladder on the roof and 'Harris Builder' painted out, but still legible on the side: an old surveillance-horse put out to grass, with steel flaps over the windows. Seeing it pull up, Jerry started forward at the same moment as the driver, a sour boy with a hare lip, shoved his spiky head through the open window.

'Where's Wilf then?' the boy demanded rudely. 'They said you got Wilf with you.'

'You'll have to make do with me,' Jerry retorted with spirit. 'Wilf's on a job.' And opening the back door he clambered straight in and slammed it: for the passenger seat in the front cab was deliberately crammed with lengths of plywood so that there was no room for him to sit there.

That was the only conversation they had, ever.

In the old days, when the Circus had a natural non-commissioned class, Jerry would have counted on some amiable small talk. No longer. When he went to Sarratt, the procedure was little different except that they bounced along for fifteen miles or so, and if he was lucky, the boy remembered to throw in a cushion to prevent the total rupture of Jerry's backside. The driver's cab was blocked off from the belly of the van where Jerry crouched, and all he had to look through, as he slid up and down the wooden bench and clutched the grab handles, were the cracks at the edges of the steel window screens, which gave at best a perforated view of the world outside, though Jerry was quick enough to read the landmarks.

On the Sarratt run he passed depressing segments of out-of-date factories resembling poorly whitewashed cinemas in the Twenties, and a brick road-house with 'wedding receptions catered for' in red neon. But his feelings were at their most intense on the first evening, and on the last, when he visited the Circus. On the first evening as he approached the fabled and familiar turrets – the moment never failed him – a sort of muddled saintliness came over him: 'This is what service is all about.' A smear of red brick was followed by the blackened stems of plane trees, a salad of coloured lights came up, a gateway flung past him and the van thudded to a stop. The van doors were slammed from outside, at the same time as he heard the gates close and a male, sergeant-major voice shout: 'Come on, man, *move* it for Christ's sake.' and that was Guillam, having a bit of fun.

'Hullo, Peter boy, how's trade? *Jesus*, it's cold!'

Not bothering to reply, Peter Guillam slapped Jerry on the shoulder briskly, as if starting him on a race, closed the door fast, locked it top and bottom, pocketed the keys and led him off at a trot down a corridor which the ferrets must have ripped apart in fury. Plaster was hacked away in clumps, exposing the lath beneath; doors had been torn from their hinges; joists and lintels were dangling; dust sheets, ladders, rubble lay everywhere.

'Had the Irish in, have you?' Jerry yelled. 'Or just an all-ranks dance?'

His questions were lost in the clatter. The two men climbed fast and competitively, Guillam bounding ahead and Jerry on his heels, laughing breathlessly, their feet thundering and scraping on the bare wood steps. A door delayed them and Jerry waited while Guillam fiddled with the locks. Then waited again the other side while he reset them.

'Welcome aboard,' said Guillam more quietly.

They had reached the fifth floor. They trod quietly now, no more romping, English subalterns called to order. The corridor turned left, then right again, then rose by a few narrow steps. A cracked fisheye mirror, steps again, two up, three down, till they came to a janitor's desk, unmanned. To their left lay the rumpus room, empty, with smoking-chairs pulled into a rough ring and a good fire burning in the grate. Thus to a long, brown-carpeted room marked 'Secretariat' but in fact the anteroom, where three mothers in pearls and twinsets quietly typed by the glow of reading lamps. At the far end of this room, one more door, shut, unpainted and very grubby round the handle. No fingerplate, no escutcheon for the lock. Just the screwholes, he noticed, and the halo where one had been. Pushing it open without knocking, Guillam shoved his head through the gap and announced something quietly into the room. Then backed away and quickly ushered Jerry past him: Jerry Westerby, into the presence.

'Gosh, super, George, hullo.'

'And don't ask him about his wife,' Guillam warned in a fast, soft murmur that hummed in Jerry's ear for a good spell afterwards.

Father and son? That kind of relationship? Brawn to brain? More exact, perhaps, would be a son to his adopted father, which in the trade is to be held the strongest tie of all.

'Sport,' Jerry muttered, and gave a husky laugh.

English friends have no real way of greeting each other, least of all across a glum civil service office with nothing more lovely to inspire them than a deal desk. For a fraction of a second Jerry laid his cricketer's fist alongside Smiley's soft, hesitant palm, then lumbered after him at a distance to the fireside, where two armchairs awaited them: old leather, cracked, and much sat in. Once again, in this erratic season, a fire burned in the Victorian grate, but very small by comparison with the fire in the rumpus room.

'And how was Lucca?' Smiley enquired, filling two glasses from a decanter.

'Lucca was great.'

'Oh dear. Then I expect it was a wrench to leave.'

'Gosh, no. Super. Cheers.'

They sat down.

'Now why *super*, Jerry?' Smiley enquired, as if *super* were not a word he was familiar with. There were no papers on the desk and the room was bare, more like a spare room than his own.

'I thought I was done for,' Jerry explained. 'On the shelf for good. Telegram took the wind right out of my sails. I thought, well, Bill's blown me sky high. Blew everyone else, so why not me?'

'Yes,' Smiley agreed, as if sharing Jerry's doubts, and peered at him a moment in frank speculation. 'Yes, yes, quite. However, on balance it seems he never got around to blowing the Occasionals. We've traced him to pretty well every other corner of the archive, but the Occasionals were filed under "friendly contacts" in the Territorials' cut, in a separate archive altogether, one to which he had no natural access. It's not that he didn't think you were important enough,' he added hastily, 'it's simply that other claims on him took priority.'

'I can live with it,' said Jerry with a grin.

'I'm glad,' said Smiley, missing the joke. Rising he refilled their glasses, then went to the fire and, taking up a brass poker, began stabbing thoughtfully at the coals. 'Lucca. Yes. Ann and I went there. Oh, eleven, twelve years ago it must have been. It rained.' He gave a little laugh. In a cramped bay at the further end of the room, Jerry glimpsed a narrow, bony-looking camp bed with a row of telephones at the head. 'We visited the *bagno*, I remember,' Smiley went on. 'It was the fashionable cure. Lord alone knows what we were curing.' He attacked the fire again and this time the flames flew alive, daubing the rounded contours of his face with strokes of orange, and making gold pools of his thick spectacles. 'Did you know the poet Heine had a great adventure there? A romance? I rather think it must be why we went, come to think of it. We thought some of it would rub off.'

Jerry grunted something, not too certain, at that moment, who Heine was.

'He went to the *bagno*, he took the waters, and while doing so he met a lady whose name alone so impressed him that he made his wife use it from then on.' The flames held him for a moment longer. 'And you had an adventure there too, didn't you?'

'Just a flutter. Nothing to write home about.'

Beth Sanders, Jerry thought automatically, as his world rocked, then righted itself. A natural, Beth was. Father a retired General, High Sheriff of the County. Old Beth must have an aunt in every secret office in Whitehall.

Stooping again, Smiley propped the poker in a corner laboriously, as if he were laying a wreath. 'We're not necessarily in competition with affection. We simply like to know where it lies.' Jerry said nothing. Over his shoulder, Smiley glanced at Jerry, and Jerry pulled a grin to please him. 'The name of Heine's lady-love, I may tell you, was *Irwin Mathilde*,' Smiley resumed and Jerry's grin became an awkward laugh. 'Yes, well it does sound better in German, I confess. And the novel, how will that fare? I'd hate to think we'd scared away your muse. I don't think I'd forgive myself, I'm sure.'

'No problem,' said Jerry.

'Finished?'

'Well, you know.'

For a moment there was no sound but the mothers' typing and the rumble of traffic from the street below.

'Then we shall make it up to you when this is over,' Smiley said. 'I insist. How did the Stubbs scene play?'

'No problem,' said Jerry again.

'Nothing more we need do for you to smooth your path?'

'Don't think so.'

From beyond the anteroom they heard the shuffle of footsteps all in one direction. It's a war party, Jerry thought, a gathering of the clans.

'And you're game and so on?' Smiliey asked. 'You're, well, *prepared*? You have the will?'

'No problem.' Why can't I say something different? he asked himself. Bloody needle's stuck.

'A lot of people haven't these days. The will. Specially in England. A lot of people see *doubt* as a legitimate philosophical posture. They think of themselves in the middle, whereas of course really, they're nowhere. No battle was ever won by spectators, was it? We understand that in this service. We're lucky. Our present war began in 1917, with the Bolshevik Revolution. It hasn't changed yet.'

Smiley had taken up a new position, across the room from him, not far from the bed. Behind him, an old and grainy photograph glittered in the new firelight. Jerry had noticed it as he came in. Now, in the strain of the moment, he felt himself to be the object of a double scrutiny: by Smiley, and by the blurred eyes of the portrait dancing in the firelight behind the glass. The sounds of preparation multiplied. They heard voices and snatches of laughter, the squeak of chairs.

'I read somewhere,' Smiley said, 'an historian, I suppose he was – an American, anyway – he wrote of generations that are born into debtor's prisons and spend their lives buying their way to freedom. I think ours is such a generation. Don't you? I still feel strongly that I owe. Don't you? I've always been grateful to this service, that it gave me a chance to pay. Is that how *you* feel? I don't think we should be afraid of . . . devoting ourselves. Is that old-fashioned of me?'

Jerry's face clamped tight shut. He always forgot this part of Smiley when he was away from him, and remembered it too late when he was with him. There was a bit of the failed priest in old George, and the older he grew, the more prominent it became. He seemed to assume that the whole blasted western world shared his worries and had to be talked round to a proper way of thinking.

'In that sense, I think we may legitimately congratulate ourselves on being a trifle old-fashioned –'

Jerry had had enough.

'Sport,' he expostulated, with a clumsy laugh, as the colour rose to his face. 'For Heaven's sake. You point me and I'll march. Okay? You're the owl, not me. Tell me the shots, I'll play them. World's chock-a-block with milk-and-water intellectuals armed with fifteen conflicting arguments against blowing their blasted noses. We don't need another. Okay? I mean, Christ.'

A sharp knock at the door announced the reappearance of Guillam.

'Peace pipes all lit, Chief.'

To his surprise, over the clatter of this interruption, Jerry thought he caught the term 'ladies' man', but whether it was a reference to himself or the poet Heine he could not say, nor did he particularly care. Smiley hesitated, frowned, then seemed to wake again to his surroundings. He glanced at Guillam, then once more at Jerry, then his eyes settled on that middle distance which is the special preserve of English academics.

'Well, then, let's start winding the clock,' he said in a withdrawn voice.

As they trooped out, Jerry paused to admire the photograph on the wall, hands in pockets, grinning at it, hoping Guillam would hang back too, which he did.

'Looks as though he's swallowed his last sixpence,' said Jerry. 'Who is he?'

'Karla,' said Guillam. 'Recruited Bill Haydon. Russian hood.'

'Sounds more like a girl's name. How you keeping?'

'It's the codename of his first network. There's a school of thought that says it's also the name of his one love.'

'Bully for him,' said Jerry carelessly and, still grinning, drifted beside him toward the rumpus room. Perhaps deliberately, Smiley had gone ahead, out of earshot of their conversation. 'Still with that loony girl, the flute-player, are you?' Jerry asked.

'She got less loony,' said Guillam. They took a few more paces.

'Bolted?' Jerry enquired sympathetically.

'Something like that.'

'And he's *all right*, is he?' Jerry asked dead casually, nodding at the solitary figure ahead of them. 'Eating well, good coat, all that stuff?'

'Never been better. Why?'

'Just asked,' said Jerry, very pleased.

From the airport Jerry rang his daughter, Cat, a thing he rarely did, but this time he had to. He knew it was a mistake before he put the money in, but he still persisted, and not even the terribly familar voice of the early wife could put him off.

'Gosh, hullo! It's me actually. Super. Listen: how's Phillie?'

Phillie was her husband, a civil servant nearly eligible for a pension, though younger than Jerry by about thirty muddled lives.

'Perfectly well, thank you,' she retorted in the frosty tone with which old wives defend new mates. 'Is that why you rang?'

'Well I did just think I might chat up old Cat, actually. Going out East for a bit, back in harness,' he said. He felt he should apologize. 'It's just the comic needs a hack out there,' he said, and heard a clatter as the receiver hit the hall chest. Oak, he remembered. Barley-twist legs. Another of old Sambo's left-overs.

'Daddy?'

'Hi!' he yelled as if the line were bad, as if she had taken him by surprise. 'Cat? Hullo, hey listen, *sport*, did you get my postcards and stuff?' He knew she had. She had thanked him regularly in her weekly letters.

Hearing nothing but 'Daddy' repeated in a questioning voice, Jerry asked jovially: 'You do still collect stamps, don't you? Only I'm going away, you see. East.'

Planes were called, others landed, whole worlds were changing places but Jerry Westerby, speaking to his daughter, was motionless in the procession.

'You used to be a demon for stamps,' he reminded her.

'I'm seventeen.'

'Sure, sure, what do you collect now? Don't tell me. Boys!' With the brightest humour he kept it going while he danced from one buckskin boot to the other, making his own jokes and supplying his own laughter. 'Listen, I'm sending you some money, Blatt and Rodney are fixing it, sort of birthday and Christmas put together, better talk to Mummy before spending it. Or maybe Phillie, what? He's a sound sort of bloke, isn't he? Turn Phillie loose on it, kind of thing he likes to get his teeth into.' He opened the kiosk door to raise an artificial flurry. ''Fraid they're calling my flight there, Cat,' he bawled over the clatter. 'Look, mind how you go, d'you hear? Watch yourself. Don't give yourself too easy. Know what I mean?'

He queued for the bar a while but at the last moment the old eastern hand in him woke up and he moved across to the cafeteria. It might be some while before he got his next glass of fresh cow's milk. Standing in the queue, Jerry had a sensation of being watched. No trick to that: at an airport everyone watches everyone, so what the hell? He thought of the orphan and wished he'd had time to get himself a girl before he left, if only to take away the bad memory of their necessary parting.

Smiley walked, one round little man in a raincoat. Social journalists with more class than Jerry, shrewdly observing his progress through the purlieus of the Charing Cross Road, would have recognized the type at once: the mackintosh brigade personified, cannonfodder of the mixed sauna parlours and the naughty bookshops. These long tramps had become a habit for him. With his new-found energy he could cover half the length of London and not notice it. From Cambridge Circus, now that he knew the byways, he could take any of twenty routes and never cross the same path twice. Having selected a beginning, he would let luck and instinct guide him while his other mind plundered the remoter regions of his soul. But this evening his journey had a pull to it, drawing him south and westward, and Smiley yielded. The air was damp and cold, hung with a harsh fog that had never seen the sun. Walking, he took his own island with him, and it was crammed with images, not people. Like an extra mantle the white walls encased him in his thoughts. In a doorway, two murderers in leather coats were whispering; under a streetlamp a dark-haired boy angrily clutched a violin case. Outside a theatre, a waiting crowd burned in the blaze of lights from the awning overhead, and the fog curled round them like fire smoke. Never had Smiley gone into battle knowing so little and expecting so much. He felt lured, and he felt pursued. Yet when he tired, and drew back for a moment, and considered the logic of what he was about, it almost eluded him. He glanced back and saw the jaws of failure waiting for him. He peered forward and through his moist spectacles saw the phantoms of great hopes dancing in the mist. He blinked around him and knew there was nothing for him where he stood. Yet he advanced without the ultimate conviction. It was no answer to rehearse the steps that had brought him to this point – the Russian goldseam, the imprint of Karla's private army, the thoroughness of Haydon's efforts to extinguish knowledge of them. Beyond the limits of these external reasons, Smiley perceived in himself the existence of a darker motive, infinitely more obscure, one which his rational mind continued to reject. He called it Karla, and it was true that somewhere in him, like a left-over legend, there burned the embers of hatred toward the man who had set out to destroy the temples of his private faith, whatever remained of them: the service that he loved, his friends, his country, his concept of a reasonable balance in human affairs. It was true also that a lifetime or two ago, in a sweltering Indian jail, the two men had actually faced each other, Smiley and Karla, across an iron table: though Smiley had no reason at the time to know he was in the presence of his destiny. Karla's head was on the block in Moscow; Smiley had tried to woo him to the West, and Karla had kept silent, preferring death or worse to an easy defection. And it was true that now and then the memory of that encounter, of Karla's unshaven face and watchful, inward eyes, came at him like an accusing spectre out of the murk of his little room, while he slept fitfully on his bunk.

But hatred was really not an emotion which he could sustain for any length of time, unless it was the obverse side of love.

He was approaching the King's Road in Chelsea. The fog was heavier because of the closeness of the river. Above him the globes of streetlights hung like Chinese lanterns in the bare branches of the trees. The traffic was sparse and cautious. Crossing the road he followed the pavement till he came to Bywater Street and turned into it, a cul-de-sac of neat flat-fronted terrace cottages. He trod discreetly now, keeping to the western side, and the shadow of the parked cars. It was the cocktail hour, and in other windows he saw talking heads and shrieking, silent mouths. Some he recognized, some she even had names for: Felix the cat, Lady Macbeth, the Puffer. He drew level

with his own house. For their return, she had had the shutters painted blue
and they were blue still. The curtains were open because she hated to be
enclosed. She sat alone at her escritoire, and she might have composed the
scene for him deliberately: the beautiful and conscientious wife, ending her
day, attends to matters of administration. She was listening to music and he
caught the echo of it carried on the fog. Sibelius. He wasn't good at music, but
he knew all her records and he had several times praised the Sibelius out of
politeness. He couldn't see the gramophone but he knew it lay on the floor,
where it had lain for Bill Haydon when she was trailing her affair with him.
He wondered whether the German dictionary lay beside it, and her anthology of German poetry. Several times, over the last decade or two, usually
during reconciliations, she had made a show of learning German so that
Smiley would be able to read aloud to her.

As he watched, she got up, crossed the room, paused in front of the pretty
gilt mirror to adjust her hair. The notes she wrote to herself were jammed
into the frame. What was it this time? he wondered. *Blast garage. Cancel lunch
Madeleine. Destroy butcher.* Sometimes when things were tense, she had sent
him messages that way: *Force George to smile, apologize insincerely for lapse.* In
very bad times, she wrote whole letters to him, and posted them there for his
collection.

To his surprise she had put out the light. He heard the bolts slide on the
front door. Drop the chain, he thought automatically. Double lock the
Banhams. How many times do I have to tell you that bolts are as weak as the
screws that hold them in place? Odd all the same: he had somehow supposed
she would leave the bolts open in case he might return. Then the bedroom
light went on, and he saw her body framed in silhouette in the window as,
angel-like, she stretched her arms to the curtains. She drew them almost to
her, stopped, and momentarily he feared that she had seen him, till he
remembered her short-sightedness and her refusal to wear glasses. She's
going out, he thought. She's going to doll herself up. He saw her head half
turn as if she had been addressed. He saw her lips move, and break into a
puckish smile as her arms lifted again, this time to the back of her neck, and
she began to unfasten the top button of her housecoat. In the same moment,
the gap between the curtains was abruptly closed by other, impatient hands.

Oh *no*, thought Smiley hopelessly. Please! Wait till I've gone!

For a minute, perhaps longer, standing on the pavement, he stared in
disbelief at the blacked-out window, till anger, shame and finally self-disgust
broke in him together like a physical anguish and he turned and hurried
blindly back toward the King's Road. Who was it this time? Another beardless
ballet dancer, performing some narcissistic ritual? Her vile cousin Miles, the
career politician? Or a one-night Adonis spirited from the nearby pub?

When the outside telephone rang Peter Guillam was sitting alone in the
rumpus room a little drunk, languishing equally for Molly Meakin's body and
George Smiley's return. He lifted the receiver at once and heard Fawn, out of
breath and furious.

'I've lost him!' he shouted. 'He's bilked me!'

'Then you're a bloody idiot,' Guillam retorted with satisfaction.

'Idiot nothing! He heads for home, right? Our usual ritual. I'm waiting for
him, I stand off, he's coming back to the main road, looks at me. Like I'm dirt.

Just *dirt*. Next thing I know I'm on my own. How does he do it? Where does he go? I'm his friend aren't I? Who the hell does he think he is? Fat little runt, I'll kill him!'

Guillam was still laughing as he rang off.

<br>

## SIX

# *the burning of Frost*

<br>

In Hong Kong it was Saturday again but the typhoons were forgotten and the day burned hot and clear and breathless. In the Hong Kong Club a serenely Christian clock struck eleven and the chimes tinkled in the panelled quiet like spoons dropped on the distant kitchen floor. The better chairs were already taken by readers of last Thursday's *Telegraph*, which gave a quite dismal picture of the moral and economic miseries of their homeland.

'Pound's in the soup again,' a crusted voice growled through a pipe. 'Electricians out. Railways out. Pilots out.'

'Who's *in*? More the question,' said another, just as crusted.

'If I was the Kremlin I'd say we were doing a first-class *job*,' said the first speaker, barking out the final word to give it a military indignation, and with a sigh ordered up a couple of dry martinis. Neither man was above twenty-five years old, but being an exiled patriot in search of a quick fortune can age you pretty fast.

The Foreign Correspondents' Club was having one of its churchy days when burghers far outnumbered newsmen. Without old Craw to hold them together, the Shanghai Bowlers had dispersed and several had left the Colony altogether. The photographers had been lured to Phnom Penh by the promise of some great new fighting now the wet season was ended. The cowboy was in Bangkok for an expected revival of student riots, Luke was at the bureau and his boss the dwarf was slouched grumpily at the bar surrounded by sonorous British suburbanites in dark trousers and white shirts discussing the eleven hundred gearbox.

'But *cold* this time. Hear that? Muchee coldee and bring it *chop chop!*'

Even the Rocker was muted. He was attended this morning by his wife, a former Bible School teacher from Borneo, a dried-out shrew in bobbed hair and ankle socks who could spot a sin before it was committed.

And a couple of miles eastward on Cloudview Road, a thirty-cent ride on the one-price city bus, in what is said to be the most populated corner of our

planet, on North Point, just where the city swells toward the Peak, on the
sixteenth floor of a highrise block called 7A, Jerry Westerby was lying on a
mattress after a short but dreamless sleep singing his own words to the tune
of 'Miami Sunrise' and watching a beautiful girl undress. The mattress was
seven feet long, intended to be used the other way on by an entire Chinese
family, and for about the first time in his life his feet didn't hang over the end.
It was longer than Pet's cot by a mile, longer even than the bed in Tuscany,
though in Tuscany it hadn't mattered because he had a real girl to curl round
and with a girl you don't lie so straight. Whereas the girl he was watching was
framed in a window opposite his own, ten yards or miles out of reach, and on
every one of the nine mornings he had woken here, she had stripped and
washed herself this way, to his considerable enthusiasm, even applause.
When he was lucky he followed the whole ceremony, from the moment when
she tipped her head sideways to let her black hair fall to her waist, until she
chastely wound a sheet about her and rejoined her ten-strong family in the
next room where they all lived. He knew the family intimately. Their washing
habits, their tastes in music, cooking and love-making, their celebrations,
their flaring, dangerous rows. The only thing he wasn't sure of was whether
she was two girls or one.

She vanished, but he kept on singing. He felt eager, which was how it took
him every time, whether he was about to gum-shoe down a back alley in
Prague to swap little packages with a terror-striken joe in a doorway or – his
finest hour, and for an Occasional unprecedented – row three miles in a
blackened dinghy to scrape a radio operator off a Caspian beach. As the
clamps tightened, Jerry discovered the same surprising mastery of himself,
the same jollity and the same alertness. And the same barking funk, not
necessarily a contradiction. It's today, he thought. The kissing's over.

There were three tiny rooms and they were parquet floored all through.
That was the first thing he noticed every morning because there was no
furniture anywhere, except the mattress and the kitchen chair and the table
where his typewriter sat, the one dinner plate, which did duty as an ashtray,
and the girlie calendar, vintage 1960, of a red-head whose charms had long
since lost their bloom. He knew the type exactly: green eyes, a temper, and a
skin so sensitive it looked like a battlefield every time you laid a finger on it.
Add on telephone, one ancient record player for seventy-eights only and two
very real opium pipes suspended from business-like nails on the wall, and he
had a complete inventory of the wealth and interests of Deathwish the Hun,
now in Cambodia, from whom Jerry had rented the apartment. And the
book-sack, his own, beside the mattress.

The gramophone had run down. He climbed happily to his feet, tightening
the makeshift sarong around his stomach. As he did so, the telephone began
ringing, so he sat again and, grabbing the flex, dragged the instrument
toward him across the floor. It was Luke as usual, wanting to play.

'Sorry, sport. Doing a story. Try solo whist.'

Dialling the speaking clock, Jerry heard a Chinese squawk, then an English
squawk and set his watch by the second. Then he went to the gramophone
and put on 'Miami Sunrise' again, loud as it would go. It was his only record,
but it drowned the gurgle of the useless airconditioner. Still humming, he
pulled open the one wardrobe, and from an old leather grip on the floor
picked out his father's yellowed tennis racket vintage nineteen thirty odd,
with S.W. in marking ink on the pommel. Unscrewing the handle he fished
from the recess four lozenges of subminiature film, a worm of grey wadding,

and a battered subminiature camera with measuring chain, which the conservative in him preferred to the flashier models which the Sarratt smudgers had tried to press on him. Loading a cassette into the camera, he set the film speed and took three sample light-readings of the red-head's bosom before slopping to the kitchen in his sandals, where he lowered himself devoutly to his knees before the fridge and loosened the Free Forresters tie which held the door in place. With a wild tearing noise, he passed his right thumb nail down the rotted rubber strips, took out three eggs and re-tied the tie. Waiting for them to boil, he lounged at the window, elbows on the sill, peering fondly through the burglar wire at his beloved rooftops which descended like giant stepping stones to the sea's edge.

The rooftops were a civilization for themselves, a breathtaking theatre of survival against the raging of the city. Within their barbed-wire compounds, sweatshops turned out anoraks, religious services were held, mah-jong was played and fortune tellers burned joss and consulted huge brown volumes. Ahead of him lay a formal garden made of smuggled earth. Below, three old women fattened Chow puppies for the pot. There were schools for dancing, reading, ballet, recreation and combat, there were schools in culture and the wonders of Mao, and this morning while Jerry's eggs boiled, an old man completed his long rigmarole of callisthenics before opening the tiny folding chair where he performed his daily reading of the great man's Thoughts. The wealthier poor, if they had no roof, built themselves giddy crow's nests, two foot by eight, on home-made cantilevers driven into their drawing room floors. Deathwish maintained there were suicides all the time. That was what grabbed him about the place he said. When he wasn't fornicating, he liked to hang out of the window with his Nikon, hoping to catch one, but he never did. Down to the right lay the graveyard, which Deathwish said was bad luck and knocked a few dollars off the rent.

While he was eating, the phone rang again.

'What story?' said Luke.

'Wanchai whores have hijacked Big Moo,' Jerry said. 'Taken him to Stonecutters Island and are holding him to ransom.'

Other than Luke, it tended to be Deathwish's women who called, but they didn't want Jerry instead. The shower had no curtain so Jerry had to squat in a tiled corner, like a boxer, in order not to flood the bathroom. Returning to the bedroom, he put on his suit, grabbed a bread knife, and counted twelve wood blocks from the corner of the room. With the knife blade he dug up the thirteenth. In a hollowed recess cut into the tar-like undersurface lay one plastic bag containing a roll of American dollar bills of large and small denominations; one escape passport, driving licence and air travel card in the name of Worrell, contractor; and one small-arm, which in defiance of every Circus regulation under the sun, Jerry had procured from Deathwish, who did not care to take it on his travels. From this treasure chest he extracted five one-hundred dollar bills and, leaving the rest untouched, replaced the wood block. He dropped the camera and two spare cassettes into his pockets then stepped on to the tiny landing whistling. His front door was guarded by a white-painted grille which would have delayed a decent burglar for ninety seconds. Jerry had picked the lock when he had nothing better to do, and that was how long it took him. He pressed the button for the lift, and it arrived full of Chinese who all got out. It happened every time. Jerry was just too big for them, too ugly and too foreign.

From scenes like these, thought Jerry, with a willed cheerfulness, as he plunged into the pitch darkness of the city-bound bus, Saint George's children go forth to save the empire.

'*Time spent in preparation is never time wasted*' runs the Nursery's laborious maxim on counter-surveillance.

Sometimes Jerry became Sarratt man and nothing else. By the ordinary logic of things he could have gone to his destination directly: he had every right. By the ordinary logic of things there was no reason on earth, particularly after their revelries of last night, why Jerry should not have taken a cab to the front door, barged gaily in, bearded his new-found bosom friend and be done with it. But this was not the ordinary logic of things, and in the Sarratt folklore, Jerry was approaching the operational moment of truth: the moment when the back door closed on him with a bang, after which there was no way out but forward. The moment when every one of his twenty years of tradecraft rose in him and shouted 'caution'. If he was walking into a trap, this was where the trap was sprung. Even if they knew his route in advance, still the static posts would be staked out ahead of him, in cars and behind windows, and the surveillance teams locked on to him in case of fumble or branch lines. If there was ever a last opportunity to test the water before he jumped, it was now. Last night, around the haunts, he could have been watched by a hundred local angels and still not have known for certain he was their quarry. But here he could weave and count the shadows: here, in theory at least, he had a chance to know.

He glanced at his watch. Exactly twenty minutes to go and even at Chinese rather than European pace he needed seven. So he sauntered, but never idly. In other countries, in almost any place in the world outside Hong Kong, he would have given himself far longer. Behind the Curtain, Sarratt lore said, half a day, preferably more. He'd have posted himself a letter, just so that he could walk halfway down the street, stop dead at the postbox and double back, checking the feet that faltered, and the faces that ducked away; looking for the classic formations, a two this side, a three across the road, a front tail who floats ahead of you.

But paradoxically, though this morning he zealously went through the steps, another side of him knew he was wasting his time: knew that in the East a roundeye could live all his life in the same block and never have the smallest notion of the secret tic-tac on his doorstep. At every corner of each teeming street he entered, men waited, lounged and watched, strenuously employed in doing nothing. The beggar who suddenly stretched his arms and yawned, the crippled shoe-shine boy who dived for his escaping feet, and having missed them drove the backs of his brushes together in a whipcrack, the old hag selling bi-racial pornography who cupped her hand and shrieked one word into the bamboo scaffolding above her: though in his mind Jerry recorded them, they were as obscure to him today as they had been when he first came east – twenty? Lord help us, twenty-five years ago. Pimps? Numbers boys? Dope pedlars pushing the coloured twists of candy paper – 'yellow two dollar, blue five dollar? You chase dragon, like quickshot?' Or were they ordering up a bowl of rice from the food stalls across the way? In the East, sport, survival is knowing you don't know.

He was using the reflections in the marble cladding of the shops: shelves of amber, shelves of jade, credit card signs, electrical gadgets and pyramids of black luggage which nobody ever seemed to carry. At Cartier's a beautiful girl was laying pearls on a velvet tray, putting them to bed for the day. Sensing his presence she lifted her eyes to him; and in Jerry, despite his preoccupation, the old Adam briefly stirred. But one glance at his shambling grin and his scruffy suit and his buckskin boots told her all she needed to know: Jerry Westerby was not a potential customer. There was news of fresh battles, Jerry noticed, passing a news-stand. The Chinese language press carried frontpage photographs of decimated children, screaming mothers and troops in American-style helmets. Whether Vietnam, or Cambodia, or Korea, or the Philippines, Jerry couldn't tell. The red characters of the headline had the effect of splashed blood. Maybe Deathwish was in luck.

Thirsty from last night's booze, Jerry cut through the Mandarin and plunged into the twilight of the Captain's Bar, but he only drank water in the Gents. Back in the lobby he bought a copy of *Time* but didn't like the way the plain-clothes crushers looked at him, and left. Joining the crowds again, he sauntered toward the post office, built 1911 and since pulled down, but in those days a rare and hideous antique made beautiful by the clumsy concrete of the buildings around it. Then he doubled through the arches into Pedder Street, passing under a green corrugated bridge where mailbags trailed like turkeys on the gibbet. Doubling yet again, he crossed to the Connaught Centre, using the footbridge to thin out the field.

In the glittering steel lobby a peasant woman was scrubbing out the teeth of a stationary escalator with a wire brush, and on the promenade a group of Chinese students gazed in respectful silence at Henry Moore's *Oval with Points*. Looking back, Jerry glimpsed the brown dome of the old law courts dwarfed by the Hilton's beehive walls: *Regina versus Westerby*, he thought, 'and the prisoner is charged with blackmail, corruption, pretended affection and a few others we shall dream up before the day is out'. The harbour was alive with shipping, most of it small. Beyond it, the New Territories, pocked with excavation, shoved vainly against muddy clouds of smog. At their feet, new godowns, and factory chimneys belching brown smoke.

Retracing his steps he passed the big Scottish business houses, Jardines, Swires, and noticed that their doors were barred. Must be a holiday, he thought. Ours or theirs? In Statue Square, a leisurely carnival was taking place with fountains, beach umbrellas, Coca-Cola sellers, and about half a million Chinese who stood in groups or shuffled past him like a barefoot army, darting glances at his size. Loudspeakers, building drills, wailing music. He crossed Jackson Road and the noise level fell a little. Ahead of him, on a patch of perfect English lawn, fifteen whiteclad figures lounged. The all-day cricket match had just begun. At the receiving end, a lank, disdainful figure in an outdated cap was fiddling with his batting gloves. Pausing, Jerry watched grinning in fond familiarity. The bowler bowled. Medium pace, bit of inswing, dead wicket. The batsman played a gracious stroke, missed and took a leg-bye in slow motion. Jerry foresaw a long dull innings to no applause. He wondered who was playing whom, and decided it was the usual Peak mafia playing itself. On the leg boundary, across the road, rose the Bank of China, a vast and fluted cenotaph festooned with crimson slogans loving Mao. At its base, granite lions looked on sightlessly while flocks of white-shirted Chinese photographed each other against their flanks.

But the bank which Jerry had his eye on stood directly behind the bowler's arm. A Union Jack was posted at its pinnacle, an armoured van more confidently at its base. The doors stood open and their burnished surfaces glittered like fool's gold. While Jerry continued his shambling arc toward it, a gang of helmeted guards, escorted by tall Indians with elephant guns, emerged suddenly from the interior blackness and nursed three black money boxes down the wide steps as if they held the Host itself. The armoured van drove away and for a sickening moment Jerry had visions of the bank's doors closing after it.

Not logical visions. Not nervous visions either. Merely that for a moment Jerry expected fumble with the same trained pessimism with which a gardener foresees drought or an athlete a foolish sprain on the eve of a great match; or a fieldman with twenty years on the clock foresees just one more unpredictable frustration. But the doors stayed open, and Jerry veered way to the left. Give the guards time to relax, he thought. Shepherding the money will have made them nervous. They'll see too sharply, they'll remember things.

Turning, he began a slow dreamy stroll toward the Hong Kong Club: Wedgwood porticoes, striped blinds and a smell of stale English food at the doorway. Cover is not a lie, they tell you. Cover is what you believe. Cover is who you are. *On Saturday morning Mr Gerald Westerby the not very distinguished journalist heads for a favourite watering hole . . .* On the Club steps Jerry paused, patted his pockets, then turned full circle and struck out purposefully for his destination, making two long sides of the square, as he watched for the last time for the slurring feet and turned down glances. *Mr Gerald Westerby, discovering he is short of weekend cash, decides on a quick visit to the bank.* Elephant guns slung carelessly at their shoulders, the Indian guards studied him without interest.

*Except, Mr Gerald Westerby doesn't!*

Cursing himself for being a damned fool, Jerry remembered that the time was after twelve o'clock, and that at twelve sharp the banking halls were closed. After twelve, it was upstairs only, and that was the way he had planned it.

Relax, he thought. You're thinking too much. Don't think: do. *In the beginning was the deed.* Who had said that to him once? Old George, for God's sake, quoting Goethe. Coming from him of all people!

As he began the run-in, a wave of dismay hit him, and he knew it was fear. He was hungry. He was tired. Why had George left him alone like this? Why did he have to do everything for himself? Before the fall, they'd have posted babysitters ahead of him – even someone inside the bank – just to watch for rain. They'd have had a reception team to skim the take almost before he left the building, and an escape car in case he had to slip away in his socks. And in London – he thought sweetly, talking himself down – they'd have had dear old Bill Haydon – wouldn't they? – passing it all to the Russians, bless him. Thinking this, Jerry willed upon himself an extraordinary hallucination, quick as the flash of camera, and as slow to fade. God had answered his prayers, he thought. The old days were here again after all, and the street was alive with a grand-slam supporting cast. Behind him a blue Peugeot had pulled up and two bullish roundeyes sat in it studying a Happy Valley racecard. Radio aerial, the works. From his left, American matrons sauntered by, laden with cameras and guidebooks, and a positive obligation to observe. And from the bank itself, as he advanced swiftly, on its portals, a couple of solemn money-men emerged, wearing just that grim stare watchers sometimes use in order to discourage an enquiring eye.

Senility, Jerry told himself. You're over the hill, sport, no question. Dotage and funk have brought you to your knees. He bounded up the steps, jaunty as a cock-robin on a hot spring day.

The lobby was as big as a railway station, the canned music as martial. The banking area was barred and he saw no one lurking, not even a phantom stand-off man. The lift was a gold cage with a spittoon filled with sand for cigarettes, but by the ninth floor the largeness of downstairs had all gone. Space was money. A narrow cream corridor led to an empty reception desk. Jerry strolled easily, marking the emergency exit and the service lift which the bearleaders had already charted for him in case he had to do a duckdive. Queer how they knew so much, he thought, with so few resources; must have dug out an architect's drawing from somewhere. On the counter, one teak sign reading Trustee Department Enquiries. Beside it, one grimy paperback on fortune-telling by the stars, open and much annotated. But no reception-ist because Saturdays are different. On Saturdays you get the best ride, they had said. He looked cheerfully round, nothing on his conscience. A second corridor ran the width of the building, office doors to the left, soggy vinyl-covered partitions to the right. From behind the partitions came the slow pat of an electric typewriter as someone typed a legal document, and the slow Saturday sing-song of Chinese secretaries without a lot to do except wait for lunch and the free afternoon. There were four glazed doors with penny-sized eyeholes for looking in or out. Jerry ambled down the corridor, glancing through each as if glancing were his recreation, hands in pockets, a slightly daft smile aloft. The fourth on the left, they had said, one door, one window. A clerk walked past him, then a secretary on dinky, clicking heels, but Jerry, though scruffy, was European and wore a suit and neither challenged him.

'Morning, gang,' he muttered, and they wished him 'Good day, sir,' in return.

There were iron bars at the end of the corridor and iron bars over the windows. A blue night-light was fixed to the ceiling, he supposed for security but he didn't know: fire, space protection, he didn't know, the bearleaders hadn't mentioned it, and stinks and bangs were not his thing. The first room was an office, unoccupied except for a few dusty sports trophies on the window-sill and an embroidered coat of arms of the bank athletics club on the pegboard wall. He passed a pile of apple boxes marked 'Trustee'. They seemed to be full of deeds and wills. The cheese-paring tradition of the old China trading houses died hard, apparently. A notice on the wall read 'Private' and another 'By Appointment Only'.

The second door gave on to a corridor and a small archive which was likewise empty. The third was a 'Directors Only' lavatory, the fourth had a staff noticeboard mounted directly beside it and a red light bulb mounted on the jamb and an important nameplate in Letraset saying 'J. Frost, Deputy Chief Trustee, Appointments Only, do NOT enter when light is ON'. But the light was not ON, and the penny-sized eyehole showed one man at his desk alone, and the only company he had was a heap of files, and scrolls of costly paper bound in green silk on the English legal pattern, and two closed-circuit television sets for the stock exchange prices, dead, and the harbour view, mandatory to the higher executive image, sliced into pencil-grey by manda-tory Venetian blinds. One shiny, podgy, prosperous little man in a sporty linen suit of Robin Hood green, working far too conscientiously for a Saturday. Moisture of his brow; black crescents beneath his arms, and – to Jerry's informed eye – the leaden immobility of a man recovering very slowly from debauch.

A corner room, thought Jerry. One door only, this one. One shove and you're away. He took a last glance up and down the empty corridor. Jerry Westerby on stage, he thought. If you can't talk, dance. The door gave immediately. He stepped gaily inside wearing his best shy smile.

'Gosh, Frostie, hullo, *super*. Am I early or late? Sport – I say – most *extraordinary* thing back there. In the corridor – nearly fell over them – lot of apple boxes full of legal bumf. "Who's Frostie's client?" I asked myself. "Cox's Orange Pippins? Or Beauty of Bath?" Beauty of Bath, knowing you. Thought it was rather a giggle, after last night's high jinks round the parlours.'

All of which, feeble though it might have sounded to the astonished Frost, got him into the room with the door closed, fast, while his broad back masked the only eyehole and his soul sent prayers of gratitude to Sarratt for a soft landing, and prayers of preservation to his Maker.

A moment of theatricality followed Jerry's entry. Frost lifted his head slowly, keeping his eyes half shut, as if the light were hurting them, which it probably was. Spotting Jerry, he winced and looked away, then looked at him again to confirm that he was flesh. Then he wiped his brow with his handkerchief.

'Christ,' he said. 'It's his nibs. What the hell are you doing here, you disgusting aristocrat?'

To which Jerry, still at the door, responded with another large grin, and a lifting of one hand in a Red Indian salute, while he marked down the worry points precisely: the two telephones, the grey box for inter-office speaking and the wardrobe safe with a keyhole but no combination lock.

'How did they let you in? I suppose you flashed your Honourable at them. What do you mean by it, barging in here?' Not half as displeased as his words suggested, Frost had left his desk and was waddling down the room. 'This isn't a cat house you know. This is a respectable bank. More or less.'

Arriving at Jerry's considerable bulk, he stuck his hands on his hips and gazed at him, shaking his head in wonder. Then patted Jerry's arm, then prodded him in the stomach, amid more shaking of the head.

'You alcoholic, dissolute, lecherous, libidinous . . .'

'Newshound,' Jerry prompted.

Frost was not above forty but nature had already printed on him the crueller marks of littleness, such as a floorwalker's fussiness about the cuffs and fingers, and a moistening of his lips and pursing of them all at once. What redeemed him was a transparent sense of fun, which leapt to his damp cheeks like sunlight.

'Here,' said Jerry. 'Poison yourself,' and offered him a cigarette.

'Christ,' said Frost again, and with a key from his chain opened an old-fashioned walnut cupboard, full of mirror and rows of cocktail sticks with artificial cherries, and trick tankards with pin-ups and pink elephants.

'Bloody Mary do you?'

'Bloody Mary would slip down grateful, sport,' Jerry assured him.

On the keychain, one brass Chubb key. The safe was also Chubb, a fine one, with a battered gold medallion fading into the old green paint.

'I'll say one thing for you blueblooded rakes,' Frost called, while he poured and shook the ingredients like a chemist. 'You do know the haunts. Drop you blindfold in the middle of Salisbury Plain, I reckon you'd find a cathouse in thirty seconds flat. My virgin sensitive nature took yet another grave jolt last night. Rocked to its frail little bearings, it was – say when! – I'll take a few addresses off you sometime, when I'm healed. If I ever am, which I doubt.'

Sauntering over to Frost's desk, Jerry riffled idly through his correspondence, then began playing with the switches of the speaking box, patting them up and down one by one with his enormous index finger, but getting no answers. A separate button was marked 'engaged'. Pressing it, Jerry saw a rose gleam in the eyehole as the caution-light went on in the corridor.

'As to those girls,' Frost was saying, his back still turned to Jerry while he rattled the sauce bottle. 'Wicked they were. Shocking.' Laughing delightedly, Frost advanced across the room, holding the glasses wide. 'What were their names? Oh dear, oh dear!'

'Seven and twenty-four,' said Jerry distractedly.

He was stooping as he spoke, looking for the alarm button he knew would be somewhere on the desk.

'Seven and twenty-four!' Frost repeated, rapturously. 'What poetry! What a memory!'

At knee level, Jerry had found a grey box screwed to the drawer-pillar. The key was vertical, at the off position. He pulled it out and dropped it into his pocket.

'I said what a wonderful memory,' Frost repeated, rather puzzled.

'You know newshounds, sport,' said Jerry, straightening. 'Worse than wives, us newshounds are, when it comes to memories.'

'Here. Come off there. That's holy ground.'

Picking up Frost's large desk diary, Jerry was studying it for the day's engagements.

'Jesus,' he said. 'It's all go, isn't it? Who's N, sport? N, eight to twelve? Not your mother-in-law is she?'

Ducking his mouth to the glass Frost drank greedily, swallowed, then make a farce of choking, writhing and recovering. 'Keep her out of this, do you mind? You nearly gave me a heart attack. Bung-ho.'

'N for nuts? N for Napoleon? Who's N?

'Natalie. My secretary. Very nice. Legs go right up to its bottom, so they tell me. Never been there myself, so I don't know. My one rule. Remind me to break it some time. Bung-ho,' he said again.

'She in?'

'I think I heard her dulcet tread, yes. Want me to give her a buzz? I'm told she puts on a very nice turn for the upper classes.'

'No thanks,' said Jerry, and setting down the diary, looked at Frost four square, man to man, though the fight was uneven, for Jerry was a whole head taller than Frost, and a lot broader.

'Incredible,' Frost declared reverently, still beaming at Jerry. 'Incredible, that's what it was.' His manner was devoted, even possessive. 'Incredible girls, incredible company. I mean why should a bloke like me bother with a bloke like you? A mere Honourable at that? Dukes are my level. Dukes and tarts. Let's do it again tonight. Come on.'

Jerry laughed.

'I mean it. Scout's honour. Let's die of it before we're too old. On me this time, the whole treat.' In the corridor, heavy footsteps sounded, coming nearer. 'Know what *I'm* going to do? Try me. I'm going to go back to the Meteor with you, and I'm going to call Madame Whoosit, and I'm going to insist on a – what's eating you? he said, catching Jerry's expression.

The footsteps slowed, then stopped. A black shadow filled the eyehole and stayed.

'Who is he?' said Jerry quietly.

'Milky.'

'Who's Milky?'

'Milky Way, my boss,' said Frost, as the footsteps moved away, and closing his eyes, crossed himself devoutly. 'Going home to his very lovely lady wife, the distinguished Mrs Way alias Moby Dick. Six foot eight and a cavalry moustache. Not him. Her.' Frost giggled.

'Why didn't he come in?'

'Thought I had a client, I suppose,' said Frost carelessly, again puzzled by Jerry's watchfulness, and by his quiet. 'Apart from the fact that Moby Dick would kick him to death if she caught him with the smell of alcohol on his evil lips at this hour of the day. Cheer up, you've got me to look after you. Have the other half. You look a bit pious today. Gives me the creeps.'

*When you get in there, go,* the bearleaders had said. *Don't feel his bones too long, don't let him get comfy with you.*

'Hey Frostie,' Jerry called, when the footsteps had quite faded. 'How's the missus?' Frost had his hand out for Jerry's glass. 'Your missus. How's she doing?'

'Still ailing nicely, thank you,' said Frost uncomfortably.

'Ring the hospital did you?'

'This morning? You're crazy. I wasn't coherent till eleven o'clock. If then. She'd have smelt my breath.'

'When are you next visiting?'

'Look. Shut up. Shut up about her. Do you mind?'

With Frost watching him, Jerry drifted to the safe. He tried the big handle but it was locked. On the top, covered in dust, lay a heavy riot stick. Taking it in both hands, he played a couple of distracted cricket shots, and put it back, while Frost's puzzled stare followed him alertly.

'I want to open an account, Frostie,' said Jerry, still at the safe.

'You?'

'Me.'

'From all you told me last night you haven't the resources to open a bloody piggy bank. Not unless your distinguished dad kept a bit in the mattress, which I somehow doubt.' Frost's world was slipping fast but he tried desperately to hold on to it. 'Look, get yourself a bloody drink and stop playing Boris Karloff on a wet Wednesday, will you? Let's go to the geegees. Happy Valley, here we come. I'll buy you lunch.'

'I didn't mean we'd open *my* account exactly, sport. I meant someone else's,' Jerry explained.

In a slow, sad comedy, the fun drained out of Frost's little face, and he muttered 'Oh *no*, oh Jerry,' under his breath, as if he were witnessing an accident in which Jerry not Frost were the victim. For the second time, footsteps approached down the corridor. A girl's, short and quick. Then a sharp knock. Then silence.

'Natalie?' said Jerry quietly. Frost nodded. 'If I was a client, would you introduce me?' Frost shook his head. 'Let her in.'

Frost's tongue, like a scared pink snake, peeked out from between his lips, looked quickly round, then vanished.

'Come!' he called, in a hoarse voice, and a tall Chinese girl with thick glasses collected some letters from his out-tray.

'Enjoy your weekend, Mr Frost,' she said.

'See you Monday,' said Frost.

The door closed again.

Coming across the room, Jerry put an arm round Frost's shoulders and guided him, unresisting, quickly to the window.

'A trust account, Frostie. Lodged in your incorruptible hands. Sharpish.'

In the square, the carnival continued. On the cricket field, somebody was out. The lank batsman in the outmoded cap had dropped into a crouch and was patiently repairing the pitch. The fieldsmen lay about and chatted.

'You set me up,' said Frost simply, trying to get used to the notion. 'I thought I had a friend at last and now you want to screw me. And you a lord.'

'Shouldn't mingle with newshounds, Frostie. Rough bunch. No sporting instinct. Shouldn't have shot your mouth off. Where do you keep the records?'

'Friends *do* shoot their mouths off,' Frost protested. 'That's what friends are for! To *tell* each other!'

'Then tell me.'

Frost shook his head. 'I'm a Christian,' he said stupidly. 'I go every Sunday, I never miss. I'm afraid it's quite out of the question. I'd rather lose my place in society than commit a breach of confidence. It's known of me, right? No go. Sorry about that.'

Jerry edged closer along the sill, till their arms were all but touching. The big window-pan was trembling from the traffic. The Venetian blinds were red with building smuts. Frost's face worked pitifully as he wrestled with the news of his bereavement.

'Here's the deal, sport,' said Jerry, very quietly. 'Listen carefully. Right? It's a stick and carrot job. If you don't play, the comic will blow the whistle on you. Front page mugshot, banner headlines, continued back page, col six, the works. "Would you buy a second-hand trust account from this man?" Hong Kong the cess-pit of corruption and Frostie the slavering monster. That line. We'd tell them how you play roundeye musical beds at the young bankers' club, just the way you told it to me, and how till recently you maintained a wicked lovenest over on Kowloonside, only it went sour on you because she wanted more bread. Before they did all that, of course, they'd check the story out with your Chairman and maybe with your missus too, if she's well enough.'

A rainstorm of sweat had broken on Frost's face without warning. One moment his sallow features had shown an oily moistness and that was all. The next they were drenched and the sweat was running unchecked off his plump chin and falling on his Robin Hood suit.

'It's the booze,' he said stupidly, trying to staunch it with his handkerchief. 'I always get this when I drink. Bloody climate, I shouldn't be exposed to it. No one should. Rotting out here. I hate it.'

'That's the *bad* news,' Jerry continued. They were still at the window, side by side, like two men loving the view. 'The good news is five hundred US into your hot little hand, compliments of Grub Street, no one any the wiser, and Frostie for Chairman. So why not sit back and enjoy it? See what I mean?'

'And may I *inquire*,' Frost said at last, with a disastrous shot at sarcasm, 'to what end or purpose you wish to peruse this file in the first place?'

'Crime and corruption, sport. The Hong Kong connection. Grub Street names the guilty men. Account number four four two. Do you keep it here?' Jerry asked, indicating the safe.

Frost made a 'No' with his lips, but no sound came out.

'Both the fours, then the two. Where is it?'

'Look,' Frost muttered. His face was a hopeless mess of fear and disappointment. 'Do me a favour, will you? Keep me out of it. Bribe one of my Chinese clerks, okay? That's the proper way. I mean I've got a position here.'

'You know the saying, Frostie. In Hong Kong even the daisies talk. I want *you.* You're here, and you're better qualified. Is it in the strong room?'

*You have to keep it moving,* they said, *you have to raise the threshold all the time. Lose the initiative once and you lose it for ever.*

As Frost dithered, Jerry affected to run out of patience. With one very large hand, he seized hold of Frost's shoulder and spun him round, and backed him till his little shoulders were flat against the safe.

'Is it in the strong room?'

'How should I know?'

'I'll tell you how,' Jerry promised, and nodded hard at Frost so that his forelock flopped up and down. 'I'll tell you, sport,' he repeated, tapping Frost's shoulder lightly with his free hand. 'Because otherwise, you're forty and on the road, with a sick wife, and bambinos to feed, and school fees, and the whole catastrophe. It's one thing or t'other, and the moment's now. Not five minutes on but now. I don't care how you do it but make it sound normal and keep Natalie out of it.'

Jerry guided him back into the middle of the room, where his desk stood, and the telephone. There are parts in life which are impossible to play with dignity. Frost's that day was one. Lifting the receiver, he dialled a single digit.

'Natalie? Oh, you haven't gone. Listen, I'll be staying on for an hour yet, I've just had a client on the phone. Tell Syd to leave the strong room on the key. I'll close up when I go, right?'

He slumped into his chair.

'Straighten your hair,' said Jerry, and returned to the window while they waited.

'Crime and corruption, my arse,' Frost muttered. 'All right, suppose he cuts a few corners. Name me a Chinese who doesn't. Name a Brit who doesn't. Do you think that brings the Island to its feet?'

'Chinese, is he? said Jerry, very sharply.

Coming back to the desk, Jerry himself dialled Natalie's number. No answer. Lifting Frost gently to his feet, Jerry led him to the door.

'Now don't go locking up,' he warned. 'We'll need to put it back before you leave.'

Frost had returned. He sat glumly at the desk, three folders before him on the blotter. Jerry poured him a vodka. Standing at his shoulder while Frost drank it, Jerry explained how a collaboration of this sort worked. Frostie wouldn't feel a thing, he said. All he had to do was leave everything where it lay, then step into the corridor, closing the door carefully after him. Beside the door was a staff noticeboard: Frostie had no doubt observed it often. Frostie should place himself before this noticeboard and read the notices diligently, all of them, until he heard Jerry give two knocks from within, when he could return. While reading he should take care to keep his body at such an angle as to obscure the peephole, so that Jerry would know he was still there, and passers-by would not be able to see in. Frost could also console himself with the thought that he had betrayed no confidences, Jerry explained. The worst that Higher Authority could ever say – or the client, for that matter – was that by abandoning his room when Jerry was inside it, he had committed a technical breach of the bank's security regulations.

'How many papers are there in the folders?'

'How should I know?' asked Frost, slightly emboldened by his unexpected innocence.

'Count 'em, will you, sport? Attaboy.'

There were fifty exactly, which was a great deal more than Jerry had bargained for. There remained the fallback against the eventuality that Jerry, despite these precautions, might be disturbed.

'I'll need application forms,' he said.

'What bloody application forms? I don't keep forms,' Frost retorted. 'I've got *girls* who bring me forms. No, I haven't. They've gone home.'

'To open my trust account with your distinguished house, Frostie. Spread here on the table, with your hospitality gold-plated fountain pen – will you? You're taking a break while I fill them in. And that's the first instalment.' he said. Drawing a little wad of American dollar bills from his hip pocket, he tossed it on the table with a pleasing slap. Frost eyed the money but did not pick it up.

Alone, Jerry worked fast. He disentangled the papers from the clasp and laid them out in pairs, photographing them two pages to a shot, keeping his big elbows close to his body for stillness, and his big feet slightly apart for balance, like a slipcatch at cricket, and the measuring chain just brushing the papers for distance. When he was not satisfied he repeated a shot. Sometimes he bracketed the exposure. Often he turned his head and glanced at the circle of Robin Hood green in the eyehole to make sure Frost was at his post and not even now, calling in the guards armoured. Once, Frost grew impatient and tapped on the glass and Jerry growled at him to shut up. Occasionally he heard footsteps approach and when that happened he left everything on the table with the money and the application forms, put the camera in his pocket and ambled to the window to gaze at the harbour and yank at his hair, like a man contemplating the great decisions of his life. And once, which is a fiddly game when you have big fingers and you're under stress, he changed the cassette, wishing the old camera's action a shade more quiet. By the time he called Frost back, the folders were once more on his desk, the money was beside the folders, and Jerry was feeling cold and just a little murderous.

'You're a bloody fool,' Frost announced, feeding the five hundred dollars into the buttondown pocket of his tunic.

'Sure,' he said. He was looking round, brushing over his traces.

'You're out of your dirty little mind,' Frost told him. His expression was oddly resolute. 'You think you can bust a man like him? You might as well try and take Fort Knox with a jemmy and a box of firecrackers as take the lid off that crowd.'

'Mister Big himself. I like that.'

'No you won't, you'll hate it.'

'Know him, do you?'

'We're like ham and eggs,' said Frost sourly. 'I'm in and out of his place every day. You know my passion for the high and mighty.'

'Who opened his account for him?'

'My predecessor.'

'Been here, has he?'

'Not in my day.'

'Ever seen him?'

'Canidrome in Macao.'

'The *where*?'

'Macao dog races. Losing his shirt. Mixing with the common crowd. I was with my little Chinese bird, the one before last. She pointed him out to me. "Him?" I said. "Him? Oh yes, well he's a client of mine." Very impressed she was.' A flicker of his former self appeared in Frost's subdued features. 'I'll tell you one thing: *he* wasn't doing badly for himself. Very nice blonde party he had with him. Roundeye. Film star by the look of her. Swedish. Lot of conscientious work on the casting couch. Here –'

Frost managed a ghostly smile.

'Hurry, sport. What is it?'

'Let's make it up. Come on. We'll go on the town. Blow my five hundred bucks. You're not really like that, are you? It's just something you do for your living.'

Groping in his pocket, Jerry dug out the alarm key and dropped it into Frost's passive hand.

'You'll need this,' he said.

On the great steps as he left stood a slender, well-dressed young man in low-cut American slacks. He was reading a serious-looking book in the hardback edition, Jerry couldn't see what. He had not got very far into it, but he was reading it intently, like somebody determined upon improving his mind.

Saratt man once more, the rest blanked out.

Heeltap, said the bearleaders. Never go there straight. If you can't cache the take, you must at least queer the scent. He took taxis, but always to somewhere specific. To the Queen's Pier, where he watched the out-island ferries loading, and the brown junks skimming between the liners. To Aberdeen, where he meandered with the sight-seers gawping at the boat people and the floating restaurants. To Stanley Village, and along the public beach, where pale-bodied Chinese bathers, a little stooped as if the city were still weighing on their shoulders, chastely paddled with their children. *Chinese never swim after the moon festival*, he reminded himself automatically, but he couldn't remember off-hand when the moon festival was. He had thought of dropping the camera at the hat-check room at the Hilton Hotel. He had thought of night safes, and posting a parcel to himself; of special messengers under journalistic cover. None worked for him – more particularly none worked for the bearleaders. It's a solo, they had said; it's a do-it-yourself or nothing. So he bought something to carry: a plastic shopping bag and a couple of cotton shirts to flesh it out. When you're hot, said the doctrine, make sure you have a distraction. Even the oldest watchers fall for it. And if they flush you and you drop it, who knows? You may even hold off the dogs long enough to get out in your socks. He kept clear of people all the same. He had a living terror of the chance pickpocket. In the hire garage on Kowloon-side, they had the car ready for him. He felt calm – he was coming down – but his vigilance was never relaxed. He felt victorious and the rest of what he felt was of no account. Some jobs are grubby.

Driving, he watched particularly for Hondas, which in Hong Kong are the poor-bloody-infantry of the watching trade. Before leaving Kowloon he made a couple of passes through sidestreets. Nothing. At Junction Road he joined the picnic convoy and continued toward Clear Water Bay for another hour, grateful for the really bad traffic, for there is nothing harder than unobtrusively ringing the changes between a trio of Hondas caught in a fifteen-mile snarl-up. The rest was watching mirrors, driving, getting there, flying solo. The afternoon heat stayed fierce. He had the airconditioning full on but couldn't feel it. He passed acres of potted plants, Seiko signs, then quilts of paddies and plots of young peach trees growing for the new year market. He came to a narrow sand lane to his left and turned sharply into it, watching his mirror. He pulled up, parked for a while with the rear lid up, pretending to let the engine cool. A pea-green Mercedes slid past him, smoked windows, one driver, one passenger up. It had been behind him for some while. But it stuck to the main road. He crossed the road to the café, dialled a number, let the phone ring four times and rang off. He dialled the number again; it rang six times and as the receiver was lifted he rang off again. He drove on, lumbering through the remnants of fishing villages to a lakeside where the rushes were threaded far out into the water, and doubled by their own reflection. Bullfrogs bellowed and light pleasure yachts switched in and out of the heat haze. The sky was dead white and reached right into the water. He got out. As he did so, an old Citroen van hobbled down the road, several Chinese aboard: Coca-Cola hats, fishing tackle, kids; but two men, no women, and the men ignored him. He made for a row of clapboard balcony-houses, very rundown and fronted with concrete lattice walls like houses on an English sea-front, but the paint on them paler because of the sun. Their names were done in heavy poker work on bits of ship's timber: Driftwood, Susy May, Dun-romin. There was a Marina at the end of the track but it was closed down and the yachts now harboured somewhere else. Approaching the houses, Jerry glanced casually at the upper windows. In the second from the left stood a lurid vase of dried flowers, their stems wrapped in silver paper. All clear, it said. Come in. Pushing open the little gate, he pressed the bell. The Citroen had stopped at the lakeside. He heard the doors slam at the same time as he heard the misused electronics over the entry-phone loudspeaker.

'What bastard's that?' a gravel voice demanded, its rich Australian tones thundering through the atmospherics, but the catch on the door was already buzzing and when he shoved it he saw the gross figure of old Craw in his kimono planted at the top of the staircase, hugely pleased, calling him 'Monsignor' and 'you thieving pommie dog', and exhorting him to haul his ugly upper-class backside up here and put a bloody drink under his belt.

The house reeked of burning joss. From the shadows of a ground floor doorway a toothless amah grinned at him, the same strange little creature whom Luke had questioned while Craw was absent in London. The drawing room was on the first floor, the grimy panelling strewn with curling photographs of Craw's old pals, journalists he'd worked with for all of fifty years of crazy oriental history. At the centre stood a table with a battered Remington where Craw was supposed to be composing his life's memoirs. The rest of the room was sparse. Craw, like Jerry, had kids and wives left over from half a dozen existences, and after meeting life's immediate needs there wasn't much money for furniture.

The bathroom had no window.

Beside the handbasin, a developing tank and brown bottles of fixer and developer. Also a small editor with a ground-glass screen for reading nega-

tives. Craw switched off the light and for numberless years in space laboured in
the total darkness, grunting and cursing and appealing to the Pope. Beside
him Jerry sweated and tried to chart the old man's actions by his swearing.
Now, he guessed, Craw was feeding the narrow ribbon from the cassette on to
the spool. Jerry imagined him holding it too lightly for fear of marking the
emulsion. In a moment he'll be doubting whether he's holding it at all,
thought Jerry. He'll be having to will his fingertips into continuing the
movement. He felt sick. In the darkness old Craw's cursing grew much
louder, but not loud enough to drown the scream of water-birds from the
lake. He's deft, thought Jerry, reassured. He can do it in his sleep. He heard
the grinding of bakelite as Craw screwed down the lid, and a muttered 'Go to
bed you little heathen bastard.' Then the strangely dry rattle as he cautiously
shook the airbubbles out of the developer. Then the safety light went on with
a snap a loud as a pistol shot, and there was old Craw himself once more, red
as a parrot from the glow, stooped over the sealed tank, quickly pouring in
the hypo, then confidently overturning the tank and setting it right again
while he watched the old kitchen timer stammer through the seconds.

Half stifled with nerves and heat, Jerry returned alone to the drawing
room, poured himself a beer and slumped into a cane chair, looking nowhere
while he listened to the steady running of the tap. From the window came the
bubbling of Chinese voices. At the lake's edge the two fishermen had set up
their tackle. The children were watching them, sitting in the dust. From the
bathroom came the scratching of the lid again, and Jerry leapt to his feet, but
Craw must have heard him, for he growled 'wait' and closed the door.

*Airline pilots, journalists, spies*, the Sarratt doctrine warned. *It's the same drag.
Blood inertia interspersed with bouts of bloody frenzy.*

He's taking the first look, thought Jerry: in case it's fumble. In the pecking
order, it was Craw, not Jerry, who has to make his peace with London. Craw,
who in the worst contingency, would order him to take a second bite of Frost.

'What are you doing in there, for Christ's sake?' Jerry yelled. 'What goes
on?'

Perhaps he's having a pee, he thought absurdly.

Slowly the door opened. Craw's gravity was awesome.

'They haven't come out,' said Jerry.

He had the feeling of not reaching Craw at all. He was going to repeat
himself in fact, loudly. He was going to dance about and make a damn scene.
So that Craw's answer, when it finally came, came just in time.

'To the contrary, my son.' The old boy took a step forward and Jerry could
see the films now, hanging behind him like black wet worms from Craw's little
clothes line, pink pegs holding them in place. 'To the contrary, sir,' he said,
'every frame is a bold and disturbing masterpiece.'

# SEVEN

## *more about horses*

In the Circus the first scraps of news of Jerry's progress arrived in the early morning, in a deadly quiet, and thereafter set the weekend upside down. Knowing what to expect, Guillam had taken himself to bed at ten and slumbered fitfully between bouts of anxiety for Jerry, and frankly lustful visions of Molly Meakin with and without her sedate swimming suit. Jerry was due to present himself to Frost just after four a.m. London time and by three-thirty Guillam was clattering in his old Porsche through the foggy streets toward Cambridge Circus. It could have been dawn or dusk. He arrived at the rumpus room to find Connie completing *The Times* crossword and Doc di Salis reading the meditations of Thomas Traherne, plucking his ear and jiggling his foot all at the same time, like a one-man percussion band. Restless as ever, Fawn flitted between them, dusting and tidying, a headwaiter impatient for the next sitting. Now and then he sucked his teeth and let out a breathy '*tah*' in barely controlled frustration. A pall of tobacco smoke hung like a raincloud across the room and there was the usual stink of rank tea from the samovar. Smiley's door was closed and Guillam saw no cause to disturb him. He opened a copy of *Country Life*. Like waiting at the bloody dentist, he thought, and sat staring mindlessly at photographs of great houses till Connie softly put down her crossword, sat bolt upright and said 'Listen'. Then he heard a quick snarl from the Cousins' green telephone before Smiley picked it up. Through the open doorway to his own room Guillam glanced at the row of electronic boxes. On one, a green caution light burned for as long as the conversation lasted. Then the pax rang in the rumpus room – pax being jargon for internal phone – and this time Guillam reached it before Fawn.

'He's entered the bank,' Smiley announced cryptically over the pax.

Guillam relayed the message to the gathering. 'He's entered the bank,' he said, but he might have been talking to the dead. Nobody gave the slightest sign of hearing.

By five Jerry had come out of the bank. Nervously contemplating the options, Guillam felt physically sick. Burning was a dangerous game and like most pros Guillam hated it, though not for reasons of scruple. First there was the quarry or, worse, the local security angels. Second there was the burn itself, and not everybody responded logically to blackmail. You got heroes, you got liars, you got hysterical virgins who put their heads back and screamed blue murder even when they were enjoying it. But the real danger came now, when the burn was over and Jerry had to turn his back on the smoking bomb and run. Which way would Frost jump? Would he telephone the police? His mother? His boss? His wife? 'Darling, I'll confess all, save me and we'll turn over a new leaf.' Guillam did not even rule out the ghastly possibility that Frost might go directly to his client: 'Sir, I have come to purge myself of a gross breach of bank confidence.'

In the fusty eeriness of early morning, Guillam shuddered, and fixed his mind resolutely on Molly.

On the next occasion the green phone sounded, Guillam didn't hear it. George must have been sitting right over the thing. Suddenly the pinlight in Guillam's room was glowing and it continued glowing for fifteen minutes. It went out and they waited, all eyes fixed on Smiley's door, willing him from his seclusion. Fawn was frozen in mid-movement, holding a plate of brown marmalade sandwiches which nobody would ever eat. Then the handle tipped and Smiley appeared with a common-or-garden search request form in his hand, already completed in his own neat script and flagged 'stripe' which meant 'urgent for Chief' and was the top priority. He gave it to Guillam and asked him to take it straight to the Queen Bee in Registry and stand over her while she looked up the name. Receiving it, Guillam recalled an earlier moment when he had been presented with a similar form, made out in the name of Worthington Elizabeth, alias Lizzie, and ending 'high-class tart'. And as he departed, he heard Smiley quietly inviting Connie and di Salis to accompany him to the throne-room, while Fawn was packed off to the unclassified library in search of the current edition of *Who's Who in Hong Kong*.

The Queen Bee had been specially summoned for the dawn shift and when Guillam walked in on her, her lair looked like a tableau from 'The Night London Burned', complete with an iron bunk and a small primus stove, though there was a coffee machine in the corridor. All she needs is a boiler suit and a portrait of Winston Churchill, he thought. The details on the trace read 'Ko, forename Drake other names unknown, date of birth 1925 Shanghai, present address Seven Gates, Headland Road, Hong Kong, occupation Chairman and Managing Director of China Airsea Ltd, Hong Kong'. The Queen Bee launched herself on an impressive paperchase but all she finally came up with was the information that Ko had been appointed to the Order of the British Empire under the Hong Kong list in 1966 for 'social and charitable services to the Colony', and that the Circus had responded 'nothing recorded against' to a vetting enquiry from the Governor's office before the award was passed up for approval. Hurrying upstairs with his glad intelligence, Guillam was awake enough to remember that China Airsea Ltd, Hong Kong, had been described by Sam Collins as the ultimate owner of that mickey-mouse airline in Vientiane which had been the beneficiary of Commercial Boris's bounty. This struck Guillam as a most orderly connection. Pleased with himself, he returned to the throne-room to be greeted by dead silence. Strewn over the floor lay not just the current edition of *Who's Who* but several backnumbers as well: Fawn as usual had overreached himself. Smiley sat at his desk and he was staring at a sheet of notes in his own handwriting, Connie and di Salis were staring at Smiley, but Fawn was absent again, presumably on another errand. Guillam handed Smiley the trace form with the Queen Bee's findings written along the middle in her best Kensington copperplate. At the same moment the green phone crackled again. Lifting the receiver Smiley began jotting on the sheet before him.

'Yes. Thanks, I have that. Go on, please. Yes, I have that also.' And so on for ten minutes, till he said: 'Good. Till this evening then,' and rang off.

Outside in the street, an Irish milkman was enthusiastically proclaiming that he never would be the wild rover no more.

'Westerby's landed the complete file,' Smiley said finally – though like everyone else he referred to him by his cryptonym. 'All the figures.' He nodded as if agreeing with himself, still studying the paper. 'The film won't be here till tonight, but the shape is already clear. Everything that was originally paid through Vientiane has found its way to the account in Hong Kong. Right from the very beginning Hong Kong was the final destination of the goldseam. All of it. Down to the last cent. No deductions, not even for bank commission. It was at first a humble figure, then rose steeply, why we may only guess. All as Collins described. Till it stopped at twenty-five thousand a month and stayed there. When the Vientiane arrangement ended, Centre didn't miss a single month. They switched to the alternative route immediately. You're right, Con. Karla never does anything without a fallback.'

'He's a professional, darling,' Connie Sachs murmured. 'Like you.'

'Not like me.' He continued studying his own jottings. 'It's a lockaway account,' he declared in the same matter-of-fact tone. 'Only one name is given and that's the founder of the trust. Ko. "Beneficiary unknown," they say. Pehaps we shall see why tonight. Not a penny has been drawn,' he said, singling out Connie Sachs. He repeated that: 'Since the payments started over two years ago, not a single penny has been drawn from the account. The balance stands in the order of half a million American dollars. With compound interest it's naturally rising fast.'

To Guillam, this last piece of intelligence was daylight madness. What the hell was the point to half a million dollar goldseam if the money was not even used when it reached the other end? To Connie Sachs and di Salis, on the other hand, it was patently of enormous significance. A crocodile smile spread slowly across Connie's face and her baby eyes fixed on Smiley in silent ecstasy.

'Oh *George*,' she breathed at last, as the revelation gathered in her. 'Darling. *Lockaway!* Well, that's quite a different kettle of fish. Well of course it had to be, didn't it! It had all the signs. From the very first *day*. And if fat, stupid Connie hadn't been so blinkered and old and doddery and idle, she'd have read them off *long* ago! You leave me alone, Peter Guillam, you lecherous young toad.' She was pulling herself to her feet, her crippled hands clamped over the chair arms. 'But who can be worth so much? Would it be a network? No, no, they'd never do it for a *network*. No precedent. Not a wholesale thing, that's unheard of. So who can it be? Whatever can he *deliver* that would be worth so much?' She was hobbling toward the door, tugging the shawl over her shoulders, slipping already from their world to her own. '*Karla* doesn't pay money like that.' They heard her mutterings follow her. She passed the mothers' lane of covered typewriters, muffled sentinels in the gloom. '*Karla's* such a mean prig he thinks his agents should work for him for *nothing*! Course he does. *Pennies* that's what he pays them. Pocket money. Inflation is all very well, but half a million dollars for one little mole. I never heard such a thing!'

In his quirkish way di Salis was no less impressed than Connie. He sat with the top part of his crabbed, uneven body tilted forward, and he was stirring feverishly in the bowl of his pipe with a silver knife as if it were a cookpot which had caught on the flame. His silver hair stood wry as a cockscomb over the dandruffed collar of his crumpled black jacket.

'Well, well, no wonder Karla wanted the bodies buried,' he blurted suddenly, as if the words had been jerked out of him. 'No wonder. Karla's a China hand too, you know. It is attested. I have it from Connie.' He clambered to his feet, holding too many things in his little hands: pipe, tobacco tin, his penknife and his Thomas Traherne. 'Not sophisticated naturally. Well one doesn't expect that. Karla's no scholar, he's a soldier. But not blind either, not by a long chalk, she tells me. *Ko.*' He repeated the name at several different levels. 'Ko. *Ko.* I must see the characters. It depends entirely on the characters. *Height . . . Tree* even, yes, I can see tree . . . or can I? . . . oh and several other concepts. "Drake" is mission school of course. Shanghainese mission boy. Well, well. Shanghai was where it all started you know. First Party cell *ever* was in Shanghai. Why did I say that? *Drake Ko.* Wonder what his real names are. We shall find all that out very shortly no doubt. Yes, good. Well, I think I might go back to my reading too. Smiley, do you think I might have a coal-scuttle in my room? Without the heating on, one simply freezes up. I've asked the housekeepers a dozen times and had nothing but impertinence for my pains. Anno domini I'm afraid, but the winter is almost upon us I suppose. You'll show us the raw material as soon as it arrives, I trust? One doesn't like to work too long on potted versions. I shall make a *curriculum vitae.* That will be my first thing. Ko. Ah, thank you, Guillam.'

He had dropped his Thomas Traherne. Accepting it he dropped his tobacco tin, so Guillam picked up that as well. 'Drake Ko. Shanghainese doesn't mean a thing of course. Shanghai was the real melting pot. Chiu Chow's the answer, judging by what we know. Still, mustn't jump the gun. Baptist. Well, the Chiu Chow Christians mostly are, aren't they? Swatownese: where did we have that? Yes, the intermediate company in Bangkok. Well, that figures well enough. Or Hakka. They're not mutually exclusive, not by any means.' He stalked after Connie into the corridor, leaving Guillam alone with Smiley, who rose and, going to an armchair, slumped into it staring sightlessly at the fire.

'Odd,' he remarked finally. 'One has no sense of shock. Why is that, Peter? You know me. Why is it?'

Guillam had the wisdom to keep quiet.

'A big fish. In Karla's pay. Lockaway accounts, the threat of Russian spies at the very centre of the Colony's life. So why no sense of shock?'

The green telephone was barking again. This time Guillam took the call. As he did so, he was surprised to see a fresh folder of Sam Collins's Far Eastern reports lying open on the desk.

That was the weekend. Connie and di Salis sank without trace; Smiley set to work preparing his submission; Guillam smoothed feathers, called in the mothers and arranged for typing in shifts. On the Monday, carefully briefed by Smiley, he telephoned Lacon's private secretary. He did it very well. 'No drumbeats,' Smiley had warned. 'Keep it very idle.' And Guillam did just that. There had been talk over dinner the other evening – he said – of convening the Intelligence Steering Group to consider certain *prima facie* evidence:

'The case has firmed up a little, so perhaps it would be sensible to fix a date. Give us the batting order and we'll circulate the document in advance.'

'A *batting order*? Firmed up? Where *ever* do you people learn your English?'

Lacon's private secretary was a fat voice called Pym. Guillam had never met him, but he loathed him quite unreasonably.

'I can only tell him,' Pym warned. 'I can tell him and I can see what he says and I can ring you back. His card is *very* heavily marked this month.'

'It's just one little waltz if he can manage it,' said Guillam and rang off in a fury.

You bloody well wait and see what hits you, he thought.

When London is having its baby, the folkelore says, the fieldman can only pace the waiting room. Airline pilots, newshounds, spies: Jerry was back with the bloody inertia.

'We're in mothballs,' Craw announced. 'The word is well done and hold your water.'

They talked every two days at least, limbo calls between two third-party telephones, usually one hotel lobby to another. They disguised their language with a mix of Sarratt wordcode and journalistic mumbo-jumbo.

'Your story is being checked out on high,' Craw said. 'When our editors have wisdom, they will impart it in due season. Meanwhile, slap your hand over it and keep it there. That's an order.'

Jerry had no idea how Craw talked to London and he didn't care as long as it was safe. He assumed some co-opted official from the huge untouchable above-the-line intelligence fraternity was playing linkman: but he didn't care.

'Your job is to put in mileage for the comic and tuck some spare copy under your belt which you can wave at Brother Stubbs when the next crisis comes,' Craw said to him. 'Nothing else, hear me?'

Drawing on his jaunts with Frost, Jerry bashed out a piece on the effect of the American military pullout on the nightlife of Wanchai: 'What's happened to Susie Wong since war-weary GIs with bulging wallets have ceased to flock in for rest and recreation?' He fabricated – or, as journalists prefer it, *hyped* – a 'dawn interview' with a disconsolate and fictitious bar-girl who was reduced to accepting Japanese customers, airfreighted his piece and got Luke's bureau to telex the number of the waybill, all as Stubbs had ordered. Jerry was by no means a bad reporter, but just as pressure brought out the best in him, sloth brought out the worst. Astonished by Stubbs's prompt and even gracious acceptance – a 'herogram' Luke called it, phoning through the text from the bureau – he cast around for other heights to scale. A couple of sensational corruption trials were attracting good houses, starring the usual crop of misunderstood policemen, but after taking a look at them, Jerry concluded they hadn't the scale to travel. England had her own these days. A 'please-matcher' ordered him to chase a story floated by a rival comic about the alleged pregnancy of Miss Hong Kong but a libel suit got there ahead of him. He attended an arid government press briefing by Shallow Throat, himself a humourless reject from a Northern Irish daily, idled away a morning researching successful stories from the past that might stand re-heating; and on the strength of rumour about army economy cuts, spent an afternoon being trailed round the Gurkha garrison by a public relations major who looked about eighteen. And no the major *didn't* know, thank you, in reply to Jerry's cheerful enquiry, what his men would do for sex when their families were sent home to Nepal. They would be visiting their villages about once every three years, he thought; and he seemed to think that was quite enough for anyone. Stretching the facts till they read as if the Gurkhas were already a community of military grass widowers, 'Cold Showers in a Hot Climate for Britain's Mercenaries', Jerry triumphantly landed himself an inside lead. He banked a couple more stories for a rainy day, lounged away the evenings at the Club and inwardly gnawed his head off while he waited for the Circus to produce its baby.

'For Christ's sake,' he protested to Craw. 'The bloody man's practically public property.'

'All the same,' said Craw firmly.

So Jerry said 'Yes, sir,' and a couple of days later, out of sheer boredom, began his own entirely informal investigation into the life and loves of Mr Drake Ko, OBE, Steward of the Royal Hong Kong Jockey Club, millionaire and citizen above suspicion. Nothing dramatic; nothing, in Jerry's book, disobedient; for there is not a fieldman born who does not at one time or another stray across the borders of his brief. He began tentatively, like journeys to a forbidden biscuit box. As it happened, he had been considering proposing to Stubbs a three-part series on the Hong Kong super-rich. Browsing in the reference shelves of the Foreign Correspondents' Club before lunch one day, he unconsciously took a leaf from Smiley's book and turned up Ko, Drake, in the current edition of *Who's Who in Hong Kong*: married, one son, died 1968; sometime law student of Gray's Inn, London, but not a successful one, apparently, for there was no record of his being called to the Bar. Then a rundown of his twenty-odd directorships. Hobbies: horseracing, cruising and jade. Well, whose aren't? Then the charities he supported, including a Baptist church, a Chiu Chow Spirit Temple and the Drake Ko Free Hospital for Children. Backed all the possibilities, Jerry reflected with amusement. The photograph showed the usual soft-eyed, twenty-year-old beautiful soul, rich in merit as well as goods, and was otherwise unrecognizable. The dead son's name was Nelson. Jerry noticed: Drake and Nelson, British admirals. He couldn't get it out of his mind that the father should be named after the first British sailor to enter the China Seas, and the son after the hero of Trafalgar.

Jerry had a lot less difficulty than Peter Guillam in making the connection betwen China Airsea in Hong Kong and Indocharter SA in Vientiane, and he was amused to read in the China Airsea company prospectus that its business was described as 'wide spread of trading and transportation activities in the South East Asian theatre' – including rice, fish, electrical goods, teak, real estate and shipping.

Devilling at Luke's bureau, he took a bolder step: the sheerest accident shoved the name of Drake Ko under his nose. True, he had looked up Ko in the card index. Just as he had looked up a dozen or twenty other wealthy Chinese in the Colony; just as he had asked the Chinese clerk, in perfectly good faith who *she* thought were the most exotic Chinese millionaires for his purpose. And while Drake might not have been one of the absolute front runners, it took very little to draw the name from her, and consequently the papers. Indeed, as he had already protested to Craw, there was something flattening, not to say dreamlike, about pursuing by hole-and-corner methods a man so publicly evident. Soviet intelligence agents, in Jerry's limited experience of the breed, normally came in more modest versions. Ko seemed king-size by comparison.

Reminds me of old Sambo, Jerry thought. It was the first time this intimation had struck him.

The most detailed offering appeared in a glossy periodical called *Golden Orient*, now out of print. In one of its last editions, an eight page illustrated feature titled 'The Red Knights of Nanyang' concerned itself with the growing number of overseas Chinese with profitable trade relations with Red China, commonly known as fat-cats. Nanyang, as Jerry knew, meant the realms south of China; and implied to the Chinese a kind of Eldorado of peace and wealth. To each chosen personality the feature devoted a page and a photograph, generally shot against a background of his possessions. The hero of the Hong Kong interview – there were pieces from Bangkok, Manila, and Singapore as well – was that 'much-loved sporting personality and Jockey

Club Steward', Mr Drake Ko, President, Chairman, Managing Director and chief shareholder of China Airsea Ltd, and he was shown with his horse Lucky Nelson at the end of a successful season in Happy Valley. The horse's name momentarily arrested Jerry's Western eye. He found it macabre that a father should christen a horse after his dead son.

The accompanying photograph revealed rather more than the spineless mugshot in *Who's Who*. Ko looked jolly, even exuberant, and he appeared, despite his hat, to be hairless. The hat was at this stage the most interesting thing about Ko, for it was one which no Chinese, in Jerry's limited experience, had ever been seen to wear. It was a beret, worn sloping, and putting Ko somewhere between a British soldier and a French onion seller. But above all, it had for a Chinese the rarest quality of all: self mockery. He was apparently tall, he was wearing a Burberry, and his long hands stuck out of the sleeves like twigs. He seemed genuinely to like the horse, and one arm rested easily on its back. Asked why he still ran a junk fleet when these were commonly held to be unprofitable, he replied: 'My people are Hakka from Chiu Chow. We breathed the water, farmed the water, slept on the water. Boats are my element.' He was fond also of describing his journey from Shanghai to Hong Kong in 1951. At that time the border was still open and there were no effective restrictions on immigration. Nevertheless, Ko chose to make the trip by fishing junk, pirates, blockades and bad weather notwithstanding: which was held at the very least to be eccentric.

'I'm a very lazy fellow,' he was reported as saying. 'If the wind will blow me for nothing, why should I walk? Now I've got a sixty-foot cruiser but I still love the sea.'

Famous for his sense of humour, said the article.

A good agent must have entertainment value, say the Sarratt bearleaders: that was something Moscow Centre also understood.

There being no one watching, Jerry ambled over to the card index and a few minutes later had taken possession of a thick folder of presscuttings, the bulk of which concerned a share scandal in 1965, in which Ko and a group of Swatownese had played a shady part. The Stock Exchange enquiry, not surprisingly, proved inconclusive and was shelved. The following year Ko got his OBE. 'If you buy people,' old Sambo used to say, 'buy them thoroughly.'

In Luke's bureau they kept a bunch of Chinese researchers, among them a convivial Cantonese named Jimmy who often appeared at the Club and was paid at Chinese rates to be the oracle on Chinese matters. Jimmy said the Swatownese were a people apart, 'like Scots or Jews', hardy, clannish and notoriously thrifty, who lived near the sea so that they could run for it when they were persecuted or starving or in debt. He said their women were sought-after, being beautiful, diligent, frugal and lecherous.

'Writing yourself another novel, your lordship?' the dwarf asked endearingly, coming out of his offfice to find out what Jerry was up to. Jerry had wanted to ask why a Swatownese should have been brought up in Shanghai, but he thought it wiser to bend course toward a less delicate topic.

Next day, Jerry borrowed Luke's battered car. Armed with a standard-size thirty-five millimetre camera he drove to Headland Road, a millionaire's ghetto between Repulse Bay and Stanley, where he made a show of rubbernecking at the outside of the villas there, as many idle tourists do. His cover story was still that feature for Stubbs on the Hong Kong super-rich: even now, even to himself, he would scarcely have admitted to going there on account of Drake Ko.

'He's raising Cain in Taipei,' Craw had told him casually in one of their limbo calls. 'Won't be back till Thursday.' Once again, Jerry accepted without question Craw's lines of communication.

He did not photograph the house called Seven Gates, but he took several long, stupid gazes at it. He saw a low, pantiled villa set well back from the road, with a big verandah on the seaward side and a pergola of white-painted pillars cut against the blue horizon. Craw had told him that Drake must have chosen the name because of Shanghai, whose old city walls were pierced with seven gates: 'Sentiment, my son. Never underrate the power of sentiment upon a slanteye, and never count on it either. Amen.' He saw lawns, including to his amusement a croquet lawn. He saw a fine collection of azaleas and hibiscus. He saw a model junk about ten feet long set on a concrete sea, and he saw a garden bar, round like a bandstand, with a blue and white striped awning over it, and a ring of empty white chairs presided over by a boy in a white coat and trousers and white shoes. The Ko's were evidently expecting company. He saw the other houseboys washing a tobacco-coloured Rolls-Royce Phantom saloon. The long garage was open, and he recorded a Chrysler station-wagon of some kind, and a Mercedes, black, with the licence plates removed, presumably as part of some repair. But he was meticulous about giving equal attention to the other houses in Headland Road and photographed three of them.

Continuing to Deep Water Bay he stood on the shore gazing at the small armada of stockbroker junks and launches which bobbed at anchor on the choppy sea, but was not able to pick out *Admiral Nelson*, Ko's celebrated ocean-going cruiser – the ubiquity of the name Nelson was becoming positively oppressive. About to give up, he heard a cry from below him, and walking down a rickety wooden causeway found an old woman in a sampan grinning up at him and pointing to herself with a yellow chicken's leg she had been sucking with her toothless gums. Clambering aboard he indicated the boats and she took him on a tour of them, laughing and chanting while she sculled, and keeping the chicken leg in her mouth. *Admiral Nelson* was sleek and low-lined. Three more boys in white ducks were diligently scouring the decks. Jerry tried to calculate Ko's monthly housekeeping bill, just for staff alone.

On the drive back, he paused to examine the Drake Ko Free Hospital for Children and established, for what it was worth, that that too was in excellent repair. Next morning early, Jerry placed himself in the lobby of a chintzy highrise office building in Central, and read the brass plates of the business companies housed there. China Airsea and its affiliates occupied the top three floors, but somewhat predictably there was no mention of Indocharter, Vientiane SA, the former recipient of twenty-five thousand US dollars on the last Friday of every month.

The cuttings folder in Luke's bureau had contained a cross-reference to US Consulate archives. Jerry had called there next day, ostensibly to check out his story on the American troops in Wanchai. Under the eye of an unreasonably pretty girl, Jerry drifted, picked at a few things, then settled on some of the oldest stuff they had, which dated from the very early Fifties when Truman had put a trade embargo on China and North Korea. The Hong Kong Consulate had been ordered to report any infringements, and this was the record of what they had unearthed. The favourite commodity, next to medicines and electrical goods, was oil, and 'the United States Agencies', as they were styled, had gone for it in a big way, setting traps, putting out gun boats, interrogating defectors and prisoners, and finally placing huge dossiers before Congressional and Senate Sub-Committees.

The year in question was 1951, two years after the Communist takeover in China and the year Ko sailed to Hong Kong from Shanghai without a cent to his name. The operation to which the bureau's reference directed him was Shanghainese, and to begin with, that was the only connection it had with Ko. Many Shanghainese immigrants in those days lived in a crowded insanitary hotel on the Des Voeux Road. The introduction said that they were like one enormous family, welded together by shared suffering and squalor. Some had escaped together from the Japanese before escaping from the Communists.

'After enduring so much at Communist hands,' one culprit told his interrogators, 'the least we could do was make a little money out of them.'

Another was more aggressive. 'The Hong Kong fat-cats are making millions out of this war. Who sells the Reds their electronic equipment, their penicillin, their rice?'

In fifty-one there were two methods open to them, said the report. One was to bribe the frontier guards and truck the oil across the New Territories and over the border. The other was taking it by ship, which meant bribing the harbour authorities.

An informant again: 'Us Hakka know the sea. We find boat, three hundred tons, we rent. We fill with drums of oil, make false manifest and false destination. We reach international waters, run like hell for Amoy. Reds call us brother, profit one hundred per cent. After a few runs we buy boat.'

'Where did the original money come from?' the interrogator demanded.

'Ritz Ballroom,' was the disconcerting answer. The Ritz was a high-class pick-up spot right down the King's Road on the waterfront, said a footnote. Most of the girls were Shanghainese. The same footnote named members of the gang. Drake Ko was one.

'Drake Ko was very tough boy,' said a witness's statement given in fine print in the appendix. 'You don't tell no fairy story to Drake Ko. He don't like politician people one piece. Chiang Kai-shek. Mao. He say they all one person. He say he big supporter of Chiang Mao-shek. One day Mr Ko lead our gang.'

As to organized crime, the investigation turned up nothing. It was a matter of history that Shanghai, by the time it fell to Mao in forty-nine, had emptied three-quarters of its underworld into Hong Kong; that the Red Gang and the Green Gang had fought enough battles over the Hong Kong protection rackets to make Chicago in the Twenties look like child's play. But not a witness could be found who admitted to knowing anything about Triads or any other criminal outfit.

Not surprisingly, by the time Saturday came round and Jerry was on his way to Happy Valley races, he possessed quite a detailed portrait of his quarry.

The taxi charged double because it was the races and Jerry paid because he knew it was the form. He had told Craw he was going and Craw had not objected. He had brought Luke along for the ride, knowing that sometimes two are less conspicuous than one. He was nervous of bumping into Frost, because roundeye Hong Kong is a very small city indeed. At the main entrance he telephoned the management to raise some influence, and in due course a Captain Grant appeared, a young official to whom Jerry explained that this was work: he was writing the place up for the comic. Grant was a witty, elegant man who smoked Turkish cigarettes through a holder, and everything Jerry said seemed to amuse him in a fond, if rather remote way.

'You're the son, then,' he said finally.

'Did you know him?' said Jerry grinning.

'Only *of* him,' Captain Grant replied, but he seemed to like what he had heard.

He gave them badges, and offered them drinks later. The second race was just over. While they talked, they heard the roar of the crowd set-to and rise and die like an avalanche. Waiting for the lift Jerry checked the noticeboard to see who had taken the private boxes. The hardy annuals were the Peak mafia: The Bank – as the Hong Kong and Shanghai Bank like to call itself – Jardine Matheson, the Governor, the Commander British Forces. Mr Drake Ko, OBE, though a Steward of the Club, was not among them.

'Westerby! Good *God*, man, who the hell ever let you in here? Listen, is it true your dad went bust before he died?'

Jerry hesitated, grinning, then belatedly drew the card from his memory: Clive Somebody, pigs-in-clover solicitor, house in Repulse Bay, overpowering Scot, all false affability and an open reputation for crookedness. Jerry had used him for background in a Macao-based gold swindle and concluded that Clive had had a slice of the cake.

'Gosh, Clive, super, marvellous.'

They exchanged banalities, still waiting for the lift.

'Here. Give us your card. Come on! I'll make your forture yet.' *Porton*, thought Jerry: Clive Porton. Tearing the racecard from Jerry's hand, Porton licked his big thumb, turned to a centre page and ringed a horse's name in ballpoint. 'Number seven in the third, you can't go wrong,' he breathed. 'Put your shirt on it, okay? Not every day I give away money, I'll tell you.'

'What did the slob sell you?' Luke enquired, when they were clear of him.

'Thing called Open Space.'

Their ways divided. Luke went off to place bets and wangle his way into the American Club upstairs. Jerry on an impulse took a hundred dollars' worth of Lucky Nelson and set a hasty course for the Hong Kong Club's luncheon room. 'If I lose,' he thought drily, 'I'll chalk it up to George.' The double doors were open and he walked straight in. The atmosphere was of dowdy wealth: a Surrey golf club on a wet weekend, except that those brave enough to risk the pickpockets wore real jewels. A group of wives sat apart, like expensive unused equipment, scowling at the closed-circuit television and moaning about servants and muggings. There was a smell of cigar smoke and sweat and departed food. Seeing him shamble in – the awful suit, the buckskin boots, 'Press' written all over him – their scowls darkened. The trouble with being exclusive in Hong Kong, their faces said, was that not enough people are thrown out. A school of serious drinkers had gathered at the bar, mainly carpet-baggers from the London merchant banks with beer-bellies and fat necks before their time. With them, the Jardine Matheson second eleven, not yet grand enough for the firm's private box: groomed, unlovable innocents for whom Heaven was money and promotion. Apprehensively, he glanced round for Frostie, but either the gee-gees hadn't drawn him today, or he was with some other crowd. With one grin and one vague flap of the hand for all of them, Jerry winkled out the under-manager, saluted him like a lost friend, talked airily of Captain Grant, slipped him twenty bucks for himself, signed up for the day in defiance of every regulation, and stepped gratefully on to the balcony with still eighteen minutes before the off: sun, the stink of dung, the feral rumble of a Chinese crowd, and Jerry's own quickening heartbeat that whispered 'horses'.

For a moment, Jerry hung there, grinning, taking in the view, because every time he saw it was the first time.

The grass at Happy Valley racecourse must be the most valuable crop on earth. There was very little of it. A narrow ring ran round the edge of what looked like a London borough recreation ground which sun and feet have beaten into dirt. Eight scuffed football pitches, one rugger pitch, one hockey, gave an air of municipal neglect. But the thin green ribbon which surrounded this dingy package in that year alone was likely to attract a cool hundred million sterling through legal betting, and the same amount again in the shade. The place was less a valley than a firebowl: glistening white stadium one side, brown hills the other, while ahead of Jerry and to his left lurked the other Hong Kong: a cardhouse Manhattan of grey sky-scraper slums crammed so tight they seemed to lean on one another in the heat. From each tiny balcony a bamboo pole stuck out like a pin put in to brace the structure. From each pole hung innumerable flags of black laundry, as if something huge had brushed against the building, leaving these tatters in its wake. It was from places like these, for all but the tiniest few that day, that Happy Valley offered the gambler's dream of instantaneous salvation.

Away to the right of Jerry shone newer, grander buildings. There, he remembered, the illegal bookies pitched their offices and by a dozen arcane methods – tic-tac, walkie-talkie, flashing lights – Sarratt would have been entranced by them – kept up their dialogue with legmen round the course. Higher again ran the spines of shaven hilltop slashed by quarries and littered with the ironmongery of electronic eavesdropping. Jerry had heard some-where that the saucers had been put there for the Cousins, so that they could track the sponsored over-flights of Taiwanese U2s. Above the hills, dump-lings of white cloud which no weather ever seemed to clear away. And above the cloud, that day, the bleached China sky aching in the sun, and one hawk slowly wheeling. All this, Jerry took in at a single grateful draught.

For the crowd it was the aimless time. The focus of attention, if anywhere, was the four fat Chinese women in fringed Hakka hats and black pyjama suits who were marching down the track with rakes, pricking the precious grass where the galloping hoofs had mussed it. They moved with the dignity of total indifference: it was as if the whole of Chinese peasantry were depicted in their gestures. For a second, in the way crowds have, a tremor of collective affinity reached out to them, and was forgotten.

The betting put Clive Porton's Open Space third favourite. Drake Ko's Lucky Nelson was in with the field at forty to one, which meant nowhere. Edging his way past a bunch of festive Australians, Jerry reached the corner of the balcony and, craning, peered over the tiers of heads to the owners' box, cut off from the common people by a green iron gate and a security guard. Shading his eyes and wishing he had brought binoculars, he made out one fat, hard-looking man in a suit and dark glasses, accompanied by a young and very pretty girl. He looked half Chinese, half Latin, and Jerry put him down as Filipino. The girl was the best that money could buy.

Must be with his horse, thought Jerry, recalling old Sambo. Most likely in the paddock, briefing his trainer and the jockey.

Striding back through the luncheon room to the main lobby, he dropped into a wide-back stairway for two floors and crossed a hall to the viewing gallery, which was filled with a vast and thoughtful Chinese crowd, all men, staring downward in devotional silence into a covered sandpit filled with noisy sparrows and three horses, each led by his permanent male groom, the mafoo. The mafoos held their charges miserably, as if sick with nerves. The elegant Captain Grant was looking on, so was an old White Russian trainer called Sacha whom Jerry loved. Sacha sat on a tiny folding chair, leaning slightly forward as if he were fishing. Sacha had trained Mongolian ponies in the treaty days of Shanghai, and Jerry could listen to him all night: how Shanghai had three race-courses, British, International and Chinese; how the British merchant princes kept sixty, even a hundred horses a-piece and sailed them up and down the coast, competing like madmen with each other from port to port. Sacha was a gentle, philosophical fellow with faraway blue eyes and an all-in wrestler's jaw. He was also the trainer of Lucky Nelson. He sat alone, watching what Jerry took to be a doorway out of his own line of sight.

A sudden hubbub from the stands caused Jerry to turn sharply toward the sunlight. A roar sounded, then one high, strangled shriek as the crowd on one tier swayed and an axehead of grey and black uniforms tore into it. An instant later and a swarm of police was dragging some wretched pickpocket, bleeding and coughing, into the tunnel stairway for a voluntary statement. Dazzled, Jerry returned his gaze to the interior darkness of the sand-paddock, and took a moment to focus on the fogged outline of Mr Drake Ko.

The identification was nowhere near immediate. The first person Jerry noticed was not Ko at all, but the young Chinese jockey standing at old Sacha's side, tall boy, thin as wire where his silks were nipped into his breeches. He was slapping his whip against his boot as if he had seen the gesture in an English sporting print, and he was wearing Ko's colours ('sky blue and sea-grey quartered' said the article in *Golden Orient*) and like Sacha he was staring at something out of Jerry's sight. Next from under the platform where Jerry stood, came a bay griffin, led by a giggly fat mafoo in filthy grey overalls. His number was hidden by a rug, but Jerry knew the horse already from its photograph, and he knew it even better now: he knew it really well, in fact. There are some horses that are simply superior to their class, and Lucky Nelson to Jerry's eye was one. Bit of quality, he thought, nice long rein, a bold eye. None of your jail-bait chestnut with a light mane and tail that take the women's vote in every race: given the local form, which is heavily restricted by the climate, Lucky Nelson was as sound as anything he'd seen here. Jerry was sure of it. For one bad moment he was anxious about the horse's condition: sweating, too much gloss on the flanks and quarters. Then he looked again at the bold eye, and his heart rose again: cunning devil's had him hosed down to make him look poorly, he thought, in joyous memory of old Sambo.

It was only at that late point, therefore, that Jerry moved his eye from the horse to its owner.

Mr Drake Ko, OBE, the recipient to date of a cool half million of Moscow Centre's American dollars, the avowed supporter of Chiang Mao-shek, stood apart from everyone, in the shadow of a white concrete pillar ten feet in diameter: an ugly but inoffensive figure at first glance, tall, with a stoop that should have been occupational: a dentist or a cobbler. He was dressed in an English way, in baggy grey flannels and a black double-breasted blazer too long in the waist, so that it emphasized the disjointedness of his legs and gave a crumpled look to his spare body. His face and neck were as polished as old leather and as hairless, and the many creases looked sharp as ironed pleats. His complexion was darker than Jerry had expected: he would almost have suspected Arab or Indian blood. He wore the same unsuitable hat of the photograph, a dark blue beret, and his ears stuck out from under it like pastry roses. His very narrow eyes were stretched still finer by its pressure. Brown Italian shoes, white shirt, open neck. No props, not even binoculars: but a marvellous half-million-dollar smile, ear to ear, partly gold, that seemed to relish everyone's good fortune as well as his own.

Except that there was a hint – some men have it, it is like a tension: headwaiters, doormen, journalists can spot it at a glance; old Sambo *almost* had it – there was a hint of resources instantly available. If things were needed, hidden people would bring them at the double.

The picture sprang to life. Over the loudspeaker the clerk of the course ordered the jockeys to mount. The giggly mafoo pulled off the rug, and Jerry to his pleasure noticed that Ko had had the bay's coat back-brushed to emphasize his supposedly poor condition. The thin jockey made the long, awkward journey to the saddle, and with nervous friendliness called down to Ko on the other side of him. Ko, already moving away, swung round and snapped something back, one inaudible syllable, without looking where he spoke or who picked it up. A rebuke? An encouragement? An order to a servant? The smile had lost none of its exuberance, but the voice was as hard as a whipcrack. Horse and rider took their leave. Ko took his, Jerry raced back up the stairs, through the lunch room to the balcony, waded to the corner, and looked down.

By then, Ko was no longer alone, but married.

Whether they arrived together on the stand, whether she followed him at a moment's distance, Jerry was never sure. She was so small. He spotted a glitter of black silk and a movement round it as men deferred – the stand was filling up – but at first he looked too high and missed her. Her head was at the level of their chests. He picked her up again at Ko's side, a tiny, immaculate Chinese wife, sovereign, elderly, pale, so groomed you could never imagine she had been any other age or worn any clothes but these Paris-tailored black silks, frogged and brocaded like a hussar's. *Wife's a handful,* Craw had said, extemporizing as they sat bemused in front of the tiny projector. *Pinches from the big stores. Ko's people have to get in ahead of her and promise to pay for whatever she nicks.*

The article in *Golden Orient* referred to her as 'an early business partner'. Reading between the lines, Jerry guessed she'd been one of the girls at the Ritz Ballroom.

The crowd's roar had gathered throat.

'Did you do him, Westerby? Did you do him, man?' Scottish Clive Porton was bearing down on him, sweating heavily from drink. 'Open Space, for God's sake! Even at those odds you'll make a dollar or two! Go on man, it's a cert!'

The 'off' spared him a reply. The roar choked, lifted and swelled. All round him a pitter-patter of names and numbers fluttered in the stands, the horses sprang from their traps, drawn forward by the din. The first lazy furlong had begun. Wait; frenzy will follow the inertia. In the dawn light when they train, Jerry remembered, their hoofs are muffled in order to spare the residents their slumbers. Sometimes in the old days, drying out between war stories, Jerry would get up early and come down here just to watch them, and if he was lucky, and found an influential friend, go back with them to the airconditioned, multi-storey stables where they lived, to watch the grooming and the cosseting. Whereas by day the howl of traffic drowned their thunder entirely and the glittering cluster that advanced so slowly made no sound at all, but floated on the thin emerald river.

'Open Space all the way,' Clive Porton announced uncertainly, as he watched through his glasses. 'The favourite's done it. Splendid. Well done, Open Space, well done, lad.' They began the long turn before the final straight. '*Come* on Open Space, stretch for it man, *ride!* Use your whip, you cretin!' Porton screamed, for by now it was clear even to the naked eye that the sky blue and sea-grey colours of Lucky Nelson were heading for the front, and that his competitors were courteously making way for him. A second horse put up a show of challenging, then flagged, but Open Space was already three lengths behind while his jockey worked furiously with his whip on the air around his mount's quarters.

'Objection!' Porton was shouting. 'Where's the Stewards for God's sake? That horse was pulled! I never saw a horse so pulled in my life!'

As Lucky Nelson loped gracefully past the post, Jerry quickly turned his gaze to the right again, and down. Ko appeared unmoved. It was not oriental unscrutability: Jerry had never subscribed to that myth. Certainly it was not indifference. It was merely that he was observing the satisfactory unfolding of a ceremony: Mr Drake Ko watches a march-past of his troops. His little mad wife stood poker-backed beside him as if, after all the struggles of her life, they were finally playing her anthem. For a second Jerry was reminded of old Pet in her prime. Just the way Pet looked, thought Jerry, when Sambo's pride came in a good eighteenth. Just the way she stood, and coped with failure.

The presentation was a moment for dreams.

While the scene lacked a cake-stall, the sunshine was certainly far beyond the expectation of the most sanguine organizer of an English village fête; and the silver cups were a great deal more lavish than the scratched little beaker presented by the squire for excellence in the three-legged race. The sixty uniformed policemen were also perhaps a trifle ostentatious. But the gracious lady in a nineteen-thirties turban who presided over the long white table was as mawkish and arrogant as the most exacting patriot would have wished. She knew the form exactly. The Chairman of the Stewards handed her the cup and she quickly held it away from her as if it were too hot for her hands. Drake Ko and his wife, both grinning hugely, Ko still in his beret, emerged from a cluster of delighted supporters and grabbed the cup, but they tripped so fast and merrily back and forth across the roped-off patch of grass that the photographer was caught unprepared and had to ask the actors to re-stage the moment of consummation. This annoyed the gracious lady quite a lot, and Jerry caught the words 'bloody bore' drawled over the chatter of the onlookers. The cup was finally Ko's, the gracious lady took sullen delivery of six hundred dollars' worth of gardenias, East and West returned gratefully to their separate cantonments.

'Do him?' Captain Grant enquired amiably. They were sauntering back toward the stands.

'Well, *yes*, actually,' Jerry confessed with a grin. 'Bit of a turn-up, wasn't it?'

'Oh, it was Drake's race, all right,' said Grant drily. They walked a little. 'Clever of you to spot it. More than we did. Do you want to talk to him?'

'Talk to who?'

'Ko. While he's flushed with victory. Perhaps you'll get something out of him for once,' said Grant with that fond smile. 'Come, I'll introduce you.'

Jerry did not falter. As a reporter he had every reason to say 'yes'. As a spy – well, sometimes they say at Sarratt that nothing is insecure but that thinking makes it so. They sauntered back to the group. The Ko party had formed a rough circle round the cup and the laughter was very loud. At the centre, closest to Ko, stood the fat Filipino with his beautiful girl, and Ko was clowning with the girl, kissing her on both cheeks, then kissing her again, while everyone laughed except Ko's wife, who withdrew deliberately to the edge and began talking to a Chinese woman her own age.

'That's Arpego,' said Grant in Jerry's ear and indicated the fat Filipino. 'He owns Manila and most of the out-islands.'

Arpego's paunch sat forward over his belt like a rock stuffed inside his shirt.

Grant did not make straight for Ko, but singled out a burly bland-faced Chinese of forty in an electric blue suit, who seemed to be some kind of aide. Jerry stood off, waiting. The plump Chinese came over to him, Grant at his side.

'This is Mr Tiu,' said Grant quietly. 'Mr Tiu, meet Mr Westerby, son of the famous one.'

'You wanna talk to Mr Ko, Mr Wessby?'

'If it's convenient.'

'Sure it's convenient,' said Tiu euphorically. His chubby hands floated restlessly in front of his stomach. He wore a gold watch on his right wrist. His fingers were curled, as if to scoop water. He was sleek and shiny and he could have been thirty or sixty. 'Mr Ko win a horse-race, everything's convenient. I bring him over. Stay here. What's your father's name?'

'Samuel,' said Jerry.

'*Lord* Samuel,' said Grant firmly, and inaccurately.

'Who is he?' Jerry asked aside, as plump Tiu returned to the noisy Chinese group.

'Ko's majordomo. Manager, chief bag carrier, bottle washer, fixer. Been with him since the start. They ran away from the Japanese together in the war.'

And his chief crusher too, Jerry thought, watching Tiu waddling back with his master.

Grant began again with the introductions.

'Sir,' he said, 'this is Westerby, whose famous father, the Lord, had a lot of very slow horses. He also bought several race-courses for the bookmakers.'

'What paper?' said Ko. His voice was harsh and powerful and deep, yet to Jerry's surprise he could have sworn he caught a trace of an English North Country accent, reminiscent of old Pet's.

Jerry told him.

'That the paper with the girls!' Ko yelled gaily. 'I used to read that paper when I was in London, during my residence there for the purpose of legal study at the famous Gray's Inn of Court. Do you know why I read your paper Mr Westerby? It is my sound opinion that the more papers which are printing pretty girls in preference to politics today, the more chance we get of a damn sight better world, Mr Westerby,' Ko declared, in a vigorous mixture of misused and boardroom English. 'Kindly tell that to your paper from me, Mr Westerby. I give it to you as free advice.'

With a laugh, Jerry opened his notebook.

'I backed your horse, Mr Ko. How does it feel to win?'

'Better than losing, I think.'

'Doesn't it wear off?'

'I like it better every time.'

'Does the same go for business.'

'Naturally.'

'Can I speak to Mrs Ko?'

'She's busy.'

Jotting, Jerry was disconcerted by a familiar smell. It was of a musky, very pungent French soap, a blend of almonds and rosewater favoured by an early wife: but also, apparently, by the shiny Tiu for his greater allure.

'What's your formula for winning, Mr Ko?'

'Hard work. No politics. Plenty sleep.'

'Are you a lot richer than you were ten minutes ago?'

'I was pretty rich ten minutes ago. You may tell your paper also I am a great admirer of the British way of life.'

'Even though we don't work hard? And make a lot of politics?'

'Just tell them,' Ko said, straight at him, and that was an order.

'What makes you so lucky, Mr Ko?'

There was a long silence.

Ko appeared not to hear this question, except that his smile slowly vanished. He was staring straight at Jerry, measuring him through his very narrow eyes, and his face hardened remarkably.

'What makes you so lucky, sir?' Jerry repeated.

'No comment,' Ko said, still into Jerry's face.

The temptation to press the question had become irresistible. 'Play fair, Mr Ko,' Jerry urged, grinning largely. 'The world's full of people who dream of being as rich as you are. Give them a clue, won't you? What makes you so lucky?'

'Mind your own damn business,' Ko told him, and without the smallest ceremony turned his back on him and walked away. At the same moment, Tiu took a leisurely half pace forward, arresting Jerry's line of advance, with one soft hand on his upper arm.

'You going to win next time round, Mr Ko?' Jerry called over Tiu's shoulder at his departing back.

'You better ask the horse, Mr Wessby,' Tiu suggested with a chubby smile, hand on Jerry's arm.

He might as well have done so, for Ko had already rejoined his friend Mr Arpego, the Filipino, and they were laughing and talking just as before. *Drake Ko was very tough boy*, Jerry remembered. *You don't tell no fairy story to Drake Ko.* Tiu doesn't do so badly either, he thought.

As they walked back toward the grandstand, Grant was laughing quietly to himself.

'Last time Ko won he wouldn't even lead the horse into the paddock after the race,' he recalled. 'Waved it away. Didn't want it.'

'Why the hell not?'

'Hadn't expected it to win, that's why. Hadn't told his Chiu Chow friends. Bad face. Maybe he felt the same when you asked him about his luck.'

'How did he get to be a Steward?'

'Oh, had Tiu buy the votes for him, no doubt. The usual thing. Cheers. Don't forget your winnings.'

Then it happened: Ace Westerby's unforeseen scoop.

The last race was over, Jerry was four thousand dollars to the good and Luke had disappeared. Jerry tried the American Club, Club Lusitano and a couple of others, but either they hadn't seen him or they'd thrown him out. From the enclosure there was only one gate, so Jerry joined the march. The traffic was chaotic. Rolls-Royces and Mercedes vied for kerb space and the crowds were shoving from behind. Deciding not to join the fight for taxis, Jerry started along the narrow pavement and saw to his surprise Drake Ko, alone, emerging from a gateway across the road, and for the first time since Jerry had set eyes on him he was not smiling. Reaching the roadside, he seemed undecided whether to cross, then settled for where he was, gazing at the on-coming traffic. He's waiting for the Rolls-Royce Phantom, thought Jerry, remembering the fleet in the garage at Headland Road. Or the Merc, or the Chrysler. Suddenly Jerry saw him whip off the beret and, clowning, hold it into the road, as if to draw rifle fire. The wrinkles flew up around his eyes and jaw, his gold teeth glittered in welcome and instead of a Rolls-Royce, or a Merc, or a Chrysler, a long red Jaguar E-Type with a soft top folded back screeched to a stop beside him, oblivious of the other cars. Jerry couldn't have missed it if he'd wanted to. The noise of the tyres alone turned every head along the pavement. His eye read the number, his mind recorded it. Ko climbed aboard with all the excitement of someone who might never have ridden in an open car before, and he was already talking and laughing before they pulled away. But not before Jerry had seen the driver, her fluttering blue headscarf, dark glasses, long blonde hair, and enough of her body, as she leaned across Drake to lock his door, to know that she was a hell of a lot of woman. Drake's hand was resting on her bare back, fingers splayed, his spare hand was waving about while he no doubt gave her a blow-by-blow account of his victory, and as they set off together he planted a very un-Chinese kiss on her cheek, and then, for good measure, two more: but all, somehow, with a great deal more sincerity than he had brought to the business of kissing Mr Arpego's escort.

On the other side of the road stood the gateway Ko had just come out of, and the iron gate was still open. His mind spinning, Jerry dodged the traffic and walked through. He was in the old Colonial Cemetery, a lush place, scented with flowers and shaded by heavy overhanging trees. Jerry had never been here and he was shocked to enter such seclusion. It was built up an opposing slope round an old chapel that was gently falling into disuse. Its cracking walls glinted in the speckled evening light. Beside it, from a chickenwire kennel, an emaciated Alsatian dog howled at him in fury.

Jerry peered round, not knowing why he was here or what he was looking for. The graves were of all ages and races and sects. There were White Russian graves and their orthodox headstones were dark and scrolled with Czarist grandeur. Jerry imagined heavy snow on them and their shape still coming through. Another stone described a restless sojourn of a Russian princess and Jerry paused to read it: Tallin to Peking, with dates, Peking to Shanghai, dates again, to Hong Kong in forty-nine to die. 'And estates in Sverdlovsk', the inscription ended defiantly. Was Shanghai the connection?

He rejoined the living: three old men in blue pyjama suits sat on a shaded bench, not talking. They had hung their cage-birds in the branches overhead, close enough to hear one another's song above the noise of traffic and

cicadas. Two gravediggers in steel helmets were filling a new grave. No
mourners watched. Still not knowing what he wanted, he reached the chapel
steps. He peered through the door. Inside was pitch dark after the sunlight.
An old woman glared at him. He drew back. The Alsatian dog howled at him
still louder. It was very young. A sign said 'Verger' and he followed it. The
shriek of the cicadas was deafening, even drowning the dog's barking. The
scent of flowers was steamy and a little rotten. An idea had struck him, almost
an intimation. He was determined to pursue it.

The verger was a kindly distant man and spoke no English. The ledgers
were very old, the entries resembled ancient bank accounts. Jerry sat at a desk
slowly turning the heavy pages, reading the names, the dates of birth, death,
and burial; lastly the map reference: the zone, and the number. Having
found what he was looking for, he stepped into the air again, and made his
way along a different path, through a cloud of butterflies, up the hill toward
the cliff-side. A bunch of schoolgirls watched him from a footbridge,
giggling. He took off his jacket and trailed it over his shoulder. He passed
between high shrubs and entered a slanted coppice of yellow grass where the
headstones were very small, the mounds only a foot or two long. Jerry sidled
past them, reading the numbers, till he found himself in front of a low iron
gate marked seven two eight. The gate was part of a rectangular perimeter,
and as Jerry lifted his eyes he found himself looking at the statue of a small
boy in Victorian knickerbockers and an Eton jacket, life size, with tousled
stone curls and rosebud stone lips, reading or singing from an open stone
book while real butterflies dived giddily round his head. He was an entirely
English child, and the inscription read *Nelson Ko in loving memory*. A lot of
dates followed, and it took Jerry a second to understand their meaning: ten
successive years with none left out and the last 1968. Then he realized they
were the ten years the boy had lived, each one to be relished. On the bottom
step of the plinth lay a large bunch of orchids, still in their paper.

Ko was thanking Nelson for his win. Now at least Jerry understood why he
did not care to be invaded with questions about his luck.

There is a kind of fatigue, sometimes, which only fieldmen know: a
temptation to gentleness which can be the kiss of death. Jerry lingered a
moment longer, staring at the orchids and the stone boy, and setting them, in
his mind, beside everything he had seen and learned of Ko till now. And he
had an overwhelming feeling – only for a moment, but dangerous at any time
– of completeness, as if he had met a family, only to discover it was his own.
He had a feeling of arrival.

Here was a man, housed this way, married that way, striving and playing in
ways Jerry effortlessly understood. A man of no particular persuasion, yet
Jerry saw him in that moment more clearly than he had ever seen himself. A
Chiu Chow poor-boy who becomes a Jockey Club Steward with an OBE, and
hoses down his horse before a race. A Hakka water-gypsy who gives his child
a Baptist burial and an English effigy. A capitalist who hates politics. A failed
lawyer, a gangboss, a builder of hospitals who runs an opium airline, a
supporter of spirit temples who plays croquet and rides about in a Rolls-
Royce. An American bar in his Chinese garden, and Russian gold in his trust
account. Such complex and conflicting insights did not, at that moment,
alarm Jerry in the least; they presaged no foreboding or paradox. Rather, he
saw them welded by Ko's own harsh endeavour into a single but many-sided
man not too unlike old Sambo. Stronger still – for the few seconds that it
lasted – he had an irresistible feeling of being in good company, a thing he

had always liked. He returned to the gate in a mood of calm munificence, as if he, not Ko, had won the race. It was not till he reached the road that reality returned him to his senses.

The traffic had cleared and he found a taxi straight away. They had driven a hundred yards when he saw Luke performing lonely pirouettes along the kerb. Jerry coaxed him aboard and dumped him outside the Foreign Correspondent's Club. From the Furama Hotel he rang Craw's home number, let it ring twice, rang it again and heard Craw's voice demanding 'Who the bloody hell is that?' He asked for a Mr Savage, received a foul rebuke and the information that he was ringing the wrong number, allowed Craw half an hour to get to another phone, then walked over to the Hilton to field the return call.

Our friend had surfaced in person, Jerry told him. Been put on public view on account of a big win. When it was over a very nice blonde party gave him a lift in her sports car. Jerry recited the licence number. They were definitely friends, he said. Very demonstrative and un-Chinese. At *least* friends, he would say.

'Roundeye?'

'Of course she was bloody well roundeye! Who the hell ever heard of a –'

'Jesus,' said Craw softly, and rang off before Jerry even had a chance to tell him about little Nelson's shrine.

# EIGHT

## *the barons confer*

The waiting room of the pretty Foreign Office conference house in Carlton Gardens was slowly filling up. People in twos and threes, ignoring each other, like mourners for a funeral. A printed notice hung on the wall saying 'Warning, no confidential matter to be discussed'. Smiley and Guillam perched disconsolately beneath it, on a bench of salmon velvet. The room was oval, the style Ministry of Works rococo. Across the painted ceiling, Bacchus pursued nymphs who were a lot more willing to be caught than Molly Meakin. Empty firebuckets stood against the wall and two goverment messengers guarded the door to the interior. Outside the curved sash windows, autumn sunlight filled the park, making each leaf crisp against the next. Saul Enderby strode in, leading the Foreign Office contingent. Guillam knew him only by name. He was a former Ambassador to Indonesia, now chief pundit on South East Asian affairs, and said to be a great supporter of the American hard line. In tow, one obedient Parliamentary Under-Secretary, a trade union appointment, and one flowery, over-dressed figure who advanced on Smiley on tiptoe, hands held horizontal, as if he had caught him napping.

'Can it be?' he whispered exuberantly. 'Is it? It *is!* George Smiley, all in your feathers. My dear, you've lost simply pounds. Who's your nice boy? Don't tell me. Peter Guillam. I've heard all about him. *Quite* unspoilt by failure, I'm told.'

'Oh *no!*' Smiley cried involuntarily. 'Oh Lord. *Roddy.*'

'What do you mean? "Oh no. Oh Lord, Roddy,"' Martindale demanded, wholly undeterred, in the same vibrant murmur. '"Oh *yes*" is what you mean! "Yes, Roddy. Divine to see you, Roddy!" Listen. Before the riff-raff come. How is the exquisite Ann? For my very own ears. Can I make a dinner for the two of you? You shall choose the guests. How's that? And yes I *am* on the list, if that's what's been going through your ratlike little mind, young Peter Guillam, I've been translated, I'm a goodie, our new masters adore me. So they should, the fuss I've made of them.'

The interior doors opened with a bang. One of the messengers shouted 'Gentlemen!' and those who knew the form stood back to let the women file ahead. There were two. The men followed and Guillam brought up the tail. For a few yards it might have been the Circus: a makeshift bottleneck at which each face was checked by janitors, then a makeshift corridor leading to what resembled a builders' cabin parked at the centre of a gutted stairwell: except that it had no windows and was suspended from wires and held tight by guy-ropes. Guillam had lost sight of Smiley entirely, and as he climbed the hardboard steps and entered the safe room he saw only shadows hovering under a blue nightlight.

'Do *do* something, somebody,' Enderby growled in the tones of a bored diner complaining about the service. 'Lights, for God's sake. *Bloody* little men.'

The door slammed behind Guillam's back, a key turned in the lock, an electronic hum did the scale and whined out of earshot, three striplights stammered to life, drenching everyone in their sickly pallor.

'Hoorah,' said Enderby, and sat down. Later, Guillam wondered how he had been so sure it was Enderby calling in the darkness, but there are voices you can hear before they speak.

The conference table was covered in a ripped green baize like a billiards table in a youth club. The Foreign Office sat one end, the Colonial Office at the other. The separation was visceral rather than legal. For six years the two departments had been formally married under the grandiose awnings of the Diplomatic Service, but no one in his right mind took the union seriously. Guillam and Smiley sat at the centre, shoulder to shoulder, each with empty chairs to the other side of him. Examining the cast, Guillam was absurdly aware of costume. The Foreign Office had come sharply dressed in charcoal suit and the secret plumage of privilege: both Enderby and Martindale wore Old Etonian ties. The Colonialists had the homeweave look of country people come to town, and the best they could offer in the way of ties was one Royal Artilleryman: honest Wilbraham, their leader, a fit lean schoolmasterly figure with crimson veins on his weatherbeaten cheeks. A tranquil woman in church-organ brown supported him, and to the other side a freshly-minted boy with freckles and a shock of ginger hair. The rest of the committee sat across from Smiley and Guillam, and had the air of seconds in a duel they disapproved of and they had come in twos for protection: dark Pretorius of the Security Service with one nameless woman bag-carrier; two pale warriors from Defence; two Treasury bankers, one of them Welsh Hammer. Oliver Lacon was alone and had set himself apart from everyone, for all the world the person least engaged. Before each pair of hands lay Smiley's submission in a pink and red folder marked 'Top Secret Withhold', like a souvenir programme. The 'withhold' meant keep it away from the Cousins. Smiley had drafted it, the mothers had typed it, Guillam himself had watched the eighteen pages come off the duplicators and supervised the hand-stitching of the twenty-four copies. Now their handiwork lay tossed around this large table, among the water glasses and the ashtrays. Lifting a copy six inches above the table, Enderby let it fall with a slap.

'All read it?' he asked. All had.

'Then let's go,' said Enderby and peered round the table with bloodshot, arrogant eyes. 'Who'll start the bowling? Oliver? You got us here. You shoot first.'

It crossed Guillam's mind that Martindale, the great scourge of the Circus and its works, was curiously subdued. His eyes were turned dutifully to Enderby, and his mouth sagged unhappily.

Lacon meanwhile was setting out his defences. 'Let me say first that I'm as much taken by surprise in this as anyone else,' he said. 'This is a real body-blow, George. It would have been helpful to have had a little preparation. It's a little uncomfortable for *me*, I have to tell you, to be the link to a service which has rather cut its links of late.'

Wilbraham said 'hear, hear.' Smiley preserved a Mandarin silence. Pretorius of the competition frowned in agreement.

'It also comes at an awkward time,' Lacon added portentously. 'I mean the thesis, your thesis *alone*, is – well, momentous. A lot to swallow. A lot to face up to, George.'

Having thus secured his back way out, Lacon made a show of pretending there might not be a bomb under the bed at all.

'Let me try to summarize the summary. May I do that? In bald terms, George. A prominent Hong Kong Chinese citizen is under suspicion of being a Russian spy. That's the nub?'

'He is known to receive very large Russian subventions,' Smiley corrected him, but talking to his hands.

'From a secret fund devoted to financing penetration agents?'

'Yes.'

'*Solely* for financing them? Or does this fund have other uses?'

'To the best of our knowledge it has no other use at all,' said Smiley in the same lapidary tone as before.

'Such as – propaganda – the informal promotion of trade – kickbacks, that kind of thing? No?'

'To the best of our knowledge: no,' Smiley repeated.

'Ah but how good's their knowledge?' Wilbraham called from below the salt. 'Hasn't been too good in the past, has it?'

'You see what I'm getting at?' Lacon asked.

'We would want *far* more corroboration,' the Colonial lady in church brown said, with a heartening smile.

'So would we,' Smiley agreed mildly. One or two heads lifted in surprise. 'It is in order to obtain corroboration that we are asking for rights and permissions.'

Lacon resumed the initiative.

'Accept your thesis for a moment. A secret intelligence fund, all much as you say.'

Smiley gave a remote nod.

'Is there any suggestion that he subverts the Colony?'

'No.'

Lacon glanced at his notes. It occurred to Guillam that he had done a lot of homework.

'He is not, for example, preaching the withdrawal of their sterling reserves from London? Which would put us a further nine hundred million pounds in the red?'

'To my knowledge: no.'

'He is not telling us to get off the Island. He is not whipping up riots or urging amalgamation with the Mainland, or waving the wretched treaty in our faces?'

'Not that we know.'

'He's not a leveller. He's not demanding effective trade unions, or a free vote, or a minimum wage, or compulsory education, or racial equality, or a separate parliament for the Chinese instead of their tame assemblies, whatever they're called?'

'Legco and Exco,' Wilbraham snapped. 'And they're not tame.'

'No, he isn't,' said Smiley.

'Then what *is* he doing?' Wilbraham interrupted excitedly. 'Nothing. That's the answer. They've got it all wrong. It's a goose-chase.'

'For what it's worth,' Lacon proceeded, as if he hadn't heard, 'he probably does as much to enrich the Colony as any other wealthy and respected Chinese businessman. Or as little. He dines with the Governor, but he is not known to rifle the contents of his safe, I assume. In fact, to all outward purposes, he is something of a Hong Kong prototype: Steward of the Jockey Club, supports the charities, pillar of the integrated society, successful, benevolent, has the wealth of Croesus and the commercial morality of the whorehouse.'

'I say, that's a bit hard!' Wilbraham objected. 'Steady on, Oliver. Remember the new housing estates.'

Again Lacon ignored him.

'Short of the Victoria Cross, a war disability pension and a baronetcy, therefore, it is hard to see how he could be a less suitable subject for harassment by a British service, or recruitment by a Russian one.'

'In my world we call that good cover,' said Smiley.

'*Touché*, Oliver,' said Enderby with satisfaction.

'Oh everything's cover these days,' said Wilbraham mournfully, but it didn't get Lacon off the hook.

Round one to Smiley, thought Guillam in delight, recalling the dreadful Ascot dinner: *Hitty-pitty within the wall, and bumps goes Pottifer*, he chanted inwardly, with due acknowledgement to his hostess.

'Hammer?' said Enderby, and the Treasury had a brief fling in which Smiley was hauled over the coals for his financial accounts, but no one except the Treasury seemed to find Smiley's transgression relevant.

'This is not the purpose for which you were granted a secret float,' Hammer kept insisting in Welsh outrage. 'That was post mortem funds only –'

'Fine, fine, so Georgie's been a naughty boy,' Enderby interrupted in the end, closing him down. 'Has he thrown his money down the drain, or has he made a cheap killing? That's the question. Chris, time the Empire had its shout.'

Thus bidden, Colonial Wilbraham formally took the floor, backed by his lady in church brown and his red-haired assistant, whose young face was already set bravely in protection of his headmaster.

Wilbraham was one of those men who are unconscious of how much time they take to think. 'Yes,' he began after an age. 'Yes. Yes, well I'd like to stay with the money, if I may, much as Lacon did, to begin with.' It was already clear that he regarded the submission as an assault upon his territory. 'Since the money is all we've got to go on,' he remarked pointedly, turning back a page in his folder. 'Yes.' And there followed another interminable hiatus. 'You say here the money first of all came from Paris through Vientiane.' Pause. 'Then the Russians switched systems, so to speak, and it was paid through a different channel altogether. A Hamburg-Vienna-Hong Kong tie-up. Endless complexities, subterfuges, all that – we'll take your word for it – right? Same amount, different hat, so to speak. Right. Now why d'you think they did that, so to speak?'

*So to speak*, Guillam recorded, who was very susceptible to verbal ticks.

'It is sensible practice to vary the routine from time to time,' Smiley replied, repeating the explanation he had already offered in the submission.

'*Tradecraft*, Chris,' Enderby put in, who liked his bit of jargon, and Martindale, still *piano*, shot him a glance of admiration.

Again Wilbraham slowly wound himself up.

'We've got to be guided by what Ko *does*,' Wilbraham declared, with puzzled fervour, and rattled his knuckles on the baize table. 'Not by what he *gets*. That's my argument. After all, I mean dash it, it's not Ko's own money is it? Legally it's nothing to do with him.' The point caused a moment's puzzled silence. 'Page two, top. Money's all in trust.' A general shuffle as everyone but Smiley and Guillam reached for their folders. 'I mean, not only is none of it being *spent*, which in itself is jolly odd – I'll come to that in a bit – it's *not Ko's money*. It's in trust, and when the claimant comes along, whoever he or she is, it will be the claimant's money. Till then it's the trust's money. So to speak. So, I mean, *what's Ko done wrong*? Opened a trust? No law against that. Done every day. Specially in Hong Kong. The *beneficiary* of the trust – oh, well, he could be anywhere! In Moscow, or Timbuctoo or –' He didn't seem able to think of a third place, so he dried up, to the discomfort of his ginger-headed assistant, who scowled straight at Guillam as if to challenge him. 'Point is: what's against Ko?'

Enderby was holding a matchstick to his mouth, and rolling it between his front teeth. Conscious, perhaps, that his adversary had made a good point badly – whereas his own speciality tended to be the reverse – he took it out and contemplated the wet end.

'Hell's all this balls about *thumbprints*, George?' he asked, perhaps in an effort to deflate Wilbraham's success. 'Like something out of Phillips Oppenheim.'

*Belgravia Cockney*, thought Guillam: the last stage of linguistic collapse.

Smiley's answers contained about as much emotion as a speaking clock.

'The use of thumbprints is old banking practice along the China coast. It dates from the days of widespread illiteracy. Many overseas Chinese prefer to use British banks rather than their own, and the structure of this account is by

no means extraordinary. The beneficiary is not named, but identifies himself
by a visual means, such as the torn half of a banknote, or in this case his left
thumbprint on the assumption that it is less worn by labour than the right.
The bank is unlikely to raise an eyebrow provided that whoever founded the
trust has indemnified the trustees against charges of accidental or wrongful
payment.'

'Thank you,' said Enderby, and did more delving with the matchstick.
'Could be Ko's *own* thumbprint, I suppose,' he suggested. 'Nothing to stop
him doing that, is there? *Then* it would be his money all right. If he's trustee
and beneficiary all at once, of *course* it's his own damn money.'

To Guillam, the issue had already taken a quite ludicrous wrong turning.

'That's pure supposition,' Wilbraham said after the usual two-minute
silence. 'Suppose Ko's doing a favour for a chum. Just suppose that for a
moment. And this chum's on the fiddle, so to speak, or doing business with
the Russians at several removes. Your Chinese *loves* a conspiracy. Get up to *all*
the tricks, even the nicest of 'em. Ko's no different, I'll be bound.'

Speaking for the first time, the red-haired boy ventured direct support.

'The submission rests on a fallacy,' he declared bluntly, speaking at this
stage more to Guillam than to Smiley. Sixth-form puritan, thought Guillam:
thinks sex weakens you and spying is immoral. '*You* say Ko is on the Russian
payroll. *We* say that's not demonstrated. We say the trust *may* contain Russian
money, but that Ko and the trust are separate entities.' In his indignation he
went on too long. 'You're talking about guilt, whereas *we* say Ko's done
nothing wrong under Hong Kong law and should enjoy the rights of a
Colonial subject.'

Several voices pounced at once. Lacon's won. 'No one is talking about guilt,'
he retorted. 'Guilt doesn't enter into it in the least degree. We're talking about
security. Solely. Security and the desirability or otherwise of investigating an
apparent threat.'

Welsh Hammer's Treasury colleague was a bleak Scot, as it turned out, with
a style as bald as the sixth-former's.

'Nobody's sizing up to infringe Ko's Colonial rights either,' he snapped. 'He
hasn't any. There's nothing in Hong Kong law *whatever* which says the
Governor cannot steam open Mr Ko's mail, tap Mr Ko's telephone, suborn
his maid or bug his house to kingdom come. Nothing whatever. There are a
few other things the Governor can do too, if he feels like it.'

'Also speculative,' said Enderby, with a glance to Smiley. 'Circus has no
local facilities for those high-jinks and anyway in the circumstances they'd be
insecure.'

'They would be scandalous,' said the red-haired boy unwisely, and
Enderby's gourmet eye, yellowed by a lifetime's luncheons, lifted to him, and
marked him down for future treatment.

So that was the second, inconclusive skirmish. They hacked about in this
way till coffee break, no victor and no corpses. Round two a draw, Guillam
decided. He wondered despondently how many rounds there would be.

'What's it all about?' he asked Smiley under the buzz. 'They won't make it
go away by talking.'

'They have to reduce it to their own size,' Smiley explained uncritically.
Beyond that, he seemed bent on oriental self-effacement, and no prodding
from Guillam was going to shake him out of it. Enderby demanded fresh
ashtrays. The Parliamentary Under-Secretary said they should try to make
progress.

'Think what it's costing the taxpayer, just having us sit here,' he urged proudly. Lunch was still two hours away.

Opening round three, Enderby moved the ticklish issue of whether to advise the Hong Kong Government of the intelligence regarding Ko. This was impish of him, in Guillam's view, since the position of the shadow Colonial Office (as Enderby referred to as his homespun *confrères*) was still that there was no crisis, and consequently nothing for anyone to be advised of. But honest Wilbraham, failing to see the trap, walked into it and said:

'Of course we should advise Hong Kong! They're self-administering. We've no alternative.'

'Oliver?' said Enderby with the calm of a man who holds good cards. Lacon glanced up, clearly irritated at being drawn into the open. 'Oliver?' Enderby repeated.

'I'm *tempted* to reply that it's Smiley's case and Wilbraham's Colony and we should let them fight it out,' he said, remaining firmly on the fence.

Which left Smiley: 'Oh well, if it were the Governor and nobody else I could hardly object,' he said. 'That is, if you feel it's not too much for him,' he added dubiously, and Guillam saw the red-head stoke himself up again.

'Why the dickens should it be too much for the Governor?' Colonial Wilbraham demanded, genuinely perplexed. 'Experienced administrator, shrewd negotiator. Find his way through anything. Why's it too much?'

This time, it was Smiley who made the pause. 'He would have to encode and decode his own telegrams, of course,' he mused, as if he were even now working his way obliviously through all the implications. 'We couldn't have him cutting his staff in on the secret, naturally. That's asking too much of anyone. Personal code books – well we can fix him up with those, no doubt. Brush up his coding if he needs it. There is also the problem, I suppose, of the Governor being forced into the position of *agent provocateur* if he continues to receive Ko socially – which he obviously must. We can't frighten the game at this stage. Would he mind that? Perhaps not. Some people take to it quite naturally.' He glanced at Enderby.

Wilbraham was already expostulating. 'But good heavens, man – if Ko's a Russian spy, which we say he isn't anyway – if the Governor has him to dinner, and perfectly naturally, in confidence, commits some minor indiscretion – well, it's damned unfair. It could ruin the man's career. Let alone what it could do to the Colony! He *must* be told!'

Smiley looked sleepier than ever.

'Well of course if he's given to being indiscreet,' he murmured meekly, 'I suppose one *might* argue that he's not a suitable person to be informed anyway.'

In the icy silence Enderby once more languidly took the matchstick from his mouth.

'Bloody odd it would be, wouldn't it, Chris,' he called cheerfully down the table to Wilbraham, 'if Peking woke up one morning to the glad news that the Governor of Hong Kong, Queen's representative and what have you, head of the troops and so forth, made a point of entertaining Moscow's ace spy at his dinner table once a month. *And* gave him a medal for his trouble. *What's* he got so far? Not a K is it?'

'An OBE,' said somebody *sotto voce*.

'Poor chap. Still he's on his way, I suppose. He'll work his way up, same as we all do.'

Enderby, as it happened, had his knighthood already, whereas Wilbraham was stuck in the bulge, owing to the growing shortage of colonies.

'There is no case,' said Wilbraham stoutly, and laid a hairy hand flat over the lurid folder before him.

A free-for-all followed, to Guillam's ear an *intermezzo*, in which by tacit understanding the minor parts were allowed to chime in with irrelevant questions in order to get themselves a mention in the minutes. The Welsh Hammer wished to establish *here and now* what would happen to Moscow Centre's half-million dollars of reptile money if by any chance they fell into British hands. There could be no question of their simply being recycled through the Circus, he warned. Treasury would have sole rights. Was that clear?

It was clear, Smiley said.

Guillam began to discern a gulf. There were those who assumed, even if reluctantly, that the investigation was a *fait accompli*; and those who continued to fight a rearguard action against its taking place. Hammer, he noticed to his surprise, seemed reconciled to the investigation.

A string of questions on 'legal' and 'illegal' residencies, though wearisome, served to entrench the fear of a red peril. Luff the parliamentarian wanted the difference spelt out to him. Smiley patiently obliged. A 'legal' or 'above-the-line' resident, he said, was an intelligence officer living under official or semi-official protection. Since the Hong Kong Government, out of deference to Peking's sensitivities about Russia, had seen fit to banish all forms of Soviet representation from the Colony – embassy, consular, Tass, Radio Moscow, Novosti, Aeroflot, Intourist and the other flags of convenience which legals traditionally sailed under – then by definition it followed that any Soviet activity on the Colony had to be carried out by an illegal or below-the-line apparatus.

It was this presumption which had directed the efforts of the Circus's researchers toward discovering the replacement money-route, he said, avoiding the jargon 'goldseam'.

'Ah well, then, we've forced the Russians into it,' said Luff with satisfaction. 'We've only ourselves to thank. We victimize the Russians, they bite back. Well, who's surprised by that? It's the *last* government's hash we're settling. Not ours at all. Go in for Russian-baiting, you get what you deserve. Natural. We're just reaping the whirlwind as usual.'

'What have the Russians got up to in Hong Kong *before* this?' asked a clever backroom-boy from the Home Office.

The Colonialists at once sprang to life. Wilbraham began feverishly leafing through a folder, but seeing his red-haired assistant straining at the leash he muttered:

'You'll do that one then, John, will you? Good,' and sat back looking ferocious. The brown-clad lady smiled wistfully at the torn baize cloth, as if she remembered when it was whole. The sixth-former made his second disastrous sally:

'We consider the precedents here very enlightening indeed,' he began aggressively. 'Moscow Centre's previous attempts to gain a toehold on the Colony have been one and all, without exception, abortive and completely low grade.' He reeled of a bunch of boring instances.

Five years ago, he said, a bogus Russian orthodox archimandrite flew in from Paris in an effort to make links with remnants of the White Russian community:

'This gentleman tried to press-gang an elderly restaurateur into Moscow Centre's service and was promptly arrested. More recently, we have had cases of ship's crew coming ashore from Russian freighters which have put in to Hong Kong for repair. They have made ham-fisted attempts to suborn longshoremen and dock workers whom they consider to be leftist oriented. They have been arrested, questioned, made complete fools of by the press, and duly confined to their ship for the rest of its stay.' He gave other equally milk-and-water examples and everyone grew sleepy, waiting for the last lap: 'Our policy has been *exactly* the same each time. As soon as they're caught, right away, culprits are put on public show. Press photographs? As many as you like, gentlemen. Television? Set up your cameras. Result? Peking hand us a nice pat on the back for containing Soviet imperialist expansionism.' Thoroughly over-excited, he found the nerve to address himself directly to Smiley. 'So you see, as to your networks of illegals, to be frank, we discount them. Legal, illegal, above-the-line, below it: our view is, the Circus is doing a bit of special pleading in order to get its nose back under the wire!'

Opening his mouth to deliver a suitable rebuke, Guillam felt a restraining touch on his elbow and closed it again.

There was a long silence, in which Wilbraham looked more embarrassed than anybody.

'Sounds more like *smoke* to me, Chris,' said Enderby drily.

'What's he driving at?' Wilbraham demanded nervously.

'Just answering the point your bully-boy made for you, Chris. Smoke. Deception. Russians are waving their sabres where you can watch 'em, and while your heads are all turned the wrong way, they get on with the dirty work t'other side of the Island. To wit, Brother Ko. Right, George?'

'Well, that is our view, yes,' Smiley conceded. 'And I suppose I *should* remind you – it's in the submission actually – that Haydon himself was always very keen to argue that the Russians had nothing going in Hong Kong.'

'Lunch,' Martindale announced without much optimism. They ate it upstairs, glumly, off plastic catering trays delivered by can. The partitions were too low, and Guillam's custard flowed into his meat.

Thus refreshed, Smiley availed himself of the after-luncheon torpor to raise what Lacon had called the panic factor. More accurately he sought to entrench in the meeting a sense of logic behind a Soviet presence in Hong Kong, even if, as he put it, Ko did not supply the example:

How Hong Kong, as Mainland China's largest port, handled forty per cent of her foreign trade.

How an estimated one out of every five Hong Kong residents travelled legally in and out of China every year: though many-time travellers doubtless raised the average.

How Red China maintained, in Hong Kong, *sub rosa*, but with the full connivance of the authorities, teams of first-class negotiators, economists and technicians to watch over Peking's interest in trade, shipping and development; and how every man jack of them constituted a natural intelligence target for 'enticement, or other forms of secret persuasion', as he put it.

How Hong Kong's fishing and junk fleets enjoyed dual registration in
Hong Kong and along the China coast, and passed freely in and out of China
waters –

Interrupting, Enderby drawled a supporting question:

'And Ko owns a junk fleet. Didn't you say he's one of the last of the brave?'

'Yes, yes he does.'

'But he doesn't visit the mainland himself?'

'No, never. His assistant goes, but not Ko, we gather.'

'Assistant?'

'He has a manager body named Tiu. They've been together for twenty
years. Longer. They share the same background, Hakka, Shanghai and so
forth. Tiu's his front man on several companies.'

'And Tiu goes to the Mainland regularly.'

'Once a year at least.'

'All over?'

'Canton, Peking, Shanghai are on record. But the record is not necessarily
complete.'

'But Ko stays home. Queer.'

There being no further questions or comments on that score, Smiley
resumed his Cook's tour of the charms of Hong Kong as a spy base. Hong
Kong was unique, he stated simply. Nowhere on earth offered a tenth of the
facilities for getting a toehold on China.

'*Facilities!*' Wilbraham echoed. 'Temptations more like.'

Smiley shrugged. 'If you like, temptations,' he agreed. 'The Soviet service is
not famous for resisting them.' And amid some knowing laughter, he went on
to recount what was known of Centre's attempts till now against the China
target as a whole: a joint précis by Connie and di Salis. He described Centre's
efforts to attack from the north, by means of the wholesale recruitment and
infiltration of her own ethnic Chinese. Abortive, he said. He described a huge
network of listening posts all along the four-and-a-half-thousand-mile Sino-
Soviet land border: unproductive, he said, since the yield was military
whereas the threat was political. He recounted the rumours of Soviet approaches to Taiwan, proposing common cause against the China threat through
joint operations and profit-sharing: rejected, he said, and probably designed
for mischief, to annoy Peking, rather than to be taken at face value. He gave
instances of the Russian use of talent-spotters among overseas Chinese
communities in London, Amsterdam, Vancouver, and San Fransisco; and
touched on Centre's veiled proposals to the Cousins some years ago for the
establishment of an 'intelligence pool' available to China's common enemies.
Fruitless, he said. The Cousins wouldn't play. Lastly he referred to Centre's
long history of savage burning and bribery operations against Peking officials
in overseas posts: product indeterminate, he said.

When he had done all this, he sat back, and restated the thesis which was
causing all the trouble.

'Sooner or later,' he repeated, 'Moscow Centre has to come to Hong Kong.'

Which brought them to Ko once more, and to Roddy Martindale, who
under Enderby's eagle eye, made the next real passage of arms.

'Well what do *you* think the money's for, George? I mean we've heard all the
things it *isn't* for, and we've heard it's not being spent. But we're no *forrarder*,
are we, bless us? We don't seem to *know* anything? It's the same old question:

how's the money being earned, how's it being spent, what should we *do*?'

'That's three questions,' said Enderby cruelly under his breath.

'It is *because* we don't know,' said Smiley woodenly, 'that we are asking permission to find out.'

Someone from the Treasury benches said: 'Is half a million a lot?'

'In my experience unprecedented,' said Smiley. 'Moscow Centre' – dutifully he avoided *Karla* – 'detests having to buy loyalty at any time. For them to buy it on this scale is unheard of.'

'But *whose* loyalty are they buying?' someone complained.

Martindale the gladiator, back to the charge: 'You're selling us short, George. I know you are. You have an inkling, of course you have. Now cut us in on it. Don't be coy.'

'Yes, can't you kick a few ideas around for us?' said Lacon, equally plaintively.

'Surely you can go down the line a *little*,' Hammer pleaded.

Even under this three-pronged attack Smiley still did not waver. The panic factor was finally paying off. Smiley himself had triggered it. Like scared patients they were appealing to him for a diagnosis. And Smiley was declining to provide one, on the grounds that he lacked the data.

'Really, I cannot do more than give you the facts as they stand. For me to speculate aloud at this stage would not be useful.'

For the first time since the meeting had begun, the Colonial lady in brown opened her mouth and asked a question. Her voice was melodious and intelligent.

'On the matter of precedents, then, Mr Smiley?' – Smiley ducked his head in a quaint little bow – 'Are there precedents for secret Russian moneys being paid to a stake-holder? In other theatres, for instance?'

Smiley did not immediately answer. Seated only a few inches from him, Guillam swore he sensed a sudden tension, like a surge of energy, passing through his neighbour. But when he glanced at the impassive profile, he saw only a deepening somnolence in his master, and a slight lowering of the weary eyelids.

'There have been a few cases of what we call *alimony*,' he conceded finally.

'*Alimony*, Mr Smiley?' the Colonial lady echoed, while her red-haired companion scowled more terribly, as if divorce were something else he disapproved of.

Smiley picked his way with extreme care. 'Clearly there are agents, working in hostile countries – hostile from the Soviet point of view – who for reasons of cover cannot enjoy their pay while they are in the field.' The brown-clad lady delicately nodded her understanding. 'The normal practice in such cases is to bank the money in Moscow and make it available to the agent when he is free to spend it. Or to his dependants if –'

'If he gets the chop,' said Martindale with relish.

'But Hong Kong is not Moscow,' the Colonial lady reminded him with a smile.

Smiley had all but come to a halt. 'In rare cases where the incentive is money, and the agent perhaps has no stomach for eventual resettlement in Russia, Moscow Centre has been known, under duress, to make a comparable arrangement in, say, Switzerland.'

'But not in Hong Kong?' she persisted.

'No. Not. And it is unimaginable, on past showing, that Moscow would contemplate parting with alimony on such a scale. For one thing, it would be an inducement to the agent to retire from the field.'

There was laughter, but when it died, the brown-clad lady had her next question ready.

'But the payments began modestly,' she persisted pleasantly. 'The inducement is only of relatively recent date?'

'Correct,' said Smiley.

Too damn correct, thought Guillam, starting to get alarmed.

'Mr Smiley, if the dividend were of sufficient value to them, do you think the Russians *would* be prepared to swallow their objections and pay such a price? After all, in absolute terms the money is entirely trivial beside the value of a great intelligence advantage.'

Smiley had simply stopped. He made no particular gesture. He remained courteous, he even managed a small smile, but he was plainly finished with conjecture. It took Enderby, with his blasé drawl, to blow the question away.

'Look, children, we'll be doing the theoreticals all day if we're not careful,' he cried, looking at his watch. 'Chris, do we wheel the Americans in here? If we're not telling the Governor, where do we stand on telling the gallant allies?'

George saved by the bell, thought Guillam.

At the mention of the Cousins, Colonial Wilbraham came in like an angry bull. Guillam guessed he had sensed the issue looming, and determined to kill it immediately it showed its head.

'Vetoed, I'm afraid,' he snapped, without any of his customary delay. 'Absolutely. Whole host of grounds. Demarcation for one. Hong Kong's our patch. Americans have no fishing rights there. None. Ko's a British subject, for another, and entitled to some protection from us. I suppose that's old-fashioned. Don't care too much, to be frank. Americans would go clean overboard. Seen it before. God knows where it would end. Three: small point of protocol.' He meant this ironically. He was appealing to the instincts of an ex-ambassador, trying to rouse his sympathy. 'Just a small point, Enderby. Telling the Americans and not telling the Governor – if *I* was the Governor, put in that position, I'd turn in my badge. That's all I can say. You would too. Know you would. You do. I do.'

'Assuming you found out,' Enderby corrected him.

'Don't worry. I'd find out. I'd have 'em ten deep crawling over his house with microphones for a start. One or two places in Africa where we let them in. Disaster. Total.' Plonking his forearms on the table, one over the other, he stared at them furiously.

A vehement chugging as if from an outboard motor announced a fault in one of the electronic bafflers. It choked, recovered and zoomed out of hearing again.

'Be a brave man who diddled you on that one, Chris,' Enderby murmured with a long admiring smile, into the strained silence.

'Endorsed,' Lacon blurted out of the blue.

They know, thought Guillam simply. George has squared them. They know he's done a deal with Martello and they know he won't say so because he's determined to lie dead. But Guillam saw nothing clearly that day. While the Treasury and Defence factions cautiously concurred on what seemed to be a straight issue – 'keep the Americans out of it' – Smiley himself appeared mysteriously unwilling to toe the line.

'But there does *remain* the headache of what to do with the raw intelligence,' he said. 'Should you decide that my service may not proceed, I mean,' he added doubtfully, to the general confusion.

Guillam was relieved to find Enderby equally bewildered:

'Hell's that mean?' he demanded, running with the hounds for a moment.

'Ko has financial interests all over South East Asia,' Smiley reminded them. 'Page one of my submission.' Business; clatter of papers. 'We have information, for example, that he controls through intermediaries and strawmen such oddities as a string of Saigon nightclubs, a Vientiane-based aviation company, a piece of a tanker fleet in Thailand . . . several of these enterprises could well be seen to have political overtones which are *far* within the American sphere of influence. I would have to have your written instruction, naturally, if I were to ignore our side of the existing bi-lateral agreements.'

'Keep talking,' Enderby ordered, and pulled a fresh match from the box in front of him.

'Oh, I think my point is made, thank you,' said Smiley politely. 'Really, it's a very simple one. Assuming we don't proceed, which Lacon tells me is the balance of probability today, what am I to do? Throw the intelligence on the scrap-heap? Or pass it to our allies under the existing barter arrangements?'

'Allies,' Wilbraham exclaimed bitterly. 'Allies? You're putting a pistol at our heads, man!'

Smiley's iron reply was all the more startling for the passivity which had preceded it.

'I have a standing instruction from this committee to repair our American liaison. It is written into my charter, by yourselves, that I am to do everything possible to nurture the special relationship and revive the spirit of mutual confidence which existed before – Haydon. "To get us back to the top table," you said . . . ' He was looking directly at Enderby.

'*Top table*,' someone echoed – a quite new voice. 'Sacrificial altar if you ask me. We already burned the Middle East and half Africa on it. All for the special relationship.'

But Smiley seemed not to hear. He relapsed once more into his posture of mournful reluctance. Sometimes, his sad face said, the burdens of his office were simply too much for him to bear.

A fresh bout of post-luncheon sulkiness set in. Someone complained of the tobacco smoke. A messenger was summoned.

'Devil's happened to the extractors?' Enderby demanded crossly. 'We're stifling.'

'It's the parts,' the messenger said. 'We put in for them months ago, sir. Before Christmas it was, sir, nearly a year come to think of it. Still you can't blame delay, can you, sir?'

'Christ,' said Enderby.

Tea was sent for. It came in paper cups which leaked on to the baize. Guillam gave his thoughts to Molly Meakin's peerless figure.

It was almost four o'clock when Lacon rode disdainfully in front of the armies and invited Smiley to state 'just exactly what it is you're asking for in practical terms, George. Let's have it all on the table and try to hack out an answer.'

Enthusiasm would have been fatal. Smiley seemed to understand that.

'One, we need rights and permissions to operate in the South East Asian theatre – deniably. So that the Governor can wash his hands of us' – a glance at the Parliamentary Under-Secretary – 'and so can our own masters here. Two, to conduct certain domestic enquiries.'

Heads shot up. The Home Office at once grew fidgety. Why? Who? How?

*What* enquiries? If it's domestic it should go to the competition. Pretorius of the Security Service was already in a ferment.

'Ko read law in London,' Smiley insisted. 'He has connections here, social and business. We should naturally have to investigate them.' He glanced at Pretorius. 'We would show the competition all our findings,' he promised. He resumed his bid.

'As regards money, my submission contains a full breakdown of what we need at once, as well as supplementary estimates for various contingencies. Finally we are asking permission, at local as well as Whitehall level, to reopen our Hong Kong residency as a forward base for the operation.'

A stunned silence greeted this last item, to which Guillam's own amazement contributed. Nowhere, in any of the preparatory discussions at the Circus, or with Lacon, had anybody, not even Smiley himself, to Guillam's knowledge, raised the slightest question of reopening High Haven or establishing its successor. A fresh clamour started.

'Failing that,' he ended, overriding the protests, 'if we cannot have our residency, we request at the very least blindeye approval to run our own below-the-line agents on the Colony. No local awareness, but approval and protection by London. Any existing sources to be retrospectively legitimized. In writing,' he ended, with a hard glance at Lacon, and stood up.

Glumly, Guillam and Smiley sat themselves once more in the waiting room on the same salmon bench where they had begun, side by side, like passengers travelling in the same direction.

'*Why?*' Guillam muttered once, but asking questions of George Smiley was not merely in bad taste that day: it was a pastime expressly forbidden by the cautionary notice which hung above them on the wall.

Of all the damn-fool ways of overplaying one's hand, thought Guillam dismally. You've thrown it, he thought. Poor old sod: finally past it. The one operation which could put us back in the game. Greed, that's what it was. The greed of an old spy in a hurry. I'll stick with him, thought Guillam. I'll go down with the ship. We'll open a chicken farm together. Molly can keep the accounts and Ann can have bucolic tangles with the labourers.

'How do you feel?' he asked.

'It's not a matter of feeling,' Smiley replied.

Thanks very much, thought Guillam.

The minutes turned to twenty. Smiley had not stirred. His chin had fallen on to his chest, his eyes had closed, he might have been at prayer.

'Perhaps you should take an evening off,' said Guillam.

Smiley only frowned.

A messenger appeared, inviting them to return. Lacon was now at the head of the table, and his manner was prefectorial. Enderby sat two away from him, conversing in murmurs with the Welsh Hammer. Pretorius glowered like a storm cloud, and his nameless lady pursed her lips in an unconscious kiss of disapproval. Lacon rustled his notes for silence and like a teasing judge began reading off the committee's detailed findings before he delivered the verdict. The treasury had entered a serious protest, on the record, regarding the misuse of Smiley's management account. Smiley should also bear in mind that any requirement for domestic rights and permissions should be cleared with the Security Service in advance and not 'sprung on them like a rabbit out of a hat in the middle of a full-dress meeting of the committee'. There could be no earthly question of reopening the Hong Kong residency. Simply on the issue of time alone, such a step was impossible. It was really a quite shameful proposal, he implied. Principle was involved, consultation would have to be at the highest level, and since Smiley had already moved specifically against advising the Governor of his findings – Lacon's doff of the cap to Wilbraham here – it was going to be very hard to make a case for re-establishing a residency in the foreseeable future, particularly bearing in mind the unhappy publicity attaching to the evacuation of High Haven.

'I must accept that view with great reluctance,' said Smiley gravely.

Oh for God's sake, thought Guillam: let's at least go down fighting!

'Accept it how you like,' said Enderby – and Guillam could have sworn he saw in the eyes of both Enderby and the Welsh Hammer a gleam of victory.

Bastards, he thought simply. No free chickens for you. In his mind he was taking leave of the whole pack of them.

'Everything else,' said Lacon, putting down a sheet of paper and taking up another, 'with certain limiting conditions and safeguards regarding desirability, money and the duration of the licence, is granted.'

The park was empty. The lesser commutters had left the field to the professionals. A few lovers lay on the damp grass like soldiers after the battle. A few flamingos dozed. At Guillam's side, as he sauntered euphorically in Smiley's wake, Roddy Martindale was singing Smiley's praises: 'I think George is simply marvellous. Indestructible. And *grip*. I adore grip. Grip is my favourite human quality. George has it in spades. One takes quite a different view of these things when one's translated. One grows to the scale of them, I admit. Your father was an Arabist, I recall?'

'Yes,' said Guillam, his mind yet again on Molly, wondering whether dinner was still possible.

'And frightfully *Almanach de Gotha*. Now was he an AD man or a BC man?'

About to give a thoroughly obscene reply, Guillam realized just in time that Martindale was enquiring after nothing more harmful than his father's scholarly preferences.

'Oh BC! – BC all the way,' he said. 'He'd have gone back to Eden if he could have done.'

'Come to dinner.'

'Thanks.'

'We'll fix a date. Who's *fun* for a change? Who do you like?'

Ahead of them floating on the dewy air, they heard the drawling voice of Enderby applauding Smiley's victory.

'*Nice* little meeting. Lot achieved. Nothing given away. *Nicely* played hand. Land this one and you can just about build an extension, I should think. And the Cousins will play ball, will they?' he bellowed as if they were still inside the safe room. 'You've tested the water there? They'll carry your bags for you and not hog the match? Bit of a cliffhanger that one, I'd have thought, but I suppose you're up to it. You tell Martello to wear his crêpe soles, if he's got any, or we'll be in deep trouble with the Colonials in no time. Pity about old Wilbraham. He'd have run India rather well.'

Beyond them again, almost out of sight among the trees, the little Welsh Hammer was making energetic gestures to Lacon, who was stooping to catch his words.

Nice little conspiracy too, thought Guillam. He glanced back and was surprised to see Fawn the babysitter hurrying after them. He seemed at first a

long way off. Shreds of mist obscured his legs entirely. Only the top of him
reached above the sea. Then suddenly he was much closer, and Guillam
heard his familiar plaintive bray calling 'Sir, sir,' trying to catch Smiley's
attention. Quickly placing Martindale out of earshot, Guillam strode up to
him.

'What the devil's the matter? Why are you bleating like that?'

'They've found a girl! Miss Sachs, sir, she sent me to tell him specially.' His
eyes shone bright and slightly crazy. '"Tell the Chief they've found the girl."
Her very words, personal for Chief.'

'Do you mean she *sent* you here?'

'Personal for Chief immediate,' Fawn replied evasively.

'I said: "did she send you here?"' Guillam was seething. 'Answer, "no, sir,
she did not." You bloody little drama queen, racing round London in your
plimsolls! You're out of your mind.' Snatching the crumpled note from
Fawn's hand, he read it cursorily. 'It's not even the same name. Hysterical
bloody nonsense. You go straight back to your hutch, do you hear? The Chief
will give the matter his attention when he returns. Don't you dare stir things
up like that again.'

'*Whoever* was he?' Martindale enquired, quite breathless with excitement, as
Guillam returned. 'What a darling little creature! Are all spies as pretty as
that? How positively Venetian. I shall volunteer at once.'

The same night a ragged conference was held in the rumpus room, and the
quality was not improved by the euphoria – in Connie's case alcoholic –
brought on by Smiley's triumph at the steering conference. After the
constraints and tensions of the last months Connie charged in all directions.
The girl! The girl was the clue! Connie had shed all her intellectual bonds.
Send Toby Esterhase to Hong Kong, house her, photograph her, trace her,
search her room! Get Sam Collins in, *now*! di Salis fidgeted, simpered, puffed
at his pipe and jiggled his feet, but for that evening he was entirely under
Connie's spell. He even spoke once of 'a natural line to the heart of things' –
meaning, yet again, the mystery girl. No wonder little Fawn had been
infected by their zeal. Guillam felt almost apologetic for his outburst in the
park. Indeed, without Smiley and Guillam to put the dampers on, an act of
collective folly could very easily have taken place that night and God knows
where it might not have led. The secret world has plenty of precedents of
sane people breaking out that way, but this was the first time Guillam had
seen the disease in action.

So it was ten o'clock or more before a brief could be drafted for old Craw,
and half past before Guillam blearily bumped into Molly Meakin on his way
to the lift. In consequence of this happy coincidence – or had Molly planned
it? he never knew – a beacon was lit in Peter Guillam's life which burned
fiercely from then on. With her customary acquiescence, Molly consented to
be driven home, though she lived in Highgate, miles out of his way, and when
they reached her doorstep she as usual invited him in for a quick coffee.
Anticipating the familiar frustrations – 'no-Peter-please-Peter-*dear*-I'm sorry'
– Guillam was on the brink of declining, when something in her eye – a
certain calm resolution as it seemed to him – caused him to change his mind.
Once inside her flat, she closed the door and put it on the chain. Then she led
him demurely to her bedroom, where she astonished him with a joyous and
refined carnality.

# NINE

## Craw's little ship

In Hong Kong it was forty-eight hours later and a Sunday evening. In the alley Craw walked carefully. Dusk had come early with the fog, but the houses were jammed too close to let it in, so it hung a few floors higher, with the washing and the cables, spitting hot polluted raindrops which raised smells of orange in the food stalls and ticked on the brim of Craw's straw hat. He was in China here, at sea level, the China he loved most, and China was waking for the festival of night: singing, honking, wailing, beating gongs, bargaining, cooking, playing tinny tunes through twenty different instruments: or watching motionless from doorways how delicately the fancy-looking Foreign Devil picked his way among them. Craw loved it all, but most tenderly he loved his *little ships*, as the Chinese called their secret whisperers, and of these Miss Phoebe Wayfarer, whom he was on his way to visit, was a classic, if modest, example.

He breathed in, savouring the familiar pleasures. The East had never failed him. 'We colonize them, your Graces, we corrupt them, we exploit them, we bomb them, sack their cities, ignore their culture and confound them with the infinite variety of our religious sects. We are hideous not only in their sight, Monsignors, but in their nostrils as well – the stink of the roundeye is abhorrent to them and we're too thick even to know it. Yet when we have done our worst, and more than our worst, my sons, we have barely scratched the surface of the Asian smile.'

Other roundeyes might not have come here so willingly alone. The peak mafia would not have known it existed. The embattled British wives in their government housing ghettos in Happy Valley would have found here every-thing they hated most about their billet. It was not a bad part of town, but it was not Europe either: the Europe of Central and Pedder Street half a mile away, of electric doors that sighed for you as they admitted you to the airconditioning. Other roundeyes, in their apprehension, might have cast inadvertent glares, and that was dangerous. In Shanghai, Craw had known more than one man die of an accidental bad look. Whereas Craw's look was at all times kindly, he deferred, he was modest in his manner, and when he stopped to make a purchase, he offered respectful greetings to the stall-holder in bad but robust Cantonese. And he paid without carping at the surcharge befitting his inferior race.

He bought orchids and lamb's liver. He bought them every Sunday, distributing his custom fairly between rival stalls and – when his Cantonese ran out – lapsing into his own ornate version of English.

He pressed the bell. Phoebe, like old Craw himself, had an entryphone. Head office had decreed they should be standard issue. She had twisted a piece of heather into her mail box for good joss, and this was a safety signal.

'Hi,' a girl's voice said, over the speaker. It could have been American or it could have been Cantonese, offering an interrogative '*Yes?*'

'Larry calls me Pete,' Craw said.

'Come on up, I have Larry with me at this moment.'

The staircase was pitch dark and stank of vomit and Craw's heels clanked like tin on the stone treads. He pressed the time switch but no light went on so he had to grope his way for three floors. There had been a move to find her somewhere better but it had died with Thesinger's departure and now there was no hope and, in a way, no Phoebe either.

'Bill,' she murmured, closing the door after him, and kissed him on both mottled cheeks, the way pretty girls may kiss kind uncles, though she was not pretty. Craw gave her the orchids. His manner was gentle and solicitous.

'My dear,' he said. 'My *dear*.'

She was trembling. There was a bedsitting room with a cooker and a handbasin, there was a separate lavatory with a shower. That was all. He walked past her to the basin, unwrapped the liver and gave it to the cat.

'Oh you spoil her, Bill,' said Phoebe, smiling at the flowers. He had laid a brown envelope on the bed but neither of them mentioned it.

'How's *William*?' she said, playing with the sound of his name.

Craw had hung his hat and stick on the door and was pouring Scotch: neat for Phoebe, soda for himself.

'How's Pheeb? That's more to the point. How's it been out there, the cold long week? Eh, Pheeb?'

She had ruffled the bed and laid a frilly nightdress on the floor because so far as the block was concerned Phoebe was the half-*kwailo* bastard who whored with the fat foreign devil. Over the crushed pillows hung her picture of Swiss Alps, the picture every Chinese girl seemed to have, and on the bedside locker the photograph of her English father, the only picture she had ever seen of him: a clerk from Dorking in Surrey, just after his arrival on the Island, rounded collars, moustache, and staring, slightly crazy eyes. Craw sometimes wondered whether it was taken after he was shot.

'It's all right *now*,' said Phoebe. 'It's fine *now*, Bill.'

She stood at his shoulder, filling the vase, and her hands were shaking badly, which they usually did on Sundays. She wore a grey tunic dress in honour of Peking, and the gold necklace given to her to commemorate her first decade of service to the Circus. In a ridiculous spurt of gallantry, Head Office had decided to have it made at Asprey's, then sent out by bag, with a personal letter to her signed by Percy Alleline, George Smiley's luckless predecessor, which she had been allowed to look at but not keep. Having filled the vase, she tried to carry it to the table but it slopped, so Craw took it.

'*Hey* now, take it easy, won't you?'

She stood for a moment, still smiling at him, then with a long slow sob reaction slumped into a chair. Sometimes she wept, sometimes she sneezed, or was very loud and laughed too much, but always she saved the moment for his arrival, however it took her.

'Bill, I get frightened sometimes.'

'I know, dear, I know.' He sat at her side, holding her hand.

'That new boy in features. He *stares* at me, Bill, he watches everything I do. I'm sure he works for someone. Bill, who does he work for?'

'Maybe he's a little amorous,' said Craw, in his softest tone, as he rhythmically patted her shoulder. 'You're an attractive woman, Phoebe. Don't forget that, my dear. You can exert an influence without knowing it.' He affected a paternal sternness. 'Now have you been flirting with him? There's another thing. A woman like you can flirt without being conscious of the fact. A man of the world can spot these things, Phoebe. He can tell.'

Last week it was the janitor downstairs. She said he was writing down the hours she came and went. The week before, it was a car she kept seeing, an Opel, always the same one, green. The trick was to calm her fears without discouraging her vigilance: because one day – as Craw never allowed himself to forget – one day, she was going to be right. Producing a bunch of handwritten notes from the bedside, she began her own de-briefing, but so suddenly that Craw was overrun. She had a pale large face which missed being beautiful in either race. Her trunk was long, her legs were short, and her hands Saxon, ugly and strong. Sitting on the edge of the bed, she looked suddenly matronly. She had put on thick spectacles to read. Canton was sending a student commissar to address Tuesday's cadre, she said, so the Thursday meeting was closed and Ellen Tuo had once more lost her chance to be secretary for an evening –

'Hey, steady down now,' Craw cried, laughing. 'Where's the fire, for God's sake!'

Opening a notebook on his knee, he tried to catch up with her. But Phoebe would not be checked, not even by Bill Craw, though she had been told he was in fact a colonel, even higher. She wanted it behind her, the whole confession. One of her routine targets was a leftist intellectual group of university students and Communist journalists which had somewhat superficially accepted her. She had reported on it weekly without much progress. Now, for some reason, the group had flared into activity. Billy Chan had been called to Kuala Lumpur for a special conference, she said, and Johnny and Belinda Fong were being asked to find a safe store for a printing press. The evening was approaching fast. While she ran on, Craw discreetly rose and put on the lamp so that the electric light would not shock her once the day faded altogether.

There was talk of joining up with the Fukienese in North Point, she said, but the academic comrades were opposed as usual. 'They're opposed to *everything*,' said Phoebe savagely, 'the snobs. And anyway that stupid bitch Belinda is months behind on her dues and we may quite well chuck her out of the Party unless she stops gambling.'

'And quite right too, my dear,' said Craw sedately.

'Johny Fong says Belinda's pregnant and it isn't his. Well I hope she is. It will shut her up . . . ' said Phoebe, and Craw thought: we had that trouble a couple of times with *you* if I remember rightly, and it didn't shut you up, did it?

Craw wrote obediently, knowing that neither London nor anyone else would ever read a word of it. In the days of its wealth the Circus had penetrated dozens of such groups, hoping in time to break into what was idiotically referred to as the Peking-Hong Kong shuttle and so get a foot in the Mainland. The ploy had withered and the Circus had no brief to act as watchdog for the Colony's security, a rôle which Special Branch jealously guarded for itself. But little ships, as Craw knew very well, cannot change course as easily as the winds that drive them. Craw played her along, pitching-in with the following questions, checking sources and subsources. Was it hearsay, Pheeb? Well, where did Billy Lee get *that* one from, Pheeb? Was it possible Billy Lee was needling the story a bit – for face, Pheeb, giving it the old needle? He used the journalistic term because, like Jerry and Craw himself, Phoebe was in her other profession a journalist, a freelance gossip writer feeding Hong Kong's English-language press with tid-bits about lifestyles of the local Chinese aristocracy.

Listening, waiting, vamping as the actors call it, Craw told himself her story, just as he had told it on the refresher course at Sarratt five years ago, when he was back there getting a rebore in the black arts. The triumph of the fortnight, they had told him afterwards. They had made it a plenary session in anticipation. Even the directing staff had come to hear him. Those who were off duty had asked for a special van to bring them in early from their Watford housing estate. Just to hear old Craw, the eastern hand, sitting under the antlers in the converted library, sum up a lifetime in the Game. *Agents who recruit themselves*, ran the title. There was a lectern on the podium but he didn't use it. Instead, he sat on a plain chair, with his jacket off and his belly hanging out and his knees apart and shadows of sweat darkening his shirt, and he told it to them the way he would have told it to the Shanghai Bowlers, on a typhoon Saturday in Hong Kong, if only circumstance had allowed.

*Agents who recruit themselves, your Graces.*

No one knew the job better, they told him – and he believed them. If the East was Craw's home, the little ships were his family, and he lavished on them all the fondness for which the overt world had somehow never given him an outlet. He raised and trained them with a love that would have done credit to a father; and it was the hardest moment in an old man's life when Tufty Thesinger did his moonlight flit and left Craw unwarned, temporarily without a purpose or a life-line.

Some people are agents from birth, Monsignors – he told them – appointed to the work by the period of history, the place, and their own natural dispositions. In their cases, it was simply a question of who got to them first, your Eminences:

'Whether it's us; whether it's the opposition; or whether it's the bloody missionaries.'

Laughter.

Then the case histories with names and places changed, and among them none other than codename Susan, a little ship of the female gender, Monsignors, South East Asian theatre, born in the year of turmoil 1941, of mixed blood. He was referring to Phoebe Wayfarer.

'Father a penniless clerk from Dorking, your Graces. Came East to join one of the Scottish houses that plundered the coast six days a week and prayed to Calvin on the seventh. Too broke to get himself a European wife, lads, so he takes a forbidden Chinese girl and sets her up for a few pence, and codename Susan is the result. Same year the Japanese appear on the scene. Call it Singapore, Hong Kong, Malaya, the story's the same, Monsignors. They appear overnight. To stay. In the chaos, codename Susan's father does a very noble thing: "To hell with caution, your Eminences," he says. "This is the time for good men and true to stand up and be counted." So he marries the lady, your Graces, a course of action I would not normally counsel, but he does, and when he's married her he christens his daughter codename Susan and joins the Volunteers, which was a fine body of heroic fools who formed a local home-guard against the Nipponese hordes. The next day, not being a natural man-at-arms, your Graces, he gets his arse shot off by the Japanese invader and promptly expires. Amen. May the clerk from Dorking rest in peace, your Graces.'

As old Craw crosses himself, gusts of laughter sweep the room. Craw does not laugh with them, but plays the straightman. There are fresh faces in the front two rows, uncut, unlined, television faces; Craw guesses they are new entrants whipped in to hear The Great One. Their presence sharpens his performance. Henceforth he has a special eye for the front rows.

'Codename Susan is still in rompers when her good father meets his *quietus*, lads, but all her life she's going to remember: when the chips are down, the British stand by their commitments. Every year that passes, she's going to love that dead hero a little more. After the war, her father's old trading house remembers her for a year or two, then conveniently forgets her. Never mind. At fifteen, she's ill from having to keep her sick mother and work the ballrooms to finance her own schooling. Never mind. A welfare worker takes up with her, fortunately a member of our distinguished brethren, your Reverends; and he guides her in our direction.' Craw mops his brow. 'Codename Susan's rise to wealth and godliness has begun, your Graces,' he declares. 'Under journalistic cover we bring her into play, give her Chinese newspapers to translate, send her on little errands, involve her, complete her education and train her in nightwork. A little money, a little patronage, a little love, a little patience and it's not too long before our Susan has seven legal trips to Mainland China to her credit, including some very windy tradecraft. Skilfully performed, your Graces. She has played courier, and made one crash approach to an uncle in Peking, which paid off. All this, lads, despite the fact she's half a *kwailo* and not naturally trusted by the Chinese.

'And who did she think the Circus was, all that time?' Craw bellowed at his enthralled audience – 'who did she think we were, lads?' The old magician drops his voice, and lifts a fat forefinger. 'Her father,' he says, in the silence. 'We're that dead clerk from Dorking. Saint George, that's who we are. Cleansing the overseas Chinese communities of *harmful elements*, whatever the hell they are. Breaking the Triads and the rice cartels and the opium gangs and the child prostitution. She even saw us, when she had to, as the secret ally of Peking, because we, the Circus, had the interest of all *good* Chinese at heart.' Craw ran a ferocious eye over the rows of child faces longing to be stern.

'Do I see someone smiling, your Graces?' he demanded, in a voice of thunder. He didn't.

'Mind you, Squires,' Craw ended, 'there's a part of her knew damn well it was all baloney. That's where *you* come in. That's where your fieldman is ever at the ready. Oh yes! We're keepers of the faith, lads. When it shakes, we stiffen it. When it falls, we've got our arms out to catch it.' He had reached his zenith. In counterpoint, he let his voice fall to a mellow murmur. 'Be the faith ever so crackpot, your Graces, never despise it. We've precious little else to offer them these days. Amen.'

All his life, in his unashamedly emotional way, old Craw would remember the applause.

Her debriefing finished, Phoebe hunched forward, her forearms on her knees, the knuckles of her big hands backed loosely against each other like tired lovers. Craw rose solemnly, took her notes from the table and burnt them at the gas ring.

'Bravo, my dear,' he said quietly. 'A sterling week if I may say so. Anything else?'

She shook her head.

'I mean, to burn,' he said.

She shook her head again.

Craw studied her. 'Pheeb, my dear,' he declared at last, as if he had reached a momentous decision. 'Get off your hunkers. It's time I took you out to dinner.' She looked round at him, confused. The drink had raced to her head, as it always did. 'An amiable dinner between fellow scribblers, once in a while, is not inconsistent with cover, I venture to suggest. How about it?'

She made him look at the wall while she put on a pretty frock. She used to have a humming bird but it died. He bought her another but it died too so they agreed the flat was bad luck for humming birds and gave up on them.

'One day I'll take you skiing,' he said, as she locked the front door behind them. It was a joke between them, to do with her snow scene over the bed.

'Only for one day?' she replied. Which was also a joke, part of the same habitual repartee.

In that year of turmoil, as Craw would say, it was still clever to eat in a sampan on Causeway Bay. The smart set had not discovered it, the food was cheap and unlike food elsewhere. Craw took a gamble and by the time they reached the waterfront the fog had lifted and the night sky was clear. He chose the sampan furthest out to sea, deep in among a cluster of small junks. The cook squatted at the charcoal brazier and his wife served, the hulls of the junks loomed over them, blotting out the stars, and the boat children scampered like crabs from one deck to another while their parents chanted slow funny catechisms across the black water. Craw and Phoebe crouched on wood stools under the furled canopy, two foot above the sea, eating mullet by lamplight. Beyond the typhoon shelters ships slid past them, lighted buildings on the march, and the junks hobbled in their wakes. Inland, the Island whined and clanged and throbbed, and the huge slums twinkled like jewelboxes opened by the deceptive beauty of the night. Presiding over them, glimpsed between the dipping fingers of the masts, sat the black Peak, Victoria, her sodden face shrouded with moonlit skeins: the goddess, the freedom, the lure of all that wild striving in the valley.

They talked the arts. Phoebe was doing what Craw thought of as her cultural number. It was very boring. One day, she said drowsily, she would direct a film, perhaps two, on the *true*, the *real* China. Recently she had seen an historical romance made by Run Run Shaw, all about the palace intrigues. She considered it excellent but a little too – well – *heroic*. Theatre, now. Had Craw heard the good news that the Cambridge Players might be bringing a new revue to the Colony in December? At present it was only a rumour, but she hoped it would be confirmed next week.

'*That* should be fun, Pheeb,' said Craw heartily.

'It will *not* be fun at all,' Phoebe retorted sternly. 'The Players specialize in biting social satire.'

In the darkness Craw smiled and poured Phoebe more beer. You can always learn, he told himself: Monsignors, you can always learn.

Till, with no prompting that she could have been aware of, Phoebe began talking about her Chinese millionaires, which was what Craw had been waiting for all evening. In Phoebe's world, the Hong Kong rich were royalty. Their foibles and excesses were handed round as freely as in other places the lives of actresses or footballers. Phoebe knew them by heart.

'So who's pig of the week this time, Pheeb?' Craw asked genially.

Phoebe was unsure. 'Whom shall we elect?' she said, affecting coquettish indecision. There was the pig PK of course, his sixty-eighth birthday on Tuesday, a third wife half his age and how does PK celebrate? Out on the town with a twenty-year-old slut.

Disgusting, Craw agreed. 'PK,' he repeated. 'PK was the fellow with the gateposts, wasn't he?'

One hundred thousand Hong Kong, said Phoebe. Dragons nine foot high, cast in fibreglass and perspex so that they lit up from inside. Or it might be the pig YY she reflected judiciously, changing her mind. YY was certainly a candidate. YY had married one month ago exactly, that nice daughter of JJ Haw, of Haw and Chan, the tanker kings, a thousand lobsters at the wedding. Night before last, he turned up at a reception with a brand new mistress, bought with his wife's money, a nobody except that he had dressed her at Saint-Laurent and decked her out in a four-string choker of Mikimoto pearls, hired of course, not given. Despite herself, Phoebe's voice faltered and softened.

'Bill,' she breathed, 'that kid looked completely fantastic beside the old frog, you should have seen.'

Or maybe Harold Tan, she pondered dreamily. Harold had been specially nasty. Harold had flown his kids home from their Swiss finishing schools for the festival, first-class return from Geneva. At four in the morning they were all cavorting naked round the pool, the kids and their friends, drunk, pouring champagne into the water while Harold tried to photograph the action.

Craw waited, in his mind holding the door wide open for her, but still she wouldn't pass through, and Craw was far too old a dog to push her. Chiu Chow were best, he said archly. 'Chiu chow wouldn't get up to all that nonsense. Eh Pheeb? Very long pockets the Chiu Chow have, and very short arms,' he advised her. 'Make a Scotsman blush, your Chiu Chow would, eh Pheeb?'

Phoebe had no place for irony. 'Do not believe it,' she retorted demurely. 'Many Chiu Chow are both generous and high-minded.'

He was willing the man on her, like a conjurer willing a card, but still she hesitated, walked round it, reached for the alternatives. She mentioned this one, that one, lost the thread, wanted more beer, and when he had all but given up she remarked, quite dreamily:

'And as for Drake Ko, he is a complete *lamb*. Against Drake Ko, no bad words at *all* please.'

Now it was Craw's turn to walk away. What did Phoebe think of old Andrew Kwok's divorce, he asked. Christ, *that* must have been a costly one! They say she would have given him the push long ago, but she wanted to wait till he'd made his pile and was really worth divorcing. Any truth in that one, Pheeb? And so on, three, five names, before he allowed himself to take the bait.

'Have you ever heard of old Drake Ko keeping a roundeye mistress at any time? They were talking about it in the Hong Kong Club only the other day. Blonde party, said to be quite a dish.'

Phoebe like to think of Craw in the Hong Kong Club. It satisfied her colonial yearnings.

'Oh *everyone* has heard,' she said wearily, as if Craw as usual were light years behind the hunt. 'There was a time when *all* the boys had them – didn't you know? PK had two, of course. Harold Tan had one, till Eustace Chow stole her, and Charlie Wu tried to take *his* to dinner at the Governor's but his *tai-tai* wouldn't let the chauffeur pick her up.'

'Where'd they get them from for Christ's sakes?' Craw asked with a laugh. 'Lane Crawford?'

'From the airlines, where do you think?' Phoebe retorted with heavy disapproval. 'Airhostesses moonlighting on their stopovers, five hundred US a night for a white-woman whore. *And* including the English lines, don't deceive yourself, the English were the worst by far. Then Harold Tan liked his so much he made an arrangement with her, and the next thing they were all moving into flats and walking round the stores like duchesses any time they came to Hong Kong for four days, enough to make you *sick*. Mind you, Liese is a different kettle of fish entirely. Liese has class. She is extremely aristocratic, her parents own fabulous estates in the South of France and also an out-island in the Bahamas and it is purely for reasons of moral independence that she refuses to accept their wealth. You only have to look at her bone structure.'

'*Liese*,' Craw repeated. '*Liese*? Kraut, eh? Don't hold with Krauts. No racial prejudices but don't care for Krauts, I'm afraid. Now what's a nice Chiu Chow boy like Drake doing with a hateful Hun for a concubine, I ask myself. Still, you should know Pheeb, you're the expert, it's your bailiwick, my dear, who am I to criticize?'

They had moved to the back of the sampan and were lying in the cushions side by side.

'Don't be utterly ridiculous,' Phoebe snapped. 'Liese is an aristocratic English girl.'

'Tra la la,' said Craw and for a while gazed at the stars.

'She has a most positive and refining influence on him.'

'Who does?' said Craw, as if he had lost the thread.

Phoebe spoke through gritted teeth. '*Liese* has a refining influence on *Drake Ko*. Bill, listen. Are you asleep? Bill, I think you should take me home. Take me home, please.'

Craw gave a low sigh. These lovers' tiffs between them were six-monthly events at least, and had a cleansing effect on their relationship.

'My dear. Phoebe. Give ear to me, will you? For one moment, right? No English girl, highborn, fine-boned or knock-kneed, can possibly be named *Liese* unless there is a Kraut at work somewhere. That's for openers. What's her other name?'

'Worth.'

'Worth what? All right, that was a joke. Forget it. Elizabeth, that's what she is. Contracted to Lizzie. Or Liza. Liza of Lambeth. You mis-heard. There's blood for you if you like: *Miss Elizabeth Worth*. I could see the bone structure there all right. Not Liese, dear. Lizzie.'

Phoebe became openly furious.

'Don't you tell me how to pronounce *anything*!' she flung at him. 'Her name is *Liese* pronounce *Leesa* and written L-I-E-S-E because I *asked* her and I wrote it *down* and I have printed that name in – oh Bill.' Her forehead fell on his shoulder. 'Oh Bill. Take me home.'

She began weeping. Craw cuddled her against him, gently patting her shoulder.

'Ah now cheer up, my dear, the fault was mine, not yours. I should have known that she was a friend of yours. A fine society woman like Liese, a woman of beauty and fortune, locked in romantic attachment to one of the Island's new nobility: how could a diligent newshound like Phoebe fail to befriend her? I was blind. Forgive me.' He allowed a decent interval. 'What happened?' he asked indulgently. 'You interviewed her, did you?'

For the second time that night, Phoebe dried her eyes with Craw's handkerchief.

'She begged me. She's not my friend. She is far too grand to be my friend.

How could she be? She begged me not to print her name. She is here incognito. Her life depends upon it. If her parents know she is here, they will send for her at once. They are fantastically influential. They have private planes, everything. The minute they know she is living with a Chinese man, they would bring fantastic pressure to bear just to get her back. "Phoebe," she said. "Of all people in Hong Kong, you will understand best what it means to live under the shadow of intolerance." She appealed to me. I promised.'

'Quite right,' said Craw stoutly. 'Don't you ever break that promise, Pheeb. A promise is a bond.' He gave an admiring sign. 'Life's byways, I always maintain, are ever stranger than life's highways. If you put that in your paper, your editor would say you were soft in the head, I dare say. And yet it's true. A shining wonderful example of human integrity for its own sake.' Her eyes had closed, so he gave her a jolt in order to keep them open. 'Now where does a match like that have its genesis, I ask myself. What star, what happy chance, could bring together two such needful souls? In Hong Kong too, for God's sake.'

'It was fate. She was not even living here. She had withdrawn from the world altogether after an unhappy love affair and she had decided to spend the rest of her life making exquisite jewellery in order to give the world something beautiful among all its suffering. She flew in for a day or two, just to buy some gold, and quite by chance, at one of Sally Cale's fabulous receptions, she met Drake Ko and that was that.'

'And thereafter the course of true love ran sweet, eh?'

'Certainly not. She met him. She loved him. But she was determined not to get embroiled, and returned home.'

'*Home?*' Craw echoed, mystified. 'Where's home for a woman of her integrity?'

Phoebe laughed. 'Not to the South of France, silly. To Vientiane. To a city no one ever visits. A city without high life, or any of the luxuries to which she was accustomed from birth. That was her chosen place. Her island. She had friends there, she was interested in Buddhism and art and antiquity.'

'And where does she hang out now? Still in some humble croft, is she, clinging to her notions of abstinence? Or has Brother Ko converted her to less frugal paths?'

'Don't be sarcastic. Drake has given her a most beautiful apartment, naturally.'

That was Craw's limit: he knew it at once. He covered the card with others, he told her stories about old Shanghai. But he didn't take another step toward the elusive Liese Worth, though Phoebe might have saved him a lot of legwork.

'Behind every painter,' he liked to say, 'and behind every fieldman, lads, there should be a colleague standing with a mallet, ready to hit him over the head when he has gone far enough.'

In the taxi home she was calm again but shivering. He saw her right to the door in style. He had forgiven her entirely. On the doorstep he made to kiss her, but she held him back from her.

'Bill. Am I really any use? Tell me. When I'm no use, you must throw me out, I insist. Tonight was nothing. You are sweet, you pretend, I try. But it was still nothing. If there is other work for me I will take it. Otherwise, you must throw me aside. Ruthlessly.'

'There'll be other nights,' he assured her, and only then did she let him kiss her.

'Thank you, Bill,' she said.

'So there you are, your Graces,' Craw reflected happily, as he took the taxi on to the Hilton. 'Codename Susan toiled and span and she was worth a little less each day, because agents are only ever as good as the target they're pointed at, and that's the truth of them. And the one time she gave us gold, pure gold, Monsignors' – in his mind's eye, he held up that same fat forefinger, one message for the uncut boys spellbound in the forward rows – 'the *one time*, she didn't even know she'd done it – and she *never could!*'

The best jokes in Hong Kong, Craw had once written, are seldom laughed at because they are too serious. That year there was the Tudor pub in the unfinished high-rise building, for instance, where geniune, sour-faced English wenches in period *décolleté* served genuine English beer at twenty degrees below its English temperature, while outside in the lobby, sweating coolies in yellow helmets toiled round the clock to finish off the elevators. Or you could visit the Italian *taverna* where a cast-iron spiral staircase pointed to Juliet's balcony but ended instead in a blank plaster ceiling; or the Scottish inn with kilted Chinese Scots who occasionally rioted in the heat, or when the fares rose on the Star Ferry. Craw had even attended an opium divan with airconditioning and Muzak churning out Greensleeves. But the most bizarre, the most contrary for Craw's money, was this rooftop bar overlooking the harbour, with its four-piece Chinese band playing Noel Coward, and its straight-faced Chinese barmen in periwigs and frock coats looming out of the darkness and enquiring in good Americanese, 'what was his drinking pleasure?'

'A beer,' Craw's guest growled, helping himself to a handful of salted almonds. 'But *cold*. Hear that? *Muchee coldee.* And bring it *chop chop.*'

'Life smiles upon your Eminence?' Craw enquired.

'Drop all that, d'you mind? Gets on my wick.'

The Superintendent's embattled face had one expression only and that was of a bottomless cynicism. If man had a choice between good and evil, his baleful scowl said, he chose evil any time: and the world was cut down the middle, between those who knew this, and accepted it, and those long-haired pansies in Whitehall who believed in Father Christmas.

'Found her file yet?'

'No.'

'She calls herself Worth. She's had her syllables removed.'

'I know what she bloody calls herself. She can call herself bloody Mata Hari for all I care. There's still no file on her.'

'But there was?'

'Right cobber, there *was*,' the Rocker simpered furiously, mimicking Craw's accent. '"*There was*, and now there isn't." Do I make myself clear or shall I write it in invisible ink on a carrier pigeon's arse for you, you heathen bloody Aussie?'

Craw sat quiet a while, sipping his drink in steady, repetitive movements.

'Would Ko have done that?'

'Done what?' The Rocker was being wilfully obtuse.

'Had her file nicked?'

'Could have done.'

'The missing-record malady appears to be spreading,' Craw commented after further pause for refreshment. 'London sneezes and Hong Kong catches cold. My professional sympathies, Monsignor. My fraternal commiserations.' He lowered his voice to a toneless murmur. 'Tell me, is the name Sally Cale music to your Grace's ear?'

'Never heard of her.'

'What's her racket?'

'Chichi antiquities limited, Kowloonside. Pillaged art treasures, quality fakes, images of the Lord Buddha.'

'Where from?'

'Real stuff comes from Burma, way of Vientiane. Fakes are home produce. Sixty-year-old dyke,' he added sourly, addressing himself cautiously to another beer. 'Keeps alsations and chimpanzees. Just up your street.'

'Any form?'

'You're joking.'

'I am advised that it was Cale who introduced the girl to Ko.'

'So what? Cale pimps the roundeye lay. The Chows like her for it and so do I. I asked her to fix me up once. Said she hadn't got anything small enough, cheeky sow.'

'Our frail beauty was here allegedly on a gold-buying kick. Does that figure?'

The Rocker looked at Craw with fresh loathing and Craw looked at the Rocker, and it was a collision of two immovable objects.

'Course it bloody figures,' said the Rocker contemptuously. 'Cale had the corner in bent gold from Macao, didn't she?'

'So where did Ko fit in the bed?'

'Ah, come off it, don't pussyfoot around. Cale was the front man. It was Ko's racket all along. That fat bulldog of his went in as partner with her.'

'Tiu?'

The Rocker had lapsed once more into beery melancholy, but Craw would not be deflected, and put his mottled head very close to the Rocker's battered ear.

'My Uncle George will be highly appreciative of all available intelligence on the said Cale. Right? He will reward merit richly. He is particularly interested in her as of the fatal moment when she introduced my little lady to her Chow protector, and up to the present day. Names, dates, track record, whatever you've got in the fridge. Hear me?'

'Well you tell your Uncle George he'll get me five bloody years in Stanley jail.'

'And you won't want for company there either, will you, squire?' said Craw pointedly.

This was an unkind reference to recent sad events in the Rocker's world. Two of his senior colleagues had been sent down for several years a-piece, and there were others dolefully waiting to join them.

'Corruption,' the Rocker muttered in fury. 'They'll be discovering bloody steam next. Bloody Boy Scouts, they make me retch.'

Craw had heard it all before, but he heard it again now, for he had the golden gift of listening, which at Sarratt they prize far higher than communication.

'Thirty thousand bloody Europeans and four million bloody slanteyes, a different bloody morality, some of the best organized bloody crime syndicates in the bloody world. What do they expect me to do? We can't stop crime, so how do we control it? We dig out the big boys and we do a deal with them, of course we do: "Right, boys. No casual crime, no territorial infringements, everything clean and decent and my daughter can walk down the street any time of day or night. I want plenty of arrests to keep the judges happy and earn me my pathetic pension, and God help anybody who breaks the rules or is disrespectful to authority." All right they pay a little squeeze. Name me one person on this whole benighted island who doesn't pay a little squeeze along the line. If there's people *paying* it, there's people *getting* it. Stands to reason. And if there's people getting it . . . Besides,' said the Rocker, suddenly bored of his own theme, 'your Uncle George knows it all already.'

Craw's lion's head lifted slowly, until his dreadful eye was fixed squarely on the Rocker's averted face.

'George knows *what*, may I enquire?'

'Sally bloody Cale. We turned her inside out for you people years ago. Planning to subvert the bloody pound sterling or some damn thing. Bullion dumping on the Zürich gold markets, I ask you. Load of old cobblers as usual, if you want my view.'

It was another half-hour before the old Australian climbed wearily to his feet, wishing the Rocker long life and felicity.

'And you keep your arse to the sunset,' the Rocker growled.


Craw did not go home that night. He had friends, a Yale lawyer and his wife, who owned one of Hong Kong's two hundred odd private houses, an elderly rambling place on Pollock's Path high up on the peak and they had given him a key. A consular car was parked in the driveway, but Craw's friends were known for their addiction to the diplomatic whirl. Entering his room Craw seemed not at all surprised to find a respectful young American seated in the wicker armchair reading a heavy novel: a blond, trim boy in a neat diplomatic-looking suit. Craw did not greet this person, or remark his presence in any way, but instead placed himself at the glass-topped writing desk and, on a single sheet of paper, in the best tradition of his Papal mentor Smiley, began blocking out a message in capital letters, personal for His Holiness, heretical hands keep off. Afterwards, on another sheet, he set out the key to match it. When he had finished, he handed both to the boy, who with great deference put them in his pocket and departed swiftly without a word. Left alone, Craw waited till he heard the growl of the limousine before opening and reading the signal which the boy had left for him. Then he burned it and washed the ash down the sink before stretching himself gratefully on the bed.

A Gideon's day, but I can surprise them yet, he thought. He was tired. Christ he was tired. He saw the serried faces of the Sarratt children. But we progress, your Graces. Inexorably we progress. Albeit at the blindman's speed, as we tap-tap along in the dark. Time I smoked a little opium, he thought. Time I had a nice little girl to cheer me up. Christ, he was tired.

Smiley was equally tired, perhaps, but the text of Craw's message, when he received it an hour later, quickened him remarkably: the more so since the file on Miss Cale, Sally, last known address Hong Kong, art faker, illicit bullion dealer and occasional heroin trafficker, was for once alive and well and intact in the Circus archives. Not only that. The cryptonym of Sam Collins, in his capacity as the Circus's below-the-line resident in Vientiane, was blazoned all over it like the bunting of a long-awaited victory.

# TEN

## *tea and sympathy*

It has been laid at Smiley's door more than once since the curtain was rung down on the Dolphin case that now was the moment when George should have gone back to Sam Collins and hit him hard and straight just where it hurt. George could have cut a lot of corners that way, say the knowing; he could have saved vital time.

They are talking simplistic nonsense.

In the first place, time was of no account. The Russian goldseam, and the operation it financed, whatever that was, had been running for years, and undisturbed would presumably run for many more. The only people who were demanding action were the Whitehall barons, the Circus itself, and indirectly Jerry Westerby, who had to eat his head off with boredom for a couple more weeks while Smiley meticulously prepared his next move. Also, Christmas was approaching, which makes everyone impatient. Ko, and whatever operation he was controlling, showed no sign of development. 'Ko and his Russian money stood like a mountain before us,' Smiley wrote later, in his departing paper on Dolphin. 'We could visit the case whenever we wished, but we could not move it. The problem was going to be, not how to stir ourselves, but how to stir Ko to the point where we could read him.'

The lesson is clear: long before anyone else, except perhaps Connie Sachs, Smiley already saw the girl as a potential lever and, as such, the most important single character in the cast – far more important, for instance, than Jerry Westerby, who was at any time replaceable. This was just one of many good reasons why Smiley made it his business to get as close to her as security considerations allowed. Another was that the whole nature of the link between Sam Collins and the girl still floated in uncertainty. It's so easy now to turn round and say 'obvious' but at that time the issue was anything but cut and dried. The Cale file gave an indication. Smiley's intuitive feeling for Sam's footwork helped fill in some blanks; hasty backbearings by Registry produced clues and the usual batch of analogous cases; the anthology of Sam's field reports was illuminating. The fact remains that the longer Smiley held Sam off, the closer he came to an independent understanding of the relationships between the girl and Ko, and between the girl and Sam; and the stronger his bargaining power when he and Sam next sat down together.

And who on earth could honestly say how Sam would have reacted under pressure? The inquisitors have had their successes, true, but also failures. Sam was a very hard nut.

One more consideration also weighed with Smiley, though in his paper he is too gentlemanly to mention it. A lot of ghosts walked in those post-fall days, and one of them was a fear that, buried somewhere in the Circus, lay Bill Haydon's chosen successor: that Bill had brought him on, recruited and educated him against the very day when he himself, one way or another, would fade from the scene. Sam was originally a Haydon nominee. His later victimization by Haydon could easily have been a put-up job. Who was to say, in that very jumpy atmosphere, that Sam Collins, manoeuvring for readmission, was not the heir elect to Haydon's treachery?

For all these reasons George Smiley put on his raincoat and got himself out on the street. Willingly, no doubt – for at heart, he was still a case man. Even his detractors give him that.

In the district of old Barnsbury, in the London borough of Islington, on the day that Smiley finally made his discreet appearance there, the rain was taking a mid-morning pause. On the slate rooftops of Victorian cottages, the dripping chimney-pots huddled like bedraggled birds among the television aerials. Behind them, held up by scaffolding, rose the outline of a public housing estate abandoned for want of funds.

'Mr –?'

'Standfast,' Smiley replied politely, from beneath his umbrella.

Honourable men recognize each other instinctively. Mr Peter Worthington had only to open his front door and run his eye over the plump, rainsoaked figure on the step – the black official briefcase, with E II R embossed on the bulging plastic flap, the diffident and slightly shabby air – for an expression of friendly welcome to brighten his kindly face.

'That's it. Jolly decent of you to come. Foreign Office is in Downing Street these days, isn't it? What did you do? Tube from Charing Cross, I suppose? Come on in, have a cuppa.'

He was a public-school man who had gone into state education because it was more rewarding. His voice was moderate and consoling and loyal. Even his clothes, Smiley noticed, following him down the slim corridor, had a sort of faithfulness. Peter Worthington might be only thirty-four years old, but his heavy tweed suit would stay in fashion – or out of it – for as long as its owner needed. There was no garden. The study backed straight on to a concrete playground. A stout grille protected the window, and the playground was divided in two by a high wire fence. Beyond it stood the school itself, a scrolled Edwardian building not unlike the Circus, except that it was possible to see in. On the ground floor, Smiley noticed children's paintings hanging on the walls. Higher up, test-tubes in wooden racks. It was playtime and, in their own half girls in gymslips were racing after a handball. But on the other side of the wire the boys stood in silent groups, like pickets at a factory gate, blacks and whites separate. The study was knee deep in exercise books. A pictorial guide to the kings and queens of England hung on the chimney breast. Dark clouds filled the sky and made the school look rusty.

'Hope you don't mind the noise,' Peter Worthington called from the kitchen. 'I don't hear it any more, I'm afraid. Sugar?'

'No, no. No sugar, thank you,' said Smiley with a confessive grin.

'Watching the calories?'

'Well, a little, a little.' Smiley was acting himself, but more so, as they say at Sarratt. A mite homelier, a mite more careworn: the gentle, decent civil servant who had reached his ceiling by the age of forty, and stayed there ever since.

'There's lemon if you want it!' Peter Worthington called from the kitchen, clattering dishes inexpertly.

'Oh, no thank you! Just the milk.'

On the threadbare study floor lay evidence of yet another, smaller child: bricks, and a scribbling book with D's and A's scrawled endlessly. From the lamp hung a Christmas star in cardboard. On the drab walls, Magi and sleds and cotton wool. Peter Worthington returned carrying a tea tray. He was big and rugged, with wiry brown hair going early to grey. After all the clattering, the cups were still not very clean.

'Clever of you to choose my free period,' he said, with a nod at the exercise books. 'If you can call it free, with that lot to correct.'

'I do think you people are very underrated,' Smiley said, mildly shaking his head. 'I have friends in the profession myself. They sit up half the night, just correcting the work, so they assure me and I've no reason to doubt them.'

'They're the conscientious ones.'

'I trust I may include you in that category.'

Peter Worthington grinned, suddenly very pleased. 'Afraid so. If a thing's worth doing it's worth doing well,' he said, helping Smiley out of his raincoat.

'I could wish that view were a little more widely held, to be frank.'

'You should have been a teacher yourself,' said Peter Worthington and they both laughed.

'What do you do with your little boy?' said Smiley, sitting down.

'Ian? Oh he goes to his Gran's. My side, not hers,' he added, as he poured. He handed Smiley a cup. 'You married?' he asked.

'Yes, yes I am, and very happily so too, if I may say so.'

'Kids?'

Smiley shook his head, allowing himself a small frown of disappointment. 'Alas,' he said.

'That's where it hurts,' said Peter Worthington, entirely reasonably.

'I'm sure it does,' said Smiley. 'Still, we'd have liked the experience. You feel it more, at our age.'

'You said on the phone there was some news of Elizabeth,' said Peter Worthington. 'I'd be awfully grateful to hear it, I must say.'

'Well nothing to be excited about,' said Smiley cautiously.

'But hopeful. One must have hope.'

Smiley stooped to the official black plastic briefcase and unlocked the cheap clasp.

'Well now, I wonder whether you'll oblige me,' he said. 'It's not that I'm holding back on you, but we do like to be sure. I'm a belt and braces man myself and I don't mind admitting it. We do exactly the same with our foreign deceases. We never commit ourselves until we're *absolutely sure*. Forenames, surname, full address, date of birth if we can get it, we go to no end of trouble. Just to be safe. Not *cause*, of course, we don't do *cause*, that's up to the local authorities.'

'Shoot ahead,' said Peter Worthington heartily. Noticing the exaggeration in his tone, Smiley glanced up, but Peter Worthington's honest face was turned away and he seemed to be studying a pile of old music stands heaped in a corner.

Licking his thumb, Smiley laboriously opened a file on his lap and turned some pages. It was the Foreign Office file, marked 'Missing Person', and obtained by Lacon on a pretext to Enderby. 'Would it be asking too much if I went through the details with you from the beginning? Only the salient ones naturally, and only what you wish to tell me, I don't have to say that, do I? My headache is, you see, I'm actually not the normal person for this work. My colleague Wendover, whom you met, is sick, I'm afraid – and, well, we don't always like to put *everything* on paper do we? He's an admirable fellow but when it comes to report writing I do find him a little *terse*. Not sloppy, far from it, but sometimes a little wanting on the human picture side.'

'I've always been absolutely frank. Always,' said Peter Worthington rather impatiently to the music stand. 'I believe in that.'

'And for *our* part, I can assure you, we at the office do respect a confidence.'

A sudden lull descended. It had not occurred to Smiley, till this moment, that the scream of children could be soothing; yet as it stopped, and the playground emptied, he had a sense of dislocation which took him a moment to get over.

'Break's over,' said Peter Worthington with a smile.

'I'm sorry?'

'Break. Milk and buns. What you pay your taxes for.'

'Now first of all there is no question here, according to my colleague Wendover's notes – nothing against him, I hasten to say – that Mrs Worthington left under any kind of constraint . . . Just a minute. Let me explain what I mean by that. Please. She left voluntarily. She left alone. She was not unduly prevailed upon, lured, or in any way the victim of unnatural pressure. Pressure for instance which, let us say, might in due course be the subject of a legal court action by yourself or others against a third party not so far named?'

Longwindedness, as Smiley knew, creates in those who must put up with it an almost unbearable urge to speak. If they do not interrupt directly, they at least counter with pent-up energy: and as a schoolmaster, Peter Worthington was not by any means a natural listener.

'She left alone, absolutely alone, and my entire position is, was, and always has been, that she was free to do so. If she had *not* left alone, if there had been others involved, men, God knows we're all human, it would have made no difference. Does that satisfy your question? Children have a right to both parents,' he ended, stating a maxim.

Smiley was writing diligently but very slowly. Peter Worthington drummed his fingers on his knee, then cracked them, one after another, in a quick impatient salvo.

'Now in the interim, Mr Worthington, can you please tell me whether a custody order has been applied for in respect of –'

'We always knew she'd wander. That was understood. I was her anchor. She called me "my anchor". Either that or "schoolmaster". I didn't mind. It wasn't badly meant. It was just, she couldn't bear to say *Peter*. She loved me as a *concept*. Not as a figure perhaps, a body, a mind, a person, not even as a partner. As a concept, a necessary adjunct to her personal, human completeness. She had an urge to please, I understand that. It was part of her insecurity, she longed to be admired. If she paid a compliment, it was because she wished for one in return.'

'I see,' said Smiley, and wrote again, as if physically subscribing to this view.

'I mean nobody could have a girl like Elizabeth as a wife and expect to have her all to himself. It wasn't natural. I've come to terms with that now. Even little Ian had to call her Elizabeth. Again I understand. She couldn't bear the chains of "Mummy". Child running after her calling "Mummy". Too much for her. That's all right, I understand that too. I can imagine it might be hard for you, as a childless man, to understand how a woman of any stamp, a mother, well cared for and loved and looked after, not even having to earn, can literally walk out on her own son and not even send him a postcard from that day to this. Probably that worries, even disgusts you. Well, I take a different view, I'm afraid. At the time, I grant you: yes, it was hard.' He glanced toward the wired playground. He spoke quietly with no hint at all of self-pity. He might have been talking to a pupil. 'We try to teach people freedom here. Freedom within citizenship. Let them develop their individuality. How could *I* tell *her* who *she* was? I wanted to be there, that's all. To be Elizabeth's friend. Her longstop: that was another of her words for me. "My longstop". The point is, she didn't *need* to go. She could have done it all here. At my side. Women need a prop, you know. Without one –'

'And you still have not received any direct word of her?' Smiley enquired meekly. 'Not a letter, not even that postcard to Ian, nothing?'

'Not a sausage.'

Smiley wrote. 'Mr Worthington, to your knowledge, has your wife ever used another name?' For some reason the question threatened to annoy Peter Worthington quite considerably. He flared, as if he were responding to impertinence in class, and his finger shot up to command silence. But Smiley hurried on. 'Her *maiden* name, for instance? Perhaps an abbreviation of her married one, which in a non-English speaking country *could* create difficulties with the natives –'

'Never. Never, *never*. You have to understand basic human behavioural psychology. She was a text-book case. She couldn't wait to get rid of her father's name. One very good reason why she married me was to have a *new* father and a *new* name. Once she'd got it, why should she give it up? It was the same with her romancing, her wild, *wild* story telling. She was trying to escape from her environment. Having done so, having succeeded, having found *me*, and the stability which I represent, she naturally no longer needed to *be* someone else. She *was* someone else. She was fulfilled. So *why go?*'

Again Smiley took his time. He looked at Peter Worthington as if in uncertainty, he looked at his file, he turned to the last entry, tipped his spectacles and read it, obviously not by any means for the first time.

'Mr Worthington, if our information is correct, and we have good reason to believe it is – I'd say our estimate was conservative eighty per cent sure, I'd go *that* far – your wife is at present using the surname *Worth*. And she is using a forename with a German spelling, curiously enough, L-I-E-S-E. Pronounced not Liza, I am told, but Leesa. I wondered whether you were in a position to confirm or deny this suggestion, also the suggestion that she is actively connected with a Far Eastern jewellery business with ramifications extending to Hong Kong and other major centres. She appears to be living in a style of affluence and good social appearance, moving in quite high circles.'

Peter Worthington absorbed very little of this, apparently. He had taken a position on the floor, but seemed unable to lower his knees. Cracking his fingers once more, he glared impatiently at the music stands crowded like skeletons into the corner of the room, and was already trying to speak before Smiley had ended.

'Look. This is what I want. That whoever approaches her should make the right kind of point. I don't want any passionate appeals, no appeals to conscience. All that's out. Just a straight statement of what's offered, and she's welcome. That's all.'

Smiley took refuge in the file.

'Well before we come to *that*, if we could just continue going through the facts, Mr Worthington –'

'There *aren't* facts,' said Peter Worthington, thoroughly irritated again. 'There are just two people. Well, three with Ian. There *aren't* facts in a thing like this. Not in *any* marriage. That's what life teaches us. Relationships are *entirely* subjective. I'm sitting on the floor. *That's* a fact. You're writing. *That's* a fact. Her mother was behind it. *That's* a fact. Follow me? Her father is a raving criminal lunatic. *That's* a fact. Elizabeth is *not* the daughter of the Queen of Sheba *or* the natural grandchild of Lloyd George. Whatever she may say. She has *not* got a degree in Sanskrit, which she chose to tell the headmistress who still believes it to this day. "When are we going to see your charming oriental wife again?" She knows no more about jewellery than I do. *That's* a fact.'

'Dates and places,' Smiley murmured to the file. 'If I could just check those for a start.'

'Absolutely,' said Peter Worthington handsomely, and from a green tin tea-pot refilled Smiley's cup. Blackboard chalk was worked into his large finger-tips. It was like the grey in his hair.

'It really was the mother that messed her up, I'm afraid, though,' he went on, in the same entirely reasonable tone. 'All that urgency about putting her on the stage, then ballet, then trying to get her into television. Her mother just wanted Elizabeth to be admired. As a substitute for herself, of course. It's perfectly natural, psychologically. Read Berne. Read anyone. That's just *her* way of defining *her* individuality. Through her daughter. One must respect that those things happen. I understand all that, now. She's okay, I'm okay, the world's okay, Ian's okay, then suddenly she's off.'

'Do you happen to know whether she communicates with her mother, incidentally?'

Peter Worthington shook his head.

'Absolutely not, I'm afraid. She'd seen through her entirely by the time she left. Broken with her completely. The one hurdle I can safely say I helped her over. My one contribution to her happiness –'

'I don't think we have her mother's address here,' said Smiley, leafing doggedly through the pages of the file. 'You don't –'

Peter Worthington gave it to him rather loud, at dictation speed.

'And now the dates and places,' Smiley repeated. '*Please.*'

She had left him two years ago. Peter Worthington repeated not just the date but the hour. There had been no scene – Peter Worthington didn't hold with scenes – Elizabeth had had too many with her mother – they'd had a happy evening, as a matter of fact, *particularly* happy. For a diversion he'd taken her to the kebab house.

'Perhaps you spotted it as you came down the road? – The Knossos, it's called, next door to the Express Dairy?'

They'd had wine and a real blow-out, and Andrew Wiltshire, the new English master had come along to make a three. Elizabeth had introduced this Andrew to yoga only a few weeks before. They had gone to classes together at the Sobell Centre and become great buddies.

'She was really *into* Yoga,' he said with an approving nod of the grizzled head. 'It was a real *interest* for her. Andrew was just the sort of chap to bring her out. Extrovert, unreflective, physical . . . perfect for her,' he said determinedly.

The three of them had returned to the house at ten, because of the babysitter, he said: himself, Andrew and Elizabeth. He'd made coffee, they'd listened to music, and around eleven Elizabeth gave them both a kiss and said she was going over to her mother's to see how she was.

'I had understood she had broken with her mother,' Smiley objected mildly, but Peter Worthington chose not to hear.

'Of course, *kisses* mean nothing with her,' Peter Worthington explained, as a matter of information. 'She kisses everybody, the pupils, her girlfriends –

she'd kiss the dustman, anyone. She's *very* outgoing. Once again, she can't leave anyone alone. I mean *every* relationship has to be a conquest. With her child, the waiter at the restaurant . . . then when she's won them, they bore her. Naturally, she went upstairs, looked at Ian and I've no doubt used the moment to collect her passport and the housekeeping money from the bedroom. She left a note saying "sorry" and I haven't seen her since. Nor's Ian,' said Peter Worthington.

'Er, has *Andrew* heard from her?' Smiley inquired, with another tilt of his spectacles.

'Why should he have done?'

'You said they were friends, Mr Worthington. Sometimes third parties become intermediaries in these affairs.'

On the word *affair*, he looked up and found himself staring directly into Peter Worthington's honest, abject eyes: and for a moment the two masks slipped simultaneously. Was Smiley observing? Or was he being observed? Perhaps it was only his embattled imagination – or did he sense, in himself and in this weak boy across the room, the stirring of an embarrassed kinship? 'There should be a *league* for deceived husbands who feel sorry for themselves. You've all got the same boring, awful charity!' Ann had once flung at him. You never knew your Elizabeth, Smiley thought, still staring at Peter Worthington: and I never knew my Ann.

'That's all I can remember really,' said Peter Worthington. 'After that, it's a blank.'

'Yes,' said Smiley, inadvertently taking refuge in Worthington's repeated assertion. 'Yes, I understand.'

He rose to leave. A little boy was standing in the doorway. He had a shrouded, hostile stare. A placid heavy woman stood behind him, holding him by both wrists above his head, so that he seemed to swing from her, though really he was standing by himself.

'Look, there's Daddy,' said the woman, gazing at Worthington with brown, attaching eyes.

'Jenny, hi. This is Mr Standfast from the Foreign Office.'

'How do you do?' said Smiley politely and after a few minutes' meaningless chatter, and a promise of further information in due course, should any become available, quietly took his leave.

'Oh and happy Christmas,' Peter Worthington called from the steps.

'Ah yes. Yes indeed. And to you too. To all of you. Happy indeed, and many more of them.'

In the transport café they put in sugar unless you asked them not to, and each time the Indian woman made a cup, the tiny kitchen filled with steam. In twos and threes, not talking, men ate breakfast, lunch or supper, depending on the point they had reached in their separate days. Here also Christmas was approaching. Six greasy coloured glass balls dangled over the counter for festive cheer, and a net stocking appealed for help for spastic kids. Smiley stared at an evening paper, not reading it. In a corner not twelve feet from him little Fawn had taken up the babysitter's classic position. His dark eyes smiled agreeably on the diners and on the doorway. He lifted his cup with his left hand, while his right idled close to his chest. Did Karla sit like this? Smiley wondered. Did Karla take refuge among the unsuspecting? Control had. Control had made a whole second, third or fourth life for himself in a two-

roomed upstairs flat, beside the Western by-pass, under the plain name of
Matthews, not filed with housekeepers as an alias. Well, 'whole' life was an
exaggeration. But he had kept clothes there, and a woman, Mrs Matthews
herself, even a cat. And taken golf lessons at an artisans' club on Thursday
mornings early, while from his desk in the Circus he poured scorn on the
great unwashed, and on golf, and on love, and on any other piffling human
pursuit which secretly might tempt him. He had even rented a garden
allotment, Smiley remembered, down by a railway siding. Mrs Matthews had
insisted on driving Smiley to see it in her groomed Morris car on the day he
broke the sad news to her. It was as big a mess as anyone else's allotment:
standard roses, winter vegetables they hadn't used, a toolshed crammed with
hosepipes and seedboxes.

Mrs Matthews was a widow, pliant but capable.

'All I want to know,' she had said, having read the figure on the cheque. 'All
I want to be sure of, Mr Standfast: is he *really* dead, or has he gone back to his
wife?'

'He is really dead,' Smiley assured her, and she believed him gratefully. He
forebore from adding that Control's wife had gone to her grave eleven years
ago, still believing her husband was something in the Coal Board.

Did Karla have to scheme in committees? Fight cabals, deceive the stupid,
flatter the clever, look in distorting mirrors of the Peter Worthington variety,
all in order to do the job?

He glanced at his watch, then at Fawn. The coinbox stood next to the
lavatory, but when Smiley asked the proprietor for change, he refused it on
the grounds that he was too busy.

'Hand it over, you awkward bastard!' shouted a long-distance driver all in
leather. The proprietor briskly obliged.

'How did it go?' Guillam asked, taking the call on the direct line.

'Good background,' Smiley replied.

'Hooray,' said Guillam.

Another of the charges later levelled against Smiley was that he wasted
time on menial matters, instead of delegating them to his subordinates.


There are blocks of flats near the Town and Country Golf Course on the
northern fringes of London that are like the superstructure of permanently
sinking ships. They lie at the end of long lawns where the flowers are never
quite in flower, the husbands man the lifeboats all in a flurry at about eight-
thirty in the morning and the women and children spend the day keeping
afloat until their menfolk return too tired to sail anywhere. These buildings
were built in the Thirties and have stayed a grubby white ever since. Their
oblong, steelframed windows look on to the lush billows of the links where
weekday women in eyeshades wander like lost souls. One such block is called
Arcady Mansions, and the Pellings lived in number seven, with a cramped
view of the ninth green which vanished when the beeches were in leaf. When
Smiley rang the bell he heard nothing except the thin electric tinkle: no
footsteps, no dog, no music. The door opened and a man's cracked voice said
'Yes?' from the darkness, but it belonged to a woman. She was tall and
stooping. A cigarette hung from her hand.

'My names is *Oates*,' Smiley said, offering a big green card encased in
cellophane. To a different cover belongs a different name.

'Oh it's you is it? Come in. Dine, see the show. You sounded younger on the telephone,' she boomed in a curdled voice striving for refinement. 'He's in here. He thinks you're a spy,' she said, squinting at the green card. 'You're not, are you?'

'No,' said Smiley. 'I'm afraid not. Just a snooper.'

The flat was all corridors. She led the way, leaving a vapour trail of gin. One leg slurred as she walked, and her right arm was stiff. Smiley guessed she had had a stroke. She dressed as if nobody had ever admired her height or sex. And as if she didn't care. She wore flat shoes and a mannish pullover with a belt that made her shoulders broad.

'He says he's never heard of you. He says he's looked you up in the telephone directory and you don't exist.'

'We like to be discreet,' Smiley said.

She pushed open a door. 'He exists,' she reported loudly, ahead of her into the room. 'And he's not a spy, he's a snooper.'

In a far chair, a man was reading the *Daily Telegraph*, holding it in front of his face so that Smiley only saw the bald head, and the dressing gown, and the short crossed legs ending in leather bedroom slippers; but somehow he knew at once that Mr Pelling was the kind of small man who would only ever marry tall women. The room carried everything he could need in order to survive alone. His television, his bed, his gas fire, a table to eat at and an easel for painting by numbers. On the wall hung an over-coloured portrait photograph of a very beautiful girl with an inscription scribbled diagonally across one corner, in the way that film stars wish love to the unglamorous. Smiley recognized it as Elizabeth Worthington. He had seen a lot of phogotraphs already.

'Mr Oates, meet Nunc,' she said, and all but curtsied.

The *Daily Telegraph* came down with the slowness of a garrison flag, revealing an aggressive, glittering little face with thick brows and managerial spectacles.

'Yes. Well just who are you precisely?' said Mr Pelling. 'Are you Secret Service or aren't you? Don't shilly shally, out with it and be done. I don't hold with snooping you see. What's that?' he demanded.

'His *card*,' said Mrs Pelling, offering it. 'Green in hue.'

'Oh, we're exchanging notes are we? I need a card too, then, Cess, don't I? Better get some printed, my dear. Slip down to Smith's will you?'

'Do you like *tea*?' Mrs Pelling asked, peering down at Smiley with her head on one side.

'What are giving him tea for?' Mr Pelling demanded, watching her plug in the kettle. 'He doesn't need tea. He's not a guest. He's not even Intelligence. I didn't ask him. Stay the week,' he said to Smiley. 'Move in if you like. Have her bed. *Bullion Universal Security Advisors*, my Aunt Fanny.'

'He wants to talk about Lizzie, darling,' said Mrs Pelling, setting a tray for her husband. 'Now be a father for a change.'

'Fat lot of good her bed would do *you*, mind,' said Mr Pelling, taking up his *Telegraph* again.

'For those kind words,' said Mrs Pelling and gave a laugh. It consisted of two notes, like a birdcall, and was not meant to be funny. A disjointed silence followed.

Mrs Pelling handed Smiley a cup of tea. Accepting it, he addressed himself to the back of Mr Pelling's newspaper. 'Sir, your daughter Elizabeth is being considered for an important appointment with a major overseas corporation. My organization has been asked in confidence – as a normal but very necessary formality these days – to approach friends and relations in this country and obtain character references.'

'That's *us* dear,' Mrs Pelling explained, in case her husband hadn't understood.

The newspaper came down with a snap.

'Are you suggesting my daughter is of bad character? Is that what you're sitting here, drinking my tea, suggesting?'

'No, sir,' said Smiley.

'No, sir,' said Mrs Pelling, unhelpfully.

A long silence followed, which Smiley was at no great pains to end.

'Mr Pelling,' he said finally, in a firm and patient voice. 'I understand that you spent many years in the Post Office, and rose to a high position.'

'Many, *many* years,' Mrs Pelling agreed.

'I worked,' said Mr Pelling from behind his newspaper once more. 'There's too much talk in the world. Not enough work done.'

'Did you employ criminals in your department?'

The newspaper rattled, then held still.

'Or Communists?' said Smiley, equally gently.

'If we did we damn soon got rid of them,' said Mr Pelling, and this time the newspaper stayed down.

Mrs Pelling snapped her fingers. 'Like *that*,' she said.

'Mr Pelling,' Smiley continued, in the same bedside manner, 'the position for which your daughter is being considered is with one of the major eastern companies. She will be specializing in air transport and her work will give her advance knowledge of large gold shipments to and from this country, as well as the movement of diplomatic couriers and classified mails. It carries an extremely high remuneration. I don't think it unreasonable – and I don't think you do – that your daughter should be subject to the same procedures as any other candidate for such a responsible – and desirable – post.'

'Who employs *you*?' said Mr Pelling. 'That's what I'm getting at. Who says *you're* responsible?'

'Nunc,' Mrs Pelling pleaded. 'Who says anyone is?'

'Don't *Nunc* me! Give him some more tea. You're hostess, aren't you? Well act like one. It's high time Lizzie was rewarded and I'm frankly displeased that it hasn't occurred before now, seeing what they owe her.'

Mr Pelling resumed his reading of Smiley's impressive green card. '"Correspondents in Asia, USA and Middle East." Pen friends I suppose *they* are. Head Office in South Molton Street. Any enquiries telephone bla bla bla. Who do I get then? Your partner in crime, I suppose.'

'If it's South Molton Street he *must* be all right,' said Mrs Pelling.

'Authority without responsibility,' Mr Pelling said, dialling the number. He spoke as if someone were holding his nostrils. 'I don't hold with it I'm afraid.'

'*With* responsibility,' Smiley corrected him. 'We as a company are pledged to indemnify our customers against any dishonesty on the part of staff we recommend. We are insured accordingly.'

The number rang five times before the Circus switchboard answered it, and Smiley hoped to God there wasn't going to be a muddle.

'Give me the Managing Director,' Mr Pelling ordered. 'I don't care if he's in conference! Has he got a name? Well what is it? Well you tell Mr Andrew Forbes-Lisle that Mr Humphrey Pelling desires a personal word with him. Now.' Long wait. *Well done thought Smiley. Nice touch.* 'Pelling here. I've got a man calling himself Oates sitting in front of me. Short, fat and worried. What do you want me to do with him?'

In the background, Smiley heard Peter Guillam's resonant, officer-like tones all but ordering Pelling to stand up when he addressed him. Mollified, Mr Pelling rang off.

'Does Lizzie know you're talking to us?' he asked.

'She'd laugh her head off if she did,' said his wife.

'She may not even know she is being considered for the post,' said Smiley. 'More and more, the tendency these days is to make the approach after clearance has been obtained.'

'It's for Lizzie, Nunc,' Mrs Pelling reminded him. 'You know you love her although we haven't heard of her for a year.'

'You don't write to her at all?' Smiley asked, sympathetically.

'She doesn't want it,' said Mrs Pelling with a glance at her husband.

The tiniest grunt escaped Smiley's lips. It could have been regret, but it was actually relief.

'Give him more tea,' her husband ordered. 'He's wolfed that lot already.'

He stared quizzically at Smiley yet again. 'I'm still not *sure* he's not Secret Service, even now,' he said. 'He may not be glamour, but that could be deliberate.'

Smiley had brought forms. The Circus printer had run them up last night, on buff paper – which was fortunate, for in Mr Pelling's world, it turned out, forms were the legitimization of everything, and buff was the respectable colour. So the men worked together like two friends solving a crossword, Smiley perched at his side and Mr Pelling doing the pencil work, while his wife sat smoking and staring through the grey net curtains, turning her wedding ring round and round. They did date and place of birth – 'Up the road at the Alexandra Nursing Home. Pulled it down now, haven't they Cess? Turned it into one of those ice-cream blocks.' They did education, and Mr Pelling gave his views on that subject.

'I never let one school have her too long, did I, Cess? Keep her mind alert. Don't let it get into a rut. A change is worth a holiday, I said. Didn't I, Cess?'

'He's read books on education,' said Mrs Pelling.

'We married late,' he said, as if explaining her presence.

'We wanted her on the stage,' she said. 'He wanted to be her manager, among other things.'

He gave other dates. There was a drama school and there was a secretarial course.

'Grooming,' Mr Pelling said. 'Preparation, not education, that's what I believe in. Throw a bit of everything at her. Make her worldly. Give her deportment.'

'Oh, she's got the deportment,' Mrs Pelling agreed, and with the click of her throat blew out a lot of cigarette smoke. '*And* the worldliness.'

'But she never *finished* secretarial college?' Smiley asked, pointing to the panel. 'Or the drama.'

'Didn't need to,' said Mr Pelling.

They came to previous employers. Mr Pelling listed half a dozen in the London area, all within eighteen months of one another.

'All bores,' said Mrs Pelling pleasantly.

'She was looking around,' said her husband airily. 'She was taking the pulse before committing herself. I made her, didn't I, Cess? They all wanted her but I wouldn't fall for it.' He flung out an arm at her. 'And don't say it didn't pay off in the end!' he yelled. 'Even if we aren't allowed to talk about it!'

'She liked the ballet best,' said Mrs Pelling. 'Teaching the children. She *adores* children. *Adores* them.'

This annoyed Mr Pelling very much. 'She's making a *career*, Cess,' he shouted slamming the form on his knee. 'God Almighty, you cretinous woman, do you want her to go back to him?'

'Now what was she doing in the Middle East exactly?' Smiley asked.

'Taking courses. Business schools. Learning Arabic,' said Mr Pelling, acquiring a sudden largeness of view. To Smiley's surprise he even stood, and gesticulating imperiously, roamed the room. 'What got her there in the first place, I don't mind telling you, was an unfortunate marriage.'

'Jesus,' said Mrs Pelling.

Upright, he had a prehensile sturdiness which made him formidable. 'But we got her back. Oh yes. Her room's always ready when she wants it. Next door to mine. She can find me any time. Oh yes. We helped her over that hurdle, didn't we, Cess? Then one day I said to her –'

'She came with a darling English teacher with curly hair,' his wife interrupted. 'Andrew.'

'Scottish,' Mr Pelling corrected her automatically.

'Andrew was a *nice* boy but no match for Nunc, was he darling?'

'He wasn't enough for her. All that Yogi-bear stuff. Swinging by your tail is what I call it. Then one day I said to her: "Lizzie: Arabs. That's where your future is." He clicked his fingers, pointing at an imaginary daughter. '"Oil. Money. Power. Away you go. Pack. Get your ticket. Off."'

'A nightclub paid her fare,' said Mrs Pelling. 'It took her for one hell of a ride too.'

'It did no such thing!' Mr Pelling retorted, hunching his broad shoulders to yell at her, but Mrs Pelling continued as if he weren't there.

'She answered this advertisement, you see. Some woman in Bradford with a soft line of talk. A bawd. "Hostesses needed, but not what you'd think," she said. They paid her air fare and the moment she landed in Bahrein they made her sign a contract giving over all her salary for the rent of her flat. From then on they'd got her, hadn't they? There was nowhere she could go, was there? The Embassy couldn't help her, no one could. She's beautiful, you see.'

'You stupid bloody hag. We're talking about a *career*! Don't you love her? Your own daughter? You unnatural mother! My God!'

'She's got her career,' said Mrs Pelling complacently. 'The best in the world.'

In desperation Mr Pelling turned to Smiley. 'Put down "reception work and picking up the language" and put down –'

'Perhaps you could tell me,' Smiley mildly interjected, as he licked his thumb and turned the page '– this might be the way to do it – of any experience she has had in the transportation industry.'

'And put down' – Mr Pelling clenched his fists and stared first at his wife, then at Smiley, and he seemed in two minds as to whether to go on or not – 'Put down "working for the British Secret Service in a high capacity." Undercover. Go on! Put it down! There. It's out now.' He swung back at his wife. 'He's in security, he said so. He's got a right to know and she's got a right to have it known of her. No daughter of mine's going to be *an unsung heroine*. *Or* unpaid! She'll get the George Medal before she's done, you mark my words!'

'Oh balls,' said Mrs Pelling wearily. 'That was just one of her *stories*. You know that.'

'Could we *possibly* take things one by one?' Smiley asked, in a tone of gentle forbearance. 'We were talking, I think, of experience in the transportation industry.'

Sage-like, Mr Pelling put his thumb and forefinger to his chin.

'Her first *commercial* experience,' he began ruminatively. 'Running her own show entirely, you understand – when everything came together, and jelled, and really began to pay off – apart from the Intelligence side I'm referring to – employing staff and handling large quantities of cash and exercising the responsibility she's capable of – came in how do you pronounce it?'

'Vi-ent-iane,' his wife droned with perfect Anglicisation.

'Capital of La-os,' said Mr Pelling, pronouncing the word to rhyme with chaos.

'And what was the name of the firm, please?' Smiley enquired, pencil poised over the appropriate panel.

'A distilling company,' said Mr Pelling grandly. 'My daughter Elizabeth owned and managed one of the major distilling concessions in that wartorn country.'

'And the name?'

'She was selling kegs of unbranded whisky to American layabouts,' said Mrs Pelling, to the window. 'On commission, twenty per cent. They bought their kegs and left them to mature in Scotland as an investment to be sold off later.'

'*They*, in this case, being . . . ?' Smiley asked.

'Then her lover went and filched the money,' Mrs Pelling said. 'It was a racket. Rather a good one.'

'Sheer unadulterated balderdash!' Mr Pelling shouted. 'The woman's insane. Disregard her.'

'And what was her address at that time, please?' Smiley asked.

'Put down "representative",' said Mr Pelling, shaking his head as if things were quite out of hand. 'Distiller's representative and secret agent.'

'She was living with a pilot,' said Mrs Pelling. 'Tiny, she called him. If it hadn't been for Tiny, she'd have starved. He was gorgeous but the war had turned him inside out. Well, of *course* it would! Same with *our* boys, wasn't it? Missions night after night, day after day.' Putting back her head, she screamed very loud: '*Scramble!*'

'She's mad,' Mr Pelling explained.

'Nervous wrecks at eighteen, half of them. But they stuck it. They loved Churchill, you see. They loved his *guts*.'

'Blind mad,' Mr Pelling repeated. 'Barking. Mad as a newt.'

'I'm sorry,' said Smiley, writing busily. 'Tiny who? The pilot? What was his name?'

'Ricardo. Tiny Ricardo. A *lamb*. He died you know,' she said, straight at her husband. 'Lizzie was *heart-broken*, wasn't she, Nunc? Still, it was probably the best way.'

'She wasn't living with *anyone*, you anthropoid ape! It was a put-up, the whole thing. She was working for the British Secret Service!'

'Oh my Christ,' said Mrs Pelling hopelessly.

'*Not* your Christ. *My* Mellon. Take that down, Oates. Let me see you write it down. *Mellon*. The name of her commanding officer in the British Secret Serice was M-E-L-L-O-N. Like the fruit but twice as many l's. Mellon. Pretending to be a plain simple trader. *And* making quite a decent thing of it. Naturally, an intelligent man, he would. But underneath' – Mr Pelling drove a fist into his open palm, making an astonishingly loud noise – 'but under-

neath the bland and affable exterior of a British businessman, this same
Mellon, two l's, was fighting a secret and lonely war against Her Majesty's
enemies and my Lizzie was helping him do it. Drug dealers, Chinese,
homosexuals, every single foreign element sworn to the subversion of our
island nation, my gallant daughter Lizzie and her friend Colonel Mellon
between them fought to check their insidious progress! And that's the honest
truth.'

'*Now* ask me where she gets it from,' said Mrs Pelling, and leaving the door
open, trailed away down the corridor grumbling to herself. Glancing after
her, Smiley saw her pause and seem to tilt her head beckoning to him from
the gloom. They heard a distant door slam shut.

'It's true,' said Pelling stoutly, but more quietly. 'She did, she did, she did.
My daughter was a senior and respected operative of our British
Intelligence.'

Smiley did not reply at first, he was too intent on writing. So for a while
there was no sound but the slow scratch of his pen on paper, and the rustle as
he turned the page.

'Good. Well then, I'll just take those details too, if I may. In confidence
naturally. We come across quite a lot of it in our work, I don't mind telling
you.'

'*Right*,' said Mr Pelling, and sitting himself vigorously on a plastic-covered
dumpty, he pulled a single sheet of paper from his wallet and thrust it into
Smiley's hand. It was a letter, hand-written, one and a half sides long. The
script was at once grandiose and childish, with high, curled I's for the first
person, while the other characters appeared more cautiously. It began 'My
dearest darling Pops' and it ended 'Your One True Daughter Elizabeth', and
the message between, the bulk of which Smiley committed to his memory, ran
like this: 'I have arrived in Vientiane which is a flat town, a bit French and
wild but don't worry, I have important news for you which I have to impart
immediately. It is possible you may not hear from me for a bit but don't worry
even if you hear bad things. I'm all right and cared for and doing it for a
Good Cause you would be proud of. As soon as I arrived I contacted the
British Trade Consul Mister Mackervoor a British and he sent me for a job to
Mellon. I'm not allowed to tell you so you'll have to trust me but that's only
half the story. Mellon is Dispatching me on a mission to Hong Kong and I'm
to investigate Bullion and Drugs, pretending otherwise, and he's got men
everywhere to look after me and his real name isn't Mellon. Mackervoor is in
on it only secretly. If anything happens to me it will be worth it anyway
because you and I know the Country matters and whats one life among so
many in Asia where life counts for naught anyway? This is good Work, Dad,
the kind we dreamed of you and me and specially you when you were in the
war fighting for your family and loved ones. Pray for me and look after Mum
I will always love you even in prison.'

Smiley handed back the letter. 'There's no date,' he objected flatly. 'Can
you give me the date, Mr Pelling? Even approximately?'

Pelling gave it not approximately but exactly. Not for nothing had he spent
his working life handling the Royal Mails.

'She's never written to me since,' said Mr Pelling proudly, folding the letter
back into his wallet. 'Not a word, not a peep have I had out of her from that
day to this. Totally unneccessary. We're one. It was said, I never alluded to it,
neither did she. She'd tipped me the wink. I knew. She knew I knew. You'll

never get finer understanding between daughter and father than that. Everything that followed: Ricardo, whatever his name was, alive, dead, who cares? Some Chinaman she's on about, forget him. Men friends, girl friends, business, disregard everything you hear. It's cover, the lot. They own her, they control her completely. She works for Mellon and she loves her father. Finish.'

'You've been very kind,' said Smiley, packing together his papers. 'Please don't worry, I'll see myself out.'

'See yourself how you like,' Mr Pelling said with a flash of his old wit.

As Smiley closed the door, he had resumed his armchair and was ostentatiously looking for his place in the *Daily Telegraph*.

In the dark corridor the smell of drink was stronger. Smiley had counted nine paces before the door slammed, so it must have been the last door on the left, and the furthest from Mr Pelling. It might have been the lavatory, except the lavatory was marked with a sign saying 'Buckingham Palace Rear Entrance'. He called her name very softly and hear her yell 'Get out'. He stepped inside and found himself in her bedroom, and Mrs Pelling sprawled on the bed with a glass in her hand, riffling through a heap of picture postcards. The room itself, like her husband's, was fitted up for a separate existence, with a cooker and a sink and a pile of unwashed plates. Round the walls were snapshots of a tall and very pretty girl, some with boy friends, some alone, mainly against oriental backgrounds. The smell was of gin and cat.

'He won't leave her alone,' Mrs Pelling said. 'Nunc won't. Never could. He tried but he never could. She's beautiful, you see,' she explained for the second time, and rolled on to her back while she held a postcard above her head to read it.

'Will he come in here?'

'Not if you dragged him, darling.'

Smiley closed the door, sat in a chair, and once more took out his notebook.

'She's got a dear sweet Chinaman,' she said, still gazing at the postcard upside down. 'She went to him to save Ricardo and then she fell in love with him. He's a real father to her, the first she ever had. It's all come out right after all. All the bad things. They're over. He calls her *Liese*,' she said. 'He thinks it's prettier for her. Funny really. We don't like Germans. We're patriotic. And now he's fiddling her a lovely job, isn't he?'

'I understand she prefers the name Worth, rather than Worthington. Is there a reason for that, that you know of?'

'Cutting that boring schoolmaster down to size I should think.'

'When you say she did it to *save* Ricardo, you mean of course that –'

Mrs Pelling let out a stage groan of pain.

'*Oh* you men. When? Who? Why? How? In the bushes, dear. In a telephone box, dear. She bought Ricardo his life, darling, with the only currency she has. She did him proud then left him. What the hell, he was a slug.' She took up another postcard, and studied the picture of palm trees and an empty beach. 'My little Lizzie went behind the hedge with half of Asia before she found her Drake. But she found him.' As if hearing a noise, she sat up sharply and stared at Smiley most intently while she straightened her hair. 'I think you'd better go, dear,' she said, in the same low voice, while she turned herself towards the mirror. 'You give me the galloping creeps to be honest. I can't do with trustworthy faces round me. Sorry darling, know what I mean?'

At the Circus, Smiley took a couple of minutes to confirm what he already knew. Mellon, with two l's exactly as Mr Pelling had insisted, was the registered workname and alias of Sam Collins.

## ELEVEN

# *Shanghai express*

In the scheme of things as they are now conveniently remembered, there is at this point a deceptive condensation of events. Somewhere around here in Jerry's life Christmas came and went in a succession of aimless drinking sessions at the Foreign Correspondents' Club, and a series of last-minute parcels to Cat clumsily wrapped in holly paper at all hours of the night. A revised trace request on Ricardo was submitted formally to the Cousins, and Smiley personally took it to the Annexe in order to explain himself more fully to Martello. But the request got snarled up in the Christmas rush – not to mention the impending collapse of Vietnam and Cambodia – and didn't complete its round of the American departments till well into the New Year, as the dates in the Dolphin file show. Indeed, the *crucial* meeting with Martello and his friends on the Drug Enforcement side did not take place till early February. The wear of this prolonged delay on Jerry's nerves was appreciated intellectually within the Circus, but not, in the continued mood of crisis, felt or acted on. For that, one may again blame Smiley, depending where one stands, but it is very hard to see what more he could have done, short of calling Jerry home: particularly since Craw continued to report in glowing terms on his general disposition. The fifth floor was working flat out all the time and Christmas was hardly noticed apart from a rather battered sherry party at midday on the twenty-fifth, and a break later while Connie and the mothers played the Queen's speech very loud in order to shame heretics like Guillam and Molly Meakin, who found it hilarious and did bad imitations of it in the corridors.

The formal induction of Sam Collins to the Circus's meagre ranks took place on a really freezing day in mid-January and it had a light side and a dark side. The light side was his arrest. He arrived at ten exactly, on a Monday morning, not in a dinner jacket, but in a dapper grey overcoat with a rose in the button-hole, looking miraculously youthful in the cold. But Smiley and Guillam were out, cloistered with the Cousins, and neither the janitors nor housekeepers had any brief to admit him, so they locked him a basement for three hours where he shivered and fumed till Smiley returned to verify the appointment. There was more comedy about his room. Smiley had put him on the fourth floor next to Connie and di Salis, but Sam wouldn't wear that and wanted the fifth. He considered it more suitable to his acting rank of co-ordinator. The poor janitors humped furniture up and down stairs like coolies.

The dark side was harder to describe, though several tried. Connie said Sam was *frigid*, a disturbing choice of adjective. To Guillam he was *hungry*, to the mothers *shifty*, and to the burrowers too *smooth by half*. The strangest thing, to those who did not know the background, was his self-sufficiency. He drew no files, he made no bids for this or that responsibility, he scarcely used the telephone, except to place racing bets or oversee the running of his club. But his smile went with him everywhere. The typists declared that he slept in it, and hand-washed it at weekends. Smiley's interviews with him took place behind closed doors, and bit by bit the product of them was communicated to the team.

Yes, the girl had fetched up in Vientiane with a couple of hippies who had overrun the Katmandu trail. Yes, when they dumped her she had asked Mackelvore to find her a job. And yes, Mackelvore had passed her on to Sam, thinking that on looks alone she must be exploitable: all, reading between the lines, much as the girl had described in her letter home. Sam had had a couple of lowgrade drug ploys mouldering on his books at the time and was otherwise, thanks to Haydon, becalmed, so he thought he might as well put her alongside the flying boys and see what came up. He didn't tell London because London at that point was killing everything. He just went ahead with her on trial and paid her out of his management fund. What came up was Ricardo. He also let her follow an old lead to the bullion racket in Hong Kong, but that was all before he realized she was a total disaster. It was a positive relief to Sam, he said, when Ricardo took her off his hands and got her a job with Indocharter.

'So what else does he know?' Guillam demanded indignantly. 'That's not much of a ticket, is it, for screwing up the pecking order, horning in on our meetings.'

'He knows *her*,' said Smiley patiently, and resumed his study of Jerry Westerby's file, which of late had become his principal reading. 'We are not above a little blackmail ourselves from time to time,' he added with a maddening tolerance, 'and it is perfectly reasonable that we should have to submit to it occasionally.' Whereas Connie, with unwonted coarseness, startled everyone by quoting – apparently – President Johnson on the subject of J. Edgar Hoover: 'George would rather have Sam Collins inside the tent pissing out than outside the tent pissing in,' she declared, and gave a schoolgirl giggle at her own audacity.

And most particularly, it was not till mid-January, in the course of his continued excursions into the minutiae of the Ko background, that Doc di Salis unveiled his amazing discovery of the survival of a certain Mr Hibbert, a China missionary in the Baptist interest, whom Ko had mentioned as a referee when he applied to read law in London.

All much more spread out, therefore, than the contemporary memory conveniently allows: and the strain on Jerry accordingly all the greater.

'There's the possibility of a knighthood,' Connie Sachs said. They had said it already on the telephone.

It was a very sober scene. Connie had bobbed her hair. She wore a dark brown hat and a dark brown suit, and she carried a dark brown handbag to contain the radio microphone. Outside in the little drive, in a blue cab with the engine and the heater on, Toby Esterhase the Hungarian pavement artist, wearing a peak cap, pretended to doze while he received and recorded the conversation on the instruments beneath his seat. Connie's extravagant shape had acquired a prim discipline. She held a Stationery Office notebook handy, and a Stationery Office ballpoint pen between her arthritic fingers. As to the remote di Salis, the art had been to modernize him a little. Under protest, he wore one of Guillam's striped shirts, with a dark tie to match. The result, somewhat surprisingly, was quite convincing.

'It's *extremely* confidential,' Connie said to Mr Hibbert speaking loud and clear. She had said that on the telephone as well.

'Enormously,' di Salis muttered in confirmation, and flung his arms about till one elbow settled awkwardly on his knobbly knee, and a crabbed hand enclosed his chin, then scratched it.

The Governor had recommended once, she said, and now it was up to the Board to decide whether or not they would pass the recommendation on to the *Palace*. And on the word *Palace* she cast a restrained glance at di Salis, who at once smiled brightly but modestly, like a celebrity at a chat show. His strands of grey hair were slicked down with cream, and looked (said Connie later) as though they had been basted for the oven.

'So you *will* understand,' said Connie, in the precise accents of a female newsreader, 'that in order to *protect* our noblest institutions against embarrassment, a very thorough inquiry has to be made.'

'The *Palace*,' Mr Hibbert echoed with a wink in di Salis's direction. 'Well I'm blowed. The Palace, hear that Doris?' He was very old. The record said eighty-one, but his features had reached the age where they were once more unweathered. He wore a clerical dog-collar and a tan cardigan with leather patches on the elbows and a shawl around his shoulders. The background of the grey sea made a halo round his white hair. '*Sir Drake Ko*,' he said. 'That's one thing I'd not thought of, I will say.' His North Country accent was so pure that, like his snowy hair, it could have been put on. '*Sir Drake*,' he repeated. 'Well I'm blowed. Eh, Doris?'

A daughter sat with them, thirty to forty-odd, blonde, and she wore a yellow frock and powder but no lipstick. Since girlhood, nothing seemed to have happened to her face, beyond a steady fading of its hopes. When she spoke she blushed, but she rarely spoke. She had made pastries, and sandwiches as thin as handkerchiefs, and seed-cake on a doily. To strain the tea she used a piece of muslin with beads to weight it stitched round the border. From the ceiling hung a pronged parchment lampshade made in the shape of a star. An upright piano stood along one wall with the score of 'Lead Kindly Light' open on its stand. A sampler of Kipling's *If* hung over the empty fire grate, and the velvet curtains on either side of the sea window were so heavy they might have been there to screen off an unused part of life. There were no books, there was not even a Bible. There was a very big colour television set and there was a long line of Christmas cards hung laterally over string, wings downward, like shot birds halfway to hitting the ground. There was nothing to recall the China coast, unless it was the shadow of the winter sea. It was a day of no weather and no wind. In the garden, cacti and shrubs waited dully in the cold. Walkers went quickly on the promenade.

They would like to take notes, Connie added: for it is Circus folklore that when the sound is being stolen, notes should be taken, both as fallback and for cover.

'Oh, you write away,' Mr Hibbert said encouragingly. 'We're not all elephants, are we, Doris? Doris is, mind, wonderful her memory is, good as her mother's.'

'So what we'd like to do first,' said Connie – careful all the same to match the old man's pace – 'if we may, is what we do with all character witnesses, as we call them, we'd like to establish exactly how long you've known Mr Ko, and the circumstances of your relationship with him.'

Describe your access to Dolphin, she was saying, in a somewhat different language.

Talking of others, old men talk about themselves, studying their image in vanished mirrors.

'I was born to the calling,' Mr Hibbert said. 'My grandfather, he was called. My father, he had, oh a *big* parish in Macclesfield. My uncle died when he was twelve, but he still took the Pledge, didn't he Doris? I was in missionary training-school at twenty. By twenty-four I'd set sail for Shanghai to join the Lord's Life Mission. The *Empire Queen* she was called. We'd more waiters than passengers the way I remember it. Oh dear.'

He aimed to spend a few years in Shanghai teaching and learning the language, he said, and then with luck transfer to the China Inland Mission and move to the interior.

'I'd have liked that. I'd have liked the challenge. I've always liked the Chinese. The Lord's Life wasn't posh, but it did a job. Now those *Roman* schools, well they were more like your monasteries, *and* with all that entails,' said Mr Hibbert.

di Salis, the sometime Jesuit, gave a dim smile.

'Now we'd got *our* kids in from the streets,' he said. 'Shanghai was a rare old hotchpotch, I can tell you. We'd everything and everyone. Gangs, corruption, prostitution galore, we'd politics, money and greed and misery. All human life was there, wasn't it, Doris? She wouldn't remember, really. We went back after the war, didn't we, Doris?' said Mr Hibbert, very conscious of speaking for both of them. 'We like the air. That's what we like.'

'Very much,' said Doris, and cleared her throat with a cough into her large fist.

'So we'd fill up with whatever we could get, that's what it came to,' he resumed. 'We had old Miss Fong. Remember Daisy Fong, Doris? Course you do – Daisy and her bell? Well she wouldn't really. My, how the time goes, though. A Pied Piper, what's what Daisy was, except it was a bell, and her not a man, and she was doing God's work even if she did fall later. Best convert I ever had, till the Japs came. She'd go down the streets, Daisy would, ringing the daylights out of that bell. Sometimes old Charlie Wan would go along with her, sometimes I'd go, we'd choose the docks or the nightclub areas – behind the Bund maybe – Blood Alley we called that street, remember, Doris? – she wouldn't really – and old Daisy would ring her bell, ring, ring!' He burst out laughing at the memory: he saw her before him quite clearly, for his hand was unconsciously making the vigorous movements of the bell. di Salis and Connie politely joined in his laughter, but Doris only frowned. 'Rue de Jaffe,

John le Carré

that was the worst spot. In the French concession not surprisingly, where the houses of sin were. Well they were everywhere really, Shanghai was jampacked with them. Sin City they called it. And they were right. Then a few kids gathered and she'd ask them: "Any of you lost your mothers?" And you'd get a couple. Not all at once, here one, there one. Some would try it on, like, for the rice supper, then get sent home with a cuff. But we'd always find a *few* real ones, didn't we, Doris, and bit by bit we had a school going, forty-four we had by the end, didn't we? Some boarders, not all. Bible Class, the three R's, a bit of geography and history. That's all we could manage.'

Restraining his impatience, di Salis had fixed his gaze on the grey sea and kept it there. But Connie had arranged her face in a steady smile of admiration, and her eyes never left the old man's face.

'That's how Daisy found the Ko's,' he went on, oblivious of his erratic sequence. 'Down in the docks, didn't she Doris, looking for their mother. They'd come up from Swatow, the two of them. When was that? Nineteen thirty-six I suppose. Young Drake was ten or eleven, and his brother Nelson was eight, thin as wire they were; hadn't had a square meal for weeks. They became rice Christians overnight, I can tell you! Mind you, they hadn't names in those days, not English, naturally. They were boat people, Chiu Chow. We never really found out about the mother, did we, Doris? "Killed by the guns," they said. "Killed by the guns." Could have been Japanese guns, could have been Kuomintang. We never got to the bottom of it, why should we? The Lord had her and that was that. Might as well stop all the questions and get on with it. Little Nelson had his arm all messed. Shocking really. Broken bone sticking through his sleeve, I suppose the guns did that as well. Drake, he was holding Nelson's good hand, and he wouldn't let it go for love nor money at first, not even for the lad to eat. We used to say they'd one good hand between them, remember, Doris? Drake would sit there at table clutching on to him, shovelling rice into him for all he was worth. We had the doctor in: *he* couldn't separate them. We just had to put up with it. "You'll be Drake," I said. "And you'll be Nelson because you're both brave sailors, how's that?" It was your mother's idea, wasn't it, Doris? She'd always wanted boys.'

Doris looked at her father, started to say something, and changed her mind.

'They used to stroke her hair,' the old man said, in a slightly mystified voice. 'Stroke your mother's hair and ring old Daisy's bell, that's what they liked. They'd never seen blond hair before. Here, Doris, how about a drop more *saw*? Mine's run cold so I'm sure theirs has. *Saw's* Shanghainese for tea,' he explained. 'In Canton they call it *cha*. We've kept some of the old words, I don't know why.'

With an exasperated hiss, Doris bounded from the room, and Connie seized the opportunity to speak.

'Now Mr Hibbert, we have no note of a *brother* till now,' she said in a slightly reproachful tone. 'He was younger, you say. Two years younger? Three?'

'No note of *Nelson*?' The old man was amazed. 'Why he loved him! Drake's whole life, Nelson was. Do anything for him. No note of *Nelson*, Doris?'

But Doris was in the kitchen, fetching *saw*.

Referring to her notes, Connie gave a strict smile.

'I'm afraid it's we who are to blame, Mr Hibbert. I see here that Government House has left a blank against *brothers and sisters*. There'll be one or two red faces in Hong Kong quite shortly, I can tell you. You don't happen to remember Nelson's date of birth, I suppose? Just to shortcut things?'

'No, my goodness! Daisy Fong would remember, of course, but she's long gone. Gave them all birthdays, Daisy did, even when they didn't know them theirselves.'

di Salis hauled on his ear lobe, pulling his head down. 'Or his Chinese forenames?' he blurted in his high voice. '*They* might be useful, if one's checking?'

Mr Hibbert was shaking his head. 'No note of Nelson! Bless my soul! You can't really think of Drake, not without little Nelson at his side. Went together like bread and cheese, we used to say. Being orphans, naturally.'

From the hall, they heard a telephone ringing and, to the secret surprise of both Connie and di Salis, a distinct 'Oh *hell*,' from Doris in the kitchen as she dashed to answer it. They heard clippings of angry conversation against the mounting whimper of a tea-kettle. 'Well, *why* isn't it? Well if it's the bloody brakes, *why* say it's the clutch? No, we *don't* want a new car. We want the old one repaired for God's sake.' With a loud 'Christ' she rang off, and returned to the kitchen and the screaming kettle.

'Nelson's Chinese forenames,' Connie prompted gently, through her smile, but the old man shook his head.

'You'd have to ask old Daisy that,' he said. 'And she's long in Heaven, bless her.' di Salis seemed about to contest the old man's claim to ignorance, but Connie shut him up with a look. *Let him run*, she was urging. *Force him and we'll lose the whole match.*

The old man's chair was on a swivel. Unconsciously, he had worked his way clockwise, and now he was talking to the sea.

'They were like chalk and cheese,' Mr Hibbert said. 'I never saw two brothers so different, nor so faithful, and that's a fact.'

'Different in what *way*?' Connie asked invitingly.

'Little Nelson now, he was frightened of the cockroaches. That was the first thing. We didn't have your modern sanitation, naturally. We'd send them down to the hut and, oh dear, those cockroaches, they flew about that hut like bullets! Nelson wouldn't go near the place. His arm was mending well enough, he was eating like a fighting cock, but that lad would hold himself in for days on end rather than go inside the hut. Your mother promised him the moon if he'd go. Daisy Fong took a stick to him and I can see his eyes still, he'd look at you sometimes and clench his one good fist and you'd think he'd turn you to stone, that Nelson was a rebel from the day he was born. Then one day we looked out of the window and there they were. Drake with his arm round little Nelson's shoulder, leading him down the path to keep him company while he did his business. Notice how they walk different, the boat children?' he asked brightly, as if he saw them now. 'Bow-legged from the cramp.'

The door was barged open and Doris came in with a tray of fresh tea, making a clatter as she set it down.

'Singing was just the same,' he said and fell silent again, gazing at the sea.

'Singing *hymns*?' Connie prompted brightly, glancing at the polished piano with its empty candleholders.

'Drake, he'd belt anything out as long as your mother was at the piano. Carols. "There is a green hill". Cut his own throat for your mother, Drake would. But young Nelson, I never heard him sing one note.'

'You heard him later all right,' Doris reminded him harshly, but he preferred not to notice her.

'You'd take his lunch away, his supper, but he'd not even say his Amens. He'd a real quarrel with God from the start.' He laughed with sudden freshness. 'Well those are your real believers, I always say. The others are just polite. There's no true conversion, not without a quarrel.'

'Damn garage,' Doris muttered, still fuming after her telephone call, as she hacked at the seed-cake.

'Here! Is your driver all right?' Mr Hibbert cried. 'Shall Doris take out to him? He must be freezing to death out there! Bring him in, go on!' But before either of them could answer, Mr Hibbert had started talking about his war. Not Drake's war, nor Nelson's, but his own, in unjoined scraps of graphic memory. 'Funny thing was, there was a lot who thought the Japs were just the ticket. Teach those upstart Chinese Nationalists where to get off. Let alone the Communists, of course. Oh, it took quite a while for the scales to fall, I can tell you. Even after the bombardments started. European shops closed, Taipans evacuated their families, Country Club became a hospital. But there were still the ones who said "don't worry". Then one day, *bang*, they'd locked us up, hadn't they, Doris. *And* killed your mother into the bargain. She'd not the stamina, had she, not after her tuberculosis. Still, those Ko brothers were better off than most, for all that.'

'Oh. Why was that?' Connie enquired, all interest.

'They'd the knowledge of Jesus to guide and comfort them, hadn't they?'

'Of course,' said Connie.

'Naturally,' di Salis chimed, linking his fingers and hauling at them. '*Indeed* they had,' he said unctuously.

So with the Japs, as he called them, the mission closed and Daisy Fong with her handbell led the children to join the stream of refugees, who by cart, bus or train, but mostly on foot, were taking the trail to Shangjao and finally to Chungking where Chiang's Nationalists had set up their temporary capital.

'He can't go on too long,' Doris warned at one point, in an aside to Connie. 'He gets gaga.'

'Oh yes I can, dear,' Mr Hibbert corrected her with a fond smile. 'I've had my share of life now. I can do what I like.'

They drank the tea and talked about the garden, which had been a problem every since they settled here.

'They tell us, get the ones with silver leaves, they stand the salt. I don't know, do we, Doris? They don't seem to take, do they?'

With his wife's death, Mr Hibbert somehow said, his own life had ended too: he was marking time until he joined her. He had had a living in the north of England for a while. After that he'd done a bit of work in London, propagating the Bible.

'Then we came south, didn't we Doris? I don't know why.'

'For the air,' she said.

'There'll be a party, will there, at the Palace?' Mr Hibbert asked. 'I suppose. Drake might even put us down for invites. Think of that, Doris. You'd like that. A Royal Garden Party. Hats.'

'But you did return to Shanghai,' Connie reminded him eventually, shuffling her notes to call him back. 'The Japanese were defeated, Shanghai was reopened and back you went. Without your wife, of course, but you returned all the same.'

'Oh ay, we went.'

'So you saw the Ko's again. You all met up and you had a marvellous old natter, I'm sure. Is that what happened, Mr Hibbert?'

For a moment it seemed he hadn't taken in the question, but suddenly with a delayed action he laughed. 'By Jove and weren't they real little men by then, too. Fly as fly they were! *And* after the girls, saving your presence, Doris. I always say Drake would have married you, dear, if you'd given him any hope.'

'Oh *honestly*, Dad,' Doris muttered and scowled at the floor.

'And Nelson, oh *my* he was the firebrand!' He drank his tea with the spoon, carefully, as if he were feeding a bird. "Where Missie?" His first question that was, Drake's. He wanted your mother. "Where Missie?" He'd forgotten all his English, so'd Nelson. I'd to give them lessons later. So I told him. He'd seen enough of death by then, *that* was for sure. Wasn't as if he didn't believe in it. "Missie dead," I said. Nothing else to say. "She's dead, Drake, and she's with God." I never saw him weep before or since, but he wept then and I loved him for it. "I lose two mothers," he says to me. "Mother dead, now Missie dead." We prayed for her, what else can you do? Little Nelson now, he didn't cry or pray. Not him. He never took to her the way Drake did. Nothing personal. She was enemy. We all were.'

'*We* being who precisely, Mr Hibbert?' di Salis asked coaxingly.

'Europeans, capitalists, missionaries: all of us carpet-baggers who were there for their souls, or their labour, or their silver. All of us,' Mr Hibbert repeated, without the least hint of rancour. 'Exploiters. That's how he saw us. Right, in a way, too.' The conversation hung awkwardly for a moment till Connie carefully retrieved it.

'So anyway, you reopened the mission, and you stayed till the Communist takeover of forty-nine, I assume, and for those four years at least you were able to keep a fatherly eye on Drake and Nelson. Is that how it went, Mr Hibbert?' she asked, pen poised.

'Oh we hung the lamp on the door again, yes. In forty-five, we were jubilant, same as anyone else. The fighting had stopped, the Japs were beaten, the refugees could come home. Hugging in the street, there was, the usual. We'd money, reparation I suppose, a grant. Daisy Fong came back, but not for long. For the first year or two the surface held, but not really, even then. We were there as long as Chiang Kai-shek could govern – well, he was never much of a one for that, was he? By forty-seven we'd the Communism out on the streets – and by forty-nine it was there to stay. International Settlement long gone of course, concessions too, and a good thing. The rest went slowly. You got the blind ones, as usual, who said the old Shanghai would go on for ever, same as you did with the Japs. Shanghai had corrupted the Manchus, they said; the warlords, the Kuomintang, the Japanese, the British. Now she'd corrupt the Communists. They were wrong of course. Doris and me – well, we didn't believe in corruption, did we, not as a solution to China's problems, nor did your mother. So we came home.'

'And the Ko's?' Connie reminded him, while Doris noisily hauled some knitting out of a brown paper bag.

The old man hesitated, and this time it was not senility, perhaps, which slowed his narrative, but doubt. 'Well, yes,' he conceded, after an awkward gap. 'Yes, rare adventures those two had, I can tell you.'

'*Adventures*,' Doris echoed angrily, as she clicked her knitting needles. 'Rampages more like.'

The light was clinging to the sea, but inside the room it was dying and the gas fire spluttered like a distant motor.

Several times, escaping from Shanghai, Drake and Nelson were separated, the old man said. When they couldn't find each other they ate their hearts out till they did. Nelson, the young one, he got all the way to Chungking without a scratch, surviving starvation, exhaustion and hellish air bombardments which killed thousands of civilians. But Drake, being older, was drafted into Chiang's army, though Chiang did nothing but run away hoping that the Communists and the Japanese would kill each other.

'Charged all over the shop, Drake did, trying to find the front and worrying himself to death about Nelson. And of course Nelson, well, he was twiddling his thumbs in Chungking wasn't he, boning up on his ideological reading. They'd even the *New China Daily* there, he told me afterwards, *and* published with Chiang's agreement. Fancy that! There was a few others of his mind around, and in Chungking they got their heads together rebuilding the world for when the war ended, and one day, thank God, it did.'

In nineteen forty-five, said Mr Hibbert simply, their separation was ended by a miracle: 'One chance in thousands, it was, millions. That road back littered with streams of lorries, carts, troops, guns all pouring towards the coast, and there was Drake running up and down like a madman: "Have you seen my brother?"'

The drama of the instant suddenly touched the preacher in him, and his voice lifted.

'And one little dirty fellow put his arm on Drake's elbow. "Here. You. Ko." Like he's asking for a light. "Your brother's two trucks back, talking the hindlegs off a bunch of Hakka Communists." Next thing, they're in each other's arms and Drake won't let Nelson out of his sight till they're back in Shanghai and *then* not!'

'So they came to see you,' Connie suggested cosily.

'When Drake got back to Shanghai, he'd only one thing in his mind and one only. Brother Nelson should have a formal education. Nothing else on God's good earth mattered to Drake except Nelson's schooling. *Nothing.* Nelson must go to school.' The old man's hand thudded on the chair arm. '*One* of the brothers at least would make the grade. Oh, he was adamant, Drake was! *And* he did it,' said the old man. 'Drake swung it. He would. He was a real fixer by then. Drake was nineteen years of age, odd, when he came back from the war. Nelson was going on seventeen, and worked night and day too – on his studies, of course. Same as Drake did, but Drake worked with his body.'

'He was a crook,' Doris said under her breath. 'He joined a gang and stole. When he wasn't pawing *me*.'

Whether Mr Hibbert heard her, or whether he was simply answering a standard objection in her was not clear.

'Now Doris, you must see those Triads in perspective,' he corrected her. 'Shanghai was a city state. It was run by a bunch of merchant princes, robber barons and worse. There were no unions, no law and order, life was cheap and hard and I doubt Hong Kong's that different today once you scratch the surface. Some of those so-called English gentlemen would have made your Lancashire mill-owner into a shining example of Christian charity by comparison.' The mild rebuke administered, he returned to Connie and his narrative. Connie was familiar to him: the archetypal lady in the front pew: big, attentive, in a hat, listening indulgently to the old man's every word.

'They'd come round to tea, see, five o'clock, the brothers. I'd to have everything ready, the food on the table, lemonade they liked, called it soda. Drake came in from the docks, Nelson from his books, and they'd eat not hardly talking, then back to work, wouldn't they, Doris? They'd dug out some legendary hero, the scholar Che Yin. Che Yin was so poor he'd had to teach himself to read and write by the light of the fireflies. They'd go on about how Nelson was to emulate him. "Come on Che Yin," I'd say, "have another bun to keep your strength up." They'd laugh a bit and away they'd go again. "Bye bye, Che Yin, off you go." Now and then when his mouth wasn't too full, Nelson would have a go at me on the politics. *My*, he'd some ideas! Nothing *we* could have taught him, I can tell you, we didn't know enough. Money the root of all evil, well I'd never deny *that*! I'd been preaching it myself for years! Brotherly love, comradeship, religion the opiate of the masses, well I couldn't go along with that, but clericalism, high church baloney, popery, idolatry – well, he wasn't too far wrong there either, the way I saw it. He'd a few bad words against us British too, not but what we deserved them, I dare say.'

'Didn't stop him eating your food, did it?' Doris said in another low-toned aside. '*Or* renouncing his religious background. Or smashing the mission to pieces.'

But the old man smiled patiently. 'Doris, my dear, I have told you before and I'll tell you again. The Lord reveals himself in many ways. So long as good men are prepared to go out and seek for truth and justice and brotherly love, He'll not be kept waiting too long outside the door.'

Colouring, Doris dug away at her knitting.

'She's right of course. Nelson *did* smash up the mission. Renounced his religion too.' A cloud of grief threatened his old face for a moment, till laughter suddenly triumphed. 'And my billy-oh didn't Drake make him smart for it! Didn't he give him a dressing down though! Oh dear, oh dear! "Politics," says Drake. "You can't eat them, you can't sell them and saving Doris's presence you can't sleep with them! All you can do with them is smash temples and kill the innocent!" I've never seen him so angry. *And* gave Nelson a hiding, he did! Drake had learned a thing or two down in the docks, I can tell you!'

'And you *must*,' di Salis hissed, snakelike in the gloom. 'You must tell us *everything*. It's your duty.'

'A student procession,' Mr Hibbert resumed. 'Torchlight, after the curfew, group of Communists out on the streets for a shindy. Early forty-nine, spring it would have been I suppose, things were just beginning to hot up.' In contrast to his earlier ramblings, Mr Hibbert's narrative style had become unexpectedly concise. 'We were sitting by the fire, weren't we, Doris? Fourteen, Doris was, or was it fifteen? We used to love a fire, even when there wasn't the need, took us home to Macclesfield. And we hear this clattering and chanting outside. Cymbals, whistles, gongs, bells, drums, oh, a shocking din. I'd a notion something like this might have been happening. Little Nelson, he was forever warning me in his English lessons. "You go home, Mr Hibbert. You're a good man," he used to say, bless him. "You're a good man but when the floodgates burst, the water will cover the good and bad alike." He'd a lovely turn of phrase, Nelson, when he wanted. It went with his faith. Not invented. *Felt*. "Daisy," I said – Daisy Fong, that was, she was sitting with us, her as rang the bell – "Daisy," you and Doris go to the back courtyard, I think we're about to have company." Next thing I knew, *smash*, someone had tossed a stone through the window. We heard voices, of course, shouting, and I picked out young Nelson even then, just from his voice. He'd the Chiu Chow *and* the Shanghainese, of course, but he was using Shanghainese to the lads, naturally. "Condemn the imperialist running dogs!" he's yelling. "Down with the religious hyenas!" Oh, the slogans they dream up! They sound all right in Chinese but shove 'em into English and they're rubbish. Then the door goes and in they come.'

'They smashed the cross,' said Doris, pausing to glare at her pattern.

It was Hibbert this time, not his daughter, who startled his audience with his earthiness.

'They smashed a damn sight more than that, Doris!' Mr Hibbert rejoined cheerfully. 'They smashed the lot. Pews, the Table, the piano, chairs, lamps, hymn books, Bibles. Oh, they'd a real old go, *I* can tell you. Proper little pigs they were. "Go on," I says. "Help yourselves. What man hath put together will perish, but you'll not destroy God's word, not if you chop the whole place up for matchwood." Nelson, he wouldn't look at me, poor lad. I could have wept for him. When they'd gone, I looked round and I saw old Daisy Fong standing there in the doorway and Doris behind her. She'd been watching, had Daisy. Enjoying it. I could see it in her eyes. She was one of them, at heart. Happy. "Daisy," I said. "Pack your things and go. In this life you give yourself or withhold yourself as you please, my dear. But never lend yourself. That way you're worse than a spy."'

While Connie beamed her agreement, di Salis gave a squeaky, offended wheeze. But the old man was really enjoying himself.

'Well, so we sat down, me and Doris here, and we'd a bit of a cry together, I don't mind admitting, hadn't we, Doris? I'm not ashamed of tears, never have been. We missed your mother sorely. Knelt down, had a pray. Then we started clearing up. Difficult to know where to begin, really. Then in comes Drake!' He shook his head in wonder. '"Good evening, Mr Hibbert," he says, in that deep voice of his, plus a bit of my North Country that always made us laugh. And behind him, there's little Nelson standing with a brush and pan in his hand. He'd still that crooked arm, I suppose he has now, smashed in the bombs when he was little, but it didn't stop him brushing, I can tell you. That's when Drake went for him, oh, cursing him like a navvy! I'd never heard him like it. Well, he *was* a navvy wasn't he, in a manner of speaking?' He smiled serenely at his daughter. 'Lucky he spoke the Chiu Chow, eh, Doris? I only understand the half of it myself, not that, but my *hat*! F-ing and blinding like I don't know what.'

He paused, and closed his eyes a moment, either in prayer or tiredness.

'It wasn't Nelson's fault, of course. Well we knew that already. He was a leader. Face was involved. They'd started marching, nowhere much in mind, then somebody calls to him: "Hey! Mission boy! Show us where your loyalties are now!" So he did. They cleaned up, we went to bed, and the two lads slept on the chapel floor in case the mob came back. Came down in the morning, there were the hymn books all piled up neatly, those that had survived, same with the Bibles. They'd fixed a cross up, fashioned it theirselves. Even patched up the piano, though not to tune it, naturally.'

Winding himself into a fresh knot, di Salis put a question. Like Connie, he had a notebook open, but he had not yet written anything in it.

'What was Nelson's *discipline* at this time?' he demanded, in his nasal, indignant way, and held his pen ready to write.

Mr Hibbert gave a puzzled frown.

'Why, the Communist Party, naturally.'

As Doris whispered 'Oh *Daddy*' into her knitting, Connie hastily translated.

'What was Nelson studying, Mr Hibbert, and where?'

'Ah *discipline. That* kind of discipline!' Mr Hibbert resumed his plainer style.

He knew the answer exactly. What else had he and Nelson to talk about in their English lessons – apart from the Communist gospel, he asked – but Nelson's own ambitions? Nelson's passion was engineering. Nelson believed that technology, not Bibles, would lead China out of feudalism.

'Shipbuilding, roads, railways, factories: that was Nelson. The Angel Gabriel with a slide-rule and a white collar and a degree. That's who *he* was, in his mind.'

Mr Hibbert did not stay in Shanghai long enough to see Nelson achieve this happy state, he said, because Nelson did not graduate till fifty-one –

di Salis's pen scratched wildly on the notebook.

'– but Drake, who'd scraped and scrounged for him those six years,' said Mr Hibbert - over Doris's renewed references to the Triads – 'Drake stuck it out, and he had his reward, same as Nelson did. He saw that vital piece of paper go into Nelson's hand, and he knew his job was done and he could get out, just like he'd always planned.'

di Salis in his excitement was growing positively avid. His ugly face had sprung fresh patches of colour and he was fidgeting desperately on his chair. 'And *after* graduating – what then?' he said urgently. 'What did he *do*? What became of him? Go on, please, *Please* go on.'

Amused by such enthusiasm, Mr Hibbert smiled. Well, according to Drake, he said, Nelson had first joined the shipyards as a draughtsman, working on blueprints and building projects, and learning like mad whatever he could from the Russian technicians who'd poured in since Mao's victory. Then in fifty-three, if Mr Hibbert's memory served him correctly, Nelson was privileged to be chosen for further training at the Leningrad University in Russia, and he stayed on there till, well, late Fifties anyway.

'Oh, he was like a dog with two tails, Drake was by the sound of him!' Mr Hibbert could not have looked more proud if it had been his own son he was talking of.

di Salis leaned suddenly forward, even presuming, despite cautionary glances from Connie, to jab his pen in the old man's direction. 'So *after* Leningrad: what did they do with him *then?*'

'Why, he came back to Shanghai, naturally,' said Mr Hibbert with a laugh. '*And* promoted he was, after the learning he'd acquired, and the standing: a shipbuilder, Russian taught, a technologist, an administrator! Oh, he loved those Russians! Specially after Korea. They'd machines, power, ideas, philosophy. His promised land, Russia was. He looked up to them like –' His voice, and his zeal, both died. 'Oh dear,' he muttered, and stopped, unsure of himself for the second time since they had listened to him. 'But that couldn't last for ever could it? Admiring Russia: how long was that fashionable in Mao's new wonderland? Doris dear, get me a shawl.'

'You're wearing it,' Doris said.

Tactlessly, stridently, di Salis still bore in on him. He cared for nothing now except the answers: not even for the notebook open on his lap.

'He returned,' he piped. 'Very well. He rose in the hierarchy. He was Russia trained, Russia oriented. Very well. *What comes next?*'

Mr Hibbert looked at di Salis for a long time. There was no guile in his face, and none in his gaze. He looked at him as a clever child might, without the hindrance of sophistication. And it was suddenly clear that Mr Hibbert didn't trust di Salis any more and, indeed, that he didn't like him.

'He's dead, young man,' Mr Hibbert said finally, and swivelling his chair, stared at the sea view. In the room it was already half dark, and most of the light came from the gas fire. The grey beach was empty. On the wicket gate a single seagull perched black and vast against the last strands of evening sky.

'You said he still had his crooked arm,' di Salis snapped straight back. 'You said you supposed he still had. You said it about *now*! I heard it in your voice!'

'Well now, I think we have taxed Mr Hibbert quite enough,' said Connie brightly and, with a sharp glance at di Salis, stooped for her bag. But di Salis would have none of it.

'I don't believe him!' he cried in his shrill voice. 'How? When did Nelson die? Give us the dates!'

But the old man only drew his shawl more closely round him, and kept his eyes to the sea.

'We were in Durham,' Doris said, still looking at her knitting, though there was not the light to knit by. 'Drake drove up and saw us in his big chauffeur-driven car. He took his henchman with him, the one he calls Tiu. They were fellow crooks together in Shanghai. Wanted to show off. Brought me a platinum cigarette lighter, and a thousand pounds in cash for Dad's church and flashed his OBE at us in its case, took me into a corner and asked me to come to Hong Kong and be his mistress, right under Dad's nose. Bloody sauce! He wanted Dad's signature on something. A guarantee. Said he was going to read law at Gray's Inn. At his age, I ask you! Forty-two! Talk about mature student! He wasn't of course. It was all just face and talk as usual. Dad said to him: "How's Nelson?" and –'

'Just one minute, please,' di Salis had made yet another ill-judged interruption. 'The date? *When* did all this happen, please? I must have *dates*!'

'Sixty-seven. Dad was almost retired, weren't you, Dad?'

The old man did not stir.

'All right, sixty-seven. What month? Be precise, please!'

He all but said 'be precise, *woman*,' and he was making Connie seriously anxious. But when she again tried to restrain him, he ignored her.

'April,' Doris said after some thought. 'We'd just had Dad's birthday. That's why he brought the thousand quid for the church. He knew Dad wouldn't take it for himself because Dad didn't like the way Drake made his money.'

'All right. Good. Well done. April. So Nelson died pre-April sixty-seven. What details did Drake supply of the circumstances? Do you remember that?'

'None. No details. I told you. Dad asked, and he just said "dead" as if Nelson was a dog. So much for brotherly love. Dad didn't know where to look. It nearly broke his heart and there was Drake not giving a hoot. "I have no brother. Nelson is dead." and Dad still praying for Nelson, weren't you, Dad?'

This time the old man spoke. With the dusk. His voice had grown considerably in force.

'I prayed for Nelson and I pray for him still,' he said bluntly. 'When he was alive I prayed that one way or another he would do God's work in the world. I believed he had it in him to do great things. Drake, he'd manage anywhere. He's tough. But the light of the door at the Lord's Life Mission would not have burned in vain, I used to think, if Nelson Ko succeeded in helping to lay the foundation of a just society in China. Nelson might *call* it Communism. Call it what he likes. But for three long years your mother and I gave him our

Christian love, and I won't have it said, Doris, not by you or anyone, that the light of God's love can be put out for ever. Not by politics, not by the sword.' He drew a long breath. 'And now he's dead, I pray for his soul, same as I do for your mother's,' he said, sounding strangely less convinced. 'If that's popery, I don't care.'

Connie had actually risen to go. She knew the limits, she had the eye, and she was scared of the way di Salis was hammering on. But di Salis on the scent knew no limits at all.

'So it was a *violent* death, was it? Politics and the sword, you said. *Which* politics? Did Drake tell you that? Actual *killings* were relatively rare, you know. I think you're holding out on us!'

di Salis was standing, but at Mr Hibbert's side, and he was yapping these questions downward at the old man's white head is if he were acting in a Sarratt playlet on interrogation.

'You've been so *very* kind,' said Connie gushingly to Doris. 'Really we've all we could possibly need *and* more. I'm sure it will all go through with the knighthood,' she said, in a voice pregnant with message for di Salis. 'Now away we go and thank you both *enormously*.'

But this time it was the old man himself who frustrated her.

'And the year after, he lost his other Nelson too, God help him, his little boy,' he said. 'He'll be a lonely man, will Drake. That was his last letter to us, wasn't it Doris? "Pray for my little Nelson, Mr Hibbert," he wrote. And we did. Wanted me to fly over and conduct the funeral. I couldn't do it, I don't know why. I never much held with money spent on funerals, to be honest.'

At this, di Salis literally pounced: and with a truly terrible glee. He stooped right over the old man, and he was so animated that he grabbed a fistful of shawl in his feverish little hand.

'Ah! Ah *now*! But did he ever ask you to pray for Nelson *senior*? Answer me that.'

'No,' the old man said simply. 'No, he didn't.'

'Why not? Unless he wasn't really dead, of course! There are more ways than one of dying in China, aren't there, and not all of them are fatal! *Disgraced*: is that a better expression?'

His squeaky words flew about the firelit room like ugly spirits.

'They're to go, Doris,' the old man said calmly to the sea.

'See that driver right, won't you, dear? I'm sure we should have taken out to him, but never mind.'

They stood in the hall, making their goodbyes. The old man had stayed in his chair and Doris had closed the door on him. Sometimes, Connie's sixth sense was frightening.

'The name *Liese* doesn't mean anything to you, does it, Miss Hibbert?' she asked, buckling her enormous plastic coat. 'We have a reference to a *Liese* in Mr Ko's life.'

Doris's unpainted face made an angry scowl.

'That's Mum's name,' she said. 'She was German Lutheran. The swine stole that too, did he?'

With Toby Esterhase at the wheel, Connie Sachs and Doc di Salis hurried home to George with their amazing news. At first, on the way, they squabbled about di Salis's lack of restraint. Toby Esterhase particularly was shocked, and Connie seriously feared the old man might write to Ko. But soon the import of their discovery overwhelmed their apprehensions, and they arrived triumphant at the gates of their secret city.

Safely inside the walls, it was now di Salis's hour of glory. Summoning his family of yellow perils once more, he set in motion a whole variety of enquiries, which sent them scurrying all over London on one false pretext or another, and to Cambridge too. At heart di Salis was a loner. No none knew him, except Connie perhaps and, if Connie didn't care for him, then no one liked him either. Socially he was discordant and frequently absurd. But neither did anyone doubt his hunter's will.

He scoured old records of the Shanghai University of Communications, in Chinese the Chiao Tung – which had a reputation for student Communist militancy after the thirty-nine forty-five war – and concentrated his interest upon the Department of Marine Studies, which included both administration and shipbuilding in its curriculum. He drew lists of Party cadre members of both before and after forty-nine, and pored over the scant details of those entrusted with the takeover of big enterprises where technological knowhow was required: in particular the Kiangnan shipyard, a massive affair from which the Kuomintang elements had repeatedly to be purged. Having drawn up lists of several thousand names, he opened files on all those who were known to have continued their studies at Leningrad University and afterwards reappeared at the shipyard in improved positions. A course of shipbuilding at Leningrad took three years. By di Salis's computation, Nelson should have been there from fifty-three to fifty-six and afterwards formally assigned to the Shanghai municipal department in charge of marine engineering, which would then have returned him to Kiangnan. Accepting that Nelson possessed not only Chinese forenames which were still unknown, but quite possibly had chosen a new surname for himself into the bargain, di Salis warned his helpers that Nelson's biography might be split into two parts, each under a different name. They should watch for dovetailing. He cadged lists of graduates and lists of enrolled students both at Chiao Tung and at Leningrad and set them side by side. China-watchers are a fraternity apart, and their common interests transcend protocol and national differences. di Salis had connections not only in Cambridge, and in every Oriental archive, but in Rome, Tokyo and Munich as well. He wrote to all of them, concealing his goal in a welter of other questions. Even the Cousins, it turned out later, had unwittingly opened their files to him. He made other enquiries even more arcane. He despatched burrowers to the Baptists, to delve among records of old pupils at the Mission Schools, on the off-chance that Nelson's Chinese names had, after all, been taken down and filed. He tracked down any chance records of the deaths of middle-ranking Shanghai officials in the shipping industry.

That was the first leg of his labours. The second began with what Connie called the Great Beastly Cultural Revolution of the mid-Sixties and the names of such Shanghainese officials who, in consequence of criminal pro-Russian leanings, had been officially purged, humiliated, or sent to a May 7th school to rediscover the virtues of peasant labour. He also consulted lists of those sent to labour reform camps, but with no great success. He looked for any references, among the Red Guards' harangues, to the wicked influence of a Baptist upbringing upon this or that disgraced official, and he played complicated games with the name *Ko*. It was at the back of his mind that, in changing his name, Nelson might have hit upon a different character which retained an internal kinship with the original – either homophonic or symphonetic. But when he tried to explain this to Connie, he lost her.

Connie Sachs was pursuing a different line entirely. Her interest centred on the activities of known Karla-trained talent-spotters working among overseas students at the University of Leningrad in the Fifties; and on rumours, never proven, that Karla, as a young Comintern agent, had been lent to the Shanghai Communist underground after the war, to help them rebuild their secret apparatus.

It was in the middle of all this fresh burrowing that a small bombshell was delivered from Grosvenor Square. Mr Hibbert's intelligence was still fresh from the presses, in fact, and the researchers of both families were still frantically at work, when Peter Guillam walked in on Smiley with an urgent message. He was as usual deep in his own reading, and as Guillam entered he slipped a file into a drawer and closed it.

'It's the Cousins,' Guillam said gently. 'About Brother Ricardo, your favourite pilot. They want to meet with you at the Annexe as soon as possible. I'm to ring back by yesterday.'

'They want *what?*'

'To meet you. But they use the preposition.'

'*Do* they? Do they *really*? Good Lord. I suppose it's the German influence. Or is it old English? Meet *with*. Well I must say.' And he lumbered off to his bathroom to shave.

Returning to his own room, Guillam found Sam Collins sitting in the soft chair, smoking one of his beastly brown cigarettes and smiling his washable smile.

'Something up?' Sam asked, very leisurely.

'Get the hell out of here,' Guillam snapped.

Sam was in general nosing around a lot too much for Guillam's liking, but that day he had a firm reason for distrusting him. Calling on Lacon at the Cabinet Office to deliver the Circus's monthly imprest account for his inspection, he had been astonished to see Sam emerging from his private office, joking easily with Lacon and Saul Enderby of the Foreign Office.

# TWELVE

# *the resurrection of Ricardo*

Before the fall, studiously informal meetings of intelligence partners to the special relationship were held as often as monthly and followed by what Smiley's predecessor Alleline had liked to call 'a jar'. If it was the American turn to play host, then Alleline and his cohorts, among them the popular Bill

Haydon, would be shepherded to a vast rooftop bar, known within the Circus as the planetarium, to be regaled with dry martinis and a view of West London they could not otherwise have afforded. If it was the British turn, then a trestle table was set up in the rumpus room, and a darned damask tablecloth spread over it, and the American delegates were invited to pay homage to the last bastion of clubland spying, and incidentally the birthplace of their own service, while they sipped South African sherry disguised by cut-glass decanters on the grounds that they wouldn't know the difference. For the discussions, there was no agenda and by tradition no notes were taken. Old friends had no need of such devices, particularly since hidden microphones stayed sober and did the job better.

Since the fall, these niceties had for a while stopped dead. Under orders from Martello's headquarters at Langley, Virginia, the 'British liaison', as they knew the Circus, was placed on the arm's length list, equating it with Jugoslavia and the Lebanon, and for a while the two services in effect passed each other on opposite pavements, scarcely lifting their eyes. They were like an estranged couple in the middle of divorce proceedings. But by the time that grey winter's morning had come along when Smiley and Guillam, in some haste, presented themselves at the front doors of the Legal Advisor's Annexe in Grosvenor Square, a marked thaw was already discernible everywhere, even in the rigid faces of the two Marines who frisked them.

The doors, incidentally, were double, with black grilles over black iron, and gilded feathers on the grilles. The cost of them alone would have kept the entire Circus ticking over for a couple more days at least. Once inside them, they had the sensation of coming from a hamlet to a metropolis.

Martello's room was very large. There were no windows and it could have been midnight. Above an empty desk an American flag, unfurled as if by a breeze, occupied half the end wall. At the centre of the floor a ring of airline chairs was clustered round a rosewood table, and in one of these sat Martello himself, a burly, cheerful-looking Yale man in a country suit which seemed always out of season. Two quiet men flanked him, each as sallow and sincere as the other.

'George this is good of you,' said Martello heartily, in his warm, confiding voice, as he came quickly forward to receive them. 'I don't need to tell you. I *know* how busy you are. I *know*. Sol.' He turned to two strangers sitting across the room so far unnoticed, the one young like Martello's quiet men, if less smooth; the other squat and tough and much older, with a slashed complexion and a crewcut; a veteran of something. 'Sol,' Martello repeated. 'I want you to meet one of the true legends of our profession, Sol: Mr George Smiley. George, this is Sol Eckland, who's high in our fine Drug Enforcement Administration, formerly the Bureau of Narcotics and Dangerous Drugs, now rechristened, right Sol? Sol, say hullo to Pete Guillam.'

The elder of the two men put out a hand and Smiley and Guillam each shook it, and it felt like dried bark.

'Sure,' said Martello, looking on with the satisfaction of a matchmaker. 'George, ah, remember Ed Ristow, also in narcotics, George? Paid a courtesy call on you over there a few months back? Well, Sol has taken over from Ristow. He has the South East Asian sphere. Cy here is with him.'

Nobody remembers names like the Americans, thought Guillam.

Cy was the young one of the two. He had sideburns and a gold watch and he looked like a Mormon missionary: devout, but defensive. He smiled as if smiling had been part of his course, and Guillam smiled in return.

'What happened to Ristow?' Smiley asked, as they sat down.

'Coronary,' growled Sol the veteran, in a voice as dry as his hand. His hair was like wire wool crimped into small trenches. When he scratched it, which he did a lot, it rasped.

'I'm sorry,' said Smiley.

'Could be permanent,' said Sol, not looking at him and drew on his cigarette.

Here, for the first time, it passed through Guillam's mind that something fairly momentous was in the air. He caught a hint of real tension between the two American camps. Unheralded replacements, in Guillam's experience of the American scene, were seldom caused by anything as banal as illness. He went so far as to wonder in what way Sol's predecessor might have blotted his copybook.

'Enforcement, ah, naturally has a strong interest in our little joint venture, ah, George,' Martello said, and with this unpromising fanfare, the Ricardo connection was indirectly announced, though Guillam detected there was still a mysterious urge, on the American side, to pretend their meeting was about something different – as witness Martello's vacuous opening comments:

'George, our people in Langley like to work very closely indeed with their good friends in narcotics,' he declared, with all the warmth of a diplomatic *note verbale*.

'Cuts both ways,' Sol the veteran growled in confirmation and expelled more cigarette smoke while he scratched his iron-grey hair. He seemed to Guillam at root a shy man, not comfortable here at all. Cy his young sidekick was a lot more at ease:

'It's parameters, Mr Smiley, sir. On a deal like this, you get some areas, they overlap entirely.' Cy's voice was a little too high for his size.

'Cy and Sol have hunted with us before, George,' Martello said, offering yet further reassurance. 'Cy and Sol are family, take my word for it. Langley cuts Enforcement in, Enforcement cuts Langley in. That's the way it goes. Right, Sol?'

'Right,' said Sol.

If they don't go to bed together soon, thought Guillam, they just *may* claw each other's eyes out instead. He glanced at Smiley and saw that he too was conscious of the strained atmosphere. He sat like his own effigy, a hand on each knee, eyes almost closed as usual, and he seemed to be willing himself into invisibility while the explanation was acted out for him.

'Maybe we should all just get ourselves up to date on the latest details, first,' Martello now suggested, as if he were inviting everyone to wash.

First before what? Guillam wondered.

One of the quiet men used the workname Murphy. Murphy was so fair he was nearly albino. Taking a folder from the rosewood table Murphy began reading from it aloud with great respect in his voice. He held each page singly between his clean fingers.

'Sir, Monday subject flew to Bangkok with Cathay Pacific Airlines, flight details given, and was picked up at the airport by Tan Lee, our reference given, in his personal limousine. They proceeded directly to the Airsea permanent suite at the Hotel Erawan.' He glanced at Sol. 'Tan is managing director of Asian Rice and General, sir, that's Airsea's Bangkok subsidiary, file references appended. They spent three hours in the suite and –'

'Ah, Murphy,' said Martello, interrupting.

'Sir?'

'All that "reference given", "reference appended". Leave that out, will you? We all know we have files on these guys. Right?'

'Right, sir.'

'Ko alone?' Sol demanded.

'Sir, Ko took his manager Tiu along with him. Tiu goes with him almost everywhere.'

Here, chancing to look at Smiley again, Guillam intercepted an enquiring glance from him directed at Martello. Guillam had a notion he was thinking of the girl – had *she* gone too? – but Martello's indulgent smile didn't waver, and after a moment Smiley seemed to accept this, and resumed his attentive pose.

Sol meanwhile had turned to his assistant and the two of them had a brief private exchange:

'Why the hell doesn't somebody bug the damn hotel suite, Cy? What's holding everyone up?'

'We already suggested that to Bangkok, Sol, but they've got problems with the party walls, they got no proper cavities or something.'

'Those Bangkok clowns are drowsy with too much ass. That the same Tan we tried to nail last year for heroin?'

'Now, that was Tan *Ha*, Sol. This one's Tan *Lee*. They have a great lot of Tans out there. Tan Lee's just a front man. He plays link to Fatty Hong in Chiang Mai. It's Hong who has the connections to the growers and the big brokers.'

'Somebody ought to go out and shoot that bastard,' Sol said. Which bastard wasn't quite clear.

Martello nodded at pale Murphy to go on.

'Sir, the three men then drove down to Bangkok port – that's Ko and Tan Lee and Tiu, sir – and they looked at twenty or thirty small coasters tied up along the bank. Then they drove back to Bangkok airport and subject flew to Manila, Philippines, for a cement conference at the Hotel Eden and Bali.'

'Tiu didn't go to Manila?' Martello asked, buying time.

'No, sir. Flew home,' Murphy replied, and once more Smiley glanced at Martello.

'Cement my ass,' Sol exclaimed. 'Those the boats that do the run up to Hong Kong, Murphy?'

'Yes, sir.'

'We know those boats,' expostulated Sol. 'We been going for those boats for years. Right, Cy?'

'Right.'

Sol had rounded on Martello, as if he were personally to blame. 'They leave harbour clean. They don't take the stuff aboard till they're at sea. Nobody knows which boat will carry, not even the captain of the selected vessel, until the launch pulls alongside, gives them the dope. When they hit Hong Kong waters, they drop the dope overboard with markers and the junks scoop it in.' He spoke slowly, as if speaking hurt him, forcing each word out hoarsely. 'We been screaming at the Brits for years to shake those junks out, but the bastards are all on the take.'

'That's all we have, sir,' said Murphy, and put down his report.

They were back to the awkward pauses. A pretty girl, armed with a tray of coffee and biscuits, provided a temporary reprieve, but when she left the silence was worse.

'Why don't you just tell him?' Sol snapped finally. 'Otherwise maybe I will.'

Which was when, as Martello would have said, they finally got down to the nitty-gritty.

Martello's manner became both grave and confiding: a family solicitor reading a will to the heirs. 'George, ah, at our request Enforcement here took a kind of a second look at the background and the record of the missing pilot Ricardo and as we half-surmised, they've dug up a fair quantity of material which till now has not come to light as it should have done, owing to various factors. There's no profit, in my view, to pointing the finger at anyone and besides Ed Ristow is a sick man. Let's just agree that, however it happened, the Ricardo thing fell into a small gap between Enforcement and ourselves. That gap has since closed and we'd like to rectify the information for you.'

'Thank you, Marty,' said Smiley patiently.

'Seems Ricardo's alive after all,' Sol declared. 'Seems like it's a prime snafu.'

'A *what*?' Smiley asked sharply, perhaps before the full significance of Sol's statement had sunk in.

Martello was quick to translate. 'Error, George. Human error. Happens to all of us. *Snafu.* Even you, okay?'

Guillam was studying Cy's shoes, which had a rubbery gloss and thick welts. Smiley's eyes had lifted to the side wall, where the benevolent features of President Nixon gazed down encouragingly on the triangular union. Nixon had resigned a good six months ago, but Martello seemed rather touchingly determined to tend his lamp. Murphy and his mute companion sat still as confirmands in the presence of the bishop. Only Sol was for ever on the move, alternately scratching at his crimped scalp or sucking on his cigarette like an athletic version of di Salis. He never smiles, thought Guillam extraneously: he's forgotten how.

Martello continued. 'Ricardo's death is formally recorded in our files as on or around August twenty-one, George, correct?'

'Correct,' said Smiley.

Martello drew a breath as tilted his head the other way as he read his notes. 'However, on September, ah, two – couple of weeks after his death, right? – it, ah, seems Ricardo made personal contact with one of the narcotics bureaux in the Asian theatre, then known as BNDD but primarily the same house, okay? Sol would, ah, prefer not to mention *which* bureau, and I respect that.' The mannersim *ah*, Guillam decided, was Martello's way of keeping talking while he thought. 'Ricardo offered the bureau his services on a sell-and-tell basis regarding an, ah, opium mission he claimed to have received to fly right over the border into, ah, Red China.'

A cold hand seemed to seize hold of Guillam's stomach at this moment and stay there. His sense of occasion was all the greater following the slow lead-in through so much unrelated detail. He told Molly afterwards that it was as if 'all the threads of the case had suddenly wound themselves together in a single skein' for him. But that was hindsight and he was boasting a little. Nevertheless the shock – after all the tiptoeing and the speculation, and the paperchases – the plain shock of being almost physically projected into the Chinese Mainland: that certainly was real, and required no exaggeration.

Martello was doing his worthy solicitor act again.

'George, I have to fill you in on, ah, a little more of the family background here. During the Laos thing, the Company used a few of the northern hilltribes for combat purposes, maybe you knew that. Right up there in Burma, know those parts, the Shans? Volunteers, follow me? Lot of those tribes were one-crop communities, ah, opium communities, and in the interests of the war there, the Company had to, ah, well turn a blind eye to what we couldn't change, follow me? These good people have to live and many knew no better and saw nothing wrong in, ah, growing that crop. Follow me?'

'Jesus Christ,' said Sol under his breath. 'Hear that, Cy?'

'I heard, Sol.'

Smiley said he followed.

'This policy, conducted, ah, by the Company, caused a very brief and very temporary rift between the Company on the one side and the, ah, Enforcement people here, formerly the Bureau of Narcotics. Because, well, while Sol's boys were out to, well, ah, suppress the abuse of drugs, and quite rightly, and, ah, ride down the shipments, which is their job, George, and their duty, it was in the Company's best interest – in the best interest of the war, that is – at this point in time, you follow, George – to, well, ah, turn a blind eye.'

'Company played godfather to the hilltribes,' Sol growled. 'Menfolk were all out fighting the war, Company people flew up to the villages, pushed their poppy crops, screwed their women and flew their dope.'

Martello was not so easily thrown. 'Well we think that's overstating things a little, Sol, but the, ah, rift was there and that's the point as far as our friend Geoge is concerned. Ricardo, well he's a tough cookie. He flew a lot of missions for the Company in Laos, and when the war ended, the Company resettled him and kissed him off and pulled up the ladder. Nobody messes around with those boys when there's no war for them any more. So, ah, maybe at that, the, ah, gamekeeper Ricardo turned into the, ah, poacher Ricardo, if you follow me –'

'Well not *absolutely*,' Smiley confessed mildly.

Sol had no such scruples about unpalatable truths. 'Long as the war was on, Ricardo carried dope for the Company to keep the home fires burning up in the hill villages. War ended, he carried it for himself. He had the connects and he knew where the bodies were buried. He went independent, that's all.'

'Thank you,' said Smiley, and Sol went back to scratching his crewcut.

For the second time, Martello backed toward the story of Ricardo's embarrassing resurrection.

They must have done a deal between them, thought Guillam. Martello does the talking. 'Smiley's our contact,' Martello would have said. 'We play him our way.'

On the second of September seventy-three, said Martello, an *un-named narcotics agent in the South East Asian theatre*, as he insisted on describing him, 'a young man quite new to the field, George,' received a nocturnal telephone call at his home from a self-styled Captain Tiny Ricardo, hitherto believed dead, formerly a Laos mercenary with Captain Rocky. Ricardo offered a sizeable quantity of raw opium at standard buy-in rates. In addition to the opium, however, he was offering hot information at what he called a bargain-basement price for a quick sale. That is to say fifty thousand US dollars in small notes, and a West German passport for a one-time journey out. The un-named narcotics agent met Ricardo later that night at a parking lot and they quickly agreed on the sale of the opium.

'You mean he *bought* it?' Smiley asked, most surprised.

'Sol tells me there is a, ah, fixed tariff for such deals, – right Sol? – known to everyone in the game, George and, ah, based upon a percentage of the street value of the haul, right?' Sol growled an affirmative. 'The, ah, un-named agent had a standing authority to buy-in at that tariff and he exercised it. No problem. The agent also, ah, expressed himself willing, subject to higher consent, to supply Ricardo with quick-expiry documentation, George' – he meant, it turned out later, a West German passport with only a few days to run – 'in the event, George – an event not yet realized, you follow me – that Ricardo's information prove to be of reasonable value, since policy is to encourage informants at all costs. But he made it clear – the agent – that the whole deal – the passport and the payment for the information – was subject to ratification and authority – of Sol's people back at headquarters. So he bought the opium, but he held on the information. Right, Sol?'

'On the button,' Sol growled.

'Sol, ah, maybe you should handle this part,' Martello said.

When Sol spoke, he kept the rest of himself still for once. Just his mouth moved.

'Our agent asked Ricardo for a teaser so's the information could be evaluated back home. What we call taking it to first base. Ricardo comes up with the story he's been ordered to fly the dope over the border into Red China and bring back an unspecified load in payment. That's what he said. His teaser. He said he knew who was behind the deal, he said he knew the Mister Big of all the Mister Bigs, they all do. He said he knew all the story, but so do they all, once more. He said he embarked on his journey for the Mainland, chickened out and hedgehopped home over Laos ducking the radar screens. That's all he said. He didn't say where he set out from. He said he owed a favour to the people who sent him, and if they ever found him they'd kick his teeth right up his throat. That's what's in the protocol, word for word. His teeth up his throat. So he was in hurry, hence the favourable price of fifty grand. He didn't say who the people were, he did not produce one scrap of positive collateral apart from the opium, but he said he had the plane still, hidden, a Beechcraft, and he offered to show this plane to our agent at the next occasion of their meeting, subject to there being serious interest back at headquarters. That's all we have,' said Sol, and devoted himself to his cigarette. 'Opium was a couple of hundred kilos. Good stuff.'

Martello deftly took back the ball:

'So the un-named narcotics agent filed his story, George. And he did what we'd all do. He took down the teaser and he sent it back to headquarters and he told Ricardo to lie low till he heard back from his people. See you in ten days, maybe fourteen. Here's your opium-money, but for information-money you have to wait a little. There's regulations. Follow me?'

Smiley nodded sympathetically, and Martello nodded back at him while he went on talking.

'So here it is. Here's where you get your human error, right? It could be worse but not much. In our game there's two views of of history: conspiracy and fuck-up. Here's where we get the fuck-up, no question at all. Sol's predecessor, Ed, now ill, evaluated the material and on the evidence – now you met him, George, Ed Ristow, a good sound guy – and on the evidence available to him, Ed decided, understandably but wrongly, not to proceed. Ricardo wanted fifty grand. Well, for a major haul I understand that's chickenfeed. But Ricardo, he wanted payment on the nail. A one-time and out. And Ed – well Ed had responsibilities, a lot of family trouble, and Ed just didn't see his way to investing that sum of public American money in a character like Ricardo, when no haul is guaranteed, who has all the passes, knows all the fast steps, and is maybe squaring up to take that field agent of Ed's, who is only a young guy, for one hell of a journey. So Ed killed it. No further action. File and forget. All squared away. Buy the opium but not the rest.'

Maybe it was a real coronary after all, Guillam reflected, marvelling. But with another part of him he knew it could have happened to himself and even had: the pedlar who has the big one, and you let it through your fingers.

Rather than waste time in recrimination, Smiley had quietly moved ahead to the remaining possibilities.

'Where is Ricardo now, Marty?' he asked.

'Not known.'

His next question was much longer in coming, and was scarcely a question so much as a piece of thinking aloud.

'To bring back an *unspecified load in payment*,' he repeated. 'Are there any theories as to what type of load that might have been?'

'We guessed gold. We don't have second vision, any more than you do,' Sol said harshly.

Here Smiley simply ceased to take part in the proceedings for a while. His face set, his expression became anxious and, to anyone who knew him, inward, and suddenly it was up to Guillam to keep the ball rolling. To do this, like Smiley, he addressed Martello.

'Ricardo did not give any hint of where he was to deliver his return load?'

'I told you, Pete. That's all we have.'

Smiley was still non-combatant. He sat staring mournfully at his folded hands. Guillam hunted for another question:

'And no hint of the anticipated *weight* of the return load, either?' he asked.

'Jesus Christ,' said Sol, and misreading Smiley's attitude slowly shook his head in wonder at the kind of deadbeat company he was obliged to keep.

'But you *are* satisfied it was Ricardo who approached your agent?' Guillam asked, still in there, throwing punches.

'One hundred per cent,' said Sol.

'Sol,' Martello suggested, leaning across to him. 'Sol, why don't you just give George a blind copy of that original field report? That way he has everything we have.'

Sol hesitated, glanced at his sidekick, shrugged, and finally with some reluctance drew a flimsy sheet of India paper from a folder on the table beside him, from which he solemnly tore off the signature.

'Off the record,' he growled, and at this point Smiley abruptly revived, and, receiving the report from Sol's hand, studied both sides intently for a while in silence.

'And, where, please, is the un-named narcotics agent who wrote this document,' he enquired finally, looking first at Martello, then at Sol.

Sol scraped his scalp. Cy began shaking his head in disapproval. Whereas Martello's two quiet men showed no curiosity whatever. Pale Murphy continued reading among his notes, and his colleague gazed blankly at the ex-President.

'Shacked up in a hippy commune north of Katmandu,' Sol growled, through a gush of cigarette smoke. 'Bastard joined the opposition.'

Martello's bright endpiece was wonderfully irrelevant: 'So, ah, that's the reason, George, why *our* computer has Ricardo dead and buried, George, when the overall record – on reconsideration by our Enforcement friends – gives no grounds for that, ah, assumption.'

So far it had seemed to Guillam that the boot was all on Martello's foot. Sol's boys had made fools of themselves, he was saying, but the Cousins were nothing if not magnanimous and they were willing to kiss and make up. In the post-coital calm which followed Martello's revelations, this false impression prevailed a little longer.

'So, ah, George, I would say that henceforward, we may count – you, we, Sol here – on the fullest cooperation of all our agencies. I would say there was a very positive side to this. Right, George? Constructive.'

But Smiley in his renewed distraction only lifted his eyebrows and pursed his lips.

'Something on your mind, George?' Martello asked. 'I said, is there something on your mind?'

'Oh. Thank you. *Beechcraft*,' Smiley said. 'Is that a single-engined plane?'

'Jesus,' said Sol under his breath.

'Twin, George, twin,' said Martello. 'Kind of executive runabout kind of thing.'

'And the weight of the opium load was four hundred kilos, the report says.'

'Just short of half of one ton, George,' said Martello at his most solicitous. 'A *metric* ton,' he added doubtfully, to Smiley's shadowed face. 'Not your English ton, George, naturally. Metric.'

'And it would be carried *where* – the opium, I mean?'

'Cabin,' said Sol. 'Most likely unscrewed the spare seats. Beechcrafts come different shapes. We don't know which this was because we never got to see it.'

Smiley peered once more at the flimsy which he still clutched in his pudgy hand. 'Yes,' he muttered. 'Yes, I suppose they would have done.' And with a gold lead-pencil he wrote a small hieroglyphic in the margin before relapsing into his private reverie.

'Well,' said Martello brightly. 'Guess us worker-bees had better get back to our hives and see where that gets us, right, Pete?'

Guillam was halfway to his feet as Sol spoke. Sol had the rare and rather terrible gift of natural rudeness. Nothing had changed in him. He was in no way out of control. This was the way he talked, this was the way he did business, and other ways patently bored him:

'Jesus *Christ*, Martello, what kind of game are we playing round here? This is the big one, right? We have put our finger on maybe the most important single narcotics target in the entire South East Asian scene. Okay, so there's liaison. The Company has finally gone to bed with Enforcement because she had to buy us off on the hilltribe thing. Don't think that makes *me* horny. Okay, so we have a hands-off deal with the Brits on Hong Kong. But Thailand's ours, so's the Philippines, so's Taiwan, so's the whole damn theatre, so's the war, and the Brits are on their ass. Four months ago the Brits came in and made their pitch. Great, so we roll it to the Brits. What they been doing all the time? Rubbing soap into their pretty faces. So when do they get to shave, for God's sakes? We got money riding on this. We got a whole apparatus standing by, ready to shake out Ko's connections across the hemisphere. We been looking *years* for a guy like this. And we can nail him. We have enough legislation – boy do we have legislation! – to pin a ten-to-thirty on him and *then* some! We got drugs on him, we got arms, we got

embargoed goods, we got the biggest damn load of Red gold we ever saw
Moscow hand to one man in our *lives*, and we got the first proof ever, if this
guy Ricardo is telling a correct story, of a Moscow-subsidized drug-subver-
sion programme which is ready and willing to carry the battle into Red China
in the hopes of doing the same for them as they've already done for us.'

The outburst had woken Smiley like a douche of water. He was sitting
forward on the edge of his chair, the narcotics agent's report crumpled in his
hand, and he was staring appalled, first at Sol, finally at Martello.

'Marty,' he muttered. 'Oh my Lord. *No.*'

Guillam showed greater presence of mind. At least he threw in an
objection:

'You'd have to spread half a ton awfully *thin*, wouldn't you, Sol, to hook
eight hundred million Chinese?'

But Sol had no use for humour, or objections either, least of all from some
pretty-faced Brit.

'And do we go for his jugular?' he demanded, keeping straight on course.
'Do we hell. We pussyfoot. We stand on the sidelines. "Play it delicate. It's a
British ballgame. Their territory, their joe, their party." So we weave, we
dance around. We float like a butterfly and sting like one. Jesus, if *we'd* been
handling this thing, we'd have had that bastard trussed over a barrel months
ago.' Slapping the table with his palm, he used the rhetorical trick of
repeating his point in different language. 'For the first time ever we have
gotten ourselves a sabre-toothed Soviet Communist corrupter in our sights,
pushing dope and screwing up the area and taking Russian money and we
can *prove* it!' It was all addressed to Martello. Smiley and Guillam might not
have been there at all. 'And you just remember another thing,' he advised
Martello in conclusion. 'We got big people wanting mileage out of this.
Impatient people. Influential. People very angry with the dubious part your
Company has indirectly played in the supply and merchandising of narcotics
to our boys in Vietnam, which is why you cut us in on this in the first place. So
maybe you better tell some of those limousine liberals back in Langley
Virginia it's time for them to shit or get off the pot. Pot in *both senses*,' he ended
in a humourless pun.

Smiley had turned so pale that Guillam was genuinely afraid for him. He
wondered whether he had had a heart attack, or was going to faint. From
where Guillam sat, his cheeks and complexion were suddenly an old man's
and his eyes, as he too addressed Martello only, had an old man's fire:

'However, there is an agreement. And so long as it stands, I trust that you
will stick to it. We have your general declaration that you will abstain from
operations in British areas unless our permission has been granted. We have
your particular promise that you will leave to us the entire development of
this case, outside surveillance and communication, *regardless of where the
development leads*. That was the contract. A complete hands-off in exchange
for a complete sight of the product. I take that to mean this: *no* action by
Langley and *no* action by any other American agency. I take that to be your
absolute word. And I take your word to be still good, and I regard that
understanding as irreducible.'

'Tell him,' said Sol, and walked out, followed by Cy, his sallow Mormon
sidekick. At the door he turned, and jabbed a finger in Smiley's direction.

'You ride our wagon, we tell you where to get off and where to stay
topsides,' he said.

The Mormon nodded: 'Sure do,' he said and smiled at Guillam as if in invitation. On Martello's nod, Murphy and his fellow quiet man followed them out of the room.

Martello was pouring drinks. In his office, the walls were also rosewood – a fake laminate, Guillam noticed, not the real thing – and when Martello pulled a handle he revealed an ice machine that vomited a steady flow of pellets in the shape of rugby balls. He poured three whiskies without asking the others what they wanted. Smiley looked all in. His plump hands were still cupped over the ends of his airline chair, but he was leaning back like a spent boxer between rounds, staring at the ceiling, which was perforated by twinkling lights. Martello set the glasses on the table.

'Thank you, sir,' Guillam said. Martello liked a 'sir'.

'You bet,' said Martello.

'Who else have your headquarters told?' Smiley said, to the stars. 'The Revenue Service? The Customs Service? The Mayor of Chicago? Their twelve best friends? Do you realize that not even my masters know we are in collaboration with you? God in heaven.'

'Ah, come on now, George. We have politics, same as you. We have promises to keep. Mouths to buy. Enforcement's out for our blood. That dope story's gotten a lot of airtime on the Hill. Senators, the House Subcommittees, the whole garbage. Kid comes back from the war a screaming junkie, first thing his Pa does is write to his Congressman. Company doesn't care for all those bad rumours. It likes to have its friends on its own side. That's showbiz, George.'

'Could I please just know what the deal is?' Smiley asked. 'Could I have it in plain words, at least.'

'Oh now, there's no *deal*, George. Langley can't deal with what she doesn't own, and this is *your* case, your property, your . . . We fish for him – you do, with a little help from us maybe – we do our best and then if, ah, we don't come up with anything, why, Enforcement will get in on the act a little and, on a very friendly and controllable basis, try their skill.'

'At which point it's open season,' Smiley said. 'My goodness, what a way to run a case.'

When it came to pacification, Martello was a very old hand indeed:

'George. *George.* Suppose they nail Ko. Suppose they fall on him out of the trees next time he leaves the Colony. If Ko's going to languish in Sing-Sing on a ten-to-thirty rap, why, we can pick him clean at will. Is that so very terrible suddenly?'

Yes it bloody well is, thought Guillam. Till it suddenly dawned on him, with a quite malignant glee, that Martello himself was not *witting* on the subject of Brother Nelson, and that George had kept his best card to his chest.

Smiley was still sitting forward. The ice in his whisky had put a damp frost round the outside of the glass, and for a time he stared at it, watching the tears slide on to the rosewood table.

'So how long have we got on our own?' Smiley asked. 'What's our head start before the narcotics people come barging in?'

'It's not rigid, George. It's not *like* that! It's parameters, like Cy said.'

'Three months?'

'That's generous, a little generous.'

'Less than three months?'

'Three months, inside of three months, ten to twelve weeks – in that *area*, George. It's fluid between friends. Three months outside, I would say.'

Smiley breathed out in a long sigh. 'Yesterday we had all the time in the world.'

Martello dropped the veil an inch or two. 'Sol is not that conscious, George' he said, careful to use Circus jargon rather than his own. 'Ah, Sol has blank areas,' he said, half by way of admission. 'We don't just throw him the whole carcass, know what I mean?'

Martello paused, then said, 'Sol goes to first echelon. No further. Believe me.'

'And what does first echelon mean?'

'He knows Ko is in funds from Moscow. Knows he pushes opium. That's all.'

'Does he know of the girl?'

'Now she's a case in point, George. The girl. That girl went with him on the trip to Bangkok. Remember Murphy describing the Bangkok trip? She stayed in the hotel suite with him. She flew on with him to Manila. I saw you read me there. I caught your eye. But we had Murphy delete that section of the report. Just for Sol's benefit.' Very slightly, Smiley seemed to revive. 'Deal stands, George,' Martello assured him munificently. 'Nothing's added, nothing's subtracted. You play the fish, we'll help you eat it. Any help along the way, you just have to pick up that green line and holler.' He went so far as to lay a consoling hand on Smiley's shoulder, but sensing that he disliked the gesture, abandoned it rather quickly. 'However, if you ever *do* want to pass us the oars, why, we would merely reverse that arrangement and –'

'Steal our thunder and get yourselves thrown off the Colony into the bargain,' said Smiley, completing the sentence for him. 'I want one more thing made clear. I want it written down. I want it to be the subject of an exchange of letters between us.'

'Your party, you choose the games,' said Martello expansively.

'My service will play the fish,' Smiley insisted, in the same direct tone. 'We will also land it, if that is the angling expression. I'm not a sportsman, I'm afraid.'

'Land it, beach it, hook it, sure.'

Martello's good will, to Guillam's suspicious eye, was tiring a little at the edges.

'I insist on it being *our* operation. Our man. I insist on first rights. To have him and to hold him, until we see fit to pass him on.'

'No problem, George, no problem at all. You take him aboard, he's yours. Soon as you want to share him, call us. It's simple as that.'

'I'll send round a written confirmation in the morning.'

'Oh don't bother to do that, George. We have people. We'll have them collect it for you.'

'I'll send it round,' said Smiley.

Martello stood up. 'George, you just got yourself a deal.'

'I had a deal already,' Smiley said. 'Langley broke it.'

They shook hands.

The case history has no other moment like this. In the trade it goes under various phrases. 'The day George reversed the controls' is one – though it took him a good week, and brought Martello's deadline that much nearer.

But to Guillam the process had something far more stately about it, far more beautiful than a mere technical re-tooling. As his understanding of Smiley's intention slowly grew, as he looked on fascinated while Smiley laid down each meticulous line, summoned this or that collaborator, put out a hook here, and took in a cleat there, Guillam had the sensation of watching the turn-round of some large ocean-going vessel as it is coaxed and nosed and gentled into facing back along its own course.

Which entailed – yes – turning the entire case upside down, or reversing the controls.

They arrived back at the Circus without a word spoken. Smiley took the last flight of stairs slowly enough to revive Guillam's fears for his health, so that as soon as he was able he rang the Circus doctor and gave him a rundown of the symptoms as he saw them, only to be told that Smiley had been round to see him a couple of days ago on an unrelated matter and showed every sign of being indestructible. The throne-room door closed, and Fawn the babysitter once more had his beloved Chief to himself. Smiley's needs, where they filtered through, had the smack of alchemy. Beechcraft aeroplanes: he wished for plans and catalogues, and also – provided they could be obtained unattributably – any details of owners, sales and purchases in the South East Asian region. Toby Esterhase duly disappeared into the murky thickets of the aircraft sales industry, and soon afterwards Fawn handed to Molly Meakin a daunting heap of backnumbers of a journal called *Transport World* with handwritten instructions from Smiley in the traditional green ink of his office to mark down any advertisements for Beechcraft planes which might have caught the eye of a potential buyer during the six-month period before the pilot Ricardo's abortive opium mission into Red China.

Again on Smiley's written orders, Guillam discreetly visited several of di Salis's burrowers and, without the knowledge of their temperamental superior, established that they were still far from putting the finger on Nelson Ko. One old fellow went so far as to suggest that Drake Ko had spoken no less than the truth in his last meeting with old Hibbert: and that Brother Nelson was dead indeed. But when Guillam took this news to Smiley he shook his head impatiently, and handed him a signal for transmission to Craw, telling him to obtain from his local police source, preferably on a pretext, all recorded details of the travel movements of Ko's manager Tiu in and out of Mainland China.

Craw's long answer was on Smiley's desk forty-eight hours later, and it appeared to give him a rare moment of pleasure. He ordered out the duty driver, and had himself taken to Hampstead, where he walked alone over the Heath for an hour, through sunlit frost, and according to Fawn stood gawping at the ruddy squirrels before returning to the throne-room.

'But don't you *see*?' he protested to Guillam, in an equally rare fit of excitement that evening – 'Don't you *understand*, Peter?' – shoving Craw's dates under his nose, actually stubbing his finger on one entry – 'Tiu went to Shanghai six weeks before Ricardo's mission. How long did he stay there? Forty-eight hours. Oh you are a dunce!'

'I'm nothing of the kind,' Guillam retorted. 'I just don't happen to have a direct line to God that's all.'

In the cellars, cloistered with Millie McCraig the head listener, Smiley replayed old Hibbert's monologues, scowling occasionally – said Millie – at di Salis's clumsy bullying. Otherwise, he read and prowled, and talked to Sam Collins in short, intensive bursts. These encounters, Guillam noticed, cost

Smiley a lot of spirit, and his bouts of ill-temper – which Lord knows were few enough for a man with Smiley's burdens – always occurred after Sam's departure. And even when they had blown over, he looked more strained and lonely than ever, till he had taken one of his long night walks.

Then on about the fourth day, which in Guillam's life was a crisis day for some reason – probably the argument with Treasury, who resented paying Craw a bonus – Toby Esterhase somehow slipped through the net of both Fawn and Guillam, and gained the throne-room undetected, where he presented Smiley with a bunch of Xeroxed contracts of sale for one brand new four-seater Beechcraft to the Bangkok firm of Aerosuis and Co., registered in Zurich, details pending. Smiley was particularly jubilant about the fact that there were four seats. The two at the rear were removable, but the pilot's and copilot's were fixed. As to the actual sale of the plane, it had been completed on the twentieth of July: a scant month, therefore, before the crazy Ricardo set off to infringe Red China's airspace, and then changed his mind.

'Even Peter can make *that* connection,' Smiley declared, with heavy skittishness. 'Sequence, Peter, sequence, come on!'

'The plane was sold two weeks after Tiu returned from Shanghai,' Guillam replied, reluctantly.

'And so?' Smiley demanded. 'And so? What do we look at next?'

'We ask ourselves who owns the firm of Aerosuis,' Guillam snapped, really quite irritated.

'Precisely. Thank you,' said Smiley in mock relief. 'You restore my faith in you, Peter. Now then. Whom do we discover at the helm of Aerosuis, do you think? The Bangkok representative, no less.'

Guillam glanced at the notes on Smiley's desk, but Smiley was too quick and clapped his hands over them.

'Tiu,' Guillam said, actually blushing.

'Hoorah. Yes. Tiu. Well done.'

But by the time Smiley sent again for Sam Collins that evening, the shadows had returned to his pendulous face.

Still the lines were thrown out. After his success in the aircraft industry, Toby Esterhase was reassigned to the liquor trade and flew to the Western Isles of Scotland, under the guise of a Value Added Tax inspector, where he spent three days making a spot check of the books of a house of whisky distillers who specialized in the forward selling of unmatured kegs. He returned – to quote Connie – leering like a successful bigamist.

The multiple climax of all this activity was an extremely long signal to Craw, drafted after a full-dress meeting of the operational directorate – The Golden Oldies, to quote Connie yet again, with Sam Collins added. The meeting followed an extended ways and means session with the Cousins, at which Smiley refrained from all mention of the elusive Nelson Ko, but requested certain additional facilities of surveillance and communication in the field. To his collaborators, Smiley explained his plans this way.

Till now the operation had been limited to obtaining intelligence about Ko and the ramifications of the Soviet goldseam. Much care had been taken to prevent Ko from becoming aware of the Circus's interest in him.

He then summarized the intelligence they had so far collected: Nelson, Ricardo, Tiu, the Beechcraft, the dates, the inferences, the Swiss-registered aviation company – which as it now turned out possessed no premises and no other aircraft. He would prefer, he said, to wait for the positive identification of Nelson, but every operation was a compromise and time, partly thanks to the Cousins, was running out.

He made no mention at all of the girl, and he never once looked at Sam Collins while he delivered his address.

Then he came to what he modestly called the *next phase*.

'Our problem is to break the stalemate. There are operations which run better for not being resolved. There are others which are worthless until they *are* resolved and the Dolphin case is one of these.' He gave a studious frown, and blinked, then whipped off his spectacles and, to the secret delight of everyone, unconsciously subscribed to his own legend by polishing them on the fat end of his tie. 'I propose to do this by turning our tactic inside out. In other words, by declaring to Ko our interest in his affairs.'

It was Connie, as ever, who put an end to the suitably dreadful silence. Her smile was also the fastest – and the most knowing.

'He's smoking him out,' she whispered to them all in ecstasy. 'Same as he did with Bill, the clever hound! Lighting a fire on his doorstep, aren't you darling, and seeing which way he runs. Oh *George*, you lovely, lovely man, the best of all my boys, I do declare!'

Smiley's signal to Craw used a different metaphor to describe the plan, one which fieldmen favour. He referred to *shaking Ko's tree*, and it was clear from the remainder of the text that, despite the considerable dangers, he proposed to use the broad back of Jerry Westerby to do it.

As a footnote to all this, a couple of days later Sam Collins vanished. Everyone was very pleased. He ceased to come in and Smiley did not refer to him. His room, when Guillam sneaked in covertly to look it over, contained nothing personal to Sam at all except a couple of unbroken packs of playing cards and some garish book matches advertising a West End nightclub. When he sounded out the housekeepers, they were for once unusually forthcoming. His price was a kiss-off gratuity, they said, and a promise to have his pension rights reconsidered. He had not really had much to sell at all. A flash in the pan, they said, never to reappear. Good riddance.

All the same, Guillam could not rid himself of a certain unease about Sam, which he often conveyed to Molly Meakin over the next few weeks. It was not just about bumping into him at Lacon's office. He was bothered about the business of Smiley's exchange of letters with Martello confirming their verbal understanding. Rather than having the Cousins collect it, with the consequent parade of a limousine and even a motor-cycle outrider in Cambridge Circus, Smiley had ordered Guillam to run it round to Grosvenor Square himself with Fawn babysitting. But Guillam was snowed under with work, as it happened, and Sam as usual was spare. So when Sam volunteered to take for him, Guillam let him and wished to God he never had. He wished it still, devoutly.

Because instead of handing George's letter to Murphy or his faceless running-mate, said Fawn, Sam had insisted on going in to Martello personally. And had spent more than an hour with him alone.

# PART TWO

# Shaking the Tree

# THIRTEEN

## *Liese*

Star Heights was the newest and tallest block in the Midlevels, built on the round, and by night jammed like a huge lighted pencil into the soft darkness of the Peak. A winding causeway led to it, but the only pavement was a line of kerbstone six inches wide between the causeway and the cliffs. At Star Heights, pedestrians were in bad taste. It was early evening and the social rush hour was nearing its height. As Jerry edged his way along the kerb, the Mercedes and Rolls-Royces brushed against him in their haste to deliver and collect. He carried a bunch of orchids wrapped in tissue: larger than the bunch which Craw had presented to Phoebe Wayfarer, smaller than the one Drake Ko had given the dead boy Nelson. These orchids were for nobody. 'When you're my size, sport, you have to have a hell of a good reason for whatever you do.'

He felt tense but also relieved that the long, long wait was over.

*A straight foot-in-the door operation, your Grace*, Craw had advised him at yesterday's protracted briefing. Shove your way in there and start pitching and don't stop till you're out the other side.

With one leg, though Jerry.

A striped awning led to the entrance hall and a perfume of women hung in the air, like a foretaste of his errand. *And just remember Ko owns the building*, Craw had added sourly, as a parting gift. The interior decoration was not quite finished. Plates of marble were missing round the mail boxes. A fibreglass fish should have been spewing water into a terrazzo fountain, but the pipes had not yet been connected and bags of cement were heaped in the basin. He headed for the lifts. A glass booth was marked 'Reception' and the Chinese porter was watching him from inside it. Jerry only saw the blur of him. He had been reading when Jerry arrived, but now he was staring at Jerry, undecided whether to challenge him, but half reassured by the orchids. A couple of American matrons in full warpaint arrived, and took up a position near him.

'Great blooms,' they said, poking in the tissue.

'Super, aren't they. Here, have them. Present! Come on! Beautiful women. Naked without them!'

Laughter. The English are a race apart. The porter returned to his reading and Jerry was authenticated. A lift arrived. A herd of diplomats, businessmen and their squaws shuffled into the lobby, sullen and bejewelled. Jerry ushered the American matrons ahead of him. Cigar smoke mingled with the scent, slovenly canned music hummed forgotten melodies. The matrons pressed the button for twelve.

'You visiting with the Hammersteins too?' they asked, still looking at the orchids.

At the fifteenth, Jerry made for the fire stairs. They stank of cat, and rubbish from the shoot. Descending he met an amah carrying a nappy bucket. She scowled at him till he greeted her, then laughed uproariously. He kept going till he reached the eighth floor where he stepped back into the plush of the residents' landing. He was at the end of a corridor. A small rotunda gave on to two gold lift doors. There were four flats, each a quadrant of the circular building, and each with its own corridor. He took up a position in the B corridor with only flowers to protect him. He was watching the rotunda, his attention on the mouth of the corridor marked C. The tissue round the orchids was damp where he'd been clutching it too tight.

'It's a firm weekly date,' Craw had assured him. 'Every Monday, flower arrangement at the American Club. Regular as clockwork. She meets a girlfriend there, Nellie Tan, works for Airsea. They take in the flower arrangement and stay for dinner afterwards.'

'So where's Ko meanwhile?'

'In Bangkok. Trading.'

'Well let's bloody well hope he stays there.'

'Amen, sir. Amen.'

With a shriek of new hinges unoiled, the door at his ear was yanked open and a slim young American in a dinner-jacket stepped into the corridor, stopped dead, and stared at Jerry and the orchids. He had blue, steady eyes and he carried a briefcase.

'You looking for me with those things?' he enquired with a Boston society drawl. He looked rich and assured. Jerry guessed diplomacy or Ivy League banking.

'Well I don't think so actually,' Jerry confessed, playing the English bloody fool. '*Cavendish*,' he said. Over the American's shoulder Jerry saw the door quietly close on a packed bookshelf. 'Friends of mine asked me to give these to a Miss *Cavendish* at 9D. Waltzed off to Manila, left me holding the orchids, sort of thing.'

'Wrong floor,' said the American strolling toward the lift. 'You want one up. Wrong corridor too. D's over the other side. Thattaway.'

Jerry stood beside him, pretending to wait for an *up* lift. The *down* lift came first, the young American stepped easily into it and Jerry resumed his post. The door marked C opened, he saw her come out, and turn to double-lock it. Her clothes were everyday. Her hair was long and ashblond but she had tied it in a pony tail at the nape. She wore a plain halter-neck dress and sandals, and though he couldn't see her face he knew already she was beautiful. She walked to the lift, still not seeing him and Jerry had the illusion of looking in on her through a window from the street.

There were women in Jerry's world who carried their bodies as if they were citadels to be stormed only by the bravest, and Jerry had married several; or perhaps they grew that way under his influence. There were women who seemed determined to hate themselves, hunching their backs and locking up their hips. And there were women who had only to walk toward him to bring him a gift. They were the rare ones and for Jerry at that moment she led the pack. She had stopped at the gold doors and was watching the lighted numbers. He reached her side as the lift arrived and she still hadn't noticed him. It was jammed full, as he had hoped it would be. He entered crabwise, intent on the orchids, apologizing, grinning and making a show of holding them high. She had her back to him, and he was standing at her shoulder. It was a strong shoulder, and bare either side of the halter, and Jerry could see small freckles and a down of tiny gold hairs disappearing down her spine. Her face was in profile below him. He peered down at it.

'Lizzie?' he said, uncertainly. 'Hey, *Lizzie*, It's me, Jerry.'

She turned sharply and stared up at him. He wished he could have backed away from her because he knew her first response would be physical fear of his size, and he was right. He saw it momentarily in her grey eyes, which flickered before holding him in their stare.

'Lizzie *Worthington*!' he declared more confidently. 'How's the whisky, remember me? One of your proud investors. Jerry. Chum of Tiny Ricardo's. One fifty-gallon keg with my name on the label. All paid and above board.'

He had kept it quiet on the assumption that he might be raking up a past she was keen to disown. He had kept it so quiet that their fellow passengers heard either 'Raindrops keep fallin' on my head' over the Muzak, or the grumbling of an elderly Greek who thought he was boxed in.

'Why, of course,' she said, and gave a bright, airhostess smile. 'Jerry!' Her voice faded as she pretended to have it on the tip of her tongue. 'Jerry – er –' She frowned and looked upward like a repertory actress doing Forgetfulness. The lift stopped at the sixth floor.

'Westerby,' he said promptly getting her off the hook. 'Newshound. You put the bite on me in the Constellation bar. I wanted a spot of loving comfort and all I got was a keg of whisky.'

'Of *course*! Jerry *darling*! How could I possibly . . . So I mean what are you doing in Hong Kong? My *God*!'

'Usual beat. Fire and pestilence, famine. How about you? Retired I should think, with your sales methods. Never had my arm twisted so thoroughly in my life.'

She laughed delightedly. The doors had opened at the third floor. An old woman shuffled in on two walking sticks.

*Lizzie Worthington sold in all a cool fifty-five kegs of the blushful Hippocrene, your Grace*, old Craw had said. *Every one of them to a male buyer and a fair number of them, according to my advisors, with service thrown in. Gives a new meaning to the term 'good measure', I venture to suggest.*

They had reached the ground floor. She got out first and he walked beside her. Through the main doors he saw her red sports car with its roof up waiting in the bay, jammed among the glistening limousines. She must have phoned down and ordered them to have it ready, he thought: if Ko owns the building he'll make damn sure she gets the treatment. She was heading for the porter's window. As they crossed the hall she went on chattering, pivoting to talk to him, one arm held wide of her body, palm upward like a fashion model. He must have asked her how she liked Hong Kong, though he couldn't remember doing so:

'I adore it, Jerry, I simply *adore* it. Vientiane seems – oh, *centuries* away. You know Ric died?' She threw this in heroically, as if she and death weren't strangers to each other. 'After Ric, I thought I'd never care for anywhere again. I was completely wrong, Jerry. Hong Kong *has* to be the most fun city in the world. Lawrence darling, I'm sailing my red submarine. It's hen night at the club.'

Lawrence was the porter, and the key to her car dangled from a large silver horseshoe which reminded Jerry of Happy Valley races.

'Thank you, Lawrence,' she said sweetly and gave him a smile that would last him all night. 'The *people* here are so marvellous, Jerry,' she confided to him in a stage whisper as they moved toward the main entrance. 'To *think* what we used to say about the Chinese in Laos! Yet here, they're just the most marvellous and outgoing and inventive people ever.' She had slipped into a stateless foreign accent, he noticed. Must have picked it up from Ricardo and stuck to it for chic. 'People think to themselves: "Hong Kong – fabulous shopping – tax free cameras – restaurants –" but honestly, Jerry, when you get under the surface, and meet the *true* Hong Kong, and the *people* – it's got everything you could possibly want from life. Don't you adore my new car?'

'So that's how you spend the whisky profits.'

He held out his open palm and she dropped the keys into it so that he could unlock the door for her. Still in dumb show he gave her the orchids to hold. Behind the black peak a full moon, not yet risen, glowed like a forest fire. She climbed in, he handed her the keys and this time he felt the contact of her hand and remembered Happy Valley again, and Ko's kiss as they drove away.

'Mind if I ride on the back?' he asked.

She laughed and pushed open the passenger door for him.

'Where are you going with those gorgeous orchids anyway?'

She started the engine, but Jerry gently switched it off again. She stared at him in surprise.

'Sport,' he said quietly. 'I cannot tell a lie. I'm a viper in your nest, and before you drive me anywhere, you'd better fasten your seat belt and hear the grisly truth.'

He had chosen this moment carefully because he didn't want her to feel threatened. She was in the driving seat of her own car, under the lighted awning of her own apartment block, within sixty feet of Lawrence the porter, and he was playing the humble sinner in order to increase her sense of security.

'Our chance reunion was not entire chance. That's point one. Point two, not to put too fine an edge on it, my paper told me to run you to earth and besiege you with many searching questions regarding your late chum Ricardo.'

She was still watching him, still waiting. On the point of her chin she had two small parallel scars like claw marks quite deep. He wondered who had made them, and what with.

'But Ricardo's dead,' she said, much too early.

'Sure,' said Jerry consolingly. 'No question. However the comic is in possession of what they're pleased to call a hot tip that he's alive after all and it's my job to humour them.'

'But that's absolutely absurd!'

'Agreed. Totally. They're out of their minds. The consolation prize is two dozen well-thumbed orchids and the best dinner in town.'

Turning away from him she gazed through the windscreen, her face in the full glare of the overhead lamp, and Jerry wondered what it must be like to inhabit such a beautiful body, living up to it twenty-four hours a day. Her grey eyes opened a little wider and he had a shrewd suspicion that he was supposed to notice the tears brimming and the way her hands grasped the steering wheel for support.

'Forgive me,' she murmured. 'It's just – when you love a man – give everything up for him – and he dies – then one evening, out of the blue –'

'Sure,' said Jerry. 'I'm sorry.'

She started the engine. 'Why should you be sorry? If he's alive, that's bonus. If he's dead, nothing's changed. We're on a pound to nothing.' She laughed. 'Ric always said he was indestructible.'

It's like stealing from a blind beggar, he thought. She shouldn't be let loose.

She drove well but stiffly and he guessed – because she inspired guesswork – that she had only recently passed her test and that the car was her prize for doing so. It was the calmest night in the world. As they sank into the city, the harbour lay like a perfect mirror at the centre of the jewel box. They talked places. Jerry suggested the Peninsula but she shook her head.

'Okay. Let's go for a drink first,' he said. 'Come on, let's blow the walls out!'

To his surprise she reached across and gave his hand a squeeze. Then he remembered Craw. She did that to everyone, he had said.

She was off the leash for a night: he had that overwhelming sensation. He remembered taking Cat, his daughter, out from school when she was young, and how they had to do lots of different things in order to make the afternoon longer. At a dark disco on Kowloonside they drank Rémy Martin with ice and soda. He guessed it was Ko's drink and she had picked up the habit to keep him company. It was early and there were maybe a dozen people, no more. The music was loud and they had to yell to hear each other, but she didn't mention Ricardo. She preferred the music, and listening with her head back. Sometimes she held his hand, and once put her head on his shoulder, and once she blew him a distracted kiss and drifted on to the floor to perform a slow, solitary dance, eyes closed, slightly smiling. The men ignored their own girls and undressed her with their eyes, and the Chinese waiters brought fresh ashtrays every three minutes so that they could look down her dress. After two drinks and half an hour she announced a passion for the Duke and the big-band sound, so they raced back to the Island to a place Jerry knew where a live Filipino band gave a fair rendering of Ellington. Cat Anderson was the best thing since sliced bread, she said. Had he heard Armstrong and Ellington together? Weren't they just the greatest? More Rémy Martin while she sang 'Mood Indigo' to him.

'Did Ricardo dance?' Jerry asked.

'Did he dance?' she replied softly, as she tapped her foot and lightly clicked her fingers to the rhythm.

'Thought Ricardo had a limp,' Jerry objected.

'*That* never stopped him,' she said, still absorbed by the music. 'I'll never go back to him, you understand. Never. That chapter's closed. And how.'

'How'd he pick it up?'

'Dancing?'

'The limp.'

With her fingers curled round an imaginary trigger she fired a shot in the air.

'It was either the war or an angry husband,' she said. He made her repeat it, her lips close to his ear.

She knew a new Japanese restaurant where they served *fabulous* Kobe beef.

'Tell me how you got those scars,' he asked as they were driving there. He touched his own chin. 'The left and the right. What did it?'

'Oh hunting innocent foxes,' she said with a light smile. 'My dear papa was horse mad. He still is, I'm afraid.'

'Where does he live?'

'Daddy? Oh the usual tumble-down schloss in Shropshire. *Miles* too big but they won't move. No staff, no money, ice cold three-quarters of the year. Mummy can't even boil an egg.'

He was still reeling when she remembered a bar where they gave heavenly curry canapés, so they drove around until they found it and she kissed the barman. There was no music but for some reason he heard himself telling her all about the orphan, till he came to the reasons for their break-up, which he deliberately fogged over.

'Ah, but Jerry darling,' she said sagely. 'With twenty-five years between you and her, what else can you expect?'

And with nineteen years and a Chinese wife between you and Drake Ko what the hell can *you* expect? he thought, with some annoyance.

They left – more kisses for the barman – and Jerry was not so intoxicated by her company, nor by the brandy-sodas, to miss the point that she made a phone call, allegedly to cancel her date, that the call took a long time, and that when she returned from it she looked rather solemn. In the car again, he caught her eye and thought he read a shadow of mistrust.

'Jerry?'

'Yes?'

She shook her head, laughed, ran her palm along his face, then kissed him. 'It's fun,' she said.

He guessed she was wondering whether, if she had really sold him that keg of unbranded whisky, she would so thoroughly have forgotten him. He guessed she was also wondering whether, in order to sell him the keg, she had thrown in any fringe benefits of the sort Craw had so coarsely referred to. But that was her problem, he reckoned. Had been from the start.

In the Japanese restaurant they were given the corner table, thanks to Lizzie's smile and other attributes. She sat looking into the room, and he sat looking at Lizzie, which was fine by Jerry but would have given Sarratt the bends. By the candlelight he saw her face very clearly and was conscious for the first time of the signs of wear: not just the claw marks on her chin, but her lines of travel, and of strain, which to Jerry had a determined quality about them, like honourable scars from all the battles against her bad luck and her bad judgment. She wore a gold bracelet, new, and a bashed tin watch with a Walt Disney dial on it, and scratched gloved hand pointing to the numerals. Her loyalty to the old watch impressed him and he wanted to know who gave it to her.

'Daddy,' she said distractedly.

A mirror was let into the ceiling above them, and he could see her gold hair and the swell of her breasts among the scalps of other diners, and the gold dust of the hairs on her back. When he tried to hit her with Ricardo, she turned guarded: it should have occurred to Jerry, but it didn't, that her attitude had changed since she made the phone call.

'What guarantee do I have that you will keep my name out of your paper?' she asked.

'Just my promise.'

'But if your editor knows I was Ricardo's girl, what's to stop him putting it in for himself?'

'Ricardo had lots of girls. You know that. They came in all shapes and sizes and ran concurrently.'

'There was only one of *me*,' she said firmly, and he saw her glance towards the door. But then she had that habit anyway, wherever she was, of looking round the room all the time for someone who wasn't there. He let her keep the initiative.

'You said your paper had a hot tip,' she said. 'What do they mean by that?'

He had boned up his answer to this with Craw. It was one they had actually rehearsed. He delivered it therefore with force if not conviction.

'Ric's crash was eighteen months ago in the hills near Pailin on the Thai-Cambodian border. That's the official line. No one found a body, no one found wreckage and there's talk he was doing an opium run. The insurance company never paid up and Indocharter never sued them. Why not? Because Ricardo had an exclusive contract to fly for them. For that matter, why doesn't someone sue Indocharter? You for instance. You were his woman. Why not go for damages?'

'That is a *very* vulgar suggestion,' she said in her duchess voice.

'Beyond that, there's rumours he's been seen recently around the haunts a little. He's grown a beard but he can't cure the limp, they say, nor his habit of sinking a bottle of Scotch a day, nor, saving your presence, chasing after everything that wears a skirt within a five mile radius of wherever he happens to be standing.'

She was forming up to argue, but he gave her the rest while he was about it.

'Head porter at the Rincome Hotel, Chiang Mai, confirmed the identification from a photograph, beard notwithstanding. All right, us roundeyes all look the same to them. Nevertheless he was pretty sure. Then only last month a fifteen-year-old girl in Bangkok, particulars to hand, took her little bundle to the Mexican Consulate and named Ricardo as the lucky father. I don't believe in eighteen month pregnancies and I assume you don't. And don't look at *me* like that, sport. It's not my idea, is it?'

It's London's, he might have added, as a neat a blend of fact and fiction as ever shook a tree. But she was actually looking past him, at the door again.

'Another thing I'm to ask you about is the whisky racket,' he said.

'It was *not* a racket, Jerry, it was a perfectly valid business enterprise!'

'Sport. *You* were straight as a die. No breath of scandal attaches. Etcetera. But if *Ric* cut a few too many corners, now, that *would* be a reason for doing the old disappearing act, wouldn't it?'

'That wasn't Ric's way,' she said finally, without any conviction at all. 'He liked to be the big man around town. It wasn't his way to run.'

He seriously regretted her discomfort. It ran quite contrary to the feelings he would have wished for her in other circumstances. He watched her and he knew that argument was something that she always lost; it planted a hopelessness in her; a resignation to defeat.

'For example,' Jerry continued – as her head fell forward in submission – 'were we to prove that your Ric, in flogging *his* kegs, had stuck to the cash and instead of passing it back to the distillery – pure hypothesis, no shred of evidence – then in that case –'

'By the time our partnership was wound up, *every* investor had a certificated contract with interest from the date of purchase. Every penny borrowed was duly accounted for.'

Till now it had all been footwork. Now he saw his goal looming, and he made for it fast.

'Not *duly*, sport,' he corrected her, while she continued to stare downwards at her uneaten food. 'Not duly at all. Those settlements were made six months *after* the due date. *Un*duly. That's a very eloquent point in my view. Question: who bailed Ric out? According to *our* information the whole world was going for him. The distillers, the creditors, the law, the local community. Every one of them had the knife sharpened for him. Till one day: *bingo!* Writs withdrawn, shades of the prison bars recede. How? Ric was on his knees. Who's the mystery angel? Who bought his debts?'

She had lifted her head while he was speaking and now, to his astonishment, a radiant smile suddenly lit her face and the next thing he knew, she was waving over his shoulder at someone he couldn't see till he looked into the ceiling mirror and caught the glitter of an electric blue suit, and a full head of black hair well greased; and between the two, a foreshortened chubby Chinese face set on a pair of powerful shoulders, and two curled hands held out in a fighter's greeting, while Lizzie piped him aboard.

'Mr Tiu! What a marvellous coincidence. It's *Mr Tiu!* Come on over! Try the beef. It's *gorgeous*. Mr Tiu, this is Jerry from Fleet Street. Jerry, this is a very good friend of mine who helps look after me. He's interviewing me, Mr Tiu! Me! It's most exciting. All about Vientiane and a poor pilot I tried to help a hundred years ago. Jerry knows everything about me. He's a miracle!'

'We met,' said Jerry, with a broad grin.

'Sure,' said Tiu, equally happy, and as he spoke, Jerry once more caught the familiar smell of almonds and rosewater mixed, the one his early wife had so much liked. 'Sure,' Tiu repeated 'You the horse-writer, okay?'

'Okay,' Jerry agreed, stretching his smile to breaking-point.

Then, of course, Jerry's vision of the world turned several somersaults, and he had a whole lot of business to worry about: such as appearing to be as tickled as everybody else by the amazing good luck of Tiu's appearance; such as shaking hands, which was like a mutual promise of future settlement; such as drawing up a chair and calling for drinks, beef and chopsticks and all the rest. But the thing that stuck in his mind even while he did all this – the memory that lodged there as permanently as later events allowed – had little to do with Tiu, or his hasty arrival. It was the expression on Lizzie's face as she first caught sight of him, for the fraction of a second before the lines of courage drew the gay smile out of her. It explained to him as nothing else could have done the paradoxes that comprised her: her prisoner's dreams, her borrowed personalities which were like disguises in which she could momentarily escape her destiny. Of course she had summoned Tiu. She had no choice. It amazed him that neither the Circus nor himself had predicted it. The Ricardo story, whatever the truth of it, was far too hot for her to handle by herself. But the expression in her grey eyes as Tiu entered the restaurant was not relief, but resignation: the doors had slammed on her again, the fun was over. 'We're like those bloody glow-worms,' the orphan had whispered to him once, raging about her childhood, 'carting the bloody fire round on our backs.'

Operationally, of course, as Jerry recognized immediately, Tiu's appearance was a gift from the gods. If information was to be fed back to Ko, then Tiu was an infinitely more impressive channel for it than Lizzie Worthington could ever hope to be.

She had finished kissing Tiu, so she handed him to Jerry.

'Mr Tiu, you're my witness,' she declared, making a great conspiracy of it. 'You must remember every word I say. Jerry, go straight on *just* as if he wasn't here. I mean, Mr Tiu's as silent as the *grave*, aren't you? *Darling*,' she said, and kissed him again. 'It's *so* exciting,' she repeated, and they all settled down for a friendly chat.

'So what you looking for, Mr Wessby?' Tiu inquired, perfectly affably, while he tucked into his beef. 'You a horse-writer, why you bother pretty girls, okay?'

'Good point, sport! Good point! Horses much safer, right?'

They all laughed richly, avoiding one another's eyes.

The waiter put a half bottle of Black Label Scotch in front of him. Tiu uncorked it and sniffed at it critically before pouring.

'He's looking for *Ricardo*, Mr Tiu. Don't you understand? He thinks Ricardo is *alive*. Isn't that wonderful? I mean, I have no vestige of feeling for Ric, now, naturally, but it would be lovely to have him back with us. Think of the party we could give!'

'Liese tell you that?' Tiu asked, pouring himself two inches of Scotch. 'She tell you Ricardo still around?'

'*Who*, old boy? Didn't get you. Didn't get the first name.'

Tiu jabbed a chopstick at Lizzie. 'She tell you he's alive? This pilot guy? This Ricardo? Liese tell you that?'

'I never reveal my sources, Mr Tiu,' said Jerry, just as affably. 'That's a journalist's way of saying he's made something up,' he explained.

'A horse-writer's way, okay?'

'That's it, that's it!'

Again Tiu laughed, and this time Lizzie laughed even louder. She was slipping out of control again. Maybe it's the drink, thought Jerry, or maybe she goes for the stronger stuff and the drink has stoked the fire. And if he calls me horse-writer again, maybe I'll take defensive action.

Lizzie again, a party-piece:

'Oh Mr Tiu, Ricardo was so *lucky*! Think who he had. Indocharter – me – everyone. There I was, working for this little airline – some dear Chinese people Daddy knew – and Ricardo like all the pilots was a shocking businessman - got into the most *frightful* debt' – with a wave of her hand she brought Jerry into the act – 'my God, he even tried to involve *me* in one of his schemes, can you imagine! – selling whisky, if you please – and suddenly my lovely, dotty Chinese friends decided they needed another charter pilot. They settled his debts, put him on a salary, they gave him an old banger to fly –'

Jerry now took the first of several irrevocable steps.

'When Ricardo went missing he wasn't flying an old banger, sport. He was flying a brand-new Beechcraft,' he corrected her deliberately . 'Indocharter never had a Beechcraft to their names. They haven't now. My editor's checked it right through, don't ask me how. Indocharter never hired one, never leased one, never crashed one.'

Tiu gave another jolly whoop of laughter.

*Tiu is a very cool bishop, your Eminence*, Craw had warned. *Ran Monsignor Ko's San Francisco diocese with exemplary efficiency for five years and the worst the narcotics artists could hang on him was washing his Rolls-Royce on a saint's day.*

'Hey Mr Wessby, maybe Liese stole them one!' Tiu cried, in his half-American accent. 'Maybe she go out nights steal aircraft from other airlines!'

'Mr Tiu, that's very naughty of you!' Lizzie declared.

'How you like that, horse-writer? How you like?'

The merriment at the table was now so loud for three people that several heads turned to peer at them. Jerry saw them in the mirrors, where he half expected to spot Ko himself, with his crooked boat-people's walk, swaying toward them through the wicker doorway. Lizzie plunged wildy on.

'Oh it was a complete fairy tale! One moment Ric can scarcely eat – *and* owed all of us money, Charlie's savings, my allowance from Daddy – Ric practically ruined us all. Of course, everyone's money just naturally belonged to him – and the next thing we knew, Ric had work, he was in the clear, life was a ball again. All those other poor pilots grounded, and Ric and Charlie flying all over the place like –'

'Like blue-arsed flies,' Jerry suggested, at which Tiu was so doubled with hilarity that he was obliged to hold on to Jerry's shoulder to keep himself afloat – while Jerry had the uncomfortable feeling of being physically measured for the knife.

'Hey, listen, that pretty good! Blue-arse fly! I like that! You pretty funny fellow, horse-writer!'

It was at this point, under the pressure of Tiu's cheerful insults, that Jerry used very good footwork indeed. Afterwards, Craw said the best. He ignored Tiu entirely, and picked up that other name which Lizzie had let slip.

'Yeah, whatever happened to old Charlie by the way, Lizzie?' he said, not having the least idea who Charlie was. 'What became of him after Ric did his disappearing number? Don't tell me he went down with his ship as well?'

Once more she floated away on a fresh wave of narrative, and Tiu patently enjoyed everything he heard, chuckling and nodding while he ate.

He's here to find out the score, Jerry thought. He's much too sharp to put the brakes on Lizzie. It's me he's worried about, not her.

'Oh, Charlie's indestructible, *completely* immortal,' Lizzie declared, and once more selected Tiu as her foil: 'Charlie *Marshall*, Mr Tiu,' she explained. 'Oh you should meet him, a fantastic half-Chinese, all skin and bones and opium and a completely brilliant pilot. His father's old Kuomintang, terrific brigand and lives up in the Shans. His mother was some poor Corsican girl – you know how the Corsicans *flocked* into Indo-China – but really he is an utterly fantastic character. Do you know why he calls himself Marshall? His father wouldn't give him his own name. So what does Charlie do? Gives himself the highest rank in the army instead. "My Dad's a general but I'm a marshal," he'd say. Isn't that cute? and *far* better than *admiral*, I mean.'

'Super,' Jerry agreed. 'Marvellous. Charlie's a prince.'

'Liese some pretty utterly fantastic character herself, Mr Wessby,' Tiu remarked handsomely, so on Jerry's insistence they drank to that – to her fantastic character.

'Hey what's all this *Liese* thing actually?' Jerry asked as he put down his glass. 'You're *Lizzie*. Who's this Liese? Mr Tiu, I don't know the lady. Why am I left out of the joke?'

Here Lizzie did definitely turn to Tiu for guidance, but Tiu had ordered himself some raw fish and was eating it rapidly and with total devotion.

'Some horse-writer ask pretty damn questions,' he remarked through a full mouth.

'New town, new leaf, new name,' Lizzie said finally, with an unconvincing smile. 'I wanted a change, so I chose a new name. Some girls get a new hair-do, I get a new name.'

'Got a new fellow to go with it?' Jerry asked.

She shook her head, eyes down, while Tiu let out a whoop of laughter.

'What's happened to this town, Mr Tiu?' Jerry demanded, instinctively covering for her. 'Chaps all gone blind or something? Crikey, I'd cross continents for her, wouldn't you? Whatever she calls herself, right?'

'Me I go from Kowloonside to Hong Kongside, no further!' said Tiu, hugely entertained by his own wit. 'Or maybe I stay Kowloonside and call her up, tell her come over see me one hour!'

At which Lizzie's eyes stayed down and Jerry thought it would be quite fun, on another occasion when they all had more time, to break Tiu's fat neck in several places.

Unfortunately, however, breaking Tiu's neck was not at present on Craw's shopping list.

*The money*, Craw had said. *When the moment's right, open up one end of the goldseam and that's your grand finale.*

So he started her off about Indocharter. Who were they, what was it like to work for them? She rose to it so fast he began to wonder whether she enjoyed this knife-edge existence more than he had realized.

'Oh it was a fabulous adventure, Jerry! You can't begin to imagine it, I assure you.' Ric's multi-national accent again: '*Airline*! Just the word is so absurd. I mean don't for a minute think of your bright new planes and your glamorous hostesses and champagne and caviar or anything like that *at all*. This was work. This was pioneering, which is what drew me in the first place. I could *perfectly* well have simply lived off Daddy, or my aunts, I mean mercifully I'm totally independent, but *who* can resist challenge? All we started out with was a couple of dreadful old DC3s *literally* stuck together with string and chewing gum. We even had to *buy* the safety certificate. Nobody would issue them. After that we flew literally anything. Hondas, vegetables, pigs – oh the boys had such a story about those poor pigs. They broke loose, Jerry. They came into the first class, even into the cabin, imagine!'

'Like passengers,' Tiu explained, with his mouth full. 'She fly first-class pigs, okay, Mr Wessby?'

'What routes?' Jerry asked when they had recovered from their laughter.

'You can see how he interrogates me, Mr Tiu? I never knew I was so glamorous! So mysterious! We flew everywhere, Jerry. Bangkok, Cambodia sometimes. Battambang, Phnom Penh, Kampong Cham when it was open. Everywhere. Awful places.'

'And who were your customers? Traders, taxi jobs – who were the regulars?'

'Absolutely anyone we could get. Amyone who could pay. Preferably in advance, naturally.'

Pausing from his Kobe beef, Tiu felt inspired to offer social chitchat.

'Your father some big lord, okay, Mr Wessby?'

'More or less,' said Jerry.

'Lords some pretty rich fellows. Why you gotta be a horse-writer, okay?'

Ignoring Tiu entirely, Jerry played his trump card and waited for the ceiling mirror to crash on to their table.

'There's a story that you people had some local Russian embassy link,' he said easily, straight at Lizzie. ' That ring a bell at all, sport? Any Reds under your bed at all, if I may ask?'

Tiu was taking care of his rice, holding the bowl under his chin and shovelling nonstop. But this time, significantly, Lizzie didn't give him half a glance.

'*Russians?*' she repeated, puzzled. 'Why on earth should Russians come to *us?* They had regular Aeroflot flights in and out of Vientiane every week.'

He would have sworn, then and later, that she was telling the truth. But toward Lizzie herself he acted not quite satisfied. 'Not even *local* runs?' he insisted. 'Fetching and carrying, courier service or whatever?'

'Never. How could we? Besides, the Chinese simply *loathe* the Russians, don't they, Mr Tiu?'

'Russians pretty bad people, Mr Wessby,' Tiu agreed. 'They smell pretty bad.'

*So do you*, thought Jerry, catching that first-wife's scent again.

Jerry laughed at his own absurdity: 'I've got editors like other people have stomach ache,' he protested. 'He's *convinced* we can do a Red-under-the-bed job. "Ricardo's Soviet Paymasters" . . . "Did Ricardo take a dive for the Kremlin?"'

'*Paymaster?*' Lizzie repeated, utterly mystified. 'Ric never received a penny from the Russians. What *are* they talking about?'

Jerry again. 'But Indocharter did, didn't they? – Unless my lords and masters have been sold a total pup, which I suspect they have been, as usual. They drew money from the local Embassy and piped it down to Hong Kong in US dollars. That's *London's* story and they're sticking to it.'

'They're mad,' she said confidently. 'I've never heard such nonsense.'

To Jerry she seemed even relieved that the conversation had taken this improbable course. Ricardo alive – there, she was drifting through a mine-field. Ko as her lover – that secret was Ko's or Tiu's to dispense, not hers. But Russian money – Jerry was as certain as he dared be that she knew nothing and feared nothing about it.

He offered to ride back with her to Star Heights, but Tiu lived that way, she said.

'See you again pretty soon, Mr Wessby,' Tiu promised.

'Look forward to it, sport,' said Jerry.

'You wanna stick to horse-writing, hear that? In my opinion, you get more money that way, Mr Wessby, okay?' There was no menace in his voice, nor in the friendly way he patted Jerry's upper arm. Tiu did not even speak as if he expected his advice to be taken as any more than a confidence between friends.

Then suddenly it was over. Lizzie kissed the headwaiter, but not Jerry. She sent Jerry, not Tiu, for her coat, so that she wouldn't be alone with him. She scarcely looked at him as she said goodbye.

*Dealing with beautiful women, your Grace*, Craw had warned, *is like dealing with known criminals, and the lady you are about to solicit undoubtedly falls within that category.* Wandering home through the moonlit streets – the long trek, beggars, eyes in doorways notwithstanding – Jerry subjected Craw's dictum to closer scrutiny. On *criminal* he really couldn't rule at all: *criminal* seemed a pretty variable sort of standard at the best of times, and neither the Circus nor its agents existed to uphold some parochial concept of the law. Craw had told him that in slump periods Ricardo had made her carry little parcels for him over frontiers. Big deal. Leave it to the owls. *Known* criminals however was quite a different matter. *Known* he would go along with absolutely. Remembering Elizabeth Worthington's caged stare at Tiu, he reckoned he had known that face, that look and that dependence, in one guise or another, for the bulk of his waking life.

It has been whispered once or twice by certain trivial critics of George Smiley that at this juncture he should somehow have seen which way the wind was blowing with Jerry, and hauled him out of the field. Effectively, Smiley was Jerry's case officer, after all. He alone kept Jerry's file, welfared and briefed him. Had he been in his prime, they say, instead of halfway down the other side, he would have read the warning signals between the lines of Craw's reports, and headed Jerry off in time. They might just as well have complained that he was a second-rate fortune-teller. The facts, as they came to Smiley, are these:

On the morning following Jerry's *pass* at Lizzie Worth or Worthington – the jargon has no sexual connotation – Craw debriefed him for more than three hours on a car pickup, and his report describes Jerry as being, quite reasonably, in a state of 'anti-climactic gloom'. He appeared, said Craw, to be afraid that Tiu, or even Ko, might blame the girl for her 'guilty knowledge' and even lay hands on her. Jerry referred more than once to Tiu's patent contempt for the girl – and for himself, and he suspected for all Europeans – and repeated his comment about travelling to Kowloonside to Hong Kong side for her and no further. Craw countered by pointing out that Tiu could at any time have shut her up; and that her knowledge, on Jerry's own testimony, did not extend even as far as the Russian goldseam, let alone to brother Nelson.

Jerry in short was producing the standard post-operational manifestations of a fieldman. A sense of guilt, coupled with foreboding, an involuntary movement of affiliation toward the target person: these are as predictable as a burst of tears in an athlete after the big race.

At their next contact – an extended limbo call on day two, at which, to buoy him up, Craw passed on Smiley's warm personal congratulations somewhat ahead of receiving them from the Circus – Jerry sounded in altogether better case, but he was worried about his daughter Cat. He had forgotten her birthday – he said it was tomorrow – and wished the Circus to send her at once a Japanese cassette player with a bunch of cassettes to start off her collection. Craw's telegram to Smiley names the cassettes, asks for immediate action by housekeepers, and requests that shoemaker section – the Circus forgers, in other words – run up an accompanying card in Jerry's hand-writing, text given: 'Darling Cat. Asked a friend of mine to post this in London. Look after yourself, my dearest, love to you now and ever, Pa.' Smiley authorized the purchase, instructing the housekeepers to dock the cost from Jerry's pay at source. He personally checked the parcel before it was sent, and approved the forged card. He also verified what he and Craw already suspected: that it was not Cat's birthday, nor anywhere near. Jerry simply had a strong urge to make a gesture of affection: once more, a normal symptom of temporary field fatigue. He cabled Craw to stay close to him but the initiative was with Jerry and Jerry made no further contact till the night of day five, when he demanded – and got – a crash meeting within the hour. This took place at their standing after-dark emergency rendezvous, an all-night roadside café in the New Territories, under the guise of a casual encounter between old colleagues. Craw's letter marked 'personal to Smiley only', was a follow-up to his telegram. It arrived at the Circus by hand of the Cousins' courier two days after the episode it describes, on day seven therefore. Writing on the assumption that the Cousins would contrive to read the text despite seals and other devices, Craw crammed it with evasions, worknames and cryptonyms, which are here restored to their real meaning:

*Westerby was very angry. He demanded to know what the hell Sam Collins was doing in Hong Kong and in what way Collins was involved in the Ko case. I have not seen him so disturbed before. I asked him what made him think Collins was around. He replied that he had seen him that very night – eleven fifteen exactly – sitting in a parked car in the Midlevels, on a terrace just below Star Heights, under a streetlamp, reading a newspaper. The position Collins had taken up, said Westerby, gave him a clear view to Lizzie Worthington's windows of the eighth floor, and it was Westerby's assumption that he was engaged in some sort of surveillance. Westerby, who was on foot at the time, insists that he 'damn nearly went up to Sam and asked him outright'. But Sarratt discipline held firm, and he kept going down the hill, on his own side of the road. But he does claim that as soon as Collins saw him, he started the car and drove up the hill at speed. Westerby has the licence number, and of course it is the correct one. Collins confirms the rest.*

*In accordance with our agreed position in this contingency (your Signal of Feb. 15th) I gave Westerby the following answers:*

*1) Even if it was Collins, the Circus had no control over his movements. Collins had left the Circus under a cloud, before the fall, he was a known gambler, drifter, wheeler-dealer etc., and the East was his natural stomping ground. I told Westerby he was being a fatheaded idiot to assume that Collins was still on the payrol, or worse, had any part in the Ko case.*

*2) Collins is facially a type, I said: regular-featured, moustached, etc., looked like half the pimps in London. I doubted whether, from across a road at eleven fifteen at night, Westerby could be certain of his identification. Westerby retorted that he had A1 vision and that Sam had his newspaper open at the racing page.*

*3) Anyway, what was Westerby himself doing, I enquired, mooning around Star Heights at eleven fifteen at night? Answer, returning from a drink with the UPI mob and hoping for a cab. At this I pretended to explode, and said that nobody who had been on a UPI thrash could see an elephant at five yards, let alone Sam Collins at twenty-five, in a car at the dead of night. Over and out – I hope.*

That Smiley was seriously concerned about the incident goes without saying. Only four people knew of the Collins ploy: Smiley, Connie Sachs, Craw and Sam himself. That Jerry shuld have stumbled on him provided an added anxiety in an operation already loaded with imponderables. But Craw was deft, and Craw believed he had talked Jerry down, and Craw was the man on the spot. Just possibly, in a perfect world, Craw might have made it his business to find out whether there had really been a UPI party in the Midlevels that night – and on learning that there had not, he might have challenged Jerry again to explain his presence in the region of Star Heights, and in that case Jerry would probably have thrown a tantrum and produced some other story that was not checkable: that he had been with a woman, for instance, and Craw could mind his own bloody business. Of which the net result would have been needless bad blood and the same take-it-or-leave-it situation as before.

It is also tempting, but unreasonable, to expect of Smiley that with so many other pressures upon him – the continued and unabating quest for Nelson, daily sessions with the Cousins, rearguard actions round the Whitehall corridors – he should have drawn the inference closest to his own lonely experience: namely that Jerry, having no taste for sleep or company that evening, had wandered the night pavements till he found himself standing outside the building where Lizzie lived, and hung about, as Smiley did, on his own nocturnal wanderings, without exactly knowing what he wanted, beyond the off-chance of a sight of her.

The rush of events which carried Smiley along was far too powerful to permit of such fanciful abstractions. Not only did the eighth day, when it came, put the Circus effectively on a war footing: it is also the pardonable vanity of lonely people everywhere to assume they have no counterparts.


# FOURTEEN

# *the eighth day*


The jolly mood of the fifth floor was a great relief after the depression of the previous gathering. A burrowers' honeymoon Guillam called it, and tonight was its highest point, its attenuated starburst of a consummation, and it came exactly eight days, in the chronology which historians afterwards impose on things, after Jerry and Lizzie and Tiu had had their full and frank exchange of views on the subject of Tiny Ricardo and the Russian goldseam – to the great delight of the Circus planners. Guillam had wangled Molly along specially. They had run in all directions, these shady night animals, down old paths and new paths and old paths grown over till they were rediscovered; and now at last, behind their twin leaders Connie Sachs alias Mother Russia, and the misted di Salis alias the Doc, they crammed themselves, all twelve of them, into the very throne-room itself, under Karla's portrait, in an obedient half circle round their chief, *bolshies* and *yellow perils* together. A plenary session then, and for people unused to such drama, a monument of history indeed. And Molly primly at Guillam's side, her hair brushed long to hide the bite marks on her neck.

di Salis does most of the talking. The other ranks feel this to be appropriate. After all, Nelson Ko is the Doc's patch entirely: Chinese to the sleeve-ends of his tunic. Reining himself right in – his spiky, wet hair, his knees, feet, and fussing fingers all but still for once, he keeps things in a low and almost deprecating key of which the inexorable climax is accordingly more thrilling. And the climax even has a name. It is Ko Sheng-hsiu, alias Ko, Nelson, later known also as Yao Kai-sheng, under which name he was later disgraced in the Cultural Revolution.

'But within these walls, gentlemen,' pipes the Doc, whose awareness of the female sex is inconsistent, 'we shall continue to call him Nelson.'

Born 1928 of humble proletarian stock, in Swatow – to quote the official sources, says the Doc – and soon afterwards removed to Shanghai. No mention, in either official or unofficial handouts, of Mr Hibbert's Lord's Life Mission school, but a sad reference to 'exploitation at the hands of western imperialists in childhood', who poisoned him with religion. When the Japanese reached Shanghai, Nelson joined the refugee trail to Chungking, all as Mr Hibbert had described. From an early age, once more according to official records, the Doc continues, Nelson secretly devoted himself to seminal revolutionary reading, and took an active part in clandestine Communist groups, despite the oppression of the loathsome Chiang Kai-shek rabble. On the refugee trail he also attempted 'on many occasions to escape to Mao but his extreme youth held him back. Returning to Shanghai he became, already as a student, a leading cadre member of the outlawed Communist movement and undertook special assignments in and around the Kiangnan shipyards to subvert the pernicious influence of KMT Fascist elements. At the University of Communications he appealed publicly for a united front of students and peasants. Graduated with conspicuous excellence in 1951 . . . '

di Salis interrupts himself, and in a sharp release of tension throws up one arm, and clenches the hair at the back of his head.

'The usual unctuous portrait, Chief, of a student hero who sees the light before his time,' he sings.

'What about Leningrad?' Smiley asks, from his desk, while he jots the occasional note.

'Nineteen fifty-three to six.'

'Yes, Connie?'

Connie is in her wheelchair again. She blames the freezing month and that toad Karla jointly.

'We have a Brother Bretlev, darling. Bretlev, Ivan Ivanovitch, Academician, Leningrad faculty of shipbuilding, old-time China hand, devilled in Shanghai for Centre's China hounds. Revolutionary war-horse, latter-day Karla-trained talent-spotter trawling the overseas students for likely lads and lasses.'

For the burrowers on the Chinese side – the yellow perils – this intelligence is new and thrilling, and produces an excited crackle of chairs and papers, till on Smiley's nod, di Salis lets go of his head and takes up his narrative once more.

'Nineteen fifty-seven returned to Shanghai and was put in charge of a railway workshop –'

Smiley again: 'But his dates at Leningrad were fifty-three to fifty-six?'

'Correct,' says di Salis.

'There seems to be a missing year.'

Now no papers crackle and no chairs either.

'A tour of Soviet shipyards is the official explanation,' says di Salis with a smirk at Connie and a mysterious knowing writhe of the neck.

'Thank you,' says Smiley and makes another note. 'Fifty-seven,' he repeats. 'Was that before or after the Sino-Soviet split, Doc?'

'Before. The split started in earnest in fifty-nine.'

Smiley asks here whether Nelson's brother receives a mention anywhere: or is Drake as much disowned in Nelson's China as Nelson is in Drake's?

'In one of the earliest official biographies Drake is referred to, but not by name. In the later ones, a brother is said to have died during the Communist takeover of forty-nine.'

Smiley makes a rare joke, which is followed by dense, relieved laughter. 'This case is littered with people pretending to be dead,' he complains. 'It will be a positive relief to me to find a real corpse somewhere.' Only hours later, this *mot* was remembered with a shudder.

'We also have a note that Nelson was a model student at Leningrad,' di Salis goes on. 'At least in Russian eyes. They sent him back with the highest references.'

Connie from her iron chair allows herself another interjection. She has brought Trot, her mangy brown mongrel, with her. He lies mis-shapenly across her vast lap, stinking and occasionally sighing, but not even Guillam, who is a dog-hater, has the nerve to banish him.

'Oh and so they would, dear, wouldn't they?' she cries. 'The Russians would praise Nelson's talents to the skies, course they would, specially if Brother Bretlev Ivan Ivanovitch has snapped him up at University, and Karla's lovelies have spirited him off to training school and all! Bright little mole like Nelson, give him a decent start in life for when he gets home to China! Didn't do him much good later though, did it, Doc? Not when the Great Beastly Cultural Revolution got him in the neck! The generous admiration of Soviet imperialist running dogs wasn't at all the thing to be wearing in your cap *then*, was it?'

Of Nelson's fall, few details are available, the Doc proclaims, speaking louder in response to Connie's outburst. 'One must assume that it was violent, and as Connie has pointed out, those who were highest in Russian favour fell the hardest.' He glances at the sheet of paper which he holds crookedly before his blotched face. 'I won't give all his appointments at the time of his disgrace, Chief, because he lost them anyway. But there is no doubt that he did indeed have effective management of most of the shipbuilding in Kiangnan, and consequently of a large part of China's naval tonnage.'

'I see,' says Smiley quietly. Jotting, he purses his lips as if in disapproval, while his eyebrows lift very high.

'His post at Kiangnan also procured him a string of seats on the naval planning committees and in the field of communication and strategic policy. By sixty-three his name is beginning to pop up regularly in the Cousins' Peking watch reports.'

'Well done, Karla,' says Guillam quietly from his place at Smiley's side, and Smiley, still writing, actually echoes this sentiment with a 'Yes.'

'The only one, Peter dear!' Connie yells, suddenly unable to contain herself. 'The only one of all those toads to see it coming! A voice in the wilderness, wasn't he, Trot? "Look out for the yellow peril," he told 'em. "One day they're going to turn round and bite the hand that's feeding 'em, sure as eggs. And when that happens you'll have eight hundred million new enemies banging on your own back door. *And* your guns will all be pointing the wrong way. Mark my words." Told 'em,' she repeats, hauling at the mongrel's ear in her emotion. 'Put it all in a paper, "Threat of deviation by emerging Socialist partner." Circulated every little brute in Moscow Centre's Collegium. Drafted it word for word in his clever little mind while he was doing a spot of bird in Siberia for Uncle Joe Stalin, bless him. "Spy on your friends today, they're certain to be your enemies tomorrow," he told them. Oldest dictum in the trade, Karla's favourite. When he was given his job back he practically nailed it up on the door in Dzezhinsky Square. No one paid a blind bit of notice. Not a scrap. Fell on barren ground, my dear. Five years later, he was proved right, and the Collegium didn't thank him for that either, *I* can tell you! He's been right a sight too often for their liking, the boobies, hasn't he, Trot! *You* know, don't you darling, *you* know what the old fool-woman's on about!' At which she lifts the dog a few inches in the air by its forepaws and lets it flop back on to her lap again.

Connie can't bear old Doc hogging the limelight, they secretly agree. She sees the logic of it, but the woman can't abide the reality.

'Very well, he was purged Doc,' Smiley says quietly, restoring calm. 'Let's go back to sixty-seven, shall we?' And puts his chin back in his hand.

In the gloom, Karla's portrait peers stodgily down as di Salis resumes. 'Well, the usual grim story, one supposes, Chief,' he chants. 'The dunce's cap no doubt. Spat on in the street. Wife and children kicked and beaten up. Indoctrination camps, labour education "on a scale commensurate with the crime". Urged to reconsider the peasant virtues. One report has him sent to a rural commune to test himself. And when he came crawling back to Shanghai they'd have made him start at the bottom again, driving bolts into a railway line, or whatever. As far as the *Russians* were concerned – if that's what we're talking about' – he hurries on before Connie can interrupt yet again – 'he was a washout. No access, no influence, no friends.'

'How long did it take him to climb back?' Smiley enquires, with a characteristic lowering of the eyelids.

'About three years ago he started to be functional again. In the long run he has what Peking needs most: brains, technical knowhow, experience. But his *formal* rehabilitation didn't really occur till the beginning of seventy-three.'

While di Salis goes on to describe the stages of Nelson's ritual reinstatement, Smiley quietly draws a folder to him and refers to certain other dates which for reasons as yet unexplained are suddenly acutely relevant to him.

'The payments to Drake have their beginnings in mid-seventy-two,' he murmurs. 'They rise steeply in mid-seventy-three.'

'With Nelson's *access*, darling,' Connie whispers after him, like a prompter from the wings. 'The more he knows, the more he tells, and the more he tells the more he gets. Karla only pays for goodies, and even then it hurts like blazes.'

By seventy-three – says di Salis – having made all the proper confessions, Nelson has been embraced into the Shanghai municipal revolutionary committee, and appointed responsible person in a naval unit of the People's Liberation Army. Six months later –

'Date?' Smiley interrupts.

'July seventy-three.'

'Then Nelson was formally rehabilitated when?'

'The process began in January seventy-three.'

'Thank you.'

Six months later, di Salis continues, Nelson is seen to be acting in an unknown capacity with the Central Committee of the Chinese Communist Party.

'Holy *smoke*,' says Guillam softly, and Molly Meakin gives his hand a hidden squeeze.

'And a report from the Cousins,' says di Salis, 'undated as usual but well attested, has Nelson down as an informal advisor to the Munitions and Ordnance Committee of the Ministry of Defence.'

Rather than orchestrate this revelation with his customary range of mannerisms, di Salis again contrives to keep rock still, to great effect.

'In terms of *eligibility*, Chief,' he goes on quietly, 'from an *operational* standpoint, we on the China side of your house would regard this as one of the key positions in the whole of the Chinese administration. If we could pick ourselves one slot for an agent inside the Mainland, Nelson's might well be the one.'

'Reasons?' Smiley enquires, still alternating between his jottings and the open folder before him.

'The Chinese Navy is still in the stone age. We do have a formal interest in Chinese technical intelligence, naturally, but our real priorities, like those of Moscow no doubt, are strategic and political. Beyond that, Nelson could supply us with the total capacity of all Chinese shipyards. Beyond that again, he could tell us the Chinese submarine potential which has been frightening the daylights out of the Cousins for years. And of ourselves too, I may add, off and on.'

'So think what it's doing for Moscow,' an old burrower murmurs out of turn.

'The Chinese are supposedly developing their own version of the Russian G-2 class submarine,' di Salis explains. 'No one knows a lot about it. Have they their own design? Have they two or four tubes? Are they are with sea to air missiles or sea to sea? What is the financial appropriation for them? There's talk of a Han class. We had word they laid one down in seventy-one. We've never had confirmation. In Dairen in sixty-four they allegedly built a G class armed with ballistic missiles, but it still hasn't been officially sighted. And so forth and so on,' says di Salis deprecatingly, for like most of the Circus he has a rooted dislike of military matters and would prefer the more artistic targets. 'For hard and fast detail on those subjects the Cousins would pay a fortune. In a couple of years Langley could spend hundreds of millions in research, overflights, satellites, listening devices and God knows what – and still not come up with an answer half as good as one photograph. So if Nelson –' He lets the sentence hang, which is somehow a lot more effective than making it finite. Connie whispers, 'Well *done*, Doc,' but still for a while nobody else speaks. They are held back by Smiley's jotting, and his continued examination of the folder.

'Good as Haydon,' Guillam mutters. 'Better. China's the last frontier. Toughest nut in the trade.'

Smiley sits back, his calculations apparently finished.

'Ricardo made his trip a few months after Nelson's formal rehabilitation,' he says.

Nobody sees fit to question this.

'Tiu travels to Shanghai and six weeks later Ricardo –'

In the far background, Guillam hears the bark of the Cousins' telephone switched through to his room, and it is a thing he afterwards avers most strongly – whether in truth or with hindsight – that the unlovable image of Sam Collins was at this point conjured out of his subconscious memory like a djini out of a lamp, and that he wondered yet again how he could ever have been so unthinking as to let Sam Collins deliver that vital letter to Martello.

'Nelson has one more string to his bow, Chief,' di Salis continues, just as everyone is assuming he is done. 'I hesitate to offer it with any confidence, but in the circumstances I dare not omit it altogether. A barter report from the West Germans, dated a few weeks ago. According to *their* sources, Nelson is lately a member of what we have for want of information dubbed The Peking Tea Club, an embryonic body which we believe has been set up to co-ordinate the Chinese intelligence effort. He came in first as an advisor on electronic surveillance, and was then co-opted as a full member. It functions, so far as we can fathom, somewhat as our own Steering Group. But I must emphasize that this is a shot in the dark. We know absolutely nothing about the Chinese services, and nor do the Cousins.'

For once at a loss for words, Smiley stares at di Salis, opens his mouth, closes it, then pulls off his glasses and polishes them.

'And Nelson's *motive?*' he asks, still oblivious to the steady bark of the Cousins' bell. 'A shot in the dark, Doc? How would you see that?'

di Salis gives an enormous shrug, so that his tallow hair bucks like a floor mop. 'Oh, anybody's guess,' he says waspishly. 'Who believes in *motive* these days? It would have been perfectly natural for him to respond to recruitment overtures in Leningrad, of course, provided they were made in the right way. Not a disloyal thing at all. Not doctrinally, anyway. Russia was China's elder brother. Nelson needed merely to be told he had been chosen as one of the special vanguard of vigilantes. I see no great art to that.'

Outside the room, the green phone just goes on ringing, which is remarkable. Martello is not usually so persistent. Only Guillam and Smiley are allowed to pick it up. But Smiley has not heard it, and Guillam is damned if he will budge while di Salis is extemporising on Nelson's possible reasons for becoming Karla's mole.

'When the Cultural Revolution came, many people in Nelson's position believed that Mao had gone mad,' di Salis explains, still reluctant to theorize. 'Even some of his own generals thought so. The humiliations Nelson suffered made him conform outwardly, but inwardly, perhaps, he remained bitter – who knows? – vengeful.'

'The alimony payments to Drake started at a time when Nelson's rehabilitation was barely complete,' Smiley objects mildly. 'What is the presumption there, Doc?'

All this is just too much for Connie and once again she brims over.

'Oh George, how can you be so naïve? *You* can find the line, *course* you can! Those poor Chinese can't afford to hang a top technician in the cupboard half his life and not use him! Karla saw the drift, didn't he, Doc? He read the wind and went with it. He kept his poor little Nelson on a string and as soon as he started to come out of the wilderness again he had his legmen get alongside him: "It's *us*, remember? Your friends! *We* don't let you down! *We* don't spit on you in the street! Let's get back to business!" You'd play it just the same way yourself, you know you would !'

'And the money?' Smiley asks. 'The half million?'

'Stick and carrot! Blackmail implicit, rewards enormous. Nelson's hooked both ways.'

But it is di Salis, Connie's outburst notwithstanding, who has the last word; 'He's Chinese. He's pragmatic. He's Drake's brother. He can't get out of China –'

'Not yet,' says Smiley softly, glancing at the folder again.

'– and he knows very well his market value to the Russian service. "You can't eat politics, you can't sleep with them," Drake liked to say, so you might as well make money out of them –'

'Against the day when you can leave China and spend it,' Smiley concludes, and – as Guillam tiptoes from the room – closes the folder and takes up his sheet of jottings. 'Drake tried to get him out once and failed, so Nelson took the Russians' money till . . . till what? Till Drake has better luck perhaps.'

In the background, the insistent snarling of the green telephone has finally ceased.

'Nelson is Karla's mole,' Smiley remarks at last, once more almost to himself. 'He's sitting on a priceless crock of Chinese intelligence. That alone we could do with. He's acting on Karla's orders. The orders themselves are of inestimable value to us. They would show us precisely how much the Russians know about their Chinese enemy, and even what they intend toward him. We could take backbearings galore. Yes, Peter?'

In the breaking of tragic news there is no transition. One minute a concept stands; the next it lies smashed, and for those affected the world has altered irrevocably. As a cushion, however, Guillam had used official Circus stationery and the written word. By writing his message to Smiley in signal form, he hoped that the sight of it would prepare him in advance. Walking quietly to the desk, the form in his hand, he laid it on the glass sheet and waited.

'*Charlie Marshall*, the other pilot, by the way,' Smiley asked of the gathering, still oblivious. 'Have the Cousins run him to earth yet, Molly?'

'His story is much the same as Ricardo's,' Molly Meakin replied, glancing queerly at Guillam. Still at Smiley's side, he looked suddenly grey and middle-agd and ill. 'Like Ricardo, he flew for the Cousins in the Laos war, Mr Smiley. They were contemporaries at Langley's secret aviation school in Oklahoma. They dumped him when Laos ended and have no further word on him. Enforcement say he has ferried opium, but they say that of all of the Cousins' pilots.'

'I think you should read that,' Guillam said, pointing firmly at the message.

'Marshall must be Westerby's next step. We have to maintain the pressure,' Smiley said.

Picking up the signal form at last, Smiley held it critically to his left side, where the reading light was brightest. He read with his eyebrows raised and his lids lowered. As always, he read twice. His expression did not change, but those nearest him said the movement went out of his face.

'Thank you, Peter,' he said quietly, laying the paper down again. 'And thank you everyone else. Connie and the Doc, perhaps you'd stay behind. I trust the rest of you will get a good night's sleep.'

Among the younger sparks this hope was greeted with cheerful laughter, for it was well past midnight already.

The girl from upstairs slept, a neat brown doll along the length of one of Jerry's legs, plump and immaculate by the orange night-light of the rain-soaked Hong Kong sky. She was snoring her head off and Jerry was staring through the window thinking of Lizzie Worthington. He thought of the twin claw marks on her chin and wondered again who had put them there. He thought of Tiu, imagining him as her jailer, and he rehearsed the name *horse-writer* until it really annoyed him. He wondered how much more waiting there was, and whether at the end of it he might have a chance with her, which was all he asked: a chance. The girl stirred, but only to scratch her rump. From next door, Jerry heard a ritual clicking as the habitual mah-jong party washed the pieces before distributing them.

The girl had not been unduly responsive to Jerry's courtship at first – a gush of impassioned notes, jammed through her letter box at all hours of the previous few days – but she did need to pay her gas bill. Officially, she was the property of a businessman, but recently his visits had become fewer and most recently had ceased altogether, with the result that she could afford neither the fortune-teller nor mah-jong, nor the stylish clothes she had set her heart on for the day she broke into Kung Fu films. So she succumbed, but on a clear financial understanding. Her main fear was of being known to consort with the hideous *kwailo* and for this reason she had put on her entire out-door equipment to descend the one floor; a brown raincoat with transatlantic brass buckles on the epaulettes, plastic yellow boots and a plastic umbrella with red roses. Now this equipment lay around the parquet floor like armour after the battle, and she slept with the same noble exhaustion. So that when the phone rang her only response was a drowsy Cantonese oath.

Lifting the receiver Jerry nursed the idiotic hope it might be Lizzie, but it wasn't.

'Get your ass down here fast,' Luke promised. 'And Stubbsie will *love* you. *Move* it. I'm doing you the favour of our career.'

'Where's here?' Jerry asked.

'Downstairs, you ape.'

He rolled the girl off him but she still didn't wake.

The roads glittered with the unexpected rain and a thick halo ringed the moon. Luke drove as if they were in a jeep, in high gear with hammer changes on the corners. Fumes of whisky filled the car.

'What have you got, for Christ's sake?' Jerry demanded. 'What's going on?'

'Great meat. Now shut up.'

'I don't want meat. I'm suited.'

'You'll want this one. *Man*, you'll want this one.'

They were heading for the harbour tunnel. A flock of cyclists without lights lurched out of a side turning and Luke had to mount the central reservation to avoid them. Look for a damn great building site, Luke said. A patrol car overtook them, all lights flashing. Thinking he was going to be stopped, Luke lowered his window.

'We're *press*, you idiots,' he screamed. 'We're *stars*, hear me?'

Inside the patrol car as it passed they had a glimpse of a Chinese sergeant and his driver, and an august-looking European perched in the back like a judge. Ahead of them, to the right of the carriageway, the promised building site sprang into view, a cage of yellow girders and bamboo scaffolding alive with sweating coolies. Cranes, glistening in the wet, dangled over them like whips. The floodlighting came from the ground and poured wastefully into the mist.

'Look for a low place, just near,' Luke ordered, slowing down to sixty. 'White. Look for a white place.'

Jerry pointed to it, a two-storey complex of weeping stucco, neither new nor old, with a twenty foot bamboo-stand by the entrance and an ambulance. The ambulance stood open and the three drivers lounged in it, smoking, watching the police who milled around the forecourt as if it were a riot they were handling.

'He's giving us an hour's start over the field.'

'Who?'

'Rocker. Rocker is. Who do you think?'

'Why?'

'Because he hit me, I guess. He loves me. He loves you too. He said to bring you specially.'

'Why?'

The rain fell steadily.

'*Why? Why? Why?*' Luke echoed, furious. 'Just hurry!'

The bamboos were out of scale, higher than the wall. A couple of orange-clad priests were sheltering against them, clapping cymbals. A third held an umbrella. There were flower stalls, mainly marigolds, and hearses, and from somewhere out of sight the sounds of leisurely incantation. The entrance lobby was a jungle swamp reeking of formaldehyde.

'Big Moo's special envoy,' said Luke.

'Press,' said Jerry.

The police nodded them through, not looking at their cards.

'Where's the Superintendent?' said Luke.

The smell of formaldehyde was awful. A young sergeant led them. They pushed through a glass door to a room where old men and women, maybe thirty of them, mostly in pyjama suits, waited phlegmatically as if for a late train, under shadowless neon lights and an electric fan. One old man was clearing out his throat, snorting on to the green tiled floor. Only the plaster wept. Seeing the giant *kwailos* they stared in polite amazement. The pathologist's office was yellow. Yellow walls, yellow blinds, closed. An airconditioner that wasn't working. The same green tiles, easily washed down.

'Great *smell*,' said Luke.

'Like home,' Jerry agreed.

Jerry wished it was battle. Battle was easier. The sergeant told them to wait while he went ahead. They heard the squeak of trolleys, low voices, the clamp of a freezer door, the low hiss of rubber soles. A volume of *Gray's Anatomy* lay next to the telephone. Jerry turned the pages, staring at the illustrations. Luke perched on a chair. An assistant in short rubber boots and overalls brought tea. White cups, green rims and the Hong Kong monogram with a crown.

'Can you tell the sergeant to hurry, please?' said Luke. 'You'll have the whole damn town here in a minute.'

'Why us?' said Jerry again.

Luke poured some tea on the tiled floor and while it ran into the gutter he topped up the cup from his whisky flask. The sergeant returned, beckoning quickly with his slender hand. They followed him back through the waiting room. This way there was no door, just a corridor, and a turn like a public lavatory, and they were there. The first thing Jerry saw was the trolley chipped to hell. There's nothing older or more derelict than worn-out hospital equipment, he thought. The walls were covered in green mould, green stalactites hung from the ceiling, a battered spittoon was filled with used tissues. They clean out the noses, he remembered, before they pull down the sheet to show you. It's a courtesy so that you aren't shocked. The fumes of formaldehyde made his eyes run. A Chinese pathologist was sitting at the window, making notes on a pad. A couple of attendants were hovering, and more police. There seemed to be a general sense of apology around. Jerry couldn't make it out. The Rocker was ignoring them. He was in a corner, murmuring to the august-looking gentleman from the back of the patrol car, but the corner wasn't far away and Jerry heard 'slur on our reputation' spoken twice in an indignant, nervous tone. A white sheet covered the body, with a blue cross on it made in two equal lengths. So that they can use it either way round, Jerry thought. It was the only trolley in the room. The big sheet. The rest of the exhibition was inside the two big freezers with the wooden doors, walk-in size, big as a butcher's shop. Luke was going out of his mind with impatience.

'Jesus, Rocker!' he called across the room. 'How much longer you going to keep the lid on this? We got work to do.'

No one bothered with him. Tired of waiting, Luke yanked back the sheet. Jerry looked and looked away. The autopsy room was next door, and he could hear the sound of sawing, like the snarling of a dog.

*No wonder they're all so apologetic,* Jerry thought stupidly. *Bringing a roundeye corpse to a place like this.*

'Jesus *Christ*,' Luke was saying. 'Holy *Christ*. Who did it to him? How do you *make* those marks? That's a Triad thing. *Jesus.*'

The dampened window gave on to the courtyard. Jerry could see the bamboo rocking in the rain and the liquid shadows of an ambulance delivering another customer, but he doubted whether any of them looked like this. A police photographer had appeared and there were flashes. A telephone extension hung on the wall. The Rocker was talking into it. He still hadn't looked at Luke, or at Jerry.

'I want him out of here,' the august gentleman said.

Soon as you like,' said the Rocker. He returned to the telephone. 'In the Walled City, sir . . . Yes, sir . . . In an alley, sir. Stripped. Lots of alcohol . . . The forensic pathologist recognized him immediately, sir. Yes sir, the bank's here already, sir.' He rang off. 'Yes sir, no sir, three bags full, sir,' he growled. He dialled a number.

Luke was making notes. 'Jesus,' he kept saying in awe 'Jesus. They must have taken *weeks* to kill him. Months.'

In actual fact, they had killed him twice, Jerry decided. Once to make him talk and once to shut him up. The things they had done to him first were all over his body, in big and small patches, the way fire hits carpet, eats holes, then suddenly gives up. Then there was the thing round his neck, a different, faster death altogether. They had done that last, when they didn't want him any more.

Luke called to the pathologist. 'Turn him over, will you? Would you mind please turning him over, *sir*?'

The Superintendent had put down the phone.

'What's the story?' said Jerry, straight at him. 'Who is he?'

'Name of Frost,' the Rocker said, staring back with his dropped eye. 'Senior official of the South Asian and China. Trustee Department.'

'Who killed him?' Jerry asked.

'Yeah, who did it? That's the point' said Luke, writing hard.

'Mice,' said the Rocker.

'Hong Kong has no Triads, no Communists, and no Kuomintang. Right, Rocker?'

'And no whores,' the Rocker growled.

The august gentleman spared the Rocker further reply.

'A vicious case of mugging,' he declared, over the policeman's shoulder. 'A filthy, vicious mugging exemplifying the need for public vigilance at all times. He was a loyal servant of the bank.'

'That's not a mugging,' said Luke, looking at Frost again. 'That's a *party*.'

'He certainly had some damned odd friends,' the Rocker said, still staring at Jerry.

'What's that supposed to mean?' said Jerry.

'What's the story so far?' said Luke.

'He was on the town till midnight. Celebrating in the company of a couple of Chinese males. One cathouse after another. Then we lose him. Till tonight.'

'The bank's offering a reward of fifty thousand dollars,' said the august man.

'Hong Kong or US?' said Luke, writing.

The august man said 'Hong Kong' very tartly.

'Now you boys go easy,' the Rocker warned. 'There's a sick wife in Stanley Hospital, and there's kids – '

'And there's the reputation of the bank,' said the august man.

'That will be our first concern,' said Luke.

They left half an hour later, still ahead of the field .

'Thanks,' said Luke to the Superintendent.

'For nothing,' said the Rocker. His dropped eyelid, Jerry noticed, leaked when he was tired.

We've shaken the tree, thought Jerry, as they drove away. Boy oh boy, have we shaken the tree.

They sat in the same attitudes, Smiley at his desk, Connie in her wheelchair, di Salis glaring into the languid smoke-coil of his pipe. Guillam stood at Smiley's side, the grate of Martello's voice still in his ears. Smiley, with a slight circular movement of his thumb, was polishing his spectacles with the end of his tie.

di Salis the Jesuit spoke first. Perhaps he had the most to disown. 'There is nothing in logic to link us with this incident. Frost was a libertine. He kept Chinese women. He was manifestly corrupt. He took our bribe without demur. Heaven knows what bribes he has not taken in the past. I will not have it laid at my door.'

'Oh *stuff*,' Connie muttered. She sat expressionless and the dog lay sleeping on her lap. Her crippled hands lay over his brown back for warmth. In the background dark Fawn was pouring tea.

Smiley spoke to the signal form. Nobody had seen his face since he had first looked down to read it.

'Connie, I want the arithmetic,' he said.

'Yes, dear.'

'Outside these four walls, who is conscious that we leaned on Frost?'

'Craw, Westerby. Craw's policeman. And if they've any *nous* the Cousins will have guessed.'

'Not Lacon, not Whitehall.'

'And *not* Karla, dear,' Connie declared, with a sharp look at the murky portrait.

'No, not Karla. I believe that.' From his voice, they could feel the intensity of the conflict as his intellect forced its will upon his emotions. 'For Karla, it would be a most exaggerated response. If a bank account is blown, all he need do is open another one elsewhere. He doesn't need *this*.' With the tips of his fingers, he precisely moved the signal form an inch up the glass. 'The ploy went as planned. The response was simply – ' He began again. 'The response was more than we expected. Operationally, nothing is amiss. Operationally, we have advanced the case.'

'We've *drawn* them, dear,' Connie said firmly.

di Salis blew up completely. 'I insist you do not speak as if we were all of us accomplices here. There is no proven link and I consider it invidious that you should suggest there is.'

Smiley remained remote in his response.

'I would consider it invidious if I suggested anything else. I ordered this initiative. I refuse not to look at the consequences merely, because they are ugly. Put it on my shoulders. But don't let's deceive ourselves.'

'Poor devil didn't know enough, did he?' Connie mused, seemingly to herself. At first nobody took her up. Then Guillam did: what did she mean by that?

'Frost had nothing to betray, darling,' she explained. 'That's the worst that can happen to anyone. What could he give them? One zealous journalist, name of Westerby. They had that already, little dears. So of course they went on. And on.' She turned in Smiley's direction. He was the only one who shared so much history with her. 'We used to make it a *rule*, remember George, when the boys and girls went in? We always gave them something they could confess, bless them.'

With loving care Fawn set down a paper cup of tea on Smiley's desk, a slice of lemon floating on the tea. His skull-like grin moved Guillam to repressed fury.

'When you've handed that round, get out,' he snapped in his ear. Still smirking, Fawn left.

'Where is Ko in his mind at this moment?' Smiley asked, still talking to the signal form. He had locked his fingers under his chin and might have been praying.

'Funk and fuzzie-headedness,' Connie declared with confidence. 'Fleet Street on the prowl, Frost dead and he's still no further forward.'

'Yes. Yes, he'll dither. "Can he hold the dam? Can he plug the leaks? Where *are* the leaks anyway?" . . . That's what we wanted. We've got it.' He made the smallest movements of his bowed head, and it pointed towards Guillam. 'Peter, you will please ask the Cousins to step up their surveillance on Tiu. Static posts only, tell them. No street work, no frightening the game, no nonsense of that kind. Telephone, mail, the easy things only. Doc, when did Tiu visit the Mainland?'

di Salis grudgingly gave a date.

'Find out the route he travelled and where he bought his ticket. In case he does it again.'

'It's on record already,' di Salis retorted sulkily, and made a most unpleasing sneer, looking to heaven and writhing with his lips and shoulder.

'Then kindly be so good as to make me a separate note of it,' Smiley replied, with unshakable forbearance. 'Westerby,' he went on in the same flat voice and for a second Guillam had the sickening feeling that Smiley was suffering from some kind of hallucination, and thought that Jerry was in the room with him to receive his orders like the rest of them. 'I pull him out – I can do that. His paper recalls him, why shouldn't it? Then what? Ko waits. He listens. He hears nothing. And he relaxes.'

'And enter the narcotics heroes,' Guillam said, glancing at the calendar. 'Sol Eckland rides again.'

'Or, I pull him out and I replace him, and another fieldman takes up the trail. Is he any less at risk than Westerby is now?'

'It never works,' Connie muttered. 'Changing horses. Never. You know that. Briefing, training, re-gearing, new relationships. Never.'

'I don't see that he *is* at risk!' di Salis asserted shrilly.

Swinging angrily round, Guillam started to slap him down, but Smiley spoke ahead of him.

'Why not, Doc?'

'Accepting your hypothesis – which I don't – Ko is not a man of violence. He's a successful businessman and his maxims are face, and expediency, and merit, and hard work. I won't have him spoken of as if he were some kind of thug. I grant you, he has people, and perhaps his people are less nice than he when it comes to method. Much as we are Whitehall's people. That doesn't make blackguards of Whitehall, I trust.'

*For Christ's sake, out with it*, thought Guillam.

'Westerby is not a Frost,' di Salis persisted in the same didactic, nasal whine. 'Westerby is not a dishonest servant. Westerby has not betrayed Ko's confidence, or Ko's money, or Ko's brother. In Ko's eyes Westerby represents a large newspaper. And Westerby has let it be known – both to Frost and to Tiu, I understand – that his paper possesses a greater degree of knowledge in the matter than he himself. Ko understands the world. By removing one journalist, he will not remove the risk. To the contrary, he will bring out the whole pack.'

'Then what is in his mind?' said Smiley.

'Uncertainty. Much as Connie said. He cannot gauge the threat. The Chinese have little place for abstracts, less still for abstract situations. He would like the threat to blow over, and if nothing concrete occurs, he will assume it has done so. That is not a habit confined to the Occident. I am extending your hypothesis.' He stood up. 'I am not endorsing it. I refuse to. I dissociate myself from it absolutely.'

He stalked out. On Smiley's nod, Guillam followed him. Only Connie stayed behind.

Smiley had closed his eyes and his brow was drawn into a rigid knot above the bridge of his nose. For a long while Connie said nothing at all. Trot lay as dead across her lap and she gazed down at him, fondling his belly.

'Karla wouldn't give two pins, would he, dearie?' she murmured. 'Not for one dead Frost, nor for ten. That's the difference, really. We can't write it much larger than that, can we, not these days? Who was it who used to say "we're fighting for the survival of Reasonable Man"? Steed-Asprey? Or was it Control? I loved that. It covered it all. Hitler. The new thing. That's who we are: reasonable. Aren't we, Trot? We're not just English. We're reasonable.' Her voice fell a little. 'Darling, what about Sam? Have you had *Thoughts*?'

It was still a long while before Smiley spoke, and when he did so, his voice was harsh, like a voice to keep her at arm's length.

'He's to stand by. Do nothing till he has the green light. He knows that. He's to wait till the green light.' He drew in a deep breath and let it out again.

'He may not even be needed. We may quite well manage without him. It all depends how Ko jumps.'

'George darling, *dear* George.'

In silent ritual she pushed herself to the grate, took up the poker and with a huge effort stirred the coals, clinging to the dog with her free hand.

Jerry stood at the kitchen window, watching the yellow dawn cut up the harbour mist. Last night there had been a storm, he remembered. Must have hit an hour before Luke telephoned. He had followed it from the mattress while the girl lay snoring along his leg. First the smell of vegetation, then the wind rustling guiltily in the palm trees, dry hands rubbed together. Then the hiss of rain like tons of molten shot being shaken into the sea. Finally the sheet lightning rocking the harbour in the long slow breaths while salvos of thunder cracked over the dancing rooftops. I killed him, he thought. Give or take a little, it was me who gave him the shove. 'It's not just the generals, it's every man who carries a gun.' Quote source and context.

The phone was ringing. Let it ring, he thought. Probably Craw, wetting his pants. He picked up the receiver. Luke, sounding even more than usually American:

'Hey, man! Big drama! Stubbsie just came through on the wire. Personal for Westerby. Eat before reading. Want to hear it?'

'No.'

'A swing through the war zones. Cambodia's airlines and the siege economy. Our man amid shot and shell! You're in luck, sailor! They want you to get your ass shot off!'

And leave Lizzie to Tiu, he thought, ringing off.

And for all I know, to that bastard Collins too, lurking in her shadow like a white slaver. Jerry had worked to Sam a couple of times while Sam was plain Mr Mellon of Vientiane, an uncannily successful trader, headman of the local roundeye crooks. He reckoned him one of the most unappetising operators he had come across.

He returned to his place at the window thinking of Lizzie again, up there on her giddy rooftop. Thinking of little Frost, and of his fondness for being alive. Thinking of the smell that had greeted him when he returned here, to his flat.

It was everywhere. It overrode the reek of the girl's deodorant, the stale cigarette smoke and the smell of gas and the smell of cooking oil from the mah-jong players next door. Catching it, Jerry had actually charted in his imagination the route Tiu had taken as he foraged: where he had lingered, and where he had skimped on his journey through Jerry's clothes, Jerry's pantry and Jerry's few possessions. A smell of rosewater and almonds mixed, favoured by an early wife.

# FIFTEEN

## *siege town*

When you leave Hong Kong it ceases to exist. When you have passed the last Chinese policeman in British ammunition boots and puttees, and held your breath as you race sixty foot above the grey slum rooftops, when the out-islands have dwindled into the blue mist, you know that the curtain has been rung down, the props cleared away, and the life you have lived there was all illusion. But this time, for once, Jerry couldn't rise to that feeling. He carried the memory of the dead Frost and the live girl with him, and they were still beside him as he reached Bangkok. As usual it took him all day to find what he was looking for; as usual, he was about to give up. In Bangkok, in Jerry's view, that happened to everyone: a tourist looking for a *wat*, a journalist for a story – or Jerry for Ricardo's friend and partner Charlie Marshall – your prize sits down the far end of some damned alley, jammed between a silted *klong* and a pile of concrete trash and it costs you five dollars US more than you expected. Also, though this was theoretically Bangkok's dry season, Jerry could not remember ever being here except in rain, which cascaded in unheralded bursts from the polluted sky. Afterwards, people always told him he got the one wet day.

He started at the airport because he was already there and because he reasoned that in the South-east no one can fly for long without flying through Bangkok. Charlie had given up flying after Ric died. Someone else said he was in jail. Someone else again that he was most likely in 'one of the dens'. A ravishing Air Vietnam hostess said with a giggle that he was making freight-hops to Saigon. She only ever saw him in Saigon.

'Out of where?' Jerry asked.

'Maybe Phnom Penh, maybe Vientiane,' she said – but Charlie's desti-nation, she insisted, was always Saigon and he never hit Bangkok. Jerry checked the telephone directory and there was no Indocharter listed. On an offchance he looked up Marshall too, discovered one – even a Marshall, C – called him, but found himself talking not to the son of a Kuomintang warlord who had christened himself with high military rank, but to a puzzled Scottish trader who kept saying 'listen but *do* come round.' He went to the jail where the *farangs* are locked up when they can't pay or have been rude to a general, and checked the record. He walked along the balconies and peered through the cage door and spoke to a couple of crazed hippies. But while they had a good deal to say about being locked up, they hadn't seen Charlie Marshall and they hadn't heard of him, and to put it delicately they didn't care about him either. In a black mood he drove to the so-called sanatorium where addicts enjoy their cold turkey, and there was a great excitement because a man in a strait-jacket had succeeded in putting his own eyes out with his fingers, but it wasn't Charlie Marshall, and no, they had no pilots, no Corsicans, no Corsican Chinese and *certainly* no son of a Kuomintang general.

So Jerry started on the hotels where pilots might hang out in transit. He didn't like the work because it was deadening and more particularly he knew that Ko had a big outfit here. He had no serious doubt that Frost had blown him;

he knew that most rich overseas Chinese legitimately run several passports and the Swatownese more than several: he knew that Ko had a Thai passport in his pocket and probably a couple of Thai generals as well. And he knew that when they were cross the Thais killed a great deal sooner and more thoroughly than almost everyone else, even though, when they condemned a man to the firing squad, they shot him through a stretched bed sheet in order not to offend the laws of the Lord Buddha. For that reason, among a good few other, Jerry felt less than comfortable shouting Charlie Marshall's name all over the big hotels.

He tried the Erawan, the Hyatt, the Miramar and the Oriental and about thirty others, and at the Erawan he trod specially lightly, remembering that China Airsea had a suite there, and Craw said Ko used it often. He formed a picture of Lizzie with her blond hair playing hostess for him or stretched out at the poolside sunning her long body while the tycoons sipped their Scotches and wondered how much would buy an hour of her time. While he drove round, a sudden rainstorm pelted fat drops so foul with smuts that they blackened the gold of the street temples. The taxi-driver aqua-planed on the flooded roads, missing the water-buffaloes by inches, the garish buses jingled and charged at them, blood-stained *Kung Fu* posters screamed at them but Marshall – Charlie Marshall – *Captain* Marshall –was not a name to anyone, though Jerry dispensed coffee-money liberally. He's got a girl, thought Jerry. He's got a girl, and uses her place, just as I would. At the Oriental he tipped the porter and arranged to collect messages and use the telephone and best of all, he obtained a receipt for two nights' lodging with which to taunt Stubbs. But his trail round the hotels had scared him, he felt exposed and at risk, so to sleep, for a dollar a night, he took a prepaid room in a nameless backstreet dosshouse, where the formalities of registration were dispensed with: a place like a row of beach huts, with all the room doors opening straight on to the pavement in order to make fornication easier, and open garages with plastic curtains that screened the number of your car. By the evening he was reduced to stomping the air-freight agencies, asking about a firm called Indocharter, though he wasn't keen to do that either, and he was seriously wondering whether to believe the Air Vietnam hostess and take up the trail in Saigon, when a Chinese girl in one of the agencies said:

'Indocharter? That's Captain Marshall's line.'

She directed him to a bookshop where Charlie Marshall bought his literature and collected his mail whenever he was in town. The shop was also run by Chinese, and when Jerry mentioned Marshall the old proprietor burst out laughing and said Charlie hadn't been in for months. The old man was very small with false teeth that grimaced.

'He owed you money? Charlie Marshall owe you money, clash a plane for you?' He once more hooted with laughter and Jerry joined in.

'Super. Great. Listen, what do you do with all the mail when he doesn't come here? Do you send it on?'

Charlie Marshall, he didn't get no mail, the old man said.

'Ah, but, sport, if a letter comes tomorrow, where will you send it?

To Phnom Penh, the old man said, pocketing his five dollars, and fished a scrap of paper from his desk so that Jerry could copy down the address.

'Maybe I should buy him a book,' said Jerry looking round. 'What does he like?'

'Flench,' the old man said automatically, and taking Jerry upstairs, showed him his sanctum for roundeye culture. For the English, pornography printed in

Brussels. For the French, row after row of tattered classics: Voltaire, Montesquieu, Hugo. Jerry bought a copy of *Candide* and slipped it into his pocket. Visitors to this room were *ex officio* celebrities apparently, for the old man produced a visitors' book and Jerry signed it *J. Westerby, newshound*. The comments column was played for laughs, so he wrote 'a most distinguished emporium.' Then he looked back through the pages and asked:

'Charlie Marshall sign here too, sport?'

The old man showed him Charlie Marshall's signature a couple of times – 'address: here', he had written.

'How about his friend?'

'Flend?'

'Captain Ricardo.'

At this the old man grew very solemn and gently took away the book.

He went round to the Foreign Correspondents' Club at the Oriental and it was empty except for a troop of Japanese who had just returned from Cambodia. They told him the state of play there as of yesterday and he got a little drunk. And as he was leaving, to his momentary horror, the dwarf appeared, in town for consultation with the local bureau. He had a Thai boy in tow, which made him particularly pert: 'Why *Westerby*! but *how's* the Secret Service today?' He played this joke on pretty well everyone, but it didn't improve Jerry's peace of mind. At the dosshouse he drank a lot more Scotch but the exertions of his fellow guests kept him awake. Finally, in self-defence, he went out and found himself a girl, a soft little creature from a bar up the road, but when he lay alone again his thoughts once more homed on Lizzie. Like it or not, she was his bed companion. How much was she consciously involved with them? he wondered. Did she know what she was playing with when she set Jerry up for Tiu? Did she know what Drake's boys had done to Frost? Did she know they might do it to Jerry? It even entered his mind that she might have been there while they did it; and that thought appalled him. No question: Frost's body was still very fresh in his memory. It was one of the worst.

By two in the morning he decided he was going to have a bout of fever, he was sweating and turning so much. Once he heard sounds of soft footsteps inside the room, and flung himself into a corner, clutching a teak table lamp ripped from its socket. At four he was woken by that amazing Asian hubbub: pig-like hawking sounds, bells, cries of old men *in extremis*, the crowing of a thousand roosters echoing in the tile and concrete corridors. He fought with the broken plumbing and began the laborious business of getting clean from a thin trickle of cold water. At five the radio was turned on full blast to get him out of bed and a whine of Asian music announced that the day had begun in earnest. By then he had shaved as if it were his wedding day and at eight he cabled his plans to the comic for the Circus to intercept. At eleven he caught the plane to Phnom Penh. As he climbed aboard the Air Cambodge Caravelle the ground hostess turned her lovely face to him and, in her best lilting English, melodiously wished him a *nice fright*.

'Thanks. Yes. Super,' he said, and chose the seat over the wing where you stood the best chance. As they slowly took off, he saw a group of fat Thais playing lousy golf on perfect links just beside the runway.

There were eight names on the flight manifest when Jerry read it at the check-in, but only one other passenger boarded the plane, a black-clad American boy with a briefcase. The rest was cargo, stacked aft in brown gunny bags and rush boxes. A siege plane, Jerry thought automatically. You fly in with the goods, you fly out with the lucky. The stewardess offered him an old *Jours de France* and a barley sugar. He read the *Jours de France* to put some French back into his mind, then remembered *Candide* and read that. He had brought Conrad because in Phnom Penh he always read Conrad, it tickled him to remind himself he was sitting in the last of the true Conrad river ports.

To land they flew in high, then pancaked through the cloud in a tight uneasy spiral to avoid random small arms fire from the jungle. There was no ground control but Jerry hadn't expected any. The stewardess didn't know how close the Khmer Rouge were to the town but the Japanese had said fifteen kilometres on all fronts and where there were no roads, less. The Japanese had said the airport was under fire but only from rockets and sporadically. No 105s – not yet, but there's always a beginning, thought Jerry. The cloud continued and Jerry hoped to heaven the altimeter was accurate. Then olive earth leapt at them and Jerry saw bomb craters spattered like eggspots, and the yellow lines from the tyre tracks of the convoys. As they landed featherlight on the pitted runway, the inevitable naked brown children splashed contentedly in a mud-filled crater.

Sun had broken through the cloud and despite the roar of aircraft Jerry had the illusion of stepping into a quiet summer's day. In Phnom Penh, like nowhere else Jerry had ever been, war took place in an atmosphere of peace. He remembered the last time he was here, before the bombing halt. A group of Air France passengers bound for Tokyo had been dawdling curiously on the apron, not realizing they had landed in a battle. No one told them take cover, no one was with them. F4s and one-elevens were screaming over the airfield, there was shooting from the perimeter, Air America choppers were landing the dead in nets like frightful catches from some red sea, and the Boeing 707, in order to take off, had to crawl across the entire airfield running the gauntlet in slow motion. Spellbound, Jerry watched her lollop out of range of the ground fire, and all the way he waited for the thump that would tell him she had been hit in the tail. But she kept going as if the innocent were immune, and disappeared sweetly into the untroubled horizon.

Now ironically, with the end so close, he noticed that the accent was on the cargo of survival. On the further side of the airfield, huge chartered all-Silver American transport planes, 707s and four-engined turbo-prop C130s marked *Transworld, Bird Airways,* or not marked at all, were landing and taking off in a clumsy, dangerous shuttle as they brought in the ammunition and rice from Thailand and Saigon, and the oil and ammunition from Thailand. On his hasty walk to the terminal Jerry saw two landings, and each time held his breath waiting for the late backcharge of the jets as they fought and shivered to a halt inside the *revêtement* of earth- filled ammunition boxes at the soft end of the landing strip. Even before they stopped, flight handlers in flak-jackets and helmets had converged like unarmed platoons to wrest their precious sacks from the holds.

Yet even these bad omens could not destroy his pleasure at being back.

'*Vous restez combien de temps, monsieur?*' the immigration officer inquired.

'*Toujours*, sport,' said Jerry. 'Long as you'll have me. Longer.' He thought of asking after Charlie Marshall then and there, but the airport was stiff with police and spooks of every sort and as long as he didn't know what he was up against it seemed wise not to advertise his interest. There was a colourful array of old aircraft with new insignia but he couldn't see any belonging to Indocharter, whose registered markings, Craw had told him at the valedictory briefing just before he left Hong Kong, were believed to be Ko's racing colours: grey and pale blue.

He took a taxi and rode in front, gently declining the driver's courteous offers of girls, shows, clubs, boys. The *flamboyants* made a luscious arcade of orange against the slate monsoon sky. He stopped at a haberdasher to change money *au cours flexible*, a term he loved. The money-changers used to be Chinese, Jerry remembered. This one was Indian. The Chinese get out early, but the Indians stay to pick the carcass. Shanty towns lay left and right of the road. Refugees crouched everywhere, cooking, dozing in silent groups. A ring of small children sat passing round a cigarette.

'*Nous sommes un village avec une population des millions,*' said the driver in his schoolroom French.

An army convoy drove at them, headlights on, sticking to the centre of the road. The taxi-driver obediently pulled in to the dirt. An ambulance brought up the rear, both doors open. The bodies were stacked feet outward, legs like pigs' trotters, marbled and bruised. Dead or alive, it scarcely mattered. They passed a cluster of stilt houses smashed by rockets, and entered a provincial French square: a restaurant, an épicerie, a charcutier, advertisements for Byrrh and Coca-Cola. On the kerb, children squatted, watching over litre wine-bottles filled with stolen petrol. Jerry remembered that too: that was what had happened in the shellings. The shells touched off the petrol and the result was a blood-bath. It would happen again this time. Nobody learned anything, nothing changed, the offal was cleared away by morning.

'Stop!' said Jerry and on the spur of the moment handed the driver the piece of paper on which he had written down the Bangkok bookshop's address for Charlie Marshall. He had imagined he should creep up on the place at dead of night, but in the sunlight, there seemed no point any more.

'Y *aller?*' the driver asked, turning to look at him in surprise.

'That's it, sport.'

'*Vous connaissez cette maison?*'

'Chum of mine.'

'*A vous? Un ami à vous?*'

'Press,' said Jerry, which explains any lunacy.

The driver shrugged and pointed the car down a long boulevard, past the French cathedral, into a mud road lined with courtyard villas which became quickly dingier as they approached the edge of town. Twice Jerry asked the driver what was special about the address, but the driver had lost his charm and shrugged away the questions. When they stopped, he insisted on being paid off, and drove away racing the gear changes in rebuke. It was just another villa, the lower half hidden behind a wall pierced with a wrought-iron gate. He pushed the bell and heard nothing. When he tried to force the gate it wouldn't move. He heard a window slam and thought, as he looked quickly up, that he saw a brown face slip away behind the mosquito wire. Then the gate buzzed and yielded and he walked up a few steps to a tiled verandah and another door, this one of solid teak with a tiny shaded grille for looking out but not in. He waited, then hammered heavily on the knocker, and heard the echoes bounding all over the house. The door was double, with a join at the centre. Pressing his face to the gap, he found himself looking on to a strip of tiled floor and two steps, presumably the last two steps of a staircase. On the lower of these stood two smooth brown feet, naked, and two bare shins, but he saw no further than the knees.

'Hullo!' he yelled, still at the gap. '*Bonjour*! Hullo!' And when the legs still did not move: '*Je suis un ami de Charlie Marshall! Madame, Monsieur, je suis un ami anglais de Charlie Marshall! Je veux lui parler.*'

He took out a five-dollar bill and shoved it through the gap but nothing bit, so he took it back and instead tore a piece of paper from his notebook. He headed his message to 'to Captain C. Marshall' and introduced himself by name as 'a British journalist with a proposal to our mutual interest', and gave the address of his hotel. Threading this note also through the gap, he looked for the brown legs again but they had vanished, so he walked till he found a *cyclo*, then rode in the cyclo till he found a cab: and no thank you, no thank you, he didn't want a girl – except that, as usual, he did.

The hotel used to be the *Royal*. Now it was the *Phnom*. A flag was flying from the mast-head, but its grandeur looked already desperate. Signing himself in, he saw living flesh basking round the courtyard pool and once more thought of Lizzie. For the girls, this was the hard school, and if she'd carried little packets for Ricardo then ten to one she'd been through it. The prettiest belonged to the richest and the richest were Phnom Penh's Rotarian crooks: the gold and rubber smugglers, the police chiefs, the big-fisted Corsicans who made neat deals with the Khmer Rouge in mid-battle. There was a letter waiting for him, the flap not sealed. The receptionist, having read it himself, politely watched Jerry do the same. A gilt-edged invitation card with an Embassy crest invited him to dinner. His host was someone he had never heard of. Mystified he turned the card over. A scrawl on the back 'Knew your friend George of the *Guardian*,' and guardian was the word that introduced. Dinner and deadletter boxes, he thought: what Sarratt scathingly called the great Foreign Office disconnection.

'*Téléphone?*' Jerry enquired.

'*Il est foutu, monsieur.*'

'*Electricité?*'

'*Aussie foutue, monsieur, mais nous avons beaucoup de l'eau.*'

'Keller?' said Jerry with a grin.

'*Dans la cour, monsieur.*'

He walked into the gardens. Among the flesh sat a bunch of warries from the Fleet Street heavies, drinking Scotch and exchanging hard stories. They looked like boy-pilots in the Battle of Britain fighting a borrowed war, and they watched him in collective contempt for his upper-class origins. One wore a white kerchief, and lank hair bravely tossed back.

'Christ, it's the Duke,' he said. 'How'd you get here? Walk on the Mekong?'

But Jerry didn't want them, he wanted Keller. Keller was permanent. He was a wireman and he was American and Jerry knew him from other wars. More particularly no *uitlander* newsman came to town without putting his cause at Keller's feet and if Jerry was to have credibility, then Keller's chop would supply it and credibility was increasingly dear to him. He found Keller in the carpark. Broad shoulders, grey-headed, one sleeve rolled down. He was standing with his sleeved arm stuffed into his pocket, watching a driver hose out the inside of a Mercedes.

'Max. Super.'

'*Ripping,*' said Keller, after glancing at him then went back to his watching. Beside him stood a pair of slim Khmer boys looking like fashion photographers in high-heeled boots and bell-bottoms and cameras dangling over their glittering, unbuttoned shirts. As Jerry looked on, the driver stopped hosing and began scrubbing the upholstery with an army pack of lint which turned brown the more he rubbed. Another American joined the group and Jerry guessed he was Keller's newest stringer. Keller went through stringer fairly fast.

'What happened?' said Jerry, as the driver began hosing again.

'Two-dollar hero caught a very expensive bullet,' said the stringer. 'That's what happened.' He was a pale Southerner with an air of being amused and Jerry was prepared to dislike him.

'Right, Keller?' Jerry said.

'Photographer,' Keller said.

Keller's wire service ran a stable of them. All the big services did: Cambodian boys, like the couple standing here. They paid them two US to go to the front and twenty for every shot printed. Jerry had heard that Keller was losing them at the rate of one a week.

'Took it clean through the shoulder while he was running and stooping,' said the stringer. 'Lost it through the lower back. Went through him like grass through a goose.' He seemed impressed.

'Where is he?' said Jerry for something to say, while the driver continued to mop and hose and scrub.

'Dying right up the road there. What happened, see, couple of weeks back those bastards in the New York bureau dug their toes in about medication. We used to ship them to Bangkok. Not now. Man, not now. Know something? Up the road they lie on the floor and have to bribe the nurses to take them water. Right, boys?'

The two Cambodians smiled politely.

'Want something, Westerby?' Keller asked.

Keller's face was grey and pitted. Jerry knew him best from the Sixties in the Congo where Keller burned his hand pulling a kid out of a lorry. Now the fingers were welded like a webbed claw, but otherwise he looked the same. Jerry remembered that incident best because he had been holding the other end of the kid.

'Comic wants me to take a look round,' Jerry said.

'Can you still do that?'

Jerry laughed and Keller laughed and they drank Scotch in the bar till the car was ready, chatting about old times. At the main entrance they picked up a girl who had been waiting all day, just for Keller, a tall Californian with too much camera and long, restless legs. As the phones weren't working Jerry insisted on stopping off at the British Embassy so that he could reply to his invitation. Keller wasn't very polite.

'You some kinda spook or something these days, Westerby, slanting your stories, ass-licking for deep background and a pension on the side or something?' There were people who said that was roughly Keller's position, but there are always people.

'Sure,' said Jerry amiably. 'Been at it for years.'

The sandbags at the entrance were new and new anti-grenade wires glistened in the teeming sunlight. In the lobby, with the spine-breaking irrelevance which only diplomats can quite achieve, a big partitioned poster recommended 'British High Performance Cars' to a city parched of fuel, and supplied cheerful photographs of several unavailable models.

'I will tell the Counsellor you have accepted,' said the receptionist solemnly.

The Mercedes smelt a little warm still from the blood but the driver had turned up the airconditioning.

'What do they do in there, Westerby?' Keller asked. 'Knit or something?'

'Or something,' Jerry smiled, mainly to the Californian girl.

Jerry sat in the front, Keller and the girl in the back.

'Okay. So hear this,' said Keller.

'Sure,' said Jerry.

Jerry had his notebook open and scribbled while Keller talked. The girl wore a short skirt and Jerry and the driver could see her thighs in the mirror. Keller had his good hand on her knee. Her name of all things was Lorraine and like Jerry she was formally taking a swing through war zones for her group of mid-West dailies. Soon they were the only car. Soon even the cyclos stopped, leaving them peasants, and bicycles, and buffaloes, and the flowered bushes of the approaching countryside.

'Heavy fighting on all the main highways,' Keller intoned, at near dictation speed. 'Rocket attacks at night, *plastics* during the day, Lon Nol still thinks he's God and the US Embassy has hot flushes supporting him then trying to throw him out.' He gave statistics, ordnance, casualties, the scale of US aid. He named generals known to be selling American arms to the Khmer Rouge, and generals who ran phantom armies in order to claim the troops' pay, and generals who did both. 'The usual snafu. Bad guys are too weak to take the towns, good guys are too crapped out to take the countryside and nobody wants to fight except the Coms. Students ready to set fire to the place soon as they're no longer exempt from the war, food riots any day now, corruption like there was no tomorrow, no one can live on his salary, fortunes being made and the place bleeding to death. Palace is unreal and the Embassy is a nut-house, more spooks than straight guys and all pretending they've got a secret. Want more?'

'How long do you give it?'

'A week. Ten years.'

'How about the airlines?'

'Airlines is all we have. Mekong's good as dead, so's the roads. Airlines have the whole ball park. We did a story on that. You see it? They ripped it to pieces. Jesus,' he said to the girl. 'Why do I have to give a re-run for the Poms?'

'More,' said Jerry, writing.

'Six months ago this town had five registered airlines. Last three months we got thirty-four new licences issued and there's like another dozen in the pipeline. Going rate is three million riels to the Minister personally and two million spread around his people. Less if you pay gold, less still if you pay abroad. We're working route thirteen,' he said to the girl. 'Thought you'd like to take a look.'

'Great,' said the girl, and pressed her knees together, entrapping Keller's one good hand.

They passed a statue with its arm shot off and after that the road followed the river bend.

'That's if Westerby here can handle it,' Keller added as an afterthought.

'Oh, I think I'm in pretty good shape,' said Jerry and the girl laughed, changing sides a moment.

'KR got themselves a new position out on the far bank there, hon,' Keller explained, talking to the girl in preference. Across the brown, fast water, Jerry saw a couple of T28s, poking around looking for something to bomb. There was a fire, quite a big one, and the smoke column rose straight into the sky like a virtuous offering.

'Where do the overseas Chinese come in?' Jerry asked. 'In Hong Kong no one's heard of this place.'

'Chinese control eighty per cent of our commerce and that includes airlines. Old or new. Cambodian's lazy, see, hon? Your Cambodian's content to take his profit out of American aid. Your Chinese aren't like that. Oh no, siree. Chinese like to work, Chinese like to turn their cash over. They fixed our money market, our transport monopoly, our rate of inflation, our siege economy. War's getting to be a wholly-owned Hong Kong subsidiary. Hey Westerby, you still got that wife you told me about, the cute one with the eyes?'

'Took the other road,' Jerry said.

'Too bad, she sounded real great. He had this great wife,' said Keller.

'How about you?' asked Jerry.

Keller shook his head and smiled at the girl. 'Care if I smoke, hon?' he asked confidingly.

There was a gap in Keller's welded claw which could have been drilled specially to hold a cigarette, and the rim of it was brown with nicotine. Keller put his good hand back on her thigh. The road turned to track and deep ruts appeared where the convoys had passed. They entered a short tunnel of trees and as they did so, a thunder of shellfire opened to their right, and the trees arched like trees in a typhoon.

'*Wow*,' the girl yelled. 'Can we slow down a little?' And she began hauling at the straps of her camera.

'Be my guest. Medium artillery,' said Keller. 'Ours,' he added as a joke. The girl lowered the window and shot off some film. The barrage continued, the trees danced, but the peasants in the paddy didn't even lift their heads. When it died, the bells of the water-buffaloes went on ringing like an echo. They drove on. On the near river bank, two kids had an old bike and were swapping rides. In the water, a shoal of them were diving in and out of an inner tube, brown bodies glistening. The girl photographed them too.

'You still speak French, Westerby? Me and Westerby did a thing together in the Congo a while back,' he explained to the girl.

'I heard,' she said knowingly.

'Poms get education, hon,' Keller explained. Jerry hadn't remembered him so talkative. 'They get *raised*. That right, Westerby? Specially lords, right? Westerby's some kind of lord.'

'That's us, sport. Scholars to a man. Not like you hayseeds.'

'Well you speak to the driver, right? We got instructions for him, you do the saying. He hasn't had time to learn English yet. Go left.'

'*A gauche*,' said Jerry.

The driver was a boy, but he already had the guide's boredom.

In the mirror, Jerry noticed that Keller's burnt hand was shaking as he drew on the cigarette. He wondered if it always did. They passed through a couple of villages. It was very quiet. He thought of Lizzie and the claw marks on her chin. He longed to do something plain with her, like taking a walk over English fields. Craw said she was a suburban drag-up. It touched him that she had a fantasy about horses.

'Westerby.'

'Yes, sport?'

'That thing you have with your fingers. Drumming them. Mind not doing that? Bugs me. It's repressive somehow.' He turned to the girl. 'They been

pounding this place for years, hon,' he said expansively. 'Years.' He blew out a
gust of cigarette smoke.

'About the airline thing,' Jerry suggested, pencil ready to write again.
'What's the arithmetic?'

'Most of the companies take drywing leases out of Vientiane. That includes
maintenance, pilot, depreciation but not fuel. Maybe you know that. Best is
own your own plane. That way you have the two things. You milk the siege
and you get your ass out when the end comes. Watch for the kids, hon,' he
told the girl, as he drew again on his cigarette. 'While there's kids around
there won't be trouble. When the kids disappear it's bad news. Means they've
hidden them. Always watch for kids.'

The girl Lorraine was fiddling with her camera again. They had reached a
rudimentary checkpoint. A couple of sentries peered in as they passed but
the driver didn't even slow down. They approached a fork and the driver
stopped.

'The river,' Keller ordered. 'Tell him to stay on the river bank.'

Jerry told him. The boy seemed surprised: seemed even about to object,
then changed his mind.

'Kids in the villages,' Keller was saying, 'kids at the front. No difference.
Either way, kids are a weathervane. Khmer soldiers take their families with
them to war as matter of course. If the father dies, there'll be nothing for the
family anyway, so they might as well come along with the military where
there's food. Another thing, hon, another thing is, the widows must be right on
hand to claim evidence of the father's death, right? That's a human interest
thing for you, right, Westerby? If they don't claim, the commanding officer
will deny it and steal the man's pay for himself. Be my guest,' he said, as she
wrote. 'But don't think anyone will print it. This war's over. Right, Westerby?'

'*Finito*,' Jerry agreed.

She would be funny, he decided. If Lizzie were here, she would definitely
see a funny side and laugh at it. Somewhere among all her imitations, he
reckoned, there was a lost original, and he definitely intended to find it. The
driver drew up beside an old woman and asked her something in Khmer, but
she put her face in her hands and turned her head away.

'Why'd she do *that* for God's sakes?' the girl cried angrily. 'We didn't want
anything bad. Jesus!'

'Shy,' said Keller, in a flattening voice.

Behind them, the artillery barrage fired another salvo and it was like a door
slamming, barring the way back. They passed a *wat* and entered a market
square made of wooden houses. Saffron-clad monks stared at them but the
girls tending the stalls ignored them and the babies went on playing with the
bantams.

'So what was the checkpoint for?' the girl asked, as she photographed. 'Are
we somewhere dangerous now?'

'Getting there, hon, getting there. Now shut up.'

Ahead of them, Jerry could hear the sound of automatic fire, M16s and
AK47s mixed. A jeep raced at them out of the trees, and at the last second
veered, banging and tripping over the ruts. At the same moment the
sunshine went out. Till now they had accepted it as their right, a liquid, vivid
light washed clean by the rainstorms. This was March and the dry season; this
was Cambodia, where war, like cricket, was played in decent weather. But
now black clouds collected, the trees closed round them like winter and the
wooden houses pulled into the dark.

'What do the Khmer Rouge dress like?' the girl asked in a quieter voice. 'Do they have *uniforms*?'

'Feather and a G-string,' Keller roared. 'Some are even bottomless.' As he laughed, Jerry heard the taut strain in his voice, and glimpsed the trembling claw as he drew on his cigarette. 'Hell, hon, they dress like farmers for Christ's sake. They just have these black pyjamas.'

'Is it always so empty?'

'Varies,' said Keller.

'And Ho Chi-minh sandals,' Jerry put in distractedly.

A pair of green water birds lifted across the track. The sound of firing was no louder.

'Didn't you have a daughter or something? What happened there?' Keller said.

'She's fine. Great.'

'Called what?'

'Catherine,' said Jerry.

'Sounds like we're going away from it,' Lorraine said, disappointed. They passed an old corpse with no arms. The flies had settled on the face-wounds in a black lava.

'Do they always do that? the girl asked, curious.

'Do what, hon?'

'Take off the boots?'

'Sometimes they take the boots off, sometimes they're the wrong damn size,' said Keller, in another queer snap of anger. 'Some cows got horns, some cows don't, and some cows is horses. Now shut up will you? Where you from?'

'Santa Barbara,' said the girl. Abruptly the trees ended. They turned a bend and were in the open again, with the brown river right beside them. Unbidden, the driver stopped, then gently backed into the trees.

'Where's he going?' the girl asked. 'Who told him to do that?'

'I think he's worried about his tyres, sport,' said Jerry, making a joke of it.

'At thirty bucks a day?' said Keller, also as a joke.

They had found a little battle. Ahead of them dominating the river bend, stood a smashed village on high waste ground without a living tree near it. The ruined walls were white and the torn edges yellow. With so little vegetation the place looked like the remnants of a Foreign Legion fort and perhaps it was just that. Inside the walls brown lorries clustered, like lorries at a building site. They heard a few shots, a light rattle. It could have been huntsmen shooting at the evening flight. Tracer flashed, a trio of mortar bombs struck, the ground shook, the car vibrated, and the driver quietly unwound his window while Jerry did the same. But the girl had opened her door and was getting out, one classic leg after the other. Rummaging in a black airbag, she produced a telefoto lens, screwed it into her camera and studied the enlarged image.

'That's all there is?' she asked doutbfully. 'Shouldn't we see the enemy as well? I don't see anything but our guys and a lot of dirty smoke.'

'Oh they're out the other side there, hon,' Keller began.

'Can't we see?' There was a small silence while the two men conferred without speaking.

'Look,' said Keller. 'This was just a tour, okay, hon? The detail of the thing gets very varied. Okay?'

'I just think it would be great to see the enemy. I want confrontation, Max. I really do. I like it.'

They started walking.

Sometimes you do it to save face, thought Jerry, other times you just do it because you haven't done your job unless you've scared yourself to death. Other times again, you go in order to remind yourself that survival is a fluke. But mostly you go because the others go; for *machismo*; and because in order to belong you must share. In the old days, perhaps, Jerry had gone for more select reasons. In order to know himself: the Hemingway game. In order to raise his threshold of fear. Because in battle, as in love, desire escalates. When you have been machine-gunned, single rounds seem trivial. When you've been shelled to pieces, the machine-gunning's child's play, if only because the impact of plain shot leaves your brain in place, where the clump of a shell blows through your ears. And there is a peace: he remembered that too. At bad times in his life – money, children, women all adrift – there had been a sense of peace that came from realizing that staying alive was his only responsibility. But this time – he thought – this time it's the most damn fool reason of all, and that's because I'm looking for a drugged-out pilot who knows a man who used to have Lizzie Worthington for his mistress. They were walking slowly because the girl in her short skirt had difficulty picking her way over the slippery ruts.

'Great chick,' Keller murmured.

'Made for it,' Jerry agreed dutifully.

With embarrassment Jerry remembered how in the Congo they used to be confidants, confessing their loves and weaknesses. To steady herself on the rutted ground, the girl was swinging her arms about.

*Don't point*, thought Jerry, *for Christ's sake don't point. That's how photographers get theirs.*

'Keep walking, hon,' Keller said shrilly. 'Don't think of anything. Walk. Want to go back, Westerby?'

They stepped round a little boy playing privately with stones in the dust. Jerry wondered whether he was gun-deaf. He glanced back. The Mercedes was still parked in the trees. Ahead, he could pick out men in low firing positions among the rubble, more men that he had realized. The noise rose suddenly. On the far bank, a couple of bombs exploded in the middle of the fire. The T28s were trying to spread the flames. A ricochet tore into the bank below them, flinging up wet mud and dust. A peasant rode past them on his bicycle, serenely. He rode into the village, through it, and out again, slowly past the ruins and into the trees beyond. No one shot at him, no one challenged him. He could be theirs or ours, thought Jerry. He came into town last night, tossed a *plastic* into a cinema, and now he's returning to his kind.

'Jesus,' cried the girl with a laugh, 'why didn't *we* think of bicycles?'

With a clatter of bricks falling, a volley of machine-gun bullets slapped round them. Below them in the river bank, by the grace of God, ran a line of empty leopard spots, shallow firing positions dug into the mud. Jerry had picked them out already. Grabbing the girl, he threw her down. Keller was already flat. Lying beside her, Jerry discerned a deep lack of interest. Better a bullet or two here than getting what Frostie got. The bullets threw up screens of mud and whined off the road. They lay low, waiting for the firing to tire. The girl was looking excitedly across the river, smiling. She was blue-eyed and flaxen and Aryan. A mortar bomb landed behind them on the verge and for the second time Jerry shoved her flat. The blast swept over them and when it was past, feathers of earth drifted down like a propitiation. But she came up still smiling. When the Pentagon thinks of civilization, thought Jerry, it thinks of you. In the fort the battle had suddenly thickened. The lorries had disappeared, a dense pall had gathered, the flash and din of mortar was incessant, light machine-gun fire challenged and answered itself with increasing swiftness. Keller's pocked face appeared white as death over the edge of his leopard spot.

'KR's got them by the balls,' he yelled. 'Across the river, ahead, and now from the other flank. We should have taken the other lane!'

Christ, Jerry thought, as the rest of the memories came back to him, Keller and I once fought over a girl, too. He tried to remember who she was, and who had won.

They waited, the firing died. They walked back to the car and gained the fork in time to meet the retreating convoy. Dead and wounded were littered along the roadside, and women crouched among them, fanning the stunned faces with palm leaves. They got out of the car again. Refugees trundled buffaloes and handcarts and one another, while they screamed at their pigs and children. One old woman screamed at the girl's camera, thinking the lens was a gun barrel. There were sounds Jerry couldn't place, like the ringing of bicycle bells and wailing, and sounds he could, like the drenched sobs of the dying and the clump of approaching mortar fire. Keller was running beside a lorry, trying to find an English-speaking officer; Jerry loped beside him yelling the same questions in French.

'Ah to hell,' said Keller, suddenly bored. 'Let's go home.' His English lordling's voice: 'The *people* and the *noise*,' he explained. They returned to the Mercedes.

For a while they were stuck in the column, with the lorries cutting them into the side and the refugees politely tapping at the window asking for a ride. Once Jerry thought he saw Deathwish the Hun riding pillion on an army motorbike. At the next fork Keller ordered the driver to turn left.

'More private,' he said, and put his good hand back on the girl's knee. But Jerry was thinking of Frost in the mortuary, and the whiteness of his screaming jaw.

'My old mother *always* told me,' Keller declared, in a folksy drawl, 'Son, don't never go back through the jungle the same way as you came. Hon?'

'Yes?'

'Hon, you just lost your cherry. My humble congratulations.' The hand slipped a little higher.

From all round them came the sound of pouring water like so many burst pipes as a sudden torrent of rain fell. They passed a settlement full of chickens running in a flurry. A barber's chair stood empty in the rain. Jerry turned to Keller.

'This siege economy thing,' he resumed, as they settled to one another again. 'Market forces and so forth. You reckon that story will go?'

'Could do,' said Keller airily. 'It's been done a few times. But it travels.'

'Who are the main operators?'

Keller named a few.

'Indocharter?'

'Indocharter's one,' said Keller.

Jerry took a long shot. 'There's a clown called Charlie Marshall flies for them, half Chinese. Somebody said he'd talk. Met him?'

'Nope.'

He reckoned that was far enough. 'What do most of them use for machines?'

'Whatever they can get. DC4s, you name it. One's not enough. You need two at least, fly one, cannibalize the second for parts. Cheaper to ground a plane and strip it than bribe the customs to release the spares.'

'What's the profit?'

'Unprintable.'

'Much opium around?'

'There's a whole damn refinery out on the Bassac, for Christ's sakes. Looks like something out of Prohibition times. I can arrange a tour, if that's what you're after.'

The girl Lorraine was at the window, staring at the rain.

'I don't see any kids, Max.' she announced. 'You said to look out for no kids, that's all. Well I've been watching and they've disappeared.' The driver stopped the car. 'It's raining and I read somewhere that when it rains Asian kids like to come out and play. So, you know, where's the kids?' she said. But Jerry wasn't listening to what she'd read. Ducking and peering through the windscreen all at once, he saw what the driver saw, and it made his throat dry.

'You're the boss, sport,' he said to Keller quietly. 'Your car, your war and your girl.'

In the mirror, to his pain, Jerry watched Keller's pumice-stone face torn between experience and incapacity.

'Drive at them slowly,' Jerry said, when he could wait no longer. '*Lentement.*'

'That's right,' Keller said. 'Do that.'

Fifty yards ahead of them, shrouded by the teeming rain, a grey lorry had pulled broadside across the track, blocking it. In the mirror a second had pulled out behind them, blocking their retreat.

'Better show our hands,' said Keller in a hoarse rush. With his good one he wound down his window. The girl and Jerry did the same. Jerry wiped the windscreen clear of mist and put his hands on the console. The driver held the wheel at the top.

'Don't smile at them, don't speak to them,' Jerry ordered.

'Jesus Christ,' said Keller. 'Holy God.'

All over Asia, thought Jerry, pressman had their favourite stories of what the Khmer Rouge did to you, and most of them were true. Even Frost at this moment would have been grateful for his relatively peaceful end. He knew newsmen who carried poison, even a concealed gun, to save themselves from just this moment. If you're caught, the first night is the only night to get out, he remembered: before they take your shoes, and your health, and God knows what other parts of you. The first night is your only chance, said the folklore. He wondered whether he should repeat it for the girl but he didn't want to hurt Keller's feelings. They were ploughing forward in first gear, engine whining. The rain was flying all over the car, thundering on the roof, smacking the bonnet and darting through the open windows. If we bog down we're finished, he thought. Still the lorry ahead had not moved and it was no more than fifteen yards away, a glistening monster in the downpour. In the dark of the lorry's cab they saw thin faces watching them. At the last minute, it lurched backward into the foliage, leaving just enough room to pass. The Mercedes tilted. Jerry had to hold the door pillar to stop himself rolling on to the driver. The two offside wheels skidded and whined, the bonnet swung and all but lurched on to the fender of the lorry.

'No licence plates,' Keller breathed. 'Holy Christ.'

'Don't hurry,' Jerry warned the driver. '*Toujours lentement.* Don't put on your lights.' He was watching in the mirror.

'And those were the black pyjamas?' the girl said excitedly. 'And you wouldn't even let me take a picture?'

No one spoke.

'What did they want? Who are they trying to ambush?' she insisted.

'Somebody else,' said Jerry. 'Not us.'

'Some bum following us,' said Keller. 'Who cares?'

'Shouldn't we warn someone?'

'There isn't the apparatus,' said Keller.

They heard shooting behind them but they kept going.

'Fucking rain,' Keller breathed, half to himself. 'Why the hell do we get rain suddenly?'

It had all but stopped.

'But Christ, Max,' the girl protested, 'if they've got us pinned out on the floor like this why don't they just finish us off?'

Before Keller could reply, the driver did it for him in French, softly and politely, though only Jerry understood.

'When they want to come, they will come,' he said, smiling at her in the mirror. 'In the bad weather. While the Americans are adding another five metres of concrete to their Embassy roof, and the soldiers are crouching in capes under their trees and the journalists are drinking whisky, and the generals are at the *fumerie*, the Khmer Rouge will come out of the jungle and cut our throats.'

'What did he say?' Keller demanded. 'Translate that, Westerby.'

'Yeah what *was* all that?' said the girl. 'It sounded really great. Like a proposition or something.'

'Didn't quite get it actually, sport. Sort of out-gunned me.'

They all broke out laughing, too loud, the driver as well.

And all through it Jerry realized, he had thought of nobody but Lizzie. Not to the exclusion of danger – quite the contrary. Like the new glorious sunshine which now engulfed them, she was the prize of his survival.

At the Phnom, the same sun was beating gaily on the poolside. There had been no rain in the town. but a bad rocket near the girls' school had killed eight or nine children. The Southern stringer had that moment returned from counting them.

'So how did Maxie make out at the bang-bangs?' he asked Jerry as they met in the hall. 'Seems to me like his nerve is cracking at the joints a little these days.'

'Take your grinning little face out of my sight,' Jerry advised. 'Otherwise actually I'll smack it.' Still grinning, the Southerner departed.

'We could meet tomorrow,' the girl said to Jerry. 'Tomorrow's free all day.'

Behind her, Keller was making his way slowly up the stairs, a hunched figure in a one-sleeved shirt, pulling himself by the banister rail.

'We could even meet tonight if you wanted,' Lorraine said.

For a while, Jerry sat alone in his room writing postcards for Cat. Then he set course for Max's bureau. He had a few more questions about Charlie Marshall. Besides, he had a notion old Max would appreciate his company. His duty done, he took a cyclo and rode up to Charlie Marshall's house again, but though he pummelled on the door and yelled, all he could see was the same bare brown legs motionless at the bottom of the stairs, this time by candlelight. But the page torn from his notebook had disappeared. He returned to the town and, still with an hour to kill, settled at a pavement café, in one of a hundred empty chairs, and drank a long Pernod, remembering how once the girls of the town ticked past him here on their little wicker carriages, whispering clichés of love in sing-song French. Tonight, the darkness trembled to nothing more lovely than the occasional thud of gunfire, while the town huddled, waiting for the blow.

Yet it was not the shelling but the silence that held the greatest fear. Like the jungle itself, this silence not gunfire, was the natural element of the approaching enemy.

When a diplomat wants to talk, the first thing he thinks of is food, and in diplomatic circles one dined early because of the curfew. Not that diplomats were subject to such rigours, but it is a charming arrogance of diplomats the world over to suppose they set an example – to whom, or of what, the devil himself will never know. The Counsellor's house was in a flat, leafy enclave bordering Lon Nol's palace. In the driveway, as Jerry arrived, an official limousine was emptying its occupants, watched over by a jeep stiff with militia. It's either royalty or religion, Jerry thought as he got out; but it was nothing more than an American diplomat and his wife arriving for a meal.

'Ah. You must be Mr Westerby,' said his hostess.

She was tall and Harrods and amused by the idea of a *journalist*, as she was amused by anyone who was not a diplomat, and of counsellor rank at that. 'John has been *dying* to meet you,' she declared brightly, and Jerry supposed she was putting him at his ease. He followed the trail upstairs. His host stood at the top, a wiry man with a moustache and a stoop and a boyishness which Jerry more usually associated with the clergy.

'Oh well done! Smashing. You're the cricketer. Well done. Mutual friends, right? We're not allowed to use the balcony tonight, I'm afraid,' he said with a naughty glance toward the American corner. 'Good men are too scarce, apparently. Got to stay under cover. Seen where you are?' He stabbed a commanding finger at a leather-framed *placement* chart showing the seating arrangement. 'Come and meet some people. Just a minute.' He drew him slightly aside, but only slightly. 'It all goes through me, right? I've made that absolutely clear. Don't let them get you into a corner, right? Quite a little *squall* running, if you follow me. Local thing. Not your problem.'

The senior American appeared at first sight small, being dark and tidy, but when he stood to shake Jerry's hand, he was nearly Jerry's height. He wore a tartan jacket of raw silk and in his other hand he held a walkie-talkie radio in a black plastic case. His brown eyes were intelligent but over-respectful, and as they shook hands, a voice inside Jerry said 'Cousin'.

'Glad to know you, Mr Westerby. I understand you're from Hong Kong. Your Governor there is a very good friend of mine. Beckie, this is Mr Westerby, a friend of the Governor of Hong Kong, and a good friend of John, our host.'

He indicated a large woman bridled in dull, handbeaten silver from the market. Her bright clothes flowed in an Asian medley.

'Oh, Mr *Westerby*,' she said. 'From Hong Kong. *Hullo*.'

The remaining guests were a mixed bag of local traders. Their womenfolk were Eurasian, French and Corsican. A houseboy hit a silver gong. The dining-room ceiling was concrete, but as they trooped in Jerry saw several eyes lift to make sure. A silver card-holder told him he was 'The Honourable

G. Westerby', a silver menu holder promised him *le roast beef à l'anglaise*, silver candlesticks held long candles of a devotional kind, Cambodian boys flitted and backed at the half-crouch with trays of food cooked this morning while the electricity was on. A much travelled French beauty sat to Jerry's right with a lace handkerchief between her breasts. She held another in her hand, and each time she ate or drank she dusted her little mouth. Her name card called her Countess Sylvia.

'*Je suis très, très, diplômée,*' she whispered to Jerry, as she pecked and dabbed. '*J'ai fait la science politique, mécanique et l'éléctricité générale.* In January I have a bad heart. Now I recover.'

'Ah well now me, I'm not qualified at *anything,*' Jerry insisted, making far too much of a joke of it. 'Jack of all trades, master of none, that's us.' To put this into French took him quite some while and he was still labouring at it when from somewhere fairly close, a burst of machine-gun fire sounded, far too long for the health of the gun. There were no answering shots. The conversation hung.

'Some bloody idiot shooting at the geckos I should think,' said the Counsellor and his wife laughed at him fondly down the table, as if the war were a little sideshow they had laid on between them for their guests. The silence returned, deeper and more pregnant than before. The little Countess put her fork on her plate and it clanged like a tram in the night.

'*Dieu,*' she said.

At once everyone started talking. The American wife asked Jerry where he was *raised* and when they had been through that she asked him where his *home* was, so Jerry gave Thurloe Square, old Pet's place, because he didn't feel like talking about Tuscany.

'We own land in Vermont,' she said firmly. 'But we haven't built on it yet.'

Two rockets fell at the same time. Jerry reckoned they were east about half a mile. Glancing round to see whether the windows were closed, Jerry caught the brown gaze of the American husband fixed on him with mysterious urgency.

'You have plans for tomorrow, Mr Westerby?'

'Not particularly.'

'If there's anything we can do, let me know.'

'Thanks,' said Jerry, but he had the feeling that wasn't the point of the question.

A Swiss trader with a wise face had a funny story. He used Jerry's presence to repeat it.

'Not long ago the whole town was alight with shooting, Mr Westerby,' he said. 'We were all going to die. Oh, *definitely*. Tonight we die! Everything: shells, tracer, poured into the sky, one million dollars' worth of ammunition, we heard afterwards. Hours on end. Some of my friends went round shaking hands with one another.' An army of ants emerged from under the table and began marching in single column across the perfectly laundered damask cloth, making a careful detour round the silver candesticks and the flower bowl brimming with hibiscus. 'The Americans radioed around, hopped up and down, we all considered very carefully our position on the evacuation list, but a funny thing, you know: the telephones were working and we even had electricity. What did the target turn out to be?' – they were already laughing hysterically – 'Frogs! Some very greedy *frogs!*'

'Toads,' somebody corrected him, but it didn't stop the laughter.

The American diplomat, a model of courteous self-criticism, supplied the amusing epilogue.

'The Cambodians have an old superstition, Mr Westerby. When there's an eclipse of the moon you must make a lot of noise. You must shoot off fireworks, you must bang tin cans, or best still, fire off a million dollars' worth of ordnance. Because if you don't, why the frogs will gobble up the moon. We *should* have known, but we *didn't* know, and in consequence we were made to look very, very silly indeed,' he said proudly.

'Yes, I'm afraid you boobed there, old boy,' the Counsellor said with satisfaction.

But though the American's smile remained frank and open, his eyes continued to impart something far more pressing –such as a message between professionals.

Someone talked about servants, and their amazing fatalism. An isolated detonation, loud and seemingly quite near, ended the performance. As the Countess Sylvia reached for Jerry's hand, their hostess smiled interrogatively at her husband down the table.

'John, darling,' she asked in her most hospitable voice, 'was that incoming or outgoing?'

'Outgoing,' he replied with a laugh. 'Oh, outgoing, definitely. Ask our journalist friend if you don't believe me. He's been through a few wars, haven't you, Westerby?'

At which the silence, yet again, joined them like a forbidden topic. The American lady clung to that piece of land in Vermont. Perhaps, after all, they *should* build on it. Perhaps, after all, it was time.

'Maybe we should just *write* to that architect,' she said.

'Maybe we should at that,' her husband agreed – at which moment, they were flung into a pitched battle. From very close a prolonged burst of pompoms lit the washing in the courtyard and a cluster of machine guns, as many as twenty, crackled in a sustained and desperate fire. By the flashes they saw the servants scurry into the house, and over the firing they heard orders given and replied to, scream for scream, and the crazy ringing of hand-gongs. Inside the room, nobody moved except the American diplomat, who lifted his walkie-talkie to his lips, drew out an aerial and murmured something before putting it to his ear. Jerry glanced downward and saw the Countess's hand battened trustingly on to his own. Her cheek brushed his shoulder. The firing faltered. He heard the clump of a small bomb close. No vibration, but the flames of the candles tilted in salute and on the mantelshelf a couple of heavy invitation cards clopped over with a slap, and lay still, the only recognizable casualties. Then as a last and separate sound, they heard the grizzle of a departing single-engined plane like the distant grousing of a child. It was capped by the Counsellor's easy laughter as he addressed his wife.

'Ah, well now, that *wasn't* the eclipse, I'm afraid, was it, Hills? That was the advantage of having Lon Nol as our neighbour. One of his pilots gets fed up with not being paid now and then so he takes up a plane and has a potshot at the palace. Darling, are you going to take the gels off to powder their noses and do whatever you all do?'

It's anger, Jerry decided, catching the senior American's eye again. He's like a man with a mission to the poor who has to waste his time with the rich.

Downstairs, Jerry, the Counsellor and the American stood silent in the ground floor study. The Counsellor had acquired a wolfish shyness.

'Yes, well,' he said. 'Now I've put you both on the map perhaps I should leave you to it. Whisky in the decanter, right, Westerby?'

'Right, John,' said the American, but the Counsellor didn't seem to hear.

'Just remember, Westerby, the mandate's *ours*, right? We're keeping the bed warm. Right?' With a knowing wag of the finger, he disappeared.

The study was candlelit, a small masculine room with no mirrors or pictures, just a ribbed teak ceiling and a green metal desk, and the feeling of deathlike quiet again in the blackness outside, though the geckos and the bullfrogs would have baffled the most sophisticated microphone.

'Hey let me get that,' said the American, arresting Jerry's progress to the sideboard, and made a show of getting the mix just right for him: 'water or soda, don't let me drown it.'

'Seems kind of a long way round to bring two friends together,' the American said, in a taut, chatty tone, from the sideboard as he poured.

'Does rather.'

'John's a great guy but he's kind of a stickler for protocol. Your people have no resources here right now, but they have certain rights, so John likes to make sure that the ball doesn't slip out of his court for good. I can understand his point of view. Just that things take a little longer sometimes.'

He handed Jerry a long brown envelope from inside the tartan jacket, and with the same pregnant intensity as before watched while he broke the seal. The paper had a smeared and photographic quality.

Somewhere a child moaned, and was silenced. The garage, he thought: the servants have filled the garage with refugees and the Counsellor is not to know.

*ENFORCEMENTS SAIGON reports Charlie* MARSHALL *rpt MARSHALL scheduled hit Battambang ETA 1930 tomorrow via Pailin . . . converted DC4 Carvair, Indocharter markings manifest quotes miscellaneous cargo . . . scheduled continue Phnom Penh.*

Then he read the time and date of transmission and anger hit him like a windstorm. He remembered yesterday's foot-slogging in Bangkok and today's hairbrained taxi ride with Keller and the girl, and with a 'Jesus *Christ*' he slammed the message back on the table between them.

'How long have you been sitting on this? That's not tomorrow. That's tonight!'

'Unfortunately our host could not arrange the wedding any earlier. He has an extremely crowded social programme. Good luck.'

Just as angry as Jerry, he quietly took back the signal, slipped it into the pocket of his jacket and disappeared upstairs to his wife, who was busy admiring her hostess's indifferent collection of pilfered Buddhas.

He stood alone. A rocket fell, and this time it was close. The candles went out and the night sky seemed finally to be splitting with the strain of this illusory, Gilbertian war. Mindlessly the machine guns joined the clatter. The little bare room with its tiled floor rattled and sang like a sound machine.

Only as suddenly to stop again, leaving the town in silence.

'Something wrong, old boy?' the Counsellor enquired genially from the doorway. 'Yank rub you up the wrong way, did he? They seem to want to run the world single-handed these days.'

'I'll need six hour options,' Jerry said. The Counsellor didn't quite follow. Having explained to him how they worked, Jerry stepped quickly into the night.

'Got transport, have you, old boy? That's the way. They'll shoot you otherwise. Mind how you go.'

He strode quickly, driven by his irritation and disgust. It was long after curfew. There were no street lamps, no stars. The moon had vanished, and the squeak of his crêpe soles ran with him like an unwanted, unseen companion. The only light came from the perimeter of the palace across the road but none spilled on to Jerry's side of the street. High walls blocked off the inner building, high wires crowned the walls, the barrels of the light anti-aircraft guns gleamed bronze against the black and soundless sky. Young soldiers dozed in groups and as Jerry stomped past them a fresh roll of gong-beats sounded: the master of the guard was keeping the sentries awake. There was no traffic, but between the sentry posts the refugees had made up their own night villages in a long column down the pavement. Some had draped themselves with strips of brown tarpaulin, some had plank bunks and some were cooking by tiny flames, though God alone knew what they had found to eat. Some sat in neat social groups, facing in upon each other. On an ox-cart, a girl lay with a boy, children Cat's age when he last had seen her in the flesh. But from the hundreds of them not one sound came, and after he had gone a distance he actually turned and peered to make sure they were there. If they were, the darkness and the silence hid them. He thought of the dinner party. It had taken place in another land, another universe entirely. He was irrelevant here, yet somehow he had contributed to the disaster.

*Just remember the mandate's ours, right? We're keeping the bed warm.*

For no reason that he knew of, the sweat began running off him and the night air made no cooling impact. The dark was as hot as the day. Ahead of him in the town a stray rocket struck carelessly, then two more. They creep into the paddies until they're within range, he thought. They lie-up, hugging their bits of drainpipe and their little bomb, then fire and run like hell for the jungle. The palace was behind him. A battery fired a salvo and for a few seconds he was able to see his way by the flashes. The road was broad, a boulevard, and as best he could he kept to the crown. Occasionally he made out the gaps of the side streets passing him in geometric regularity. If he stooped he could even see the treetops retreating into the paler sky. Once a cyclo pattered by, toppling nervously out of the turning, hitting the kerb, then steadying. He thought of shouting to it but he preferred to keep on striding. A male voice greeted him doubtfully out of the darkness – a whisper, nothing indiscreet.

'*Bon soir? Monsieur? Bon soir?*'

The sentries stood every hundred metres in ones or twos, holding their carbines in both hands. Their murmurs came to him like invitations, but Jerry was always careful and kept his hands wide of his pockets where they could watch them. Some, seeing the enormous sweating roundeye, laughed and waved him on. Others stopped him at pistol point and gazed up at him earnestly by the light of bicycle lamps while they asked him questions in order to practise their French. Some requested cigarettes, and these he gave. He tugged off his drenched jacket and ripped his shirt open to the waist, but still the air wouldn't cool him and he wondered again whether he had a fever, and whether, like last night in Bangkok, he would wake up in his bedroom crouching in the darkness waiting to brain someone with a table lamp.

The moon appeared, lapped by the foam of the rainclouds. By its light his hotel resembled a locked fortress. He reached the garden wall and followed it leftward along the trees until it turned again. He threw his jacket over the wall and with difficulty climbed after it. He crossed the lawn to the steps, pushed open the door to the lobby and stepped back with a sick cry of disgust. The lobby was in pitch blackness except for a single moonbeam, which shone like a spotlight on to a huge luminous chrysalis spun around the naked brown larva of a human body.

'*Vous désirez, monsieur?*' a voice asked softly.

It was the night watchman in his hammock, asleep under a mosquito net.

The boy handed him a key and a note and silently accepted his tip. Jerry struck his lighter and read the note. '*Darling, I'm in room twenty-eight and lonely. Come and see me. L.*'

What the hell? he thought: maybe it'll put the bits back together again. He climbed the stairs to the second floor, forgetting her terrible banality, thinking only of her long legs and her tilting rump as she negotiated the ruts along the river bank; her cornflower eyes and her regular all-American gravity as she lay in the leopard spot; thinking only of his own yearning for human touch. Who gives a damn about Keller? he thought. To hold someone is to exist. Perhaps she's frightened too. He knocked on the door, waited, gave it a shove.

'Lorrraine? It's me. Westerby.'

Nothing happened. He lurched toward the bed, conscious of the absence of any female smell, even face powder or deodorant. On his way there he saw by the same moonlight the dreadfully familiar sight of blue jeans, heavy beanboots and a tattered Olivetti portable not unlike his own.

'Come one step nearer and it's statutory rape,' said Luke, uncorking the bottle on his bedside table.

# SIXTEEN

# *friends of Charlie Marshall*

He crept out before light, having slept on Luke's floor. He took his typewriter and shoulder bag though he expected to use neither. He left a note for Keller asking him to wire Stubbs that he was following the siege story out to the provinces. His back ached from the floor and his head from the bottle.

Luke had come for the bang-bangs, he said: bureau was giving him a rest from Big Moo. Also Jake Chiu, his irate landlord, had finally thrown him out of his apartment.

'I'm destitute, Westerby!' he had cried, and began wailing round the room, '*destitute*', till Jerry, to buy himself some sleep, and stop the neighbours' banging, slipped his spare flat-key off its ring and flung it at him.

'Until I get back,' he warned. 'Then *out*. Understood?'

Jerry asked about the Frost thing. Luke had forgotton all about it and had to be reminded. Ah *him*, he said. *Him*. Yeah, well there were stories he'd been cheeky to the Triads and maybe in a hundred years they would all come true, but meanwhile who gave a damn?

But sleep hadn't come so easy, even then. They discussed today's arrangements. Luke had proposed to do whatever Jerry was doing. Dying alone was a bore, he had insisted. Better they got drunk and found some whores. Jerry had replied that Luke would have to wait a while before the two of them went into the sunset together, because he was going fishing for the day, and he was going alone.

'Fishing for what, for hell's sakes? If there's a story, share it. Who gave you Frost for free? Where can you go that is not more beautiful for Brother Lukie's presence?'

Pretty well anywhere, Jerry had said unkindly, and managed to leave without waking him.

He made first for the market and sipped a *soupe chinoise*, studying the stalls and shop fronts. He selected a young Indian who was offering nothing but plastic buckets, water bottles and brooms, yet looking very prosperous on the profits.

'What else to you sell, sport?'

'Sir, I sell all things to all gentlemen.'

They foxed around. No, said Jerry, it was nothing to smoke that he wanted, and nothing to swallow, nothing to sniff and nothing for the wrists either. And no, thank you, with all respect to the many beautiful sisters, cousins and young men of his circle, Jerry's other needs were also taken care of.

'Then, oh gladness, sir, you are a most happy man.'

'I was *really* looking for something for a friend,' said Jerry.

The Indian boy looked sharply up and down the street and he wasn't foxing any more.

'A *friendly* friend, sir?'

'Not very.'

They shared a cyclo. The Indian had an uncle who sold Buddhas in the silver market, and the uncle had a back room, with locks and bolts on the door. For thirty American dollars Jerry bought a neat brown Walther automatic with twenty rounds of ammunition. The Sarratt bearleaders, he reckoned as he climbed back into the cyclo, would have fallen into a deep swoon. First, for what they called improper dressing, a crime of crimes. Second because they preached the hardy nonsense that small guns gave more trouble than use. But they'd have had a bigger fit still if he'd carted his Hong Kong Webley through customs to Bangkok and thence to Phnom Penh, so in Jerry's view they could count themselves lucky, because he wasn't walking into this one naked whatever their doctrine of the week. At the airport there was no plane to Battambang, but there was never a plane to anywhere. There were the all-silver rice jets howling on and off the landing strip, and there were new *revêtements* being built after a fresh fall of rockets in the night. Jerry watched the earth arriving in lorryloads, and the coolies filling ammunition boxes frantically. In another life, he decided, I'll go into the sand business and flog it to beseiged cities.

In the waiting room, Jerry found a group of stewardesses drinking coffee and laughing, and in his breezy way he joined them. A tall girl who spoke English made a doubtful face and disappeared with his passport and five dollars.

'*C'est impossible*,' they all assured him, while they waited for her. '*C'est tout occupé*.'

The girl returned smiling. 'The pilot is *very* susceptible,' she said. 'If he don't like you, he don't take you. But I show him your photograph and he has agreed to *surcharger*. He is allowed to take only thirty-one *personnes* but he take you, he don't care, he do it for friendship if you give him one thousand five hundred riels.'

The plane was two-thirds empty, and the bullet holes in the wings wept dew like undressed wounds.

At that time, Battambang was the safest town left in Lon Nol's dwindling archipelago, and Phnom Penh's last farm. For an hour, they lumbered over supposedly Khmer Rouge-infested territory without a soul in sight. As they circled, someone shot lazily from the paddies and the pilot pulled a couple of token turns to avoid being hit, but Jerry was more concerned to mark the ground layout before they touched down: the park-bays; which runways were civil and which were military; the wired-off enclave which contained the freight huts. They landed in an air of pastoral affluence. Flowers grew round the gun emplacements, fat brown chickens scurried in the shell holes, water and electricity abounded, though a telegram to Phnom Penh already took a week.

Jerry trod very carefully now. His instinct for cover was stronger than ever. *The Honourable Gerald Westerby, the distinguished hack, reports on the siege economy.* When you're my size, sport, you have to have a hell of a good reason for whatever you're doing. So he put out smoke, as the jargon goes. At the enquiry desk, watched by several quiet men, he asked for the names of the best hotels in town and wrote down a couple while he continued to study the groupings of planes and buildings. Meandering from one office to another he asked what facilities existed to air-freight news copy to Phnom Penh and no one had the least idea. Continuing his discreet reconnaissance he waved his cablecard around and enquired how to get to the governor's palace, implying that he might have business with the great man personally. By now he was the most distinguished reporter who have ever been to Battambang. Meanwhile he noted the doors marked 'crew' and the doors marked 'private', and the position of the men's rooms, so that later, when he was clear, he could make himself a sketch plan of the entire concourse, with emphasis on the exits to the wired-off part of the airfield. Finally he asked who was in town just now among the pilots. He was friendly with several, he said, so his simplest plan – should it become necessary – was probably to ask one of them to take his copy in his flightbag. A stewardess gave names from a list and while she did this Jerry gently turned the list round and read off the rest. The Indocharter flight was listed but no pilot was mentioned.'

'Captain Andreas still flying for Indocharter?' he enquired.

'Le Capitaine *qui*, monsieur?'

'Andreas. We used to call him André. Little fellow, always wore dark glasses.

Did the Kampong Cham run.'

She shook her head. Only Captain Marshall and Captain Ricardo, she said, flew for Indocharter, but le Capitaine *Ric* had immolated himself in an accident. Jerry affected no interest, but established in passing that Captain Marshall's Carvair was due to take off in the afternoon, as forecast in last night's signal, but there was no freight space available, everything was taken, Indocharter was always fully contracted.

'Know where I can reach him?'

'Captain Marshall never flies in the mornings, monsieur.'

He took a cab into town. The best hotel was a flea-bitten dug-out in the main street. The street itself was narrow, stinking and deafening, an Asian boomtown in the making, pounded by the din of Hondas and crammed with the frustrated Mercedes of the quick rich. Keeping his cover going, he took a room and paid for it in advance, to include 'special service' which meant nothing more exotic than clean sheets as opposed to those which still bore the marks of other bodies. He told his driver to return in an hour. By force of habit he secured an inflated receipt. He showered, changed and listened courteously while the houseboy showed him where to climb in after curfew, then he went out to find breakfast because it was still only nine in the morning.

He carried his typewriter and shoulder bag with him. He saw no other roundeyes. He saw basket-makers, skin-sellers and fruit-sellers, and once again the inevitable bottles of stolen petrol laid along the pavement waiting for an attack to touch them off. In a mirror hung in a tree, he watched a dentist extract teeth from a patient tied in a high chair, and the red-tipped tooth being solemnly added to the thread which displayed the day's catch. All of these things Jerry ostentatiously recorded in his notebook, as became a zealous reporter of the social scene. And from a pavement café, as he consumed cold beer and fresh fish, he watched the dingy half-glazed offices marked 'Indocharter' across the road, and waited for someone to come and unlock the door. No one did. *Captain Marshall never flies in the mornings, monsieur.* At a chemist's shop which specialized in children's bicycles he bought a roll of sticking plaster and back in his room taped the Walther to his ribs rather than have it waving around in his waistband. Thus equipped, the intrepid journalist set forth to live some more cover – which sometimes, in the psychology of a fieldman, is no more than a gratuitous act of self-legitimization as the heat begins to gather.

The governor lived on the edge of town, behind a verandah and French colonial portals and a secretariat seventy strong. The vast concrete hall led to a waiting room never finished, and to much smaller offices behind, and in one of these, after a fifty-minute wait, Jerry was admitted to the diminutive presence of a tiny, very senior black-suited Cambodian sent by Phnom Penh to handle noisome correspondents. Word said he was the son of a general and managed the Battambang end of the family opium business. His desk was much too big for him. Several attendants lounged about and they all looked very severe. One wore uniform with a lot of medal ribbons. Jerry asked for deep background and made a list of several charming dreams: that the Communist enemy was all but beaten; that there was serious discussion about reopening the entire national road system; that tourism was the growth industry of the province. The general's son spoke slow and beautiful French and it clearly gave him great pleasure to hear himself, for he kept his eyes half closed and smiled as he spoke, as if listening to beloved music.

'I may conclude, monsieur, with a word of warning to your country. You are American?'

'English.'

'It is the same. Tell your government, sir. If you do not help us to continue the fight against the Communists, we shall go to the Russians and ask them to replace you in our struggle.'

Oh, mother, thought Jerry. Oh boy. Oh God.

'I will give them that message,' he promised, and made to go.

'*Un instant, monsieur*,' said the senior official sharply, and there was a stirring among his dozing courtiers. He opened a drawer and pulled out an imposing folder. Frost's will, Jerry thought. My death warrant. Stamps for Cat.

'You are a writer?'

'Yes.'

Ko's putting the arm on me. The pen tonight, and wake up with my throat cut tomorrow.

'You were at the Sorbonne, monsieur?' the official enquired.

'Oxford.'

'Oxford in London?'

'Yes.'

'Then you have read the great French poets, monsieur?'

'With intense pleasure,' Jerry replied fervently. The courtiers were looking extremely grave.

'Then perhaps *monsieur* will favour me with his opinion of the following few verses?' In his dignified French, the little official began to read aloud, slowly conducting with his palm.

'*Deux amants assis sur la terre*
'*Regardaient la mer*,'

he began, and continued for perhaps twenty excruciating lines while Jerry listened in mystification.

'*Voila*,' said the official finally, and put the file aside. '*Vous l'aimez?*' he inquired, severely fixing his eye upon a neutral part of the room.

'*Superbe*,' said Jerry with a gush of enthusiasm. '*Merveilleux*. The sensitivity.'

'They are by whom would you think?'

Jerry grabbed a name at random. 'By Lamartine?'

The senior official shook his head. The courtiers were observing Jerry even more closely.

'Victor Hugo?' Jerry ventured.

'They are by me,' said the official and with a sigh returned his poems to the drawer. The courtiers relaxed. 'See that this literary person has every facility,' he ordered.

Jerry returned to the airport to find it a milling, dangerous chaos. Mercedes raced up and down the approach as if someone had invaded their nest, the forecourt was a turmoil of beacons, motorcycles and sirens; and the hall, when he argued his way through the cordon, was jammed with scared people fighting to read noticeboards, yell at each other and hear the blaring loudspeakers all at the same time. Forcing a path to the information desk, Jerry found it closed. He leapt on the counter and saw the airfield through a hole in the anti-blast board. A squad of armed soldiers was jog-trotting down the empty runway towards a group of white poles where the national flags drooped in the windless air. They lowered two of the flags to half mast, and inside the hall the loudspeakers interrupted themselves to blare a few bars of the national anthem. Over the seething heads, Jerry searched for someone he might talk to. He selected a lank missionary with cropped yellow hair and glasses and a six-inch silver cross pinned to the pocket of his brown shirt. A pair of Cambodians in dog-collars stood miserably beside him.

'*Vous parlez francais?*'

'Yes, but I also speak English!'

A lilting, corrective tone. Jerry guessed he was a Dane.

'I'm press. What's the fuss?' He was shouting at the top of his voice.

'Phnom Penh is closed,' the missionary bellowed in reply. 'No planes may leave or land.'

'Why?'

'Khmer Rouge have hit the ammunition dump in the airport. The town is closed till morning at the least.'

The loudspeaker began chattering again. The two priests listened. The missionary stooped nearly double to catch their murmured translation.

'They have made a great damage and devastated half a dozen planes already. Oh yes! They have laid them waste entirely. The authority is also suspecting sabotage. Maybe she also takes some prisoners. Listen, why are they putting an ammunition house inside the airport in the first case? That was most dangerous. What is the reason here?'

'Good question,' Jerry agreed.

He ploughed across the hall. His master plan was already dead, as his master plans usually were. The 'crew only' door was guarded by a pair of very serious crushers and in the tension he saw no chance of brazening his way through. The thrust of the crowd was toward the passenger exit, where harrassed ground staff were refusing to accept boarding tickets, and harassed police were being besieged with letters of *laissez passer* designed to put the prominent outside their reach. He let it carry him. At the edges, a team of French traders was screaming for a refund, and the elderly were preparing to settle for the night. But the centre pushed and peered and exchanged fresh rumours, and the momentum carried him steadily to the front. Reaching it, Jerry discreetly took out his cable card and climbed over the improvised barrier. The senior policeman was sleek and well-covered and he watched Jerry disdainfully while his surbordinates toiled. Jerry strode up to him, his shoulder bag dangling from his hand and pressed the cable card under his nose.

'*Securité americaine*,' he roared in awful French, and with a snarl at the two men on the swing doors, barged his way on to the tarmac and kept going, while his back waited all the time for a challenge or a warning shot or, in the trigger-happy atmosphere, a shot that was not even a warning. He walked angrily, with rough authority, swinging his shoulder bag, Sarratt-style, to distract. Ahead of him – sixty yards, soon fifty – stood a row of single-engined military trainers without insignia. Beyond lay the caged enclosure, and the freight huts, numbered nine to eighteen, and beyond the freight huts Jerry saw a cluster of hangars and park bays, marked prohibited in just about every language except Chinese. Reaching the trainers, Jerry strode imperiously along the line of them as if he were carrying out an inspection. They were anchored with bricks on wires. Pausing but not stopping, he stabbed irritably at a brick with his buckskin boot, yanked at an aileron and shook his head.

From their sandbagged emplacement, to his left, an anti-aircraft guncrew watched him indolently.

'*Qu'est-ce-que vous fâites?*'

Half turning, Jerry cupped his hand to his mouth. 'Watch the damn sky for Christ's sakes,' he yelled in good American, pointing angrily to heaven, and kept going till he reached the high cage. It was open and the huts lay ahead of him. Once past them he would be out of sight of both terminal and the control tower. He was walking on smashed concrete with couch-grass in the cracks. There was nobody in sight. The huts were weatherboard, thirty feet long, ten high, with palm roofs. He reached the first. The boarding on the windows read 'Bomb Cluster Fragmentation Without Fuses.' A trodden dust-path led to the hangars on the other side. Through the gap Jerry glimpsed the parrot colours of parked cargo planes.

'Got you,' Jerry muttered aloud, as he emerged on the safe side of the huts, because there ahead of him, clear as day, like a first sight of the enemy after months of lonely marching, a battered blue-grey DC4 Carvair, fat as a frog, squatted on the crumbling tarmac with her nose cone open. Diesel oil was dripping in a fast black rain from both her starboard engines and a spindly Chinese in a sailing cap laden with military insignia stood smoking under the loading bay while he marked an inventory. Two coolies scuried back and forth with sacks, and a third worked the ancient loading lift. At his feet, chickens scrabbled petulantly. And on the fuselage, in flaming crimson against Drake Ko's faded racing colours, ran the letters OCHART. The others had been lost in a repair job.

*Oh, Charlie's indestructible,* completely *immortal! Charlie* Marshall, *Mr Tiu, a fantastic half Chinese, all skin and bones and opium and a completely brilliant pilot . . .*

He'd bloody well better be, sport, thought Jerry with a shudder, as the coolies loaded sack after sack through the open nose and into the battered belly of the plane.

*The Reverend Ricardo's lifelong Sancho Panza, your Grace,* Craw had said, in extension of Lizzie's description. *Half Chow, as the good lady advised us, and the proud veteran of many futile wars.*

Jerry remained standing, making no attempt to conceal himself, dangling the bag from his fist and wearing the apologetic grin of an English stray. Coolies now seemed to be converging on the plains from several points at once: there were many more than two. Turning his back on them, Jerry repeated his routine of strolling along the line of huts, much as he had walked along the line of trainers, or along the corridor toward Frost's room peering through cracks in the weatherboard and seeing nothing but the occasional broken packing case. *The concession to operate out of Battambang costs half a million US renewable,* Keller had said. At that price, who pays for redecoration? The line of huts broke and he came on four army lorries loaded high with fruit, vegetables and unmarked gunny bags. Their tailboards faced the plane and they sported artillery insignia. Two soldiers stood in each lorry, handing the gunny bags down to the coolies. The sensible thing would have been to drive the lorries on to the tarmac, but a mood of discretion prevailed. *The army likes to be in on things,* Keller had said. *The navy can make millions out of one convoy down the Mekong, the air force is sitting pretty: bombers fly fruit and the choppers can airlift the rich Chinese instead of the wounded out of the siege towns.*

*Fighter boys go a little hungry because they have to land where they take off. But the army really has to scratch around to make a living.*

Jerry was closer to the plane now and could hear the squawking as Charlie Marshall fired commands at the coolies.

The huts began again. Number eighteen had double doors and the name *Indocharter* daubed in green down the woodwork, so that from any distance the letters looked like Chinese characters. In the gloomy interior, a Chinese peasant couple squatted on the dust floor. A tethered pig lay with its head on the old man's slippered foot. Their other possession was a long rush parcel meticulously bound with string. It could have been a corpse. A water jar stood in one corner with two rice bowls at its base. There was nothing else in the hut. 'Welcome to the Indocharter transit lounge,' Jerry thought. With the sweat running down his ribs, he tagged himself to the line of coolies till he drew alongside Charlie Marshall, who went on squawking in Khmer at the top of his voice while his shaking pen checked each load on the inventory.

He wore an oily white short-sleeved shirt with enough gold stripes on the epaulettes to make a full general in anybody's air force. Two American combat patches were stitched on his shirt front, amid an amazing collection of medal ribbons and Communist red stars. One patch read 'Kill a Commie for Christ', and the other 'Christ was a Capitalist at Heart'. His head was turned down and his face was in the shadow of his huge sailing cap, which slopped freely over his ears. Jerry waited for him to look up. The coolies were already yelling for Jerry to move on, but Charlie Marshall kept his head turned stubbornly down while he added and wrote on the inventory and squawked furiously back at them.

'Captain Marshall, I'm doing a story on Ricardo for a London newspaper,' said Jerry quietly. 'I want to ride with you as far as Phnom Penh and ask you some questions.'

As he spoke, he gently laid the volume of *Candide* on top of the inventory, with three one-hundred dollar bills poking outward in a discreet fan. When you want a man to look one way, says the Sarratt school of illusionists, always point him in the other.

'They tell me you like Voltaire,' he said.

'I don't like anybody,' Charlie Marshall retorted in a scratchy falsetto at the inventory, while the cap slipped still lower over his face. 'I hate the whole human race, hear me?' His vituperation, despite its Chinese cadence, was unmistakably French-American. 'Jesus Christ, I hate mankind so damn much that if it don't hurry and blow itself to pieces I'm personally going to buy some bombs and go out there *myself*!'

He had lost his audience. Jerry was halfway up the steel ladder before Charlie Marshall had completed his thesis.

'Voltaire didn't know a damn bloody thing!' he screamed at the next coolie. 'He fought the wrong damn war, hear me? Put it over there you lazy coon and grab another handful! *Dépêche toi, crétin, oui?*'

But all the same he jammed Voltaire into the back pocket of his baggy trousers.

The inside of the plane was dark and roomy and cool as a cathedral. The seats had been removed, and perforated green shelves like Meccano had been fitted to the walls. Carcasses of pig and guinea fowl hung from the roof. The rest of the cargo was stowed in the gangway, starting from the tail end, which gave Jerry no good feeling about taking off, and consisted of fruit and vegetable and the gunny bags which Jerry had spotted in the army trucks, marked 'grain', 'rice', 'flour', in letters large enough for the most illiterate narcotics agent to read. But the sticky smell of yeast and molasses which already filled the hold required no label at all. Some of the bags had been arranged in a ring, to make a siting area for Jerry's fellow passengers. Chief of these were two austere Chinese men, dressed very poorly in grey, and from their sameness and their demure superiority Jerry at once inferred an expertise of some kind. He remembered explosives-wallahs and pianists he had occasionally ferried thanklessly in and out of badland. Next to them, but respectfully apart, four hillsmen armed to the teeth sat smoking, and cropping from their rice bowls. Jerry guessed Meo or one of the Shan tribes from the northern borders where Charlie Marshall's father had his army, and he guessed from their ease that they were part of the permanent help. In a separate class altogether sat the quality: the colonel of artillery himself, who had thoughtfully supplied the transport and the troop escort, and his companion a senior officer of customs, without whom nothing could have been achieved. They reclined regally in the gangway, on chairs specially provided, watching proudly while the loading continued, and they wore their best uniforms as the ceremony demanded.

There was one other member of the party and he lurked alone on top of the cases in the tail, head almost against the roof, and it was not possible to make him out in any detail. He sat with a bottle of whisky to himself, and even a glass to himself. He wore a Fidel Castro hat and a full beard. Gold links glittered on his dark arms, known in those days (to all but those who wore them) as CIA bracelets, on the happy assumption that a man ditched in hostile country could buy his way to safety by doling out a link at a time. But his eyes as they watched Jerry along the well-oiled barrel of an AK47 automatic rifle had a fixed brightness. 'He was covering me through the nose cone,' thought Jerry. 'He had a bead on me from the moment I left the hut.'

The two Chinese were cooks, he decided in a moment of inspiration: *cooks* being the underworld nickname for chemists. Keller had said that the Air Opium lines had taken to bringing in the raw base and refining it in Phnom Penh, but were having hell's own job persuading the cooks to come and work in siege conditions.

'Hey you! Voltaire!'

Jerry hurried forward to the edge of the hold. Looking down he saw the old peasant couple standing at the bottom of the ladder and Charlie Marshall trying to wrench the pig from them while he shoved the old woman up the steel ladder.

'When she come up you gotta reach out and grab her, hear me?' he called, holding the pig in his arms. 'She fall down and break her ass we gotta whole lot more trouble with the coons. You some crazy narcotics hero, Voltaire?'

'No.'

'Well, you grab hold of her completely, hear me?'

She started up the ladder. When she had gone a few rungs she began croaking and Charlie Marshall contrived to get the pig under his arm while he gave her a sharp crack on the rump and screamed at her in Chinese. The husband scurried up after her and Jerry hauled them both to safety. Finally Charlie Marshall's own clown's head appeared though the cone, and though it was swamped by the hat, Jerry had first glimpse of the face beneath: skeletal and brown, with sleepy Chinese eyes and a big French mouth which twisted all ways when he squawked. He shoved the pig through, Jerry grabbed it and carted it, screaming and wriggling, to the old peasants. Then Charlie hauled his own fleshless frame aboard, like a spider climbing out of a drain. At once, the officer of customs and the colonel of artillery stood up, brushed the seats of their uniforms, and progressed swiftly along the gangway to the shadowed man in the Castro hat squatting on the packing cases. Reaching him, they waited respectfully, like sidesmen taking the offertory to the altar.

The linked bracelets flashed, an arm reached down, once, twice, and a devout silence descended while the two men carefully counted a lot of bank notes and everybody watched. In rough unison they returned to the top of the ladder where Charlie Marshall waited with the manifest. The officer of customs signed it, the colonel of artillery looked on approvingly, then they both saluted and disappeared down the ladder. The nose cone juddered to an almost-closed position, Charlie Marshall gave it a kick, flung some matting across the gap, and clambered quickly over the packing cases to an inside stairway leading himself to the cabin. Jerry clambered after him, and having settled into the co-pilot's seat, he silently totted up his blessings.

'We're about five hundred tons overweight. We're leaking oil. We're carrying an armed bodyguard. We're forbidden to take off. We're forbidden to land, Phnom Penh airport's probably got a hole the size of Buckingham-shire. We have an hour and a half of Khmer Rouge between us and salvation, and if anybody turns sour on us the other end, ace operator Westerby is caught with his knickers round his ankles and about two hundred gunny bags of opium base in his arms.'

'You know how to fly this thing?' Charlie Marshall yelled, as he struck at a row of mildewed switches. 'You some kinda great flying hero, Voltaire?'

'I hate it all.'

'Me too.'

Seizing a swat, Charlie Marshall flung himself upon a huge bottle-fly that was buzzing round the windscreen, then started the engines one by one, until the whole dreadful plane was heaving and rattling like a London bus on its last journey home up Clapham Hill. The radio cracked and Charlie Marshall took time off to give an obscene instruction to the control tower, first in Khmer and afterwards, in the best aviation tradition, in English. Heading for the far end of the runway, they passed a couple of gun emplacements and for a moment Jerry expected an over zealous crew to loose off at the fuselage, till in gratitude he remembered the army colonel and his lorries and his pay-off. Another bottle-fly appeared and this time Jerry took possession of the fly swat. The plane seemed to be gathering no speed at all, but half the instruments read zero so he couldn't be sure. The din of the wheels on the runway seemed louder than the engines. Jerry remembered old Sambo's chauffeur driving him back to school: the slow, inevitable progress down the Western by-pass toward Slough and finally Eton.

A couple of the hillmen had come forward to see the fun and were laughing their heads off. A clump of palm trees came hopping toward them but the plane kept its feet firmly on the ground. Charlie Marshall absently pulled back the stick and retracted the landing gear. Uncertain whether the nose had really lifted, Jerry thought of school again, and competing in the long jump, and recalled the same sensation of not rising, yet ceasing to be on the earth. He felt the jolt and heard the swish of leaves as the underbelly cropped the trees. Charlie Marshall was screaming at the plane to pull itself into the damn air, and for an age they made no height at all, but hung and wheezed a few feet above a winding road which climbed inexorably into a ridge of hills. Charlie Marshall was lighting a cigarette so Jerry held the wheel in front of him and felt the live kick of the rudder. Taking back the controls, Charlie Marshall pointed the plane into a slow bank at the lowest point of the range. He held the turn, crested the range and went on to make a complete circle. As they looked down on the brown rooftops and the river and the airport Jerry reckoned they had an altitude of a thousand feet. As far as Charlie Marshall was concerned, that was a comfortable cruising height, for now at last he took his hat off and, with the air of a man who had done a good job well, treated himself to a large glass of Scotch from the bottle at his feet. Below them dusk was gathering, and the brown earth was fading softly into mauve.

'Thanks,' said Jerry, accepting the bottle. 'Yes, I think I might.'

Jerry kicked off with a little small-talk – if it is possible to talk small while you are shouting at the top of your voice.

'Khmer Rouge just blew up the airport ammunition dump!' he bellowed. 'It is closed for landing and take-off.'

'They did?' For the first time since Jerry had met him, Charlie Marshall seemed both pleased and impressed.

'They say you and Ricardo were great buddies.'

'We bomb everything. We killed half the human race already. We see more dead people than alive people. Plain of Jars, Da Nang, we're such big damn heroes that when we die Jesus Christ going to come down personally with a chopper and fish us out of the jungle.'

'They tell me Ric was a great guy for business!'

'Sure! He the greatest! Know how many offshore companies we got, me and Ricardo? Six. We got foundations in Liechtenstein, corporations in Geneva, we got a bank manager in the Dutch Antilles, lawyers, Jesus. Know how much money I got?' He slapped his back pocket. 'Three hundred US exactly. Charlie Marshall and Ricardo killed half the whole damn human race together. Nobody give us no money. My father killed the other half and he got plenty *plenty* money. Ricardo he always got these crazy schemes always. Shell cases. Jesus. We're going to pay the coons to collect up all the shell cases in Asia, sell 'em for the next war!' The nose dropped and he hauled it up again with a foul French oath. 'Latex! We gotta steal all the latex out of Kampong Cham! We fly to Kampong Cham, we got big choppers, red crosses. So what do we do? We bring out the damn wounded. Hold still, you crazy bastard, hear me?' He was talking to the plane again. In the nose cone, Jerry noticed a long line of bullet holes which had not been very well patched *Tear here*, he thought absurdly. '*Human hair*. We were gonna be millionaires out of hair. All the coon-girls in the villages got to grow long hair and we're going to cut it off and fly it to Bangkok for wigs.'

'Who was it paid Ricardo's debts so that he could fly for Indocharter?'

'Nobody!'

'Somebody told me it was Drake Ko.'

'I never heard of Drake Ko. On my deathbed I tell my mother, my father: bastard Charlie, the General's boy, he never heard of Drake Ko in his life.'

'What did Ricardo do for Ko that was so special that Ko paid all his debts?'

Charlie Marshall drank some whisky straight from the bottle, then handed it to Jerry. His fleshless hands shook wildly whenever he took them off the stick, and his nose ran all the while. Jerry wondered now many pipes a day he was up to. He had once known a *pied-noir* Corsican hotelier in Luang Prabang who needed sixty to do a good day's work. *Captain Marshall never flies in the mornings*, he thought.

'Americans always in a hurry,' Charlie Marshall complained, shaking his head. 'Know why we gotta take this stuff to Phnom Pneh now? Everybody impatient. Everybody want quickshot these days. Nobody got time to smoke. Everybody got to turn on quick. You wanta kill the human race, you gotta take time, hear me?'

Jerry tried again. One of the four engines had given up, but another had developed a howl as if from a broken silencer, so that he had to yell even louder than before.

'What did Ricardo do for all that money?' he repeated.

'Listen, Voltaire, okay? I don't like politics, I'm just a simple opium smuggler, okay? You like politics you go back below and talk to those crazy Shans. "You can't eat politics. You can't screw politics. You can't smoke politics." He tell my father.'

'Who did?'

'Drake Ko tell my father, my father tell me and me I tell the whole damn human race! Drake Ko some philosopher, hear me?'

For its own reasons the plane had begun falling steadily till it was a couple of hundred feet above the paddies. They saw a village and cooking fires burning and figures running wildly towards the trees, and Jerry wondered seriously whether Charlie Marshall had noticed. But at the last minute, like a patient jockey, he hauled and leaned and finally got the horse's head up and they both had some more Scotch.

'You know him well?'

'Who?'

'Ko.'

'I never met him in my life, Voltaire. You wanna talk about Drake Ko, you go ask my father. He cut your throat.'

'How about Tiu? – Tell me, who's the couple with the pig?' Jerry yelled, to keep the conversation going while Charlie took back the bottle for another pull.

'Haw people, down from Chiang Mai. They worried about their lousy son in Phnom Penh. They think he too damn hungry so they take him a pig.'

'So how about Tiu?'

'I never heard of Mr Tiu, hear me?'

'Ricardo was seen up in Chiang Mai three months ago,' Jerry yelled.

'Yeah, well Ric's a damn fool,' said Charlie Marshall with feeling. 'Ric's gotta keep his ass out of Chiang Mai or somebody shoot it right off. Anybody lying dead they gotta keep their damn mouth shut, hear me? I say to him: "Ric, you my partner. Keep you damn mouth shut and your ass out of sight or certain people get personally pretty mad with you."'

The plane entered a raincloud and at once began losing height fast. Rain raced over the iron deck and down the insides of the windows. Charlie Marshall flicked some switches up and down, there was a bleeping from the controls panel and a couple of pinlights came on, which no amount of swearing could put out. To Jerry's amazement they began climbing again, though in the racing cloud he doubted his judgement of the angle. Glancing behind him in order to check, he was in time to glimpse the bearded figure of the dark-skinned paymaster in the Fidel Castro cap retreating down the cabin ladder, holding his AK47 by the barrel. They continued climbing, the rain ended and the night surrounded them like another country. The stars broke suddenly above them, they jolted over the moonlit crevasses of the cloud tops, they lifted again, the cloud vanished for good, and Charlie Marshall put on his hat and announced that both starboard engines had now ceased to play any part in the festivities. In this moment of respite, Jerry asked his maddest question.

'So where's Ricardo now, sport? Got to find him, see. Promised my paper I'd have a word with him. Can't disappoint them, can we?'

Charlie Marshall's sleepy eyes had all but closed. He was sitting in a half-trance, with his head against the seat and the brim of his hat over his nose.

'What that, Voltaire? You speak at all?'

'Where is Ricardo now?'

'Ric?' Charlie Marshall repeated, glancing at Jerry in a sort of wonder. 'Where Ricardo is, Voltaire?'

'That's it, sport. Where is he? I'd like to have an exchange of views with him. That's what the three hundred bucks were about. There's another five hundred if you could find the time to arrange an introduction.'

Springing suddenly to life, Charlie Marshall delved for the *Candide* and slammed it into Jerry's lap while he delivered himself of a furious outburst.

'I don't know where Ricardo is *ever*, hear me? I never don't want a friend in my life. If I see that crazy Ricardo I shoot his balls right off in the street, hear me? He dead. So he can stay dead till he dies. He tell everyone he got killed. So maybe for once in my life I'm going to believe that bastard!'

Pointing the plane angrily into the cloud, he let it fall toward the slow flashes of Phnom Penh's artillery batteries to make a perfect three point landing in what to Jerry was pitch darkness. He waited for the burst of machine-gun fire from the ground defences, he waited for the sickening free-fall as they nose-dived into a mammoth crater, but all he saw, quite suddenly, was a newly assembled *revêtement* of the familiar mud-filled ammunition boxes, arms open and palely lit, waiting to receive them. As they taxied toward it a brown jeep pulled in front of them with a green light winking on the back, like a flashlight being turned on and off by hand. The plane was humping over grass. Hard beside the *revêtement* Jerry could see a pair of green lorries, and a tight knot of waiting figures, looking anxiously toward them, and behind them the dark shadow of a twin-engined sports plane. They parked, and Jerry heard at once from the hold beneath their penthouse the creak of the nose cone opening, followed by the clatter of feet on the iron ladder and the quick call and answer of voices. The speed of their departure took him by surprise. But he heard something else that turned his blood cold, and made him charge down the steps to the belly of the plane.

'Ricardo!' he yelled 'Stop! Ricardo!'

But the only passengers left were the old couple clutching their pig and their parcel. Seizing the steel ladder, he let himself fall, jolting his spine as he hit the tarmac. The jeep had already left with the Chinese cooks and their Shan bodyguard. As he ran forward, Jerry could see the jeep racing for an open gateway at the perimeter of the airfield. It passed through, two sentries slammed the gates and took up their position as before. Behind him, the helmeted flight-handlers were already swarming toward the Carvair. A couple of lorryloads of police looked on and for a moment the western fool in Jerry was seduced into thinking they might be playing some restraining rôle, till he realized they were Phnom Penh's guard-of-honour for a three-ton load opium. But his main eye was for one figure only, and that was the tall bearded man with the Fidel Castro hat and the AK47 and the heavy limp that sounded like a hard-soft drumbeat as the rubber-soled flying boots hobbled down the steel ladder. Jerry saw him just. The door of the little Beechcraft waited open for him, and there were two ground-crew poised to help him in. As he reached them, they held out their hands for the rifle but Ricardo waved them aside. He had turned and was looking for Jerry. For a second they saw each other. Jerry was falling and Ricardo was lifting the gun, and for twenty seconds Jerry reviewed his life from birth till now while a few more bullets ripped and whined round the battletorn air field. By the time Jerry looked up again the firing had stopped, Ricardo was inside the plane and his helpers were pulling away the chocks. As the little plane lifted into the flashes, Jerry ran like the devil for the darkest part of the perimeter before anybody else decided that his presence was obstructive to good trading.

*Just a lovers' tiff*, he told himself, sitting in the cab, as he held his hands over his head and tried to damp down the wild shaking of his chest. That's what you get for trying to play footsy-footsy with an old flame of Lizzie Worthington.

Somewhere a rocket fell and he didn't give a damn.

He allowed Charlie Marshall two hours, though he reckoned one was generous. It was past curfew but the day's crisis had not ended with the dark, there were traffic checks all the way to le Phnom and the sentries held their machine pistols at the ready. In the square, two men were screaming at each other by torchlight before a gathering crowd. Further down the boulevard, troops had surrounded a floodlit house and were leaning against the wall of it, fingering their guns. The driver said the secret police had made an arrest there. A colonel and his people were still inside with a suspected agitator. In the hotel forecourt, tanks were parked, and in his bedroom he found Luke lying on the bed drinking contentedly.

'Any water?' Jerry asked.

'Yip.'

He turned on the bath and started to undress until he remembered the Walther.

'Filed?' he asked.

'Yip,' said Luke again. 'And so have you.'

'Ha ha.'

'I had Keller cable Stubbsie under your byline.'

'The airport story?'

Luke handed him a tearsheet. 'Added some true Westerby colour. How the buds are bursting in the cemeteries. Stubbsie loves you.'

'Well thanks.'

In the bathroom Jerry unstuck the Walther from the plaster and slipped it in the pocket of his jacket where he would be able to get at it.

'Where we going tonight?' Luke called, through the closed door.

'Nowhere.'

'Hell's that mean?'

'I've got a date.'

'A woman?'

'Yes.'

'Take Lukie. Three in a bed.'

Jerry sank gratefully into the tepid water. 'No.'

'Call her. Tell her to whip a whore for Lukie. Listen, there's that hooker from Santa Barbara downstairs. I'm not proud. I'll bring her.'

'No.'

'For Christ's sakes,' Luke shouted, now serious. 'Why the hell not?' He had come right to the locked door to make his protest.

'Sport, you've got to get off my back,' Jerry advised. 'Honest. I love you but you're not everything to me, right? So stay off.'

'Thorn in your breeches, huh?' Long silence. 'Well don't get your ass shot off, pardner, it's a stormy night out there.'

When Jerry returned to the bedroom, Luke lay on the bed in the foetal position staring at the wall and drinking methodically.

'You know you're worse than a bloody woman,' Jerry told him, pausing at the door to look back at him.

The whole childish exchange would not have caused him another moment's thought, had it not been for the way things turned out afterwards.

This time Jerry didn't bother with the bell on the gate, but climbed the wall and grazed his hands on the broken glass that ran along the top of it. He didn't make for the front door either, or go through the formality of watching the brown legs standing on the bottom stair. Instead, he stood in the garden waiting for the clump of his heavy landing to fade and for his eyes and ears to catch a sign of habitation from the big villa which loomed darkly above him with the moon behind it.

A car drew up without lights and two figures got out, by their size and quietness Cambodian. They pressed the gate bell, and at the front door murmured the magic password through the crack, and were instantly, silently admitted. Jerry tried to fathom the layout. It puzzled him that no telltale smell escaped either from the front of the house or into the garden where he stood. There was no wind. He knew that for a large *divan* secrecy was vital, not because the law was punitive, but because the bribes were. The villa possessed a chimney and a courtyard and two floors: a place to live comfortably as a French *colon*, with a little family of concubines and half-caste children. The kitchen, he guessed, would be given over to preparation. The safest place to smoke would undoubtedly be upstairs, in rooms which looked on to the courtyard. And since there was no smell from the front door, Jerry reckoned that they were using the rear of the courtyard rather than the wings or the front.

He trod soundlessly till he came to the paling which marked the rear boundary. It was lush with flowers and creeper. A barred window gave a first foothold to his buckskin boot, and overflow pipe a second, a high extractor fan a third, and as he climbed past it to the upper balcony he caught the smell he expected: warm and sweet and beckoning. On the balcony there was still no light, though the two Cambodian girls who squatted there were easily visible in the moonlight, and he could see their scared eyes fixing him as he appeared out of the sky. Beckoning them to their feet, he walked them ahead of him, led by the smell. The shelling had stopped, leaving the night to the geckos. Jerry remembered that Cambodians liked to gamble on the number of times they cheeped: tomorrow will be a lucky day; tomorrow won't; tomorrow I will take a bride; no, the day after. The girls were very young and they must have been waiting for the customers to send for them. At the rush door they hesitated and stared unhappily back at him. Jerry signalled and they began pulling aside layers of matting until a pale light gleamed on to the balcony, no stronger than a candle. He stepped inside, keeping the girls ahead of him.

The room must once have been the master bedroom, with a second, smaller room connecting. He had his hand on the shoulder of one girl. The other followed submissively. Twelve customers lay in the first room, all men. A few girls lay between them, whispering. Barefooted coolies ministered, moving with great deliberation from one recumbent body to the next, threading a pellet on to the needle, lighting it and holding it across the bowl of the pipe while the customer took a long steady draught and the pellet burned itself out. The conversation was slow and murmured and intimate, broken by soft ripples of grateful laughter. Jerry recognized the wise Swiss from the Counsellor's dinner party. He was chatting to a fat Cambodian. No one was interested in Jerry. Like the orchids at Lizzie Worthington's apartment block, the girls authenticated him.

'Charlie Marshall,' Jerry said quietly. A coolie pointed to the next room. Jerry dismissed the two girls and they slipped away. The second room was smaller and Marshall lay in the corner, while a Chinese girl in an elaborate *cheongsam* crouched over him preparing his pipe. Jerry supposed she was the daughter of the house, and that Charlie Marshall was getting the grand treatment because he was both an habitué and a supplier. He knelt the other side of him. An old man was watching from the doorway. The girl watched also, the pipe still in her hands.

'What you want, Voltaire? Why don't you leave me be?'

'Just a little stroll, sport. Then you can come back.'

Taking his arm, Jerry lifted him gently to his feet, while the girl helped.

'How much has he had?' he asked the girl. She held up three fingers.

'And how many does he like?' he asked.

She lowered her head, smiling, A whole lot more, she was saying.

Charlie Marshall walked shakily at first, but by the time they reached the balcony he was prepared to argue, so Jerry lifted him up and carried him across his body like a fire victim down the wooden steps and across the courtyard. The old man bowed them obligingly through the front door, a grinning coolie held the gate on to the street, and both were clearly very thankful to Jerry for showing so much tact. They had gone perhaps fifty yards when a pair of Chinese boys came rushing down the road at them, yelling and waving sticks like small paddles. Setting Charlie Marshall upright but holding him firmly with his left hand, Jerry let the first boy strike, deflected the paddle then hit him at half strength with a two-knuckle punch just below the eye. The boy ran away, his friend after him. Still clutching Charlie Marshall, Jerry walked him till they came to the river, and a heavy patch of darkness, then he sat him down on the bank like a puppet in the sloped, dry grass.

'You gonna blow my brains out, Voltaire?'

'We're going to have to leave that to the opium, sport,' said Jerry.

Jerry liked Charlie Marshall and in a perfect world he would have been glad to spend an evening with him at the *fumerie* and hear the story of his wretched but extraordinary life. But now his fist grasped Charlie Marshall's tiny arm remorselessly lest he took it into his hollow head to bolt; for he had a feeling Charlie could run very fast when he became desperate. He half-lay, therefore, much as he had lounged among the magic mountain of possessions in old Pet's place, on his left haunch and his left elbow, holding Charlie Marshall's wrist into the mud, while Charlie Marshall lay flat on his back. From the river thirty feet below them came the murmured chant of the sampans as they drifted like long leaves across the golden moon-path. From the sky – now in front, now behind them – came the occasional ragged flashes of outgoing gunfire as some bored battery commander decided to justify his existence. Now and then, from much nearer, came the lighter, sharper snap as the Khmer Rouge replied, but once more these were only tiny interludes between the racket of the geckos, and the greater silence beyond. By the moonlight Jerry looked at his watch, then at the crazed face, trying to calculate the strength of Charlie Marshall's cravings. Like a baby's feed, he thought. If Charlie was a night smoker and slept in the mornings, then his needs must come on fast. The wet on his face was already unearthly. It flowed from the heavy pores and from the stretched eyes, and from the sniffing, weeping nose. It channelled itself meticulously along the engraved creases, making neat reservoirs in the caverns.

'Jesus, Voltaire. Ricardo's my friend. He got a lot of philosophy, that guy. You want to hear him talk, Voltaire. You wanna hear his ideas.'

'Yes,' Jerry agreed 'I do.'

Charlie Marshall grabbed hold of Jerry's hand.

'Voltaire, these are good guys, hear me? Mr Tiu . . . Drake Ko. They don't want to hurt nobody. They wanna do business. They got something to sell, they got people buying it! It's a service! Nobody gets his ricebowl broken. Why you want to screw that up? You're a nice guy, yourself. I saw. You carry the old boy's pig, okay? Whoever saw a roundeye carry a slanteye pig before? But Jesus, Voltaire, you screw it out of me, they will kill you very completely because Mr Tiu, he's businesslike and very philosophical gentleman, hear me? They kill *me*, they kill *Ricardo*, they kill *you*, they kill the whole damn human race!'

The artillery fired a barrage, and this time the jungle replied with a small salvo of missiles, perhaps six, which hissed over their heads like whirring boulders from a catapult. Moments later they heard the detonations somewhere in the centre of the town. After them, nothing. Not the wail of a fire engine, not the siren of an ambulance.

'Why would they kill *Ricardo*?' Jerry asked. 'What's *Ricardo* done wrong?'

'Voltaire! Ricardo's my friend! Drake Ko my father's friend! Those old men big brothers, they fight some lousy war together in Shanghai about two hundred and fifty years ago okay? I go see my father. I tell him: "Father, you gotta love me once. You gotta quit calling me your spider-bastard, and you gotta tell your good friend Drake Ko to take the heat off Ricardo. You gotta say 'Drake Ko, that Ricardo and my Charlie, they are like you and me. They brothers, same as us. They learn to fly together in Oklahoma, they kill the human race together. And they some pretty good friends. And that's a fact.'" My father hate me very bad, okay.'

'Okay.'

'But he send Drake Ko a damn long personal message all the same.'

Charlie Marshall breathes in, on and on, as if his little breast could scarcely hold enough air to feed him. 'That Lizzie. She some woman. Lizzie, she go personally to Drake Ko herself. Also on a very private basis. And she say to him: "Mr Ko, you gotta take the heat off Ric." That's a very delicate situation there, Voltaire. We all got to hold on to each other tight or we fall off the crazy mountain top, hear me? Voltaire, let me go. I beg! I completely beg for Christ's sake, *je m'abîme*, hear me? That's all I know!'

Watching him, listening to his racked outbursts, how he collapsed and rallied and broke again and rallied less, Jerry felt he was witnessing the last martyred writhing of a friend. His instinct was to lead Charlie slowly and let him ramble. His dilemma was that he didn't know how much time he had before whatever happens to an addict happened. He asked questions but often Charlie didn't seem to hear them. At other times he appeared to answer questions Jerry hadn't put. And sometimes a delayed action mechanism threw out an answer to a question which Jerry had long abandoned. At Sarratt, the inquisitors said, a broken man was dangerous because he paid you money he didn't have in order to buy your love. But for whole precious minutes Charlie could pay nothing at all.

'Drake Ko never went to Vientiane in his life!' Charlie yelled suddenly. 'You crazy, Voltaire! A big guy like Ko bothering with a dirty little Asian town? Drake Ko some philosopher, Voltaire! You wanna watch that guy pretty careful!' Everyone, it seemed, was some philosopher – or everyone but Charlie Marshall. 'In Vientiane nobody even hear Ko's name! Hear me, Voltaire?'

At another point, Charlie Marshall wept and seized Jerry's hands and inquired between sobs whether Jerry also had had a father.

'Yes, sport, I did,' said Jerry patiently. 'And in his way, he was a general too.'

Over the river two white flares shed an amazing daylight, inspiring Charlie to reminisce on the hardships of their early days together in Vientiane. Sitting bolt upright, he drew a house in diagram in the mud. That's where Lizzie and Ric and Charlie Marshall lived, he said proudly: in a stinking flea-hut on the edge of town, a place so lousy even the geckos got sick from it. Ric and Lizzie had the royal suite, which was the only room this flea-hut contained and Charlie's job was to keep out of the way and pay the rent and fetch the booze. But the memory of their dreadful economic plight moved Charlie suddenly to a fresh storm of tears.

'So what did you live on, sport?' Jerry asked, expecting nothing from the question. 'Come on. It's over now. What did you live on?'

More tears while Charlie confessed to a monthly allowance from his father, whom he loved and revered.

'That crazy Lizzie' – said Charlie through his grief – 'that crazy Lizzie she make trips to Hong Kong for Mellon.'

Somehow Jerry contrived to keep himself steady in order not to shake Charlie from his course.

'*Mellon*. Who's this Mellon?' he asked. But the soft tone made Charlie sleepy, and he started playing with the mud-house, adding a chimney and smoke.

'Come on damn you! *Mellon. Mellon!*' Jerry shouted straight into Charlie's face, trying to shock him into replying. '*Mellon*, you hashed-out wreck! Trips to Hong Kong!' Lifting Charlie to his feet he shook him like a rag doll, but it took a lot more shaking to produce the answer, and in the course of it Charlie Marshall implored Jerry to understand what it was like to love, really to love, a crazy roundeye hooker and know you could never have her, even for a night.

Mellon was a creepy English trader, nobody knew what he did. A little of this, a little of that, Charlie said. People were scared of him. Mellon said he could get Lizzie into the bigtime heroin trail. 'With your passport and your body,' Mellon had told her, 'you can go in and out of Hong Kong like a princess.'

Exhausted, Charlie sank to the ground and crouched before his mud-house. Squatting beside him, Jerry fastened his fist on the back of Charlie's collar, careful not to hurt him.

'So she did that for him did she, Charlie? Lizzie carried for Mellon.' With this palm, he gently tipped Charlie's head round till his lost eyes were staring straight at him.

'Lizzie don't carry for *Mellon*, Voltaire,' Charlie corrected him. 'Lizzie carry for *Ricardo*. Lizzie don't love Mellon. She love *Ric* and me.'

Staring glumly at the mud-house, Charlie burst suddenly into raucous dirty laughter, which then petered out with no explanation.

'You louse it up, Lizzie!' Charlie called teasingly, poking a finger into the mud door. 'You louse it up as usual, honey! You talk too much. Why you tell everyone you Queen of England? Why you tell everyone you some great spook-lady? Mellon get very very mad with you, Lizzie. Mellon throw you out, right out on your ass. Ric got pretty mad too, remember? Ric smash you up real bad and Charlie have to take you to the doctor in the middle of the damn night, remember? You got one hell of a big mouth, Lizzie, hear me? You my sister, but you got the biggest damn mouth *ever*!'

Till Ricardo closed it for her, Jerry thought, remembering the grooves on her chin. Because she spoiled the deal with Mellon.

Still crouching at Charlie's side and clutching him by the scruff, Jerry watched the world around him vanish and in place of it he saw Sam Collins sitting in his car below Star Heights, with a clear view of the eighth floor, while he studied the racing page of the newspaper at eleven o'clock at night. Not even the clump of a rocket falling quite close could distract him from that freezing vision. Also he heard Craw's voice above the mortar fire, intoning on the subject of Lizzie's criminality. When funds were low, Craw had said, Ricardo had made her carry little parcels across frontiers for him.

And how did London-town learn *that*, your Grace – he would have liked to ask old Craw – if not from Sam Collins alias Mellon himself?

A three-second rainstorm had washed away Charlie's house and he was furious about it. He was splashing around on all fours looking for it, weeping and cursing frantically. The fit passed, and he started talking about his father again, and how the old man had found employment for his natural son with a certain distinguished Vientiane airline – though Charlie till then had been quite keen to get out of flying for good on account of losing his nerve.

One day, it seemed, the General just lost patience with Charlie. He called together his bodyguard and came down from his hilltop in the Shans to a little opium town called Fang not far inside the Thai border. There, after the fashion of patriarchs the world over, the General rebuked Charlie for his spendthrift ways.

Charlie had a special squawk for his father, and a special way of puffing out his wasted cheeks in military disapproval:

'"So you better do some proper damn work for a change hear me, you *kwailo* spider-bastard? You better stay away from horse gambling, hear me, and strong liquor, and opium. And you better take those Commie stars off your tits and sack that stink-friend Ricardo of yours. And you better cease financing his woman, hear me? Because I don't gonna keep you one day more, not one *hour*, you spider-bastard, and I hate you so much one day I kill you because you remind me of that Corsican whore your mother!'"

Then the job itself, and Charlie's father the General still speaking:

"'Certain very fine Chiu Chow gentlemen who are pretty good friends of pretty good friends of mine, hear me, happen to have a controlling interest in a certain aviation company. Also I got certain shares in that company. Also this company happens to bear the distinguished title of Indocharter Aviation. Why you laugh, you *kwailo* ape! Don't laugh at me! So these good friends, they do me a favour to assist me in my disgrace for my three-legged spider-bastard son and I pray sincerely you may fall out of the sky and break your *kwailo* neck.'"

So Charlie flew his father's opium for Indocharter: one, two flights a week at first, but regular, honest work and he liked it. His nerve came back, he steadied down, and he felt real gratitude toward his old man. He tried, of course, to get the Chiu Chow boys to take Ricardo too but they wouldn't. After a few months they did agree to pay Lizzie twenty bucks a week to sit in the front office and sweetmouth the clients. These were the golden days, Charlie implied. Charlie and Lizzie earned the money, Ricardo wasted it on ever crazier enterprises, everybody was happy, everybody was employed. Till one evening, like a Nemesis, Tiu appeared and screwed the whole thing up. He appeared just as they were locking up the company's offices, straight off the pavement without an appointment, asking for Charlie Marshall by name and describing himself as part of the company's Bangkok management. The Chiu Chow boys came out of the back office, took one look at Tiu, vouched for his good faith, and made themselves scarce.

Charlie broke off in order to weep on Jerry's shoulder.

'Now listen to me carefully, sport,' Jerry urged. 'Listen. This is the bit I like, okay? You tell me this bit carefully, and I'll take you home. Promise. *Please.*'

But Jerry had it wrong. It was no longer a matter of making Charlie talk. Jerry was now the drug on which Charlie Marshall depended. It was no longer a matter of holding him down, either. Charlie Marshall clutched Jerry's breast as if it were the last raft on his lonely sea, and their conversation had become a desperate monologue from which Jerry stole his facts while Charlie Marshall cringed and begged and howled for his tormentor's attention, making jokes and laughing at them through his tears. Downriver one of Lon Nol's machine guns which had not yet been sold to the Khmer Rouge was firing tracer into the jungle by the light of another flare. Long golden bolts flowed in streams above and below the water, and lit a small cave where they disappeared into the trees.

Charlie's sweat-soaked hair was pricking Jerry's chin and Charlie was gabbling and dribbling all at the same time.

'Mr Tiu don't wanna talk in no office, Voltaire. Oh no! Mr Tiu don't dress too good, either. Tiu very Chiu Chow person, he use Thai passport like Drake Ko, he use crazy name and keep a very very low appearance when he come to Vientiane. "Captain Marshall," he say to me, "how you like earn a lot of extra cash by performing certain interesting and varied work outside the Company's hours, tell me? How you like fly a certain unconventional journey for me once? They tell me you some pretty damn fine pilot these days, very steady. How you like to earn yourself not less than maybe four to five thousand bucks for one day's work, not even a whole day? How would that personally attract you, Captain Marshall?" "Mr Tiu," I tell him' – Charlie is shouting hysterically now – '"without in any way prejudicing my negotiating position, Mr Tiu, for five thousand bucks US in my present serene mood I go down to hell for you and I bring you the devil's balls back." Mr Tiu say he come back one day and I gotta keep my damn mouth shut.'

Suddenly Charlie had changed to his father's voice and he was calling himself a spider-bastard and the son of a Corsican whore: till gradually it dawned on Jerry that Charlie was describing the next episode in the story.

Amazingly, it turned out, Charlie had kept to himself the secret of Tiu's offer until he next saw his father, this time in Chiang Mai for a celebration of the Chinese New Year. He had not told Ric, and he had not even told Lizzie, maybe because at this point they weren't getting on too well any more, and Ric was having himself a lot of women on the side.

The General's counsel was not encouraging.

"'Don't you touch that horse! That Tiu got some pretty highly big connections, and they all a bit too special for a crazy little spider-bastard like you, hear me! Jesus Christ, who ever heard of a Swatownese give five thousand dollars to a lousy half-*kwailo* to improve his mind with travel!'"

'So you passed the deal to Ric, right?' said Jerry quickly. 'Right, Charlie? You told Tiu "sorry but try Ricardo". Is that how it went?'

But Charlie Marshall was missing believed dead. He had fallen straight off Jerry's chest and lay flat in the mud with his eyes closed and only his occasional gulps for breath – greedy, rasping draughts of it – and the crazy beating of his pulse where Jerry held his wrist, testified to the life inside the frame.

'Voltaire,' Charlie whispered. 'On the Bible, Voltaire. You're a good man. Take me home. Jesus, take me home, Voltaire.'

Stunned, Jerry stared at the prone and broken figure and knew that he had to ask one more question, even if it was the last in both their lives. Reaching down, he dragged Charlie to his feet for the last time. And there, for an hour in the black road, struggling on his arm, while more aimless barrages stabbed the darkness, Charlie Marshall screamed and begged, and swore he would love Jerry always if only he didn't have to reveal what arrangements his friend Ricardo had made for his survival. But Jerry explained that without that, the mystery was not even half revealed. And perhaps Charlie Marshall, in his ruin and despair, as he sobbed out the forbidden secrets, understood Jerry's reasoning: that in a city about to be given back to the jungle, there was no destruction unless it was complete.

As gently as he could, Jerry carried Charlie Marshall down the road, back to the villa and up the steps, where the same silent faces gratefully received him. I should have got more, he thought. I should have told him more as well: I didn't tend the two-way traffic in the way they ordered. I stayed too long with the business of Lizzie and Sam Collins. I did it upside-down, I foozled my shopping list, I loused it up like Lizzie. He tried to feel sorry about that but he couldn't, and the things he remembered best were the things that weren't on the list at all, and they were the same things that stood up in his mind like monuments while he typed his message to dear old George.

He typed with the door locked and the gun in his belt. There was no sign of Luke, so Jerry assumed he had gone off to a whorehouse still in his drunken sulk. It was a long signal, the longest of his career: 'Know this much in case you don't hear from me again.' He reported his contact with the Counsellor, he gave his next port of call, and gave Ricardo's address, and a portrait of Charlie Marshall, and of the three-sided household in the flea-hut, but only in the most formal terms, and he left out entirely his newfound knowledge regarding the rôle played by the unsavoury Sam Collins. After all, if they knew it already what was the point of telling it to them again? He left out the place names and the proper names and made a separate key of them then spent another hour putting the two messages into a first-base code which wouldn't fool a cryptographer for five minutes, but was beyond the ken of ordinary mortals, and of mortals like his host the British Counsellor. He ended with a reminder to housekeepers to check whether Blatt and Rodney had made that latest money-draft to Cat. He burned the *en clair* texts, rolled the encoded versions into a newspaper, then lay on the newspaper and dozed, the gun awkwardly at his side. At six he shaved, transferred his signals to a paperback novel which he felt able to part with, and took himself for a walk in the morning quiet. In the *place*, the Counsellor's car was parked conspicuously. The Counsellor himself was parked equally conspicuously on the terrace of a pretty bistro, wearing a Riviera straw hat reminiscent of Craw, and treating himself to hot croissants and *café au lait*. Seeing Jerry, he gave an elaborate wave. Jerry wandered over to him.

'Morning,' said Jerry.

'Ah, you've got it! Good man!' the Counsellor cried, bounding to his feet. 'Been *longing* to read it ever since it came out!'

Parting with the signal, conscious only of its omissions, Jerry had a feeling of end-of-term. He might come back, he might not, but things would never be quite the same, again.

The exact circumstances of Jerry's departure from Phnom Penh are relevant because of Luke, later.

For the first part of the morning that remained, Jerry pursued his obsessional search for cover, which was the natural antidote, perhaps, to his increasing sense of nakedness. Diligently he went on the stomp for refugee and orphan stories which he filed through Keller at midday, together with a quite decent atmosphere piece on his visit to Battambang, which though never used has at least a place in his dossier. There were two refugee camps at that time, both blossoming, one in an enormous hotel on the Bassac, Siha-nouk's personal and unfinished dream of paradise; one in the marshalling yards near the airport, two or three families packed in each carriage. He visited both and they were the same; young Australian heroes struggling with the impossible, the only water filthy, a rice handout twice a week and the children chirruping 'hi' and 'bye bye' after him, while he trailed his Cambo-dian interpreter up and down their lines, besieging everyone with questions, acting large and looking for that extra something that would melt Stubbsie's heart.

At a travel office he noisily booked a passage to Bangkok in a feeble attempt to brush over his tracks. Making for the airport, he had a sudden sense of *déjà vu*. Last time I was here, I went water-skiing, he thought. The roundeye traders kept houseboats moored along the Mekong. And for a moment he saw himself – and the city – in the days when the Cambodian war still had a certain ghastly innocence: ace operator Westerby, risking mono for the first time, bouncing boyishly over the brown water of the Mekong, towed by a jolly

Dutchman in a speed launch which burned enough petrol to feed a family for a week. The greatest hazard was the two-foot wave, he remembered, which rolled down the river every time the guards on the bridge let off a depth charge to prevent Khmer Rouge divers from blowing it up. But now the river was theirs, so was the jungle. And so, tomorrow or the next day, was the town.

At the airport, he ditched the Walther in a rubbish bin and at the last minute bribed his way aboard a plane to Saigon which was his destination. Taking off, he wondered who had the longer expectation of survival: himself or the city.

Luke, on the other hand, with the key to Jerry's Hong Kong flat nestling in his pocket presumably – or more properly to Deathwish the Hun's flat – flew to Bangkok, and as luck had it he flew unwittingly under Jerry's name, since Jerry was on the flight list, and Luke was not, and the remaining places were all taken. In Bangkok he attended a hasty bureau conference at which the magazine's local manpower was carved up between various bits of the crumbling Vietnam front. Luke got Hue and Da Nang, and accordingly left for Saigon next day, and thence north by connecting midday plane.

Contrary to later rumour, the two men did not meet in Saigon.

Nor did they meet in the course of the Northern rollback.

The last they saw of each other, in any mutual sense, was on that final evening in Phnom Penh, when Jerry had bawled Luke out and Luke had sulked, and that is a fact – a commodity which was afterwards notoriously hard to come by.

# SEVENTEEN

# *Ricardo*

At no time in the entire case did George Smiley hold the ring with such tenacity as now. In the Circus, nerves were stretched to snapping point. The bloody inertia and the bouts of frenzy which Sarratt habitually warned against became one and the same. Each day that brought no hard news from Hong Kong was another day of disaster. Jerry's long signal was put under the microscope and held to be ambiguous, then neurotic. Why had he not pressed Marshall harder? Why had he not raised the Russian spectre again? He should have grilled Charlie about the goldseam, he should have carried on where he left off with Tiu. Had he forgotten that his main job was to sow alarm and only afterwards to obtain information? As to his obsession with that wretched daughter of his – God Almighty, doesn't the fellow *know* what signals cost? (They seemed to forget it was the Cousins who were footing the bill.) And what was all this about having no more to do with the British Embassy officials standing proxy for the absent Circus resident? All right, there had been a delay in the pipeline in getting the signal across from the Cousins' side of the house. Jerry had still run Charlie Marshall to earth, hadn't he? It was absolutely no part of a fieldman's job to dictate the do's and don'ts to London. Housekeeping Section, who had arranged the contact, wanted him rebuked by return.

Pressure from outside the Circus was even fiercer. Colonial Wilbraham's faction had not been idle, and the Steering Group, in a startling about-turn, decided that the Governor of Hong Kong should after all be informed of the case, and soon. There was high talk of calling him back to London on a pretext. The panic had arisen because Ko had once more been received at Government House, this time at one of the Governor's talk-in suppers, at which influential Chinese were invited to air their opinions off the record.

By contrast, Saul Enderby and his fellow hardliners pulled the opposite way: 'To hell with the Governor. What we want is full partnership with the Cousins immediately!' George should go to Martello *today*, said Enderby, and make a clean breast of the whole case, and invite them to take over the last stage of development. He should stop playing hide-and-seek about Nelson, he should admit that he had no resources, he should let the Cousins compute the possible intelligence dividend for themselves, and if they brought the job off, so much the better: let them claim the credit on Capitol Hill, to the confusion of their enemies. The result of this generous and timely gesture, Enderby argued – coming bang in the middle of the Vietnam fiasco – would be an indissoluble intelligence partnership for years to come, a view which in his shifty way, Lacon seemed to support. Caught in the crossfire, Smiley suddenly found himself saddled with a double reputation. The Wilbraham set branded him as anti-colonial and pro-American, while Enderby's men accused him of ultra-conservatism in the handling of the special relationship. Much more serious, however, was Smiley's impression that some hint of the row had reached Martello by other routes, and that he would be able to exploit it. For example, Molly Meakin's sources spoke of a burgeoning relationship between Enderby and Martello at the personal level, and not just because their children were all being educated at the Lycée in South Kensington. It seemed that the two men had taken to fishing together in Scotland at weekends, where Enderby had a bit of water. Martello supplied the plane, said the joke later, and Enderby supplied the fish. Smiley also learned around this time, in his unworldly way, what everyone else had known from the beginning and assumed he knew too. Enderby's third and newest wife was American, and rich. Before their marriage she had been a considerable hostess of the Washington establishment, a rôle she was now repeating with some success in London.

But the underlying cause of everybody's agitation was finally the same. On the Ko front, nothing ultimately was happening. Worse still, there was an agonizing shortage of operational intelligence. Every day now, at ten o'clock, Smiley and Guillam presented themselves at the Annexe, and every day came away less satisfied. Tiu's domestic telephone line was tapped, so was Lizzie Worthington's. The tapes were locally monitored, then flown back to London for detailed processing. Jerry had sweated Charlie Marshall on a Wednesday. On the Friday, Charlie was sufficiently recovered from his ordeal to ring Tiu from Bangkok and pour out his heart to him. But after listening for less than thirty seconds Tiu cut him short with an instruction to 'get in touch with Harry right away' which left everybody mystified: nobody had a Harry anywhere. On the Saturday there was drama because the watch on Ko's home number had him cancelling his regular Sunday morning golf date with Mr Arpego. Ko pleaded a pressing business engagement. This was it! This was the breakthrough! Next day, with Smiley's consent, the Hong Kong Cousins locked a surveillance van, two cars and a Honda on to Ko's Rolls-Royce as it entered town. What secret mission, at five thirty on a Sunday morning, was so important to Ko that he would abandon his weekly golf? The answer turned out to be his fortune-teller, a venerable old Swatownese who operated from a seedy spirit temple in a side street off the Hollywood Road. Ko spent more than an hour with him before returning home, and though some zealous child inside one of the Cousins' vans trained a concealed directional microphone on the temple window for the entire session, the only sounds he recorded apart from the traffic turned out to be cluckings from the old man's henhouse. Back at the Circus, di Salis was called in. What on earth would anyone be going to the fortune-teller at six in the morning for, least of all a millionaire?

Greatly amused by their perplexity, di Salis twirled his hair in delight. A man of Ko's standing would insist on being the first client in a fortune-teller's day, he said, while the great man's mind was still clear to receive the intimations of the spirits.

Then nothing happened for five weeks. Nothing. The mail and phone checks spewed out wads of indigestible raw material, which when refined produced not a single intelligence lead. Meanwhile, the artificial deadline imposed by the Enforcement Agency drew steadily nearer, on which day Ko should become open game for whoever could pin something on him soonest.

Yet Smiley kept his head. He resisted all recriminations, both of his own handling of the case, and of Jerry's. The tree had been shaken, he maintained, Ko was running scared, time would show they were right. He refused to be hustled into some dramatic gesture to Martello, and he held resolutely to the terms of the deal which he had outlined in his letter, and of which a copy now lodged with Lacon. He also refused, as his charter allowed him, to enter into any discussion of operational detail, either God or the forces of logic or better, the forces of Ko's except where issues of protocol or local mandate were concerned. To give way on this, he knew very well, would only have meant providing the doubters with fresh ammunition with which to shoot him down.

He held this line for five weeks and on the thirty-sixth day, either God or the forces of logic, or, better, the forces of Ko's human chemistry, delivered to Smiley a substantial, if mysterious, consolation. Ko took to the water. Accompanied by Tiu and an unknown Chinese later identified as the lead captain of Ko's junk fleet, he spent the better part of three days touring the Hong Kong out-islands, returning each evening at dusk. Where they went, there was as yet no telling. Martello proposed a series of helicopter overflights to observe their course but Smiley turned down the suggestion flat. Static surveillance from the quayside confirmed that they apparently left and returned by a different route each day, and that was all. And on the last day, the fourth, the boat did not return at all.

Panic. Where had it gone? Martello's masters in Langley, Virginia, flew into a complete spin and decided that Ko and the *Admiral Nelson* had deliberately strayed into China waters. Even that they had been abducted. Ko would never be seen again, and Enderby, going downhill fast, actually telephoned Smiley and told him it would be 'your damn fault if Ko pops up in Peking yelling the odds about secret service persecution'. Even Smiley, for one agonizing day, secretly wondered whether, against all reason, Ko had indeed gone to join his brother.

Then, of course, next morning early, the launch calmly sailed back into the main harbour looking as if it had just returned from a regatta, and Ko gaily disembarked, following his beautiful Liese down the gangway, her gold hair trailing in the sunlight like a soap commercial.

It was this intelligence which, after very long thought and a renewed and detailed reading of Ko's file – not to mention much tense debate with Connie and di Salis – determined Smiley to take two decisions at once, or in gambler's terms, to play the only two cards that were left to him.

One: Jerry should advance to the 'last stage', by which Smiley meant Ricardo. He hoped by this step to maintain the pressure on Ko, and provide Ko, if he needed it, with the final proof that he must act.

Two: Sam Collins should 'go in'.

This second decision was reached in consultation with Connie Sachs alone. It finds no mention on Jerry's main dossier, but only in a secret appendix later released, with deletions, for wider scrutiny.

The fragmenting effect upon Jerry of these delays and hesitations was something not the greatest intelligence chief on earth could have included in his calculations. To be aware of it was one thing – and Smiley undoubtedly was, and even took one or two steps to forestall it. To be guided by it, to set it on the same plane as the factors of high policy which he was having daily fired at him, would have been downright irresponsible. A general is nothing without priorities.

The fact remains that Saigon was the worst place on earth for Jerry to be kicking his heels. Periodically, as the delays dragged on, there was talk at the Circus of sending him somewhere more salubrious, for instance to Singapore or Kuala Lumpur, but the arguments of expediency and cover always kept him where he was: besides, tomorrow everything might change. There was also the matter of his personal safety. Hong Kong was not to be considered, and in both Singapore and Bangkok Ko's influence was sure to be strong. Then cover again: with the collapse approaching, where more natural than Saigon? Yet it was a half life Jerry lived, and in a half town. For forty years, give or take, war had been Saigon's staple industry, but the American pullout of seventy-three had produced a slump from which, to the end, the city never properly recovered, so that even this long-awaited final act, with its cast of millions, was playing to quite poor audiences. Even when he took his obligatory rides to the sharp end of the fighting, Jerry had a sense of watching a rained-off cricket match where the contestants wanted only to go back to the pavilion. The Circus forbade him to leave Saigon on the grounds that he might be needed elsewhere at any moment, but the injunction, literally observed, would have made him look ridiculous, and he ignored it. Xuan Loc was a boring French rubber town fifty miles out, on what was now the city's tactical perimeter. For this was a different war entirely from Phnom Penh's, more technical and more European in inspiration. Where the Khmer Rouge had no armour, the North Vietnamese had Russian tanks and 130 millimetre artillery which they drew up on the classic Russian pattern wheel to wheel, as if they were about to storm Berlin under Marshal Zhukov, and nothing would move till the last gun was laid and primed. He found the town half deserted, and the Catholic church empty except for one French priest.

'*C'est terminé*,' the priest explained to him simply. The South Vietnamese would do what they always did, he said. They would stop the advance, then turn and run.

They drank wine together staring at the empty square.

Jerry filed the story saying the rot this time was irreversible and Stubbsie shoved it on the spike with a laconic, 'Prefer people to prophecies Stubbs.'

Back in Saigon, on the steps of the Hotel Caravelle, begging children peddled useless garlands of flowers. Jerry gave them money and took their flowers to save them face, then dumped them in the wastepaper basket in his room. When he sat downstairs they tapped on the window and sold him *Stars and Stripes*. In the empty bars where he drank, the girls collected round him desperately as if he was their last chance before the end. Only the police were in their element. They stood at every corner in white helmets and fresh white gloves, as if already waiting to direct the victorious enemy traffic when it arrived. In white jeeps, they rode like monarchs past the refugees in their birdcoops on the pavement. He returned to his hotel room and Hercule rang, Jerry's favourite Vietnamese, whom he had been avoiding for all he was worth. Hercule, as he called himself, was anti-establishment and anti-Thieu and had made a quiet living supplying British journalists with information on the Vietcong, on the questionable grounds that the British were not involved in the war. 'The British are my friends!' he begged into the phone. 'Get me out! I need papers, I need money!'

Jerry said 'Try the Americans' and rang off hopelessly.

The Reuters office, when Jerry filed his stillborn copy, was a monument to forgotten heroes and the romance of failure. Under the glass desktops lay the photographed heads of tousled boys, on the walls famous rejection slips and samples of editorial fury; in the air, a stink of old newsprint, and the Somewhere-in-England sense of makeshift habitation which enshrines the secret nostalgia of every exiled correspondent. There was a travel agent just round the corner, and later it turned out that Jerry had twice in that period booked himself passages to Hong Kong, then not appeared at the airport. He was serviced by an earnest young Cousin named Pike who had Information cover and occasionally came to the hotel with signals in yellow envelopes marked RUSH PRESS for authenticity. But the message inside was the same: no decision, stand by, no decision. He read Ford Madox Ford and a truly terrible novel about old Hong Kong. He read Greene and Conrad and T. E. Lawrence, and still no word came. The shellings sounded worst at night, and the panic was everywhere, like a spreading plague.

In search of Stubbsie's people not prophecies, he went down to the American Embassy where ten thousand-odd Vietnamese were beating at the doors in an effort to prove their American citizenship. As he watched, a South Vietnamese officer rode up in a jeep, leapt out and began yelling at the women, calling them whores and traitors – picking, as it happened, a group of *bona fide* US wives to bear the brunt.

Again Jerry filed, and again Stubbs threw his story out, which no doubt added to his depression.

A few days later the Circus planners lost their nerve. As the rout continued, and worsened, they signalled Jerry to fly at once to Vientiane and keep his head down till ordered otherwise by a Cousins' postman. So he went, and took a room at the Constellation, where Lizzie had liked to hang out, and he drank at the bar where Lizzie had liked to drink, and he occasionally chatted to Maurice the proprietor, and he waited. The bar was of concrete, two foot deep, so that if need arose it could do duty as a bomb shelter or firing position. Each night, in the mournful dining room attached to it, one old *colon* ate and drank fastidiously, a napkin tucked into his collar. Jerry sat reading at another table. They were the only diners, ever, and they never spoke. In the streets, the Pathet Lao – not long down from the hills – walked righteously in pairs, wearing Maoist caps and tunics, and avoiding the glances of the girls. They had commandeered the corner villas, and the villas along the road to the airport. They had camped in immaculate tents which peeked over the walls of the overgrown gardens.

'Will the coalition hold?' Jerry asked Maurice once.

Maurice was not a political man.

'It's the way it is,' he replied in a French accent, and in silence handed Jerry a ballpoint pen as a consolation. It had *Lowenbräu* written on it: Maurice owned the concession for the whole of Laos, selling – it was said – several bottles a year. Jerry avoided absolutely the street which housed the Indo-charter offices, just as he restrained himself from taking a look, out of curiosity, at the flea-hut on the edge of town which, on Charlie Marshall's testimony, had housed their *ménage à trois*. When asked, Maurice said there were very few Chinese left in town these days. 'Chinese do not like,' he said with another smile, tilting his head at the Pathet Lao on the pavement outside.

There remains the mystery of the telephone transcripts. Did Jerry ring Lizzie from the Constellation, or not? And if he did ring her, did he mean to talk to her, or only to listen to her voice? And if he intended to talk to her, then what did he propose to say? Or was the very act of making the phone call – like the act of booking airline passages in Saigon – in itself sufficient catharsis to hold him back from the reality?

What is certain is that nobody, neither Smiley nor Connie nor anyone else who read the crucial transcripts, can be seriously accused of failing in their duty, for the entry was at best ambivalent:

'*0055 hrs HK time. Incoming overseas call, personal for subject. Operator on the line. Subject accepts call, says* "hullo" *several times.*

Operator: Speak up please, caller!

Subject: Hullo? Hullo?

Operator: Can you hear me caller? Speak up, please!

Subject: Hullo? Liese Worth here. Who's calling, please? *Call disconnected from caller's end.*'

The transcript nowhere mentions Vientiane as the place of origin and it is even doubtful whether Smiley saw it, since his cryptonym does not appear in the signing panel.

Anyway, whether it was Jerry who made the call or someone else, the next day a pair of Cousins, not one, brought him his marching orders, and at long, long last the welcome relief of action. The bloody inertia, however many interminable weeks of it, had ended finally – and as it happened for good.

He spent the afternoon fixing himself visas and transport, and next morning at dawn he crossed the Mekong into North East Thailand, carrying his shoulder bag and his typewriter. The long wooden ferryboat was crammed with peasants and shrieking pigs. At the shack which controlled the crossing point he pledged himself to return to Laos by the same route. Documentation would otherwise be impossible, the officials warned him severely. If I return at all, he thought. Looking back to the receding shores of Laos, he saw an American car parked on the towpath, and beside it two slender stationary figures watching. The Cousins we have always with us.

On the Thai bank, everything was immediately impossible. Jerry's visa was not enough, his photographs bore no likeness, the whole area was forbidden to *farangs*. Ten dollars secured a revised opinion. After the visa, the car. Jerry had insisted on an English-speaking driver and the rate had been fixed accordingly, but the old man who waited for him spoke nothing but Thai and little of that. By bawling English phrases into the nearby rice shop, Jerry finally hooked a fat supine boy who had some English and said he could drive. A laborious contract was drawn up. The old man's insurance did not cover another driver and anyway it was out of date. An exhausted travel clerk issued a new policy while the boy went home to make his arrangements. The car was a clapped-out red Ford with bald tyres. Of all the ways Jerry didn't intend to die in the next day or two, this was one of them. They haggled, Jerry put up another twenty dollars. At a garage full of chickens he watched every move of the mechanics till the new tyres were in place.

Having thus wasted an hour they set out at a breakneck speed south-eastward over flat farm country. The boy played 'the lights are always out in Massachusetts' five times before Jerry asked for silence.

The road was tarmac but deserted. Occasionally a yellow bus came side-winding down the hill toward them and at once the driver accelerated and stayed on the crown till the bus had yielded a foot and thundered past. Once, while he was dozing, Jerry was startled by the crunch of bamboo fencing and woke in time to see a fountain of splinters lift into the sunlight just ahead of him, and a pick-up truck rolling into the ditch in slow motion. He saw the door float upward like a leaf and the flailing driver follow it through the fence and into the high grass. The boy hadn't even slowed down, though his laughter made them swerve all over the road. Jerry shouted 'Stop!' but the boy would have none of it.

'You want to get blood on your suit? You leave that to the doctors,' he advised sternly. 'I look after you, okay? This very bad country here. Lot of Commies.'

'What's your name?' said Jerry resignedly.

It was unpronounceable, so they settled on Mickey.

It was two more hours before they hit the first barrier. Jerry dozed again, rehearsing his lines. There's always one more door you have to put your foot in, he thought. He wondered whether a day would come – for the Circus – for the comic – when the old entertainer would not be able to pull the gags any more, when just the sheer energy of bare-arsing his way over the threshold would defeat him, and he would stand there flaccid, sporting his friendly salesman's grin, while the words died in his throat. Not this time, he thought hastily. Dear God, not this time, please.

They stopped, and a young monk scurried out of the trees carrying a *wat* bowl and Jerry dropped a few *haht* into it. Mickey opened the boot. A police sentry peered inside, then ordered Jerry out and led him over to a captain who sat in a shaded hut all his own. The captain took a long while to notice Jerry at all.

'He ask you American?' said Mickey.

Jerry produced his papers.

On the other side of the barrier, the perfect tarmac road ran straight as a pencil over the flat scrubland.

'He says what you want here?' Mickey said.

'Business with the colonel.'

Driving on, they passed a village and a cinema. Even the latest films up here are silents, Jerry recalled. He had once done a story about them. Local actors made the voices, and invented whatever plots came into their heads. He remembered John Wayne with a squeaky Thai voice, and the audience ecstatic, and the interpreter explaining to him that they were hearing an imitation of the local mayor who was a famous queen. They were passing forest but the shoulders of the road had been cleared fifty yards on either side to cut the risk of ambush. Occasionally, they came on sharp white lines which had nothing to do with earthbound traffic. The road had been laid by the Americans with an eye to auxiliary landing strips.

'You know this colonel guy?' Mickey asked.

'No,' said Jerry.

Mickey laughed in delight. 'Why you want?'

Jerry didn't bother to answer.

The second roadblock came twenty miles later, in the centre of a small village given over to police. A cluster of grey trucks stood in the courtyard of the *wat*, four jeeps were parked beside the roadblock. The village lay at a junction. At right-angles to their road, a yellow dust-path crossed the plain and snaked into the hills to either side. This time Jerry took the initiative, leaping from the car immediately with a merry cry of 'Take me to your leader!' Their leader turned out to be a nervous young captain with the anxious frown of a man trying to keep abreast of matters beyond his learning. He sat in the police station with his pistol on the desk. The police station was temporary, Jerry noticed. Out of the window, he saw the bombed ruins of what he took to be the last one.

'My colonel is a busy man,' the captain said, through Mickey the driver.

'He is also a very brave man,' Jerry said.

There was dumb show till they had established 'brave'.

'He has shot many Communists,' Jerry said. 'My paper wishes to write about this brave Thai colonel.'

The captain spoke for quite a while and suddenly Mickey began hooting with laughter.

'The captain say we don't got no Commies! We only got Bangkok! Poor people up here don't know nothing, because Bangkok don't give them no schools so the Commies come talk to them in the night and the Commies tell them all their sons all go Moscow, learn be big doctors, so they blow up the police station.'

'Where can I find the colonel?'

'Captain say we stay here.'

'Will he ask the colonel to come to us?'

'Colonel very busy man.'

'Where is the colonel?'

'He next village.'

'What is the name of the next village?'

The driver once more collapsed with laughter.

'It don't got no name. That village all dead.'

'What was the village called before it died?'

Mickey said a name.

'Is the road open as far as this dead village?'

'Captain say military secret. That mean he don't know.'

'Will the capatin let us through to take a look?'

A long exchange followed.

'Sure,' said Mickey finally. 'He say we go.'

'Will the captain radio the colonel and tell him we are coming?'

'Colonel very busy man.'

'Will he radio him?'

'Sure,' said the driver, as if only a hideous *farang* could have made a meal of such a patently obvious detail.

They climbed back into the car. The boom lifted and they continued along the perfect tarmac road with its cleared shoulders and occasional landing marks. For twenty minutes they drove without seeing another living thing but Jerry wasn't consoled by the emptiness. He had heard that for every Communist guerrilla fighting with a gun in the hills, it took five in the plains to produce the rice, the ammunition and the infrastructure, and these were the plains. They came to a dust-path on their right, and the dust of it was smeared across the tarmac from recent use. Mickey swung down it, following the heavy tyre tracks, playing 'The lights are always out in Massachusetts' very loud, Jerry notwithstanding.

'This way the Commies think we plenty people,' he explained amid more laughter, thus making it impossible for him to object. To Jerry's surprise he also produced a huge, long-barrelled .45 target pistol from the bag beneath his seat. Jerry ordered him sharply to shove it back where it came from. Minutes later, they smelt burning, then they drove through wood-smoke, then they reached what was left of the village: clusters of cowed people, a couple of acres of burnt teak trees like a petrified forest, three jeeps, twenty-odd police, and a stocky lieutenant-colonel at their centre. Villagers and police alike were gazing at a patch of smouldering ash sixty yards across, in which a few charred beams sketched the outline of the burned houses. The colonel watched them park and he watched them walk over. He was a fighting man. Jerry saw it immediately. He was squat and strong and he neither smiled nor scowled. He was swarthy and greying and he could have been Malay, except that he was thicker in the trunk. He wore parachute wings and flying wings and a couple of rows of medal ribbons. He wore battle drill and a regulation automatic in a leather holster on his right thigh, and the restraining straps hung open.

'You the newsman?' he asked Jerry, in flat, military American.

'That's right.'

The colonel's eye turned to the driver. He said something, and Mickey walked hastily back to his car, got into it and stayed there.

'What do you want?'

'Anybody die here?'

'Three people. I just shot them. We got thirty-eight million.'

His functional American-English, all but perfect, came as a growing surprise.

'Why did you shoot them?'

'At night the CTs held classes here. People come from all around to hear the CTs.'

*Communist Terrorists*, thought Jerry. He had an inkling it was originally a British phrase. A string of lorries was nosing down the dust-path. Seeing them, the villagers began picking up their bedrolls and children. The colonel gave an order and his men formed them into a rough file while the lorries turned round.

'We find them a better place,' the colonel said. 'They start again.'

'Who did you shoot?'

'Last week two of my men got bombed. The CTs operated from this village.' He picked out a sullen woman at that moment clambering on the lorry and called her back so that Jerry could take a look at her. She stood with her head bowed.

'They stay in her house,' he said. 'This time I shoot her husband. Next time I shoot her.'

'And the other two?' Jerry asked.

He asked because to keep asking is to stay punching, but it was Jerry, not the colonel, who was under interrogation. The colonel's brown eyes were hard and appraising and held a lot in reserve. They looked at Jerry inquiringly but without anxiety.

'One of the CTs sleep with a girl here,' he said simply. 'We're not only the police. We're the judge and courts as well. There's no one else. Bangkok don't care for a lot of public trials up here.'

The villagers had boarded the lorries. They drove away without looking back. Only the children waved over the tailboards. The jeeps followed, leaving the three of them, and the two cars, and a boy, perhaps fifteen.

'Who's he?' said Jerry.

'He comes with us. Next year, year after maybe, I shoot him too.'

Jerry rode in the jeep beside the colonel, who drove. The boy sat impassively in the back murmuring yes and no while the colonel lectured him in a firm, mechanical tone. Mickey followed in the taxi. On the floor of the jeep, between the seat and the pedals, the colonel kept four grenades in a cardboard carton. A small machine gun lay along the rear seat, and the colonel didn't bother to move it for the boy. Above the driving mirror beside the votive pictures hung a postcard portrait of John Kennedy with the legend 'Ask not what your country can do for you. Ask rather what you can do for your country.' Jerry had taken his notebook out. The lecture to the boy continued.

'What are you saying to him?'

'I am explaining the principles of democracy.'

'What are they?'

'No Communism and no generals,' he replied and laughed.

At the main road they turned right, further into the interior, Mickey following in the red Ford.

'Dealing with Bangkok is like climbing that big tree,' the colonel said to Jerry, interrupting himself to point at the forest. 'You climb one branch, go up a bit, change branches, the branch breaks, you go up again. Maybe one day, you get to the top general. Maybe never.'

Two small kids flagged them down and the colonel stopped to let them squeeze in beside the boy.

'I don't do that too often,' he said with another sudden smile. 'I do that to show you I'm a nice guy. The CTs get to know you stop for kids, they put out kids to stop you. You got to vary yourself. That way you stay alive.'

He had turned into the forest again. They drove a few miles and let the small children out, but not the sullen boy. The trees stopped and gave way to desolate scrubland. The sky grew white, with the shadows of the hills just breaking thought the mist.

'What's he done?' Jerry asked.

'Him? He's a CT,' the colonel said. 'We catch him.' In the forest Jerry saw a flash of gold, but it was only a *wat*. 'Last week one of my police turns informer to CT. I send him on patrol, shoot him, make him a big hero. I fix the wife a pension, I buy a big flag for the body, I make a great funeral and the village gets a bit richer. That guy's not an informer any more. He's a folk hero. You got to win the hearts and minds of the people.'

'No question,' Jerry agreed.

They had reached a wide dry paddy field, with two women hoeing at the centre, and otherwise nothing in sight but a far hedge, and rocky dune-land fading into the white sky. Leaving Mickey in the Ford, Jerry and the colonel began walking across the field, the sullen boy trailing behind them.

'You British?'

'Yes.'

'I was at Washington International Police Academy,' said the colonel. 'Very nice place. I read law enforcement at Michigan State. They showed us a good time. You want to keep clear of me a little?' he asked politely, as they trod meticulously over a plough. 'They shoot me, not you. They shoot a *farang*, they get too much trouble here. They don't want that. Nobody shoots a *farang* in my territory.'

They had reached the women. The colonel spoke to them, walked a distance, stopped, looked back at the sullen boy and returned to the women and spoke to them a second time.

'What's that about?' said Jerry.

'I ask them if there's any CTs around. They tell me no. Then I think: maybe the CTs want this boy back. So I go back and tell them: "If anything goes wrong, we shoot you women first."' They had reached the hedge. The dunes lay ahead of them, overgrown with high bushes and palms like swordblades. The colonel cupped his hands and yelled until an answering call came.

'I learn that in the jungle,' he explained with another smile. 'When you're in the jungle, always call first.'

'What jungle was that?' said Jerry.

'Stand near to me now please. Smile when you speak to me. They like to see you very clear.'

They had reached a small river. Around it, a hundred or more men and boys picked indifferently at the rocks with picks and spades, or humped bags of cement from one vast pile to another. A handful of armed police looked negligently on. The colonel called up the boy and spoke to him, and the boy bowed his head and the colonel boxed him sharply on the ears. The boy muttered something and the colonel hit him again, then patted him on the shoulder, whereupon like a freed but crippled bird he scuffled away to join the labour force.

'You write about CTs, you write about my dam too,' the colonel ordered, as they started their return walk. 'We're going to make this fine pasture here. They will name it after me.'

'What jungle did you fight in?' Jerry repeated, as they started back.

'Laos. Very hard fighting.'

'You volunteered?'

'Sure. I got kids, need the money. I join PARU. Heard of PARU? The Americans ran it. They got it made. I write a letter resigning from the Thai police. They put it in a drawer. If I get killed, they pull out the letter to prove I resigned before I joined PARU.'

'That where you met Ricardo?'

'Sure. Ricardo my friend. We fought together, shoot a lot of badguys.'

'I want to see him,' said Jerry. 'I met a girl of his in Saigon. She told me he had a place up here. I want to make a business proposition.'

They passed the women again. The colonel waved at them but they ignored him. Jerry was watching his face but he could as soon have watched a boulder back on the dunes. The colonel climbed into the jeep. Jerry jumped in after him.

'I thought maybe you could take me to him. I could even make him rich for a few days.'

'This for your paper?'

'It's private.'

'A private business proposition?' the colonel asked.

'That's right.'

As they drove back to the road, two yellow cement mixer lorries came toward them and the colonel had to back to let them pass. Automatically, Jerry noticed the name painted on the yellow sides. As he did so, he caught the colonel's eye watching him. They continued toward the interior, driving as fast as the jeep would go, in order to beat anybody's bad intentions along the way. Faithfully, Mickey followed behind.

'Ricardo is my friend and this is my territory,' the colonel repeated in his excellent American. The statement, though familiar, was this time an entirely explicit warning. 'He lives here under my protection, according to an arrangement we have. Everybody here know that. The villagers know it, CT knows it. Nobody hurts Ricardo or I'll shoot every CT on the dam.'

As they turned off the main road into the dust-path, Jerry saw the light skidmarks of a small plane written on the tarmac.

'This where he lands?'

'Only in the rainy season.' The colonel continued outlining his ethical position in the matter. 'If Ricardo kills you, that's his business. One *farang* shoots another on my territory, that's natural.' He could have been explaining basic arithmetic to a child. 'Ricardo is my friend,' he repeated without embarrassment. 'My comrade.'

'He expecting me?'

'Please pay attention to him. Captain Ricardo is sometimes a sick man.'

*Tiu make a special place for him*, Charlie Marshall had said, *a place where only crazy people go. Tiu say to him, 'you stay alive, you keep the plane, you ride shotgun for Charlie Marshall any time you like, carry money for him, watch his back for him, if that's the way Charlie wants it. That's the deal and Drake Ko don't never break a deal,' he say. But if Ric make trouble, or if Ric louses up, or if Ric shoot his big mouth off about certain matters, Tiu and his people kill that crazy bastard so completely he don't know who he is.*

'Why doesn't Ric just take the plane and run for it?' Jerry had asked.

*Tiu got Ric's passport, Voltaire. Tiu buy Ric's debts and his business enterprises and his police record. Tiu pinned about fifty tons of opium on him and Tiu got the proof all ready for the narcs for if ever he need it. Ric, he's free to walk out any damn time he wants. They got prisons waiting for him all over the damn world.*

The house stood on stilts at the centre of a wide dust-path with a balcony all round it and a small stream beside it and a couple of Thai girls under it, and one of them was feeding her baby while the other stirred a cookpot. Behind the house lay a flat brown field with a shed at one end big enough to house a small plane – say a Beechcraft – and there was a silvered track of pressed grass down the field where one might recently have landed. There were no trees near the house, and it stood on a small rise. It had all-round vision and broad windows not very high, which Jerry guessed had been altered to provide a wide angle of fire from inside. Short of the house, the colonel told Jerry to get out, and walked back with him to Mickey's car. He spoke to Mickey and Mickey leapt out and unlocked the boot. The colonel reached under the car-seat and pulled out the target pistol and tossed it contemptuously into the jeep. He frisked Jerry, then Mickey, then he searched the car for himself. Then he told them both to wait, and he climbed the steps to the first floor. The girls ignored him.

'He fine colonel,' said Mickey.

They waited.

'England rich country,' said Mickey.

'England a very *poor* country,' Jerry retorted as they continued to watch the house.

'Poor country, rich people,' said Mickey. He was still shaking with laughter at his own good joke as the colonel came out of the house, climbed into the jeep, and drove away.

'Wait here,' said Jerry. He walked slowly to the foot of the steps, cupped his hands to his mouth and called upwards.

'My name's Westerby. You may remember shooting at me in Phnom Penh a few weeks ago. I'm a poor journalist with expensive ideas.'

'What do you want, Voltaire? Somebody told me you were dead already.'

A Latin American voice, deep and feathered from the darkness above.

'I want to blackmail Drake Ko. I reckon that between us we could sting him for a couple of million bucks and you could buy your freedom.'

In the darkness of the trap above him, Jerry saw a single gun barrel, like a cyclopic eye, wink, then settle its gaze on him again.

'*Each,*' Jerry called. 'Two for you, two for me. I've got it all worked out. With my brains and your information and Lizzie Worthington's figure, I reckon it's a dead cert.'

He started walking slowly up the steps. *Voltaire,* he thought. When it came to spreading the word, Charlie Marshall didn't hang around. As to being dead already – give it a little time, he thought.

As Jerry climbed through the trap, he moved from the dark into the light, and the Latin American voice said, 'Stay right there.' Doing as he was told, Jerry was able to look round the room, which was a mix between a small armaments museum and an American PX. On the centre table on a tripod stood an AK47 similar to the one Ricardo had already fired at him, and as Jerry had suspected it covered all four approaches through the windows. But in case it didn't, there were a couple of spares, and beside each gun a decent pile of ammunition clips. Grenades lay about like fruit, in clusters of three and four, and on the hideous walnut cocktail cabinet under a plastic effigy of the Madonna lay a selection of pistols and automatics for all occasions. There was only one room but it was large, with a low bed with japanned and lacquered ends, and Jerry had a silly moment wondering how the devil Ricardo had ever got it into his Beechcraft. There were two refrigerators and an icemaker, and there were painfully-worked oil paintings of nude Thai girls, drawn with the sort of erotic inaccuracy that usually comes with too little access to the subject. There was a filing cabinet with a Luger on it and there was a bookshelf with works on company law, international taxation, and sexual technique. On the walls hung several locally carved icons of saints, the Virgin, and the Christ child. On the floor lay a steel scaffold of a rowing boat, with a sliding seat for improving the figure.

At the centre of all this, in much the same pose in which Jerry had first set eyes on him, sat Ricardo in a senior executive's swivel chair, wearing his CIA bracelets and a sarong and a gold cross on his handsome bare chest. His beard was a lot less full than when Jerry had seen it last and he guessed the girls had clipped it for him. He wore no cap, and his crinkly black hair was threaded into a small gold ring at the back of his neck. He was broad-shouldered and muscular and his skin was tanned and oily and his chest was matted.

He also had a bottle of Scotch at his elbow, and a jug of water, but no ice because there was no electricity for the refrigerators.

'Take off your jacket please, Voltaire,' Ricardo ordered, so Jerry did, and with a sigh Ricardo stood up, and picked an automatic from the table, and walked slowly round Jerry studying his body while he gently probed it for weapons.

'You play tennis?' he enquired from behind him, running one hand very lightly down Jerry's back. 'Charlie said you got muscles like a gorilla.' But Ricardo did not really ask questions of anyone but himself. 'I like very much tennis. I am an extremely good player. I win always. Here unfortunately I have little opportunity.' He sat down again. 'Sometimes you got to hide with the enemy to get away from your friends. I ride horses, box, shoot, I got degrees, I fly an aeroplane, I know a lot of things about life, I'm very intelligent, but owing to unforeseen circumstances I live in the jungle like a monkey.' The automatic lay casually in his left hand. 'That what you call a paranoid, Voltaire? Somebody who think everybody his enemy?'

'I rather think it is.'

To produce the well-trodden witticism, Ricardo laid a finger to his bronzed and oiled breast.

'Well this paranoid got real enemies,' he said.

'With two million bucks,' said Jerry, still standing where Ricardo had left him, 'I'm sure most of them could be eliminated.'

'Voltaire, I must tell you honestly that I regard your business proposition as crap.'

Ricardo laughed. That was to say, he made a fine display of his white teeth against the newly clipped beard, and flexed his stomach muscles a little, and kept his eyes fixed dead level on Jerry's face while he sipped his glass of whisky. He's got a brief, thought Jerry, same as I have.

*If he shows up, you hear him out,* Tiu had no doubt said to him. And when Ricardo had heard him out – then what?

'I definitely understood you had an accident, Voltaire,' said Ricardo sadly, and shook his head as if complaining about the poor quality of his information. 'You want a drink?'

'I'll pour it for myself,' said Jerry. The glasses were in a cabinet, all different colours and sizes. Deliberately, Jerry walked over to it and helped himself to a long pink tumbler with a dressed girl outside and a naked girl inside. He poured a couple of fingers of Scotch into it, added a little water, and sat down opposite Ricardo at the table while Ricardo studied him with interest.

'You do exercises, weight-lifting, something?' he enquired confidingly.

'Just the odd bottle,' said Jerry.

Ricardo laughed inordinately, still examining him very closely with his flickering bedroom eyes.

'That was a very bad thing you did to little Charlie, you know that? I don't like you to sit on my friend's head in the darkness while he catch cold turkey. Charlie going to take a long while to recover. That's no way to make friends with Charlie's friends, Voltaire. They say you even been rude to Mr Ko. Took my little Lizzie out to dinner. That true?'

'I took her out to dinner.'

'You screw her?'

Jerry didn't answer. Ricardo gave another burst of laughter, which stopped as suddenly as it had started. He took a long draught of whisky and sighed.

'Well, I hope she's grateful, that's all.' He was at once a much misunderstood man. 'I forgive her. Okay? You see Lizzie again: tell her I, Ricardo, forgive her. I train her. I put her on the right road. I tell her a lot of things, art, culture, politics, business, religion, I teach her how to make love, and I send her into the world. Where would she be without my connections? Where? Living in the jungle with Ricardo like a monkey. She owes me everything. *Pygmalion*: know that movie? Well, I'm the professor. I tell her some things – know what I mean? – I tell her things no man can tell her but Ricardo. Seven years in Vietnam. Two years in Laos. Four thousand dollars a month from CIA and me a Catholic. You think I can't tell her some things, a girl like that from nowhere, an English scrubber? She got a kid, you know that? Little boy in London. She walk out on him, imagine. Such a mother huh? Worse than a whore.'

Jerry found nothing useful to say. He was looking at the two large rings side by side on the middle fingers of Ricardo's heavy right hand, and in his memory measuring them against the twin scars on Lizzie's chin. It was a downward blow, he decided, a right cross while she was below him. It seemed strange he hadn't broken her jaw. Perhaps he had, and she'd had a lucky mend.

'You gone deaf, Voltaire? I said outline to me your business proposition. Without prejudice, you understand. Except I don't believe a word of it.'

Jerry helped himself to some more whisky. 'I thought maybe if you told me what it was Drake Ko wanted you to do that time you flew for him, and if Lizzie could get me alongside Ko, and we all kept our hands on the table, we'd have a good chance of taking him to the cleaners.'

Now he said it, it sounded even lamer than when he had rehearsed it, but he didn't particularly care.

'You crazy, Voltaire. Crazy. You're making pictures in the air.'

'Not if Ko was asking you to fly into the China Mainland for him, I'm not. Ko can own the whole of Hong Kong for all I care, but if the Governor ever got to hear of that little adventure, I reckon he and Ko would stop kissing overnight. That's for openers. There's more.'

'What are you talking about, Voltaire? China? What nonsense is this you are telling me? The China *Mainland*?' He shrugged his glistening shoulders and drank, smirking into his glass. 'I do not read you, Voltaire. You talk through your ass. What makes you think I fly to China for Ko? Ridiculous. Laughable.'

As a liar, Jerry reckoned, Ricardo was about three leagues lower down the chart than Lizzie which was saying quite a lot.

'My editor makes me think it, sport. My editor is a very sharp fellow. Lot of influential and knowledgeable friends. They tell him things. Now for instance, my editor has a very good hunch that not long after you died so tragically in that aircrash of yours you sold a damn great load of raw opium to a friendly American purchaser engaged in the suppression of dangerous drugs. Another hunch of his tells him it was Ko's opium, not yours to sell at all, and that it was addressed to the China Mainland. Only, you decided to play the angles instead.' He went straight on, while Ricardo's eyes watched him over the top of his whisky glass. 'Now if that were so, and Ko's ambition were, let us say, to reintroduce the opium habit to the Mainland – slowly, but gradually creating new markets, you follow me – well, I reckon he would go a very long distance to prevent that information making the front pages of the world's press. That's not all, either. There's another aspect altogether, even more lucrative.'

'What's that, Voltaire?' Ricardo asked, and continued watching him as fixedly as if he had him in the sights of his rifle. 'What are these other aspects you refer to? Kindly tell me, please.'

'Well I think I'll hold back on that one,' said Jerry with a frank smile. 'I think I'll keep it warm while you give me a little something in return.'

A girl came silently up the stairs carrying bowls of rice and lemon grass and boiled chicken. She was trim and entirely beautiful. They could hear voices from underneath the house, including Mickey's, and the sound of the baby laughing.

'Who you got down there, Voltaire?' Ricardo asked vaguely, half waking from his reverie. 'You got some damn bodyguard or something?'

'Just the driver.'

'He got guns?'

Receiving no reply, Ricardo shook his head in wonder.

'You're some crazy fellow,' he remarked, as he waved at the girl to get out. 'You're some really crazy fellow.' He handed Jerry a bowl and chopsticks. 'Holy Maria. That Tiu, he's a pretty rough guy, I'm a pretty rough guy myself. But those Chinese can be very hard people, Voltaire. You mess with a guy like Tiu, you get pretty big trouble.'

'We'll beat them at their own game,' said Jerry. 'We'll use English lawyers. We'll stack it so high a board of bishops couldn't knock it down. We'll collect witnesses. You, Charlie Marshall, whoever else knows. Give dates and times of what he said and did. We'll show him a copy and we'll bank the others and we'll make a contract with him. Signed, sealed, and delivered. Legal as hell. That's what he likes. Ko's a very legal-minded man. I've been into his business affairs. I've seen his bank statements, his assets. The story's pretty good as it stands. But with the other aspects I'm talking about, I reckon it's cheap at five million. Two for you. Two for me. One for Lizzie.'

'For her, nothing.'

Ricardo was stooping over the filing cabinet. Pulling open a drawer, he began picking through the contents, studying brochures and correspondence.

'You ever been to Bali, Voltaire?'

Solemnly pulling on a pair of reading glasses, Ricardo sat at the table again and began studying the file. 'I bought some land there a few years back. A deal I made. I make many deals. Walk, ride, I got a Honda seven fifty there, a girl. In Laos we kill everybody, in Vietnam we burn the whole damn countryside, so I buy this land in Bali, bit of land we don't burn for once and a girl we don't kill, know what I mean? Fifty acres of scrub. Here, come here.'

Peering over his shoulder, Jerry saw a planner's mimeographed diagram of an isthmus broken into numbered building plots, and in the bottom left corner the words 'Ricardo and Worthington Ltd, Dutch Antilles.'

'You come into business with me, Voltaire. We develop this thing together, okay? Build fifty houses, have one each, nice people, put Charlie Marshall out there as manager, get some girls, make a colony maybe, artists, concerts sometimes: you like music, Voltaire?'

'I need hard facts,' Jerry insisted firmly. 'Dates, times, places, witnesses' statements. When you've told me, I'll trade you. I'll explain those other aspects to you – the lucrative ones. I'll explain the whole deal.'

'Sure,' said Ricardo distractedly, still studying the map. 'We screw him. Sure we do.'

This is how they lived together, Jerry thought: with one foot in fairyland and the other in jail, bolstering each other's fantasies, a beggars' opera with a cast of three.

For a while now, Ricardo fell in love with his sins and there was nothing Jerry could do to stop him. In Ricardo's simple world, to talk about himself was to get to know the other person better. So he talked about his big soul, about his great sexual potency and his concern for its continuation but most of all he talked about the horrors of war, a subject on which he considered himself uniquely well informed. 'In Vietnam, I fall in love with a girl, Voltaire. I, Ricardo, I fall in love. This is very rare and holy to me. Black hair, straight back, face like a Madonna, little tits. Each morning I stop the jeep as she walks to school, each morning she says "no". "Listen," I tell her, "Ricardo is not American. He is Mexican." She never even heard of Mexico. I go crazy, Voltaire. For weeks I, Ricardo, live like a monk. The other girls, I don't touch them any more. Every morning. Then one day I'm in first gear already and she throws up her hand – stop! She gets in beside me. She leaves school, goes out to live in a kampong, I tell you one day the name. The B52s go in and flatten the village. Some hero doesn't read the map too good. Little villages, they're like stones on the beach, each one the same. I'm in the chopper behind. Nothing's stopping me. Charlie Marshall's beside me and he's screaming me I'm crazy. I don't care. I go down, land, I find her. The whole village dead. I find her. She's dead too, but I find her. I get back to base, the military police beat me up, I get seven weeks in solitary, lose my service stripes. Me. Ricardo.'

'You poor thing,' said Jerry, who had played these games before and hated them – disbelieved or believed them, but always hated them.

'You are right,' said Ricardo, acknowledging Jerry's homage with a bow. 'Poor is the correct word. They treat us like peasants. Me and Charlie, we fly everything. We were never properly rewarded. Wounded, dead, bits of bodies, dope. For nothing. Jesus, that was shooting, that war. Twice I fly into Yunnan province. I am fearless. Totally. Even my good looks do not make me afraid for myself.'

'Counting Drake Ko's trip,' Jerry reminded him. 'You would have been there three times, wouldn't you?'

'I train pilots for the Cambodian air force. For nothing. The Cambodian air force, Voltaire! Eighteen generals, fifty-four planes – and Ricardo. End of your time, you get the life insurance, that's the deal. A hundred thousand US. Only you. Ricardo die, his next of kin get nothing, that's the deal. Ricardo make it, he get it all. I talk to some friends from the French Foreign Legion once, they know the racket, they warn me. "Take care, Ricardo. Soon they send you to bad spots you can't get out of. That way they don't have to pay you." Cambodians want me to fly on half fuel. I got wing-tanks and refuse. Another time they fix my hydraulics. I engineer the plane myself. That way they don't kill me. Listen, I snap my fingers, Lizzie come back to me. Okay?'

Lunch was over.

'So how did it go with Tiu and Drake?' said Jerry. With confession, they say at Sarratt, all you have to do is tilt the stream a little.

For the first time, it seemed to Jerry, Ricardo stared at him with the full intensity of his animal stupidity.

'You confuse me, Voltaire. If I tell you too much, I have to shoot you. I'm a very talkative person, you follow me? I get lonely up here, it is my disposition always to be lonely. I like a guy, I talk to him, then I regret myself. I remember my business commitments, follow me?'

An inner stillness came over Jerry now, as Sarratt man became Sarratt recording angel, with no part to play but to receive and to remember. Operationally, he knew, he stood close to journey's end: even if the journey back was, at best, imponderable. Operationally, by any precedents he understood, muted bells of triumph should have been sounding in his awe-struck ear. But that didn't happen. And the fact that it didn't was an early warning to him, even then that his quest was no longer, in every respect, on all fours with that of the Sarratt bearleaders.

At first – with allowances for Ricardo's vaulting ego – the story went much as Charlie Marshall had said it went. Tiu came to Vientiane dressed like a coolie and smelling of cat-scent and asked around for the finest pilot in town and naturally he was at once referred to Ricardo, who as it happened was resting between business commitments and available for certain specialized and highly rewarded work in the aviation field.

Unlike Charlie Marshall, Ricardo told his story with a studious directness, as if he expected to be dealing with intellects inferior to his own. Tiu introduced himself as a person with wide contacts in the aviation industry, mentioned his undefined link with Indocharter, and went over the ground he had already covered with Charlie Marshall. Finally he came to the project in hand – which is to say that, in fine Sarratt style, he fed Ricardo the cover story. A certain major Bangkok trading company with which Tiu was proud to be associated, he said, was in the throes of an extremely legitimate deal with certain officials in a neighbouring friendly foreign country.

'I ask him, Voltaire, very seriously. "Mr Tiu, maybe you just discovered the moon. I never heard yet an Asian country with a friendly foreign neighbour." Tiu laughed at my joke. He naturally considered it a witty contribution,' said Ricardo very seriously, in one of his strange outbreaks of business-school English.

Before consummating their profitable and legitimate deal, however – Tiu explained, in Ricardo's language – his business associates were faced with the problem of paying off certain officials and other parties inside that friendly foreign country who had cleared away tiresome bureaucratic obstacles.

'Why was this a problem?' Ricardo had asked, not unnaturally.

Suppose, said Tiu, the country was Burma. Just suppose. In modern Burma, officials were not allowed to enrich themselves, nor could they easily bank money. In such a case, some other means of payment would have to be found.

Ricardo suggested gold. Tiu, said Ricardo, regretted himself: in the country he had in mind, even gold was difficult to negotiate. The currency selected in this case was therefore to be opium, he said: four hundred kilos of it. The distance was not great, the inside of a day would see Ricardo there and back; the fee was five thousand dollars, and the remaining details would be vouchsafed to him just before departure in order to avoid 'a needless erosion of the memory', as Ricardo put it, in another of those bizarre linguistic flourishes which must have formed a major part of Lizzie's education at his hands. Upon Ricardo's return from what Tiu was certain would be a painless and instructive flight, five thousand US dollars in convenient denominations would at once be his – subject of course to Ricardo producing, in whatever form should prove convenient, confirmation that the consignment had reached its destination. A receipt, for example.

Ricardo, as he described his own footwork, now showed a crude cunning in his dealings with Tiu. He told him he would think about this offer. He spoke of other pressing commitments and his ambitions to open his own airline. Then he set to work to find out who the hell Tiu was. He discovered at once that, following their interview, Tiu had returned not to Bangkok but to Hong Kong on the direct flight. He made Lizzie pump the Chiu Chow boys at Indocharter, and one of them let slip that Tiu was a big cat in China Airsea, because when he was in Bangkok he stayed in the China Airsea suite at the Erawan Hotel. By the time Tiu returned to Vientiane to hear Ricardo's answer, Ricardo therefore knew a lot more about him – even, though he made little of it, that Tiu was right-hand man to Drake Ko.

Five thousand US dollars for a one-day trip, he now told Tiu at this second interview, was either too little or too much. If the job was as soft as Tiu insisted, it was too much. If it was as totally crazy as Ricardo suspected, it was too little. Ricardo suggested a different arrangement: 'a business compromise,' he said. He was suffering, he explained – in a phrase he had no doubt used often – from 'a temporary problem of liquidity.' In other words (Jerry interpreting) he was broke as usual, and the creditors were at his throat. What he required immediately was a regular income, and this was best obtained by Tiu arranging for him to be taken on by Indocharter as a pilot-consultant for a year at an agreed salary of twenty-five thousand US dollars.

Tiu did not seem too shocked by the idea, said Ricardo. Upstairs in the stilt-house, the room grew very quiet.

Secondly, instead of being paid five thousand dollars on delivery of the consignment, Ricardo wanted an advance of twenty thousand US dollars now to settle his outstanding commitments. Ten thousand would be considered earned as soon as he had delivered the opium, and the other ten thousand would be deductible 'at source' – another Ricardo *nom de guerre* – from his Indocharter salary over the remaining months of his employment. If Tiu and his associates couldn't manage this, Ricardo explained, then unfortunately he would have to leave town before he could make the opium delivery.

Next day, with variations, Tiu agreed to the terms. Rather than advance Ricardo twenty thousand dollars, Tiu and his associates proposed to buy Ricardo's debts directly from his creditors. That way, he explained, they would feel more comfortable. The same day, the arrangement was 'sancti-fied' – Ricardo's religious convictions were never far away – by a formidable contract, drawn in English and signed by both parties. Ricardo – Jerry silently recorded – had just sold his soul.

'What did Lizzie think of the deal?' Jerry asked.

He shrugged his glistening shoulders. 'Women,' Ricardo said.

'Sure,' said Jerry, returning his knowing smile.

Ricardo's future thus secured, he resumed a 'suitable professional life-style', as he called it. A scheme to float an all-Asian football pool claimed his attention, so did a fourteen-year-old girl in Bangkok named Rosie whom, on the strength of his Indocharter salary, he periodically visited for the purpose of training her for life's great stage. Occasionally, but not often, he flew the odd run for Indocharter, but nothing demanding:

'Chiang Mai couple of times. Saigon. Couples of times into the Shans visit Charlie Marshall's old man, collect a little mud maybe, take him a few guns, rice, gold. Battambang, maybe.'

'Where's Lizzie meanwhile?' Jerry asked, in the same easy, man-to-man tone as before.

The same contemptuous shrug. 'Sitting in Vientiane. Does her knitting. Scrubs a little at the Constellation. That's an old woman already, Voltaire. I need youth. Optimism. Energy. People who respect me. It is my nature to give. How can I give to an old woman?'

'Until?' Jerry asked.

'Huh?'

'So when did the kissing stop?'

Misunderstanding the phrase, Ricardo looked suddenly very dangerous, and his voice dropped to a low warning. 'What the hell you mean?'

Jerry soothed him with the friendliest of smiles.

'How long did you draw your pay and kick around before Tiu collected on the contract?'

Six weeks, said Ricardo, recovering his composure. Maybe eight. Twice the trip was on, then cancelled. Once, it seemed, he was ordered to Chiang Mai and loafed for a couple of days till Tiu called to say the people at the other end weren't ready. Increasingly Ricardo had the feeling he was mixed up in something deep, he said, but history, he implied, had always cast him for the great rôles of life and at least the creditors were off his back.

Ricardo broke off, and once more studied Jerry closely, scratching his beard in contemplation. Finally he sighed, and pouring them both a whisky, pushed a glass across the table. Below them, the perfect day was preparing its own slow death. The green trees had grown heavy. The wood-smoke from the girls' cookpot smelt damp.

'Where you go from here, Voltaire?'

'Home,' said Jerry.

Ricardo let out a fresh burst of laughter.

'You stay the night, I send you one of my girls.'

'I'll make my own damn way, actually sport,' Jerry said. Like fighting animals, the two men surveyed each other, and for a moment the spark of battle was very close indeed.

'You some crazy fellow, Voltaire,' Ricardo muttered.

But Sarratt man prevailed. 'Then one day the trip was on, right?' Jerry said. 'And nobody cancelled. Then what? Come on, sport, let's have the story.'

'Sure,' said Ricardo. 'Sure, Voltaire,' and drank, still watching him. 'How it happened,' he said. 'Listen, I tell you how it happened, Voltaire.'

And then I'll kill you, said his eyes.

Ricardo was in Bangkok. Rosie was being demanding. Tiu had insisted Ricardo should always be within reach and one morning early, maybe five o'clock, a messenger arrived at their love-nest summoning him to the Erawan immediately. Ricardo was impressed by the suite. He would have wished it for himself.

'Ever seen Versailles, Voltaire? A desk so big as a B52. This Tiu is a very different human individual to the cat-scent coolie who came to Vientiane, okay? This is a very influential person. "Ricardo," he tell me, "this time is for certain. This time we deliver."'

His orders were simple. In a few hours there was a commercial flight to Chiang Mai. Ricardo should take it. Rooms had been booked for him at the Hotel Rincome. He should stay the night there. Alone. No drink, no women, no society.

'"You better take plenty to read, Mr Ricardo," he tell me. "Mr Tiu," I tell him. "You tell me where to fly. You don't tell me where to read. Okay?" This guy is very arrogant behind his big desk, understand me, Voltaire? I am obliged to teach him manners.'

Next morning, someone would call for Ricardo at six o'clock at his hotel announcing himself as a friend of Mr. Johnny. Ricardo should go with him.

Things went as planned. Ricardo flew to Chiang Mai, spent an abstemious night at the Rincome, and at six o'clock two Chinese, not one, called for him and drove him north for some hours till they came to a Hakka village. Leaving the car, they walked for half an hour till they reached an empty field with a hut at one end of it. Inside the hut stood 'a dandy little Beechcraft', brand new, and inside the Beechcraft sat Tiu with a lot of maps and documents on his lap, in the seat beside the pilot's. The rear seats had been removed to make space for the gunny bags. A couple of Chinese crushers stood off watching, and the overall mood, Ricardo implied, was not all he would have liked.

'First I got to empty my pockets. My pockets are very personal to me, Voltaire. They are like a lady's handbag. Mementos. Letters. Photographs. My Madonna. They retain everything. My passport, my pilot's licence, my money . . . even my bracelets,' he said, and lifted his brown arms so that the gold links jingled.

After that, he said with a frown of disapproval, there were yet more documents to sign. Such as a power of attorney, signing over whatever bits of Ricardo's life were left to him after his Indocharter contract. Such as various confessions to 'previous technically illegal undertakings', several of them – Ricardo asserted in considerable outrage – performed on behalf of Indocharter. One of the Chinese crushers even turned out to be a lawyer. Ricardo considered this particularly unsporting.

Only then did Tiu unveil the maps, and the instructions, which Ricardo now reproduced in a blend of his own style and Tiu's: '"You head north, Mr Ricardo, and you keep heading north. Maybe you clip the edge off Laos, maybe you stay over the Shans, I don't give a damn. Flying is your business,

not mine. Fifty miles inside the China border, you pick up the Mekong and
follow it. Then you keep going north till you find a little hill town called
Tienpao, stuck on a tributary of that very famous river. Head due east twenty
miles, you find a landing strip, one white flare, one green, you do me a favour
please. You land there. A man will be waiting for you. He speaks very lousy
English, but he speaks it. Here is half one dollar bill. This man will have the
other half. Unload the opium. This man will give you a package, and certain
particular instructions. The package is your receipt, Mr Ricardo. When you
return, bring it with you and obey all instructions most absolutely, including
especially your place of landing. Do you understand me entirely, Mr
Ricardo?"'

'What kind of package?' Jerry asked.

'He don't say and I don't care. "You do that," he tell me, "and keep your big
mouth shut, Mr Ricardo, and my associates will look after you all your life like
you are their son. Your children, they look after, your girls. Your girl in Bali.
All your life they will be grateful men. But you screw them, or you go big-
mouthing round town, they definitely kill you, Mr Ricardo, believe me. Not
tomorrow, maybe, not the next day, but they definitely kill you. We got a
contract, Mr Ricardo. My associates don't never break a contract. They are
very legal men." I got sweat on me, Voltaire. I am in perfect condition, a fine
athlete, but I sweat. "Don't you worry, Mr Tiu," I tell him. "Mr Tiu, sir, any
time you want to fly opium into Red China, Ricardo's your man." Voltaire,
believe me, I was very concerned.'

Ricardo squeezed his nose as if it were smarting with sea water.

'Hear this, Voltaire. Listen most attentively. When I was young and crazy, I
flew twice into Yunnan province for the Americans. To be a hero, one must
do certain crazy things, and if you crash, maybe one day they get you out. But
each time I flew, I look down at the lousy brown earth and I see Ricardo in a
wood cage. No women, extremely lousy food, no place to sit, no place to stand
or sleep, chains on my arms, no status or position assured to me. "See the
imperialist spy and running dog." Voltaire, I do not like this vision. To be
locked all my life in China for pushing opium? I am not enthusiastic. "Sure,
Mr Tiu! Bye-bye! See you this afternoon!" I have to consider most seriously.'

The brown haze of the sinking sun suddenly filled the room. On Ricardo's
chest, despite the perfection of his condition, the same sweat had gathered. It
lay in beads over the matted black hair and on his oiled shoulders.

'Where was Lizzie in all this?' Jerry asked again.

Ricardo's answer was nervous and already angry.

'In Vientiane! On the moon! In bed with Charlie! What the hell do I care?'

'Did she know of the deal with Tiu?'

Ricardo gave only a scowl of contempt.

Time to go, Jerry thought. Time to light the last fuse and run. Below,
Mickey was making a great hit with Ricardo's women. Jerry could hear his
sing-song chattering, broken by their high-pitched laughter, like the laughter
of a whole class at a girl's school.

'So away you flew,' he said. He waited, but Ricardo remained lost in
thought.

'You took off and headed north,' Jerry said.

Lifting his eyes a little, Ricardo held Jerry in a bullish, furious stare, till the
invitation to describe his own heroic feat finally got the better of him.

'I never flew so good in my life. Never. I was magnificent. That little black Beechcraft. North a hundred miles because I don't trust nobody. Maybe those clowns have got me locked on a radar screen somewhere? I don't take no chances. The east, but very slowly, very low over the mountains, Voltaire. I fly between the cow's legs, okay? In the war we have little landing strips up there, crazy listening places in the middle of badland. I flew those places, Voltaire. I know them. I find one right at the top of a mountain, you can reach it only from the air. I take a look, I see the fuel dump, I land, I refuel, I take a sleep, it's crazy. But Jesus, Voltaire, it's not Yunnan province, okay? It's not China, and Ricardo, the American war criminal and opium smuggler, is not going to spend the rest of his life hanging from a hen-hook in Peking okay? Listen, I brought that plane back south again. I know places, I know places I could lose a whole air force, believe me.'

Ricardo became suddenly very vague about the next few months of his life. He had heard of the Flying Dutchman, and he said that was what he became. He flew, hid again, flew, resprayed the Beechcraft, changed the registration once a month, sold the opium in small lots in order not to be conspicuous, a kilo here, fifty there, bought a Spanish passport from an Indian but had no faith in it, kept away from everyone he knew, including Rosie in Bangkok, and even Charlie Marshall. It was also the time, Jerry remembered from his briefing by old Craw, when Ricardo sold Ko's opium to the Enforcement heroes, but got the cold shoulder on his story. On Tiu's orders, said Ricardo, the Indocharter boys had been quick to post him dead, and changed his flight-route southward to distract attention. Ricardo heard of this and did not object to being dead.

'What did you do about Lizzie?' Jerry asked.

Again, Ricardo flared. '*Lizzie, Lizzie!* You got some fixation about that scrubber, Voltaire, that you throw *Lizzie* in my face all the time? I never knew a woman so irrelevant. Listen, I give her to Drake Ko, okay? I make her fortune.' Seizing his whisky glass, he drank from it, still glowering.

She was lobbying for him, Jerry thought. She and Charlie Marshall. Plodding the pavements trying to buy Ricardo's neck for him.

'You referred boastingly to other lucrative aspects of the case,' Ricardo said, in a peremptory resumption of his business-school English. 'Kindly advise me what they are, Voltaire.'

Sarratt man had this part off pat.

'Number one: Ko was being paid large sums by the Russian Embassy in Vientiane. The money was siphoned through Indocharter and ended up in a slush account in Hong Kong. We've got the proof. We've got photostats of the bank statements.'

Richardo pulled a face as if his whisky didn't taste right, then went on drinking.

'Whether the money was for reviving the opium habit in Red China or for some other service, we don't yet know,' said Jerry. 'But we will. Point two. Do you want to hear it or am I keeping you awake?'

Ricardo had yawned.

'Point two,' Jerry continued. 'Ko has a younger brother in Red China. Used to be called Nelson. Ko pretends he's dead, but he's now a big beef with the Peking administration. Ko's been trying to get him out for years. Your job was to take in opium and bring back out a package. The package was brother

Nelson. That's why Ko was going to love you like his own son if you brought him out. And that's why he was going to kill you if you didn't. If that's not a five million dollar touch what is?'

Nothing much happened to Ricardo as Jerry watched him in the failing light, except that the slumbering animal in him visibly woke. To set down his glass, he leaned forward slowly, but he couldn't conceal the tautness of his shoulders or the knotting of the muscles of his stomach. To flash a smile of exceptional goodwill at Jerry, he turned quite languidly, but his eyes had a brightness that was like a signal to attack; so that when he reached forward and patted Jerry's cheek affectionately with his right hand, Jerry was quite ready to fall straight back with it, if necessary, on the offchance he would manage to throw Ricardo across the room.

'Five million bucks, Voltaire!' Ricardo exclaimed with steely-bright excitement. 'Five million! Listen – we got to do something for poor old Charlie Marshall, okay? For love. Charlie's always broke. Maybe we put him in charge of the football pool once. Wait a minute. I get some more Scotch, we celebrate.' He stood up, his head tilted to one side, he held out his naked arms. 'Voltaire,' he said softly. '*Voltaire!*' Affectionately, he took Jerry by the cheeks and kissed him. 'Listen, that's some research you guys did! That's some pretty smart editor you work for. You be my business partner. Like you say. Okay? I need an Englishman in my life. I got to be like Lizzie once, marry a schoolmaster. You do that for Ricardo, Voltaire? You hold me down a little?'

'No problem,' said Jerry, smiling back.

'You play with the guns a minute okay?'

'Sure.'

'Personal family thing.'

'I'll be here.'

From the top of the trap Jerry looked urgently down after him. Mickey the driver was dandling the baby on his arm, chucking it under the ear. In a mad world you keep the fiction going, he thought. Stick to it till the bitter end and leave the first bite to him. Returning to the desk, Jerry took Ricardo's pencil and his pad of paper and wrote out a non-existent address in Hong Kong where he could be reached at any time. Ricardo had still not returned, but when Jerry stood he saw him coming out of the trees behind the car. He likes contracts, he thought. Give him something to sign. He took a fresh sheet of paper: *I Jerry Westerby do solemnly swear to share with my friend Captain Tiny Ricardo all proceeds relating to our joint exploitation of his life story*, he wrote, and signed his name. Ricardo was coming up the steps. Jerry thought of helping himself from the private armoury but he guessed Ricardo was waiting for him to do just that. While Ricardo poured more whisky, Jerry handed him the two sheets of paper.

'I'll draft a legal deposition,' he said, looking straight into Ricardo's burning eyes. 'I have an English lawyer in Bangkok whom I trust entirely. I'll have him check it over and bring it back to you to sign. After that we'll plan the march-route and I'll talk to Lizzie. Okay?'

'Sure. Listen, it's dark out there. They got a lot of badguys in that forest. You stay the night. I talk to the girls. They like you. They say you very strong man. Not so strong as me, but strong.'

Jerry said something about not wasting time. He'd like to make Bangkok by tomorrow, he said. To himself, he sounded as lame as a three-legged mule, good enough to get in, maybe, but never to get out. But Ricardo seemed content to the point of serenity. Maybe it's the ambush deal, thought Jerry, something the colonel is arranging.

'Go well, horse-writer. Go well, my friend.'

Ricardo put both hands on the back of Jerry's neck and let his thumbpoints settle into Jerry's jaw, then drew Jerry's head forward for another kiss and Jerry let it happen. Though his heart thumped and his wet spine felt sore against his shirt, Jerry let it happen. Outside it was half dark. Ricardo did not see them to the car but watched them indulgently from under the stilts, the girls sitting at his feet, while he waved with both naked arms. From the car Jerry turned and waved back. The last sun lay dying in the teak trees. My last ever, he thought.

'Don't start the engine,' he told Mickey quietly. 'I want to check the oil.'

Perhaps it's just me who's mad. Perhaps I really got myself a deal, he thought.

Sitting in the driver's seat, Mickey released the catch and Jerry pulled up the bonnet but there was no little *plastic*, no leaving present from his new friend and partner. He pulled up the dipstick and pretended to read it.

'You want oil, horse-writer?' Ricardo yelled down the dustpath.

'No, we're all right. So long!'

'So long.'

He had no torch, but when he crouched and groped under the chassis in the gloom, he again found nothing.

'You lost something, horse-writer?' Ricardo called again, cupping his hands to his mouth.

'Start the engine,' Jerry said and got into the car.

'Lights on, Mister?'

'Yes, Mickey. Lights on.'

'Why he call you horse-writer?'

'Mutual friends.'

If Ricardo has tipped off the CTs, thought Jerry, it won't make any damn difference either way. Mickey put on the lights, and inside the car the American dashboard lit up like a small city.

'Let's go,' said Jerry.

'Quick-quick?'

'Yes, quick-quick.'

They drove five miles, seven, nine. Jerry was watching them on the indicator, reckoning twenty to the first checkpoint and forty-five to the second. Mickey had hit seventy and Jerry was in no mood to complain. They were on the crown of the road and the road was straight and beyond the ambush strips the tall teaks slid past them like orange ghosts.

'Fine man,' Mickey said. 'He plenty fine lover. Those girls say he some pretty fine lover.'

'Watch for wires,' Jerry said.

On the right the trees broke and a red dust-track disappeared into the cleft.

'He get pretty good time in there,' said Mickey. 'Girls, he get kids, he get whisky, PX. He get real good time.'

'Pull in, Mickey. Stop the car. Here in the middle of the road where it's level. Just do it, Mickey.'

Mickey began laughing.

'Girls get good time too,' Mickey said. 'Girls get candy, little baby get candy, everybody get candy!'

'Stop the damn car!'

Taking his own good time, Mickey brought the car to a halt, still giggling about the girls.

'Is that thing accurate?' Jerry asked, his finger pressed to the petrol gauge.

'Accurate?' Mickey echoed, puzzled by the English.

'Petrol. Gas. Full? Or half full? Or three-quarters? Has it been reading right on the journey?'

'Sure. He right.'

'When we arrived at the burnt village, Mickey, you had half-full gas. You still have half-full gas.'

'Sure.'

'You put any in? From a can? You fill car?'

'No.'

'Get out.'

Mickey began protesting but Jerry leaned across him opened his door, shoved Mickey straight through it on to the tarmac and followed him. Seizing Mickey's arm, he jammed it into his back and frogmarched him at a gallop, straight across the road to the edge of the wide soft shoulder, and twenty yards into it, then threw him into the scrub and fell half beside him, half on to him, so that the wind went out of Mickey's stomach in a single astonished hiccup, and it took him all of half a minute before he was able to give vent to an indignant 'Why for?' But Jerry by that time was pushing his face back into the earth to keep it out of the blast. The old Ford seemed to burn first and explode afterwards, finally lifting into the air in one last assertion of life, before collapsing dead and flaming on its side. While Mickey gasped in admiration, Jerry looked at his watch. Eighteen minutes since they had left the stilt-house. Maybe twenty. Should have happened sooner, he thought. Not suprising Ricardo was keen for us to go. At Sarratt they wouldn't even have seen it coming. This was an eastern treat, and Sarratt's natural soul was with Europe and the good old days of the cold war: Czecho, Berlin and the old fronts. Jerry wondered which brand of grenade it was. The Vietcong preferred the American type. They loved its double action. All you needed, they said, was a wide throat to the petrol tank. You took out the pin, you put an elastic band over the spring, you slipped the grenade into the petrol tank, and you waited patiently for the petrol to eat its way through the rubber. The result was one of those western inventions it took the Vietcong to discover. Ricardo must have used fat elastic bands, he decided.

They made the first checkpoint in four hours, walking on the road. Mickey was extremely happy about the insurance situation, assuming that since Jerry had paid the premium, the money was automatically theirs to squander. Jerry could not deter him from this view. But Mickey was also scared: first of CTs, then of ghosts, then of the colonel. So Jerry explained to him that neither the ghosts nor the CTs would venture near the road after that little episode. As for the colonel, though Jerry didn't mention this to Mickey – well, he was a father and a soldier and he had a dam to build: not for nothing was he building it with Drake Ko's cement and China Airsea's transport.

At the checkpoint, they eventually found a truck to take Mickey home. Riding with him a distance, Jerry promised the comic's support in any insurance haggle but Mickey in his euphoria was deaf to doubts. Amid much laughter, they exchanged addresses, and many hearty handshakes, then

Jerry dropped off at a roadside café to wait half a day for the bus that would carry him eastward toward a fresh field of war.

Need Jerry have ever gone to Ricardo in the first place? Would the outcome, for himself, have been different if he had not? Or did Jerry, as Smiley's defenders to this day insist, by his pass at Ricardo, supply the last crucial heave which shook the tree and caused the coveted fruit to fall? For the Smiley Supporters' Club there is no question: the visit to Ricardo was the final straw and Ko's back broke under it. Without it, he might have gone on dithering until the open season started, by which time Ko himself, and the intelligence on him, would be up for grabs. End of argument. And on the face of it, the facts demonstrate a wonderful causality. For this is what happened. A mere six hours after Jerry and his driver Mickey had picked themselves out of the dust of that roadside in north-east Thailand, the whole of the Circus fifth floor exploded into a blaze of ecstatic jubilation which would have out-shone the pyre of Mickey's borrowed Ford car any night. In the rumpus room, where Smiley announced the news, Doc di Salis actually danced a stiff little jig, and Connie would unquestionably have joined him if her arthritis had not held her to that wretched chair. Trot howled, Guillam and Molly embraced, and only Smiley, amid so much revelry, preserved his usual slightly startled air, though Molly swore she saw him redden as he blinked around the company.

He had just had word, he said. A flash communication from the Cousins. At seven this morning, Hong Kong time, Tiu had telephoned Ko at Star Heights, where he had been spending the night relaxing with Lizzie Worth. Lizzie herself took the call in the first instance, but Ko came in on the extension and sharply ordered Lizzie to ring off, which she did. Tiu had proposed breakfast in town at once: 'At George's place,' said Tiu, to the great entertainment of the transcribers. Three hours later, Tiu was on the phone to his travel agent making hasty plans for a business trip to Mainland China. His first stop would be Canton, where China Airsea kept a representative, but his ultimate destination was Shanghai.

So how did Ricardo get through to Tiu so fast without the telephone? The most likely theory is the colonel's police link to Bangkok. And from Bangkok? Heaven knows. Trade telex, the exchange-rate network, anything is possible. The Chinese have their own ways of doing these things.

On the other hand, it may just be that Ko's patience chose this moment to snap of its own accord – and that the breakfast 'at George's place' was about something entirely different. Either way, it was the breakthrough they had all been dreaming of, the triumphant vindication of Smiley's footwork. By lunchtime, Lacon had called in person to offer his congratulations, and by early evening Saul Enderby had made a gesture nobody from the wrong side of Trafalgar Square had ever made before.

He had sent round a crate of champagne from Berry Brothers and Rudd, a vintage Krug, a real beauty. Attached to it was a note to George saying 'to the first day of summer'. And indeed, though late April, it seemed to be just that. Through the thick net curtains of the lower floors, the plane trees were already in leaf. Higher up, a cluster of hyacinths had bloomed in Connie's window box. 'Red,' she said, as she drank Saul Enderby's health. 'Karla's favourite colour, bless him.'

# EIGHTEEN

## *the river bend*

The airbase was neither beautiful nor victorious. Technically it was under Thai command, and in practice the Thais were allowed to collect the garbage and occupy the stockade close to the perimeter. The checkpoint was a separate town. Amid smells of charcoal, urine, pickled fish and calor gas, chains of collapsing tin hovels plied the historic trades of military occupation. The brothels were manned by crippled pimps, the tailor shops offered wedding tuxedos, the bookshops offered pornography and travel, the bars were called Sunset Strip, Hawaii and Lucky Time. At the MP hut Jerry asked for Captain Urquhart of public relations and the black sergeant squared to throw him out when he said he was press. On the base telephone, Jerry heard a lot of clicking and popping before a slow Southern voice said, 'Urquhart isn't around just now. My name is Masters. Who's this again?'

'We met last summer at General Crosse's briefing,' Jerry said.

'Well now, so we did, man.' said the same amazingly slow voice, reminding him of Deathwish. 'Pay off your cab. Be right down. Blue jeep. Wait for the whites of its eyes.'

A long silence followed, presumably while the codewords Urquhart and Crosse were hunted down in the contingency book.

A flow of airforce personnel was passing in and out of the camp, blacks and whites, in scowling segregated groups. A white officer passed. The blacks gave him the black power salute. The officer warily returned it. The enlisted men wore Charlie-Marshall-style patches on their uniforms, mostly in praise of drugs. The mood was sullen, defeated and innately violent. The Thai troops greeted nobody. Nobody greeted the Thais.

A blue jeep with lights flashing and siren wailing pulled up with a ferocious skid the other side of the boom. The sergeant waved Jerry through. A moment later he was careering over the runway at breakneck speed toward a long string of low white huts at the centre of the airfield. His driver was a lanky boy with all the signs of a probationer.

'You Masters?' Jerry asked.

'No, sir. Sir, I just carry the major's bags,' he said.

They passed a ragged baseball game, siren wailing all the time, lights still flashing.

'Great cover,' said Jerry.

'What's that, sir?' the boy yelled above the din.

'Forget it.'

It was not the biggest base. Jerry had seen larger. They passed lines of Phantoms and helicopters and as they approached the white huts he realized they comprised a separate spook encampment with their own compound and aerial masts, and their own cluster of little black-painted small planes – weirdos, they used to be called – which before the pullout had dropped and collected God knew whom in God knew where.

They entered by a side door which the boy unlocked. The short corridor was empty and soundless. A door stood ajar at the end of it, made of traditional fake rosewood. Masters wore a short-sleeved airforce uniform with few insignia. He had medals and the rank of major and Jerry guessed he was the paramilitary type of Cousin, maybe not even career. He was sallow and wiry with resentful tight lips and hollow cheeks. He stood before a faked fireplace, under an Andrew Wyeth reproduction, and there was something strangely still about him, and disconnected. He was like a man being deliberately slow because everyone else was in a hurry. The boy made the introductions and hesitated. Masters stared at him until he left, then turned his colourless gaze to the rosewood table where the coffee was.

'Look like you need breakfast,' Masters said.

He poured coffee and proffered a plate of doughnuts, all in slow motion.

'Facilities,' he said.

'Facilities,' Jerry agreed.

An electric typewriter lay on the desk, and plain paper beside it. Masters walked stiffly to a chair and perched on the arm. Taking up a copy of *Stars and Stripes*. 'Well now.'

Setting up his portable in preference to the electric, Jerry stabbed out his report in a series of quick smacks which to his own ear grew louder as he laboured. Perhaps to Masters's ear also, for he looked up frequently, though only as far as Jerry's hands, and the toy-town portable.

Jerry handed him his copy.

'Your orders are to remain here,' Masters said, articulating each word with great deliberation. 'Your orders are to remain here while we despatch your signal. Man, will we despatch that signal. Your orders are to stand by for confirmation and further instructions. That figure? Does that figure, *sir?*'

'Sure,' said Jerry.

'Heard the glad news by any chance?' Masters enquired. They were facing each other. Not three feet lay between them. Masters was staring at Jerry's signal but his eyes did not appear to be scanning the lines.

'What news is that, sport?'

'We just lost the war, Mr Westerby. Yes, sir. Last of the brave just had themselves scraped off the roof of the Saigon Embassy by chopper like a bunch of rookies caught with their pants down in a whorehouse. Maybe that doesn't affect you. Ambassador's dog survived, you'll be relieved to hear. Newsman took it out on his damn lap. Maybe that doesn't affect you either. Maybe you're not a dog-lover. Maybe you feel about dogs same way I personally feel about newsmen, Mr Westerby, sir.'

Jerry had by now caught the smell of brandy on Masters's breath which no amount of coffee could conceal, and he guessed he had been drinking for a long time without succeeding in getting drunk.

'Mr Westerby, sir?'

'Yes, old boy.'

Masters held out his hand.

'*Old boy*, I want you to shake me by the hand.'

The hand stuck between them, thumb upward.

'What for?' said Jerry.

'I want you to extend the hand of welcome, sir. The United States of America has just applied to join the club of second class powers, of which I understand your own fine nation to be chairman, president and oldest member. *Shake it!*'

'Proud to have you aboard,' said Jerry and obligingly shook the major's hand.

He was at once rewarded by a brilliant smile of false gratitude.

'Why sir, I call that *real* handsome of you, Mr Westerby. Anything we can do to make your stay with us more comfortable, I invite you to let me know. If you want to rent the place, no reasonable offer refused, we say.'

'You could shove a little Scotch through the bars,' Jerry said, pulling a dead grin.

'Mah pleasure,' said Masters, in a drawl so long it was like a slow punch. 'Man after my own heart. Yes, sir.'

Masters left him with a half bottle of J & B, from the cupboard, and some backnumbers of *Playboy*.

'We keep these handy for English gentlemen who didn't see fit to lift a damn finger to help us,' he explained confidingly.

'Very thoughtful of you,' said Jerry.

'I'll go send your letter home to Mummy. How is the Queen, by the way?'

Masters didn't turn a key but when Jerry tested the door handle it was locked. The windows overlooking the airfield were smoked and double glazed. On the runway, aircraft landed and took off without making a sound. This is how they tried to win, Jerry thought: from inside soundproof rooms, through smoked glass, using machines at arm's length. This is how they lost. He drank, feeling nothing. So it's over, he thought, and that was all. So what was his next stop? Charlie Marshall's old man? Little swing through the Shans, heart to heart chat with the General's bodyguard? He waited, his thoughts crowding formlessly. He sat down, then lay on the sofa and for a while slept, he never knew how long. He woke abruptly to the sound of canned music occasionally interrupted by an announcement of homely-wise assurance. Would Captain somebody do so and so? Once the speaker offered higher education. Once cut-price washing machines. Once, prayer. Jerry prowled the room made nervous by the crematorium quiet and the music.

He crossed to the other window, and in his mind Lizzie's face bobbed along at his shoulder, the way once the orphan's had, but no more. He drank more whisky. I should have slept in the truck, he thought. Altogether I should sleep more. So they've lost the war at last. The sleep had done him no good. It seemed a long time since he'd slept the way he'd like to. Old Frostie had rather put an end to that. His hand was shaking: Christ, look at that. He thought of Luke. Time we went on a bend together. He must be back by now, if he hasn't had his arse shot off. Got to stop the old brain a bit, he thought. But sometimes the old brain hunted on its own these days. Bit too much, actually. Got to tie it down, he told himself sternly. *Man*. He thought of Ricardo's grenades. Hurry up, he thought. Come on, let's have a decision. *Where* next? *Who* now? No whys. His face was dry and hot, and his hands moist. He had a headache just above the eyes. Bloody music, he thought. Bloody, bloody end-of-world music. He was casting round urgently for somewhere to switch it off when he saw Masters standing in the doorway, an envelope in his hand and nothing in his eyes. Jerry read the signal. Masters settled on the chair arm again.

'"Son, come home,"' Masters intoned, mocking his own Southern drawl. '"Come directly home. Do not pass *go*. Do not collect two hundred dollars." The Cousins will fly you to Bangkok. From Bangkok you will proceed immediately to London, England, *not* repeat not London, Ontario, by a flight of *your* choosing. You will on no account return to Hong Kong. You will not! No *sir*! Mission accomplished, *son*. Thank you and well done. Her Majesty is *so thrilled*. So hurry home to dinner, we got hominy grits and turkey, and *blue-*

berry pie. Sounds like a bunch of fairies you're working for, *man*.'

Jerry re-read the signal.

'Plane leaves for Bangkok one one hundred,' Masters said. He wore his watch on the inside of his wrist, so that information was private to himself. 'Hear me?'

Jerry grinned. 'Sorry, sport. Slow reader. Thanks. Too many big words. Lot to get the old mind round. Look, left my things at the hotel.'

'My houseboys are at your royal command.'

'Thanks, but if you don't mind, I'd prefer to avoid the official connection.'

'Please yourself, sir, please yourself.'

'I'll find a cab at the gates. There and back in an hour. Thanks,' he repeated.

'Thank *you*.'

Sarratt man provided a smart piece of tradecraft for the kiss-off. 'Mind if I leave that there?' he asked, nodding to his scruffy portable, where it lay beside Masters's golf-ball IBM.

'Sir, it shall be our most treasured possession.'

If Masters had bothered to look at him at that moment, he might have hesitated when he saw the purposeful brightness in Jerry's eye. If he had known Jerry's voice better perhaps, or noticed its particularly friendly huskiness, he might also have hesitated. If he had seen the way Jerry clawed at his forelock, forearm across his body in an attitude of instinctive self-concealment, or responded to Jerry's sheepish grin of thanks as the probationer returned to drive him to the gates in the blue jeep: well, again he might have had his doubts. But Major Masters was not only an embittered professional with a lot of disillusionment to his credit. He was a Southern gentleman suffering the stab of defeat at the hands of unintelligible savages; and he hadn't too much time just then for the contortions of a bone-weary overdue Brit who used his expiring spookhouse as a post office.

A mood of festivity attended the leavetaking of the Circus's Hong Kong operations party, and it was only enriched by the secrecy of the arrangements. The news of Jerry's reappearance triggered it. The content of his signal intensified it, and coincided with word from the Cousins that Drake Ko had cancelled all his social and business engagements and withdrawn to the seclusion of his house Seven Gates in Headland Road. A photograph of Ko, taken in longshot from the Cousins' surveillance van, showed him in quarter profile, standing in his own large garden, at the end of an arbour of rose trees, staring out to sea. The concrete junk was not visible but he was wearing his floppy beret.

'Like a latter-day Jay Gatsby, my dear!' Connie Sachs cried in delight, as they pored over it. 'Mooning at the blasted light at the end of the pier or whatever the ninny did!'

When the van returned that way two hours later, Ko was in the identical pose so they didn't bother to re-shoot. More significant was the fact that Ko had ceased to use the telephone altogether – or, at the very least, those lines on which the Cousins ran a tap.

Sam Collins also sent a report, the third in a stream, but by far his longest to date. As usual, it arrived in a special cover addressed to Smiley personally, and as usual he discussed its contents with nobody but Connie Sachs. And at the very moment when the party was leaving for London Airport, a last-minute message from Martello advised them that Tiu had returned from China, and was at present closeted with Ko in Headland Road.

But the most important ceremony, then and later, in Guillam's recollection, and the most disturbing, was a small war-party held in Martello's rooms in the Annexe, which exceptionally was attended not only by the usual quintet of Martello, his two quiet men, Smiley and Guillam, but by Lacon and Saul Enderby as well, who significantly arrived in the same official car. The purpose of the ceremony – called by Smiley – was the formal handing over of the keys. Martello was now to receive a complete portrait of the Dolphin case, including the all-important link with Nelson. He was to be indoctrinated, with certain minor omissions, which only showed up later, as a full partner in the enterprise. How Lacon and Enderby muscled in on the occasion Guillam never quite knew and Smiley was afterwards understandably reticent about it. Enderby declared flatly that he had come along in the 'interest of good order and military discipline'. Lacon looked more than usually wan and disdainful. Guillam had the strongest impression they were up to something, and this was strengthened by his observation of the interplay between Enderby and Martello: in short, these new-found buddies cut each other so dead they put Guillam in mind of two secret lovers meeting at communal breakfast in a country house, a situation in which he often found himself.

It was the *scale* of the thing, Enderby explained at one point. Case was blowing up so big he really thought there ought to be a few official flies on the wall. It was the Colonial lobby, he explained at another. Wilbraham was raising a stink with Treasury.

'All right, so we've heard the dirt,' said Enderby, when Smiley had finished his lengthy summary, and Martello's praises had all but brought the roof down. 'Now whose finger's on the trigger, George, point one?' he demanded to know, and after that the meeting became very much Enderby's show, as meetings with Enderby usually did. 'Who calls the shots when it gets hot? You, George? Still? I mean you've done a good planning job, I grant you, but it's old Marty here who's providing the artillery, isn't it?'

At which Martello had another bout of deafness, while he beamed upon all the great and lovely British people he was privileged to be associated with, and let Enderby go on doing his hatchet-work for him.

'Marty, how do *you* see this one?' Enderby pressed, as if he really had no idea; as if he never went fishing with Martello, or gave lavish dinners for him, or discussed top secret matters out of school.

A strange insight came to Guillam at this moment, though he kicked himself afterwards for making too little of it. *Martello knew.* The revelations about Nelson, which Martello had affected to be dazzled by, were not revelations at all, but re-statements of information which he and his quiet men already possessed. Guillam read it in their pale, wooden faces and their watchful eyes. He read it in Martello's fulsomeness. *Martello knew.*

'Ah technically this is George's show, Saul,' Martello reminded Enderby loyally, in answer to his question, but with just enough spin on the *technically* to put the rest in doubt. 'George is on the bridge, Saul. We're just there to stoke the engines.'

Enderby staged an unhappy frown and shoved a match between his teeth.

'George, how does that grab *you*? You content to let that happen, are you? Let Marty chuck in the cover, the accommodation out there, communications, all the cloak and dagger stuff, surveillance, charging round Hong Kong and whatnot? While you call the shots? Crikey. Bit like wearing someone else's dinner jacket, I'd have thought.'

Smiley was firm enough but, to Guillam's eye, a deal too concerned with the question, and not nearly concerned enough with the thinly-veiled collusion.

'Not at all,' said Smiley. 'Martello and I have a clear understanding. The spearhead of the operation will be handled by ourselves. If supportive action is required, Martello will supply it. The product is then shared. If one is thinking in terms of a dividend for the American investment, it comes with the partition of the product. The responsibility for obtaining it remains ours.' He ended strongly. 'The letter of agreement setting all this out has of course long been on file.'

Enderby glanced at Lacon. 'Oliver, you said you'd send me that. Where is it?'

Lacon put his long head on one side and pulled a dreary smile at nothing in particular. 'Kicking around your Third Room I should think, Saul.'

Enderby tried another tack. 'And you two guys can see the deal holding up in all contingencies, can you? I mean, who's handling the safe houses, all that? Burying the body, sort of thing?'

Smiley again. 'Housekeeping Section has already rented a cottage in the country, and is preparing it for occupation,' he said stolidly.

Enderby took the wet matchstick from his mouth and broke it into the ashtray. 'Could have had my place if you'd asked,' he muttered absently. 'Bags of room. Nobody ever there. Staff. Everything.' But he went on worrying at his theme. 'Look here. Answer me this one. Your man panics. He cuts and runs through the back streets of Hong Kong. Who plays cops and robbers to get him back?'

Don't answer it! Guillam prayed. He has absolutely no business to plumb around like this! Tell him to get lost!

Smiley's answer, though effective, lacked the fire Guillam longed for.

'Oh I suppose one can always invent a *hypothesis*,' he objected mildly. 'I think the best one can say is that Martello and I would at that stage pool our thoughts and act for the best.'

'George and I have a fine working relationship, Saul,' Martello declared handsomely. 'Just fine.'

'Much *tidier*, you see, George,' Enderby resumed, through a fresh matchstick. 'Much *safer* if it's an all-Yank do. Marty's people make a balls and all they do is apologize to the Governor, post a couple of blokes to Walla-Walla and promise not to do it again. That's it. What everyone expects of 'em anyway. Advantage of a disgraceful reputation, right, Marty? Nobody's surprised if you screw the housemaid.'

'Why, *Saul*,' said Martello and laughed richly at the great British sense of humour.

'Much more tricky if *we're* the naughty boys,' Enderby went on. 'Or *you* are, rather. Governor could blow you down with one puff, the way it's set up at the moment. Wilbraham's crying all over his desk already.'

Against Smiley's distracted obduracy, there was however no progress to be made, so for the while Enderby bowed out and they resumed their discussion of the 'meat-and-potatoes', which was Martello's amusing phrase for modalities. But before they finished Enderby had one last shot at dislodging Smiley from his primacy, choosing again the issue of the efficient handling and aftercare of the catch.

'George, who's going to manage all the grilling and stuff? You using that funny little Jesuit of yours, the one with the smart name?'

'di Salis will be responsible for the Chinese aspects of the debriefing and our Soviet Research Section for the Russian side.'

'That the crippled don-woman, is it, George? The one bloody Bill Haydon shoved out to grass for drinking?'

'It is they, between them, who have brought the case this far,' said Smiley.

Inevitably, Martello sprang into the breach.

'Ah now George, I won't have that! Sir, I will not! Saul, Oliver, I wish you to know that I regard the Dolphin case, in all its aspects, Saul, as a personal triumph for George here, and for George *alone*!'

With a big hand all round for dear old George, they made their way back to Cambridge Circus.

'Gunpowder, treason and plot!' Guillam expostulated. 'Why's Enderby selling you down the river? What's all that tripe about losing the letter?'

'Yes,' said Smiley at last, but from far away. 'Yes, that's very careless of them. I thought I'd send them a copy actually. Blind, by hand, for information only. Enderby seemed so *woolly*, didn't he. Will you attend to that, Peter, ask the mothers?'

The mention of the letter of agreement – *heads* of agreement as Lacon called it – revived Guillam's worst misgivings. He remembered how he had foolishly allowed Sam Collins to be the bearer of it, and how, according to Fawn, he had spent more than an hour cloistered with Martello under the pretext of delivering it. He remembered Sam Collins also as he had glimpsed him in Lacon's anteroom, the mysterious confidant of Lacon and Enderby, lazing around Whitehall like a blasted Cheshire cat. He remembered Enderby's taste for backgammon, which he played for very high stakes, and it even passed through his head, as he tried to sniff out the conspiracy, that Enderby might be a client of Sam Collins's club. From that notion he soon pulled back, discounting it as too absurd. But ironically it later turned out to be true. And he remembered his fleeting conviction – based on little but the physiognomy of the three Americans, and therefore soon also to be dismissed – that they knew already what Smiley had come to tell them.

But Guillam did not pull back from the notion of Sam Collins as the ghost at that morning's feast, and as he boarded the plane at London Airport, exhausted by his long and energetic farewell from Molly, the same ghost grinned at him through the smoke of Sam's infernal brown cigarette.

The flight was uneventful, except in one respect. They were three strong, and in the seating arrangements Guillam had won a small battle in his running war with Fawn. Over Housekeeping Section's dead body, Guillam and Smiley flew first class, while Fawn the babysitter took an aisle seat at the front of the tourist compartment, cheek by jowl with the airline security guards, who slept innocently for most of the journey while Fawn sulked. There had never been any suggestion, fortunately, that Martello and his quiet men would fly with them, for Smiley was determined that that should not on any account happen. As it was, Martello flew west, staging in Langley for instructions, and continuing through Honolulu and Tokyo in order to be on hand in Hong Kong for their arrival.

As an unconsciously ironic footnote to their departure, Smiley left a long handwritten note to Jerry, to be presented to him on his arrival at the Circus, congratulating him on his first-rate performance. The carbon copy is still on Jerry's dossier. Nobody has thought to remove it. Smiley speaks of Jerry's 'unswerving loyalty', and of 'setting the crown on more than thirty years of service'. He includes an apocryphal message from Ann 'who joins me in wishing you an equally distinguished career as a novelist'. And he winds up rather awkwardly with the sentiment that 'one of the privileges of our work is that it provides us with such wonderful colleagues. I must tell you that we all think of you in those terms.'

Certain people do still ask why no anxious word about Jerry's whereabouts had reached the Circus before take-off. He was after all several days overdue. Once more they look for ways of blaming Smiley, but there is no evidence of a lapse on the Circus's side. For the transmission of Jerry's report from the airbase in North East Thailand – his last – the Cousins had cleared a line through Bangkok direct to the Annexe in London. But the arrangement was valid for one signal and one answer-back only, and a follow-up was not envisaged. Accordingly the grizzle, when it came, was routed first to Bangkok on the military network, thence to the Cousins in Hong Kong on their network – since Hong Kong was held to have a total lien on all Dolphin-starred material – and only then, marked 'routine', repeated by Hong Kong to London, where it kicked around in several laminated rosewood in-trays before anybody noted its significance. And it must be admitted that the languid Major Masters had attached very little significance to the no-show, as he later called it, of some travelling English fairy. 'ASSUME EXPLANATION YOUR END' his message ends. Major Masters now lives in Norman, Oklahoma, where he runs a small automobile repair business.

Nor did Housekeeping Section have any reason to panic – or so they still plead. Jerry's instructions, on reaching Bangkok, were to find himself a plane, any plane, using his air-travel card, and get himself to London. No date was mentioned, and no airline. The whole purpose was to leave things fluid. Most likely he had stopped over somewhere for a bit of relaxation. Many homing fieldmen do, and Jerry was on record as sexually voracious. So they kept their usual watch on flight lists and made a provisional booking at Sarratt for the two weeks' drying-out and re-cycling ceremony, then returned their attention to the far more urgent business of setting up the Dolphin safe house. This was a charming millhouse, quite remote, though situated in the commuter town of Maresfield in Sussex, and on most days they found a reason for going down there. As well as di Salis and a sizeable part of his Chinese archive, a small army of interpreters and transcribers had to be accommodated, not to mention technicians, babysitters and a Chinese-speaking doctor. In no time at all, the residents were complaining noisily to the police about the influx of Japanese. The local paper carried a story that they were a visiting dance troupe. Housekeeping Section had inspired the leak.

Jerry had nothing to collect at the hotel, and as it happened no hotel, but he reckoned he had an hour to get clear, perhaps two. He had no doubt the Americans had the whole town wired, and he knew there would be nothing easier, if London asked for it, than for Major Masters to have Jerry's name and description broadcast as an American deserter travelling on a false-flag passport. Once his taxi was clear of the gates, therefore, he took it to the southern edge of town, waited, then took a second taxi and pointed it due north. A wet haze lay over the paddies and the straight road ran into it endlessly. The radio pumped out female Thai voices like an endless slow motion nursery rhyme. They passed an American electronics base, a circular grid a quarter of a mile wide floating in the haze and known locally as the Elephant Cage. Giant bodkins marked the perimeter, and at the middle, surrounded by webs of strung wire, burned a single infernal light, like the promise of a future war. He had heard there were twelve hundred language students inside the place, but not one soul was to be seen.

He needed time, and in the event he helped himself to more than one week. Even now, he needed that long to bring himself to the point, because Jerry at heart was a soldier and voted with his feet. *In the beginning was the deed*, Smiley liked to say to him, in his failed-priest mood, quoting from one of his German poets. For Jerry, that simple maxim had become a pillar of his uncomplicated philosophy. What a man thinks is his own business. What matters is what he does.

Reaching the Mekong by early evening, he selected a village and strolled idly for a couple of days up and down the river bank, trailing his shoulder bag and kicking at an empty Coca-Cola tin with the toe of his buckskin boot. Across the river, behind the brown ant-hill mountains, lay the Ho Chi-minh trail. He had once watched a B52 strike from this very point, three miles away in Central Laos. He remembered how the ground shook under his feet and the sky emptied and burned, and he had known, he had really for a moment known, what it was like to be in the middle of it.

The same night, to use his own jolly phrase, Jerry Westerby blew the walls out, much along the lines the housekeepers expected of him, if not in quite the circumstances. In a riverside bar where they played old tunes on a nickelodeon, he drank black market PX Scotch and night after night drove himself into oblivion, leading one laughing girl after another up the unlit staircase to a tattered bedroom, till finally he stayed there sleeping, and didn't come down. Waking with a jolt, clear-headed at dawn, to the screaming of roosters and the clatter of the river traffic, Jerry forced himself to think long and generously of his chum and mentor, George Smiley. It was an act of will that made him do this, almost an act of obedience. He wished, quite simply, to rehearse the articles of his Creed, and his Creed till now had been old George. At Sarratt, they have a very worldly and relaxed attitude to the motives of a fieldman, and no patience at all for the fiery-eyed zealot who grinds his teeth and says 'I hate Communism'. If he hates it that much, they argue, he's most likely in love with it already. What they really like – and what Jerry possessed, what he was, in effect – was the fellow who hadn't a lot of time for flannel but loved the service and knew – though God forbid he should make a fuss of it – that *we* were right. *We* being a necessarily flexible notion, but to Jerry it meant George and that was that.

Old George. Super. Good morning.

He saw him as he liked to remember him best, the first time they met, at Sarratt, soon after the war. Jerry was still an army subaltern, his time nearly up and Oxford looming, and he was bored stiff. The course was for London Occasionals: people who, having done the odd bit of skulduggery without going formally on to the Circus payroll, were being groomed as an auxiliary reserve. Jerry had already volunteered for full-time employment, but Circus personnel had turned him down, which scarcely helped his mood. So when Smiley waddled into the paraffin-heated lecture hut in his heavy overcoat and spectacles, Jerry inwardly groaned and prepared himself for another creaking fifty minutes of boredom – on good places to look for dead letter-boxes, most likely – followed by a sort of clandestine nature ramble through Rickmansworth trying to spot hollow trees in graveyards. There was comedy while the Directing Staff fought to crank the lectern lower so that George could see over the top. In the end, he stood himself a little fussily at the side of it and declared that his subject this afternoon was 'problems of maintaining courier lines inside enemy territory'. Slowly it dawned on Jerry that he was talking not from the textbook but from experience: that this owlish little pedant with the diffident voice and the blinking, apologetic manner had sweated out three years in some benighted German town, holding the threads of a very respectable network, while he waited for the boot through the door panel or the pistol butt across the face that would introduce him to the pleasures of interrogation.

When the meeting was over, Smiley asked to see him. They met in a corner of an empty bar, under the antlers where the darts board hung.

'I'm so sorry we couldn't have you,' he said. 'I think our feeling was, you needed a little more time *outside* first.' Which was their way of saying he was immature. Too late, Jerry remembered Smiley as one of the non-speaking members of the Selection Board which had failed him. 'Perhaps if you could get your degree, and make your way a little in a different walk of life, they would change their way of thinking. Don't lose touch, will you?'

After which, somehow, old George had always been there. Never surprised, never out of patience, old George had gently but firmly rejigged Jerry's life till it was Circus property. His father's empire collapsed: George was waiting with his hand out to catch him. His marriages collapsed: George would sit all night for him, hold his head.

'I've always been grateful to this service that it gave me a chance to pay,' Smiley had said. 'I'm sure one should feel that. I don't think we should be afraid of . . . devoting ourselves. Is that old-fashioned of me?'

'You point me, I'll march', Jerry had replied. 'Tell me the shots and I'll play them.'

There was still time. He knew that. Train to Bangkok, hop on a plane home, and the worst he would get was a flea in his ear for jumping ship for a few days. Home, he repeated to himself. Bit of a problem. Home to Tuscany, and the yawning emptiness of the hilltop without the orphan? Home to old Pet, sorry about the bust teacup? Home to dear old Stubbsie, key appointment as desk jockey with special responsibility for the spike? Or home to the Circus: 'We think you'd be happiest in Banking Section.' Even – great thought – home to Sarratt, training job, winning the hearts and minds of new entrants while he commuted dangerously from a maisonette in Watford.

On the third or fourth morning he woke very early. Dawn was just rising over the river, turning it first red, then orange, now brown. A family of water-buffaloes wallowed in the mud, their bells jingling. In midstream, three sampans were linked in a long and complicated trawl. He heard a hiss and saw a net curl, then fall like hail on the water.

Yet it's not for want of a future that I'm here, he thought. It's for want of a present.

Home's where you go when you run out of homes, he thought. Which brings me to Lizzie. Vexed issue. Shove it on the back burner. Spot of breakfast.

Sitting on the teak balcony munching eggs and rice Jerry remembered George breaking the news to him about Haydon. El Vino's bar, Fleet Street, a rainy midday. Jerry had never found it possible to hate anyone for very long, and after the initial shock there had really not been much more to say.

'Well, no point in crying in the old booze, is there, sport? Can't leave the ship to the rats. Soldier on, that's the thing.'

To which Smiley agreed: yes, that was the thing, to soldier on, grateful for the chance to pay. Jerry had even found a sort of rum comfort in the fact that Bill was one of the clan. He had never seriously doubted, in his vague way, that his country was in a state of irreversible decline, nor that his own class was to blame for the mess. 'We *made* Bill,' ran his argument, 'so it's right we should carry the brunt of his betrayal.' Pay in fact. Pay. What old George was on about.

Pottering beside the river again, breathing the free warm air, Jerry chucked flat stones to make them bounce.

Lizzie, he thought. Lizzie Worthington, suburban bolter. Ricardo's pupil and punchball. Charlie Marshall's big sister and earth mother and unattainable whore. Drake Ko's cagebird. My dinner companion for all of four hours. And to Sam Collins – to repeat the question – what had she been to him? For Mr Mellon, Charlie's 'creepy British trader' of eighteen months ago, she was a courier working the Hong Kong heroin trail. But she was more than that. Somewhere along the line Sam had shown her a bit of ankle and told her she was working for Queen and country. Which glad news Lizzie had promptly shared with her admiring circle of friends. To Sam's fury, and he dropped her like a hot brick. So Sam had set her up as a patsy of some kind. A coat-trailer on probation. In one way this thought amused Jerry very much, for Sam had a reputation as an ace operator, whereas Lizzie Worthington might well star at Sarratt as the archetypal Woman Never to Be Recruited as Long as She Can Speak or Breathe.

Less funny was the question of what she meant to Sam now. What kept him skulking in her shadow like a patient murderer, smiling his grim iron smile? That question worried Jerry very much. Not to put too fine a point on it, he was obsessed by it. He definitely did not wish to see Lizzie taking another of her dives. If she went anywhere from Ko's bed, it was going to be into Jerry's. For some while, off and on – ever since he had met her, in fact – he had been thinking how much Lizzie would benefit from the bracing Tuscan air. And while he didn't know the how's and why's of Sam Collins's presence in Hong Kong, nor even what the Circus at large intended for Drake Ko, he had the strongest possible impression – and here was the nub of the thing – that by pushing off to London at this moment, far from carting Lizzie away on his white charger, Jerry was leaving her sitting on a very large bomb.

Which struck him as unacceptable. In other times, he might have been prepared to leave that problem to the owls, as he had left so many other problems in his day. But these were not other times. This time, as he now realized, it was the Cousins who were paying the piper, and while Jerry had no particular quarrel with the Cousins, their presence made it a much rougher ball-game. So that whatever vague notions he had about George's humanity did not apply.

Also, he cared about Lizzie. Urgently. There was nothing imprecise in his feelings at all. He ached for her, warts and all. She was his kind of loser, and he loved her. He had worked it out and drawn the line, and that, after several days of counting on beads, was his net, unalterable solution. He was a little awed, but very pleased by it.

Gerald Westerby, he told himself. You were present at your birth. You were present at your several marriages and at some of your divorces and you will certainly be present at your funeral. High time, in our considered view, that you were present at certain other crucial moments in your history.

Taking a bus up-river a few miles, he walked again, rode on cycles, sat in bars, made love to the girls, thinking only of Lizzie. The inn where he stayed was full of children and one morning he woke to find two of them sitting on his bed, marvelling at the enormous length of the *farang's* legs and giggling at the way his bare feet hung over the end. Maybe I'll just stay here, he thought. But by then he was fooling, because he knew that he had to go back and ask her; even if the answer was a custard pie. From the balcony he launched paper aeroplanes for the children, and they clapped and danced, watching them float away.

He found a boatman and when evening came he crossed the river to Vientiane, avoiding the formalities of immigration. Next morning, also without formality, he wangled himself aboard an unscheduled Royal Air Lao DC8, and by afternoon he was airborne, and in possession of a delicious warm whisky and chatting merrily to a couple of friendly opium dealers. As they landed, black rain was falling and the windows of the airport bus were foul with dust. Jerry didn't mind at all. For the first time in his life, returning to Hong Kong was quite like coming home after all.

Inside the reception area, nevertheless, Jerry played a cautious hand. No trumpets, he told himself: definitely. The few days' rest had done wonders for his presence of mind. Having taken a good look round he made for the men's room instead of the immigration desks and lay up there till a big load of Japanese tourists arrived, then barged over to them and asked who spoke English. Having cut out four of them, he showed them his Hong Kong press card and while they stood in line waiting for their passport check he besieged them with questions about why they were here and what they proposed to do, and with whom, and wrote wildly on his pad before choosing four more, and repeating the process. Meanwhile he waited for the police on duty to change watch. At four o'clock they did and he at once made for a door signed 'No Entry' which he had marked earlier. He banged on it till it was opened, and started to walk through to the other side.

'Where the hell are you going?' asked an outraged Scottish police inspector.

'Home to the comic, sport. Got to file the dirt on our friendly Japanese visitors.'

He showed his press card.

'Well go through the damn gates like everyone else.'

'Don't be bloody silly. I haven't got my passport. That's why your distinguished colleague brought me through this way in the first place.'

Bulk, a ranking voice, a patently British appearance, an affecting grin, won him a space in a city-bound bus five minutes later. Outside his apartment block, he dawdled but saw no one suspicious, but this was China and who could tell? The lift as usual emptied for him. Riding in it he hummed Deathwish the Hun's one record in anticipation of a hot bath and change of clothes. At his front door, he had a moment's anxiety when he noticed the tiny wedges he had left in place lying on the floor, till he belatedly remembered Luke, and smiled at the prospect of their reunion. He unlocked the burglar door and as he did so he heard the sound of humming from inside, a droning monotone, which could have been airconditioner, but not Deathwish's, it was too useless and ineffecient. Bloody idiot Luke has left the gramophone on, he thought, and it's about to brew up. Then he thought: I'm doing him an injustice, it's that fridge. Then he opened the door and saw Luke's dead body strewn across the floor with half his head shot to pieces, and half the flies in Hong Kong swarming over it and round it; and all he could think of to do, as he quickly closed the door behind him, and jammed his handkerchief over his mouth, was run into the kitchen in case there was still someone there. Returning to the living room, he pushed Luke's feet aside and dug up the parquet brick where he had cached his forbidden sidearm and his escape kit, and put them in his pocket before he vomited.

Of course, he thought. That's why Ricardo was so certain the horse-writer was dead.

Join the club, he thought, as he stood out in the street again, with the rage and grief pounding in his ears and eyes. Nelson Ko's dead but he's running China. Ricardo's dead, but Drake Ko says he can stay alive as long as he sticks to the shady side of the street. Jerry Westerby the horse-writer is also completely dead, except that Ko's stupid pagan vicious bastard of a henchman, Mr bloody Tiu, was so thick he shot the wrong roundeye.

# NINETEEN

## *golden thread*

The inside of the American Consulate in Hong Kong could have been the inside of the Annexe, right down to the ever-present fake rosewood and bland courtesy and the airport chairs and the heartening portrait of the President, even if this time it was Ford. Welcome to your Howard Johnson spookhouse, Guillam thought. The section they worked in was called the isolation ward and had its own doorway to the street, guarded by two marines. They had passes in false names – Guillam's was Gordon – and for the duration of their stay there, except on the telephone, they never spoke to a soul inside the building except one another. 'We're not just deniable, gentlemen,' Martello had told them proudly in the briefing, 'we're also invisible as well.' That was how it was going to be played, he said. The US Consul General could put his hand on the Bible and swear to the Governor they weren't there and his staff were not involved, said Martello. 'Blindeye right down the line.' After that, he handed over to George because: 'George this is your show from soup to nuts.'

Downhill they had five minutes' walk to the Hilton, where Martello had booked them rooms. Uphill, though it would have been hard going, they had ten minutes' walk to Lizzie Worth's apartment block. They had been here five days and now it was evening, but they had no way of telling because there were no windows in the operations room. There were maps and sea-charts instead, and a couple of telephones manned by Martello's quiet men, Murphy and his friend. Martello and Smiley had a big desk each. Guillam, Murphy and his friend shared the table with the telephones and Fawn sat moodily at the centre of an empty row of cinema chairs along the back wall, like a bored critic at a preview, sometimes picking his teeth and sometimes yawning but refusing to take himself off, as Guillam repeatedly advised him. Craw had been spoken to and ordered to keep clear of everything: a total duckdive. Smiley was frightened for him since Frost's death, and would have preferred him evacuated, but the old boy wouldn't leave.

It was also, for once, the hour of the quiet men: 'our final detailed briefing', Martello had called it. 'Ah, that's if it's okay by *you*, George.' Pale Murphy, wearing a white shirt and blue trousers, was standing on the raised podium before a wall chart soliloquizing from pages of notes. The rest of them, including Smiley and Martello, sat at his feet and listened mainly in silence. Murphy could have been describing a vacuum cleaner, and to Guillam that made his monologue the more hypnotic. The chart showed largely sea, but at the top and to the left hung a lace-fringe of the South China coast. Behind Hong Kong, the spattered outskirts of Canton were just visible below the batten which held the chart in place, and due south of Hong Kong at the very mid-point of the chart stretched the green outline of what looked to be a cloud divided into four sections marked A, B, C and D respectively. These, said Murphy reverently, were the fishing beds and the cross at the centre was Centre Point, sir. Murphy spoke only to Martello, whether it was George's show from soup to nuts or not.

'Sir, basing on the last occasion Drake exited Red China, sir, and updating our assessment to the situation as of now, we and navy int. between us, sir –'

'Murphy, Murphy,' put in Martello quite kindly, 'ease off a little, will you, friend? This isn't training school any more, okay? Loosen your girdle, will you, son?'

'Sir. One. Weather,' Murphy said, quite untouched by this appeal. 'April and May are the transitional months, sir, between the north-east monsoons and the beginning of the south-west monsoons. Forecasts day-to-day are unpredictable, sir, but no extreme conditions are foreseen for the trip.' He was using the pointer to show the line from Swatow southward to the fishing beds, then from the fishing beds north-west past Hong Kong up the Pearl River to Canton.

'Fog?' Martello said.

'Fog is traditional for the season and cloud is anticipated at six to seven oktas, sir.'

'What the hell's an *okta*, Murphy?'

'One okta is one eighth of sky area covered, sir. Oktas have replaced the former tenths. No typhoons have been recorded in April for over fifty years and navy int. call typhoons unlikely. Wind is easterly, nine to ten knots but any fleet that runs with it must count on periods of calm, also contrary winds too, sir. Humidity around eighty per cent, temperature fifteen to twenty-four centigrade. Sea conditions calm with a small swell. Currents around Swatow tend to run north-east through the Taiwan Strait, at around three sea miles per day. But further westward – on *this* side, sir –'

'That's one thing I do know Murphy,' Martello put in sharply. 'I know where west is, dammit.' Then he grinned at Smiley as if to say 'these young whipper-snappers'.

Murphy was again unmoved. 'We have to be prepared to calculate the speed factor and consequently the progress of the fleet at any one point in its journey, sir.'

'Sure, sure.'

'Moon, sir,' Murphy continued. 'Assuming the fleet to have exited Swatow on the night of Friday April twenty-fifth, the moon would be three days off of full –'

'Why do we assume that, Murphy?'

'Because that's when the fleet exited Swatow, sir. We had confirmation from navy int. one hour ago. Column of junks sighted at the eastern end of fishing bed C and easing westward with the wind, sir. Positive identification of the lead junk confirmed.'

There was a prickly pause. Martello coloured.

'You're a clever boy, Murphy,' Martello said, in a warning tone. 'But you should have given me that information a little earlier.'

'Yes, sir. Assuming also that the intention of the junk containing Nelson Ko is to hit Hong Kong waters on the night of May four, the moon will be in its last quarter, sir. If we follow precedents right down the line –'

'We do,' said Smiley firmly. 'The escape is to be an exact repetition of Drake's own journey in fifty-one.'

Once more, no one doubted him, Guillam noticed. Why not? It was utterly bewildering.

'– then our junk should hit the southernmost out-island of Po Toi at twenty hundred hours tomorrow, and rejoin the fleet up along the Pearl River in time to make Canton harbour between zero ten thirty and twelve hundred hours following day, May five, sir.'

While Murphy droned on, Guillam covertly kept his eye on Smiley, thinking, as he often thought, that he knew him no better today than when he first met him back in the dark days of the cold war in Europe. Where did he slip away to at all odd hours? Mooning about Ann? About Karla? What company did he keep that brought him back to the hotel at four in the morning? Don't tell me George is having a second spring, he thought. Last night at eleven there had been a scream from London, so Guillam had trailed up here to unbutton it. Westerby adrift, they said. They were terrified Ko had had him murdered or, worse, abducted and tortured, and that the operation would abort in consequence. Guillam thought it more likely Jerry was holed up with a couple of airhostesses somewhere en route to London but with that priority on the signal he had no option but to wake Smiley and tell him. He rang his room and got no answer so he dressed and banged on Smiley's door and finally he was reduced to picking the lock, for now it was Guillam's turn to panic: he thought Smiley might be ill.

But Smiley's room was empty and his bed unslept in, and when Guillam went through his things he was fascinated to see that the old fieldman had gone to the length of sewing false name-tapes in his shirts. That was all he discovered, however. So he settled in Smiley's chair and dozed and didn't wake till four when he heard a tiny flutter and opened his eyes to see Smiley stooped and peering at him about six inches away. How he got into the room so silently, God alone knew.

'Gordon?' he asked softly. 'What can I do for you?' – for they were on an operational footing, of course, and lived with the assumption the rooms were bugged. For the same reason Guillam did not speak, but handed Smiley the envelope containing Connie's message, which he read and re-read, then burned. Guillam was impressed how seriously he took the news. Even at that hour, he insisted on going straight up to the Consulate to attend to it, so Guillam went along to carry his bags.

'Instructive evening?' he asked lightly, as they plodded the short way up the hill.

'I? Oh, to a point, thank you, to a point,' Smiley replied, doing his disappearing act, and that was all Guillam or anyone could get out of him about his nocturnal or other ambles. Meanwhile, without the smallest explanation of his source, George was bringing in hard operational data in a manner which brooked no enquiry from anyone.

'Ah George, we can count on that, can we?' Martello asked in bewilderment, on the first occasion that this happened.

'What? Oh yes, yes, indeed you may.'

'Great. Great footwork, George. I admire you,' said Martello heartily, after a further puzzled silence, and from then on they had gone along with it, they had no choice. For nobody, not even Martello, quite dared to challenge his authority.

'How many days' fishing is that, Murphy?' Martello was asking.

'Fleet will have had seven days' fishing and hopefully make Canton with full holds, sir.'

'That figure, George?'

'Yes, oh yes, nothing to add, thank you.'

Martello asked what time the fleet would have to leave the fishing beds in order for Nelson's junk to make tomorrow evening's rendezvous on time.

'I have put it at eleven tomorrow morning,' Smiley said, without looking up from his notes.

'Me too,' said Murphy.

'This rogue junk, Murphy,' Martello said, with another deferential glance at Smiley.

'Yes sir,' said Murphy.

'Can it break away from the pack that easy? What would be its cover for entering Hong Kong waters, Murphy?'

'Happens all the time, sir. Red Chinese junk fleets operate a collective catch system without profit motivation, sir. Consequence of that, you get the single junks that break away at night time and come in without lights and sell their fish to the out-islanders for money.'

'*Literally* moonlighting!' Martello exclaimed, much amused by the felicity of the expression.

Smiley had turned to the map of Po Toi island on the other wall and was tilting his head in order to intensify the magnification of his spectacles.

'What size of junk are we talking of?' Martello asked.

'Twenty-eight man long-liners, sir, baited for shark, golden thread and conger.'

'Did Drake use that type also?'

'Yes,' said Smiley, still watching the map. 'Yes, he did.'

'And she can come that close in, can she? Provided the weather allows?'

Again it was Smiley who answered. Till today, Guillam had not heard him so much as speak of a boat in his life.

'The draw of a long-liner is less than five fathoms,' he remarked. 'She can come in as close as she wishes, provided always that the sea is not too rough.'

From the back bench, Fawn gave an immoderate laugh. Wheeling round in his chair Guillam shot him a foul look. Fawn leered and shook his head, marvelling at his master's omniscience.

'How many junks make up a fleet?' Martello asked.

'Twenty to thirty,' said Smiley.

'Check,' said Murphy meekly.

'So what does Nelson do, George? Kind of get out to the edge of the pack there, and stray a little?'

'He'll hang back,' said Smiley. 'The fleets like to move in column astern. Nelson will tell his skipper to take the rear position.'

'Will he, by God,' Martello muttered under his breath. 'Murphy, what identifications are traditional?'

'Very little known in that area, sir. Boat people are notoriously evasive. They have no respect for marine regulations. Out to sea they show no lights at all, mostly for fear of pirates.'

Smiley was lost to them again. He had sunk into a wooden immobility, and though his eyes stayed fixed on the big sea chart, his mind, Guillam knew, was anywhere but with Murphy's dreary recitation of statistics. Not so Martello.

'How much coastal trade do we have overall, Murphy?'

'Sir, there are no controls and no data.'

'Any quarantine checks as the junks enter Hong Kong waters, Murphy?' Martello asked.

'Theoretically all vessels should stop and have themselves checked, sir.'

'And in practice, Murphy?'

'Junks are a law to themselves, sir. Technically Chinese junks are forbidden to sail between Victoria Island and Kowloon Point, sir, but the last thing the Brits want is a hassle with the Mainland over rights of way. Sorry, sir.'

'Not at all,' said Smiley politely, still gazing at the chart. 'Brits we are and Brits we shall remain.'

It's his Karla expression, Guillam decided: the one that comes over him when he looks at the photograph. He catches sight of it, it surprises him and for a while he seems to study it, its contours, its blurred and sightless gaze. Then the light slowly goes out of his eyes, and somehow the hope as well, and you feel he's looking inward, in alarm.

'Murphy, did I hear you mention navigation lights?' Smiley inquired, turning his head, but still staring toward the chart.

'Yes, sir.'

'I expect Nelson's junk to carry three,' said Smiley. 'Two green lights vertically on the stern mast and one red light to starboard.'

'Yes, sir.'

Martello tried to catch Guillam's eye but Guillam wouldn't play.

'But it may not,' Smiley warned as an afterthought. 'It may carry none at all, and simply signal from close in.'

Murphy resumed. A new heading: Communications.

'Sir, in the communications area, sir, few junks have their own transmitters but most all have receivers. Once in a while you get a skipper who buys a cheap walkie-talkie with range about one mile to facilitate the trawl, but they've been doing it so long they don't have much call to speak to each other,

I guess. Then as to finding their way, well navy int. says that's near enough a mystery. We have reliable information that many long-liners operate on a primitive compass, a hand lead-and-line, or even just a rusty alarm clock for finding true north.'

'Murphy, how the *hell* do they work *that*, for God's sakes?' Martello cried.

'Line with a lead plumb and wax stuck to it, sir. They sound the bed, and know where they are from what sticks to the wax.'

'Well they *really* do it the hard way,' Martello declared.

A phone rang. Martello's other quiet man took the call, listened, then put his hand over the mouthpiece.

'Quarry Worth's just gotten back, sir,' he said to Smiley. 'Party drove around for an hour, now she's checked in her car back at the block. Mac says sounds like she's running a bath so maybe she plans going out again later.'

'And she's alone,' Smiley said impassively. It was a question.

'She alone there, Mac?' He gave a hard laugh. 'I'll bet you would, you dirty bastard. Yes, *sir,* lady's all alone taking a bath, and Mac there says when will we ever get to use video as well. Is the lady *singing* in the bath, Mac?' He rang off. 'She's not singing.'

'Murphy, get on with the war,' Martello snapped.

Smiley would like the interception plans rehearsed once more, he said.

'Why George! Please! It's your show, remember?'

'Perhaps we could look again at the big map of Po Toi island, could we? And then Murphy could break it down for us, would you mind?'

'*Mind*, George, *mind*!' Martello cried, so Murphy began again, this time using a pointer. Navy int. observation posts *here*, sir . . . constant two-way communication with base, sir . . . no presence at all within two sea-miles of the landing zone . . . Navy int. to advise base the moment the Ko launch starts back for Hong Kong, sir . . . interception will take place by regular British police vessel as the Ko launch enters harbour . . . US to supply op. int. and stand off only, for unforeseen supportive situation . . .

Smiley monitored every detail with a prim nod of his head.

'After all, Marty,' he put in, at one point, 'once Ko has Nelson aboard, there's nowhere else he *can* go is there? Po Toi is right at the edge of China waters. It's us or nothing.'

One day thought Guillam, as he continued listening, one of two things will happen to George. He'll cease to care, or the paradox will kill him. If he ceases to care, he'll be half the operator he is. If he doesn't, that little chest will blow up from the struggle of trying to find the explanation for what we do. Smiley himself, in a disastrous off-the-record chat to senior officers, had put the names to his dilemma, and Guillam, with some embarrassment, recalled them to this day. To be *inhuman in defence of our humanity,* he had said, *harsh in defence of compassion.* To be *single-minded in defence of our disparity.* They had filed out in a veritable ferment of protest. Why didn't George just do the job and shut up instead of taking his faith out and polishing it in public till the flaws showed? Connie had even murmured a Russian aphorism in Guillam's ear which she insisted on attributing to Karla.

'There'll be no war, will there, Peter darling?' she had said reassuringly, squeezing his hand as he led her along the corridor. 'But in the struggle for peace not a single stone will be left standing, bless the old fox. I'll bet they didn't thank him for *that* one in the Collegium either.'

A thud made Guillam swing round. Fawn was changing cinema seats again. Seeing Guillam, he flared his nostrils in an insolent sneer.

'He's off his head,' thought Guillam with a shiver.

Fawn too, for different reasons, was now causing Guillam serious anxiety. Two days ago, in Guillam's company, he had been the author of a disgusting incident. Smiley as usual had gone out alone. To kill time, Guillam had hired a car and driven Fawn up to the China border, where he had sniggered and puffed at the mysterious hills. Returning, they were waiting at some country traffic lights when a Chinese boy drew alongside on a Honda. Guillam was driving. Fawn had the passenger set. Fawn's window was lowered, he had taken his jacket off and was resting his left arm on the door where he could admire a new gilt watch he had bought himself in the Hilton shipping concourse. As they pulled away, the Chinese boy ill-advisedly made a dive for the watch, but Fawn was much too quick for him. Catching hold of the boy's wrist instead, he held on to it, towing him beside the car while the boy struggled vainly to break free. Guillam had driven fifty yards or so before he realized what had happened and he at once stopped the car, which was what Fawn was waiting for. He jumped out before Guillam could stop him, lifted the boy straight off his Honda, led him to the side of the road and broke both his arms for him, then returned smiling to the car. Terrified of a scandal, Guillam drove rapidly from the scene, leaving the boy screaming and staring at his dangling arms. He reached Hong Kong determined to report Fawn to George immediately, but luckily for Fawn it was eight hours before Smiley surfaced, and by then Guillam reckoned George had enough on his plate already.

Another phone was ringing, the red. Martello took the call himself. He listened a moment then burst into a loud laugh.

'They found him,' he told Smiley, holding the phone to him.

'Found whom?'

The phone hovered between them.

'Your *man*, George. Your Weatherby –'

'Westerby,' Murphy corrected him, and Martello shot him a venomous look.

'They got him,' said Martello.

'Where is he?'

'Where *was* he, you mean! George, he just had himself the time of his life in two cathouses up along the Mekong. If our people are not exaggerating, he's the hottest thing since Barnum's baby elephant left town in forty-nine!'

'And where is he now, please?'

Martello handed him the phone. 'Why don't you just have 'em read you the signal, okay? They have some story that he crossed the river.' He turned to Guillam, and winked. 'They tell me there's a couple of places in Vientiane where he might find himself a little action too,' he said, and went on laughing richly while Smiley sat patiently with the telephone to his ear.

Jerry chose a cab with two wing-mirrors and sat in the front. In Kowloon he hired a car from the biggest outfit he could find, using the escape passport and driving licence because marginally he thought the false name was safer, if only by an hour. As he headed up the Midlevels it was dusk and still raining and huge haloes hung from the neon lights that lit the hillside. He passed the American Consulate and drove past Star Heights twice, half expecting to see Sam Collins, and on the second occasion he knew for sure he had found her flat and that her light was burning: an arty Italian affair by the look of it, that hung across the picture window in a gracious droop, three hundred dollars' worth of pretension. Also the frosted glass of a bathroom was lit. The third time he passed he saw her pulling a wrap over her shoulders and instinct or something about the formality of her gesture told him she was once more preparing to go out for the evening, but that this time she was dressed to kill.

Every time he allowed himself to remember Luke, a darkness covered his eyes and he imagined himself doing the noble, useless things like telephoning Luke's family in California, or the dwarf at the bureau, or even for whatever purpose the Rocker. Later, he thought. Later, he promised himself, he would mourn Luke in fitting style.

He coasted slowly into the driveway which led to the entrance till he came to the sliproad to the carpark. The park was three tiers deep and he idled round it till he found her red Jaguar stowed in a safe corner behind a chain to discourage careless neighbours from approaching its peerless paintwork. She had put a mock leopardskin cover on the steering wheel. She just couldn't do enough for the damn car. Get pregnant, he thought, in a burst of fury. Buy a dog. Keep mice. For two pins he'd have smashed the front in, but those two pins had held Jerry back more times that he liked to count. If she's not using it, then he's sending a limousine for her, he thought. Maybe with Tiu riding shotgun, even. Or maybe he'll come himself. Or maybe she's just getting herself dolled up for the evening sacrifice and not going out at all. He wished it was Sunday. He remembered Craw saying that Drake Ko spent Sunday with his family, and that on Sundays Lizzie had to make her own running. But it wasn't Sunday and neither did he have dear old Craw at his elbow telling him, on what evidence Jerry could only guess, that Ko was away in Bangkok or Timbuctoo conducting his business.

Grateful that the rain was turning to fog, he headed back up the slipway to the drive and at the junction found a narrow piece of shoulder where, if he parked hard against the barrier, the other traffic could complain but squeeze past. He grazed the barrier and didn't care. From where he now sat he could watch the pedestrians coming in and out under the striped awning to the block, and the cars joining or leaving the main road. He felt no sense of caution at all. He lit a cigarette and the limousines crackled past him both ways but none belonged to Ko. Occasionally, as a car edged by him, the driver paused to hoot or shout a complaint and Jerry ignored him. Every few seconds his eyes took in the mirrors and once when a plump figure not unlike Tiu padded guiltily up behind him he actually dropped the safety catch of the pistol in his jacket pocket before admitting to himself that the man lacked Tiu's brawn. Probably been collecting gambling debts from the *pak-pai* drivers, he thought, as the figure went by him.

He remembered being with Luke at Happy Valley. He remembered being with Luke.

He was still looking in the mirror when the red Jaguar hissed up the slipway behind him, just the driver and the roof closed, no passenger, and the one thing he hadn't thought of was that she might take the lift right down to the carpark and collect the car herself rather than have the porter bring it to the door for her as he did before. Pulling out after her, he glanced up and saw the lights still burning in her window. Had she left somebody behind? Or did she propsoe to come back shortly? Then he thought, Don't be so damn clever, she's just careless about lights.

The last time I spoke to Luke, it was to tell him to get out of my hair, he thought, and the last time he spoke to me was to tell me he'd covered my back with Stubbsie.

She had turned down the hill toward the town. He headed down after her and for a space nothing followed him, which seemed unnatural, but these were unnatural hours, and Sarratt man was dying in him faster than he could handle. She was heading for the brightest part of town. He supposed he still loved her, though just now he was prepared to suspect anybody of anything. He kept close behind her remembering that she used her mirror seldom. In this dusky fog she would only see his headlights anyway. The fog hung in patches and the harbour looked as if it was on fire, with the shafts of cranelight playing like waterhoses on the crawling smoke. In Central she ducked into another basement garage, and he drove straight in after her and parked six bays away, but she didn't notice him. Remaining in the car, she paused to repair her make-up and he actually saw her working on her chin, powdering the scars. Then she got out and went through the ritual of locking, though a kid with a razor blade could have cut through the soft-top in one easy movement. She was dressed in a silk cape of some kind and a long silk dress, and as she walked toward the stone spiral stair she raised both her hands and carefully lifted her hair, which was gathered at the neck, and laid the pony tail down the outside of the cape. Getting out after her he followed her as far as the hotel lobby, and turned aside in time to avoid being photographed by a bi-sexual drove of chattering fashion journalists in satins and bows.

Hanging back in the comparative safety of the corridor, Jerry pieced the scene together. It was a large private party and Lizzie had joined it from the blind side. The other guests were arriving at the front entrance, where the Rolls-Royces were so thick on the ground that nobody was special. A woman with blue-grey hair presided, swaying about and speaking gin-sodden French. A prim Chinese public relations girl with a couple of assistants made up the receiving line, and as the guests filed in, the girl and her cohorts came forward frightfully cordially and asked for names and sometimes invitation cards before consulting a list and saying 'Oh yes, of *course*.' The blue-grey woman smiled and growled. The cohorts handed out lapel-pins for the men and orchids for the women, then lighted on the next arrivals.

Lizzie Worthington went through this screening woodenly. Jerry gave her a minute to clear, watched her through the double doors marked *soirée* with a Cupid's arrow, then attached himself to the queue. The public relations girl was bothered by his buckskin boots. His suit was disgusting enough but it was the boots that bothered her. On her course of training, he decided while she stared at them, she had been taught to place a lot of value on shoes. Millionaires may be tramps from the socks up but a pair of two hundred dollar Guccis is a passport not to be missed. She frowned at his presscard, then at her guest list, then at his presscard again, and once more at his boots and she threw a lost glance at the blue-grey lush, who kept on smiling and growling. Jerry guessed she was drugged clean out of her mind. Finally the girl put up her own special smile for the marginal consumer and handed him a disc the size of a coffee saucer painted fluorescent pink with PRESSE an inch high in white.

'Tonight we are making everybody beautiful, Mr Westerby,' she said.

'Have a job with me, sport.'

'You like my *parfum*, Mr Westerby?'

'Sensational,' said Jerry.

'It is called *juice of the vine*, Mr Westerby, one hundred Hong Kong for a little bottle but tonight Maison Flaubert gives free samples to all our guests. Madame Montifiori . . . oh, of *course*, welcome to House of Flaubert. You like my parfum, Madam Montifiori?'

A Eurasian girl in a *cheongsam* held out a tray and whispered 'Flaubert wishes you an exotic night.'

'For Christ's sake,' Jerry said.

Inside the double doors a second receiving line was manned by three pretty boys flown in from Paris for their charm, and a posse of security men that would have done credit to a President. For a moment he thought they might frisk him and he knew that if they tried he was going to pull down the temple with him. They eyed Jerry without friendliness, counting him part of the help, but he was light-haired and they let him go.

'The press is in the third row back from the catwalk,' said a hermaphrodite blond in a cowboy leather suit, handing him a presskit. 'You have no camera, monsieur?'

'I just do the captions,' Jerry said, jamming a thumb over his shoulder, 'Spike here does the pictures,' and walked into the reception room peering round him, grinning extravagantly, waving at whoever caught his eye.

The pyramid of champagne glasses was six feet tall with black satin steps so that the waiters could take them from the top. In sunken ice-coffins lay magnums awaiting burial. There was a wheelbarrow full of cooked lobsters and a wedding cake of *pâté de foie gras* with *Maison Flaubert* done in aspic on the top. Space music was playing and there was even conversation under it, if only the bored drone of the extremely rich. The catwalk stretched from the foot of the long window to the centre of the room. The window faced the harbour, but the fog broke the view into patches. The airconditioning was turned up so that the women could wear their mink without sweating. Most of the men wore dinner jackets but the young Chinese playboys sported New-York-style slacks and black shirts and gold chains. The British *taipans* stood in one sodden circle with their womenfolk, like bored officers at a garrison get-together.

Feeling a hand on his shoulder Jerry swung fast, but all he found in front of him was a little Chinese queer called Graham who worked for one of the local gossip rags. Jerry had once helped him out with a story he was trying to sell to the comic. Rows of armchairs faced the catwalk in a rough horseshoe, and Lizzie was sitting in the front between Mr Arpego and his wife or paramour. Jerry recognized them from Happy Valley. They looked as though they were chaperoning Lizzie for the evening. The Arpegos talked to her but she seemed barely to hear them. She sat straight and beautiful and she had taken off her cape and from where Jerry sat she could have been stark naked except for her pearl collar and her pearl earrings. At least she's still intact, he thought. She hasn't rotted or got cholera or had her head shot off. He remembered the line of gold hairs running down her spine as he stood over her that first evening in the lift. Queer Graham sat next to Jerry, and Phoebe Wayfarer sat two along. He knew her only vaguely but gave her a fat wave.

'Gosh. Super. Pheeb. You look terrific. Should be up there on the catwalk, sport, showing a bit of leg.'

He thought she was a bit tight, and perhaps she thought he was, though he'd drunk nothing since the plane. He took out a pad and wrote on it, playing the professional, trying to rein himself in. Easy as you go. Don't frighten the game. When he read what he had written, he saw the words

'Lizzie Worthington' and nothing else. Chinese Graham read it too and
laughed.

'My new byline,' said Jerry, and they laughed together, too loud, so that
people in the front turned their heads as the lights began to dim. But not
Lizzie, though he thought she might have recognized his voice.

Behind them, the doors were being closed and as the lights went lower.
Jerry had a mind to fall asleep in this soft and kindly chair. The space music
gave way to a jungle beat brushed out on a cymbal, till only a single chandelier
flickered over the black catwalk, answering the churned and patchy lights of
the harbour in the window behind. The drumbeat rose in a slow crescendo
from amplifiers everywhere. It went on a long time, just drums, very well
played, very insistent, till gradually grotesque human shadows became visible
against the harbour window. The drumbeats stopped. In a racked silence two
black girls strode flank against flank down the catwalk, wearing nothing but
jewels. Their skulls were shaven and they wore round ivory earrings and
diamond collars like the iron rings of slave girls. Their oiled limbs shone with
clustered diamonds, pearls and rubies. They were tall, and beautiful, and
lithe, and utterly unexpected, and for a moment they cast over the whole
audience the spell of absolute sexuality. The drums recovered and soared,
spotlights raced over jewels and limbs. They writhed out of the steaming
harbour and advanced on the spectators with the anger of sensuous enslave-
ment. They turned and walked slowly away, challenging and disdaining with
their haunches. Lights came on, there was a crash of nervous applause
followed by laughter and drinks. Everyone was talking at once and Jerry was
talking loudest: to Miss Lizzie Worthington the well-known aristocratic
society beauty whose mother couldn't even boil an egg, and to the Arpegos
who owned Manila and one or two of the out-islands, as Captain Grant of the
Jockey Club had once assured him. Jerry was holding his notebook like a
headwaiter.

'Lizzie Worthington, *gosh*, all Hong Kong at your feet, ma'am, if I may say
so. My paper is doing an exclusive on this event, Miss Worth or Worthington,
and we're hoping to feature you, your fascinating life-style and your even
more facinating friends. My photographers are bringing up the rear.' He
bowed to the Arpegos. 'Good evening, madame. Sir. Proud to have you with
us I'm sure. This your first visit to Hong Kong?'

He was doing his big-puppy number, the boyish soul of the party. A waiter
brought champagne and he insisted on transferring the glasses to their hands
rather than let them help themselves. The Arpegos were much amused by
this performance. Craw said they were crooks. Lizzie was staring at him and
there was something in her eyes he couldn't make out, something real and
appalled, as if she, not Jerry, had just opened the door on Luke.

'Mr Westerby has already done one story on me, I understand,' she said. 'I
don't think it was ever printed, was it, Mr Westerby?'

'Who you write for?' Mr Arpego demanded suddenly. He wasn't smiling
any more. He looked dangerous and ugly, and she had clearly reminded him
of something he had heard about and didn't like. Something Tiu had warned
him of, for instance.

Jerry told him.

'Then go write for them. Leave this lady alone. She don't give interviews.
You got work to do, you work somewhere else. You didn't come here to play.
Earn your money.'

'Couple of questions for *you*, then, Mr Arpego. Just before I go. How can I write you down sir? As a rude Filipino millionaire? Or only half a millionaire?'

'For God's sake,' Lizzie breathed, and by a mercy the lights went out again, the drumbeat began, everyone went back to his corner and a woman's voice with a French accent began a soft commentary on the loudspeaker. At the back of the catwalk the two black girls were performing long insinuating shadow dances. As the first model appeared, Jerry saw Lizzie stand up ahead of him in the darkness, pull her cape over her shoulders, and walk fast and softly up the aisle past him and toward the doors, head bowed. Jerry went after her. In the lobby she half turned as if to look at him and it crossed his mind she was expecting him. Her expression was the same and it reflected his own mood. She looked haunted and tired and utterly confused.

'Lizzie!' he called, as if he had just sighted an old friend, and ran quickly to her side before she could reach the powder room door. 'Lizzie! My God! It's been years! A lifetime! Super!'

A couple of security guards looked on meekly as he flung his arms round her for the kiss of long friendship. He had slipped his left hand under her cape and as he bent his laughing face to hers, he laid the small revolver against the bare flesh of her back, the barrel just below her nape, and in that way, linked to her with bonds of old affection, led her straight into the street, chatting gaily all the way, and hailed a cab. He hadn't wanted to produce the gun, but he couldn't risk having to manhandle her. That's the way it goes, he thought. You come back to tell her you love her, and end up by marching her off at gun point. She was shivering and furious but he didn't think she was afraid, and he didn't even think she was sorry to be leaving that awful gathering.

'That's all I need,' she said, as they wound up the hill again, through the fog. 'Perfect. Bloody perfect.'

She wore a scent that was strange to him, but he thought it smelt a deal better than juice of the vine.

Guillam was not bored exactly, but neither was his capacity for concentration infinite, as George's appeared to be. When he wasn't wondering what the devil Jerry Westerby was up to, he found himself basking in the erotic deprival of Molly Meakin or else remembering the Chinese boy with his arms inside out, whining like a half-shot hare after the disappearing car. Murphy's theme was now the island of Po Toi and he was dilating on it remorselessly.

Volcanic, sir, he said.

Hardest rock substance of the whole Hong Kong group, sir, he said.

And the most southerly of the islands, he said, and right there on the edge of China waters.

Seven hundred and ninety feet high, sir, fishermen use it as a navigation point from far out to sea, sir, he said.

Technically not one island but a group of six islands, the other five being barren and treeless and uninhabited.

Fine temple, sir. Great antiquity. Fine wood carvings but little natural water.

'Jesus Christ, Murphy, we're not *buying* the damn place, are we?' Martello expostulated. With action close, and London far away, Martello had lost a lot of his gloss, Guillam noticed, and all his Englishness. His tropical suits were honest-to-cornball American, and he needed to talk to people, preferably his own. Guillam suspected that even London was an adventure for him, and Hong Kong was already enemy territory. Whereas under stress Smiley went quite the other way: he became private, and rigidly polite.

Po Toi itself has a shrinking population of one hundred and eighty farmers and fishermen, mostly Communist, three living villages and three dead ones, sir, said Murphy. He droned on. Smiley continued to listen intently but Martello impatiently doodled on his pad.

'And *tomorrow*, sir,' said Murphy, '*tomorrow* is the night of Po Toi's annual festival intended to pay homage to Tin Hau, the goddess of the sea, sir.'

Martello stopped doodling. 'These people really believe that crap?'

'Everybody has a right to his religion, sir.'

'They teach you that at training college too, Murphy?' Martello returned to his doodling.

There was an uncomfortable silence before Murphy valiantly took up his pointer and laid the tip on the southern edge of the island's coastline.

'This festival of Tin Hau, sir, is concentrated in the one main harbour, sir, right here on the south-west point where the ancient temple is situated. Mr Smiley's informed prediction, sir, has the Ko landing operation taking place *here*, away from the main bay, in a small cove on the east side of the island. By landing on that side of the island which has *no* habitation, *no* natural access to the sea, at a point in time when the diversion of the island festival in the *main* bay –'

Guillam never heard the ring. He just heard the voice of Martello's other quiet man answering the call: '*Yes, Mac*,' then the squeak of his airline chair as he sat bolt upright, staring at Smiley 'Right, *Mac*. Sure, *Mac*. Right now. Yes. Hold it. Right beside me. Hold everything.'

Smiley was already standing over him, his hand held out for the phone. Martello was watching Smiley. On the podium Murphy had his back turned while he pointed out further intriguing features of Po Toi, not quite registering the interruption.

'This island is also known to seamen as Ghost Rock, sir,' he explained in the same dreary voice. 'But nobody seems to know why.'

Smiley listened briefly then put down the telephone.

'Thank you, Murphy,' he said courteously. 'That was very interesting.'

He stood dead still a moment, his fingers to his upper lip, in a Pickwickian posture of deliberation. 'Yes,' he repeated. 'Yes, very.'

He walked as far as the door, then paused again.

'Marty, forgive me, I shall have to leave you for a while. Not above an hour or two, I trust. I shall telephone you in any event.'

He reached for the door handle, then turned to Guillam.

'Peter, I think you had better come along too, would you mind? We may need a car and you seem admirably unmoved by the Hong Kong traffic. Did I see Fawn somewhere? Ah, there you are.'

On Headland Road the flowers had a hairy brilliance, like ferns sprayed for Christmas. The pavement was narrow and seldom used, except by amahs to exercise the children, which they did without talking to them as if they were walking dogs. The Cousins' surveillance van was a deliberately forgettable brown Mercedes lorry, battered looking, with clay dust on the wings and the letters H. K. DEVp. and BLDg. SURVEY Ltd sprayed on one side. An old aerial with Chinese streamers trailing from it drooped over the cab, and as the lorry nosed its lugubrious way past the Ko residence – for the second, or was it the fourth time that morning? – nobody gave it a thought. In Headland Road, as everywhere in Hong Kong, somebody is always building.

Stretched inside the lorry, on rexine-covered bunks fitted for the purpose, the two men watched intently from among a forest of lenses, cameras and radio telephone appliances. For them also, their progress past Seven Gates was becoming something of a routine.

'No change?' said the first.

'No change,' the second confirmed.

'No change,' the first repeated, into the radio telephone, and heard the assuring voice of Murphy the other end, acknowledging the message.

'Maybe they're waxworks,' said the first, still watching. 'Maybe we should go give them a prod and see if they holler.'

'Maybe we should at that,' said the second.

In all their professional lives, they were agreed, they had never followed anything that kept so still. Ko stood where he always stood, at the end of the rose-arbour, his back to them as he stared out to sea. His little wife sat apart from him, dressed as usual in black, on a white garden chair, and she seemed to be staring at her husband. Only Tiu made any movement. He also was sitting, but to Ko's other side, and he was munching what looked like a doughnut.

Reaching the main road, the lorry lumbered toward Stanley, pursuing for cover reasons its fictional reconnaissance of the region.

# TWENTY

## *Liese's lover*

Her flat was big and unreconciled: a mix of airport lounge, executive suite and tart's boudoir. The drawing room ceiling was raked to a lopsided point, like the nave of a subsiding church. The floor changed levels restlessly, the carpet was as thick as grass and left shiny footprints where they walked. The enormous windows gave limitless but lonely views, and when she closed the blinds and drew the curtains, the two of them were suddenly in a suburban bungalow with no garden. The amah had gone to her room behind the kitchen and when she appeared Lizzie sent her back there. She crept out scowling and hissing. Wait till I tell the master, she was saying.

He put the chains across the front door and after that he took her with him, steering her from room to room, making her walk a little ahead of him on his left side, open the doors for him and even the cupboards. The bedroom was a television stage-set for a *femme fatale*, with a round, quilted bed and a sunken round bath behind Spanish screens. He looked through the bedside lockers for a smallarm because though Hong Kong is not particularly gun-ridden, people who have lived in Indo China usually have something. Her dressing room looked as though she'd emptied one of the smart Scandinavian décor shops in Central by telephone. The dining room was done in smoked glass, polished chrome and leather, with fake Gainsborough ancestors staring soggily at the empty chairs: all the mummies who couldn't boil eggs, he thought. Black tigerskin steps led to Ko's den and here Jerry lingered, staring round, fascinated despite himself, seeing the man in everything, and his kinship with old Sambo. The king-sized desk with the *bombé* legs and ball-and-claw feet, the presidential cutlery. The inkwells, the sheathed paper-knife and scissors, the untouched works of legal reference, the very ones old Sambo trailed around with him: Simons on Tax, Charlesworth on Company Law. The framed testimonials on the wall. The citation for his Order of the British Empire beginning 'Elizabeth the Second by the Grace of God . . . ' The medal itself, embalmed in satin, like the arms of a dead knight. Group photographs of Chinese elders on the steps of a spirit temple. Victorious racehorses. Lizzie laughing to him. Lizzie in a swimsuit, looking stunning. Lizzie in Paris. Gently, he pulled open the desk drawers and discovered the embossed staionery of a dozen different companies. In the cupboards, empty files, an IBM electric typewriter with no plug on it, an address book with no addresses entered. Lizzie naked from the waist up, glancing round at him over her long back. Lizzie, God help her, in a wedding dress, clutching a posy of gardenias. Ko must have sent her to a bridal parlour for the photograph.

There were no photographs of gunny-bags of opium.

The executive sanctuary, Jerry thought, standing there. Old Sambo had several: girls who had flats from him, one even a house, yet saw him only a few times a year. But always this one secret, special room, with the desk and the unused telephones and the instant-momentos, a physical corner carved off someone else's life, a shelter from his other shelters.

'Where is he?' Jerry asked, remembering Luke again.

'Drake?'

'No, Father Christmas.'

'You tell me.'

He followed her to the bedroom.

'Do you often not know?' he asked.

She was pulling off her earrings, dropping them in a jewellery box. Then her clasp, her necklace and bracelets.

'He rings me wherever he is, night or day, we never care. This is the first time he's cut himself off.'

'Can you ring him?'

'*Any* bloody time,' she retorted with savage sarcasm. 'Course I can. Number One Wife and me get on just *great*. Didn't you know?'

'What about at the office?'

'He's not going to the office.'

'What about Tiu?'

'Sod Tiu.'

'Why?'

'Because he's a pig,' she snapped pulling open a cupboard.

'He could pass on messages for you.'

'If he felt like it, which he doesn't.'

'Why not?'

'How the hell should I know?' She hauled out a pullover and some jeans and chucked them on the bed. 'Because he resents me. Because he doesn't trust me. Because he doesn't like roundeyes horning in on Big Sir. Now get out while I change.'

So he wandered into the dressing room again, keeping his back to her, hearing the rustle of silk and skin.

'I saw Ricardo,' he said. 'We had a full and frank exchange of views.'

He needed very much to hear whether they had told her. He needed to absolve her from Luke. He listened, then went on:

'Charlie Marshall gave me his address, so I popped up and had a chat with him.'

'Great,' she said. 'So now you're family.'

'They told me about Mellon. Said you carried dope for him.'

She didn't speak so he turned to look at her and she was sitting on the bed with her head in her hands. In the jeans and pullover she looked about fifteen years old, and half a foot shorter.

'What the hell do you want?' she whispered at last, so quietly she might have been putting the question to herself.

'You,' he said. 'For keeps.'

He didn't know whether she heard, because all she did was let out a long breath and whisper 'Oh Jesus' at the end of it.

'Mellon a friend of yours?' she asked finally.

'No.'

'Does Arpego know where Ko is?'

She shrugged.

'So when did you last hear from him?'

'A week.'

'What did he say?'

'He had things to arrange.'

'What things?'

'For Christ's sake stop asking questions! The whole sodding world is asking questions, so just don't join the queue, right?'

He stared at her and her eyes were alight with anger and despair. He opened the balcony door and stepped outside.

I need a brief, he thought bitterly. Sarratt bearleaders, where are you now I need you? It hadn't dawned on him till now that when he cut the cable, he was also dropping the pilot.

The balcony ran along three sides. The fog had temporarily cleared. Behind him hung the Peak, its shoulders festooned in gold lights. Banks of running cloud made changing caverns round the moon. The harbour had dug out all its finery. At its centre an American aircraft carrier, floodlit and dressed overall, basked like a pampered woman amid a cluster of attendant launches. On her deck, a line of helicopters and small fighters reminded him of the airbase in Thailand. A column of ocean-going junks drifted past her, headed for Canton.

'Jerry?'

She was standing in the open doorway, watching him down a line of tub trees.

'Come on in. I'm hungry,' she said.

It was a kitchen where nobody cooked or ate, but it had a Bavarian corner, with pine settles, alpine pictures and ashtrays saying *Carlsberg*. She gave him coffee from an ever-ready percolator, and he noticed how, when she was on guard, she kept her shoulders forward and her forearms across her body, the way the orphan used to. She was shivering. He thought she had been shivering ever since he laid the gun on her and he wished he hadn't done that, because it was beginning to dawn on him that she was in as bad a state as he was, and perhaps a damn sight worse, and that the mood between them was like two people after a disaster, each in a separate hell. He fixed her a brandy and soda and the same for himself and sat her in the drawing room where it was warmer, and he watched her while she hugged herself and drank the brandy, staring at the carpet.

'Music?' he asked.

She shook her head.

'I represent myself,' he said. 'No connection with any other firm.'

She might not have heard.

'I'm free and willing,' he said. 'It's just that a friend of mine died.'

He saw her nod, but only in sympathy. He was sure it rang no bell with her at all.

'The Ko thing is getting very grubby,' he said. 'It's not going to work out well. They're very rough boys you're mixed up with. Ko included. Looked at cold, he's a grade A public enemy. I thought maybe you'd like a leg out of it all. That's why I came back. Mr Galahad act. It's just I don't quite know what's gathering around you. Mellon, all that. Maybe we should unbutton it together and see what's there.'

After which not very articulate explanation, the telephone rang. It had one of those throttled croaks which are designed to spare the nerves.

The telephone was across the room on a gilded trolley. A pinlight winked on it with each dull note and the rippled glass shelves picked up the reflection. She glanced at it, then at Jerry and her face was at once alert with hope. Jumping to his feet he pushed the trolley over to her and its wheels stammered in the deep pile. The flex uncoiled behind him as he walked, till it was like a child's scribble across the room. She lifted the receiver quickly and said 'Worth' in the slightly rude tone which women learn when they live alone. He thought of telling her the line was bugged but he didn't know what he was warning her against: he had no position any more, this side or that side. He didn't know what the sides were, but his head was suddenly full of Luke again and the hunter in him was wide awake.

She had the telephone to her ear but she hadn't spoken again. Once she said 'yes', as if she were acknowledging instructions and once she said 'no' strongly. Her expression had turned blank, her voice told him nothing. But he sensed obedience, and he sensed concealment, and as he did so, the anger lit in him completely and nothing else mattered.

'No,' she said to the phone, 'I left the party early.'

He knelt beside her, trying to listen, but she kept the receiver pressed hard against her.

Why didn't she ask him where he was? Why didn't she ask when she would see him? Whether he was all right? Why he hadn't phoned? Why did she look at Jerry like this, show no relief?

His hand on her cheek, he forced her head round and whispered to the other ear.

'Tell him you *must* see him! You'll come to him. *Anywhere.*'

'Yes,' she said again into the phone. 'All right. Yes.'

'Tell him! Tell him you must see him!'

'I must see you,' she said finally. 'I'll come to you wherever you are.'

The receiver was still in her hand. She made a shrug, asking for instruction and her eyes were still turned to Jerry – not as her Sir Galahad, but as just another part of a hostile world that encircled her.

'*I love you!*' he whispered. 'Say what you say!'

'I love you,' she said shortly, with her eyes closed, and rang off before he could stop her.

'He's coming here,' she said. 'And damn you.'

Jerry was still kneeling beside her. She stood up in order to get clear of him.

'Does he know?' Jerry asked.

'Know what?'

'That I'm here?'

'Perhaps.' She lit a cigarette.

'Where is he now?'

'I don't know.'

'When will he be here?'

'He said soon.'

'Is he alone?'

'He didn't say.'

'Does he carry a gun?'

She was across the room from him. Her strained grey eyes still held him in their furious, frightened glare. But Jerry was indifferent to her mood. A feverish urge for action had overcome all other feelings.

'Drake Ko. The nice man who set you up here. Does he carry a gun? Is he going to shoot me? Is Tiu with him? Just questions that's all.'

'He doesn't wear it in bed, if that's what you mean.'

'Where are you going?'

'I thought you two men would prefer to be left alone.'

Leading her back to the sofa, he sat her facing the double doors at the far end of the room. They were panelled with frosted glass and on the other side of them lay the hall and the front entrance. He opened them, clearing her line of view to anybody coming in.

'Do you have rules about letting people in, you two?' She didn't follow his question. 'There's a peephole here. Does he insist you check every time before you open?'

'He'll ring on the house phone from downstairs. Then he'll use his door key.'

The front door was laminated hardboard, not solid but solid enough. Sarratt folklore said, if you are taking a lone intruder unawares, don't get behind the door or you'll never get out again. For once Jerry was inclined to agree. Yet to keep to the open side was to be a sitting duck for anyone aggressively inclined, and Jerry was by no means sure that Ko was either unaware, or alone. He considered going behind the sofa but if there was to be shooting he didn't want the girl to be in the line of it, he definitely didn't. Her new-found passivity, her lethargic stare, did nothing to reassure him. His brandy glass was beside hers on the table and he put it quietly out of sight behind a vase of plastic orchids. He emptied the ashtray, and set an open copy of *Vogue* in front of her on the table.

'You play music when you're alone?'

'Sometimes.'

He chose Ellington.

'Too loud?'

'Louder,' she said. Suspicious, he turned down the sound, watching her. As he did so the house phone whistled twice from the hall.

'Take care,' he warned, and gun in hand moved to the open side of the front door, the sitting-duck position, three feet from the arc, close enough to spring forward, far enough to shoot and throw himself, which was what he had in mind as he dropped into the half crouch. He held the gun in his left hand and nothing in his right because at that distance he couldn't miss with either hand, whereas if he had to strike he wanted his right hand free. He remembered the way Tiu carried his hands curled, and he warned himself not to get in close. Whatever he did, to do it from a distance. A groin kick but don't follow it in. Stay outside those hands.

'You say "come on up",' he told her.

'Come on up,' Lizzie repeated into the phone. She rang off and unhooked the chain.

'When he comes in, smile for the camera. Don't shout.'

'Go to hell.'

From the lift-well, to his sharpened ear, came the clump of a lift arriving and the monotonous 'ping' of the bell. He heard footsteps approaching the door, one pair only, steady, and remembered Drake Ko's comic, slightly ape-like gait at Happy Valley, how the knees tipped through the grey flannels. A key slid into the lock, one hand came round the door, and the rest with no apparent forethought followed. By then, Jerry had sprung with all his weight, flattening the unresisting body against the wall. A picture of Venice fell, the glass smashed, he slammed the door, all in the same moment as he found a throat and jammed the barrel of the pistol straight into the deep flesh. Then the door was unlocked a second time from outside, very fast, the wind went out of his body, his feet flew upward, a crippling shock of pain spread from his kidneys and felled him on the thick carpet, a second blow caught him in the groin and made him gasp as he jerked his knees to his chin. Through his streaming eyes he saw the little, furious figure of Fawn the babysitter standing over him, shaping for a third strike, and the rigid grin of Sam Collins as he peered calmly over Fawn's shoulder to see what the damage was. And still in the doorway, wearing an expression of grave apprehension as he straightened his collar after Jerry's unprovoked assault on him, the flustered figure of his one-time guide and mentor Mr George Smiley, breathlessly calling his leashdogs to order.

Jerry was able to sit, but only if he leaned forward. He held both hands in front of him, his elbows jammed into his lap. The pain was all over his body, like poison spreading from a central source. The girl watched from the hall doorway. Fawn was lurking, hoping for another excuse to hit him. Sam Collins was at the other end of the room, sitting in a winged armchair with his legs crossed. Smiley had poured Jerry a neat brandy, and was stooping over him, poking the glass into his hand.

'What are you doing here, Jerry?' Smiley said. 'I don't understand.'

'Courting,' said Jerry, and closed his eyes as a wave of black pain swept over him. 'Developed an unscheduled affection for our hostess there. Sorry about that.'

'That was a very dangerous thing to do, Jerry,' Smiley objected. 'You could have wrecked the entire operation. Suppose I had been Ko. The consequences would have been disastrous.'

'I'll say they would.' He drank some brandy. 'Luke's dead. Lying in my flat with his head shot off.'

'Who's Luke?' Smiley asked, forgetting their meeting at Craw's house.

'No one. Just a friend.' He drank again. 'American journalist. A drunk. No loss to anyone.'

Smiley glanced at Sam Collins but Sam shrugged.

'Nobody *we* know,' he said.

'Ring them all the same,' said Smiley.

Sam picked up the mobile telephone and walked out of the room with it because he knew the layout.

'Put the burn on her have you?' Jerry said, with a nod of his head toward Lizzie. 'About the only thing left in the book that hasn't been done to her, I should think.' He called over to her. 'How are you doing there, sport? Sorry about the tussle. Didn't break anything, did we?'

'No', she said.

'Put the bite on you about your wicked past, did they? Stick and carrot? Promised to wipe the slate clean? Silly girl, Lizzie. Not allowed a past in this game. Can't have a future either. *Verboten.*'

He turned back to Smiley:

'That's all it was, George. No philosophy to it. Old Lizzie just got under my skin.'

Tilting back his head, he studied Smiley's face through half closed eyes. And with the clarity which pain sometimes brings, he observed that by his action he had put Smiley's own existence under threat.

'Don't worry,' he said gently. 'Won't happen to *you*, that's for sure.'

'Jerry,' said Smiley.

'Yessir,' said Jerry and made a show of sitting to attention.

'Jerry, you don't understand what's going on. How much you could upset things. Billions of dollars and thousands of men could not obtain a part of what we stand to gain from this one operation. A war general would laugh himself silly at the thought of such a tiny sacrifice for such an enormous dividend.'

'Don't ask *me* to get you off the hook, old boy,' Jerry said, looking up into his face again. 'You're the owl, remember? Not me.'

Sam Collins returned. Smiley glanced at him in question.

'He's not one of theirs either,' said Sam.

'They were aiming for me,' said Jerry. 'They got Lukie instead. He's a big bloke. Or was.'

'And he's in your flat?' Smiley asked. 'Dead. Shot. And in your flat?'

'Been there some while.'

Smiley to Collins: 'We shall have to brush over the traces, Sam. We can't risk a scandal.'

'I'll get back to them now,' Collins said.

'And find out about planes,' Smiley called after him. 'Two first class.'

Collins nodded.

'Don't like that fellow one bit,' Jerry confessed. 'Never did. Must be his moustache.' He shoved a thumb toward Lizzie. 'What's she got that's so hot for you all, anyway, George? Ko doesn't whisper his inmost secrets to her. She's a roundeye.' He turned to Lizzie. 'Does he?'

She shook her head.

'If he did, she wouldn't remember,' he went on. 'She's thick as hell about those things. She's probably never even heard of Nelson.' He called to her again. 'You. Who's Nelson? Come on, who is he? Ko's little dead son, isn't he? That's right. Named his boat after him, didn't he? And his gee-gee.' He turned back to Smiley. 'See? Thick. Leave her out of it, that's my advice.'

Collins had returned with a note of flight times. Smiley read it, frowning through his spectacles. 'We shall have to send you home at once, Jerry,' he said. 'Guillam's waiting downstairs with a car. Fawn will go along as well.'

'I'd just like to be sick again, if you don't mind.'

Reaching upward, Jerry took hold of Smiley's arm for support and at once Fawn sprang forward, but Jerry shot out a warning at him, as Smiley ordered him back.

'You keep your distance, you poisonous little leprechaun,' Jerry advised. 'You're allowed one bite and that's all. The next one won't be so easy.'

He moved in a crouch, trailing his feet slowly, hands clutched over his groin. Reaching the girl he stopped in front of her.

'Did they have pow-wows up here, Ko and his lovelies, sport? Ko bring his boyfriends up here for a natter, did he?'

'Sometimes.'

'And you helped with the mikes did you, like the good little housewife? Let the sound boys in, tended the lamp? Course you did.'

She nodded.

'Still not enough,' he objected, as he hobbled to the bathroom. 'Still doesn't answer my question. Must be more to it than that. *Far* more.'

In the bathroom he held his face under cold water, drank some, and immediately vomited. On the way back, he looked for the girl again. She was in the drawing room and in the way that people under stress look for trivial things to do, she was sorting the gramophone records, putting each in its proper sleeve. In a distant corner Smiley and Collins were quietly conferring. Closer at hand, Fawn was waiting at the door.

'Bye, sport,' he said to her. Putting his hand on her shoulder he drew her round till her grey eyes looked straight at him.

'Goodbye,' she said, and kissed him, not in passion exactly, but at least with more deliberation than the waiters got.

'I was a sort of accessory before the fact,' he explained. 'I'm sorry about that. I'm not sorry about anything else. You'd better look after that sod Ko, too. Because if they don't manage to kill him, I may.'

He touched the lines on her chin, then shuffled toward the door where Fawn stood, and turned round to take his leave of Smiley, who was alone again. Collins had been sent off to telephone. Smiley stood as Jerry remembered him best, his expression at once apologetic and enquiring, as if he'd just left his umbrella on the underground. The girl had turned away from both of them, and was still sorting the records.

'Love to Ann then,' Jerry said.

'Thank you.'

'You're wrong. sport. Don't know how, don't know why, but you're wrong. Still, too late for that I suppose.' He felt sick again and his head was shrieking from the pains in his body. 'You come any nearer than that,' he said to Fawn, 'and I will definitely break your bloody neck, you understand?' He turned back to Smiley who stood in the same posture and gave no sign of having heard.

'Season of the year to you then,' said Jerry.

With a last nod but none to the girl Jerry limped into the corridor, Fawn following. Waiting for the lift he saw the elegant American standing at his open doorway, watching his departure.

'Ah yeah I forgot about you,' he called very loudly. 'You're running the bug on her flat, aren't you? The Brits blackmail her and the Cousins bug her, lucky girl gets it all ways.'

The American vanished, closing the door quickly after him. The lift came and Fawn shoved him in.

'Don't do that,' Jerry warned him. 'This gentleman's name is Fawn,' he told the other occupants of the lift, in a very loud voice. They mostly wore dinner jackets and sequinned dresses. 'He's a member of the British Secret Service and he's just kicked me in the balls. The Russians are coming,' he added, to their doughy, indifferent faces. 'They're going to take away all your bloody money.'

'Drunk,' said Fawn in disgust.

In the lobby Lawrence the porter watched with keen interest. In the forecourt, a Peugeot saloon waited, blue. Peter Guillam was sitting in the driving seat.

'Get in,' he snapped.

The passenger door was locked. Jerry climbed into the back, Fawn after him.

'What the hell do you think you're up to?' Guillam demanded through clenched teeth. 'Since when did half-arsed London Occasionals cut anchor in mid-operation?'

'Keep clear,' Jerry warned Fawn. 'Just the hint of a frown from you right now is enough to get me going. I mean that. I warn you. Official.'

The ground mist had returned, rolling over the bonnet. The passing city offered itself like the framed glimpses of a junk yard: a painted sign, a shop window, strands of cable strung across a neon, a clump of suffocated foliage; the inevitable building site, floodlit. In the mirror, Jerry saw a black Mercedes following, male passenger, male driver.

'Cousins bringing up the tail,' he announced.

A spasm of pain in the abdomen almost blacked him out, and for a moment he actually thought Fawn had hit him again, but it was only an after-effect of the first time. In Central, he made Guillam pull up and was sick in the gutter in full public view, leaning his head through the window while Fawn crouched tensely over him. Behind them, the Mercedes stopped too.

'Nothing like a spot of pain,' he exclaimed, settling in the car again, 'for getting the old brain out of mothballs once in a while. Eh Peter?'

In his black anger Guillam made an obscene answer.

*You don't understand what's going on,* Smiley had said. *How much you could upset things. Billions of dollars and thousands of men could not obtain a part of what we stand to gain . . .'*

*How?* he kept asking himself. Gain *what?* His knowledge of Nelson's position inside Chinese affairs was sketchy. Craw had told him only the minimum he needed to know. *Nelson has access to the Crown jewels of Peking, your Grace. Whoever gets his hooks on Nelson has earned a lifetime's merit for himself and his noble house.*

They were skirting the harbour, heading for the tunnel. From sea level the American aircraft carrier looked strangely small against the merry backdrop of Kowloon.

'How's Drake getting him out by the way?' he asked Guillam chattily. 'Not trying to fly him again, *that's* for sure. Ricardo put the lid on that one for good, didn't he?'

'Suction,' Guillam snapped – which was very silly of him, thought Jerry jubilantly, he should have kept his mouth shut.

'Swimming?' Jerry asked. 'Nelson on the Mirs Bay ticket. That's not Drake's way is it? Nelson's too old for that one anyway. Freeze to death, even if the sharks didn't get his whatnots. How about the pig-train, come out with the grunters? Sorry you've got to miss the big moment, sport, all on account of me.'

'So am I, as a matter of fact. I'd like to kick your teeth in.'

Inside Jerry's brain, the sweet music of rejoicing sounded. *It's true!* he told himself. *That's what's happening! Drake's bringing Nelson out and they're all queuing up for the finish!*

Behind Guillam's lapse – just one word, but in Sarratt terms totally unforgivable, indivisibly wrong – there lay nevertheless a revelation as dazzling as anything which Jerry was presently enduring, and in some respects vastly more bitter. If anything mitigates the crime of indiscretion – and in Sarratt terms nothing does – then Guillam's experiences of the last hour – half of it spent driving Smiley frantically through rush-hour traffic, and half of it waiting, in desperate indecision, in the car outside Star Heights – would surely qualify. Everything he had feared in London, the most Gothic of his apprehensions regarding the Enderby-Martello connection, and the supporting rôles of Lacon and Sam Collins, had in these sixty minutes been proven to him beyond all reasonable doubt as right, and true, and justified, and if anything somewhat understated.

They had driven first to Bowen Road in the Midlevels, to an apartment block so blank and featureless and large that even those who lived there must have had to look twice at the number before they were sure they were entering the right one. Smiley pressed a bell marked *Mellon* and, idiot that he was, Guillam asked 'Who's Mellon?' at exactly the same time as he remembered that it was Sam Collins's workname. Then he did a double take and asked himself – but not Smiley, they were in the lift by now – what maniac, after Haydon's ravages, could conceivably award himself the same workname which he had used before the fall? Then Collins opened the door to them, wearing his Thai silk dressing gown, a brown cigarette jammed into a holder, and his washable non-iron smile, and the next thing was, they were grouped in a parquet drawing room with bamboo chairs and Sam had switched two transistor radios to different programmes, one voice, the other music, to provide rudimentary anti-bug security while they talked. Sam listened, ignoring Guillam entirely, then promptly phoned Martello direct – Sam had a *direct line* to him, please note, no dialling, nothing, a straight landline apparently – to ask in veiled language 'how things stood with chummy'. Chummy – Guillam learned later – being gambling slang for a mug. Martello replied that the surveillance van had just reported in. Chummy and Tiu were presently sitting in Causeway Bay aboard the *Admiral Nelson*, said the watchers, and the directional mikes (as usual) were picking up so much bounce from the water that the transcribers would need days if not weeks to clean off the extraneous sound and find out whether the two men had ever said anything interesting. Meanwhile they had dropped one man at the quayside as a static post, with orders to advise Martello immediately should the boat weigh anchor or either of the two quarries disembark.

'Then we must go there at once,' said Smiley, so they piled back into the car, and while Guillam drove the short distance to Star Heights, seething and listening impotently to their terse conversation, he became with every moment more convinced that he was looking at a spider's web, and that only George Smiley, obsessed by the promise of the case and the image of Karla, was myopic enough, and trusting enough, and in his own paradoxical way innocent enough, to bumble straight into the middle of it.

George's age, thought Guillam. Enderby's political ambitions, his fondness for the hawkish, pro-American stance – not to mention the crate of champagne and his outrageous courtship of the fifth floor. Lacon's tepid support of Smiley, while he secretly cast around for a successor. Martello's stopover in Langley. Enderby's attempt, *only days ago*, to prise Smiley away from the case and hand it to Martello on a plate. And now, most eloquent and ominous of all, the reappearance of Sam Collins as the joker in the pack with a private line to Martello! And Martello, Heaven help us, acting dumb about where George got his information from – the direct line notwithstanding.

To Guillam all these threads added up to one thing only, and he could not wait to take Smiley aside and by any means at his command deflect him sufficiently from the operation, just for one moment, for him to see where he was heading. To tell him about the letter. About Sam's visit to Lacon and Enderby in Whitehall.

Instead of which? He was to return to England. Why was he to return to England? Because a genial thick-skulled hack named Westerby had had the gall to slip the leash.

Even without his crying awareness of impending disaster, the disappointment to Guillam would have been scarcely supportable. He had endured a great deal for this moment. Disgrace and exile to Brixton under Haydon, poodling for old George instead of getting back to the field, putting up with George's obsessive secretiveness, which Guillam privately considered both humiliating and self-defeating – but at least it had been a journey with a destination, till bloody Westerby, of all people, had robbed him even of that. But to return to London knowing that for the next twenty-two hours at least, he was leaving Smiley and the Circus to a bunch of wolves, without even the chance to warn him – to Guillam it was the crowning cruelty of a frustrated career, and if blaming Jerry helped, then damn him, he would blame Jerry or anybody else.

'Send Fawn!'

'Fawn's not a gentleman,' Smiley would have replied – or words that meant the same.

You can say *that* again too, thought Guillam, remembering the broken arms.

Jerry was equally conscious of abandoning someone to the wolves, even if it was Lizzie Worthington rather than George Smiley. As he gazed through the rear window of the car, it seemed to him that the very world that he was moving through had been abandoned also. The street markets were deserted, the pavements, even the doorways. Above them, the Peak loomed fitfully, its crocodile spine daubed by a ragged moon. It's the Colony's last day, he decided. Peking has made its proverbial telephone call. 'Get out, party over.' The last hotel was closing, he saw the empty Rolls-Royces lying like scrap around the harbour, and the last blue-rinse roundeye matron, laden with her tax-free furs and jewellery, tottering up the gangway of the last cruise-ship, the last China-watcher frantically feeding his last miscalculations into the shredder, the looted shops, the empty city waiting like a carcass for the hordes. For a moment it was all one vanishing world – here, Phnom Penh, Saigon, London, a world on loan, with the creditors standing at the door and Jerry himself, in some unfathomable way, a part of the debt that was owed.

*I've always been grateful to this service that it gave me a chance to pay. Is that how you feel? Now? As a survivor, so to speak?*

Yes, George, he thought. Put the words into my mouth, old boy. That's how I feel. But perhaps not quite in the sense *you* mean it, sport. He saw Frost's cheerful, fond little face as they drank and fooled. He saw it the second time, locked in that awful scream. He felt Luke's friendly hand upon his shoulder, and saw the same hand lying on the floor, flung back over his head to catch a ball that would never come, and he thought: trouble is, sport, the paying is actually done by the other poor sods.

Like Lizzie for instance.

He'd mention that to George one day, if they ever, over a glass, should get back to that sticky little matter of just why we climb the mountain. He'd make a point there – nothing aggressive, not rocking the boat you understand, sport – about the selfless and devoted way in which we sacrifice other people, such as Luke and Frost and Lizzie. George would have a perfectly good answer, of course. Reasonable. Measured. Apologetic. George saw the bigger picture. Understood the imperatives. Of course he did. He was an owl.

The harbour tunnel was approaching and he was thinking of her shivering last kiss, and remembering the drive to the mortuary all at the same time, because the scaffold of a new building rose ahead of them out of the fog, and like the scaffold on the way to the mortuary it was floodlit, and glistening coolies were swarming over it in yellow helmets.

Tiu doesn't like her either, he thought. Doesn't like roundeyes who spill the beans on Big Sir.

Forcing his mind in other directions he tried to imagine what they would do with Nelson: stateless, homeless, a fish to be devoured or thrown back into the sea at will. Jerry had seen a few of those fish before: he had been present for their capture; at their swift interrogation; he had led more than one of them back across the border they had so recently crossed, for hasty *recycling*, as the Sarratt jargon had it so charmingly – 'quick before they notice he has left home'. And if they didn't put him back? If they kept him, this great prize they all so coveted? Then after the years of his debriefing – two, three even – he had heard some ran for five – Nelson would become one more Wandering Jew of the spy trade, to be hidden, and moved again, and hidden, to be loved not even by those to whom he had betrayed his trust.

*And what will Drake do with Lizzie* – he wondered – *while that little drama unfolds? Which particular scrapheap is she headed for this time?*

They were at the mouth of the tunnel and they had slowed almost to a halt. The Mercedes lay right behind them. Jerry let his head fall forward. He put both hands over his groin while he rocked himself and grunted in pain. From an improvised police box, like a sentry post, a Chinese constable watched curiously.

'If he comes over to us, tell him we've got a drunk on our hands,' Guillam snapped. 'Show him the sick on the floor.'

They crawled into the tunnel. Two lanes of north-bound traffic were bunched nose to bumper by the bad weather. Guillam had taken the right-hand stream. The Mercedes drew up beside them on their left. In the mirror, through half-closed eyes, Jerry saw a brown lorry grind down the hill after them.

'Give me some change,' Guillam said. 'I'll need change as I come out.'

Fawn delved in his pockets, but using one hand only.

The tunnel pounded to the roar of engines. A hooting match started. Others began joining in. To the encroaching fog was added the stench of exhaust fumes. Fawn closed his window. The din rose and echoed till the car trembled to it. Jerry put his hands to his ears.

'Sorry, sport. Going to bring up again I'm afraid.'

But this time he leaned towards Fawn, who with a muttered 'Filthy bastard' started hastily to wind his window down again, until Jerry's head crashed into the lower part of his face, and Jerry's elbow hacked down into his groin. For Guillam, caught between driving and defending himself, Jerry had one pounding chop on the point where the shoulder socket meets the collarbone. He started the strike with the arm quite relaxed, converting the speed into power at the last possible moment. The impact made Guillam scream 'Christ!' and lifted him straight out of his seat as the car veered to the right. Fawn had an arm round Jerry's neck and with his other hand he was trying to press Jerry's head over it, which would definitely have killed him. But there is a blow they teach at Sarratt for cramped spaces which is called a tiger's claw, and is delivered by driving the heel of the hand upward into the opponent's windpipe, keeping the arm crooked and the fingers pressed back for tension. Jerry did that now, and Fawn's head hit the back window so hard that the safety glass starred. In the Mercedes, the two Americans went on looking ahead of them, as if they were driving to a state funeral. He thought of squeezing Fawn's windpipe with his finger and thumb but it didn't seem necessary. Recovering his gun from Fawn's waistband, Jerry opened the right-hand door. Guillam made one desperate dive for him, ripping the sleeve of his faithful but very old blue suit to the elbow. Jerry swung the gun on to his arm and saw his face contort with pain. Fawn got a leg out but Jerry slammed the door on it and heard him shout 'Bastard!' again and after that he just kept running back toward town, against the stream. Bounding and weaving between the land-locked cars, he pelted out of the tunnel and up the hill until he reached the little sentry hut. He thought he heard Guillam yelling. He thought he heard a shot but it could have been a car backfiring. His groin was hurting amazingly, but he seemed to run faster under the impetus of the pain. A policeman on the kerb shouted at him, another held out his arms, but Jerry brushed them aside, and they gave him the final indulgence of the roundeye. He ran until he found a cab. The driver spoke no English so he had to point the way. 'That's it, sport. Up there. Left, you bloody idiot. That's it –' until they reached her block.

He didn't know whether Smiley and Collins were still there, or whether Ko had turned up, perhaps with Tiu, but there was very little time to play games finding out. He didn't ring the bell because he knew the mikes would pick it up. Instead he fished a card from his wallet, scribbled on it, shoved it through the letterbox and waited in a crouch, shivering and sweating and panting like a dray-horse while he listened for her tread and nursed his groin. He waited an age and finally the door opened and she stood there staring at him while he tried to get upright.

'Christ, it's Galahad,' she muttered. She wore no make-up and Ricardo's claw marks were deep and red. She wasn't crying; he didn't think she did that, but her face looked older than the rest of her. To talk, he drew her into the corridor and she didn't resist. He showed her the door leading to the firesteps.

'Meet me the other side of it in five seconds flat, hear me? *Don't* telephone anybody, *don't* make a clatter leaving, and *don't* ask any bloody silly questions. Bring some warm clothes. Now do it, sport. Don't dither. *Please.*'

She looked at him, at his torn sleeve, and sweat-stained jacket; at his mop of forelock hanging over his eye.

'It's me or nothing,' he said. 'And believe me, it's a big nothing.'

She walked back to her flat alone, leaving the door ajar. But she came out much faster and for safety's sake she didn't even close the door. On the firestairs he led the way. She carried a shoulder bag and wore a leather coat. She had brought a cardigan for him to replace the torn jacket, he supposed Drake's because it was miles too small, but he managed to squeeze into it. He emptied his jacket pockets into her handbag and chucked the jacket down the rubbish chute. She was so quiet following him that he twice looked back to make sure she was still there. Reaching the ground floor, he peered through the glass mesh window and drew back in time to see the Rocker in person accompanied by a heavy subordinate, approach the porter in his kiosk and show him his police pass. They followed the stair as far as the car park and she said, 'Let's take the red canoe.'

'Don't be bloody stupid, we left it in town.'

Shaking his head, he led her past the cars into a squalid open-air compound full of refuse and building junk, like the backyard at the Circus. From here, between walls of weeping concrete, a giddy stairway fell toward the town, overhung by black branches and cut into sections by the winding road. The jarring of the downward steps hurt his groin a lot. The first time they reached the road, Jerry took her straight across it. The second time, alerted by the blood-red flash of an alarm light in the distance, he hauled her into the trees to avoid the beam of a police car whining down the hill at speed. At the underpass they found a *pak-pai* and Jerry gave the address.

'Where the hell's that?' she said.

'Somewhere you don't have to register,' said Jerry. 'Just shut up and let me be masterful, will you? How much money have you got with you?'

She opened her bag and counted from a fat wallet.

'I won it off Tiu at mah-jong,' she said and for some reason he sensed she was romancing.

The driver dropped them at the end of the alley and they walked the short distance to the low gateway. The house had no lights, but as they approached the front door it opened and another couple flitted past them out of the darkness. They entered the hall and the door closed behind them and they followed a handborne pinlight through a short maze of brick walls until they reached a smart interior lobby in which piped music played. On the serpentine sofa in the centre sat a trim Chinese lady with a pencil and a notebook on her lap, to all the world a model châtelaine. She saw Jerry and smiled, she saw Lizzie and her smile broadened.

'For the whole night,' Jerry said.

'Of course,' she replied.

They followed her upstairs to a small corridor. The open doors gave glimpses of silk counterpanes, low lights, mirrors. Jerry chose the least suggestive, declined the offer of a second girl to make up the numbers, gave her money and ordered a bottle of Rémy Martin. Lizzie followed him in, chucked her shoulder bag on the bed and while the door was still open broke into a taut laugh of relief.

'Lizzie Worthington,' she announced, 'this is where they said you'd end up, you brazen bitch, and blow me if they weren't right!'

There was a chaise-longue and Jerry lay on it, staring at the ceiling, feet crossed, the brandy glass in his hand. Lizzie took the bed and for a time neither spoke. The place was very still. Occasionally from the floor above, they heard a cry of pleasure or muffled laughter, once of protest. She went to the window and peered out.

'What's out there?' he asked.

'Bloody brick wall, about thirty cats, stack of empties.'

'Foggy?'

'Vile.'

She sauntered to the bathroom, poked around, came out again.

'Sport,' said Jerry quietly.

She paused, suddenly wary.

'Are you sober and of sound judgment?'

'Why'

'I want you to tell me everything you told them. When you've done that, I want you tell me everything they asked you, whether you could answer it or not. And when you've done that, we'll try to take a little thing called a backbearing and work out where those bastards all are in the scheme of the universe.'

'It's a replay,' she said finally.

'What of?'

'I don't know. It's all to be exactly the way it happened before.'

'So what happened before?'

'Whatever it was,' she said wearily, 'it's going to happen again.'

# TWENTY-ONE

# *Nelson*

It was one in the morning. She had bathed. She came out of the bathroom wearing a white wrap and no shoes and her hair in a towel, so that the proportions of her were all suddenly different.

'They've even got those bits of paper stretched across the loo,' she said.

'And toothmugs in cellophane bags.'

She dozed on the bed and he on the sofa, and once she said, 'I'd like to but it doesn't work,' and he replied that after being kicked where Fawn had kicked him the libido tended to be a bit quiescent anyway. She told him about her schoolmaster – Mr Bloody Worthington, she called him – and 'her one shot at going straight,' and about the child she had borne him out of politeness. She talked about her terrible parents, and about Ricardo and what a sod he was, and how she had loved him, and how a girl in the Constellation Bar had advised her to poison him with laburnum, so one day after he had beaten her half to death she put a 'damn great dose in his coffee'. But perhaps she hadn't got the right stuff, she said, because all that happened was that he was sick for days and 'the one thing worse than Ricardo healthy was Ricardo at death's door'. How another time she actually got a knife into him while he was in the bath but all he did was stick a bit of plaster over it and swipe her again.

How when Ricardo did his disappearing act she and Charlie Marshall refused to accept that he was dead, and mounted a Ricardo Lives! campaign, as they called it, and how Charlie went and badgered his old man, all just as he had described to Jerry. How Lizzie packed up her rucksack and went down to Bangkok, where she barged straight into the China Airsea suite at the Erawan, intending to beard Tiu, and found herself face to face with Ko instead, having met him only once before, very briefly, at a bunfight in Hong Kong given by one Sally Cale, a blue-rinse bull-dyke in the antique trade who pushed heroin on the side. And how that was quite a scene she played, beginning with Ko's sharp instruction to get out, and ending with 'Nature taking her course' as she put it cheerfully: 'Another step on Lizzie Worthington's unswerving road to perdition.' So that slowly and deviously, with Charlie Marshall's old man pulling, 'and Lizzie pushing, as you might say,' they put together a very Chinese contract, to which the main signatories were Ko and Charlie's old man, and the commodities to be transacted were, one, Ricardo and, two his recently retired life partner, Lizzie.

In which said contract, Jerry learned with no particular surprise, both she and Ricardo gratefully acquiesced.

'You should have let him rot,' said Jerry, remembering the twin rings on his right hand, and the Ford car blown to bits.

But Lizzie hadn't seen it that way at all, and she didn't now.

'He was one of us,' she said. 'Although he was a sod.'

But having bought his life, she felt free of him.

'Chinese arrange marriages every day. So why shouldn't Drake and Liese?'

What was all the *Liese* stuff? Jerry asked. Why *Liese* instead of *Lizzie*?

She didn't know. Something Drake didn't talk about, she said. There had once been a Liese in his life, he told her, and his fortune-teller had promised him that one day he would get another, and he reckoned Lizzie was near enough, so they gave it a shove and called it Liese and while she was about it she pared her surname to plain Worth.

'Blonde bird,' she said absently.

The name-change had a practical purpose too, she said. Having chosen a new name for her, Ko took the trouble to have the local police record of her old one destroyed.

'Till that sod Mellon marches in and says he'll get them to rewrite it, with a special mention about me carrying his bloody heroin,' she said.

Which brought them back to where they were now. And why.

To Jerry, their sleepy wanderings occasionally had the calm of after-love.

He lay on the divan, wide awake, but Lizzie talked between dozes, taking up her story dreamily where she had left it when she fell asleep, and he knew that near enough she was telling him the truth because it made nothing of her that he did not already know, and understand. He realized also that, with time, Ko had become an anchor for her. He gave her the authority from which to survey her Odyssey, somewhat as the schoolmaster had.

'Drake never broke a promise in his life,' she said once, as she rolled over and sank back into a fitful sleep. He remembered the orphan: just never lie to me.

Hours, lifetimes later, she was woken by a squawk of ecstasy next door.

'Christ,' she declared appreciatively. 'She *really* hit the moon.' The squawk repeated itself. 'Uha! Faking it.' Silence.

'You awake?' she asked.

'Yes.'

'What are you going to do?'

'Tomorrow?'

'Yes.'

'I don't know,' he said.

'Join the club,' she whispered, and seemed to fall asleep again.

I need that Sarratt brief again, he thought. Very badly I need it. Put in a limbo call to Craw, he thought. Ask dear old George for a spot of that philosophical advice he's taken to doling out these days. He must be around. Somewhere.

Smiley was around but at that moment he could not have given Jerry any help at all. He would have traded all his knowledge for a little understanding. The isolation ward had no night-time and they lay or lounged under the punctured daylight of the ceiling, the three Cousins and Sam one side of the room, Smiley and Guillam the other, and Fawn striding up and down the line of the cinema seats, looking caged and furious and squeezing what appeared to be a squash-ball in each tiny fist. His lips were black and swollen and one eye was shut. A clot of blood under his nose refused to go away. Guillam had his right arm strapped to his shoulder and his eyes were on Smiley all the while. But so were the eyes of everyone, or everyone but Fawn. A phone rang but it was the communications room upstairs saying Bangkok had reported Jerry traced for certain as far as Vientiane.

'Tell them the trail's cold, Murphy,' Martello ordered, his eyes still on Smiley. 'Tell them any damn thing. Just get them off our backs. Right, George?'

Smiley nodded.

'Right,' said Guillam firmly, speaking for him.

'The trail's cold, honey,' Murphy echoed into the phone. The *honey* came as a surprise. Murphy had not till now shown such signs of human tenderness. 'You want to make a signal or do I have to do it for you? We're not interested, right? Kill it.'

He rang off.

'Rockhurst has found her car,' Guillam said for the second time, while Smiley still stared ahead of him. 'In an underground carpark in Central. There is a hire car down there too. Westerby rented it. Today. In his workname. George?'

Smiley gave a nod so slight it might have been no more than an attack of sleepiness which he had staved away.

'At least he's doing something, George,' said Martello pointedly, down the room from his own small caucus of Collins and the quiet men. 'Some people would say, when you have a rogue elephant, best thing to do is go out there and shoot him.'

'You have to find him first,' snapped Guillam, whose nerves were at breaking point.

'I'm not even sure George wants to do that, Peter,' Martello said in a reprise of his avuncular style. 'I think George may be lifting his eye from the ball a little on this, to the grave peril of our common enterprise.'

'What do you want George to do?' Guillam rejoined tartly. 'Walk the streets till he finds him? Have Rockhurst circulate his name and description so that every journalist in town knows there's a manhunt for him?'

At Guillam's side, Smiley remained hunched and inert, like an old man.

'Westerby's a professional,' Guillam insisted. 'He's not a natural but he's good. He can lie up for months in a town like this and Rockhurst wouldn't get a scent of him.'

'Not even with the girl in tow?' said Murphy.

His strapped arm notwithstanding Guillam stooped to Smiley.

'It's your operation,' he whispered urgently. 'If you say we've got to wait, we'll wait. Just give the order. All these people want is an excuse to take over. Anything but a vacuum. Anything.'

Prowling the line of the cinema chairs, Fawn gave bent to a sarcastic murmur.

'Talk, talk, talk. That's all they can do.'

Martello tried again.

'George. Is this island British or is it not? You guys can shake this town out any time.' He pointed to a windowless wall. 'We have a man out there – your man – who seems bent on running amok. Nelson Ko is the biggest catch you or I are ever likely to land. The biggest of my career, and I will stake my wife, my grandmother and the deeds of my plantation, the biggest even of yours.'

'No takers,' said Sam Collins the gambler, through his grin.

Martello stuck to his guns.

'Are we going to let him rob us of the prize, George, while we sit here passively asking one another how it came about that Jesus Christ was born on Christmas Day and not on December twenty-six or seven?'

Smiley peered at Martello at last, then up at Guillam who stood stiffly at his side, tipping back his shoulders to support the sling, and finally he looked downward at his own, locked, conflicting hands and for a period quite meaningless in time he studied himself in his mind, and reviewed his quest for Karla, whom Ann called *his black Grail*. He thought of Ann and her repeated betrayals of him in the name of her own Grail, which she called love. He recalled how, against his better judgment, he had tried to share her faith, and like a true believer, renew it each day, despite her anarchic interpretations of its meaning. He thought of Haydon, steered at Ann by Karla. He thought of Jerry and the girl, and he thought of Peter Worthington her husband, and the doglike look of kinship which Worthington had bestowed on him, when he called to interview him in the terrace house in Islington: 'You and I are the ones they leave behind,' ran the message.

He thought of Jerry's other tentative loves along his untidy trail, the half-paid bills the Circus had picked up for him, and it would have been handy to lump Lizzie in with them as just one more, but he couldn't do that. He was not Sam Collins, and he had not the smallest doubt that at this moment Jerry's feeling for the girl was a cause which Ann would warmly have espoused. But he was not Ann either. For a cruel moment, nevertheless, as he sat, still locked in indecision, he did honestly wonder whether Ann was right, and his striving had become nothing other than a private journey among the beasts and villains of his own insufficiency, in which he ruthlessly involved simplistic minds like Jerry's.

*You're wrong, sport. Don't know how, don't know why, but you're wrong.*

*The fact that I am wrong,* he had once replied to Ann in the midstream of one of their endless arguments, *does not make you right.*

He heard Martello again, speaking in present time.

'George, we have people waiting with *open arms* for what we can give them. What Nelson can.'

A phone was ringing. Murphy took the call and relayed the message to the silent room: 'Landline from the aircraft carrier, sir. Navy int. has the junks dead on schedule, sir. South wind favourable and good fishing along the way. Sir, I don't even think Nelson's riding with them. I don't see why he should.'

The focus shifted abruptly to Murphy, who had never before been heard to express an opinion.

'What the hell's *that*, Murphy?' Martello demanded, quite astonished. 'You been to the fortune-teller too, son?'

'Sir, I was down on the ship this morning and those people have a lot of data. They can't figure why anybody who lives in Shanghai would ever want to exit out of Swatow. They would do it all different, sir. They would fly or train to Canton, then take the bus maybe to Waichow. They say that's a lot safer, sir.'

'These are Nelson's people,' Smiley said, as the heads swung sharply back on him. 'They're his clan. He would rather be at sea with them, even if he's at risk. He trusts them.' He turned to Guillam. 'We'll do this,' he said. 'Tell Rockhurst to distribute a description of Westerby and the girl together. You say he hired the car under his workname? Used his escape papers?'

'Yes.'

'Worrell?'

'Yes.'

'The police are looking for a Mr and Mrs Worrell then, British. No photographs, and make sure the descriptions are vague enough not to arouse suspicion. Marty.'

Martello was all attentiveness.

'Is Ko still on his boat?' Smiley asked.

'Nestled right in there with Tiu, George.'

'It is just possible Westerby may try to reach him. You have a static post at the quayside. Put more men down there. Tell them to keep eyes in the back of their heads.'

'What are they looking for?'

'Trouble. The same goes for surveillance on his house. Tell me –' he sank into his thoughts a moment, but Guillam need not have worried. 'Tell me – can you simulate a fault on Ko's home telephone line?'

Martello glanced at Murphy.

'Sir, we don't have the apparatus handy,' Murphy said, 'but I guess we could . . .'

'Then cut it,' Smiley said simply. 'Cut the whole cable if necessary. Try and do it near some roadworks.'

Having dispensed his orders, Martello came lightly across the room, and sat himself at Smiley's side.

'Ah George, about tomorrow, now. Do you think we might, ah, put a little hardware on standby, as well?' From the desk where he was telephoning Rockhurst, Guillam watched the dialogue most intently. From across the room, so did Sam Collins. 'Just seems there's no telling what your man Westerby might do, George. We have to be prepared for all emergencies, right?'

'By all means stand anything by. But for the time being, if you don't mind, we'll leave the interception plans as they are. And the competence with me.'

'Sure, George. Sure,' said Martello fulsomely, and with the same church-like reverence tiptoed back to his own camp.

'What did he want?' Guillam demanded in a low voice, crouching at Smiley's side. 'What's he trying to get you to agree to?'

'I will not have it, Peter,' Smiley warned, also under his breath. He was suddenly very angry. 'I shall not hear you again. I shall not tolerate your Byzantine notions of a palace plot. These people are our hosts and our allies. We have a written agreement with them. We have quite enough to worry about already without grotesque, and, I may tell you honestly, paranoid fancies. Now please –'

'I tell *you!*' Guillam began, but Smiley closed him down.

'I want you to get hold of Craw. Call on him if necessary. Perhaps the journey would do you good. Tell him Westerby's on the rampage. He's to let us know at once if he has word of him. He'll know what to do.'

Still walking the line of seats, Fawn watched Guillam leave, while his fists continued restlessly kneading whatever was inside them.

In Jerry's world it was also three in the morning, and the madame had found him a razor, but no fresh shirt. He had shaved and cleaned himself up as best he could, but his body still ached from head to toe. He stood over Lizzie where she lay on the bed and promised to be back in a couple of hours but he doubted whether she even heard him. *More papers print girls instead of news,* he remembered, *and the world be a damn sight better place, Mr Westerby.*

He took *pak-pais*, knowing they were less under the thumb of the police. Otherwise he walked, and the walking helped his body and his mystical processs of decision taking, because back there on the divan it had suddenly become impossible. He needed to move in order to find direction. He was heading for Deep Water Bay, and he knew he was entering badland. Now that he was on the loose they would be on to that launch like leeches. He wondered who they had, what they were using. If it was the Cousins he would look for too much hardware, and overmanning. Rain was coming on and he feared it would clear the fog. Above him, the moon was already partly free and as he padded silently down the hill he could make out by its pale light the nearest stockbroker junks groaning and tugging at their moorings. A south-east wind, he noticed, and rising. If it's a static observation post, they'll go for height, he thought, and sure enough, there on the promontory to his right, he saw a battered-looking Mercedes van tucked between the trees, and the aerial with its Chinese streamers. He waited, watching the fog roll, till a car came down the hill with its lights full on, and as soon as it was past him he darted across the road, knowing that not all the hardware in the world would enable them to see him behind the advancing headlights. At the water's level the visibility was down to zero, and he had to grope in order to pick out the rickety wooden causeway he remembered from his previous reconnaissance. Then he found what he was looking for. The same toothless old woman sat in her sampan grinning up at him through the fog.

'Ko,' he whispered. *'Admiral Nelson, Ko?'*

The echo of her cackle bounded away across the water.

'Po Toi!' she screamed. 'Tin Hau! Po Toi!'

'Today?'

'Today!'

'Tomorrow?'

'Tomollow!'

He tossed her a couple of dollars and her laughter followed him as he crept away.

I'm right, Lizzie's right, *we're* right, he thought. He's going to the festival. He hoped to God Lizzie was staying put. If she woke up, he wouldn't put it past her to wander.

He walked, trying to stamp away the aching in his groin and back. Take it stage by stage, he thought. Nothing big. Just play it as it comes. The fog was like a corridor leading to different rooms. Once he met an invalid car crawling along the kerb, as its owner exercised his Alsation dog. Once, two old men in undervests performing their morning exercises. In a public garden small children stared at him from a rhododendron bush which they seemed to have made their home, for their clothes, were draped over the branches and they were as naked as the refugee kids in Phnom Penh.

She was sitting up waiting for him when he returned and she looked terrible.

'Don't do that again,' she warned, and shoved her arm through his as they set out to find some breakfast and a boat. 'Don't ever bloody walk out on me without warning.'

Hong Kong at first possessed no boats at all that day. Jerry would not contemplate the big out-island ferries which took the trippers. He knew the Rocker would have them sewn up. He refused to go down to the bays and make conspicuous enquiries. When he telephoned the listed water-taxi firms, whatever they had was either rented or too small for the voyage. Then he remembered Luigi Tan the fixer, who was a myth at the Foreign Correspondents' Club: Luigi could get you anything from a Korean dance troupe to a cutprice airticket faster than any fixer in town. They took a taxi to the other side of Wanchai, where Luigi had his lair, then walked. It was eight in the morning but the hot fog had not lifted. The unlit signs sprawled over the narrow lanes like spent lovers: Happy Boy, Lucky Place, Americana. The crowded food stalls added their warm smells to the reek of petrol fumes and smuts. Through splits in the wall they sometimes glimpsed a canal. 'Anyone tell you where to find me,' Luigi Tan liked to say. 'Ask for the big guy with one leg.'

They found him behind the counter of his shop, just tall enough to look over it, a tiny, darting half-Portuguese who had once earned a living Chinese boxing in the grimy booths of Macao. The front of the shop was six foot wide. His wares were new motorbikes and relics of the old China Service, which he called antiques; daguerreotypes of hatted ladies in tortoiseshell frames, a battered travelling box, an opium clipper's log. Luigi knew Jerry already but he liked Lizzie much better, and insisted that she go ahead so that he could study her hind quarters while he ushered them under a washing line, to an outhouse marked *private*, with three chairs and a telephone on the floor. Crouching till he was rolled into a neat ball, Luigi talked Chinese to the telephone and English to Lizzie. He was a grandfather, he said, but virile, and had four sons, all good. Even number four son was off his hands. All good drivers, good workers and good husbands. Also, he said to Lizzie, he had a Mercedes complete with stereo.

'Maybe I take you ride in it one day,' he said.

Jerry wondered whether she realized that he was proposing marriage, or perhaps something slightly less.

And yes, Luigi thought he had a boat as well.

After two phone calls he knew he had a boat, which he only ever lent to friends, at a nominal cost. He gave Lizzie his credit-card case to count the number of cards, then his wallet to admire the family snaps, one of which showed a lobster caught by number four son on the day of his recent wedding, though the son was not visible.

'Po Toi bad place,' said Luigi Tan to Lizzie, still on the telephone. 'Very dirty place. Rough sea, lousy festival, bad food. Why you want to go there?'

For Tin Hau of course, Jerry said patiently, answering for her. For the famous temple and the festival.

Luigi Tan preferred to speak to Lizzie.

'You go Lantau,' he advised. 'Lantau good island. Nice food, good fish, nice people. I tell them you go Lantau, eat at Charlie's, Charlie my friend.'

'Po Toi,' said Jerry firmly.

'Po Toi hell of a lot of cash.'

'We've got a hell of a lot of cash,' said Lizzie with a lovely smile, and Luigi looked at her again, contemplatively, the long up and down look.

'Maybe I come with you,' he said to her.

'No,' said Jerry.

Luigi drove them to Causeway Bay and rode with them on the sampan. The boat was a fourteen-foot power boat, common as driftwood, but Jerry reckoned she was sound and Luigi said she had a deep keel. A boy lounged on the stern, trailing one foot in the water.

'My nephew,' said Luigi, ruffling the boy's hair proudly. 'He got mother in Lantau. He take you Lantau, eat Charlie's place, give you good time. You pay me later.'

'Old boy,' said Jerry patiently. 'Sport. We don't want Lantau. We want Po Toi. Only Po Toi. Po Toi or nothing. Drop us there and go.'

'Po Toi bad weather, bad festival. Bad place. Too near China water. Lot of Commies.'

'Po Toi or nothing,' Jerry said.

'Boat too small,' said Luigi, with a frightful loss of face, and it took all Lizzie's charm to build him up again.

For another hour the boys primed the boat and all Jerry and Lizzie could do was sit in the half cabin keeping out of sight and sip judicious shots of Rémy Martin. Periodically one or other of them sank into a private reverie. When Lizzie did this, she hugged herself and rocked slowly on her haunches, head down. Whereas Jerry yanked at his forelock, and once he yanked so hard she touched his arm to stop him, and he laughed.

Almost carelessly they pulled away from the harbour.

'Stay out of sight,' Jerry ordered, and for safety's sake put his arm round her to keep her in the meagre shelter of the open cabin.

The American aircraft carrier had stripped off her ornamental garb and lay grey and menacing, like an unsheathed knife above the water. At first, they had nothing but the same sticky calm. On the shore, shelves of mist pressed on to the grey highrises, and brown smoke columns slid into a white expressionless sky. On the flat water their boat felt high as a balloon. But as they slipped the shelter and headed east, the waves slapped her sides hard enough to wind her, the bow pitched and cracked, and they had to brace themselves to keep upright. With the little bow lifting and tugging like a bad horse, they tumbled past cranes and godowns and factories and the stumps of quarried hillsides. They were running straight into the wind and spray was flying on all sides. The coswain at the wheel was laughing and crowing to his mate, and Jerry supposed it was the mad roundeyes they were laughing at, who chose to do their courting in a pitching tub. A giant tanker passed them, not seeming to move, brown junks running in her wake. From the dockyards, where a freighter was laid-to, the white flashes of the welders' lamps signalled to them across the water. The boys' laughter eased and they began to talk sensibly because they were at sea. Looking back between the swaying walls of transport ships Jerry saw the Island drawing slowly away from him, cut like a table mountain by the cloud. Once more, Hong Kong was ceasing to exist.

They passed another headland. As the sea roughened, the pitching steadied and the cloud above them dropped until its base was only a few feet above them dropped until its base was only a few feet above their mast, and for a while they stayed in this lower, unreal world, advancing under cover of its protective blanket. The fog ended suddenly and left them in dancing sunlight. Southward, on hills of violent lushness, an orange navigation lamp winked at them through the clear air.

'What do we do now?' she asked softly, looking through the porthole.

'Smile and pray,' said Jerry.

'I'll smile, you pray,' she said.

A pilot's launch was pulling alongside and for a moment he definitely expected to see the hideous face of the Rocker glowering down on him, but the crew ignored them entirely.

'Who are they?' she whispered. 'What do they think?'

'It's routine,' said Jerry. 'It's meaningless.'

The launch veered away. That's it, thought Jerry, with no particular feeling, they've spotted us.

'You sure it was just routine?' she asked.

'Hundreds of boats go to the festival,' he said.

The boat bucked violently, and kept bucking. Great seaworthiness, he thought, hanging on to Lizzie. Great keel. If this goes on, we won't have anything to decide. The sea will do it for us. It was one of those trips where if you made it nobody noticed, and if you didn't they'd say you threw your life away. The east wind could swirl right round on itself at any moment, he thought. In the season between west monsoons, nothing was ever sure. He listened anxiously to the erratic galloping of the engine. If it gives up we'll finish on the rocks.

Suddenly his nightmares multiplied unreasonably. *The butane,* he thought. *Christ the butane!* While the boys were preparing the boat, he had glimpsed two cylinders stowed in the front hold beside the watertanks, presumably for cooking Luigi's lobsters. Fool that he was, he had made nothing of them till now. He worked it out. Butane is heavier than air. All cylinders leak. It's just a question of degree. With this sea pounding the bows they leak faster, and the escaped gas will now be lying in the bilge about two feet from the spark for the engine, with a nice blend of oxygen to assist combustion. Lizzie had slipped from his grasp and stood astern. The sea was suddenly crowded. Out of nowhere, a fleet of fishing junks had gathered, and she was gazing at them earnestly. Grabbing her arm he hauled her back to the cover of the cabin.

'Where do you think you are?' he shouted. 'Bloody Cowes?'

She studied him a moment, then gently kissed him, then kissed him again.

'You calm down,' she warned. She kissed him a third time, muttered 'Yes,' as if her expectations had been fulfilled, then sat quiet for a while, looking at the deck but keeping hold of his hand.

Jerry reckoned they were making five knots into the wind. A small plane zoomed overhead. Holding her out of sight he looked up sharply, but was too late to read the markings.

'And good morning to *you*,' he thought.

They were rounding the last point, tossing and groaning in the spray. Once, the propellers lifted clean out of the water with a roar. As they hit the sea again, the engine faltered, choked, but decided to stay alive. Touching Lizzie's shoulder Jerry pointed ahead of them to where the bare, steep island of Po Toi loomed like a cutout against the cloud-torn sky: two peaks, sheer from the water, the larger to the south, and a saddle between. The sea had turned iron blue and the wind ripped over it, slapping the breath from their mouths and hurling spray at them like hail. On the port bow lay Beaufort Island: a lighthouse, a jetty, no inhabitants. The wind dropped as though it had never been. Not a breeze greeted them as they entered the unruffled water of the island's lee. The sun's heat was direct and harsh. Ahead of them, perhaps a mile, lay the mouth of Po Toi's main bay, and behind it, the low brown ghosts of China's islands. Soon they could make out a whole untidy fleet of junks and cruise boats jamming the bay, as the first jingle of drums and cymbals and unco-ordinated chanting floated to them across the water. On the hill behind lay the shanty village, its tin roofs twinkling, and on its own small headland stood one solid building, the temple of Tin Hau, with a bamboo scaffold lashed round it in a rudimentary grandstand, and a large crowd with a pall of smoke hanging over it and dabs of gold between.

'Which side was it?' he asked her.

'I don't know. We climbed to a house and walked from there.'

Each time he spoke to her he looked at her, but now she avoided his gaze. Tapping the coxswain on the shoulder he pointed the course he wanted him to take. The boy at once began protesting. Squaring to him, Jerry showed him a bunch of money, pretty well all he had left. With an ill grace, the boy swung across the mouth of the harbour, weaving between the boats toward a small granite headland where a tumbledown jetty offered a risky landing. The din of the festival was much louder. They could smell charcoal and suckling pig, and hear concerted bursts of laughter, but for the time being the crowd was out of sight to them, as they were to the crowd.

'Here! he yelled. 'Put in here. Now! *Now!*'

The jetty leaned drunkenly as they clambered onto it. They had not even reached land before their boat had turned for home. Nobody said goodbye. They climbed up the rock, hand in hand, and walked straight into a money game that was being watched by a large and laughing crowd. At the centre stood a clownish old man with a bag of coins and he was throwing them down the rock one by one while barefooted boys hurled themselves after them, pushing each other almost to the cliff-edge in their zeal.

'They took a boat,' Guillam said. 'Rockhurst has interviewed the proprietor. The proprietor is a friend of Westerby, and yes it was Westerby and a beautiful girl, and they wanted to go to Po Toi for Tin Hau.'

'And how did Rockhurst play that?' Smiley asked.

'Said in that case it wasn't the couple he was looking for. Bowed out. Disappointed. The harbour police have also belatedly reported sighting it on a course for the festival.'

'Want us to put up a spotter plane, George?' Martello asked nervously. 'Navy int. have all sorts standing by.'

Murphy had a bright suggestion. 'Why don't we just go right in with choppers and scoop Nelson off that end junk?' he demanded.

'Murphy, shut up,' Martello said.

'They're making for the island,' Smiley said firmly. 'We know they are. I don't think we need aircover to prove it.'

Martello was not satisfied. 'Then maybe we should send a couple of people out to that island, George. Maybe we ought to do a little interfering finally.'

Fawn was standing stock still. Even his fists had stopped working.

'No,' said Smiley.

At Martello's side Sam Collins's grin grew a little thinner.

'Any reason?' Martello asked.

'Right up to the last minute, Ko has one sanction. He can signal his brother not to come ashore,' Smiley said. 'The merest hint of a disturbance on the island could persuade him to do that.'

Martello gave a nervous, angry sigh. He had put aside the pipe he sometimes smoked and was drawing heavily on Sam's supply of brown cigarettes, which seemed to be endless.

'George, what does this man *want*?' he demanded in exasperation. 'Is this a blackmail thing now, a disruption? I don't see a category here.' A dreadful thought struck him. His voice dropped and he pointed with the full length of his arm across the room. 'Now just don't tell me we got one of these new ones on our hands, for Christ's sakes! Don't tell me he's one of those cold-war converts with a middle-aged mission to wash his soul in public. Because if he is, and we are going to read this guy's frank life story in *The Washington Post* next week, George, I personally am going to put the whole Fifth Fleet on that island, if that's what it takes to hold him down.' He turned to Murphy. 'I have contingencies, right?'

'Right.'

'George, I want a landing party on standby. You guys can come aboard or stay home. Please yourselves.'

Smiley stared at Martello, then at Guillam with his strapped and useless arm, then at Fawn, who was poised like a diver at the end of a springboard, eyes half closed and heels together, while he lifted himself slowly up and down on his toes.

'Fawn and Collins,' Smiley said at last.

'You two boys take them down to the aircraft carrier and hand them right over to the people there. Murphy comes back.'

A smoke-cloud marked the place where Collins had been sitting. Where Fawn had stood, two squash balls slowly rolled a distance before coming to a halt.

'Gold help us all,' somebody murmured fervently. It was Guillam, but Smiley ignored him.

The lion was three-men long and the crowd was laughing because it nipped at them and because self-appointed picadors were prodding it with sticks while it lolloped in dance-steps down the narrow path, to the clatter of the drums and cymbals. Reaching the headland, the procession slowly turned itself and started to retrace its steps, and at this point Jerry drew Lizzie quickly into the middle of it, bending low in order to make less of his height. The track was mud and full of puddles. Soon the dance was leading them past the temple and down concrete steps toward a sand beach where the suckling pigs were being roasted.

'Which way?' he asked her.

She guided him quickly left, out of the dance, along the back of a shanty village and over a wooden bridge across an inlet. They climbed along a fringe of cypress trees, Lizzie leading, until they were alone again, standing over the perfect horseshoe bay, looking down on Ko's *Admiral Nelson* where she lay at the very centre, like a grand lady among the hundreds of pleasure boats and junks around her. There was nobody visible on deck, not even crew. A clutch of grey police boats, five or six of them, was anchored further out to sea.

And why not, thought Jerry, since this was a festival?

She had let go his hand and, when he turned to her, she was still staring at Ko's launch and he saw the shadow of confusion in her face.

'Is this really the way he brought you?' he asked.

It was the way, she said, and turned to him to look, to confirm or weigh things in her mind. Then with her forefinger she gravely traced his lips, at the centre of them where she had kissed them. 'Jesus,' she said, and as gravely shook her head.

They started climbing again. Glancing up, Jerry saw the brown island peak deceptively near, and on the hillside, groups of rice terraces gone to ruin. They entered a small village populated by nothing but surly dogs, and the bay vanished from sight. The school house was open and empty. Through the doorway, they saw charts of fighting aircraft. Washing jars stood on the step. Cupping her hands, Lizzie rinsed her face. The huts were slung with wire and brick to anchor them against typhoons. The path turned to sand and the going grew harder.

'Still right?' he asked.

'It's just *up*,' she said, as if she were sick of telling him. 'It's just *up*, and then the *house*, and bingo. I mean, Christ, what do you think I am, a bloody nitwit?'

'I didn't say a thing,' said Jerry. He put his arm round her and she pressed in to him, giving herself exactly as she had done on the dance floor.

They heard a blare of music from the temple as somebody tested the loudspeakers, and after it the wail of a slow tune. The bay was in view again. A crowd had gathered on the shore. Jerry saw more puffs of smoke and, in the windless heat of this side of the island, caught a whiff of joss. The water was blue and clear and calm. Round it, white lights burned on poles. The Ko launch had not stirred, nor had the police.

'See him?' he asked.

She was studying the crowd. She shook her head.

'Probably having a kip after lunch,' she said carelessly.

The beating of the sun was ferocious. When they entered the shadow of the hillside it was like a sudden dusk, and when they reached the sunlight it stung their faces like the heat of a close fire. The air was alive with dragonflies, the hillside strewn with big boulders, but where bushes grew they wound and straggled everywhere, producing rich trumpets, red and white and yellow.

Old picnic cans lay in profusion.

'And that's the house you meant?'

'I told you,' she said.

It was a ruin: a broken brown-plastered villa with gaping walls and a view. It had been built with some grandeur above a dried-up stream and was reached by a concrete foot bridge. The mud stank and hummed with insects. Between palms and bracken the remains of a verandah gave a vast prospect of the sea and of the bay. As they crossed the footbridge he took her arm.

'So let's play it from here,' he said. 'No interrogations. Just tell.'

'We walked up here, like I said. Me, Drake and bloody Tiu. The boys brought a basket and the booze. I said "where are we going?" and he said "picnic". Tiu didn't want me but Drake said I could come. "You *hate* walking," I said. "I've never even seen you cross a *road* before!" "Today we walk," he says, doing his Captain of Industry Act. So I tag along and shut up.'

A thick cloud was already obscuring the peak above them and rolling slowly down the hill. The sun had vanished. In moments the cloud reached them, and they were alone at the world's end, unable to see even their feet. They groped their way into the house. She sat apart from him, on a bust roof beam. Chinese slogans were daubed in red paint down the door pillars. The floor was littered with picnic refuse and long twists of lining paper.

'He tells the boys to hop it so they hop it, him and Tiu have a long earnest natter in whatever they're speaking this week, and halfway through lunch he breaks into English and tells me Po Toi's *his* island. It's where he first landed when he left China. The boat people dumped him here. "My people", he calls them. That's why he comes to the festival every year and that's why he gives money to the temple, and that's why we've sweated up the bloody hill for a picnic. They then go back into Chinese, and I get the feeling Tiu is tearing him off a strip for talking too much, but Drake's all excited and little-boy and won't listen. Then they go on up.'

'*Up?*'

'Up to the top. "Old ways are the best," he says to me. "We shall stick to what is proven" – then his Baptist bit – "hold fast to that which is good, Liese. That is what God likes."'

Jerry glanced into the fog-bank above him, and he could have sworn he heard the crackle of a small plane, but at the moment he didn't mind too much whether it was there or not, because he had the two things he most badly needed. He had the girl with him, and he had the information: for now he finally understood exactly what she had been worth to Smiley and Sam Collins, and how she had unconsciously betrayed to them the vital clue to Ko's intentions.

'So they went on to the top. Did you go with them?'

'No.'

'Did you see where they went?'

'To the top. I told you.'

'Then what?'

'They looked down the other side. Talked. Pointed. More talk, more pointing, then down they come again and Drake's even more excited, the way he gets when he's brought off a big deal and Number One's not there to disapprove. Tiu looks dead solemn, and that is the way he gets when Drake acts fond of me. Drake wants to stay and have a couple of brandies so Tiu goes back to Hong Kong in a huff. Drake gets amorous and decides we'll spend the night on the boat and go home in the morning, so that's what we do.'

'Where does he moor the boat? Here? In the bay?'
'No.'
'Where?'
'Off Lantau.'
'You went straight there, did you?'
She shook her head.
'We did a round of the island.'
'*This* island?'
'There was a place he wanted to look at in the dark. A bit of coast round the other side. The boys had to shine the lamps on it. "That's where I land in fifty-one," he said. "The boat people were frightened to put into the main harbour. They were frightened of police and ghosts and pirates and customs men. They say the islanders will cut their throats."'
'And in the night?' said Jerry softly. 'While you were moored off Lantau?'
'He told me he had a brother and loved him.'
'That was the first time he told you?'
She nodded.
'He tell you where the brother was?'
'No.'
'But you knew?'
This time she didn't even nod.
From below, the clatter of the festival rose criss-cross through the cloud. He lifted her gently to her feet.
'Bloody questions,' she muttered.
'They're nearly over,' he promised. He kissed her and she let him, but did not otherwise take part.
'Let's go up and take a look,' he said.
Ten minutes more and the sunlight returned and blue sky opened above them. With Lizzie leading, they scrambled quickly over several false peaks toward the saddle. The sounds from the bay stopped and the colder air filled with screaming, wheeling gulls. They approached the crest, the path widened, they walked side by side. A few steps more and the wind had hit them with a force that made them gasp and reel back. They were at the knife-edge, looking down into an abyss. At their very feet the cliff fell vertical to a boiling sea, and the foam smothered the headlands. Dumpling clouds were blowing from the east and behind them the sky was black. Perhaps two hundred metres down lay an inlet which the breakers did not cover. Fifty yards out from it, a brown shoal of rock checked the sea's force, and the spume washed it in white rings.
'That it?' he yelled above the wind. 'He landed there? That bit of coast?'
'Yes.'
'Shone the lights on it?'
'Yes.'
Leaving her where she stood, he moved slowly up the knife-edge, crouching almost double while the wind rushed over his ears and covered his face in a sticky salt sweat and his stomach screamed in pain from what he supposed was a punctured gut or internal bleeding or both. At the inmost point before the cliff cut back into the sea, he once more looked down and now he thought he could just make out a skimpy path, sometimes no more than a seam of rock, or a ridge of rough grass, eking its way cautiously toward the inlet. There was no sand in the inlet but some of the rocks looked dry. Returning to her, he led her away from the knife-edge. The wind dropped,

and they heard the din of the festival again much louder than before. The snap of firecrackers made a toy war.

'It's his brother Nelson,' he explained. 'In case you hadn't gathered, Ko's bringing him out of China. Tonight's the night. Trouble is, he's a much sought-after character. Lot of people would like a chat with him. That's where Mellon came in.' He took a breath. 'My view is that you should get the hell out of here. How do you see that? Drake's not going to want you around, that's for sure.'

'Is he going to want you?' she asked.

'I think, what you should do, you should go back to the harbour,' he said. 'Are you listening?'

She managed, 'Of course I am.'

'You look for a nice friendly-looking roundeye family. Choose the woman for once and not the bloke. Tell her you've had a row with your boyfriend and can they take you home in their boat? If they'll have you, stay the night with them, otherwise go to a hotel. Spin them one of your stories. Christ, *that's* no problem is it?'

A police helicopter pattered overhead in a long curve, presumably to observe the festival. Instinctively he grabbed her shoulders and drew her into the rock.

'Remember the second place we went – the big band sound – the bar?' He was still holding her.

She said, 'Yes.'

'I'll pick you up there tomorrow night.'

'I don't know,' she said.

'Be there anyway at seven. At seven, got it?'

She pushed him gently away from her, as if she were determined to stand alone.

'Tell him I kept faith,' she said. 'It's what he cares about most. I stuck to the deal. If you see him, tell him, "Liese stuck to the deal."'

'Sure.'

'Not *sure*. *Yes*. Tell him. He did everything he promised. He said he'd look after me. He did. He said he'd let Ric go. He did that too. He always stuck to a deal.'

He lifted her head, holding it with both his hands, but she insisted on going on.

'And tell him – and tell him – tell him they made it impossible. They fenced me in.'

'Be there from seven on,' he said. 'Even if I'm a bit late. Now come on, that's not too difficult, is it? You don't need a university degree to hoist that aboard.' He was gentling her, battling for a smile, striving for a last complicity before they separated.

She nodded.

She wanted to say something else but it didn't work. She took a few steps, turned and looked back at him and he waved – one big flap of the arm. She took a few more and kept going till she was below the line of the hill, but he did hear her shout 'Seven then', or thought he did. Having watched her out of sight, Jerry returned to the knife-edge, where he sat down for a bit of a breather before the Tarzan stuff. A snatch of John Donne came back to him, one of the few things he had picked up at school, though somehow he never got quotations completely right, or thought he didn't:

> *On a huge hill*
> *Cragged and steep, Truth stands, and he that will*
> *Reach her, about must, and about must go.*

Or something. For an hour, deep in thought, two hours, he lay in the lee of the rock and watched the daylight turn to dusk over the Chinese islands a few miles into the sea. The he pulled off his buckskin boots, and re-threaded the laces in a herringbone, the way he used to thread them for his cricket boots. Then he put them on again and tied them as tight as they would go. It could be Tuscany again, he thought, and the five hills which he used to gawp at from the hornet field. Except that this time he wasn't proposing to walk out on anyone. Not the girl. Not Luke. Not even himself. Even if it took a lot of footwork.

'Navy int. has the junk fleet making around six knots and slap on course,' Murphy announced. 'Quit the beds right on one one hundred, just like they were following our projection.'

From somewhere he had scrounged a set of bakelite toy boats which he could fix to the chart. Standing, he pointed them proudly in a single column at Po Toi island.

Murphy had returned, but his colleague had stayed with Sam Collins and Fawn, so they were four.

'And Rockhurst has found the girl,' said Guillam quietly, putting down the other phone. His shoulder was playing up, and he was extremely pale.

'Where?' said Smiley.

Still at the chart Murphy turned. At his desk, where he was keeping a log of events, Martello put down his pen.

'Picked her up at Aberdeen harbour as she landed,' Guillam went on. 'She'd cadged a lift back from Po Toi with a clerk and his wife from the Hong Kong and Shanghai Bank.'

'So what's the story?' Martello demanded before Smiley could speak. 'Where's Westerby?'

'She doesn't know,' said Guillam.

'Ah come on!' Martello protested.

'She says they had a row and left in different boats. Rockhurst says give him another hour with her.'

Smiley spoke. 'And Ko?' he asked. 'Where's he?'

'His launch is still in Po Toi harbour,' Guillam replied. 'Most of the other boats have already left. But Ko's is where it was this morning. Sitting pretty, Rockhurst says, and everyone below.'

Smiley peered at the sea chart, then at Guillam, then at the map of Po Toi. 'If she told Westerby what she told Collins,' he said, 'then he's stayed on the island.'

'With what in mind?' Martello demanded, very loud. 'George for what purpose is *that* man remaining on *that* island?'

An age went by for all of them.

'He's waiting,' Smiley said.

'For *what*, may I enquire?' Martello persisted in the same determined tone.

Nobody saw Smiley's face. It had found its own bit of shadow. They saw his shoulders hunch, they saw his hand rise to his spectacles as if to remove them, they saw it fall back empty in defeat, on to the rosewood table.

'Whatever we do, we must let Nelson land,' he said firmly.

'And whatever *do* we do?' Martello demanded, getting up and coming round the table. 'Weatherby's not *here*, George. He never entered the Colony. He can leave by the same damn route!'

'Please don't shout at me,' Smiley said.

Martello ignored him. 'Which is it going to be, that's all? The conspiracy or the fuck-up?'

Guillam was standing his height, barring the way, and for an extraordinary moment it seemed possible that, broken shoulder notwithstanding, he proposed physically to restrain Martello from coming any closer to where Smiley sat.

'Peter,' Smiley said quietly. 'I see there's a telephone behind you. Perhaps you'd be good enough to pass it to me.'

With the full moon, the wind had dropped and the sea settled. Jerry had not descended all the way to the inlet but made a last camp thirty feet above it, in the cover of a shrub, where he had protection. His hands and knees were cut to ribbons and a branch had grazed his cheek, but he felt good: hungry and alert. In the sweat and danger of the scramble he had forgotten his pain. The inlet was larger than he imagined when he had looked down on it from higher up, and the granite cliffs at sea level were pierced with caves. He was trying to guess Drake's plan – for since Lizzie, he now thought of him as Drake. He had been trying all day. What Drake had to do, he would do from the sea because he was not capable of the nightmarish climb down the cliff. Jerry wondered at first whether Drake might try to intercept Nelson before he landed, but could see no safe way for Nelson to slip the fleet and make a sea-meeting with his brother.

The sky darkened, the stars came, and the moon-path grew brighter. And Westerby? he thought: what does *A* do now? *A* was one hell of a long way from the syndicate solutions of Sarratt, *that* was for sure.

Drake would also be a fool to attempt to bring his launch to this side of the island, he decided. She was unwieldy and drew too much water to come inshore on a windward coast. A small boat was better and a sampan or a rubber dinghy best. Clambering down the cliff till his boots hit pebbles, Jerry huddled against the rock, watching the breakers thump and the sparks of phosphorus riding with the spume.

'She'll be back by now,' he thought. With any luck she's talked her way into someone's house and is charming the kids and wrapping herself round a cup of Bovril. *Tell him I kept faith*, she said.

The moon lifted, and still Jerry waited, training his eyes on the darkest spots in an effort to improve his vision. Then over the clatter of the sea he could have sworn he heard the awkward slap of water on a wooden hull and the short grumble of an engine switched on and off again. He saw no light. Edging his way along the shadowed rock he crept as close to the water's edge as he dared and once more crouched, waiting. As the wave of surf soaked him to the thighs, he saw what he was waiting for: against the path of the moon, not twenty yards from him, the arched cabin and curled prow of a single sampan rocking on its anchor. He heard a splash and a muffled order, and as he sank as low as the slope allowed, he picked out against the starstrewn sky the unmistakable shape of Drake Ko in his Anglo-French beret wading cautiously ashore, followed by Tiu carrying an M16 machine gun across both arms. So there you are, thought Jerry, addressing himself, rather than Drake Ko. End of the long trail. Luke's killer, Frostie's killer – whether by proxy or in the flesh is immaterial – Lizzie's lover, Nelson's father, Nelson's brother. Welcome to the man who never broke a deal in his life.

Drake also had a burden but it was less ferocious, and Jerry knew long before he made it out that it was a lamp and a power pack, pretty much like the ones he had used in the Circus watergames on the Helford Estuary, except that the Circus favoured ultra-violet, and shoddy wire-framed spectacles which were useless in rain or spray.

Reaching the beach, the two men made their way grunting over the shingle until they reached the highest point, then like himself they merged against the black rock. He reckoned they were sixty feet from him. He heard a grunt, and saw the flame of a cigarette lighter, then the red glow of two cigarettes followed by the murmur of Chinese voices. Wouldn't mind one myself, thought Jerry. Stooping, he spread out one large hand and began loading it with pebbles until it was full, then padded as stealthily as he could manage along the base of the rock toward the two red embers. By his calculation he was eight paces from them. He had the pistol in his left hand and the pebbles in his right, and he was listening to the clump of the waves, how they gathered, tottered and fell, and he was thinking that it was going to be a lot easier to have a chat with Drake once Tiu was out of the way.

Very slowly, in the classic posture of the outfielder, he leaned back, raised his left elbow in front of him and crooked his right arm behind him, prepared for a throw at full stretch. A wave fell, he heard the shuffle of the undertow, the grumble as another gathered. Still he waited, right arm back, palm sweating as he clasped the pebbles. Then as the wave reached its height he hurled them high up the cliff using all his strength, before ducking to a crouch, gaze fixed upon the embers of the two cigarettes. He waited, then heard the pebbles patter against the rock above him, and the hailstorm gather as they tumbled down. In the next instant he heard Tiu's short curse and saw one ember fly into the air as he leapt to his feet, machine gun in hand, barrel lifted to the cliff and his back to Jerry. Drake was scrambling for cover.

First Jerry hit Tiu very hard with the pistol, taking care to keep his fingers inside the guard. Then he hit him again with his closed right hand, a two-knuckle strike at full force, with the fist turned down and turning, as they say at Sarratt, and a lot of follow-through at the end. As Tiu went down, Jerry caught his cheekbone with the whole weight of his swinging right boot, and heard the snap of his closing jaw. And as he stooped to pick up the M16 he smashed the butt of it into Tiu's kidneys, thinking very angrily of both Luke and Frost, but also of that cheap crack he had made about Lizzie not rating more than the journey from Kowloonside to Hong Kongside. Greetings from the horse-writer, he thought.

Then he looked toward Drake, who, having stepped forward, was still no more than a black shape against the sea: a crooked silhouette with piecrust ears sticking out below the line of his odd beret. A strong wind had risen again, or perhaps Jerry was only now aware of it. It rattled in the rocks behind them, and made Drake's broad trousers billow.

'That Mr Westerby, the English newsman?' he enquired, in precisely the deep, harsh tones he had used at Happy Valley.

'The same,' said Jerry.

'You're a very political man, Mr Westerby. What the hell do you want here?'

Jerry was recovering his breath and for a moment he didn't feel quite ready to answer.

'Mr Ricardo tells my people it is your aim to blackmail me. Is money your aim, Mr Westerby?'

'Message from your girl,' Jerry said, feeling he should discharge that promise first. 'She says she keeps faith. She's on your side.'

'I don't have a side, Mr Westerby. I'm an army of one. What do you want? Mr Marshall tells my people you are some kind of hero. Heroes are very political persons, Mr Westerby. I don't care for heroes.'

'I came to warn you. They want Nelson. You mustn't take him back to Hong Kong. They've got him all sewn up. They've got plans that will last him the rest of his life. And you as well. They're queuing up for both of you.'

'What do you *want*, Mr Westerby?'

'A deal.'

'Nobody wants a deal. They want a commodity. The deal obtains for them the commodity. What do you want?' Drake repeated, raising his voice in command. 'Tell me please.'

'You bought yourself the girl with Ricardo's life,' said Jerry. 'I thought I might buy her back with Nelson's. I'll speak to them for you. I know what they want. They'll settle.'

That's the last foot in the last door for me, he thought.

'A *political* settlement, Mr Westerby? With *your* people? I made many political settlements with them. They told me God loved children. Did you ever notice God love an Asian child, Mr Westerby? They told me God was a *kwailo* and his mother had yellow hair. They told me God was a peaceful man, but I read once that there have never been so many civil wars as in the Kingdom of Christ. They told me –'

'Your brother's right behind you, Mr Ko.'

Drake swung round. On their left, heading from the east, a dozen or more junks in full sail trembled southward across the moon-path in ragged column, lights prickling in the water. Dropping to his knees, Drake began frantically groping for the lamp. Jerry found the tripod, wrenched it open, Drake stood the lamp on it but his hands were shaking wildly and Jerry had to help him. Jerry seized the flexes, struck a match and clipped the cables to the terminals. They were staring out to sea, side by side. Drake flashed the lamp once, then again, first red then green.

'Wait,' Jerry said softly. 'You're too soon. Go easy or you'll muck it all up.'

Moving him gently aside, Jerry bent to the eyepiece and scanned the busy line of boats.

'Which one?' Jerry asked.

'The last,' said Ko.

Holding the last junk in view, though it was still only a shadow, Jerry signalled again, one red, one green, and a moment later heard Drake let out a cry of joy as an answering flicker darted back across the water.

'Can he fix on that?' said Jerry.

'Sure,' said Ko, still looking out to sea. 'Sure. He will fix on that.'

'Then leave it alone. Don't do any more.'

Ko turned to him, and Jerry saw the excitement in his face, and felt his dependence.

'Mr Westerby. I am advising you sincerely. If you have played a trick on me for my brother Nelson, your Christian Baptist hell will be a very comfortable place by comparison with what my people do to you. But if you help me I give you everything. That is my contract and I never broke a contract in my life. My brother also made certain contracts.' He looked out to sea.

The forward junks were out of sight. Only the tail-enders remained. From far away Jerry fancied he heard the uneven rumble of an engine, but he knew his mind was all over the place and it could have been the tumble of the waves. The moon passed behind the peak and the shadow of the mountain fell like a black knife-point on to the sea, leaving the far fields silver. Stooped to the lamp, Drake gave another cry of pleasure.

'Here! Here! Take a look, Mr Westerby.'

Through the eyepiece, Jerry made out a single phantom junk, unlit except for three pale lamps, two green ones on the mast, red to starboard, making its way toward them. It passed from the silver into the blackness and he lost it. From behind him, he heard a groan from Tiu. Ignoring it, Drake remained stooped to the eyepiece, one arm held wide like a Victorian photographer while he began calling softly in Chinese. Running up the shingle Jerry pulled the pistol from Tiu's belt, picked up the M16 and, taking both to the sea's edge, chucked them in. Drake was preparing to repeat the signal again but mercifully he couldn't find the button and Jerry was in time to stop him. Once more Jerry thought he heard the rumble, not of one engine but of two. Running out on to the headland, he peered anxiously north and south in search of a patrol boat, but again he saw nothing, and again he blamed the surf and his strained imagination. The junk was nearer, beating in toward the island, her brown batwing sail suddenly tall and terribly conspicuous against the sky. Drake had run to the water's edge and was waving and yelling across the sea.

'Keep your voice down!' Jerry hissed from beside him.

But Jerry had become an irrelevance. Drake's whole life was for Nelson. From the shelter of the near headland, Drake's sampan tottered alongside the rocking junk. The moon came out of hiding and for a moment Jerry forgot his anxiety as a little grey-clad figure, small and sturdy, in stature Drake's antithesis, in a kapok coat and bulging proletarian cap, lowered himself over the side and leapt for the waiting arms of the sampan's crew. Drake gave another cry, the junk filled its sails and slid behind the headland till only the green lights on its masthead remained visible above the rocks, and then vanished. The sampan was making for the beach and Jerry could see Nelson's stocky frame as he stood on the bow waving with both hands and Drake Ko in his beret wild on the beach, dancing like a madman, waving back.

The throb of engines grew steadily louder, but still Jerry couldn't place them. The sea was empty, and when he looked upward he saw only the hammerhead cliff and its peak black against the stars. The brothers met, and embraced, and stayed locked in each other's arms, not moving. Seizing hold of both of them, pummelling them, Jerry cried out for all his life.

'Get back in the boat! Hurry!'

They saw no one but each other. Running back to the water's edge Jerry grabbed the sampan's prow and held it, still calling to them as he saw the sky behind the peak turn yellow, then quickly brighten as the throb of the engines swelled to a roar and three blinding searchlights burst on them from blackened helicopters. The rocks danced to the whirl of landing lights, the sea furrowed and the pebbles bounced and flew around in storms. For a fraction of a second Jerry saw Drake's face turn to him beseeching help: as if, too late, he had recognized where help lay. He mouthed something, but the din drowned it. Jerry hurled himself forward. Not for Nelson's sake, still less for Drake's; but for what linked them, and what linked him to Lizzie. But long before he reached them, a dark swarm closed on the two men, tore them apart and bundled the baggy shape of Nelson into the helicopter's hold. In the mayhem Jerry had drawn his gun and held it in his hand. He was screaming, though he could not hear himself above the hurricanes of war. The helicopter was lifting. A single figure remained in the open doorway, looking down, and perhaps it was Fawn, for he looked dark and mad. Then an orange flash broke from the doorway, then a second and a third and after that Jerry wasn't counting any more. In fury he threw up his hands, his open mouth still calling, his face still silently imploring. Then he fell, and lay there, till there was once more no sound but the surf flopping on the beach and Drake Ko's hopeless, choking grief against the victorious armadas of the West, which had stolen his brother and left their hard-pressed soldier dead at his feet.

## TWENTY-TWO

# *born again*

In the Circus a mood of wild triumph broke out when the grand news came through from the Cousins. Nelson landed, Nelson bagged! Not a hair of his head injured! For two days there was speculation about medals, knighthoods and promotions. They must do *something* for George, at last, they *must*! Not so, said Connie shrewdly from the touchline. They would never forgive him for raking up Bill Haydon.

The euphoria was followed by certain perplexing rumours. Connie and Doc di Salis, for instance, who were eagerly ensconced in the Maresfield safe house, now dubbed the *Dolphinarium*, waited a full week for their body to arrive and waited in vain. So did the interpreters, transcribers, inquisitors, babysitters and allied trades who made up the rest of the reception and interrogation unit there.

The match was rained off, said the housekeepers. Another date was fixed. Stand by, they said. But quite soon a source at the local estate agent in the neighbouring town of Uckfield revealed that the housekeepers were trying to renege on the lease. Sure enough, after another week the team was stood down 'pending policy decisions'. It was never reassembled.

Next, word filtered out that Enderby and Martello jointly – the combination even then seemed odd – were chairing an Anglo-American processing committee. It would meet alternately in Washington and London and have responsibility for simultaneous distribution of the Dolphin product, code-name CAVIAR, on either side of the Atlantic.

Quite incidentally, it emerged that Nelson was somewhere in the United States, in an armed compound already prepared for him in Philadelphia. The explanation was even slower in coming. It was *felt* – presumably *by* somebody, but feelings are hard to trace among so many corridors – that Nelson would be safer there. Physically safer. Think of the Russians. Think of the Chinese. Also, the housekeepers insisted, the Cousins' processing and evaluation units were more of a scale to handle the unprecedented take which was expected. Also, they said, the Cousins could afford the cost.

*Also* –

'Also gammon and spinach!' Connie stormed, when she heard the news.

She and di Salis waited moodily to be invited to join the Cousins' team. Connie even got herself the injections to be ready, but no call came.

More explanations. The Cousins had a new man at Harvard, the housekeepers said, when Connie sailed in on them in her wheelchair.

'Who?' she demanded in a fury.

A professor somebody, young, a Moscow-gazer. He had made a *life specialty* of the dark side of Moscow Centre, they said, and had recently published a paper for private distribution only, but based on Company archives, in which he had referred to the *mole principle* and even in veiled terms to Karla's private army.

'Of course he did, the maggot!' she blurted at them, through her bitter tears of frustration. 'And he hogged it all from Connie's blasted reports, didn't he? Culpepper, that's his name, and he knows as much about Karla as my left toe!'

The housekeepers were unmoved, however, by thoughts of Connie's toe. It was Culpepper, not Sachs, who had the new committee's vote.

'Wait till George gets back!' Connie warned them in a voice of thunder. The threat left them strangely unaffected.

di Salis fared no better. China-watchers were two a penny in Langley, he was told. A glut on the market, old boy. Sorry, but Enderby's orders, said housekeepers.

*Enderby's?* di Salis echoed.

The committee's, they said vaguely. It was a joint decision.

So di Salis took his cause to Lacon, who liked to think of himself as a poor man's ombudsman in such matters, and Lacon in turn took di Salis to luncheon, at which they split the bill down the middle because Lacon did not hold with civil servants treating one another at the taxpayers' expense.

'How do you all *feel* about Enderby by the by?' he asked, at some point in the meal, interrupting di Salis's plaintive monologue about his familiarity with the Chiu Chow and Hakka dialects. *Feeling* was playing a large part just at the moment. 'Does he go down well over there? I'd have thought you liked his way of seeing things. Isn't he rather sound, wouldn't you say?'

*Sound* in the Whitehall vocabulary in those days meant hawkish.

Rushing back to the Circus, di Salis duly reported this amazing question to Connie Sachs – as Lacon, of course, wished him to – and Connie was thereafter seen little. She spent her time quietly 'packing her trunk' as she called it: that is to say, preparing her Moscow Centre archive for posterity. There was a new young burrower she favoured, a goatish but obliging youth called Doolittle. She made this Doolittle sit at her feet while she gave him of her wisdom.

'The old order's hoofing it,' she warned whoever would listen. 'That twerp Enderby is oiling through the back door. It's a pogrom.'

They treated her at first with much the same derision as Noah had to put up with when he started building his ark. No slouch at tradecraft still, Connie meanwhile secretly took Molly Meakin aside and persuaded her to put in a letter of resignation. 'Tell the housekeepers you're looking for something more fulfilling, dear,' she advised, with much winking and pinching. 'They'll give you a rise at the very least.'

Molly had fears of being taken at her word, but Connie knew the game too well. So she wrote her letter, and was at once ordered to stay behind after hours. Certain changes were in the air, the housekeepers told her in great confidence. There was a move to create a younger and more vigorous service with closer links to Whitehall. Molly solemnly promised to reconsider her decision, and Connie Sachs resumed her packing with fresh determination.

Then where *was* George Smiley all this while? In the Far East? No, in Washington! Nonsense! He was back home and skulking down in the country somewhere – Cornwall was his favourite – taking a well-earned rest and mending his fences with Ann!

Then one of the housekeepers let slip that George might be *suffering from a spot of strain,* and this phrase struck a chill everywhere, for even the dimmest little gnome in Banking Section knew that strain, like old age, was a disease for which there was only one known remedy, and it did not entail recovery.

Guillam came back eventually, but only to sweep Molly off on leave, and he refused to say anything at all. Those who saw him on his swift passage through the fifth floor said he looked shot-about, and obviously in need of a break. Also he seemed to have had an accident to his collar bone: his right shoulder was all strapped up. From housekeepers it became known that he had spent a couple of days in the care of the Circus leech at his private clinic in Manchester Square. But still there was no Smiley, and the housekeepers showed only a steely bonhomie when asked when he would return. The housekeepers in these cases become the Star Chamber, feared but needed. Unobtrusively, Karla's portrait disappeared, the wits ironically said for cleaning.

What was odd, and in a way rather terrible, was that none of them thought to drop in on the little house in Bywater Street and simply ring the door bell. If they had done so, they would have found Smiley there, most likely in his dressing gown, either clearing up plates or preparing food he didn't eat. Sometimes, usually at dusk, he took himself for a solitary walk in the park and peered at people as if he half recognized them, so that they peered in return, and then looked down. Or he would go and sit himself in one of the cheaper cafés in the King's Road, taking a book for company, and sweet tea for refreshment – for he had abandoned his good intentions about sticking to saccharine for his waistline. They would have noticed that he spent a deal of time looking at his hands, and polishing his spectacles on his tie, or re-reading the letter Ann had left for him, which was very long, but only because of repetitions.

Lacon called on him, and so did Enderby, and once Martello came along with them, dressed in his London character again, for everyone agreed, and none with greater sincerity than Smiley, that in the interests of the service the handover should be as smooth and painless as possible. Smiley made certain requests regarding staff, and these were carefully noted by Lacon, who let him understand that toward the Circus – if toward no one else – Treasury was at present in a spending mood. In the secret world at least, sterling was on the up. It was not merely the success of the Dolphin affair which accounted for this change of heart, Lacon said. The American enthusiasm for Enderby's appointment had been overwhelming. It had been *felt* even at the highest diplomatic levels. *Spontaneous applause* was how Lacon described it.

'Saul really knows how to talk to them,' he said.

'Oh, does he? Ah, good. Well, good,' Smiley said, and bucked his head in approval, as the deaf do.

Even when Enderby confided to Smiley that he proposed to appoint Sam Collins as his head of operations, Smiley showed nothing but courtesy toward the suggestion. Sam was a *hustler*, Enderby explained, and *hustlers* were what Langley liked these days. The silk shirt crowd had taken a real nosedive, he said.

'No doubt,' said Smiley.

The two men agreed that Roddy Martindale, though he had bags of entertainment value, was *not* cut out for the game. Old Roddy really was *too* queer, said Enderby, and the Minister was scared stiff of him. Nor did he exactly go down swimmingly with the Americans, even those who happened to be that way themselves. Also, Enderby was a bit chary of taking in any more Etonians. Gave the wrong impression.

A week later, the housekeepers re-opened Sam's old room on the fifth floor and removed the furniture. Collins's ghost laid for good, said certain unwise voices with relish. Then on the Monday an ornate desk arrived, with a red leather top, and several fake hunting prints from the walls of Sam's club, which was in the process of being taken over by one of the larger gambling syndicates, to the satisfaction of all parties.

Little Fawn was not seen again. Not even when several of the more muscular London outstations were revived, including the Brixton scalp-hunters to whom he had formerly belonged, and the Acton lamplighters under Toby Esterhase. But he was not missed either. Like Sam Collins, somehow, he had stalked the story without ever quite belonging to it. But unlike Sam, he stayed in the thickets when it ended, and never reappeared.

To Sam Collins, also, on his first day back in harness, fell the task of breaking the sad news of Jerry's death. He did it in the rumpus room, just a small, unaffected speech, and everyone agreed he did it well. They had not thought he had it in him.

'For fifth floor ears only,' he told them. His audience was appalled, then proud. Connie wept, and tried to claim him as another of Karla's victims, but she was held back in this for want of information about who or what had killed him. It was operational, went the word, and it was noble.

Back in Hong Kong, the Foreign Correspondents' Club showed much initial concern for its missing children Luke and Westerby. Thanks to heavy lobbying by its members, a full-scale confidential enquiry was set up, under the chairmanship of the vigilant Superintendent Rockhurst, to solve the double riddle of their disappearance. The authorities promised full publication of all findings and the United States Consul General offered five thousand dollars of his own money to anyone coming forward with helpful information. As a gesture to local feeling, he included Jerry Westerby's name in the offer. The two became known as The Missing Newsmen, and suggestions of a disgraceful attachment between them were rampant. Luke's bureau matched the five-thousand-dollar figure, and the dwarf, though he was inconsolable, entered a strong bid to have the moneys paid to him. It was he, after all, working on both fronts at once, who had learned from Deathwish that the Cloudview Road apartment, which Luke had last used, had been redecorated from floor to ceiling before the Rocker's sharp-eyed investigators got round to visiting it. Who ordered this? Who paid? Nobody knew. It was the dwarf also, who collected first-hand reports that Jerry had been seen at Kai Tak airport interviewing Japanese package tourists. But the Rocker's committee of enquiry was obliged to reject them. The Japanese concerned were *willing but unreliable witnesses*, they said, when it came to identifying a roundeye who sprang at them after a long journey. As to Luke: well, the way he had been going, they said, he was heading for some kind of breakdown anyway. The knowing spoke of amnesia, brought on by alcohol and fast living. After a while, even the best stories grow cold. Rumours went out that the two men had been seen hunting together during the Hue collapse – or was it Da Nang? – and drinking together in Saigon. Another had them sitting side by side on the waterfront at Manila.

'Holding hands?' the dwarf asked.

'Worse,' was the reply.

The Rocker's name was also in wide circulation, thanks to his success in a recent spectacular narcotics trial mounted with the help of the American Drug Enforcement Administration. Several Chinese and a glamorous English adventuress, a heroin carrier, were featured and though as usual the Mr Big was never brought to justice, it was said the Rocker came within an ace of nailing him. 'Our tough but honest troubleshooter,' wrote the *South China Morning Post* in an editorial praising his astuteness. 'Hong Kong could do with more like him.'

For other distractions, the Club could turn to the dramatic reopening of High Haven, behind a twenty-foot floodlit wire perimeter patrolled by guard dogs. But there were no free lunches any more and the joke soon faded.

As to old Craw, for months he was not seen and not spoken of. Till one night he appeared looking much aged and soberly dressed, and sat in his former corner gazing into space. A few were still left who recognized him. The Canadian cowboy suggested a rubber of Shanghai bowling, but he declined. Then a strange thing happened. An argument broke out concerning a silly point of Club protocol. Nothing serious at all: whether some item of tradition about signing chits was still useful to the Club's running. As trifling as that. But for some reason it made the old fellow absolutely furious. Rising to his feet, he stomped toward the lifts, tears pouring down his face while he hurled one insult after another at them.

'Don't change anything,' he advised them, shaking his stick in fury. 'The old order changeth *not*, let it all run on. You won't stop the wheel, not together, not divided, you snivelling, arselicking novices! You're a bunch of suicidal tits to try!'

Past it, they agreed, as the doors closed on him. Poor fellow. Embarrassing.

Was there really a conspiracy against Smiley, of the scale that Guillam supposed? And if so, how was it affected by Westerby's own maverick intervention? No information is available, and even those who trust each other well are not disposed to discuss the question. Certainly there was a secret understanding between Enderby and Martello that the Cousins should have first bite of Nelson – as well as joint credit for procuring him – against their championship of Enderby for chief. Certainly Lacon and Collins, in their vastly different spheres, were party to it. But at what point they proposed to seize Nelson for themselves and by what means – for instance the more conventional recourse of a concerted *démarche* at ministerial level in London – will probably never be known. But there can be no doubt, as it turned out, that Westerby was a blessing in disguise. He gave them the excuse they were looking for.

And did Smiley *know* of the conspiracy, deep down? Was he aware of it, and did he secretly even welcome the solution? Peter Guillam, who has since had three good years in exile in Brixton to consider his opinion, insists that the answer to both questions is a firm *yes*. There is a letter George wrote to Ann Smiley – he says – in the heat of the crisis, presumably in one of the long waiting periods in the isolation ward. Guillam leans heavily on it for his theory. Ann showed it to him when he called on her in Wiltshire in the hope of bringing about a reconciliation, and though the mission failed, she produced it from her handbag in the course of their talk. Guillam memorized a part, he claims, and wrote it down as soon as he got back to the car. Certainly the style flies a lot higher than anything Guillam would aspire to for himself.

> *I honestly do wonder, without wishing to be morbid, how I reached this present pass. So far as I can ever remember of my youth, I chose the secret road because it seemed to lead straightest and furthest toward my country's goal. The enemy in those days was someone we could point at and read about in the papers. Today, all I know is that I have learned to interpret the whole of life in terms of conspiracy. That is the sword I have lived by, and as I look round me now I see it is the sword I shall die by as well. These people terrify me but I am one of them. If they stab me in the back, then at least that is the judgment of my peers.*

As Guillam points out, the letter was essentially from Smiley's blue period.

These days, he says, the old boy is much more himself. Occasionally he and Ann have lunches, and Guillam personally is convinced that they will simply get together one day and that will be that. But George never mentions Westerby. And nor does Guillam, for George's sake.

# SMILEY'S PEOPLE

# ONE

Two seemingly unconnected events heralded the summons of Mr. George Smiley from his dubious retirement. The first had for its background Paris, and for a season the boiling month of August, when Parisians by tradition abandon their city to the scalding sunshine and the bus-loads of packaged tourists.

On one of these August days – the fourth, and at twelve o'clock exactly, for a church clock was chiming and a factory bell had just preceded it – in a *quartier* once celebrated for its large population of the poorer Russian émigrés, a stocky woman of about fifty, carrying a shopping bag, emerged from the darkness of an old warehouse and set off, full of her usual energy and purpose, along the pavement to the bus-stop. The street was grey and narrow, and shuttered, with a couple of small *hôtels de passe* and a lot of cats. It was a place, for some reason, of peculiar quiet. The warehouse, since it handled perishable goods, had remained open during the holidays. The heat, fouled by exhaust fumes and unwashed by the slightest breeze, rose at her like the heat from a lift-shaft, but her Slavic features registered no complaint. She was neither dressed nor built for exertion on a hot day, being in stature very short indeed, and fat, so that she had to roll a little in order to get along. Her black dress, of ecclesiastical severity, possessed neither a waist nor any other relief except for a dash of white lace at the neck and a large metal cross, well fingered but of no intrinsic value, at the bosom. Her cracked shoes, which in walking tended outwards at the points, set a stern tattoo rattling between the shuttered houses. Her shabby bag, full since early morning, gave her a slight starboard list and told clearly that she was used to burdens. There was also fun in her, however. Her grey hair was gathered in a bun behind her, but there remained one sprightly forelock that flopped over her brow to the rhythm of her waddle. A hardy humour lit her brown eyes. Her mouth, set above a fighter's chin, seemed ready, given half a reason, to smile at any time.

Reaching her usual bus-stop, she put down her shopping bag and with her right hand massaged her rump just where it met the spine, a gesture she made often these days though it gave her little relief. The high stool in the warehouse where she worked every morning as a checker possessed no back, and increasingly she was resenting the deficiency. 'Devil', she muttered to the offending part. Having rubbed it, she began plying her black elbows behind her like an old town raven preparing to fly. 'Devil', she repeated. Then, suddenly aware of being watched, she wheeled round and peered upward at the heavily built man towering behind her.

He was the only other person waiting, and indeed, at that moment, the only other person in the street. She had never spoken to him, yet his face was already familiar to her: so big, so uncertain, so sweaty. She had seen it yesterday, she had seen it the day before, and for all she knew, the day before that as well – my Lord, she was not a walking diary! For the last three or four days, this weak, itchy giant, waiting for a bus or hovering on the pavement outside the warehouse, had become a figure of the street for her; and what was more, a figure of a recognisable type, though she had yet to put her finger on which. She thought he looked *traqué* – hunted – as so many Parisians did these days. She saw so much fear in their faces; in the way they walked yet dared not greet each other. Perhaps it was the same everywhere, she wouldn't know. Also, more than once, she had felt *his* interest in *her*. She had wondered whether he was a policeman. She had even considered asking him, for she had this urban cockiness. His lugubrious build suggested the police, so did the sweaty suit and the needless raincoat that hung like a bit of old uniform from his forearm. If she was right, and he *was* police, then, high time too, the idiots were finally doing something about the spate of pilfering that had made a bear-garden of her stock-checking for months.

By now the stranger had been staring down at her for some time, however. And he was staring at her still.

'I have the misfortune to suffer in my back, monsieur,' she confided to him finally, in her slow and classically enunciated French. 'It is not a large back but the pain is disproportionate. You are a doctor, perhaps? An osteopath?'

Then she wondered, looking up at him, whether he was ill, and her joke out of place. An oily gloss glistened on his jaw and neck, and there was an unseeing self-obsession about his pallid eyes. He seemed to see beyond her to some private trouble of his own. She was going to ask him this – You are perhaps in love, monsieur? Your wife is deceiving you? – and she was actually considering steering him into a café for a glass of water or a *tisane* when he abruptly swung away from her and looked behind him, then over her head up the street the other way. And it occurred to her that he really was afraid, not just *traqué* but frightened stiff; so perhaps he was not a policeman at all, but a thief, though the difference, she knew well, was often slight.

'Your name is Maria Andreyevna Ostrakova?' he asked her abruptly, as if the question scared him.

He was speaking French but she knew that it was not his mother tongue any more than it was her own, and his correct pronunciation of her name, complete with Patronymic, already alerted her to his origin. She recognised the slur at once and the shapes of the tongue that made it, and she identified too late, and with a considerable inward start, the type she had not been able to put her finger on.

'If it is, who on earth are *you?*' she asked him in reply, sticking out her jaw and scowling.

He had drawn a pace closer. The difference in their heights was immediately absurd. So was the degree to which the man's features betrayed his unpleasing character. From her low position Ostrakova could read his weakness as clearly as his fear. His damp chin had set in a grimace, his mouth had twisted to make him look strong, but she knew he was only banishing an incurable cowardice. He is like a man steeling himself for a heroic act, she thought. Or a criminal one. He is a man cut off from all spontaneous acts, she thought.

'You were born in Leningrad on May 8, 1927?' the stranger asked.

Probably she said yes. Afterwards she was not sure. She saw his scared gaze lift and stare at the approaching bus. She saw an indecision near to panic seize him, and it occurred to her – which in the long run was an act of near clairvoyance – that he proposed to push her under it. He didn't, but he did put his next question in Russian – and in the brutal accents of Moscow officialdom.

'In 1956, were you granted permission to leave the Soviet Union for the purpose of nursing your sick husband, the traitor Ostrakov? Also for certain other purposes?'

'Ostrakov was not a traitor,' she replied, cutting him off. 'He was a patriot.' And by instinct she took up her shopping bag and clutched the handle very tight.

The stranger spoke straight over this contradiction, and very loudly, in order to defeat the clatter of the bus: 'Ostrakova, I bring you greetings from your daughter Alexandra in Moscow, also from certain official quarters! I wish to speak to you concerning her! Do not board this car!'

The bus had pulled up. The conductor knew her and was holding his hand out for her bag. Lowering his voice, the stranger added one more terrible statement: 'Alexandra has serious problems which require the assistance of a mother.'

The conductor was calling to her to get a move on. He spoke with pretended roughness, which was the way they joked. 'Come on, mother! It's too hot for love! Pass us your bag and let's go!' cried the conductor.

Inside the bus there was laughter; then someone shouted an insult – old woman, keeps the world waiting! She felt the stranger's hand scrabbling inexpertly at her arm, like a clumsy suitor groping for the buttons. She pulled herself free. She tried to tell the conductor something but she couldn't; she opened her mouth but she had forgotten how to speak. The best she could manage was to shake her head. The conductor yelled at her again, then waved his hands and shrugged. The insults multiplied – old woman, drunk as a whore at midday! Remaining where she was, Ostrakova watched the bus out of sight, waiting for her vision to clear and her heart to stop its crazy cavorting. Now it is I who need a glass of water, she thought. From the strong I can protect myself. God preserve me from the weak.

She followed him to the café, limping heavily. In a forced-labour camp, exactly twenty-five years before, she had broken her leg in three places in a coal slip. On this August 4th – the date had not escaped her – under the extreme duress of the stranger's message to her, the old sensation of being crippled came back to her.

The café was the last in the street, if not in all Paris, to lack both a juke-box and neon lighting – and to remain open in August – though there were bagatelle tables that bumped and flashed from dawn till night. For the rest, there was the usual mid-morning hubbub, of grand politics, and horses, and whatever else Parisians talked; there was the usual trio of prostitutes murmuring among themselves, and a sullen young waiter in a soiled shirt who led them to a table in a corner that was reserved with a grimy Campari sign. A moment of ludicrous banality followed. The stranger ordered two coffees, but the waiter protested that at midday one does not reserve the best table in the house merely in order to drink coffee; the *patron* had to pay the rent, monsieur! Since the stranger did not follow this flow of patois, Ostrakova had to translate it for him. The stranger blushed and ordered two ham omelettes with *frites*, and two Alsatian beers, all without consulting Ostrakova. Then he took himself to the men's room to repair his courage – confident, presumably, she would not run way – and when he returned his face was dry and his ginger hair combed, but the stink of him, now they were indoors, reminded Ostrakova of Moscow subways, and Moscow trams, and Moscow interrogation rooms. More eloquently than anything he could ever have said to her, that short walk back from the men's room to their table had convinced her of what she already feared. He was one of them. The suppressed swagger, the deliberate brutalization of the features, the ponderous style in which he now squared his forearms on the table and with feigned reluctance helped himself to a piece of bread from the basket as if he were dipping a pen in ink – they revived her worst memories of living as a disgraced woman under the weight of Moscow's malevolent bureaucracy.

'So,' he said, and started eating the bread at the same time. He selected a crusty end. With hands like that he could have crushed it in a second, but instead he chose to prise ladylike flakes from it with his fat finger-ends, as if that were the official way of eating. While he nibbled, his eyebrows went up and he looked sorry for himself, me a stranger in this foreign land. 'Do they know here that you have lived an immoral life in Russia?' he asked finally. 'Maybe in a town full of whores they don't care.'

Her answer lay ready on the tip of her tongue: *My life in Russia was not immoral. It was your system which was immoral.*

But she did not say it, she kept rigidly silent. Ostrakova had already sworn to herself that she would restrain both her quick temper and her quick tongue, and she now physically enjoined herself to this vow by grabbing a piece of skin on the soft inside of her wrist and pinching it through her sleeve with a fierce, sustained pressure under the table, exactly as she had done a hundred times before, in the old days, when such questionings were part of her daily life – When did you last hear from your husband, Ostrakov, the traitor? Name all persons with whom you have associated in the last three months! With bitter experience she had learned the other lessons of interrogation too. A part of her was rehearsing them at this minute, and though they belonged, in terms of history, to a full generation earlier, they appeared to her now as bright as yesterday and as vital: never to match rudeness with rudeness, never to be provoked, never to score, never to be witty or superior or intellectual, never to be deflected by fury, or despair, or the surge of sudden hope that an occasional question might arouse. To match dullness with dullness and routine with routine. And only deep, deep down to preserve the two secrets that made all these humiliations bearable: her hatred of them; and her hope that one day, after endless drips of water on the stone, she would wear them down, and by a reluctant miracle of their own elephantine processes, obtain from them the freedom they were denying her.

He had produced a notebook. In Moscow it would have been her file but here in a Paris café it was a sleek black leatherbound notebook, something that in Moscow even an official would count himself lucky to possess.

File or notebook, the preamble was the same: 'You were born Maria Andreyevna Rogova in Leningrad on May 8, 1927,' he repeated. 'On September 1, 1948, aged twenty-one, you married the traitor Ostrakov Igor, a captain of infantry in the Red Army, born of an Estonian mother. In 1950, the said Ostrakov, being at the time stationed in East Berlin, traitorously defected to Fascist Germany through the assistance of reactionary Estonian émigrés, leaving you in Moscow. He took up residence, and later French citizenship, in Paris, where he continued his contact with anti-Soviet elements. At the time of his defection you had no children by this man. Also you were not pregnant. Correct?'

'Correct,' she said.

In Moscow it would have been 'Correct, Comrade Captain,' or 'Correct, Comrade Inspector,' but in this clamorous French café such formality was out of place. The fold of skin on her wrist had gone numb. Releasing it, she allowed the blood to return, then took hold of another.

'As an accomplice to Ostrakov's defection you were sentenced to five years' detention in a labour camp, but were released under an amnesty following the death of Stalin in March, 1953. Correct?'

'Correct.'

'On your return to Moscow, despite the improbability that your request would be granted, you applied for a foreign travel passport to join your husband in France. Correct?'

'He had cancer,' she said. 'If I had not applied, I would have been failing in my duty as his wife.'

The waiter brought the plates of omelette and *frites* and the two Alsatian beers, and Ostrakova asked him to bring a *thé citron*: she was thirsty, but did not care for beer. Addressing the boy, she tried vainly to make a bridge to him, with smiles and with her eyes. But his stoniness repulsed her; she realised she was the only woman in the place apart from the three prostitutes. Holding his notebook to one side like a hymnal, the stranger helped himself to a forkful, then another, while Ostrakova tightened her grasp on her wrist, and Alexandra's name pulsed in her mind like an unstaunched wound, and she contemplated a thousand different *serious problems* that required *the assistance of a mother*.

The stranger continued his crude history of her while he ate. Did he eat for pleasure or did he eat in order not to be conspicuous again? She decided he was a compulsive eater.

'Meanwhile,' he announced, eating.

'Meanwhile,' she whispered involuntarily.

'Meanwhile, despite your pretended concern for your husband, the traitor Ostrakov,' he continued through his mouthful, 'you nevertheless formed an adulterous relationship with the so-called music student Glikman Joseph, a Jew with four convictions for anti-social behaviour whom you had met during your detention. You cohabited with this Jew in his apartment. Correct or false?'

'I was lonely.'

'In consequence of this union with Glikman you bore a daughter, Alexandra, at The Lying-in Hospital of the October Revolution in Moscow. The certificate of parentage was signed by Glikman Joseph and Ostrakova Maria. The girl was registered in the name of the Jew Glikman. Correct or false?'

'Correct.'

'Meanwhile, you persisted in your application for a foreign travel passport. Why?'

'I told you. My husband was ill. It was my duty to persist.'

He ate again, so grossly that she had a sight of his many bad teeth. 'In January, 1956, as an act of clemency you were granted a passport on condition the child Alexandra was left behind in Moscow. You exceeded the permitted time limit and remained in France, abandoning your child. Correct or false?'

The doors to the street were glass, the walls too. A big lorry parked outside them and the café darkened. The young waiter slammed down her tea without looking at her.

'Correct,' she said again, and managed this time to look at her interrogator, knowing what would follow, forcing herself to show him that on this score at least she had no doubts, and no regrets. 'Correct,' she repeated defiantly.

'As a condition of your application being favourably considered by the authorities, you signed an undertaking to the organs of State Security to perform certain tasks for them during your residence in Paris. One, to persuade your husband, the traitor Ostrakov, to return to the Soviet Union –'

'To *attempt* to persuade him,' she said with a faint smile. 'He was not amenable to this suggestion.'

'Two, you undertook also to provide information concerning the activities and personalities of revanchist anti-Soviet émigré groups. You submitted two reports of no value and afterwards nothing. Why?'

'My husband despised such groups and had given up his contact with them.'

'You could have participated in the groups without him. You signed the document and neglected its undertaking. Yes or no?'

'Yes.'

'For this you abandon your child in Russia? To a Jew? In order to give your attention to an enemy of the people, a traitor of the State? For this you neglect your duty? Outstay the permitted period, remain in France?'

'My husband was dying. He needed me.'

'And the child Alexandra? She did not need you? A dying husband is more important than a living child? A traitor? A conspirator against the people?'

Releasing her wrist, Ostrakova deliberately took hold of her tea and watched the glass rise to her face, the lemon floating on the surface. Beyond it, she saw a grimy mosaic floor and beyond the floor, the loved, ferocious and kindly face of Glikman pressing down on her, exhorting her to sign, to go, to swear to anything they asked. The freedom of one is more than the slavery of three, he had whispered; a child of such parents as ourselves cannot prosper in Russia whether you stay or go; leave and we shall do our best to follow; sign anything, leave, and live for all of us; if you love me, go . . .

'They were the hard days, still,' she said to the stranger finally, almost in a tone of reminiscence. 'You are too young. They were the hard days, even after Stalin's death: still hard.'

'Does the criminal Glikman continue to write to you?' the stranger asked in a superior, knowing way.

'He never wrote,' she lied. 'How could he write, a dissident, living under restriction? The decision to stay in France was mine alone.'

Paint yourself black, she thought; do everything possible to spare those within their power.

'I have heard nothing from Glikman since I came to France more than twenty years ago,' she added, gathering courage. 'Indirectly, I learned that he was angered by my anti-Soviet behaviour. He did not wish to know me any more. Inwardly he was already wishing to reform by the time I left him.'

'He did not write concerning your common child?'

'He did not write, he did not send messages. I told you this already.'

'Where's your daughter now?'

'I don't know.'

'You have received communications from her?'

'Of course not. I heard only that she had entered a State orphanage and acquired another name. I assume she does not know I exist.'

The stranger ate again with one hand, while the other held the notebook. He filled his mouth, munched a little, then swilled his food down with the beer. But the superior smile remained.

'And now it is the criminal Glikman who is dead,' the stranger announced, revealing his little secret. He continued eating.

Suddenly, Ostrakova wished the twenty years were two hundred. She wished that Glikman's face had never, after all, looked down on her, that she had never loved him, never cared for him, never cooked for him, or got drunk with him day after day in his one-roomed exile where they lived on the charity of their friends, deprived of the right to work, to do anything but make music and love, get drunk, walk in the woods, and be cut dead by their neighbours.

'Next time I go to prison or you do, they will take her anyway. Alexandra is forfeit in any case,' Glikman had said. 'But you can save yourself.'

'I will decide when I am there,' she had replied.

'Decide now.'

'When I am there.'

The stranger pushed aside his empty plate and once more took the sleek French notebook in both hands. He turned a page, as if approaching a new chapter.

'Concerning now your criminal daughter Alexandra,' he announced, through his food.

'*Criminal?*' she whispered.

To her astonishment the stranger was reciting a fresh catalogue of crimes. As he did so, Ostrakova lost her final hold upon the present. Her eyes were on the mosaic floor and she noticed the husks of langoustine and crumbs of bread. But her mind was in the Moscow law court again, where her own trial was being repeated. If not hers, then Glikman's – yet not Glikman's either. Then whose? She remembered trials which the two of them had attended as unwelcome spectators. Trials of friends, if only friends by accident: such as people who had questioned the absolute right of the authorities; or had worshipped some unacceptable god; or had painted criminally abstract pictures; or had published politically endangering love-poems. The chattering customers in the café became the jeering claque of the State police; the slamming of the bagatelle tables, the crash of iron doors. On this date, for escaping from the State orphanage on something street, so many months' corrective detention. On that date, for insulting organs of State Security, so many more months, extended for bad behaviour, followed by so many years' internal exile. Ostrakova felt her stomach turn and thought she might be sick. She put her hands to her glass of tea and saw the red pinch marks on her wrist. The stranger continued his recitation and she heard her daughter awarded another two years for refusing to accept employment at the something factory, God help her, and why shouldn't she? Where had she learnt it? Ostrakova asked herself, incredulous. What had Glikman taught the child, in the short time before they took her away from him, that had stamped her in his mould and defeated all the system's efforts? Fear, exultation, amazement jangled in Ostrakova's mind, till something that the stranger was saying to her blocked them out.

'I did not hear,' she whispered after an age. 'I am a little distressed. Kindly repeat what you just said.'

He said it again and she looked up and stared at him, trying to think of all the tricks she had been warned against, but they were too many and she was no longer clever. She no longer had Glikman's cleverness – if she had ever had it – about reading their lies and playing their games ahead of them. She knew only that to save herself and be reunited with her beloved Ostrakov, she had committed a great sin, the greatest a mother can commit. The stranger had begun threatening her, but for once the threat seemed meaningless. In the event of her non-collaboration – he was saying – a copy of her signed undertaking to the Soviet authorities would find its way to the French police. Copies of her useless two reports (done, as he well knew, solely in order to keep the brigands quiet) would be circulated among the surviving Paris émigrés – though, God knows, there were few enough of *them* about these days! Yet why should she have to submit to *pressure* in order to accept a gift of such immeasurable value – when, by some inexplicable act of clemency, this man, this system, was holding out to her the chance to redeem herself, and her child? She knew that her nightly and daily prayers for forgiveness had been answered, the thousands of candles, the thousands of tears. She made him say it a third time. She made him pull his notebook away from his gingery face, and she saw that his weak mouth had lifted into a half smile and that, idiotically, she seemed to require her absolution, even while he repeated his insane, God-given question.

'Assuming it has been decided to rid the Soviet Union of this disruptive and unsocial element, how would you like your daughter Alexandra to follow your footsteps here to France?'

For weeks after that encounter, and through all the hushed activities which accompanied it – furtive visits to the Soviet Embassy, form-filling, signed affidavits – *certificats d'hébergement* – the laborious trail through successive French ministries – Ostrakova followed her own actions as if they were someone else's. She prayed often, but even with her prayers she adopted a conspiratorial attitude, dividing them among several Russian Orthodox churches so that in none would she be observed suffering an undue assault of piety. Some of the churches were no more than little private houses scattered round the 15th and 16th districts, with distinctive twice-struck crosses in plywood, and old, rain-sodden Russian notices on the doors, requesting cheap accommodation and offering instruction in the piano. She went to the Church of the Russian Abroad, and the Church of the Apparition of the Holy Virgin, and the Church of Saint Seraphin of Sarov. She went everywhere. She rang the bells till someone came, a verger or a frail-faced woman in black; she gave them money, and they let her crouch in the damp cold before candle-lit icons, and breathe the thick incense till it made her half drunk. She made promises to the Almighty, she thanked Him, she asked Him for advice, she practically asked Him what *He* would have done if the stranger had approached Him in similar circumstances, she reminded Him that anyway she was under pressure, and they would destroy her if she did not obey. Yet at the same time, her indomitable common sense asserted itself and she asked herself over and again *why* she of all people, wife of the traitor Ostrakov, lover of the dissident Glikman, mother – so she was given to believe – of a turbulent and anti-social daughter, should be singled out for such untypical indulgence?

In the Soviet Embassy, when she made her first formal application, she was treated with a regard she would never have dreamed possible, which was suited neither to a defector and renegade spy nor to the mother of an untamable hell-raiser. She was not ordered brusquely to a waiting-room, but escorted to an interviewing-room, where a young and personable official showed her a positively Western courtesy, even helping her, where her pen or courage faltered, to a proper formulation of her case.

And she told nobody, not even her nearest – though her nearest was not very near. The gingery man's warning rang in her ears day and night: any indiscretion and your daughter will not be released.

And who was there, after all, apart from God, to turn to? To her half-sister Valentina who lived in Lyons and was married to a car salesman? The very thought that Ostrakova had been consorting with a secret official from Moscow would send her rushing to her smelling salts. In a *café*, Maria? In *broad daylight*, Maria? Yes, Valentina, and what he said is true. I had a bastard daughter by a Jew.

It was the nothingness that scared her most. The weeks passed; at the Embassy they told her that her application was receiving 'favoured attention'; the French authorities had assured her that Alexandra would quickly qualify for French citizenship; the gingery stranger had persuaded her to backdate Alexandra's birth so that she could be represented as an Ostrakova, not a Glikman; he said the French authorities would find this more acceptable; and it seemed that they had done so, even though she had never so much as mentioned the child's existence at her naturalisation interviews. Now, suddenly, there were no more forms to fill in, no more hurdles to be cleared, and Ostrakova waited without knowing what she was waiting for. For the gingery stranger to reappear? He no longer existed. One ham omelette and *frites*, some Alsatian beer, two pieces of crusty bread had satisfied all his needs, apparently. What he was in relation to the Embassy she could not imagine: he had told her to present herself there, and that they would be expecting her; he was right. But when she referred to 'your gentleman,' even 'your blond, large gentleman who first approached me,' she met with smiling incomprehension.

Thus gradually whatever she was waiting for ceased to exist. First it was ahead of her, then it was behind her, and she had had no knowledge of its passing, no moment of fulfilment. Had Alexandra already arrived in France? Obtained her papers, moved on or gone to ground? Ostrakova began to think she might have done. Abandoned to a new and inconsolable sense of disappointment, she peered at the faces of young girls in the street, wondering what Alexandra looked like. Returning home, her eyes would fall automatically to the doormat in the hope of seeing a handwritten note or a *pneumatique*: 'Mama, it is I. I am staying at the so-and-so hotel . . .' A cable giving a flight number, arriving Orly tomorrow, tonight; or was it not Orly airport but Charles de Gaulle? She had no familiarity with airlines, so she visited a travel agent, just to ask. It was both. She considered going to the expense of having a telephone installed so that Alexandra could ring her up. Yet what on earth was she expecting, after all these years? Tearful reunions with a grown child to whom she had never been united? The wishful remaking, more than twenty years too late, of a relationship she had deliberately turned her back on? I have no right to her, Ostrakova told herself severely; I have only my debts and my obligations. She asked at the Embassy but they knew nothing more. The formalities were complete, they said. That was all they knew. And if Ostrakova wished to send her daughter money? she asked cunningly – for her fares, for instance, for her visa? – could they give her an address perhaps, an office that would find her?

We are not a postal service, they told her. Their new chilliness scared her. She did not go any more.

After that, she fell once more to worrying about the several muddy photographs, each the same, which they had given to her to pin to her application forms. The photographs were all she had ever seen. She wished now that she had made copies, but she had never thought of it; stupidly, she had assumed she would soon be meeting the original. She had not had them in her hand above an hour! She had hurried straight from the Embassy to the Ministry with them, and by the time she left the Ministry the photographs were already working their way through another bureaucracy. But she had studied them! My Lord, how she had studied those photographs, whether they were each the same or not! On the Métro, in the Ministry waiting-room, even on the pavement before she went in, she had stared at the lifeless depiction of her child, trying with all her might to see in the expressionless grey shadows some hint of the man she had adored. And failing. Always, till then, whenever she had dared to wonder, she had imagined Glikman's features as clearly written on the growing child as they had been on the new-born baby. It had seemed impossible that a man so vigorous would not plant his imprint deeply and for good. Yet Ostrakova saw nothing of Glikman in that photograph. He had worn his Jewishness like a flag. It was part of his solitary revolution. He was not orthodox, he was not even religious, he disliked Ostrakova's secret piety nearly as much as he disliked the Soviet bureaucracy – yet he had borrowed her tongs to curl his sideburns like the Hasidim, just to give focus, as he put it, to the anti-Semitism of the authorities. But in the face in the photograph she recognised not a drop of his blood, not the least spark of his fire – though his fire, according to the stranger, burned in her amazingly.

'If they had photographed a corpse to get the picture,' thought Ostrakova aloud in her apartment, 'I would not be surprised.' And with this downright observation, she gave her first outward expression of the growing doubt inside her.

Toiling in her warehouse, sitting alone in her tiny apartment in the long evenings, Ostrakova racked her brains for someone she could trust; who would not condone and not condemn; who would see round the corners of the route she had embarked on; above all, who would not talk and thus wreck – she had been assured of it – wreck her chances of being reunited with Alexandra. Then one night, either God or her own striving memory supplied her with an answer: The General! she thought, sitting up in bed and putting on the light. Ostrakov himself had told her of him! Those émigré groups are a catastrophe, he used to say, and you must avoid them like the pest. The only one you can trust is Vladimir the General; he is an old devil, and a womaniser, but he is a man, he has connections and knows how to keep his mouth shut.

But Ostrakov had said this some twenty years ago, and not even old generals are immortal. And besides – Vladimir who? She did not even know his other name. Even the name Vladimir – Ostrakov had told her – was something he had put on for the military service; since his real name was Estonian, and not suitable for Red Army usage. Nevertheless, next day, she went down to the bookshop beside the Cathedral of St. Alexander Nevsky, where information about the dwindling Russian population was often to be had, and made her first enquiries. She got a name and even a phone number, but no address. The phone was disconnected. She went to the Post Office, cajoled the assistants, and finally came up with a 1956 telephone directory listing the Movement for Baltic Freedom, followed by an address in Montparnasse. She was not stupid. She looked up the address and found no less than four other organisations listed there also; the Riga Group, the Association of Victims of Soviet Imperialism, the Forty-Eight Committee for a Free Latvia, the Tallinn Committee of Freedom. She remembered vividly Ostrakov's scathing opinions of such bodies, even though he had paid his dues to them. All the same, she went to the address and rang the bell, and the house was like one of her little churches: quaint, and very nearly closed for ever. Eventually an old White Russian opened the door wearing a cardigan crookedly buttoned, and leaning on a walking stick, and looking superior.

They've gone, he said, pointing his stick down the cobbled road. Moved out. Finished. Bigger outfits put them out of business, he added with a laugh. Too few of them, too many groups, and they squabbled like children. No wonder the Tsar was defeated! The old White Russian had false teeth that didn't fit, and thin hair plastered all over his scalp to hide his baldness.

But the General? she asked. Where was the General? Was he still alive, or had he –'

The old Russian smirked and asked whether it was business.

It was not, said Ostrakova craftily, remembering the General's reputation for philandering, and contrived a shy woman's smile. The old Russian laughed, and his teeth rattled. He laughed again and said, 'Oh, the General!' Then he came back with an address in London, stamped in mauve on a bit of card, and gave it to her. The General would never change, he said; when he got to Heaven, he'd be chasing after the angels and trying to up-end them, no question. And that night while the whole neighbourhood slept, Ostrakova sat at her dead husband's desk and wrote to the General with a frankness which lonely people reserve for strangers, using French rather than Russian as an aid to greater detachment. She told him about her love for Glikman and took comfort from the knowledge that the General himself loved women just as Glikman had. She admitted immediately that she had come to France as a spy, and she explained how she had assembled the two trivial reports that were the squalid price of her freedom. It was *à contre-cœur*, she said; invention and evasion, she said; a nothing. But the reports existed, so did her signed undertaking, and they placed grave limits on her freedom. Then she told him of her soul, and of her prayers to God all round the Russian churches. Since the gingery stranger's approach to her, she said, her days had become unreal; she had a feeling of being denied a natural explanation of her life, even if it had to be a painful one. She kept nothing back from him, for whatever guilty feelings she had, they did not relate to her efforts to bring Alexandra to the West, but rather to her decision to stay in Paris and take care of Ostrakov until he died – after which event, she said, the Soviets would not let her come back anyway; she had become a defector herself.

'But, General,' she wrote, 'if tonight I had to face my Maker in person, and tell Him what is deepest in my heart, I would tell Him what I now tell you. My child Alexandra was born in pain. Days and nights she fought me and I fought her back. Even in the womb she was her father's child. I had no time to love her; I only ever knew her as the little Jewish warrior her father made. But, General, this I do know: the child in the photograph is neither Glikman's, nor is she mine. They are putting the wrong egg into the nest, and though there is a part of this old woman that would like to be deluded, there is a stronger part that hates them for their tricks.'

When she had finished the letter, she sealed it immediately in its envelope so that she would not read it and change her mind. Then she stuck too many stamps on it deliberately, much as she might have lit a candle to a lover.

For the next two weeks, exactly, following the posting of this document, nothing happened, and in the strange ways of women the silence was a relief to her. After the storm had come the calm, she had done the little she could do – she had confessed her weaknesses and her betrayals and her one great sin – the rest was in the hands of God, and of the General. A disruption of the French postal services did not dismay her. She saw it rather as another obstacle which those who were shaping her destiny would have to overcome if their will was strong enough. She went to work contentedly and her back ceased to trouble her, which she took as an omen. She even managed to become philosophical again. It is this way or that way, she told herself: either Alexandra was in the West and better off – if indeed it *was* Alexandra – or Alexandra was where she had been before, and no worse off. But gradually, with another part of her, she saw through this false optimism. There was a third possibility, and that was the worst and by degrees the one she considered most likely: namely, that Alexandra was being used for a sinister and perhaps wicked purpose; that they were forcing her somehow, exactly as they had forced Ostrakova, misusing the humanity and courage that her father, Glikman, had given her. So that on the fourteenth night, Ostrakova broke into a profound fit of weeping, and with the tears streaming down her face walked half-way across Paris looking for a church, any church that was open, until she came to the Cathedral of Alexander Nevsky itself. It was open. Kneeling, she prayed for long hours to St Joseph, who was after all a father and protector, and the giver of Glikman's first name, even if Glikman would have scoffed at the association. And on the day following these spiritual exertions, her prayer was answered. A letter came. It had no stamp or postmark. She had added her address at work as a precaution, and the letter was there waiting for her when she arrived, delivered by hand, presumably, some time in the night. It was a very short letter and carried neither the name of the sender nor his address. It was unsigned. Like her own, it was in a stilted French and handwritten, in the sprawl of an old and dictatorial hand, which she knew at once was the General's.

*Madame!* – it began, like a command – *Your letter has reached the writer safely. A friend of our cause will call upon you very soon. He is a man of honour and he will identify himself by handing to you the other half of the enclosed postcard. I urge you to speak to nobody concerning this matter until he arrives. He will come to your apartment between eight and ten o'clock in the evening. He will ring your doorbell three times. He has my absolute confidence. Trust him entirely, Madame, and we shall do everything to assist you.*

Even in her relief, she was secretly entertained by the writer's melodramatic tone. Why not deliver the letter directly to her flat? she wondered; and why should I feel safer because he gives me half an English picture? For the piece of postcard showed a part of Piccadilly Circus and was torn, not cut, with a deliberate roughness, diagonally. The side to be written on was blank.

To her astonishment the General's envoy came that night.

He rang the bell three times, as the letter promised, but he must have known she was in her apartment – must have watched her enter, and the lights go on – for all she heard was a snap of the letter-box, a snap much louder than it normally made, and when she went to the door she saw the piece of torn postcard lying on the mat, the same mat she had looked at so often when she was longing for word of her daughter Alexandra. Picking it up, she ran to the bedroom for her Bible, where her own half already lay, and yes, the pieces matched, God was on her side, St. Joseph had interceded for her. (But what a needless piece of nonsense, all the same!) And when she opened the door to him, he slipped past her like a shadow: a little hobgoblin of a fellow, in a black overcoat with velvet tabs on the collar, giving him an air of operatic conspiracy. They have sent me a midget to catch a giant, was her first thought. He had arched eyebrows and a grooved face and flicked-up horns of black hair above his pointed ears, which he prinked with his little palms before the hall mirror as he took off his hat – so bright and comic that on a different occasion Ostrakova would have laughed out loud at all the life and humour and irreverence in him.

But not tonight.

Tonight he had a gravity that she sensed immediately was not his normal way. Tonight, like a busy salesman who had just stepped off an aeroplane – she had the feeling also about him that he was brand new in town: his cleanliness, his air of travelling light – tonight he wished only to do business.

'You received my letter safely, madame?' He spoke Russian swiftly, with an Estonian accent.

'I had thought it was the General's letter,' she replied, affecting – she could not save herself – a certain sternness with him.

'It is I who brought it for him,' he said gravely. He was delving in an inside pocket and she had a dreadful feeling that, like the big Russian, he was going to produce a sleek black notebook. But he drew out instead a photograph, and one look was quite enough: the pallid, glossy features, the expression that despised all womanhood, not just her own; the suggestion of longing, but not daring to take.

'Yes,' she said. 'This is the stranger.'

Seeing his happiness increase, she knew immediately that he was what Glikman and his friends called 'one of us' – not a Jew necessarily, but a man with heart and meat to him. From that moment on she called him in her mind 'the magician.' She thought of his pockets as being full of clever tricks, and of his merry eyes as containing a dash of magic.

For half the night, with an intensity she hadn't experienced since Glikman, she and the magician talked. First, she told it all again, reliving it exactly, secretly surprised to discover how much she had left out of her letter, which the magician seemed to know by heart. She explained her feelings to him, and her tears, her terrible inner turmoil; she described the crudeness of her perspiring tormentor. He was so *inept* – she kept repeating, in wonder – as if it were the first time, she said – he had no finesse, no assurance. So odd to think of the Devil as a fumbler! She told about the ham omelette and the *frites* and the Alsatian beer and he laughed; about her feeling that he was a man of dangerous timidity and inhibition – not a woman's man at all – to most of which the little magician agreed with her cordially, as if he and the gingery man were already well acquainted. She trusted the magician entirely, as the General had told her to; she was sick and tired of suspicion. She talked, she thought afterwards, as frankly as she once had talked to Ostrakov when they were young lovers in her own home town, on the nights they thought they might never meet again, clutching each other under siege, whispering to the sound of approaching guns; or to Glikman, while they waited for the hammering on the door that would take him back to prison yet again. She talked to his alert and understanding gaze, to the laughter in him, to the suffering which she sensed immediately was the better side of his unorthodox and perhaps anti-social nature. And gradually, as she went on talking, her woman's instinct told her that she was feeding a passion in him – not a love this time, but a sharp and particular hatred that gave thrust and sensibility to every little question he asked. What or whom it was that he hated, exactly, she could not say, but she feared for any man, whether the gingery stranger or anybody else, who had attracted this tiny magician's fire. Glikman's passion, she recalled, had been a universal, sleepless passion against injustice, fixing itself almost at random upon a range of symptoms, small or large, But the magician's was a single beam, fixed upon a spot she could not see.

It is in any case a fact that by the time the magician left – my Lord, she thought, it was nearly time for her to go to work again! – Ostrakova had told him everything she had to tell, and the magician in return had woken feelings in her which for years, until this night, had belonged only to her past. Tidying away the plates and bottles in a daze, she managed, despite the complexity of her feelings, regarding Alexandra, and herself, and her two dead men, to burst out laughing at her woman's folly.

'And I do not even know his name!' she said aloud, and shook her head in mockery. 'How shall I reach you?' she had asked. 'How can I warn you if he returns?'

She could not, the magician had replied. But if there was a crisis she should write to the General again, under his English name and at a different address. 'Mr. Miller,' he said gravely, pronouncing it as French, and gave her a card with a London address printed by hand in capitals. 'But be discreet,' he warned. 'You must be indirect in your language.'

All that day, and for many days afterwards, Ostrakova kept her last departing image of the magician at the forefront of her memory as he slipped away from her and down the ill-lit staircase. His last fervid stare, taut with purpose and excitement: 'I promise to release you. Thank you for calling me to arms.' His little white hand, running down the broad banister of the stairwell, like a handkerchief waved from a train window, round and round in a dwindling circle of farewell, till it disappeared into the darkness of the tunnel.

# TWO

The second of the two events that brought George Smiley from his retirement occurred a few weeks after the first, in early autumn of the same year: not in Paris at all, but in the once ancient, free, and Hanseatic city of Hamburg, now almost pounded to death by the thunder of its own prosperity; yet it remains true that nowhere does the summer fade more splendidly than along the gold and orange banks of the Alster, which nobody as yet has drained or filled with concrete. George Smiley, needless to say, had seen nothing of its languorous autumn splendour. Smiley, on the day in question, was toiling obliviously, with whatever conviction he could muster, at his habitual desk in the London Library in St. James's Square, with two spindly trees to look at through the sash-window of the reading-room. The only link to Hamburg he might have pleaded – if he had afterwards attempted the connection, which he did not – was in the Parnassian field of German baroque poetry, for at the time he was composing a monograph on the bard Opitz, and trying loyally to distinguish true passion from the tiresome literary convention of the period.

The time in Hamburg was a few moments after eleven in the morning, and the footpath leading to the jetty was speckled with sunlight and dead leaves. A candescent haze hung over the flat water of the Aussenalster, and through it the spires of the Eastern bank were like green stains dabbed on the wet horizon. Along the shore, red squirrels scurried, foraging for the winter. But the slight and somewhat anarchistic-looking young man standing on the jetty wearing a track suit and running shoes had neither eyes nor mind for them. His red rimmed gaze was locked tensely upon the approaching steamer, his hollow face darkened by a two-day stubble. He carried a Hamburg news-paper under his left arm, and an eye as perceptive as George Smiley's would have noticed at once that it was yesterday's edition, not today's. In his right hand he clutched a rush shopping basket better suited to the dumpy Madame Ostrakova than to this lithe, bedraggled athlete who seemed any minute about to leap into the lake. Oranges peeked out of the top of the basket, a yellow Kodak envelope with English printing lay on top of the oranges. The jetty was otherwise empty, and the haze over the water added to his solitude. His only companions were the steamer timetable and an archaic notice, which must have survived the war, telling him how to revive the half-drowned; his only thoughts concerned the General's instructions, which he was continu-ously reciting to himself like a prayer.

The steamer glided alongside and the boy skipped aboard like a child in a dance game – a flurry of steps, then motionless until the music starts again. For forty-eight hours, night and day, he had had nothing to think of but this moment: now. Driving, he had stared wakefully at the road, imagining, between glimpses of his wife and little girl, the many disastrous things that could go wrong. He knew he had a talent for disaster. During his rare breaks for coffee, he had packed and repacked the oranges a dozen times, laying the envelope lengthways, sideways – no, this angle is better, it is more appropri-ate, easier to get hold of. At the edge of town he had collected small change so that he would have the fare exactly – what if the conductor held him up, engaged him in casual conversation? There was so little time to do what he had to do! He would speak no German, he had worked it out. He would mumble, smile, be reticent, apologise, but stay mute. Or he would say some of his few words of Estonian – some phrase from the Bible he could still remember from his Lutheran childhood, before his father insisted he learn Russian. But now, with the moment so close upon him, the boy suddenly saw a snag in this plan. What if his fellow passengers then came to his aid? In polyglot Hamburg, with the East only a few miles away, any six people could muster as many languages between them! Better to keep silent, be blank.

He wished he had shaved. He wished he was less conspicuous.

Inside the main cabin of the steamer, the boy looked at nobody. He kept his eyes lowered; *avoid eye contact* the General had ordered. The conductor was chatting to an old lady and ignored him. He waited awkwardly, trying to look calm. There were about thirty passengers. He had an impression of men and women dressed alike in green overcoats and green felt hats, all disapproving of him. It was his turn. He held out a damp palm. One mark, a fifty-pfennig piece, a bunch of little brass tens. The conductor helped himself, not speaking. Clumsily, the boy groped his way between the seats, making for the stern. The jetty was moving away. They suspect me of being a terrorist, thought the boy. There was engine oil on his hands and he wished he'd washed it off. Perhaps it's on my face as well. *Be blank*, the General had said. *Efface yourself. Neither smile nor frown. Be normal.* He glanced at his watch, trying to keep the action slow. He had rolled back his left cuff in advance, specially to leave the watch free. Ducking, though he was not tall, the boy arrived suddenly in the stern section, which was open to the weather, protected only by a canopy. It was a case of seconds. Not of days or kilometres any more; nor hours. Seconds. The timing hand of his watch flickered past the six. The next time it reaches six, you move. A breeze was blowing but he barely noticed it. The time was an awful worry to him. When he got excited – he knew – he lost all sense of time completely. He was afraid the seconds hand would race through a double circuit before he had realised, turning one minute into two. In the stern section all seats were vacant. He made jerkily for the last bench of all, holding the basket of oranges over his stomach in both hands, clamping the newspaper to his armpit at the same time: it is I, read my signals. He felt a fool. The oranges were too conspicuous by far. Why on earth should an unshaven young man in a track suit be carrying a basket of oranges and yesterday's paper? The whole boat must have noticed him! 'Captain – that young man – there – he is a bomber! He has a bomb in his basket, he intends to hijack us or sink the ship!' A couple stood arm in arm at the railing with their backs to him, staring into the mist. The man was very small, shorter than the woman. He wore a black overcoat with a velvet collar. They ignored him. *Sit as far back as you can, be sure you sit next to the aisle*, the General had said. He sat down, praying it would work first time, that none of the fallbacks would be needed. 'Beckie, I do this for *you*,' he whispered secretly, thinking of his daughter, and remembering the General's words. His Lutheran origins notwithstanding, he wore a wooden cross round his neck, a present to him from his mother, but the zip of his tunic covered it. Why had he hidden the cross? So that God would not witness his deceit? He didn't know. He wanted only to be driving again, to drive and drive till he dropped or was safely home.

*Look nowhere*, he remembered the General saying. He was to look nowhere but ahead of him: *you are the passive partner. You have nothing to do but supply the opportunity. No code word, nothing; just the basket and the oranges and the yellow envelope and the newspaper under your arm.* I should never have agreed to it, he thought. I have endangered my daughter Beckie. Stella will never forgive me. I shall lose my citizenship, I have put everything at risk. *Do it for our cause*, the General had said. General, I haven't got one: it was not my cause, it was your cause, it was my father's; that is why I threw the oranges overboard.

But he didn't. Laying the newspaper beside him on the slatted bench, he saw that it was drenched in sweat – that patches of print had worn off when he clutched it. He looked at his watch. The seconds hand was standing at ten. It's stopped! Fifteen seconds since I last looked – that simply is not possible! A frantic glance at the shore convinced him they were already in mid-lake. He looked at the watch again and saw the seconds hand jerking past eleven. Fool, he thought, calm yourself. Leaning to his right, he affected to read the newspaper while he kept the dial of his watch constantly in view. Terrorists. Nothing but terrorists, he thought, reading the headlines for the twentieth time. No wonder the passengers think I'm one of them. *Grossfahndung.* That was their word for massive search. It amazed him that he remembered so much German. *Do it for our cause.*

At his feet the basket of oranges was leaning precariously. *When you get up, put the basket on the bench to reserve your seat,* the General had said. What if it falls over? In his imagination he saw the oranges rolling all over the deck, the yellow envelope upside down among them, photographs everywhere, all of Beckie. The seconds hand was passing six. He stood up. *Now.* His midriff was cold. He tugged his tunic down to cover it and inadvertently exposed his mother's wooden cross. He closed the zip. *Saunter. Look nowhere. Pretend you are the dreamy sort,* the General had said. *Your father would not have hesitated a moment,* the General had said. *Nor will you.* Cautiously lifting the basket on to the bench, he steadied it with both hands, then leaned it towards the back to give it extra stability. Then tested it. He wondered about the *Abendblatt.* To take it, to leave it where it was? Perhaps his contact had still not seen the signal? He picked it up and put it under his arm.

He returned to the main cabin. A second couple moved into the stern section, presumably to take the air, older, very sedate. The first couple were a sexy pair, even from behind – the little man, the shapely girl, the trimness of them both. You knew they had a good time in bed, just to look at them. But the second couple were like a pair of policemen to him; the boy was certain they got no pleasure from their love-making at all. Where is my mind going? he thought crazily. To my wife, Stella, was the answer. To the long exquisite embraces we may never have again. Sauntering as he had been ordered to, he advanced down the aisle towards the closed-off area where the pilot sat. Looking at nobody was easy; the passengers sat with their backs to him. He had reached as far forward as passengers were allowed. The pilot sat to his left, on a raised platform. *Go to the pilot's window and admire the view. Remain there one minute exactly.* The cabin roof was lower here; he had to stoop. Through the big windscreen, trees and buildings on the move. He saw a rowing eight switch by, followed by a lone blonde goddess in a skiff. Breasts like a statue's, he thought. For greater casualness, he propped one running shoe on the pilot's platform. Give me a woman, he thought desperately, as the moment of crisis came; give me my Stella, drowsy and desiring, in the half-light of early morning. He had his left wrist forward on the railing, his watch constantly in view.

'We don't clean boots here,' the pilot growled.

Hastily the boy replaced his foot on the deck. Now he knows I speak German, he thought, and felt his face prickle in embarrassment. But they know anyway, he thought stupidly, for why else would I carry a German newspaper?

It was time. Swiftly standing to his full height again, he swung round too fast and began the return journey to his seat, and it was no use any more remembering not to stare at faces because the faces stared at him, disapproving of his two days' growth of beard, his track suit and his wild look. His eyes left one face, only to find another. He thought he had never seen such a chorus of mute ill-will. His track suit had parted at the midriff again and showed a line of black hair. Stella washed them too hot, he thought. He tugged the tunic down again and stepped into the air, wearing his wooden cross like a medal. As he did so, two things happened almost at the same time. On the bench, next to the basket, he saw the yellow chalk mark he was looking for, running over two slats, bright as a canary, telling him that the hand-over had taken place successfully. At the sight of it, a sense of glory filled him, he had known nothing like it in his life, a release more perfect than any woman could provide.

Why must we do it this way? he had asked the General; why does it have to be so elaborate?

*Because the object is unique in the whole world*, the General had replied. *It is a treasure without a counterpart. Its loss would be a tragedy to the free world.*

And he chose *me* to be his courier, thought the boy proudly: though he still, at the back of his mind, thought the old man was overdoing it. Serenely picking up the yellow envelope, he dropped it into his tunic pocket, drew the zip and ran his finger down the join to make sure it had meshed.

At the same instant exactly, he realised he was being watched. The woman at the railing still had her back to him and he noticed again that she had very pretty hips and legs. But her sexy little companion in the black overcoat had turned all the way round to face him, and his expression put an end to all the good feelings the boy had just experienced. Only once had he seen a face like that, and that was when his father lay dying in their first English home, a room in Ruislip, a few months after they had reached England. The boy had seen nothing so desperate, so profoundly serious, so bare of all protection, in anyone else, ever. More alarming still, he knew – precisely as Ostrakova had known – that it was a desperation in contrast with the natural disposition of the features, which were those of a comedian – or as Ostrakova had it, a magician. So that the impassioned stare of this little, sharp-faced stranger, with its message of furious entreaty – 'Boy, you have no idea what you are carrying! Guard it with your life!' – was a revelation of that same comedian's soul.

The steamer had stopped. They were on the other bank. Seizing his basket, the boy leapt ashore and, almost running, ducked between the bustling shoppers from one side-street to another without knowing where they led.

All through the drive back, while the steering-wheel hammered his arms and the engine played its pounding scale in his ears, the boy saw that face before him in the wet road, wondering as the hours passed whether it was something he had merely imagined in the emotion of the hand-over. Most likely the real contact was someone completely different, he thought, trying to soothe himself. One of those fat ladies in the green felt hats – even the conductor. I was overstrung, he told himself. At a crucial moment, an unknown man turned round and looked at me and I hung an entire history on him, even imagining he was my dying father.

By the time he reached Dover he almost believed he had put the man out of his mind. He had dumped the cursed oranges in a litter bin; the yellow envelope lay snug in the pouch of his tunic, one sharp corner pricking his skin, and that was all that mattered. So he had formed theories about his secret accomplice? Forget them. And even if, by sheer coincidence, he was right, and it *was* that hollowed, glaring face – *then* what? All the less reason to go blabbing about it to the General, whose concern with security the boy likened to the unchallengable passion of a seer. The thought of Stella became an aching need to him. His desire sharpened with every noisy mile. It was early morning still. He imagined waking her with his caresses; he saw her sleepy smile slowly turn to passion.

The summons came to Smiley that same night, and it is a curious fact, since he had an overall impression of not sleeping at all well during this late period of his life, that the phone had to ring a long time beside the bed before he answered it. He had come home straight from the library, then dined poorly at an Italian restaurant in the King's Road, taking the *Voyages of Olearius* with him for protection. He had returned to his house in Bywater Street and resumed work on his monograph with the devotion of a man who had nothing else to do. After a couple of hours he had opened a bottle of red Burgundy and drunk half of it, listening to a poor play on the radio. Then dozed, wrestling with troubled dreams. Yet the moment he heard Lacon's voice, he had the feeling of being hauled from a warm and treasured place, where he wished to remain undisturbed for ever. Also, though in fact he was moving swiftly, he had the sensation of taking a long time to dress; and he wondered whether that was what old men did when they heard about a death.

# THREE

'Knew him personally at all, did you sir?' the Detective Chief Superintendent of Police asked respectfully in a voice kept deliberately low. 'Or perhaps I shouldn't enquire.'

The two men had been together for fifteen minutes but this was the Superintendent's first question. For a while Smiley did not seem to hear it, but his silence was not offensive, he had the gift of quiet. Besides, there is a companionship about two men contemplating a corpse. It was an hour before dawn on Hampstead Heath, a dripping, misty, no-man's hour, neither warm or cold, with a heaven tinted orange by the London glow, and the trees glistening like oilskins. They stood side by side in an avenue of beeches and the Superintendent was taller by a head: a young giant of a man, prematurely grizzled, a little pompous perhaps, but with a giant's gentleness that made him naturally befriending. Smiley was clasping his pudgy hands over his belly like a mayor at a cenotaph, and had eyes for nothing but the body lying at his feet in the beam of the Superintendent's torch. The walk this far had evidently winded him, for he puffed a little as he stared. From the darkness round them, police receivers crackled on the night air. There were no other lights at all; the Superintendent had ordered them extinguished.

'He was just somebody I worked with,' Smiley explained after a long delay.

'So I was given to understand, sir,' the Superintendent said.

He waited hopefully but nothing more came. 'Don't even speak to him,' the Deputy Assistant Commissioner (Crime and Ops) had said to him. 'You never saw him and it was two other blokes. Just show him what he wants and drop him down a hole. Fast.' Till now, the Detective Chief Superintendent had done exactly that.He had moved, in his own estimation, with the speed of light. The photographer had photographed, the doctor had certified life extinct, the pathologist had inspected the body *in situ* as a prelude to conducting his autopsy – all with an expedition quite contrary to the proper pace of things, merely in order to clear the way for the visiting *irregular*, as the Deputy Assistant Commissioner (Crime and Ops) had liked to call him. The irregular had arrived – with about as much ceremony as a meter-reader, the Superintendent noted – and the Superintendent had led him over the course at a canter. They had looked at foot-prints, they had tracked the old man's route till here. The Superintendent had made a reconstruction of the crime, as well as he was able in the circumstances, and the Superintendent was an able man. Now they were in the dip, at the point where the avenue turned, where the rolling mist was thickest. In the torchbeam the dead body was the centre-piece of everything. It lay face downward and spreadeagled, as if it had been crucified to the gravel, and the plastic sheet emphasised its lifelessness. It was the body of an old man, but broad-shouldered still, a body that had battled and endured. The white hair was cut to stubble. One strong, veined hand still grasped a sturdy walking-stick. He wore a black overcoat and rubber overshoes. A black beret lay on the ground beside him, and the gravel at his head was black with blood. Some loose change lay about, and a pocket handkerchief, and a small penknife that looked more like a keepsake than a tool. Most likely they had started to search him and given up, sir, the Superintendent had said. Most likely they were disturbed, Mr. Smiley, sir; and Smiley had wondered what it must be like to touch a warm body you had just shot.

'If I might possibly take a look at his face, Superintendent,' Smiley said.

This time it was the Superintendent who caused the delay. 'Ah, now are you sure about that, sir?' He sounded slightly embarrassed. 'There'll be better ways of identifying him than *that*, you know.'

'Yes. Yes, I am sure,' said Smiley earnestly, as if he really had given the matter great thought.

The Superintendent called softly to the trees, where his men stood among their blacked-out cars like a next generation waiting for its turn.

'You there. Hall. Sergeant Pike. Come here at the double and turn him over.'

*Fast*, the Deputy Assistant Commissioner (Crime and Ops) had said.

Two men slipped forward from the shadows. The elder wore a black beard. Their surgical gloves of elbow length shone ghostly grey. They wore blue overalls and thigh-length rubber boots. Squatting, the bearded man cautiously untucked the plastic sheet while the younger constable laid a hand on the dead man's shoulder as if to wake him up.

'You'll have to try harder than that, lad,' the Superintendent warned in an altogether crisper tone.

The boy pulled, the bearded sergeant helped him, and the body reluctantly rolled over, one arm stiffly waving, the other still clutching the stick.

'Oh Christ,' said the constable. 'Oh bloody hell!' – and clapped a hand over his mouth. The sergeant grabbed his elbow and shoved him away. They heard the sound of retching.

'I don't hold with politics,' the Superintendent confided to Smiley inconse-
quentially, staring downwards still. 'I don't hold with politics and I don't hold
with politicians either. Licensed lunatics most of them, in my view. That's why
I joined the Force, to be honest.' The sinewy mist curled strangely in the
steady beam of his torch. 'You don't happen to know what did it, do you, sir? I
haven't seen a wound like that in fifteen years.'

'I'm afraid ballistics are not my province,' Smiley replied, after another
pause for thought.

'No, I don't expect they would be, would they? Seen enough, sir?'
Smiley apparently had not.

'Most people expect to be shot in the chest really, don't they, sir?' the
Superintendent remarked brightly. He had learned that small talk sometimes eased the atmosphere on such occasions. 'Your neat round bullet that
drills a tasteful hole. That's what most people expect. Victim falls gently to his
knees to the tune of celestial choirs. It's the telly that does it, I suppose.
Whereas your real bullet these days can take off an arm or a leg, so my friends
in brown tell me.' His voice took on a more practical tone. 'Did he have a
moustache at all, sir? My sergeant fancied a trace of white whisker on the
upper jaw.'

'A military one,' said Smiley after a long gap, and with his thumb and
forefinger absently described the shape upon his own lip while his gaze
remained locked upon the old man's body. 'I wonder, Superintendent,
whether I might just examine the contents of his pockets, possibly?'

'Sergeant Pike.'

'Sir!'

'Put that sheet back and tell Mr. Murgotroyd to have his pockets ready for
me in the van, will you, what they've left of them. At the double,' the
Superintendent added, as a matter of routine.

'Sir!'

'And come here.' The Superintendent had taken the sergeant softly by the
upper arm. 'You tell that young Constable Hall that I can't stop him sicking
up but I won't have his irreverent language.' For the Superintendent on his
home territory was a devoutly Christian man and did not care who knew it.
'This way, Mr. Smiley, sir,' he added, recovering his gentler tone.

As they moved higher up the avenue, the chatter of the radios faded, and
they heard instead the angry wheeling of rooks and the growl of the city. The
Superintendent marched briskly, keeping to the left of the roped-off area.
Smiley hurried after him. A windowless van was parked between the trees, its
back doors open, and a dim light burning inside. Entering, they sat on hard
benches. Mr. Murgotroyd had grey hair and wore a grey suit. He crouched
before them with a plastic sack like a transparent pillowcase. The sack had a
knot at the throat, which he untied. Inside, smaller packages floated. As Mr.
Murgotroyd lifted them out, the Superintendent read the labels by his torch
before handing them to Smiley to consider.

'One scuffed leather coin purse Continental appearance. Half inside his
pocket, half out, left-side jacket. You saw the coins by his body – seventy-two
pence. That's all the money on him. Carry a wallet at all, did he, sir?'

'I don't know.'

'Our guess is they helped themselves to the wallet, started on the purse,
then ran. One bunch keys domestic and various, right hand trousers . . .' He
ran on but Smiley's scrutiny did not relax. Some people *act* a memory, the
Superintendent thought, noticing his concentration, others *have* one. In the

Superintendent's book, memory was the better half of intelligence, he prized it highest of all mental accomplishments; and Smiley, he knew, possessed it. 'One Paddington Borough Library Card in the name of V. Miller, one box Swan Vesta matches partly used, overcoat left. One Aliens' Registration Card, number as reported, also in the name of Vladimir Miller. One bottle tablets, overcoat left. What would the tablets be for, sir, any views on that at all? Name of Sustac, whatever that is, to be taken two or three times a day?'

'Heart,' said Smiley.

'And one receipt for the sum of thirteen pounds from the Straight and Steady Minicab Service of Islington, North.'

'May I look?' said Smiley, and the Superintendent held it out so that Smiley could read the date and the driver's signature, J. Lamb, in a copy-book hand wildly underlined.

The next bag contained a stick of school chalk, yellow and miraculously unbroken. The narrow end was smeared brown as if by a single stroke, but the thick end was unused.

'There's yellow chalk powder on his left hand too,' Mr Murgotroyd said, speaking for the first time. His complexion was like grey stone. His voice too was grey, and mournful as an undertaker's. 'We did *wonder* whether he might be in the teaching line, actually,' Mr. Murgotroyd added, and Smiley, either by design or oversight, did not answer Mr. Murgotroyd's implicit question, and the Superintendent did not pursue it.

And a second cotton handkerchief, proffered this time by Mr. Murgotroyd, part bloodied, part clean, and carefully ironed into a sharp triangle for the top pocket.

'On his way to a party, we wondered,' Mr. Murgotroyd said, this time with no hope at all.

'Crime and Ops on the air, sir,' a voice called from the front of the van.

Without a word the Superintendent vanished into the darkness, leaving Smiley to the depressed gaze of Mr. Murgotroyd.

'You a specialist of some sort, sir?' Mr. Murgotroyd asked after a long sad scrutiny of his guest.

'No. No, I'm afraid not,' said Smiley.

'Home Office, sir?'

'Alas, not Home Office either,' said Smiley with a benign shake of his head, which somehow made him party to Mr. Murgotroyd's bewilderment.

'My superiors are a little worried about the press, Mr. Smiley,' the Superintendent said, poking his head into the van again. 'Seems they're heading this way, sir.'

Smiley clambered quickly out. The two men stood face to face in the avenue.

'You've been very kind,' Smiley said. 'Thank you.'

'Privilege,' said the superintendent.

'You don't happen to remember which pocket the *chalk* was in do you?' Smiley asked.

'Overcoat left,' the Superintendent replied in some surprise.

'And the searching of him – could you tell me again how you see *that* exactly?'

'They hadn't time or didn't care to turn him over. Knelt by him, fished for his wallet, pulled at his purse. Scattered a few objects as they did so. By then they'd had enough.'

'Thank you,' said Smiley again.

And a moment later, with more ease than his portly figure might have suggested him capable of, he had vanished among the trees. But not before the Superintendent had shone the torch full upon his face, a thing he hadn't done till now for reasons of discretion. And taken an intense professional look at the legendary features, if only to tell his grandchildren in his old age: how George Smiley, sometime Chief of the Secret Service, by then retired, had one night come out of the woodwork to peer at some dead foreigner of his who had died in highly nasty circumstances.

Not *one* face at all actually, the Superintendent reflected. Not when it was lit by the torch like that indirectly from below. More your whole range of faces. More your patchwork of different ages, people and endeavours. Even – thought the Superintendent – of different faiths.

'The best I ever met,' old Mendel, the Superintendent's one-time superior, had told him over a friendly pint not long ago. Mendel was retired now, like Smiley. But Mendel knew what he was talking about and didn't like Funnies any better than the Superintendent did – interfering la-di-da amateurs most of them, and devious with it. But not Smiley. Smiley was different, Mendel had said. Smiley was the best – simply the best case man Mendel had ever met – and old Mendel knew what he was talking about.

An abbey, the Superintendent decided. That's what he was, an abbey. He would work that into his sermon the next time his turn came around. An abbey, made up of all sorts of conflicting ages and styles and convictions. The Superintendent liked that metaphor the more he dwelt on it. He would try it out on his wife when he got home: man as God's architecture, my dear, moulded by the hand of ages, infinite in his striving and diversity . . . But at this point the Superintendent laid a restraining hand upon his own rhetorical imagination. Maybe not, after all, he thought. Maybe we're flying a mite too high for the course, my friend.

There was another thing about that face the Superintendent wouldn't easily forget either. Later, he talked to old Mendel about it, as he talked to him later about lots of things. The moisture. He'd taken it for dew at first – yet if it was dew why was the Superintendent's own face bone dry? It wasn't dew and it wasn't grief either, if his hunch was right. It was a thing that happened to the Superintendent himself occasionally and happened to the lads too, even the hardest; it crept up on them and the Superintendent watched for it like a hawk. Usually in kids' cases, where the pointlessness suddenly got through to you – your child batterings, your criminal assaults, your infant rapes. You didn't break down or beat your chest or any of those histrionics. No. You just happened to put your hand to your face and find it damp and you wondered what the hell Christ bothered to die for, if He ever died at all.

And when you had *that* mood on you, the Superintendent told himself with a slight shiver, the best thing you could do was give yourself a couple of days off and take the wife to Margate, or before you knew where you were you found yourself getting a little too rough with people for your own good health.

'Sergeant!' the Superintendent yelled.

The bearded figure loomed before him.

'Switch the lights on and get it back to normal,' the Superintendent ordered. 'And ask Inspector Hallowes to slip up here and oblige. At the double.'

# FOUR

They had unchained the door to him, they had questioned him even before they took his coat: tersely and intently. Were there any compromising materials on the body, George? Any that would link him with us? My God, you've been a time! They had shown him where to wash, forgetting that he knew already. They had sat him in an armchair and there Smiley remained, humble and discarded, while Oliver Lacon, Whitehall's Head Prefect to the intelligence services, prowled the threadbare carpet like a man made restless by his conscience, and Lauder Strickland said it all again in fifteen different ways to fifteen different people, over the old upright telephone in the far corner of the room – 'Then get me back to police liaison, woman, *at once*' – either bullying or fawning, depending on rank and clout. The Superintendent was a life ago, but in time ten minutes. The flat smelt of old nappies and stale cigarettes and was on the top floor of a scrolled Edwardian apartment house not two hundred yards from Hampstead Heath. In Smiley's mind, visions of Vladimir's burst face mingled with these pale faces of the living, yet death was not a shock to him just now, but merely an affirmation that his own existence too was dwindling; that he was living against the odds. He sat without expectation. He sat like an old man at a country railway station, watching the express go by. But watching all the same. And remembering old journeys.

This is how crises always were, he thought; ragtag conversations with no centre. One man on the telephone, another dead, a third prowling. The nervous idleness of slow motion.

He peered around, trying to fix his mind on the decaying things outside himself. Chipped fire extinguishers, Ministry of Works issue. Prickly brown sofas – the stains a little worse. But safe flats, unlike old generals, never die, he thought. They don't even fade away.

On the table before him lay the cumbersome apparatus of agent hospitality, there to revive the unrevivable guest. Smiley took the inventory. In a bucket of melted ice, one bottle of Stolichnaya vodka, Vladimir's recorded favourite brand. Salted herrings, still in their tin. Pickled cucumber, bought loose and already drying. One mandatory loaf of black bread. Like every Russian Smiley had known, the old boy could scarcely drink his vodka without it. Two Marks & Spencer vodka glasses, could be cleaner. One packet of Russian cigarettes, unopened: if he had come, he would have smoked the lot; he had none with him when he died.

Vladimir had none with him when he died, he repeated to himself, and made a little mental stammer of it, a knot in his handkerchief.

A clatter interrupted Smiley's reverie. In the kitchen, Mostyn the boy had dropped a plate. At the telephone Lauder Strickland wheeled round, demanding quiet. But he already had it again. What was Mostyn preparing anyway? Dinner? Breakfast? Seed-cake for the funeral? And what was Mostyn? *Who* was Mostyn? Smiley had shaken his damp and trembling hand, then promptly forgotten what he looked like except that he was so young. And yet for some reason Mostyn was known to him, if only as a type. Mostyn is our grief, Smiley decided arbitrarily.

Lacon, in the middle of his prowling, came to a sudden halt.

'George! You look worried. Don't be. We're all in the clear on this. All of us!'

'I'm not worried, Oliver.'

'You look as though you're reproaching yourself. I can tell!'

'When agents die –' said Smiley, but left the sentence incomplete, and anyway Lacon couldn't wait for him. He strode off again, a hiker with miles to go. Lacon, Strickland, Mostyn, thought Smiley as Strickland's Aberdonian brogue hammered on. One Cabinet Office factotum, one Circus fixer, one scared boy. Why not real people? Why not Vladimir's case officer, whoever he is? Why not Saul Enderby, their Chief?

A couplet of Auden's rang in his mind from the days when he was Mostyn's age: *let us honour if we can the vertical man, though we value none but the horizontal one.* Or something.

And why Smiley? he thought. Above all, why me? Of all people, when as far as they're concerned I'm deader than old Vladimir.

'Will you have tea, Mr. Smiley, or something stronger?' called Mostyn through the open kitchen doorway. Smiley wondered whether he was naturally so pale.

'He'll have tea only, thank you, Mostyn!' Lacon blurted, making a sharp about-turn. 'After shock, tea is a deal safer. With sugar, right, George? Sugar replaces lost energy. Was it *gruesome*, George? How perfectly awful for you.'

No, it wasn't awful, it was the truth, thought Smiley. He was shot and I saw him dead. Perhaps you should do that too.

Apparently unable to leave Smiley alone, Lacon had come back down the room and was peering at him with clever, uncomprehending eyes. He was a mawkish creature, sudden but without spring, with youthful features cruelly aged and a raw unhealthy rash around his neck where his shirt had scuffed the skin. In the religious light between dawn and morning his black waistcoat and white collar had the glint of the soutane.

'I've hardly said hullo,' Lacon complained, as if it were Smiley's fault. 'George. Old friend. My goodness.'

'Hullo, Oliver,' said Smiley.

Still Lacon remained there, gazing down at him, his long head to one side, like a child studying an insect. In his memory Smiley replayed Lacon's fervid phone call of two hours before.

*It's an emergency, George. You remember Vladimir? George, are you awake? You remember the old General, George? Used to live in Paris?*

Yes, I remember the General, he had replied. Yes, Oliver, I remember Vladimir.

*We need someone from his past, George. Someone who knew his little ways, can identify him, damp down potential scandal. We need you, George. Now. George, wake up.*

He had been trying to. Just as he had been trying to transfer the receiver to his better ear, and sit upright in a bed too large for him. He was sprawling in the cold space deserted by his wife, because that was the side where the telephone was.

You mean he's been shot? Smiley had repeated.

*George, why can't you listen? Shot dead. This evening. George, for Heaven's sake wake up, we need you!*

Lacon loped off again, plucking at his signet ring as if it were too tight. *I need you*, thought Smiley, watching him gyrate. *I love you, I hate you, I need you.* Such apocalyptic statements reminded him of Ann when she had run out of money or love. The heart of the sentence is the subject, he thought. It is not the verb, least of all the object. It is the ego, demanding its feed.

Need me what for? he thought again. To console them? Give them absolution? What have they done that they need my past to redress their future?

Down the room, Lauder Strickland was holding up an arm in Fascist salute while he addressed Authority.

'Yes, Chief, he's with us at this moment, sir . . . I shall tell him that, sir . . . Indeed, sir . . . I shall convey to him that message . . . Yes, sir . . .'

Why are Scots so attracted to the secret world? Smiley wondered, not for the first time in his career. Ships' engineers, Colonial administrators, spies . . . Their heretical Scottish history drew them to distant churches, he decided.

'George!' Strickland, suddenly much louder, calling Smiley's name like an order. 'Sir Saul sends you his warmest personal salutations, George!' He had swung round, still with his arm up. 'At a quieter moment he will express his gratitude to you more fittingly.' Back to the phone: 'Yes, Chief, Oliver Lacon is also with me and his opposite number at the Home Office is at this instant in parley with the Commissioner of Police regarding our former interest in the dead man and the preparation of the D-Notice for the press.'

*Former interest*, Smiley recorded. A former interest with his face shot off and no cigarettes in his pocket. Yellow chalk. Smiley studied Strickland frankly: the awful green suit, the shoes of brushed pigskin got up as suède leather. The only change he could observe in him was a russet moustache not half as military as Vladimir's when he had still had one.

'Yes, sir, "an extinct case of purely historic concern", sir,' Strickland went on, into the telephone. Extinct is right, thought Smiley. Extinct, extinguished, put out. 'That is precisely the terminology,' Strickland continued. 'And Oliver Lacon proposed to have it included word for word in the D-Notice. Am I on target there, Oliver?'

'*Historical*,' Lacon corrected him irritably. 'Not *historic* concern. That's the last thing we want! Historical.' He stalked across the room, ostensibly to peer through the window at the coming day.

'It *is* still Enderby in charge, is it, Oliver?' Smiley asked, of Lacon's back.

'Yes, yes, it is still Saul Enderby, your old adversary, and he is doing marvels,' Lacon retorted impatiently. Pulling at the curtain, he unseated it from its runners. 'Not your style, I grant you – why should he be? He's an Atlantic man.' He was trying to force the casement. 'Not an easy thing to be under a government like this one, I can tell you.' He gave the handle another savage shove. A freezing draught raced round Smiley's knees. 'Takes a lot of footwork. Mostyn, where's tea? We seem to have been waiting for ever.'

All our lives, thought Smiley.

Over the sound of a lorry grinding up the hill, he heard Strickland again, interminably talking to Saul Enderby. 'I think the point with the press is not to play him down *too far*, Chief. Dullness is all, in a case like this. Even the private-life angle is a dangerous one, here. What we want is absolute lack of contemporary relevance of any sort. Oh true, true indeed, Chief, right –' On he droned, sycophantic but alert.

'Oliver –' Smiley began, losing patience. 'Oliver, do you mind, just –'

But Lacon was talking, not listening: 'How's Ann?' he asked vaguely, at the window, stretching his forearms on the sill. 'With you and so forth, I trust? Not roaming, is she? *God*, I hate autumn.'

'Fine, thank you. How's –' He struggled without success to remember the name of Lacon's wife.

'*Abandoned* me, dammit. Ran off with her pesky riding instructor, blast her. Left me with the children. The girls are farmed out to boarding-schools, thank God.' Leaning over his hands, Lacon was staring up at the lightening sky. 'Is that Orion up there, stuck like a golf ball between the chimney pots?' he asked.

Which is another death, thought Smiley sadly, his mind staying briefly with Lacon's broken marriage. He remembered a pretty, unworldly woman and a string of daughters jumping ponies in the garden of their rambling house in Ascot.

'I'm sorry, Oliver,' he said.

'Why should you be? Not *your* wife. She's mine. It's every man for himself in love.'

'Could you close the window, please!' Strickland called, dialling again. 'It's bloody arctic down this end.'

Irritably slamming the window, Lacon strode back into the room.

Smiley tried a second time: 'Oliver, what's going on?' he asked. 'Why did you need me?'

'Only one who knew him for a start. Strickland, are you nearly done? He's like one of those airport announcers,' he told Smiley with a stupid grin. '*Never* done.'

You could break, Oliver, thought Smiley, noticing the estrangement of Lacon's eyes as he came under the light. You've had too much, he thought in unexpected sympathy. We both have.

From the kitchen the mysterious Mostyn appeared with tea: an earnest, contemporary-looking child with flared trousers and a mane of brown hair. Seeing him set down the tray, Smiley finally placed him in the terms of his own past. Ann had had a lover like him once, an ordinand from Wells Theological College. She gave him a lift down the M4 and later claimed to have saved him from going queer.

'What section are you in, Mostyn?' Smiley asked him quietly.

'Oddbins, sir.' He crouched, level to the table, displaying an Asian suppleness. 'Since your day, actually, sir. It's a sort of operational pool. Mainly probationers waiting for overseas postings.'

'I see.'

'I heard you lecture at the Nursery at Sarratt, sir. On the new entrant's course. "Agent handling in the field." It was the best thing of the whole two years.'

'Thank you.'

But Mostyn's calf eyes stayed on him intently.

'Thank you,' said Smiley again, more puzzled than before.

'Milk, sir, or lemon, sir? The lemon was for *him*,' Mostyn added in a low aside, as if that were a recommendation for the lemon.

Strickland had rung off and was fiddling with the waistband of his trousers, making it looser or tighter.

'Yes, well, we have to temper truth, George!' Lacon bellowed suddenly, in what seemed to be a declaration of personal faith. 'Sometimes people are innocent but the circumstances can make them appear quite otherwise. There was never a golden age. There's only a golden mean. We have to remember that. Chalk it on your shaving mirrors.'

In yellow, Smiley thought.

Strickland was waddling down the room: 'You. Mostyn. Young Nigel. You, sir!'

Mostyn lifted his grave brown eyes in reply.

'Commit nothing to paper whatever,' Strickland warned him, wiping the back of his hand on his moustache as if one or the other were wet. 'Hear me? That's an order from on high. There was no encounter so you've no call to fill in the usual encounter sheet or any of that stuff. You've nothing to do but keep your mouth shut. Understand? You'll account for your expenses as general petty-cash disbursements. To me, direct. No file reference. Understand?'

'I understand,' said Mostyn.

'And no whispered confidences to those little tarts in Registry, or I'll know. Hear me? Give us some tea.'

Something happened inside George Smiley when he heard this conversation. Out of the formless indirection of these dialogues, out of the horror of the scene upon the Heath, a single shocking truth struck him. He felt a pull in his chest somewhere and he had the sensation of momentary disconnection from the room and the three haunted people he had found in it. *Encounter* sheet? No *encounter*? *Encounter* between Mostyn and Vladimir? *God in Heaven*, he thought, squaring the mad circle. *The Lord preserve, cosset and protect us. Mostyn was Vladimir's case officer! That old man, a General, once our glory, and they farmed him out to this uncut boy!* Then another lurch, more violent still, as his surprise was swept aside in an explosion of internal fury. He felt his lips tremble, he felt his throat seize up in indignation, blocking his words, and when he turned to Lacon his spectacles seemed to mist over from the heat:

'Oliver, I wonder if you'd mind finally telling me what I'm doing here,' he heard himself suggesting for the third time, hardly above a murmur.

Reaching out an arm he removed the vodka bottle from its bucket. Still unbidden, he broke the cap and poured himself a rather large tot.

Even then, Lacon dithered, pondered, hunted with his eyes, delayed. In Lacon's world, direct questions were the height of bad taste but direct answers were worse. For a moment, caught in mid-gesture at the centre of the room, he stood staring at Smiley in disbelief. A car stumbled up the hill, bringing news of the real world outside the window. Lauder Strickland slurped his tea. Mostyn was seating himself primly on a piano-stool to which there was no piano. But Lacon with his jerky gestures could only scratch about for words sufficiently elliptical to disguise his meaning.

'George,' he said. A shower of rain crashed against the window, but he ignored it. 'Where's Mostyn?' he asked.

Mostyn, no sooner settled, had flitted from the room to cope with a nervous need. They heard the thunder of the flush, loud as a brass band, and the gurgle of pipes all down the building.

Lacon raised a hand to his neck, tracing the raw patches. Reluctantly, he began: 'Three years ago, George – let us start there – soon after you left the Circus – your successor Saul Enderby – your *worthy* successor – under pressure from a concerned Cabinet – by *concerned* I mean newly formed – decided on certain far-reaching changes of intelligence practice. I'm giving you the *background*, George,' he explained, interrupting himself. 'I'm doing this because you're who you are, because of old times, and because' – he jabbed a finger at the window – 'because of out there.'

Strickland had unbuttoned his waistcoat and lay dozing and replete like a first-class passenger on a night plane. But his small watchful eyes followed every pass that Lacon made. The door opened and closed, admitting Mostyn, who resumed his perch on the piano-stool.

'Mostyn, I expect you to close your ears to this. I am talking high, high policy. One of these *far-reaching* changes, George, was the decision to form an inter-ministerial Steering Committee. A *mixed* committee' – he composed one in the air with his hands – 'part Westminster, part Whitehall, representing Cabinet as well as the major Whitehall customers. Known as the Wise Men. But placed – George – placed *between* the intelligence fraternity and Cabinet. As a channel, as a filter, as a brake.' One hand had remained outstretched, dealing these metaphors like cards. 'To look over the Circus's shoulder. To exercise control, George. Vigilance and accountability in the interest of a more open government. You don't like it. I can tell by your face.'

'I'm out of it,' Smiley said. 'I'm not qualified to judge.'

Suddenly Lacon's own face took on an appalled expression and his tone dropped to one of near despair.

'You should *hear* them, George, our new masters! You should *hear* the way they talk about the Circus! I'm their dog's-body, damn it: I *know*, get it every day! Gibes. Suspicion. Mistrust at every turn, even from Ministers who should know better. As if the Circus were some rogue animal outside their comprehension. As if British Intelligence were a sort of wholly owned subsidiary of the Conservative Party. Not their ally at all but some autonomous viper in their Socialist nest. The thirties all over again. Do you know, they're even reviving all that talk about a British Freedom of Information Act on the American pattern? From *within* the Cabinet? Of open hearings, revelations, all for the public sport? You'd be shocked, George. Pained. Think of the effect such a thing would have on morale alone. Would Mostyn here ever have joined the Circus after that kind of notoriety in the press and wherever? Would you, Mostyn?'

The question seemed to strike Mostyn very deep, for his grave eyes, made yet darker by his sickly colour, became graver, and he lifted a thumb and finger to his lip. But he did not speak.

'Where was I, George?' Lacon asked, suddenly lost.

'The Wise Men,' said Smiley sympathetically.

From the sofa, Lauder Strickland threw in his own pronouncement on that body: 'Wise, my Aunt Fanny. Bunch of left-wing flannel merchants. Rule our lives for us. Tell us how to run the shop. Smack our wrists when we don't do our sums right.'

Lacon shot Strickland a glance of rebuke but did not contradict him.

'One of the *less* controversial exercises of the Wise Men, George – one of their first duties – conferred upon them specifically by our masters – enshrined in a jointly drafted charter – was *stock-taking*. To review the Circus's resources world-wide and set them beside legitimate present-day targets. Don't ask me what constitutes a legitimate present-day target in their sight. That is a very moot point. However, I must not be disloyal.' He returned to his text. 'Suffice it to say that over a period of six months a review was conducted, and an axe duly laid.' He broke off, staring at Smiley. 'Are you with me, George?' he asked in a puzzled voice.

But it was hardly possible at that moment to tell whether Smiley was with anybody at all. His heavy lids had almost closed, and what remained visible of his eyes was clouded by the thick lenses of his spectacles. He was sitting upright but his head had fallen forward till his plump chins rested on his chest.

Lacon hesitated a moment longer, then continued: 'Now as a result of this axe-laying – this stock-taking, if you prefer – on the part of our Wise Men – certain categories of clandestine operation have been ruled *ipso facto* out of bounds. *Verboten.* Right?'

Prone on his sofa, Strickland incanted the unsayable: 'No coat-trailing. No honey-traps. No doubles. No stimulated defections. No émigrés. No bugger all.'

'What's that?' said Smiley, as if sharply waking from a deep sleep. But such straight talk was not to Lacon's liking and he overrode it.

'Let us not be simplistic please, Lauder. Let us reach things organically. Conceptual thinking is essential here. So the Wise Men composed a *codex,* George,' he resumed to Smiley. 'A catalogue of proscribed practices. Right?' But Smiley was waiting rather than listening. 'Ranged the whole field – on the uses and abuses of agents, on our fishing rights in Commonwealth countries – or lack of them – all sorts. Listeners, surveillance overseas, false-flag operations – a mammoth task, bravely tackled.' To the astonishment of everyone but himself, Lacon locked his fingers together, turned down the palms, and cracked the joints in a defiant staccato.

He continued: '*Also* included in their forbidden list – and it *is* a crude instrument, George, no respecter of tradition – are such matters as the classic use of double agents. *Obsession,* our new masters were pleased to call it in their findings. The old games of coat-trailing – turning and playing back our enemies' spies – in your day the very meat and drink of counter-intelligence – today, George, in the collective opinion of the Wise Men – today they are ruled obsolete. Uneconomic. Throw them out.'

Another lorry thundered giddily down the hill, or up it. They heard the bump of its wheels on the kerb.

'Christ,' Strickland muttered.

'Or – for example – I strike another blow at random – the over-emphasis on exile groups.'

This time there was no lorry at all: only the deep, accusing silence that had followed in its wake. Smiley sat as before, receiving not judging, his concentration only on Lacon, hearing him with the sharpness of the blind.

'Exile groups, you will want to know,' Lacon went on – 'or more properly the Circus's time-honoured connections with them – the Wise Men prefer to call it *dependence,* but I think that a trifle strong – I took issue with them, but was overruled – are today ruled provocative, anti-détente, inflammatory. An expensive indulgence. Those who tamper with them do so *on pain of excommunication.* I mean it, George. We have got thus far. This is the extent of their mastery. Imagine.'

With a gesture of baring his breast for Smiley's onslaught, Lacon opened his arms, and remained standing, peering down at him as he had done before, while in the background Strickland's Scottish echo once again told the same truth more brutally.

'The groups have been dustbinned, George,' Strickland said. 'The lot of them. Orders from on high. No contact, not even arm's length. The late Vladimir's death-and-glory artists included. Special two-key archive for 'em on the fifth floor. No officer access without consent in writing from the Chief. Copy to the weekly float for the Wise Men's inspection. Troubled times, George, I tell you true, troubled times.'

'George, now steady,' Lacon warned uneasily, catching something the others had not heard.

'What utter nonsense,' Smiley repeated deliberately.

His head had lifted and his eyes had turned full on Lacon, as if emphasising the bluntness of his contradiction. 'Vladimir wasn't *expensive*. He wasn't an indulgence either. Least of all was he uneconomic. You know perfectly well he loathed taking our money. We had to force it on him or he'd have starved. As to inflammatory – anti-détente, whatever those words mean – well, we had to hold him in check once in a while as one does with most good agents, but when it came down to it he took our orders like a lamb. You were a fan of his, Oliver. You know as well as I do what he was worth.'

The quietness of Smiley's voice did not conceal its tautness. Nor had Lacon failed to notice the dangerous points of colour in his cheeks.

Sharply, Lacon turned upon the weakest member present: 'Mostyn, I expect you to forget all this. Do you hear? Strickland, tell him.'

Strickland obliged with alacrity: 'Mostyn, you will present yourself to Housekeepers this morning at ten-thirty precisely and sign an indoctrination certificate which I personally shall compose and witness!'

'Yes, sir,' Mostyn said, after a slightly eerie delay.

Only now did Lacon respond to Smiley's point: 'George, I admired the *man*. Never his Group. There is an absolute distinction here. The man, yes. In many ways, a heroic figure, if you will. But not the company he kept: the fantasists, the down-at-heel princelings. Nor the Moscow Centre infiltrators they enfolded so warmly to their breasts. Never. The Wise Men have a point and you can't deny it.'

Smiley had taken off his spectacles and was polishing them on the thick end of his tie. By the pale light now breaking through the curtains, his plump face looked moist and undefended.

'Vladimir was one of the best agents we ever had,' Smiley said baldly.

'Because he was yours, you mean?' Strickland sneered, behind Smiley's back.

'Because he was good!' Smiley snapped, and there was a startled silence everywhere, while he recovered himself. 'Vladimir's father was an Estonian and a passionate Bolshevik, Oliver,' he resumed in a calmer voice. 'A professional man, a lawyer. Stalin rewarded his loyalty by murdering him in the purges. Vladimir was born Voldemar but he even changed his name to Vladimir out of allegiance to Moscow and the Revolution. He still wanted to believe, despite what they had done to his father. He joined the Red Army and by God's grace missed being purged as well. The war promoted him, he fought like a lion, and when it was over, he waited for the great Russian liberalisation that he had been dreaming of, and the freeing of his own people. It never came. Instead, he witnessed the ruthless repression of his homeland by the government he had served. Scores of thousands of his fellow Estonians went to the camps, several of his own relatives among them.'

Lacon opened his mouth to interrupt, but wisely closed it. 'The lucky ones escaped to Sweden and Germany. We're talking of a population of a million sober, hardworking people, cut to bits. One night, in despair, he offered us his services. Us, the British. In Moscow. For three years after that he spied for us from the very heart of the capital. Risked everything for us, every day.'

'And needless to say, our George here ran him,' Strickland growled, still somehow trying to suggest that this very fact put Smiley out of court. But Smiley would not be stopped. At his feet, young Mostyn was listening in a kind of trance.

'We even gave him a medal, if you remember, Oliver. Not to wear or to

592    John le Carré

possess, of course. But somewhere, on a bit of parchment that he was occasionally allowed to look at, there was a signature very like the Monarch's.'

'George, this is history,' Lacon protested weakly. 'This is not *today*.'

'For three long years, Vladimir was the best source we ever had on Soviet capabilities and intentions – and at the height of the cold war. He was close to their intelligence community and reported on that too. Then one day on a service visit to Paris, he took his chance and jumped, and thank God he did, because otherwise he'd have been shot a great deal sooner.'

Lacon was suddenly quite lost. 'What *do* you mean?' he asked. 'How *sooner*? What are you saying now?'

'I mean that in those days the Circus was largely run by a Moscow Centre agent,' Smiley replied with deadly patience. 'It was the sheerest luck that Bill Haydon happened to be stationed abroad while Vladimir was working for us. Another three months and Bill would have blown him sky-high.'

Lacon found nothing to say at all, so Strickland filled in for him.

'Bill Haydon this, Bill Haydon that,' he sneered. 'Just because you had the extra involvement with him –' He was going to continue but thought better of it. 'Haydon's dead, damn it,' he ended sullenly, 'so's that whole era.'

'And so is Vladimir,' said Smiley quietly, and once again there was a halt in the proceedings.

'George,' Lacon intoned gravely, as if he had belatedly found his place in the prayer book. 'We are *pragmatists*, George. We *adapt*. We are *not* keepers of some sacred flame. I ask you, I commmend you, to remember this!'

Quiet but resolute, Smiley had not quite finished the old man's obituary, and perhaps he sensed already that it was the only one he was ever going to get.

'And when he did come out, all right, he was a declining asset, as all ex-agents are,' he continued.

'I'll say,' said Strickland *sotto voce*.

'He stayed on in Paris and threw himself whole-heartedly into the Baltic independence movement. All right, it was a lost cause. It so happens that to this very day, the British have refused *de jure* recognition to the Soviet annexation of the three Baltic States – but never mind that either. Estonia, you may not know, Oliver, maintains a perfectly respectable Legation and Consulate General in Queen's Gate. We don't mind supporting lost causes once they're fully lost, apparently. Not before.' He drew a sharp breath. 'And all right, in Paris he formed a Baltic Group, and the Group went downhill, as émigré groups and lost causes always will – let me go on, Oliver, I'm not often long!'

'My dear fellow,' said Lacon, and blushed. 'Be as long as you like,' he said, quelling another groan from Strickland.

'His Group split up, there were quarrels. Vladimir was in a hurry and wanted to bring all the factions under one hat. The factions had their vested interests and didn't agree. There was a pitched battle, some heads got broken and the French threw him out. We moved him to London with a couple of his lieutenants. Vladimir in his old age returned to the Lutheran religion of his forefathers, exchanging the Marxist Soviet for the Christian Messiah. We're supposed to encourage that too, I believe. Or perhaps that is not policy any more. He has now been murdered. Since we are talking background, that is Vladimir's. Now why am I here?'

The ringing of the bell could not have been more timely. Lacon was still quite pink, and Smiley, breathing heavily, was once more polishing his spectacles. Reverently, Mostyn the acolyte unchained the door and admitted a tall motor-cycle messenger dangling a bunch of keys in his gloved hand. Reverently, Mostyn bore the keys to Strickland, who signed for them and made an entry in his log. The messenger, after a long and even doting glance at Smiley, departed, leaving Smiley with the guilty feeling that he should have recognised him even under all his paraphernalia. But Smiley had more pressing insights to concern him. With no reverence at all, Strickland dumped the keys into Lacon's open palm.

'All right, Mostyn, tell him!' Lacon boomed suddenly. 'Tell him in your own words.'

# FIVE

Mostyn sat with a quite particular stillness. He spoke softly. To hear him, Lacon had withdrawn to a corner, and bunched his hands judicially under his nose. But Strickland had sat himself bolt upright and seemed, like Mostyn himself, to be patrolling the boy's words for lapses.

'Vladimir telephoned the Circus at lunch-time today, sir,' Mostyn began, leaving some unclarity as to which 'sir' he was addressing. 'I happened to be Oddbins duty officer and took the call.'

Strickland corrected him with unpleasant haste: 'You mean *yesterday*. Be precise, can't you?'

'I'm sorry, sir. Yesterday,' said Mostyn.

'Well, get it right,' Strickland warned.

To be Oddbins duty officer, Mostyn explained, meant little more than covering the lunch-hour gap and checking desks and wastebins at closing time. Oddbins personnel were too junior for night duty, so there was just this roster for lunch-times and evenings.

And Vladimir, he repeated, came through in the lunch-hour, using the lifeline.

'*Lifeline?*' Smiley repeated in bewilderment. 'I don't think I quite know what you mean.'

'It's the system we have for keeping in touch with dead agents, sir,' said Mostyn, then put his fingers to his temple and muttered, 'Oh, my Lord.' He started again: 'I mean agents who have run their course but are still on the welfare roll, sir,' said Mostyn unhappily.

'So he rang and you took the call,' said Smiley kindly. 'What time was that?'

'One-fifteen exactly, sir. Oddbins is like a sort of Fleet Street news-room, you see. There are these twelve desks and there's the section head's hen-coop at the end, with a glass partition between us and him. The lifeline's in a locked box and normally it's the section head who keeps the key. But in the lunch-hour he gives it to the duty dog. I unlocked the box and heard this foreign voice saying "Hullo."'

'Get on with it, Mostyn,' Strickland growled.

'I said "Hullo" back, Mr. Smiley. That's all we do. We don't give the number. He said. "This is Gregory calling for Max. I have something very urgent for him. Please get me Max immediately." I asked him where he was calling from, which is routine, but he just said he had plenty of change. We have no brief to trace incoming calls, and anyway it takes too long. There's an electric card selector by the lifeline, it's got all the worknames on it. I told him to hold on and typed out "Gregory." That's the next thing we do after asking where they're calling from. Up it came on the selector. "Gregory equals Vladimir, ex-agent, ex-Soviet General, ex-leader of the Riga Group." Then the file reference. I typed out "Max" and found you, sir.' Smiley gave a small nod. '"Max equals Smiley." Then I typed out "Riga Group" and realised you were their last vicar, sir.'

'Their *vicar*?' said Lacon, as if he had detected heresy. 'Smiley their last *vicar*, Mostyn? What on earth –'

'I thought you had heard all this, Oliver,' Smiley said, to cut him off.

'Only the essence,' Lacon retorted. 'In a crisis one deals only with essentials.'

In his pressed-down Scottish, without letting Mostyn from his sight, Strickland provided Lacon with the required explanation: 'Organisations such as the Group had by tradition two case officers. The postman, who did the nuts and bolts for them, and the vicar who stood above the fight. Their father figure,' he said, and nodded perfunctorily towards Smiley.

'And who was carded as his most recent postman, Mostyn?' Smiley asked, ignoring Strickland entirely.

'Esterhase, sir. Workname Hector.'

'And he didn't ask for him?' said Smiley to Mostyn, speaking straight past Strickland yet again.

'I'm sorry, sir?'

'Vladimir didn't ask for Hector? His postman? He asked for me. Max. Only Max. You're sure of that?'

'He wanted you and nobody else, sir,' said Mostyn earnestly.

'Did you make notes?'

'The lifeline is taped automatically, sir. It's also linked to a speaking clock, so that we get the exact timing as well.'

'Damn you, Mostyn, that's a confidential matter,' Strickland snapped. 'Mr. Smiley may be a distinguished ex-member, but he's no longer family.'

'So what did you do next, Mostyn?' Smiley asked.

'Standing instructions gave me very little latitude, sir,' Mostyn replied, showing once again, like Smiley, a studied disregard for Strickland. 'Both "Smiley" and "Esterhase" were wait-listed, which meant that they could be contacted only through the fifth floor. My section head was out to lunch and not due back till two-fifteen.' He gave a light shrug. 'I stalled. I told him to try again at two-thirty.'

Smiley turned to Strickland. 'I thought you said that all the émigré files had been consigned to special keeping?'

'Correct.'

'Shouldn't there have been something on the selector card to that effect?'

'There should and there wasn't,' Strickland said.

'That is just the point, sir,' Mostyn agreed, talking only to Smiley.

'At that stage there was no suggestion that Vladimir or his Group was out of bounds. From the card, he looked just like any other pensioned-off agent raising a wind. I assumed he wanted a bit of money, or company, or something. We get quite a few of those. Leave him to the section head, I thought.'

'Who shall remain nameless, Mostyn,' Strickland said. 'Remember that.'

It crossed Smiley's mind at this point that the reticence in Mostyn – his air of distastefully stepping round some dangerous secret all the time he spoke – might have something to do with protecting a negligent superior. But Mostyn's next words put paid to this, for he went out of his way to imply that his superior was at fault.

'The trouble was, my section head didn't get back from lunch till three-fifteen, so that when Vladimir rang in at two-thirty, I had to put him off again. He was furious,' said Mostyn. 'Vladimir was, I mean. I asked whether there was anything I could do in the meantime and he said, "Find Max. Just find me Max. Tell Max I have been in touch with certain friends, also through friends with neighbours." There were a couple of notes on the card about his word code and I saw that "neighbour" meant Soviet Intelligence.'

A mandarin impassivity had descended over Smiley's face. The earlier emotion was quite gone.

'All of which you duly reported to your section head at three-fifteen?'

'Yes, sir.'

'Did you play him the tape?'

'He hadn't time to hear it,' said Mostyn mercilessly. 'He had to leave straight away for a long weekend.'

The stubborn brevity in Mostyn was now so strong that Strickland apparently felt obliged to fill the gaps.

'Yes, well, there's no question but that if we're looking for scapegoats, George, that section head of Mostyn's made a monumental fool of himself, no question at all,' Strickland declared brightly. 'He omitted to send for Vladimir's papers – which would not, of course, have been forthcoming. He omitted to acquaint himself with standing orders on the handling of émigrés. He also appears to have succumbed to a severe dose of weekend fever, leaving no word of his whereabouts should he be required. God help him on Monday morning, says I. Oh, yes. Come Mostyn, we're waiting, boy.'

Mostyn obediently took back the story. Vladimir rang for the third and last time at three-forty-three, sir, he said, speaking even more slowly than before. It should have been quarter to four, but he jumped the gun by two minutes. Mostyn had by then a rudimentary brief from his section head, which he now repeated to Smiley: 'He called it a bromide job. I was to find out what, if anything, the old boy really wanted and, if all else failed, make a rendezvous with him to cool him down. I was to give him a drink, sir, pat him on the back, and promise nothing except to pass on whatever message he brought me.'

'And the "neighbours"?' Smiley asked. 'They were not an issue to your section head?'

'He rather thought that was just a bit of agent's histrionics, sir.'

'I see. Yes, I see.' Yet his eyes, in contradiction, closed completely for a moment. 'So how did the dialogue with Vladimir go this third time?'

'According to Vladimir, it was to be an immediate meeting or nothing, sir. I tried out the alternatives on him as instructed – "Write us a letter – is it money you want? Surely it can wait till Monday" – but by then he was shouting at me down the phone. "A meeting or nothing. Tonight or nothing. Moscow Rules. I insist Moscow Rules. Tell this to Max —"'

Interrupting himself, Mostyn lifted his head and with unblinking eyes returned Lauder Strickland's hostile stare.

'Tell *what* to Max?' said Smiley, his gaze moving swiftly from one to the other of them.

'We were speaking French, sir. The card said French was his preferred second language and I'm only Grade B in Russian.'

'Irrelevant,' Strickland snapped.

'Tell *what* to Max?' Smiley persisted.

Mostyn's eyes searched out a spot on the floor a yard or two beyond his own feet: 'He meant: Tell Max I insist it's Moscow Rules.'

Lacon, who had stayed uncharacteristically quiet these last minutes, now chimed in: 'There's an important point here, George. The Circus were not the suitors here. *He* was. The ex-agent. He was doing *all* the pressing, making *all* the running. If he'd accepted our suggestion, written out his information, none of this need ever have happened. He brought it on himself entirely. George, I insist you take the point!'

Strickland was lighting himself a fresh cigarette.

'Whoever heard of Moscow Rules in the middle of bloody Hampstead anyway?' Strickland asked, waving out the match.

'Bloody Hampstead is right,' Smiley said quietly.

'Mostyn, wrap the story up,' Lacon commanded, blushing scarlet.

They had agreed a time, Mostyn resumed woodenly, now staring at his left palm as if he were reading his own fortune in it: 'Ten-twenty, sir.'

They had agreed Moscow Rules, he said, and the usual contact procedures, which Mostyn had established earlier in the afternoon by consulting the Oddbins encounter index.

'And what *were* the contact procedures exactly?' Smiley asked.

'A copy-book rendezvous, sir,' Mostyn replied. 'The Sarratt training course all over again, sir.'

Smiley felt suddenly crowded by the intimacy of Mostyn's respectfulness. He did not wish to be this boy's hero, or to be caressed by his voice, his gaze, his 'sirs.' He was not prepared for the claustrophobic admiration of this stranger.

'There's a tin pavilion on Hampstead Heath, ten minutes' walk from East Heath Road, overlooking a games field on the south side of the avenue, sir. The safety signal was one new drawing-pin shoved high in the wood support on the left as you entered.'

'And the counter-signal?' Smiley asked.

But he knew the answer already.

'A yellow chalk line,' said Mostyn. 'I gather yellow was the sort of Group trade mark from the old days.' He had adopted a tone of ending. 'I put up the pin and came back here and waited. When he didn't show up, I thought, "Well, if he's secrecy-mad I'll have to go up to the hut again and check out his counter-signal, then I'll know whether he's around and proposes to try the fallback."'

'Which was what?'

'A car pick-up near Swiss Cottage underground at eleven-forty, sir. I was about to go out and take a look when Mr. Strickland rang through and ordered me to sit tight until further orders.' Smiley assumed he had finished but this was not quite true. Seeming to forget everyone but himself, Mostyn slowly shook his handsome head. 'I never met him,' he said, in amazement. 'He was my first agent, I never met him, I'll never know what he was trying to tell me,' he said. 'My first agent, and he's dead. It's incredible. I feel like a complete Jonah.' His head continued shaking long after he had finished speaking.

Lacon added a brisk postscript: 'Yes, well, Scotland Yard has a computer these days, George. The Heath Patrol found the body and cordoned off the area and the moment the name was fed into the computer a light came up or a lot of digits or something, and immediately they knew he was on our special watch list. From then on it went like clockwork. The Commissioner phoned the Home Office, the Home Office phoned the Circus –'

'And you phoned me,' said Smiley. 'Why, Oliver? Who suggested you bring me in on this?'

'George, does it matter?'

'Enderby?'

'If you insist, yes, it was Saul Enderby. George, listen to me.'

It was Lacon's moment at last. The issue, whatever it might be, was before them, circumscribed if not yet actually defined. Mostyn was forgotten. Lacon was standing confidently over Smiley's seated figure and had assumed the rights of an old friend.

'George, as things can stand, I can go to the Wise Men and say: "I have investigated and the Circus's hands are clean." I can say that. "The Circus gave no encouragement to these people, nor to their leader. For a whole year they have neither paid nor welfared him!" Perfectly honestly. They don't own his flat, his car, they don't pay his rent, educate his bastards, send flowers to his mistress or have any other of the old – and lamentable – connections with him or his kind. His only link was with the past. His case officers have left the stage for good – yourself and Esterhase, both old 'uns, both off the books. I can say that with my hand on my breast. To the Wise Men, and if necessary to my Minister personally.'

'I don't follow you,' Smiley said with deliberate obtuseness. 'Vladimir was our agent. He was trying to tell us something.'

'Our *ex*-agent, George. How do we *know* he was trying to tell us something? We gave him no *brief*. He spoke of urgency – even of Soviet Intelligence – so do a lot of ex-agents when they're holding out their caps for a subsidy!'

'Not Vladimir,' Smiley said.

But sophistry was Lacon's element. He was born to it, he breathed it, he could fly and swim in it, nobody in Whitehall was better at it.

'George, we cannot be held responsible for every ex-agent who takes an injudicious nocturnal walk in one of London's increasingly dangerous open spaces!' He held out his hands in appeal. 'George. What is it to be? Choose. *You* choose. On the one hand, Vladimir asked for a chat with you. Retired buddies – a chin-wag about old times – why not? And in order to raise a bit of wind, as any of us might, he pretended he had something for you. Some nugget of information. Why not? They all do it. On that basis my Minister will back us. No heads need roll, no tantrums, Cabinet hysteria. He will help us bury the case. Not a cover-up, naturally. But he will use his judgment. If I catch him in the right mood he may even decide that there is no point in troubling the Wise Men with it at all.'

'Amen,' Strickland echoed.

'On the other hand,' Lacon insisted, mustering all his persuasiveness for the kill, 'if things were to come unstuck, George, and the Minister got it into his head that we were engaging his good offices in order to clean up the traces of some unlicensed adventure which has aborted' – he was striding again, skirting an imaginary quagmire – 'and there was a scandal, George, and the Circus were proved to be currently involved – your old service, George, one you still love, I am sure – with a notoriously revanchist émigré outfit – volatile, talkative, violently anti-détente – with all manner of anachronistic fixations – a total hangover from the worst days of the cold war – the very archetype of everything our masters have told us to avoid' – he had reached his corner again, a little outside the circle of light – 'and there had been a death, George – and an attempted cover-up, as they would no doubt call it – with all the attendant publicity – well, it could be just one scandal too many. The service is a weak child still, George, a sickly one, and in the hands of these new people desperately delicate. At this stage in its rebirth, it could die of the common cold. If it does, your generation will not be least to blame. You have a duty, as well as we all do. A loyalty.'

Duty to *what*? Smiley wondered, with that part of himself which sometimes seemed to be a spectator to the rest. Loyalty to *whom*? 'There is no loyalty without betrayal,' Ann liked to tell him in their youth when he had ventured to protest at her infidelities.

For a time nobody spoke.

'And the weapon?' Smiley asked finally, in the tone of someone testing a theory. 'How do you account for that, Oliver?'

'What weapon? There was no weapon. He was shot. By his own buddies most likely, knowing their cabals. Not to mention his appetite for other people's wives.'

'Yes, he was shot,' Smiley agreed. 'In the face. At extremely close range. With a soft-nosed bullet. And cursorily searched. Had his wallet taken. That is the police diagnosis. But our diagnosis would be different, wouldn't it, Lauder?'

'No way,' said Strickland, glowering at him through a cloud of cigarette smoke.

'Well mine would.'

'Then let's hear it, George,' said Lacon handsomely.

'The weapon used to kill Vladimir was a standard Moscow Centre assassination device,' Smiley said. 'Concealed in a camera, a brief-case, or whatever. A soft-nosed bullet is fired at point-blank range. To obliterate, to punish, and to discourage others. If I remember rightly they even had one on display at Sarratt in the black museum next to the bar.'

'They still have. It's horrific,' said Mostyn.

Strickland vouchsafed Mostyn a foul glance.

'But George!' Lacon cried.

Smiley waited, knowing that in this mood, Lacon could swear away Big Ben.

'These people – these émigrés – of whom this poor chap was one – don't they *come* from Russia? Haven't half of them been in *touch* with Moscow Centre – with or without our knowledge? A weapon like that – I'm not saying you're right, of course – a weapon like that, in their world, could be as common as cheese!'

Against stupidity, the gods themselves fight in vain, thought Smiley: but

Schiller had forgotten the bureaucrats. Lacon was addressing Strickland.

'Lauder. There is the question of the D-Notice to the press outstanding.' It was an order. 'Perhaps you would have another shot at them, see how far it's got.'

In his stockinged feet, Strickland obediently padded down the room and dialled a number.

'Mostyn, perhaps you should take these things out to the kitchen. We don't want to leave needless traces, do we?'

With Mostyn also dismissed, Smiley and Lacon were suddenly alone.

'It's a yes or no, George,' Lacon said. 'There's cleaning up to be done. Explanations to be given to tradesmen, who do I know? Mail. Milk. Friends. Whatever such people have. No one knows the course as you do. No one. The police have promised you a head start. They will not be dilatory but they will observe a certain measured order about things and let routine play its part.' With a nervous bound Lacon approached Smiley's chair and sat awkwardly on the arm. 'George. You were their vicar. Very well, I'm asking you to go and read the Office. He wanted *you*, George. Not us. You.'

From his old place at the telephone, Strickland interrupted: 'They're asking for a signature for that D-Notice, Oliver. They'd like it to be yours, if it's all the same to you.'

'Why not the Chief's?' Lacon demanded warily.

'Seem to think yours will carry a spot more weight, I fancy.'

'Ask him to hold a moment,' Lacon said, and with a windmill gesture drove a fist into his pocket: 'I may give you the keys, George?' He dangled them in front of Smiley's face. 'On terms. Right?' The keys still dangled. Smiley stared at them and perhaps he asked 'What terms?' or perhaps he just stared; he wasn't really in a mood for conversation. His mind was on Mostyn, and missing cigarettes; on phone calls about neighbours; on agents with no faces; on sleep. Lacon was counting, He attached great merit to numbering his paragraphs. 'One, that you are a private citizen, Vladimir's Executor, not ours. Two, that you are of the past, not the present, and conduct yourself accordingly. The *sanitised* past. That you will pour oil on the waters, not muddy them. That you will suppress your old professional interest in him, naturally, for that means ours. On those terms may I give you the keys? Yes? No?'

Mostyn was standing in the kitchen doorway. He was addressing Lacon, but his earnest eyes veered constantly towards Smiley.

'What is it, Mostyn?' Lacon demanded. 'Be quick!'

'I just remembered a note on Vladimir's card, sir. He had a wife in Tallinn. I wondered whether she should be informed. I just thought I'd better mention it.'

'The card is once more not accurate,' said Smiley, returning Mostyn's gaze. 'She was with him in Moscow when he defected, she was arrested and taken to a forced labour camp. She died there.'

'Mr. Smiley must do whatever he thinks fit about such things,' Lacon said swiftly, anxious to avoid a fresh outbreak, and dropped the keys into Smiley's passive palm. Suddenly everything was in movement. Smiley was on his feet, Lacon was already half-way down the room and Strickland was holding out the phone to him. Mostyn had slipped to the darkened hallway and was unhooking Smiley's raincoat from the stand.

'What else did Vladimir say to you on the telephone, Mostyn?' Smiley asked quietly, dropping one arm into the sleeve.

'He said, "Tell Max that it concerns the Sandman. Tell him I have two proofs and can bring them with me. Then perhaps he will see me." He said it twice. It was on the tape but Strickland erased it.'

'Do you know what Vladimir meant by that? Keep your voice down.'

'No, sir.'

'Nothing on the card?'

'No, sir.'

'Do _they_ know what he meant?' Smiley asked, tilting his head swiftly towards Strickland and Lacon.

'I think Strickland may. I'm not sure.'

'Did Vladimir really not ask for Esterhase?'

'No, sir.'

Lacon was finishing on the phone. Strickland took back the receiver from him and spoke into it himself. Seeing Smiley at the door, Lacon bounded down the room to him.

'George! Good man! Fare you well! Listen, I want to talk to you about marriage some time . A seminar with no holds barred. I'm counting on you to tell me the art of it, George!'

'Yes. We must get together,' Smiley said.

Looking down, he saw that Lacon was shaking his hand.

A bizarre postscript to this meeting confounds its conspiratorial purpose. Standard Circus tradecraft requires that hidden microphones be installed in safe houses. Agents in their strange way accept this, even though they are not informed of it, even though their case officers go through motions of taking notes. For his rendezvous with Vladimir, Mostyn had quite properly switched on the system in anticipation of the old man's arrival, and nobody, in the subsequent panic, thought to turn it off. Routine procedures brought the tapes to transcriber section, who in good faith put out several texts for the general Circus reader. The luckless head of Oddbins got a copy, so did the Secretariat, so did the heads of Personnel, Operations and Finance. It was not till a copy landed in Lauder Strickland's in-tray that the explosion occurred and the innocent recipients were sworn to secrecy under all manner of dreadful threats. The tape is perfect. Lacon's restless pacing is there, so are Strickland's _sotto voce_ asides, some of them obscene. Only Mostyn's flustered confessions in the hall escaped.

As to Mostyn himself, he played no further part in the affair. He resigned of his own accord a few months later, part of the wastage rate that gets everyone so worried these days.

# SIX

The same uncertain light that greeted Smiley as he stepped gratefully out of the safe flat into the fresh air of that Hampstead morning greeted Ostrakova also, though the Paris autumn was further on, and only a few leaves clung like old dusters to the plane trees. Like Smiley's too, her night had not been restful. She had risen in the dark and dressed with care, and she had deliberated, since the morning looked colder, whether this was the day on which to get out her winter boots, because the draught in the warehouse could be cruel and affected her legs the most. Still undecided, she had fished them out of the cupboard and wiped them down, and even polished them, but she still had not been able to make up her mind whether to wear them or not. Which was how it always went with her when she had one big problem to grapple with: the small ones became impossible. She knew all the signs, she could feel them coming on, but there was nothing she could do. She would mislay her purse, botch her book-keeping at the warehouse, lock herself out of the flat and have to fetch the old fool of a concierge, Madame la Pierre, who pecked and snuffled like a goat in a nettle patch. She could quite easily, when the mood was on her, after fifteen years of taking the same route, catch the wrong bus and finish up, furious, in a strange neighbourhood. Pulling on the boots, finally – muttering to herself 'old fool, cretin,' and the like – and, carrying the heavy shopping bag that she had prepared the previous night, she set off along her usual route, passing her three usual shops and neglecting to enter any of them, while she tried to work out whether or not she was going off her head.

*I am mad. I am not mad. Somebody is trying to kill me, somebody is trying to protect me. I am safe. I am in mortal danger.* Back and forth.

In the four weeks since she had received her little Estonian confessor, Ostrakova had been aware of many changes in herself and for most of them she was not at all ungrateful. Whether she had fallen in love with him was neither here nor there: his appearance was timely, and the privacy in him had revived her sense of opposition at a moment when it was in danger of going out. He had rekindled her, and there was enough of the alley cat in him to remind her of Glikman and other men as well; she had never been particularly continent. And since, on top of this, she thought, the magician is a man of looks, and knows women, and steps into my life armed with a picture of my oppressor and the determination, apparently, to eliminate him – why then, it would be positively indecent, lonely old fool that I am, if I did *not* fall in love with him on the spot!

But it was his gravity which had impressed her even more than his magic. 'You must not *decorate*,' he had told her, with uncharacteristic sharpness, when for the sake of entertainment or variety she had allowed herself to deviate just a little from the version she had written to the General. 'Merely because you yourself feel more at ease, do not make the mistake of supposing that the danger is over.'

She had promised to improve herself.

'The danger is absolute,' he had told her as he left. 'It is not yours to make greater or make less.'

People had talked to her about danger before, but when the magician talked about it, she believed him.

'Danger to my daughter?' she had asked. 'Danger to Alexandra?'

'Your daughter plays no part in this. You may be sure she knows nothing of what is going on.'

'Then danger to whom?'

'Danger to all of us who have knowledge of this matter,' he had replied, as she happily conceded, in the doorway, to their one embrace. 'Danger most of all to you.'

And now, for the last three days – or was it two? or was it ten? – Ostrakova swore she had seen the danger gather round her like an army of shadows at her own deathbed. The danger that was absolute; that was not hers to make greater or less. And she saw it again this Saturday morning as she clumped along in her polished winter boots, swinging the heavy shopping bag at her side: the same two men, pursuing her, the weekend notwithstanding. Hard men. Harder than the gingery man. Men who sit about at headquarters listening to the interrogations. And never speak a word. The one was walking five metres behind her, the other was keeping abreast of her across the street, at this moment passing the doorway of that vagabond Mercier the chandler, whose red-and-green awning hung so low it was a danger even to someone of Ostrakova's humble height.

She had decided, when she had first allowed herself to notice them, that they were the General's men. That was Monday, or was it Friday? General Vladimir has turned out his bodyguard for me, she thought with much amusement, and for a dangerous morning she plotted the friendly gestures she would make to them in order to express her gratitude: the smiles of complicity she would vouchsafe to them when there was nobody else looking; even the *soupe* she would prepare and take to them, to help them while away their vigil in the doorways. Two hulking great bodyguards, she had thought, just for one lady! Ostrakov had been right: that General was a man! On the second day she decided they were not there at all, and that her desire to appoint such men was merely an extension of her desire to be reunited with the magician: I am looking for links to him, she thought; just as I have not yet brought myself to wash up the glass from which he drank his vodka, or to puff up the cushions where he sat and lectured me on danger.

But on the third – or was it the fifth? – day she took a different and harsher view of her supposed protectors. She stopped playing the little girl. On whichever day it was, leaving her apartment early in order to check a particular consignment to the warehouse, she had stepped out of the sanctuary of her abstractions straight into the streets of Moscow, as she had too often known them in her years with Glikman. The ill-lit, cobbled street was empty but for one black car parked twenty metres from her doorway. Most likely it had arrived that minute. She had a notion, afterwards, of having seen it pull up, presumably in order to deliver the sentries to their beat. Pull up sharply, just as she came out. And douse its headlights. Resolutely she had begun walking down the pavement. 'Danger most of all to *you*,' she kept remembering; 'danger to all of us who know.'

The car was following her.

They think I am a whore, she thought vainly, one of those old ones who work the early-morning market.

Suddenly her one aim had been to get inside a church. Any church. The nearest Russian Orthodox church was twenty minutes away, and so small that to pray in it at all was like a séance; the very proximity of the Holy Family offered a forgiveness by itself. But twenty minutes was a lifetime. Non-

Orthodox churches she eschewed, as a rule, entirely – they were a betrayal of her nationhood. That morning, however, with the car crawling along behind her, she had suspended her prejudice and ducked into the very first church she came to, which turned out to be not merely Catholic, but *modern* Catholic as well, so that she heard the whole Mass twice through in bad French, read by a worker-priest who smelt of garlic and worse. But by the time she left, the men were nowhere to be seen and that was all that mattered – even though when she arrived at the warehouse she had to promise them two extra hours to make up for the inconvenience she had caused them by her lateness.

Then for three days nothing, or was it five? Ostrakova had become as incapable of hoarding time as money. Three or five, they had gone, they had never existed. It was all her 'decoration,' as the magician had called it, her stupid habit of seeing too much, looking too many people in the eye, inventing too much incident. Till today again, when they were back. Except that today was about fifty thousand times worse, because today was *now*, and the street today was as empty as on the Last Day or the First, and the man who was five metres behind her was drawing closer, and the man who had been under Mercier's outrageously dangerous awning was crossing the street to join him.

What happened next, in such descriptions or imaginings as had come Ostrakova's way, was supposed to happen in a flash. One minute you were upright, walking down the pavement, the next, with a flurry of lights and a wailing of horns, you were wafted to the operating table surrounded by surgeons in various-coloured masks. Or you were in Heaven, before the Almighty, mumbling excuses about certain lapses which you did not really regret; and neither – if you understood Him at all – did He. Or worst of all, you came round, and were returned, as walking wounded, to your apartment, and your boring half-sister Valentina dropped everything, with an extremely ill grace, in order to come up from Lyons and be a non-stop scold at your bedside.

Not one of these expectations was fulfilled.

What happened took place with the slowness of an under-water ballet. The man who was gaining on her drew alongside her, taking the right, or inside position. At the same moment, the man who had crossed the road from Mercier's camp came up on her left, walking not on the pavement, but in the gutter, incidentally splashing her with yesterday's rain-water as he strode along. With her final habit of looking into people's eyes Ostrakova stared at her two unwished-for companions and saw faces she had already recognised and knew by heart. They had hunted Ostrakov, they had murdered Glikman, and in her personal view they had been murdering the entire Russian people for centuries, whether in the name of the Czar, or God, or Lenin. Looking away from them, she saw the black car which had followed her on her way to church, heading slowly down the empty road towards her. Therefore she did exactly what she had planned to do all night through, what she had lain awake picturing. In her shopping bag she had put an old flat-iron, a bit of junk that Ostrakov had acquired in the days when the poor dying man had fancied he might make a few extra francs by dealing in antiques. Her shopping bag was of leather – green and brown in a patchwork – and stout. Drawing it back, she swung it round her with all her strength at the man in the gutter – at his groin, the hated centre of him. He swore – she could not hear in which language – and crumpled to his knees. Here her plan went adrift. She had not expected a villain on either side of her, and she needed time to recover her own balance and get the iron swinging at the second man. He did not allow her to do this. Throwing his arms round both of hers, he gathered her together like the fat sack she was, and lifted her clean off her feet. She saw the bag fall and heard the chime as the flat-iron slipped from it onto a drain cover. Still looking down, she saw her boots dangling ten centimetres from the ground, as if she had hanged herself like her brother Niki – his feet, exactly, turned into each other like a simpleton's. She noticed that one of her toe-caps, the left, was already scratched in the scuffle. Her assailant's arms now locked themselves even harder across her breast and she wondered whether her ribs would crack before she suffocated. She felt him draw her back, and she presumed that he was shaping to swing her into the car, which was now approaching at a good speed down the road: that she was being kidnapped. This notion terrified her. Nothing, least of all death, was as appalling to her at that moment as the thought that these pigs would take her back to Russia and subject her to the kind of slow, doctrinal prison death which she was certain had killed Glikman. She struggled with all her force, she managed to bite his hand. She saw a couple of bystanders who seemed as scared as she was. Then she realised that the car was not slowing down, and that the men had something quite different in mind: not to kidnap her at all, but to kill her.

He threw her.

She reeled but did not fall, and as the car swerved to knock her down, she thanked God and all His angels that she had, after all, decided on the winter boots, because the front bumper hit her at the back of the shins, and when she saw her feet again, they were straight up in front of her face, and her bare thighs were parted as for childbirth. She flew for a while, then hit the road with everything at once – with her head, her spine and her heels – then rolled like a sausage over the cobbles. The car had passed her but she heard it screech to a stop and wondered whether they were going to reverse and drive over her again. She tried to move but felt too sleepy. She heard voices and car doors slamming, she heard the engine roaring, and fading, so that either it was going away or she was losing her hearing.

'Don't touch her,' someone said.

No, *don't*, she thought.

'It's a lack of oxygen,' she heard herself say. 'Lift me to my feet and I'll be all right.'

Why on earth did she say that? Or did she only think it?

'*Aubergines*,' she said. 'Get the *aubergines*.' She didn't know whether she was talking about her shopping, or the female traffic wardens for whom aubergine was the Paris slang.

Then a pair of woman's hands put a blanket over her, and a furious Gallic argument started about what one did next. Did anyone get the number? she wanted to ask. But she was really too sleepy to bother, and besides she had no oxygen – the fall had taken it out of her body for good. She had a vision of half-shot birds she had seen in the Russian countryside, flapping helplessly on the ground, waiting for the dogs to reach them. General, she thought, did you get my second letter? Drifting off, she willed him, begged him to read it, and to respond to its entreaty. General, read my second letter.

She had written it a week before in a moment of despair. She had posted it yesterday in another.

# SEVEN

There are Victorian terraces in the region of Paddington Station that are painted as white as luxury liners on the outside, and inside are dark as tombs. Westbourne Terrace that Saturday morning gleamed as brightly as any of them, but the service road that led to Vladimir's part of it was blocked at one end by a heap of rotting mattresses, and by a smashed boom, like a frontier post, at the other.

'Thank you, I'll get out here,' said Smiley politely, and paid the cab off at the mattresses.

He had come straight from Hampstead and his knees ached. The Greek driver had spent the journey lecturing him on Cyprus, and out of courtesy he had crouched on the jump seat in order to hear him over the din of the engine. Vladimir, we should have done better by you, he thought, surveying the filth on the pavements, the poor washing trailing from the balconies. The Circus should have shown more honour to its vertical man.

*It concerns the Sandman,* he thought. *Tell him I have two proofs and can bring them with me.*

He walked slowly, knowing that early morning is a better time of day to come out of a building than go into it. A small queue had gathered at the bus-stop. A milkman was going his rounds, so was a newspaper boy. A squadron of grounded sea-gulls scavenged gracefully at the spilling dustbins. If sea-gulls are taking to the cities, he thought, will pigeons take to the sea? Crossing the service road, he saw a motor-cyclist with a black official-looking side-car parking his steed a hundred yards down the kerb. Something in the man's posture reminded him of the tall messenger who had brought the keys to the safe flat – a similar fixity, even at that distance; a respectful attentiveness, of an almost military kind.

Shedding chestnut trees darkened the pillared doorway, a scarred cat eyed him warily. The doorbell was the topmost of thirty but Smiley didn't press it and when he shoved the double doors they swung open too freely, revealing the same gloomy corridors painted very shiny to defeat graffiti writers, and the same linoleum staircase which squeaked like a hospital trolley. He remembered it all. Nothing had changed, and now nothing ever would. There was no light switch and the stairs grew darker the higher he climbed. Why didn't Vladimir's murderers steal his keys? he wondered, feeling them nudging against his hip with every step. Perhaps they didn't need them. Perhaps they had their own set already. He reached a landing and squeezed past a luxurious perambulator. He heard a dog howling and the morning news in German and the flushing of a communal lavatory. He heard a child screaming at its mother, then a slap and the father screaming at the child. *Tell Max it concerns the Sandman.* There was a smell of curry and cheap fat frying, and disinfectant. There was a smell of too many people with not much money jammed into too little air. He remembered that too, Nothing had changed.

If we'd treated him better, it would never have happened, Smiley thought. The neglected are too easily killed, he thought, in unconscious affinity with Ostrakova. He remembered the day they had brought him here, Smiley the vicar, Toby Esterhase the postman. They had driven to Heathrow to fetch him: Toby the fixer, dyed in all the oceans, as he would say of himself. Toby drove like the wind but they were almost late, even then. The plane had landed. They hurried to the barrier and there he was: silvered and majestic, towering stock-still in the temporary corridor from the arrivals bay, while the common peasants swept past him. He remembered their solemn embrace – 'Max, my old friend, it is really you?' 'It's me, Vladimir, they've put us together again.' He remembered Toby spiriting them through the large back alleys of the immigration service, because the enraged French police had confiscated the old boy's papers before throwing him out. He remembered how they had lunched at Scott's, all three of them, the old boy too animated even to drink but talking grandly of the future they all knew he didn't have: 'It will be Moscow all over again, Max. Maybe we even get a chance at the Sandman.' Next day they went flat-hunting, 'just to show you a few possibilities, General,' as Toby Esterhase had explained. It was Christmas time and the resettlement budget for the year was used up. Smiley appealed to Circus Finance. He lobbied Lacon and the Treasury for a supplementary estimate, but in vain. 'A dose of reality will bring him down to earth,' Lacon had pronounced. 'Use your influence with him, George. That's what you're there for.' Their first dose of reality was a tart's parlour in Kensington, their second overlooked a shunting yard near Waterloo. Westbourne Terrace was their third, and as they squeaked up these stairs, Toby leading, the old man had suddenly halted, and put back his great mottled head, and wrinkled his nose theatrically:

*Ah! So if I get hungry I have only to stand on the corridor and sniff and my hunger is gone!* he had announced in his thick French. *That way I don't have to eat for a week!*

By then even Vladimir had guessed they were putting him away for good.

Smiley returned to the present. The next landing was musical, he noticed, as he continued his solitary ascent. Through one door came rock music played at full blast, through another Sibelius and the smell of bacon. Peering out of the window he saw two men loitering between the chestnut trees who were not there when he had arrived. A team would do that, he thought. A team would post look-outs while the others went inside. Whose team was another question. Moscow's? The Superintendent's? Saul Enderby's? Farther down the road, the tall motor-cyclist had acquired a tabloid newspaper and was sitting on his bike reading it.

At Smiley's side a door opened and an old woman in a dressing gown came out holding a cat against her shoulder. He could smell last night's drink on her breath even before she spoke to him.

'Are you a burglar, dearie?' she asked.

'I'm afraid not,' Smiley replied with a laugh. 'Just a visitor.'

'Still, it's nice to be fancied, isn't it, dearie?' she said.

'It is indeed,' said Smiley politely.

The last flight was steep and very narrow and lit by real daylight from a wired skylight on the slant. There were two doors on the top landing, both closed, both very cramped. On one, a typed notice faced him: 'Mr. V. Miller, Translations.' Smiley remembered the argument about Vladimir's alias now he was to become a Londoner and keep his head down. 'Miller' was no problem. For some reason, the old boy found Miller rather grand. 'Miller, *c'est bien*,' he had declared. 'Miller I like, Max.' But 'Mr.' was anything but good. He pressed for General, then offered to settle for Colonel. But Smiley in his rôle as vicar was on this point unbudgeable: Mr. was a lot less trouble than a bogus rank in the wrong army, he had ruled.

He knocked boldly, knowing that a soft knock is more conspicuous than a loud one. He heard the echo, and nothing else. He heard no footfall, no sudden freezing of a sound. He called 'Vladimir' through the letter-box as though he were an old friend visiting. He tried one Yale from the bunch and it stuck, he tried another and it turned. He stepped inside and closed the door, waiting for something to hit him on the back of the head but preferring the thought of a broken skull to having his face shot off. He felt dizzy and realised he was holding his breath. The same white paint, he noticed; the same prison emptiness exactly. The same queer hush, like a phone box; the same mix of public smells.

This is where we stood, Smiley remembered – the three of us, that afternoon. Toby and myself like tugs, nudging at the old battleship between us. The estate agent's particulars had said 'penthouse.'

'Hopeless,' Toby Esterhase had announced in his Hungarian French, always the first to speak, as he turned to open the door and leave. 'I mean completely awful. I mean, I should have come and taken a look first, I was an idiot,' said Toby when Vladimir still didn't budge. 'General, please accept my apologies. This is a complete insult.'

Smiley added his own assurances. We can do better for you than this Vladi; much; we just have to persist.

But the old man's eyes were on the window, as Smiley's were now, on this dotty forest of chimney-pots and gables and slate roofs that flourished beyond the parapet. And suddenly he had thumped a gloved paw on Smiley's shoulder:

'Better you keep your money to shoot those swine in Moscow, Max,' he had advised.

With tears running down his cheeks, and the same determined smile, Vladimir had continued to stare at the Moscow chimneys; and at his fading dreams of ever again living under a Russian sky.

'*On reste ici,*' he had commanded finally, as if he were drawing up a last-ditch defence.

A tiny divan bed ran along one wall, a cooking ring stood on the sill. From the smell of putty Smiley guessed that the old man had kept whiting the place himself, painting out the damp and filling the cracks. On the table he used for typing and eating lay on old Remington upright and a pair of worn dictionaries. His translating work, he thought: the few extra pennies that fleshed out his pension. Pressing back his elbows as if he were having trouble with his spine, Smiley drew himself to his full if diminutive height and launched himself upon the familiar death rites of a departed spy. An Estonian Bible lay on the pine bedside locker. He probed it delicately for cut cavities then dangled it upside down for scraps of paper or photographs. Pulling open the locker drawer he found a bottle of patent pills for rejuvenating the sexually jaded and three Red Army gallantry medals mounted on a chrome bar. So much for cover, thought Smiley, wondering how on earth Vladimir and his many paramours had managed on such a tiny bed. A print of Martin Luther hung at the bedhead. Next to it, a coloured picture called the 'Red Roofs of Old Tallinn,' which Vladimir must have torn from something and backed on cardboard. A second picture showed 'The Kazari Coast,' a third 'Windmills and a Ruined Castle.' He delved behind each. The bedside light caught his eye. He tried the switch and when it didn't work he unplugged it, took out the bulb and fished in the wood base, but without result. Just a dead bulb he thought. A sudden shriek from outside sent him pulling back against the wall but when he had collected himself he realised it was more of those land-borne sea-gulls: a whole colony had settled round the chimney-pots. He glanced over the parapet into the street again. The two loiterers had gone. They're on their way up, he thought: my head start is over. They're not police at all, he thought; they're assassins. The motor-bike with its black side-car stood unattended. He closed the window, wondering whether there was a special Valhalla for dead spies where he and Vladimir would meet and he could put things right; telling himself he had lived a long life and that this moment was as good as any other for it to end. And not believing it for one second.

The table drawer contained sheets of plain paper, a stapler, a chewed pencil, some elastic bands and a recent quarterly telephone bill, unpaid, for the sum of seventy-eight pounds, which struck him as uncharacteristically high for Vladimir's frugal lifestyle. He opened the stapler and found nothing. He put the phone bill in his pocket to study later and kept searching, knowing it was not a real search at all, that a real search would take three men several days before they could say with certainty they had found whatever was to be found. If he was looking for anything in particular, then it was probably an address book or a diary or something which did duty for one, even if it was only a scrap of paper. He knew that sometimes old spies, even the best of them, were a little like old lovers; as age crept up on them, they began to cheat, out of fear that their powers were deserting them. They pretended they had it all in the memory, but in secret they were hanging on to their virility, in secret they wrote things down, often in some home-made code which, if they only knew it, could be unbuttoned in hours or minutes by anyone who knew the game. Names and addresses of contacts, sub-agents. Nothing was holy. Routines, times and places of meetings, worknames, phone numbers, even safe combinations written out as social-security numbers and birthdays. In his time Smiley had seen entire networks put at risk that way because one agent no longer dared to trust his head. He didn't believe Vladimir would have done that, but there was always a first time.

*Tell him I have two proofs and can bring them with me . . .*

He was standing in what the old man would have called his kitchen: the window-sill with the gas ring on it, the tiny home-made food-store with holes drilled for ventilation. We men who cook for ourselves are half creatures, he thought as he scanned the two shelves, tugged out the saucepan and the frying-pan, poked among the cayenne and paprika. Anywhere else in the house – even in bed – you can cut yourself off, read your books, deceive yourself that solitude is best. But in the kitchen the signs of incompleteness are too strident. Half of one black loaf. Half of one coarse sausage. Half an onion. Half a pint of milk. Half a lemon. Half a packet of black tea. Half a life. He opened anything that would open, he probed with his finger in the paprika. He found a loose tile and prised it free, he unscrewed the wooden handle of the frying-pan. About to pull open the clothes cupboard, he stopped as if listening again, but this time it was something he had seen that held him, not something he had heard.

On top of the food-store lay a whole parcel of Gauloises Caporal cigarettes, Vladimir's favourites when he couldn't get his Russians. Tipped, he noticed, reading the different legends. 'Duty free.' *'Filtre.'* Marked *'Exportation'* and 'Made in France.' Cellophane wrapped. He took them down. Of the ten original packets, one already missing. In the ashtray, three stubbed-out cigarettes of the same brand. In the air, now that he sniffed for it over the smell of food and putty, a faint aroma of French cigarettes.

*And no cigarettes in his pocket*, he remembered.

Holding the blue parcel in both hands, slowly turning it, Smiley tried to understand what it meant to him. Instinct – or better, a submerged perception yet to rise to the surface – signalled to him urgently that something about these cigarettes was wrong. Not their appearance. Not that they were stuffed with microfilm or high explosive or soft-nosed bullets or any other of those weary games.

Merely the fact of their presence, here and nowhere else, was wrong.

So new, so free of dust, one packet missing, three smoked.

*And no cigarettes in his pocket.*

He worked faster now, wanting very much to leave. The flat was too high up. It was too empty and too full. He had a growing sense of something being out of joint. Why didn't they take his keys? He pulled open the cupboard. It held clothes as well as papers but Vladimir possessed few of either. The papers were mostly cyclostyled pamphlets in Russian and English and in what Smiley took to be one of the Baltic languages. There was a folder of letters from the Group's old headquarters in Paris, and posters reading, 'REMEMBER LATVIA,' 'REMEMBER ESTONIA,' 'REMEMBER LITHUANIA,' presumably for display at public demonstrations. There was a box of school chalk, yellow, a couple of pieces missing. And Vladimir's treasured Norfolk jacket, lying off its hook on the floor. Fallen there, perhaps, as Vladimir closed the cupboard door too fast.

And Vladimir so vain? thought Smiley. So military in his appearance? Yet dumped his best jacket in a heap on the cupboard floor? Or was it that a more careless hand than Vladimir's had not replaced it on the hanger?

Picking the jacket up, Smiley searched the pockets, then hung it back in the cupboard and slammed the door to see if it fell off its hook.

It did.

They didn't take the keys, and they didn't search his flat, he thought. They searched Vladimir, but in the Superintendent's opinion they had been disturbed.

*Tell him I have two proofs and can bring them with me.*

Returning to the kitchen area he stood before the food-store and took another studied look at the blue parcel lying on top of it. Then peered in the waste-paper basket. At the ashtray again, memorising. Then in the garbage bucket, just in case the missing packet, crumpled up, was there. It wasn't, which for some reason pleased him.

Time to go.

But he didn't, not quite. For another quarter of an hour, with his ear cocked for interruptions, Smiley delved and probed, lifting and replacing, still on the look-out for the loose floor-board, or the favoured recess behind the shelves. But this time he wanted *not* to find. This time, he wanted to confirm an absence. Only when he was as satisfied as circumstance allowed him did he step quietly on to the landing and lock the door behind him. At the bottom of the first flight he met a temporary postman wearing a GPO armband emerging from another corridor. Smiley touched his elbow.

'If you've anything at all for flat 6B, I can save you the climb,' he said humbly.

The postman rummaged and produced a brown envelope. Postmark Paris, dated five days ago, the 15th district. Smiley slipped it into his pocket. At the bottom of the second flight stood a fire-door with a push-bar to open it from the inside only. He had made a mental note of it on his way up. He pushed, the door yielded, he descended the vile concrete staircase and crossed an interior courtyard to a deserted mews, still pondering the omission. Why didn't they search his flat? he wondered. Moscow Centre, like any other large bureaucracy, had its fixed procedures. You decide to kill a man. So you station pickets outside his house, you stake out his route with static posts, you put in your assassination team and you kill him. In the classic method. Then why not search his flat as well? – Vladimir, a bachelor, living in a building constantly overrun with strangers? – why not send in the pickets the moment he is on his way? *Because they knew he had it with him*, thought Smiley. And the body search, which the Superintendent regarded as so cursory? Suppose they were not disturbed, but had found what they were looking for?

He hailed a taxi, telling the driver 'Bywater Street in Chelsea, please, off the King's Road.'

Go home, he thought. Have a bath, think it through. Shave. *Tell him I have two proofs and can bring them with me.*

Suddenly, leaning forward, he tapped on the glass partition and changed his destination. As they made the U-turn, the tall motor-cyclist screeched to a stop behind them, dismounted and solemnly shunted his large black bike and side-car into the opposite lane. A footman, thought Smiley, watching him. A footman, wheeling in the trolley for tea. Like an official escort, arch-backed and elbows spread, the motor-cyclist followed them through the outer reaches of Camden, then, still at a regulation distance, slowly up the hill. The cab drew up, Smiley leaned forward to pay his fare. As he did so, the dark figure processed solemnly past them, one arm lifted from the elbow in a mail-fist salute.

# EIGHT

He stood at the mouth of the avenue, gazing into the ranks of beech trees as they sank away from him like a retreating army into the mist. The darkness had departed reluctantly, leaving an indoor gloom. It could have been dusk already: tea-time in an old country house. The street lights either side of him were poor candles, illuminating nothing. The air felt warm and heavy. He had expected police still, and a roped-off area. He had expected journalists or curious bystanders. It never happened, he told himself, as he stared slowly down the slope. No sooner had I left the scene than Vladimir clambered merrily to his feet, stick in hand, wiped off the gruesome make-up and skipped away with his fellow actors for a pot of beer at the police station.

*Stick in hand*, he repeated to himself, remembering something the Superintendent had said to him. Left hand or right hand? 'There's yellow chalk powder on his left hand too,' Mr. Murgotroyd had said inside the van.

'Thumb and first two fingers.'

He advanced and the avenue darkened round him, the mist thickened. His footsteps echoed tinnily ahead of him. Twenty yards higher, brown sunlight burned like a slow bonfire in its own smoke. But down here in the dip the mist had collected in a cold fog, and Vladimir was very dead after all. He saw tyre marks where the police cars had parked. He noticed the absence of leaves and the unnatural cleanness of the gravel. What do you do? he wondered. Hose the gravel down? Sweep the leaves into yet more plastic pillowcases?

His tiredness had given way to a new and mysterious clarity. He continued up the avenue wishing Vladimir good morning and good night and not feeling a fool for doing so, thinking intently about drawing-pins and chalk and French cigarettes and Moscow Rules, looking for a tin pavilion by a playing field. Take it in sequence, he told himself. Take it from the beginning. Leave the Caporals on their shelf. He reached an intersection of paths and crossed it, still climbing. To his right, goal-posts appeared, and beyond them a green pavilion of corrugated iron, apparently empty. He started across the field, rain-water seeping into his shoes. Behind the hut ran a steep mud bank scoured with children's slides. He climbed the bank, entered a coppice, and kept climbing. The fog had not penetrated the trees and by the time he reached the brow it had cleared. There was still no one in sight. Returning, he approached the pavilion through the trees. It was a tin box, no more, with one side to the field. The only furniture was a rough wood bench slashed and written on with knives, the only occupant a prone figure stretched on it, with a blanket pulled over his head and brown boots protruding. For an undisciplined moment Smiley wondered whether he too had had his face blown off. Girders held up the roof; earnest moral statements enlivened the flaking green paint. 'Punk is destructive. Society does not need it.' The assertion caused him a moment's indecision. 'Oh, but society *does*,' he wanted to reply; 'society is an association of minorities.' The drawing-pin was where Mostyn said it was, at head height exactly, in the best Sarratt tradition of regularity, its Circus-issue brass head as new and as unmarked as the boy who had put it there.

*Proceed to the rendezvous*, it said, *no danger sighted.*

Moscow Rules, thought Smiley yet again. Moscow, where it could take a fieldman three days to post a letter to a safe address. Moscow, where all minorities are punk.

*Tell him I have two proofs and can bring them with me . . .*

Vladimir's chalked acknowledgement ran close beside the pin, a wavering yellow worm of a message scrawled all down the post. Perhaps the old man was worried about rain, thought Smiley. Perhaps he was afraid it could wash his mark away. Or perhaps in his emotional state he leaned too heavily on the chalk, just as he had left his Norfolk jacket lying on the floor. *A meeting or nothing . . . he had told Mostyn . . . Tonight or nothing . . . Tell him I have two proofs and can bring them with me . . .* Nevertheless only the vigilant would ever have noticed that mark, heavy though it was, or the shiny drawing-pin either, and not even the vigilant would have found them odd, for on Hampstead Heath people post bills and messages to each other ceaselessly, and not all of them are spies. Some are children, some are tramps, some are believers in God and organisers of charitable walks, some have lost pets, and some are looking for variations of love and having to proclaim their needs from a hilltop. And not all of them, by any means, get their faces blown off at point-blank range by a Moscow Centre assassination weapon.

And the purpose of this acknowledgment? In Moscow, when Smiley from his desk in London had had the ultimate responsibility for Vladimir's case – in Moscow these signs were devised for agents who might disappear from hour to hour; they were the broken twigs along a path that could always be their last. *I see no danger and am proceeding as instructed to the agreed rendezvous,* read Vladimir's last – and fatally mistaken – message to the living world.

Leaving the hut, Smiley moved a short distance back along the route he had just come. And as he walked, he meticulously called to mind the Superintendent's reconstruction of Vladimir's last journey, drawing upon his memory like an archive.

Those rubber overshoes are a Godsend, Mr. Smiley, the Superintendent had declared piously: North British Century, diamond-pattern soles, sir, and barely walked on – why, you could follow him through a football crowd if you had to!

'I'll give you the authorised version,' the Superintendent had said, speaking fast because they were short of time. 'Ready, Mr. Smiley?'

Ready, Smiley had said.

The Superintendent changed his tone of voice. Conversation was one thing, evidence another. As he spoke, he shone his torch in phases on to the wet gravel of the roped-off area. A lecture with magic lantern, Smiley had thought; at Sarratt I'd have taken notes: 'Here he is, coming down the hill now, sir. See him there? Normal pace, nice heel and toe movement, normal progress, everything above board. See, Mr Smiley?'

Mr. Smiley had seen.

'And the stick mark there, do you see, in his right hand, sir?'

Smiley had seen that too, how the rubber-ferruled walking stick had left a deep round rip with every second footprint.

'Whereas of course he had the stick in his *left* when he was shot, correct? You saw that, too, sir, I noticed. Happen to know which side his bad leg was at all, sir, if he had one?'

'The right,' Smiley had said.

'Ah. Then most likely the right was the side he normally held the stick, as well. Down here, please, sir, that's the way! Walking normal still, please note,' the Superintendent had added, making a rare slip of grammar in his distraction.

For five more paces the regular diamond imprint, heel and toe, had continued undisturbed in the beam of the Superintendent's torch. Now, by daylight, Smiley saw only the ghost of them. The rain, other feet, and the tyre tracks of illicit cyclists had caused large parts to disappear. But by night, at the Superintendent's lantern show, he had seen them vividly, as vividly as he saw the plastic-covered corpse in the dip below them, where the trail had ended.

'*Now*,' the Superintendent had declared with satisfaction, and halted, the cone of his torchbeam resting on a single scuffed area of ground.

'How old did you say he was, sir?' the Superintendent asked.

'I didn't, but he owned to sixty-nine.'

'Plus your recent heart attack, I gather. Now, sir. First he stops. In sharp order. Don't ask me why, perhaps he was spoken to. My guess is he heard something. Behind him. Notice the way the pace shortens, notice the position of the feet as he makes the half-turn, looks over his shoulder or whatever? Anyway he *turns* and that's why I say "behind him." And whatever he saw or didn't see – or heard or didn't hear – he decided to run. Off he goes, look!' the Superintendent urged, with the sudden enthusiasm of the sportsman.

'Wider stride, heels not hardly on the ground at all. A new print entirely, and going for all he's worth. You can even see where he shoved himself off with his stick for the extra purchase.'

Peering now by daylight, Smiley no longer with any certainty *could* see, but he had seen last night – and in his memory saw again this morning – the sudden desperate gashes of the ferrule thrust downward then thrust at an angle.

'Trouble was,' the Superintendent commented quietly, resuming his courtroom style, 'whatever killed him was out in front, wasn't it? Not behind him at all.'

It was both, thought Smiley now, with the advantage of the intervening hours. They *drove* him, he thought, trying without success to recall the Sarratt jargon for this particular technique. They knew his route, and they *drove* him. The frightener behind the target drives him forward, the finger man loiters ahead undetected till the target blunders into him. For it was a truth known also to Moscow Centre murder teams that even the oldest hands will spend hours worrying about their backs, their flanks, the cars that pass and the cars that don't, the streets they cross and the houses that they enter. Yet still fail, when the moment is upon them, to recognise the danger that greets them face to face.

'Still running,' the Superintendent said, moving steadily nearer the body down the hill. 'Notice how his pace gets a little longer because of the steeper gradient now? Erratic too, see that? Feet flying all over the shop. Running for dear life. Literally. And the walking stick still in his right hand. See him veering now, moving towards the verge? Lost his bearings, I wouldn't wonder. Here we go. Explain *that* if you can!'

The torchbeam rested on a patch of footprints close together, five or six of them, all in a very small space at the edge of the grass between two high trees.

'Stopped again,' the Superintendent announced. 'Not so much a total *stop* perhaps, more your stutter. Don't ask me why. Maybe he just wrong-footed himself. Maybe his heart got him if you tell me it was dicky. Then off he goes again same as before.'

'With the stick in his left hand,' Smiley had said quietly.

'Why? That's what I ask myself, sir, but perhaps you people know the answer. Why? Did he hear something again? Remember something? Why – when you're running for your life – why pause, do a duck-shuffle, change hands and then run on again? Straight into the arms of whoever shot him? Unless of course whatever was behind him *overtook* him there, came round through the trees perhaps, made an arc as it were? Any explanation from *your* side of the street, Mr. Smiley?'

And with that question still ringing in Smiley's ears they had arrived at last at the body, floating like an embryo under its plastic film.

But Smiley, on this morning after, stopped short of the dip. Instead, by placing his sodden shoes as best he could upon each spot exactly, he set about trying to imitate the movements the old man might have made. And since Smiley did all this in slow motion, and with every appearance of concentration, under the eye of two trousered ladies walking their Alsatians, he was taken for an adherent of the new fad in Chinese martial exercises, and accounted mad accordingly.

First he put his feet side by side and pointed them down the hill. Then he put his left foot forward, and moved his right foot round until the toe pointed directly towards a spinney of young saplings. As he did so, his right shoulder followed naturally, and his instinct told him that this would be the likely moment for Vladimir to transfer the stick to his left hand. But *why*? As the Superintendent had also asked, why transfer the stick at all? Why, in this most extreme moment of his life, why solemnly move a walking stick from the right hand to the left? Certainly not to defend himself – since, as Smiley remembered, he was right handed. To defend himself, he would only have seized the stick more firmly. Or clasped it with *both* his hands, like a club.

Was it in order to leave his right hand free? But free for what?

Aware this time of being observed, Smiley peered sharply behind him and saw two small boys in blazers who had paused to watch this round little man in spectacles performing strange antics with his feet. He glowered at them in his most schoolmasterly manner, and they moved hastily on.

To leave his right hand free for what? Smiley repeated to himself. And why start running again a moment later?

Vladimir turned to the right, thought Smiley, once again matching his action to the thought. Vladimir turned to the right. He faced the spinney, he put his stick in his left hand. For a moment, according to the Superintendent, he stood still. *Then* he ran on.

*Moscow Rules*, Smiley thought, staring at his own right hand. Slowly he lowered it into his raincoat pocket. Which was empty, as Vladimir's right-hand coat pocket was also empty.

Had he meant to write a message perhaps? Smiley was teasing himself with the theory he was determined to hold at bay. To write a message with the *chalk* for instance? Had he recognised his pursuer, and wished to chalk a name somewhere, or a sign? But what *on*? Not on these wet tree trunks for sure. Not on the clay, the dead leaves, the gravel! Looking round him, Smiley became aware of a peculiar feature of his location. Here, almost between two trees, at the very edge of the avenue, at the point where the fog was approaching its thickest, he was as good as out of sight. The avenue descended, yes, and lifted ahead of him. But it also curved, and from where he stood the upward line of sight in both directions was masked by tree trunks and a dense thicket of saplings. Along the whole path of Vladimir's last frantic journey – a path he knew well, remember, had used for similar meetings – this was the one point, Smiley realised with increasing satisfaction, where the fleeing man was out of sight from both ahead of him and behind him.

And had stopped.

Had freed his right hand.

Had put it – let us say – in his pocket.

For his heart tablets? No. Like the yellow chalk and the matches, they were in his left pocket, not his right.

For something – let us say – that was no longer in the pocket when he was found dead.

For what then?

*Tell him I have two proofs and can bring them with me . . . Then perhaps he will see me . . . This is Gregory asking for Max. I have something for him, please . . .*

Proofs. Proofs too precious to post. He was bringing something. Two somethings. Not just in his head – in his pocket. And was playing Moscow Rules. Rules that had been drummed into the General from the very day of his recruitment as a defector in place. By Smiley himself, no less, as well as his case officer on the spot. Rules that had been invented for his survival; and the survival of his network. Smiley felt the excitement seize his stomach like a nausea. Moscow Rules decree that, if you physically *carry* a message, you must also carry the means to discard it! That, however it is disguised or concealed – microdot, secret writing, undeveloped film, any one of the hundred risky, finicky ways – still as an *object* it must be the first and lightest thing that comes to hand, the least conspicuous when jettisoned!

Such as a medicine bottle full of tablets, he thought, calming a little. Such as a box of matches.

*One box Swan Vesta matches partly used, overcoat left*, he remembered. A smoker's match, note well.

And in the safe flat, he thought relentlessly – tantalising himself, staving off the final insight – there on the table waiting for him, one packet of cigarettes, Vladimir's favourite brand. And in Westbourne Terrace on the food safe, nine packets of Gauloises Caporal. Out of ten.

But no cigarettes in his pockets. None, as the good Superintendent would have said, on his person. Or not when they found him, that is to say.

So the premise, George? Smiley asked himself, mimicking Lacon – brandishing Lacon's prefectorial finger accusingly in his own intact face – the premise? The premise is thus far, Oliver, that a smoker, a habitual smoker, in a state of high nervousness, sets off on a crucial clandestine meeting equipped with matches but not even so much as an *empty* packet of cigarettes, though he possesses quite demonstrably a whole stock of them. So that either the assassins found it, and removed it – the proof, or proofs, which Vladimir was speaking of, or – or what? Or Vladimir changed his stick from his right hand to his left in time. And put his right hand in his pocket in time. And took it out again, also in time, at the very spot where he could not be seen. And got rid of it, or them, according to Moscow Rules.

Having satisfied his own insistence upon a logical succession, George Smiley stepped cautiously into the long grass that led to the spinney, soaking his trousers from the knees down. For half an hour or more he searched, groping in the grass and among the foliage, retreading his tracks, cursing his own blundering, giving up, beginning again, answering the fatuous enquiries of passers-by, which ranged from the obscene to the excessively attentive. There were even two Buddhist monks from a local seminary, complete with saffron robes and lace-up boots and knitted woollen caps, who offered their assistance. Smiley courteously declined it. He found two broken kites, a quantity of Coca-Cola tins. He found scraps of the female body, some in colour, some in black and white, ripped from magazines. He found an old running shoe, black, and shreds of an old burnt blanket. He found four beer bottles, empty, and four empty cigarette packets so sodden and old that after one glance he discounted them. And in a branch, slipped into the fork just where it joined its parent trunk, the fifth packet, or better perhaps the tenth – that was not even empty; a relatively dry packet of Gauloises Caporal, *Filtre* and Duty Free, high up. Smiley reached for it as if it were forbidden fruit, but like forbidden fruit it stayed outside his grasp. He jumped for it and felt his back rip: a distinct and unnerving parting of tissue that smarted and dug at him for days afterwards. He said 'damn' out loud and rubbed the spot, much as Ostrakova might have done. Two typists, on their way to work, consoled him with their giggles. He found a stick, poked the packet free, opened it. Four cigarettes remained.

And behind those four cigarettes, half concealed, and protected by its own skin of cellophane, something he recognised but dared not even disturb with his wet and trembling fingers. Something he dared not even contemplate until he was free of this appalling place, where giggling typists and Buddhist monks innocently trampled the spot where Vladimir had died.

They have one, I have the other, he thought. I have shared the old man's legacy with his murderers.

Braving the traffic, he followed the narrow pavement down the hill till he came to South End Green, where he hoped for a café that would give him tea. Finding none open so early, he sat on a bench across from a cinema instead, contemplating an old marble fountain and a pair of red telephone boxes, one filthier than the other. A warm drizzle was falling; a few shopkeepers had started lowering their awnings; a delicatessen store was taking delivery of bread. He sat with hunched shoulders, and the damp points of his mackintosh collar stabbed his unshaven cheeks whenever he turned his head. 'For God's sake, mourn!' Ann had flung at Smiley once, infuriated by his apparent composure after yet another friend had died. 'If you won't grieve for the dead, how can you love the living?' Sitting on his bench, pondering his next step, Smiley now transmitted to her the answer he had failed to find at the time. 'You are wrong,' he told her distractedly. 'I mourn the dead sincerely, and Vladimir, at this moment, deeply. It's loving the living which is sometimes a bit of a problem.'

He tried the telephone boxes and the second worked. By a miracle, even the S–Z directory was intact and, more amazing still, the Straight and Steady Minicab Service of Islington North had paid for the privilege of heavy type. He dialled the number and while it rang out he had a panic that he had forgotten the name of the signatory on the receipt in Vladimir's pocket. He rang off, recovering his two pence. Lane? Lang? He dialled again.

A female voice answered him in a bored singsong: 'Straight-and-Stead-ee! Name-when-and-where-*to*, please?'

'I'd like to speak to Mr. J. Lamb, please, one of your drivers,' Smiley said politely.

'Sorr-ee, no personal calls on this line,' she sang and rang off.

He dialled a third time. It wasn't personal at all, he said huffily, now surer of his ground. He wanted Mr. Lamb to drive for him, and nobody but Mr. Lamb would do. 'Tell him it's a long journey. Stratford-on-Avon' – choosing a town at random – 'tell him I want to go to Stratford.' *Sampson*, he replied, when she insisted on a name. Sampson with a 'p'.

He returned to his bench to wait again.

To ring Lacon? For what purpose? Rush home, open the cigarette packet, find out its precious contents ? It was the first thing Vladimir threw away, he thought: in the spy trade we abandon first what we love the most. I got the better end of the bargain after all. An elderly couple had settled opposite him. The man wore a stiff Homburg hat and was playing war tunes on a tin whistle. His wife grinned inanely at the passers-by. To avoid her gaze, Smiley remembered the brown envelope from Paris, and tore it open, expecting what? A bill probably, some hangover from the old boy's life there. Or one of those cyclostyled battle-cries that émigrés send each other like Christmas cards. But this was neither a bill nor a circular but a personal letter: an appeal, but of a very special sort. Unsigned, no address for the sender. In French, handwritten very fast. Smiley read it once and he was reading it a second time when an overpainted Ford Cortina, driven by a boy in a polo neck pullover, skidded to a giddy halt outside the cinema. Returning the letter to his pocket, he crossed the road to the car.

'Sampson with a "p"?' the boy yelled impertinently through the window, then shoved open the back door from inside. Smiley climbed in. A smell of aftershave mingled with the stale cigarette smoke. He held a ten-pound note in his hand and he let it show.

'Will you please switch off the engine?' Smiley asked.

The boy obeyed, watching him all the time in the mirror. He had brown Afro hair. White hands, carefully manicured.

'I'm a private detective,' Smiley explained. 'I'm sure you get a lot of us and we're a nuisance but I would be happy to pay for a little bit of information. You signed a receipt yesterday for thirteen pounds. Do you remember who your fare was?'

'Tall party. Foreign. White moustache and a limp.'

'Old?'

'Very. Walking stick and all.'

'Where did you pick him up?' Smiley asked.

'Cosmo Restaurant, Praed Street, ten-thirty, morning,' the boy said, gabbling deliberately.

Praed Street was five minutes' walk from Westbourne Terrace.

'And where did you take him, please?'

'Charlton.'

'Charlton in south-east London?'

'Saint Somebody's Church off of Battle-of-the-Nile Street. Ask for a pub called The Defeated Frog.'

'Frog?'

'Frenchman.'

'Did you leave him there?'

'One hour wait, then back to Praed Street.'

'Did you make any other stops?'

'Once at a toy-shop going, once at a phone-box coming back. Party bought a wooden duck on wheels.' He turned and, resting his chin on the back of the seat, insolently held his hands apart, indicating size. 'Yellow job,' he said. 'The phone call was local.'

'How do you know?'

'I lent him twopence, didn't I? Then he come back and borrows himself two ten p's, for in-case.'

*I asked him where he was calling from but he just said he had plenty of change,* Mostyn had said.

Passing the boy the ten-pound note, Smiley reached for the door handle.

'You can tell your firm I didn't turn up,' he said.

'Tell 'em what I bloody like, can't I?'

Smiley climbed quickly out, just managing to close the door before the boy drove away at the same frightful speed. Standing on the pavement, he completed his second reading of the letter, and by then he had it in his memory for good. A woman, he thought, trusting his first instinct. And she thinks she's going to die. Well, so do we all, and we're right. He was feigning light-headedness to himself, indifference. Each man has only a quantum of compassion, he argued, and mine is used up for the day. But the letter scared him all the same, and re-charged his sense of urgency.

*General, I do not wish to be dramatic but some men are watching my house and I do not think they are your friends or mine. This morning I had an impression that they were trying to kill me. Will you not send me your magic friend once more?*

He had things to hide. To *cache*, as they insisted on saying at Sarratt. He took buses, changing several times, watching his back, dozing. The black motor-cycle with its side-car had not reappeared; he could discern no other surveillance. At a stationer's shop in Baker Street he bought a large cardboard box, some daily newspapers, some wrapping paper and a reel of Scotch tape. He hailed a taxi, crouched in the back making up his parcel. He put Vladimir's packet of cigarettes into the box, together with Ostrakova's letter, and he padded out the rest of the space with newspaper. He wrapped the box and got his fingers tangled in the Scotch tape. Scotch tape had always defeated him. He wrote his own name on the lid, 'To be called for.' He paid off the cab at the Savoy Hotel, where he consigned the box to the men's-cloakroom attendant, together with a pound note.

'Not heavy enough for a bomb, is it, sir?' the attendant asked, and facetiously held the parcel to his ear.

'I wouldn't be so sure,' said Smiley and they shared a good laugh together.

*Tell Max that it concerns the Sandman*, he thought. Vladimir, he wondered wistfully, what was your other proof?

# NINE

The low skyline was filled with cranes and gasometers; lazy chimneys spouted ochre smoke into the rainclouds. If it had not been Saturday, Smiley would have used public transport but on Saturdays he was prepared to drive, though he lived on terms of mutual hatred with the combustion engine. He had crossed the river at Vauxhall Bridge. Greenwich lay behind him. He had entered the flat, dismembered hinterland of the docks. While the wiper blades shuddered, large raindrops crept through the bodywork of his unhappy little English car. Glum children, sheltering in a bus-stop, said, 'Keep straight on, luv.' He had shaved and bathed, but he had not slept. He had sent Vladimir's telephone bill to Lacon, requesting a breakdown of all traceable calls as a matter of urgency. His mind, as he drove, was clear, but prey to anarchic changes of mood. He was wearing a brown tweed overcoat, the one he used for travelling. He navigated a roundabout, mounted a rise, and suddenly a fine Edwardian pub stood before him, under the sign of a red-faced warrior. Battle-of-the-Nile Street rose away from it towards an island of worn grass, and on the island stood St. Saviour's Church, built of stone and flint, proclaiming God's message to the crumbling Victorian warehouses. Next Sunday's preacher, said the poster, was a female major in the Salvation Army, and in front of the poster stood the lorry: a sixty-foot giant trailer, crimson, its side windows fringed with football pennants and a motley of foreign registration stickers covering one door. It was the biggest thing in sight, bigger even than the church. Somewhere in the background he heard a motor-bike engine slow down and then start up again, but he didn't even bother to look back. The familiar escort had followed him since Chelsea; but fear, as he used to preach at Sarratt, is always a matter of selection.

Following the footpath, Smiley entered a graveyard with no graves. Lines of headstones made up the perimeter, a climbing frame and three standard-pattern new houses occupied the central ground. The first house was called Zion, the second had wide windows but Number Three had lace curtains, and when he pushed the gate all he saw was one shadow upstairs. He saw it stationary then he saw it sink and vanish as if it had been sucked into the floor, and for a second he wondered, in a quite dreadful way, whether he had just witnessed another murder. He rang the bell and angel chimes exploded inside the house. The door was made of rippled glass. Pressing his eye to it, he made out brown stair carpet and what looked like a perambulator. He rang the bell again and heard a scream. It started low and grew louder and at first he thought it was a child, then a cat, then a whistling kettle. It reached its zenith, held it, then suddenly stopped, either because someone had taken the kettle off the boil or because it had blown its nozzle off. He walked round to the back of the house. It was the same as the front, except for the drain-pipes and a vegetable patch, and a tiny goldfish pond made of pre-cast slab. There was no water in the pond, and consequently no goldfish either, but in the concrete bowl lay a yellow wooden duck on its side. It lay with its beak open and its staring eye turned to Heaven and two of its wheels were still going round.

'Party bought a wooden duck on wheels,' the minicab driver had said, turning to illustrate with his white hands. 'Yellow job.'

The back door had a knocker. He gave a light tap with it and tried the door handle, which yielded. He stepped inside and closed the door carefully behind him. He was standing in a scullery which led to a kitchen and the first thing he noticed in the kitchen was the kettle off the gas with a thin line of steam curling from its silent whistle. And two cups and a milk jug and a teapot on a tray.

'Mrs. Craven?' he called softly. 'Stella?'

He crossed the dining-room and stood in the hall, on the brown carpet beside the perambulator, and in his mind he was making pacts with God: just no more deaths, no more Vladimirs and I will worship You for the rest of our respective lives.

'Stella? It's me. Max.' he said.

He pushed open the drawing-room door and she was sitting in the corner on an easy chair between the piano and window, watching him with cold determination. She was not scared, but she looked as if she hated him. She was wearing a long Asian dress and no make-up. She was holding the child to her, boy or girl he couldn't tell and couldn't remember. She had its tousled head pressed against her shoulder and her hand over its mouth to stop it making a noise, and she was watching him over the top of its head, challenging and defying him.

'Where's Villem?' he asked.

Slowly she took her hand away and Smiley expected the child to scream but instead it stared at him in salute.

'His name's William,' she said quietly. 'Get that straight, Max. That's his choice. William Craven. British to the core. Not Estonian, not Russian. British.' She was a beautiful woman, black-haired and still. Seated in the corner holding her child, she seemed permanently painted against the dark background.

'I want to talk to him, Stella. I'm not asking him to do anything. I may even be able to help him.'

'I've heard that before, haven't I? He's out. Gone to work where he belongs.'

Smiley digested this.

'Then what's the lorry doing outside?' he objected gently.

'He's gone to the depot. They sent a car for him.'

Smiley digested this also.

'Then who's the second cup for in the kitchen?'

'He's got nothing to do with it,' she said.

He went upstairs and she let him. There was a door straight ahead of him and there were doors to his left and right, both open, one to the child's room, one to the main bedroom. The door ahead of him was closed and when he knocked there was no answer.

'Villem, it's Max,' he said. 'I have to talk to you, please. Then I'll go and leave you in peace, I promise.'

He repeated this word for word then went down the steep stairs again to the drawing-room. The child had begun crying loudly.

'Perhaps if you made that tea,' he suggested between the child's sobs.

'You're not talking to him alone, Max. I'm not having you charm him off the tree again.'

'I never did that. That was not my job.'

'He still thinks the world of you. That's enough for me.'

'It's about Vladimir,' Smiley said.

'I know what it's about. They've been ringing half the night, haven't they?'

'Who have?'

'"Where's Vladimir? Where's Vladi?" What do you think William is? Jack the Ripper? He hasn't had sound nor sight of Vladi for God knows how long. Oh Beckie, darling, *do* be quiet!' Striding across the room she found a tin of biscuits under a heap of washing and shoved one forcibly into the child's mouth. 'I'm not usually like this,' she said.

'*Who's* been asking for him?' Smiley insisted gently.

'Mikhel, who else? Remember Mikhel, our Freedom Radio ace, Prime Minister designate of Estonia, betting tout? Three o'clock this morning while Beckie's cutting a tooth, the bloody phone goes. It's Mikhel doing his heavy-breathing act. "Where's Vladi, Stella? Where's our Leader?" I said to him: "You're daft, aren't you? You think it's harder to tap the phone when people only whisper? You're barking mad," I said to him. "Stick to racehorses and get out of politics," I told him.'

'Why was he so worried?' Smiley asked.

'Vladi owed him money, that's why. Fifty quid. Probably lost it on a horse together, one of their many losers. He'd promised to bring it round to Mikhel's place and have a game of chess with him. In the middle of the night, mark you. They're insomniacs apparently, as well as patriots. Our leader hadn't shown up. Drama. "Why the hell should William know where he is?" I ask him. "Go to sleep." An hour later who's back on the line? Breathing as before? Our Major Mikhel once more, hero of the Royal Estonian Cavalry, clicking our heels and apologising. He's been round to Vladi's pad, banged on the door, rung the bell. There's nobody at home. "Look, Mikhel," I said, "he's not here, we're not hiding him in the attic, we haven't seen him since Beckie's christening, we haven't heard from him. Right? William's just in from Hamburg, he needs sleep, and I'm not waking him."'

'So he rang off again,' Smiley suggested.

'Did he hell! He's a leech. "Villem is Vladi's favourite." he says. "What for?" I say. "The three-thirty at Ascot? Look, go to bloody sleep!" "Vladimir always said to me, if ever anything went wrong, I should go to Villem," he said. "So what do you want him to do?" I said. "Drive up to town in the trailer and bang on Vladi's door as well?" Jesus!'

She sat the child on a chair. Where she stayed, contentedly cropping her biscuit.

There was the sound of a door slammed violently, followed by fast footsteps coming down the stairs.

'William's right out of it, Max,' Stella warned, staring straight at Smiley. 'He's not political and he's not slimy, and he's got over his dad being a martyr. He's a big boy now and he's going to stand on his own feet. Right? I said "Right?"'

Smiley had moved to the far end of the room to give himself distance from the door. Villem strode in purposefully, still wearing his track suit and running shoes, about ten years Stella's junior and somehow too slight for his own safety. He perched himself on the sofa, at the edge, his intense gaze switching between his wife and Smiley as if wondering which of them would spring first. His high forehead looked strangely white under his dark, swept-back hair. He had shaved, and shaving had filled out his face, making him even younger. His eyes, red-rimmed from driving, were brown and passionate.

'Hullo, Villem,' Smiley said.

'William,' Stella corrected him.

Villem nodded tautly, acknowledging both forms.

'Hullo, Max,' said Villem. On his lap, his hands found and held each other. 'How you doing, Max? That's the way, huh?'

'I gather you've already heard the news about Vladimir,' Smiley said.

'News? What news, please?'

Smiley took his time. Watching him, sensing his stress.

'That he's disappeared,' Smiley replied quite lightly, at last. 'I gather his friends have been ringing you up at unsocial hours.'

'Friends?' Villem shot a dependent glance at Stella. 'Old émigrés, drink tea, play chess all day, politics? Talk crazy dreams? Mikhel is not my friend, Max.'

He spoke swiftly, with impatience for this foreign language which was such a poor substitute for his own. Whereas Smiley spoke as if he had all day.

'But *Vladi* is your friend,' he objected. 'Vladi was your father's friend before you. They were in Paris together. Brothers-in-arms. They came to England together.'

Countering the weight of this suggestion, Villem's small body became a storm of gestures. His hands parted and made furious arcs, his brown hair lifted and fell flat again.

'Sure! Vladimir, he was my father's friend. His good friend. Also of Beckie the godfather, okay? But not for politics. Not any more.' He glanced at Stella, seeking her approval. 'Me, I am William Craven. I got English home, English wife, English kid, English name. Okay?'

'And an English job,' Stella put in quietly, watching him.

'A good job! Know how much I earn, Max? We buy house. Maybe a car, okay?'

Something in Villem's manner – his glibness perhaps, or the energy of his protest – had caught the attention of his wife, for now Stella was studying him as intently as Smiley was, and she began to hold the baby distractedly, almost without interest.

'When did you last see him, William?' Smiley asked.

'Who, Max? See who? I don't understand you, please.'

'Tell him, Bill,' Stella ordered her husband, not moving her eyes from him for a moment.

'When did you last see Vladimir?' Smiley repeated patiently.

'Long time, Max.'

'Weeks?'

'Sure. Weeks.'

'Months?'

'Months. Six months! Seven! At christening. He was godfather, we make a party. But no politics.'

Smiley's silences had begun to produce an awkward tension.

'And not since?' he asked at last.

'No.'

Smiley turned to Stella, whose gaze had still not flinched.

'What time did William get back yesterday?'

'Early,' she said.

'As early as ten o'clock in the morning?'

'Could have been. I wasn't here. I was visiting Mother.'

'Vladimir drove down here yesterday by taxi,' he explained, still to Stella. 'I think he saw William.'

Nobody helped him, not Smiley, not his wife. Even the child kept still.

'On his way here Vladimir bought a toy. The taxi waited an hour down the lane and took him away again, back to Paddington where he lives,' Smiley said, still being very careful to keep the present tense.

Villem had found his voice at last: 'Vladi is of Beckie the godfather!' he protested with another flourish, as his English threatened to desert him entirely. 'Stella don't like him, so he must come here like a thief, okay? He bring my Beckie toy, okay? Is a crime already, Max? Is a law, an old man cannot bring to his godchild toys?'

Once again neither Smiley nor Stella spoke. They were both waiting for the same inevitable collapse.

'Vladi is old man, Max! Who knows when he sees his Beckie again? He is friend of family!'

'Not of this family,' said Stella. 'Not any more.'

'He was friend of my father! Comrade! In Paris they fight together Bolshevism. So he brings to Beckie a toy. Why not, please? Why not, Max?'

'You said you bought the bloody thing yourself,' said Stella. Putting a hand to her breast, she closed a button as if to cut him off.

Villem swung to Smiley, appealing to him: 'Stella don't like the old man, okay? Is afraid I make more politics with him, okay? So I don't tell Stella. She goes to see her mother in Staines hospital and while she is away Vladi makes a small visit to see Beckie, say hullo, why not?' In desperation he actually leapt to his feet, flinging up his arms in too much protest. 'Stella!' he cried.'Listen to me! So Vladi don't get home last night? Please, I am so sorry! But it is not my fault, okay? Max! That Vladi is an old man! Lonely. So maybe he finds a woman once, Okay? So he can't do much with her, but he still likes her company. For this he was pretty famous, I think! Okay? Why not?'

'And *before* yesterday?' Smiley asked, after an age. Villem seemed not to understand, so Smiley paced out the question again: 'You saw Vladimir yesterday. He came by taxi and brought a yellow wooden duck for Beckie. On wheels.'

'Sure.'

'Very well. But before yesterday – not counting yesterday – when did you last see him?'

Some questions are hazard, some are instinct, some – like this one – are based on a premature understanding that is more than instinct, but less than knowlege.

Villem wiped his lips on the back of his hand. 'Monday,' he said miserably. 'I see him Monday. He ring me, we meet. Sure.'

Then Stella whispered, 'Oh William,' and held the child upright against her, a little soldier, while she peered downward at the haircord carpet waiting for her feelings to right themselves.

The phone began ringing. Like an infuriated infant Villem sprang at it, lifted the receiver, slammed it back on the cradle, then threw the whole telephone on to the floor and kicked the receiver clear. He sat down.

Stella turned to Smiley: 'I want you to go,' she said. 'I want you to walk out of here and never come back. Please Max. Now.'

For a time Smiley seemed to consider this request quite seriously. He looked at Villem with avuncular affection; he looked at Stella. Then he delved in his inside pocket and pulled out a folded copy of the day's first edition of the *Evening Standard* and handed it to Stella rather than to Villem, partly because of the language barrier and partly because he guessed that Villem would break down.

'I'm afraid Vladi's disappeared for good, William,' he said in a tone of simple regret. 'It's in the papers. He's been shot dead. The police will want to ask you questions. I have to hear what happened and tell you how to answer them.'

Then Villem said something hopeless in Russian and Stella, moved by his tone if not his words, put down one child and went to comfort the other, and Smiley might not have been in the room at all. So he sat for a while quite alone, thinking of Vladimir's piece of negative film – indecipherable until he turned it to positive – nestling in its box in the Savoy Hotel with the anonymous letter from Paris that he could do nothing about. And of the second proof, wondering what it was, and how the old man had carried it, and supposing it was in his wallet; but believing also that he would never know.

Villem sat bravely as if he were already attending Vladimir's funeral. Stella sat at his side with her hand on his, Beckie the child lay on the floor and slept. Occasionally as Villem talked, tears rolled unashamedly down his pale cheeks.

'For the others I give nothing,' said Villem. 'For Vladi everything. I love this man.' He began again: 'After the death of my father, Vladi become father to me. Sometimes I even say him: "my father." Not uncle. Father.'

'Perhaps we could start with Monday,' Smiley suggested. 'With the first meeting.'

Vladi had telephoned, said Villem. It was the first time Villem had heard from him or from anybody in the Group for months. Vladi telephoned Villem at the depot, out of the blue, while Villem was consolidating his load and checking his trans-shipment papers with the office before leaving for Dover. That was the arrangement, Villem said, that was how it had been left with the Group. He was out of it, as they all were, more or less, but if he was ever urgently needed he could be reached at the depot on a Monday morning, not at home because of Stella. Vladi was Beckie's godfather and as godfather could ring the house any time. But not on business. Never.

'I ask him: "Vladi! What do you want? Listen, how are you?"'

Vladimir was in a call box down the road. He wanted a personal conversation immediately. Against all the employers' regulations Villem picked him up at the roundabout and Vladimir rode half the way to Dover with him: 'black,' said Villem – meaning 'illegally.' The old boy was carrying a rush basket full of oranges, but Villem had not been of a mood to ask him why he should saddle him with pounds of oranges. At first Vladimir had talked about Paris and Villem's father, and the great struggles they had shared; then he talked about a small favour Villem could do for him. For the sake of old times a small favour. For the sake of Villem's dead father, whom Vladimir had loved. For the sake of the Group, of which Villem's father had once been such a hero.

'I tell him: "Vladi, this small favour is impossible for me. I promise Stella: is impossible!"'

Stella's hand left her husband's side and she sat alone, torn between wishing to console him for the old man's death and her hurt at his broken promise.

Just a small favour, Vladimir had insisted. Small, no trouble, no risk, but very helpful to our cause: also Villem's duty. Then Vladi produced snaps he had taken of Beckie at the christening. They were in a yellow Kodak envelope, the prints on one side and the negatives in protective cellophane on the other and the chemist's blue docket still stapled to the outside, all as innocent as the day.

For a while they admired them till Vladimir said suddenly: 'It is for Beckie, Villem. What we do, we do for Beckie's future.'

Hearing Villem repeat this, Stella clenched her fists, and when she looked up again she was resolute and somehow much older, with islands of tiny wrinkles at the corner of each eye.

Villem went on with his story: 'Then Vladimir tell to me, "Villem. Every Monday you are driving to Hanover and Hamburg, returning Monday. How long you stay in Hamburg, please?"'

To which Villem had replied as short a time as possible, depending on how long it took him to unload, depending on whether he delivered to the agent or to the addressee, depending what time of day he arrived and how many hours he already had on his sheet. Depending on his return load, if he had one. There were more questions of this sort, which Villem now related, many trivial – where Villem slept on the journey, where he ate – and Smiley knew that the old man in a rather monstrous way was doing what he would have done himself; he was talking Villem into a corner, making him answer as a prelude to making him obey. And only after this did Vladimir explain to

Villem, using all his military and family authority, just what he wished Villem to do:

'He say to me: "Villem, take these oranges to Hamburg for me. Take this basket." "What for?" I ask him. "General, why do I take this basket?" Then he give me fifty pounds. "For emergencies," he tell to me. "In emergency, here is fifty pounds." "But why do I take this basket?" I ask him. "What emergency is considered here, General?"'

Then Vladimir recited to Villem his instructions, and they included fallbacks and contingencies – even, if necessary, staying an extra night on the strength of the fifty pounds – and Smiley noticed how the old man had insisted upon Moscow Rules, exactly as he had with Mostyn, and how there was *too much*, as there always had been – the older he got, the more the old boy had tied himself up in the skeins of his own conspiracies. Villem should lay the yellow Kodak envelope containing Beckie's photographs on the top of the oranges, he should take his stroll down to the front of the cabin – all as Villem, in the event had done, he said – and the envelope was the letter-box, and the sign that it had been filled would be a chalk mark 'also yellow like the envelope, which is the tradition of our Group,' said Villem.

'And the safety signal?' Smiley asked. 'The signal that says "I am not being followed"?'

'Was Hamburg newspaper from yesterday,' Villem replied swiftly – but on this subject, he confessed, he had had a small difference with Vladimir, despite all the respect he owed to him as a leader, as a General, and as his father's friend.

'He tell to me, "Villem, you carry this newspaper in your pocket." But I tell to him: "Vladi, please, look at me, I have only track suit, no pockets." So he say, "Villem, then carry the newspaper under your arm."'

'Bill,' Stella breathed, with a sort of awe. 'Oh Bill, you stupid bloody fool.' She turned to Smiley. 'I mean, why didn't they just put it in the bloody post, whatever it is, and be done with it?'

Because it was a negative, and only negatives are acceptable by Moscow Rules. Because the General had a terror of betrayal, Smiley thought. The old boy saw it everywhere, in everyone around him. And if death is the ultimate judge, he was right.

'And it worked?' Smiley said finally to Villem with great gentleness. 'The hand-over worked?'

'Sure! It work fine,' Villem agreed heartily, and darted Stella a defiant glance.

'And did you have any idea, for instance, who might have been your contact at this meeting?'

Then with much hesitation, and after much prompting, some of it from Stella, Villem told that also: about the hollowed face that had looked so desperate and had reminded him of his father; about the warning stare which was either real or he had imagined it because he was so excited. How sometimes, when he watched football on the television, which he liked to do very much, the camera caught somone's face or expression, and it stuck in your memory for the rest of the match, even if you never saw it again – and how the face on the steamer was of this sort exactly. He described the flicked horns of hair and with his fingertips he lightly drew deep grooves in his own unmarked cheeks. He described the man's smallness, and even his sexiness – Villem said he could tell. He described his own feelings of being *warned* by the man, warned to take care of a precious thing. Villem would look the same way himself – he told Stella with a sudden flourish of imagined tragedy – if there was another war, and fighting, and he had to give away Beckie to a stranger to look after! And this was the cue for more tears, and more reconciliation, and more lamentations about the old man's death, to which Smiley's next question inevitably contributed.

'So you brought the yellow envelope back, and yesterday when the General came down with Beckie's duck, you handed him the envelope,' he suggested, as mildly as he knew how, but it was still some while before a plain narrative emerged.

It was Villem's habit, he said, before driving home on Fridays, to sleep at the depot for a few hours in the cab, then shave and drink a cup of tea with the boys so that he arrived home feeling steady, rather than nervous and bad-tempered. It was a trick he had learned from the older hands, he said: not to rush home, you only regret it. But yesterday was different, he said, and besides – lapsing suddenly into monosyllabic nicknames – Stella had taken Beck to Staines to see her mum. So he for once came straight home, rang Vladimir and gave him the code word which they had agreed on in advance.

'Rang him where?' Smiley asked, softly interrupting.

'At flat. He told me: "Phone me only at flat. Never at library. Mikhel is good man, but he is not informed."'

And, Villem continued, within a short time – he forgot how long – Vladimir had arrived at the house by minicab, a thing he had never done before, bringing the duck for Beck. Villem handed him the yellow envelope of snapshots and Vladimir took them to the window and very slowly, 'like they were sacred from a church, Max,' with his back to Villem, Vladimir held the negatives one after the other to the light till he apparently found the one he was looking for, and after that he went on gazing at it for a long time.

'Just one?' Smiley asked swiftly – his mind upon the two proofs again – '*One* negative?'

'Sure.'

'One frame, or one strip?'

Frame: Villem was certain. One small frame. Yes, thirty-five millimetre, like his own Agfa automatic. No, Villem had not been able to see what it contained, whether writing or what. He had seen Vladimir, that was all.

'Vladi was red, Max. Wild in the face, Max, bright with his eyes. He was old man.'

'And on your journey,' Smiley said, interrupting Villem's story to ask this crucial question. 'All the way home from Hamburg, you never once thought to look?'

'Was secret, Max. Was military secret.'

Smiley glanced at Stella.

'He wouldn't,' she said in answer to his unspoken question 'He's too straight.'

Smiley believed her.

Villem took up his story again. Having put the yellow envelope in his pocket, Vladimir took Villem into the garden and thanked him, holding Villem's hand in both of his, telling him that it was a great thing he had done, the best; that Villem was his father's son, a finer soldier even than his father – the best Estonian stock, steady, conscientious and reliable; that with this photograph they could repay many debts and do great damage to the

Bolsheviks; that the photograph was a *proof*, a proof impossible to ignore. But of what, he did not say – only that Max would see it, and believe, and remember. Villem didn't quite know why they had to go into the garden but he supposed that the old man in his excitement had become scared of microphones, for he was already talking a lot about security.

'I take him to gate but not to taxi. He tell me I must not come to taxi. "Villem, I am old man," he say to me. We speak Russian. "Next week maybe I fall dead. Who cares? Today we have won great battle. Max will be greatly proud of us."'

Struck by the aptness of the General's last words to him, Villem again bounded to his feet in fury, his brown eyes smouldering. 'Was Soviets!' he shouted. 'Was Soviet spies, Max *they* kill Vladimir! He know too much!'

'So do you,' said Stella, and there was a long and awkward silence. 'So do we all,' she added, with a glance at Smiley.

'That's all he said?' Smiley asked. 'Nothing else, about the value of what you had done, for instance? Just that Max would believe?'

Villem shook his head.

'About there being other proofs, for instance?'

Nothing, said Villem: no more.

'Nothing to explain how he had communicated with Hamburg in the first place, set up the arrangements? Whether others of the Group were involved? Please think.'

Villem thought, but without result.

'So who have you told this to, William, apart from me?' Smiley asked.

'Nobody! Max, nobody!'

'He hasn't had time,' said Stella.

'Nobody! On journey I sleep in cab, save ten pounds a night subsistence. We buy house with this money! In Hamburg I tell *nobody*! At depot *nobody*!'

'Had Vladimir told anyone – anyone that you know of, that is?'

'From the Group nobody, only Mikhel, which was necessary, but not all, even to Mikhel. I ask to him: "Vladimir, who knows I do this for you?" "Only Mikhel a very little," he say. "Mikhel lends me money, lends me photocopier, he is my friend. But even to friends we cannot trust. Enemies I do not fear, Villem. But friends I fear greatly."'

Smiley spoke to Stella: 'If the police *do* come here,' he said. '*If* they do, they will only know that Vladimir drove down here yesterday. They'll have got on to the cab driver, as I did.'

She was watching him with her large shrewd eyes.

'So?' she asked.

'So don't tell them the rest. They know all they need. Any more could be an embarrassment to them.'

'To them or to you?' Stella asked.

'Vladimir came here yesterday to see Beckie and bring her a present. That's the cover story, just as William first told it. He didn't know you'd taken her to see your mother. He found William here, they talked old times and strolled in the garden. He couldn't wait too long because of the taxi, so he left without seeing either you or his god-daughter. That's all there was.'

'Were *you* here?' Stella was still watching him.

'If you ask about me, yes. I came here today and gave you the bad news. The police don't mind that Villem belonged to the Group. It's only the present that matters to them.'

Smiley returned his attention to Villem. 'Tell me, did you bring anything else for Vladimir?' he asked. 'Apart from what was in the envelope? A present perhaps? Something he liked and couldn't buy himself?

Villem concentrated energetically upon the question before replying. 'Cigarettes!' he cried suddenly. 'On boat, I buy him French cigarettes as gift. Gauloises, Max. He like very much! "Gauloises Caporal, with filter, Villem." Sure!'

'And the fifty pounds he had borrowed from Mikhel?' Smiley asked.

'I give back. Sure.'

'All?' said Smiley.

'All. Cigarettes was gift. Max, I love this man.'

Stella saw him to the door and at the door he gently took her arm and led her a few steps into the garden out of earshot of her husband.

'You're out of date,' she told him. 'Whatever it is you're doing, sooner or later one side or the other will have to stop. You're like the Group.'

'Be quiet and listen,' said Smiley. 'Are you listening?'

'Yes.'

'William's to speak to no one about this. Whom does he like to talk to at the depot?'

'The whole world.'

'Well, do what you can. Did anyone else ring apart from Mikhel? A wrong-number call even? Ring – then ring off?'

She thought, then shook her head.

'Did anyone come to the door? Salesman, market researcher, religious evangelist. Canvasser. Anyone? You're sure?'

As she continued staring at him her eyes seemed to acquire real knowledge of him, and appreciation. Then again she shook her head, denying him the complicity he was asking for.

'Stay away, Max. All of you. Whatever happens, however bad it is. He's grown up. He doesn't need a vicar any more.'

She watched him leave, perhaps to make sure he really went. For a while as he drove, the notion of Vladimir's piece of negative film nestling in its box consumed him like hidden money – whether it was still safe, whether he should inspect it or convert it, since it had been brought through the lines at the cost of life. But by the time he approached the river he had other thoughts and purposes. Eschewing Chelsea, he joined the northbound Saturday traffic, which consisted mainly of young families with old cars. And one motor-bike with a black side-car, clinging faithfully to his tail all the way to Bloomsbury.

# TEN

The free Baltic Library was on the third floor over a dusty antiquarian bookshop that specialised in the Spirit. Its little windows squinted into a forecourt of the British Museum. Smiley reached the place by way of a winding wooden staircase, passing on his ponderous climb several aged hand-drawn signs pulling at their drawing-pins and a stack of brown toiletry boxes belonging to a chemist's shop next door. Gaining the top, he discovered himself thoroughly out of breath and wisely paused before pressing the bell. Waiting, he was assailed in his momentary exhaustion by a hallucination. He had the delusion that he kept visiting the same high place over and over again: the safe flat in Hampstead, Vladimir's garret in Westbourne Terrace, and now this haunted backwater from the fifties, once a rallying point of the so-called Bloomsbury Irregulars. He fancied they were all a single place, a single proving ground for virtues not yet stated. The illusion passed, and he gave three short rings, one long, wondering whether they had changed the signal, doubting it; still worrying about Villem or perhaps Stella, or perhaps just the child. He heard a close creak of floor-boards and guessed he was being examined through a spyhole by someone a foot away from him. The door swiftly opened, he stepped into a gloomy hall as two wiry arms hugged him in their grip. He smelt body-heat and sweat and cigarette smoke and an unshaven face pressed against his own – left cheek, right cheek, as if to bestow a medal – once more to the left for particular affection.

'Max,' Mikhel murmured in a voice that was itself a requiem. 'You came. I am glad. I had hoped but I did not dare expect. I was waiting for you nevertheless. I waited all day till now. He loved you, Max. You were the best. He said so always. You were his inspiration. He told me. His example.'

'I'm sorry, Mikhel,' Smiley said. 'I'm really sorry.'

'As we all are, Max. As we all are. Inconsolable. But we are soldiers.'

He was dapper, and hollow-backed, and trim as the ex-major of horse he professed to be. His brown eyes, reddened by the night watch, had a becoming droopiness. He wore a black blazer over his shoulders like a cloak and black boots much polished which could indeed have been for riding. His grey hair was groomed with military correctness, his moustache thick but carefully clipped. His face was at first glance youthful and only a close look at the crumbling of its pale surface into countless tiny deltas revealed his years. Smiley followed him to the library. It ran the width of the house and was divided by alcoves into vanished countries – Latvia, Lithuania, and not least Estonia – and in each alcove were a table and a flag and at several tables there were chess sets laid out for play, but nobody was playing, nobody was reading either; nobody was there, except for one blonde, broad woman in her forties wearing a short skirt and ankle socks. Her yellow hair, dark at the roots, was knotted in a severe bun, and she lounged beside a samovar reading a travel magazine showing birch forests in the autumn. Drawing level with her, Mikhel paused and seemed about to make an introduction, but at the sight of Smiley, her glance flared with an intense and unmistakable anger. She looked at him, her mouth curled in contempt, she looked away through the rain-smeared window. Her cheeks were shiny from weeping and there were olive bruises under her heavy-lidded eyes.

'Elvira loved him also very much,' Mikhel observed by way of explanation when they were out of hearing. 'He was a brother to her. He instructed her.'

'Elvira?'

'My wife, Max. After many years we are married. I resisted. It is not always good for our work. But I owe her this security.'

They sat down. Around them and along the walls hung martyrs of forgotten movements. This one already in prison, photographed through wire. That one dead and – like Vladimir – they had pulled back the sheet to expose his bloodied face. A third, laughing, wore the baggy cap of a partisan and carried a long-barrelled rifle. From down the room they heard a small explosion followed by a rich Russian oath. Elvira, bride of Mikhel, was lighting the samovar.

'I'm sorry,' Smiley repeated.

*Enemies I do not fear, Villem,* thought Smiley. *But friends I fear greatly.*

They were in Mikhel's private alcove that he called his office. An old-fashioned telephone lay on the table beside a Remington upright typewriter like the one in Vladimir's flat. Somebody must once have bought lots of them, thought Smiley. But the focus was a high hand-carved chair with barley-twist legs and a monarchic crest embroidered on the back. Mikhel sat on it primly, knees and boots together, a proxy king too small for his throne. He had lit a cigarette, which he held vertically from below. Above him a pall of tobacco smoke hung exactly where Smiley remembered it. In the waste-paper basket, Smiley noticed several discarded copies of *Sporting Life*.

'He was a leader, Max, he was a hero,' Mikhel declared. 'We must try to profit from his courage and example.' He paused as if expecting Smiley to write this down for publication. 'In such cases it is natural to ask oneself how one can possibly carry on. Who is worthy to follow him? Who has his stature, his honour, his sense of destiny? Fortunately our movement is a continuing process. It is greater than any one individual, even than any one group.'

Listening to Mikhel's polished phrases, staring at his polished boots, Smiley found himself marvelling at the man's age. The Russians occupied Estonia in 1940, he recalled. To have been a cavalry officer, Mikhel would have to be sixty if a day. He tried to assemble the rest of Mikhel's turbulent biography – the long road through foreign wars and untrusted ethnic brigades, all the chapters of history contained in this one little body. He wondered how old the boots were.

'Tell me about his last days, Mikhel,' Smiley suggested. 'Was he active to the very end?'

'Completely active, Max, active in all respects. As a patriot. As a man. As a leader.'

Her expression as contemptuous as before, Elvira put the tea before them, two cups with lemon, and small marzipan cakes. In motion she was insinuating, with fluid haunches and a sullen hint of challenge. Smiley tried to remember her background also, but it eluded him or perhaps he had never known it. *He was a brother to her,* he thought. *He instructed her.* But something from his own life had long ago warned him to mistrust explanations, particularly of love.

'And as a member of the Group?' Smiley asked when she had left them.

'Also active?'

'Always,' said Mikhel gravely.

There was a small pause while each man politely waited for the other to continue.

'Who do you think did it, Mikhel? Was he betrayed?'

'Max, you know as well as I do who did it. We are all of us at risk. All of us. The call can come any time. Important is, we must be ready for it. Myself I am a soldier, I am prepared, I am ready. If I go, Elvira has her security. That is all. For the Bolshevites we exiles remain enemy number one. Anathema. Where they can, they destroy us. Still. As once they destroyed our churches and our villages and our schools and our culture. And they are right, Max., They are right to be afraid of us. Because one day we shall defeat them.'

'But why did they choose this particular moment?' Smiley objected gently after this somewhat ritualistic pronouncement. 'They could have killed Vladimir years ago.'

Mikhel had produced a flat tin box with two tiny rollers on it like a mangle, and a packet of coarse yellow cigarette-papers. Having licked a paper, he laid it on the rollers and poured in black tobacco. A snap, the mangle turned, and there on the silvered surface lay one fat, loosely packed cigarette. He was about to help himself to it when Elvira came over and took it. He rolled another and returned the box to his pocket.

'Unless Vladi was *up* to something, I suppose,' Smiley continued after these staged manoeuvres. 'Unless he *provoked* them in some way – which he might have done, knowing him.'

'Who can tell?' Mikhel said and blew some more smoke carefully into the air above them.

'Well, *you* can, Mikhel, if anyone can. Surely he confided in *you*. You were his right-hand man for twenty years or more. First Paris, then here. Don't tell me he didn't trust *you*,' said Smiley ingenuously.

'Our leader was a secretive man, Max. This was his strength. He had to be. It was a military necessity.'

'But not towards *you*, surely?' Smiley insisted, in his most flattering tone. 'His Paris adjutant. His aide-de-camp. His confidential secretary? Come, you do yourself an injustice!'

Leaning forward in his throne, Mikhel placed a small hand strictly across his heart. His brown voice took on an even deeper tone.

'Max. Even towards me. At the end, even towards Mikhel. It was to shield me. To spare me dangerous knowledge. He said to me even: "Mikhel, it is better that you – even you – do not know what the past has thrown up." I implored him. In vain. He came to me one evening. Here. I was asleep upstairs. He gave the special ring on the bell: "Mikhel, I need fifty pounds."'

Elvira returned, this time with an empty ashtray, and as she put it on the table Smiley felt a surge of tension like the sudden working of a drug. He experienced it driving sometimes, waiting for a crash that didn't happen. And he experienced it with Ann, watching her return from some supposedly innocuous engagement and knowing – simply knowing – it was not.

'When was this?' he asked when she had left again.

'Twelve days ago. One week last Monday. From his manner I am able to discern immediately that this is an official affair. He has never before asked me for money. "General," I say to him. "You are making a conspiracy. Tell me what it is." But he shakes his head. "Listen," I tell him, "if this is a conspiracy, take my advice, go to Max." He refused. "Mikhel," he tells me. "Max is a good man, but he does not have confidence any more in our Group. He wishes, even, that we end our struggle. But when I have landed the big fish I am hoping for, then I shall go to Max and claim our expenses and perhaps many things besides. But this I do afterwards, not before. Meanwhile I cannot conduct my business in a dirty shirt. Please, Mikhel. Lend me fifty pounds. In all my life this is my most important mission. It reaches far into our past." His words exactly. In my wallet I had fifty pounds – fortunately I had that day made a successful investment – I give them to him. "General," I said. "Take all I have. My possessions are yours. Please,"' said Mikhel and to punctuate this gesture – or to authenticate it – drew heavily at his yellow cigarette.

In the grimy window above them Smiley had glimpsed the reflection of Elvira standing half-way down the room, listening to their conversation. Mikhel had also seen her and had even shot her an evil frown, but he seemed unwilling, and perhaps unable, to order her away.

'That was very good of you,' Smiley said after a suitable pause.

'Max, it was my duty. From the heart. I know no other law.'

She despises me for not helping the old man, thought Smiley. She was in on it, she knew, and now she despises me for not helping him in his hour of need. *He was a brother to her*, he remembered. *He instructed her.*

'And this approach to you – this request for operational funds,' and Smiley. 'It came out of the blue? There'd been nothing before, to tell you he was up to something big?'

Again Mikhel frowned, taking his time, and it was clear that Mikhel did not care too much for questions.

'Some months ago, perhaps two, he received a letter,' he said cautiously. 'Here, to this address.'

'Did he receive so few?'

'This letter was special,' said Mikhel, with the same air of caution, and suddenly Smiley realised that Mikhel was in what the Sarratt inquisitors called the loser's corner, because he did not know – he could only guess – how much or how little Smiley knew already. Therefore Mikhel would give up his information jealously, hoping to read the strength of Smiley's hand while he did so.

'Who was it from?'

Mikhel, as so often, answered a slightly different question.

'It was from Paris, Max, a long letter, many pages, handwritten. Addressed to the General personally, not Miller. To General Vladimir, most personal. On the envelope was written Most Personal, in French. The letter arrived, I locked it in my desk; at eleven o'clock he walks in as usual: "Mikhel, I salute you." Sometimes, believe me, we even saluted each other. I hand him the letter, he sat' – he pointed towards Elvira's end of the room – 'he sat down, opened it quite carelessly, as if he had no expectation from it, and I saw him gradually become preoccupied. Absorbed. I would say fascinated. Impassioned even. I spoke to him. He didn't answer. I spoke again – you know his ways – he ignored me totally. He went for a walk. "I shall return," he said.'

'Taking the letter?'

'Of course. It was his fashion, when he had a great matter to consider, to go for a walk. When he returned, I noticed a deep excitement in him. A tension. "Mikhel." You know how he spoke. All must obey. "Mikhel. Get out the photocopier. Put some paper in it for me. I have a documentary to copy." I asked him how many copies. One. I ask him how many sheets. "Seven. Please stand at five paces' distance while I operate the machine," he tells me. "I cannot involve you in this matter."'

Once again, Mikhel indicated the spot as if it proved the absolute veracity of his story. The black copier stood on its own table, like an old steam-engine, with rollers, and holes for pouring in the different chemicals. 'The General was not mechanical, Max. I set up the machine for him – then I stood – here – so –calling out instructions to him across the room. When he had finished, he stood over the copies while they dried, then folded them into his pocket.'

'And the original?'

'This also he put in his pocket.'

'So you never read the letter?' Smiley said, in a tone of light commiseration.

'No, Max. I am sad to tell you I did not.'

'But you saw the envelope. You had it here to give to him when he arrived.'

'I told you, Max. It was from Paris.'

'Which district?'

The hesitation again: 'The fifteenth,' said Mikhel. 'I believe it was the fifteenth. Where many of our people used to be.'

'And the date? Can you be more precise about it? You said about two months.'

'Early September. I would say early September. Late August is possible. Say six weeks ago, around.'

'The address on the envelope was also handwritten?'

'It was, Max. It was.'

'What colour was the envelope?'

'Brown.'

'And the ink?'

'I suppose blue.'

'Was it sealed?'

'Please?'

'Was the envelope sealed with sealing-wax or adhesive tape? Or was it just gummed in the ordinary way?'

Mikhel shrugged, as if such details were beneath him.

'But the sender had put his name on the outside, presumably?' Smiley persisted lightly.

If he had, Mikhel was not admitting it.

For a moment Smiley allowed his mind to dwell upon the brown envelope cached in the Savoy cloakroom, and the passionate plea for help it had contained. *This morning I had an impression that they were trying to kill me. Will you not send me your magic friend once more?* Postmark Paris, he thought. The 15th district. After the first letter, Vladimir gave the writer his home address, he thought. Just as he gave his home telephone number to Villem. After the first letter, Vladimir made sure he bypassed Mikhel.

A phone rang and Mikhel answered it at once, with a brief 'Yes?' then listened.

'Then put me five each way,' he muttered, and rang off with magisterial dignity.

Approaching the main purpose of his visit to Mikhel, Smiley took care to proceed with great respect. He remembered that Mikhel – who by the time he joined the Group in Paris had seen the inside of half the interrogation centres of Eastern Europe – had a way of slowing down when he was prodded, and by this means in his day had driven the Sarratt inquisitors half mad.

'May I ask you something, Mikhel?' Smiley said, selecting a line that was oblique to the main thrust of his enquiry.

'Please.'

'That evening when he called here to borrow money from you, did he stay?

Did you make him tea? Play a game of chess perhaps? Could you paint it for me a little, please, that evening?'

'We played chess, but not with concentration. He was preoccupied, Max.'

'Did he say any more about the big fish?'

The drooped eyes considered Smiley soulfully.

'Please, Max?'

'The big fish. The operation he said he was planning. I wondered whether he enlarged upon it in any way.'

'Nothing. Nothing at all, Max. He was entirely secretive.'

'Did you have the impression it involved another country?'

'He spoke only of having no passport. He was wounded – Max, I tell you this frankly – he was hurt that the Circus would not trust him with a passport. After such service, such devotion – he was hurt.'

'It was for his own good, Mikhel.'

'Max, *I* understand entirely. I am a younger man, a man of the world, flexible. The General was at times impulsive, Max. Steps had to be taken – even by those who admired him – to contain his energies. Please. But for the man himself, it was incomprehensible. An insult.'

From behind him Smiley heard the thud of feet as Elvira stomped contemptuously back to her corner.

'So who did he think should do his travelling for him?' Smiley asked, again ignoring her.

'Villem,' said Mikhel with obvious disapproval. 'He does not tell me in as many words but I believe he sends Villem. That was my impression. Villem would go. General Vladimir spoke with much pride of Villem's youth and honour. Also of his father. He even made an historical reference. He spoke of bringing in the new generation to avenge the injustices of the old. He was very moved.'

'Where did he send him? Did Vladi give any hint of that?'

'He does not tell me. He tells me only, "Villem has a passport, he is a brave boy, a good Balt, steady, he can travel, but it is also necessary to protect him." I do not probe, Max. I do not pry. That is not my way. You know that.'

'Still you did form an impression, I suppose,' Smiley said. 'The way one does. There are not so many places Villem would be free to go to, after all. Least of all on fifty pounds. There was Villem's job too, wasn't there? Not to mention his wife. He couldn't just step into the blue when he felt like it.'

Mikhel made a very military gesture. Pushing out his lips till his moustache was almost on its back, he tugged shrewdly at his nose with his thumb and forefinger. 'The General also asked me for maps,' he said finally. 'I was in two minds whether to tell you this. You are his vicar, Max, but you are not of our cause. But as I trust you, I shall.'

'Maps of where?'

'Street maps.' He flicked a hand towards the shelves as if ordering them closer. 'City plans. Of Danzig. Hamburg. Lübeck. Helsinki. The northern seaboard. I asked him, "General, sir. Let me help you," I said to him. "Please. I am your assistant for everything. I have a right, Vladimir. Let me help you." He refused me. He wished to be entirely private.'

Moscow Rules, Smiley thought yet again. Many maps and only one of them is relevant. And once again, he noted, towards his trusted Paris adjutant Vladimir was taking measures to obscure his purpose.

'After which he left?' he suggested.

'Correct.'

'At what time?'

'It was late.'

'Can you say how late?'

'Two. Three. Even four maybe. I am not sure.'

Then Smiley felt Mikhel's gaze lift fractionally over his shoulder and beyond it and stay there and an instinct which he had lived by for as long as he could remember made him ask: 'Did Vladimir come here alone?'

'Of course, Max. Who would he bring?'

They were interrupted by a clank of crockery as Elvira at the other end of the room went clumsily back to her chores. Daring to glance at Mikhel just then, Smiley saw him staring after her with an expression he recognised but for a split second could not place: hopeless and affectionate at once, torn between dependence and disgust. Till, with sickening empathy, Smiley found himself looking into his own face as he had glimpsed it too often, red-eyed like Mikhel's, in Ann's pretty gilt mirrors in their house in Bywater Street.

'So if he wouldn't let you help him, what did you do?' Smiley asked with the same studied casualness. 'Sit up and read – play chess with Elvira?'

Mikhel's brown eyes held him a moment, slipped away and came back to him.

'No, Max,' he replied with great courtesy. 'I gave him the maps. He desired to be left alone with them. I wished him goodnight. I was asleep by the time he left.'

But not Elvira, apparently, Smiley thought. Elvira stayed behind for instruction from her proxy brother. *Active as a patriot, as a man, as a leader,* Smiley rehearsed. *Active in all respects.*

'So what contact have you had with him since?' Smiley asked and Mikhel came suddenly to yesterday. Nothing till yesterday, Mikhel said.

'Yesterday afternoon he called me on the telephone. Max, I swear to you I had not heard him so excited for many years. Happy, I would say ecstatic. "Mikhel! Mikhel!" Max, that was a delighted man. He would come to me that night. Last night. Late maybe but he will have my fifty pounds. "General," I tell him. "What is fifty pounds? Are you well? Are you safe? Tell me." "Mikhel, I have been fishing and I am happy. Stay awake," he says to me. "I shall be with you at eleven o'clock. soon after. I shall have the money. Also it is necessary I beat you at chess to calm my nerves." I stay awake, make tea, wait for him. And wait. Max, I am a soldier, for myself I am not afraid. But for the General – for that old man, Max – I was afraid. I phone the Circus, an emergency. They hang up on me. Why? Max, why did you do that, please?'

'I was not on duty,' Smiley said, now watching Mikhel as intently as he dared. 'Tell me, Mikhel,' he began.

'Max.'

'What did you think Vladimir was going to be doing after he rang you with the good news – and before he came to repay you fifty pounds?'

Mikhel did not hesitate. 'Naturally I assumed he would be going to Max,' he said. 'He had landed his big fish. Now he would go to Max, claim his expenses, present him with his great news. Naturally,' he repeated, looking a little too straight into Smiley's eyes.

*Naturally,* thought Smiley; and you knew to the minute when he would leave his apartment, and to the metre the route he would take to reach the Hampstead flat.

'So he failed to appear, you rang the Circus and we were unhelpful,' Smiley resumed. 'I'm sorry. So what did you do next?'

'I phone Villem. First to make sure the boy is all right, also to ask him, where is our Leader? That English wife of his bawled me out. Finally I went to his flat. I did not like to – it was an intrusion – his private life is his own – but I went. I rang the bell. He did not answer. I came home. This morning at eleven o'clock Jüri rings.I had not read the early edition of the evening papers, I am not fond of English newspapers. Jüri had read them. Vladimir our leader was dead,' he ended.

Elvira was at his elbow. She had two glasses of vodka on a tray.

'Please,' said Mikhel. Smiley took a glass, Mikhel the other.

'To life!' said Mikhel, very loud, and drank, as the tears started to his eyes.

'To life,' Smiley repeated while Elvira watched them.

She went with him, Smiley thought. She forced Mikhel to the old man's flat, she dragged him to the door.

'Have you told anyone else of this, Mikhel?' Smiley asked when she had once more left.

'Jüri I don't trust,' said Mikhel, blowing his nose.

'Did you tell Jüri about Villem?'

'Please?

'Did you mention Villem to him? Did you suggest to Jüri in any way that Villem might have been involved with Vladimir?'

Mikhel had committed no such sin, apparently.

'In this situation you should trust no one,' Smiley said, in a more formal tone, as he prepared to take his leave. 'Not even the police. Those are the orders. The police must not know that Vladimir was doing anything operational when he died. It is important for security. Yours as well as ours. He gave you no message otherwise? No words for Max, for instance?'

*Tell Max that it concerns the Sandman,* he thought.

Mikhel smiled his regrets.

'Did Vladimir mention Hector recently, Mikhel?'

'Hector was no good for him.'

'Did Vladimir say that?'

'Please, Max. I have nothing against Hector personally. Hector is Hector, he is not a gentleman, but in our work we must use many varieties of mankind. This was the General speaking. Our leader was an old man. "Hector," Vladimir says to me. "Hector is no good. Our good postman Hector is like the City banks. When it rains, they say, the banks take away your umbrella. Our postman Hector is the same." Please. This is Vladimir speaking. Not Mikhel. "Hector is no good."'

'When did he say this?'

'He said it several times.'

'Recently?'

'Yes.'

'How recently?'

'Maybe two months. Maybe less.'

'After he received the Paris letter, or before?'

'After. No question.'

Mikhel escorted him to the door, a gentleman even if Toby Esterhase was not. At her place again beside the samovar, Elvira sat smoking before the same photograph of birch trees. And as he passed her, Smiley heard a sort of hiss, made through the nose or mouth, or both at once, as a last statement of her contempt.

'What will you do now?' he asked of Mikhel in the way one asks such things of the bereaved. Out of the corner of his eye he saw her head lift at his question and her fingers spread across the page.

A last thought struck him: 'And you didn't recognise the handwriting?' Smiley asked.

'What handwriting is this, Max?'

'On the envelope from Paris?'

Suddenly he had no time to wait for an answer; suddenly he was sick of evasion.

'Goodbye, Mikhel.'

'Go well, Max.'

Elvira's head sank again to the birch trees.

I'll never know, Smiley thought, as he made his way quickly down the wooden staircase. None of us will. Was he Mikhel the traitor who resented the old man sharing his woman, and thirsted for the crown that had been denied him for too long? Or was he Mikhel the selfless officer and gentleman, Mikhel the ever-loyal servant? Or was he perhaps, like many loyal servants, both?

He thought of Mikhel's cavalry pride, as terribly tender as any other hero's manhood. His pride in being the General's keeper, his pride in being his satrap. His sense of injury at being excluded. His pride again – how it split so many ways! But how far did it extend? To a pride in giving nobly to each master, for instance? *Gentlemen, I have served you both well*, says the perfect double agent in the twilight of his life. And says it with pride, too, thought Smiley, who had known a number of them.

He thought of the seven-page letter from Paris. He thought of second proofs. He wondered who the photocopy had gone to – maybe Esterhase? He wondered where the original was. So who went to Paris? he wondered. If Villem went to Hamburg, who was the little magician? He was bone tired. His tiredness hit him like a sudden virus. He felt it in the knees, the hips, his whole subsiding body. But he kept walking, for his mind refused to rest.

# ELEVEN

To walk was just possible for Ostrakova, and to walk was all she asked. To walk and wait for the magician. Nothing was broken. Though her dumpy little body, when they had given her a bath, was shaping up to become as blackened and patchy as a map of the Siberian coalfields, nothing was broken. And her poor rump, which had given her that bit of trouble at the warehouse, looked already as though the assembled secret armies of Soviet Russia had booted her from one end of Paris to the other: still, nothing was broken. They had X-rayed every part of her, they had prodded her like questionable meat for signs of internal bleeding. But in the end, they had gloomily declared her to be the victim of a miracle.

They had wanted to keep her, for all that. They had wanted to treat her for shock, sedate her – at least for one night! The police, who had found six witnesses with seven conflicting accounts of what had happened (The car was grey or was it blue? The registration number was from Marseilles, or was it foreign?), the police had taken one long statement from her, and threatened to come back and take another.

Ostrakova had nevertheless discharged herself.

Then had she at least children to look after her? they had asked. Oh, but she had a mass of them! she said. Daughters who would pander to her smallest whim, sons to assist her up and down the stairs! Any number – as many as they wished! To please the sisters, she even made up lives for them, though her head was beating like a war-drum. She had sent out for clothes. Her own were in shreds and God Himself must have blushed to see the state she was in when they found her. She gave a false address to go with her false name; she wanted no follow-up, no visitors. And somehow, by sheer will-power, at the stroke of six that evening, Ostrakova became just another ex-patient, stepping cautiously and extremely painfully down the ramp of the great black hospital, to rejoin the very world which that same day had done its best to be rid of her for good. Wearing her boots, which like herself were battered but mysteriously unbroken; and she was quaintly proud of the way they had supported her.

She wore them still. Restored to the twilight of her own apartment, seated in Ostrakov's tattered armchair while she patiently wrestled with his old army revolver, trying to fathom how the devil it loaded, cocked, and fired itself, she wore them like a uniform. 'I am an army of one.' To stay alive: that was her one aim, and the longer she did it, the greater would be her victory. To stay alive until the General came, or sent her the magician.

To escape from them, like Ostrakov? Well, she had done that. To mock them, like Glikman, to force them into corners where they had no option but to contemplate their own obscenity? In her time, she liked to think, she had done a little of that as well. But to survive, as neither of her men had done; to cling to life, against all the efforts of that soulless, numberless universe of brutalized functionaries; to be a thorn to them every hour of the day, merely by staying alive, by breathing, eating, moving, and having her wits about her – that, Ostrakova had decided, was an occupation worthy of her mettle, and her faith, and of her two loves. She had set about it immediately, with appropriate devotion. Already she had sent the fool concierge to shop for her: disability had its uses.

'I have had a small *attack*, Madame la Pierre' – whether of the heart, the stomach or the Russian secret police she did not divulge to the old goat. 'I am advised to leave off work for several weeks and rest completely. I am exhausted, madame – there are times when one wishes only to be alone. And here, take this, madame – not like the others, so grasping and over-vigilant.' Madame la Pierre took the note in her fist, and looked at just one corner of it before tucking it away at her waist somewhere. 'And listen, madame, if anyone asks for me, do me a favour and say I am away. I shall burn no lights on the street side. We women of sensitivity are entitled to a little peace, you agree? But, madame, please, remember who they are, these visitors, and tell me – the gasman, people from the charities – tell me everything. I like to hear that life is going on around me.'

The concierge concluded she was mad, no doubt, but there was no madness to her money, and money was what the concierge liked best, and besides, she was mad herself. In a few hours, Ostrakova had become more cunning even than in Moscow. The concierge's husband came up – a brigand himself, worse than the old goat – and, encouraged by further payments, fixed chains to her front door. Tomorrow he would fit a peep-hole, also for money. The concierge promised to receive her mail for her, and deliver it only at certain agreed times – exactly eleven in the morning, six in the evening, two short rings – for money. By forcing open the tiny ventilator in the back lavatory, and standing on a chair, Ostrakova could look down into the courtyard whenever she wanted, at whoever came and went. She had sent a note to the warehouse saying she was indisposed. She could not move her double bed, but with pillows and her feather coverlet she made up the divan and positioned it so that it pointed like a torpedo through the open door of the drawing-room at the front door beyond it, and all she had to do was lie on it with her boots aimed at the intruder and shoot down the line of them, and if she didn't blow her own foot off, she would catch him in the first moment of surprise as he attempted to burst in on her: she had worked it out. Her head throbbed and caterwauled, her eyes had a way of darkening over when she moved her head too fast, she had a raging temperature and sometimes she half fainted. But she had worked it out, she had made her dispositions, and till the General or the magician came, it was Moscow all over again. 'You're on your own, you old fool,' she told herself aloud. 'You've nobody to rely on but yourself, so get on with it.'

With one photograph of Glikman and one of Ostrakov on the floor beside her, and an icon of the Virgin under the coverlet, Ostrakova embarked upon her first night's vigil, praying steadily to a host of saints, not least of them St. Joseph, that they would send her her redeemer, the magician.

Not a single message tapped to me over the water-pipes, she thought. Not even a guard's insult to wake me up.

# TWELVE

And still it was the same day; there was no end to it, no bed. For a while after leaving Mikhel, George Smiley let his legs lead him, not knowing where, too tired, too stirred to trust himself to drive, yet bright enough to watch his back, to make the vague yet sudden turnings which catch would-be followers off guard. Bedraggled, heavy-eyed, he waited for his mind to come down, trying to unwind, to step clear of the restless thrust of his twenty-hour marathon.

The Embankment had him, so did a pub off Northumberland Avenue, probably The Sherlock Holmes, where he gave himself a large whisky and dithered over telephoning Stella – was she all right? Deciding there was no point – he could hardly phone her every night asking whether she and Villem were alive – he walked again until he found himself in Soho, which on Saturday nights was even nastier than usual. Beard Lacon, he thought. Demand protection for the family. But he had only to imagine the scene to know the idea was stillborn. If Vladimir was not the Circus's responsibility, then still less could Villem be. And how, pray, do you attach a team of baby-sitters to a long-distance Continental lorry driver? His one consolation was that Vladimir's assassins had apparently found what they were looking for: that they had no other needs. Yet what about the woman in Paris? What about the writer of the two letters?

Go home, he thought. Twice, from phone boxes, he made dummy calls, checking the pavement. Once he entered a cul-de-sac and doubled back, watching for the slurred step, the eye that ducked his glance. He considered taking a hotel room. Sometimes he did that, just for a night's peace. Sometimes his house was too much of a dangerous place for him. He thought of the piece of negative film: time to open the box. Finding himself gravitating by instinct towards his old headquarters at Cambridge Circus, he cut hastily away eastward, finishing by his car again. Confident that he was not observed, he drove to Bayswater, well off his beaten track, but he still watched his mirror intently. From a Pakistani ironmonger who sold everything, he bought two plastic washing-up bowls and a rectangle of commercial glass three and a half inches by five; and from a cash-and-carry chemist not three doors down, ten sheets of Grade 2 resin-coated paper of the same size, and a children's pocket torch with a spaceman on the handle and a red filter that slid over the lens when you pushed a nickel button. From Bayswater, by a painstaking route, he drove to the Savoy, entering from the Embankment side. He was still alone. In the men's cloakroom, the same attendant was on duty, and he even remembered their joke.

'I'm still waiting for it to explode,' he said with a smile, handing back the box. 'I thought I heard it ticking once or twice, and all.'

At his front door the tiny wedges he had put up before his drive to Charlton were still in place. In his neighbours' windows he saw Saturday-evening candle-light and talking heads; but in his own, the curtains were still drawn as he had left them, and in the hall, Ann's pretty little grandmother clock received him in deep darkness, which he hastily corrected.

Dead weary, he nevertheless proceeded methodically.

First he tossed three fire-lighters into the drawing-room grate, lit them, shovelled smokeless coal over them and hung Ann's indoor clothes-line across the hearth. For an overall he donned an old kitchen apron, tying the cord firmly round his ample midriff for additional protection. From under the stairs he exhumed a pile of green black-out material and a pair of kitchen steps, which he took to the basement. Having blacked out the window, he went upstairs again, unwrapped the box, opened it, and no, it was not a bomb, it was a letter and a packet of battered cigarettes with Vladimir's piece of negative film fed into it. Taking it out, he returned to the basement, put on the red torch, and went to work, though Heaven knows he possessed no photographic flair whatever, and could perfectly well – in theory – have had the job done for him in a fraction of the time, through Lauder Strickland, by the Circus's own photographic section. Or for that matter he could have taken it to any one of half a dozen 'tradesmen', as they are known in the jargon: marked collaborators in certain fields who are pledged, if called upon at any time, to drop everything and, asking no questions, put their skills at the service's disposal. One such tradesman actually lived not a stone's throw from Sloane Square, a gentle soul who specialized in wedding photographs. Smiley had only to walk ten minutes and press the man's doorbell and he could have had his prints in half an hour. But he didn't. He preferred instead the inconvenience, as well as imperfection, of taking a contact print in the privacy of his home, while upstairs the telephone rang and he ignored it.

He preferred the trial and error of exposing the negative for too long, then for too little, under the main room light. Of using as a measure the cumbersome kitchen timer, which ticked and grumbled like something from *Coppélia*. He preferred grunting and cursing in irritation and sweating in the dark and wasting at least six sheets of resin-coated paper before the developer in the washing-up bowl yielded an image even half-way passable, which he laid in the rapid fixer for three minutes. And washed it. And dabbed it with a clean tea-cloth, probably ruining the cloth for good, he wouldn't know. And took it upstairs and pegged it to the clothes-line. And for those who like a heavy symbol, it is a matter of history that the fire, despite the fire-lighters, was all but out, since the coal consisted in great measure of damp slag, and that George Smiley had to puff at the flames to prevent it from dying, crouching on all fours for the task. Thus it might have occurred to him – though it didn't, for with his curiosity once more aroused he had put aside his introspective mood – that the action was exactly contrary to Lacon's jangling order to douse the flames and not to fan them.

Next, with the print safely suspended over the carpet, Smiley addressed himself to a pretty marquetry writing-desk in which Ann kept her 'things' with embarrassing openness. Such as a sheet of writing-paper on which she had written the one word 'Darling' and not continued, perhaps uncertain which darling to write to. Such as book-matches from restaurants he had never been to and letters in handwriting he did not know. From among such painful bric-à-brac he extracted a large Victorian magnifying glass with a mother-of-pearl handle, which she employed for reading clues to crosswords never completed. Thus armed – the sequence of these actions, because of his fatigue, lacked the final edge of logic – he put on a record of Mahler, which Ann had given him, and sat himself in the leather reading chair which was equipped with a mahogany book-rest designed to swivel like a bed tray across the occupant's stomach. Tired to death again, he unwisely allowed his eyes to close while he listened, part to the music, part to the occasional *pat-pat* of the dripping photograph, and part to the grudging crackle of the fire. Waking with a start thirty minutes later, he found the print dry, and the Mahler revolving mutely on its turntable.

He stared, one hand to his spectacles, the other slowly rotating the magnifying glass over the print.

The photograph showed a group, but it was not political, nor was it a bathing party, since nobody was wearing a swimming-suit. The group consisted of a quartet, two men and two women, and they were lounging on quilted sofas round a low table laden with bottles and cigarettes. The women were naked and young and pretty. The men, scarcely better covered, were sprawled side by side, and the girls had twined themselves dutifully around their elected mates. The lighting of the photograph was sallow and unearthly, and from the little Smiley knew of such matters he concluded that the negative was made on fast film, for the print was also grainy. Its texture, when he pondered it, reminded him of the photographs one saw too often of terrorists' hostages, except that the four in the photograph were concerned with each other, whereas hostages have a way of staring down the lens as if it were a gun barrel. Still in quest of what he would have called operational intelligence, he passed to the probable position of the camera and decided it must have been high above the subjects. The four appeared to be lying at the centre of a pit with the camera looking down on them. A shadow, very black – a balustrade, or perhaps it was a window-sill, or merely the shoulder of somebody in front – obtruded across the lower foreground. It was as if, despite the vantage point, only half the lens had dared to lift its head above the eye-line.

Here Smiley drew his first tentative conclusion. A step – not a large one; but he had enough large steps on his mind already. A technical step, call it: a modest, technical step. The photograph had every mark of being what the trade called *stolen*. And stolen moreover with a view to *burning*, meaning 'blackmail.' But the blackmail of whom? To what end?

Weighing the problem, Smiley probably fell asleep. The telephone was on Ann's little desk, and it must have rung three or four times before he was aware of it.

'Yes, Oliver?' said Smiley cautiously.

'Ah. George. I tried you earlier. You got back all right, I trust?'

'Where from?' asked Smiley.

Lacon preferred not to answer the question. 'I felt I owed you a call, George. We parted on a sour note. I was brusque. Too much on my plate. I apologise. How are things? You are done? Finished?'

In the background Smiley heard Lacon's daughters squabbling about how much rent was payable on a hotel in Park Lane. He's got them for the weekend, thought Smiley.

'I've had the Home Office on the line again, George,' Lacon went on in a lower voice, not bothering to wait for his reply. 'They've had the pathologist's report and the body may be released. An early cremation is recommended. I thought perhaps if I gave you the name of the firm that is handling things, you might care to pass it on to those concerned. Unattributably, of course. You saw the press release? What did you think of it? I thought it was apt. I thought it caught the tone exactly.'

'I'll get a pencil,' Smiley said and fumbled in the drawer once more until he found a pear-shaped plastic object with a leather thong which Ann sometimes wore around her neck. With difficulty he prised it open, and wrote to Lacon's dictation: the firm, the address, the firm again, followed yet again by the address.

'Got it? Want me to repeat it? Or should you read it back to me, make assurance double sure?'

'I think I have it, thank you,' Smiley said. Somewhat belatedly, it dawned on him that Lacon was drunk.

'Now, George, we have a date, don't forget. A seminar on marriage with no holds barred. I have cast you as my elder statesman here. There's a very decent steak-house downstairs and I shall treat you to a slap-up dinner while you give me of your wisdom. Have you a diary there? Let's pencil something in.'

With dismal foreboding Smiley agreed a date. After a lifetime of inventing cover stories for every occasion, he still found it impossible to talk his way out of a dinner invitation.

'And you found nothing?' Lacon asked, on a more cautious note. 'No snags, hitches, loose ends. It was a storm in a teacup, was it, as we suspected?'

A lot of answers crossed Smiley's mind, but he saw no use to any of them.

'What about the phone bill?' Smiley asked.

'Phone bill? What phone bill? Ah, you mean *his*. Pay it and send me the receipt. No problem. Better still, slip it in the post to Strickland.'

'I already sent it to you,' said Smiley patiently. 'I asked you for a breakdown of traceable calls.'

'I'll get on to them at once,' Lacon replied blandly. 'Nothing else?'

'No. No, I don't think so. Nothing.'

'Get some sleep. You sound all in.'

'Good night,' said Smiley.

With Ann's magnifying glass in his plump fist once more, Smiley went back to his examination. The floor of the pit was carpeted, apparently in white; the quilted sofas were formed in a horseshoe following the line of the drapes that comprised the rear perimeter. There was an upholstered door in the background and the clothes the two men had discarded – jackets, neckties, trousers – were hanging from it with hospital neatness. There was an ashtray on the table and Smiley set to work trying to read the writing round the edge. After much manipulation of the glass he came up with what the lapsed philologist in him described as the asterisk (or putative) form of the letters 'A-C-H-T,' but whether as a word in their own right – meaning 'eight' or 'attention' as well as certain other more remote concepts – or as four letters from a larger word, he could not tell. Nor did he at this stage exert himself to find out, preferring simply to store the intelligence in the back of his mind until some other part of the puzzle forced it into play.

Ann rang. Once again, perhaps, he had dozed off, for his recollection ever afterwards was that he did not hear the ring of the phone at all, but simply her voice as he slowly lifted the receiver to his ear: 'George, George,' as if she had been crying for him a long time, and he had only now summoned the energy or the caring to answer her.

They began their conversation as strangers, much as they began their love-making.

'How are you?' she asked.

'Very well, thank you. How are you? What can I do for you?'

'I mean it,' Ann insisted. 'How are you? I want to know.'

'And I told you I was well.'

'I rang you this morning. Why didn't you answer?'

'I was out.'

Long silence while she appeared to consider this feeble excuse. The telephone had never been a bother to her. It gave her no sense of urgency.

'Out working?' she asked.

'An administrative thing for Lacon.'

'He begins his administration early these days.'

'His wife's left him,' Smiley said by way of explanation.

No answer.

'You used to say she would be wise to,' he went on. 'She should get out fast, you used to say, before she became another Civil Service geisha.'

'I've changed my mind. He needs her.'

'But she, I gather, does not need him,' Smiley pointed out, taking refuge in an academic tone.

'Silly woman,' said Ann, and another longer silence followed, this time of Smiley's making while he contemplated the sudden unwished-for mountain of choice she had revealed to him.

To be together again, as she sometimes called it.

To forget the hurts, the list of lovers; to forget Bill Haydon, the Circus traitor, whose shadow still fell across her face each time he reached for her, whose memory he carried in him like a constant pain. Bill his friend, Bill the flower of their generation, the jester, the enchanter, the iconoclastic conformer; Bill the born deceiver, whose quest for the ultimate betrayal led him into the Russians' bed, and Ann's. To stage yet another honeymoon, fly away to the South of France, eat the meals, buy the clothes, all the let's-pretend that lovers play. And for how long? How long before her smile faded and her eyes grew dull and those mythical relations started needing her to cure their mythical ailments in far-off places?

'Where are you?' he asked.

'Hilda's.'

'I thought you were in Cornwall.'

Hilda was a divorced woman of some speed. She lived in Kensington, not twenty minutes' walk away.

'So where's Hilda?' he asked when he had come to terms with this intelligence.

'Out.'

'All night?'

'I expect so, knowing Hilda. Unless she brings him back.'

'Well then I suppose you must entertain yourself as well as you can without her,' he said, but as he spoke he heard her whisper 'George.'

A profound and vehement fear seized hold of Smiley's heart. He glared across the room at the reading chair and saw the contact photograph still on the book-rest beside her magnifying glass; in a single surge of memory, he reconstructed all the things that had hinted and whispered to him throughout the endless day; he heard the drum-beats of his own past, summoning him to one last effort to externalise and resolve the conflict he had lived by; and he wanted her nowhere near him. *Tell Max that it concerns the Sandman.* Gifted with the clarity that hunger, tiredness and confusion can supply, Smiley knew for certain she must have no part in what he had to do. He knew – he was barely at the threshold – yet he still knew that it was just possible, against all the odds, that he had been given, in late age, a chance to return to the rained-off contests of his life and play them after all. If that was so, then no Ann, no false peace, no tainted witness to his actions, should disturb his lonely quest. He had not known his mind till then. But now he knew it.

'You mustn't,' he said. 'Ann? Listen. You mustn't come here. It has nothing to do with choice. It's to do with practicalities. You mustn't come here.' His own words rang strangely to him.

'Then come here,' she said.

He rang off. He imagined her crying, then getting out her address book to see who from her First Eleven, as she called them, might console her in his place. He poured himself a neat whisky, the Lacon solution. He went to the kitchen, forgot why, and wandered into his study. Soda, he thought. Too late. Do without. I must have been mad, he thought. I'm chasing phantoms, there is nothing there. A senile General had a dream and died for it. He remembered Wilde: the fact that a man dies for a cause does not make that cause right. A picture was crooked. He straightened it, too much, too little, stepping back each time. *Tell him it concerns the Sandman.* He returned to the reading chair and his two prostitutes, fixing on them through Ann's magnifying glass with a ferocity which would have sent them scurrying to their pimps.

Clearly they were from the upper end of their profession, being fresh-bodied and young and well-groomed. They seemed also – but perhaps it was coincidence – to be deliberately distinguished from one another by whoever had selected them. The girl at the left was blonde and fine and even classical in build, with long thighs and small high breasts. Whereas her companion was dark-haired and stubby, with spreading hips and flared features, perhaps Eurasian. The blonde, he recorded, wore earrings in the shape of anchors, which struck him as odd because, in his limited experience of women, earrings were what they took off first. Ann had only to go out of the house without wearing them for his heart to sink. Beyond that he could think of nothing very clever to say about either girl and so, having swallowed another large gulp of raw Scotch, he transferred his attention to the men, once more – which was where it had been, if he would admit it, ever since he had started looking at the photograph in the first place. Like the girls, they were sharply differentiated from each other, though in the men – since they were a deal older – the differences had the appearance of greater depth and legibility of character. The man supporting the blonde girl was fair and at first sight dull, while the man supporting the dark girl was not merely dark-complexioned but had a Latin, even Levantine, alertness in his features, and an infectious smile that was the one engaging feature of the photograph. The fair man was large and sprawling, the dark man was small and bright enough to be his jester: a little imp of a fellow, with a kind face and flicked-up horns of hair above his ears.

A sudden nervousness – in retrospect perhaps foreboding – made Smiley take the fair man first. It was a time to feel safer with strangers.

The man's torso was burly but not athletic, his limbs ponderous without suggesting strength. The fairness of his skin and hair emphasised his obesity. His hands, one splayed on the girl's flank, the other round her waist, were fatty and artless. Lifting the magnifying glass slowly over the naked chest, Smiley reached the head. By the age of forty, someone clever had written ominously, a man gets the face he deserves. Smiley doubted it. He had known poetic souls condemned to life imprisonment behind harsh faces, and delinquents with the appearance of angels. Nevertheless, it was not an asset as a face, nor had the camera caught it at its most appealing. In terms of character, it appeared to be divided into two parts: the lower, which was pulled into a grin of crude high spirits as, open-mouthed, he addressed something to his male companion; the upper, which was ruled by two small and pallid eyes round which no mirth had gathered at all and no high spirits either, but which seemed to look out of their doughy surroundings with the cold, unblinking blandness of a child. The nose was flat, the hair-style full and mid-European.

Greedy, Ann would have said, who was given to passing absolute judgment on people merely by studying their portraits in the press. Greedy, weak, vicious. Avoid. A pity she had not reached the same conclusion about Haydon, he thought; or not in time.

Smiley returned to the kitchen and rinsed his face, then remembered that he had come to fetch water for his whisky. Settling again in the reading chair, he trained the magnifying glass on the second of the men, the jester. The whisky was keeping him awake, but it was also putting him to sleep. Why doesn't she ring again? he thought. If she rings again, I'll go to her. But in reality his mind was on this second face, because its familiarity disturbed him in much the way that its urgent complicity had disturbed Villem and Ostrakova before him. He gazed at it and his tiredness left him, he seemed to draw energy from it. Some faces, as Villem had suggested this morning, are known to us before we see them; others we see once and remember all our lives; others we see every day, and never remember at all. But which was this?

A Toulouse-Lautrec face, Smiley thought, peering in wonder – caught as the eyes slid away to some intense and perhaps erotic distraction. Ann would have taken to him immediately; he had the dangerous edge she liked. A Toulouse-Lautrec face, caught as a stray shard of fair-ground light fired one gaunt and travelled cheek. A hewn face, peaked and jagged, of which the brow and nose and jaw seemed all to have succumbed to the same eroding gales. A Toulouse-Lautrec face, swift and attaching. A waiter's face, never a diner's. With a waiter's anger burning brightest behind a subservient smile. Ann would like that side less well. Leaving the print where it lay, Smiley clambered slowly to his feet in order to keep himself awake, and lumbered round the room, trying to place it, failing, wondering whether it was all imagining. Some people *transmit*, he thought. Some people – you meet them, and they bring you their whole past as a natural gift. Some people are intimacy itself.

At Ann's writing-table he paused to stare at the telephone again. Hers, Hers and Haydon's. Hers and everybody's. Trimline, he thought. Or was it Slimline? Five pounds extra to the Post Office for the questionable pleasure of its outmoded, futuristic lines. *My tart's phone*, she used to call it. *The little warble for my little loves, the loud woo-hoo for my big ones.* He realised it was ringing. Had been ringing a long while, the little warble for the little loves. He put down his glass, still staring at the telephone while it trilled. She used to leave it on the floor among her records when she was playing music, he remembered. She used to lie with it – there, by the fire, over there – one haunch carelessly lifted in case it needed her. When she went to bed, she unplugged it and took it with her, to comfort her in the night. When they made love, he knew he was the surrogate for all the men who hadn't rung. For the First Eleven. For Bill Haydon, even though he was dead.

It had stopped ringing.

What does she do now? Try the Second Eleven? *To be beautiful and Ann is one thing*, she had said to him not long ago; *to be beautiful and Ann's age will soon be another.* And to be ugly and mine is another again, he thought furiously. Taking up the contact print, he resumed, with fresh intensity, his contemplations.

Shadows, he thought. Smudges of light and dark, ahead of us, behind us, as we lurch along our ways. Imp's horns, devil's horns, our shadows so much larger than ourselves. Who is he? Who was he? I met him. I refused to. And if I refused to, how do I know him? He was a supplicant of some kind, a man with something to sell – Intelligence, then? Dreams? Wakefully now, he stretched out on the sofa – anything rather than go upstairs to bed – and with the print before him, began plodding through the long galleries of his professional memory, holding the lamp to the half-forgotten portraits of charlatans, gold-makers, fabricators, pedlars, middlemen, hoods, rogues and occasionally heros who made up the supporting cast of his multitudinous acquaintance; looking for the one hallowed face that, like a secret sharer, seemed to have swum out of the little contact photograph to board his faltering consciousness. The lamp's beam flitted, hesitated, returned. I was deceived by the darkness, he thought. I met him in the light. He saw a ghastly, neon-lit hotel bedroom – Muzak and tartan wallpaper, and the little stranger perched smiling in a corner, calling him Max. A little ambassador – but representing what cause, what country? He recalled an overcoat with velvet tabs and hard little hands, jerking out their own dance. He recalled the passionate, laughing eyes, the crisp mouth opening and closing swiftly, but he heard no words. He felt a sense of loss – of missing the target – of some other, looming shadow being present while they spoke.

Maybe, he thought. Everything is maybe. Maybe Vladimir was shot by a jealous husband after all, he thought, as the front doorbell screamed at him like a vulture, two rings.

She's forgotten her key as usual, he thought. He was in the hall before he knew it, fumbling with the lock. Her key would do no good, he realised; like Ostrakova, he had chained the door. He fished at the chain, calling 'Ann. Hang on!' and feeling nothing in his fingers. He slammed a bolt along its runner and heard the whole house tingle to the echo. 'Just coming!' he shouted. 'Wait! Don't go!'

He heaved the door wide open, swaying on the threshold, offering his plump face as a sacrifice to the midnight air, to the shimmering black leather figure, crash helmet under his arm, standing before him like death's sentinel.

'I didn't mean to *alarm* you, sir, I'm sure,' the stranger said.

Clutching the doorway, Smiley could only stare at his intruder. He was tall and close cropped, and his eyes reflected unrequited loyalty.

'Ferguson, sir. You remember me, sir, Ferguson? I used to manage the transport pool for Mr. Esterhase's lamplighters.'

His black motor-cycle with its side-car was parked on the kerb behind him, its lovingly polished surface glinting under the street lamp.

'I thought lamplighter section had been disbanded,' Smiley said, still staring at him.

'So they have, sir. Scattered to the four winds, I regret to say. The cameraderie, the spirit, gone for ever.'

'So who employs you?'

'Well, no one, sir. Not officially, as you might say. But still on the side of the angels, all the same.'

'I didn't know we had any angels.'

'No, well that's true, sir. All men are fallible, I do say. Specially these days.' He was holding a brown envelope for Smiley to take. 'From certain friends of yours, sir, put it that way. I understand it relates to a telephone account you were enquiring about. We get a good response from the Post Office generally, I will say. Goodnight, sir. Sorry to bother you. Time you had some shut-eye, isn't it? Good men are scarce, I always say.'

'Good night,' said Smiley.

But still his visitor lingered, like someone asking for a tip. 'You did remember me really, didn't you sir? It was just a lapse, wasn't it?'

'Of course.'

There were stars, he noticed as he closed the door. Clear stars swollen by the dew. Shivering, he took out one of Ann's many photograph albums and opened it at the centre. It was her habit, when she liked a snap, to wedge the negative behind it. Selecting a picture of the two of them in Cap Ferrat – Ann in a bathing-dress, Smiley prudently covered – he removed the negative and put Vladimir's behind it. He tidied up his chemicals and equipment and slipped the print into the tenth volume of his 1961 Oxford English dictionary, under Y for Yesterday. He opened Ferguson's envelope, glanced wearily at the contents, registered a couple of entries and the word 'Hamburg,' and tossed the whole lot into a drawer of the desk. Tomorrow, he thought; tomorrow is another riddle. He climbed into bed, never sure, as usual, which side to sleep on. He closed his eyes and at once the questions bombarded him, as he knew they would, in crazy uncoordinated salvoes.

Why didn't Vladimir ask for Hector? he wondered for the hundredth time. Why did the old man liken Esterhase, alias Hector, to the City banks who took your umbrella away when it rained?

*Tell Max it concerns the Sandman.*

To ring her? To throw on his clothes and hurry round there, to be received as her secret lover, creeping away with the dawn?

Too late. She was already suited.

Suddenly, he wanted her dreadfully. He could not bear the spaces round him that did not contain her, he longed for her laughing trembling body as she cried to him, calling him her only true, her best lover, she wanted none other, ever. 'Women are lawless, George,' she had told him once, when they lay in rare peace. 'So what am I?' he had asked, and she said, 'My law.' So what was Haydon?' he had asked. And she laughed and said, 'My anarchy.'

He saw the little photograph again, printed, like the little stranger himself, in his sinking memory. A small man, with a big shadow. He remembered Villem's description of the little figure on the Hamburg ferry, the horns of flicked-up hair, the grooved face, the warning eyes. *General*, he thought chaotically, *will you not send me your magic friend once more?*

Maybe. Everything is maybe.

Hamburg, he thought, and got quickly out of bed and put on his dressing gown. Back at Ann's desk, he set to work seriously to study the breakdown of Vladimir's telephone account, rendered in the copperplate script of a post-office clerk. Taking a sheet of paper, he began jotting down dates and notes.

Fact: in early September, Vladimir received the Paris letter, and removed it from Mikhel's grasp.

Fact: at about the same date, Vladimir makes a rare and costly trunk-call to Hamburg, operator-dialled, presumably so that he can later claim the cost.

Fact: three days after that again, the eighth, Vladimir accepts a reverse-charge call from Hamburg, at a cost of two pounds eighty, origin, duration and time all given, and the origin is the same number that Vladimir had called three days before.

Hamburg, Smiley thought again, his mind flitting once more to the imp in the photograph. The reversed telephone traffic had continued intermittently till three days ago; nine calls, totalling twenty-one pounds, and all of them from Hamburg to Vladimir. But who was calling him? From Hamburg? Who?

Then suddenly he remembered.

The looming figure in the hotel room, the imp's vast shadow, was Vladimir himself. He saw them standing side by side, both in black coats, the giant and the midget. The vile hotel with Muzak and tartan wallpaper was near Heathrow Airport, where the two men, so ill-matched, had flown in for a conference at the very moment of Smiley's life when his professional identity was crashing round his ears. *Max we need you. Max, give us the chance.*

Picking up the telephone, Smiley dialled the number in Hamburg, and heard a man's voice the other end: the one word 'Yes,' spoken softly in German, followed by a silence.

'I should like to speak to Herr Dieter Fassbender,' Smiley said, selecting a name at random. German was Smiley's second language, and sometimes his first.

'We have no Fassbender,' said the same voice coolly after a moment's pause, as if the speaker had consulted something in the meantime. Smiley could hear faint music in the background.

'This is Leber,' Smiley persisted. 'I want to speak to Herr Fassbender urgently. I'm his partner.'

There was yet another delay.

'Not possible,' said the man's voice flatly after another pause – and rang off.

Not a private house, thought Smiley, hastily jotting down his impressions – the speaker had too many choices. Not an office, for what kind of office plays soft background music and is open at midnight on a Saturday? A hotel? Possibly, but a hotel, if it was of any size, would have put him through to reception, and displayed a modicum of civility. A restaurant? Too furtive, too guarded – and surely they would have announced themselves as they picked up the phone?

Don't force the pieces, he warned himself. Store them away. Patience. But how to be patient when he had so little time?

Returning to bed, he opened a copy of Cobbett's *Rural Rides* and tried to read it while he loosely pondered, among other weighty matters, his sense of *civitas* and how much, or how little, he owed to Oliver Lacon: 'Your *duty*, George.' Yet who could seriously be Lacon's man? he asked himself. Who could regard Lacon's fragile arguments as Caesar's due?

'Émigrés in, émigrés out. Two legs good, two legs bad,' he murmured aloud.

All his professional life, it seemed to Smiley, he had listened to similar verbal antics signalling supposedly great changes in Whitehall doctrine; signalling restraint, self-denial, always another reason for doing nothing. He had watched Whitehall's skirts go up, and come down again, her belts being tightened, loosened, tightened. He had been the witness, or victim – or even reluctant prophet – of such spurious cults as lateralism, parallelism, separatism, operational devolution, and now, if he remembered Lacon's most recent meanderings correctly, of integration. Each new fashion had been hailed as a panacea: 'Now we shall vanquish, now the machine will work!' Each had gone out with a whimper, leaving behind it the familiar English muddle, of which, more and more, in retrospect, he saw himself as a lifelong moderator. He had forborne, hoping others would forbear, and they had not. He had toiled in back rooms while shallower men held the stage. They held it still. Even five years ago he would never have admitted to such sentiments. But today, peering calmly into his own heart, Smiley knew that he was unled, and perhaps unleadable; that the only restraints upon him were those of his own reason, and his own humanity. As with his marriage, so with his sense of public service. I invested my life in institutions – he thought without rancour – and all I am left with is myself.

And with Karla, he thought; with my black Grail.

He could not help himself: his restless mind would not leave him alone. Staring ahead of him into the gloom, he imagined he saw Karla standing before him, breaking and reforming in the shifting specks of dark. He saw the brown, attendant eyes appraising him, as once they had appraised him from the darkness of the interrogation cell in Delhi jail a hundred years before: eyes that at first glance were sensitive and seemed to signal companionship; then like molten glass slowly hardened till they were brittle and unyielding. He saw himself stepping onto the dusk-driven runway of Delhi airport, and wincing as the Indian heat leapt up at him from the tarmac: Smiley alias Barraclough, or Standfast, or whatever name he had fished from the bag that week – he forgot. A Smiley of the Sixties, anyway, Smiley the commercial traveller, they called him, charged by the Circus to quarter the globe, offering resettlement terms to Moscow Centre officers who were thinking of jumping ship. Centre was holding one of its periodical purges at the time, and the woods were thick with Russian field officers scared of going home. A Smiley who was Ann's husband and Bill Haydon's colleague, whose last illusions were still intact. A Smiley close to inner crisis all the same, for it was the year Ann lost her heart to a ballet dancer: Haydon's turn was yet to come.

Still in the darkness of Ann's bedroom, he relived the rattling, honking jeep-ride to the jail, the laughing children hanging to the tailboard; he saw the ox-carts and the eternal Indian crowds, the shanties on the brown river bank. He caught the smells of dung and ever-smouldering fires – fires to cook and fires to cleanse; fires to remove the dead. He saw the iron gateway of the old prison engulf him, and the perfectly pressed British uniforms of the warders as they waded knee-deep through the prisoners:

'This way, your honour, sir! Please be good enough to follow us, your excellency!'

One European prisoner, calling himself Gerstmann.

One grey-haired little man with brown eyes and a red calico tunic, resembled the sole survivor of an extinguished priesthood.

With his wrists manacled: 'Please undo them, officer, and bring him some cigarettes,' Smiley had said.

One prisoner, identified by London as a Moscow Centre agent, and now awaiting deportation to Russia. One little Cold War infantryman, as he appeared, who knew – knew for certain – that to be repatriated to Moscow was to face the camps or the firing squad or both; that to have been in enemy hands was in Centre's eyes to have become the enemy himself: to have talked or to have kept his secrets was immaterial.

Join us, Smiley had said to him across the iron table.

Join us and we will give you life.

Go home and they will give you death.

His hands were sweating – Smiley's, in the prison. The heat was dreadful. Have a cigarette, Smiley had said – here, use my lighter. It was a gold one, smeared by his own damp hands. Engraved. A gift from Ann to compensate some misdemeanour. *To George from Ann with all my love.* There are little loves and big loves, Ann liked to say, but when she had composed the inscription she awarded him both kinds. It was probably the only occasion when she did.

Join us, Smiley had said. Save yourself. You have no right to deny yourself survival. First mechanically, then with passion, Smiley had repeated the familiar arguments while his own sweat fell like raindrops onto the table. Join us. You have nothing to lose. Those in Russia who love you are already lost. Your return will make things worse for them, not better. Join us. I beg. Listen to me, listen to the arguments, the philosophy.

And waited, on and on, vainly, for the slightest response to his increasingly desperate entreaty. For the brown eyes to flicker, for the rigid lips to utter a single word through the billows of cigarette smoke – yes, I will join you. Yes, I will agree to be debriefed. Yes, I will accept your money, your promises of resettlement, and the leftover life of a defector. He waited for the freed hands to cease their restless fondling of Ann's lighter, to George from Ann with all my love.

Yet the more Smiley implored him, the more dogmatic Gerstmann's silence became. Smiley pressed answers on him, but Gerstmann had no questions to support them. Gradually Gerstmann's completeness was awesome. He was a man who had prepared himself for the gallows; who would rather die at the hands of his friends than live at the hands of his enemies. Next morning they parted, each to his appointed fate: Gerstmann, against all odds, flew back to Moscow to survive the purge and prosper. Smiley, with a high fever, returned to his Ann and not quite all her love; and to the later knowledge that Gerstmann was none other than Karla himself, Bill Haydon's recruiter, case officer, mentor; and the man who had spirited Bill into Ann's bed – this very bed where he now lay – in order to cloud Smiley's hardening vision of Bill's greater treason, against the service and its agents.

Karla, he thought, as his eyes bored into the darkness, what do you want with me now? *Tell Max it concerns the Sandman.*

Sandman, he thought: why do you wake me up when you are supposed to put me back to sleep?

Still incarcerated in her little Paris apartment, tormented equally in spirit and body, Ostrakova could not have slept even if she had wanted. Not all the Sandman's magic would have helped her. She turned on her side and her squeezed ribs screamed as if the assassin's arms were still flung round them while he prepared to sling her under the car. She tried her back and the pain in her rump was enough to make her vomit. And when she lay on her belly, her breasts became as sore as when she had tried to feed Alexandra in the months before she abandoned her, and she hated them.

It is God's punishment, she told herself, without too much conviction. Not till morning came, and she was back in Ostrakov's armchair, with his pistol across her knees, did the waking world, for an hour or two, release her from her thoughts.

# THIRTEEN

The gallery was situated in what the art trade calls the naughty end of Bond Street, and Smiley arrived on its doorstep that Monday morning long before any respectable art dealer was out of bed.

His Sunday had passed in mysterious tranquillity. Bywater Street had woken late, and so had Smiley. His memory had served him while he slept, and it continued to serve him in modest spasms of enlightenment throughout the day. In terms of memory at least, his black Grail had drawn a little nearer. His telephone had not rung once, a slight but persistent hangover had kept him in the contemplative mood. There was a club he belonged to, against his better judgment, near Pall Mall, and he lunched there in imperial solitude on warmed-up steak-and-kidney pie. Afterwards, from the head porter, he had requested his box from the club safe and discreetly abstracted a few illicit possessions, including a British passport in his former work name of Standfast, which he had never quite managed to return to Circus Housekeepers; an international driving licence to match; a sizeable sum of Swiss francs, his own certainly, but equally certainly retained in defiance of the Exchange Control Act. He had them in his pocket now.

The gallery had a dazzling whiteness and the canvases in its armoured glass window were much the same: white upon white, with just the faintest outline of a mosque or St. Paul's Cathedral – or was it Washington? – drawn with a finger in the thick pigment. Six months ago the sign hanging over the pavement had proclaimed The Wandering Snail Coffee Shop. Today it read 'ATELIER BENATI, GOÛT ARABE, PARIS, NEW YORK, MONACO,' and a discreet menu on the door proclaimed the new chef's specialities: *'Islam classique-moderne. Conceptual Interior Design. Contracts catered. Sonnez.'*

Smiley did as he was bidden, a buzzer screamed, the glass door yielded. A shop-worn girl, ash blonde and half-awake, eyed him warily over a white desk.

'If I could just look round,' said Smiley.

Her eyes lifted slightly towards an Islamic heaven. 'The little red spots mean sold,' she drawled, and, having handed him a typed price-list, sighed and went back to her cigarette and her horoscope.

For a few moments Smiley shuffled unhappily from one canvas to another till he stood in front of the girl again.

'If I could possibly have a word with Mr. Benati,' he said.

'Oh, I'm afraid Signor Benati is *fully* involved right now. That's the trouble with being international.'

'If you could tell him it's Mr. Angel,' Smiley proposed in the same diffident style. 'If you could just tell him that. Angel, Alan Angel, he does know me.'

He sat himself on the S-shaped sofa. It was priced at two hundred pounds and covered in protective cellophane which squeaked when he moved. He heard her lift the phone and sigh into it.

'Got an angel for you,' she drawled, in her pillow-talk voice. 'As in Paradise, got it, angel?'

A moment later he was descending a spiral staircase into darkness. He reached the bottom and waited. There was a click and half a dozen picture lights sprang on to empty spaces where no pictures hung. A door opened revealing a small and dapper figure, quite motionless. His full white hair was swept back with bravado. He wore a black suit with a broad stripe and shoes with pantomime buckles. The stripe was definitely too big for him. His right fist was in his jacket pocket, but when he saw Smiley he drew it slowly out, and held it at him like a dangerous blade.

'Why, Mr. Angel,' he declared in a distinctly mid-European accent, with a sharp glance up the staircase as if to see who was listening. 'What pure pleasure, sir. It has been far too long. Come in, please.'

They shook hands, each keeping his distance.

'Hullo, Mr. Benati,' Smiley said, and followed him to an inner room and through it to a second, where Mr. Benati closed the door and gently leaned his back against it, perhaps as a bulwark against intrusion. For a while after that, neither man spoke at all, each preferring to study the other in a silence bred of mutual respect. Mr. Benati's eyes were brown and swift and they looked nowhere long and nowhere without a purpose. The room had the atmosphere of a sleazy boudoir, with a chaise longue and a pink handbasin in one corner.

'So how's trade, Toby?' Smiley asked.

Toby Esterhase had a special smile for that question and a special way of tilting his little palm.

'We have been lucky, George. We have a good opening, we had a fantastic summer. Autumn, George' – the gesture again – 'autumn I would say is on the slow side. One must live off one's hump actually. Some coffee, George? My girl can make some.'

'Vladimir's dead,' said Smiley after another longish gap. 'Shot dead on Hampstead Heath.'

'Too bad. That old man, huh? Too bad.'

'Oliver Lacon has asked me to sweep up the bits. As you were the Group's postman, I thought I'd have a word with you.'

'Sure,' said Toby agreeably.

'You knew, then? About his death?'

'Read it in the papers.'

Smiley let his eye wander round the room. There were no newspapers anywhere.

'Any theories about who did it?' Smiley asked.

'At *his* age, George? After a lifetime of disappointments, you might say? No family, no prospects, the Group all washed up – I assumed he had done it himself. Naturally.'

Cautiously Smiley sat himself on the chaise longue and, watched by Toby, picked up a bronze maquette of a dancer that stood on the table.

'Shouldn't this be *numbered* if it's a Degas, Toby?' Smiley asked.

'Degas, that's a very grey area, George. You got to know exactly what you are dealing with.'

'But this one is genuine?' Smiley asked, with an air of really wishing to know.

'Totally.'

'Would you sell it to me?'

'What's that?'

'Just out of academic interest. Is it for sale? If I offered to buy it, would I be out of court?'

Toby shrugged, slightly embarrassed.

'George listen, we're talking thousands, know what I mean? Like a year's pension or something.'

'When was the last time you had anything to do with Vladi's network, actually, Toby?' Smiley asked, returning the dancer to its table.

Toby digested this question at his leisure.

'Network?' he echoed incredulously at last. 'Did I hear network, George?' Laughter in the normal run played little part in Toby's repertoire but now he did manage a small if tense outburst. 'You call that crazy Group a network? Twenty cuckoo Balts, leaky like a barn, and they make a *network* already?'

'Well, we have to call them something,' Smiley objected equably.

'Something, sure. Just not network, okay?'

'So what's the answer?'

'What answer?'

'When did you last have dealings with the Group?'

'Years ago. Before they sacked me. Years ago.'

'How many years?'

'I don't know.'

'Three?'

'Maybe.'

'Two?'

'You trying to pin me down, George?'

'I suppose I am. Yes.'

Toby nodded gravely as if he had suspected as much all along: 'And have you forgotten, George, how it was with us in lamplighters? How overworked we were? How my boys and I played postman to half the networks in the Circus? Remember? In one week how many meetings, pick-ups? Twenty, thirty? In the high season once – forty? Go to Registry, George. If you've got Lacon behind you, go to Registry, draw the file, check the encounter sheets. That way you see exactly. Don't come here trying to trip me up, know what I mean? Degas, Vladimir – I don't like these questions. A friend, an old boss, my own house – it upsets me, okay?'

His speech having run for a deal longer than either of them apparently expected, Toby paused, as if waiting for Smiley to provide the explanation for his loquacity. Then he took a step forward, and turned up his palms in appeal.

'George,' he said reproachfully. 'George, my name is Benati, okay?'

Smiley seemed to have lapsed into dejection. He was peering gloomily at the stacks of grimy art catalogues strewn over the carpet.

'I'm not called Hector, definitely not Esterhase,' Toby insisted. 'I got an alibi for every day of the year – hiding from my bank manager. You think I want trouble round my neck? Émigrés, police even? This an interrogation, George?'

'You know me, Toby.'

'Sure. I know you, George. You want matches so you can burn my feet?'

Smiley's gaze remained fixed upon the catalogue. 'Before Vladimir died – hours before – he rang the Circus,' he said. 'He said he wanted to give us information.'

'But this Vladimir was an old man, George!' Toby insisted – protesting, at least to Smiley's ear, altogether too much. 'Listen, there's a lot of guys like him. Big background, been on the pay-roll too long; they get out, soft in the head, start writing crazy memoirs, seeing world plots everywhere, know what I mean?'

On and on, Smiley contemplated the catalogues, his round head supported on his clenched fists.

'Now why do you say that exactly, Toby?' he asked critically. 'I don't follow your reasoning.'

'What do you mean, why I say it? Old defectors, old spies, they get a bit cuckoo. They hear voices, talk to the dicky-birds. It's normal.'

'Did Vladimir hear voices?'

'How should I know?'

'That's what I was asking you, Toby,' Smiley explained reasonably, to the catalogues. 'I told you Vladimir claimed to have news for us, and *you* replied to me that he was going soft in the head. I wondered how you knew. About the softness of Vladimir's head. I wondered how recent was your information about his state of mind. And why you pooh-poohed whatever he might have had to say. That's all.'

'George, these are very old games you are playing. Don't twist my words. Okay? You want to ask me, ask me. Please. But don't twist my words.'

'It wasn't suicide, Toby,' Smiley said, still without a glance at him. 'It *definitely* wasn't suicide. I saw the body, believe me. It wasn't a jealous husband either – not unless he was equipped with a Moscow Centre murder weapon. What used we to call them, those gun things? "Inhumane killers," wasn't it? Well, that's what Moscow used. An inhumane killer.'

Smiley once more pondered, but this time – even if it was too late – Toby had the wit to wait in silence.

'You see, Toby, when Vladimir made that phone call to the Circus he demanded *Max*. Myself, in other words. Not his postman, which would have been you. Not Hector. He demanded his vicar, which for better or worse was me. Against all protocol, against all training, and against all precedent. Never done it before. I wasn't there of course, so they offered him a substitute, a silly little boy called Mostyn. It didn't matter because in the event they never met anyway. But can *you* tell me why he didn't ask for Hector?'

'George, I mean *really*! These are shadows you are chasing! Should I know why he *doesn't* ask for me? We are responsible for the omissions of others, suddenly? What is this?'

'Did you quarrel with him? Would that be a reason?'

'Why should I quarrel with Vladimir? He was being dramatic, George. That's how they are, these old guys when they retire.' Toby paused as if to imply that Smiley himself was not above these foibles. 'They get bored, they miss the action, they want stroking, so they make up some piece of mickey-mouse.'

'But not all of them get shot, do they, Toby? That's the worry, you see: the cause and effect. Toby quarrels with Vladimir one day, Vladimir gets shot with a Russian gun the next. In police terms that's what one calls an embarrassing chain of events. In our terms too, actually.'

'George, are you crazy? What the hell is quarrel? I told you: I never quarrel with the old man in my life!'

'Mikhel said you did.'

'Mikhel? You go talking to *Mikhel*?'

'According to Mikhel, the old man was very bitter about you. "Hector is no good," Vladimir kept telling him. He quoted Vladimir's word exactly. "Hector is no good." Mikhel was very surprised. Vladimir used to think highly of you. Mikhel couldn't think what had been going on between the two of you that could produce such a severe change of heart. "Hector is no good." *Why* weren't you any good, Toby? What happened that made Vladimir so passionate about you? I'd like to keep it away from the police if I could, you see. For all our sakes.'

But the fieldman in Toby Esterhase was by now fully awake, and he knew that interrogations, like battles, are never won but only lost.

'George, this is absurd,' he declared with pity rather than hurt. 'I mean it's so obvious you are fooling me. Know that? Some old man builds castles in the air, so you want to go to the police already? Is that what Lacon is hiring you for? Are these the bits you are sweeping up? George?'

This time, the long silence seemed to create some resolution in Smiley, and when he spoke again it was as if he had not much time left. His tone was brisk, even impatient.

'Vladimir came to see you. I don't know when but within the last few weeks. You met him or you talked to him over the phone – call box to call box, whatever the technique was. He asked you to do something for him. You refused. That's why he demanded Max when he rang the Circus on Friday night. He'd had Hector's answer already and it was no. That's also why Hector was "no good." You turned him down.'

This time Toby made no attempt to interrupt.

'And if I may say so, you're scared,' Smiley resumed, studiously not looking at the lump in Toby's jacket pocket. 'You know enough about who killed Vladimir to think they might kill you too. You even thought it possible I wasn't the right Angel.' He waited, but Toby didn't rise. His tone softened. '*You* remember what we used to say at Sarratt, Toby – about fear being information without the cure? How we should respect it? Well I respect yours, Toby. I want to know more about it. Where it came from. Whether I should share it. That's all.'

Still at the door, his little palms pressed flat against the panels, Toby Esterhase studied Smiley more attentively and without the smallest decline in his composure. He even contrived to suggest, by the depth and question of his glance, that his concern was now for Smiley rather than himself. Next, in line with this solicitous approach, he took a pace, then another, into the room – but tentatively, and somewhat as if he were visiting an ailing friend in hospital. Only then, with a passable imitation of a bedside manner, did he respond to Smiley's accusations with a most perceptive question, one which Smiley himself, as it happened, had deliberated in some depth over the last two days.

'George. Kindly answer me something. Who is speaking here actually? Is it George Smiley? Is it Oliver Lacon? Mikhel? Who is speaking, please?' Receiving no immediate answer, he continued his advance as far as a grimy satin-covered stool where he perched himself with a catlike trimness, one hand over each knee. 'Because for an official fellow, George, you are asking some pretty damn unofficial questions, it strikes me. You are taking rather an unofficial attitude, I think.'

'You saw Vladimir and you spoke to him. What happened?' Smiley asked, quite undeflected by this challenge. 'You tell me that, and I'll tell you who is speaking here.'

In the farthest corner of the ceiling there was a yellowed patch of glass about a metre square and the shadows that played over it were the feet of passers-by in the street. For some reason Toby's eyes had fixed on this strange spot and he seemed to read his decision there, like an instruction flashed on a screen.

'Vladimir put up a distress rocket,' Toby said in exactly the same tone as before, of neither conceding nor confiding. Indeed, by some trick of tone or inflection, he even managed to bring a note of warning to his voice.

'Through the Circus?'

'Through friends of mine,' said Toby.

'When?'

Toby gave a date. Two weeks ago. A crash meeting. Smiley asked where it took place.

'In the Science Museum,' Toby replied with new-found confidence. 'The café on the top floor, George. We drank coffee, admired the old aeroplanes hanging from the roof. You going to report all this to Lacon, George? Feel free, okay? Be my guest. I got nothing to hide.'

'And he put the proposition?'

'Sure. He put me a proposition. He wanted me to do a lamplighter job. To be his camel. That was our joke, back in the old Moscow days, remember? To collect, carry across the desert, to deliver. "Toby I got no passport. *Aidez-moi. Mon ami, aidez-moi.*" You know how he talked. Like de Gaulle. We used to call him that – "The other General." Remember?'

'Carry what?'

'He was not precise. It was documentary, it was small, no concealment was needed. This much, he tells me.'

'For somebody putting our feelers, he seems to have told you a lot.'

'He was asking a hell of a lot too,' said Toby calmly, and waited for Smiley's next question.

'And the where?' Smiley asked. 'Did Vladimir tell you that too?'

'Germany.'

'Which one?'

'Ours. The north of it.'

'Casual encounter? Dead letter-boxes? Live? What sort of meeting?'

'On the fly. I should take a train ride. From Hamburg north. The hand-over to be made on the train, details on acceptance.'

'And it was to be a private arrangement. No Circus, no Max?'

'For the time being very private, George.'

Smiley picked his words with tact. 'And the compensation for your labours?'

A distinct scepticism marked Toby's answer: 'If we get the document – that's what he called it, okay? Document. If we get the document, and the document is genuine, which he swore it was, we win immediately a place in Heaven. We take first the document to Max, tell Max the story. Max would know its meaning, Max would know the crucial importance – of the document. Max would reward us. Gifts, promotion, medals, Max will put us in the House of Lords. Sure. Only problem was, Vladimir didn't know Max was on the shelf and the Circus has joined the Boy Scouts.'

'Did he know that Hector was on the shelf?'

'Fifty-five, George.'

'What does that mean?' Then with a 'never mind', Smiley cancelled his own question and again lapsed into prolonged thought.

'George, you want to drop this line of enquiry,' Toby said earnestly. 'That is my strong advice to you, abandon it,' he said, and waited.

Smiley might not have heard. Momentarily shocked, he seemed to be pondering the scale of Toby's error.

'The point is, you sent him packing,' he muttered and remained staring into space. 'He appealed to you and you slammed the door in his face. How could you do that, Toby? You of all people?'

The reproach brought Toby furiously to his feet, which was perhaps what it was meant to do. His eyes lit up, his cheeks coloured, the sleeping Hungarian in him was wide awake.

'And you want to hear why, maybe? You want to know why I told him, "Go to hell, Vladimir. Leave my sight, please, you make me sick."? You want to know who his connect is out there – this magic guy in North Germany with the crock of gold that's going to make millionaires of us overnight, George – you want to know his full identity? Remember the name Otto Leipzig, by any chance? Holder many times of our Creep of the Year award? Fabricator, intelligence pedlar, confidence man, sex maniac, pimp, also various sorts of criminal? Remember *that* great hero?'

Smiley saw the tartan walls of the hotel again, and the dreadful hunting prints of Jorrocks in full cry; he saw the two black-coated figures, the giant and the midget, and the General's huge mottled hand resting on the tiny shoulder of his protégé. '*Max, here is my good friend Otto. I have brought him to tell his own story.*' He heard the steady thunder of the planes landing and taking off at Heathrow Airport.

'Vaguely,' Smiley replied equably. 'Yes, vaguely I do remember an Otto Leipzig. Tell me about him. I seem to remember he had rather a *lot* of names. But then so do we all, don't we?'

'About two hundred, but Leipzig he ended up with. Know why? Leipzig in East Germany: he liked the jail there. He was that kind of crazy joker. Remember the stuff he peddled, by any chance?' Believing he had the initiative, Toby stepped boldly forward and stood over the passive Smiley while he talked down at him: 'George, do you not even remember the incredible and total bilge which year after year that creep would push out under fifteen different source names to our West European stations, mainly German? Our expert on the new Estonian order? Our top source on Soviet arms shipments out of Leningrad? Our inside ear at Moscow Centre, our principal Karla-watcher, even?' Smiley did not stir. 'How he took our Berlin resident alone for two hundred Deutschmarks for a rewrite from *Stern* magazine? How he foxed that old General, worked on him like a sucking-leech, time and again – "Us fellow Balts" – that line? "General, I just got the Crown jewels for you – only trouble, I don't have the air fare"? Jesus!'

'It wasn't *all* fabrication, though, was it, Toby?' Smiley objected mildly. 'Some of it, I seem to remember – in certain areas, at least – turned out to be rather good stuff.'

'Count it on one finger.'

'His Moscow Centre material, for instance. I don't remember that we faulted him on that, ever?'

'Okay! So Centre gave him some decent chicken-feed occasionally, so he could pass us the other crap! How else does anyone play a double, for God's sake?'

Smiley seemed about to argue this point, then changed his mind.

'I see,' he said finally, as if overruled. 'Yes, I see what you mean. A plant.'

'Not a plant, a creep. A little of this, a little of that. A dealer. No principles. No standards. Work for anyone who sweetens his pie.'

'I take the point,' said Smiley gravely, in the same diminished tone. 'And of course he settled in North Germany, too, didn't he? Up towards Travemünde somewhere.'

'Otto Leipzig never settled anywhere in his life,' said Toby with contempt. 'George, that guy's a drifter, a total bum. Dresses like he was a Rothschild, owns a cat and a bicycle. Know what his last job was, this great spy? Night-watchman in some lousy Hamburg cargo house somewhere! Forget him.'

'And he had a partner,' Smiley said, in the same tone of innocent reminiscence. 'Yes, that comes back to me too. An immigrant, an East German.'

'Worse than East German: Saxon. Name of Kretzschmar, first name was Claus. Claus with a "C," don't ask me why. I mean these guys have got no logic at all. Claus was also a creep. They stole together, pimped together, faked reports together.'

'But that was long ago, Toby,' Smiley put in gently.

'Who cares? It was a perfect marriage.'

'Then I expect it didn't last,' said Smiley, in an aside to himself. But perhaps Smiley had for once overdone his meekness; or perhaps Toby simply knew him too well. For a warning light had come up in his swift, Hungarian eye, and a tuck of suspicion formed on his bland brow. He stood back and, contemplating Smiley, passed one hand thoughtfully over his immaculate white hair.

'George,' he said. 'Listen, who are you fooling, okay?'

Smiley did not speak, but lifted the Degas, and turned it round, then put it down.

'George, listen to me once. Please! Okay George? Maybe I give you once a lecture.'

Smiley glanced at him, then looked away.

'George, I owe you. You got to hear me. So you pulled me from the gutter once in Vienna when I was a stinking kid. I was a Leipzig. A bum. So you got me my job with the Circus. So we had a lot of times together, stole some horses. You remember the first rule of retirement, George? "No moonlighting. No fooling with loose ends? No private enterprise ever?" You remember who preached this rule? At Sarratt? In the corridors? George Smiley did. "When it's over, it's over. Pull down the shutters, go home!" So now what do you want to do, suddenly? Play kiss-kiss with an old crazy General who's dead but won't lie down and a five-sided comedian like Otto Leipzig! What is this? The last cavalry charge on the Kremlin suddenly? We're over, George. We got no licence. They don't want us any more. Forget it.' He hesitated, suddenly embarrassed. 'So okay, Ann gave you a bad time with Bill Haydon. So there's Karla, and Karla was Bill's big daddy in Moscow. George, I mean this gets very crude, know what I mean?'

His hands fell to his sides. He stared at the still figure before him. Smiley's eyelids were nearly closed. His head had dropped forward. With the shifting of his cheeks deep crevices had appeared round his mouth and eyes.

'We never faulted Leipzig's reports on Moscow Centre,' Smiley said, as if he hadn't heard the last part. 'I remember distinctly that we never faulted them. Nor on Karla. Vladimir trusted him implicitly. On the Moscow stuff, so did we.'

'George, whoever faulted a report on Moscow Centre? Please? So okay, once in a while we got a defector, he tells you: "This thing is crap and that thing is maybe true." So where's the collateral? Where's the hard base, you used to say? Some guy feeds you a story: "Karla just built a new spy nursery in Siberia." So who's to say they didn't? Keep it vague enough, you can't lose.'

'That was why we put up with him,' Smiley went on, as if he hadn't heard. 'Where the Soviet Service was involved, he played a straight game.'

'George,' said Toby softly, shaking his head. 'You got to wake up. The crowds have all gone home.'

'Will you tell me the rest of it now, Toby? Will you tell me exactly what Vladimir said to you? Please?'

So in the end, as a reluctant gift of friendship, Toby told it as Smiley asked, straight out, with a frankness that was like defeat.

The Maquette which might have been by Degas portrayed a ballerina with her arms above her head. Her body was curved backward and her lips were parted in what might have been ecstasy and there was no question but that, fake or genuine, she bore an uncomfortable if superficial resemblance to Ann. Smiley had taken her in his hands again and was slowly turning her, gazing at her this way and that with no clear appreciation. Toby was back on his satin stool. In the ceiling window, the shadowed feet walked jauntily.

Toby and Vladimir had met in the café of the Science Museum on the aeronautical floor, Toby repeated. Vladimir was in a state of high excitement and kept clutching Toby's arm, which Toby didn't like, it made him conspicuous. Otto Leipzig had managed the impossible, Vladimir kept saying. It was the big one, the chance in a million, Toby; Otto Leipzig had landed the one Max had always dreamed of, 'the full settlement of all our claims,' as Vladimir had put it. When Toby asked him somewhat acidly what claims he had in mind, Vladimir either wouldn't or couldn't say: 'Ask Max,' he insisted. 'If you do not believe me, ask Max, tell Max it is the big one.'

'So what's the deal?' Toby had asked – knowing, he said, that where Otto Leipzig was concerned the bill came first and the goods a long, long way behind. 'How much does he want, the great hero?'

Toby confessed to Smiley that he had found it hard to conceal his scepticism – 'which put a bad mood on the meeting from the start.' Vladimir outlined the terms. Leipzig had the story, said Vladimir, but he also had certain material proofs that the story was true. There was first a document and the document was what Leipzig called a *Vorspeise*, or appetizer. There was also a second proof, a letter, held by Vladimir. There was then the story itself, which would be given by other materials which Leipzig had entrusted to safe keeping. The document showed how the story was obtained, the materials themselves were incontrovertible.

'And the subject?' Smiley asked.

'Not revealed,' Toby replied shortly. 'To Hector, not revealed. Get Max and okay – then Vladimir reveals the subject. But Hector for the time being got to shut up and run the errands.'

For a moment Toby appeared about to launch upon a second speech of discouragement. 'George, I mean look here, the old boy was just totally cuckoo,' he began. 'Otto Leipzig was taking him a complete ride.' Then he saw Smiley's expression, so inward and inaccessible, and contented himself instead with a repetition of Otto Leipzig's totally outrageous demands.

'The document to be taken personally to Max by Vladimir, Moscow Rules at all points, no middle men, no correspondence. The preparations they made already on the telephone –'

'Telephone between London and Hamburg?' Smiley interrupted, suggesting by his tone that this was new and unwelcome information.

'They used word code, he tells me. Old pals, they know how to fox around. But not with the proof, says Vladi; with the proof there's no foxing at all. No phones, no mails, no trucks, they got to have a camel, period. Vladi's security-crazy, okay, this we know already. From now on, only Moscow Rules apply.'

Smiley remembered his own phone call to Hamburg of Saturday night, and wondered again what kind of establishment Otto Leipzig had been using as his telephone exchange.

'Once the Circus had declared its interest,' Toby continued, 'they pay a down payment to Otto Leipzig of five thousand Swiss for an audition fee. George! Five thousand Swiss! For openers! Just to be in the game! Next – George, you got to hear this – next, Otto Leipzig to be flown to a safe house in England for the audition. George, I mean I never heard such craziness. You want the rest? If, following the audition, the Circus wants to buy the material itself – you want to hear how much?'

Smiley did.

'Fifty grand Swiss. Maybe you want to sign me a cheque?'

Toby waited for a cry of outrage but none came.

'All for Leipzig?'

'Sure. They were Leipzig's terms. Who else would be so cuckoo?'

'What did Vladimir ask for himself?'

A small hesitation. 'Nothing,' said Toby reluctantly. Then, as if to leave that point behind, set off on a fresh wave of indignation.

'*Basta*. So now all Hector got to do is fly to Hamburg at his own expense, take a train north and play rabbit for some crazy entrapment game that Otto Leipzig had lined up for himself with the East Germans, the Russians, the Poles, the Bulgarians, the Cubans, and also no doubt, being modern, the Chinese. I said to him – George, listen to me – I said to him: "Vladimir, old friend, excuse me, pay attention to me once. Tell me what in life is so important that the Circus pays five thousand Swiss from its precious reptile fund for one lousy audition with Otto Leipzig? Maria Callas never got so much and believe me she sang a damn lot better than Otto does." He's holding my arm. Here.' Demonstrating, Toby grasped his own bicep. 'Squeezing me like I am an orange. That old boy had some strength still, believe me. "Fetch the document for me, Hector." He is speaking Russian. That's a very quiet place, that museum. Everyone has stopped to listen to him. I had a bad feeling. He is weeping. "For the sake of God, Hector, I am an old man. I got no legs, no passport, no one I can trust but Otto Leipzig. Go to Hamburg and fetch the document. When he sees the proof, Max will believe me, Max has faith." I try to console him, make some hints. I tell him émigrés are bad news these days, change of policy, new government. I advise him, "Vladimir, go home, play some chess. Listen, I come round to the library one day, have a game maybe." Then he says to me: "Hector, I began this. It was me sent the order to Otto Leipzig telling him to explore the position. Me who sent the money to him for the groundwork, all I had." Listen, that was an old, sad man. Past it.'

Toby made a pause but Smiley did not stir. Toby stood up, went to a cupboard, poured two glasses of an extremely indifferent sherry, and put one on the table beside the Degas maquette. He said 'Cheers' and drank back his glass, but still Smiley did not budge. His inertia rekindled Toby's anger.

'So I killed him, George, okay? It's Hector's fault, okay? Hector is personally and totally responsible for the old man's death. That's all I need.' He flung out both hands, palms upward. 'George! Advise me! George, for this story I should go to Hamburg, unofficial, no cover, no baby-sitter? Know where the East German border is up there? From Lübeck two kilometres? Less? Remember? In Travemünde you got to stay on the left of the street or you've defected by mistake.' Smiley did not laugh. 'And in the unlikely event I come back, I should call up George Smiley, go round to Saul Enderby with him, knock on the back door like a bum – "Let us in, Saul, please, we got hot information totally reliable from Otto Leipzig, only five grand Swiss for an audition concerning matters totally forbidden under the Boy Scout laws?" I should do this, George?'

From an inside pocket, Smiley drew a battered packet of English cigarettes. From the packet he drew the home-made contact print which he passed silently across the table for Toby to look at.

'Who's the second man?' Smiley asked.

'I don't know.'

'Not his partner, the Saxon, the man he stole with in the old days? Kretzschmar?'

Shaking his head, Toby Esterhase went on looking at the picture.

'So who's the second man?' Smiley asked again.

Toby handed back the photograph. 'George, pay attention to me, please,' he said quietly. 'You listening?'

Smiley might have been and might not. He was threading the print back into the cigarette packet.

'People forge things like that these days, you know that? That's very easy done, George. I want to put a head on another guy's shoulders, I got the equipment, it takes me maybe two minutes. You're not a technical guy, George, you don't understand these matters. You don't buy photographs from Otto Leipzig, you don't buy Degas from Signor Benati, follow me?'

'Do they forge negatives?'

'Sure. You forge the print, then you photograph it, make a new negative – why not?'

'Is this a forgery?' Smiley asked.

Toby hesitated a long time. 'I don't think so.'

'Leipzig travelled a lot. How did we raise him if we needed him?' Smiley asked.

'He was strictly arm's length. Totally.'

'So how did we raise him?'

'For a routine rendezvous the *Hamburger Abendblatt* marriage ads. Petra, aged twenty-two, blonde, petite, former singer – that crap. George, Listen to me. Leipzig is a dangerous bum with very many lousy connections, mostly still in Moscow.'

'What about emergencies? Did he have a house, a girl?'

'He never had a house in his life. For crash meetings, Claus Kretzschmar played key-holder. George, for God's sake, hear me once –'

'So how did we reach Kretzschmar?'

'He's got a couple of night-clubs. Cat houses. We left a message there.'

A warning buzzer rang and from upstairs they heard the sound of voices raised in argument.

'I'm afraid Signor Benati has a conference in Florence today,' the blonde girl was saying. 'That's the trouble with being international.'

But the caller refused to believe her; Smiley could hear the rising tide of his protest. For a fraction of a second Toby's brown eyes lifted sharply to the sound; then with a sigh he pulled open a wardrobe and drew out a grimy raincoat and a brown hat, despite the sunlight in the ceiling window.

'What's it called?' Smiley asked. 'Kretzschmar's night-club – what's it called?'

'The Blue Diamond. George, don't do it, okay? Whatever it is, drop it. So the photo is genuine, then what? The Circus has a picture of some guy rolling in the snow, courtesy of Otto Leipzig. You think that's a gold-mine suddenly? You think that makes Saul Enderby horny?'

Smiley looked at Toby, and remembered him, and remembered also that in all the years they had known each other and worked together, Toby had never once volunteered the truth, that information was money to him; even when he counted it valueless, he never threw it away.

'What else did Vladimir tell you about Leipzig's information?' Smiley asked.

'He said it was some old case come alive. Years of investment. Some crap about the Sandman. He was a child again, remembering fairy tales, for God's sake. See what I mean?'

'What about the Sandman?'

'To tell you it concerned the Sandman. That's all. The Sandman is making a legend for a girl. Max will understand. George, he was weeping, for Christ's sake. He'd have said anything that came into his head. He wanted the action. He was an old spy in a hurry. You used to say they were the worst.'

Toby was at the far door, already half-way gone. But he turned and came back despite the approaching clamour from upstairs, because something in Smiley's manner seemed to trouble him – 'a definitely harder stare,' he called it afterwards, 'like I'd completely insulted him somehow.'

'George? George, this is Toby, remember? If you don't get the hell out of here, that guy upstairs will sequester you in part-payment, hear me?'

Smiley hardly did. 'Years of investment and the Sandman was making a legend for a girl?' he repeated. 'What else? Toby, what else?'

'He was behaving like a crazy man again.'

'The General was? Vladi was?'

'No, the Sandman. George, listen. "The Sandman is behaving like a crazy man again, the Sandman is making a legend for a girl, Max will understand," *Finito*. The total garbage. I've told you every word. Go easy now, hear me?'

From upstairs, the sounds of argument grew still louder. A door slammed, they heard footsteps stamping towards the staircase. Toby gave Smiley's arm a last, swift pat.

'Goodbye, George. Hear me. You want a Hungarian babysitter some day, call me. Hear that? You're messing around with a creep like Otto Leipzig, then you better have a creep like Toby look after you. Don't go out alone nights, you're too young.'

Climbing the steel ladder back to the gallery, Smiley all but knocked over an irate creditor on his way down. But this was not important to Smiley; neither was the insolent sigh of the ash-blonde girl as he stepped into the street. What mattered was that he had put a name to the second face in the photograph; and to the name, the story, which like an undiagnosed pain had been nagging at his memory for the last thirty-six hours – as Toby might have said, the story of a legend.

And that, indeed, is the dilemma of those would-be historians who are concerned, only months after the close of the affair, to chart the interplay of Smiley's knowledge and his actions. Toby told him this much, they say, so he did that much. Or: if so-and-so had not occurred, then there would have been no resolution. Yet the truth is more complex than this, and far less handy. As a patient tests himself on coming out of the anaesthetic – this leg, that leg, do the hands still close and open? – so Smiley by a succession of cautious movements grew into his own strength of body and mind, probing the motives of his adversary as he probed his own.


# FOURTEEN


He was driving on a high plateau and the plateau was above the tree-line because the pines had been planted low in the valley's cleft. It was early evening of the same day and in the plain the first lights were pricking the wet gloom. On the horizon lay the city of Oxford, lifted by ground mist, an academic Jerusalem. The view from that side was new to him and increased his sense of unreality, of being conveyed rather than determining his own journey; of being in the grasp of thoughts which were not his to command. His visit to Toby Esterhase had fallen, arguably, within the crude guide-lines of Lacon's brief; but his journey, he knew, led for better, for worse to the forbidden province of his secret interest. Yet he was aware of no alternative, and wanted none. Like an archaeologist who has delved all his life in vain, Smiley had begged for one last day, and this was it.

At first he had watched his rear-view mirror constantly, how the familiar motor cycle had hung behind him like a gull at sea. But when he left the last roundabout the man called Ferguson had not followed him, and when he pulled up to read the map nothing passed him either, so either they had guessed his destination or, for some arcane reason of procedure, they had forbidden their man to cross the county border. Sometimes, as he drove, a trepidation gripped him. Let her be, he thought. He had heard things; not much, but enough to guess the rest. Let her be, let her find her own peace where she can. But he knew that peace was not his to give, that the battle he was involved in must be continuous to have any meaning at all.

The kennel sign was like a painted grin: 'MERRILEE BOARDING ALL PETS WELCOME EGGS.' A daubed yellow dog wearing a top hat pointed one paw down a cart-track; the track, when he took it, led so steeply downward that it felt like a free fall. He passed a pylon and heard the wind howling in it; he entered the plantation. First came the young trees; then the old ones darkened over him and he was in the Black Forest of his German childhood heading for some unrevealed interior. He switched on his head-lights, rounded a steep bend, and another, and a third, and there was the cabin much as he had imagined it – her *dacha*, as she used to call it. Once she had had the house in Oxford and the *dacha* as a place away from it. Now there was only the *dacha*; she had quitted towns for ever. It stood in its own clearing of tree trunks and trodden mud, with a ramshackle veranda and a wood-shingle roof and a tin chimney with smoke coming out of it. The clapboard walls were blackened with creosote, a galvanised iron feed-tub almost blocked the front porch. On a bit of lawn stood a home-made bird-table with enough bread to feed an ark, and dotted round the clearing, like allotment huts, stood the asbestos sheds and wire runs which held the chickens and all the pets welcome without discrimination.

Karla, he thought. What a place to look for you.

He parked, and his arrival set loose a bedlam as dogs sobbed in torment and thin walls thundered to desperate bodies. He walked to the house, carrier-bag in hand, the bottles bumping against his legs. Above the din he heard his own feet rattling up the six steps of the veranda. A notice on the door read: 'If OUT do NOT leave pets on spec.' and underneath, seemingly added in a fury, 'No bloody monkeys.'

The bell-pull was a donkey's tail in plastic. He reached for it but the door had already opened and a frail pretty woman peered at him from the interior darkness of the cabin. Her eyes were timid and grey, she had that period English beauty which had once been Ann's: accepting, and grave. She saw him and stopped dead. 'Oh, Lord,' she whispered. 'Gosh.' Then looked downward at her brogues, brushing back her forelock with one finger, while the dogs barked themselves hoarse at him from behind their wire.

'I'm sorry, Hilary,' said Smiley, with great gentleness. 'It's only for an hour, I promise. That's all it is. An hour.'

A deep, masculine voice, very slow, issued out of the darkness behind her. 'What is it, Hils?' growled the voice. 'Bog-weevil, budgie or giraffe?'

The question was followed by a slow thud like the movement of cloth over something hollow.

'It's human, Con,' Hilary called over her shoulder, and went back to looking at her brogues.

'*She* human or the other thing?' the voice demanded.

'It's George, Con. Don't be cross, Con.'

'*George*? Which *George*? George the Lorry, who waters my coal, or George the Meat, who poisons my dogs?'

'It's just some questions,' Smiley assured Hilary in the same deeply compassionate tone. 'An old case. Nothing momentous, I promise you.'

'It doesn't matter, George,' Hilary said, still looking downward. 'Honestly. It's fine.'

'Stop all that flirting!' the voice from inside the house commanded. 'Unhand her, whoever you are!'

As the thudding drew gradually nearer Smiley leaned past Hilary and spoke into the doorway. 'Connie, it's me,' he said. And once again, his voice did everything possible to signal his goodwill.

First came the puppies – four of them, probably whippets – in a fast pack. Next came a mangy old mongrel with barely life enough to reach the veranda and collapse. Then the door shuddered open to its fullest extent and revealed a mountainous woman propped crookedly between two thick wooden crutches, which she did not seem to hold. She had white hair clipped short as a man's, and watery, very shrewd eyes that held him fiercely in their stare. So long was her examination of him, in fact, so leisured and minute – his earnest face, his baggy suit, the plastic carrier-bag dangling from his left hand, his whole posture of waiting meekly to be admitted – that it gave her an almost regal authority over him, to which her stillness, and her troubled breathing, and her crippled state only contributed greater strength.

'Oh my giddy aunts,' she announced, still studying him, and blew out a stream of air. 'Jumping whatevers. Damn you, George Smiley. Damn you and all who sail in you. Welcome to Siberia.'

Then she smiled, and her smile was so sudden, and fresh, and little-girl, that it almost washed away the long questioning that had gone before it.

'Hullo, Con,' said Smiley.

Her eyes, notwithstanding her smile, stayed on him still. They had the pallor of a new-born baby's.

'Hils,' she said, at last. 'I said *Hils!*'

'Yes, Con?'

'Go feed the doggy-wogs, darling. When you've done that, feed the filthy chickadees. Glut the brutes. When you've done that, mix tomorrow's meal, and when you've done *that*, bring me the humane killer so that I can despatch this interfering whatsit to an early Paradise. George, follow me.'

Hilary smiled but seemed unable to move till Connie softly pushed an elbow into her to get her going.

'Hoof it, darling. There's nothing he can do to you now. He's shot his bolt, and so have you, and, God knows, so have I.'

It was a house of day and night at once. At the centre, on a pine table littered with the remains of toast and Marmite, an old oil lamp shed a globe of yellow light, intensifying the darkness round it. The gleam of blue rain clouds, streaked by sunset, filled the far French windows. Gradually, as Smiley followed Connie's agonisingly slow procession, he realised that this one wooden room was all there was. For an office, they had the roll-top desk laden with bills and flea powder; for a bedroom the brass double bedstead with its heap of stuffed toy animals lying like dead soldiers between the pillows; for a drawing-room Connie's rocking-chair and a crumbling wicker sofa; for a kitchen a gas ring fired from a cylinder; and for decoration the unclearable litter of old age.

'Connie's not coming back, George,' she called as she hobbled ahead of him. 'Wild horses can puff and blow their snivelling hearts out, the old fool has hung up her boots for good.' Reaching her rocking-chair, she began the ponderous business of turning herself round until she had her back to it. 'So if that's what you're after, you can tell Saul Enderby to shove it up his smoke and pipe it.' She held out her arms to him and he thought she wanted him to kiss her. 'Not *that*, you sex maniac. Batten on to my hands!'

He did so, and lowered her into the rocking-chair.

'That's not what I came for, Con,' said Smiley. 'I'm not trying to woo you away, I promise.'

'For one good reason, she's dying,' she announced firmly, not seeming to notice his interjection. 'The old fool's for the shredder, and high time too. The leech tries to fool me, of course. That's because he's a funk. Bronchitis. Rheumatism. Touch of the weather. Balls, the lot of it. It's death, that's what I'm suffering from. The systematic encroachment of the big D. Is that booze you're toting in that bag?'

'Yes. Yes, it is,' said Smiley.

'Goody. Let's have lots. How's the demon Ann?'

On the draining-board, amid a permanent pile of washing -up, he found two glasses, and half filled them.

'Flourishing, I gather,' he replied.

Reciprocating, by his own kindly smile, her evident pleasure at his visit, he held out a glass to her and she grappled it between her mittened hands.

'You gather,' she echoed. 'Wish you *would* gather. Gather her up for good is what you should do. Or else put powdered glass in her coffee. All right, what are you after?' she demanded, all in the same breath. 'I never knew you yet do anything without a reason. Mud in your eye.'

'And in yours, Con,' said Smiley.

To drink, she had to lean her whole trunk towards the glass. And as her huge head lurched into the glare of the lamplight, he saw – he knew from too much experience – that she was telling no less than the truth, and her flesh had the leprous whiteness of death.

'Come on. Out with it,' she ordered, in her sternest tone. 'I'm not sure I'll help you, mind. I've discovered love since we parted. Addles the hormones. Softens the teeth.'

He had wanted time to know her again. He was unsure of her.

'It's one of our old cases, Con, that's all,' he began apologetically. 'It's come alive again, the way they do.' He tried to raise the pitch of his voice to make it sound casual. 'We need more details. You know how you used to be about keeping records,' he added, teasingly.

Her eyes did not stir from his face.

'*Kirov*,' he went on, pronouncing the name very slowly. 'Kirov, first name Oleg. Ring a bell? Soviet Embassy, Paris, three or four years ago, Second Secretary? We thought he was some sort of Moscow Centre man.'

'He was,' she said, and sat back a little, still watching him.

She motioned for a cigarette. A packet of ten lay on the table. He wedged one between her lips and lit it, but still her eyes would not leave his face.

'Saul Enderby threw that case out of the window,' she said and, forming her lips as if to play a flute, blew a lot of smoke straight downward in order to avoid his face.

'He ruled it should be dropped,' Smiley corrected her.

'What's the difference?'

Smiley had not expected to find himself defending Saul Enderby.

'It ran awhile, then in the transition time between my tenure and his, he ruled, quite understandably, that it was unproductive,' Smiley said, picking his words with measured care.

'And now he's changed his mind,' she said.

'I've got bits, Con. I want it all.'

'You always did,' she said. 'George,' she muttered. 'George Smiley. Lord alive. Lord bless us and preserve us. *George*,' Her gaze was half possessive, half disapproving, as if he were an erring son she loved. It held him a while longer, then switched to the French windows, and the darkening sky outside.

'Kirov,' he said again, reminding her, and waited, wondering seriously whether it was all up with her; whether her mind was dying with her body, and this was all there was.

'Kirov, Oleg,' she repeated, in a musing tone. 'Born Leningrad October, 1929, according to his passport, which doesn't mean a damn thing except that he probably never went near Leningrad in his life.' She smiled, as if that were the way of the wicked world. 'Arrived Paris June 1, 1974, in the rank and quality of Second Secretary, Commercial. Three or four years ago, you say? Dear Lord, it could be twenty. That's right, darling, he was a hood. 'Course he was. Identified by the Paris lodge of the poor old Riga Group, which didn't help us any, specially not on the fifth floor. What was his real name? *Kursky*. Of course it was. Yes, I think I remember Oleg Kirov, né Kursky, all right.' Her smile returned, and was once more very pretty. 'Must have been Vladimir's last case, near enough. How is the old stoat?' she asked, and her moist clever eyes waited for his answer.

'Oh, fighting fit,' said Smiley.

'Still terrifying the virgins of Paddington?'

'I'm sure he is.'

'Bless you, darling,' said Connie, and turned her head till it was in profile to him, very dark except for the one fine line from the oil lamp, while she again stared out of the French windows.

'Go and see how the mad bitch is, will you, heart?' she asked fondly. 'Make sure the idiot hasn't thrown herself into the mill-race or drunk the universal weed-killer.'

Stepping outside, Smiley stood on the veranda, and in the thickening gloom made out the figure of Hilary loping awkwardly among the coops. He heard the clanking of her spoon on the bucket, and shreds of her well-bred voice on the night air as she called out childish names: Come on Whitey, Flopsy, Bo.

'She's fine,' said Smiley, coming back. 'Feeding the chickens.'

'I should tell her to bugger off, shouldn't I, '"Go forth into the world, Hils my dear." That's what I should say. "Don't tie yourself to a rotting old hulk like Con. Marry a chinless fool, spawn brats, fulfil your foul womanhood."' She had voices for everybody, he remembered: even for herself. She had them still. 'I'll be damned if I will, George. I want her. Every gorgeous bit of her. I'd take her with me if I'd half a chance. You want to try it some time.' A break. 'How *are* all the boys and girls?'

For a second, he didn't understand her question; his thoughts were with Hilary still, and Ann.

'His Grace Saul Enderby is still top of the heap, I take it? Eating well, I trust? Not moulting?'

'Oh, Saul goes from strength to strength, thanks.'

'That toad Sam Collins still Head of Operations?'

There was an edge to her questions, but he had no choice except to answer.

'Sam's fine too,' he said.

'Toby Esterhase still oiling round the corridors?'

'It's all pretty much as usual.'

Her face was now so dark to him that he could not tell whether she was proposing to speak again. He heard her breathing and the rasp of her chest. But he knew he was still the object of her scrutiny.

'*You'd* never work for that bunch, George,' she remarked at last, as if it were the most self-evident of platitudes. 'Not you. Give me another drink.'

Glad of the movement, Smiley went down the room again.

'*Kirov*, you said?' Connie called to him.

'That's right,' said Smiley cheerfully, and returned with her glass replenished.

'That little ferret Otto Leipzig was the first hurdle,' she remarked with relish, when she had taken a deep draught. 'The fifth floor wouldn't believe *him*, would they? Not our little Otto – *oh* no! Otto was a fabricator, and that was that!'

'But I don't think Leipzig ever lied to us about the *Moscow* target,' Smiley said, taking up her tone of reminiscence.

'No, darling, he did *not*,' she said with approval. 'He had his weaknesses, I'll grant you. But when it came to the big stuff he always played a straight bat. And *you* understood that, alone of all your tribe, I'll say that for you. But you didn't get much support from the *other* barons, did you?'

'He never lied to Vladimir, either,' Smiley said, 'It was Vladimir's escape lines that got him out of Russia in the first place.'

'Well, well,' said Connie, after another long silence. 'Kirov, né Kursky, the Ginger Pig.'

She said it again – 'Kirov, né Kursky' – a rallying call spoken to her own mountainous memory. As she did so, Smiley saw in his mind's eye the airport hotel room again, and the two strange conspirators seated before him in their black overcoats: the one so huge, the other tiny; the old General using all his bulk to enforce his passionate imploring; little Leipzig, an angry leash-dog at his side.

She was seduced.

The glow of the oil lamp had grown into a smoky light-ball, and Connie in her rocking-chair sat at the edge of it, Mother Russia herself, as they had called her in the Circus, her wasting face hallowed with reminiscence as she unfolded the story of just one of her unnumbered family of erring children. Whatever suspicions she was harbouring about Smiley's motive in coming here, she had suspended them: this was what she had lived for; this was her song, even if it was her last; these monumental acts of recollection were her genius. In the old days, Smiley remembered, she would have teased him, flirted with her voice, taken huge arcs through seemingly extraneous chunks of Moscow Centre history, all to lure him nearer. But tonight her narrative had acquired an awesome sobriety, as if she knew she had very little time.

Oleg Kirov arrived in Paris direct from Moscow, she repeated – that June, darling, same as I told you – the one when it poured and poured and the annual Sarratt cricket match had to be scrapped three Sundays in a row. Fat Oleg was listed as single, and he didn't replace anyone. His desk was on the second floor overlooking the Rue Saint-Simon – trafficky but *nice*, darling – whereas the Moscow Centre Residency hogged the third and fourth, to the rage of the Ambassador, who felt he was being squeezed into a cupboard by his unloved neighbours. To outward appearances, therefore, Kirov looked at first sight like that rare creature of the Soviet diplomatic community – namely, a straight diplomat. But it was the practice in Paris in those days – and for all Connie knew in *these* days too, heart – whenever a new face showed up at the Soviet Embassy, to distribute his photograph among the émigré tribal chiefs. Brother Kirov's photograph duly found its way to the groups, and in no time that old devil Vladimir was banging on his case officer's door in a state of fine excitement – Steve Mackelvore had Paris in those days, bless him, and dropped dead of a heart attack soon after, but that's another story – insisting that 'his people' had identified Kirov as a former *agent provocateur* named Kursky, who, while a student at Tallinn Polytechnical Institute, had formed a circle of dissident Estonian dock workers, something called 'the unaligned discussion club,' then shopped its members to the secret police. Vladimir's source, presently visiting Paris, had been one of those unfortunate workers, and for his sins he had personally befriended Kursky right up to the moment of his betrayal.

So far so good, except that Vladi's source – said Connie – was none other than wicked little Otto, which meant that the fat was in the fire from the start.

As Connie went on speaking, Smiley's memory once again began to supplement her own. He saw himself in his last months as caretaker Chief of the Circus, wearily descending the rickety wooden staircase from the fifth floor for the Monday meeting, a bunch of dog-eared files jammed under his arm. The Circus in those days was like a bombed-out building, he remembered; its officers scattered, its budget hamstrung, its agents blown or dead or laid off. Bill Haydon's unmasking was an open wound in everyone's mind: they called it the Fall and shared the same sense of primeval shame. In their secret hearts, perhaps, they even blamed Smiley for having caused it, because it was Smiley who had nailed Bill's treachery. He saw himself at the head of the conference, and the ring of hostile faces already set against him as one by one the week's cases were introduced, and subjected to the customary questions: Do we or do we not develop this? Shall we give it another week? Another month? Another year? Is it a trap, is it deniable, is it within our Charter? What resources will be needed and are they better applied elsewhere? Who will authorise? Who will be informed? How much will it cost? He remembered the intemperate outburst which the mere name, or workname, of Otto Leipzig immediately called forth among such uncertain judges as Lauder Strickland, Sam Collins and their kind. He tried to recall who else would have been there apart from Connie and her cohorts from Soviet Research. Director of Finance, director Western Europe, director Soviet Attack, most of them already Saul Enderby's men. And Enderby himself, still nominally a Foreign Servant, put in by his own palace guard in the guise of Whitehall linkman, but whose smile was already their language, whose frown, their disapproval. Smiley saw himself listening to the submission – Connie's own – much as she now repeated it, together with the results of her preliminary researches.

Otto's story figured, she had insisted. This far, it couldn't be faulted. She had shown her workings:

Her own Soviet Research Section had confirmed from printed sources that one Oleg Kursky, a law student, was at Tallinn Polytechnic during the relevant period, she said.

Foreign Office contemporary archives spoke of unrest in the docks.

A defector report from the American Cousins gave a Kursky query Karsky, lawyer, first name Oleg, as graduating from a Moscow Centre training course at Kiev in 1971.

The same source, though suspect, suggested Kursky had later changed his name on the advice of his superiors, 'owing to his previous field experience.'

Routine French liaison reports, though notoriously unreliable, indicated that for a Second Secretary, Commercial, in Paris, Kirov did indeed enjoy unusual freedoms, such as shopping alone and attending Third World receptions without the customary fifteen companions.

All of which, in short – Connie had ended, far too vigorously for the fifth-floor taste – all of which confirmed the Leipzig story, and the suspicion that Kirov had an intelligence rôle. Then she had slapped the file on the table and passed round her photographs – the very stills, picked up as a matter of routine by French surveillance teams, that had caused the original uproar in the Riga Group headquarters in Paris. Kirov enters an Embassy car. Kirov emerges from the Moscow Narodny carrying a brief-case. Kirov pauses at the window of a saucy bookshop in order to scowl at the magazine covers.

But none, Smiley reflected – returning to the present – none showing Oleg Kirov and his erstwhile victim Otto Leipzig disporting themselves with a pair of ladies.

'So that was the *case*, darling,' Connie announced, when she had taken a long pull at her drink. 'We had the evidence of little Otto with plenty on his file to prove him right. We had a spot of collateral from other sources, not oodles, I grant you, but a start. Kirov was a hood, he was newly appointed, but what *sort* of hood was anybody's guess. And that made him *interesting*, didn't it darling?'

'Yes,' Smiley said distractedly. 'Yes, Connie, I remember that it did.'

'He wasn't residency mainstream, we knew that from day one. He didn't ride about in residency cars, do night-shifts or twin up with identified fellow hoods, or use their cipher room or attend their weekly prayer-meetings or feed the residency cat or whatever. On the other hand, Kirov wasn't Karla's man either, was he, heart? That was the rum thing.'

'Why not?' Smiley asked, without looking at her.

But Connie looked at Smiley all right. Connie made one of her long pauses in order to consider him at her leisure, while outside in the dying elms, the rooks wisely chose the sudden lull to sound a Shakespearean omen of screams. 'Because Karla already *had* his man in Paris, darling,' she explained patiently. 'As you are very well aware. That old stickler Pudin, the assistant military attaché. *You* remember how Karla always loved a soldier. Still does, for all I know.' She broke off, in order once more to study his impassive face. He had put his chin in his hands. His eyes half closed, were turned towards the floor. 'Besides, Kirov was an idiot, and the one thing Karla *never* did like was idiots, did he? You weren't too kindly towards them either, come to think of it. Oleg Kirov was foul-mannered, stank, sweated, and stuck out like a fish in a tree wherever he went. Karla would have run a *mile* before hiring an oaf like that.' Again she paused. 'So would you,' she added.

Lifting a palm, Smiley placed it against his brow, fingers upwards, like a child at an exam. 'Unless,' he said.

'Unless *what*? Unless he'd gone off his turnip, I suppose! That'll be the day, I must say.'

'It was the time of the rumours,' Smiley said from far inside his thoughts.

'What rumours? There were always rumours, you dunderhead.'

'Oh, just defector reports,' he said disparagingly. 'Stories of strange happenings in Karla's court. Secondary sources, of course. But didn't they –'

'Didn't they what?'

'Well, didn't they suggest that he was taking rather strange people onto his pay-roll? Holding interviews with them at dead of night? It was all low-grade stuff, I know. I only mention it in passing.'

'And we were ordered to discount them,' Connie said very firmly. 'Kirov was the target. Not Karla. That was the fifth-floor ruling, George, and you were party to it. "Stop moon-gazing and get on with earthly matters," says you.' Twisting her mouth and putting back her head, she produced an uncomfortably realistic likeness of Saul Enderby: '"This Service is in the business of collectin' intelligence,"' she drawled. '"*Not* conductin' feuds agin the opposition." Don't tell me he's changed his tune, darling. Has he? *George?*' she whispered. 'Oh *George*, you are bad!'

He fetched her another drink and when he came back he saw her eyes glistening with mischievous excitement. She was plucking at the tufts of her white hair the way she used to when she wore it long.

'The point is, we licensed the operation, Con,' said Smiley, in a factual tone intended to rein her in. 'We overruled the doubters, and we gave you permission to take Kirov to first base. How did it run after that?'

The drink, the memories, the revived excitement of the chase were driving her at a speed he could not control. Her breathing had quickened. She was rasping like an old engine with the restraints dangerously removed. He realised she was telling Leipzig's story the way Leipzig had told it to Vladimir. He had thought he was in the Circus with her still, with the operation against Kirov just about to be launched. But in her imagination she had leapt instead to the ancient city of Tallinn more than a quarter of a century earlier. In her extraordinary mind, she had been there; she had known both Leipzig and Kirov in the time of their friendship. A love story, she insisted. Little Otto and fat Oleg. This was the pivot, she said; let the old fool tell it the way it was, she said, and you pursue your wicked purposes as I go along, George.

'The tortoise and the hare, darling, that's who they were. Kirov the big sad baby, reading away at his law books at the Poly, and using the beastly secret police as Daddy; and little Otto Leipzig the proper devil, a finger in all the rackets, bit of prison behind him, working in the docks all day, at night preaching sedition to the unaligned. They met in a bar and it was love at first sight. Otto pulled the girls, Oleg Kirov slip-streamed along behind him, picking up his leavings. What are you trying to do, George? Joan-of-Arc me?'

He had lighted a fresh cigarette for her and put it into her mouth in the hope of calming her, but her feverish talking had already burned it low enough to scorch her. Taking it quickly from her, he stubbed it on the tin lid she used for an ashtray.

'They even shared a girl-friend for a time,' she said, so loud she was nearly yelling. 'And *one* day, if you can believe it, the poor ninny came to little Otto and warned him outright. "Your fat friend is jealous of you and he's a toady of the secret police," says she. "The unaligned discussion club is for the high jump. Beware the Ides of March!"'

'Go easy, Con,' Smiley warned her anxiously. 'Con, come down!'

Her voice grew still louder: 'Otto threw the girl out and a week later the whole bunch were arrested. Including fat Oleg, of course, who's set them up – but they knew. Oh *they* knew!' She faltered as if she had lost her way. 'And the fool girl who'd tried to warn him died,' she said. 'Missing believed interrogated. Otto combed the forests for her till he found someone who'd been with her in the cells. Dead as a dodo. Two dodos. Dead as I'll be, damn soon.'

'Let's go on later,' Smiley said.

He would have stopped her, too – made tea, talked weather, anything to halt the mounting speed of her. But she had taken a second leap and was already back in Paris, describing how Otto Leipzig, with the fifth floor's grudging approval and the old General's passionate help, set about arranging the reunion, after all those lost years, with Second Secretary Kirov, whom she dubbed the Ginger Pig. Smiley supposed it was her name for him at the time. Her face was scarlet and her breath was not enough for her story, so that it kept running out in a wheeze, but she forced herself to continue.

'Connie,' he begged her again, but it was not enough either, and perhaps nothing would have been.

First, she said, in search of the Ginger Pig, little Otto trotted along to the various Franco-Soviet friendship societies that Kirov was known to frequent.

'That poor little Otto must have seen *The Battleship Potemkin* fifteen times, but the Ginger Pig never showed up once.'

Word came that Kirov was showing a serious interest in émigrés, and even representing himself as their secret sympathiser, enquiring whether, as a junior official, there was anything he could do to help their families in the Soviet Union. With Vladimir's help Leipzig tried to put himself in Kirov's path, but once more luck was against him. Then Kirov started travelling – travelling everywhere, my dear, a positive flying Dutchman – so that Connie and her boys began to wonder whether he was some sort of clerical administrator for Moscow Centre, not on the operational side at all: the accountant-auditor for a group of Western residencies, for instance, with Paris as their centre – Bonn, Madrid, Stockholm, Vienna.

'For Karla or for the mainstream?' Smiley asked quietly.

Whisper who dares, said Connie, but for her money, it was for Karla. Even though Pudin was already there. Even though Kirov was an idiot, and not a soldier; it still *had* to be for Karla, Connie said, perversely doubling back upon her own assertions to the contrary. If Kirov had been visiting the mainstream residencies, he would have been entertained and put up by identified intelligence officers. But instead, he lived his cover, and stayed only with his national counterparts as the Commercial sections, she said.

Anyway, the flying did it, said Connie. Little Otto waited till Kirov had booked himself on a flight to Vienna, made sure he was travelling alone, then boarded the same flight, and they were in business.

'A straight copy book honey-trap, that's what we were aiming for,' Connie sang, very loud indeed. 'Your real old-fashioned burn. A big operator might laugh it off, but not Brother Kirov, least of all if he was on Karla's books. Naughty photographs and information with menaces, that was what we were after. And when we'd done with him, and found out what he was up to, and who his nasty friends were, and who was giving him all that heady freedom, we'd either buy him in as a defector or bung him back in the pond, depending on how much was left of him!'

She stopped dead. She opened her mouth, closed it, drew some breath, held out her glass to him.

'Darling, get the old soak another drinkie, double-quick, will you? Connie's getting her lurgies. No, don't. Stay where you are.'

For a fatal second, Smiley was lost.

'George?'

'Connie, I'm here! What is it?'

He was fast but not fast enough. He saw the stiffening of her face, he saw her distorted hands fly out in front of her, and her eyes screw up in disgust, as if she had seen a horrible accident.

'Hils, quick!' she cried. 'Oh, my hat!'

He embraced her and felt her forearms lock over the back of his neck to hold him tighter. Her skin was cold, she was shaking, but from terror not from chill. He stayed against her, smelling Scotch and medicated powder and old lady, trying to comfort her. Her tears were all over his cheeks, he could feel them and taste their salty sting as she pushed him away from her. He found her handbag and opened it for her, then went quickly back to the veranda and called to Hilary. She ran out of the darkness with her fists half clenched, elbows and hips rotating, in a way that makes men laugh. She hurried past him, grinning with shyness, and he stayed on the veranda, feeling the night cold pricking his cheeks while he stared at the gathering rain-clouds and the pine trees silvered by the rising moon. The dogs' screaming had subsided. Only the wheeling rooks sounded their harsh warnings. Go, he told himself. Get out of here. Bolt. His car waited not a hundred feet from him, frost already forming on the roof. He imagined himself leaping into it and driving up the hill, through the plantation, and away, never to return. But he knew he couldn't.

'She wants you back now, George,' Hilary said sternly from the doorway, with the special authority of those who nurse the dying.

But when he went back, everything was fine.

# FIFTEEN

Everything was fine. Connie sat powdered and austere in her rocking-chair, and her eyes, as he entered, were as straight upon him as when he had first come here. Hilary had calmed her, Hilary had sobered her, and now Hilary stood behind her with her hands on Connie's neck, thumbs inward, while she gently massaged the nape.

'Spot of *timor mortis*, darling,' Connie explained. 'The leech prescribes Valium but the old fool prefers the juice. You won't mention that bit to Saul Enderby when you report back, will you, heart?'

'No, of course not.'

'When *will* you be reporting back, by the by, darling?'

'Soon,' said Smiley.

'Tonight, when you get home?'

'It depends what there is to tell.'

'Con did write it all *up* you know, George. The old fool's accounts of the case were very *full*, I thought. Very *detailed*. Very *circumstantial*, for once. But you haven't consulted them.' Smiley said nothing. 'They're lost. Destroyed. Eaten by mealy-bugs. You haven't had time. Well, well. And you such a devil for the paperwork. *Higher*, Hils,' she ordered, without taking her gleaming eyes away from Smiley. 'Higher, darling. The bit where the vertebrae get stuck in the tonsils.'

Smiley sat down on the old wicker sofa.

'I used to love those double-double games,' Connie confessed dreamily, rolling her head in order to caress Hilary's hands with it. 'Didn't I, Hils? All human life was there. You wouldn't know that any more, would you? Not

since you blew your gasket.'

She returned to Smiley. 'Want me to go on, dearie?' she asked in her East End tart's voice.

'If you could just take me through it briefly,' Smiley said. 'But not if it's –'

'Where were we? I know. Up in the aeroplane with the Ginger Pig. He's on his way to Vienna, he's got his trotters in a trough of beer. Looks up, and who does he see standing in front of him like his own bad conscience but his dear old buddy of twenty-five years ago, little Otto, grinning like Old Nick. What does Brother Kirov né Kursky *feel*? we ask ourselves, assuming he's got any feelings. Does Otto *know* – he wonders – that it was naughty me who sold him into the Gulag? So what does he do?'

'What does he do?' said Smiley, not responding to her banter.

'He decides to play it hearty, dearie. Doesn't he, Hils? Whistles up the caviare, and says "Thank God."' She whispered something and Hilary bent her head to catch it, then giggled. '"Champagne!" he says. And my God they have it, and the Ginger Pig pays for it, and they drink it, and they share a taxi into town, and they even have a quick snifter in a café before the Ginger Pig goes about his furtive duties. Kirov *likes* Otto,' Connie insisted. '*Loves* him, doesn't he, Hils? They're a proper pair of raving whatsits, same as us. Otto's sexy, Otto's fun, Otto's dishy, and anti-authoritarian, and light on his feet – and – oh, everything the Ginger Pig could never be, not in a thousand years! Why did the fifth floor always think people had to have one motive only?'

'I'm sure I didn't,' said Smiley fervently.

But Connie was back talking to Hilary, not to Smiley at all. 'Kirov was *bored*, heart. Otto was life for him. Same as you are for me. You put the spring into my stride, don't you, lovey? Hadn't prevented him from shopping Otto, of course, but that's only Nature, isn't it?'

Still gently swaying at Connie's back, Hilary nodded in vague assent.

'And what did Kirov mean to Otto Leipzig?' Smiley asked.

'Hate, my darling,' Connie replied, without hesitation. 'Pure, undiluted hatred. Plain, honest-to-God, black loathing. Hate and money. Those were Otto's two best things. Otto always felt he was *owed* for all those years he'd spent in the slammer. He wanted to collect for the girl, too. His great dream was that one day he would sell Kirov né Kursky for lots of money. Lots and lots and *lots* of money. Then spend it.'

*A waiter's anger*, Smiley thought, remembering the contact print. Remembering the tartan room again, at the airport, and Otto's quiet German voice with its caressing edge; remembering his brown, unblinking eyes, that were like windows on his smouldering soul.

After the Vienna meeting, said Connie, the two men had agreed to meet again in Paris, and Otto wisely played a long hand. In Vienna, Otto had not asked a single question to which the Ginger Pig could take exception; Otto was a pro, said Connie. Was Kirov married? he had asked. Kirov had flung up his hands and roared with laughter at the question, indicating that he was prepared not to be at any time. *Married but wife in Moscow*, Otto had reported – which would make a honey-trap that much more effective. Kirov had asked Leipzig what his job was these days, and Leipzig had replied magnanimously 'import-export,' proposing himself as a bit of a wheeler-dealer, Vienna one day, Hamburg the next. In the event, Otto waited a whole month – after twenty-five years, said Connie, he could afford to take his time – and during that one month, Kirov was observed by the French to make three separate passes at elderly Paris-based Russian émigrés: one a taxi-driver, one a shopkeeper, one a restaurateur, all three with dependants in the Soviet Union. He offered to take letters, messages, addresses; he even offered to take money and, if they were not too bulky, gifts. And to operate a two-way service next time he returned. Nobody took him up. In the fifth week Otto rang Kirov at his flat, said he had just flown in from Hamburg, and suggested they had some fun. Over dinner, picking his moment, Otto said the night was on him; he had just made a big killing on a certain shipment to a certain country, and had money to burn.

'This was the bait we had worked out for him, darling,' Connie explained, addressing Smiley directly at last. 'And the Ginger Pig rose to it, didn't he, as they all do, don't they, bless them, salmon to the fly every time?'

What sort of shipment? Kirov had asked Otto. What sort of country? For reply, Leipzig had drawn in the air a hooked nose on the end of his own, and broken out laughing. Kirov laughed too, but he was clearly very interested. To *Israel*? he said; then what sort of shipment? Leipzig pointed his same forefinger at Kirov and pretended to pull a trigger. *Arms* to Israel? Kirov asked in amazement, but Leipzig was a pro and would say no more. They drank, went to a strip club, and talked old times. Kirov even referred to their shared girl-friend, asking whether Leipzig knew what had become of her. Leipzig said he didn't. In the early morning, Leipzig had proposed they pick up some company and take it to his flat, but Kirov, to his disappointment, refused: not in Paris, too dangerous. In Vienna or Hamburg, sure. But not in Paris. They parted, drunk, at breakfast time, and the Circus was a hundred pounds poorer.

'Then the bloody infighting started,' said Connie, suddenly changing track completely. 'The Great Head Office Debate. Debate, my arse. You were away, Saul Enderby put one manicured hoof in, and the rest of them promptly got the vapours – that's what happened.' Her baron's voice again: '"Otto Leipzig's taking us for a ride . . . We haven't cleared the operation with the Frogs . . . Foreign Office worried about implications . . . Kirov is a plant . . . the Riga Group a totally unsound base from which to make a ploy of this scale." Where were you, anyway? Beastly Berlin, wasn't it?'

'Hong Kong.'

'Oh, there,' she said vaguely, and slumped in her chair while her eyelids drooped.

Smiley had sent Hilary to make tea, and she was clanking dishes at the other end of the room. He glanced at her, wondering whether he should call her, and saw her standing exactly as he had last seen her in the Circus the night they sent for him – her knuckles backed against her mouth, supporting a silent scream. He had been working late – it was about that time; yes, he was preparing his departure to Hong Kong – when suddenly his internal phone rang and he heard a man's voice, very strained, asking him to come immediately to the cipher room, Mr. Smiley, sir, it's urgent. Moments later he was hurrying down a bare corridor, flanked by two worried janitors. They pushed open the door for him, he stepped inside, they hung back. He saw the smashed machinery, the files and card indices and telegrams flung around the room like rubbish at a football ground, he saw the filthy graffiti daubed in lipstick on the wall. And at the centre of it all, he saw Hilary herself, the culprit – exactly as she was now – staring through the thick net curtains at the free white sky outside: Hilary our Vestal, so well bred; Hilary our Circus bride.

'Hell are you up to, Hils?' Connie demanded roughly from her rocking-chair.

'Making tea, Con. George wants a cup of tea.'

'To hell with what *George* wants,' she retorted, flaring. 'George is *fifth floor*. George put the kibosh on the Kirov case and now he's trying to get it right, flying solo in his old age. Right, George? Right? Even lied to me about the old devil Vladimir, who walked into a bullet on Hampstead Heath, according to the newspapers, which he apparently doesn't read, any more than my reports!'

They drank the tea. A rainstorm was getting up. The first hard drops were hammering on the wood roof.

Smiley had charmed her, Smiley had flattered her, Smiley had willed her to go on. She had drawn the thread half-way out for him. He was determined that she should draw it all the way.

'I've got to have it all, Con,' he repeated. 'I've got to hear everything, just as you remember it, even if the end is painful.'

'The end bloody well *is* painful,' she retorted.

But already her voice, her face, the very lustre of her memory were flagging , and he knew it was a race against time.

Now it was Kirov's turn to play the classic card, she said, wearily. At this next meeting, which was in Brussels a month later, Kirov referred to the Israeli arms shipment thing and said he had happened to mention their conversation to a friend of his in the Commercial Section of the Embassy who was contributing to a special study of the Israeli military economy, and even had funds available for researching it. Would Leipzig consider – no, but seriously, Otto! – talking to the fellow or, better still, giving the story to his old buddy Oleg here and now, who might even get a little credit for it on his own account? Otto said, 'Provided it pays, and didn't hurt anyone.' Then he solemnly fed Kirov a bag of chicken-feed prepared by Connie and the Middle Eastern people – all of it true, of course, and eminently checkable, even if it wasn't a lot of use to anyone – and Kirov solemnly wrote it all down, though both of them, as Connie put it, knew perfectly well that neither Kirov nor his master, whoever that was, had the smallest interest in Israel, or arms, or shipments, or her military economy – not in *this* case anyway. What Kirov was aiming to do was create a conspiratorial relationship, as their next meeting back in Paris showed. Kirov evinced huge enthusiasm for the report, insisted that Otto accept five hundred dollars for it, against the minor formality of signing a receipt. And when Otto had done this, and was squarely hooked, Kirov sailed straight in with all the crudity he could command – which was a lot, said Connie – and asked Otto how well placed he was with the local Russian émigrés.

'Please, Con,' he whispered. 'We're almost there!' She was so near but he could feel her drifting farther and farther away.

Hilary was lying on the floor with her head against Connie's knees. Absently, Connie's mittened hands had taken hold of her hair for comfort, and her eyes had fallen almost shut.

'Connie!' he repeated.

Opening her eyes, Connie gave a tired smile.

'It was only the fan dance, darling,' she said. 'The he-knows-I-know-you-know. The usual fan dance,' she repeated indulgently, and her eyes closed again.

'So how did Leipzig answer him? *Connie!*'

'He did what we'd do, darling,' she murmured. 'Stalled. Admitted he was well in with the émigré groups, and hugger-mugger with the General. Then stalled. Said he didn't visit Paris that much. "Why not hire someone local?" he said. He was teasing, Hils, darling, you see. Asked again: Would it hurt anyone? Asked what the job was, anyway? What did it pay? Get me some booze, Hils.'

'No,' said Hilary.

'Get it.'

Smiley poured two fingers of whisky and watched her sip.

'What did Kirov want Otto to do with the émigrés?' he said.

'Kirov wanted a legend,' she replied. 'He wanted a legend for a girl.'

Nothing in Smiley's manner suggested he had heard the phrase from Toby Esterhase only a few hours ago. Four years ago, Oleg Kirov wanted a legend, Connie repeated. Just as the Sandman, according to Toby and the General – thought Smiley – wanted one today. Kirov wanted a cover story for a female agent who could be infiltrated into France. That was the nub of it, Connie said. Kirov didn't say this, of course; he put it quite differently, in fact. He told Otto that Moscow had issued a secret instruction to all Embassies announcing that split Russian families might in certain circumstances be reunited abroad. If enough families could be found who wished it, said the instruction, then Moscow would go public with the idea and thus enhance the Soviet Union's image in the field of human rights. Ideally, they wanted cases with a compassionate ring: daughters in Russia, say, cut off from their families in the West, single girls, perhaps of marriageable age. Secrecy was essential, said Kirov, until a list of suitable cases had been assembled – think of the outcry there would be, Kirov said, if the story leaked ahead of time!

The Ginger Pig made his pitch so badly, said Connie, that Otto had at first to deride the proposal simply for the sake of verisimilitude: it was too crazy, too hole-in-corner, he said – secret lists, what nonsense! Why didn't Kirov approach the émigré organisations themselves and swear them to secrecy? Why employ a total outsider to do his dirty work? As Leipzig teased, Kirov grew more heated. It was not Leipzig's job to make fun of Moscow's secret edicts, said Kirov. He began shouting at him, and somehow Connie discovered the energy to shout too, or at least to lift her voice above its weary level, and to give it the guttural Russian ring she thought Kirov ought to have: '"Where is your compassion?" he says. "Don't you want to help people? Why do you sneer at a human gesture merely because it comes from Russia!"' Kirov said he had approached some families himself, but found no trust, and made no headway. He began to put pressure on Leipzig, first of a personal kind – 'Don't you want to help me in my career?' – and when this failed, he suggested to Leipzig that since he had already supplied secret information to the Embassy for money, he might consider it prudent to continue, lest the West German authorities somehow got to hear of this connection and threw him out of Hamburg – maybe out of Germany altogether. How would Otto like that? And finally, said Connie, Kirov offered money, and that was where the wonder lay. 'For each successful reunion effected, ten thousand U.S. dollars,' she announced. 'For each suitable candidate, whether a reunion takes place or not, one thousand U.S. on the nail. Cash-cash.'

At which point, of course, said Connie, the fifth floor decided Kirov was off his head, and ordered the case abandoned immediately.

'And I returned from the Far East,' said Smiley.

'Like poor King Richard from the Crusades, you did, darling!' Connie agreed. '*And* found the peasants in uproar and your nasty brother on the throne. Serves you right.' She gave a gigantic yawn. 'Case dustbinned,' she declared. 'The Kraut police wanted Leipzig extradited from France; we could perfectly well have begged them off but we didn't. No honey-trap, no dividend, no bugger-all. Fixture cancelled.'

'And how did Vladimir take all that?' Smiley asked, as if he really didn't know.

Connie opened her eyes with difficulty. 'Take what?'

'Cancelling the fixtures.'

'Oh, *roared*, what do you expect? Roar, roar. Said we'd spoilt the kill of the century. Swore to continue the war by other means.'

'What *kind* of kill?'

She missed his question. 'It's not a *shooting* war any more, George,' she said, as her eyes closed again. 'That's the trouble. It's grey. Half-angels fighting half-devils. No one knows where the lines are. No bang-bangs.'

Once again, Smiley in his memory saw the tartan hotel bedroom and the two black overcoats side by side, as Vladimir appealed desperately to have the case reopened: 'Max, hear us one more time, hear what has happened since you ordered us to stop!' They had flown from Paris at their own expense to tell him, because Finance Section on Enderby's orders had closed the case account. 'Max, hear us, please,' Vladimir had begged.'Kirov summoned Otto to his apartment late last night. They had another meeting, Otto and Kirov. Kirov got drunk and said amazing things!'

He saw himself back in his old room at the Circus, Enderby already installed in his desk. It was the same day, just a few hours later.

'Sounds like little Otto's last-ditch effort at keeping out of the hands of the Huns,' Enderby said when he had heard Smiley out. 'What do they want him for over there, theft or rape?'

'Fraud,' Smiley had replied hopelessly, which was the wretched truth.

Connie was humming something. She tried to make a song of it, then a limerick. She wanted more drink but Hilary had taken away her glass.

'I want you to go,' Hilary said, straight into Smiley's face.

Leaning forward on the wicker sofa, Smiley asked his last question. He asked it, one might have thought, reluctantly; almost with distaste. His soft face had hardened with determination, but not enough to conceal the marks of disapproval. 'Do you remember a story old Vladimir used to tell, Con? One we never shared with anyone? Stored away, as a piece of private treasure? That Karla had a mistress, someone he loved?'

'His Ann,' she said dully.

'That in all the world, she was his one thing, that she made him act like a crazy man?'

Slowly her head came up, and he saw her face clear, and his voice quickened and gathered strength.

'How that was the rumour they passed around in Moscow Centre – those in the know? Karla's invention – his creation, Con? How he found her when she was a child, wandering in a burnt-out village in the war? Adopted her, brought her up, fell in love with her?'

He watched her and despite the whisky, despite her deathly weariness, he saw the last excitement, like the last drop in the bottle, slowly rekindle her features.

'He was behind the German lines,' she said. 'It was the forties. There was a team of them, raising the Balts. Building networks, stay-behind groups. It was a big operation. Karla was boss. She became their mascot. They carted her from pillar to post. A kid. Oh, George!'

He was holding his breath to catch her words. The din on the roof grew louder, he heard the rising growl of the forest as the rain came down on it. His face was near to hers, very; its animation matched her own.

'And then what?' he said.

'Then he bumped her off, darling. That's what.'

'Why?' He drew still closer, as if he feared her words might fail her at the crucial moment. '*Why*, Connie? Why kill her when he loved her?'

'He'd done everything for her. Found foster-parents for her. Educated her. Had her all got up to be his ideal hag. Played Daddy, played lover, played God. She was his toy. Then one day she ups and gets ideas above her station.'

'What sort of ideas?'

'Soft on revolution. Mixing with bloody intellectuals. Wanting the State to wither away. Asking the big "Why?" and the big "Why not?" He told her to shut up. She wouldn't. She had a devil in her. He had her shoved in the slammer. Made her worse.'

'And there was a child,' Smiley prompted, taking her mittened hand in both of his. 'He gave her a child, remember?' Her hand was between them, between their faces. 'You researched it, didn't you, Con? One silly season, I gave you your head. "Track it down, Con," I said to you. "Take it wherever it leads." Remember?'

Under Smiley's intense encouragement, her story had acquired the fervour of a last love. She was speaking fast, eyes streaming. She was backtracking, zigzagging everywhere in her memory. Karla had this hag . . yes, darling, that was the story, do you hear me? – Yes, Connie, go on, I hear you. – Then listen. He brought her up, made her his mistress, there was a brat, and the quarrels were about the brat. George, darling, do you love me like the old days? – Come on, Con, give me the rest, yes of course I do. – He accused her of warping its precious mind with dangerous ideas, like freedom for instance. Or love. A girl, her mother's image, said to be a beauty. In the end the old despot's love turned to hatred and he had his ideal carted off and spavined: end of story. We had it from Vladimir first, then a few scraps, never the hard base. Name unknown, darling, because he destroyed all records of her, killed whoever might have heard, which is Karla's way, bless him, isn't it, darling, always was? Others said she wasn't dead at all, the story of her murder was disinformation to end the trail. There, she did it, didn't she? The old fool remembered!

'And the child?' Smiley asked. 'The girl in her mother's image? There was a defector report – what was *that* about?' She didn't pause. She had remembered that as well, her mind was galloping ahead of her, just as her voice was outrunning her breath.

A don of some sort from Leningrad University, said Connie. Claimed he'd been ordered to take on a weird girl for special political instruction in the evenings, a sort of private patient who was showing anti-social tendencies, the daughter of a high official. Tatiana, he was only allowed to know her as Tatiana. She'd been raising hell all over town, but her father was a big beef in Moscow and she couldn't be touched. The girl tried to seduce him, probably did, then told him some story about how Daddy had had Mummy killed for showing insufficient faith in the historical process. Next day his professor called him in and said if he ever repeated a word of what had happened at that interview, he would find himself tripping on a very big banana skin . . .

Connie ran on wildly, describing clues that led nowhere, the sources that vanished at the moment of discovery. It seemed impossible that her racked and drink-sodden body could have once more summoned so much strength.

'Oh, George, darling, take me with you! That's what you're after, I've got it! Who killed Vladimir, and why! I saw it in your ugly face the moment you walked in. I couldn't place it, now I can. You've got your Karla look! Vladi had opened up the vein again, so Karla had him killed! That's your banner, George. I can see you marching. Take me with you, George, for God's sake! I'll leave Hils. I'll leave anything, no more of the juice, I swear. Get me up to London and I'll find his hag for you, even if she doesn't exist, if it's the last thing I do!'

'Why did Vladimir call him the Sandman?' Smiley asked, knowing the answer already.

'It was his joke. A German fairy tale Vladi picked up in Estonia from one of his Kraut forebears. "Karla is our Sandman. Anyone who comes too close to him has a way of falling asleep." We never knew, darling, how could we? In the Lubianka, someone had met a man who'd met a woman, who'd met her. Someone else knew someone who'd helped to bury her. That hag was Karla's shrine, George. And she betrayed him. Twin cities, we used to say you were, you and Karla, two halves of the same apple. George, darling, don't! Please!'

She had stopped, and he realised that she was staring up at him in fear, that her face was somehow beneath his own; he was standing, glaring down at her. Hilary was against the wall, calling 'Stop, stop!' He was standing over her, incensed by her cheap and unjust comparison, knowing that neither Karla's methods nor Karla's absolutism were his own. He heard himself say '*No, Connie!*' and discovered that he had lifted his hands to the level of his chest, palms downward and rigid, as if he were pressing something into the ground. And he realised his passion had scared her; that he had never betrayed so much conviction to her – or so much feeling – before.

'I'm getting old,' he muttered, and gave a sheepish smile.

He relaxed, and as he did so, slowly Connie's own body became limp also, and the dream died in her. The hands which had clutched him seconds earlier lay on her lap like bodies in a trench.

'It was all bilge,' she said sullenly. A deep and terminal listlessness descended over her. 'Bored émigrés, crying into their vodka. Drop it, George. Karla's beaten you all ends up. He foxed you, he made a fool of your time. *Our* time.' She drank, no longer caring what she said. Her head flopped forward again and for a moment he thought she really was asleep. 'He foxed *you*, he foxed *me*, and when you smelt a rat he got Bloody Bill Haydon to fox Ann and put you off the scent.' With difficulty she lifted her head to stare at him one more time. 'Go home, George. Karla won't give you back your past. Be like the old fool here. Get yourself a bit of love and wait for Armageddon.'

She began coughing again, hopelessly, one hacking retch after another.

The rain had stopped. Gazing out of the French windows, Smiley saw again the moonlight on the cages, touching the frost on the wire; he saw the frosted crowns of the fir trees climbing the hill into a black sky; he saw a world reversed, with the light things darkened into shadow, and the dark things picked out like beacons on the white ground. He saw a sudden moon, stepping clear before the clouds, beckoning him into seething crevices. He saw one black figure in Wellington boots and a headscarf running up the lane, and realised it was Hilary; she must have slipped out without his noticing. He remembered he had heard a door slam. He went back to Connie and sat on the sofa beside her. Connie wept and drifted, talking about love. Love was a positive power, she said vaguely – ask Hils. But Hilary was not there to ask. Love was a stone thrown into the water, and if there were enough stones and we all loved together, the ripples would eventually be strong enough to reach across the sea and overwhelm the haters and the cynics – 'even beastly Karla, darling,' she assured him. 'That's what Hils says. Bilge, isn't it? It's bilge, Hils!' she yelled.

The Connie closed her eyes again, and after a while, by her breathing, appeared to doze off. Or perhaps she was only pretending in order to avoid the pain of saying goodbye to him. He tiptoed into the cold evening. The car's engine, by a miracle, started; he began climbing the lane, keeping a look-out for Hilary. He rounded a bend and saw her in the headlights. She was cowering among the trees, waiting for him to leave before she went back to Connie. She had her hands to her face again and he thought he saw blood; perhaps she had scratched herself with her finger-nails. He passed her and saw her in the mirror, staring after him in the glow of his rear lights, and for a moment she resembled for him all those muddy ghosts who are the real victims of conflict: who lurch out of the smoke of war, battered and starved and deprived of all they ever had or loved. He waited until he saw her start down the hill again, towards the lights of the *dacha*.

At Heathrow airport he bought his air ticket for the next morning, then lay on his bed in the hotel, for all he knew the same one, though the walls were not tartan. All night long the hotel stayed awake, and Smiley with it. He heard the clank of plumbing and the ringing of phones and the thud of lovers who would not or could not sleep.

*Max, hear us one more time,* he rehearsed; *it was the Sandman himself who sent Kirov to the émigrés to find the legend.*

# SIXTEEN

Smiley arrived in Hamburg in mid-morning and took the airport bus to the city centre. Fog lingered and the day was very cold. In the Station Square, after repeated rejections, he found an old, thin terminus hotel with a lift licensed for three persons at a time. He signed in as Standfast, then walked as far as a car-rental agency, where he hired a small Opel, which he parked in an underground garage that played softened Beethoven out of loudspeakers. The car was his back door. He didn't know whether he would need it, but he knew it needed to be there. He walked again, heading for the Alster, sensing everything with a particular sharpness: the manic traffic, the toy-shops for millionaire children. The din of the city hit him like a fire-storm, causing him to forget the cold. Germany was his second nature, even his second soul. In his youth, her literature had been his passion and his discipline. He could put on her language like a uniform and speak with its boldness. Yet he sensed danger in every step he took, for Smiley as a young man had spent half the war here in the lonely terror of the spy, and the awareness of being on enemy territory was lodged in him for good. In boyhood he had known Hamburg as a rich and graceful shipping town, which hid its volatile soul behind a cloak of Englishness; in manhood as a city smashed into medieval darkness by thousand-bomber air raids. He had seen it in the fifty years of peace, one endless smouldering bomb-site and the survivors tilling the rubble like fields. And he saw it today, hurtling into the anonymity of canned music, high-rise concrete and smoked glass.

Reaching the sanctuary of the Alster he walked the pleasant footpath to the jetty where Villem had boarded the steamer. On weekdays, he recorded, the first ferry was at 7:10, the last at 20:15, and Villem had been here on a weekday. There was a steamer due in fifteen minutes. Waiting for it, he watched the sculls and the red squirrels much as Villem had done, and when the steamer arrived he sat in the stern where Villem had sat, in the open air under the canopy. His companions consisted of a crowd of schoolchildren and three nuns. He sat with his eyes almost closed by the dazzle, listening to their chatter. Half-way across he stood, walked through the cabins to the forward window, looked out, apparently to confirm something, glanced at his watch, then returned to his seat until the Jungfernstieg, where he landed.

Villem's story tallied. Smiley had not expected otherwise, but in a world of perpetual doubt, reassurance never came amiss.

He lunched then went to the main Post Office and studied old telephone directories for an hour, much as Ostrakova had done in Paris, though for different reasons. His researches complete, he settled himself gratefully in the lounge of the Four Seasons Hotel and read newspapers till dusk.

In a Hamburg guide to houses of pleasure, the Blue Diamond was not listed under night-clubs but under 'amour' and earned three stars for exclusivity and cost. It was situated in St. Pauli, but discreetly apart from the main beat, in a cobbled alley that was tilted and dark and smelt of fish. Smiley rang the doorbell and it opened on an electric switch. He stepped inside and stood at once in a trim ante-room filled with grey machinery manned by a young smart man in a grey suit. On the wall, grey reels of tape turned slowly, though the music they played was mostly somewhere else. On the desk an elaborate telephone system, also grey, flickered and ticked.

'I should like to pass some time here,' Smiley said.

This is where they answered my phone call, he thought, when I telephoned Vladimir's Hamburg correspondent.

The smart young man drew a printed form from his desk and in a confiding manner explained the procedure, much as a lawyer would, which possibly was his daytime profession anyway. Membership cost one hundred and seventy-five marks, he said softly. This was a one-time annual subscription entitling Smiley to enter free for a full year, as many times as he wished. The first drink would cost him a further twenty-five marks and thereafter prices were high but not unreasonable. A first drink was obligatory and, like the membership fee, payable before entry. All other forms of entertainment came without charge, though the girls received gifts appreciatively. Smiley should complete the form in whatever name he wished. It would be filed here by the young man personally. All he had to do on his next visit was remember the name under which he had joined and he would be admitted without formalities.

Smiley put down his money and added one more false name to the dozens he had used in his lifetime. He descended a staircase to a second door which once more opened electronically, revealing a narrow passage giving on to a row of cubicles, still empty because in that world the night was only now beginning. At the end of the passage stood a third door and, once through it, he entered total darkness filled with the full blast of the music from the smart young man's tape-recorders. A male voice spoke to him, a pin-light led him to a table. He was handed a list of drinks. 'Proprietor C.Kretzschmar,' he read at the foot of the page in small print. He ordered whisky.

'I wish to remain alone. No company.'

'I shall advise the house, sir,' the waiter said with confiding dignity, and accepted his tip.

'Concerning Herr Kretzschmar. He is from Saxony, by any chance?'

'Yes, sir.'

*Worse than East German*, Toby Esterhase had said. *Saxon, They stole together, pimped together, faked reports together. It was a perfect marriage.*

He sipped his whisky, waiting for his eyes to grow accustomed to the light. From somewhere a blue glow shone, picking out cuffs and collars eerily. He saw white faces and white bodies. There were two levels. The lower, where he sat, was furnished with tables and armchairs. The upper consisted of six *chambres séparées*, like boxes at the theatre, each with its own blue glow. It was in one of these, he decided, that, knowingly or not, the quartet had posed for its photograph. He recalled the angle from which the picture had been taken. It was from above – from well above. But 'well above' meant somewhere in the blackness of the upper walls where no eye could penetrate, not even Smiley's.

The music died and over the same speakers a cabaret was announced. The title, said the *compére*, was Old Berlin, and the *compére's* voice was also Old Berlin: hectoring, nasal and suggestive. The smart young man has changed the tape, thought Smiley. A curtain lifted revealing a small stage. By the light it released, he peered quickly upward again and this time saw what he was looking for: a small observation window of smoked glass set very high in the wall. The photographer used special cameras, he thought vaguely; these days, he had been told, darkness was no longer a hindrance. I should have asked Toby, he thought; Toby knows those gadgets by heart. On the stage, a demonstration of love-making had begun, mechanical, pointless, dispiriting. Smiley turned his attention to his fellow members scattered round the room. The girls were beautiful and naked and young, in the way the girls in the photograph were young. Those who had partners sat entwined with them, seemingly delighted by their senility and ugliness. Those who had none sat in a silent group like American footballers waiting to be called. The noise from the speakers grew very loud, a mixture of music and hysterical narrative. And in Berlin they are playing Old Hamburg, Smiley thought. On the stage the couple increased their efforts, but to little account Smiley wondered whether he would recognise the girls in the photograph if they should appear. He decided he would not. The curtain closed. He ordered another whisky in relief.

'Is Herr Kretzschmar in the house tonight?' he asked the waiter.

Herr Kretzschmar was a man of commitments, the waiter explained. Herr Kretzschmar was obliged to divide his time between several establishments.

'If he comes, have the goodness to let me know.'

'He will be here at eleven exactly, sir.'

At the bar, naked couples had begun dancing. He endured another half-hour of this before returning to the front office by way of the cubicles, some of which were not occupied. The smart young man asked whom he might announce.

'Tell him it's a special request,' Smiley said.

The smart young man pressed a button and spoke extremely quietly, much as he had spoken to Smiley.

The upstairs office was clean as a doctor's surgery with a polished plastic desk and a lot more machinery. A closed-circuit television supplied a daylight version of the scene downstairs. The same observation window that Smiley had already noticed looked down into the *séparées*. Herr Kretzschmar was what the Germans call a serious person. He was fiftyish, groomed and thickset, with a dark suit and a pale tie. His hair was straw blond like a good Saxon's, his bland face neither welcomed nor rejected. He shook Smiley's hand briskly and motioned him to a chair. He seemed well accustomed to dealing with special requests.

'Please,' Herr Kretzschmar said, and the preliminaries were over.

There was nowhere to go but forward.

'I understand you were once business partner to an acquaintance of mine named Otto Leipzig,' Smiley said, sounding a little too loud to himself. 'I happen to be visiting Hamburg and I wondered whether you could tell me where he is. His address does not appear to be listed anywhere.'

Herr Kretzschmar's coffee was in a silver pot with a paper napkin round the handle to protect his fingers when he poured. He drank and put his cup down carefully, to avoid collision.

'Who are you, please?' Herr Kretzschmar asked. The Saxon twang made his voice flat. A small frown enhanced his air of respectability.

'Otto called me Max,' Smiley said.

Herr Kretzschmar did not respond to this information but he took his time before putting his next question. His gaze, Smiley noticed again, was strangely innocent. *Otto never had a house in his life*, Toby had said. *For crash meetings, Kretzschmar played key-holder.*

'And your business with Herr Leipzig, if I may ask?'

'I represent a large company,' Smiley said. 'Among other interests, we own a literary and photographic agency for freelance reporters.'

'So?'

'In the distant past, my parent company has been pleased to accept occasional offerings from Herr Leipzig – through intermediaries – and pass them out to our customers for processing and syndication.'

'So?' Herr Kretzschmar repeated. His head had lifted slightly, but his expression had not altered.

'Recently the business relationship between my parent company and Herr Leipzig was revived.' He paused slightly. 'Initially by means of the telephone,' he said, but Herr Kretzschmar might never have heard of the telephone. 'Through intermediaries again, he sent us a sample of his work which we were pleased to place for him. I came here to discuss terms and to commission further work. Assuming of course that Herr Leipzig is in a position to provide it.'

'Of what nature was this work, please – that Herr Leipzig sent you – please, Herr Max?'

'It was a negative photograph of erotic content. My firm always insists on negatives. Herr Liepzig knew this, naturally.' Smiley pointed carefully across the room. 'I rather think it must have been taken from the window. A peculiarity of the photograph is that Herr Leipzig himself was modelling in it. One therefore assumes that a friend or business partner may have operated the camera.'

Herr Kretzschmar's blue gaze remained as direct and innocent as before. His face, though strangely unmarked, struck Smiley as courageous, but he didn't know why.

*You're messing around with a creep like Leipzig, then you better have a creep like me to look after you*, Toby had said.

'There is another aspect,' Smiley said.

'Yes?'

'Unhappily the gentleman who was acting as intermediary on this occasion met with a serious accident shortly after the negative was put into our care. The usual line of communcation with Herr Leipzig was therefore severed.'

Herr Kretzschmar did not conceal his anxiety. A frown of what seemed to be genuine concern clouded his smooth face and he spoke quite sharply.

'How so an accident? What sort of accident?'

'A fatal one. I came to warn Otto and talk to him.'

Herr Kretzschmar owned a fine gold pencil. Taking it deliberately from an inside pocket he popped out the point and, still frowning, drew a pure circle on the pad before him. Then he set a cross on top, then he drew a line through his creation, then he tutted and said 'Pity,' and when he had done all this he straightened up, and spoke tersely into a machine. 'No disturbances,' he said. In a murmur, the voice of the grey receptionist acknowledged the instruction.

'You said Herr Leipzig was an old acquaintance of your parent company?' Herr Kretzschmar resumed.

'As I believe you yourself were, long ago, Herr Kretzschmar.'

'Please explain this more closely,' Herr Kretzschmar said, turning the pencil slowly in both hands as if studying the quality of the gold.

'We are talking old history, of course,' said Smiley deprecatingly.

'This I understand.'

'When Herr Leipzig first escaped from Russia he came to Schleswig-Holstein,' Smiley said. 'The organisation which had arranged his escape was based in Paris, but as a Balt, he preferred to live in northern Germany. Germany was still occupied and it was difficult for him to make a living.'

'For anyone,' Herr Kretzschmar corrected him. 'For anyone at all to make a living. Those were fantastically hard times. The young of today have no idea.'

'None,' Smiley agreed. 'And they were particularly hard for refugees. Whether they came from Estonia or from Saxony, life was hard for them.'

'This is absolutely correct. The refugees had it worst. Please continue.'

'In those days there was a considerable industry in information. Of all kinds. Military, industrial, political, economic. The victorious powers were prepared to pay large sums of money for enlightening material about each other. My parent company was involved in this commerce, and kept a representative here whose task was to collect such material and pass it back to London. Herr Leipzig and his partner became occasional clients. On a freelance basis.'

News of the General's fatal accident notwithstanding, a swift and most unexpected smile passed like a breeze across the surface of Herr Kretzschmar's features.

'Free lance,' he said, as if he liked the words, and were new to them. 'Free lance,' he repeated. 'That's what we were.'

'Such relationships are naturally of a temporary nature,' Smiley continued.'But Herr Leipzig, being a Balt, had other interests and continued over a long period to correspond with my firm through intermediaries in Paris.' He paused. 'Notably a certain General. A few years ago, following a dispute, the General was obliged to move to London, but Otto kept in touch with him. And the General on his side remained the intermediary.'

'Until his accident,' Herr Kretzschmar put in.

'Precisely,' Smiley said.

'It was a traffic accident? An old man – a bit careless?'

'He was shot,' said Smiley and saw Herr Kretzschmar's face once more wince with displeasure. 'But murdered,' Smiley added, as if to reassure him. 'It wasn't suicide or an accident or anything like that.'

'Naturally,' said Herr Kretzschmar, and offered Smiley a cigarette. Smiley declined, so he lit one for himself, took a few puffs, and stubbed it out. His pale complexion was a shade paler.

'You have met Otto? You know him?' Herr Kretzschmar asked in the tone of one making light conversation.

'I have met him once.'

'Where?'

'I am not at liberty to say.'

Herr Kretzschmar frowned, but in perplexity rather than disapproval.

'Tell me, please. If your parent company – okay, London – wanted to reach Herr Leipzig directly, what steps did it take?' Herr Kretzschmar asked.

'There was an arrangement involving the *Hamburger Abendblatt*.'

'And if they wished to contact him very urgently?'

'There was you.'

'You are police?' Herr Kretzschmar asked quietly. 'Scotland Yard?'

'No.' Smiley stared at Herr Kretzschmar and Herr Kretzschmar returned his gaze.

'Have you brought me something?' Herr Kretzschmar asked. At a loss, Smiley did not immediately reply. 'Such as a letter of introduction? A card, for instance?'

'No.'

'Nothing to show? That's a pity.'

'Perhaps when I have seen him, I shall understand your question better.'

'But you have seen it evidently, this photograph? You have it with you, maybe?'

Smiley took out his wallet, and passed the contact print across the desk. Holding it by the edges, Herr Kretzschmar studied it for a moment, but only by way of confirmation, then laid it on the plastic surface before him. As he did so, Smiley's sixth sense told him that Herr Kretzschmar was about to make a statement, in the way that Germans sometimes do make statements – whether of philosophy, or personal exculpation, or in order to be liked, or pitied. He began to suspect that Herr Kretzschmar in his own estimation at least, was a companionable if misunderstood man; a man of heart; even a good man; and that his initial taciturnity was something he wore like a professional suit, reluctantly, in a world which he frequently found unsympathetic to his affectionate character:

'I wish to explain to you that I run a decent house here,' Herr Kretzschmar remarked, when he had once more, by the clinical modern lamp, glanced at the print on his desk. 'I am not in the habit of photographing clients. Other people sell ties, I sell sex. The important thing to me is to conduct my business in an orderly and correct manner. But this was not business. This was friendship.'

Smiley had the wisdom to keep silent.

Herr Kretzschmar frowned. His voice dropped and became confiding: 'You knew him, Herr Max? That old General? You were personally connected with him?'

'Yes.'

'He was something, I understand?'

'He was indeed.'

'A lion, huh?'

'A lion.'

'Otto is still crazy about him. My name is Claus. "Claus," he would say to me. "That Vladimir, I love that man." You follow me? Otto is a very loyal fellow. The General too?'

'He was,' said Smiley.

'A lot of people do not believe in Otto. Your parent company also, they do not always believe in him. This is understandable. I make no reproach. But the General, he believed in Otto. Not in every detail. But in the big things.' Holding up his forearm, Herr Kretzschmar clenched his fist and it was suddenly a very big fist indeed. 'When things got hard, the old General believed in Otto absolutely. I too believe in Otto, Herr Max. In the big things. But I am German, I am not political, I am a businessman. These refugee stories are finished for me. You follow me?'

'Of course.'

'But not for Otto. Never. Otto is a fanatic. I can use that word. Fanatic. This is one reason why our lives have diverged. Nevertheless he is my friend. Anyone harms him, they get a bad time from Kretzschmar.' His face clouded in momentary mystification. 'You are sure you have nothing for me, Herr Max?'

'Beyond the photograph, I have nothing for you.'

Reluctantly Herr Kretzschmar once more dismissed the matter, but it took him time; he was uneasy.

'The old General was shot in England?' he asked finally.

'Yes.'

'But you consider nevertheless that Otto too is in danger?'

'Yes, but I think he has chosen to be.'

Herr Kretzschmar was pleased with this answer and nodded energetically twice.

'So do I. I also. This is my clear impression of him. I told him many times: "Otto, you should have been a high-wire acrobat." To Otto, in my opinion, no day is worth living unless it threatens on at least six separate occasions to be his last. You permit me to make certain observations on my relationship with Otto?'

'Please,' said Smiley politely.

Putting his forearms on the plastic surface, Herr Kretzschmar settled himself into a more comfortable posture for confession.

'There was a time when Otto and Claus Kretzschmar did everything together – stole a lot of horses, as we say. I was from Saxony, Otto came from the East. A Balt. Not Russia – he would insist – Estonia. He had had a tough time, studied the interior of a good few prisons, some bad fellow had betrayed him back in Estonia. A girl had died, and he was pretty mad about that. There was an uncle near Kiel but he was a swine. I may say that. A swine. We had no money, we were comrades and fellow thieves. This was normal, Herr Max.'

Smiley acknowledged the instructive point.

'One of our lines of business was to sell information. You have said correctly that information was a valuable commodity in those days. For example, we would hear of a refugee who had just come over and had not yet been interviewed by the Allies. Or maybe a Russian deserted. Or the master of a cargo ship. We hear about him, we question him. If we are ingenious, we contrive to sell the same report in different versions to two or even three different buyers. The Americans, the French, the British. The Germans themselves, already back in the saddle, yes. Sometimes, as long as it was inaccurate, even *five* buyers.' He gave a rich laugh. 'But only if it was inaccurate, okay? On other occasions, when we were out of sources, we invented – no question. We had maps, good imagination, good contacts. Don't misunderstand me: Kretzschmar is an enemy of Communism. We are talking old history, like you said. Herr Max. It was necessary to survive. Otto had the idea, Kretzschmar did the work. Otto was not the inventor of work, I would say.' Herr Kretzschmar frowned. 'But in one respect Otto was a very serious man. He had a debt to settle. Of this he spoke repeatedly. Maybe against the fellow who betrayed him and killed his girl, maybe against the whole human race. What do I know? He had to be active. Politically active. So for this purpose he went to Paris, on many occasions. Many.'

Herr Kretzschmar allowed himself a short period of reflection.

'I shall be frank,' he announced.

'And I shall respect your confidence,' said Smiley.

'I believe you. You are Max. The General was your friend, Otto told me this. Otto met you once, he admired you. Very well. I shall be frank with you.

Many years ago Otto Leipzig went to prison for me. In those days I was not respectable. Now that I have money I can afford to be. We stole something, he was caught, he lied and took the whole rap. I wanted to pay him. He said, "What the hell? if you are Otto Leipzig, a year in prison is a holiday." I visited him every week, I bribed the guards to take him special food – even once a woman. When he came out, I again tried to pay him. He declined my offers. "One day I'll ask you something," he said. "Maybe your wife." "You shall have her," I told him. "No problem." Herr Max, I assume you are an Englishman. You will appreciate my position.'

Smiley said he did.

'Two months ago – what do I know, maybe more, maybe less – the old General comes through on the telephone. He needs Otto urgently. "Not tomorrow, but tonight." Sometimes he used to call that way from Paris, using code-names, all this nonsense. The old General is a secretive fellow. So is Otto. Like children, know what I mean? Never mind.'

Herr Kretzschmar made an indulgent sweep of his big hand across his face, as if he were wiping away a cobweb. '"Listen," I tell him. "I don't know where Otto is. Last time I heard of him, he was in bad trouble with some business he started. I've got to find him, it will take time. Maybe tomorrow, maybe ten days." Then the old man tells me "I sent you a letter for him. Guard it with your life." Next day a letter comes, express for Kretzschmar, postmark London. Inside, a second envelope. "Urgent and top secret for Otto." *Top Secret*, okay? So the old guy's crazy. Never mind. You know that big hand-writing of his, strong like an army order?'

Smiley did.

'I find Otto. He's hiding from trouble again, no money. One suit he's got, but dresses like a film star. I give him the old man's letter.'

'Which is a fat one,' Smiley suggested, thinking of the seven pages of photocopy paper. Thinking of Mikhel's black machine parked like an old tank in the library.

'Sure. A long letter. He opened it while I was there –'

Herr Kretzschmar broke off and stared at Smiley and from his expression seemed, reluctantly, to recognise a restraint.

'A long letter,' he repeated. 'Many pages. He read it, he got pretty excited. "Claus," he said. "Lend me some money. I got to go to Paris." I lend him some money, five hundred marks, no problem. After this I don't see him much for a time. A couple of occasions he comes here, makes a phone call. I don't listen. Then a month ago he came to see me.' Again he broke off, and again Smiley felt his restraint. 'I am being frank,' he said, as if once again enjoining Smiley to secrecy. 'He was – well, I would say excited.'

'He wanted to use the night-club,' Smiley suggested helpfully.

'"Claus," he said. "Do what I ask and you have paid your debt to me." He called it a honey-trap. He would bring a man to the club, an Ivan, someone he knew well, had been cultivating for many years, he said, a very particular swine. This man was the target. He called him "the target". He said it was the chance of his life, everything he had waited for. The best girls, the best champagne, the best show. For one night, courtesy of Kretzschmar. The climax of his efforts, he said. The chance to pay old debts and make some money as well. He was owed, he said. Now he would collect. He promised there would be no repercussions. I said "No problem." "Also, Claus, I wish you to photograph us," he tells me. I said "No problem" again. So he came. And brought his target.'

Herr Kretzschmar's narrative had suddenly become uncharacteristically sparse. In the hiatus, Smiley slipped in a question, of which the purpose went far beyond the context: 'What language did they speak?'

Herr Kretzschmar hesitated, frowned, but finally answered: 'At first his target pretended to be French, but the girls did not speak much French so he spoke German to them. But with Otto he spoke Russian. He was disagreeable, this target. Smelt a lot, sweated a lot, and was in certain other ways not a gentleman. The girls did not like to stay with him. They came to me and complained. I sent them back but they still grumbled.'

He seemed embarrassed.

'Another small question,' said Smiley, as the awkwardness returned.'

'Please.'

'How could Otto Leipzig promise there would be no repercussions since he was presumably setting out to blackmail this man?'

'The target was not the *end*,' Herr Kretzschmar said, pursing his lips to assist the intellectual point. 'He was the means.'

'The means to someone else?'

'Otto was not precise. "A step on the General's ladder," was his expression. "For me, Claus, the target is enough. The target and afterwards the money. But for the General, he is only a step on the ladder. For Max also." For reasons I did not understand, the money was also dependent upon the General's satisfaction. Or perhaps yours.' He paused, as if hoping Smiley might enlighten him. Smiley did not. 'It was not my wish to ask questions or make conditions,' Herr Kretzschmar continued, picking his words with much greater severity. 'Otto and his target were admitted by the back entrance, and shown straight to a *séparée*. We arranged to display nothing that would indicate the name of the establishment. Not long ago, a night-club down the road went bankrupt,' Herr Kretzschmar said, in a tone which suggested he might not be wholly desolated by the event. 'Place called the Freudenjacht. I had bought certain equipment at the sale. Matches. Plates, we spread them around the *séparée*.' Smiley remembered the letters ACHT on the ashtray in the photograph.

'Can you tell me what the two men discussed?'

'No.' He changed his answer: 'I have no Russian,' he said. He made the same disowning wave of his hand. 'In German they talked about God and the world. Everything.'

'I see.'

'That's all I know.'

'How was Otto in his manner?' Smiley asked. 'Was he still excited?'

'I never saw Otto like that before in my life. He was laughing like an executioner, speaking three languages at once, not drunk but extremely animated, singing, telling jokes, I don't know what. That's all I know,' Herr Kretzschmar repeated, with embarrassment.

Smiley glanced discreetly at the observation window and at the grey boxes of machinery. He glimpsed once more in Herr Kretzschmar's little television screen the soundless twining and parting of the white bodies on the other side of the wall. He saw his last question, he recognised its logic, he sensed the wealth it promised. Yet the same lifetime's instinct that had brought him this far now held him back. Nothing at this moment, no short-term dividend, was worth the risk of alienating Kretzschmar, and closing the road to Otto Leipzig.

'And Otto gave you no other description of his target?' Smiley asked, for the sake of asking something; to help him run their conversation down.

'During the evening he came to me once. Up here. He excused himself from the company and came up here to make sure the arrangements were in order. He looked at the screen there and laughed. "Now I have taken him over the edge and he can't get back," he said. I did not ask any more. That is all that happened.'

Herr Kretzschmar was writing his instructions for Smiley on a leather-backed jotting pad with gold corners.

'Otto lives in bad circumstances,' he said. 'One cannot alter that. Giving him money does not improve his social standards. He remains' – Herr Kretzschmar hesitated – 'he remains at heart, Herr Max, a *gypsy*. Do you understand me.'

'Will you warn him that I am coming?'

'We have agreed not to use the telephone. The official link between us is completely closed.' He handed him the sheet of paper. 'I strongly advise you to take care,' Herr Kretzschmar said. 'Otto will be very angry when he hears the old General has been shot.' He saw Smiley to the door. 'What did they charge you down there?'

'I'm sorry?'

'Downstairs. How much did they take from you?'

'A hundred and seventy-five marks for membership.'

'With the drinks inside, at least two hundred. I'll tell them to give it back to you at the door. You English are poor these days. Too many trade unions. How'd you like the show?'

'It was very artistic,' said Smiley.

Herr Kretzschmar was once again very pleased with Smiley's answer. He patted Smiley on the shoulder: 'Maybe you should have more fun in life.'

'Maybe I should have done,' Smiley agreed.

'Greet Otto for me,' said Herr Kretzschmar.

'I will,' Smiley promised.

Herr Kretzschmar hesitated, and the same momentary bewilderment came over him.

'And you have nothing for me?' he repeated. 'No papers for example?'

'No.'

'Pity.'

As Smiley left, Herr Kretzschmar was already at the telephone, attending to other special requests.

He returned to the hotel. A drunken night porter opened the doors to him, full of suggestions about the wonderful girls he could send to Smiley's room. He woke, if he had ever slept, to the chime of church bells and the honk of shipping in the harbour, carried to him on the wind. But there are nightmares that do not go away with daylight, and as he drove northward over the fens in his hired Opel, the terrors which hovered in the mist were the same as those that had plagued him in the night.

# SEVENTEEN

The roads were as empty as the landscape. Through breaks in the mist, he glimpsed now a patch of cornfield, now a red farmhouse crouched low against the wind. A blue notice said 'KAI.' He swung sharply in a slip-road, dropping two flights, and saw ahead of him the wharf, a complex of low grey barracks dwarfed by the decks of cargo ships. A red-and-white pole guarded the entrance, there was a customs notice in several languages, but not a human soul in sight. Stopping the car, Smiley got out and walked lightly to the barrier. The red push-button was as big as a saucer. He pressed it and the shriek of its bell set a pair of herons flapping into the white mist. A control tower stood to his left on tubular legs. He heard a door slam and a ring of metal and watched a bearded figure in blue uniform stomp down the iron staircase to the bottom step. The man called to him, 'What do you want then?' Not waiting for an answer, he released the boom and waved Smiley through. The tarmac was like a vast bombed area cemented in, bordered by cranes and pressed down by the fogged white sky. Beyond it, the low sea looked too frail for the weight of so much shipping. He glanced in the mirror and saw the spires of a sea town etched like an old print half-way up the page. He glanced out to sea and saw through the mist the line of buoys and winking lamps that marked the water border to East Germany and the start of seven and a half thousand miles of Soviet Empire. That's where the herons went, he thought. He was driving at a crawl between red-and-white traffic cones towards a container-park heaped with car tyres and logs. 'Left at the container-park', Herr Kretzschmar had said. Obediently, Smiley swung slowly left, looking for an old house, though an old house in this Hanseatic dumping ground seemed a physical impossibility. But Herr Kretzschmar had said, 'Look for an old house marked "Office,"' and Herr Kretzschmar did not make errors.

He bumped over a railway track and headed for the cargo ships. Beams of morning sun had broken through the mist, making their white paintwork dazzle. He entered an alley comprised of control rooms for the cranes, each like a modern signal-box, each with green levers and big windows. And there at the end of the alley, exactly as Herr Kretzschmar had promised, stood the old tin house with a high tin gable cut like fretwork and crowned with a peeling flag-post. The electric wires that led into it seemed to hold it up; there was an old water pump beside it, dripping, with a tin mug chained to its pedestal. On the wooden door, in faded Gothic lettering, stood the one word 'BUREAU,' in the French spelling, not the German, above a newer notice saying, 'P. K. BERGEN, IMPORT-EXPORT.' *He works there as the night clerk,* Herr Kretzschmar had said. *What he does by day only God and the Devil know.*

He rang the bell, then stood well back from the door, very visible. He was keeping his hands clear of his pockets and they were very visible too. He had buttoned his overcoat to the neck. He wore no hat. He had parked the car sideways to the house so that anyone indoors could see the car was empty. *I am alone and unarmed,* he was trying to say. *I am not their man, but yours.* He rang the bell again and called 'Herr Leipzig!' An upper window opened, and a pretty woman looked out blearily, holding a blanket round her shoulders.

'I'm sorry,' Smiley called up to her politely. 'I was looking for Herr Leipzig. It's rather important.'

'Not here,' she replied, and smiled.

A man joined her. He was young and unshaven with tattoo marks on his arms and chest. They spoke together a moment, Smiley guessed in Polish.

'*Nix hier*,' the man confirmed guardedly. '*Otto nix hier*.'

'We're just the temporary tenants,' the girl called down. 'When Otto's broke he moves to his country villa and rents us the apartment.'

She repeated this to her man, who this time laughed.

'*Nix hier*,' he repeated. 'No money. Nobody has money.'

They were enjoying the crisp morning, and the company.

'How long since you saw him?' Smiley asked.

More conference. Was it this day or that day? Smiley had the impression they had lost track of time.

'Thursday,' the girl announced, smiling again.

'Thursday,' her man repeated.

'I've got good news for him,' Smiley explained cheerfully, catching her mood. He patted his side pocket. 'Money, *Pinka-pinka*. All for Otto. He's earned it in commission. I promised to bring it to him yesterday.'

The girl interpreted all this and the man argued with her, and the girl laughed again.

'My friend says don't give it to him or Otto will come back and move us out and we'll have nowhere to make love!'

Try the water camp, she suggested, pointing with her bare arm. Two kilometres along the main road, over the railway and past the windmill, then right – she looked at her hands, then curved one prettily towards her lover – yes, right; right towards the lake, though you don't see the lake till you get to it.

'What is the place called?' Smiley asked.

'It has no name,' she said: 'It's just a place. Ask for holiday houses to let, then drive on towards the boats. Ask for Walther. If Otto is around, Walther will know where to find him.'

'Thank you.'

'Walther knows everything!' she called. 'He is like a professor!'

She translated this also, but this time her man looked angry.

'*Bad* professor!' he called down. 'Walther bad man!'

'Are you a professor too?' the girl asked Smiley.

'No. No, unfortunately not.' He laughed and thanked them, and they watched him get into his car as if they were children at a celebration. The day, the spreading sunshine, his visit – everything was fun for them. He lowered the window to say goodbye and heard her say something he couldn't catch.

'What was that?' he called up to her, still smiling.

'I said, "Then Otto is twice lucky for a change!"' The girl repeated.

'Why?' asked Smiley, and stopped the engine. 'Why is he twice lucky?'

The girl shrugged. The blanket was slipping from her shoulders and the blanket was all she wore. Her man put an arm around her and pulled it up again for decency.

'Last week the unexpected visit from the East,' she said, 'And today the money.' She opened her hands. 'Otto is Sunday's child for once. That's all.'

Then she saw Smiley's face, and the laughter went clean out of her voice.

'Visitor?' Smiley repeated. 'Who was the visitor?'

'From the East,' she said.

Seeing her dismay, terrified she might disappear altogether, Smiley with difficulty resurrected his appearance of good humour.

'Not his brother, was it?' he asked gaily, all enthusiasm. He held out one hand, cupping it over the mythical brother's head. 'A small chap? Spectacles like mine?'

'No, *no*! A big fellow. With a chauffeur. Rich.'

Smiley shook his head, affecting light-hearted disappointment. 'Then I don't know him,' he said. 'Otto's brother was certainly never rich.' He succeeded laughing outright. 'Unless he was the chauffeur, of course,' he added.

He followed her directions exactly, with the secret calmness of emergency. To be conveyed. To have no will of his own. To be conveyed, to pray, to make deals with your Maker. Oh God, don't make it happen, not another Vladimir. In the sunlight the brown fields had turned to gold, but the sweat on Smiley's back was like a cold hand stinging his skin. He followed her directions seeing everything as if it were his last day, knowing the big fellow with the chauffeur had gone ahead of him. He saw the farmhouse with the old horse-plough in the barn, the faulty beer sign with its neon blinking, the window-boxes of geraniums like blood. He saw the windmill like a giant pepper-mill and the field full of white geese all running with the gusty wind. He saw the herons skimming like sails over the fens. He was driving too fast. I should drive more often, he thought; I'm out of practice, out of control. The road changed from tarmac to gravel, gravel to dust and the dust blew up round the car like a sandstorm. He entered some pine trees and on the other side of them saw a sign saying 'HOLIDAY HOUSES TO LET,' and a row of shuttered asbestos bungalows waiting for their summer paint. He kept going and in the distance saw a coppice of masts, and brown water low in its basin. He headed for the masts, bumped over a pot-hole and heard a frightful crack from under the car. He supposed it was the exhaust, because the noise of his engine was suddenly much louder, and half the water birds in Schleswig-Holstein had taken fright at his arrival.

He passed a farm and entered the protective darkness of trees, then emerged in a stark and brilliant frame of whiteness of which a broken jetty and a few faint olive-coloured reeds made up the foreground, and an enormous sky the rest. The boats lay to his right, beside an inlet. Shabby caravans were parked along the track that led to them, grubby washing hung between the television aerials. He passed a tent in its own vegetable patch and a couple of broken huts that had once been military. On one, a psychedelic sunshine had been painted, and it was peeling. Three old cars and some heaped rubbish stood beside it. He parked and followed a mud path through the reeds to the shore. In the grass harbour lay a cluster of improvised houseboats, some of them converted landing-craft from the war. It was colder here, and for some reason darker. The boats he had seen were day boats, moored in a huddle apart, mostly under tarpaulins. A couple of radios played, but at first he saw nobody. Then he noticed a back-water and a blue dinghy made fast in it. And, in the dinghy, one gnarled old man in a sailcloth jacket and a black peaked cap, massaging his neck as if he had just woken up.

'Are you Walther?' Smiley asked.

Still rubbing his neck the old man seemed to nod.

'I'm looking for Otto Leipzig. They told me at the wharf I might find him here.'

'Walther's eyes were cut almond-shaped into the crumpled down paper of his skin.

'*Isadora*,' he said.

He pointed at a rickety jetty farther down the shore. The *Isadora* lay at the end of it, a forty-foot motor launch down on her luck, a Grand Hotel awaiting demolition. The portholes were curtained, one of them was smashed, another was repaired with Scotch tape. The planks of the jetty yielded alarmingly to Smiley's tread. Once he nearly fell, and twice, to bridge the gaps, he had to stride much wider than seemed safe to his short legs. At the end of the jetty, he realised that the *Isadora* was adrift. She had slipped her moorings at the stern and shifted twelve feet out to sea, which was probably the longest journey she would ever make. The cabin doors were closed, their windows curtained. There was no small boat.

The old man sat sixty yards off, resting on his oars. He had rowed out of the backwater to watch. Smiley cupped his hands and yelled: 'How do I get to him?'

'If you want him, call him,' the old man replied, not seeming to lift his voice at all.

Turning to the old launch, Smiley called, 'Otto.' He called softly, then more loudly, but inside the *Isadora* nothing stirred. He watched the curtains. He watched the oily water tossing against the rotting hull. He listened and thought he heard music like the music in Herr Kretzschmar's club, but it might have been echo from another boat. From the dinghy, Walther's brown face still watched him.

'Call again,' he growled. 'Keep calling, if you want him.'

But Smiley had an instinct against being commanded by the old man. He could feel his authority and his contempt and he resented both.

'Is he in here or not?' Smiley called. 'I said, "Is he in here?"'

The old man did not budge.

'Did you see him come aboard?' Smiley insisted.

He saw the brown head turn and knew the old man was spitting into the water.

'The wild pig comes and goes,' Smiley heard him say. 'What the hell do I care?'

'So when did he come last?'

At the sound of their voices a couple of heads had lifted out of other boats. They stared at Smiley without expression: the little fat stranger standing at the end of the broken jetty. On the shore a ragtag group had formed: a girl in shorts, an old woman; two blond teen-aged boys dressed alike. There was something that linked them in their disparity: a prison look; submission to the same bad laws.

'I'm looking for Otto Leipzig,' Smiley called to all of them. 'Can anyone tell me, please, whether he's around?' On a houseboat not too far away, a bearded man was lowering a bucket into the water. Smiley's eye selected him. 'Is there anyone aboard the *Isadora*?' he asked.

The bucket gurgled and filled. The bearded man pulled it out, but didn't speak.

'You should see his car,' a woman shouted shrilly from the shore, or perhaps it was a child. 'They took it to the wood.'

The wood lay a hundred yards back from the water, mostly saplings and birch trees.

'Who did?' Smiley asked. 'Who took it there?'

Whoever had spoken chose not to speak again. The old man was rowing himself towards the jetty. Smiley watched him approach, watched him back the stern towards the jetty steps. Without hesitating, Smiley clambered aboard. The old man pulled him the few strokes to the *Isadora's* side. A cigarette was jammed between his cracked old lips, and, like his eyes, it shone unnaturally against the evil gloom of his weathered face.

'Come far?' the old man asked.

'I'm a friend of his,' Smiley said.

There was rust and weed on the *Isadora's* ladder, and as Smiley reached the deck it was slippery with dew. He looked for signs of life and saw none. He looked for footprints in the dew, in vain. A couple of fixed fishing-lines hung into the water, made fast to the rusted balustrade, but they could have been there for weeks. He listened, and heard again, very faintly, the strains of slow band music. From the shore? Or from farther out? From neither. The sound came from under his feet, and it was as if someone were playing a seventy-eight record on thirty-three.

He looked down and saw the old man in his dinghy, leaning back, and the peak of his cap pulled over his eyes, while he slowly conducted to the beat. He tried the cabin door and it was locked, but the door did not seem strong – nothing did – so he walked around the deck till he found a rusted screwdriver to use as a jemmy. He shoved it into the gap, worked it backwards and forwards, and suddenly to his surprise the whole door went, frame, hinges, lock, and everything else, with a bang like an explosion, followed by a shower of red dust from the rotten timber. A big slow moth thudded against his cheek and left it stinging strangely for a good while afterwards, till he began to wonder whether it was a bee. Inside, the cabin was pitch dark, but the music was a little louder. He was on the top rung of the ladder and even with the daylight behind him the darkness below remained absolute. He pressed a light switch. It didn't work, so he stepped back and spoke to the old man in his dinghy: 'Matches.'

For a moment Smiley nearly lost his temper. The peaked cap didn't stir, nor did the conducting cease. He shouted, and this time a box of matches landed at his feet. He took them into the cabin and lit one, and saw the exhausted transister radio that was still putting out music with the last of its energy, and it was about the only thing intact, the only thing still functioning, in all the devastation round it.

The match had gone out. He pulled the curtains, but not on the landward side, before he lit another. He didn't want the old man looking in. In the grey sideways light, Leipzig was ridiculously like his tiny portrait in the photograph taken by Herr Kretzschmar. He was naked, he was lying where they had trussed him, even if there was no girl and no Kirov either. The hewn Toulouse-Lautrec face, blackened with bruising and gagged with several strands of rope, was as jagged and articulate in death as Smiley had remembered it in life. They must have used the music to drown the noise while they tortured him, Smiley thought. But he doubted whether the music would have been enough. He went on staring at the radio as a point of reference, a thing to go back to with his ears and eyes when the body became too much to look at before the match went out. Japanese, he noticed. Odd, he thought. Fix on the oddness of it. How odd of the technical Germans to buy Japanese radios. He wondered whether the Japanese returned the compliment. Keep wondering, he urged himself ferociously; keep your whole mind on this interesting economic phenomenon of the exchange of goods between highly industrialized nations.

Still staring at the radio, Smiley righted a folding stool and sat on it. Slowly, he returned his gaze to Leipzig's face. Some dead faces, he reflected, have the dull, even stupid look of a patient under anaesthetic. Others preserve a single mood of the once varied nature – the dead man as lover, as father, as car driver, bridge player, tyrant. And some, like Vladimir's, have ceased to preserve anything. But Leipzig's face, even with the ropes across it, had a mood, and it was anger: anger intensified by pain, turned to fury by it; anger that had increased and become the whole man as the body lost its strength.

Hate, Connie had said.

Methodically, Smiley peered about him, thinking as slowly as he could manage, trying, by his examination of the debris, to reconstruct their progress. First the fight before they overpowered him, which he deduced from the smashed table-legs and chairs and lamps and shelves, and anything else that could be ripped from its housing and either wielded or thrown. Then the search, which took place after they had trussed him and in the intervals while they questioned him. Their frustration was written every-where. They had ripped out wall-boards and floor-boards and cupboard drawers and clothes and mattresses and by the end anything that came apart, anything that was not a minimal component, as Otto Leipzig still refused to talk. He noticed also that there was blood in surprising places – in the wash-basin, over the stove. He liked to think it was not all Otto Leipzig's. And finally, in desperation, they had killed him, because those were Karla's orders, that was Karla's way. 'The killing comes first, the questioning second,' Vladimir used to say.

*I too believe in Otto*, Smiley thought stupidly, recalling Herr Kretzschmar's words. *Not in every detail but in the big things*. So do I, he thought. He believed in him, at that moment, as surely as he believed in death, and in the Sandman. As for Vladimir, so for Otto Leipzig: death had ruled that he was telling the truth.

From the direction of the shore, he heard a woman yelling: 'What's he found? Has he found something? Who is he?'

He returned aloft. The old man had shipped his oars and let the dinghy drift. He sat with his back to the ladder, head hunched into his big shoulders. He had finished his cigarette and lit a cigar as if it were Sunday. And at the same moment as Smiley saw the old man, he saw also the chalk mark. It was in the same line of vision, but very close to him, swimming in the misted lenses of his spectacles. He had to lower his head and look over the top of them to fix on it. A chalk mark, sharp and yellow. One line, carefully drawn over the rust of the balustrade, and a foot away from it the reel of fishing-line, made fast with a sailor's knot. The old man was watching him; so, for all he knew, was the growing group of watchers on the shore, but he had no option. He pulled at the line and it was heavy. He pulled steadily, hand over hand, till the line changed to gut, and he found himself pulling that instead. The gut grew suddenly tight. Cautiously he kept pulling. The people on the shore had grown expectant; he could feel their interest even across the water. The old man had put back his head and was watching through the black shadow of his cap. Suddenly, with a plop, the catch jumped clear of the water and a peal of ribald laughter rose from the spectators: one old gym-shoe, green, with the lace still in it, and the hook which held it to the line was big enough to beach a shark. The laughter slowly died. Smiley unhooked the shoe. Then, as if he had other business there, he lumbered back into the cabin till he was out of sight, leaving the door ajar for light.

But happening to take the gym-shoe with him.

An oilskin packet was hand-stitched into the toe of the shoe. He pulled it out. It was a tobacco pouch, stitched along the top and folded several times. *Moscow Rules*, he thought woodenly. *Moscow Rules all the way*. How many more dead men's legacies must I inherit? he wondered. *Though we value none but the horizontal one*. He had unpicked the stitching. Inside the pouch was another wrapping, this time a latex rubber sheath knotted at the throat. And secreted inside the sheath, one hard wad of cardboard smaller than a book of matches. Smiley spread it open. It was half a picture postcard. Black-and-white, not even coloured. Half a dull picture of Schlewig-Holstein landscape with half a herd of Friesian cattle grazing in grey sunlight. Ripped with a deliberate jaggedness. No writing on the back, no address, no stamp. Just half a boring, unposted postcard; but they had tortured him, then killed him for it, and still not found it, or any of the treasures it unlocked. Putting it, together with its wrapping, into the inside pocket of his jacket, he returned to the deck. The old man in his dinghy had drawn alongside. Without a word, Smiley climbed slowly down the ladder. The crowd of camp people on the shore had grown still larger.

'Drunk?' the old man asked. 'Sleeping it off?'

Smiley stepped into the dinghy and, as the old man pulled away, looked back at the *Isadora* once more. He saw the broken porthole, he thought of the wreckage in the cabin, the paper-thin sides that allowed him to hear the very shuffle of feet on the shore. He imagined the fight and Leipzig's screams filling the whole camp with their din. He imagined the silent group standing where they were standing now, without a voice or a helping hand between them.

'It was a party,' the old man said carelessly while he made the dinghy fast against the jetty. 'Lots of music, singing. They warned us it would be loud.' He tugged at a knot. 'Maybe they quarrelled. So what? Many people quarrel. They made some noise, played some jazz. So what? We are musical people here.'

'They were police,' a woman called from the group on the shore. 'When police go about their business it is the duty of the citizen to keep his trap shut.'

'Show me his car,' Smiley asked.

They moved in a rabble, no one leading. The old man strode at Smiley's side, half custodian, half bodyguard, making a way for him with facetious ceremony. The children ran everywhere but they kept well clear of the old man. The Volkswagen stood in a coppice and it was ripped apart like the cabin of the *Isadora*. The roof lining hung in shreds, the seats had been pulled out and split open. The wheels were missing but Smiley guessed that had happened since. The camp people stood round it reverently as if it were their show-piece. Someone had tried to burn it but the fire had not caught.

'He was scum,' the old man explained. 'They all are. Look at them. Polacks, criminals, subhumans.'

Smiley's Opel stood where he had parked it, at the edge of the track, close to the dustbins, and the two blond boys who were dressed alike were standing over the boat beating the lid with hammers. As he walked towards them he could see their forelocks bouncing with each blow. They wore jeans and black boots studded with love-daisies.

'Tell them to stop hitting my car,' Smiley said to the old man.

The camp people were following at a distance. He could hear again the furtive shuffle of their feet, like a refugee army. He reached his car and had the keys in his hand, and the two boys were still bent over the back hitting with all their might. But when he walked round to take a look, all they had done was beat the lid of the boot right off its hinges, then fold it and beat it flat again till it lay like a crude parcel on the floor. He looked at the wheels but nothing seemed amiss. He didn't know what else to look for. Then he saw that they had tied a dustbin to the rear bumper with string. Keeping clear, he tugged at the string to break it, but it refused to yield. He tried it with his teeth, without success. The old man lent him a penknife and he cut it, keeping clear of the boys with their hammers. The camp people had made a half ring and they were holding up their children for the farewell. Smiley got into the car and the old man slammed the door afer him with a tremendous heave. Smiley had the key in the ignition but by the time he turned it, one of the boys had draped himself over the bonnet as languidly as a model at a motorshow and the other was tapping politely at the window.

Smiley lowered the window.

'What do you want?' Smiley asked.

The boy held out his palm. 'Repairs,' he explained. 'Your boot didn't shut properly. Time and materials. Overheads. Parking.' He indicated his thumb-nail. 'My colleague here hurt his hand. It could have been serious.'

Smiley looked at the boy's face and saw no human instinct that he understood.

'You have repaired nothing. You have done damage. Ask your friend to get off the car.'

The boys conferred, seeming to disagree. They did this under the full gaze of the crowd, in a reasoned manner, slowly pushing each other's shoulders and making rhetorical gestures which did not coincide with their words. They talked about nature and about politics, and their Platonic dialogue might have gone on indefinitely if the boy who was on the car had not stood up in order to make the best of a debating point. As he did so, he broke off a windscreen wiper as if it were a flower and handed it to the old man. Driving away, Smiley looked in his mirror and saw a ring of faces staring after him with the old man at their centre. Nobody waved goodbye.

He drove without haste, weighing the chances, while the car clanged like an old fire-engine. He supposed they had done something else to it as well; something he had failed to notice. He had left Germany before, he had come and gone illicitly, he had hunted while on the run, and though he was old now and in a different Germany, he felt as if he had been returned to the wild. He had no way of knowing whether anybody from the water camp had tele-phoned the police, but he took it for an accomplished fact. The boat was open and its secret out. Those who had looked away would now be the first to come forward as good citizens. He had seen that before as well.

He entered a sea town, the boot – if it *was* the boot – still clanking behind him. Or perhaps it's the exhaust, he thought; the pot-hole I crashed into on the way to the camp. A hot, unseasonable sun had replaced the morning mists. There were no trees. An amazing brilliance was opening around him. It was still early, and empty horse carriages stood waiting for the first tourists. The sand was a pattern of craters dug in the summer by sun-worshippers to escape the wind. He could hear the tinny echo of his own progress bouncing between the painted shop-fronts and the sunlight seemed to make it even louder. When he passed people, he saw their heads lift to stare after him because of the row the car made.

'They'll know the car,' he thought. Even if nobody at the water camp remembered the number, the smashed boot would give him away. He turned off the main street. The sun was really very bright indeed. 'A man came, Herr Wachtmeister,' they would be saying to the police patrol. 'This morning, Herr Wachtmeister. He said he was a friend. He looked at the boat and then drove away. He asked us nothing, Captain. He was unmoved. He fished a shoe, Herr Wachtmeister. Imagine – a shoe!'

He was heading for the railway station, following the signs, looking for a place where you could park a car all day. The station was red brick and massive, he supposed from before the war. He passed it and found a big car-park to his left. A line of shedding trees ran through it, and there were leaves on some of the cars. A machine took his money and issued him with a ticket to stick on his windscreen. He backed into the middle of a line, the boot as far out of sight as possible against a mud bank. He stepped out and the extraordinary sun hit him like a slap. There was not a breath of wind. He locked the car and put the keys in the exhaust-pipe, he didn't quite know why, except that he felt apologetic towards the hire company. He kicked up the leaves and sand till the front number-plate was almost hidden. In an hour, in this St. Luke's summer, there would be a hundred and more cars in the park.

He had noticed a men's clothes shop in the main street. He bought a linen jacket there but nothing more, because people who buy whole outfits are remembered. He did not wear it, but carried it in a plastic bag. In a side-street full of boutiques he bought a gaudy straw hat and, from a stationer's, a holiday map of the area, and a railway timetable of the region Hamburg, Schleswig-Holstein and Lower Saxony. He didn't wear the hat either, but kept it in its bag like the jacket. He was sweating from the unexpected heat. The heat was upsetting him; it was as absurd as snow in summer. He went to a telephone box and again consulted local directories. Hamburg had no Claus Kretzschmar, but one of the Schleswig-Holstein directories had a Kretzschmar who lived in a place Smiley had never heard of. He studied his map and found a small town by that name on the main railway line to Hamburg. This pleased him very much.

Calmly, all other thoughts bound down with iron bands, Smiley once more did his sums. Within moments of finding the car, the police would be talking to the hire firm in Hamburg. As soon as they had spoken to the hire firm and obtained his name and description, they would put a watch on the airport and other crossing places. Kretzschmar was a night-bird and would sleep late. The town where he lived was an hour away by stopping train.

He returned to the railway station. The main concourse was a Wagnerian fantasy of a Gothic court, with an arched roof, and a huge stained-glass window that poured out coloured sunbeams onto the ceramic floor. From a telephone box, he rang Hamburg Airport, giving his name as 'Standfast, initial J,' which was the name on the passport he had collected from his London club. The first available flight to London was this evening at six but only first-class was open. He booked a first-class seat and said he would upgrade his economy ticket on arrival at the airport. The girl said, 'Then please come half an hour before check-in.' Smiley promised he would – he wanted to make an impression – but no, alas, Mr. Standfast had no phone number where he could be reached meanwhile. There was nothing in her tone to suggest she had a security officer standing behind her with a telex in his hand, whispering instructions in her ear, but he guessed that within a couple of hours Mr. Standfast's seat reservation was going to ring a lot of bells, because it was Mr. Standfast who had hired the Opel car. He stepped back into the concourse, and the shafts of coloured light. There were two ticket counters and two short queues. At the first, an intelligent girl attended him and he bought a second-class single ticket to Hamburg. But it was a deliberately laboured purchase, full of indecision and nervousness, and when he had made it he insisted on writing down times of departure and arrival: also on borrowing her ball-point and a pad of paper.

In the men's room, having first transferred the contents of his pockets, beginning with the treasured piece of postcard from Leipzig's boat, he changed into the linen jacket and straw hat, then went to the second ticket counter where, with a minimum of fuss, he bought a ticket on the stopping train to Kretzschmar's town. To do this, he avoided looking at the attendant at all, concentrating instead on the ticket and his change, from under the brim of his loud straw hat. Before leaving he took one last precaution. He made a wrong-number phone call to Herr Kretzschmar and established from an indignant wife that it was a scandal to telephone anybody so early. As a last measure, he folded the plastic carrier-bags into his pocket.

The town was leafy and secluded, the lawns large, the houses carefully zoned. Whatever there had been of country life had long fallen before the armies of suburbia, but the brilliant sunlight made everything beautiful. Number 8 was on the right-hand side, a substantial two-storey residence with steep Scandinavian roofs, a double garage and a wide selection of young trees planted much too close together. There was a swing chair in the garden with a flowered plastic seat and a new fish-pond in the romantic idiom. But the main attraction, and Herr Kretzschmar's pride, was an outdoor swimming-pool in its own patio of shrieking red tile, and it was there that Smiley found him, in the bosom of his family, on this unlikely autumn day, entertaining a few neighbours at an impromptu party. Herr Kretzschmar himself, in shorts, was preparing the barbecue and as Smiley dropped the latch on the gate he paused from his labours and looked round to see who had come. But the new straw hat and the linen jacket confused him and he called instead to his wife.

Frau Kretzschmar strode down the path bearing a champagne glass. She was clad in a pink bathing-dress and a diaphanous pink cape, which she allowed to flow behind her daringly.

'Who *is* that then? Who *is* the nice surprise?' she kept asking in a playful voice. She could have been talking to her puppy.

She stopped in front of him. She was tanned and tall and, like her husband, built to last. He could see little of her face, for she wore dark glasses with a white plastic beak to protect her nose from burning.

'Here is family Kretzschmar, going about its pleasures,' she said not very confidently, when he had still not introduced himself. 'What can we do for you, sir? In what way can we *serve*?'

'I have to speak to your husband,' Smiley said. It was the first time he had spoken since he bought his ticket, and his voice was thick and unnatural.

'But Cläuschen does no business in the daytime,' she said firmly, still smiling. 'In the daytime by family decree the profit motive has its sleep. Shall I put handcuffs on him to prove to you he is our prisoner till sunset?'

Her bathing-dress was in two parts and her smooth, full belly was oily with lotion. She wore a gold chain round her waist, presumably as a further sign of naturalness. And gold sandals with very high heels.

'Kindly tell your husband that this is not business,' Smiley said. 'This is friendship.'

Frau Kretzschmar took a sip of her champagne, then removed her dark glasses and beak, as if she were declaring herself at the *bal masqué*. She had a snub nose. Her face, though kindly, was a good deal older than her body.

'But how can it be friendship when I don't know your name?' she demanded, no longer sure whether to be winsome or discouraging.

But by then Herr Kretzschmar himself had walked down the path after her, and stopped before them, staring from his wife to Smiley, then at Smiley again. And perhaps the sight of Smiley's set face and manner, and the fixity of his gaze, warned Herr Kretzschmar of the reason for his coming.

'Go and take care of the cooking,' he said curtly.

Guiding Smiley by the arm, Herr Kretzschmar led him to a drawing-room with brass chandeliers and a picture window full of jungle cacti.

'Otto Leipzig is dead,' Smiley said without preliminary as soon as the door was closed. 'Two men killed him at the water camp.'

Herr Kretzschmar's eyes opened very wide; then unashamedly he swung his back to Smiley and covered his face with his hands.

'You made a tape-recording,' Smiley said, ignoring this display entirely. 'There was the photograph which I showed you, and somewhere there is also a tape-recording which you are keeping for him.' Herr Kretzschmar's back showed no sign that he had heard. 'You talked about it to me yourself last night,' Smiley went on, in the same sentinel tone. 'You said they discussed God and the world. You said Otto was laughing like an executioner, speaking three languages at once, singing, telling jokes. You took the photographs for Otto, but you also recorded their conversation for him. I suspect you also have the letter which you received on his behalf from London.'

Herr Kretzschmar had swung round and he was staring at Smiley in outrage.

'Who killed him?' he asked. 'Herr Max, I ask you as a soldier!'

Smiley had taken the torn piece of picture postcard from his pocket.

'Who killed him?' Herr Kretzschmar repeated. 'I insist!'

'This is what you expected me to bring last night,' said Smiley ignoring the question. 'Whoever brings it to you may have the tapes and whatever else you were keeping for him. That was the way he worked it out with you.'

Kretzschmar took the card.

'He called it his Moscow Rules,' Kretzschmar said. 'Both Otto and the General insisted on it, though it struck me personally as ridiculous.'

'You have the other half of the card?' Smiley asked.

'Yes,' said Kretzschmar.

'Then make the match and give me the material. I shall use it exactly as Otto would have wished.'

He had to say this twice in different ways before Kretzschmar answered. 'You promise this?' Kretzschmar demanded.

'Yes.'

'And the killers? What will you do with them?'

'Most likely they are already safe across the water,' Smiley said. 'They have only a few kilometres to drive.'

'Then what good is the material?'

'The material is an embarrassment to the man who sent the killers,' Smiley said, and perhaps at this moment the iron quietness of Smiley's demeanour advised Herr Kretzschmar that his visitor was as distressed as he was –

perhaps, in his own very private fashion, more so.

'Will it kill him also?' Herr Kretzschmar asked.

Smiley took quite a time to answer this question. 'It will do worse than kill him,' he said.

For a moment Herr Kretzschmar seemed disposed to ask what was worse than being killed; but he didn't. Holding the half postcard lifelessly in his hand, he left the room. Smiley waited patiently. A perpetual brass clock laboured on its captive course, red fish gazed at him from an aquarium. Kretzschmar returned. He held a white cardboard box, Inside it, padded in hygienic tissue, lay a folded wad of photocopy paper covered with a now familiar handwriting, and six miniature cassettes, blue plastic, of a type favoured by men of modern habits.

'He entrusted them to me,' Herr Kretzschmar said.

'He was wise,' said Smiley.

Herr Kretzschmar laid a hand on Smiley's shoulder. 'If you need anything let me know,' he said. 'I have my people. These are violent times.'

From a call box Smiley once more rang Hamburg Airport, this time to re-confirm Standfast's flight to London Heathrow. This done, he bought stamps and a strong envelope and wrote on it a fictional address in Adelaide, Australia. He put Mr. Standfast's passport inside it and dropped it in a letter-box. Then, travelling as plain Mr. George Smiley, profession, clerk, he returned to the railway station, passing without incident across the border into Denmark. During the journey, he took himself to the lavatory and there read Ostrakova's letter, all seven pages of it, the copy made by the General himself on Mikhel's antiquated liquid copier in the little library next door to the British Museum. What he read, added to what he had that day already seen, filled him with a growing and almost uncontainable alarm. By train, ferry and finally taxi, he hastened to Copenhagen's Castrup Airport. From Castrup he caught a mid-afternoon plane to Paris and, though the flight lasted only an hour, in Smiley's world it took a lifetime, conveying him across an entire range of his memories, emotions, and anticipation. His anger and revulsion at Leipzig's murder, till now suppressed, welled over, only to be set aside by his fears for Ostrakova: if they had done so much to Leipzig and the General, what would they not do to her? The dash through Schleswig-Holstein had given him the swiftness of revived youth, but now, in the anti-climax of escape, he was assailed by the incurable indifference of age. With death so close, he thought, so ever-present, what is the point of struggling any longer? He thought of Karla again, and of his absolutism, which at least gave point to the perpetual chaos that was life's condition; point to voilence, and to death; of Karla for whom killing had never been more than the necessary adjunct of a grand design.

How can I win? he asked himself; alone, restrained by doubt and a sense of decency – how can any of us – against this remorseless fusilade?

The plane's descent – and the promise of the renewed chase – restored him. There are two Karlas, he reasoned, remembering again the stoic face, the patient eyes, the wiry body waiting philosophically upon its own destruc-tion. There is Karla the professional, so self-possessed that he could allow, if need be, ten years for an operation to bear fruit: in Bill Haydon's case, twenty; Karla the old spy, the pragmatist, ready to trade a dozen losses for one great win.

And there is this other Karla, Karla of the human heart after all, of the one great love, the Karla flawed by humanity. I should not be deterred if, in order to defend his weakness, he resorts to the methods of his trade.

Reaching in the compartment above him for his straw hat, Smiley happened to remember a cavalier promise he had once made concerning Karla's eventual downfall. 'No,' he had replied, in answer to a question much like the one he had just put to himself. 'No, Karla is not fireproof. Because he's a fanatic. And one day, if I have anything to do with it, that lack of moderation will be his downfall.'

Hastening to the cab rank, he recalled that his remark had been made to one Peter Guillam, who at this present moment happened to be much upon his mind.

# EIGHTEEN

Lying on the divan, Ostrakova glanced at the twilight and seriously wondered whether it signalled the world's end.

All day long the same grey gloom had hung over the courtyard, consigning her tiny universe to a perpetual evening. At dawn a sepia glow had thickened it; at midday, soon after the men came, it was a celestial power-cut, deepening to a cavernous black in anticipation of her own end. And now, at evening, fog had further strengthened the grip of darkness upon the retreating forces of light. And so it goes with Ostrakova also, she decided without bitterness: with my bruised, black-and-blue body, and my siege, and my hopes for the second coming of the redeemer; so it goes exactly, an ebbing of my own day.

She had woken this morning to find herself seemingly bound hand and foot. She had tried to move one leg and, immediately, burning cords had tightened round her thighs and chest and stomach. She had raised an arm, but only against the tugging of iron ligatures. She had taken a lifetime to crawl to the bathroom and another to get herself undressed and into the warm water. And when she entered it, she was frightened that she had fainted from the pain, her flailed flesh hurt so terribly where the road had grazed it. She heard a hammering and had thought it was inside her head, till she realised it was the work of a furious neighbour. When she counted the church clock's chimes, they stopped at four, so no wonder the neighbour was protesting at the thunder of running water in the old pipes. The labour of making coffee had exhausted her but sitting down was suddenly unbearable, lying down just as bad. The only way to rest was to lean herself forward, elbows on the draining-board. From there she could watch the courtyard, as a pastime and as a precaution, and from there she had seen the men, the two creatures of darkness, as she now thought of them, mouthing to the concierge, and the old goat of a concierge, Madame la Pierre, mouthing back, shaking her fool head – 'No, Ostrakova is not here, not here' – not here in ten different ways, that echoed like an aria round the courtyard – *is not here* – drowning the clipping of carpet-beaters and the clatter of children and the gossip of the two turbaned old wives on the third floor, leaning out of their windows two metres apart – *is not here!* Till a child would not have believed her.

If she wanted to read, she had to put the book on the draining-board, which after the men came, was where she kept the gun as well, till she noticed the swivel on the butt-end, and with a woman's practicality improvised a lanyard out of kitchen string. In that way, with the pistol round her neck, she had both her arms free when she needed to hand herself across the room. But when it prodded her breasts she thought she would retch from the agony. After the men left again, she had started reciting aloud while she went about the chores she had promised herself she would observe during her imprisonment. 'One *tall* man, one leather *coat*, one Homburg *hat*,' she had murmured, helping herself to a generous ration of vodka to restore her. 'One *broad* man, one balding *pate*, grey *shoes* with perforations!' Make songs of my memory, she had thought; sing them to the magician, to the General – oh, why don't they answer my second letter?

She was a child again, falling off her pony, and the pony came back and trampled her. She was a woman again, trying to be a mother. She remembered the three days of impossible pain in which Alexandra fiercely resisted being born into the grey and dangerous light of an unwashed Moscow nursing home – the same light that was outside her window now, and lay like unnatural dust over the polished floors of her apartment. She heard herself calling for Glikman – 'Bring him to me, bring him to me.' She remembered how it had seemed to her that sometimes it was he, Glikman her lover, whom she was bearing, and not their child at all – as if his whole sturdy, hairy body were trying to fight its way out of her – or was it into her? – as if to give birth at all would be to deliver Glikman into the very captivity she dreaded for him.

Why was he not there, why would he not come? she wondered, confusing Glikman with the General and the magician equally. Why don't they answer my letter?

She knew very well why Glikman had not come to her as she wrestled with Alexandra. She had begged him to keep away. 'You have the courage to suffer, and that is enough,' she had told him. 'But you have not the courage to witness the suffering of others, and for that I love you also. Christ had it too easy,' she told him. 'Christ could cure the lepers, Christ could make the blind see and the dead come alive. He could even die in a sensible cause. But you are not Christ, you are Glikman, and there's nothing you can do about my pain except watch and suffer too, which does nobody any good whatever.'

But the General and his magician were different, she argued, with some resentment; they have set themselves up as the physicians of my disease, and I have a right to them!

At her appointed time, the cretinous, braying concierge had come up, complete with her troglodyte husband with his screwdriver. They were full of excitement for Ostrakova, and joy at being able to bring such heartening news. Ostrakova had composed herself carefully for the visit, putting on music, making up her face, and heaping books beside the divan, all to create an atmosphere of leisured introspection.

'Visitors, madame, *men* . . . No, they would not leave their names . . . here for a short visit from abroad . . . knew your *husband*, madame. Emigrés, they were, like yourself . . . No, they wished to keep it a *surprise*, madame . . . They said they had *gifts* for you from relations, madame . . . a secret, madame, and one of them so big and strong and good-looking . . . No, they will come back another time, they are here on business, many appointments, they said . . . No, by taxi, and they kept it waiting – the expense, imagine!'

Ostrakova had laughed, and put her hand on the concierge's arm, physically drawing her into a great secret, while the troglodyte stood and puffed cigarette and garlic over both of them.

'Listen,' she said. 'Both of you. Attend to me, Monsieur and Madame la Pierre. I know very well who they are, these rich and handsome visitors. They are my husband's no-good nephews from Marseilles, lazy devils and great vagabonds. If they are bringing a present for me, you may be sure they will also want beds and most likely dinner too. Be so kind and tell them I am away in the country for a few more days. I love them dearly, but I must have my peace.'

Whatever doubts or disappointments remained in their goatish heads, Ostrakova bought them away with money, and now she was alone again – the lanyard round her neck. She was stretched out on the divan, her hips hoisted into a position that was half-way tolerable. The gun was in her hand and pointed at the door, and she could hear the footsteps coming up the stairs, two pairs, the one heavy, the other light.

She rehearsed: 'One *tall* man, one leather *coat* . . . One *broad* man, grey *shoes* with perforations . . .'

Then the knocking, timid as a childhood proposition of love. And the unfamiliar voice, speaking French with an unfamiliar accent, slow and classical like her husband Ostrakov's and with the same alluring tenderness.

'Madame Ostrakova. Please admit me. I am here to help you.'

With a sense of everything ending, Ostrakova deliberately cocked her dead husband's pistol, and advanced with firm if painful steps, upon the door. She advanced crabwise and she wore no shoes and she mistrusted the fish-eye peep-hole. Nothing would convince her it couldn't peep in both directions. Therefore she made this detour round the room in the hope of escaping its eyeline, and on the way she passed Ostrakov's blurry portrait and resented very much that he had had the selfishness to die so early instead of staying alive so that he could protect her. Then she thought: No. I have turned the corner. I possess my own courage.

And she did possess it. She was going to war, every minute could be her last, but the pains had vanished, her body felt as ready as it had been for Glikman, always, any time; she could feel his energy running into her limbs like reinforcements. She had Glikman beside her and she remembered his strength without wishing for it. She had a Biblical notion that all his tireless love-making had invigorated her for this moment. She had the calm of Ostrakov and the honour of Ostrakov; she had his gun. But her desperate, solitary courage was finally her own, and it was the courage of a mother roused, and deprived, and furious: Alexandra! The men who had come to kill her were the same men who had taunted her with her secret motherhood, who had killed Ostrakov and Glikman, and would kill the whole poor world if she did not stop them.

She wanted only to aim before she fired, and she had realised that as long as the door was closed and chained and the peep-hole was in place, she could aim from very close – and the closer she aimed, the better, for she was sensibly modest about her marksmanship. She put her finger over the peep-hole to stop them looking in, then she put her eye to it to see who they were, and the first thing she saw was her own foolish concierge, very close, round as an onion in the distorted lens, with green hair from the glow of the ceramic tiles in the landing, and a huge rubber smile and a nose that came out like a duck's bill. And it occurred to Ostrakova that the light foot-steps had been hers – lightness, like pain and happiness, being always relative to whatever has come before, or after. And the second thing she saw was a small gentleman in spectacles, who in the fish-eye was as fat as the Michelin tyre man. And while she watched him, he earnestly removed a straw hat that came straight out of a novel by Turgenev, and held it at his side as if he had just heard his national anthem being played. And she inferred from this gesture that the small gentleman was telling her that he knew she was afraid, and knew that a shadowed face was what she was afraid of most, and that by baring his head he was in some way revealing his goodwill to her.

His stillness and gravity had a sense of dutiful submission about them, which, like his voice, again reminded her of Ostrakov; the lens might make him into a frog, but it could not take away his bearing. His spectacles also reminded her of Ostrakov, being as necessary to vision as a walking-stick to a cripple. All this, with a thumping heart but a very steady eye, Ostrakova took in at her first long inspection, while she kept the gun barrel clamped to the door and her finger on the trigger, and considered whether or not to shoot him then and there, straight through the door – 'Take *that* for Glikman, *that* for Ostrakov, *that* for Alexandra!'

For, in her state of suspicion, she was ready to believe that they had selected the man for his very air of humanity; because they knew that Ostrakov himself had had this same capacity to be at once fat and dignified.

'I do not need help,' Ostrakova called back at last, and watched in terror to see what effect her words would have on him. But while she watched, the fool concierge decided to start yelling on her own account.

'Madame, he is a gentleman! He is English! He is concerned for you! You are ill, madame, the whole street is frightened for you! Madame, you cannot lock yourself away like this any more.' And pause. 'He is a doctor, madame – aren't you, monsieur? A distinguished doctor for maladies of the spirit!' Then Ostrakova heard the idiot whisper to him: 'Tell her, monsieur. Tell her you're a doctor.'

But the stranger shook his head in disapproval, and replied: 'No. It is not true.'

'Madame, open up or I shall fetch the police!' the concierge cried. 'A Russian, making such a scandal!'

'*I do not need help*,' Ostrakova repeated, much louder.

But she knew already that help, more than anything else, was what she did need; that without it she would never kill, any more than Glikman would have killed. Not even if she had the Devil himself in her sights could she kill another woman's child.

As she continued her vigil, the little man took a slow step forward till his face, distorted like a face under water, was all she could see in the lens; and she saw for the first time the fatigue in it, the redness of the eyes behind the spectacles, the heavy shadows under them; and she sensed in him a passionate caring for herself that had nothing to do with death, but with survival; she sensed that she was looking at a face that was concerned, rather than one that had banished sympathy for ever. The face came closer still and the snap of the letter-box alone almost made her pull the trigger by mistake and this appalled her. She felt the convulsion in her hand and stayed it only at the very instant of completion; then stooped to pick the envelope from the mat. It was her own letter, addressed to the General – her second, saying 'Someone is trying to kill me,' written in French. As a last-ditch gesture of resistance, she pretended to wonder whether the letter was a trick, and they had intercepted it, or bought it, or stolen it, or done whatever deceivers do. But seeing the letter, recognising its opening words and its despairing tone, she became utterly weary of deceit, and weary of mistrust, and weary of trying to read evil where she wished more than anything to read good. She heard the fat man's voice again, and a French well-taught but a little rusty, and it reminded her of rhymes from school she half remembered. And if it was a lie he was telling, then it was the most cunning lie she had ever heard in her life.

'The magician is dead, madame,' he said, fogging the fist-eye with his breath. 'I have come from London to help you in his place.'

For years afterwards, and probably for all his life, Peter Guillam would relate, with varying degrees of frankness, the story of his home-coming that same evening. He would emphasize that the circumstances were particular. He was in a bad temper – one – he had been so all day. Two – his Ambassador had publicly rebuked him at the weekly meeting for a remark of unseemly levity about the British balance of payments. He was newly married – three – and his very young wife was pregnant. Her phone call – four – came moments after he had decoded a long and extremely boring signal from the Circus reminding him for the fifteenth time that no, repeat *no* operations could be undertaken on French soil without advance permission in writing from Head Office. And – five – *le tout Paris* was having one of its periodical scares about kidnapping. Last, the post of Circus head resident in Paris was widely known to be a laying-out place for officers shortly to be buried, offering little more than the opportunity to lunch interminably with a variety of very corrupt, very boring chiefs of rival French Intelligence services who spent more time spying on each other than on their supposed enemies. All of these factors, Guillam would afterwards insist, should be taken into account before anyone accused him of impetuosity. Guillam, it may be added, was an athlete, half French, but more English on account of it: he was slender, and near enough handsome – but though he fought it every inch of the way, he was also close on fifty, which is the watershed that few careers of ageing fieldmen survive. He also owned a brand-new German Porsche car, which he had acquired, somewhat shamefacedly, at diplomatic rates, and parked, to the Ambassador's strident disapproval, in the Embassy car-park.

Marie-Claire Guillam, then, rang her husband at six exactly, just as Guillam was locking away his code-books. Guillam had two telephone lines to his desk, one of them in theory operational and direct. The second went through the Embassy switchboard. Marie-Claire rang on the direct line, a thing they had always agreed she would only ever do in emergency. She spoke French, which, true, was her native language, but they had recently been communi-

He heard at once the tension in her voice.

'Marie-Claire? What is it?'

'Peter, there's someone here. He wants you to come at once.'

'Who?'

'I can't say. It's important. Please come home at once,' she repeated and rang off.

Guillam's chief clerk, a Mr. Anstruther, had been standing at the strong-room door when the call came, waiting for him to spin the combination lock before they each put in their keys. Through the open doorway to Guillam's office he saw him slam down the phone, and the next thing he knew, Guillam had tossed to Anstruther – a long, throw, probably fifteen feet – the Head Resident's sacred *personal key*, near enough the symbol of his office, and Anstruther by a miracle had caught it: put up his left hand and caught it in his palm, like an American baseball player; he couldn't have done it again if he'd tried it a hundred times, he told Guillam later.

'Don't budge from here till I ring you!' Guillam shouted. 'You sit at my desk and you man those phones. Hear me?'

Anstruther did, but by then Guillam was half-way down the absurdly elegant spiral staircase of the Embassy, barging between typists and Chancery guards and bright young men setting out on the evening cocktail round. Seconds later, he was at the wheel of his Porsche, revving the engine like a racing driver, which in another life he might well have been. Guillam's house was in Neuilly, and in the ordinary way these sporting dashes through the rush hour rather amused him, reminding him twice a day – as he put it – that however mind-bendingly boring the Embassy routine, life around him was hairy, quarrelsome, and fun. He was even given to timing himself over the distance. If he took the Avenue Charles de Gaulle and got a fair wind at the traffic-lights, twenty-five minutes through the evening traffic was not unreasonable. Late at night or early in the morning, with empty roads and CD plates, he could cut it to fifteen, but in the rush hour thirty-five minutes was fast going and forty the norm. That evening, hounded by visions of Marie-Claire held at pistol point by a bunch of crazed nihilists, he made the distance in eighteen minutes cold. Police reports later submitted to the Ambassador had him jumping three sets of lights and touching around a hundred and forty kilometres as he entered the home stretch; but these were of necessity something of a reconstruction, since no one felt inclined to try to keep up with him. Guillam himself remembers little of the drive, beyond a near squeak with a furniture van, and a lunatic cyclist who took it into his head to turn left when Guillam was a mere hundred and fifty metres behind him.

His apartment was in a villa, on the third floor. Braking hard before he reached the entrance, he cut the engine and coasted to a halt in the street outside, then pelted to the front door as quietly as haste allowed. He had expected a car parked somewhere close, probably with a get-away driver waiting at the wheel, but to his momentary relief there was none in sight. A light was burning in their bedroom, however, so that he now imagined Marie-Claire gagged and tied to the bed, and her captors sitting over her, waiting for Guillam to arrive. If it was Guillam they wanted, he did not propose to disappoint them. He had come unarmed; he had no choice. The Circus

Housekeepers had a holy terror of weapons, and his illicit revolver was in the bedside locker, where no doubt they had by now found it. He climbed the three flights silently and at the front door threw off his jacket and dropped it on the floor beside him. He had his door-key in his hand, and now, as softly as he knew how, he fed it into the lock, then pressed the bell and called '*Facteur*' – postman – through the letter-box and then '*Exprès.*' His hand on the key, he waited till he heard approaching footsteps, which he knew at once were not those of Marie-Claire. They were slow, even ponderous, and, to Guillam's ear, too self-assured by half. And they came from the direction of the bedroom. What he did next, he did all at once. To open the door from inside, he knew, required two distinct movements: first the chain must be shot, then the spring catch must be freed. In a half-crouch, Guillam waited till he heard the chain slip, then used his own weapon of surprise: he turned his own key and threw all his weight against the door and, as he did so, had the intense satisfaction of seeing a plump male figure spin wildly back against the hall mirror, knocking it clean off its moorings, while Guillam seized his arm and swung it into a vicious breaking lock – only to see the startled face of his lifelong friend and mentor, George Smiley, staring helplessly at him.

The aftermath of that encounter is described by Guillam somewhat hazily; he had, of course, no forewarning of Smiley's coming, and Smiley – perhaps out of fear of microphones – said little inside the flat to enlighten him. Marie-Claire was in the bedroom, but neither bound nor gagged; it was Ostrakova who, at Marie-Claire's insistence, was lying on the bed, still in her old black dress, and Marie-Claire was ministering to her in any way she could think of – jellied breast of chicken, mint tea, all the invalid foods she had diligently laid in for the wonderful day, alas not yet at hand, when Guillam would fall ill on her. Ostrakova, Guillam noticed (though he had yet to learn her name) seemed to have been beaten up. She had broad grey bruises round the eyes and lips, and her fingers were cut to bits where she had apparently tried to defend herself. Having briefly admitted Guillam to this scene – the battered lady tended by the anxious child bride – Smiley conducted Guillam to his own drawing-room and, with all the authority of Guillam's old chief, which he indeed had been, rapidly set out his requirements. Only now, it developed, was Guillam's earlier haste warranted. Ostrakova – Smiley referred to her only as 'our guest' – should leave Paris tonight, he said. The station's safe house outside Orléans – he called it 'our country mansion' – was not safe enough; she needed somewhere that provided care and protection. Guillam remembered a French couple in Arras, a retired agent and his wife, who in the past provided shelter for the Circus's occasional birds of passage. It was agreed he would telephone them, but not from the apartment: Smiley sent him off to find a public call box. By the time Guillam had made the necessary arrangements and returned, Smiley had written out a brief signal on a sheet of Marie-Claire's awful notepaper with its grazing bunnies, which he wished Guillam to have transmitted immediately to the Circus, 'Personal for Saul Enderby, decipher yourself.' The text, which Smiley insisted that Guillam should read (but not aloud), politely asked Enderby – 'in view of a second death no doubt by now reported to you' – for a meeting at Ben's Place forty-eight hours hence. Guillam had no idea where Ben's Place was.

'And, Peter.'

'Yes, George,' said Guillam, still dazed.

'I imagine there exists an official directory of locally accredited diplomats. Do you happen to have such a thing in the house by any chance?'

Guillam did. Indeed, Marie-Claire lived by it. She had no memory for names at all, so it lay beside the bedroom telephone for every time a member of a foreign embassy telephoned her with yet another invitation to drinks, to dinner, or, most ghastly of all, to a National Day festivity. Guillam fetched it, and a moment later was peering over Smiley's shoulder. 'Kirov,' he read – but not, once more, aloud – as he followed the line of Smiley's thumb-nail – 'Kirov, Oleg, Second Secretary (Commercial), Unmarried.' Followed by an address in the Soviet Embassy ghetto in the 7th district.

'Ever bumped into him?' Smiley asked.

Guillam shook his head. 'We took a look at him a few years back. He's marked "hands off,"' he replied.

'When was this list compiled?' Smiley asked. The answer was printed on the cover: December of the previous year.

Smiley said, 'Well, when you get to the office –'

'I'll take a look at the file,' Guillam promised.

'There is also *this*,' said Smiley sharply, and handed Guillam a plain carrier-bag containing, when he looked later, several micro-cassettes and a fat brown envelope.

'By first bag tomorrow, please,' Smiley said. 'The same grading and the same addressee as the telegram.'

Leaving Smiley still poring over the list, and the two women cloistered in the bedroom, Guillam hastened back to the Embassy and, having released the bemused Anstruther from his vigil at the telephones, consigned the carrier-bag to him, together with Smiley's instructions. The tension in Smiley had affected Guillam considerably, and he was sweating. In all the years he had known George, he said later, he had never known him so inward, so intent, so elliptical, so desperate. Re-opening the strong-room, he personally encoded and despatched the telegram, waiting only as long as it took him to receive the Head Office acknowledgment before drawing the file on Soviet Embassy movements and browsing through back numbers of old watch lists. He had not far to look. The third serial, copied to London, told him all that he needed to know. Kirov, Oleg, Second Secretary (Commercial), described this time as 'married but wife not en poste,' had returned to Moscow two weeks ago. In the panel reserved for miscellaneous comments, the French liaison service had added that, according to informed Soviet sources, Kirov had been 'recalled to the Soviet Ministry of Foreign Affairs at short notice in order to take up a senior appointment which had become vacant unexpectedly.' The customary farewell parties had therefore not been feasible.

Back in Neuilly, Smiley received Guillam's intelligence in utter silence. He did not seem surprised, but he seemed in some way appalled, and when he finally spoke – which did not occur until they were all three in the car and speeding towards Arras – his voice had an almost hopeless ring. 'Yes,' he said – as if Guillam knew the whole history inside out. 'Yes, that is of course exactly what he *would* do, isn't it? He would call Kirov back under the pretext of a promotion, in order to make sure he really came.'

George had not sounded that way, said Guillam – no doubt with the wisdom of hindsight – since the night he unmasked Bill Haydon as Karla's mole as well as Ann's lover.

Ostrakova also, in retrospect, had little coherent recollection of that night, neither of the car journey, on which she contrived to sleep, nor of the patient but persistent questioning to which the little plump man subjected her when she woke late the next morning. Perhaps she had temporarily lost her capacity to be impressed – and, accordingly, to remember. She answered his questions, she was grateful to him, she gave him – without the zest or 'decoration' – the same information that she had given to the magician, though he seemed to possess most of it already.

'The magician,' she said once. 'Dead. My God.'

She asked after the General, but scarcely heeded Smiley's non-committal reply. She was thinking of Ostrakov, then Glikman, now the magician – and she never knew his name. Her host and hostess were kind to her also, but as yet made no impression on her. It was raining and she could not see the distant fields.

Little by little, all the same, as the weeks passed, Ostrakova permitted herself an idyllic hibernation. The deep winter came early and she let its snow embrace her; she walked a little, and then a great deal, retired early, spoke seldom, and as her body repaired itself so did her spirit. At first a pardonable confusion reigned in her mind, and she found herself thinking of her daughter in the terms of which the gingery stranger had described her: as the tearaway dissenter and untameable rebel. Then slowly the logic of the matter presented itself to her. Somewhere, she argued, there was the real Alexandra who lived and had her being, as before. Or who, as before, did not. In either case, the gingery man's lies concerned a different creature altogether, one whom they had invented for their own needs. She even managed to find consolation in the likelihood that her daughter, if she lived at all, lived in complete ignorance of their machinations. Perhaps the hurts which had been visited on her – of the mind as well as of the body – did what years of prayer and anxiety had failed to do, and purged her of her self-recriminations regarding Alexandra. She mourned Glikman at her leisure, she was conscious of being quite alone in the world, but in the winter landscape her solitude was not disagreeable to her. A retired brigadier proposed marriage to her but she declined. It turned out later that he proposed to everybody. Peter Guillam visited her at least every week and sometimes they walked together for an hour or two. In faultless French he talked to her mainly of landscape gardening, a subject on which he possessed an inexhaustible knowledge. That was Ostrakova's life, where it touched upon this story. And it was lived out in total ignorance of the events that her own first letter to the General had set in train.

'Do you know his name really *is* Ferguson?' Saul Enderby drawled in that lounging Belgravia cockney which is the final vulgarity of the English upper class.

'I never doubted it,' Smiley said.

'He's about all we've got left of that whole lamplighter stable. Wise Men don't hold with domestic surveillance these days. Anti-Party or some damn thing.' Enderby continued his study of the bulky document in his hand. 'So what's *your* name, George? Sherlock Holmes dogging his poor old Moriarty? Captain Ahab chasing his big white whale? Who are you?'

Smiley did not reply.

'Wish I had an enemy, I must say,' Enderby remarked, turning a few pages. 'Been looking for one for donkey's years. Haven't I, Sam?'

'Night and day, Chief,' Sam Collins agreed heartily, and sent his master a confiding grin.

Ben's Place was the back room of a dark hotel in Knightsbridge and the three men had met there an hour ago. A notice on the door said 'MANAGE-MENT STRICTLY PRIVATE' and inside was an ante-room for coats and hats and privacy, and beyond it lay this oak-panelled sanctum full of books and musk, which in turn gave on to its own rectangle of walled garden stolen from the park, with a fish-pond and a marble angel and a path for contemplative walks. Ben's identity, if he ever had one, was lost in the unwritten archives of Circus mythology. But this place of his remained, as an unrecorded perquisite of Enderby's appointment, and of George Smiley's before him – and as a trysting ground for meetings that afterwards have not occurred.

'I'll read it again, if you don't mind,' Enderby said. 'I'm a bit slow on the uptake this time of day.'

'I think that would be jolly helpful, actually, Chief,' said Collins.

Enderby shifted his half-lens spectacles, but only by way of peering over the top of them, and it was Smiley's secret theory that they were plain glass anyway.

'Kirov is doing the talking. This is after Leipzig has put the bite on him, right, George?' Smiley gave a distant nod. 'They're still sitting in the cat house with their pants down, but it's five in the morning and the girls have been sent home. First we get Kirov's tearful how-could-you-do-this-to-me? "I thought you were my friend, Otto!" he says. Christ, he picked a wrong 'un there! Then comes his statement, put into bad English by the translators. They've made a concordance – that the word, George? Um's and ah's omitted.'

Whether it was the word or not, Smiley offered no answer. Perhaps he was not expected to. He sat very still in a leather armchair leaning forward over his clasped hands, and he had not taken off his brown tweed overcoat. A set of the Kirov typescripts lay at his elbow. He looked drawn, and Enderby remarked later that he seemed to have been on a diet. Sam Collins, Head of Operations, sat literally in Enderby's shadow, a dapper man with a dark moustache and a flashy, ever-ready smile. There had been a time when Collins was the Circus hard-man, whose years in the field had taught him to despise the cant of the fifth floor. Now he was the poacher turned game-keeper, nurturing his own pension and security in the way he had once nurtured his networks. A wilful blankness had overcome him; he was smoking brown cigarettes down to the half-way mark, then stubbing them into a cracked sea shell, while his doglike gaze rested faithfully on Enderby, his master. Enderby himself stood propped against the pillar of French windows, silhouetted by the light outside, and he was using a bit of matchstick to pick his teeth. A silk handkerchief peeked from his left sleeve and he stood with one knee forward and slightly bent as if he were in the members' enclosure at Ascot. In the garden, shreds of mist lay stretched like fine gauze across the lawn. Enderby put back his head and held the document away from him like a menu.

'Here we go. I'm Kirov. "As a finance officer working in Moscow Centre from 1970 to 1974 it was my duty to unearth irregularities in the accounts of overseas residencies and bring the culprits to book."' He broke off and peered over his glasses again. 'This is all before Kirov was posted to Paris, right?'

'Dead right,' said Collins keenly and glanced at Smiley for support, but got none.

'Just working it out, you see, George,' Enderby explained. 'Just getting my ducks in a row. Haven't got your little grey cells.'

Sam Collins smiled brightly at his chief's show of modesty.

Enderby continued: '"As a result of conducting these extremely delicate and confidential enquiries, which in some cases led to the punishment of senior officers of Moscow Centre, I made the acquaintance of the head of the independent Thirteenth Intelligence Directorate, subordinated to the Party's Central Committee, who is known throughout Centre only by his workname Karla. This is a woman's name and is said to belong to the first network he controlled." That right, George?'

'It was during the Spanish Civil War,' said Smiley.

'The great playground. Well, well. To continue. "The Thirteenth Directorate is a separate service within Moscow Centre, since its principal duty is the recruitment, training and placing of illegal agents under deep cover in Fascist countries, known also as moles . . . blah . . . blah . . . blah. Often a mole will take many years to find his place inside the target country before he becomes active in secret work." Shades of Bloody Bill Haydon. "The task of servicing such moles is not entrusted to normal overseas residencies but to a Karla representative, as he is known, usually a military officer, whose daywork is to be an attaché of an Embassy. Such representatives are hand-picked by Karla personally and constitute an élite . . . blah . . . blah . . . enjoying privileges of trust and freedom not given to other Centre officers, also travel and money. They are accordingly objects of jealousy to the rest of the service."'

Enderby affected to draw breath: '*Christ*, these translators!' he exclaimed. 'Or maybe it's just Kirov being a perishing little bore. You'd think a man making his deathbed confession would have the grace to keep it brief, wouldn't you? But not our Kirov, oh no. How you doing, Sam?'

'Fine, Chief, fine.'

'Here we go again,' said Enderby, and resumed his ritual tone: '"In the course of my general investigations into financial irregularities, the integrity of a Karla resident came into question, the resident in Lisbon, Colonel Orlov. Karla convened a secret tribunal of his own people to hear the case, and as a result of my evidence Colonel Orlov was liquidated in Moscow on June 10, 1973." That checks, you say, Sam?'

'We have an unconfirmed defector report that he was shot by firing-squad,' said Collins breezily.

'Congratulations, Comrade Kirov, the embezzler's friend. Jesus. What a snake pit. Worse than us.' Enderby continued: '"For my part in bringing the criminal Orlov to justice I was personally congratulated by Karla, and also sworn to secrecy, since he considered the irregularity of Colonel Orlov a shame on his Directorate, and damaging to his standing with Moscow Centre. Karla is known as a comrade of high standards of integrity, and for this reason has many enemies among the ranks of the self-indulgent."'

Enderby deliberately paused, and yet again glanced at Smiley over the top of his half-lenses.

'We all spin the ropes that hang us, right, George?'

'We're a bunch of suicidal spiders, Chief,' said Collins heartily, and flashed an even broader smile at a place somewhere between the two of them.

But Smiley was lost in his reading of Kirov's statement and not accessible to pleasantries.

'Skip the next year of Brother Kirov's life and loves, and let's come to his next meeting with Karla,' Enderby proposed, undeterred by Smiley's taciturnity. 'The nocturnal summons . . . that's standard, I gather.' He turned a couple of pages. Smiley, following Enderby, did the same. 'Car pulls up outside Kirov's Moscow apartment – why can't they say *flat* for God's sake, like anyone else? – he's hauled out of bed and driven to an unknown destination. They lead a rum life, don't they, those gorillas in Moscow Centre, never knowing whether they're getting a medal or a bullet?' He referred to the report again. 'All that tallies, does it. George? The journey and stuff? Half an hour by car, small plane, and so forth?'

'The Thirteenth Directorate has three or four establishments, including a large training camp near Minsk,' Smiley said.

Enderby turned some more pages.

'So here's Kirov back in Karla's presence again: middle of nowhere, the same night. Karla and Kirov totally alone. Small wooden hut, monastic atmosphere, no trimmings, no witnesses – or none visible. Karla goes straight to the nub. How would Kirov like a posting to Paris? Kirov would like one very much, sir –' He turned another page. 'Kirov always admired the Thirteenth Directorate, sir, blah, blah – always been a great fan of Karla's – creep, crawl, creep. Sounds like you, Sam. Interesting that Kirov thought Karla looked tired – notice that point? – twitchy. Karla under stress, smoking like a chimney.'

'He always did that,' said Smiley.

'Did what?'

'He was always an excessive smoker,' Smiley said.

'Was he, by God? Was he?'

Enderby turned another page. 'Now Kirov's brief,' he said, 'Karla spells it out for him. "For my daywork I should have the post of a Commercial officer for the Embassy, and for my special work I would be responsible for the control and conduct of financial accounts in all outstations of the Thirteenth Directorate in the following countries . . ." Kirov goes on to list them. They include Bonn, but not Hamburg. With me, Sam?'

'All the way, Chief.'

'Not losing you in the labyrinth?'

'Not a bit, Chief.'

'Clever blokes, these Russkies.'

'Devilish.'

'Kirov again: "He impressed upon me the extreme importance of my task –

blah, blah – reminded me of my excellent performance in the Orlov case, and advised me that in view of the great delicacy of the matters I was handling, I would be reporting directly to Karla's private office and would have a separate set of ciphers . . ." Turn to page fifteen.'

'Page fifteen it is, Chief,' Collins said.

Smiley had already found it.

'"In addition to my work as West European auditor to the Thirteenth Directorate outstations, however, Karla also warned me that I would be required to perform certain clandestine activities with a view to finding cover backgrounds, or legends for future agents. All members of his Directorate took a hand in this, he said, but legend work was extremely secret nevertheless, and I should not under any circumstances discuss it with anybody at all. Not my Ambassador, nor with Major Pudin who was Karla's permanent operational representative inside our Embassy in Paris. I naturally accepted the appointment and, having attended a special course in security and communications, took up my post. I had not been in Paris long when a personal signal from Karla advised me that a legend was required urgently for a female agent, age about twenty-one years." Now we're at the bone,' Enderby commented with satisfaction. '"Karla's signal referred me to several émigré families who might be persuaded by pressure to adopt such an agent as their own child, since blackmail is considered by Karla a preferable technique to bribery." Damn right it is,' Enderby assented heartily. 'At the present rate of inflation, blackmail's about the only bloody thing that keeps its value.'

Sam Collins obliged with a rich laugh of appreciation.

'Thank you, Sam,' said Enderby pleasantly. 'Thanks very much.'

A lesser man than Enderby – or a less thick-skinned one – might have skated over the next two pages, for they consisted mainly of a vindication of Connie Sachs's and Smiley's pleas of three years ago that the Leipzig–Kirov relationship should be exploited.

'Kirov dutifully trawls the émigrés, but without result,' Enderby announced, as if he were reading out subtitles at the cinema. 'Karla exhorts Kirov to greater efforts, Kirov strives still harder, and goofs again.'

Enderby broke off, and looked at Smiley, this time very straight. 'Kirov was no bloody good, was he, George?' he said.

'No,' said Smiley.

'Karla couldn't trust his own chaps, that's your point. He had to go out into the sticks and recruit an irregular like Kirov.'

'Yes.'

'A clod. Sort of bloke who'd never make Sarratt.'

'That's right.'

'Having set up his apparatus, in other words, trained it to accept his iron rules, you might say, he didn't dare use it for this particular deal. That your point?'

'Yes,' said Smiley. 'That is my point.'

Thus, when Kirov bumped into Leipzig on the plane to Vienna – Enderby resumed, paraphrasing Kirov's own account now – Leipzig appeared to him as the answer to all his prayers. Never mind that he was based in Hamburg, never mind that there's been a bit of nastiness back in Tallinn: Otto was an émigré, in with the groups. Otto the Golden Boy. Kirov signalled urgently to Karla proposing that Leipzig be recruited as an émigré source and talent-spotter. Karla agreed.

'Which is another rum thing, when you work it out,' Enderby remarked. 'Jesus, I mean who'd back a horse with Leipzig's record when he was sober and of sound mind? Specially for a job like that?'

'Karla was under stress,' Smiley said, in a tone of such casual exoneration that Enderby glanced at him quite sharply.

'You're bloody forgiving these days, aren't you, George?' said Enderby suspiciously.

'Am I?' Smiley sounded puzzled by the question. 'If you say so, Saul.'

'And bloody meek, too.' He returned to the transcript. 'Page twenty-one and we're home free.' He read slowly to give the passage extra point. 'Page twenty-one,' he repeated. '"Following the successful recruitment of Ostrakova, and the formal issuing of a French permit to her daughter Alexandra, I was instructed to set aside immediately ten thousand American dollars a month from the Paris imprest for the purpose of servicing this new mole, who was henceforth awarded the workname KOMET. The agent KOMET also received the highest classification of secrecy within the Directorate, requiring all communications regarding her to be sent to the Director personally, using person-to-person ciphers, and without intermeediaries. Preferably, however, such communications should go by courier, since Karla is an opponent of the excessive use of radio." Any truth in that one, George?' Enderby asked casually.

'It was how we caught him in India,' said Smiley without lifting his head from the script. 'We broke his codes and he later swore that he would never use radio again. Like most promises, it was subject to review.'

Enderby bit off a bit of matchstick, and smeared it onto the back of his hand. 'Don't you want to take your coat off, George?' he asked. 'Sam, ask him what he wants to drink.'

Sam asked, but Smiley was too absorbed in the script to answer.

Enderby resumed his reading aloud: '"I was also instructed to make sure that no reference to KOMET appeared on the annual accounts for Western Europe which, as auditor, I was obliged to sign and present to Karla for submission to the Collegium of Moscow Centre at the close of each financial year . . . No, I never met the agent KOMET, nor do I know what became of her, or in which country she is operating. I know only that she is living under the name of Alexandra Ostrakova, the daughter of naturalised French parents . . ."' More turning of pages. '"The monthly payment of ten thousand dollars was not expended by myself, but transferred to a bank in Thun in the Swiss canton of Berne. The transfer is made by standing orders to the credit of a Dr. Adolf Glaser. Glaser is the nominal account holder, but I believe that Dr. Glaser is only the workname for a Karla operative at the Soviet Embassy in Berne, whose real name is Grigoriev. I believe this because once when I sent money to Thun, the sending bank made an error, and it did not arrive; when this became known to Karla, he ordered me to send a second sum immediately to Grigoriev personally while bank enquiries were continuing. I did as I was ordered and later recovered the duplicated amount. This is all I know. Otto, my friend, I beg you to preserve these confidences, they could kill me." He's bloody right. They did.' Enderby chucked the transcript on to a table, and it made a loud slap. 'Kirov's last will and testament, as you might say. That's it. George.'

'Yes, Saul.'

'Really no drink?'

'Thank you, I'm fine.'

'I'm still going to spell it out because I'm thick. Watch my arithmetic. It's nowhere near as good as yours. Watch my *every move*.' Recalling Lacon, he held up a white hand and spread the fingers as a prelude to counting on them.

'One, Ostrakova writes to Vladimir. Her message rings old bells. Probably Mikhel intercepted and read it, but we'll never know. We could sweat him, but I doubt if it would help, and it would most certainly put the cat among Karla's pigeons in a big way if we did.' He grabbed a second finger. 'Two, Vladimir sends a copy of Ostrakova's letter to Otto Leipzig, urging him to re-warm the Kirov relationship double-quick. Three, Leipzig roars off to Paris, sees Ostrakova, gets himself alongside his dear old buddy Kirov, tempts him to Hamburg – where Kirov is free to go, after all, since Leipzig is still down in Karla's books as Kirov's agent. Now there's a thing, George.'

Smiley waited.

'In Hamburg, Leipzig burns Kirov rotten. Right? Proof right here in our sweaty hands. But I mean – how?'

Did Smiley really not follow, or was he merely intent upon making Enderby work a little harder? In either case, he preferred to take Enderby's question as rhetorical.

'*How* does Leipzig burn him precisely?' Enderby insisted. 'What's the pressure? Dirty pix – well, okay. Karla's a puritan, so's Kirov. But I mean, Christ, this isn't the fifties, is it? Everyone's allowed a bit of leg-sliding these days, what?'

Smiley offered no comment on Russian mores; but on the subject of pressure he was as precise as Karla might have been: 'It's a different ethic to ours. It suffers no fools. We think of ourselves as more susceptible to pressure than the Russians. It's not true. It's simply not true.' He seemed very sure of this. He seemed to have given the matter a lot of recent thought:

'Kirov had been incompetent and indiscreet. For his indiscretion alone, Karla would have destroyed him. Leipzig had the proof of that. You may remember that when we were running the original operation against Kirov, Kirov got drunk and talked out of turn about Karla. He told Leipzig that it was Karla personally who had ordered him to compose the legend for a female agent. You discounted the story at the time, but it was true.'

Enderby was not a man to blush, but he did have the grace to pull a wry grin before fishing in his pocket for another matchstick.

'*And he that rolleth a stone, it will return upon him,*' he remarked contentedly, though whether he was referring to his own dereliction or to Kirov's was unclear. '"Tell us the rest, buddy, or I'll tell Karla what you've told me already," says little Otto to the fly. Jesus, you're right, he really *did* have Kirov by the balls!'

Sam Collins ventured a soothing interjection. 'I think George's point meshed pretty neatly with the reference on page two, Chief,' he said. 'There's a passage where Leipzig actually refers to "our discussions in Paris." Otto's twisting the Karla knife there, no question. Right, George?'

But Sam Collins might have been speaking in another room for all the attention either of them paid him.

'Leipzig also had Ostrakova's letter,' Smiley added. 'Its contents did not speak well for Kirov.'

'Another thing,' said Enderby.

'Yes, Saul?'

'Four years, right? It's fully four years since Kirov made his original pass at Leipzig. Suddenly he's all over Ostrakova, wanting the same thing. Four years later. You suggesting he's been swanning around with the same brief from Karla all this time, and got no forrader?'

Smiley's answer was curiously bureaucratic. 'One can only suppose that Karla's requirement ceased and was then revived,' he replied primly, and Enderby had the sense not to press him.

'Point is, Leipzig burns Kirov rotten and gets word to Vladimir that he's done so,' Enderby resumed as the spread fingers came up again for counting. 'Vladimir dispatches Villem to play courier. Meanwhile back at the Moscow ranch, Karla is either smelling a rat or Mikhel has peached, probably the latter. In either case, Karla calls Kirov home under the pretext of promotion and swings him by his ears. Kirov sings, as I would, fast. Karla tries to put the toothpaste back in the tube. Kills Vladimir while he's on the way to our rendezvous armed with Ostrakova's letter. Kills Leipzig. Takes a pot at the old lady, and fluffs it. What's his mood now?'

'He's sitting in Moscow waiting for Holmes or Captain Ahab to catch up with him,' Sam Collins suggested, in his velvet voice, and lit yet another of his brown cigarettes.

Enderby was unamused. 'So why doesn't Karla dig up his treasure, George? Put it somewhere else? If Kirov has confessed to Karla what he's confessed to Leipzig, Karla's first move should be to brush over the traces!'

'Perhaps the treasure is not movable,' Smiley replied. 'Perhaps Karla's options have run out.'

'But it would be daylight madness to leave the bank account intact!'

'It was daylight madness to use a fool like Kirov,' Smiley said, with unusual harshness. 'It was madness to let him recruit Leipzig and madness to approach Ostrakova, and madness to believe that by killing three people he could stop the leak. Presumptions of sanity are therefore not given. Why should they be?' He paused. 'And Karla *does* believe it, apparently, or Grigoriev would not still be in Berne. Which you say he is, I gather?' The smallest glance at Collins.

'As of today he's sitting pretty,' Collins said, through his all-weather grin.

'Then moving the bank account would hardly be a logical step,' Smiley remarked. And he added: 'Even for a madman.'

And it was strange – as Collins and Enderby afterwards privily agreed – how everything that Smiley said seemed to pass through the room like a chill; how in some way that they failed to understand, they had removed themselves to a higher order of human conduct for which they were unfit.

'So who's his dark lady?' Enderby demanded. 'Who's worth ten grand a month and his whole damn career? Forcing him to use boobies instead of his own regular cut-throats? Must be quite a gal.'

Again there is mystery about Smiley's decision not to reply to this question. Perhaps only his wilful inaccessibility can explain it; or perhaps we are staring at the stubborn refusal of the born caseman to reveal anything to his controller that is not essential to their collaboration. Certainly there was philosophy in his decision. In his mind already, Smiley was accountable to nobody but himself: why should he act as if things were otherwise? 'The threads lead all of them into my own life,' he may have reasoned. 'Why pass the ends to my adversary merely so that he can manipulate me?' Again, he may well have assumed – and probably with justice – that Enderby was as familiar as Smiley was with the complexities of Karla's background; and that even if he was not, he had had his Soviet Research Section burrowing all night until they found the answers he required.

In any case, the fact is that Smiley kept his counsel.

'George?' said Enderby, finally.

An aeroplane flew over quite low.

'It's simply a question of whether you want the product,' Smiley said at last. 'I can't see that anything else is ultimately of very much importance.'

'Can't you, by God!' said Enderby, and pulled his hand from his mouth and the matchstick with it. 'Oh I *want* him all right,' he went on, as if that were only half the point. 'I *want* the Mona Lisa, and the Chairman of the Chinese People's Republic, and next year's winner of the Irish Sweep. I *want* Karla sitting on the hot seat at Sarratt, coughing out his life story to the inquisitors. I *want* the American Cousins to eat out of my hand for years to come. I *want* the whole ball game, of course I do. Still doesn't get me off the hook.'

But Smiley seemed curiously unconcerned by Enderby's dilemma.

'Brother Lacon told you the facts of life, I suppose? The stalemate and all?' Enderby asked. 'Young, idealistic Cabinet, mustard for détente, preaching open government, all that balls? Ending the conditioned reflexes of the cold war? Sniffing Tory conspiracies under every Whitehall bed, ours specially? Did he? Did he tell you they're proposing to launch a damn great Anglo-Bolshie peace initiative, yet another, which will duly fall on its arse around Christmas next?'

'No. No, he didn't tell me that part.'

'Well, they are. And we're not to jeopardise it, tra-la. Mind you, the very chaps who go hammering the peace-drums are the ones who scream like hell when we don't deliver the goods. I suppose that stands to reason. They're already asking what the Soviet posture will be, even now. Was it always like that?'

Smiley took so long to answer that he might have been passing the Judgment of Ages. 'Yes. I suppose it was. I suppose that in one form or another it always *was* like that,' he said at last, as if the answer mattered to him deeply.

'Wish you'd warned me.'

Enderby sauntered back towards the centre of the room and poured himself some plain soda from the sideboard; he stared at Smiley with what seemed to be honest indecision. He stared at him, he shifted his head and stared again, showing all the signs of being faced with an insoluble problem.

'It's a tough one, Chief, it really is,' said Sam Collins, unremarked by either man.

'And it's not all a wicked Bolshie plot, George, to lure us to our ultimate destruction – you're sure of *that*?'

'I'm afraid we're no longer worth the candle, Saul,' Smiley said, with an apologetic smile.

Enderby did not care to be reminded of the limitations of British grandeur, and for a moment his mouth set into a sour grimace.

'All right, Maud,' he said finally. 'Let's go into the garden.'

They walked side by side. Collins, on Enderby's nod, had stayed indoors. Slow rain puckered the surface of the pool and made the marble angel glisten in the dusk. Sometimes a breeze passed and a chain of water slopped from the hanging branches onto the lawn, soaking one or the other of them. But Enderby was an English Gentleman, and while God's rain might be falling on the rest of mankind, he was damned if it was going to fall on him. The light came at them in bits. From Ben's French windows, yellow rectangles fell across the pond. From over the brick wall, they had the sickly green glow of a modern street lamp. They completed a round in silence before Enderby spoke.

'Led us a proper dance, you did, George, I'll tell you that for nothing. Villem, Mikhel, Toby, Connie. Poor old Ferguson hardly had time to fill in his expense claims before you were off again. "Doesn't he ever sleep?" he asked me. "Doesn't he ever drink?"'

'I'm sorry,' said Smiley, for something to say.

'Oh, no, you're not,' said Enderby, and came to a sudden halt. '*Bloody* laces,' he muttered, stooping over his boot, 'they always do this with suède. Too few eyeholes, that's the problem. You wouldn't think even the bloody Brits would manage to be mean with *holes*, would you?'

Enderby replaced one foot and lifted the other.

'I want his body, George, hear me? Hand me a live, talking Karla and I'll accept him and make my excuses later. Karla asks for asylum? Well, um, yes, most reluctantly he can have it. By the time the Wise Men are loading their shot-guns for me I'll have enough out of him to shut them up for good. His body or nothing, you got me?'

They were strolling again, Smiley trailing behind, but Enderby, though he was speaking, did not turn his head.

'Don't you ever go thinking they'll go away, either,' he warned. 'When you and Karla are stuck on your ledge on the Reichenbach Falls and you've got your hands round Karla's throat, Brother Lacon will be right there behind you holding your coat-tails and telling you not to be beastly to the Russians. Did you get that?'

Smiley said yes, he had got it.

'What have you got on him so far? Misuse of the facilities of his office, I suppose. Fraud. Peculation of public funds, the very thing he topped that Lisbon fellow for. Unlawful operations abroad, including a couple of assassination jobs. I suppose there's a whole bloody bookful when you work it out. *Plus* all those jealous beavers at Centre longing for an excuse to knife him. He's right: blackmail's a *bloody* sight better than bribery.'

Smiley said, yes, it seemed so.

'You'll need people. Baby-sitters, lamplighters, all the forbidden toys. Don't talk to me about it, find your own. Money's another matter. I can lose you in the accounts for years the way these clowns in Treasury work. Just tell me when and how much and where, and I'll do a Karla for you and fiddle the accounts. How about passports and stuff? Need some addresses?'

'I think I can manage, thank you.'

'I'll watch you day and night. If the ploy aborts and there's a scandal, I'm not going to have people telling me I should have staked you out. I'll say I suspected you might be slipping the leash on the Vladimir thing and I decided to have you checked in case. I'll say the whole catastrophe was a ludicrous piece of private enterprise by a senile spy who's lost his marbles.'

Smiley said he thought that was a good idea.

'I may not have much to put on the street, but I can still tap your phone, steam open your mail, and if I want to, I'll bug your bedroom too. We've been listening in since Saturday as it is. Nothing of course, but what do you expect?'

Smiley gave a small nod of sympathy.

'If your departure abroad strikes me as hasty or mysterious, I shall report it. I also need a cover story for your visits to the Circus Registry. You'll go at night but you may be recognised and I'm not having *that* catch up with me, either.'

'There was a project once to commission an in-house history of the service,' Smiley said helpfully. 'Nothing for publication, obviously, but some sort of continuing record which could be available to new entrants and certain liaison services.'

'I'll send you a formal letter,' Enderby said. 'I'll bloody well backdate it too. If you happen to misuse your licence while you're inside the building, it's no fault of mine. That chap in Berne whom Kirov mentioned. Grigoriev, Commercial Counsellor. The chap who's been getting the cash?'

Smiley seemed lost in thought. 'Yes, yes, of course,' he said. 'Grigoriev?'

'I suppose he's your next stop, is he?'

A shooting star ran across the sky and for a second they both watched it.

Enderby pulled a plain piece of folded paper from his inside pocket. 'Well, that's Grigoriev's pedigree, far as we know it. He's clean as a whistle. One of the very rare ones. Used to be an economics don at some Bolshie university. Wife's a harridan.'

'Thank you,' said Smiley politely. 'Thank you very much.'

'Meanwhile, you have my totally deniable blessing,' said Enderby as they started back towards the house.

'Thank you,' said Smiley again.

'Sorry you've become an instrument of the imperial hypocrisy, but there's rather a lot of it about.'

'Not at all,' said Smiley.

Enderby stopped to let Smiley draw up beside him.

'How's Ann?'

'Well, thank you.'

'How much –' He was suddenly off his stroke. 'Put it this way, George,' he suggested, when he had savoured the night air for a moment. 'You travelling on business, or for pleasure in this thing? Which is it?'

Smiley's reply was also slow in coming, and as indirect: 'I was never conscious of pleasure,' he said. 'Or perhaps I mean: of the distinction.'

'Karla still got that cigarette-lighter she gave you? It's true, isn't it? That time you interviewed him in Delhi – tried to get him to defect – they say he pinched your cigarette-lighter. Still got it, has he? Still using it? Pretty grating, I'd find that, if it was mine.'

'It was just an ordinary Ronson,' Smiley said. 'Still, they're made to last, aren't they?'

They parted without saying goodbye.

# TWENTY

In the weeks that followed this encounter with Enderby, George Smiley found himself in a complex and variable mood to accompany his many tasks of preparation. He was not at peace; he was not, in a single phrase, definable as a single person, beyond the one constant thrust of his determination. Hunter, recluse, lover, solitary man in search of reassurance – Smiley was by turns each one of them, and sometimes more than one. Among those who remembered him later – old Mendel, the retired policeman, one of his few confidants; a Mrs. Gray, the landlady of the humble bed-and-breakfast house for gentlemen only, in Pimlico, which for security reasons he made his temporary headquarters; or Toby Esterhase, alias Benati, the distinguished dealer in Arab art – most, in their various ways spoke of an ominous *going in*, *a quietness*, an economy of words and glance, and they described it according to their knowledge of him, and their station in life.

Mendel, a loping, dourly observant man with a taste for keeping bees, said outright that George was pacing himself before his big fight. Mendel had been in the amateur ring in his time, he had boxed middleweight for the Division, and he claimed to recognise the eve-of-match signs: a sobriety, a clarifying loneliness, and what he called a staring sort of look, which showed that Smiley was 'thinking about his hands.' Mendel seems to have taken him in occasionally, and fed him meals. But Mendel was too perceptive not to observe the other side of him also: the perplexity, often cloaked as social inhibition; his habit of slipping away, on a frail excuse, as if the sitting-still had suddenly become too long for him; as if he needed movement in order to escape himself.

To his landlady, Mrs. Gray, Smiley was, quite simply, bereaved. She knew nothing of him as a man, except that his name was Lorimer and he was a retired librarian by trade. But she told her other gentlemen she could feel he had had a *loss*, which was why he left his bacon, why he went out a lot but always alone, and why he slept with his light on. He reminded her of her father, she said, 'after Mother went.' And this was perceptive of Mrs Gray, for the aftermath of the two violent deaths hung heavily on Smiley in the lull, though it did the very reverse of slow his hand. She was also right when she called him *divided*, constantly changing his mind about small things; like Ostrakova, Smiley found life's lesser decisions increasingly difficult to take.

Toby Esterhase, on the other hand, who dealt with him a great deal, took a more informed view, and one that was naturally brightened by Toby's own excitement at being back in the field. The prospect of playing Karla 'at the big table,' as he insisted on describing it, had made a new man of Toby. Mr. Benati had become international indeed. For two weeks, he toured the byways of Europe's seedier cities, mustering his bizarre army of discarded specialists – the pavement artists, the sound-thieves, the drivers, the photographers – and every day, from wherever he happened to be, using an agreed word code, he telephoned Smiley at a succession of numbers within walking distance of the boarding-house in order to report his progress. If Toby was passing through London, Smiley would drive to an airport hotel, and debrief him in one of its now familiar bedrooms. George – Toby declared – was making a *Flucht nach vorn*, which nobody has ever quite succeeded in translating. Literally it means 'an escape forward,' and it implies a desperation certainly, but also a weakness at one's back, if not an actual burning of boats. Quite what this weakness was, Toby could not describe. 'Listen,' he would say, 'George always bruised easy, know what I mean? You see a lot – your eyes get very painful. George saw too much, maybe.' And he added, in a phrase which found a modest place in Circus folklore – 'George has got too many heads under his hat.' Of his generalship, on the other hand, Toby had no doubt whatever. 'Meticulous to a fault,' he declared respectfully – even if the fault included checking Toby's imprest down to the last Swiss *Rappen*, a discipline he accepted with a rueful grace. George was nervous, he said, as they all were; and his nervousness came to a natural head as Toby began concentrating his teams, in twos and threes, on the target city of Berne, and very, very cautiously taking the first steps towards the quarry. 'He got too detailed,' Toby complained. 'Like he wanted to be on the pavement with us. A case man, he finds it hard to delegate, know what I mean?'

Even when the teams were all assembled, all accounted for and briefed, Smiley from his London base still insisted on three days of virtual inactivity while everybody 'took the temperature of the city,' as he called it, acquired local clothes and transport, and rehearsed the systems of communication. 'It's lace curtain all the way, Toby,' he repeated anxiously. 'For every week that nothing happens, Karla will feel that much more secure. But frighten the game just once, and Karla will panic and we're done for.' After the first operational swing Smiley summoned Toby home to report yet again: 'Are you sure there was no eye contact? Did you ring the changes enough? Do you need more cars, more people?' Then, said Toby, he had to take him through the whole manoeuvre yet again, using street maps and still photographs of the target house, explaining exactly where the static posts were laid, where the one team had peeled off to make room for the next. 'Wait till you've got his pattern,' said Smiley as they parted. 'When you've got his behaviour pattern, I'll come. Not before.'

Toby says he made damn sure to take his time.

Of Smiley's visits to the Circus during this trying period there is, naturally, no official memory at all. He entered the place like his own ghost, floating as if invisible down the familiar corridors. At Enderby's suggestion he arrived at a quarter past six in the evening, just after the day-shift had ended, and before the night staff had got into its stride. He had expected barriers; he had queasy notions of janitors he had known for twenty years telephoning the fifth floor for clearance. But Enderby had arranged things differently, and when Smiley presented himself, passless, at the hardboard chicane, a boy he had never seen before nodded him carelessly to the open lift. From there, he made his way unchallenged to the basement. He got out, and the first thing he saw was the welfare club notice-board and they were the same notices from his own days exactly, word for word: free kittens available to good home; the junior staff drama group would read *The Admirable Crichton*, misspelt, on Friday in the canteen. The same squash competition, with players enrolled under work-names in the interest of security. The same ventilators emitting their troubled hum. So that, by the time he pushed the wired-glass door of Registry, and scented the printing-ink and library dust, he half expected to see his own rotund shape bowed over the corner desk in the glow of the chipped green reading-lamp, as it had been often enough in the days when he was charting Bill Haydon's rampages of betrayal, and trying, by a reverse process of logic, to point to the weaknesses in Moscow Centre's armour.

'Ah, now, you're writing up our glorious past, I hear,' the night registrar sang indulgently. She was a tall girl and county, with Hilary's walk: she seemed to topple even when she sat. She plonked on old tin deed-box on the table. 'Fifth floor sent you this lot with their love,' she said. 'Squeal if you need ferrying around, won't you?'

The label on the handle read 'Memorabilia.' Lifting the lid, Smiley saw a heap of old buff files bound together with green string. Gently, he untied and lifted the cover of the first volume, to reveal Karla's misted photograph staring up at him like a corpse from the darkness of its coffin. He read all night, he hardly stirred. He read as far into his own past as into Karla's, and sometimes it seemed to him that the one life was merely the complement to the other; that they were causes of the same incurable malady. He wondered, as so often before, how he would have turned out if he had had Karla's childhood, had been fired in the same kilns of revolutionary upheaval. He tried but, as so often before, failed to resist his own fascination at the sheer scale of the Russian suffering, its careless savagery, its flights of heroism. He felt small in the face of it, and soft by comparison, even though he did not consider his own life wanting in its pains. When the night-shift ended, he was still there, staring into the yellow pages 'the way a horse sleeps standing up,' said the same night registrar, who rode in gymkhanas. Even when she took the files from him to return them to the fifth floor, he went on staring till she gently touched his elbow.

He came the next night and the next; he disappeared, and returned a week later without explanation. When he had done with Karla, he drew the files on Kirov, on Mikhel, or Villem, and on the Group at large, if only to give, in retrospect, a solid documentary heart to all he had heard and remembered of the Leipzig-Kirov story. For there was yet another part of Smiley, call it pedant, call it scholar, for which the file was the only truth, and all the rest a mere extravagance until it was matched and fitted to the record. He drew the files on Otto Leipzig and the General, too, and, as a service to their memory, if nothing else, added to each a memorandum which calmly set out the true circumstances of his death. The last file he drew was Bill Haydon's. There was hesitation at first about releasing it, and the fifth-floor duty officer, whoever he was that night, called Enderby out of a private ministerial dinner party in order to clear it with him. Enderby, to his credit, was furious: 'God Almighty man, he *wrote* the damn thing in the first place, didn't he? If George can't read his own reports, who the hell can?' Smiley didn't really *read* it, even then, the registrar reported, who had a secret watching brief on everything he drew. It was more *browsing*, she said – and described a slow and speculative turning of the pages, 'like someone looking for a picture they'd seen and couldn't find again.' He only kept the file for an hour or so, then gave it back with a polite 'Thank you very much.' He did not come again after that, but there is a story the janitors tell that some time after eleven on the same night, when he had tidied away his papers and cleared his desk space and consigned his few scribbled notes to the bin for secret waste, he was observed to stand for a long time in the rear courtyard – a dismal place, all white tiles and black drainpipes and a stink of cat – staring at the building he was about to take his leave of, and at the light that was burning weakly in his former room, much as old men will look at the houses where they were born, the schools where they were educated, and the churches where they were married. And from Cambridge Circus – it was by then eleven-thirty – he startled everybody, took a cab to Paddington and caught the night sleeper to Penzance, which leaves just after midnight. He had not bought a ticket in advance, nor ordered one by telephone; nor did he have any night things with him, not even a razor, though in the morning he did manage to borrow one from the attendant. Sam Collins had put together a ragtag team of watchers by then, an amateurish lot admittedly, and all they could say afterwards was that he made a call from a phone box, but there was no time for them to do anything about it.

'Bloody queer moment to take a holiday, isn't it?' Enderby remarked petulantly, when this intelligence was brought to him, together with a string of moans from the staff-side about overtime, travelling time, and allowances for unsocial hours. Then he remembered, and said, 'Oh my Christ, he's visiting his bitch goddess. Hasn't he got enough problems, taking on Karla single-handed?' The whole episode annoyed Enderby strangely. He fumed all day and insulted Sam Collins in front of everyone. As a former diplomat, he had great contempt for abstracts, even if he took refuge in them constantly.

The house stood on a hill, in a coppice of bare elms still waiting for the blight. It was granite and very big, and crumbling, with a crowd of gables that clustered like torn black tents above the tree tops. Acres of smashed greenhouses led to it; collapsed stables and an untended kitchen garden lay below it in the valley. The hills were olive and shaven, and had once been hill-forts. 'Harry's Cornish heap,' she called it. Between the hills ran the line of the sea, which that morning was hard as slate under the lowering cloud banks. A taxi took him up the bumpy drive, an old Humber like a wartime staff car. This is where she spent her childhood, thought Smiley; and where she adopted mine. The drive was very pitted; stubs of felled trees lay like yellow tombstones either side. She'll be in the main house, he thought. The cottage where they had passed their holidays together lay over the brow, but on her own she stayed in the house, in the room she had had as a girl. He told the driver not to wait, and started towards the front porch, picking his way between the puddles with his London shoes, giving the puddles all his attention. It's not my world any more, he thought. It's hers, it's theirs. His watcher's eyes scanned the many windows of the front façade, trying to catch a glimpse of her shadow. She'd have picked me up at the station, only she muddled the time, he thought, giving her the benefit of the doubt. But her car was parked in the stables with the morning frost still on it; he had spotted it while he was still paying off the taxi. He rang the bell and heard her footsteps on the flagstones, but it was Mrs. Tremedda who opened the door and showed him to one of the drawing-rooms – smoking-room, morning-room, drawing-room, he had never worked them out. A log fire was burning.

'I'll get her,' Mrs. Tremedda said.

At least I haven't got to talk about Communists to mad Harry, Smiley thought, while he waited. At least I haven't got to hear how all the Chinese waiters in Penzance are standing by for the order from Peking to poison their customers. Or how the bloody strikers should be put up against a wall and shot – where's their sense of service, for Christ's sake? Or how Hitler may have been a blackguard, but he had the right idea about the Jews. Or some similar monstrous, but seriously held, conviction.

She's told the family to keep clear, he thought.

He could smell honey through the wood-smoke and wondered, as he always did, where it came from. The furniture wax? Or was there, something in the catacombs, a honey room, just as there was a gunroom and a fishing-room and a box-room and, for all he knew, a love room? He looked for the Tiepolo drawing that used to hang over the fireplace, a scene of Venice life. They've sold it, he thought. Each time he came, the collection had dwindled by one more pretty thing. What Harry spent the money on was anybody's guess – certainly not the upkeep of the house.

She crossed the room to him and he was glad it was she who was doing the walking, not himself, because he would have stumbled into something. His mouth was dry and he had a lump of cactus in his stomach; he didn't want her near him, her reality was suddenly too much for him. She was looking beautiful and Celtic, as she always did down here, and as she came towards him her brown eyes scanned him, looking for his mood. She kissed him on the mouth, putting her fingers along the back of his neck to guide him, and Haydon's shadow fell between them like a sword.

'You didn't think to pick up a morning paper at the station, did you?' she enquired. 'Harry's stopped them again.'

She asked whether he had breakfast and he lied and said he had. Perhaps they could go for a walk instead, she suggested, as if he were someone waiting to see round the estate. She took him to the gunroom where they rummaged for boots that would do. There were boots that shone like conkers and boots that looked permanently damp. The coast footpath led in both directions out of the bay. Periodically, Harry threw barbed-wire barricades across it, or put up notice saying 'DANGER LANDMINES.' He was fighting a running battle with the Council for permission to make a camping site, and their refusal sometimes drove him to a fury. They chose the north shoulder and the wind, and she had taken his arm to listen. Then north was windier, but on the south you had to go single-file through the gorse.

'I'm going away for a bit, Ann,' he said, trying to use her name naturally. 'I didn't want to tell you over the telephone.' It was his wartime voice and he felt an idiot when he heard himself using it. 'I'm going off to blackmail a lover,' he should have said.

'Away to somewhere particular, or just away from me?'

'There's a job I have to do abroad,' he said, still trying to escape his Gallant Pilot rôle, and failing. 'I don't think you should go to Bywater Street while I'm away.'

She had locked her fingers through his own, but then she did those things: she handled people naturally, all people. Below them in the rocks' cleft, the sea broke and formed itself furiously in patterns of writhing foam.

'And you've come all this way just to tell me the house is out of bounds?' she asked.

He didn't answer.

'Let me try it differently,' she proposed when they had walked a distance. 'If Bywater Street had been *in* bounds, would you have suggested that I *did* go there? Or are you telling me it's out of bounds for good?'

She stopped and gazed at him, and held him away from her, trying to read his answer. She whispered, 'For godness' sake,' and he could see the doubt, the pride, and the hope in her face all at once, and wondered what she saw in his, because he himself had no knowledge of what he felt, except that he belonged nowhere near her, nowhere near this place; she was like a girl on a floating island that was swiftly moving away from him with the shadows of all her lovers gathered round her. He loved her, he was indifferent to her, he observed her with the curse of detachment, but she was leaving him. If I do not know myself, he thought, how can I tell who you are? He saw the lines of age and pain and striving that their life together had put there. She was all he wanted, she was nothing, she reminded him of someone he had once known a long time ago; she was remote to him, he knew her entirely. He saw the gravity in her face and one minute wondered that he could ever have taken it for profundity; the next, he despised her dependence on him, and wanted only to be free of her. He wanted to call out 'Come back' but he didn't do it; he didn't even put out a hand to stop her from slipping away.

'You used to tell me never to stop looking,' he said. The statement began like the preface to a question, but no question followed.

She waited, then offered a statement of her own. 'I'm a comedian, George,' she said. 'I need a straight man. I need you.'

But he saw her from a long way off.

'It's the job,' he said.

'I can't live with them. I can't live without them.' He supposed she was talking about her lovers again. 'There's one thing worse than change and that's the status quo. I hate the choice. I love you. Do you understand?' There was a gap while he must have said something. She was not relying on him, but she was leaning on him while she wept, because the weeping had taken away her strength. 'You never knew how free you were, George,' he heard her say. 'I had to be free for both of us.'

She seemed to realise her own absurdity and laughed.

She let go his arm and they walked again while she tried to right the ship by asking plain questions. He said weeks, perhaps longer. He said 'In a hotel,' but didn't say which city or country. She faced him again, and the tears were suddenly running anywhere, worse than before, but they still didn't move him as he wished they would.

'George, this is all there is, I promise you,' she said, halting to make her entreaty. 'The whistle's gone, in your world and in mine. We're landed with each other. There isn't any more. According to the averages, we're the most contented people on earth.'

He nodded, seeming to take the point that she had been somewhere he had not, but not regarding it as conclusive. They walked a little more, and he noticed that when she didn't speak he was able to relate to her, but only in the sense that she was another living creature moving along the same path as himself.

'It's to do with the people who ruined Bill Haydon,' he said to her, either as a consolation, or an excuse for his retreat. But he thought: 'Who ruined you.'

He had missed his train and there were two hours to kill. The tide was out so he walked along the shore near Marazion, scared by his own indifference. The day was grey, the seabirds were very white against the slate sea. A couple of brave children were splashing in the surf. I am a thief of the spirit, he thought despondently. Faithless, I am pursuing another man's convictions; I am trying to warm myself against other people's fires. He watched the children, and recalled some scrap of poetry from the days when he read it:

> To turn as swimmers into cleanness leaping,
> Glad from a world grown old and cold and weary.

Yes, he thought glumly. That's me.

'Now George,' Lacon demanded. 'Do you think we set our women up too high, is *that* where we English middle-class chaps go wrong? Do you think – I'll put it this way – that we English, with our traditions and our schools, expect our womenfolk to stand for *far* too much, then *blame* them for not standing up at all – if you follow me? We see them as *concepts*, rather than flesh and blood. Is that our hangup?'

Smiley said it might be.

'Well if it *isn't* why does Val *always* fall for shits?' Lacon snapped aggressively, to the surprise of the couple sitting at the next-door table.

Smiley did not know the answer to that either.

They had dined, appallingly, in the steak-house Lacon had suggested. They had drunk Spanish burgundy out of a carafe, and Lacon had raged wildly over the British political dilemma. Now they were drinking coffee and a suspect brandy. The anti-Communist phobia was overdone: Lacon had declared himself sure of it. Communists were only *people*, after all. They weren't red-toothed monsters, not any more. Communists wanted what everyone wanted: prosperity and a bit of peace and quiet. A chance to take a breather from all this damned hostility. And if they didn't – well, what could we do about it anyway? he had asked. Some problems – take Ireland – were insoluble, but you would never get the Americans to admit *anything* was insoluble. Britain was ungovernable; so would everywhere else be in a couple of years. Our future was with the collective, but our survival was with the individual, and the paradox was killing us every day.

'Now, George, how do *you* see it? You're out of harness after all. You have the objective view, the overall perspective.'

Smiley heard himself muttering something inane about a spectrum.

And now the topic that Smiley had dreaded all evening was finally upon them: their seminar on marriage had begun.

'*We* were always taught that women had to be cherished,' Lacon declared resentfully. 'If one didn't make 'em feel loved every minute of the day, they'd go off the rails. But this chap Val's with – well if she annoys him, or speaks out of turn, he'll like as not give her a black eye. You and I never do that, do we?'

'I'm sure we don't,' said Smiley.

'Look here. Do you reckon if I went and saw her – bearded her in his house – took a really tough line – threatened legal action and so forth – it might tip the scales? I mean I'm bigger than he is, God knows. I'm not without clout, whichever way you read me!'

They stood on the pavement under the stars, waiting for Smiley's cab.

'Well have a good holiday anyway. You've deserved it,' Lacon said. 'Going somewhere warm?'

'Well, I thought I might just take off and wander.'

'Lucky you. My God, I envy you your freedom! Well, you've been jolly useful, anyway. I shall follow your advice to the letter.'

'But, Oliver, I didn't *give* you any advice,' Smiley protested, slightly alarmed.

Lacon ignored him. 'And that other thing is all squared away, I hear,' he said serenely. 'No loose ends, no messiness. Good of you, that, George. Loyal. I'm going to see if we can get you a bit of recognition for it. What have you got already, I forget? Some chap the other day in the Athenaeum was saying you deserve a K.'

The cab came, and to Smiley's embarrassment Lacon insisted on shaking hands. 'George. Bless you. You've been a brick. We're birds of a feather,

George. Both patriots, givers, not takers. Trained to our services. Our country. We must pay the price. If Ann had been your agent instead of your wife, you'd probably have run her pretty well.'

The next afternoon, following the telephone call from Toby to say that 'the deal was just about ready for completion,' George Smiley quietly left for Switzerland, using the workname Barraclough. From Zurich airport he took the Swissair bus to Berne and made straight for the Bellevue Palace Hotel, an enormous, sumptuous place of mellowed Edwardian quiet, which on clear days looks across the foothills to the glistening Alps, but that evening was shrouded in a cloying winter fog. He had considered smaller places; he had considered using one of Toby's safe flats. But Toby had persuaded him that the Bellevue was best. It had several exits, it was central, and it was the first place in Berne where anyone would think to find him, and therefore the last where Karla, if he was looking out for him, would expect him to be. Entering the enormous hall, Smiley had the feeling of stepping onto an empty liner far out at sea.

# TWENTY-ONE

His room was a tiny Swiss Versailles. The *BOMBÉ* writing-desk had brass inlay and a marble top, a Bartlett print of Lord Byron's Childe Harold hung above the pristine twin beds. The fog outside the window made a grey wall. He unpacked and went downstairs again to the bar where an elderly pianist was playing a medley of hits from the Fifties, things that had been Ann's favourites, and, he supposed, his. He ate some cheese and drank a glass of Fendant, thinking: *Now*. Now is the beginning. From now on there is no shrinking back, no space for hesitation. At ten he made his way to the old city, which he loved. The streets were cobbled; the freezing air smelt of roast chestnuts and cigar. The ancient fountains advanced on him through the fog, the mediaeval houses were the backdrop to a play he had no part in. He entered the arcades, passing art galleries and antique shops, and doorways tall enough to ride a horse through. At the Nydegg Bridge he came to a halt, and stared into the river. So many nights, he thought. So many streets still here. He thought of Hesse: *strange to wander in the fog . . . no tree knows another.* The frozen mist curled low over the racing water; the weir burned creamy yellow.

An orange Volvo estate car drew up behind him, Berne registration, and briefly doused its lights. As Smiley started towards it, the passenger door was pushed open from inside, and by the interior light he saw Toby Esterhase in the driving seat, and in the back, a stern-looking woman in the uniform of a

Bernese housewife, dandling a child on her knee. He's using them for cover, Smiley thought; for what the watchers called the silhouette. They drove off and the woman began talking to the child. Her Swiss German had a steady note of indignation: 'See there the crane, Eduard . . . Now we are passing the bear-pit, Eduard . . . Look Eduard, a tram . . .' Watchers are always dissatisfied, he remembered; it's the fate of every voyeur. She was moving her hands about, directing the child's eye to anything. *A family evening, Officer*, said the scenario. *We are going visiting in our fine orange Volvo, Officer. We are going home.* And the men, naturally, Officer, seated in the front.

They had entered Elfenau, Berne's diplomatic ghetto. Through the fog, Smiley glimpsed tangled gardens white with frost, and the garden porticos of villas. The headlights picked out a brass plate proclaiming an Arab state, and two bodyguards protecting it. They passed an English church and a row of tennis-courts; they entered an avenue lined with bare beeches. The street lights hung in them like white balloons.

'Number eighteen is five hundred metres on the left,' said Toby softly. 'Grigoriev and his wife occupy the ground floor.' He was driving slowly, using the fog as his excuse.

'Very rich people live here, Eduard!' the woman was singing from behind them. 'All from foreign places.'

'Most of the Iron Curtain crowd live in Muri, not Elfenau,' Toby went on. 'It's a commune, they do everything in groups. Shop in groups, go for walks in groups, you name it. The Grigorievs are different. Three months ago, they moved out of Muri and rented this apartment on a personal basis. Three thousand five hundred a month, George, he pays it in person to the landlord.'

'Cash?'

'Monthly in one-hundred notes.'

'How are the rest of the Embassy hirings paid for?'

'Through the Mission accounts. Not Grigoriev's. Grigoriev is the exception.'

A police-patrol car overtook them with the slowness of a river barge; Smiley saw its three heads turned to them.

'Look, Eduard, police!' the woman cried, and tried to make the child wave at them.

Toby too was careful not to stop talking. 'The police boys are worried about bombs,' he explained. 'They think the Palestinians are going to blow the place sky high. That's been good and bad for us, George. If we're clumsy, Grigoriev can tell himself we're local angels. The same doesn't go for the police. One hundred metres, George. Look for a black Mercedes in the forecourt. Other staff use the Embassy car pool. Not Grigoriev. Grigoriev drives his own Mercedes.'

'When did he get it?' Smiley asked.

'Three months ago, second-hand. Same time as he moved out of Muri. That was a big leap for him, George. Like a birthday, so many things. Car, house, promotion from First Secretary to Counsellor.'

It was a stucco villa, set in a large garden that had no back because of the fog. In a bay window at the front Smiley glimpsed a light burning behind curtains. There was a children's slide in the garden, and what appeared to be an empty swimming pool. On the gravel sweep stood a black Mercedes with CD plates.

'All Soviet Embassy car numbers end with 73,' said Toby. 'The Brits have 72. Grigorieva got herself a driving licence two months ago. There are only two women in the Embassy with licences. She's one and she's a terrible driver, George. And I mean terrible.'

'Who occupies the rest of the house?'

'The landlord. A professor at Berne University, a creep. A while ago the Cousins got alongside him and said they'd like to run a couple of probe mikes into the ground floor, offered him money. The professor took the money and reported them to the Bundespolizei like a good citizen. The Bundespolizei got a scare. They'd promised the Counsins to look the other way in exchange for a sight of the product. Operation abandoned. Seems the Cousins had no particular interest in Grigoriev, it was just routine.'

'Where are the Grigoriev children?'

'In Geneva at Soviet Mission School, weekly boarders. They get home Friday nights. Weekends the family make excursions. Romp in the woods, langlauf, play badminton. Collect mushrooms. Grigorieva's a fresh-air freak. Also they have taken up bicycling,' he added, with a glance.

'Does Grigoriev go with the family on these excursions?'

'Saturdays he works, George – and, I am certain, only to escape them.' Toby had formed decided views on the Grigoriev marriage, Smiley noticed. He wondered whether it had echoes of one of Toby's own.

They had left the avenue and entered a side-road. 'Listen, George,' Toby was saying, still on the subject of Grigoriev's weekends. 'Okay? Watchers imagine things. They got to, it's their job. There's a girl works in the Visa Section. Brunette and, for a Russian, sexy. The boys call her "little Natasha." Her real name's something else but for them she's Natasha. Saturdays she comes in to the Embassy. To work. Couple of times, Grigoriev drives her home to Muri. We took some pictures, not bad. She got out of the car short of her apartment and walked the last five hundred metres. Why? Another time he took her nowhere – just a drive round the Gurten, but talking very cosy. Maybe the boys just want it to be that way, on account of Grigorieva. They like the guy, George. You know how watchers are. It's love or hate all the time. They like him.

He was pulling up. The lights of a small café glowed at them through the fog. In its courtyard stood a green Citroën deuxchevaux, Geneva registration. Cardboard boxes were heaped on the back seat, like trade samples. A foxtail dangled from the radio aerial. Springing out, Toby pulled open the flimsy door and hustled Smiley into the passenger seat: then handed him a trilby hat, which he put on. For himself, Toby had a Russian -style fur. They drove off again, and Smiley saw their Bernese matron climbing into the front of the orange Volvo they had just abandoned. Her child waved at them despondently through the back window as they drove.

'How is everyone?' Smiley said.

'Great. Pawing the earth, George, every one of them. One of the Sartor brothers had a sick kid, had to go home to Vienna. It nearly broke his heart. Otherwise great. You're Number One for all of them. This is Harry Slingo coming up on the right. Remember Harry? Used to be my sidekick back in Acton.'

'I read that his son had won a scholarship to Oxford,' Smiley said.

'Physics. Wadham, Oxford. The boy's a genius. Keep looking down the road, George, don't move your head.'

They passed a van with '*Auto-Schnelldienst*' painted in breezy letters on the side, and a driver dozing at the wheel.

'Who's in the back?' Smiley asked when they were clear.

'Pete Lusty, used to be a scalp-hunter. Those guys have been having it very bad, George. No work, no action. Peter signed up for the Rhodesian Army. Killed some guys, didn't care for it, came back. No wonder they love you.'

They were passing Grigoriev's house again. A light was burning in the other window.

'The Grigorievs go to bed early,' Toby said in a sort of awe.

A parked limousine lay ahead of them with Zurich consular plates. In the driving seat, a chauffeur was reading a paperback book.

'That's Canada Bill,' Toby explained. 'Grigoriev leaves the house, turns right, he passes Pete Lusty. Turns left, he passes Canada Bill. They're good boys. Very vigilant.'

'Who's behind us?'

'The Meinertzhagen girls. The big one got married.'

The fog made their progress private, very quiet. They descended a gentle hill, passing the British Ambassador's residence on their right, and his Rolls-Royce parked in the sweep. The road led left and Toby followed it. As he did so, the car behind overtook them and conveniently put up its headlights. By their beam, Smiley found himself looking into a wooded cul-de-sac ending in a pair of tall closed gates guarded on the inside by a small huddle of men. The trees cut off the rest entirely.

'Welcome to the Soviet Embassy, George,' Toby said, very softly. 'Twenty-four diplomats, fifty other ranks – cipher clerks, typists, and some very lousy drivers, all home-based. The trade delegation's in another building, Schanze-neckstrasse 17. Grigoriev visits there a lot. In Berne we got also Tass and Novosti, mostly mainstream hoods. The parent residency is Geneva, U.N. cover, about two hundred strong. This place is a side-show: twelve, fifteen altogether, growing but only slow. The Consulate is tacked onto the back of the Embassy. You go into it through a door in the fence, like it was an opium den or a cat house. They got a closed-circuit television camera on the path and scanners in the waiting-room. Try applying for a visa once.'

'I think I'll give it a miss, thanks,' said Smiley, and Toby gave one of his rare laughs.

'Embassy grounds,' Toby said, as the headlights flashed over steep woods falling away to the right. 'That's where Grigorieva plays her volley-ball, gives political instruction to the kids. George, believe me, that's a very distorting woman. Embassy kindergarten, the indoctrination classes, the Ping-Pong club, women's badminton – that woman runs the whole show. Don't take my word for it, hear my boys talk about her.' As they turned out of the cul-de-sac, Smiley lifted his glance towards the upper window of the corner house and saw a light go out, and then come on again.

'And that's Pauli Skordeno saying "Welcome to Berne,"' said Toby. 'We managed to rent the top floor last week. Pauli's a Reuters stringer. We even faked a press pass for him. Cable cards, everything.'

Toby had parked near the Thunplatz. A modern clock tower was striking eleven. Fine snow was falling but the fog had not dispersed. For a moment neither man spoke.

'Today was a model of last week, last week was a model of the week before, George,' said Toby. 'Every Thursday it's the same. After work he takes the Mercedes to the garage, fills it with petrol and oil, checks the batteries, asks for a receipt. He goes home. Six o'clock, a little after, the Embassy car arrives at his front door and out gets Krassky, the regular Thursday courier from Moscow. Alone. That's a very itchy fellow, a professional. In all other situations, Krassky don't go anywhere without his companion, Bogdanov. Fly together, carry together, eat together. But to visit Grigoriev, Krassky breaks ranks and goes alone. Stays half an hour, leaves again. Why? That's very irregular in a courier, George. Very dangerous, if he hasn't got the backing, believe me.'

'So what do you make of Grigoriev, Toby?' Smiley asked. 'What is he?'

Toby made his tilting gesture with his outstretched palm. 'A trained hood Grigoriev isn't, George. No tradecraft, actually a complete catastrophe. But he's not straight either. A half-breed, George.'

So was Kirov, Smiley thought.

'Do you think we've got enough on him?' Smiley asked.

'Technically no problem. The bank, the false identity, little Natasha even: technically we got a hand of aces.'

'And you think he'll burn,' said Smiley, more as confirmation than a question.

In the darkness, Toby's palm once more tilted, this way, that way.

'Burning, George, that's always a hazard, know what I mean? Some guys get heroic and want to die for their countries suddenly. Other guys roll over and lie still the moment you put the arm on them. Burning, that touches the stubbornness in certain people. Know what I mean?'

'Yes. Yes, I think I do,' said Smiley. And he remembered Delhi again, and the silent face watching him through the haze of cigarette smoke.

'Go easy, George. Okay? You got to put your feet up now and then?'

'Good night,' said Smiley.

He caught the last tram back to the town centre. By the time he had reached the Bellevue, the snow was falling heavily: big flakes, milling in the yellow light, too wet to settle. He set his alarm for seven.

# TWENTY-TWO

The young woman they called Alexandra had been awake one hour exactly when the morning bell sounded for assembly, but when she heard it she immediately drew up her knees inside her calico night-suit, crammed her eyelids together, and swore to herself she was still asleep, a child who needed rest. The assembly bell, like Smiley's alarm clock, went off at seven, but already at six she had heard the chiming of the valley clocks, first the Catholics, then the Protestants, then the Town Hall, and she didn't believe in any of them. Not this God, not that God, and least of all the burghers with their butchers' faces, who at the annual festival had stood to attention with their stomachs stuck out while the fire-brigade choir moaned patriotic songs in dialect.

She knew about the annual festival because it was one of the few Permitted Expeditions, and she had recently been allowed to attend it as a privilege, her first, and to her huge amusement it was devoted to the celebration of the common onion. She had stood between Sister Ursula and Sister Beatitude and she knew they were both alert in case she tried to run away or snap inside and start a fit, and she had watched an hour of the most boring speechifying ever, then an hour's singing to the accompaniment of boring martial music by the brass band. Then a march past of people dressed in village costume and carrying strings of onions on long sticks, headed by the village flag-swinger, who on other days brought the milk to the lodge and – if he could slip by – right up to the hostel door, in the hope of getting a sight of a girl through the window, or perhaps it was just Alexandra trying to get a sight of him.

After the village clocks had chimed the six, Alexandra from deep, deep in her bed had decided to count the minutes till eternity. In her self-imposed rôle as child, she had done this by counting each second in a whisper: 'One -thousand-and-*one*, one-thousand-and-*two*.' At twelve minutes past, by her childish reckoning, she heard Mother Felicity's pompous Moped snorting down the drive on her way back from Mass, telling everyone that Felicity-Felicity – pop-pop – and no one else – pop-pop – was our Superintendent and Official Starter of the Day; nobody else – pop-pop – would do. Which was funny because her real name was not Felicity at all; Felicity was what she had chosen for the other nuns. Her real name, she had told Alexandra as a secret, was Nadezhda, meaning 'Hope.' So Alexandra had told Felicity that *her* real name was Tatiana, not Alexandra at all. Alexandra was a *new* name, she explained, put on to wear in Switzerland specially. But Felicity-Felicity had told her sharply not to be a silly girl.

After Mother Felicity's arrival, Alexandra had held the white bed sheet to her eyes and decided that time was not passing at all, that she was in a child's white limbo where everything was shadowless, even Alexandra, even Tatiana. White light bulbs, white walls, a white iron bed frame. White radiators. Through the high windows, white mountains against a white sky.

Dr. Rüedi, she thought, here is a new dream for you when we have our next little Thursday talk, or is it Tuesday?

Now listen carefully, Doctor. Is your Russian good enough? Sometimes you pretend to understand more than you really do. Very well, I will begin. My name is Tatiana and I am standing in my white night-suit in front of the white Alpine landscape, trying to write on the mountain face with a stick of Felicity-Felicity's white chalk, whose real name is Nadezhda. I am wearing nothing underneath. You pretend you are indifferent to such things, but when I talk to you about how I love my body you pay close attention, don't you, Dr. Rüedi? I scribble with the chalk in the mountain face. I stub with it like a cigarette. I think of the filthiest words I know – yes, Dr. Rüedi, *this* word, *that* word – but I fear your Russian vocabulary is unlikely to include them. I try to write them also, but white on white, what impact can a little girl make, I ask you, Doctor?

Doctor, it's terrible, you must never have my dreams. Do you know I was once a whore called Tatiana? That I can do no wrong? That I can set fire to things, even myself, vilify the State, and *still* the wise ones in authority will not punish me? But instead, they let me out of the back door – 'Go, Tatiana, go' – do you know this?

Hearing footsteps in the corridor, Alexandra pulled herself deeper under the bedclothes. The French girl is being led to the toilets, she thought. The French girl was the most beautiful in the place. Alexandra loved her, just for her beauty. She beat the whole system with it. Even when they put her in the coat – for clawing or messing herself or smashing something – her angel's face still gazed at them like one of their own icons. Even when she wore her shapeless night-suit with no buttons, her breasts lifted it up in a crisp bridge and there was nothing anyone could do, not even the most jealous, not even Felicity-Felicity whose secret name was Hope, to prevent her from looking like a film star. When she tore her clothes off, even the nuns stared at her with a kind of covetous terror. Only the American girl had matched her for looks, and the American girl had been taken away, she was too bad. The French girl was bad enough with her naked tantrums and her wrist-cutting and her fits of rage at Felicity-Felicity, but she was nothing beside the American girl by the time she left. The sisters had to fetch Kranko from the lodge to hold her down, just for the sedation. They had to close the entire rest-wing while they did it, but when the van took the American girl off, it was like a death in the family and Sister Beatitude wept all through evening prayers. And afterwards, when Alexandra forced her to tell, she called her by her pet name, Sasha, a sure sign of her distress.

'The American girl has gone to Untersee,' she said through her tears when Alexandra forced her to tell. 'Oh, Sasha, Sasha, promise me you will never go to Untersee.' Just as in the life she could not mention, they had begged her: 'Tatiana, do not do these mad and dangerous things!'

After that, Untersee became Alexandra's worst terror, a threat that silenced her at any time, even her naughtiest: 'If you are bad you will go to Untersee, Sasha. If you tease Dr. Rüedi, pull up your skirt, and cross your legs at him, Mother Felicity will have to send you to Untersee. Hush, or they'll send you to Untersee.'

The footsteps returned along the corridor. The French girl was being taken to be dressed. Sometimes she fought them and ended up in the coat instead. Sometimes Alexandra would be sent to calm her, which she did by brushing the French girl's hair over and over again, not talking, till the French girl relaxed and stared to kiss her hands. Then Alexandra would be taken away again because love was not, was not, was *not* on the curriculum.

The door flew open and Alexandra heard Felicity-Felicity's courtly voice, harrying her like an old nurse in a Russian play: 'Sasha! You must get up immediately! Sasha, wake up immediately! Sasha, wake up! Sasha!'

She came a step nearer. Alexandra wondered whether she was going to pull back the sheets and yank her to her feet. Mother Felicity could be rough as a soldier, for all her aristocratic blood. She was not a bully, but she was blunt and easily provoked.

'Sasha, you will be late for breakfast. The other girls will look at you and laugh, and say that we stupid Russians are always late. Sasha? Sasha, do you want to miss prayers? God will be very angry with you, Sasha. He will be sad and He will cry. He may have to think of ways of punishing you.'

Sasha, do you want to go to Untersee?

Alexandra pressed her eyelids closer together. I am six years old and need my sleep, Mother Felicity. God make me five, God make me four. I am three years old and need my sleep, Mother Felicity.

'Sasha, have you forgotten it is your special day? Sasha, have you forgotten you have your *visitor* today?'

God make me two, God make me one, God make me nothing and unborn.

No, I have not forgotten my visitor, Mother Felicity. I remembered my visitor before I went to sleep, I dreamt of him, I have thought of nothing else since I woke. But, Mother Felicity, I do not want my visitor today, or any other day. I cannot, cannot live the lie, I don't know how, and that is why I shall not, shall not, *shall* not let the day begin!

Obediently, Alexandra clambered out of bed.

'*There*,' said Mother Felicity, and gave her a distracted kiss before bustling off down the corridor, calling 'Late again! Late again!' and clapping her hands – 'Shoo, shoo!' – just as she would to a flock of silly hens.

# TWENTY-THREE

The train journey to Thun took half an hour and from the station Smiley drifted, window-shopping, making little detours. *Some guys get heroic and want to die for their countries*, he thought . . . *Burning, that touches the stubbornness in people* . . . He wondered what it would touch in himself.

It was a day of darkening blankness. The few pedestrians were slow shadows against the fog, and lake steamers were frozen in the locks. Occasionally the blankness parted enough to offer him a glimpse of castle, a tree, a piece of city wall. Then swiftly closed over them again. Snow lay in the cobble and in the forks of the knobbly spa trees. The few cars drove with their lights on, their tyres crackling in the slush. The only colours were in shop-windows: gold watches, ski clothes like national flags. 'Be there by eleven earliest,' Toby had said; 'eleven is already too early, George, they won't arrive till twelve.' It was only ten-thirty but he wanted the time, he wanted to circle before he settled; time, as Enderby would say, to get his ducks in a row. He entered a narrow street and saw the castle lift directly above him. The arcade became a pavement, then a staircase, then a steep slope, and he kept climbing. He passed an English Tea-Room, an American-Bar, an Oasis Night-Club, each hyphenated, each neon-lit, each a sanitized copy of a lost original. But they could not destroy his love of Switzerland. He entered a square and saw the bank, the very one, and straight across the road the little hotel exactly as Toby had described it, with its café-restaurant on the ground floor and its barracks of rooms above. He saw the yellow mail van parked boldly in the no-parking bay, and he knew it was Toby's static post. Toby had a lifelong faith in mail vans; he stole them wherever he went, saying nobody noticed or remembered them. He had fitted new number-plates but they looked older than the van. Smiley crossed the square. A notice on the bank door said 'OPEN MONDAY TO THURSDAY 07.45–17.00, FRIDAY 07.45–18.15.' 'Grigoriev likes the lunch-hour because in Thun nobody wastes his lunch hour going to the bank,' Toby had explained. 'He has completely mistaken quiet for security, George. Empty places, empty times, Grigoriev is so conspicuous he's embarrassing.' He crossed a foot-bridge. The time was ten to eleven. He crossed the road and headed for the little hotel with its unencumbered view of Grigoriev's bank. Tension in a vacuum, he thought, listening to the clip of his own feet and the gurgle of water from the gutters; the town was out of season and out of time. *Burning, George, that's always a hazard.* How would Karla do it? he wondered. What would the absolutist do which we are not doing ourselves? Smiley could think of nothing, short of straight physical abduction. Karla would collect the operational intelligence, he thought, then he would make his approach – risking the hazard. He pushed the café door and the warm air sighed to him. He made for a window table marked 'RESERVED.' 'I'm waiting for Mr. Jacobi,' he told the girl. She nodded disapprovingly, missing his eye. The girl had a cloistered pallor, and no expression at all. He ordered *café-crème* in a glass, but she said that if it came in a glass, he would have to have schnapps with it.

'Then in a cup,' he said, capitulating.

Why had he asked for a glass in the first place?

Tension in a vacuum, he thought again, looking round. Hazard in a blank place.

The café was modern Swiss antique. Crossed plastic lances hung from stucco pillars. Hidden speakers played harmless music; the confiding voice changed language with each announcement. In a corner, four men played a silent game of cards. He looked out of the window, into the empty square. Rain had started again, turning white to grey. A boy cycled past, wearing a red wooden cap, and the cap went down the road like a torch until the fog put it out. The bank's doors were double, he noticed, opened by electronic eye. He looked at his watch. Eleven-ten. A till murmured. A coffee machine hissed. The card-players were dealing a new hand. Wooden plates hung on the wall: dancing couples in national costume. What else was there to look at? The lamps were wrought iron but the illumination came from a ring of strip lighting round the ceiling and it was very harsh. He thought of Hong Kong, with its Bavarian beer cellars on the fifteenth floor, the same sense of waiting for explanations that would never be supplied. And today is only preparation, he thought: today is not even the approach. He looked at the bank again. Nobody entered, nobody leaving. He remembered waiting all his life for something he could no longer define: call it resolution. He remembered Ann, and their last walk. Resolution in a vacuum. He heard a chair squeak, saw Toby's hand held out for him, Swiss style, to shake, and Toby's bright face sparkling as if he'd just come in from a run.

'The Grigorievs left the house in Elfenau five minutes ago,' he said quietly. 'Grigorieva's driving. Most likely they die before they get here.'

'And the bicycles?' Smiley said anxiously.

'Like normal,' said Toby, pulling up a chair.

'Did she drive last week?'

'Also the week before. She insists. George, I mean that woman is a monster.' The girl brought him a coffee unbidden. 'Last week, she actually hauled Grigoriev out of the driving seat, then drove the car into the gate post, clipped the wing. Pauli and Canada Bill were laughing so much we thought we'd get static on the whisperers.' He put a friendly hand on Smiley's shoulder. 'Listen, it's going to be a nice day. Believe me. Nice light, a nice layout, all you got to do is sit back and enjoy the show.'

The phone rang, and the girl called 'Herr Jacobi!' Toby walked easily to the counter. She handed him the receiver and blushed at something he whispered to her. From the kitchen, the chef came in with his small son: 'Herr Jacobi!' The chrysanthemums on Smiley's table were plastic but someone had put water in the vase.

'*Ciao*,' Toby called cheerfully into the phone, and came back. 'Everyone in position, everyone happy,' he announced with satisfaction. 'Eat something, okay? Enjoy yourself, George. This is Switzerland.'

Toby stepped gaily into the street. *Enjoy the show*, thought Smiley. That's right. I wrote it, Toby produced it, and all I can do now is watch. No, he thought, correcting himself: Karla wrote it, and sometimes that worried him quite a lot.

Two girls in hiking kit were entering the double doors of the bank. A moment later and Toby had followed them in. He's packing the bank, thought Smiley. He'll man every counter two-deep. After Toby, a young couple, arm in arm, then a stubby woman with two shopping bags. The yellow mail van had not budged: nobody moves a mail van. He noticed a public phone box, and two figures huddled into it, perhaps sheltering from the rain. Two people are less conspicuous than one, they liked to say at Sarratt, and three are less conspicuous than a pair. An empty tour coach passed. A clock struck twelve and, right on cue, a black Mercedes lurched out of the fog, its dipped headlights glittering on the cobble. Bumping clumsily on to the kerb, it stopped outside the bank, six feet from Toby's mail van. *Soviet Embassy car numbers end with* 73, Toby had said. *She drops him and drives round the block a couple of times till he comes out.* But today, in the filthy weather, the Grigorievs had apparently decided to flout the parking laws and Karla's laws too, and rely on their CD plates to keep them out of trouble. The passenger door opened and a stocky figure in a dark suit and spectacles scampered for the bank entrance, carrying a brief-case. Smiley had just time to record the thick grey hair and rimless spectacles of Grigoriev's photographs before a lorry masked his view. When it moved on, Grigoriev had disappeared, but Smiley had a clear sight of the formidable bulk of Grigorieva herself, with her red hair and learner-driver scowl, seated alone at the steering-wheel. *George, believe me, that's a very distorting woman.* Seeing her now, her jaw set, her bullish glare, Smiley was able for the first time, if cautiously, to share Toby's optimism. If fear was the essential concomitant of a successful burn, Grigorieva was certainly someone to be afraid of.

In his mind's eye Smiley now imagined the scene that was playing inside the bank, exactly as he and Toby had planned. The bank was a small one, a team of seven could flood it. Toby had opened a private account for himself: Herr Jacobi, a few thousand francs. Toby would take one counter and occupy it with small transactions. The foreign-exchange desk was also no problem. Two of Toby's people, armed with a spread of currencies, could keep them on the run for minutes. He imagined the hubbub of Toby's hilarity, causing Grigoriev to raise his voice. He imagined the two girl hikers doing a double act, one rucksack dumped carelessly at Grigoriev's feet, recording whatever he happened to say to the cashier; and the hidden cameras snapping away from toggle bags, rucksacks, brief-cases, bedrolls, or wherever they were stowed. 'It's the same as the firing-squad, George,' Toby explained, when Smiley said he was worried about the shutter noise. 'Everybody hears the click except the quarry.'

The bank doors slid open. Two businessmen emerged, adjusting their raincoats as if they had been to the lavatory. The stubby woman with the two shopping bags followed them out, and Toby came after her, chatting volubly to the girl hikers. Next came Grigoriev himself. Oblivious of everything, he hopped into the black Mercedes and planted a kiss on his wife's cheek before she had time to turn away. He saw her mouth show criticism of him, and Grigoriev's placatory smile as he replied. Yes, Smiley thought, he certainly has something to be guilty about; yes, he thought, remembering the watchers' affection for him: yes, I understand that too. But the Grigorievs did not leave; not yet. Grigoriev had hardly closed the door before a tall, vaguely familiar woman in a green Loden coat came striding down the pavement, tapped fiercely on the passenger window and delivered herself of what seemed to be a homily upon the sins of parking on pavements. Grigoriev was embarrassed, Grigorieva leaned across him and bawled at her – Smiley even heard the word *Diplomat* in heavy German rise above the sound of the traffic – but the woman remained where she was, her handbag under her arm, still swearing at them as they drove away. She'll have snapped them in the car with the bank doors in the background, he thought. They photograph through perforations: half a dozen pinholes and the lens can see perfectly.

Toby had returned and was sitting beside him at the table. He had lit a small cigar. Smiley could feel him trembling like a dog after the chase.

'Grigoriev drew his normal ten thousand,' he said. His English had become a little rash. 'Same as last week, same as the week before. We got it, George, the whole scene. The boys are very happy, the girls too. George, I mean they are fantastic. Completely the best. I never had so good. What do you think of him?'

Surprised to be asked, Smiley actually laughed.

'He's certainly henpecked,' he agreed.

'And a nice fellow, know what I mean? Reasonable. I think he'll act reasonable too. That's my view, George. The boys are the same.'

'Where do the Grigorievs go from here?'

A sharp male voice interrupted them. 'Herr Jacobi!'

But it was only the chef, holding up a glass of schnapps to drink Toby's health. Toby returned the toast.

'Lunch at the station buffet, first-class,' he continued. 'Grigorieva takes pork chop and chips, Grigoriev steak, a glass of beer. Maybe they take also a couple of vodkas.'

'And after lunch?'

Toby gave a brisk nod, as if the question required no elucidation.

'Sure,' he said. 'That's where they go. George, cheer up. That guy will fold, believe me. You never had a wife like that. And Natasha's a cute kid.' He lowered his voice. 'Karla's his meal ticket, George. You don't always understand the simple things. You think she'd let him give up the new apartment? The Mercedes?'

Alexandra's weekly visitor arrived, always punctual, always at the same time, which was on Fridays after rest. At one o'clock came lunch, which on Fridays consisted of cold meat and *Rösti* and *Kompott* of apples or perhaps plums, depending on the season, but she couldn't eat it and sometimes she made a show of sicking it up or running to the lavatory or calling Felicity-Felicity and complaining, in the basest language, about the quality of the food. This never failed to annoy her. The hostel took great pride in growing its own fruit, and the hostel's brochures in Felicity-Felicity's office contained many photographs of fruit and blossom and Alpine streams and mountains indiscriminately, as if God, or the sisters, or Dr. Rüedi, had grown the whole lot specially for the inmates. After lunch came an hour's rest and on Fridays this daily hour was Alexandra's worst, her worst of the whole week, when she had to lie on the white iron bedstead and pretend she was relaxing, while she prayed to any God that would have her that Uncle Anton might be run over or have a heart attack, or, best of all, cease to exist – locked away with her own past and her own secrets and her own name of Tatiana. She thought of his rimless spectacles and in her imagination she drove them into his head and out the other side, taking his eyes with them, so that instead of his soggy gaze to stare at, she would see straight through him to the world outside.

And now at last rest had ended, and Alexandra stood in the empty dining hall in her best frock, watching the lodge through the window while two of the Marthas scoured the tiled floor. She felt sick. Crash, she thought. Crash on your silly bicycle. Other girls had visitors, but they came on Saturdays and none had Uncle Anton, few had men of any sort; it was mainly wan aunts and bored sisters who attended. And none got Felicity-Felicity's study to sit in, either, with the door closed and nobody present but the visitor; that was a privilege which Alexandra and Uncle Anton enjoyed alone, as Sister Beatitude never tired of pointing out. But Alexandra would have traded all of those privileges, and a good more besides, for the privilege of not having Uncle Anton's visit at all.

The lodge gates opened and she began trembling on purpose, shaking her hands from the wrists as if she had seen a mouse, or a spider, or a naked man aroused for her. A tubby figure in a brown suit began cycling down the drive. He was not a natural cyclist, she could tell from his self-consciousness. He had not cycled here from any distance, bringing a breath of outside. It could be baking hot, but Uncle Anton neither sweated nor burned. It could be raining heavily, but Uncle Anton's mackintosh and hat, when he reached the main door, would scarcely be wet, and his shoes were never muddied. Only when the giant snowfall had come, three weeks ago, or call it years, and put a metre's thickness of extra padding round the dead castle, did Uncle Anton look anything like a real man living in the real elements; in his thick knee-boots and anorak and fur hat, skirting the pine trees as he plodded up the track, he stepped straight out of the memories she was never to mention. And when he had embraced her, calling her 'my little daughter,' slapping his big gloves down on Felicity-Felicity's highly polished table, she felt such a surge of kinship and hope that she would catch herself smiling for days afterwards.

'He was so warm,' she confided to Sister Beatitutde in her bit of French. 'He held me like a friend! Why does the snow make him so fond?'

But today there was only sleet and fog and big floppy flakes that would not settle on the yellow gravel.

He comes in a car, Sasha – Sister Beatitude told her once – with a *woman*, Sasha. Beatitude had seen them. Twice. Watched them, naturally. They had two bicycles strapped to the roof of the car, upside down, and the woman did the driving, a big strong woman, a bit like Mother Felicity but not so Christian, with hair red enough to scare a bull. When they reached the edge of the village, they parked the car behind Andreas Gertsch's barn, and Uncle Anton untied his bicycle and rode it to the lodge. But the woman stayed in the car and smoked, and read *Schweizer Illustrierte*, sometimes scowling at the mirror, and her bicycle never left the roof; it stayed there like an upturned sow while she read her magazine! And guess what! Uncle Anton's bicycle was *illegal!* The bicycle – as a good Swiss, Sister Beatitude had checked the point quite naturally – Uncle Anton's bicycle had no *plaque*, no licence, he was a criminal at large, and so was the woman, though she was probably too fat to ride it!

But Alexandra cared nothing for illegal bicycles. It was the car she wanted to know about. What type? Rich or poor? What colour, and above all, where did it come from? Was it from Moscow, from Paris, where? But Sister Beatitude was a country girl and simple, and in the world beyond the mountains most foreign places were alike to her. Then what letters were on the number-plate, for goodness' sake, silly? Alexandra had cried. Sister Beatitude had not noticed such matters. Sister Beatitude shook her head like the dumb dairymaid she was. Bicycles and cows she understood. Cars were beyond her mark.

Alexandra watched Grigoriev arrive, she waited for the moment when he leaned his head forward over the handlebars and raised his ample bottom in the air and swung one short leg over the crossbars as if he were climbing off a woman. She saw how the short ride had reddened his face, she watched him unfasten the brief-case from the rack over the back wheel. She ran to the door and tried to kiss him, first on the cheek, then on the lips, for she had an idea of putting her tongue into his mouth as an act of welcome, but he scurried past her with his head down as if he were already going back to his wife.

'Greetings, Alexandra Borisovna,' she heard him whisper, all of a flurry, uttering her Patronymic as if it were a state secret.

'Greetings, Uncle Anton,' she replied; then Sister Beatitude caught her by the arm and whispered to her to behave herself or else.

Mother Felicity's study was at once both sparse and sumptuous. It was small and bare and very hygienic, and the Marthas scrubbed it and polished it every day so that it smelt like a swimming-pool. Yet her little pieces of Russia glistened like caskets. She had icons, and she had richly framed sepia photographs of princesses she had loved, and bishops she had served, and on her saint's day – or was it her birthday or the bishop's? – she had taken them all down and made a theatre of them with candles and a Virgin and a Christ-child. Alexandra knew this because Felicity had called her in to sit with her, and had read old Russian prayers to her aloud, and chanted bits of liturgy in a marching rhythm to her, and given her sweet cake and a glass of sweet wine, all to have Russian company on her saint's day – or was it Easter or Christmas? Russians were the best in the world, she said. Gradually, though she had had a lot of pills, Alexandra had realised that Felicity-Felicity was stone drunk, so she lifted up her old feet and put a pillow for her, and kissed her hair and let her fall asleep on the tweed sofa where parents sat when they came to enrol fresh patients. It was the same sofa where Alexandra sat now, staring at Uncle Anton while he pulled the little notebook from his pocket. He was having one of his brown days, she noticed: brown suit, brown tie, brown shirt.

'You should buy yourself brown cycle clips,' she told him in Russian.

Uncle Anton did not laugh. He kept a piece of black elastic like a garter round his notebook and he was unwinding it with a shrewd, reluctant air while he moistened his official lips. Sometimes Alexandra thought he was a policeman, sometimes a priest disguised, sometimes a lawyer or school-master, sometimes even a special kind of doctor. But whatever he was, he clearly wished her to know, by means of the elastic and the notebook, and by the expressions of nervous benevolence, that there was a Higher Law for which neither he nor she was personally responsible, that he did not mean to be her jailer, that he wished her forgiveness – if not her actual love – for locking her away. She knew also that he wished her to know that he was sad and even lonely, and assuredly that he was fond of her, and that in a better world he would have been the uncle who brought her birthday presents, Christmas presents faithfully, and each year chucked her under the chin, 'My-*my*, Sasha, aren't you growing up,' followed by a restrained pat on some rounded part of her, meaning 'My-*my*, Sasha, you'll soon be ready for the pot.'

'How is your reading progressing, Alexandra?' he asked her while he flattened the notebook in front of him and turned the pages looking for his list. This was small talk. This was not the Higher Law. This was like talk about the weather, or what a pretty dress she was wearing, or how happy she appeared today – not at all like last week.

'My name is Tatiana and I come from the moon,' she replied.

Uncle Anton acted as though this statement had not been made, so perhaps she only said it to herself, silently in her mind, where she said a lot of things.

'You have finished the novel by Turgenev I brought you?' he asked. 'You were reading *Torrents of Spring*, I think.'

'Mother Felicity was reading it to me but she has a sore throat,' said Alexandra.

'So.'

This was a lie. Felicity-Felicity had stopped reading to her as a punishment for throwing her food on the floor.

Uncle Anton had found the page of his notebook with the list on it, and he had found his pencil too, a silver one with a top you pressed; he appeared inordinately proud of it.

'So,' he said. '*So* then, Alexandra!'

Suddenly Alexandra did not want to wait for his questions. Suddenly she could not. She thought of pulling down his trousers and making love to him. She thought of messing in a corner like the French girl. She showed him the blood on her hands where she had chewed them. She needed to explain to him, through her own divine blood, that she did not want to hear his first question. She stood up, holding out one hand for him while she dug her teeth into the other. She wanted to demonstrate to Uncle Anton, for once and for ever, that the question he had in mind was obscene to her, and insulting, and unacceptable, and mad, and to do this she had chosen Christ's example as the nearest and best: did He not hang on Felicity-Felicity's wall, straight ahead of her, with blood running down His wrists? *I have shed this for you, Uncle Anton*, she explained, thinking of Easter now, of Felicity-Felicity going round the castle breaking eggs. *Please. This is my blood, Uncle Anton. I have shed it for you.* But with her other hand jammed in her mouth, all she could manage in her speaking voice was a sob. So finally she sat down, frowning, with her hands linked on her lap, not actually *bleeding*, she noticed, but at least wet with her saliva.

Uncle Anton held the notebook open with his right hand and was holding the pop-top pencil in his left. He was the first left-handed man she had known and sometimes, watching him write, she wondered whether he was a mirror image, with the real version of him sitting in the car behind Andreas

Gertsch's barn. She thought what a wonderful way that would be of handling what Doctor Rüedi called the 'divided nature' – to send one half away on a bicycle while the other half stayed put in the car with the redheaded woman who drove him. Felicity-Felicity, if you lend me your pop-pop bicycle, I will send the bad part of me away on it.

Suddenly she heard herself talking. It was a wonderful sound. It made her like all the strong and healthy voices around her: politicians on the radio, doctors when they looked down on her in bed.

'Uncle Anton, where do you come from, please?' she heard herself enquire, with measured curiosity. 'Uncle Anton, pay attention to me, please, while I make a statement. Until you have told me who you are and whether you are my real uncle, and what is the registration number of your big black car, I shall refuse to answer any of your questions. I regret this, but it is necessary. Also, is the red headed woman your wife or is she Felicity-Felicity with her hair dyed, as Sister Beatitude advises me?'

But too often Alexandra's mind spoke words which her mouth did not transmit, with the result that the words stayed flying around inside her and she became their unwilling jailer, just as Uncle Anton pretended to be hers.

'Who gives you the money to pay Felicity-Felicity for my detention here? Who pays Dr. Rüedi? Who dictates what questions go into your notebook every week? To whom do you pass my answers which you so meticulously write down?'

But once again, the words flew around inside her skull like the birds in Kranko's greenhouse in the fruit season, and there was nothing that Alexandra could do to persuade them to come out.

'*So*, then?' said Uncle Anton a third time, with the watery smile that Dr. Rüedi wore when he was about to give her an injection. 'Now first you must please tell me your full name, Alexandra.'

Alexandra held up three fingers and counted on them like a good child. 'Alexandra Borisovna Ostrakova,' she said in an infantile voice.

'Good. And how have you been feeling this week, Sasha?'

Alexandra smiled politely in response: 'Thank you, Uncle Anton. I have been feeling much better this week. Dr. Rüedi tells me that my crisis is already far behind me.'

'Have you received by any means – post, telephone, or word of mouth – any communication from outside persons?'

Alexandra had decided she was a saint. She folded her hands on her lap, and tilted her head to one side, and imagined she was one of Felicity-Felicity's Russian Orthodox saints on the wall behind the desk. Vera, who was faith; Liubov, who was love, Sofia, Olga, Irina, or Xenia – all the names that Mother Felicity had taught her during that evening when she had confided that her own real name was Hope – whereas Alexandra's was Alexandra or Sasha, but never, never Tatiana, and just remember it. Alexandra smiled at Uncle Anton and she knew her smile was sublime, and tolerant, and wise; and that she was hearing God's voice, not Uncle Anton's; and Uncle Anton knew it too, for he gave a long sigh and put away his notebook, then reached for the bell button to summon Mother Felicity for the ceremony of the money.

Mother Felicity came hastily and Alexandra guessed she had not been far from the other side of the door. She had the account ready in her hand. Uncle Anton considered it and frowned, as he always did, then counted notes onto the desk, blue ones and orange ones singly, so that each was for a moment transparent under the beam of the reading lamp. Then Uncle

Anton patted Alexandra on the shoulder as if she were fifteen instead of twenty-five, or twenty, or however old she was when she had clipped away the forbidden bits of her life. She watched him waddle out of the door again and on to his bike. She watched his rump strive and gather rhythm as he rode away from her, through the lodge, past Kranko, and away down the hill towards the village. And as she watched she saw a strange thing, a thing that had never happened before: not to Uncle Anton, at least. From nowhere, two purposeful figures materialised – a man and a woman, wheeling a motor-bike. They must have been sitting on the summer bench the other side of the lodge, keeping out of sight, perhaps in order to make love. They moved into the lane, and stared after him, but they didn't mount the motor-bike, not yet. Instead, they waited till Uncle Anton was almost out of sight before setting off after him down the hill. Then Alexandra decided to scream, and this time she found her talking voice and the scream split the whole house from roof to floor before Sister Beatitude bore down on her to quell her with a heavy smack across the mouth.

'They're the same people,' Alexandra shrieked.

'Who are?' Sister Beatitude demanded, drawing back her hand in case she needed to use it again. 'Who are the same people, you bad girl?'

'They're the people who followed my mother before they dragged her away to kill her.'

Sister Beatitude gave a snort of disbelief. 'On black horses, I suppose!' she sneered. 'Dragged her on a sledge, too, didn't he, all across Siberia!'

Alexandra had spun these tales before. How her father was a secret prince more powerful than the Tsar. How he ruled at night, as the owls rule while the hawks are at rest. How his secret eyes followed her wherever she went, how his secret ears heard every word she spoke. And how, one night, hearing her mother praying in her sleep, he sent his men for her and they took her into the snow and she was never seen again: not even by God, He was looking for her still.

# TWENTY-FOUR

The burning of Tricky Tony, as it afterwards became known in the Circus mythology – such being Grigoriev's whimsical codename among the watchers – was one of those rare operations where luck, timing and preparation come together in a perfect marriage. They had all known from early on that the problem would be to find Grigoriev alone at a moment which allowed for his speedy reintroduction into normal life a few hours later. Yet by the weekend following the coverage of the Thun bank, intensive researches into Grigoriev's behaviour pattern had produced no obvious pointers as to when this moment might be. In desperation Skordeno and de Silsky, Toby's hard men, dreamed up a wildcat scheme to snatch him on his way to work, along the few hundred metres of pavement between his house and the Embassy. Toby killed it at once. One of the girls offered herself as a decoy: perhaps she could hitch a lift from him somehow? Her altruism was applauded, but it did not answer the practicalities.

The main problem was that Grigoriev was under double guard. Not only did the Embassy security staff keep check on him as a matter of routine; so did his wife. The watchers had no doubt that she suspected him of a tenderness for little Natasha. Their fears were confirmed when Toby's listeners contrived to tamper with the junction box at the corner of the road. In one day's watch, Grigorieva telephoned her husband no less than three times, to no apparent purpose other than to establish that he was indeed at the Embassy.

'George, I mean that woman is a total monster,' Toby stormed when he heard this. 'Love – I mean, all right. But possession, for its own sake, this I absolutely condemn. It's a matter of principle for me.'

The one chink was Grigoriev's Thursday-afternoon drives in the garage, when he took the Mercedes to have it checked. If a practised car coper such as Canada Bill could introduce an engine fault during the Wednesday night – one that kept the car mobile, but only just – then might not Grigoriev be snatched from the garage while he was waiting for the mechanic to trace it? The plan bristled with imponderables. Even if everything worked, how long would they have Grigoriev to themselves? Then again, on Thursdays Grigoriev must be back home in time to receive his weekly visit from the courier Krassky. Nevertheless, it remained the only plan they had – their worst except for the others, said Toby – and accordingly they settled to an apprehensive wait for five days while Toby and his team leaders plotted fallbacks for the many unpleasant contingencies should the plot abort: everyone to be signed out of his hotel and packed; escape papers and money to be carried at all times; radio equipment to be boxed and cached under American identity in the vaults of one of the major banks, so that any clues left behind would point to the Cousins rather than themselves; no forms of assembly other than walk-and-talk encounters on the pavement; wavelengths to be changed every four hours. Toby knew his Swiss police, he said. He had hunted here before. If the balloon went up, he said, then the fewer of his boys and girls around to answer questions, the better. 'I mean thank God the Swiss are only neutral, know what I mean?'

As a somewhat forlorn consolation, and as a boost to the delicate morale of the watchers, Smiley and Toby decreed that the surveillance of Grigoriev should be kept at full pitch throughout the expected days of waiting. The observation post in the Brunnadernrain would be manned round the clock; car and cycle patrols would be increased; everyone should be on his toes for the remote chance that God, in an uncharacteristic moment, would favour the just.

What God did, in fact, was send idyllic Sunday weather, and it proved decisive. By ten o'clock that Sunday it was as if the Alpine sun had come down from the Oberland to brighten the lives of the fog-ridden lowlanders. In the Bellevue Palace, which on Sundays has a quite overwhelming calm, a waiter had just spread a napkin on Smiley's lap for him. He was drinking a leisurely coffee, trying to concentrate on the weekend edition of the *Herald Tribune*, when, looking up, he saw the gentle figure of Franz the head porter standing before him.

'Mr. Barraclough, sir, the telephone, I am sorry. A Mr. Anselm.'

The cabins were in the main hall, the voice was Toby's, and the name Anselm signified urgency: 'The Geneva bureau has just advised us that the managing director is on his way to Berne at this very moment.'

The Geneva bureau was word code for the Brunnadernrain observation post.

'Is he bringing his wife?' said Smiley.

'Unfortunately, Madame is obliged to make an excursion with the children,' Toby replied. 'Perhaps if you could come down to the office, Mr. Barraclough?'

Toby's office was a sun pavilion situated in an ornamental garden next to the Bundeshaus. Smiley was there in five minutes. Below them lay the ravine of the green river. In the distance, under a blue sky, the peaks of the Bernese Oberland lifted splendidly in the sunlight.

'Grigoriev left the Embassy on his own five minutes ago, wearing a hat and coat,' Toby said as soon as Smiley arrived. 'He's heading for the town on foot. It's like the first Sunday we watched him. He walks to the Embassy, ten minutes later he sets off for the town. He's going to watch the chess game, George, no question. What do you say?'

'Who's with him?'

'Skordeno and de Silsky on foot, a back-up car behind, two more ahead. One team's heading for the Cathedral Close right now. Do we go, George, or don't we?'

For a moment, Toby was aware of that disconnection which seemed to afflict Smiley whenever the operation gathered speed: less indecision, than a mysterious reluctance to advance.

He pressed him: 'The green light, George? Or not? George, please! We are speaking of seconds here!'

'Is the house still covered for when Grigorieva and the children get back?'

'Completely.'

For a moment longer Smiley hesitated. For a moment, he weighed the method against the prize, and the grey and distant figure of Karla seemed actually to admonish him.

'The green light, then,' said Smiley. 'Yes. Go.'

He had barely finished speaking before Toby was standing in the telephone kiosk not twenty metres from the pavilion. 'With my heart going like a complete steam engine,' as he later claimed. But also with the light of battle in his eyes.

There is even a scale model of the scene at Sarratt, and occasionally the directing staff will dig it out and tell the tale.

The old city of Berne is best described as a mountain, a fortress, and a peninsula all at once, as the model shows. Between the Kirchenfeld and Kornhaus bridges, the Aare runs in a horseshoe cut into a giddy cleft, and the old city roosts prudently inside it, in rising foothills of medieval streets, till it reached the superb late-Gothic spire of the Cathedral, which is both the mountain peak and its glory. Next to the Cathedral, at the same height, stands the Platform, from whose southern perimeter the unwary visitor may find himself staring down a hundred feet of sheer stone face, straight into the swirling river. It is a place where, according to popular history, a pious man was thrown from his horse and, though he fell the whole awesome distance, survived by God's deliverance to serve the church for another thirty years, dying peacefully at a great age. The rest of the Platform makes a tranquil spot, with benches and ornamental trees and a children's playground – and, in recent years, a place for public chess. The pieces are two foot or more in height, light enough to move, but heavy enough to withstand the occasional thrust of a south wind that whips off the surrounding hills. The scale model even runs to replicas of them.

By the time Toby Esterhase arrived there that Sunday morning, the unexpected sunshine had drawn a small but tidy body of the game's enthusiasts, who stood or sat around the chequered pavement. And at their centre, a mere six feet from where Toby stood, as oblivious to his surroundings as could be wished, stood Counsellor (Commercial) Anton Grigoriev of the Soviet Embassy in Berne, a truant from both work and family, intently following, through his rimless spectacles, each move the players made. And behind Grigoriev stood Skordeno and his companion de Silsky, watching Grigoriev. The players were young and bearded and volatile – if not art students, then certainly they wished to be taken for them. and they were very conscious of fighting a duel under the public gaze.

Toby had been this close to Grigoriev before, but never when the Russian's attention was so firmly locked elsewhere. With the calm of impending battle, Toby appraised him and confirmed what he had all along maintained: Anton Grigoriev was not a fieldman. His rapt attention, the unguarded frankness of his expression as each move was played or contemplated, had an innocence which could never have survived the infighting of Moscow Centre.

Toby's personal appearance was another of those happy chances of the day. Out of respect for the Bernese Sunday, he had donned a dark overcoat and his black fur hat. He was therefore, at this crucial moment of improvisation, looking exactly as he would have wished had he planned everything to the last detail: a man of position takes his Sunday relaxation.

Toby's dark eyes lifted to the Cathedral Close. The get-away cars were in position.

A ripple of laughter went out. With a flourish, one of the bearded players lifted his queen and, pretending it was a most appalling weight, reeled with it a couple of steps and dumped it with a groan. Grigoriev's face darkened into a frown as he considered this unexpected move. On a nod from Toby, Skordeno and de Silsky drew one to either side of him, so close that Skordeno's shoulder was actually nudging the quarry's, but Grigoriev paid no heed. Taking this as their signal, Toby's watchers began sauntering into the crowd, forming a second echelon behind de Silsky and Skordeno. Toby waited no longer. Placing himself directly in front of Grigoriev, he smiled and lifted his hat. Grigoriev returned the smile – uncertainly, as one might to a diplomatic colleague half-remembered – and lifted his hat in return.

'How are you today, Counsellor?' Toby asked in Russian, in a tone of quiet jocularity.

More mystified than ever, Grigoriev said thank you, he was well.

'I hope you enjoyed your little excursion to the country on Friday,' said Toby in the same easy, but very quiet voice, as he slipped his arm through Grigoriev's. 'The old city of Thun is not sufficiently appreciated, I believe, by members of our distinguished diplomatic community here. In my view it is to be recommended both for its antiquity, and its banking facilities. Do you not agree?'

This opening sally was long enough, and disturbing enough, to carry Grigoriev unresisting to the crowd's edge. Skordeno and de Silsky were packing close behind.

'My name is Kurt Siebel, sir,' Toby confided in Grigoriev's ear, his hand still on his arm. 'I am chief investigator to the Bernese Standard Bank of Thun. We have certain questions relating to Dr. Adolf Glaser's private account with us. You would do well to pretend you know me.' They were still moving. Behind them, the watchers followed in a staggered line, like rugger players poised to block a sudden dash. 'Please do not be alarmed,' Toby continued, counting the steps as Grigoriev kept up his progress. 'If you could spare us an hour, sir, I am sure we could arrange matters without troubling your domestic or professional position. Please.'

In the world of a secret agent, the wall between safety and extreme hazard is almost nothing, a membrane that can be burst in a second. He may court a man for years, fattening him for the pass. But the pass itself – the 'will you, won't you?' – is a leap from which there is either ruin or victory, and for a moment Toby thought he was looking ruin in the face. Grigoriev had finally stopped dead and turned round to stare at him. He was pale as an invalid. His chin lifted, he opened his mouth to protest a monstrous insult. He tugged at his captive arm in order to free himself but Toby held it firm. Skordeno and de Silsky were hovering, but the distance to the car was still fifteen metres, which was a long way, in Toby's book, to drag one stocky Russian. Meanwhile, Toby kept talking; all his instinct urged him to.

'There are irregularities, Counsellor. Grave irregularities. We have a dossier upon your good self which makes lamentable reading. If I placed it before the Swiss police, not all the diplomatic protests in the world would protect you from the most acute public embarrassment, I need hardly mention the consequence to your professional career. Please. I said *please*.'

Grigoriev had still not budged. He seemed transfixed with indecision. Toby pushed at his arm, but Grigoriev stood rock solid and seemed unaware of the physical pressure of him. Toby shoved harder, Skordeno and de Silsky drew closer, but Grigoriev had the stubborn strength of the demented. His mouth opened, he swallowed, his gaze fixed stupidly on Toby.

'What irregularities?' he said at last. Only the shock and the quietness in his voice gave cause for hope. His thick body remained rigidly set against further movement. 'Who is this Glaser you speak of?' he demanded huskily, in the same stunned tone. 'I am not Glaser. I am a diplomat, Grigoriev. The account you speak of has been conducted with total propriety. As Commercial Counsellor I have immunity. I also have the right to own foreign bank accounts.'

Toby fired his only other shot. *The money and the girl*, Smiley had said. *The money and the girl are all you have to play with.*

'There is also the delicate matter of your marriage, sir,' Toby resumed with a show of reluctance. 'I must advise you that your philanderings in the Embassy have put your domestic arrangements in grave danger.' Grigoriev started, and was heard to mutter '*banker*' – whether in disbelief or derision will never be sure. His eyes closed and he was heard to repeat the word, this time – according to Skordeno – with a particularly vile obscenity. But he started walking again. The rear door of the car stood open. The back-up car waited behind it. Toby was talking some nonsense about the withholding tax payable on the interest accruing from Swiss bank accounts, but he knew that

Grigoriev was not really listening. Slipping ahead, de Silsky jumped into the back of the car and Skordeno threw Grigoriev straight in after him, then sat down beside him and slammed the door. Toby took the passenger seat; the driver was one of the Meinertzhagen girls. Speaking German, Toby told her to go easy and for God's sake remember it was a Bernese Sunday. No English in his hearing, Smiley had said.

Somewhere near the station Grigoriev must have had second thoughts, because there was a short scuffle and when Toby looked in the mirror Grigoriev's face was contorted with pain and he had both hands over his groin. They drove to the Länggass-strasse, a long dull road behind the university. The door of the apartment house opened as they pulled up outside it. A thin housekeeper waited on the doorstep. She was Millie McCraig, an old Circus trooper. At the sight of her smile, Grigoriev bridled and now it was speed, not cover, that mattered. Skordeno jumped onto the pavement, seized one of Grigoriev's arms and nearly pulled it out of its socket; de Silsky must have hit him again, though he swore afterwards it was an accident, for Grigoriev came out doubled up, and between them they carried him over the threshold like a bride, and burst into the drawing-room in a bunch. Smiley was seated in a corner waiting for them. It was a room of brown chintzes and lace. The door closed, the abductors allowed themselves a brief show of festivity. Skordeno and de Silsky burst out laughing in relief. Toby took off his fur hat and wiped the sweat away.

'*Ruhe*,' he said softly, ordering quiet. They obeyed him instantly.

Grigoriev was rubbing his shoulder, seemingly unaware of anything but the pain. Studying him, Smiley took comfort from this gesture of self-concern: subconsciously, Grigoriev was declaring himself to be one of life's losers. Smiley remembered Kirov, his botched pass at Ostrakova and his laborious recruitment of Otto Leipzig. He looked at Grigoriev and read the same incurable mediocrity in everything he saw: in the new but ill-chosen striped suit that emphasised his portliness; in the treasured grey shoes, punctured for ventilation but too tight for comfort; in the prinked, waved hair. All these tiny, useless acts of vanity communicated to Smiley an aspiration to greatness which he knew – as Grigoriev seemed to know – would never be fulfilled.

*A former academic*, he remembered, from the document Enderby had handed him at Ben's Place. *Appears to have abandoned university teaching for the larger privileges of officialdom.*

*A pincher*, Ann would have said, weighing his sexuality at a single glance. *Dismiss him.*

But Smiley could not dismiss him. Grigoriev was a hooked fish: Smiley had only moments in which to decide how best to land him. He wore rimless spectacles and was running to fat round the chin. His hair oil, warmed by the heat of the body, gave out a lemon vapour. Still kneading his shoulder, he started peering round at his captors. Sweat was falling from his face like raindrops.

'Where am I?' he demanded truculently, ignoring Smiley and selecting Toby as the leader. His voice was hoarse and high pitched. He was speaking German, with a Slav sibilance.

*Three years as First Secretary (Commercial), Soviet Mission to Potsdam*, Smiley remembered. *No apparent intelligence connection.*

'I demand to know where I am. I am a senior Soviet diplomat. I demand to speak to my Ambassador immediately.'

The continuing action of his hand upon his injured shoulder took the edge off his indignation.

'I have been kidnapped! I am here against my will! If you do not immediately return me to my Ambassador there will be a grave international incident!'

Grigoriev had the stage to himself, and he could not quite fill it. Only George will ask questions, Toby had told his team. Only George will answer them. But Smiley sat still as an undertaker; nothing, it seemed, could rouse him.

'You want ransom?' Grigoriev called, to all of them. An awful thought appeared to strike him. 'You are terrorists?' he whispered. 'But if you are terrorists, why do you not bind my eyes? Why do you let me see your faces?' He stared round at de Silsky, then at Skordeno. 'You must cover your faces. Cover them! I want no knowledge of you!'

Goaded by the continuing silence, Grigoriev drove a plump fist into his open palm and shouted 'I demand' twice. At which point Smiley, with an air of official regret, opened a notebook on his lap, much as Kirov might have done, and gave a small, very official sigh: 'You are Counsellor Grigoriev of the Soviet Embassy in Berne?' he asked in the dullest possible voice.

'Grigoriev! I am Grigoriev! Yes, well done, I am Grigoriev! Who are you, please? Al Capone? Who are you? Why do you rumble at me like a commissar?'

Commissar could not have described Smiley's manner better: it was leaden to the point of indifference.

'Then, Counsellor, since we cannot afford to delay, I must ask you, to study the incriminating photographs on the table behind you,' Smiley said, with the same studied dullness.

'Photographs? What photographs? How can you incriminate a diplomat? I demand to telephone my Ambassador immediately!'

'I would advise the Counsellor to look at the photographs first,' said Smiley, in a glum, regionless German. 'When he has looked at the photographs, he is free to telephone whomever he wants. Kindly start at the left,' he advised. 'The photographs are arranged from left to right.'

A blackmailed man has the dignity of all our weaknesses, Smiley thought, covertly watching Grigoriev shuffling along the table as if he were inspecting one more diplomatic buffet. A blackmailed man is any one of us caught in the door as we try to escape the trap. Smiley had arranged the layout of the pictures himself; he had imagined, in Grigoriev's mind, an orchestrated succession of disasters. The Grigorievs parking their Mercedes outside the bank. Grigorieva, with her perpetual scowl of discontent, waiting alone in the driving seat, clutching the wheel in case anyone tried to take it from her. Grigoriev and little Natasha in long shot, sitting very close to each other on a bench. Grigoriev inside the bank, several pictures, culminating in a superb over-the-shoulder shot of Grigoriev signing a cashier's receipt, the full name Adolf Glaser clearly typed on the line above his signature. There was Grigoriev looking uncomfortable on his bicycle, about to enter the sanatorium; there was Grigorieva roosting crossly in the car again, this time beside Gertsch's barn, her own bicylce still strapped to the roof. But the photograph that held Grigoriev longest, Smiley noticed, was the muddy long shot stolen by the Meinertzhagen girls. The quality was not good but the two heads in the car, though they were locked mouth to mouth, were recognisable enough. One was Grigoriev's. The other, pressed down on him as if she would eat him alive, was little Natasha's.

'The telephone is at your disposal, Counsellor,' Smiley called to him quietly, when Grigoriev still did not move.

But Grigoriev remained frozen over this last photograph, and to judge by his expression, his desolation was complete. He was not merely a man found out, thought Smiley; he was a man whose very dream of love, till now vested in secrecy, had suddenly become public and ridiculous.

Still using his glum tone of official necessity, Smiley set about explaining what Karla would have called the pressures. Other inquisitors, says Toby, would have offered Grigoriev a choice, thereby inevitably mustering the Russian obstinacy in him, and the Russian *penchant* for self-destruction: the very impulses, he says, which could have invited catastrophe. Other inquisitors, he insists, would have menaced, raised their voices, resorted to histrionics, even physical abuse. Not George, he says: never. George acted out the low-key official time-server, and Grigoriev, like Grigorievs the world over, accepted him as his unalterable fate. George by-passed choice entirely, says Toby. George calmly made clear to Grigoriev why it was that he had no choice at all: the important thing, Counsellor – said Smiley, as if he were explaining a tax demand – was to consider what impact these photographs would have in the places where they would very soon be studied if nothing was done to prevent their distribution. There were first the Swiss authorities, who would obviously be incensed by the misuse of a Swiss passport on the part of an accredited diplomat, not to mention the grave breach of banking laws, said Smiley. They would register the strongest official protest, and the Grigorievs would be returned to Moscow overnight, all of them, never again to enjoy the fruits of a foreign posting. Back in Moscow, however, Grigoriev would not be well regarded either, Smiley explained. His superiors in the Foreign Ministry would take a dismal view of his behaviour, 'both in the private and professional spheres'. Grigoriev's prospects for an official career would be ended. He would be an *exile* in his own land, said Smiley, and his family with him. All his family. 'Imagine facing the wrath of Grigorieva twenty-four hours a day in the wastes of outer Siberia,' he was saying in effect.

At which Grigoriev slumped into a chair and clapped his hands on to the top of his head, as if scared it would blow off.

'But finally,' said Smiley, lifting his eyes from his notebook, though only for a moment – and what he read there, said Toby, God knows, the pages were ruled but otherwise blank – 'finally, Counsellor, we have also to consider the effect of these photographs upon certain organs of State security.'

And here Grigoriev released his head and drew the handkerchief from his top pocket and began wiping his brow, but as hard as he wiped, the sweat came back again. It fell as fast as Smiley's own in the interrogation cell in Delhi, when he had sat face to face with Karla.

Totally committed to his part as bureaucratic messenger of the inevitable, Smiley sighed once more and primly turned to another page of his notebook.

'Counsellor, may I ask you what time you expect your wife and family to return from their picnic?'

Still dabbing with the handkerchief, Grigoriev appeared too preoccupied to hear.

'Grigorieva and the children are taking a picnic in the Elfenau woods,' Smiley reminded him. 'We have some questions to ask you, but it would be unfortunate if your absence from home were to cause concern.'

Grigoriev put away the handkerchief. 'You are spies?' he whispered. 'You are Western spies?'

'Counsellor, it is better that you do not know who we are,' said Smiley earnestly. 'Such information is a dangerous burden. When you have done as we ask, you will walk out of here a free man. You have our assurance. Neither your wife, nor even Moscow Centre, will ever be the wiser. Please tell me what time your family returns from Elfenau –' Smiley broke off.

Somewhat half-heartedly, Grigoriev was affecting to make a dash for it. He stood up, he took a bound towards the door. Paul Skordeno had a lanquid air for a hard-man, but he caught the fugitive in an armlock even before he had taken a second step, and returned him gently to his chair, careful not to mark him. With another stage groan, Grigoriev flung up his hands in vast despair. His heavy face coloured and became convulsed, his broad shoulders started heaving as he broke into a mournful torrent of self-recrimination. He spoke half in Russian, half in German. He cursed himself with a slow and holy zeal, and after that, he cursed his mother, his wife and his bad luck and his own dreadful frailty as a father. He should have stayed in Moscow, in the Trade Ministry. He should never have been wooed away from academia merely because his fool wife wanted foreign clothes and music and privileges. He should have divorced her long ago but he could not bear to relinquish the children, he was a fool and a clown. He should be in the asylum instead of the girl. When he was sent for in Moscow, he should have said no, he should have resisted the pressure, he should have reported the matter to his Ambassador when he turned.

'Oh, Grigoriev!' he cried. 'Oh, Grigoriev! You are so weak, so weak!'

Next, he delivered himself of a tirade against conspiracy. Conspiracy was anathema to him, several times in the course of his career he had been obliged to collaborate with the hateful '*neighbours*' in some crackpot enterprise, every time it was a disaster. Intelligence people were criminals, charlatans and fools, a masonry of monsters. Why were Russians so in love with them? Oh, the fatal flaw of secretiveness in the Russian soul!

'Conspiracy has replaced religion!' Grigoriev moaned to all of them, in German. 'It is our mystical substitute! Its agents are our Jesuits, these swine, they ruin everything!'

Bunching his fists now, he pushed them into his cheeks, pummelling himself in his remorse, till with a movement of the notepad on his lap, Smiley brought him dourly back to the matter in hand: 'Concerning Grigorieva and your children, Counsellor,' he said. 'It really is essential that we know what time they are due to return home.'

In every successful interrogation – as Toby Esterhase likes to pontificate concerning this moment – there is one slip which cannot be recovered; one gesture, tacit or direct, even if it is only a half smile, or the acceptance of a cigarette, which marks the shift away from resistance, towards collaboration. Grigoriev, in Toby's account of the scene, now made his crucial slip. 'She will be home at one o'clock,' he muttered, avoiding both Smiley's eye, and Toby's.

Smiley looked at his watch. To Toby's secret ecstasy, Grigoriev did the same.

'But perhaps she will be late?' Smiley objected.

'She is never late,' Grigoriev retorted moodily.

'Then kindly begin by telling me of your relationship with the girl Ostrakova,' said Smiley, stepping right into the blue – says Toby – yet contriving to imply that the question was the most natural sequel to the issue of Madame Grigorieva's punctuality. Then he held his pen ready, and in such a way, says Toby, that a man like Grigoriev would feel positively obliged to give him something to write down.

For all this, Grigoriev's resistance was not quite evaporated. His *amour propre* demanded at least one further outing. Opening his hands, therefore, he appealed to Toby: '*Ostrakova!*' he repeated with exaggerated scorn. 'He asks me about some woman called *Ostrakova*? I know no such person. Perhaps he does, but I do not. I am a diplomat. Release me immediately, I have important engagements.'

But the steam, as well as the logic, was fast going out of his protests. Grigoriev knew this as well as anyone.

'Alexandra Borisovna Ostrakova,' Smiley intoned, while he polished his spectacles on the fat end of his tie. 'A Russian girl, but has a French passport.' He replaced his spectacles. 'Just as you are Russian, Counsellor, but have a Swiss passport. Under a false name. Now how did you come to get involved with her, I wonder?'

'*Involved*? Now he tells me I was *involved* with her! You think I am so base I sleep with mad girls? I was blackmailed. As you blackmail me now, so I was *blackmailed*. Pressure! Always pressure, always Grigoriev!'

'Then tell me how they blackmailed you,' Smiley suggested, with barely a glance at him.

Grigoriev peered into his hands, lifted them, but let them drop back on to his knees again, for once unused. He dabbed his lips with his handkerchief. He shook his head at the world's iniquity.

'I was in Moscow,' he said, and in Toby's ears, as he afterwards declares, angel choirs sang their hallelujahs. George had turned the trick, and Grigoriev's confession had begun.

Smiley, on the other hand, betrayed no such jubilation at his achievement. To the contrary, a frown of irritation puckered his plump face.

'The *date*, please, Counsellor,' he said, as if the place were not the issue. 'Give the *date* when you were in Moscow. Henceforth, please give dates at all points.'

This too is classic, Toby likes to explain: the wise inquisitor will always light a few false fires.

'September,' said Grigoriev, mystified.

'Of which year?' said Smiley, writing.

Grigoriev looked plaintively to Toby again. 'Which year! I say September, he asks me *which* September. He is a historian? I think he is a historian. *This* September,' he said sulkily to Smiley. 'I was recalled to Moscow for an urgent commercial conference. I am an expert in certain highly specialized economic fields. Such a conference would have been meaningless without my presence.'

'Did your wife accompany you on this journey?'

Grigoriev let out a hollow laugh. 'Now he thinks we are capitalists!' he commented to Toby. 'He thinks we go flying our wives around for two-week conferences, first class Swissair.'

'"In September of this year, I was ordered to fly alone to Moscow in order to attend a two-week economic conference,"' Smiley proposed, as if he were reading Grigoriev's statement aloud. '"My wife remained in Berne." Please describe the purpose of the conference.'

'The subject of our high-level discussions was extremely secret,' Grigoriev replied with resignation. 'My Ministry wished to consider ways of giving teeth to the official Soviet attitude towards nations who were selling arms to China. We were to discuss what sanctions could be used against the offenders.'

Smiley's faceless style, his manner of regretful bureaucratic necessity, were by now not merely established, says Toby, they were perfected: Grigoriev had adopted them wholesale, with philosophic, and very Russian, pessimism. As to the rest of those present, they could hardly believe, afterwards, that he had not been brought to the flat already in a mood to talk.

'Where was the conference held?' Smiley asked, as if secret matters concerned him less than formal details.

'At the Trade Ministry. On the fourth floor . . . in the conference room. Opposite the lavatory,' Grigoriev retorted, with hopeless facetiousness.

'Where did you stay?'

At a hostel for senior officials, Grigoriev replied. He gave the address and even, in sarcasm, his room number. Sometimes, our discussions ended late at night, he said, by now liberally volunteering information; but on the Friday, since it was still summer weather and very hot they ended early in order to enable those who wished to leave for the country. But Grigoriev had no such plans. Grigoriev proposed to stay in Moscow for the weekend and with reason: 'I had arranged to pass two days in the department of a girl called Evdokia, formerly my secretary. Her husband was away on military service,' he explained, as if this were a perfectly normal transaction among men of the world, one which Toby at least, as a fellow soul, would appreciate even if soulless commissars would not. Then, to Toby's astonishment, he went straight on. From his dalliance with Evdokia he passed without warning or preamble to the very heart of their enquiry:

'Unfortunately, I was prevented from adhering to these arrangements by the intervention of members of the Thirteenth Directorate of Moscow Centre known also as the Karla Directorate. I was summoned to attend an interview immediately.'

At which moment the telephone rang. Toby took the call, rang off, and spoke to Smiley.

'She's arrived back at the house,' he said, still in German.

Without demur, Smiley turned straight to Grigoriev: 'Counsellor, we are advised that your wife has returned home. It has now become necessary for you to telephone her.'

'Telephone her?' Horrified, Grigoriev swung round on Toby. 'He tells me, telephone her! What do I say? "Grigorieva, here is loving husband! I have been kidnapped by Western spies!" Your commissar is mad! Mad!'

'You will please tell her you are unavoidably delayed,' Smiley said.

His placidity added fuel to Grigoriev's outrage: 'I tell this to my wife? To Grigorieva? You think she will believe me? She will report me to the Ambassador immediately. "Ambassador, my husband has run away! Find him!"'

'The courier Krassky brings you weekly orders from Moscow, does he not?' Smiley asked.

'The commissar knows everything,' Grigoriev told Toby, and wiped his hand across his chin. 'If he knows everything, why doesn't he speak to Grigorieva himself?'

'You are to adopt an official tone with her, Counsellor,' Smiley advised. 'Do not refer to Krassky by name, but suggest that he has ordered you to meet him for a conspiratorial discussion somewhere in the town. An emergency. Krassky has changed his plans. You have no idea when you will be back, or what he wants. If she protests, rebuke her. Tell her it is a secret of State.'

They watched him worry, they watched him wonder. Finally, they watched a small smile settle over his face.

'A secret,' Grigoriev repeated to himself. 'A secret of State. Yes.'

Stepping boldly to the telephone, he dialled a number. Toby stood over him, one hand discreetly poised to slam the cradle should he try some trick, but Smiley with a small shake of the head signalled him away. They heard Grigorieva's voice saying 'Yes?' in German. They heard Grigoriev's bold reply, followed by his wife – it is all on tape – demanding sharply to know where he was. They saw him stiffen and lift his chin, and put on an official face; they heard him snap out a few short phrases, and ask a question to which there was apparently no answer. They saw him ring off again, bright-eyed and pink with pleasure, and his short arms fly in the air with delight, like someone who has scored a goal. The next thing they knew, he had burst out laughing, long, rich gusts of Slav laughter, up and down the scale. Uncontrollably, the others began laughing with him – Skordeno, de Silsky, and Toby. Grigoriev was shaking Toby's hand.

'Today I like very much conspiracy!' Grigoriev cried, between further gusts of cathartic laugher. 'Conspiracy is very good today!'

Smiley had not joined in the general festivity, however. Having cast himself deliberately as the killjoy, he sat turning the pages of his notebook, waiting for the fun to end.

'You were describing how you were approached by members of the Thirteenth Directorate,' Smiley said, when all was quiet again. 'Known also as the Karla Directorate. Kindly continue with your narrative, Counsellor.'

# TWENTY-FIVE

Did Grigoriev sense the new alertness round him – the discreet freezing of gestures? Did he notice how the eyes of Skordeno and de Silsky both hunted out Smiley's impassive face and held it in their gaze? How Millie McCraig slipped silently to the kitchen to check her tape recorders yet again, in case, by an act of a malevolent god, both the main set and the reserve had failed at once? Did he notice Smiley's now almost Oriental self-effacement – the very opposite of interest – the retreat of his whole body into the copious folds of his brown tweed travelling coat, while he patiently licked his thumb and finger and turned a page?

Toby, at least, noticed these things. Toby in his dark corner by the telephone had a grandstand seat from which he could observe everyone and remain as good as unobserved himself. A fly could not have crossed the floor, but Toby's watchful eyes would have recorded its entire odyssey. Toby even describes his own symptoms – a hot feeling around the neckband, he says, a knotting of the throat and stomach muscles – Toby not only endured these discomforts, but remembered them faithfully. Whether Grigoriev was responsive to the atmosphere is another matter. Most likely he was too consumed by his central rôle. The triumph of the telephone call had stimulated him, and revived his self-confidence; and it was significant that his first statement, when he once more had the floor, concerned not the Karla Directorate, but his prowess as the lover of little Natasha: 'Fellows of our age *need* a girl like that,' he explained to Toby with a wink. 'They make us into young men again, like we used to be!'

'Very well, you flew to Moscow alone,' Smiley said, quite snappishly. 'The conference got under way, you were approached for an interview. Please continue from there. We have not got all afternoon, you know.'

The conference started on the Monday, Grigoriev agreed, obediently resuming his official statement. When the Friday afternoon came, I returned to my hostel in order to fetch my belongings and take them to Evdokia's apartment for our little weekend together. Instead of this, however, I was met by three men who ordered me into their car with even less explanation than you did – a glance at Toby – saying to me only that I was required for a special task. During the journey they advised me that they were members of the Thirteenth Directorate of Moscow Centre, which everybody in official Moscow knows to be the élite. I formed the impression that they were intelligent men, above the common run of their profession, which, saving your presence, sir, is not high. I had the impression they could be officers rather than mere lackeys. Nevertheless I was not unduly worried. I assumed that my professional expertise was being required for some secret matter, that was all. They were courteous and I was even somewhat flattered . . .

'How long was the journey?' Smiley interrupted, as he continued writing.

Across town, Grigoriev replied vaguely. Across town, then into countryside till dark. Till we reached this one little man like a monk, sitting in a small room, who seemed to be their master.

Once again, Toby insists on bearing witness here to Smiley's unique mastery of the occasion. It was the shortest proof yet of Smiley's tradecraft, says Toby – as well as of his command of Grigoriev altogether – that throughout Grigoriev's protracted narrative, he never once, whether by an over-hasty follow-up question or the smallest false inflection of his voice, departed from the faceless rôle he had assumed for the interrogation. By his self-effacement, Toby insists, George held the whole scene 'like a thrush's egg in his hand.' The slightest careless movement on his part could have destroyed everything, but he never made it. And as the crowning example, Toby likes to offer this crucial moment, when the actual figure of Karla was for the first time introduced. Any other inquisitor, he says, at the very mention of a 'little man like a monk who seemed to be their master,' would have pressed for a description – his age, rank, what was he wearing, smoking, how did you know he was their master? Not Smiley. Smiley with a suppressed exclamation of annoyance tapped his ballpoint pen on his pad, and in a long-suffering voice invited Grigoriev, then and for the future, kindly *not* to foreshorten factual detail:

'Let me put the question again. How long was the journey? Please describe it precisely as you remember it and let us proceed from there.'

Crestfallen, Grigoriev actually apologised. He would say they drove for four hours at speed, sir; perhaps more. He remembered now that they twice stopped to relieve themselves. After four hours they entered a guarded area – no, sir, I saw no shoulder-boards, the guards wore plain clothes – and drove for at least another half hour into the heart of it. Like a nightmare, sir.

Yet again, Smiley objected, determined to keep the temperature as low as possible. How could it have been a nightmare, he wanted to know, since Grigoriev had only a moment before claimed that he was not frightened?

Well, not a nightmare exactly, sir, more a dream. At this stage, Grigoriev had had an impression he was being taken to the *landlord* – he used the Russian word, and Toby translated it – while he himself felt increasingly like a poor peasant. Therefore he was not frightened, sir, because he had no control over events, and accordingly nothing for which to reproach himself. But when the car finally stopped, and one of the men put a hand on his arm, and addressed a warning to him: at this point, his attitude changed entirely, sir: 'You are about to meet a great Soviet fighter and a powerful man,' the man told him 'If you are disrespectful to him, or attempt to tell lies, you may never again see your wife and family.'

'What is the name of this man?' Grigoriev had asked.

But the men replied, without smiling, that this great Soviet fighter had no name. Grigoriev asked whether he was Karla himself; knowing that Karla was the code name for the head of the Thirteenth Directorate. The men only repeated that the great fighter had no name.

'So that was when the dream became a nightmare, sir,' said Grigoriev humbly. 'They told me also that I could say goodbye to my weekend of love. Little Evdokia would have to get her fun elsewhere, they said. Then one of them laughed.'

Now a great fear had seized Grigoriev, he said, and by the time he had entered the first room and advanced upon the second door, he was so scared his knees were shaking. He even had time to be scared for his beloved Evdokia. Who could this supernatural person be, he wondered in awe, that he could know almost before Grigoriev himself knew, that he was pledged to meet Evdokia for the weekend?

'So you knocked on the door,' said Smiley, as he wrote.

And I was ordered to enter! Grigoriev went on. His enthusiasm for confession was mounting, so was his dependence upon his interrogator. His voice had become louder, his gestures more free. It was as if, says Toby, he was trying physically to coax Smiley out of his posture of reticence; whereas in reality it was Smiley's feigned indifference which was coaxing Grigoriev into the open. And I found myself not in a large and splendid office at all, sir, as became a senior official and a great Soviet fighter, but in a room so barren it would have done duty for a prison cell, with a bare wood desk at the centre, and a hand chair for a visitor to sit on:

'Imagine, sir, a great Soviet fighter and a powerful man! And all he had was a bare desk, which was illuminated only by a most inferior light! And behind it sat this priest, sir, a man of no affectation or pretence at all – a man of deep experience, I would say – a man from the very roots of his country – with small, straight eyes, and short grey hair, and a habit of holding his hands together while he smoked.'

'Smoked *what*?' Smiley asked, writing.

'Please?'

'What did he smoke? The question is plain enough. A pipe, cigarette, cigar?'

'Cigarettes, American, and the room was full of their aroma. It was like Potsdam again, when we were negotiating with the American officers from Berlin. "If this man smokes American all the time," I thought, "then he is certainly a man of influence."' Rounding on Toby again in his excitement, Grigoriev put the same point to him in Russian. To smoke American, chain smoke them, he said: imagine the cost, the influence necessary to obtain so many packets!

Then Smiley, true to his pedantic manner, asked Grigoriev to demonstrate what he meant by 'holding his hands together' while he smoked. And he looked on impassively while Grigoriev took a brown wood pencil from his pocket and linked his chubby hands in front of his face, and held the pencil in both of them, and sucked at it in caricature, like someone drinking two-handed from a mug.

'So!' he explained, and with another volatile switch of mood, shouted something in high laughter to Toby in Russian, which Toby did not see fit, at the time, to translate, and in the transcription is rendered only as 'obscene'.

The priest ordered Grigoriev to sit, and for ten minutes described to him the most intimate details of Grigoriev's love affair with Evdokia, and also of his indiscretions with two other girls, who had both worked for him as secretaries, one in Potsdam and one in Bonn, and had ended up, unknown to Grigorieva, by sharing his bed. At which point, if Grigoriev was to be believed, he made a show of courage, and rose to his feet, demanding to know whether he had been brought halfway across Russia in order to attend a court of morals: 'To sleep with one's secretary was not an unknown phenomenon, I told him, even in the Politburo! I assured him that I had never been indiscreet with foreign girls, only Russians. "This too I know," he says. "But Grigorieva is unlikely to appreciate the distinction."'

And then, to Toby's continuing amazement, Grigoriev gave vent to another burst of throaty laughter; and though both de Silsky and Skordeno discreetly joined in, Grigoriev's mirth outlived everybody's, so that they had to wait for it to run down.

'Kindly tell us, please, why the man you call the priest summoned you,' Smiley said, from deep in his brown overcoat.

'He advised me that he had special work for me in Berne on behalf of the Thirteenth Directorate. I should reveal it to nobody, not even to my Ambassador, it was too secret for any of them. "But," says the priest, "you shall tell your wife. Your personal circumstances render it impossible for you to make a conspiracy without the knowledge of your wife. This I know, Grigoriev. So tell her." And he was right,' Grigoriev commented. 'This was wise of him! This was clear evidence that the man was familiar with the human condition.'

Smiley turned a page and continued writing. 'Go on, please,' he said.

First, said the priest, Grigoriev was to open a Swiss bank account. The priest handed him a thousand Swiss francs in one hundred notes and told him to use them as the first payment. He should open the account not in Berne, where he was known, nor in Zurich, where there was a Soviet trade bank.

'The Vozhod,' Grigoriev explained gratuitously. 'This bank is used for many official and unofficial transactions.'

Not in Zurich, then, but in the small town of Thun, a few kilometres outside Berne. He should open the account under the name of Glaser, a Swiss subject: 'But I am a Soviet diplomat!' Grigoriev had objected. 'I am not Glaser, I am Grigoriev!'

Undeterred, the priest handed him a Swiss passport in the name of Adolf Glaser. Every month, said the priest, the account would be credited with several thousand Swiss francs, sometimes even ten or fifteen. Grigoriev would now be told what use to make of them. It was very secret, the priest repeated patiently, and to the secrecy belonged both a reward, and a threat. Very much as Smiley himself had done an hour before, the priest baldly set out each in turn. 'Sir, you should have observed his composure towards me,' Grigoriev told Smiley incredulously. 'His calmness, his authority in all circumstances! In a chess game he would win everything, merely by his nerves.'

'But he was not playing chess,' Smiley objected drily.

'Sir, he was not,' Grigoriev agreed, and with a sad shake of his head resumed his story.

A reward, and a threat, he repeated.

The threat was that Grigoriev's parent Ministry would be advised that he was unreliable on account of his philandering, and that he should therefore be barred from further foreign postings. This would cripple Grigoriev's career, also his marriage. So much for the threat.

'This would be extremely terrible for me,' Grigoriev added, needlessly.

Next the reward, and the reward was substantial. If Grigoriev acquitted himself well, and with absolute secrecy, his career would be furthered, his indiscretions overlooked. In Berne he would have an opportunity to move to more agreeable quarters, which would please Grigorieva; he would be given funds with which to buy himself an imposing car which would be greatly to Grigorieva's taste; also he would be independent of Embassy drivers, most of whom were *neighbours*, it was true, but were not admitted to this great secret. Lastly, said the priest, his promotion to Counsellor would be accelerated in order to explain the improvement in his living standards.

Grigoriev looked at the heap of Swiss francs lying on the desk between them, then at the Swiss passport, then at the priest. And he asked what would happen to him if he said he would rather not take part in his conspiracy. The priest nodded his head. He too, he assured Grigoriev, had considered this third possibility, but unfortunately the urgency of the need did not provide for such an option.

'So tell me what I must do with this money,' Grigoriev had said.

It was routine, the priest replied, which was another reason why Grigoriev had been selected: 'In matters of routine, I am told you are excellent,' he said. Grigoriev, though he was by now scared halfway out of his skin by the priest's words, had felt flattered by this commendation.

'He had heard good reports of me,' he explained to Smiley with pleasure.

Then the priest told Grigoriev about the mad girl.

Smiley did not budge. His eyes as he wrote were almost closed, but he wrote all the time – though God knows *what* he wrote, said Toby, for George would never have dreamed of consigning anything of even passing confidentiality to a notepad. Now and then, says Toby, while Grigoriev continued talking, George's head lifted far enough out of his coat collar for him to study the speaker's hands, or even his face. In every other respect he appeared remote from everything and everybody inside the room. Millie McCraig was in the doorway, de Silsky and Skordeno kept still as statues, while Toby prayed only for Grigoriev to 'keep talking, I mean talking at any price, who cares? We were hearing of Karla's tradecraft from the horse's mouth.'

The priest proposed to conceal nothing, he assured Grigoriev – which, as everyone in the room but Grigoriev at once recognised, was a prelude to concealing something.

In a private psychiatric clinic in Switzerland, said the priest, there was confined a young Russian girl who was suffering from an advanced state of schizophrenia: 'In the Soviet Union this form of illness is not sufficiently understood,' said the priest. Grigoriev recalled being strangely touched by the priest's finality. 'Diagnosis and treatment are too often complicated by political considerations,' the priest went on. 'In four years of treatment in our hospitals, the child Alexandra has been accused of many things by her doctors. "Paranoid reformist and delusional ideas . . . An over-estimation of her own personality . . . Poor adaptation to the social environment . . . Over-inflation of her capabilities . . . A bourgeois decadence in her sexual behaviour." Soviet doctors have repeatedly ordered her to renounce her incorrect ideas. This is not medicine,' said the priest unhappily to Grigoriev. 'It is politics. In Swiss hospitals, a more advanced attitude is taken to such matters.' It was essential that the child Alexandra should go to Switzerland.

It was by now clear to Grigoriev that the high official was personally committed to the girl's problem, and familiar with every aspect of it. Grigoriev himself was already beginning to feel sad for her. She was the daughter of a Soviet hero – said the priest – and a former official of the Red Army who, in the guise of a traitor to Russia, was living in penurious circumstances among counter-revolutionary Tsarists in Paris.

'His name,' the priest said, admitting Grigoriev to the greatest secret of all, 'his name,' he said, 'is Colonel Ostrakov. He is one of our finest and most active secret agents. We rely on him totally for our information regarding counter-revolutionary conspirators in Paris.'

Nobody in the room, said Toby, showed the least surprise at this sudden deification of a dead Russian deserter.

The priest, said Grigoriev, now proceeded to sketch the manner of the heroic agent Ostrakov's life, at the same time initiating Grigoriev into the mysteries of secret work. In order to escape the vigilance of imperialist counter-intelligence, the priest explained, it was necessary to invent for an agent a legend or false biography which would make him acceptable to anti-Soviet elements. Ostrakov was therefore in appearance a Red Army defector who had 'escaped' into West Berlin, and thence to Paris, abandoning his wife and one daughter in Moscow. But in order to safeguard Ostrakov's standing among the Paris émigrés, it was logically necessary that the wife should suffer for the traitorous actions of her husband.

'For after all,' said the priest, 'if imperialist spies were to report that Ostrakova, the wife of a deserter and renegade, was living in good standing in Moscow – receiving her husband's salary, for example, or occupying the same apartment – imagine the effect this would have upon the credibility of Ostrakov!'

Grigoriev said he could imagine this well. The priest, he explained in parenthesis, was in no sense authoritarian in his manner, but rather treated Grigoriev as an equal, doubtless out of respect for his academic qualifications.

'Doubtless,' Smiley said, and made a note.

Therefore, said the priest somewhat abruptly, Ostrakova and her daughter Alexandra, with the full agreement of her husband, were transferred to a far province and given a house to live in, and different names, and even – in their modest and selfless way – of necessity, their own legend also. Such, said the priest, was the painful reality of those who devoted themselves to special work. And consider, Grigoriev – he went on intently – consider the effect that such deprivation, and subterfuge, and even duplicity, might have upon a sensitive and perhaps already unbalanced daughter: an absent father whose very name had been eradicated from her life! A mother, who before being removed to safety, was obliged to endure the full brunt of public disgrace! Picture to yourself, the priest insisted – you, a father – the strains upon the young and delicate nature of a maturing girl!

Bowing to such forceful eloquence, Grigoriev was quick to say that as a father he could picture such strains easily and it occurred to Toby at that moment, and probably to everybody else as well, that Grigoriev was exactly what he claimed to be: a humane and decent man caught in the net of events beyond his understanding or control.

For the last several years, the priest continued in a voice heavy with regret, the girl Alexandra – or, as she used to call herself, Tatiana – had been, in the Soviet province where she lived, a wanton and a social outcast. Under the pressures of her situation she had performed a variety of criminal acts, including arson and theft in public places. She had sided with pseudo-intellectual criminals and the worst imaginable anti-social elements. She had given herself freely to men, often several in a day. At first, when she was arrested, it had been possible for the priest and his assistants to stay the normal processes of law. But gradually, for reasons of security, this protection had to be withdrawn, and Alexandra had more than once been confined to State psychiatric clinics that specialised in the treatment of congenital social malcontents – with the negative results which the priest had already described.

'She has also on several occasions been detained in a common prison,' said the priest in a low voice. And, according to Grigoriev, he summoned up this sad story as follows: 'You will readily appreciate, dear Grigoriev, as an academic, a father, as a man of the world, how tragically the ever-worsening news of his daughter's misfortunes affected the usefulness of our heroic agent Ostrakov in his lonely exile in Paris.'

Yet again, Grigoriev had been impressed by the remarkable sense of feeling – he would call it even a sense of direct personal responsibility – that the priest, through his story, inspired.

His voice arid as ever, Smiley made another interruption.

'And the mother is by now *where*, Counsellor, according to your priest?' he asked.

'Dead,' Grigoriev replied. 'She died in the province. The province to which she had been sent. She was buried under another name, naturally. According to the story as he told it to me, she died of a broken heart. This also placed a great burden on the priest's heroic agent in Paris,' he added. 'And upon the authorities in Russia.'

'Naturally,' said Smiley, and his solemnity was shared by the four motionless figures stationed round the room.

At last, said Grigoriev, the priest came to the precise reason why Grigoriev had been summoned. Ostrakova's death, coupled with the dreadful fate of Alexandra, had produced a grave crisis in the life of Moscow's heroic foreign agent. He was even for a short time tempted to give up his vital work in Paris in order to return to Russia and take care of his deranged amd motherless child. Eventually, however, a solution was agreed upon. Since Ostrakov could not come to Russia, his daughter must come to the West, and be cared for in a private clinic where she was accessible to her father whenever he cared to visit her. France was too dangerous for this purpose, but in Switzerland across the border, treatment could take place far from the suspicious eye of Ostrakov's counter-revolutionary companions. As a French citizen, the father would claim the girl and obtain the necessary papers. A suitable clinic had already been located and it was a short drive from Berne. What Grigoriev must now do was take over the welfare of this child, and report weekly to Moscow on her progress, so that the information could at once be relayed to her father. This was the purpose of the bank account, and of what the priest referred to as Grigoriev's Swiss identity.

'And you agreed,' said Smiley, as Grigoriev paused, and they heard his pen scratching busily over the paper.

'Not immediately. I asked him first two questions,' said Grigoriev, with a queer flush of vanity. 'We academics are not deceived so easily, you understand. First, I naturally asked him why this task could not be undertaken by one of the many Swiss-based representatives of our State Security.'

'An excellent question,' Smiley said, in a rare mood of congratulation. 'How did he reply to it?'

'It was too secret. Secrecy, he said, was a matter of compartments. He did not wish the name of Ostrakov to be associated with the people of the Moscow Centre mainstream. As things were now, he said, he would know that if ever there was a leak, Grigoriev alone was personally responsible. I was not grateful for this distinction,' said Grigoriev, and smirked somewhat wanly at Nick de Silsky.

'And what was your second question, Counsellor?'

'Concerning the father in Paris: how often he would visit. If the father was visiting frequently, then surely my own position as a substitute father was redundant. Arrangements could be made to pay the clinic directly, the father could visit from Paris every month and concern himself with his own daughter's welfare. To this the priest replied that the father could come only very seldom and should never be spoken of in discussions with the girl Alexandra. He added, without consistency, that the topic of the daughter was also acutely painful to the father and that conceivably he would never visit her at all. He told me I should feel honoured to be performing an important service on behalf of a secret hero of the Soviet Union. He grew stern. He told me it was not my place to apply the logic of an amateur to the craft of professionals. I apologised. I told him I indeed felt honoured. I was proud to assist however I could in the anti-imperialist struggle.'

'Yet you spoke without inner conviction?' Smiley suggested, looking up again and pausing in his writing.

'That is so.'

'Why?'

At first, Grigoriev seemed unsure why. Perhaps he had never before been invited to speak the truth about his feelings.

'Did you perhaps not *believe* the priest?' Smiley suggested.

'The story had many inconsistencies,' Grigoriev repeated with a frown. 'No doubt in secret work this was inevitable. Nevertheless I regarded much of it as unlikely or untrue.'

'Can you explain why?'

In the catharsis of confession, Grigoriev once more forgot his own peril, and gave a smile of superiority.

'He was emotional,' he said. 'I asked myself. Afterwards, with Evdokia, next day, lying at Evdokia's side, discussing the matter with her, I asked myself: What was it between the priest and this Ostrakov? Are they brothers? Old comrades? This great man they had brought me to see, so powerful, so secret – all over the world he is making conspiracies, putting pressure, taking special action. He is a ruthless man, in a ruthless profession. Yet when I, Grigoriev, am sitting with him, talking about some fellow's deranged daughter, I have the feeling I am reading this man's most intimate love letters. I said to him: "Comrade. You are telling me too much. Don't tell me what I do not need to know. Tell me only what I must do." But he says to me: "Grigoriev, you must be a friend to the child. Then you will be a friend to me. Her father's twisted life has had a bad effect on her. She does not know who she is or where she belongs. She speaks of freedom without regard to its meaning. She is the victim of pernicious bourgeois fantasies. She uses foul language not suitable to a young girl. In lying, she has the genius of madness. None of this is her fault." Then I ask him: "Sir, have you met the girl?" And he says to me only, "Grigoriev, you must be a father to her. Her mother was in many ways not an easy mother either. You have sympathy for such matters. In her later life she became embittered, and even supported her daughter in some of her anti-social fantasies."'

Grigoriev fell silent a moment and Toby Esterhase, still reeling from the knowledge that Grigoriev had discussed Karla's proposition with his occasional mistress within hours of its being made, was grateful for the respite.

'I felt he was dependent on me,' Grigoriev resumed. 'I felt he was concealing not only facts, but feelings.'

There remained, said Grigoriev, the practical details. The priest supplied them. The overseer of the clinic was a White Russian woman, a nun, formerly of the Russian Orthodox community in Jerusalem, but a good-hearted woman. In these cases, we should not be too scrupulous politically, said the priest. This woman had herself met Alexandra in Paris and escorted her to Switzerland. The clinic also has the services of a Russian-speaking doctor. The girl, thanks to the ethnic connections of her mother, also spoke German, but frequently refused to do so. These factors, together with the remoteness of the place, accounted for its selection. The money paid into the Thun bank would be sufficient for the clinic's fees and for medical attention up to one thousand francs a month, and as a hidden subsidy for the Grigoriev's new lifestyle. More money was available if Grigoriev thought it necessary; he should keep no bills or receipts; the priest would know soon enough if Grigoriev was cheating. He should visit the clinic weekly to pay the bill and inform himself of the girl's welfare; the Soviet Ambassador in Berne would be informed that the Grigoriev's had been entrusted with secret work, and that he should allow them flexibility.

The priest then came to the question of Grigoriev's communication with Moscow.

'He asked me: "Do you know the courier Krassky?" I reply, naturally I know this courier; Krassky comes once, sometimes twice a week to the

Embassy in the company of his escort. If you are friendly with him, he will maybe bring you a loaf of black bread direct from Moscow.'

In future, said the priest, Krassky would make a point of contacting Grigoriev privately each Thursday evening during his regular visit to Berne, either in Grigoriev's house or in Grigoriev's room in the Embassy, but preferably his house. No conspiratorial discussions would take place, but Krassky would hand to Grigoriev an envelope containing an apparently personal letter from Grigoriev's aunt in Moscow. Grigoriev would take the letter to a safe place and treat it at prescribed temperatures with three chemical solutions freely available on the open market – the priest named them and Grigoriev now repeated them. In the writing thus revealed, said the priest, Grigoriev would find a list of questions he should put to Alexandra on his next weekly visit. At the same meeting with Krassky, Grigoriev should hand him a letter to be delivered to the same aunt, in which he would pretend to be writing in detail about his wife Grigorieva's welfare, whereas in fact he would be reporting to the priest on the welfare of the girl Alexandra. This was called word code. Later, the priest would if necessary supply Grigoriev with materials for a more clandestine communication, but for the time being the word code letter to Grigoriev's aunt would do.

The priest then handed Grigoriev a medical certificate, signed by an eminent Moscow doctor.

'While here in Moscow, you have suffered a minor heart attack as a consequence of stress and overwork,' said the priest. 'You are advised to take up regular cycling in order to improve your physical condition. Your wife will accompany you.'

By arriving at the clinic by bicycle or on foot, the priest explained, Grigoriev would be able to conceal the diplomatic registration of his car.

The priest then authorised him to purchase two second-hand bicycles. There remained the question of which day of the week would be best suited to Grigoriev's visits to the clinic. Saturday was the normal visiting day but this was too dangerous; several of the inmates were from Berne and there was always the risk that 'Glaser' would be recognised. The overseer had therefore been advised that Saturdays were impracticable, and had consented, exceptionally, to a regular Friday-afternoon visit. The Ambassador would not object, but how would Grigoriev reconcile his Friday absence with Embassy routine?

There was no problem, Grigoriev replied. It was always permissible to trade Fridays for Saturdays, so Grigoriev would merely apply to work on Saturdays instead; then his Fridays would be free.

His confession over, Grigoriev treated his audience to a swift, over-lit smile.

'On Saturdays, a certain young lady also happened to be working in the Visa Section,' he said, with a wink at Toby. 'It was therefore possible we could enjoy some privacy together.'

This time the general laughter was not quite as hearty as it might have been. Time, like Grigoriev's story, was running out.

They were back where they had started, and suddenly there was only Grigoriev himself to worry about, only Grigoriev to administer, only Grigoriev to secure. He sat smirking on the sofa, but the arrogance was ebbing from him. He had linked his hands submissively and he was looking from one to the other of them, as if expecting orders.

'My wife cannot ride a bicycle,' he remarked with a sad little smile. 'She tried many times.' Her failure seemed to mean whole volumes to him. 'The priest wrote to me from Moscow: "Take your wife to her. Maybe Alexandra needs a mother also."' He shook his head, bemused. 'She cannot ride it,' he said to Smiley. 'In such a great conspiracy, how can I tell Moscow that Grigorieva cannot ride a bicycle?' Perhaps there was no greater test of Smiley's rôle as the responsible functionary in charge, than the way in which he now almost casually transformed Grigoriev the one-time source into Grigoriev the defector-in-place.

'Counsellor, whatever your long-term plans may be, you will please remain at the Embassy for at least another two weeks,' he announced, precisely closing his note pad. If you do as I propose, you will find a warm welcome should you elect to make a new life somewhere in the West.' He dropped the pad into his pocket. 'But next Friday you will on no account visit the girl Alexandra. You will tell your wife that this was the substance of today's meeting with Krassky. When Krassky the courier brings you Thursday's letter, you will accept it normally but you will afterwards continue to maintain to your wife that Alexandra is not to be visited. Be mysterious towards her. Blind her with mystery.'

Accepting his instructions, Grigoriev nodded uneasily.

'I must warn you however that if you make the smallest error or, on the other hand, try some trick, the priest will find out and destroy you. You will also forfeit your chances of a friendly reception in the West. Is that clear to you?'

There were telephone numbers for Grigoriev to ring, there were call box to call box procedures to be explained, and against all the laws of the trade, Smiley allowed Grigoriev to write the whole lot down, for he knew that he would not remember them otherwise. When all this was done, Grigoriev took his leave in a spirit of brooding dejection. Toby drove him to a safe dropping point, then returned to the flat and held a curt meeting of farewell.

Smiley was in his same chair, hands clasped on his lap. The rest of them, under Millie McCraig's orders, were busily tidying up the traces of their presence, polishing, dusting, emptying ashtrays and wastepaper baskets. Everyone present except himself and Smiley was getting out today, said Toby, the surveillance teams as well. Not tonight, not tomorrow. Now. They were sitting on a king-sized time bomb, he said: Grigoriev might at this very moment, under the continued impulse of confession, be describing the entire episode to his awful wife. If he had told Evdokia about Karla, who was to say he would not tell Grigorieva, or for that matter little Natasha, about his pow-wow with George today? Nobody should feel discarded, nobody should feel left out, said Toby. They had done a great job, and they would be meeting again soon to set the crown on it. There were handshakes, even a tear or two, but the prospect of the final act left everybody cheerful at heart.

And Smiley, sitting so quiet, so immobile, as the party broke up around him, what did he feel? On the face of it, this was a moment of high achievement for him. He had done everything he had set out to do, and more, even if he had resorted to Karla's techniques for the purpose. He had done it alone; and today as the record would show, he had broken and turned Karla's hand-picked agent in the space of a couple of hours. Unaided, even hampered by those who had called him back to service, he had fought his way through to the point where he could honestly say he had burst the last important lock. He was in late age, yet his tradecraft had never been better; for the first time in his career, he held the advantage over his old adversary.

On the other hand, that adversary had acquired a human face of disconcerting clarity. It was no brute whom Smiley was pursuing with such mastery, no unqualified fanatic after all, no automaton. It was a man; and one whose downfall, if Smiley chose to bring it about, would be caused by nothing more sinister than excessive love, a weakness with which Smiley himself from his own tangled life was eminently familiar.

# TWENTY-SIX

To every clandestine operation, says the folklore, belong more days of waiting than are numbered in Paradise, and for both George Smiley and Toby Esterhase, in their separate ways, the days and nights between Sunday evening and Friday seemed often numberless, and surely bore no relation to the Hereafter.

They lived not so much by Moscow Rules, said Toby, as by George's war rules. Both changed hotels and identities that same Sunday night, Smiley decamping to a small *hôtel garni* in the old town, the Arca, and Toby to a distasteful motel outside the town. Thereafter the two men communicated between call boxes according to an agreed rota, and if they needed to meet, they selected crowded outdoor places, walking a short distance together before parting. Toby had decided to change his tracks, he said, and was using cars as sparingly as possible. His task was to keep the watch on Grigoriev. All week he clung to his stated conviction that, having so recently enjoyed the luxury of one confession, Grigoriev was sure to treat himself to another. To forestall this, he kept Grigoriev on as short a rein as possible, but to keep up with him at all was a nightmare. For example, Grigoriev left his house at quarter to eight each morning and had a five-minute walk to the Embassy. Very well: Toby would make one car sweep down the road at seven-fifty exactly. If Grigoriev carried his brief-case in his right hand, Toby would know that nothing was happening. But the left hand meant 'emergency,' with a crash meeting in the gardens of the Elfenau palace, and a fallback in the town. On the Monday and Tuesday, Grigoriev went the distance using his right hand only. But on the Wednesday it was snowing, he wished to clear his spectacles, and therefore he stopped to locate his handkerchief, with the result that Toby first saw the brief-case in his left hand, but when he raced round the block again to check, Grigoriev was grinning like a madman and waving the brief-case at him with his right. Toby, according to his own account, had 'a total heart attack.' The next day, the crucial Thursday, Toby achieved a car meeting with Grigoriev in the little village of Allmendingen, just outside the town, and was able to talk to him face to face. An hour earlier, the courier Krassky had arrived, bringing Karla's weekly orders: Toby had seen him enter the Grigoriev residence. So where were the instructions from Moscow? Toby asked. Grigoriev was cantankerous and a little drunk. He demanded ten thousand dollars for the letter, which so enraged Toby that he threatened Grigoriev with exposure then and there; he would make a citizen's arrest and take him straight down to the police station and charge him personally with posing as a Swiss national, abusing his diplomatic status, evading Swiss tax laws, and about fifteen other things, including venery and espionage. The bluff worked, Grigoriev produced the letter, already treated, with the secret writing showing between the handwritten lines. Toby took several photographs of it, then returned it to Grigoriev.

Karla's questions from Moscow, which Toby showed to Smiley late that night in a rare meeting at a country inn, had a beseeching ring: '. . . report more fully on Alexandra's appearance and state of mind . . . Is she lucid? Does she laugh and does her laughter make a happy or a sad impression? Is she clean in her personal habits, clean finger-nails, brushed hair? What is the doctor's latest diagnosis; does he recommend some other treatment?'

But Grigoriev's main preoccupations at their rendezvous in Allmendingen turned out not to be with Krassky, nor with the letter, nor its author. His lady-friend of the Visa Section had been demanding outright to know about his Friday excursions, he said. Hence his depression and drunkenness. Grigoriev had answered her vaguely, but now he suspected her of being a Moscow spy, put there either by the priest or, worse, by some other frightful organ of Soviet Security. Toby, as it happened, shared this belief, but did not feel that much would be served by saying so.

'I have told her I shall not make love to her again until I completely trust her,' Grigoriev said earnestly. 'Also I have not yet decided whether she shall be permitted to accompany me in my new life in Australia.'

'George, this is a madhouse!' Toby told Smiley in a furious mixture of images, while Smiley continued to study Karla's solicitous questions, even though they were written in Russian. 'Listen, I mean how long can we hold the dam? This guy is a total crazy!'

'When does Krassky return to Moscow?' Smiley asked.

'Saturday midday.'

'Grigoriev must arrange a meeting with him before he leaves. He's to tell Krassky he will have a special message for him. An urgent one.'

'Sure,' said Toby. 'Sure, George.' And that was that.

Where had George gone in his mind? Toby wondered, watching him vanish into the crowd once more. Karla's instructions to Grigoriev seemed to have upset Smiley quite absurdly. 'I was caught between one total loony and one complete depressive,' Toby claims of this taxing period.

While Toby, however, could at least agonise over the vagaries of his master and his agent, Smiley had less substantial fare with which to occupy his time, which may have been his problem. On the Tuesday, he took a train to Zurich and lunched quietly at the Kronenhalle with Peter Guillam, who had flown in by way of London at Saul Enderby's behest. Their discussion was restrained, and not merely on the grounds of security. Guillam had taken it upon himself to speak to Ann while he was in London, he said, and was keen to know whether there was any message he might take back to her. Smiley said icily that there was none, and came as near as Guillam could remember to bawling him out. On another occasion – he suggested – perhaps Guillam would be good enough to keep his damned fingers out of Smiley's private affairs? Guillam switched the topic hastily to business. Concerning Grigoriev, he said, Saul Enderby had a notion to sell him to the Cousins as found rather than process him at Sarratt. How did George feel about that one? Saul had a sort of hunch that the glamour of a senior Russian defector would give the Cousins a much-needed lift in Washington, even if he hadn't anything to tell, while Grigoriev in London might, so to speak, mar the pure wine to come. How did George feel on that one, actually?

'Quite,' said Smiley.

'Saul also rather wondered whether your plans for next Friday were strictly necessary,' said Guillam, with evident reluctance.

Picking up a table-knife, Smiley stared along the blade.

'She's worth his career to him,' he said at last, with a most unnerving tautness. 'He steals for her, lies for her, risks his neck for her. He has to know whether she cleans her finger-nails and brushes her hair. Don't you think we owe her a look?'

Owe to whom? Guillam wondered nervously as he flew back to London to report. Had Smiley meant that he owed it to himself? Or did he mean to Karla? But he was far too cautious to air these theories to Saul Enderby.

From a distance, it might have been a castle, or one of those small farmsteads which sit on hilltops in the Swiss wine country, with turrets, and moats with covered bridges lending to inner courtyards. Closer to, it took on a more utilitarian appearance, with an incinerator, and an orchard, and modern outbuildings with rows of small windows rather high. A sign at the edge of the village pointed to it, praising its quiet position, its comfort, and the solicitude of its staff. The community was described as 'interdenominational Christian theosophist,' and foreign patients were a speciality. Old, heavy snow cluttered fields and roof-tops, but the road which Smiley drove was clear. The day was all white; sky and snow had merged into a single, uncharted void. From the gatehouse a dour porter telephoned ahead of him and, receiving somebody's permission, waved him through. There was a bay marked 'DOCTORS' and a bay marked 'VISITORS' and he parked in the second. When he pressed the bell, a dull-looking woman in a grey habit opened the door to him, blushing even before she spoke. He heard crematorium music, and the clanking of crockery from the kitchen, and human voices all at once. It was a house with hard floors and no curtains.

'Mother Felicity is expecting you,' said Sister Beatitude in a shy whisper.

A scream would fill the entire house, thought Smiley. He noticed pot plants out of reach. At a door marked 'OFFICE' his escort thumped lustily, then shoved it open. Mother Felicity was a large, inflamed-looking woman with a disconcerting worldliness in her gaze. Smiley sat opposite her. An ornate cross rested on her large bosom, and while she spoke, her heavy hands consoled it with a couple of touches. Her German was slow and regal.

'So,' she said. 'So, you are Herr *Lachmann*, and Herr Lachmann is an acquaintance of Herr *Glaser*, and Herr Glaser is this week indisposed.' She played on these names as if she knew as well as he did they were lies. 'He was not so indisposed that he could not telephone, but he was so indisposed that he could not bicycle. That is correct?'

Smiley said it was.

'Please do not lower your voice merely because I am a nun. We run a noisy house here and nobody is the less pious for it. You look pale. You have a flu?'

'No. No, I am well.'

'Then you are better off than Herr Glaser who has succumbed to a flu. Last year we had an Egyptian flu, the year before it was an Asian flu, but this year the *malheur* seems to be our own entirely. Does Herr Lachmann have documents, may I ask, which legitimize him for who he is?'

Smiley handed her a Swiss identity card.

'Come. Your hand is shaking. But you have no flu. "By occupation, *professor*," she read aloud. 'Herr Lachmann hides his light. He is *Professor* Lachmann. Of which subject is he professor, may one ask?'

'Of philology.'

'So. Philology. And Herr *Glaser*, what is *his* profession? He has never revealed it to me.'

'I understand he is in business,' Smiley said.

'A businessman who speaks perfect Russian. You also speak perfect Russian, Professor?'

'Alas, no.'

'But you are friends.' She handed back the identity card. 'A Swiss-Russian businessman and a modest professor of philology are friends. So. Let us hope the friendship is a fruitful one.'

'We are also neighbours,' Smiley said.

'We are all neighbours, Herr Lachmann. Have you met Alexandra before?'

'No.'

'Young girls are brought here in many capacities. We have god-children. We have wards. Nieces. Orphans. Cousins. Aunts, a few. A few sisters. And now a Professor. But you would be very surprised how few *daughters* there are in the world. What is the family relationship between Herr Glaser and Alexandra, for example?'

'I understand he is a friend of Monsieur Ostrakov.'

'Who is in Paris. But is invisible. As also is Madame Ostrakova. Invisible. As also, today, is Herr Glaser. You see how difficult it is for us to come to grips with the world, Herr Lachmann? When we ourselves scarcely know who we are, how can we tell *them* who *they* are? You must be very careful with her.' A bell was ringing for the end of rest. 'Sometimes she lives in the dark. Sometimes she sees too much. Both are painful. She has grown up in Russia. I don't know why. It is a complicated story, full of contrasts, full of gaps. If it is not the cause of her malady, it is certainly, let us say, the framework. You do not think Herr Glaser is the father for instance?'

'No.'

'Nor do I. Have you *met* the invisible Ostrakov? You have not. Does the invisible Ostrakov exist? Alexandra insists he is a phantom. Alexandra will have a quite different parentage. Well, so would many of us!'

'May I ask what you have told her about me?'

'All I know. Which is nothing. That you are a friend of Uncle Anton, whom she refuses to accept as her uncle. That Uncle Anton is ill, which appears to delight her, but probably it worries her very much. I have told her it is her father's wish to have someone visit her every week, but she tells me her father is a brigand and pushed her mother off a mountain at dead of night. I have told her to speak German but she may still decide that Russian is best.'

'I understand,' said Smiley.

'You are lucky, then,' Mother Felicity retorted. 'For I do not.'

Alexandra entered and at first he saw only her eyes: so clear, so defence-less. In his imagination, he had drawn her, for some reason, larger. Her lips were full at the centre, but at the corners already thin and too agile, and her smile had a dangerous luminosity. Mother Felicity told her to sit, said something in Russian, give her a kiss on her flaxen head. She left, and they heard her keys jingle as she strode off down the corridor, yelling at one of the sisters in French to have this mess cleared up. Alexandra wore a green tunic with long sleeves gathered at the wrists and a cardigan over her shoulders like a cape. She seemed to carry her clothes rather than wear them, as if someone had dressed her for the meeting.

'Is Anton dead?' she asked, and Smiley noticed that there was no natural link between the expression on her face and the thoughts in her head.

'No, Anton has a bad flu,' he replied.

'Anton says he is my uncle but he is not,' she explained. Her German was good, and he wondered whether, despite what Karla had said to Grigoriev, she had that from her mother too, or whether she had inherited her father's gift for languages, or both. 'He also pretends he has no car.' As her father had once done, she watched him without emotion, and without commitment. 'Where is your list?' she asked. 'Anton always brings a list.'

'Oh, I have my questions in my head.'

'It is forbidden to ask questions without a list. Questions out of the head are all completely forbidden by my father.'

'Who is your father?' Smiley asked.

For a time he saw only her eyes again, staring at him out of their private lonely place. She picked up a roll of Scotch tape from Mother Felicity's desk, and lightly traced the shiny surface with her finger.

'I saw your car,' she said. '"Be" stands for Berne.'

'Yes, it does,' said Smiley.

'What kind of car does Anton have?'

'A Mercedes. A black one. Very grand.'

'How much did he pay for it?'

'He bought it second-hand. About five thousand francs, I should imagine.'

'Then why does he come and see me on a bicycle?'

'Perhaps he needs the exercise.'

'No,' she said. 'He has a secret.'

'Have *you* got a secret, Alexandra?' Smiley asked.

She heard his question, and smiled at it, and nodded a couple of times as if to someone a long way off. 'My secret is called Tatiana.'

'That's a good name,' said Smiley. '*Tatiana.* How did you come by that?'

Raising her head, she smiled radiantly at the icons on the wall. 'It is forbidden to talk about it,' she said. 'If you talk about it, nobody will believe you, but they put you in a clinic.'

'But you are in a clinic already,' Smiley pointed out.

Her voice did not lift, it only quickened. She remained so absolutely still that she seemed not even to draw breath between her words. Her lucidity and her courtesy were awesome. She respected his kindness, she said, but she knew that he was an extremely dangerous man, more dangerous than teachers or police. Dr. Rüedi had invented property and prison and many of the clever arguments by which the world lived out its lies, she said. Mother Felicity was too close to God, she did not understand that God was somebody who had to be ridden and kicked like a horse till he took you in the right direction.

'But you, Herr Lachmann, represent the forgiveness of the authorities. Yes, I am afraid you do.'

She sighed, and gave him a tired smile of indulgence, but when he looked at the table he saw that she had seized hold of her thumb, and was forcing it back upon itself till it looked like snapping.

'Perhaps *you* are my father, Herr Lachmann,' she suggested with a smile.

'No, alas, I have no children,' Smiley replied.

'Are you God?'

'No, I'm just an ordinary person.'

'Mother Felicity says that in every ordinary person, there is a part that is God.'

This time it was Smiley's turn to take a long while to reply. His mouth opened, then with uncharacteristic hesitation closed again.

'I have heard it said too,' he replied, and looked away from her a moment.

'You are supposed to ask me whether I have been feeling better.'

'Are you feeling better, Alexandra?'

'My name is Tatiana,' she said.

'Then how does Tatiana feel?'

She laughed. Her eyes were delightfully bright. 'Tatiana is the daughter of a man who is too important to exist,' she said. 'He controls the whole of Russia, but he does not exist. When people arrest her, her father arranges for her to be freed. He does not exist but everyone is afraid of him. Tatiana does not exist either,' she added. 'There is only Alexandra.'

'What about Tatiana's mother?'

'She was punished,' said Alexandra calmly, confiding this information to the icons rather than to Smiley. 'She was not obedient to history. That is to say, she believed that history had taken a wrong course. She was mistaken. The people should not attempt to change history. It is the task of history to change the people. I would like you to take me with you, please. I wish to leave this clinic.'

Her hands were fighting each other furiously while she continued to smile at the icons.

'Did Tatiana ever meet her father?' he asked.

'A small man used to watch the children walk to school,' she replied. He waited but she said no more.

'And then?' he asked.

'From a car. He would lower the window but he looked only at me.'

'Did you look at him?'

'Of course. How else would I know he was looking at me?'

'What was his appearance? His manner? Did he smile?'

'He smoked. Feel free, if you wish. Mother Felicity likes a cigarette occasionally. Well, it's only natural, isn't it? Smoking calms the conscience, I am told.'

She had pressed the bell: reached out and pressed it for a long time. He heard the jingle of Mother Felicity's keys again, coming towards them down the bare corridor, and the shuffle of her feet at the door as she paused to unlock it, just like the sounds of any prison in the world.

'I wish to come with you in your car,' said Alexandra.

Smiley paid her bill and Alexandra watched him count the notes out under the lamp, exactly the way Uncle Anton did it. Mother Felicity intercepted Alexandra's studious look and perhaps, she sensed trouble, for she glanced sharply at Smiley as if she suspected some misconduct in him. Alexandra accompanied him to the door and helped Sister Beatitude open it, then shook Smiley's hand in a very stylish way, lifting her elbow up and outwards, and bending her front knee. She tried to kiss his hand but Sister Beatitude prevented her. She watched him to the car and she began waving, and he was already moving when he heard her screaming from very close, and saw that she was trying to open the car door and travel with him, but Sister Beatitude hauled her off and dragged her, still screaming, back into the house.

Half an hour later in Thun, in the same café from which he had observed Grigoriev's visit to the bank a week before, Smiley silently handed Toby the letter he had prepared. Grigoriev was to give it to Krassky tonight or whenever they met, he said.

'Grigoriev wants to defect tonight,' Toby objected.

Smiley shouted. For once in his life, shouted. He opened his mouth very wide, he shouted, and the whole café sat up with a jolt – which is to say, that the barmaid looked up from her marriage advertisements, and of the four card-players in the corner, one at least turned his head.

'*Not yet!*'

Then, to show that he had himself completely under control, he repeated the words quietly: 'Not yet, Toby. Forgive me. Not yet.'

Of the letter which Smiley sent to Karla by way of Grigoriev, no copy exists, which is perhaps what Smiley intended, but there can be little doubt of the substance, since Karla himself was anyway a self-professed exponent of the arts of what he liked to call pressure. Smiley would have set out the bare facts: that Alexandra was known to be his daughter by a dead mistress of manifest anti-Soviet tendencies, that he had arranged her illegal departure from the Soviet Union by pretending that she was his secret agent; that he had misappropriated public money and resources; that he had organised two murders and perhaps also the conjectured official execution of Kirov, all in order to protect his criminal scheme. Smiley would have pointed out that the accumulated evidence of this was quite sufficient, given Karla's precarious position within Moscow Centre, to secure his liquidation by his peers in the Collegium; and that if this were to happen, his daughter's future in the West – where she was residing under false pretences – would be uncertain, to say the least. There would be no money for her, and Alexandra would become a perpetual and ailing exile, ferried from one public hospital to another, without friends, proper papers, or a penny to her name. At worst, she would be brought back to Russia, to have visited upon her the full wrath of her father's enemies.

After the stick, Smiley offered Karla the same carrot he had offered him more than twenty years before, in Delhi: save your skin, come to us, tell us what you know, and we will make a home for you. A straight replay, said Saul Enderby later, who liked a sporting metaphor. Smiley would have promised Karla immunity from prosecution for complicity in the murder of Vladimir, and there is evidence that Enderby obtained a similar concession through his German liaison regarding the murder of Otto Leipzig. Without a question, Smiley also threw in general guarantees about Alexandra's future in the West – treatment, maintenance, and if necessary, citizenship. Did he take the line of kinship, as he had done before, in Delhi? Did he appeal to Karla's humanity, now so demonstrably on show? Did he add some clever seasoning, calculated to spare Karla humiliation, and knowing his pride, head him off perhaps from an act of self-destruction?'

Certainly, he gave Karla very little time to make up his mind. For that too is an axiom of pressure, as Karla was well aware: time to think is dangerous, except that in this case, there is reason to suppose that it was dangerous to Smiley also, though for vastly different reasons; he might have relented at the eleventh hour. Only the immediate call to action, says the Sarratt folklore, will force the quarry to slip the ropes of his restraint, and against every impulse born or taught to him, sail into the blue. The same, on this occasion, may be said to have applied equally to the hunter.

# TWENTY-SEVEN

It's like putting all your money on black, thought Guillam, staring out of the window of the café: everything you've got in the world, your wife, your unborn child. Then waiting, hour by hour, for the croupier to spin the wheel.

He had known Berlin when it was the world capital of the cold war, when every crossing point from East to West had the tenseness of a major surgical operation. He remembered how on nights like these, clusters of Berlin policemen and Allied soldiers used to gather under the arc lights, stamping their feet, cursing the cold, fidgeting their rifles from shoulder to shoulder, puffing clouds of frosted breath into each other's faces. He remembered how the tanks waited, growling to keep their engines warm, their gun barrels picking targets on the other side, feigning strength. He remembered the sudden wail of the alarm klaxons and the dash to the Bernauerstrasse or wherever the latest escape attempt might be. He remembered the fire brigade ladders going up; the orders to shoot back; the orders not to; the dead, some of them agents. But after tonight, he knew that he would remember it only like this: so dark you wanted to take a torch with you into the street, so still you could have heard the cocking of a rifle from across the river.

'What cover will he use?' he asked.

Smiley sat opposite him across the little plastic table, a cup of cold coffee at his elbow. He looked somehow very small inside his over-coat.

'Something humble,' Smiley said. 'Something that fits in. Those who cross here are mostly old-age pensioners, I gather.' He was smoking one of Guillam's cigarettes and it seemed to take all his attention.

'What on earth do pensioners want here?' Guillam asked.

'Some work. Some visit dependents. I didn't enquire very closely, I'm afraid.'

Guillam remained dissatisfied.

'We pensioners tend to keep ourselves to ourselves,' Smiley added, in a poor effort at humour.

'You're telling me,' said Guillam.

The café was in the Turkish quarter because the Turks are now the poor whites of West Berlin, and property is worst and cheapest near the Wall. Smiley and Guillam were the only foreigners. At a long table sat a whole Turkish family, chewing flat bread and drinking coffee and Coca-Cola. The children had shaven heads and the wide, puzzled eyes of refugees. Islamic music was playing from an old tape-recorder. Strips of coloured plastic hung from the hardboard arch of an Islamic doorway.

Guillam returned his gaze to the window, and the bridge. First came the piers of the overhead railway, next the old brick house that Sam Collins and his team had discreetly requisitioned as an observation centre. His men had been moving in surreptitiously these last two days. Then came the halo of sodium arc lights, and behind it lay a barricade, a pillbox, then the bridge. The bridge was for pedestrians only, and the only way over it was a corridor of steel fencing like a bird walk, sometimes one man's width and sometimes three. Occasionally one crossed, keeping a meek appearance and a steady pace in order not to alarm the sentry tower, then stepping into the sodium halo as he reached the West. By daylight the bird walk was grey; by night for some reason yellow, and strangely bright. The pillbox was a yard or two inside the border, its roof just mastering the barricade, but it was the tower that dominated everything, one iron-black rectangular pillar at the bridge's centre. Even the snow avoided it. There was snow on the concrete teeth that blocked the bridge to traffic, snow swarmed round the halo and the pillbox and made a show of settling on the wet cobble; but the sentry tower was immune, as if not even the snow would go near it of its own free will. Just short of the halo, the bird walk narrowed to a last gateway and a cattle pen. But the gateway, said Toby, could be closed electrically at a moment's notice from inside the pillbox.

The time was ten-thirty but it could have been three in the morning, because along its borders, West Berlin goes to bed with the dark. Inland, the island-city may chat and drink and whore and spend its money; the Sony signs and rebuilt churches and conference halls may glitter like a fairground; but the dark shores of the borderland are silent from seven in the evening. Close to the halo stood a Christmas tree, but only the upper half of it was lit, only the upper half was visible from across the river. It is a place of no compromise, thought Guillam, a place of no third way. Whatever reservations he might occasionally have about the Western freedom, here, at this border, like most other things, they stopped dead.

'George?' said Guillam softly, and cast Smiley a questioning glance.

A labourer had lurched into the halo. He seemed to rise into it as they all did the moment they stepped out of the bird walk, as if a burden had fallen from their backs. He was carrying a small briefcase and what looked like a rail man's lamp. He was slight of built. But Smiley, if he had noticed the man at all, had already returned to the collar of his brown overcoat and his lonely, far-away thoughts. 'If he comes, he'll come on time,' Smiley had said. Then why do we get here two hours early? Guillam had wanted to ask. Why do we sit here, like two strangers, drinking sweet coffee out of little cups, soaked in the steam of this wretched Turkish kitchen, talking platitudes? But he knew the answer already. Because we *owe*, Smiley would have said if he had been in a talking mood. Because we owe the caring and the waiting, we owe this vigil over one man's effort to escape the system he has helped create. For as long as he is trying to reach us, we are his friends. Nobody else is on his side.

He'll come, Guillam thought. He won't. He may. If this isn't prayer, he thought, what is?'

'More coffee, George?'

'No, thank you, Peter. No, I don't think so. No.'

'They seem to have soup of some sort. Unless that was the coffee.'

'Thank you, I think I've consumed about all I can manage,' said Smiley, in quite a general tone, as if anyone who wished to hear was welcome.

'Well, maybe I'll just order something for rent,' said Guillam.

'Rent? I'm sorry. Of course. God knows what they must live on.'

Guillam ordered two more coffees and paid for them. He was paying as he went, deliberately, in case they had to leave in a hurry.

Come for George's sake, he thought; come for mine. Come for all our damn sakes, and be the impossible harvest we have dreamed of for so long.

'When did you say the baby was due, Peter?'

'March.'

'Ah. March. What will you call it?'

'We haven't really thought.'

Across the road, by the glow of a furniture shop that sold reproduction wrought iron and brocade and fake muskets and pewter, Guillam made out the muffled figure of Toby Esterhase in his Balkan fur hat, affecting to study the wares. Toby and his team had the streets, Sam Collins had the observation post: that was the deal. For the escape cars, Toby had insisted on taxis, and there they stood, three of them, suitably shabby, in the darkness of the station arches, with notices in their windscreens saying 'OUT OF SERVICE,' and their drivers standing at the *Imbiss*-stand, eating sausages in sweet sauce out of paper dishes.

*The place is a total minefield, Peter*, Toby had warned. *Turks, Greeks, Yugoslavs, a lot of crooks – even the damn cats are wired, no exaggeration.*

*Not a whisper anywhere*, Smiley had ordered. *Not a murmur, Peter, Tell Collins.*

Come, thought Guillam urgently. We're all rooting for you. Come.

From Toby's back, Guillam lifted his gaze slowly to the top-floor window of the old house where Collins' observation post was sited. Guillam had done his Berlin stint, he had been part of it a dozen times. The telescopes and cameras, the directional microphones, all the useless hardware that was supposed to make the waiting easier; the crackle of the radios, the stink of coffee and tobacco; the bunk-beds. He imagined the co-opted West German policeman who had no idea why he had been brought here, and would have to stay till the operation was abandoned or successful – the man who knew the bridge by heart and could tell the regulars from the casuals and spot the smallest bad omen the moment it occurred: the silent doubling of the watch, the Vopo sharpshooters easing softly into place.

And if they shoot him? thought Guillam. If they arrest him? If they leave him – which they would surely like to, and had done before to others – bleeding to death, face downward in the bird walk not six feet from the halo?

*Come*, he thought, less certainly, willing his prayers into the black skyline of the East. Come all the same.

A fine, very bright pin-light flitted across the west-facing upper window of the observation house, bringing Guillam to his feet. He turned round to see

Smiley already half-way to the door. Toby Esterhase was waiting for them on the pavement.

'It's only a possibility, George,' he said softly, in the tone of a man preparing them for disappointment. 'Just a thin chance, but he could be our man.'

They followed him without another word. The cold was ferocious. They passed a tailor's shop with two dark-haired girls stitching in the window. They passed wall posters offering cheap ski holidays, death to Fascists, and to the Shah. The cold made them breathless. Turning his face from the swirling snow, Guillam glimpsed a children's adventure playground made of old railway sleepers. They passed between black, dead buildings, then right, across the cobbled road, in pitch-frozen darkness to the river bank, where an old timber bullet-shelter with rifle-slits offered them the whole span of the bridge. To their left, black against the hostile river, a tall wooden cross, garnished with barbed wire, bore memory to an unknown man who had not quite escaped.

Toby silently extracted a pair of field-glasses from his overcoat and handed them to Smiley.

'George. Listen. Good luck, okay?'

Toby's hand closed briefly over Guillam's arm. Then he darted away again, into the darkness.

The shelter stank of leaf-mould and damp. Smiley crouched to the rifle slit, the skirts of his tweed coat trailing in the mud, while he surveyed the scene before him as if it held the very reaches of his own long life. The river was broad and slow, misted with cold. Arc lights played over it, and the snow danced in their beams. The bridge spanned it on fat stone piers, six or eight of them, which swelled into crude shoes as they reached the water. The spaces between them were arched, all but the centre, which was squared off to make room for shipping, but the only ship was a grey patrol boat moored at the Eastern bank, and the only commerce that it offered was death. Behind the bridge, like its vastly bigger shadow, ran the railway viaduct, but like the river it was derelict, and no trains ever crossed. The warehouses of the far bank stood monstrous as the hulks of an earlier barbaric civilisation, and the bridge with its yellow bird walk seemed to leap from half-way up them, like a fantastic light-path out of darkness. From his vantage point, Smiley could scan the whole length of it with his field-glasses, from the floodlit white barrack house on the Eastern bank, up to the black sentry tower at the crest, then slightly downhill again towards the Western side: to the cattle pen, the pillbox that controlled the gateway, and finally the halo.

Guillam stood but a few feet behind him, yet Guillam could have been back in Paris for all the awareness Smiley had of him: he had seen the solitary black figure start his journey; he had seen the glimmer of the cigarette-end as he took one last pull, the spark of it comet towards the water as he tossed it over the iron fencing of the bird walk. One small man, in a worker's half-length coat, with a worker's satchel slung across his little chest, walking neither fast nor slowly, but walking like a man who walked a lot. One small man, his body a fraction too long for his legs, hatless despite the snow. That is all that happens, Smiley thought; one little man walks across a bridge.

'Is it him?' Guillam whispered. 'George, tell me! Is it Karla?'

*Don't come,* thought Smiley. *Shoot,* Smiley thought, talking to Karla's people, not to his own. There was suddenly something terrible in his foreknowledge that this tiny creature was about to cut himself off from the black castle behind him. Shoot him from the sentry tower, shoot him from the pillbox, from the white barrack hut, from the crow's-nest on the prison warehouse, slam the gate on him, cut him down, your own traitor, kill him! In his racing imagination, he saw the scene unfold: the last-minute discovery by Moscow Centre of Karla's infamy; the phone calls to the frontier – 'Stop him at any cost!' And the shooting, never too much – enough to hit a man a time or two, and wait.

'It's him!' Guillam whispered. He had taken the binoculars from Smiley's unresisting hand. 'It's the same man! The photograph that hung on your wall in the Circus! George, you miracle!'

But Smiley in his imagination saw only the Vopo's searchlights converging on Karla as if he were a hare in the headlights, so dark against the snow; and Karla's hopeless old man's run before the bullets threw him like a rag doll over his own feet. Like Guillam, Smiley had seen it all before. He looked across the river into the darkness again, and an unholy vertigo seized him as the very evil he had fought against seemed to reach out and possess him and claim him despite his striving, calling him a traitor also; mocking him, yet at the same time applauding his betrayal. On Karla has descended the curse of Smiley's compassion; on Smiley the curse of Karla's fanaticism. I have destroyed him with the weapons I abhorred, and they are his. We have crossed each other's frontiers, we are the no-men of this no-man's-land.

'Just keep moving,' Guillam was murmuring. 'Just keep moving, let nothing stop you.'

Approaching the blackness of the sentry tower, Karla took a couple of shorter steps and for a moment Smiley really thought he might change his mind and give himself up to the East Germans. Then he saw a cat's tongue of flame as Karla lit a fresh cigarette. With a match or a lighter? he wondered. *To George from Ann with all my love.*

'Christ, he's cool!' said Guillam.

The little figure set off again, but at a slower pace, as if he had grown weary. He is stoking up his courage for the last step, thought Smiley, or he is trying to damp his courage down. He thought of Vladimir and Otto Leipzig and the dead Kirov; he thought of Haydon and his own life's work ruined; he thought of Ann, permanently stained for him by Karla's cunning, and Haydon's scheming embrace. He recited in his despair a whole list of crimes – the tortures, the killings, the endless ring of corruption – to lay upon the frail shoulders of this one pedestrian on the bridge, but they would not stay there: he did not want these spoils, won by these methods. Like a chasm, the jagged skyline beckoned to him yet again, the swirling snow made it an inferno. For a second longer, Smiley stood on the brink at the smouldering river's edge.

They had started walking along the tow-path, Guillam leading, Smiley reluctantly following. The halo burned ahead of them, glowing as they approached it. *Like two ordinary pedestrians*, Toby had said. *Just walk to the bridge and wait, it's normal.* From the darkness around them, Smiley heard whispered voices and the swift, damped sounds of hasty movement under tension. 'George,' someone whispered. 'George.' From a yellow phone box, an unknown figure lifted a hand in discreet salute, and he heard the word 'triumph' smuggled to him on the wet freezing air. The snow was blurring his glasses, he found it hard to see. The observation post stood to their right, not a light burning in the windows. He made out a van parked at the entrance, and realised it was a Berlin mail van, one of Toby's favourites. Guillam was hanging back. Smiley heard something about 'claiming the prize.'

They had reached the edge of the halo. An orange rampart blocked the bridge and the chicane from sight. They were out of the eye-line of the sentry-box. Perched above the Christmas tree, Toby Esterhase was standing on the observation scaffold with a pair of binoculars, calmly playing the cold-war tourist. A plump female watcher stood at his side. An old notice warned them they were there at their own risk. On the smashed brick viaduct behind them Smiley picked out a forgotten armorial crest. Toby made a tiny motion with his hand: *thumbs up, it's our man now.* From beyond the rampart, Smiley heard light footsteps and the vibration of an iron fence. He caught the smell of an American cigarette as the icy wind wafted it ahead of the smoker. There's still the electric gateway, he thought; he waited for the clang as it slammed shut, but none came. He realised he had no real name by which to address his enemy: only a code-name and a woman's at that. Even his military rank was a mystery. And still Smiley hung back, like a man refusing to go on stage.

Guillam had drawn alongside him and seemed to be trying to edge him forward. He heard soft footsteps as Toby's watchers gathered to the edge of the halo, safe from view in the shelter of the rampart, waiting with bated breath for a sight of the catch. And suddenly, there he stood, like a man slipping into a crowded hall unnoticed. His small right hand hung flat and naked at his side, his left held the cigarette timidly across his chest. One little man, hatless, with a satchel. He took a step forward and in the halo Smiley saw his face, aged and weary and travelled, the short hair turned to white by a sprinkling of snow. He wore a grimy shirt and a black tie: he looked like a poor man going to the funeral of a friend. The cold had nipped his cheeks low down, adding to his age.

They faced each other; they were perhaps a yard apart, much as they had been in Delhi jail. Smiley heard more footsteps and this time it was the sound of Toby padding swiftly down the wooden ladder of the scaffold. He heard soft voices and laughter; he thought he even heard the sound of gentle clapping, but he never knew; there were shadows everywhere, and once inside the halo, it was hard for him to see out. Paul Skordeno slipped forward and stood himself one side of Karla; Nick de Silsky stood the other. He heard Guillam telling someone to get him back. He heard the ring of something metal falling onto the icy cobble, and knew it was Ann's cigarette-lighter, but nobody else seemed to notice it. They exchanged one more glance and perhaps each for that second did see in the other something of himself. He heard the crackle of car tyres and the sounds of doors opening, while the engine kept running. De Silsky and Skordeno moved towards it and Karla went with them, though they didn't touch him; he seemed to have acquired already the submissive manner of a prisoner; he had learned it in a hard school. Smiley stood back and the three of them marched softly past him, all somehow too absorbed by the ceremony to pay attention to him. The halo was empty. He heard the quiet closing of the car's doors and the sound of it driving away. He heard two other cars leave after it, or with it. He didn't watch them go. He felt Toby Esterhase fling his arms round his shoulders, and saw that his eyes were filled with tears.

'George,' he began. 'All your life. Fantastic!'

Then something in Smiley's stiffness made Toby pull away, and Smiley himself stepped quickly out of the halo, passing very close to Ann's lighter on his way. It lay at the halo's very edge, tilted slightly, glinting like fool's gold on the cobble. He thought of picking it up, but somehow there seemed no point and no one else appeared to have seen it. Someone was shaking his hand, someone else was clapping him on the shoulder. Toby quietly restrained them.

'Take care, George,' Toby said. 'Go well, hear me?'

Smiley heard Toby's team leave one by one until only Peter Guillam remained. Walking a short way back along the embankment, almost to where the cross stood, Smiley took another look at the bridge, as if to establish whether anything had changed, but clearly it had not, and though the wind appeared a little stronger, the snow was still swirling in all directions.

Peter Guillam touched his arm.

'Come on, old friend,' he said. 'It's bedtime.'

From long habit, Smiley had taken off his spectacles and was absently polishing them on the fat end of his tie, even though he had to delve for it among the folds of his tweed coat.

'George, you won,' said Guillam as they walked slowly towards the car.

'Did I?' said Smiley. 'Yes. Yes, well I suppose I did.'